Rufus Griswol

The Poets and Poetry of America

Rufus Griswold

The Poets and Poetry of America

Reprint of the original, first published in 1874.

1st Edition 2024 | ISBN: 978-3-36884-700-5

Verlag (Publisher): Outlook Verlag GmbH, Zeilweg 44, 60439 Frankfurt, Deutschland
Vertretungsberechtigt (Authorized to represent): E. Roepke, Zeilweg 44, 60439 Frankfurt, Deutschland
Druck (Print): Books on Demand GmbH, In de Tarpen 42, 22848 Norderstedt, Deutschland

FITZ-GREENE HALLECK.

THE POETS AND POETRY OF AMERICA.

BY RUFUS WILMOT GRISWOLD.

WITH ADDITIONS BY R. H. STODDARD.

HERE THE FREE SPIRIT OF MANKIND AT LENGTH
THROWS ITS LAST FETTERS OFF; AND WHO SHALL PLACE
A LIMIT TO THE GIANT'S UNCHAINED STRENGTH?
BRYANT.

ERE LONG, THINE EVERY STREAM SHALL FIND A TONGUE,
LAND OF THE MANY WATERS! *HOFFMAN.*

THIS BE THE POET'S PRAISE!
THAT HE HATH EVER BEEN OF LIBERTY
THE STEADIEST FRIEND; OF JUSTICE AND OF TRUTH
FIRMEST OF ALL SUPPORTERS.
AMERICAN PROSPECTS—1768.

CAREFULLY REVISED, MUCH ENLARGED, AND CONTINUED TO THE PRESENT TIME.

With Portraits, on Steel, from Original Pictures,

OF RICHARD H. DANA, WILLIAM C. BRYANT, JAMES G. PERCIVAL, HENRY W. LONGFELLOW, WILLIAM D. GALLAGHER, EDGAR A. POE, PHILIP PENDLETON COOKE, JAMES RUSSELL LOWELL, AND BAYARD TAYLOR.

NEW YORK:
JAMES MILLER, PUBLISHER, 647 BROADWAY.
1874.

Preface to the Sixteenth Edition.

By the publication of "The Female Poets of America," in 1849, this survey of American Poetry was divided into two parts. From "The Poets and Poetry of America" were omitted all reviewals of our female poets, and their places were supplied with notices of other authors. The entire volume was also revised, re-arranged, and in other respects improved.

The book was in the first place too hastily prepared. There was difficulty in procuring materials, and in deciding, where so many had some sort of claim to the title, whom to regard as Poets. There had been published in this country about five hundred volumes of rhythmical compositions of various kinds and degrees of merit, nearly all of which I read, with more or less attention. From the mass I chose about one fifth, as containing writings not unworthy of notice in such an examination of this part of our literature as I proposed to make. I have been censured, perhaps justly, for the wide range of my selections. But I did not consider all the contents of the volume Poetry. I aimed merely to show what had been accomplished toward a Poetical Literature by our writers in verse before the close of the first half century of our national existence. With much of the first order of excellence more was accepted that was comparatively poor. But I believe nothing was admitted inferior to passages in the most celebrated foreign works of like character. I have also been condemned for omissions. But on this score I have no regrets. I can think of no name not included in the first edition which I would now admit without better credentials than were before me when that edition was printed.

The value of books of this description has been recognised from an early period. Besides the few leading authors in every literature whose works are indispensable in libraries to be regarded as in any degree complete, there are a far greater number of too little merit to render the possession of all their productions desirable. The compilations of English poetry by Mr. Southey, Mr. Hazlitt, Mr. Campbell, and Mr. S. C. Hall, embrace as many as most readers wish to read of the effusions of more than half the writers quoted in them; and of the qualities of all such, indications are given in criticisms or specimens as will intelligibly guide the lover of poetry to more comprehensive studies. In our own country, where there are comparatively few poets of a high rank, the majority would have little chance of a just appreciation but for such reviewals.

The earliest project for a general collection of Specimens of American Poetry was that of JAMES RIVINGTON, the celebrated royalist printer of New York, who in January, 1773, sent a printed circular on the subject to several persons in the colonies who had reputations as poets, and soon after published in his "Royal Gazette" the following advertisement:

"THE public is hereby notified that the printer of this paper has it in contemplation to publish with all convenient speed a COLLECTION OF POEMS by the FAVORITES of the MUSES in America, on the same plan with DODSLEY'S celebrated *English Compilation*. Such ladies and gentlemen, therefore, as will please to honour the attempt with their productions, (which will be treated with the utmost impartiality by a gentleman who hath undertaken to conduct the publication,) will confer a favor on the public in general, and particularly on their much obliged and very humble servant. JAMES RIVINGTON.

The execution of RIVINGTON'S design was prevented by the approaching revolution, and no such book appeared until 1791, when MATTHEW CAREY brought out his "Beauties of Poetry, British and American," in which selections are given from nineteen native writers. In 1793 the first of a proposed series of volumes of "American Poems, Selected and Original," was printed in Litchfield, Connecticut, under the editorial supervision of RICHARD ALSOP. It is curious and interesting, and students in our literary history will regret that its sale did not warrant a completion of the undertaking. In 1794 "The Columbian Muse, a Selection of American Poetry by various Authors of established Reputation," appeared from the press of J. CAREY, in New York. The next publication of this kind was the comprehensive and judicious "Specimens of American Poetry, with Critical and Biographical Notices," in three volumes, by Mr. SAMUEL KETTELL, in 1829; followed in 1831 by Dr. CHEEVER'S "American Common-Place Book of Poetry, with occasional Notes;" in 1839 by "The Poets of America, illustrated by one of her Painters," edited by Mr. KEESE, and in the same year by "Selections from the American Poets," by Mr. BRYANT.

Since the reconstruction of the present work, in the eleventh edition, the sale has been still greater than previously, and I have now added many new authors, and notices of the new productions of authors already mentioned, with additional extracts.

No. 22, WEST TWENTYTHIRD STREET, NEW YORK, 1855.

PREFACE TO THIS EDITION.

Thirty years have passed since the publication of the first edition of the POETS OF AMERICA, and every year has added to the materials of which it was composed. DR. GRISWOLD made such ample use of these additional materials in the different editions through which his work went, that the last issued during his life may be said to have brought the work down to that time. Such being the case, the present editor has confined himself to the period which has since elapsed, and which may be said to have commenced in 1855. His first intention was to have revised DR. GRISWOLD's volume, correcting any errors that he might discover, and substituting later, and, in some cases, perhaps, better specimens of the authors quoted; but a little reflection convinced him that it was not advisable to do so. DR. GRISWOLD had done this work, and whether it was well done, or ill done, it had taken its place among standard works of the same character. It was an authority, and as such it was not to be rashly disturbed. Had its preparation fallen originally to the present editor, he would probably have given it a different form, and would certainly have dissented from some of DR. GRISWOLD's critical opinions. Fortunately for him, however, this arduous and thankless task was accomplished, and but little remained to be done. Whether this, which was simply to continue DR. GRISWOLD's work to the present time, has been satisfactorily performed, is not for him to decide. He has avoided one fault, or what might have been considered a fault in him; he has expressed no opinions concerning the poets whom he has added to DR. GRISWOLD's collection.

The reasons which determined this omission on his part, as well as his intention to leave DR. GRISWOLD's own work intact, were submitted to some of his literary friends, who acquiesed in their justice. "If I were in your place," was the advice one gave, "I should not mix my work and GRISWOLD's, but leave the latter precisely as he left it. Every reader now will want GRISWOLD's book (at least I do), with his biographies, critical remarks, and selections. The latter are as good as necessary, giving, in almost all cases, the author's best and most characteristic poems; while his criticisms would lose their historical value if meddled with. To be sure he got into a good deal of hot water (there, by the way, is a warning to you, in dealing with the new names,) but all that has passed away. No one can complain if you let his articles stand, while there might be a great deal of complaint if you meddle with them."

"You think of proceeding," another wrote, "in the additions you are to make to GRISWOLD'S AMERICAN POETS, just as I should were I in your place. It would not become a poet to assign to his contemporary brethren the place which they are to hold in our literature, and it would be most ungracious in you to intercept any praise which might otherwise come to them, and to which they would naturally think that they have a fair claim. Poets are a sensitive race, as has been said a million times, beginning with HORACE, and you could not speak disparagingly of any, except the most modest of the tribe, without being suspected, by them at least, of a disposition to stand in the way of rival merit."

The editor returns his thanks to the poets whom he has added to this collection for information furnished in regard to themselves and their writings, and for permission to select what he chose from the latter. His thanks are especially due to MESSRS. J. R. OSGOOD & Co. for the liberal use they have enabled him to make of various volumes of which they are the publishers, without which this collection could not have been completed.

R. H. STODDARD.

NEW YORK, Aug. 15th, 1872.

Contents.

CONTENTS.

The Poets and Poetry of America.

BEFORE THE REVOLUTION.

The literary annals of this country before the revolution present few names entitled to a permanent celebrity. Many of the earlier colonists of New England were men of erudition, profoundly versed in the dogmas and discussions of the schools, and familiar with the best fruits of ancient genius and culture, and they perpetuated their intellectual habits and accomplishments among their immediate descendants; but they possessed neither the high and gentle feeling, the refined appreciation, the creating imagination, nor the illustrating fancy of the poet, and what they produced of real excellence was nearly all in those domains of experimental and metaphysical religion in which acuteness and strength were more important than delicacy or elegance. The "renowned" Mr. THOMAS SHEPHERD, the "pious" Mr. JOHN NORTON, and our own "judicious" Mr. HOOKER, are still justly esteemed in the churches for soundness in the faith and learned wisdom, as well as for all the practical Christian virtues, and in their more earnest "endeavours" they and several of their contemporaries frequently wrote excellent prose, an example of which may be found in the "attestation" to COTTON MATHER'S "Magnalia," by JOHN HIGGINSON, of Salem, which has not been surpassed in stately eloquence by any modern writing on the exodus of the Puritans. In a succeeding age that miracle of dialectical subtlety, EDWARDS, with MAYHEW, CHAUNCEY, BELLAMY, HOPKINS, and others, demonstrated the truth that there was no want of energy and activity in American mind in the direction to which it was most especially determined; but our elaborate metrical compositions, formal, pedantic, and quaint, of the seventeenth century and the earlier part of the eighteenth, are forgotten except by curious antiquaries, who see in them the least valuable relics of the first ages of American civilization.

The remark has frequently been quoted from Mr. JEFFERSON, that when we can boast as long a history as that of England, we shall not have cause to shrink from a comparison of our literatures; but there is very little reason in such a suggestion, since however unfavourable to the cultivation of any kind of refinement are the necessarily prosaic duties of the planters of an empire in wilderness countries, in our case, when the planting was accomplished, and our ancestors chose to turn their attention to mental luxuries, they had but to enter at once upon the most advanced condition of taste, and the use of all those resources in literary art acquired or invented by the more happily situated scholars to whom had been confided in a greater degree the charge of the English language. When, however, the works of CHAUCER, SPENSER, SHAKSPEARE, and MILTON were as accessible as now, and the living harmonies of DRYDEN and POPE were borne on every breeze that fanned the cheek of an Englishman, the best praise which could be awarded to American verses was that they were ingeniously grotesque. There were displayed in them none of the graces which result from an æsthetical sensibility, but only such ponderous oddities, laborious conceits, and sardonic humors, as the slaves of metaphysical and theological scholasticism might be expected to indulge when yielding to transient and imperfect impulses of human nature. Our fathers were like the labourers of an architect; they established deeply and strongly in religious virtue and useful science the foundations of an edifice, not dreaming how great and magnificent it was to be. They did well their part; it was not for them to fashion the capitals and adorn the arches of the temple.

The first poem composed in this country was a description of New England, in Latin, by the Reverend WILLIAM MORRELL, who came to the Plymouth colony in 1623, and returned to London in the following year. It has been reprinted, with an English translation made by the author, in the collections of the Massachusetts Historical Society.

Mr. GEORGE SANDYS, while "treasurer for the colony in Virginia," about the year 1625, wrote probably the earliest English verse produced in America. MICHAEL DRAYTON, author of the "Polyolbion," addressed to him an epistle in which he says—

"My worthy George, by industry and use,
Let's see what lines Virginia will produce;
Go on with OVID, as you have begun
With the first five books: let your numbers run
Glib as the former: so, it shall live long
And do much honor to the English tongue."

SANDYS completed in Virginia his translation of the "Metamorphoses," dating hence his dedication to the king, and probably wrote here all his "Paraphrase upon the Psalms," and "Songs selected out of the Old and New Testaments." DRYDEN and POPE unite in praising his poems, and his version of the Book of Psalms has been described as incomparably the most poetical in the English language.

The oldest rhythmical composition from the hand of a colonist which has come down to us is believed to have been written about the year 1630. The name of the author has been lost:

"New England's annoyances, you that would know them,
Pray ponder these verses which briefly do show them.

"The place where we live is a wilderness wood,
Where grass is much wanting that 's fruitful and good:
Our mountains and hills and our valleys below
Being commonly cover'd with ice and with snow:
And when the northwest wind with violence blows,
Then every man pulls his cap over his nose:
But if any 's so hardy and will it withstand,
He forfeits a finger, a foot, or a hand.

"But when the spring opens, we then take the hoe,
And make the ground ready to plant and to sow;
Our corn being planted and seed being sown,
The worms destroy much before it is grown;
And when it is growing some spoil there is made
By birds and by squirrels that pluck up the blade;
And when it is come to full corn in the ear,
It is often destroy'd by raccoon and by deer.

"And now do our garments begin to grow thin,
And wool is much wanted to card and to spin;
If we get a garment to cover without,
Our other in-garments are clout upon clout:
Our clothes we brought with us are apt to be torn,
They need to be clouted soon after they 're worn;
But clouting our garments they hinder us nothing,
Clouts double are warmer than single whole clothing.

"If fresh meat be wanting, to fill up our dish,
We have carrots and pumpkins and turnips and fish:
And is there a mind for a delicate dish,
We repair to the clam banks, and there we catch fish.
'Stead of pottage and puddings and custards and pies,
Our pumpkins and parsnips are common supplies:
We have pumpkins at morning and pumpkins at noon;
If it was not for pumpkins we should be undone.

"If barley be wanting to make into malt,
We must be contented and think it no fault;
For we can make liquor to sweeten our lips
Of pumpkins and parsnips and walnut-tree chips. . . . .

"Now while some are going let others be coming,
For while liquor 's boiling it must have a scumming;
But I will not blame them, for birds of a feather,
By seeking their fellows, are flocking together.
But you whom the LORD intends hither to bring,
Forsake not the honey for fear of the sting;
But bring both a quiet and contented mind,
And all needful blessings you surely will find."

The first book published in British America was "The Psalms, in Metre, faithfully Translated, for the Use, Edification and Comfort of the Saints, in Public and Private, especially in New England," printed at Cambridge, in 1640. The version was made by THOMAS WELDE, of Roxbury, RICHARD MATHER, of Dorchester, and JOHN ELIOT, the famous apostle to the Indians. The translators seem to have been aware that it possessed but little poetical merit. "If," say they, in their preface, "the verses are not always so smooth and elegant as some may desire and expect, let them consider that GOD's altar needs not our polishings; for we have respected rather a plain translation, than to smooth our verses with the sweetness of any paraphrase, and so have attended to conscience rather than elegance, and fidelity rather than poetry, in translating Hebrew words into English language, and DAVID's poetry into English metre." COTTON MATHER laments the inelegance of the version, but declares that the Hebrew was most exactly rendered. After a second edition had been printed, President DUNSTER,* of Harvard College, assisted by Mr. RICHARD LYON, a tutor at Cambridge, attempted to improve it, and in their advertisement to the godly reader they state that they "had special eye both to the gravity of the phrase of sacred writ and sweetness of the verse." DUNSTER's edition was reprinted twenty-three times in America, and several times in Scotland and England, where it was long used in the dissenting congregations. The following specimen is from the second edition:

PSALM CXXXVII.

"The rivers on of Babilon
There when wee did sit downe,
Yea, even then, wee mourned when
Wee remembered Sion.

"Our harp wee did hang it amid,
Upon the willow tree,
Because there they that us away
Led in captivitee

"Requir'd of us a song, and thus
Askt mirth us waste who laid,
Sing us among a Sion's song,
Unto us then they said.

"The LORD's song sing can wee, being
In stranger's land? then let
Lose her skill my right hand if I
Jerusalem forget.

"Let cleave my tongue my pallate on
If mind thee doe not I,
If chiefe joyes o're I prize not more
Jerusalem my joy.

"Remember, LORD, Edom's sons' word,
Unto the ground, said they,
It rase, it rase, when as it was
Jerusalem her day.

"Blest shall he be that payeth thee,
Daughter of Babilon,
Who must be waste, that which thou hast
Rewarded us upon.

"O happie hee shall surely bee
That taketh up, that eke
The little ones against the stones
Doth into pieces breake.

Mrs. ANNE BRADSTREET, "the mirror of her age and glory of her sex," as she is styled by a contemporary admirer, came to America with her husband, Governor SIMON BRADSTREET, in 1630,

* HENRY DUNSTER was the first president of Harvard College, and was inaugurated on the twenty-seventh of August, 1640. In 1654 he became unpopular on account of his public advocacy of anti-pædobaptism, and was compelled to resign. When he died, in 1659, he bequeathed legacies to the persons who were most active in causing his separation from the College. In the life of DUNSTER, in the *Magnalia*, is the following admonition, by Mr. SHEPHERD, to the authors of the New Psalm Book:

"You *Roxb'ry* poets keep clear of the crime
Of missing to give us very good rhyme.
And you of *Dorchester*, your verses lengthen,
But with *the texts' own words* you will them strengthen.'

and ten years afterward published her celebrated volume of "Several Poems, compiled with great variety of wit and learning, full of delight; wherein especially is contained a compleat Discourse and Description of the four Elements, Constitutions, Ages of Man, and Seasons of the Year, together with an exact Epitome of the Three First Monarchies, viz.: the Assyrian, Persian, and Grecian; and the Roman Commonwealth, from the beginning, to the end of the last King; with divers other Pleasant and Serious Poems." NORTON declares her poetry so fine that were MARO to hear it he would condemn his own works to the fire; the author of the "Magnalia" speaks of her poems as a "monument for her memory beyond the stateliest marble;" and JOHN ROGERS, one of the presidents of Harvard College, in some verses addressed to her, says—

"Your only hand those poesies did compose:
Your head the source, whence all those springs did flow:
Your voice, whence change's sweetest notes arose:
Your feet that kept the dance alone, I trow:
Then vail your bonnets, poetasters all,
Strike, lower amain, and at these humbly fall,
And deem yourselves advanced to be her pedestal.

"Should all with lowly congees laurels bring,
Waste Flora's magazine to find a wreath,
Or Pineus' banks, 't were too mean offering;
Your muse a fairer garland doth bequeath
To guard your fairer front; here 't is your name
Shall stand immarbled: this your little frame
Shall great Colossus be, to your eternal fame."

She died in September, 1672. Of her history and writings a more ample account may be found in my "Female Poets of America."

WILLIAM BRADFORD, the second governor of Plymouth, who wrote a "History of the People and Colony from 1602 to 1647," composed also "A Descriptive and Historical Account of New England, in Verse," which is preserved in the Collections of the Massachusetts Historical Society.

When JOHN COTTON, an eminent minister of Boston, died, in 1652, BENJAMIN WOODBRIDGE, the first graduate of Harvard College, and afterward one of the chaplains of CHARLES the Second, wrote an elegiac poem, from a passage in which it is supposed FRANKLIN borrowed the idea of his celebrated epitaph on himself. COTTON, says WOODBRIDGE, was

"A living, breathing Bible; tables where
Both covenants at large engraven were;
Gospel and law in 's heart had each its column,
His head an index to the sacred volume,
His very name a title-page, and next
His life a commentary on the text.
O, what a monument of glorious worth,
When in a new edition he comes forth,
Without erratas, may we think he 'll be,
In leaves and covers of eternity!"

The lines of the Reverend JOSEPH CAPEN, on the death of Mr. JOHN FOSTER, an ingenious mathematician and printer, are yet more like the epitaph of FRANKLIN:

"Thy body which no activeness did lack,
Now 's laid aside like an old almanack;
But for the present only 's out of date,
'T will have at length a far more active state:
Yea, though with dust thy body soiled be,
Yet at the resurrection we shall see
A fair edition, and of matchless worth,
Free from *erratas*, new in heaven set forth;
'T is but a word from GOD the great Creator,
It shall be done when he saith *Imprimatur*."

The excellent President URIAN OAKES, styled "the LACTANTIUS of New England," was one of the most distinguished poets of his time. The following verses are from his elegy on the death of THOMAS SHEPARD, minister of Charlestown:

"Art, nature, grace, in him were all combined
To show the world a matchless paragon;
In whom of radiant virtues no less shined,
Than a whole constellation; but hee 's gone!
Hee 's gone, alas! down in the dust must ly
As much of this rare person, as could die.

"To be descended well, doth that commend?
Can sons their fathers' glory call their own?
Our SHEPARD justly might to this pretend,
(His blessed father was of high renown,
Both Englands speak him great, admire his name,)
But his own personal worth 's a better claim

"His look commanded reverence and awe,
Though mild and amiable, not austere;
Well humour'd was he, as I ever saw,
And ruled by love and wisdom more than fear.
The muses and the graces too, conspired,
To set forth this rare piece to be admired.

"He breathed love, and pursued peace in his day,
As if his soul were made of harmony:
Scarce ever more of goodness crowded lay
In such a piece of frail mortality.
Sure Father WILSON'S genuine son was he,
New-England's PAUL had such a TIMOTHY.

"My dearest, inmost, bosome friend is gone!
Gone is my sweet companion, soul's delight!
Now in a huddling crowd, I 'm all alone,
And almost could bid all the world good-night
Blest be my rock! GOD lives: O! let him be
As he is all, so all in all to me."

At that period the memory of every eminent person was preserved in an ingenious elegy, epitaph, or anagram. SHEPARD, mourned in the above verses by OAKES, on the death of JOHN WILSON, "the Paul of New England," and "the greatest anagrammatizer since the days of LYCOPHRON," wrote—

"*John Wilson, anagr. John Wilson.*
"O, change it not! No sweeter name or thing,
Throughout the world, within our ears shall ring."

THOMAS WELDE, a poet of some reputation in his day, wrote the following epitaph on SAMUEL DANFORTH, a minister of Roxbury, who died soon after the completion of a new meeting-house:

"Our new-built church now suffers too by this,
Larger its windows, but its lights are less."

PETER FOULGER, a schoolmaster of Nantucket, and the maternal grandfather of Doctor FRANKLIN, in 1676 published a poem entitled "A Looking-glass for the times," addressed to men in authority, in which he advocates religious liberty, and implores the government to repeal the uncharitable laws against the Quakers and other sects. He says—

"The rulers in the country I do owne them in the Lord
And such as are for government, with them I do accord

But that which I intend thereby, is that they would keep
bound;
And meddle not with GOD's worship, for which they have
no ground.
And I am not alone herein, there's many hundreds more,
That have for many years ago spoke much more upon that
score.
Indeed, I really believe, it's not your business,
To meddle with the church of GOD in matters more or less."

In another part of his "Looking Glass"—

"Now loving friends and countrymen, I wish we may be
wise;
'T is now a time for every man to see with his own eyes.
'T is easy to provoke the LORD to send among us war;
'T is easy to do violence, to envy and to jar;
To show a spirit that is high; to scold and domineer;
To pride it out as if there were no GOD to make us fear;
To covet what is not our own; to cheat and to oppress;
To live a life that might free us from acts of righteousness;
To swear and lie and to be drunk; to backbite one another;
To carry tales that may do hurt and mischief to our bro-
ther;
To live in such hypocrisy, as men may think us good,
Although our hearts within are full of evil and of blood.
All these, and many evils more, are easy for to do;
But to repent and to reform we have no strength thereto."

The following are the concluding lines:

"I am for peace, and not for war, and that's the reason why
I write more plain than some men do, that use to daub and lie.
But I shall cease and set my name to what I here insert:
Because to be a libeller, I hate with all my heart.
From Sherbonton, where now I dwell, my name I do put
here,
Without offence, your real friend, it is PETER FOULGER."

Probably the first native bard was he who is described on a tombstone at Roxbury as "BENJAMIN THOMSON, learned schoolmaster and physician, and ye renowned poet of New England." He was born in the town of Dorchester, (now Quincy,) in 1640, and educated at Cambridge, where he received a degree in 1622. His principal work, "New England's Crisis," appears to have been written during the famous wars of PHILIP, sachem of the Pequods, against the colonists, in 1675 and 1676. The following is the prologue, in which he laments the growth of luxury among the people:

"The times wherein old POMPION was a saint,
When men fared hardly, yet without complaint,
On vilest cates: the dainty Indian-maize
Was eat with clamp-shells out of wooden trayes,
Under thatched huts, without the cry of rent,
And the best sawce to every dish, content.
When flesh was food and hairy skins made coats,
And men as well as birds had chirping notes;
When Cimnels were accounted noble blood,
Among the tribes of common herbage food,
Of CERES' bounty formed was many a knack,
Enough to fill poor ROBIN's Almanack.
These golden times (too fortunate to hold)
Were quickly sin'd away for love of gold.
'T was then among the bushes, not the street,
If one in place did an inferior meet,
"Good-morrow, brother, is there aught you want?
Take freely of me, what I have you ha'nt."
Plain TOM and DICK would pass as current now,
As ever since, "Your servant, Sir," and bow.
Deep-skirted doublets, puritanick capes,
Which now would render men like upright apes,
Were comelier wear, our wiser fathers thought,
Than the last fashions from all Europe brought.
'T was in those dayes an honest grace would hold
Till an hot pudding grew at heart a cold,
And men had better stomachs at religion,
Than I to capon, turkey-cock, or pigeon;
When honest sisters met to pray, not prate,
About their own and not their neighbour's state.
During Plain Dealing's reign, that worthy stud
Of the ancient planters' race before the flood,
Then times were good, merchants cared not a rush
For other fare than jonakin and mush.
Although men fared and lodged very hard,
Yet innocence was better than a guard.
'T was long before spiders and worms had drawn
Their dingy webs, or hid with cheating lawne
New England's beautys, which still seem'd to me
Illustrious in their own simplicity.
'T was ere the neighboring Virgin-Land had broke
The hogsheads of her worse than hellish smoak.
'T was ere the Islands sent their presents in,
Which but to use was counted next to sin.
'T was ere a barge had made so rich a fraight
As chocolate, dust-gold, and bitts of eight;
Ere wines from France, and Muscovadoe too,
Without the which the drink will scarsely doe:
From western isles ere fruits and delicasies
Did rot maids' teeth and spoil their handsome faces.
Or ere these times did chance, the noise of war
Was from our towns and hearts removed far.
No bugbear comets in the chrystal air
Did drive our Christian planters to despair.
No sooner pagan malice peeped forth
But valour snib'd it. Then were men of worth,
Who by their prayers slew thousands; angel-like,
Their weapons are unseen with which they strike.
Then had the churches rest; as yet the coales
Were covered up in most contentious souls:
Freeness in judgment, union in affection,
Dear love, sound truth, they were our grand protection.
Then were the times in which our councells sate
These gave prognosticks of our future fate.
If these be longer liv'd our hopes increase,
These warrs will usher in a longer peace.—
But if New England's love die in its youth,
The grave will open next for blessed truth.
This theame is out of date, the peacefull hours
When castles needed not, but pleasant bowers.
Not ink, but bloud and tears now serve the turn
To draw the figure of New England's urne.
New England's hour of passion is at hand;
No power except divine can it withstand.
Scarce hath her glass of fifty years run out,
But her old prosperous steeds turn heads about,
Tracking themselves back to their poor beginnings,
To fear and fare upon their fruits of sinnings.
So that the mirror of the Christian world
Lyes burnt to heaps in part, her streamers furl'd.
Grief sighs, joyes flee, and dismal fears surprize
Not dastard spirits only, but the wise.
Thus have the fairest hopes deceiv'd the eye
Of the big-swoln expectant standing by:
Thus the proud ship after a little turn,
Sinks into NEPTUNE's arms to find its urne;
Thus hath the heir to many thousands born
Been in an instant from the mother torn:
Even thus thine infant cheeks begin to pale,
And thy supporters through great losses fail.
This is the *Prologue* to thy future woe,
The *Epilogue* no mortal yet can know."

THOMSON died in April, 1714, aged 74. He wrote besides his "great epic," three shorter poems, neither of which have much merit.

ROGER WILLIAMS, whose best verses appear in his book on the Indian languages, NATHANIEL PITCHER, and many others were in this period known as poets. The death of PITCHER was cecelebrated in some verses entitled "Pitchero Threnodia," in which he was compared to PINDAR, HORACE, and other poets of antiquity.

The most remarkable character of his age in this country was the Reverend COTTON MATHER, D.D. and F.R.S., who was born in Boston on the nieth of February, 1662. When twelve years of age he was qualified for admission to the college at Cambridge; at sixteen composed systems of logic and physics; and on receiving his master's degree, chose for his thesis "Puncta Hebraica sunt originis divinæ." The president, in his Latin oration, at commencement, said, "MATHER is named *Cotton* MATHER. What a name! but I am wrong: I should have said, what *names!* I shall say nothing of his reverend father, since I dare not praise him to his face; but should he represent and resemble his venerable grandfathers, JOHN COTTON and RICHARD MATHER,* in piety, learning, and elegance of mind, solid judgment, prudence, and wisdom, he will bear away the palm; and I trust that in him COTTON and MATHER will be united and flourish again." In his eighteenth year he was invited to become a colleague of his father in the ministry of the "North Church," but declined the place for three years. In 1684 he was married, and from this period devoted himself with untiring assiduity to professional and literary duties. During the last days of the disgraceful administration of Sir EDMUND ANDROS he took an active part in politics, and twice by his eloquence and wisely temperate counsels saved the city from riot and revolution. In 1692 he was unfortunately conspicuous in the terrible scenes connected with the witchcraft superstition, and he has been unjustly ridiculed and condemned for the credulity and cruelty he then manifested. But he was no more credulous or cruel than under similar circumstances were Sir MATTHEW HALE, and many others, whose intellectual greatness and moral excellence are unquestioned; and in an age when tens of thousands believe in the puerile, ridiculous, and contemptible stuff called "spiritualism," the silliest and most disgusting delusion that ever illustrated the weakness of the human understanding, it certainly should not be a cause of surprise that the strange phenomena which he undoubtedly witnessed led MATHER into the far more respectable as well as time-honored error of a visible and punishable complicity of men and women with devils. In the reaction of the popular excitement an attempt was made to show that he was responsible for the excesses which had tarnished the fame of the colony; but a candid examination of the subject will lead to a different conclusion; participating, as it must be confessed he did, in the melancholy infatuation, he yet counselled caution and moderation, and evinced a willingness to sacrifice his convictions as to demoniacal interference rather than hazard the lives of any of the accused.

Although his mind was not of the first order for clearness and solidity, he was nevertheless a man of genius, and of extraordinary erudition, facility in literary execution, and perseverance. He wrote readily in seven languages, and was the author of three hundred and eighty-three separate publications, besides unpublished manuscripts sufficient for half a dozen folio volumes. The "Magnalia," "Christian Philosopher," "Essays to do Good," "Wonders of the Invisible World," and many more, however disfigured by those striking faults of style which at the time were a prevailing fashion, contain passages of eloquence not less attractive than peculiar. With all their pedantry, their anagrams, puns, and grotesque conceits, they are thoughtful and earnest, and abound in original and shrewd observations of human nature, religious obligation, and providence.

In 1718 Doctor MATHER published "Psalterum Americanum: the Book of Psalms, in a Translation exactly conformed to the Original, but all in Blank Verse, fitted unto the Tunes commonly used in our Churches: Which pure Offering is accompanied with Illustrations, digging for hidden Treasures in it, and Rules to employ it upon the glorious Intentions of it." Other poetical "composures" are scattered through nearly all his works, and they are generally as harsh and turgid as the worst verses of his contemporaries. The following lines from his "Remarks on the Bright and the Dark Side of that American Pillar, the Reverend Mr. WILLIAM THOMSON," are characteristic:

"APOLLYON, owing him a cursed spleen
Who an APOLLOS in the church had been—
Dreading his traffic here would be undone
By numerous proselytes he daily won—
Accused him of imaginary faults,
And pushed him down, so, into dismal vaults—
Vaults, where he kept long ember-weeks of grief,
Till Heaven, alarméd, sent him a relief.
Then was a DANIEL in the lion's den,
A man, oh, how beloved of GOD and men!
By his bedside an Hebrew sword there lay,
With which at last he drove the devil away.
Quakers, too, durst not bear his keen replies,
But fearing it, half drawn, the trembler flies.
Like LAZARUS, new-raised from death, appears
The saint that had been dead for many years.
Our NEHEMIAH said, 'Shall such as I
Desert my flock, and like a coward fly!'
Long had the churches begg'd the saint's release;
Released at last, he dies in glorious peace.
The night is not so long, but Phosphor's ray
Approaching glories doth on high display.
Faith's eye in him discerned the morning star,
His heart leap'd: sure the sun cannot be far.
In ecstacies of joy, he ravish'd cries,
'Love, love the LAMB, the LAMB!' in whom he dies."

There are however glimpses of nature even in the poems of COTTON MATHER. After having mentioned the sad fate of the Lady ARBELLA JOHNSON, whose religious ardor brought her to America, and who sunk under the fatigues and privations of exile, he adds, with touching pathos: "And for her virtuous husband, ISAAC JOHNSON,

"he tried
To live without her—liked it not—and died!"

COTTON MATHER himself died on the thirteenth of February, 1724, in the sixty-fifth year of his age.

ROGER WOLCOTT, a major-general at the capture of Louisburg, and afterward governor of Connecticut, published a volume of verses at New London, in 1725. His principal work is "A Brief Account of the Agency of the Honorable

* An epitaph upon RICHARD MATHER runs thus:
"Under this stone lies RICHARD MATHER,
Who had a son, greater than his father,
And eke a *grandson* greater than either."

JOHN WINTHROP, Esquire, in the Court of King CHARLES the Second, Anno Domini 1662, when he obtained a Charter for the Colony of Connecticut." In this he describes a miracle by one of WINTHROP'S company, on the return voyage.

"The winds awhile
Are courteous, and conduct them on their way,
To near the midst of the Atlantic sea,
When suddenly their pleasant gales they change
For dismal storms that o'er the ocean range.
For faithless ÆOLUS, meditating harms,
Breaks up the peace, and priding much in arms,
Unbars the great artillery of heaven,
And at the fatal signal by him given,
The cloudy chariots threatening take the plains:
Drawn by wing'd steeds hard pressing on their reins.
These vast battalions, in dire aspect raised,
Start from the barriers — night with lightning blazed,
Whilst clashing wheels, resounding thunders crack,
Strike mortals deaf, and heavens astonished shake.
"Here the ship captain, in the midnight watch,
Stamps on the deck, and thunders up the hatch,
And to the mariners aloud he cries,
'Now all from safe recumbency arise!
All hands aloft, and stand well to your tack,
Engendering storms have clothed the sky with black,
Big tempests threaten to undo the world:
Down topsail, let the mainsail soon be furled:
Haste to the foresail, there take up a reef:
'Tis time boys, now if ever, to be brief;
Aloof for life; let's try to stem the tide,
The ship's much water, thus we may not ride:
Stand roomer then, let's run before the sea,
That so the ship may feel her steerage way:
Steady at the helm!' Swiftly along she scuds
Before the wind, and cuts the foaming suds.
Sometimes aloft she lifts her prow so high,
As if she'd run her bowsprit through the sky;
Then from the summit ebbs and hurries down,
As if her way were to the centre shown.
"Meanwhile our founders in the cabin sat,
Reflecting on their true and sad estate;
Whilst holy WARHAM'S sacred lips did treat
About GOD'S promises and mercies great.
"Still more gigantic births spring from the clouds,
Which tore the tattered canvass from the shrouds,
And dreadful balls of lightning fill the air,
Shot from the hand of the great THUNDERER.
"And now a mighty sea the ship o'ertakes,
Which falling on the deck, the bulk-head breaks;
The sailors cling to ropes, and frightened cry,
'The ship is foundered, we die! we die!'
"Those in the cabin heard the sailors screech;
All rise, and reverend WARHAM do beseech,
That he would now lift up to heaven a cry
For preservation in extremity.
He with a faith sure bottom'd on the word
Of Him that is of sea and winds the LORD,
His eyes lifts up to heaven, his hands extends,
And fervent prayers for deliverance sends.
The winds abate, the threatening waves appease,
And a sweet calm sits regent on the seas.
They bless the name of their deliverer,
Whom now they found a GOD that heareth prayer.
"Still further westward on they keep their way,
Ploughing the pavement of the briny sea,
Till the vast ocean they had overpast,
And in Connecticut their anchors cast."

In a speech to the king, descriptive of the valley of the Connecticut, WINTHROP says —

"The grassy banks are like a verdant bed,
With choicest flowers all enamelled,
O'er which the winged choristers do fly,
And wound the air with wondrous melody.
Here Philomel, high perched upon a thorn,
Sings cheerful hymns to the approaching morn.
The song once set, each bird tunes up his lyre,
Responding heavenly music through the quire. . . .
"Each plain is bounded at its utmost edge
With a long chain of mountains in a ridge,
Whose azure tops advance themselves so high,
They seem like pendants hanging in the sky."

In an account of King PHILIP'S wars, he tells how the soldier —

"met his amorous dame,
Whose eye had often set his heart in flame.
Urged with the motives of her love and fear,
She runs and clasps her arms about her dear,
Where, weeping on his bosom as she lies,
And languishing, on him she sets her eyes,
Till those bright lamps do with her life expire,
And leave him welt'ring in a double fire."

In the next page he paints the rising of the sun —

"By this AURORA doth with gold adorn
The ever-beauteous eyelids of the morn;
And burning TITAN his exhaustless rays
Bright in the eastern horizon displays;
Then, soon appearing in majestic awe,
Makes all the starry deities withdraw —
Vailing their faces in deep reverence,
Before the throne of his magnificence."

WOLCOTT retired from public life, after having held many honorable offices, in 1755, and died in May, 1767, in the eighty-ninth year of his age.

The next American verse-writer of much reputation was the Reverend MICHAEL WIGGLESWORTH, (1631, 1707.) He was graduated at Harvard College soon after entering upon his twentieth year, became a minister, and when rendered unable to preach, by an affection of the lungs, amused himself with writing pious poems. One of his volumes is entitled "Meat out of the Eater, or Meditations concerning the necessity and Usefulness of Affliction unto God's Children, all tending to prepare them for, and comfort them under, the Cross." His most celebrated performance, "The Day of Doom, or a Poetical Description of the Great and Last Judgment, with a short Discourse about Eternity," passed through six editions in this country, and was reprinted in London. A few verses will show its quality —

"Still was the night, serene and bright,
When all men sleeping lay;
Calm was the season, and carnal reason
Thought so 't would last for aye.
'Soul, take thine ease, let sorrow cease,
Much good thou hast in store:'
This was their song, their cups among,
The evening before."

After the "sheep" have received their reward, the several classes of "goats" are arraigned before the judgment-seat, and, in turn, begin to excuse themselves. When the infants object to damnation on the ground that

"Adam is set free
And saved from his trespass,
Whose sinful fall hath spilt them all,
And brought them to this pass," —

the Puritan theologist does not sustain his doctrine very well, nor quite to his own satisfaction even: and the judge, admitting the palliating circumstances, decides that although

"In bliss
They may not hope to dwell,
Still unto them He will allow
The easiest room in hell."

At length the general sentence is pronounced, and the condemned begin to

"wring their hands, their caitiff-hands,
And gnash their teeth for terror;
They cry, they roar, for anguish sore,
And gnaw their tongues for horror.
But get away, without delay,
CHRIST pities not your cry:
Depart to hell, there may ye yell,
And roar eternally."

The Reverend BENJAMIN COLMAN, D.D., "married in succession three widows, and wrote three poems;" but though his diction was more elegant than that of most of his contemporaries, he had less originality. His only daughter, Mrs. JANE TURELL, wrote verses which were much praised by the critics of her time.

The "Poems, on several Occasions, Original and Translated, by the late Reverend and Learned JOHN ADAMS, M.A.," were published in Boston in 1745, four years after the author's death. The volume contains paraphrases of the Psalms, the Book of Revelation in heroic verse, translations from HORACE, and several original compositions, of which the longest is a "Poem on Society," in three cantos. The following picture of parental tenderness is from the first canto:

"The parent, warm with nature's tender fire,
Does in the child his second self admire;
The fondling mother views the springing charms
Of the young infant smiling in her arms,
And when imperfect accents show the dawn
Of rising reason, and the future man,
Sweetly she hears what fondly he returns,
And by this fuel her affection burns.
But when succeeding years have fixed his growth,
And sense and judgment crown the ripened youth,
A social joy thence takes its happy rise,
And friendship adds its force to nature's ties."

The conclusion of the second canto is a description of love—

"But now the Muse in softer measure flows,
And gayer scenes and fairer landscapes shows:
The reign of Fancy, when the sliding hours
Are past with lovely nymphs in woven bowers,
Where cooly shades, and lawns forever green,
And streams, and warbling birds, adorn the scene;
Where smiles and graces, and the wanton train
Of Cytherea, crown the flowery plain.
What can their charms in equal numbers tell—
The glow of roses, and the lily pale;
The waving ringlets of the flowing hair;
The snowy bosom, and the killing air;
Their sable brows in beauteous arches bent;
The darts which from their vivid eyes are sent,
And, fixing in our easy-wounded hearts,
Can never be removed by all our arts.
'T is then with love, and love alone possest—
Our reason fled, that passion claims our breast.
How many evils then will fancy form!
A frown will gather, and discharge a storm;
Her smile more soft and cooling breezes brings
Than zephyrs fanning with their silken wings.
But love, where madness reason does subdue,
E'en angels, were they here, might well pursue.
Lovely the sex, and moving are their charms,
But why should passion sink us to their arms?
Why should the female to a goddess turn,
And flames of love to flames of incense burn?
Either by fancy fired, or fed by lies,
Be all distraction, or all artifice?
True love does flattery as much disdain
As, of its own perfections, to be vain.
The heart can feel whate'er the lips reveal,
Nor syren's smiles the destined death conceal.
Love is a noble and a generous fire;
Esteem and virtue feed the just desire;
Where honour leads the way it ever moves,
And ne'er from breast to breast, inconstant, roves.
Harbour'd by one, and only harbour'd there,
It likes, but ne'er can love, another fair.
Fix'd upon one supreme, and her alone,
Our heart is, of the fair, the constant throne.
Nor will her absence, or her cold neglect,
At once, expel her from our just respect:
Inflamed by virtue, love will not expire,
Unless contempt or hatred quench the fire."

ADAMS died on the twenty-second of January, 1740. The following letter from a correspondent at Cambridge, which shows the estimation in which he was held by his contemporaries, is copied from the "Boston Weekly Newsletter,"* printed the day after his interment:

"Last Wednesday morning expired, in this place, in the thirty-sixth year of his age, and this day was interred, with a just solemnity and respect, the reverend and learned JOHN ADAMS, M.A., only son of the Honourable JOHN ADAMS, Esquire. The corpse was carried and placed in the center of the college hall, from whence, after a portion of Holy Scripture, and a prayer very suitable to the occasion, by the learned head of that society, it was taken and deposited within sight of the place of his own education. The pall was supported by the fellows of the college, the professor of mathematics, and another master of arts And, next to a number of sorrowful relatives, the remains of this great man were followed by his honour the lieutenant-governor, with some of his majesty's council and justices; who, with the reverend the president, the professor of divinity, and several gentlemen of distinction from this and the neighbouring towns, together with all the members and students of the college, composed the train that attended in an orderly procession, to the place that had been appointed for his mournful interment. The character of this excellent person is too great to be comprised within the limits of a paper of intelligence. It deserves to be engraven in letters of gold on a monument of marble, or rather to appear and shine forth from the works of some genius, of an uncommon sublimity, and equal to his own. But sufficient to perpetuate his memory to the latest posterity, are the immortal writings and composures of this departed gentleman; who, for his genius, his learning, and his piety, ought to be enrolled in the highest class in the catalogue of Fame."

In the Middle Colonies literature was cultivated as industriously as in New England, and generally in a more liberal spirit, though Quakerism, when its ascendancy was absolute, was much more intolerant than Puritanism, as may be learned from the interesting history of WILLIAM BRADFORD, the first printer in Pennsylvania. The founder of the colony, indeed, had been unwilling to have a printing-press set up in Philadelphia, and was perhaps delighted when BRADFORD was driven away.

The earliest attempt at poetry in the region drained by the Delaware, was probably "A True Relation of the Flourishing State of Pennsylvania," by JOHN HOLME, of Holmesburg, first pub-

* This was the first newspaper published in America. The first number was issued the twenty-fourth of April, 1704, and the first sheet printed was taken damp from the press by Chief Justice SEWEL, to exhibit as a curiosity to President WILLARD, of Harvard University. The "News letter" was continued seventy-two years

lished, from the original manuscript in my possession, by the Pennsylvania Historical Society, in 1848. It is exceedingly curious. The author says:

"I have often travelled up and down,
And made my observations on each town;
The truth of matters I well understand,
And thereby know how to describe this land;"

and after nearly a thousand lines in this style gives us the following pleasant picture of the state of the country:

"Poor people here stand not in fear
The nuptial knot to tie;
The working hand in this good land
Can never want supply.

"If children dear increase each year
So do our crops likewise,
Of stock and trade such gain is made
That none do want supplies.

"Whoe'er thou art, take in good part
These lines which I have penned;
It is true love which me doth move
Them unto thee to send.

"Some false reports hinder resorts
Of those who would come here;
Therefore, in love, I could remove
That which puts them in fear.

"Here many say they bless the day
That they did see PENN's wood;
To cross the ocean back home again
They do not think it good.

"But here they 'll bide and safely bide
Whilst Europe broils in war;
The fruit of the curse, which may prove worse
Than hath been yet, by far.

"For why should we, who quiet be,
Return into the noise
Of fighting men, which now and then
Great multitudes destroys?

"I bid farewell to all who dwell
In England or elsewhere,
Wishing good speed when they indeed
Set forward to come here."

About the year 1695 Mr. HENRY BROOKE, a son of Sir HENRY BROOKE, of York, was appointed to a place in the customs, at Lewiston, in Delaware, and for many years was much in the best society of Philadelphia. One of his poetical pieces is a "Discourse concerning Jests," addressed to ROBERT GRACIE, whom FRANKLIN describes as a young man of fortune — generous, animated, and witty — fond of epigrams, and more fond of his friends. A specimen is here quoted:

"I prithee, BOB, forbear, or if thou must
Be talking still, yet talk not as thou do'st:
Be silent or speak well; and oh, detest
That darling bosom sin of thine, a jest.
Believe me, 't is a fond pretence to wit,
To say what's forced, unnatural, unfit,
Frigid, ill-timed, absurd, rude, petulant —
''T is so,' you say, 'all this I freely grant;'
Yet such were those smart turns of conversation,
When late our Kentish friends, in awkward fashion,
Grinned out their joy, and I my indignation.
Oh, how I hate that time! all, all that feast,
When, fools or mad, we scoured the city last!
All the false humour of our giddy club,
The tread, the watch, the windows, door, or tub. . . . .
These, though my hate — and these GOD knows I hate
Much more than JONES or STORY do debate
More than all shapes of action, corporation,
Remonstrances, a Whig or Tory nation,
Reviews, or churches, in or out of fashion,
The BRADBURYS, DINTONS, RIDPATHS, 'Observators,'
Or true-born DANIELS, unpoetic satyrs, —
From wine's enchanting power have some excuse;
But for a man in 's wits, unpoisoned with the juice,
To indulge so wilfully in empty prate,
And sell rich time at such an under-rate,
This hath no show nor colour of defence,
And wants so much of wit, it fails of common sense."

The entire performance is in the same respectable style. It is possible that one of the "Kentish friends" referred to was the author of "The Invention of Letters," of whom some account will be given on another page. That the excellences of BROOKE were appreciated by his literary associates is evident from a passage in a satire entitled "The Wits and Poets of Pennsylvania," —

"In BROOKE's capacious heart the muses sit,
Enrobed with sense polite and poignant wit."

When FRANKLIN arrived in Philadelphia, in 1723, there were several persons in the city distinguished for talents and learning. ANDREW HAMILTON, the celebrated lawyer, and JAMES LOGAN, whose translation of CICERO's "Cato Major" is the most elegant specimen we have of FRANKLIN's printing, were now old men; but THOMAS GODFREY, the inventor of the quadrant, JOHN BARTRAM, who won from LINNÆUS the praise of being the "greatest natural botanist in the world," and JOHN MORGAN, afterward a member of the Royal Society, were just coming forward; and there were a large number of persons, for so small a town, who wrote clever verses and prose essays. GEORGE WEBB, an Oxford scholar working in the printing office of KEIMER, whose eccentric history is given in FRANKLIN's Memoirs, was as confident as any succeeding Philadelphia writer of the destined supremacy of the city, and in a poem published in 1727 gives this expression to his sanguine anticipations:

"'T is here APOLLO does erect his throne:
This his Parnassus, this his Helicon:
Here solid sense does every bosom warm —
Here noise and nonsense have forgot to charm.
Thy seers, how cautious! and how gravely wise
Thy hopeful youth in emulation rise,
Who, if the wishing muse inspired does sing,
Shall liberal arts to such perfection bring,
Europe shall mourn her ancient fame declined,
And Philadelphia be the Athens of mankind."

In the same production he implores the goddess of numbers so to aid him that he may sing the attractions of his theme in verses

"Such as from BRIENTNALL's pen were wont to flow,
Or more judicious TAYLOR's used to show."

FRANKLIN describes BRIENTNALL as "a great lover of poetry, reading every thing that come in his way, and writing tolerably well; ingenious in many little trifles, and of an agreeable conversation." JACOB TAYLOR, schoolmaster, physician, surveyor, almanac-maker, and poet,

"With years oppressed, and compassed with woes,"

gave to the public the last and best of his works, "Pennsylvania," a descriptive poem, in 1728. In the same year THOMAS MAKIN, who nearly half a century before had been an usher in the school kept by the famous GEORGE KEITH, dedicated to JAMES LOGAN a Latin poem called "Encomium Pennsylvaniæ," and in the year following another, "In laudes Pennsylvaniæ," of both of which PROUD, the historian, gives specimens and translations.

Among FRANKLIN'S more intimate associates, was JAMES RALPH, a young printer, characterized by him as "ingenious, genteel in his manners, and extremely eloquent." He had been a schoolmaster in Maryland, and a clerk in Philadelphia, and now had such confidence in his literary abilities that he was disposed to abandon the pursuit of printing entirely for that of authorship. CHARLES OSBORNE, another acquaintance, endeavoured to dissuade him from attempting a literary life, assuring him that his capacities were better suited for his trade; but it was in vain, and FRANKLIN soon after assisted in a little scheme of deception, the result of which confirmed him in all the suggestions of his vanity. FRANKLIN, RALPH, OSBORNE, and JOSEPH WATSON, agreed to write verses for each other's criticism, as a means of mutual improvement; and as FRANKLIN had no inclination for the business, he was persuaded to offer as his own a piece by RALPH, who believed that OSBORNE had depreciated his talents from personal envy. The stratagem succeeded; the production was warmly applauded by OSBORNE, and RALPH enjoyed his triumph. RALPH accompanied FRANKLIN to England, and was very badly treated by him there, as FRANKLIN admits. He became a prolific author, in prose and verse. His longest poem, "Zeuma, or the Love of Liberty," was partly written in Philadelphia, and was first published in London, in 1729. A few lines from it will sufficiently display his capacities in this way:

"Tlascala's vaunt, great ZAOMAR'S martial son,
Extended on the rack, no more complains
That realms are wanting to employ his sword;
But, circled with innumerable ghosts,
Who print their keenest vengeance on his soul,
For all the wrongs, and slaughters of his reign,
Howls out repentance to the deafen'd skies,
And shakes hell's concave with continual groans."

In the following fifteen years he wrote several plays, some of which were acted at Drury Lane. Among his shorter poems were two called "Cynthia" and "Night," and a satire in which he abused POPE, SWIFT, and GAY. This procured him the distinction of a notice in "The Dunciad,"—

"Silence, ye wolves! while RALPH to 'Cynthia' howls,
And makes 'Night' hideous: answer him, ye owls!"

His book on "The Use and Abuse of Parliaments" was much talked of, and his "History of England during this Reign of William the Third" is praised by HALLAM as "accurate and faithful," and led FOX to refer to him as "a historian of great acuteness and diligence." His last work was "The Case of Authors stated, with regard to Booksellers, the Stage, and the Public." He died on the twenty-fourth of January, 1762.

The poems written by FRANKLIN himself are not very poetical. The best of them is the amusing little piece entitled

"PAPER.

"SOME wit of old—such wits of old there were—
Whose hints showed meaning, whose allusions care,
By one brave stroke to mark all human kind,
Called clear blank paper every infant mind,
Where still, as opening sense her dictates wrote,
Fair virtue put a seal, or vice a blot.

"The thought was happy, pertinent, and true;
Methinks a genius might the plan pursue.
I—can you pardon my presumption?—I,
No wit, no genius, yet for once will try.

"Various the papers various wants produce—
The wants of fashion, elegance, and use;
Men are as various; and, if right I scan,
Each sort of *paper* represents some *man*.

"Pray, note the fop—half powder and half lace—
Nice as a bandbox were his dwelling-place;
He 's the *gilt paper*, which apart you store,
And lock from vulgar hands in the scrutoire.

"Mechanics, servants, farmers, and so forth,
Are *copy paper*, of inferior worth;
Less prized, more useful, for your desk decreed,
Free to all pens, and prompt at every need.

"The wretch whom avarice bids to pinch and spare,
Starve, cheat, and pilfer, to enrich an heir,
Is coarse *brown paper;* such as pedlers choose
To wrap up wares, which better men will use.

"Take next the miser's contrast, who destroys
Health, fame and fortune, in a round of joys.
Will any paper match him? Yes, throughout,
He 's a true *sinking paper*, past all doubt.

"The retail politician's anxious thought
Deems *this* side always right, and *that* stark naught;
He foams with censure—with applause he raves—
A dupe to rumours, and a tool of knaves:
He 'll want no type his weakness to proclaim,
While such a thing as *fools-cap* has a name.

"The hasty gentleman whose blood runs high,
Who picks a quarrel, if you step awry,
Who can't a jest, or hint, or look endure:
What is he? What? *touch-paper* to be sure.

"What are the poets, take them as they fall,
Good, bad, rich, poor, much read, not read at all?
Them and their works in the same class you 'll find;
They are the mere *waste paper* of mankind.

"Observe the maiden, innocently sweet,
She 's fair *white paper*, an unsullied sheet;
On which the happy man, whom fate ordains,
May write his *name*, and take her for his pains.

"One instance more, and only one, I 'll bring;
'T is the *great man*, who scorns a little thing—
Whose thoughts, whose deeds, whose maxims are his own,
Formed on the feelings of his heart alone:
True, genuine *royal paper* is his breast;
Of all the kinds most precious, purest, best."

The "General Magazine," published by FRANKLIN, from January to June, in 1741, contained a few original and a much larger number of selected poems, most of the latter being from the "Virginia Gazette." The "American Magazine, and Monthly Chronicle for the British Colonies," established by WILLIAM BRADFORD, a nephew of the first printer west of Boston, and published for twelve months, was a periodical of far higher character than FRANKLIN'S, or indeed than any that had yet been attempted on the continent. In the preface the editor says of his contributors,

"Some are grave and serious, while others are gay and facetious; some have a turn for matters of state and government, while others are led to the study of commerce, agriculture, or the mechanic arts; some indulge themselves in the belles-lettres, and in productions of art and fancy, while others are wrapt up in speculation and wholly beset on the abstruser parts of philosophy and science." The principal poetical contributors to the "American Magazine" were an anonymous writer, of Kent, in Maryland, whose name I have not been able to discover, and JOSEPH SHIPPEN, THOMAS GODFREY, NATHANIEL EVANS, FRANCIS HOPKINSON, and JOHN BEVERIDGE, the professor of ancient languages in the Philadelphia college.

The anonymous writer here mentioned was the son of an officer distinguished in the military service, in Ireland, Spain, and Flanders. In early life he had been intimate with MR. POPE, upon whose death, in 1744, he wrote a pastoral, which makes between two and three hundred lines, besides numerous learned notes. Anticipating BISHOP BERKLEY's famous verses on the prospect of the arts in America, he says in his invocation:

"Pierian nymphs that haunt Sicilian plains,
And first inspired to sing in rural strains,
A western course has pleased you all along:
Greece, Rome, and Britain, flourish all in song.
Keep on your way, and spread a glorious fame;
Around the earth let all admire your name.
Chuse in our plains or forests soft retreats;
For here the muses boast no antient seats.
Here fertile fields, and fishy streams abound;
Nothing is wanting but poetic ground.
Bring me that pipe with which ALEXIS charm'd
The eastern world, and every bosom warm'd.
Our western climes shall henceforth own your power;
THETIS shall hear it from her wat'ry bower;
Even PHŒBUS listen as his chariot flies,
And smile propitious from his flaming skies.
"Haste, lovely nymphs! and quickly come away,
Our sylvan gods lament your long delay;
The stately oaks that dwell on Delaware,
Rear their tall heads to view you from afar;
The naiads summon all their scaly crew,
And at Henlopen anxious wait for you.
Haste, lovely nymphs! and quickly reach our shore;
Th' impatient river heeds his tides no more,
Forsakes his banks, and where he joins the main,
Heaps waves on waves to usher in your train.
"But hark! they come! the dryads crowd the shore,
The waters rise, I hear the billows roar!
Hoarse Delaware the joyful tidings brings,
And all his swans, transported, clap their wings.
Our mountains ring with all their savage host—
Thrice welcome, lovely nymphs, to India's coast!
Not more Parnassian rocks Phœbus admire,
Nor Thracian mountains ORPHEUS' tuneful lyre;
Not more sad lovers court the darkling note
Of Philomela's mournful warbling throat;
Not more the morning lark delights the swains,
Than you, sweet maids, our Pennsylvania plains!"

He had recommended to Mr. POPE the discovery of printing as a subject worthy of his genius, and when that poet died, without having made use of the suggestion, he wrote from the banks of the Delaware, in 1749, his own "Poem on the Invention of Letters," which is inscribed to Mr. RICHARDSON, "the author of 'Sir Charles Grandison,' and other works for the promotion of religion, virtue, and polite manners, in a corrupted age," whom he describes as "himself the Grandison he paints:"

"These lays, ye Great! to RICHARDSON belong;
His Art and Virtues have inspired the song.
Forgive the bard—who dares transfer, from you,
A tribute to superior merit due—
Who, midst war's tumults, in flagitious times,
And regions distant from maternal climes,
Industriously obscure, to heaven resign'd,
Salutes the friend and patron of mankind."

Colonel JOSEPH SHIPPEN, who in 1759 wrote "The Glooms of Ligonier," an amatory song much in vogue for a quarter of a century, was the author of the following early recognition of the genius of BENJAMIN WEST:*

"ON SEEING A PORTRAIT OF MISS —, BY MR. WEST.

"SINCE GUIDO's skilful hand, with mimic art,
Could form and animate so sweet a face,
Can nature still superior charms impart,
Or warmest fancy add a single grace?

"The enliven'd tints in due proportion rise,
Her polish'd cheeks with deep vermilion glow;
The shining moisture swells into her eyes,
And from such lips nectareous sweets must flow.

"The easy attitude, the graceful dress,
The soft expression of the perfect whole,
Both GUIDO's judgment and his skill confess,
Informing canvas with a living soul.

"How fixt, how steady, yet how bright a ray
Of modest lustre beams in every smile!
Such smiles as must resistless charms convey,
Enliven'd by a heart devoid of guile.

"Yet sure his flattering pencil's unsincere,
His fancy takes the place of bashful truth,
And warm imagination pictures here
The pride of beauty and the bloom of youth.

"Thus had I said, and thus, deluded, thought,
Had lovely STELLA still remained unseen,
Whose grace and beauty, to perfection brought,
Make every imitative art look mean."

THOMAS GODFREY, a son of the inventor of the quadrant, was esteemed a prodigy of youthful genius. He was a lieutenant in the expedition against Fort Du Quesne in 1759, and on the disbanding of the colonial forces went to New Providence, and afterward to North Carolina, where he died, on the third of August, 1763, in the twenty-seventh year of his age. His poems were published in Philadelphia in 1765, in a quarto volume of two hundred and thirty pages. His "Prince of Parthia" was the first tragedy written in America. "The Court of Fancy," which the editor of the "American Magazine" thought evinced "an elevated and daring genius," is in smooth but feeble heroic verse, and betrays very little inventive capacity. Some of his shorter poems are more striking. The following is from an "Ode to Wine:"

"Haste, ye mortals! leave your sorrow;
Let pleasure crown to-day—to-morrow,

* In the "American Magazine" for February, 1758, occurs, probably, the first paragraph ever printed in commendation of the genius of WEST. The editor says, introducing the above poem on one of his portraits:

"We are glad of this opportunity of making known to the world the name of so extraordinary a genius as Mr. WEST. He was born in Chester county in this province, and without the assistance of any master, has acquired such a delicacy and correctness of expression in his paintings, joined to such a laudable thirst of improvement, that we are persuaded, when he shall have obtained more experience and proper opportunities of viewing the productions of able masters, he will become truly eminent in his profession."

Yield to fate.
Join the universal chorus —
BACCHUS reigns, ever great —
BACCHUS reigns, ever glorious —
Hark! the joyful groves rebound,
Sporting breezes catch the sound,
And tell to hill and dale around,
BACCHUS reigns! while far away,
The busy echoes die away."

One of GODFREY'S most intimate friends was NATHANIEL EVANS, a native of Philadelphia, admitted to holy orders by the Bishop of London in 1765. He died in October, 1767, in the twenty-sixth year of his age, and his poems, few of which had been printed in his lifetime, were soon afterward by his direction collected and published under the editorial supervision of the Reverend WILLIAM SMITH, and Miss ELIZABETH GRÆME, subsequently so well known as Mrs. FERGUSON. EVANS was preparing a collection of his poems for the press, and had written part of the preface, in which, after having referred to the unhappy fortunes of many men of genius, he said: "Sometimes, alas! the iron hand of death cuts them suddenly off, as their beauties are just budding into existence, and leaves but the fair promise of future excellences." These were his last words; and Doctor SMITH suggests that they were so applicable to his case that he should have feared to publish them as from the mind of the deceased poet, if he had neglected to preserve the autograph to show that they had not been accommodated to that event. The most carefully finished of the pieces by EVANS is an "Ode on the Prospect of Peace," written in 1761, but several in a lighter vein were more pleasing. In the following, we have a glimpse of our great philosopher, in his middle age:

"TO BENJAMIN FRANKLIN, ESQ., LL.D.
"ON HEARING HIM PLAY ON THE HARMONICA.

"IN grateful wonder lost, long had we view'd
Each gen'rous act thy patriot-soul pursued;
Our little state resounds thy just applause,
And, pleased, from thee new fame and honour draws;
In thee those various virtues are combined,
That form the true preëminence of mind.
"What wonder struck us when we did survey
The lambent lightnings innocently play;
And down thy rods beheld the dreaded fire
In a swift flame descend —— and then expire;
While the red thunders, roaring loud around,
Burst the black clouds, and harmless smote the ground.
Blest use of art! applied to serve mankind —
The noble province of the sapient mind!
For this the soul's best faculties were given,
To trace great nature's laws from earth to heaven.
"Yet not these themes alone thy thoughts command;
Each softer science owns thy fostering hand;
Aided by thee, URANIA'S heavenly art
With finer raptures charms the feeling heart;
Th' *Harmonica* shall join the sacred choir,
Fresh transports kindle, and new joys inspire.
Hark! the soft warblings, sounding smooth and clear,
Strike with celestial ravishment the ear,
Conveying inward, as they sweetly roll,
A tide of melting music to the soul;
And sure if aught of mortal-moving strain,
Can touch with joy the high angelic train,
'Tis this enchanting instrument of thine,
Which speaks in accents more than half divine!"

Among some trifles inscribed to Miss GRÆME, who had rallied him on his indisposition to marry, was a new version of the story of

"ORPHEUS AND EURYDICE.

"ORPHEUS, of old, as poets tell,
Took a fantastic trip to hell,
To seek his wife, as wisely guessing
She must be there, since she was missing.
Downward he journeyed, wonderous gay,
And, like a lark, sang all the way.
The reason was — or they belied him,
His yoke-fellow was not beside him.
Whole grottoes, as he pass'd along,
Danced to the music of his song.
So I have seen, upon the plains,
A fiddler captivate the swains,
And make them caper to his strains.
To PLUTO'S court at last he came,
Where the god sat enthroned in flame,
And ask'd if his lost love was there —
EURYDICE, his darling fair?
The fiends, who listening round him stood,
At the odd question laugh'd aloud:
'This must some mortal madman be —
We fiends are happier far than he.'
But music's sounds o'er hell prevail;
Most mournfully he tells his tale,
Soothes with soft arts the monarch's pain,
And gets his bargain back again.
'Thy prayers are heard,' grim PLUTO cries,
'On this condition take thy prize:
Turn not thine eyes upon the fair —
If once thou turn'st, she flies in air.'
In amorous chat they climb th' ascent —
ORPHEUS, as order'd, foremost went;
(Though, when two lovers downwards steer,
The man, as fit, falls in the rear;)
Soon the fond fool turns back his head —
As soon, in air, his spouse was fled!
If 'twas designed, 'twas wonderous well;
But, if by chance, more lucky still.
Happy the man, all must agree,
Who once from wedlock's noose gets free;
But he who from it twice is freed
Has most prodigious luck indeed!"

A portrait of EVANS, by his young friend WEST, is preserved in Philadelphia. Among the subscribers for his volume of poems, was Dr. GOLDSMITH, with whom he had probably become acquainted while visiting London for ordination.

The celebrated wit, lawyer, and statesman, FRANCIS HOPKINSON, born in 1737, made his first appearance as a poet in BRADFORD'S "American Magazine," one of his earlier contributions to which was a tribute to the genius of WOLLASTON,* the painter, then living in Philadelphia, from which the following is an extract:

"To you, famed WOLLASTON, these strains belong,
And be your praise the subject of my song
When your soft pencil bids the canvas shine
With mimic life, with elegance divine,
The enraptured muse, fond to partake thy fire,
With equal sweetness strives to sweep the lyre,
With equal justice fain would paint your praise,
And by your name immortalize her lays.
"Ofttimes with wonder and delight I stand
To view the amazing conduct of your hand.
At first unlabored sketches lightly trace
The glimmering outlines of a human face,
Then, by degrees, the liquid life o'erflows
Each rising feature — the rich canvas glows
With heightened charms — the forehead rises fair —
In glossy ringlets twines the nut brown hair,

* WOLLASTON is honorably mentioned in HORACE WALPOLE'S "Anecdotes." The finest of his known American portraits is that of MARTHA DANDRIDGE, afterward the wife of WASHINGTON.

And sparkling eyes give meaning to the whole,
And seem to speak the dictates of the soul.....
Thus the gay flowers, that paint the embroidered plain,
By rising steps their glowing beauties gain.
No leaves at first their burning glories show,
But wrapt in simple forms, unnoticed grow,
Till, ripened by the sun's meridian ray,
They spread perfection to the blaze of day.
"Nor let the muse forget thy name, O, WEST!
Loved youth, by virtue, as by nature blest.
If such the radiance of thy early morn,
What bright effulgence must thy noon adorn!
Hail, sacred genius! mayst thou ever tread
The pleasing paths your WOLLASTON has led;
Let his just precepts all your works refine,
Copy each grace, and learn like him to shine.
So shall some future muse her sweeter lays
Swell with your name, and give you all *his* praise!"

This poem is not reprinted in the collection of HOPKINSON'S Works, published in Philadelphia in 1793. His "Battle of the Kegs," a satirical ballad, is the most celebrated of his productions; and several pieces of humorous prose, written by him before the revolution, are among the familiar and popular examples of early American literature.

JOHN BEVERIDGE, the author of numerous Latin poems in the "American Magazine" and other miscellanies of that period, was a native of Scotland, and had studied under "the great RUDDIMAN" in Edinburgh. He emigrated in 1752 to New England, where he remained five years, and became intimate with Doctor JONATHAN MATHEW and other scholars. In 1757 he proceeded to Philadelphia, and was appointed professor of languages in the college there. An entertaining account of him is given in Captain ALEXANDER GRAYDON'S admirably written "Memoirs of a Life passed chiefly in Pennsylvania." In 1765 he published by subscription his volume entitled "Epistolæ Familiares et alia quædam Miscellanea," several of which were translated by ALEXANDER ALEXANDER, who prefixes some verses "on Mr. BEVERIDGE'S poetical performances," wherein he says —

"If music sweet delight your ravished ear,
No music's sweeter than the numbers here.
In former times famed MARO smoothly sung,
But still he warbled in his native tongue,
His towering thoughts and soft enchanting lays
Long since have crowned him with enduring bays,
But ne'er did MARO such high glory seek
As to excel MÆONIDES in Greek.
Here you may view a bard of modern time,
Who claims fair Scotland as his native clime,
Contend with FLACCUS on the Roman lyre,
His humor catch, and glow with kindred fire."

While in Boston BEVERIDGE addressed the following epistle to one of his friends in Scotland:

"AD REV. JACOB INNESIUM, V.D.M.

"Tædium longi maris et viarum,
Bella ventorum varias vicesque,
Et procellosi rabiem profundi,
Jam superavi.
"Atque tranquillus requiesco pace,
Lætus ad ripam viridantis amnis,
Tuta quà Casco sinuosus offert
Littora nautis;
"Gratior qua sol radiis refulget,
Aptior tellus avidis colonis,
Lenior gratis zephyri susurris
Murmurat aura.
"Dama fœcundis levis errat agris,
Piscium puris genus omne rivis,
Alites sylvis, aviumque turba
Plurima dumis.
"Æstuet vultu Boreas minaci,
Sæviat diris Aquilo procellis,
Eurus algentes glacialis imbres
Spiret ab ortu;
"Hic tamen vitæ liceat beatæ
Mî bonis uti, pariter saventis
Læta fortunæ, masa seu minantis
Ferre parato.
"Nam juvant sylvis operum labores,
Gratus et sudor fluit, atra bilis
Cura nec vanis animum querelis
Anxia turbat.
"Attamen torquet male nunc, amice,
Talus intortus: glacies sesellit
Lævis incautum, subitusque lapsu
Volvor iniquo.
"Cæterum vivunt reliqui valentque,
Omnibus ridet locus, atque ridet
Capium spondens inarata cornu
Terra benigno.
"Scire nunce hæc te volui. Tabellas
Mitteram longas; sed aquam bibenti
Scripta sunt ævi brevis, ut probavit
Carmine FLACCUS."*

JOHN OSBORN, son of a schoolmaster of Sandwich, in Massachusetts, who was born in 1713 and died in 1753, wrote a "Whaling Song," which was well known in the Pacific for more than half a century. While in college, in 1735, he addressed an elegiac epistle to one of his sisters, on the death of a member of the family, of which the following is a specimen:

* The following is a translation of the above Ode, by the Reverend Doctor JONATHAN MATHEW, of Boston:

"TO THE REVEREND MR. J. INNES, &c.

"I've now o'ercome the long fatigue
Of seas extended many a league,
The war of winds, their rage and sleep,
And all the madness of the deep;
Once more in joyous peace abide
Upon a river's verdant side,
Where *Casco's* shore, of winding form,
Invites the sailor from the storm;
Where shoots the sun a milder ray,
And scatters round the genial day:
Where a more kind and generous soil
Invites the eager lab'rer's toil;
Where murmuring zephyrs still I hear
And gentle breezes fan the air.
"Here the light deer still take their round,
And o'er the fruitful valleys bound;
Here purer streams alive I find,
With finny swarms of every kind;
The woods with feather'd life abound
Of every size, of every sound,
And airy music warbles round.
"With angry face, let Boreas storm,
Let northern blasts the heav'ns deform,
Let Eurus rage with all his power,
And headlong drive the snowy shower;
Yet I can here enjoy my rest,
A life with nature's bounty blest;
Alike prepared, if fortune lend
Precarious bliss, or evil send,
To live contented to the end.
"For in these groves, from morn to night,
Sweat grateful flows, and toils delight;
Black choler here no place can find,
Nor fruitless cares distract the mind.
"Yet, friend, my ancle by a sprain,
At present gives unwelcome pain:
Along incautious as I stray'd,
The slippery ice my heels betray'd,
And, while I dreamt no harm at all,
Gave me a base dishonest fall.
"Excepting this, all friends are well,
Charm'd with the country where we dwell;
And charm'd, while here the bounteous field
Spontaneous promises, untill'd,
With copious horn, its stores to yield.
"I thought it could not much displease
To tell a friend such things as these:
And should have writ a longer letter,
Only his verse, whose drink is water,
Can live but for a moment's time,
As *Horace* proved long since in rhyme."

"Dear sister, see the smiling spring
In all its beauties here;
The groves a thousand pleasures bring:
A thousand grateful scenes appear.
With tender leaves the trees are crown'd,
And scatter'd blossoms, all around,
Of various dyes
Salute your eyes,
And cover o'er the speckled ground.
Now thickets shade the glassy fountains,
Trees o'erhang the purling streams,
Whisp'ring breezes brush the mountains,
Grots are fill'd with balmy steams.
"But, sister, all the sweets that grace
The spring, and blooming nature's face—
The chirping birds,
Nor lowing herds;
The woody hills,
Nor murm'ring rills;
The sylvan shades,
Nor flowery meads,
To me their former joys dispense.
Though all their pleasures court my sense,
But melancholy damps my mind;
I lonely walk the field,
With inward sorrow fill'd,
And sigh to every breathing wind."

The facetious MATHER BYLES was in his time equally famous as a poet and wit. A contemporary bard exclaims—

"Would but APOLLO'S genial touch inspire
Such sounds as breathe from BYLES'S warbling lyre,
Then might my notes in melting measures flow,
And make all nature wear the signs of wo."

And his humor is celebrated in a poetical account of the clergy of Boston, copied by Mr. LORING in his "Hundred Orators of Boston:"

"There's punning BYLES, provokes our smiles,
A man of stately parts.
He visits folks to crack his jokes,
Which never mends their hearts.

"With strutting gait, and wig so great,
He walks along the streets;
And throws out wit, or what's like it,
To every one he meets."

BYLES was graduated at Cambridge in 1725, and ordained the first minister of the church in Hollis street, in 1732. He soon became eminent as a preacher, and King's College at Aberdeen conferred on him the degree of Doctor in Divinity. He was one of the authors of "A Collection of Poems by several Hands," which appeared in 1744, and of numerous essays and metrical compositions in "The New England Weekly Journal," the merit of which was such as to introduce him to the notice of POPE and other English scholars. One of his poems is entitled, "The Conflagration;" and it is "applied to that grand catastrophe of our world when the face of nature is to be changed by a deluge of fire." The following lines are from this effusion:

"Yet shall ye, flames, the wasting globe refine,
And bid the skies with purer splendor shine.
The earth, which the prolific fires consume,
To beauty burns, and withers into bloom;
Improving in the fertile flame it lies,
Fades into form, and into vigor dies:
Fresh-dawning glories blush amidst the blaze,
And nature all renews her flowery face.
With endless charms the everlasting year
Rolls round the seasons in a full career;
Spring, ever-blooming, bids the fields rejoice,
And warbling birds try their melodious voice;
Where'er she treads, lilies unbidden blow,
Quick tulips rise, and sudden roses glow:
Her pencil paints a thousand beauteous scenes,
Where blossoms bud amid immortal greens:
Each stream, in mazes, murmurs as it flows,
And floating forests gently bend their boughs.
Thou, autumn, too, sitt'st in the fragrant shade,
While the ripe fruits blush all around thy head:
And lavish nature, with luxuriant hands,
All the soft months in gay confusion blends."

BYLES was earnestly opposed to the revolution, and in the spring of 1777 was denounced in the public assemblies as a Tory, and compelled to give bonds for his appearance before a court for trial. In the following June he was convicted of treasonable conversation, and hostility to the country, and sentenced to be imprisoned forty days on board a guard-ship, and at the end of that period to be sent with his family to England. The board of war however took his case into consideration, and commuted the punishment to a short confinement under a guard in his own house; but, though he continued to reside in Boston during the remainder of his life he never again entered a pulpit, nor regained his ante-revolutionary popularity. He died in 1788, in the eighty-second year of his age.

He was a favorite in every social or convivial circle, and no one was more fond of his society than the colonial governor, BELCHER, on the death of whose wife he wrote an elegy ending with—

"Meantime my name to thine allied shall stand,
Still our warm friendship, mutual flames extend;
The muse shall so survive from age to age,
And BELCHER'S name protect his BYLES'S page."

The doctor had declined an invitation to visit with the governor the province of Maine, and BELCHER resorted to a stratagem to secure his company. Having persuaded him to drink tea with him on board the Scarborough ship of war, one Sunday afternoon, as soon as they were seated at the table the anchor was weighed, the sails set, and before the punning parson had called for his last cup, the ship was too far at sea for him to think of returning to the shore. As every thing necessary for his comfort had been thoughtfully provided, he was easily reconciled to the voyage. While making preparations for religious services, the next Sunday, it was discovered that there was no hymn-book on board, and he wrote the following lines, which were sung instead of a selection from STERNHOLD and HOPKINS—

"Great God, thy works our wonder raise;
To thee our swelling notes belong;
While skies and winds, and rocks and seas,
Around shall echo to our song.

"Thy power produced this mighty frame,
Aloud to thee the tempests roar,
Or softer breezes tune thy name
Gently along the shelly shore.

"Round thee the scaly nation roves,
Thy opening hands their joys bestow,
Through all the blushing coral groves,
These silent gay retreats below.

"See the broad sun forsake the skies,
Glow on the waves, and downward glide
Anon heaven opens all its eyes,
And star-beams tremble o'er the tide

"Each various scene, or day or night,
Lord! points to thee our nourish'd soul;
Thy glories fix our whole delight;
So the touch'd needle courts the pole.

Joseph Green, a merchant of Boston, who had been a classmate of Byles at Cambridge, was little less celebrated than the doctor for humour; and some of his poetical compositions were as popular a hundred years ago as more recently have been those of "Croaker & Co.," which they resemble in spirit and playful ease of versification. The abduction of the Hollis street minister was the cause of not a little merriment in Boston; and Green, between whom and Byles there was some rivalry, as the leaders of opposing social factions, soon after wrote a burlesque account of it:

"In David's Psalms an oversight
Byles found one morning at his tea,
Alas! that he should never write
A proper psalm to sing at sea.

"Thus ruminating on his seat,
Ambitious thoughts at length prevail'd
The bard determined to complete
The part wherein the prophet fail'd.

"He sat awhile, and stroked his Muse,*
Then taking up his tuneful pen,
Wrote a few stanzas for the use
Of his seafaring bretheren.

"The task perform'd, the bard content—
Well chosen was each flowing word—
On a short voyage himself he went,
To hear it read and sung on board.

"Most serious Christians do aver,
(Their credit sure we may rely on,)
In former times that after prayer,
They used to sing a song of Zion.

"Our modern parson having pray'd,
Unless loud fame our faith beguiles,
Sat down, took out his book and said,
"Let's sing a psalm of Mather Byles."

"At first, when he began to read,
Their heads the assembly downward hung,
But he with boldness did proceed,
And thus he read, and thus they sung.

"THE PSALM.

"With vast amazement we survey
The wonders of the deep,
Where mackerel swim, and porpoise play,
And crabs and lobsters creep.

"Fish of all kinds inhabit here,
And throng the dark abode.
Here haddock, hake, and flounders are,
And eels, and perch, and cod.

"From raging winds and tempests free,
So smoothly as we pass,
The shining surface seems to be
A piece of Bristol glass.

"But when the winds and tempests rise,
And foaming billows swell,
The vessel mounts above the skies
And lower sinks than hell.

"Our heads the tottering motion feel
And quickly we become
Giddy as new-dropp'd calves, and reel
Like Indians drunk with rum.

"What praises then are due that we
Thus far have safely got,
Amarescoggin tribe to see,
And tribe of Penobscot.

* Byles's favorite cat, so named by his friends.

In 1750 Green published "An Entertainment for a Winter Evening," in which he ridicules the freemasons; and afterward "The Sand Bank," "A True Account of the Celebration of St. John the Baptist," and several shorter pieces, all of which I believe were satirical. His epigrams are the best written in this country before the revolution; and many anecdotes are told to show the readiness of his wit and his skill as an improvisator. On one occasion, a country gentleman, knowing his reputation as a poet, procured an introduction to him, and solicited a "first-rate epitaph," for a favorite servant, who had lately died. Green asked what were the man's chief qualities, and was told that "Cole excelled in all things, but was particularly good at raking hay, which he could do faster than anybody, the present company, of course, excepted." Green wrote immediately:

"Here lies the body of John Cole,
His master loved him like his soul;
He could rake hay, none could rake faster
Except that raking dog, his master."

In his old age he left Boston for England, rather from the infirmities of age, than indifference to the cause of liberty.

The most remarkable book of poems printed in this country during the eighteenth century is the "*Pietas et Gratulatio Collegii Cantabrigiensis apud Novanglos*," (1761,) in which the president and fellows of Harvard College celebrated the death of George II. and the accession of his grandson. It was handsomely printed in a quarto of one hundred and six pages, and the copy in my possession, one of two that were sent to the king, is very richly bound, in red morocco, profusely gilt. Dr. Holyoke, who was then president of the college, and whose contribution, "*Adhortatio Præsidis*," which the "Monthly Review" for 1763 praises as truly Horatian, is the first piece in the collection, describes it in a letter to Thomas Hollis as "an attempt of several young gentlemen here with us, and educated in this college, to show their pious sorrow on account of the death of our late glorious king, their attachment to his royal house, the joy they have in the accession of his present majesty to the British throne, and in the prospect they have of the happiness of Britain from the royal progeny which they hope for from his alliance with the illustrious house of Mechlenburg." The "Critical Review" for October, 1763, expresses an opinion that "the verses from Harvard College already seem to bid fair for a rivalship with the productions of Cam and Isis." The prose introduction has been ascribed both to Governor Hutchinson and to Governor Francis Bernard, but was probably from the pen of the latter, who was a very accomplished scholar. Numbers ii. in Latin and xxv. in English were by John Lovell; iii. xii. xiv. and xxiii. in Latin, xv. and xvi. in Greek, and v. in English, by Stephen Sewell; vii. in English by John Lowell; x. in English by Samuel Deane; xi. by Doctor Benjamin Church; xiii. by Doctor Samuel Cooper; xviii. in Greek, xix. a Latin translation of it, xx. the same in English, and xxi. in Latin, by Governor Bernard; xxvi in Latin, and xxii., an English version of it, by Doctor JOHN WINTHROP; and xxix. by THOMAS OLIVER, afterwards lieutenant-governor. A writer in the "Monthly Anthology" for 1809 gives the authorship of these pieces from MS. notes in a copy which had been owned by Mr. SEWELL, and believes, from internal evidence, that xxviii., an English lyric, was by Doctor COOPER. Mr. KETTELL, says Governor JAMES BOWDOIN, was also a contributor.

The best English poem in the *Pietas et Gratulatio* is that of the celebrated Doctor BENJAMIN CHURCH. He was born in Boston in 1739, and graduated at Cambridge when in the sixteenth year of his age. After finishing his professional education, he established himself as a physician in his native city, and soon became eminent by his literary and political writings. At the commencement of the revolutionary troubles he was chosen a member of the Massachusetts legislature, and after the battle of Lexington was appointed surgeon-general of the army. In the autumn of 1775 he was suspected of treasonable correspondence with the enemy, arrested by order of the commander-in-chief, tried by the general court, and found guilty. By direction of the Congress, to whom the subject of his punishment was referred, he was confined in a prison in Connecticut; but after a few months, on account of the condition of his health, was set at liberty; and in the summer of 1776 embarked at Newport for the West Indies, in a ship which was never heard of after the day on which it sailed. The concluding lines of his address to GEORGE III., to which allusion has been made, are as follows:

"May one clear calm attend thee to thy close,
One lengthen'd sunshine of complete repose
Correct our crimes, and beam that Christian mind
O'er the wide wreck of desolate mankind;
To calm-brow'd Peace, the maddening world restore,
Or lash the demon thirsting still for gore;
Till nature's utmost bound thy arms restrain,
And prostrate tyrants bite the British chain."

CHURCH also wrote "The Times," "The Choice," and "Elegies on GEORGE WHITFIELD and Doctor MAYHEW." He was a man of various and decided talents, but his poetical writings possess only a moderate degree of excellence.

WILLIAM LIVINGSTON, a member of the first Congress, and the first republican governor of New Jersey, was born in New York in 1723, and graduated at Yale College in 1741. His "Philosophic Solitude, or the Choice of a Rural Life," written while he was a student, was first printed in 1747. It is in smoothly flowing verse, evinces a careful study of good models, and may be regarded as the most chaste and agreeable poem of considerable length produced in America before the close of the first half of the last century. Its prevailing tone is indicated in the opening lines:

"Let ardent heroes seek renown in arms,
Pant after fame, and rush to war's alarms;
To shining palaces let fools resort,
And dunces cringe to be esteem'd at court:
Mine be the pleasure of a rural life,
From noise remote, and ignorant of strife;
Far from the painted belle, and white-gloved beau,
The lawless masquerade, and midnight show,
From ladies, lap-dogs, courtiers, garters, stars,
Fops, fiddlers, tyrants, emperors, and czars."

Mr. LIVINGSTON was an able and manly writer on public affairs before the revolution and during the war, and continued in old age occasionally to indulge his early predilection for poetical composition. When more than sixty he addressed a poem, marked by generous feeling and good sense, to WASHINGTON, with whom he had maintained the most friendly relations. He died in 1790.

ROBERT BOLLING, of Buckingham county, Virginia, born in 1738, wrote with facility in Latin, Italian, and French, and some of his poetical pieces in these languages and in English have been printed. He left in manuscript two volumes of verses, which a writer in the "Columbian Magazine" for 1787 describes as "Horatian." His poems which have been submitted to the public hardly justify this praise.

Another southern poet of the same period was ROWLAND RUGELY. In June, 1782, while MATTHEW CAREY contemplated the publication of an extensive American Anthology, TRUMBULL, the author of "MacFingal," wrote to him: "RUGELY, of South Carolina, is a poet certainly better than EVANS. He published a volume of poems in London near twenty years ago, chiefly in the manner of PRIOR, many of which are well worth preserving; and since that a travestie of the fourth book of Virgil, which for delicacy and true humor is superior to COTTON'S." I have examined RUGELY'S volume published at Oxford in 1763, and cannot quite concur in Judge TRUMBULL'S estimate of its merits.

GULIAN VERPLANCK, of New York, after completing his education, travelled abroad, and while in England, in 1773, wrote the following prophetic lines on the destiny of this country:

"Hail, happy Britain, Freedom's blest retreat!
Great is thy power, thy wealth, thy glory great,
But wealth and power have no immortal day,
For all things ripen only to decay;
And when that time arrives—the lot of all—
When Britain's glory, power, and wealth shall fall,
Then shall thy sons by Fate's unchanged decree
In other worlds another Britain see,
And what thou art, America shall be."

In 1774 Mr. VERPLANCK published "Vice, a Satire," written with elegance and spirit.

Dr. PRIME, also of New York, finished his professional education in Europe, and on returning applied for a commission in the army, but did not succeed in obtaining one. He alludes to his disappointment in an elegy on the death of a friend, Doctor SCUDDER, who was slain in the skirmish at Shrewsbury in New Jersey:

"So bright, bless'd shade! thy deeds of virtue shine:
So, rich, no doubt, thy recompense on high!
My lot's far more lamentable than thine—
Thou liv'st in death, while I in living die.

"With great applause hast thou perform'd thy part,
Since thy first entrance on the stage of life,
Or in the labors of the healing art,
Or in fair Liberty's important strife. . . .

"But I, alas! like some unfruitful tree,
That useless stands, a cumberer of the plain,
My faculties unprofitable see,
And five long years have lived almost in vain.

"While all around me, like the busy swarms
That ply the fervent labors of the hive,
Or guide the state, with ardor rush to arms,
Or some less great but needful business drive,

"I see my time inglorious glide away,
Obscure and useless, like an idle drone:
And unconducive each revolving day
Or to my country's interest or my own."

A manuscript satire of the Welsh, in Latin and English, entitled "Muscipula sive Cambromyomachia," was found among Doctor PRIME's papers after his death, and published with a collection of his poetical writings: but it has been discovered that he was not the author of it. On the passage of the stamp act he composed "A Song for the Sons of Liberty," which is superior to any patriotic lyric up to that time written here.

JAMES ALLEN, a native of Boston, born in 1739, published in 1782 "Lines on the Massacre," which are in a fluent style, and display an ardent devotion to the popular cause. He afterward wrote many other pieces, but his indolent habits prevented their appearance in print. BRISSOT de Warville, in his "Travels in the United States," after remarking that poets must be more rare among us than other writers,—an opinion in which he seems to have been mistaken—says, "They speak however in Boston of an original but lazy poet named ALLEN; his verses are said to be full of fire and force; they mention particularly a manuscript poem of his on the famous battle of Bunker Hill; but he will not print it; he has for his reputation and his money the carelessness of LAFONTAINE."

MACPHERSON's "Ossian" was reprinted in Philadelphia soon after its first publication, and had for many years a decided influence upon poetical taste in this country. Among those who attempted to paraphrase it was JONATHAN MITCHELL SEWELL, of New Hampshire, who began the task of turning it into heroic verse in 1770, and afterward submitted to the public specimens of his completed work, but their reception did not encourage him to a further expenditure in that way. SEWELL was the author of an epilogue to ADDISON's "Cato," containing the often quoted lines:

"No pent-up Utica contracts our powers,
But the whole boundless continent is ours,"

and in the early part of the revolution wrote a patriotic song called "War and WASHINGTON," which had for many years extraordinary popularity.

JOSEPH BROWN LADD, M.D., of Rhode Island, author of "The Poems of Arouet," began to write during the early days of the revolution. His productions have very little merit. He lost his life in a duel, at Charleston, in 1785.

Among the emigrants from the mother country within a few years of the commencement of the war was JOHN LOWE, a native of Scotland, born in 1752, who arrived in Virginia in 1773, and became a successful teacher at Fredericksburg. He wrote there the celebrated song entitled "Mary's Dream." He died in 1798.

The year following that in which LOWE came to America, THOMAS PAINE followed, and settled in Philadelphia, where he was employed by ROBERT AITKIN, in 1775, to edit "The Pennsylvania Magazine," in which he published several poetical pieces, one of which is "On the Death of General WOLFE," and another is a song entitled "The Liberty Tree."*

The ballads and songs relating to "tragedies in the wilderness," to the Indian wars, the "old French war," and the revolution—of which I have succeeded in collecting more than a thousand—though many of them are extremely rude, are upon the whole far more fresh, vigorous and poetical than might be supposed. Enough for a volume refer to the single event of the taking of Louisburg, in 1747. On the approach of the period in which the colonies separated from Great Britain the newspapers and magazines were filled with lyrical appeals to the patriotism of the people, some of which were by the most dignified public characters. JOHN DICKINSON, author of "The Farmer's Letters," inclosing to JAMES OTIS, in 17 4, a copy of the famous song commencing—

"Come, join hand in hand, brave Americans all,
And rouse your bold hearts at Liberty's call,"

informs him that it was his own production, except eight lines, which were by his friend ARTHUR LEE, of Virginia. General WARREN's song of "Free America," is well known. A much better piece, "American Taxation," is supposed to have been written by a Connecticut schoolmaster named ST. JOHN. In a paper on "The Minstrelsy of the Revolution," in "Graham's Magazine," for 1842, I have given a considerable number of the compositions which illustrate this subject, and it is my intention hereafter to present the public a large collection of our historical verses, with suitable introductions and notes.

Of the American women known as poets during our colonial era, notices may be found in "The Female Poets of America." The leading poets of the revolution—FRENEAU, BARLOW, DWIGHT, TRUMBULL, and HUMPHRIES,—are subjects of separate articles in the following pages.

* Of British and other foreign poets who have written in this country since the revolution I have given no specimens in the following pages, though, perhaps, I should have quoted from ALEXANDER WILSON his spirited poem on "The Blue Bird," and other pieces from Mr. DA PONTE, Dr. FRANCIS LIEBER, Mr. HENRY WILLIAM HERBERT, and a few others who have made their homes in the United States. But "Mary's Dream" and the lyrics of THOMAS PAINE are as little entitled to be called American poems as the verses of MYLES COOPER, Sir JOHN BURGOYNE, or Major ANDRE, or those in which THOMAS MOORE celebrated his visits to the Dismal Swamp and the Schuylkill.

PHILIP FRENEAU.

[Born 1752. Died 1832.]

THE first attempts to establish in America a refuge for French Protestants were made under the direction of the Admiral Coligny in 1652. It was not, however, until Louis the Fourteenth revoked the edict of Nantz, in 1685, that there was any considerable emigration of the Reformers to this country. From that period, for many years, Massachusetts, New York, Pennsylvania, Virginia, and the Carolinas, received some of the best elements of their subsequent civilization in the polite, industrious and variously skilful exiles whom the intolerance of the Roman Catholics compelled to abandon the soil of France. Those who settled in New York founded the old church of Saint Esprit, which was long the centre of the Huguenot influence on this continent. Among the principal families connected with it were the DE LANCEYS, JAYS, PINTARDS, ALLAIRES, and FRESNEAUS. In 1712 we find the latter name written without the s, and four years later ANDRE FRENEAU is referred to in the Journal of JEAN FONTAINE, as a leading citizen, and a frequenter of the French club. This ANDRE FRENEAU was the grandfather of PHILIP, who was born in New York on the thirteenth of January, (the second, old style,) 1752. His mother was a native of New Jersey, and his elder brother, PETER,* was born in that colony, to which the family appears to have returned after the death of the poet's father, in 1754.

Young FRENEAU entered Nassau Hall, then known as the New Jersey "Log College," in 1767, so far advanced in classical studies that the acting president made his proficiency the subject of a congratulatory letter to one of his relations. His room-mate here was JAMES MADISON, and HUGH H. BRECKENRIDGE, who afterwards wrote "Modern Chivalry," was also in the same class. MADISON, BRECKENRIDGE, and FRENEAU, were intimate friends; and being all gifted with unusual satirical powers, which they were fond of displaying as frequently as there were fair occasions, they joined in lampooning, not only the leaders of adverse parties in the college, but also those prominent public characters who opposed the growing enthusiasm of the people for liberty. I have before me a considerable manuscript volume of personal and political satires, written by them in about equal proportions, and in which they exhibit nearly equal abilities, though MADISON'S have the least coarseness, and the least spirit. Several theological students, particularly two or three whose family connections were very humble, were objects of their continual ridicule. In the class below were AARON BURR, and the refined and elegant WILLIAM BRADFORD, whose occasional verses show that he might have equalled any of his American contemporaries as a poet, if such had been the aim of his ambition. FRENEAU graduated on the nineteenth of September, 1771, being then a few months over twenty years of age. The earliest of his printed poems is "The Poetical History of the Prophet Jonah," in four cantos, dated in 1768, the year after he went to Princeton. While in college he also formed the plan of an epic on the discovery of this continent, of which an "Address to Ferdinand," and a series of sixteen "Pictures of Columbus," are probably fragments. His valedictory exercise was a dialogue, in blank verse, on "The Rising Glory of America," in the composition and recitation of which he was associated with BRECKENRIDGE. It was printed in 1772, in an octavo pamphlet, at Philadelphia, where FRENEAU went to reside, with an intention of studying the law. It has been stated that he was on terms of familiar intimacy, while here, with Judge HOPKINSON, author of "The Battle of the Kegs," but the late venerable Dr. MEASE, who had been well acquainted with FRENEAU, remarks in a letter to me that "the humourist knew him only as a young scapegrace."

For some cause he appears to have abandoned the design of becoming a lawyer, and an irregular and aimless life of two or three years ended in his going to sea, but in what capacity, at first, I cannot ascertain. In 1774 and 1775 he was living in New York, where, during this period, he began to publish those pieces of political burlesque and invective which made his name familiar and popular throughout the country during the revolutionary war. His style was pointed, and he was successful in representing the exploits of the enemy in a ludicrous light, and in ridiculing the characters and conduct of the neutrals, loyalists, and others who were obnoxious to the prejudices of the Whigs. The speeches of the king and his ministers, and the proclamations of the royal governors and generals, he parodied and travestied in an amusing manner, and every memorable event, on land or sea, was celebrated by him in verses easily understood, and none the less admired, perhaps, for a dash of coarseness by which most of them were distinguished.

In 1776 he passed several months in the Danish West Indies, and wrote there two of his longest poems, "The House of Night," and "The Beauties of Santa Cruz." In 1778 he was in Bermuda, and during the following year we find him in Phila-

* PETER FRENEAU occasionally wrote verses, though I believe nothing of more pretension than a song or an epigram. He was a man of wit and education; was one of Mr. JEFFERSON'S warmest adherents; and when the democratic party came into power in South Carolina, was made Secretary of State there. THOMAS, in his "Reminiscences," says that "his style of writing combined the beauty and smoothness of ADDISON with the simplicity of COBBETT." He died in 1814.

delphia, editing for FRANCIS BAILEY "The United States Magazine." This periodical was not successful, and on its discontinuance he again turned his attention to the sea. He sailed for St. Eustatia in May, 1780, in the ship Aurora, which soon after leaving the Delaware was captured by a British cruiser. FRENEAU with his companions was taken to New York, and in the hot weather of June and July confined seven weeks on board the Scorpion, and the Hunter, those floating hells in which so many of our countrymen experienced the extremest horrors of the war. On being released he returned to Philadelphia, and in the family of his friend BAILEY gradually regained the health lost during his confinement. He now published "The British Prison Ship," in four cantos, in which he described, with indignant energy, the brutalities to which he had been subjected, and urged the people to new efforts against the cruel and remorseless enemy.

On the twenty-fifth of April, 1781, appeared the first number of "The Freeman's Journal," printed and published by BAILEY, and edited or in a large degree written by FRENEAU. For three or four years his hand is apparent in its most pungent paragraphs of prose, as well as in numerous pieces of verse, on public characters and passing events, and particularly in a succession of satires on the New York printers, HUGH GAINE and JAMES RIVINGTON, whom he delighted in assailing with all the resources of his abusive wit. Of GAINE, a sort of Vicar of Bray, "who lied at the sign of the Bible and Crown," he wrote a "Biography," and of RIVINGTON, who edited "The Royal Gazette," in which the Whigs were treated with every species of absurd and malicious vituperation, he gave the "Reflections," the "Confessions," the "Last Will and Testament," &c. The following lines are characteristic of these productions:

"*Occasioned by the title of Mr. Rivington's Royal Gazette being scarcely legible.*

Says Satan to Jemmy, "I hold you a bet,
That you mean to abandon our Royal Gazette;
Or, between you and me, you would manage things better
Than the title to print in so sneaking a letter.
Now, being connected so long in the art,
It would not be prudent at present to part;
And the people, perhaps, would be frightened, and fret
If the devil alone carried on the Gazette."
Says Jemmy to Satan, (by way of a wipe,)
"Who gives me the matter, should furnish the type;
And why you find fault I can scarcely divine,
For the types, like the printer, are certainly thine."

A remonstrance against the worn-out vignette—the *king's arms*—is too gross for quotation, but when the appearance of the "Gazette" was sufficiently improved—

"From the regions of night, with his head in a sack,
Ascended a person, accoutred in black,"

who looks over the paper, and the printing-room, and expresses his approbation of the change:

"My mandates are fully complied with at last,
New arms are engraved, and new letters are cast;
I therefore determine and fully accord,
This servant of mine shall receive his reward."
Then turning about, to the printer he said,
"Who late was my *servant*, shall now be my *aid*;
Kneel down! for your merits I dub you a knight;
From a passive subaltern I bid you to rise—
The inventor, as well as the printer, of lies."

In 1783, a few months after its appearance in Paris, FRENEAU translated and published in Philadelphia, the *Nouveau Voyage dans l'Amerique Septentrionale en l'année* 1781, by the Abbe ROBIN, a chaplain in the army of the Count de ROCHAMBEAU, and he was much occupied during this and the two following years in various literary services for Mr. BAILEY, who was his warm friend as well as liberal employer.

In 1784 he left Philadelphia, and after a few months spent in travel, and in visiting his old friends, become master of a vessel which sailed between New York and the West Indies, and New York and Charleston. In a letter to BAILEY he gives a striking account of a disastrous shipwreck which he suffered in one of his voyages, in the summer of 1788. Writing from Norfolk in Virginia, he says:

"After leaving New York, on the twenty-first of July, I had the misfortune to have my vessel dismasted, thrown on her beam ends, the bulk of her cargo shifted and ruined, and every sail, mast, spar, boat, and almost every article upon deck, lost, on the Wednesday afternoon following, in one of the hardest gales that ever blew on this coast. Captain William Cannon, whom I think you know, and who was going passenger with me to Charleston, and Josiah Stillwell, a lad of a reputable family in the state of New Jersey, were both washed overboard and drowned, notwithstanding every effort to save them. All my people besides except an old man who stuck fast in one of the scuttles were several times overboard, but had the luck to regain the wreck, and, with considerable difficulty, save their lives. As to myself, when I found the vessel no longer under my guidance, I took refuge in the main weather shrouds, where, indeed, I saved myself from being washed into the sea, but was almost staved to pieces in a violent fall I had upon the main deck—the main mast having given way six feet above, and gone overboard. I was afterwards knocked in the head by a violent stroke of the tiller, which entirely deprived me of sensation, for, I was told, near a quarter of an hour. Our pumps were now so choked with corn that they would no longer work. Upwards of four feet of water was in the hold. Fortunately our bucket was saved, and with this we went to bailing, which alone prevented us from foundering, in one of the most dismal nights that ever man witnessed. The next morning the weather had cleared, and the wind come round to the north-east—during the gale having been east-north-east. The land was now in sight, about five miles distant, latitude at noon 36° 17′. I soon rigged out a broken boom, and set the fore topsail—the only sail remaining—and steered for Cape Henry, making however but little way, the vessel being very much on one side, and ready to sink with her heavy cargo of iron and other weighty articles. We were towed in next day, Friday, by the friendly aid of Captain Archibald Bell, of the ship Betsy, from London. I have since arrived at this port, by the assistance of a Potomac pilot. Nothing could exceed our distress: no fire, no candle, our beds soaked with sea-water, the cabin torn to pieces, a vast quantity of corn damaged and poisoning us to death, &c. &c. As we entered Norfolk, on the twenty-ninth of July, the very dogs looked at us with an eye of commiseration, the negroes pitied us, and almost every one showed a disposition to relieve us. In the midst of all our vexation the crew endeavored to keep up their spirits with a little grog, while I had recourse to my old expedient of philosophy and reflection. I have unloaded my cargo, partly damaged, partly otherwise. This day I shall also begin to refit my vessel, and mean to proceed back to New York as soon as refitted. It is possible, however, that I may be ordered to sell the vessel here. If so, I shall take a passage to Baltimore, and go to New York by way of Philadelphia, to look out for another and a more fortunate barque than that which I now command.

Yours, &c. P. FRENEAU."

After FRENEAU left Philadelphia BAILEY issued the first collection of his poems, in a volume of more than four hundred pages, entitled "The Poems of PHILIP FRENEAU, written chiefly during the late War." In his advertisement, dated the sixth of June, 1786, the publisher says:

"The pieces now collected and printed in the following sheets were left in my hands by the author, above a year ago, with permission to publish them whenever I thought proper. A considerable number of the performances contained in this volume, as many will recollect, have appeared at different times in newspapers, (particularly the Freeman's Journal) and other periodical publications in the different states of America, during the late war, and since; and from the avidity and pleasure with which they generally appear to have been read by persons of the best taste, the printer now the more readily gives them to the world in their present form, (without troubling the reader with any affected apologies for their supposed or real imperfections,) in hopes they will afford a high degree of satisfaction to the lovers of poetical wit, and elegance of expression."

In the following October notice was given in the Freeman's Journal, that "An Additional Collection of Entertaining Original Performances, in Prose and Verse, by PHILIP FRENEAU," would be issued as soon as a sufficient number of copies should be subscribed for; but such a time did not arrive, and it was not until the twenty-seventh of April, 1788, that Mr. BAILEY gave the public "The Miscellaneous Works of PHILIP FRENEAU, containing his Essays and Additional Poems." Nearly half the copies of this volume were subscribed for in Charleston.

On the twenty-fourth of April, 1789, General WASHINGTON arrived in New York from Mount Vernon, to enter upon his duties as President of the United States. As the procession of boats by which he was attended from Elizabethtown Point approached the city, it is mentioned in the journals of the day, that the schooner Columbia, Captain PHILIP FRENEAU, eight days from Charleston, came up the bay. This was the poet's last voyage for several years. He now engaged with the printers, CHILDS and SWAINE, to edit the New York "Daily Advertiser," and continued in this employment until the removal of the government to Philadelphia, when he became a translating clerk in the Department of State, under Mr. JEFFERSON, and editor of the "National Gazette," which gained an infamous reputation by its attacks on WASHINGTON'S administration. FRENEAU made oath to a statement that Mr. JEFFERSON did not compose or suggest any of the contents of his paper, but in his old age he acknowledged to Dr. JOHN W. FRANCIS that the Secretary wrote or dictated the most offensive articles against WASHINGTON and his friends, and to Dr. JAMES MEASE he exhibited a file of the "Gazette," in which what were alleged to be his contributions were marked. This matter has been much and angrily debated, but it has not been denied that the conduct of the clerk was in the main, at least, approved by his employer. The President could not forbear speaking to Mr. JEFFERSON of FRENEAU'S abuse, and requesting him, as a member of his cabinet, to administer him some rebuke. Mr. JEFFERSON tells us in his "Anas" what course he chose to pursue. At a cabinet council, he says, WASHINGTON remarked that "That rascal, FRENEAU, sent him three copies of his papers every day, as if he thought he (WASHINGTON) would become the distributor of them; that he could see in this nothing but an impudent design to insult him: he ended in a high tone." Again, speaking of the President, Mr. JEFFERSON says, "He adverted to a piece in FRENEAU'S paper of yesterday; he said he despised all their attacks on him personally, but that there had never been an act of the government, not meaning in the executive line only, but in any line, which that paper had not abused. He was evidently sore and warm, and I took his intention to be, that I should interpose in some way with FRENEAU, perhaps withdraw his appointment of translating clerk in my office. But I will not do it. His paper has saved our Constitution, which was galloping fast into monarchy, and has been checked by no one means so powerfully as by that paper. It is well and universally known that it has been that paper which has checked the career of the monocrats," &c.

During the prevalence of the yellow fever in Philadelphia, in 1793, the publication of the "National Gazette" was suspended; and Mr. JEFFERSON having retired from the cabinet, it was not resumed. FRENEAU was for a few months without any regular occupation. I have seen two letters, one written by JEFFERSON and the other by MADISON, in which he is commended to certain citizens of New York, for his "extensive information, sound discretion," and other qualities, as a candidate for the editorship of a journal which it was intended to establish in that city. The project was abandoned, or his application unsuccessful, and on the second of May, 1795, he commenced "The Jersey Chronicle," at Mount Pleasant, near Middletown Point, in New Jersey, which was continued every week for one year, the fifty-second number having appeared on the thirtieth of April, 1796. In the "Chronicle" he maintained his opposition to the administration of WASHINGTON, and the unpopularity of its politics with the reading classes doubtless prevented its success. He now again turned his attention to New York, and on the thirteenth of March, 1797, issued there the first number of "The Time-Piece and Literary Companion," which was published tri-weekly, and devoted more largely than any other paper in the country to belles-lettres, while it embraced news and frequent discussions of public affairs. FRENEAU himself contributed to almost every number one or more copies of verses, and he had many poetical correspondents. After six months, MATTHEW L. DAVIS, then a very young man, became his partner, and at the end of the first year "The Time-Piece" was resigned entirely to his direction.*

* "The Time-Piece" was afterwards edited by JOHN D'OLEY BURKE, an Irishman, who, in 1798, was arrested under the Alien and Sedition law. Burke was a noisy Democrat, and possessed of but moderate abilities. He wrote "Bunker Hill, or the Death of Warren," a play; "The Columbiad, an Epic Poem;" "The History of Virginia," &c., and was killed in a duel, in 1808

In 1798 FRENEAU went again to South Carolina, and, becoming master of a merchant ship, he made several voyages, of which we have some souvenirs in his subsequently published poems. In 1799 and in 1801 he visited St. Thomas; in 1803 he was in the island of Madeira; in 1804 he declines in a copy of verses an invitation to visit a nunnery in Teneriffe, and in 1806 he leaves New York, in command of the sloop Industry, for Savannah, Charleston, and the West Indies. From some lines "To Hezekiah Salem," a name by which he frequently describes himself, it may be inferred that he also made a voyage to Calcutta.

While conducting the "Jersey Chronicle," at Monmouth, in 1795, he had published a second edition of his collection of poems, in a closely-printed octavo volume; and in 1809, after his final abandonment of the life of a sailor, he issued a third edition, in Philadelphia, in two duodecimo volumes, entiled "Poems written and published during the American Revolutionary War, and now republished from the original Manuscripts, interspersed with Translations from the Ancients, and other Pieces not heretofore in Print." In the last-mentioned year he addressed a short poem to his friend Mr. JEFFERSON, on his retirement from the Presidency of the United States, and celebrated in another the death of THOMAS PAINE, of whom he was an ardent admirer.

When the second war with Great Britain came on, he restrung his lyre, and commemorated in characteristic verses the triumphs of our arms, especially our naval victories; and his songs and ballads relating to these events are still reprinted in "broadsides," and sold in every port. They were for the most part included in two small volumes which he published in New York, after the peace, under the title of "A Collection of Poems on American Affairs, and a Variety of other Subjects, chiefly Moral and Political, written between 1797 and 1815." He afterwards contemplated a complete edition of his works, and in a letter to Dr. MEASE inquires whether there is "still enough of the old spirit of patriotism abroad to insure the safety of such an adventure." His house at Mount Pleasant was destroyed by fire in 1815 or 1816, and he laments to the same correspondent the loss, by that misfortune, of some of his best compositions, which had never been given to the public.

In his old age FRENEAU resided in New Jersey, but made occasional visits to Philadelphia, where he was always welcomed by Mrs. LYDIA R. BAILEY, who was the daughter-in-law of his early friend and publisher, FRANCIS BAILEY, and had herself been his publisher in 1809. More frequently he passed a few days in New York, where he found living many of the companions of his active and ambitious life. Here too he became intimate with Dr. JOHN W. FRANCIS, to whom he was wont to recount the incidents of his varied history, and to discourse of his ancient associations, with a careless enthusiasm, such as only the genial inquisition of a FRANCIS could awaken. Mrs. BAILEY, who still carries on the printing house which her father-in-law established three-quarters of a century ago, has described to me the poet as he appeared to her in his prime. "He was a small man," she says, "very gentleman-like in his manners, very entertaining in his conversation, and withal a great favourite with the ladies;" the venerable ex-manager of the Philadelphia theatre, Mr. WILLIAM B. WOOD, now (in 1855) seventy-seven years old, also remembers him, and concurs in this description. Dr. FRANCIS's recollections of the bard are of a later date; he describes him as having dressed, in his later years, like a farmer, and as having had "a fine expression of countenance for so old a man—mild, pensive, and intelligent."

FRENEAU perished in a snow-storm, in his eightieth year, during the night of the eighteenth of December, 1832, near Freehold. On the approach of evening he had left an inn of that village for his home, a mile and a half distant. He was unattended, and it is supposed he lost his way. The next morning, says Mr. WILLIAM LLOYD of Freehold, in a letter to Dr. MEASE, from which I derive these particulars, his body was found, partially covered by the snow, in a meadow, a little aside from his direct path.

FRENEAU was unquestionably a man of considerable genius, and among his poems are illustrations of creative passion which will preserve his name long after authors of more refinement and elegance are forgotten. His best pieces were for the most part written in early life, when he was most ambitious of literary distinction. Of these, "The Dying Indian," "The Indian Student," and others copied into the following pages, are finely conceived and very carefully finished. It is worthy of notice that he was the first of our authors to treat the "ancients of these lands" with a just appreciation, and in a truly artistical spirit. His song of "Alknomock" had long the popularity of a national air. Mr. WASHINGTON IRVING informs me that when he was a youth it was familiar in every drawing-room, and among the earliest theatrical reminiscences of Mr. WILLIAM B. WOOD is its production, in character, upon the stage. The once well-known satire, entitled "A New England Sabbath-day Chase," was so much in vogue when Mr. IRVING was a school-boy, that he committed it to memory as an exercise in declamation. The political odes and pasquinades which he wrote during the revolution possess much historical interest, and, with his other works, they will some time undoubtedly be collected and edited with the care due to unique and curious souvenirs of so remarkable an age.

In an address "To the Americans of the United States," first published in November, 1797, FRENEAU himself evinces a sense of the proper distinction of his writings: "Catching our subjects," he says,

——"from the varying scene,
Of human things, a mingled work we draw,
Chequered with fancies odd and figures strange,
Such as no courtly poet ever saw
Who writ, beneath some great man's ceiling placed,—
Traveled no lands, nor roved the watery waste."

THE DYING INDIAN.

"On yonder lake I spread the sail no more!
Vigour, and youth, and active days are past—
Relentless demons urge me to that shore
On whose black forests all the dead are cast:—
Ye solemn train, prepare the funeral song,
For I must go to shades below,
Where all is strange and all is new;
Companion to the airy throng!—
What solitary streams,
In dull and dreary dreams,
All melancholy, must I rove along!

To what strange lands must Chequi take his way!
Groves of the dead departed mortals trace:
No deer along those gloomy forests stray,
No huntsmen there take pleasure in the chase,
But all are empty, unsubstantial shades,
That ramble through those visionary glades;
No spongy fruits from verdant trees depend,
But sickly orchards there
Do fruits as sickly bear,
And apples a consumptive visage shew,
And withered hangs the whortleberry blue.

Ah me! what mischiefs on the dead attend!
Wandering a stranger to the shores below,
Where shall I brook or real fountain find!
Lazy and sad deluding waters flow—
Such is the picture in my boding mind!
Fine tales, indeed, they tell
Of shades and purling rills,
Where our dead fathers dwell
Beyond the western hills;
But when did ghost return his state to shew;
Or who can promise half the tale is true!

I too must be a fleeting ghost!—no more—
None, none but shadows to those mansions go;
I leave my woods, I leave the Huron shore,
For emptier groves below!
Ye charming solitudes,
Ye tall ascending woods
Ye glassy lakes and purling streams,
Whose aspect still was sweet,
Whether the sun did greet,
Or the pale moon embraced you with her beams—
Adieu to all!
To all, that charm'd me where I strayed,
The winding stream, the dark sequester'd shade;
Adieu all triumphs here!
Adieu the mountain's lofty swell,
Adieu, thou little verdant hill,
And seas, and stars, and skies—farewell,
For some remoter sphere!

Perplex'd with doubts, and tortured with despair,
Why so dejected at this hopeless sleep?
Nature at last these ruins may repair, [weep;
When fate's long dream is o'er, and she forgets to
Some real world once more may be assigned,
Some new-born mansion for the immortal mind!
Farewell, sweet lake; farewell, surrounding woods:
To other groves, through midnight glooms I stray,
Beyond the mountains and beyond the floods,
Beyond the Huron bay!
Prepare the hollow tomb, and place me low,
My trusty bow and arrows by my side,
The cheerful bottle and the venison store,
For long the journey is that I must go,
Without a partner, and without a guide."

He spoke, and bid the attending mourners weep,
Then closed his eyes, and sunk to endless sleep!

THE INDIAN BURYING-GROUND.

In spite of all the learn'd have said,
I still my old opinion keep;
The *posture* that *we* give the dead,
Points out the soul's eternal sleep.

Not so the ancients of these lands—
The Indian, when from life released,
Again is seated with his friends,
And shares again the joyous feast.*

His imaged birds, and painted bowl,
And venison, for a journey dressed,
Bespeak the nature of the soul,
Activity that knows no rest.

His bow, for action ready bent,
And arrows, with a head of stone,
Can only mean that life is spent,
And not the old ideas gone.

Thou, stranger, that shalt come this way,
No fraud upon the dead commit—
Observe the swelling turf, and say,
They do not *lie*, but here they *sit*.

Here still a lofty rock remains,
On which the curious eye may trace
(Now wasted, half, by wearing rains,)
The fancies of a ruder race.

Here still an aged elm aspires,
Beneath whose far-projecting shade
(And which the shepherd still admires)
The children of the forest played!

There oft a restless Indian queen
(Pale Shebah, with her braided hair)
And many a barbarous form is seen
To chide the man that lingers there.

By midnight moons, o'er moistening dews,
In habit for the chase arrayed,
The hunter still the deer pursues,—
The hunter and the deer, a shade!†

And long shall timorous fancy see
The painted chief and pointed spear,
And Reason's self shall bow the knee
To shadows and delusions here.

* The North American Indians bury their dead in a sitting posture; decorating the corpse with wampum, the images of birds, quadrupeds, &c.: and (if that of a warrior) with bows, arrows, tomahawks, and other military weapons.

† Campbell appropriated this line, in his beautiful poem entitled "O'Conor's Child:"

"Now o'er the hills in chase he flits—
The hunter and the deer—a shade."

TO AN OLD MAN.

Why, dotard, wouldst thou longer groan
  Beneath a weight of years and wo;
Thy youth is lost, thy pleasures flown,
  And age proclaims, "'T is time to go."

To willows sad and weeping yews
  With us a while, old man, repair,
Nor to the vault thy steps refuse;
  Thy constant home must soon be there.

To summer suns and winter moons
  Prepare to bid a long adieu;
Autumnal seasons shall return,
  And spring shall bloom, but not for you.

Why so perplex'd with cares and toil
  To rest upon this darksome road?
'T is but a thin, a thirsty soil,
  A barren and a bleak abode.

Constrain'd to dwell with pain and care,
  These dregs of life are bought too dear;
'T is better far to die, than bear
  The torments of life's closing year.

Subjected to perpetual ills,
  A thousand deaths around us grow:
The frost the tender blossom kills,
  And roses wither as they blow.

Cold, nipping winds your fruits assail;
  The blasted apple seeks the ground;
The peaches fall, the cherries fail;
  The grape receives a mortal wound.

The breeze, that gently ought to blow,
  Swells to a storm, and rends the main;
The sun, that charm'd the grass to grow,
  Turns hostile, and consumes the plain;

The mountains waste, the shores decay,
  Once purling streams are dead and dry—
'T was Nature's work—'t is Nature's play,
  And Nature says that all must die.

Yon flaming lamp, the source of light,
  In chaos dark may shroud his beam,
And leave the world to mother Night,
  A farce, a phantom, or a dream.

What now is young, must soon be old:
  Whate'er we love, we soon must leave;
'T is now too hot, 't is now too cold—
  To live, is nothing but to grieve.

How bright the morn her course begun!
  No mists bedimm'd the solar sphere;
The clouds arise—they shade the sun,
  For nothing can be constant here.

Now hope the longing soul employs,
  In expectation we are bless'd;
But soon the airy phantom flies,
  For, lo! the treasure is possess'd.

Those monarchs proud, that havoc spread,
  (While pensive Reason dropt a tear,)
Those monarchs have to darkness fled,
  And ruin bounds their mad career.

The grandeur of this earthly round,
  Where folly would forever stay,
Is but a name, is but a sound—
  Mere emptiness and vanity.

Give me the stars, give me the skies,
  Give me the heaven's remotest sphere,
Above these gloomy scenes to rise
  Of desolation and despair.

Those native fires, that warm'd the mind,
  Now languid grown, too dimly glow,
Joy has to grief the heart resign'd,
  And love itself, is changed to wo.

The joys of wine are all your boast,—
  These, for a moment, damp your pain
The gleam is o'er, the charm is lost—
  And darkness clouds the soul again.

Then seek no more for bliss below,
  Where real bliss can ne'er be found;
Aspire where sweeter blossoms blow,
  And fairer flowers bedeck the ground;

Where plants of life the plains invest,
  And green eternal crowns the year:—
The little god, that warms the breast,
  Is weary of his mansion here.

Like Phospher, sent before the day,
  His height meridian to regain,
The dawn arrives—he must not stay
  To shiver on a frozen plain.

Life's journey past, for fate prepare,—
  'T is but the freedom of the mind;
Jove made us mortal—his we are,
  To Jove be all our cares resign'd.

THE WILD HONEYSUCKLE

Fair flower that dost so comely grow,
  Hid in this silent, dull retreat,
Untouch'd thy honey'd blossoms blow,
  Unseen thy little branches greet:
    No roving foot shall crush thee here,
    No busy hand provoke a tear.

By Nature's self in white arrayed,
  She bade thee shun the vulgar eye,
And planted here the guardian shade,
  And sent soft waters murmuring by;
    Thus quietly thy summer goes—
    Thy days declining to repose.

Smit with those charms, that must decay,
  I grieve to see your future doom;
They died—nor were those flowers more gay—
  The flowers that did in Eden bloom;
    Unpitying frosts and Autumn's power
    Shall leave no vestige of this flower.

From morning suns and evening dews
  At first thy little being came:
If nothing once, you nothing lose,
  For when you die you are the same;
    The space between is but an hour,
    The frail duration of a flower.

TO THE MEMORY OF THE AMERICANS WHO FELL AT EUTAW.*

At Eutaw Springs the valiant died;
Their limbs with dust are cover'd o'er;
Weep on, ye springs, your tearful tide—
How many heroes are no more!
If, in this wreck of ruin, they
Can yet be thought to claim the tear,
Oh smite your gentle breast and say,
The friends of freedom slumber here!

Thou who shalt trace this bloody plain,
If goodness rules thy generous breast,
Sigh for the wasted rural reign;
Sigh for the shepherds, sunk to rest!
Stranger, their humble graves adorn;
You too may fall, and ask a tear;
'T is not the beauty of the morn
That proves the evening shall be clear.

They saw their injured country's wo—
The flaming town, the wasted field,
Then rush'd to meet the insulting foe;
They took the spear, but left the shield.†
Led by the conquering genius, Greene,
The Britons they compell'd to fly:
None distant viewed the fatal plain;
None grieved, in such a cause, to die.

But like the Parthians, famed of old,
Who, flying, still their arrows threw;
These routed Britons, full as bold,
Retreated, and retreating slew.
Now rest in peace, our patriot band;
Though far from Nature's limits thrown,
We trust they find a happier land,
A brighter sunshine of their own.

INDIAN DEATH-SONG.

The sun sets at night and the stars shun the day,
But glory remains when their lights fade away.
Begin, ye tormentors! your threats are in vain,
For the son of Alknomock can never complain.

Remember the woods where in ambush he lay,
And the scalps which he bore from your nation away.
Why do ye delay? 'till I shrink from my pain?
Know the son of Alknomock can never complain.

Remember the arrows he shot from his bow;
Remember your chiefs by his hatchet laid low.
The flame rises high—you exult in my pain!
But the son of Alknomock will never complain.

I go to the land where my father has gone;
His ghost shall exalt in the fame of his son.
Death comes like a friend; he relieves me from pain,
And thy son, oh Alknomock! has scorned to complain.

* The Battle of Eutaw, South Carolina, fought September 8, 1781.

† Sir Walter Scott adopted this line in the introduction to the third canto of "Marmion:"

"When Prussia hurried to the field,
And snatched *the spear, but left the shield*."

THE PROSPECT OF PEACE.

Though clad in winter's gloomy dress
All Nature's works appear,
Yet other prospects rise to bless
The new returning year.
The active sail again is seen
To greet our western shore,
Gay plenty smiles, with brow serene,
And wars distract no more.

No more the vales, no more the plains
An iron harvest yield;
Peace guards our doors, impels our swains
To till the grateful field:
From distant climes, no longer foes,
(Their years of misery past,)
Nations arrive, to find repose
In these domains at last.

And if a more delightful scene
Attracts the mortal eye,
Where clouds nor darkness intervene,
Behold, aspiring high,
On freedom's soil those fabrics plann'd,
On virtue's basis laid,
That makes secure our native land,
And prove our toils repaid.

Ambitious aims and pride severe,
Would you at distance keep,
What wanderer would not tarry here,
Here charm his cares to sleep?
Oh, still may health her balmy wings
O'er these fair fields expand,
While commerce from all climates brings
The products of each land.

Through toiling care and lengthened views,
That share alike our span,
Gay, smiling hope her heaven pursues,
The eternal friend of man:
The darkness of the days to come
She brightens with her ray,
And smiles o'er Nature's gaping tomb,
When sickening to decay!

HUMAN FRAILTY.

Disasters on disasters grow,
And those which are not sent we make,
The good we rarely find below,
Or, in the search, the road mistake.

The object of our fancied joys
With eager eye we keep in view·
Possession, when acquired, destroys
The object and the passion too.

The hat that hid Belinda's hair
Was once the darling of her eye;
'T is now dismiss'd, she knows not where
Is laid aside, she knows not why.

Life is to most a nauseous pill,
A treat for which they dearly pay:
Let 's take the good, avoid the ill,
Dis arge the debt, and walk away.

EXTRACTS FROM "GAINE'S LIFE."

Now, if I was ever so given to lie,
My dear native country I would n't deny;
(I know you love Teagues) and I shall not conceal,
That I came from the kingdom where PHELIM O'NEAL
And other brave worthies ate butter and cheese,
And walked in the clover-fields up to their knees:
Full early in youth, without basket or burden,
With a staff in my hand, I pass'd over Jordan,
(I remember, my comrade was Doctor MAGRAW,
And many strange things on the waters we saw,
Sharks, dolphins and sea dogs, bonettas and whales,
And birds at the tropic, with quills in their tails,)
And came to your city and government seat,
And found it was true, you had something to eat!
When thus I wrote home: "The country is good,
They have plenty of victuals and plenty of wood;
The people are kind, and whate'er they may think,
I shall make it appear I can swim where they'll sink;
And yet they're so brisk, and so full of good cheer,
By my soul! I suspect they have always New Year,
And, therefore, conceive it is good to be here."
So said, and so acted: I put up a press,
And printed away with amazing success;
Neglected my person and looked like a fright,
Was bothered all day, and was busy all night,
Saw money come in, as the papers went out,
While PARKER and WEYMAN were driving about,
And cursing and swearing and chewing their cuds,
And wishing HUGH GAINE and his press in the suds.
Thus life ran away, so smooth and serene—
Ah! these were the happiest days I had seen!
But the saying of JACOB I've found to be true,
"The days of thy servant are evil and few!"
The days that to me were joyous and glad,
Are nothing to those which are dreary and sad!
The feuds of the stamp act foreboded foul weather,
And war and vexation, all coming together.
Those days were the days of riots and mobs,
Tar, feathers, and tories, and troublesome jobs—
Priests preaching up war for the good of our souls,
And libels, and lying, and liberty-poles,
From which when some whimsical colors you waved
We had nothing to do, but look up and be saved!
But this was the season that I must lament;
I first was a whig, with an honest intent—
Yes, I *was* a whig, and a whig from my heart—
But still was unwilling with Britain to part.
I thought to oppose her was foolish and vain,
I thought she would turn and embrace us again,
And make us as happy as happy could be,
By renewing the era of mild sixty-three;
And yet, like a cruel, undutiful son,
Who evil returns for the good to be done,
Unmerited odium on Britain to throw,
I printed some treason for PHILIP FRENEAU! ....
At this time arose a certain king SEARS,
Who made it his study to banish our fears.
He was, without doubt, a person of merit,
Great knowledge, some wit, and abundance of spirit,
Could talk like a lawyer, and that without fee,
And threatened perdition to all who drank tea.
Long sermons did he against Scotchmen prepare
And drank like a German, and drove away care,
Ah! don't you remember what a vigorous hand he put
To drag off the great guns, and plague Captain VANDEPUT,
That night when the hero (his patience worn out)
Put fire to his cannon, and folks to the rout,
And drew up his ship with a spring on his cable,
And gave us a second confusion of Babel! ....
For my part, I hid in a cellar, (as sages
And Christians were wont, in the primitive ages.)
Yet I hardly could boast of a moment of rest,
The dogs were a howling, the town was distrest. ....
From this very day till the British came in,
We lived, I may say, in the Desert of Sin; ...
We townsmen, like women, of Britons in dread,
Mistrusted their meaning, and foolishly fled;
Like the rest of the dunces, I mounted my steed,
And galloped away with incredible speed;
To Newark I hastened—but trouble and care
Got up on the crupper, and followed me there! ....
So, after remaining one cold winter season,
And stuffing my papers with something like treason,
I, cursing my folly and idle pursuits,
Returned to the city and hung up my boots! .

LITERARY IMPORTATION.

HOWEVER we wrangled with Britain awhile
We think of her now in a different style,
And many fine things we receive from her isle:
Among all the rest,
Some demon possess'd
Our dealers in knowledge and sellers of sense
To have a good BISHOP imported from thence.

The words of SAM CHANDLER were thought to be vain,
When he argued so often and proved it so plain,
That SATAN must flourish till bishops should reign:
Though he went to the wall
With his project and all,
Another bold SAMMY, in bishop's array,
Has got something more for his pains than his pay

It seems we had spirit to humble a throne,
Have genius for science inferior to none,
But never encourage a plant of our own:
If a college be planned,
'T is all at a stand
'Till to Europe we send at a shameful expense,
To bring us a pedant to teach us some sense.

Can we never be thought to have learning or grace
Unless it be brought from that horrible place
Where tyranny reigns with her impudent face,
And popes and pretenders,
And sly faith-defenders,
Have ever been hostile to reason and wit,
Enslaving a world that shall conquer them yet!

'T is a folly to fret at the picture I draw:
And I say what was said by a Doctor MAGRAW;
"If they give us their teachers, they'll give us their law."
How that will agree
With such people as we,
I leave to the learn'd to reflect on awhile,
And say what they think in a handsomer style.

THE INDIAN STUDENT: OR, FORCE OF NATURE.

FROM Susquehanna's farthest springs,
  Where savage tribes pursue their game,
(His blanket tied with yellow strings,)
  A shepherd of the forest came. ....

Some thought he would in law excel,
  Some said in physic he would shine;
And one that knew him passing well,
  Beheld in him a sound divine.

But those of more discerning eye,
  Even then could other prospects show,
And saw him lay his VIRGIL by,
  To wander with his dearer bow.

The tedious hours of study spent,
  The heavy moulded lecture done,
He to the woods a hunting went—
  Through lonely wastes he walked, he run.

No mystic wonders fired his mind
  He sought to gain no learned degree,
But only sense enough to find
  The squirrel in the hollow tree

The shady bank, the purling stream,
  The woody wild his heart possessed,
The dewy lawn his morning dream
  In fancy's gayest colors drest.

"And why," he cried, "did I forsake
  My native woods for gloomy walls?
The silver stream, the limpid lake
  For musty books and college halls?

"A little could my wants supply—
  Can wealth and honor give me more!
Or, will the sylvan god deny
  The humble treat he gave before?

"Let seraphs gain the bright abode,
  And heaven's sublimest mansions see;
I only bow to Nature's god—
  The land of shades will do for me.

"These dreadful secrets of the sky
  Alarm my soul with thrilling fear—
Do planets in their orbits fly?
  And is the earth indeed a sphere?

"Let planets still their course pursue,
  And comets to the centre run:
In him my faithful friend I view,
  The image of my GOD—the sun.

"Where nature's ancient forests grow,
  And mingled laurel never fades,
My heart is fixed, and I must go
  To die among my native shades."

He spoke, and to the western springs,
  (His gown discharged, his money spent,
His blanket tied with yellow strings,)
  The shepherd of the forest went.

A BACCHANALIAN DIALOGUE.

WRITTEN IN 1808.

ARRIVED at Madeira, the island of vines,
  Where mountains and valleys abound,
Where the sun the mild juice of the cluster refines,
  To gladden the magical ground:

As pensive I strayed, in her elegant shade,
  Now halting, and now on the move,
Old BACCHUS I met, with a crown on his head,
  In the darkest recess of a grove.

I met him with awe, but no symptom of fear,
  As I roved by his mountains and springs,
When he said with a sneer, "How dare you come here,
  You hater of despots and kings?

"Do you know that a prince and a regent renown'd
  Presides in this island of wine?
Whose fame on the earth has encircled it round
  And spreads from the pole to the line?

"Haste away with your barque; on the foam of the main
  To Charleston I bid you repair;
There drink your Jamaica, that maddens the brain;
  You shall have no Madeira—I swear!"

"Dear BACCHUS," I answered, for BACCHUS it was
  That spoke in this menacing tone:
I knew by the smirk, and the flush on his face,
  It was BACCHUS and BACCHUS alone—

"Dear BACCHUS," I answered, "ah, why so severe?
  Since your nectar abundantly flows,
Allow me one cargo—without it I fear
  Some people will soon come to blows:

"I left them in wrangles, disorder, and strife
  Political feuds were so high—
I was sick of their quarrels, and sick of my life,
  And almost requested to die."

The deity smiling, replied, "I relent:
  For the sake of your coming so far,
Here, taste of my choicest: go, tell them repent,
  And cease their political war.

"With the cargo I send, you may say I intend
  To hush them to peace and repose;
With this present of mine, on the wings of the wind
  You shall travel, and tell them, 'Here goes—

"'*A health to old BACCHUS!*' who sends them the best
  Of the nectar his island affords,
The soul of the feast, and the joy of the guest,
  Too good for your monarchs and lords.

"No rivals have I in this insular waste,
  Alone will I govern the isle.
With a king at my feet, and a court to my taste,
  And all in the popular style.

"But a spirit there is in the order of things,
  To me it is perfectly plain,
That will strike at the sceptres of despots and kings,
  And only king BACCHUS remain."

ST. GEORGE TUCKER.

[Born about 1750. Died 1827.]

St. George Tucker was born in Bermuda about the middle of the last century. His family had been in that island ever since it was settled, and one of his ancestors, Daniel Tucker, who had lived a while in Virginia, was its governor in 1616. His father came into Virginia while still a young man, but spent much of his time in England, where he was agent for the colony. He there met Dr. Franklin, with whom he occasionally corresponded. He had four sons, two of whom adhered to England on the breaking out of the revolution, and two joined the Americans, and continued through life stanch republicans. These were Thomas Tudor Tucker, many years representative of South Carolina in Congress, and St. George, who lived and died in Virginia. The latter was graduated at the College of William and Mary, and afterwards studied the law, but, tired of the silence of the courts, on the approach of the war, resorted to arms. In the early part of the contest he is said to have planned a secret expedition to Bermuda, where he knew there was a large amount of military stores, in a fortification feebly garrisoned. The perilous enterprise proved entirely successful, and it appears from a recent biography of his nephew, Henry St. George Tucker, one of the directors of the East India Company, that he personally aided in it. He was with the army at Yorktown, holding the rank of lieutenant-colonel, and received during the siege a slight scratch in the face, from the explosion of a bomb; upon which General Washington, in a more jocular mood than was his wont, congratulated him on his honorable scar. He was soon afterwards appointed to a seat in the General Court; while a judge, was professor of law in the College of William and Mary; was next advanced to the Court of Appeals; and finally to the District Court of the United States. He was one of the commissioners of Virginia who met at Annapolis, in 1796, and recommended the convention which formed the present federal constitution.

By his first wife, Mrs. Randolph, mother of John Randolph, he has numerous descendants; by his second, he had none who survived him.

Judge Tucker had a ready talent for versification, which he exercised through life, and he was particularly successful in *vers de société*, when that species of literary accomplishment was more practised and admired than it is at the present day. His rhymed epistles, epigrams, complimentary verses, and other bagatelles, would fill several volumes; but he gave only one small collection of them to the public in this form. When Dr. Wolcott's satires on George the Third, written under the name of "Peter Pindar," obtained both in this country and in England a popularity far beyond their merits, Judge Tucker, who admired them, was induced to publish in Freneau's "National Gazette" a series of similar odes, under the signature of "Jonathan Pindar," by which he at once gratified his political zeal and his poetical propensity. His object was to assail John Adams and other leading federalists, for their supposed monarchical predilections. His pieces might well be compared with Wolcott's for poetical qualities, but were less playful, and had far more acerbity. Collected into a volume, they continued to be read by politicians, and had the honour of a volunteer reprint from one of the earliest presses in Kentucky.

Judge Tucker was capable of better things than these political trifles. He wrote a poem entitled "Liberty," in which the leading characters and events of the revolution are introduced. Of his numerous minor pieces some are characterized by ease, sprightliness, and grace. One of them, entitled "Days of My Youth," so affected John Adams, in his old age, that he declared he would rather have written it than any lyric by Milton or Shakspeare. He little dreamed it was by an author who in earlier years had made him the theme of his satirical wit.

In prose also Judge Tucker was a voluminous writer. His most elaborate performance was an edition of Blackstone's "Commentaries," with copious notes and illustrative dissertations. He lived to a great age, and through life had numerous and warm friends. He was an active and often an intolerant politician, yet such was the predominance of his kindly affections and companionable qualities, that some of his most cherished friends were of the party which in the mass he most cordially hated.

DAYS OF MY YOUTH.

Days of my youth, ye have glided away:
Hairs of my youth, ye are frosted and gray:
Eyes of my youth, your keen sight is no more:
Cheeks of my youth, ye are furrowed all o'er;
Strength of my youth, all your vigour is gone:
Thoughts of my youth, your gay visions are flown.

Days of my youth, I wish not your recall:
Hairs of my youth, I'm content ye should fall:
Eyes of my youth, you much evil have seen:
Cheeks of my youth, bathed in tears you have been:
Thoughts of my youth, you have led me astray:
Strength of my youth, why lament your decay?

Days of my age, ye will shortly be past:
Pains of my age, yet awhile you can last:
Joys of my age, in true wisdom delight:
Eyes of my age, be religion your light:
Thoughts of my age, dread ye not the cold sod:
Hopes of my age, be ye fixed on your God.

JOHN TRUMBULL.

[Born 1750. Died 1831.]

John Trumbull, LL.D., the author of "McFingal," was born in Waterbury, Connecticut, on the twenty-fourth day of April, 1750. His father was a Congregational clergyman, and for many years one of the trustees of Yale College. He early instructed his son in the elementary branches of education, and was induced by the extraordinary vigour of his intellect, and his unremitted devotion to study, to give him lessons in the Greek and Latin languages before he was six years old. At the age of seven, after a careful examination, young Trumbull was declared to be sufficiently advanced to merit admission into Yale College. On account of his extreme youth, however, at that time, and his subsequent ill health, he was not sent to reside at New Haven until 1763, when he was in his thirteenth year. His college life was a continued series of successes. His superior genius, attainments and industry enabled him in every trial to surpass his competitors for academic honours; and such of his collegiate exercises as have been printed evince a discipline of thought and style rarely discernible in more advanced years, and after greater opportunities of improvement. He was graduated in 1767, but remained in the college three years longer, devoting his attention principally to the study of polite letters. In this period he became acquainted with Dwight, then a member of one of the younger classes, who had attracted considerable attention by translating in a very creditable manner two of the finest odes of Horace, and contracted with him a lasting friendship. On the resignation of two of the tutors in the college in 1771, Trumbull and Dwight were elected to fill the vacancies, and exerted all their energies for several years to introduce an improved course of study and system of discipline into the seminary. At this period the ancient languages, scholastic theology, logic, and mathematics were dignified with the title of "solid learning," and the study of belles lettres was decried as useless and an unjustifiable waste of time. The two friends were exposed to a torrent of censure and ridicule, but they persevered, and in the end were successful. Trumbull wrote many humorous prose and poetical essays while he was a tutor, which were published in the gazettes of Connecticut and Massachusetts, and with Dwight produced a series in the manner of the "Spectator," which extended to more than forty numbers. The "Progress of Dulness" was published in 1772. It is the most finished of Trumbull's poems, and was hardly less serviceable to the cause of education than "McFingal" was to that of liberty. The puerile absurdity of regarding a knowledge of the Greek and Hebrew languages as of more importance to a clergyman than the most perfect acquaintance with rhetoric and belles lettres, then obtained more generally than now, and dunces had but to remain four years in the neighbourhood of a university to be admitted to the fellowship of scholars and the ministers of religion. In the satire, Tom Brainless, a country clown, too indolent to follow the plough, is sent by his weak-minded parents to college, where a degree is gained by residence, and soon after appears as a full-wigged parson, half-fanatic, half-fool, to do his share toward bringing Christianity into contempt. Another principal person is Dick Hairbrain, an impudent fop, who is made a master of arts in the same way; and in the third part is introduced a character of the same description, belonging to the other sex.

During the last years of his residence at College, Trumbull paid as much attention as his other avocations would permit to the study of the law, and in 1773 resigned his tutorship and was admitted to the bar of Connecticut. He did not seek business in the courts, however, but went immediately to Boston, and entered as a student the office of John Adams, afterward President of the United States, and at that time an eminent advocate and counsellor. He was now in the focus of American politics. The controversy with Great Britain was rapidly approaching a crisis, and he entered with characteristic ardour into all the discussions of the time, employing his leisure hours in writing for the gazettes and in partisan correspondence. In 1774, he published anonymously his "Essay on the Times," and soon after returned to New Haven, and with the most flattering prospects commenced the practice of his profession.

The first gun of the revolution echoed along the continent in the following year, and private pursuits were abandoned in the general devotion to the cause of liberty. Trumbull wrote the first part of "McFingal," which was immediately printed in Philadelphia, where the Congress was then in session, and soon after republished in numerous editions in different parts of this country and in England. It was not finished until 1782, when it was issued complete in three cantos at Hartford, to which place Trumbull had removed in the preceding year.

"McFingal" is in the Hudibrastic vein, and much the best imitation of the great satire of Butler that has been written. The hero is a Scottish justice of the peace residing in the vicinity of Boston at the beginning of the revolution, and the first two cantos are principally occupied with a discussion between him and one Honorius on the course of the British government, in which McFingal, an unyielding loyalist, endeavours to make proselytes, while all his arguments are directed against himself. His zeal and his logic are together irresistibly ludicrous, but there is nothing in the character unnatural, as it is common for men who read more than they think, or attempt to discuss questions they do not understand, to use arguments which refute the positions they wish to defend. The meeting ends with a riot, in which McFINGAL is seized, tried by the mob, convicted of violen toryism, and tarred and feathered. On being set at liberty, he assembles his friends around him in his cellar, and harangues them until they are dispersed by the whigs, when he escapes to Boston, and the poem closes. These are all the important incidents of the story, yet it is never tedious, and few commence reading it who do not follow it to the end and regret its termination. Throughout the three cantos the wit is never separated from the character of the hero.

After the removal of TRUMBULL to Hartford a social club was established in that city, of which BARLOW, Colonel HUMPHRIES, Doctor LEMUEL HOPKINS, and our author, were members. They produced numerous essays on literary, moral, and political subjects, none of which attracted more applause than a series of papers in imitation of the "Rolliad," (a popular English work, ascribed to FOX, SHERIDAN, and their associates,) entitled "American Antiquities" and "Extracts from the Anarchiad," originally printed in the New Haven Gazette for 1786 and 1787. These papers have never been collected, but they were republished from one end of the country to the other in the periodicals of the time, and were supposed to have had considerable influence on public taste and opinions, and by the boldness of their satire to have kept in abeyance the leaders of political disorganization and infidel philosophy. TRUMBULL also aided BARLOW in the preparation of his edition of WATTS's version of the Psalms and wrote several of the paraphrases in that work which have been generally attributed to the author of "The Columbiad."

TRUMBULL was a popular lawyer, and was appointed to various honourable offices by the people and the government. From 1795, in consequence of ill health, he declined all public employment, and was for several years an invalid. At length, recovering his customary vigour, in 1800 he was elected a member of the legislature, and in the year following a judge of the Superior Court. In 1808 he was appointed a judge of the Supreme Court of Errors, and held the office until 1819, when he finally retired from public life. His poems were collected and published in 1820, and in 1825 he removed to Detroit, where his daughter, the wife of the Honourable WILLIAM WOODBRIDGE, recently a member of the United States Senate for Michigan, was residing, and died there in May, 1831, in the eighty-first year of his age.

ODE TO SLEEP.

I.

COME, gentle Sleep!
Balm of my wounds and softener of my woes,
And lull my weary heart in sweet repose,
And bid my sadden'd soul forget to weep,
And close the tearful eye;
While dewy eve, with solemn sweep,
Hath drawn her fleecy mantle o'er the sky,
And chased afar, adown the ethereal way,
The din of bustling care and gaudy eye of day.

II.

Come, but thy leaden sceptre leave,
Thy opiate rod, thy poppies pale,
Dipp'd in the torpid fount of Lethe's stream,
That shroud with night each intellectual beam,
And quench the immortal fire, in deep Oblivion's wave.
Yet draw the thick, impervious veil
O'er all the scenes of tasted wo;
Command each cypress shade to flee;
Between this toil-worn world and me
Display thy curtain broad, and hide the realms below.

III.

Descend, and, graceful, in thy hand,
With thee bring thy magic wand,
And thy pencil, taught to glow
In all the hues of Iris' bow.
And call thy bright, aerial train,
Each fairy form and visionary shade,
That in the Elysian land of dreams,
The flower-enwoven banks along,
Or bowery maze, that shades the purple streams,
Where gales of fragrance breathe the enamour'd song,
In more than mortal charms array'd,
People the airy vales and revel in thy reign.

IV.

But drive afar the haggard crew,
That haunt the guilt-encrimson'd bed,
Or dim before the frenzied view
Stalk with slow and sullen tread;
While furies, with infernal glare,
Wave their pale torches through the troubled air
And deep from Darkness' inmost womb,
Sad groans dispart the icy tomb,
And bid the sheeted spectre rise,
Mid shrieks and fiery shapes and deadly fantasies

* See a note on this subject appended to the Life of BARLOW in this volume.

V.

Come and loose the mortal chain,
That binds to clogs of clay the ethereal wing;
And give the astonish'd soul to rove,
Where never sunbeam stretch'd its wide domain;
And hail her kindred forms above,
In fields of uncreated spring,
Aloft where realms of endless glory rise,
And rapture paints in gold the landscape of the skies.

VI.

Then through the liquid fields we'll climb,
Where Plato treads empyreal air,
Where daring Homer sits sublime,
And Pindar rolls his fiery car;
Above the cloud-encircled hills,
Where high Parnassus lifts his airy head,
And Helicon's melodious rills
Flow gently through the warbling glade;
And all the Nine, in deathless choir combined,
Dissolve in harmony the enraptured mind,
And every bard, that tuned the immortal lay,
Basks in the ethereal blaze, and drinks celestial day.

VII.

Or call to my transported eyes
Happier scenes, for lovers made;
Bid the twilight grove arise,
Lead the rivulet through the glade.
In some flowering arbour laid,
Where opening roses taste the honey'd dew,
And plumy songsters carol through the shade,
Recall my long-lost wishes to my view.
Bid Time's inverted glass return
The scenes of bliss, with hope elate,
And hail the once expected morn,
And burst the iron bands of fate
Graced with all her virgin charms,
Attractive smiles and past, responsive flame,
Restore my ***** to my arms,
Just to her vows and faithful to her fame.

VIII.

Hymen's torch, with hallow'd fire,
Rising beams the auspicious ray.
Wake the dance, the festive lyre
Warbling sweet the nuptial lay;
Gay with beauties, once alluring,
Bid the bright enchantress move,
Eyes that languish, smiles of rapture,
And the rosy blush of love.
On her glowing breast reclining,
Mid that paradise of charms,
Every blooming grace combining,
Yielded to my circling arms,
I clasp the fair, and, kindling at the view,
Press to my heart the dear deceit, and think the transport true.

IX.

Hence, false, delusive dreams,
Fantastic hopes and mortal passions vain
Ascend, my soul, to nobler themes
Of happier import and sublimer strain.
Rising from this sphere of night,
Pierce yon blue vault, ingemm'd with golden fires:
Beyond where Saturn's languid car retires,
Or Sirius keen outvies the solar ray,
To worlds from every dross terrene refined,
Realms of the pure, ethereal mind,
Warm with the radiance of unchanging day:
Where cherub-forms and essences of light,
With holy song and heavenly rite,
From rainbow clouds their strains immortal pour;
An earthly guest, in converse high,
Explore the wonders of the sky,
From orb to orb with guides celestial soar,
And take, through heaven's wide round, the universal tour;

X.

And find that mansion of the blest,
Where, rising ceaseless from this lethal stage,
Heaven's favourite sons, from earthly chains released,
In happier Eden pass the eternal age.
The newborn soul beholds the angelic face
Of holy sires, that throng the blissful plain,
Or meets his consort's loved embrace,
Or clasps the son, so lost, so mourn'd in vain.
There, charm'd with each endearing wile,
Maternal fondness greets her infant's smile;
Long-sever'd friends, in transport doubly dear,
Unite and join the interminable train—
And, hark! a well-known voice I hear
I spy my sainted friend! I meet my Howe* again

XI.

Hail, sacred shade! for not to dust consign'd,
Lost in the grave, thine ardent spirit lies,
Nor fail'd that warm benevolence of mind
To claim the birthright of its native skies.
What radiant glory and celestial grace,
Immortal meed of piety and praise!
Come to my visions, friendly shade,
'Gainst all assaults my wayward weakness arm,
Raise my low thoughts, my nobler wishes aid,
When passions rage, or vain allurements charm;
The pomp of learning and the boast of art,
The glow, that fires in genius' boundless range,
The pride, that wings the keen, satiric dart,
And hails the triumph of revenge.
Teach me, like thee, to feel and know
Our humble station in this vale of wo,
Twilight of life, illumed with feeble ray,
The infant dawning of eternal day;
With heart expansive, through this scene improve
The social soul of harmony and love;
To heavenly hopes alone aspire and prize
The virtue, knowledge, bliss, and glory of the skies.

* Rev. Joseph Howe, pastor of a church in Boston, some time a fellow-tutor with the author at Yale College. He died in 1775. The conclusion of the ode was varied by inserting this tribute of affection.

THE COUNTRY CLOWN.*

Bred in distant woods, the clown
Brings all his country airs to town;
The odd address, with awkward grace,
That bows with all-averted face;
The half-heard compliments, whose note
Is swallow'd in the trembling throat;
The stiffen'd gait, the drawling tone,
By which his native place is known;
The blush, that looks, by vast degrees,
Too much like modesty to please;
The proud displays of awkward dress,
That all the country fop express:
The suit right gay, though much belated,
Whose fashion 's superannuated;
The watch, depending far in state,
Whose iron chain might form a grate
The silver buckle, dread to view,
O'ershadowing all the clumsy shoe;
The white-gloved hand, that tries to peep
From ruffle, full five inches deep;
With fifty odd affairs beside,
The foppishness of country pride.
Poor Dick! though first thy airs provoke
The obstreperous laugh and scornful joke,
Doom'd all the ridicule to stand,
While each gay dunce shall lend a hand;
Yet let not scorn dismay thy hope
To shine a witling and a fop.
Blest impudence the prize shall gain,
And bid thee sigh no more in vain.
Thy varied dress shall quickly show
At once the spendthrift and the beau.
With pert address and noisy tongue,
That scorns the fear of prating wrong
'Mongst listening coxcombs shalt thou shine,
And every voice shall echo thine.

THE FOP.†

How blest the brainless fop, whose praise
Is doom'd to grace these happy days,
When well-bred vice can genius teach,
And fame is placed in folly's reach;
Impertinence all tastes can hit,
And every rascal is a wit.
The lowest dunce, without despairing,
May learn the true sublime of swearing;
Learn the nice art of jests obscene,
While ladies wonder what they mean;
The heroism of brazen lungs,
The rhetoric of eternal tongues;
While whim usurps the name of spirit,
And impudence takes place of merit.
And every money'd clown and dunce
Commences gentleman at once.
For now, by easy rules of trade,
Mechanic gentlemen are made!
From handicrafts of fashion born;
Those very arts so much their scorn.
To tailors half themselves they owe,
Who make the clothes that make the beau.
Lo! from the seats, where, fops to bless,
Learn'd artists fix the forms of dress,
And sit in consultation grave
On folded skirt, or straiten'd sleeve,
The coxcomb trips with sprightly haste,
In all the flush of modern taste;
Oft turning, if the day be fair,
To view his shadow's graceful air;
Well pleased, with eager eye runs o'er
The laced suit glittering gay before;*
The ruffle, where from open'd vest
The rubied brooch adorns the breast;
The coat, with lengthening waist behind
Whose short skirts dangle in the wind;
The modish hat, whose breadth contains
The measure of its owner's brains;
The stockings gay, with various hues;
The little toe-encircling shoes;
The cane, on whose carved top is shown
A head, just emblem of his own;
While, wrapp'd in self, with lofty stride,
His little heart elate with pride,
He struts in all the joys of show
That tailors give, or beaux can know.
And who for beauty need repine,
That's sold at every barber's sign;
Nor lies in features or complexion,
But curls disposed in meet direction,
With strong pomatum's grateful odour,
And *quantum sufficit* of powder?
These charms can shed a sprightly grace
O'er the dull eye and clumsy face;
While the trim dancing-master's art
Shall gestures, trips, and bows impart,
Give the gay piece its final touches,
And lend those airs, would lure a duchess.
Thus shines the form, nor aught behind,
The gifts that deck the coxcomb's mind;
Then hear the daring muse disclose
The sense and piety of beaux.
To grace his speech, let France bestow
A set of compliments for show.
Land of politeness! that affords
The treasure of new-fangled words,
And endless quantities disburses
Of bows and compliments and curses;
The soft address, with airs so sweet,
That cringes at the ladies' feet;
The pert, vivacious, play-house style,
That wakes the gay assembly's smile;
Jests that his brother beaux may hit,
And pass with young coquettes for wit,
And prized by fops of true discerning,
Outface the pedantry of learning.
Yet learning too shall lend its aid
To fill the coxcomb's spongy head;
And studious oft he shall peruse
The labours of the modern muse.
From endless loads of novels gain
Soft, simpering tales of amorous pain,

* From the "Progress of Dulness."
† From the same.

* This passage alludes to the mode of dress then in fashion.

With double meanings, neat and handy,
From ROCHESTER and TRISTRAM SHANDY.*
The blundering aid of weak reviews,
That forge the fetters of the muse,
Shall give him airs of criticising
On faults of books, he ne'er set eyes on.
The magazines shall teach the fashion,
And commonplace of conversation,
And where his knowledge fails, afford
The aid of many a sounding word.
Then, lest religion he should need,
Of pious HUME he'll learn his creed,
By strongest demonstration shown,
Evince that nothing can be known;
Take arguments, unvex'd by doubt,
On VOLTAIRE's trust, or go without;
'Gainst Scripture rail in modern lore,
As thousand fools have rail'd before;
Or pleased a nicer art display
To expound its doctrines all away,
Suit it to modern tastes and fashions
By various notes and emendations;
The rules the ten commands contain,
With new provisos well explain;
Prove all religion was but fashion,
Beneath the Jewish dispensation.
A ceremonial law, deep hooded
In types and figures long exploded;
Its stubborn fetters all unfit
For these free times of gospel light,
This rake's millennium, since the day
When Sabbaths first were done away;
Since pander-conscience holds the door,
And lewdness is a vice no more;
And shame, the worst of deadly fiends,
On virtue, as its squire, attends.
Alike his poignant wit displays
The darkness of the former days,
When men the paths of duty sought,
And own'd what revelation taught;
Ere human reason grew so bright,
Men could see all things by its light,
And summon'd Scripture to appear,
And stand before its bar severe,
To clear its page from charge of fiction,
And answer pleas of contradiction;
Ere miracles were held in scorn,
Or BOLINGBROKE, or HUME were born.
And now the fop, with great energy,
Levels at priestcraft and the clergy,
At holy cant and godly prayers,
And bigots' hypocritic airs;
Musters each veteran jest to aid,
Calls piety the parson's trade;
Cries out 't is shame, past all abiding,
The world should still be so priest-ridden;
Applauds free thought that scorns control,
And generous nobleness of soul,
That acts its pleasure, good or evil,
And fears nor deity nor devil.
These standing topics never fail
To prompt our little wits to rail,
With mimic drollery of grimace,
And pleased impertinence of face,
'Gainst virtue arm their feeble forces,
And sound the charge in peals of curses.
Blest be his ashes! under ground
If any particles be found,
Who, friendly to the coxcomb race,
First taught those arts of commonplace,
Those topics fine, on which the beau
May all his little wits bestow,
Secure the simple laugh to raise,
And gain the dunce's palm of praise.
For where 's the theme that beaux could hit
With least similitude of wit,
Did not religion and the priest
Supply materials for the jest;
The poor in purse, with metals vile
For current coins, the world beguile;
The poor in brain, for genuine wit
Pass off a viler counterfeit;
While various thus their doom appears,
These lose their souls, and those their ears;
The want of fancy, whim supplies,
And native humour, mad caprice.
Loud noise for argument goes off,
For mirth polite, the ribald's scoff;
For sense, lewd drolleries entertain us,
And wit is mimick'd by profaneness.

* STERNE's Tristram Shandy was then in the highest vogue, and in the zenith of its transitory reputation.

CHARACTER OF McFINGAL.*

WHEN Yankees, skill'd in martial rule,
First put the British troops to school;
Instructed them in warlike trade,
And new manœuvres of parade;
The true war-dance of Yankee-reels,
And *manual exercise* of heels;
Made them give up, like saints complete,
The arm of flesh, and trust the feet,
And work, like Christians undissembling,
Salvation out by fear and trembling;
Taught Percy fashionable races,
And modern modes of Chevy-Chaces:†
From Boston, in his best array,
Great SQUIRE McFINGAL took his way,
And, graced with ensigns of renown,
Steer'd homeward to his native town.
His high descent our heralds trace
To Ossian's famed Fingalian race;
For though their name some part may lack,
Old FINGAL spelt it with a Mac;
Which great McPHERSON, with submission,
We hope will add the next edition.
His fathers flourish'd in the Highlands
Of Scotia's fog-benighted island;
Whence gain'd our squire two gifts by right,
Rebellion and the second-sight.

* From "McFingal."

† LORD PERCY commanded the party that was first opposed by the Americans at Lexington. This allusion to the family renown of Chevy-Chace arose from the precipitate manner of his quitting the field of battle, and returning to Boston.

Of these the first, in ancient days,
Had gain'd the noblest palms of praise;
'Gainst kings stood forth, and many a crown'd head
With terror of its might confounded;
Till rose a king with potent charm
His foes by goodness to disarm;
Whom every Scot and Jacobite
Straight fell in love with—at first sight;
Whose gracious speech, with aid of pensions,
Hush'd down all murmurs of dissensions,
And with the sound of potent metal,
Brought all their blust'ring swarms to settle;
Who rain'd his ministerial mannas,
Till loud sedition sung hosannas;
The good lords-bishops and the kirk
United in the public work;
Rebellion from the northern regions,
With Bute and Mansfield swore allegiance,
And all combined to raze, as nuisance,
Of church and state, the constitutions;
Pull down the empire, on whose ruins
They meant to edify their new ones;
Enslave the American wildernesses,
And tear the provinces in pieces.
For these our squire, among the valiant'st,
Employ'd his time, and tools, and talents;
And in their cause, with manly zeal,
Used his first virtue—to rebel;
And found this new rebellion pleasing
As his old king-destroying treason.
  Nor less avail'd his optic sleight,
And Scottish gift of second-sight.
No ancient sibyl, famed in rhyme,
Saw deeper in the womb of time;
No block in old Dodona's grove
Could ever more oracular prove.
Nor only saw he all that was,
But much that never came to pass;
Whereby all prophets far outwent he,
Though former days produced a plenty:
For any man with half an eye
What stands before him may espy;
But optics sharp it needs, I ween,
To see what is not to be seen.
As in the days of ancient fame,
Prophets and poets were the same,
And all the praise that poets gain
Is but for what they invent and feign:
So gain'd our squire his fame by seeing
Such things as never would have being;
Whence he for oracles was grown
The very tripod of his town.
Gazettes no sooner rose a lie in,
But straight he fell to prophesying;
Made dreadful slaughter in his course,
O'erthrew provincials, foot and horse;
Brought armies o'er by sudden pressings
Of Hanoverians, Swiss, and Hessians;*
Feasted with blood his Scottish clan,
And hang'd all rebels to a man;
Divided their estates and pelf,
And took a goodly share himself.
All this, with spirit energetic,
He did by second-sight prophetic.
  Thus stored with intellectual riches,
Skill'd was our squire in making speeches,
Where strength of brains united centres
With strength of lungs surpassing Stentor's.
But as some muskets so contrive it,
As oft to miss the mark they drive at,
And, though well aim'd at duck or plover,
Bear wide and kick their owners over:
So fared our squire, whose reas'ning toil
Would often on himself recoil,
And so much injured more his side,
The stronger arguments he applied;
As old war-elephants, dismay'd,
Trod down the troops they came to aid,
And hurt their own side more in battle
Than less and ordinary cattle:
Yet at town meetings ev'ry chief
Pinn'd faith on great McFingal's sleeve.
And, as he motioned, all, by rote,
Raised sympathetic hands to vote.
  The town, our hero's scene of action,
Had long been torn by feuds of faction;
And as each party's strength prevails,
It turn'd up different heads or tails;
With constant rattling, in a trice
Show'd various sides, as oft as dice:
As that famed weaver, wife to Ulysses,
By night each day's work pick'd in pieces
And though she stoutly did bestir her,
Its finishing was ne'er the nearer:
So did this town, with steadfast zeal,
Weave cobwebs for the public weal;
Which when completed, or before,
A second vote in pieces tore.
They met, made speeches full long-winded,
Resolved, protested, and rescinded;
Addresses sign'd, then chose committees,
To stop all drinking of Bohea-teas;
With winds of doctrine veer'd about,
And turn'd all Whig committees out.
Meanwhile our hero, as their head,
In pomp the Tory faction led,
Still following, as the squire should please
Successive on, like files of geese.

EXTREME HUMANITY *

Thus Gage's arms did fortune bless
With triumph, safety, and success:
But mercy is without dispute
His first and darling attribute;
So great, it far outwent, and conquer'd,
His military skill at Concord.
There, when the war he chose to wage,
Shone the benevolence of Gage;

* This prophecy, like some of the prayers of Homer's heroes, was but half accomplished. The Hanoverians, &c., indeed came over, and much were they feasted with blood; but the hanging of the rebels and the dividing their estates remain unfulfilled. This, however, cannot be the fault of the hero, but rather the British ministers who left off the war before the work was completed.

* From "McFingal."

Sent troops to that ill-omen'd place
On errands mere of special grace,
And all the work he chose them for
Was to prevent a civil war;
And for that purpose he projected
The only certain way to effect it,
To take your powder, stores, and arms,
And all your means of doing harms:
As prudent folks take knives away,
Lest children cut themselves at play.
And yet, though this was all his scheme,
This war you still will charge on him;
And though he oft has swore and said it,
Stick close to facts, and give no credit,
Think you, he wish'd you'd brave and beard him?
Why, 'twas the very thing that scared him.
He'd rather you should all have run,
Than stay'd to fire a single gun.
And for the civil law you lament,
Faith, you yourselves must take the blame in't;
For had you then, as he intended,
Given up your arms, it must have ended;
Since that's no war, each mortal knows,
Where one side only gives the blows,
And the other bear 'em; on reflection
The most you'll call it, is correction.
Nor could the contest have gone higher,
If you had ne'er return'd the fire;
But when you shot and not before,
It then commenced a civil war.
Else GAGE, to end this controversy,
Had but corrected you in mercy:
Whom mother Britain, old and wise,
Sent o'er the colonies to chastise;
Command obedience on their peril
Of ministerial whip and ferule,
And, since they ne'er must come of age,
Govern'd and tutor'd them by GAGE.
Still more, that this was all their errand
The army's conduct makes apparent.
What though at Lexington you can say
They kill'd a few they did not fancy,
At Concord then, with manful popping,
Discharg'd a round, the ball to open—
Yet, when they saw your rebel-rout
Determined still to hold it out;
Did they not show their love to peace,
And wish that discord straight might cease,
Demonstrate, and by proofs uncommon,
Their orders were to injure no man!
For did not every regular run
As soon as e'er you fired a gun?
Take the first shot you sent them greeting,
As meant their signal for retreating;
And fearful, if they stay'd for sport,
You might by accident be hurt,
Convey themselves with speed away
Full twenty miles in half a day;
Race till their legs were grown so weary,
They'd scarce suffice their weight to carry?
Whence GAGE extols, from general hearsay,
The great activity of LORD PERCY,
Whose brave example led them on,
And spirited the troops to run;
And now may boast, at royal levees,
A Yankee chace worth forty Cherys.
Yet you, as vile as they were kind,
Pursued, like tigers, still behind;
Fired on them at your will, and shut
The town, as though you'd starve them out;
And with parade preposterous hedged,
Affect to hold him there besieged.

THE DECAYED COQUETTE.*

NEW beauties push her from the stage;
She trembles at the approach of age,
And starts to view the alter'd face
That wrinkles at her in her glass:
So Satan, in the monk's tradition,
Fear'd, when he met his apparition.
At length her name each coxcomb cancels
From standing lists of toasts and angels;
And slighted where she shone before,
A grace and goddess now no more,
Despised by all, and doom'd to meet
Her lovers at her rival's feet,
She flies assemblies, shuns the ball,
And cries out, vanity, on all;
Affects to scorn the tinsel-shows
Of glittering belles and gaudy beaux;
Nor longer hopes to hide by dress
The tracks of age upon her face.
Now careless grown of airs polite,
Her noonday nightcap meets the sight:
Her hair uncomb'd collects together,
With ornaments of many a feather;
Her stays for easiness thrown by,
Her rumpled handkerchief awry,
A careless figure half undress'd,
(The reader's wits may guess the rest;)
All points of dress and neatness carried,
As though she'd been a twelvemonth married
She spends her breath, as years prevail,
At this sad wicked world to rail,
To slander all her sex *impromptu*,
And wonder what the times will come to.

* From the "Progress of Dulness."

TIMOTHY DWIGHT.

[Born 1752. Died 1817.]

Timothy Dwight, D. D., LL. D., was born in Northampton, Massachusetts, on the fourteenth of May, 1752. His father was a merchant, of excellent character and liberal education; and his mother, a daughter of the great Jonathan Edwards, was one of the noblest matrons of her time, distinguished not less for her maternal solicitude, ardent temperament, and patriotism, than for the intellectual qualities which made so illustrious the name of the New England metaphysician. She early perceived the indications of superior genius in her son; and we are told by his biographers that under her direction he became familiar with the rudiments of the Latin language before he was six years old, and at the same early period laid the foundation of his remarkable knowledge of history, geography, and the kindred departments of learning. When thirteen years old he entered Yale College. His previous unremitted attention to study had impaired his health, and he made little progress during the first two years of his residence at New Haven; but his subsequent intense and uninterrupted application enabled him to graduate in 1769, the first scholar in the institution. Immediately after obtaining the degree of bachelor of arts, he opened a grammar-school in New Haven, in which he continued two years, at the end of which time he was elected a tutor in his *alma mater*. Yale College was established in the year 1700 by several Congregational clergymen, and had, before the period at which Dwight returned to it, become generally unpopular, in consequence of the alleged illiberality of the trustees towards other denominations of Christians. At this time two of the tutors had resigned, leaving in office Mr. Joseph Howe, a man of erudition and liberal sentiments, and Dwight and John Trumbull were chosen in their places. The regeneration of the seminary now commenced; the study of belles lettres was successfully introduced; its character rapidly rose, and so popular did Dwight become with the students, that when, at the age of twenty-five, he resigned his office, they drew up and almost unanimously signed a petition to the corporation that he might be elected to the presidency. He, however, interfered and prevented the formal presentation of the application.

In 1771, Dwight commenced writing the "Conquest of Canaan," an "epic poem in eleven books," which he finished in 1774, before he was twenty-three years of age. The subject probably was not the most fortunate that could have been chosen, but a poet with passion and a brilliant imagination, by attempting to paint the manners of the time and the natural characteristics of the oriental world, might have treated it more successfully. Dwight "endeavoured to represent such manners as are removed from the peculiarities of any age or country, and might belong to the amiable and virtuous of any period; elevated without design, refined without ceremony, elegant without fashion, and agreeable because they are ornamented with sincerity, dignity, and religion;" his poem therefore has no distinctive features, and with very slight changes would answer as well for any other land or period as for Judea at the time of its conquest by Joshua. Its versification is harmonious, but monotonous, and the work is free from all the extravagances of expression and sentiment which so frequently lessen the worth of poetry by youthful and inexperienced writers. Some of the passages which I have quoted from the "Conquest of Canaan" are doubtless equal to any American poetry produced at this period.

In 1777, the classes in Yale College were separated on account of the war, and, in the month of May, Dwight repaired with a number of students to Weathersfield, in Connecticut, where he remained until the autumn, when, having been licensed to preach as a Congregational minister, he joined the army as a chaplain. In this office he won much regard by his professional industry and eloquence, and at the same time exerted considerable influence by writing patriotic songs, which became popular throughout New England. The death of his father, in 1778, induced him to resign his situation in the army, and return to Northampton, to assist his mother to support and educate her family. He remained there five years, labouring on a farm, preaching, and superintending a school, and was in that period twice elected a member of the Legislature of Massachusetts. Declining offers of political advancement, he was, in 1783, ordained a minister in the parish of Greenfield, in Connecticut, where he remained twelve years, discharging his pastoral duties in a manner that was perfectly satisfactory to his people, and taking charge of an academy, established by himself, which soon become the most popular school of the kind that had ever existed in America.

The "Conquest of Canaan," although finished ten years before, was not printed until the spring of 1785. It was followed by "Greenfield Hill," a descriptive, historical, and didactic poem, which was published in 1794. This work is divided into seven parts, entitled "The Prospect," "The Flourishing Village," "The Burning of Fairfield," "The Destruction of the Pequods," "The Clergyman's Advice to the Villagers," "The Farmer's Advice to the Villagers," and "The Vision, or Prospect of the Future Happiness of America." It contains some pleasing pictures of rural life, but added little to the author's reputation as a poet. The "Triumph of Infidelity," a satire, occasioned by the appearance of a defence of Universalism, was his next attempt in poetry. It was printed anonymously, and his fame would not have been less had its authorship been still a secret.

On the death of Dr. STYLES, in 1795, DWIGHT was elected to the presidency of Yale College, which at this time was in a disordered condition, and suffering from pecuniary embarrassments. The reputation of the new president as a teacher soon brought around him a very large number of students; new professorships were established, the library and philosophical apparatus were extended, the course of study and system of government changed, and the college rapidly rose in the public favour. Besides acting as president, DWIGHT was the stated preacher, professor of theology, and teacher of the senior class, for nearly twenty-one years, during which time the reputation of the college was inferior to that of no other in America.

Dr. DWIGHT died at his residence in New Haven on the eleventh of January, 1817, in the sixty-fifth year of his age. The following catalogue of his works is probably complete: "America," a poem in the style of Pope's "Windsor Forest," 1772; "The History, Eloquence and Poetry of the Bible," 1772; "The Conquest of Canaan," a poem, 1785; "An Election Sermon," 1791; "The Genuineness and Authenticity of the New Testament," 1793; "Greenfield Hill," a poem, 1794; "The Triumph of Infidelity," a satire, and two "Discourses on the Nature and Danger of Infidel Philosophy," 1797; "The Duty of Americans in the Present Crisis," 1798; "Discourse on the Character of Washington," 1800; "Discourse on some Events in the last Century," 1801; "Sermons," on the death of E. G. Marsh, 1804; on Duelling, 1805; at the Andover Theological Seminary, 1808; on the ordination of E. Pearson, 1808; on the death of Governor Trumbull, 1809; on Charity, 1810; at the ordination of N. W. Taylor, 1812; on two days of public fasting, 1812; and before the American Board of Foreign Missions, 1813; "Remarks on a Review of Inchiquin's Letters," 1815; "Observations on Language," and an "Essay on Light," 1816; and "Theology Explained and Defended," in a series of sermons, and "Travels in New England and New York," in which is given an account of various spring and autumn vacation excursions, each in four volumes, published after his death.

The merits of Dr. DWIGHT as a poet are eminently respectable. COWPER, who wrote a criticism of his "Conquest of Canaan" in "The Analytical Review," for 1789, says: "His numbers imitate pretty closely those of POPE, and therefore cannot fail to be musical; but he is chiefly to be commended for the animation with which he writes, and which rather increases as he proceeds than suffers any abatement..... A strain of fine enthusiasm runs through the whole seventh book, and no man who has a soul impressible by a bright display of the grandest subjects that revelation furnishes, will read it without some emotion."

AN INDIAN TEMPLE.

THERE too, with awful rites, the hoary priest,
Without, beside the moss-grown altar stood,
(His sable form in magic cincture dress'd,)
And heap'd the mingled offering to his god.
What time with golden light calm evening glow'd,
The mystic dust, the flower of silver bloom
And spicy herb, his hand in order strew'd;
Bright rose the curling flame, and rich perfume
On smoky wings upflew or settled round the tomb.

Then o'er the circus danced the maddening throng
As erst the Thyas roam'd dread Nysa round,
And struck to forest notes the ecstatic song,
While slow beneath them heaved the wavy ground.
With a low, lingering groan of dying sound,
The woodland rumbled; murmur'd deep each stream;
Shrill sung the leaves; the ether sigh'd profound;
Pale tufts of purple topp'd the silver flame,
And many-colour'd forms on evening breezes came:

Thin, twilight forms, attired in changing sheen
Of plumes, high-tinctured in the western ray—
Bending, they peep'd the fleecy folds between,
Their wings light-rustling in the breath of May;
Soft-hovering round the fire in mystic play,
They snuff'd the incense waved in clouds afar,
Then silent floated toward the setting day;
Eve redden'd each fine form, each misty car,
And through them faintly gleam'd, at times, the western star.

Then—so tradition sings—the train behind,
In plumy zones of rainbow beauty dress'd,
Rode the Great Spirit, in the obedient wind,
In yellow clouds slow-sailing from the west.
With dawning smiles the god his votaries blest,
And taught where deer retired to ivy dell;
What chosen chief with proud command t' invest,
Where crept the approaching foe, with purpose fell,
And where to wind the scout, and war's dark storm dispel.

There, on her lover's tomb in silence laid,
While still and sorrowing shower'd the moon's pale beam,
At times expectant, slept the widow'd maid,
Her soul far-wandering on the sylph-wing'd dream.
Wafted from evening skies on sunny stream,
Her darling youth with silver pinions shone;
With voice of music, tuned to sweetest theme,
He told of shell-bright bowers beyond the sun,
Where years of endless joy o'er Indian lovers run

ENGLAND AND AMERICA.*

Soon fleets the sunbright form, by man adored!—
Soon fell the head of gold to Time a prey,
The arms, the trunk, his cankering tooth devour'd,
And whirlwinds blew the iron dust away.
Where dwelt imperial Timur, far astray
Some lonely-musing pilgrim now inquires;
And, rack'd by storms and hastening to decay,
Mohammed's mosque foresees its final fires,
And Rome's more lordly temple day by day expires.

As o'er proud Asian realms the traveller winds,
His manly spirit, hush'd by terror, falls
When some forgotten town's lost site he finds;
Where ruin wild his pondering eye appals,
Where silence swims along the moulder'd walls,
And broods upon departed Grandeur's tomb,
Through the lone, hollow aisles, sad Echo calls
At each slow step; deep sighs the breathing gloom,
And weeping fields around bewail their empress' doom.

Where o'er a hundred realms the throne uprose
The screech-owl nests, the panther builds his home;
Sleep the dull newts, the lazy adders doze
Where pomp and luxury danced the golden room;
Low lies in dust the sky-resembled dome,
Tall grass around the broken column waves,
And brambles climb and lonely thistles bloom;
The moulder'd arch the weedy streamlet laves,
And low resound, beneath, unnumber'd sunken graves.

In thee, O Albion! queen of nations, live [known;
Whatever splendours earth's wide realms have
In thee proud Persia sees her pomp revive,
And Greece her arts, and Rome her lordly throne;
By every wind thy Tyrian fleets are blown;
Supreme, on Fame's dread roll, thy heroes stand;
All ocean's realms thy naval sceptre own;
Of bards, of sages, how august thy band!
And one rich Eden blooms around thy garden'd land.

But, O how vast thy crimes! Through Heaven's great year,
When few centurial suns have traced their way;
When Southern Europe, worn by feuds severe,
Weak, doting, fallen, has bow'd to Russian sway,
And setting Glory beam'd her farewell ray,
To wastes, perchance, thy brilliant fields shall turn;
In dust thy temples, towers, and towns decay;
The forest howl where London turrets burn,
And all thy garlands deck thy sad funereal urn.

Some land, scarce glimmering in the light of fame,
Scepter'd with arts and arms, (if I divine,)
Some unknown wild, some shore without a name,
In all thy pomp shall then majestic shine.
As silver-headed Time's slow years decline,
Not ruins only meet the inquiring eye;
Where round yon mouldering oak vain brambles
The filial stem, already towering high, [twine,
Ere long shall stretch his arms, and nod in yonder sky.

Where late resounded the wild woodland roar
Now heaves the palace, now the temple smiles;
Where frown'd the rude rock and the desert shore
Now Pleasure sports, and Business want beguiles,
And Commerce wings her flight to thousand isles;
Culture walks forth, gay laugh the loaded fields,
And jocund Labour plays his harmless wiles;
Glad Science brightens, Art her mansion builds,
And Peace uplifts her wand, and HEAVEN his blessing yields.

* The extract above and the one which precedes it are from the canto on the destruction of the Pequod Indians, in "Greenfield Hill."

THE SOCIAL VISIT.*

YE Muses! dames of dignified renown,
Revered alike in country and in town,
Your bard the mysteries of a visit show;
(For sure your ladyships those mysteries know:)
What is it, then, obliging sisters! say,
The debt of social visiting to pay?
'Tis not to toil before the idol pier;
To shine the first in fashion's lunar sphere;
By sad engagements forced abroad to roam,
And dread to find the expecting fair at home!
To stop at thirty doors in half a day,
Drop the gilt card, and proudly roll away;
To alight, and yield the hand with nice parade;
Up stairs to rustle in the stiff brocade;
Swim through the drawing-room with studied air,
Catch the pink'd beau, and shade the rival fair;
To sit, to curb, to toss with bridled mien,
Mince the scant speech, and lose a glance between;
Unfurl the fan, display the snowy arm,
And ope, with each new motion, some new charm:
Or sit in silent solitude, to spy
Each little failing with malignant eye;
Or chatter with incessancy of tongue,
Careless if kind or cruel, right or wrong;
To trill of us and ours, of mine and me,
Our house, our coach, our friends, our family,
While all the excluded circle sit in pain,
And glance their cool contempt or keen disdain:
To inhale from proud Nanking a sip of tea,
And wave a courtesy trim and flirt away:
Or waste at cards peace, temper, health, and life,
Begin with sullenness, and end in strife;
Lose the rich feast by friendly converse given,
And backward turn from happiness and heaven.
It is in decent habit, plain and neat,
To spend a few choice hours in converse sweet,
Careless of forms, to act the unstudied part,
To mix in friendship, and to blend the heart;
To choose those happy themes which all must feel
The moral duties and the household weal,
The tale of sympathy, the kind design,
Where rich affections soften and refine,
To amuse, to be amused, to bless, be bless'd,
And tune to harmony the common breast;
To cheer with mild good-humour's sprightly ray,
And smooth life's passage o'er its thorny way;
To circle round the hospitable board,
And taste each good our generous climes afford,
To court a quick return with accents kind,
And leave, at parting, some regret behind.

* From "Greenfield Hill."

THE COUNTRY PASTOR.*

Ah! knew he but his happiness, of men†
Not the least happy he, who, free from broils
And base ambition, vain and bustling pomp,
Amid a friendly cure, and competence,
Tastes the pure pleasures of parochial life.
What though no crowd of clients, at his gate,
To falsehood and injustice bribe his tongue,
And flatter into guilt!—what though no bright
And gilded prospects lure ambition on
To legislative pride, or chair of state?
What though no golden dreams entice his mind
To burrow, with the mole, in dirt and mire?
What though no splendid villa, Eden'd round
With gardens of enchantment, walks of state,
And all the grandeur of superfluous wealth,
Invite the passenger to stay his steed,
And ask the liveried foot-boy, "Who dwells here?"
What though no swarms, around his sumptuous
board,
Of soothing flatterers, humming in the shine
Of opulence, and honey from its flowers
Devouring, till their time arrives to sting,
Inflate his mind; his virtues round the year
Repeating, and his faults, with microscope
Inverted, lessen, till they steal from sight?—
Yet from the dire temptations these present
His state is free; temptations, few can stem;
Temptations, by whose sweeping torrent hurl'd
Down the dire steep of guilt, unceasing fall
Sad victims, thousands of the brightest minds
That time's dark reign adorn; minds, to whose grasp
Heaven seems most freely offer'd; to man's eye,
Most hopeful candidates for angels' joys.
His lot, that wealth, and power, and pride forbids,
Forbids him to become the tool of fraud,
Injustice, misery, ruin; saves his soul
From all the needless labours, griefs, and cares,
That avarice and ambition agonize;
From those cold nerves of wealth, that, palsied, feel
No anguish, but its own; and ceaseless lead
To thousand meannesses, as gain allures.
Though oft compell'd to meet the gross attack
Of shameless ridicule and towering pride,
Sufficient good is his; good, real, pure,
With guilt unmingled. Rarely forced from home,
Around his board his wife and children smile;
Communion sweetest, nature here can give,
Each fond endearment, office of delight,
With love and duty blending. Such the joy
My bosom oft has known. His, too, the task
To rear the infant plants that bud around;
To ope their little minds to truth's pure light;
To take them by the hand, and lead them on
In that straight, narrow road where virtue walks;
To guard them from a vain, deceiving world,
And point their course to realms of promised life.
His too the esteem of those who weekly hear
His words of truth divine; unnumber'd acts
Of real love attesting to his eye
Their filial tenderness. Where'er he walks,
The friendly welcome and inviting smile
Wait on his steps, and breathe a kindred joy.
Oft too in friendliest association join'd,
He greets his brethren, with a flowing heart,
Flowing with virtue; all rejoiced to meet,
And all reluctant parting; every aim,
Benevolent, aiding with purpose kind;
While, season'd with unblemish'd cheerfulness,
Far distant from the tainted mirth of vice,
Their hearts disclose each contemplation sweet
Of things divine; and blend in friendship pure,
Friendship sublimed by piety and love.
All virtue's friends are his: the good, the just,
The pious, to his house their visits pay,
And converse high hold of the true, the fair,
The wonderful, the moral, the divine:
Of saints and prophets, patterns bright of truth,
Lent to a world of sin, to teach mankind
How virtue in that world can live and shine;
Of learning's varied realms; of Nature's works;
And that bless'd book which gilds man's darksome
way
With light from heaven; of bless'd Messiah's throne
And kingdom; prophecies divine fulfill'd,
And prophecies more glorious yet to come
In renovated days; of that bright world,
And all the happy trains which that bright world
Inhabit, whither virtue's sons are gone:
While God the whole inspires, adorns, exalts;
The source, the end, the substance, and the soul.
This too the task, the bless'd, the useful task,
To invigour order, justice, law, and rule;
Peace to extend, and bid contention cease;
To teach the words of life; to lead mankind
Back from the wild of guilt and brink of wo
To virtue's house and family; faith, hope,
And joy to inspire; to warm the soul
With love to God and man; to cheer the sad,
To fix the doubting, rouse the languid heart;
The wandering to restore; to spread with down
The thorny bed of death; console the poor,
Departing mind, and aid its lingering wing.
To him her choicest pages Truth expands,
Unceasing, where the soul-entrancing scenes
Poetic fiction boasts are real all:
Where beauty, novelty, and grandeur wear
Superior charms, and moral worlds unfold
Sublimities transporting and divine.
Not all the scenes Philosophy can boast,
Though them with nobler truths he ceaseless blends,
Compare with these. They, as they found the mind,
Still leave it; more inform'd, but not more wise.
These wiser, nobler, better, make the man.
Thus every happy mean of solid good
His life, his studies, and profession yield.
With motives hourly new, each rolling day
Allures, through wisdom's path and truth's fair field,
His feet to yonder skies. Before him heaven
Shines bright, the scope sublime of all his prayers
The meed of every sorrow, pain, and toil

* From "Greenfield Hill."

† Ah! knew he but his happiness, of men
The happiest he, &c. THOMSON.

O fortunatos nimium sua si bona norint,
Agricolas! VIRGIL, *Georg.* 2.

THE COUNTRY SCHOOLMASTER.*

Where yonder humble spire salutes the eye,
Its vane slow-turning in the liquid sky,
Where, in light gambols, healthy striplings sport,
Ambitious learning builds her outer court;
A grave preceptor, there, her usher stands,
And rules without a rod her little bands.
Some half-grown sprigs of learning graced his brow:
Little he knew, though much he wish'd to know;
Enchanted hung o'er Virgil's honey'd lay,
And smiled to see desipient Horace play;
Glean'd scraps of Greek; and, curious, traced afar,
Through Pope's clear glass the bright Mæonian star.
Yet oft his students at his wisdom stared,
For many a student to his side repair'd;
Surprised, they heard him Dilworth's knots untie,
And tell what lands beyond the Atlantic lie.
Many his faults; his virtues small and few;
Some little good he did, or strove to do;
Laborious still, he taught the early mind,
And urged to manners meek and thoughts refined;
Truth he impress'd, and every virtue praised;
While infant eyes in wondering silence gazed;
The worth of time would day by day unfold,
And tell them every hour was made of gold.

THE BATTLE OF AI.†

Now near the burning domes the squadrons stood,
Their breasts impatient for the scenes of blood:
On every face a death-like glimmer sate,
The unbless'd harbinger of instant fate.
High through the gloom, in pale and dreadful spires,
Rose the long terrors of the dark-red fires;
Torches, and torrent sparks, by whirlwinds driven,
Stream'd through the smoke, and fired the clouded heaven;
As oft tall turrets sunk, with rushing sound,
Broad flames burst forth, and sweep the ethereal round;
The bright expansion lighten'd all the scene,
And deeper shadows lengthen'd o'er the green.
Loud through the walls, that cast a golden gleam,
Crown'd with tall pyramids of bending flame,
As thunders rumble down the darkening vales,
Roll'd the deep, solemn voice of rushing gales:
The bands, admiring, saw the wondrous sight,
And expectation trembled for the fight.
At once the sounding clarion breathed alarms;
Wide from the forest burst the flash of arms;
Thick gleam'd the helms; and o'er astonish'd fields,
Like thousand meteors rose the flame-bright shields.
In gloomy pomp, to furious combat roll'd
Ranks sheath'd in mail, and chiefs in glimmering gold;
In floating lustre bounds the dim-seen steed,
And cars unfinish'd, swift to cars succeed:
From all the host ascends a dark-red glare,
Here in full blaze, in distant twinklings there;
Slow waves the dreadful light, as round the shore
Night's solemn blasts with deep confusion roar:
So rush'd the footsteps of the embattled train,
And send an awful murmur o'er the plain.
Tall in the opposing van, bold Irad stood,
And bid the clarion sound the voice of blood.
Loud blew the trumpet on the sweeping gales,
Rock'd the deep groves, and echoed round the vales·
A ceaseless murmur all the concave fills,
Waves through the quivering camp, and trembles o'er the hills.
High in the gloomy blaze the standards flew;
The impatient youth his burnish'd falchion drew,
Ten thousand swords his eager bands display'd,
And crimson terrors danced on every blade.
With equal rage, the bold, Hazorian train
Pour'd a wide deluge o'er the shadowy plain;
Loud rose the songs of war, loud clang'd the shields,
Dread shouts of vengeance shook the shuddering fields;
With mingled din, shrill, martial music rings,
And swift to combat each fierce hero springs.
So broad, and dark, a midnight storm ascends,
Bursts on the main, and trembling nature rends;
The red foam burns, the watery mountains rise,
One deep, unmeasured thunder heaves the skies;
The bark drives lonely; shivering and forlorn,
The poor, sad sailors wish the lingering morn:
Not with less fury rush'd the vengeful train;
Not with less tumult roar'd the embattled plain.
Now in the oak's black shade they fought conceal'd;
And now they shouted through the open field;
The long, pale splendours of the curling flame
Cast o'er their polish'd arms a livid gleam;
An umber'd lustre floated round their way,
And lighted falchions to the fierce affray.
Now the swift chariots 'gainst the stubborn oak
Dash'd; and the earth re-echoes to the shock.
From shade to shade the forms tremendous stream,
And their arms flash a momentary flame.
Mid hollow tombs as fleets an airy train,
Lost in the skies, or fading o'er the plain;
So visionary shapes, around the fight,
Shoot through the gloom, and vanish from the sight;
Through twilight paths the maddening coursers bound,
The shrill swords crack, the clashing shields resound.
There, lost in grandeur, might the eye behold
The dark-red glimmerings of the steel and gold;
The chief; the steed; the nimbly-rushing car;
And all the horrors of the gloomy war.
Here the thick clouds, with purple lustre bright,
Spread o'er the long, long host, and gradual sun in night;
Here half the world was wrapp'd in rolling fires,
And dreadful valleys sunk between the spires.
Swift ran black forms across the livid flame,
And oaks waved slowly in the trembling beam:
Loud rose the mingled noise; with hollow sound,
Deep rolling whirlwinds roar, and thundering flames resound.
As drives a blast along the midnight heath,
Rush'd raging Irad on the scenes of death;
High o'er his shoulder gleam'd his brandish'd blade,
And scatter'd ruin round the twilight shade.

* From "Greenfield Hill."

† This and the three following extracts are from "The Conquest of Canaan."

Full on a giant hero's sweeping car
He pour'd the tempest of resistless war;
His twinkling lance the heathen raised on high,
And hurl'd it, fruitless, through the gloomy sky;
From the bold youth the maddening coursers wheel,
Gash'd by the vengeance of his slaughtering steel;
'Twixt two tall oaks the helpless chief they drew;
The shrill car dash'd; the crack'd wheels rattling flew;
Crush'd in his arms, to rise he strove in vain,
And lay unpitied on the dreary plain.

THE LAMENTATION OF SELIMA.

Canst thou forget, when, call'd from southern bowers,
Love tuned the groves, and spring awaked the flowers,
How, loosed from slumbers by the morning ray,
O'er balmy plains we bent our frequent way?
On thy fond arm, with pleasing gaze, I hung,
And heard sweet music murmur o'er thy tongue;
Hand lock'd in hand, with gentle ardour press'd,
Pour'd soft emotions through the heaving breast;
In magic transport heart with heart entwined,
And in sweet languor lost the melting mind.
'T was then thy voice, attuned to wisdom's lay,
Show'd fairer worlds, and traced the immortal way;
In virtue's pleasing paths my footsteps tried,
My sweet companion and my skilful guide;
Through varied knowledge taught my mind to soar,
Search hidden truths, and new-found walks explore:
While still the tale, by nature learn'd to rove,
Slid, unperceived, to scenes of happy love.
Till, weak and lost, the faltering converse fell,
And eyes disclosed what eyes alone could tell;
In rapturous tumult bade the passions roll,
And spoke the living language of the soul.
With what fond hope, through many a blissful hour,
We gave the soul to fancy's pleasing power;
Lost in the magic of that sweet employ
To build gay scenes, and fashion future joy!
We saw mild peace o'er fair Canaan rise,
And shower her pleasures from benignant skies.
On airy hills our happy mansion rose,
Built but for joy, nor room reserved for woes.
Round the calm solitude, with ceaseless song,
Soft roll'd domestic ecstasy along:
Sweet as the sleep of innocence, the day,
By raptures number'd, lightly danced away:
To love, to bliss, the blended soul was given,
And each, too happy, ask'd no brighter heaven.
Yet then, even then, my trembling thoughts would rove,
And steal an hour from Irad, and from love,
Through dread futurity all anxious roam,
And cast a mournful glance on ills to come. . . .
And must the hours in ceaseless anguish roll?
Must no soft sunshine cheer my clouded soul?
Spring charm around me brightest scenes, in vain,
And youth's angelic visions wake to pain!
O, come once more; with fond endearments come
Burst the cold prison of the sullen tomb;
Through favourite walks thy chosen maid attend,
Where well known shades for thee their branches bend;
Shed the sweet poison from thy speaking eye,
And look those raptures lifeless words deny!
Still be the tale rehearsed, that ne'er could tire,
But, told each eve, fresh pleasure could inspire;
Still hoped those scenes which love and fancy drew,
But, drawn a thousand times, were ever new!
Again all bright shall glow the morning beam,
Again soft suns dissolve the frozen stream,
Spring call young breezes from the southern skies,
And, clothed in splendour, flowery millions rise—
In vain to thee! No morn's indulgent ray
Warms the cold mansion of thy slumbering clay
No mild, ethereal gale, with tepid wing,
Shall fan thy locks, or waft approaching spring:
Unfelt, unknown, shall breathe the rich perfume,
And unheard music wave around thy tomb.
A cold, dumb, dead repose invests thee round;
Still as a void, ere Nature form'd a sound.
O'er thy dark region, pierced by no kind ray,
Slow roll the long, oblivious hours away.
In these wide walks, this solitary round,
Where the pale moonbeam lights the glimmering ground,
At each sad turn, I view thy spirit come,
And glide, half-seen, behind a neighbouring tomb;
With visionary hand, forbid my stay,
Look o'er the grave, and beckon me away.

PREDICTION TO JOSHUA RELATIVE TO AMERICA.

Far o'er yon azure main thy view extend,
Where seas and skies in blue confusion blend:
Lo, there a mighty realm, by Heaven design'd
The last retreat for poor, oppress'd mankind;
Form'd with that pomp which marks the hand divine,
And clothes yon vault where worlds unnumber'd shine.
Here spacious plains in solemn grandeur spread,
Here cloudy forests cast eternal shade;
Rich valleys wind, the sky-tall mountains brave,
And inland seas for commerce spread the wave.
With nobler floods the sea-like rivers roll,
And fairer lustre purples round the pole.
Here, warm'd by happy suns, gay mines unfold
The useful iron and the lasting gold;
Pure, changing gems in silence learn to glow,
And mock the splendours of the covenant bow
On countless hills, by savage footsteps trod,
That smile to see the future harvest nod,
In glad succession plants unnumber'd bloom,
And flowers unnumber'd breathe a rich perfume.
Hence life once more a length of days shall claim,
And health, reviving, light her purple flame.
Far from all realms this world imperial lies,
Seas roll between, and threat'ning tempests rise
Alike removed beyond ambition's pale,
And the bold pinions of the venturous sail:

Till circling years the destined period bring,
And a new Moses lift the daring wing,
Through trackless seas an unknown flight explores,
And hails a new Canaan's promised shores.
On yon far strand behold that little train
Ascending venturous o'er the unmeasured main;
No dangers fright, no ills the course delay;
'Tis virtue prompts, and God directs the way.
Speed—speed, ye sons of truth! let Heaven befriend,
Let angels waft you, and let peace attend.
O! smile, thou sky serene; ye storms, retire;
And airs of Eden every sail inspire.
Swift o'er the main behold the canvass fly,
And fade and fade beneath the farthest sky;
See verdant fields the changing waste unfold;
See sudden harvests dress the plains in gold;
In lofty walls the moving rocks ascend,
And dancing woods to spires and temples bend. . .
Here empire's last and brightest throne shall rise,
And Peace, and Right, and Freedom greet the skies;
To morn's far realms her trading ships shall sail,
Or lift their canvass to the evening gale:
In wisdom's walks her sons ambitious soar,
Tread starry fields, and untried scenes explore.
And, hark! what strange, what solemn breaking strain
Swells, wildly murmuring, o'er the far, far main!
Down Time's long, lessening vale the notes decay,
And, lost in distant ages, roll away.

EVENING AFTER A BATTLE.

Above tall western hills, the light of day
Shot far the splendours of his golden ray;
Bright from the storm, with tenfold grace he smiled,
The tumult soften'd, and the world grew mild.
With pomp transcendent, robed in heavenly dyes,
Arch'd the clear rainbow round the orient skies;
Its changeless form, its hues of beam divine—
Fair type of truth and beauty—endless shine
Around the expanse, with thousand splendours rare;
Gay clouds sail wanton through the kindling air;
From shade to shade unnumber'd tinctures blend,
Unnumber'd forms of wondrous light extend;
In pride stupendous, glittering walls aspire,
Graced with bright domes, and crown'd with towers of fire;
On cliffs cliffs burn; o'er mountains mountains roll:
A burst of glory spreads from pole to pole:
Rapt with the splendour, every songster sings,
Tops the high bough, and claps his glistening wings;
With new-born green reviving nature blooms,
And sweeter fragrance freshening air perfumes.
Far south the storm withdrew its troubled reign,
Descending twilight dimm'd the dusky plain;
Black night arose, her curtains hid the ground:
Less roar'd, and less, the thunder's solemn sound;
The bended lightning shot a brighter stream,
Or wrapp'd all heaven in one wide, mantling flame;
By turns, o'er plains, and woods, and mountains spread
Faint, yellow glimmerings, and a deeper shade.
From parting clouds, the moon out-breaking shone
And sate, sole empress, on her silver throne;
In clear, full beauty, round all nature smiled,
And claimed, o'er heaven and earth, dominion mild
With humbler glory, stars her court attend,
And bless'd, and union'd, silent lustre blend.

COLUMBIA

Columbia, Columbia, to glory arise,
The queen of the world and the child of the skies;
Thy genius commands thee; with rapture behold,
While ages on ages thy splendours unfold.
Thy reign is the last and the noblest of time;
Most fruitful thy soil, most inviting thy clime;
Let the crimes of the east ne'er encrimson thy name;
Be freedom and science, and virtue thy fame.

To conquest and slaughter let Europe aspire;
Whelm nations in blood and wrap cities in fire;
Thy heroes the rights of mankind shall defend,
And triumph pursue them, and glory attend.
A world is thy realm; for a world be thy laws,
Enlarged as thine empire, and just as thy cause;
On Freedom's broad basis that empire shall rise,
Extend with the main, and dissolve with the skies.

Fair Science her gates to thy sons shall unbar,
And the east see thy morn hide the beams of her star;
New bards and new sages, unrivall'd, shall soar
To fame, unextinguish'd when time is no more;
To thee, the last refuge of virtue design'd,
Shall fly from all nations the best of mankind;
Here, grateful, to Heaven with transport shall bring
Their incense, more fragrant than odours of spring.

Nor less shall thy fair ones to glory ascend,
And genius and beauty in harmony blend;
The graces of form shall awake pure desire,
And the charms of the soul ever cherish the fire:
Their sweetness unmingled, their manners refined,
And virtue's bright image enstamp'd on the mind,
With peace and soft rapture shall teach life to glow,
And light up a smile in the aspect of wo.

Thy fleets to all regions thy power shall display,
The nations admire, and the ocean obey;
Each shore to thy glory its tribute unfold,
And the east and the south yield their spices and gold.
As the day-spring unbounded, thy splendour shall flow,
And earth's little kingdoms before thee shall bow,
While the ensigns of union, in triumph unfurl'd,
Hush the tumult of war, and give peace to the world.

Thus, as down a lone valley, with cedars o'erspread,
From war's dread confusion I pensively stray'd—
The gloom from the face of fair heaven retired,
The winds ceased to murmur, the thunders expired
Perfumes, as of Eden, flow'd sweetly along,
And a voice, as of angels, enchantingly sung:
"Columbia, Columbia, to glory arise,
The queen of the world, and the child of the skies"

DAVID HUMPHREYS.

[Born 1753. Died 1818.]

David Humphreys, LL.D., was the son of a Congregational clergyman, at Derby, in Connecticut, where he was born in 1753. He was educated at Yale College, with Dwight, Trumbull, and Barlow, and soon after being graduated, in 1771, joined the revolutionary army, under General Parsons, with the rank of captain. He was for several years attached to the staff of General Putnam, and in 1780 was appointed aid-de-camp to General Washington, with the rank of colonel. He continued in the military family of the commander-in-chief until the close of the war, enjoying his friendship and confidence, and afterward accompanied him to Mount Vernon, where he remained until 1784, when he went abroad with Franklin, Adams, and Jefferson, who were appointed commissioners to negotiate treaties of commerce with foreign powers, as their secretary of legation.* Soon after his return to the United States, in 1786, he was elected by the citizens of his native town a member of the Legislature of Connecticut, and by that body was appointed to command a regiment to be raised by order of the national government. On receiving his commission, Colonel Humphreys established his head-quarters and recruiting rendezvous at Hartford; and there renewed his intimacy with his old friends Trumbull and Barlow, with whom, and Doctor Lemuel Hopkins, he engaged in writing the "Anarchiad," a political satire, in imitation of the "Rolliad," a work attributed to Sheridan and others, which he had seen in London. He retained his commission until the suppression of the insurrection in 1787, and in the following year accepted an invitation to visit Mount Vernon, where he continued to reside until he was appointed minister to Portugal, in 1790. He remained in Lisbon seven years, at the end of which period he was transferred to the court of Madrid, and in 1802, when Mr. Pinckney was made minister to Spain, returned to the United States. From 1802 to 1812, he devoted his attention to agricultural and manufacturing pursuits; and on the breaking out of the second war with Great Britain, was appointed commander of the militia of Connecticut, with the rank of brigadier-general. His public services terminated with the limitation of that appointment. He died at New Haven, on the twenty-first day of February, 1818, in the sixty-fifth year of his age.

The principal poems of Colonel Humphreys are an "Address to the Armies of the United States," written in 1772, while he was in the army; "A Poem on the Happiness of America," written during his residence in London and Paris, as secretary of legation; "The Widow of Malabar, or The Tyranny of Custom, a Tragedy, imitated from the French of M. Le Mierre," written at Mount Vernon; and a "Poem on Agriculture," written while he was minister at the court of Lisbon. The "Address to the Armies of the United States" passed through many editions in this country and in Europe, and was translated into the French language by the Marquis de Chastellux, and favourably noticed in the Parisian gazettes. The "Poem on the Happiness of America" was reprinted nine times in three years; and the "Widow of Malabar" is said, in the dedication of it to the author of "McFingal," to have met with "extraordinary success" on the stage. The "Miscellaneous Works of Colonel Humphreys" were published in an octavo volume, in New York, in 1790, and again in 1804. The Works contain, besides the author's poems, an interesting biography of his early friend and commander, General Putnam, and several orations and other prose compositions. They are dedicated to the Duke de Rochefoucault, who had been his intimate friend in France. In the dedication he says: "In presenting for your amusement the trifles which have been composed during my leisure hours, I assume nothing beyond the negative merit of not having ever written any thing unfavourable to the interests of religion, humanity, and virtue." He seems to have aimed only at an elegant mediocrity, and his pieces are generally simple and correct, in thought and language. He was one of the "four bards with Scripture names," satirized in some verses published in London, commencing

"David and Jonathan, Joel and Timothy,
Over the water, set up the hymn of the"—etc.,

and is generally classed among the "poets of the Revolution." The popularity he enjoyed while he lived, and his connection with Trumbull, Barlow, and Dwight, justify the introduction of a sketch of his history and writings into this volume. The following extracts exhibit his style. The first alludes to the departure of the British fleet from New York.

* In a letter to Doctor Franklin, written soon after the appointment of Humphreys to this office, General Washington, says: "His zeal in the cause of his country, his good sense, prudence, and attachment to me, have rendered him dear to me; and I persuade myself you will find no confidence which you may think proper to repose in him, misplaced. He possesses an excellent heart, good natural and acquired abilities, and sterling integrity, as well as sobriety, and an obliging disposition. A full conviction of his possessing all these good qualities makes me less scrupulous of recommending him to your patronage and friendship."—Sparks's *Life of Washington*, vol. ix. p. 46.

ON THE PROSPECT OF PEACE.

E'en now, from half the threaten'd horrors freed,
See from our shores the lessening sails recede;
See the proud flags that, to the wind unfurl'd,
Waved in proud triumph round a vanquish'd world,
Inglorious fly; and see their haggard crew,
Despair, shame, rage, and infamy pursue.

Hail, heaven-born peace! thy grateful blessings pour
On this glad land, and round the peopled shore;
Thine are the joys that gild the happy scene,
Propitious days, and happy nights serene;
With thee gay Pleasure frolics o'er the plain,
And smiling Plenty leads the prosperous train.

Then, O blest land! with genius unconfined,
With polish'd manners, and the illumined mind,
Thy future race on daring wing shall soar,
Each science trace, and all the arts explore
Till bright religion, beckoning to the skies,
Shall bid thy sons to endless glory rise.

WESTERN EMIGRATION.

With all that's ours, together let us rise,
Seek brighter plains, and more indulgent skies;
Where fair Ohio rolls his amber tide,
And nature blossoms in her virgin pride;
Where all that Beauty's hand can form to please
Shall crown the toils of war with rural ease.
The shady coverts and the sunny hills,
The gentle lapse of ever-murmuring rills,
The soft repose amid the noontide bowers,
The evening walk among the blushing flowers,
The fragrant groves, that yield a sweet perfume,
And vernal glories in perpetual bloom
Await you there; and heaven shall bless the toil:
Your own the produce, and your own the soil.
There, free from envy, cankering care and strife,
Flow the calm pleasures of domestic life;
There mutual friendship soothes each placid breast:
Blest in themselves, and in each other blest.
From house to house the social glee extends,
For friends in war in peace are doubly friends.
There cities rise, and spiry towns increase,
With gilded domes and every art of peace.
There Cultivation shall extend his power,
Rear the green blade, and nurse the tender flower;
Make the fair villa in full splendours smile,
And robe with verdure all the genial soil.
There shall rich Commerce court the favouring gales,
And wondering wilds admire the passing sails,
Where the bold ships the stormy Huron brave,
Where wild Ontario rolls the whitening wave,
Where fair Ohio his pure current pours,
And Mississippi laves the extended shores.
And thou Supreme! whose hand sustains this ball,
Before whose nod the nations rise and fall,
Propitious smile, and shed diviner charms
On this blest land, the queen of arts and arms;
Make the great empire rise on wisdom's plan,
The seat of bliss, and last retreat of man.

AMERICAN WINTER.

Then doubling clouds the wintry skies deform,
And, wrapt in vapour, comes the roaring storm;
With snows surcharged, from tops of mountains sails,
Loads leafless trees, and fills the whiten'd vales.
Then Desolation strips the faded plains,
Then tyrant Death o'er vegetation reigns;
The birds of heaven to other climes repair,
And deepening glooms invade the turbid air.
Nor then, unjoyous, winter's rigours come,
But find them happy and content with home;
Their granaries fill'd—the task of culture past
Warm at their fire, they hear the howling blast.
While pattering rain and snow, or driving sleet,
Rave idly loud, and at their window beat·
Safe from its rage, regardless of its roar,
In vain the tempest rattles at the door.
'Tis then the time from hoarding cribs to feed
The ox laborious, and the noble steed;
'Tis then the time to tend the bleating fold,
To strew with litter, and to fence from cold.
The cattle fed, the fuel piled within
At setting day the blissful hours begin;
'Tis then, sole owner of his little cot,
The farmer feels his independent lot;
Hears, with the crackling blaze that lights the wall,
The voice of gladness and of nature call;
Beholds his children play, their mother smile,
And tastes with them the fruit of summer's toil.
From stormy heavens the mantling clouds unroll'd,
The sky is bright, the air serenely cold.
The keen north-west, that heaps the drifted snows,
For months entire o'er frozen regions blows;
Man braves his blast; his gelid breath inhales,
And feels more vigorous as the frost prevails.

REVOLUTIONARY SOLDIERS.

O, what avails to trace the fate of war
Through fields of blood, and paint each glorious scar!
Why should the strain your former woes recall,
The tears that wept a friend's or brother's fall,
When by your side, first in the adventurous strife,
He dauntless rush'd, too prodigal of life!
Enough of merit has each honour'd name,
To shine untarnish'd on the rolls of fame,
To stand the example of each distant age,
And add new lustre to the historic page;
For soon their deeds illustrious shall be shown
In breathing bronze or animated stone,
Or where the canvass, starting into life,
Revives the glories of the crimson strife.
And soon some bard shall tempt the untried themes,
Sing how we dared, in fortune's worst extremes,
What cruel wrongs the indignant patriot bore,
What various ills your feeling bosoms tore,
What boding terrors gloom'd the threatening hour
When British legions, arm'd with death-like power,
Bade desolation mark their crimson'd way,
And lured the savage to his destined prey.

JOEL BARLOW.

[Born 1755. Died 1812.]

The author of the "Columbiad" was born in the village of Reading, in Connecticut, in 1755. He was the youngest in a family of ten, and his father died while he was yet a child, leaving to him property sufficient only to defray the costs of his education. On the completion of his preparatory studies he was placed by his guardians at Dartmouth College, but was soon induced to remove to New Haven, where he was graduated, in 1778. Among his friends here were Dwight, then a college tutor, Colonel Humphreys, a revolutionary bard of some reputation, and Trumbull, the author of "McFingal." Barlow recited an original poem, on taking his bachelor's degree, which is preserved in the "American Poems," printed at Litchfield in 1793. It was his first attempt of so ambitious a character, and possesses little merit. During the vacations of the college he had on several occasions joined the army, in which four of his brothers were serving; and he participated in the conflict at White Plains, and a number of minor engagements, in which he is said to have displayed much intrepidity.

For a short time after completing his academic course, Barlow devoted his attention chiefly to the law; but being urged by his friends to qualify himself for the office of chaplain, he undertook the study of theology, and in six weeks became a licensed minister. He joined the army immediately, and remained with it until the establishment of peace, cultivating the while his taste for poetry, by writing patriotic songs and ballads, and composing, in part, his "Vision of Columbus," afterward expanded into the "Columbiad." When the army was disbanded, in 1783, he removed to Hartford, to resume his legal studies; and to add to his revenue established "The Mercury," a weekly gazette, to which his writings gave reputation and an immediate circulation. He had previously married at New Haven a daughter of the Honourable Abraham Baldwin, and had lost his early patron and friend, the Honourable Titus Hosmer, on whom he wrote an elegant elegy. In 1785 he was admitted to the bar, and in the same year, in compliance with the request of an association of Congregational ministers, he prepared and published an enlarged and improved edition of Watts's version of the Psalms,* to which were appended a collection of hymns, several of which were written by himself.

"The Vision of Columbus" was published in 1787. It was dedicated to Louis XVI., with strong expressions of admiration and gratitude, and in the poem were corresponding passages of applause; but Barlow's feelings toward the amiable and unfortunate monarch appear to have changed in after time, for in the "Columbiad" he is coldly alluded to, and the adulatory lines are suppressed. The "Vision of Columbus" was reprinted in London and Paris, and was generally noticed favourably in the reviews. After its publication the author relinquished his newspaper and established a bookstore, principally to sell the poem and his edition of the Psalms, and as soon as this end was attained, resumed the practice of the law. In this he was, however, unfortunate, for his forensic abilities were not of the most popular description, and his mind was too much devoted to political and literary subjects to admit of the application to study and attention to business necessary to secure success. He was engaged with Colonel Humphreys, John Trumbull, and Dr. Lemuel Hopkins, a man of some wit, of the coarser kind, in the "Anarchiad," a satirical poem published at Hartford, which had considerable political influence, and in some other works of a similar description; but, obtaining slight pecuniary advantage from his literary labours, he was induced to accept a foreign agency from the "Sciota Land Company," and sailed for Europe, with his family, in 1788. In France he sold some of the lands held by this association, but deriving little or no personal benefit from the transactions, and becoming aware of the fraudulent character of the company, he relinquished his agency and determined to rely on his pen for support.

* Of the psalms omitted by Watts and included in this edition, only the eighty-eighth and one hundred and thirty-seventh were paraphrased by Barlow. His version of the latter added much to his reputation, and has been considered the finest translation of the words of David that has been written, though they have received a metrical dress from some of the best poets of England and America. Recently the origin of this paraphrase has been a subject of controversy, but a memorandum found among the papers of the late Judge Trumbull, who aided in the preparation of the Connecticut edition of Watts, settles the question in favour of Barlow. The following is the version to which we have alluded:

THE BABYLONIAN CAPTIVITY.

Along the banks where Babel's current flows,
Our captive bands in deep despondence stray'd;
Where Zion's fall in sad remembrance rose,—
Her friends, her children, mingled with the dead.

The tuneful harp that once with joy we strung,
When praise employ'd and mirth inspired the lay,
In mournful silence on the willows hung,
And growing grief prolong'd the tedious day.

Our proud oppressors, to increase our wo,
With taunting smiles a song of Zion claim;
Bid sacred praise in strains melodious flow,
While they blaspheme the great Jehovah's name.

But how, in heathen chains, and lands unknown,
Shall Israel's sons the sacred anthems raise?
O hapless Salem! God's terrestrial throne,
Thou land of glory, sacred mount of praise!

If e'er my memory lose thy lovely name,
If my cold heart neglect my kindred race,
Let dire destruction seize this guilty frame!
My hands shall perish and my voice shall cease!

Yet shall the Lord who hears when Zion calls,
O'ertake her foes with terror and dismay;
His arm avenge her desolated walls,
And raise her children to eternal day.

In 1791, Barlow published in London "Advice to the Privileged Orders," a work directed against the distinguishing features of kingly and aristocratic governments; and in the early part of the succeeding year, "The Conspiracy of Kings," a poem of about four hundred lines, educed by the first coalition of the continental sovereigns against republican France. In the autumn of 1792, he wrote a letter to the French National Convention, recommending the abolition of the union between the church and the state, and other reforms; and was soon after chosen by the "London Constitutional Society," of which he was a member, to present in person an address to that body. On his arrival in Paris he was complimented with the rights of citizenship, an "honour" which had been previously conferred on Washington and Hamilton. From this time he made France his home. In the summer of 1793, a deputation, of which his friend Gregorie, who before the Revolution had been Bishop of Blois, was a member, was sent into Savoy, to organize it as a department of the republic. He accompanied it to Chamberry, the capital, where, at the request of its president, he wrote an address to the inhabitants of Piedmont, inciting them to throw off allegiance to "the man of Turin who called himself their king." Here too he wrote "Hasty Pudding," the most popular of his poems.

On his return to Paris, Barlow's time was principally devoted to commercial pursuits, by which, in a few years, he obtained a considerable fortune. The atrocities which marked the progress of the Revolution prevented his active participation in political controversies, though he continued under all circumstances an ardent republican. Toward the close of 1795, he visited the North of Europe, on some private business, and on his return to Paris was appointed by Washington consul to Algiers, with power to negotiate a commercial treaty with the dey, and to ransom all the Americans held in slavery on the coast of Barbary. He accepted and fulfilled the mission to the satisfaction of the American Government, concluding treaties with Algiers, Tunis, and Tripoli, and liberating more than one hundred Americans, who were in prisons or in slavery to the Mohammedans. He then returned to Paris, where he purchased the splendid hotel of the Count Clermont de Tonnere, and lived several years in a fashionable and costly manner, pursuing still his fortunate mercantile speculations, revising his "great epic," and writing occasionally for the political gazettes.

Finally, after an absence of nearly seventeen years, the poet, statesman, and philosopher returned to his native country. He was received with kindness by many old friends, who had corresponded with him while abroad or been remembered in all his wanderings; and after spending a few months in travel, marking, with patriotic pride, the rapid progress which the nation had made in greatness, he fixed his home on the banks of the Potomac, near the city of Washington, where he built the splendid mansion, known afterward as "Kalorama," and expressed an intention to spend there the remainder of his life. In 1806, he published a prospectus of a National Institution, at Washington, to combine a university with a naval and military school, academy of fine arts, and learned society. A bill to carry his plan into effect was introduced into Congress, but never became a law.

In the summer of 1808, appeared the "Columbiad," in a splendid quarto volume, surpassing in the beauty of its typography and embellishments any work before that time printed in America. From his earliest years Barlow had been ambitious to raise the epic song of his nation. The "Vision of Columbus," in which the most brilliant events in American history had been described, occupied his leisure hours when in college, and afterward, when, as a chaplain, he followed the standard of the liberating army. That work was executed too hastily and imperfectly, and for twenty years after its appearance, through every variety of fortune, its enlargement and improvement engaged his attention.

The events of the Revolution were so recent and so universally known, as to be inflexible to the hand of fiction; and the poem could not therefore be modelled after the regular epic form, which would otherwise have been chosen. It is a series of visions, presented by Hesper, the genius of the western continent, to Columbus, while in the prison at Valladolid, where he is introduced to the reader uttering a monologue on his ill-requited services to Spain. These visions embrace a vast variety of scenes, circumstances, and characters. Europe in the middle ages, with her political and religious reformers; Mexico and the South American nations, and their imagined history; the progress of discovery; the settlement of the states now composing the federation; the war of the Revolution, and establishment of republicanism; and the chief actors in the great dramas which he attempts to present.

The poem, having no unity of fable, no regular succession of incidents, no strong exhibition of varied character, lacks the most powerful charms of a narrative; and has, besides, many dull and spiritless passages, that would make unpopular a work of much more faultless general design. The versification is generally harmonious, but mechanical and passionless, the language sometimes incorrect, and the similes often inappropriate and inelegant. Yet there are in it many bursts of eloquence and patriotism, which should preserve it from oblivion. The descriptions of nature and of personal character are frequently condensed and forceful; and passages of invective, indignant and full of energy. In his narrative of the expedition against Quebec, under Arnold, the poet exclaims:

Ah, gallant troop! deprived of half the praise
That deeds like yours in other times repays,
Since your prime chief (the favourite erst of Fame,)
Hath sunk so deep his hateful, hideous name,
That every honest muse with horror flings
It forth unsounded from her sacred strings,
Else what high tones of rapture must have told
The first great actions of a chief so bold!

These lines are characteristic of his manner.

The "Columbiad" was reprinted in Paris and London. and noticed in the leading critical gazettes, but generally with little praise. The London "Monthly Magazine" attempted in an elaborate article to prove its title to a place in the first class of epics, and expressed a belief that it was surpassed only by the "Illiad," the "Æneid" and "Paradise Lost." In America, however, it was regarded by the judicious as a failure, and reviewed with even more wit and severity than in England. Indeed, the poet did not in his own country receive the praise which he really merited; and faults were imputed to his work which it did not possess. Its sentiments were said to be hostile to Christianity,* and the author was declared an infidel; but there is no line in the "Columbiad" unfavourable to the religion of New England, the Puritan faith which is the basis of the national greatness; and there is no good reason for believing that BARLOW at the time of his death doubted the creed of which in his early manhood he had been a minister.

After the publication of the "Columbiad," BARLOW made a collection of documents, with an intention to write a history of the United States; but, in 1811, he was unexpectedly appointed minister plenipotentiary to the French government, and immediately sailed for Europe. His attempts to negotiate a treaty of commerce and indemnification for spoliations were unsuccessful at Paris; and in the autumn of 1812 he was invited by the Duke of BASSANO to a conference with NAPOLEON at Wilna, in Poland. He started from Paris, and travelled without intermission until he reached Zarnowitch, an obscure village near Cracow, where he died, from an inflammation of the lungs, induced by fatigue and exposure in an inhospitable country, in an inclement season, on the twenty-second day of December, in the fifty-fourth year of his age. In Paris, honours were paid to his memory as an important public functionary and a man of letters; his eulogy was written by DUPONT DE NEMOURS, and an account of his life and writings was drawn up and published, accompanied by a canto of the "Columbiad," translated into French heroic verse. In America, too, his death was generally lamented, though without any public exhibition of mourning.

BARLOW was much respected in private life for his many excellent social qualities. His manners were usually grave and dignified, though when with his intimate friends he was easy and familiar. He was an honest and patient investigator, and would doubtless have been much more successful as a metaphysical or historical writer than as a poet. As an author he belonged to the first class of his time in America; and for his ardent patriotism, his public services, and the purity of his life, he deserves a distinguished rank among the men of our golden age.

THE HASTY PUDDING.

CANTO I.

YE Alps audacious, through the heavens that rise,
To cramp the day and hide me from the skies;
Ye Gallic flags, that, o'er their heights unfurl'd,
Bear death to kings and freedom to the world,
I sing not you. A softer theme I choose,
A virgin theme, unconscious of the muse,
But fruitful, rich, well suited to inspire
The purest frenzy of poetic fire.

Despise it not, ye bards to terror steel'd,
Who hurl your thunders round the epic field;
Nor ye who strain your midnight throats to sing
Joys that the vineyard and the stillhouse bring;
Or on some distant fair your notes employ,
And speak of raptures that you ne'er enjoy.
I sing the sweets I know, the charms I feel,
My morning incense, and my evening meal,—
The sweets of Hasty Pudding. Come, dear bowl,
Glide o'er my palate, and inspire my soul.
The milk beside thee, smoking from the kine,
Its substance mingled, married in with thine,
Shall cool and temper thy superior heat,
And save the pains of blowing while I eat.

O! could the smooth, the emblematic song
Flow like thy genial juices o'er my tongue,
Could those mild morsels in my numbers chime,
And, as they roll in substance, roll in rhyme,
No more thy awkward, unpoetic name
Should shun the muse or prejudice thy fame;
But, rising grateful to the accustom'd ear,
All bards should catch it, and all realms revere!

Assist me first with pious toil to trace
Through wrecks of time thy lineage and thy race;

* It is now generally believed that BARLOW, while in France, abjured the Christian religion. The Reverend THOMAS ROBBINS, a venerable clergyman of Rochester, Massachusetts, in a letter written in 1840, remarks that "BARLOW's deistical opinions were not suspected previous to the publication of his 'Vision of Columbus,' in 1787;" and further, that "when at a later period he *lost his character*, and became an open and bitter reviler of Christianity, his psalm-book was laid aside; but for that cause only, as competent judges still maintained that no revision of WATTS possesses as much poetic merit as BARLOW's." I have seen two letters written by BARLOW during the last year of his life, in which he declares himself "a sincere believer of Christianity, divested of its corruptions." In a letter to M. GREGOIRE, published in the second volume of DENNIE's "Port Folio," pages 471 to 479, he says, "the sect of Puritans, in which I was born and educated, *and to which I still adhere*, for the same reason that you adhere to the Catholics, *a conviction that they are right*," etc. The idea that BARLOW disbelieved in his later years the religion of his youth, was probably first derived from an engraving in the "Vision of Columbus," in which the cross, by which he intended to represent monkish superstition, is placed among the "symbols of prejudice." He never "lost his character" as a man of honourable sentiments and blameless life; and I could present numerous other evidences that he did not abandon his religion, were not the above apparently conclusive.

Declare what lovely squaw, in days of yore,
(Ere great Columbus sought thy native shore,)
First gave thee to the world; her works of fame
Have lived indeed, but lived without a name.
Some tawny Ceres, goddess of her days,
First learn'd with stones to crack the well-dried maize,
Through the rough sieve to shake the golden shower,
In boiling water stir the yellow flour:
The yellow flour, bestrew'd and stirr'd with haste,
Swells in the flood and thickens to a paste,
Then puffs and wallops, rises to the brim,
Drinks the dry knobs that on the surface swim;
The knobs at last the busy ladle breaks,
And the whole mass its true consistence takes.
Could but her sacred name, unknown so long,
Rise, like her labours, to the son of song,
To her, to them I'd consecrate my lays,
And blow her pudding with the breath of praise.
Not through the rich Peruvian realms alone
The fame of Sol's sweet daughter should be known,
But o'er the world's wide clime should live secure,
Far as his rays extend, as long as they endure.
Dear Hasty Pudding, what unpromised joy
Expands my heart, to meet thee in Savoy!
Doom'd o'er the world through devious paths to roam,
Each clime my country, and each house my home,
My soul is soothed, my cares have found an end:
I greet my long-lost, unforgotten friend.
For thee through Paris, that corrupted town,
How long in vain I wander'd up and down,
Where shameless Bacchus, with his drenching hoard,
Cold from his cave usurps the morning board.
London is lost in smoke and steep'd in tea;
No Yankee there can lisp the name of thee;
The uncouth word, a libel on the town,
Would call a proclamation from the crown.
For climes oblique, that fear the sun's full rays,
Chill'd in their fogs, exclude the generous maize:
A grain whose rich, luxuriant growth requires
Short, gentle showers, and bright, ethereal fires.
But here, though distant from our native shore,
With mutual glee, we meet and laugh once more.
The same! I know thee by that yellow face,
That strong complexion of true Indian race,
Which time can never change, nor soil impair,
Nor Alpine snows, nor Turkey's morbid air;
For endless years, through every mild domain,
Where grows the maize, there thou art sure to reign.
But man, more fickle, the bold license claims,
In different realms to give thee different names.
Thee the soft nations round the warm Levant
Polanta call; the French, of course, *Polante.*
E'en in thy native regions, how I blush
To hear the Pennsylvanians call thee *Mush!*
On Hudson's banks, while men of Belgic spawn
Insult and eat thee by the name *Suppawn.*
All spurious appellations, void of truth;
I've better known thee from my earliest youth:
Thy name is *Hasty Pudding!* thus our sires
Were wont to greet thee fuming from the fires·
And while they argued in thy just defence
With logic clear, they thus explained the sense:
"In *haste* the boiling caldron, o'er the blaze,
Receives and cooks the ready powder'd maize;
In *haste* 'tis served, and then in equal *haste,*
With cooling milk, we make the sweet repast.
No carving to be done, no knife to grate
The tender ear and wound the stony plate;
But the smooth spoon, just fitted to the lip,
And taught with art the yielding mass to dip,
By frequent journeys to the bowl well stored,
Performs the *hasty* honours of the board."
Such is thy name, significant and clear,
A name, a sound to every Yankee dear,
But most to me, whose heart and palate chaste
Preserve my pure, hereditary taste.
There are who strive to stamp with disrepute
The luscious food, because it feeds the brute;
In tropes of high-strain'd wit, while gaudy prigs
Compare thy nursling man to pamper'd pigs;
With sovereign scorn I treat the vulgar jest,
Nor fear to share thy bounties with the beast.
What though the generous cow gives me to quaff
The milk nutritious; am I then a calf?
Or can the genius of the noisy swine,
Though nursed on pudding, thence lay claim to mine!
Sure the sweet song I fashion to thy praise,
Runs more melodious than the notes they raise.
My song, resounding in its grateful glee,
No merit claims: I praise myself in thee.
My father loved thee through his length of days
For thee his fields were shaded o'er with maize;
From thee what health, what vigour he possess'd,
Ten sturdy freemen from his loins attest;
Thy constellation ruled my natal morn,
And all my bones were made of Indian corn.
Delicious grain! whatever form it take,
To roast or boil, to smother or to bake,
In every dish 'tis welcome still to me,
But most, my *Hasty Pudding*, most in thee.
Let the green succotash with thee contend;
Let beans and corn their sweetest juices blend;
Let butter drench them in its yellow tide,
And a long slice of bacon grace their side;
Not all the plate, how famed soe'er it be,
Can please my palate like a bowl of thee.
Some talk of *Hoe-Cake*, fair Virginia's pride!
Rich *Johnny-Cake* this mouth hath often tried;
Both please me well, their virtues much the same
Alike their fabric, as allied their fame,
Except in dear New England, where the last
Receives a dash of pumpkin in the paste,
To give it sweetness and improve the taste.
But place them all before me, smoking hot,
The big, round dumpling, rolling from the pot;
The pudding of the bag, whose quivering breast,
With suet lined, leads on the Yankee feast;
The *Charlotte* brown, within whose crusty sides
A belly soft the pulpy apple hides;
The yellow bread, whose face like amber glows,
And all of Indian that the bakepan knows,—
You tempt me not; my favourite greets my eyes,
To that loved bowl my spoon by instinct flies.

CANTO II.

To mix the food by vicious rules of art,
To kill the stomach and to sink the heart,
To make mankind to social virtue sour,
Cram o'er each dish, and be what they devour;
For this the kitchen muse first framed her book,
Commanding sweat to stream from every cook;
Children no more their antic gambols tried,
And friends to physic wonder'd why they died.
Not so the Yankee: his abundant feast,
With simples furnish'd and with plainness dress'd,
A numerous offspring gathers round the board,
And cheers alike the servant and the lord; [taste,
Whose well-bought hunger prompts the joyous
And health attends them from the short repast.
While the full pail rewards the milkmaid's toil,
The mother sees the morning caldron boil;
To stir the pudding next demands their care;
To spread the table and the bowls prepare:
To feed the children as their portions cool,
And comb their heads, and send them off to school.
Yet may the simplest dish some rules impart,
For nature scorns not all the aids of art.
E'en *Hasty Pudding*, purest of all food,
May still be bad, indifferent, or good,
As sage experience the short process guides,
Or want of skill, or want of care presides.
Whoe'er would form it on the surest plan,
To rear the child and long sustain the man;
To shield the morals while it mends the size,
And all the powers of every food supplies,—
Attend the lesson that the muse shall bring;
Suspend your spoons, and listen while I sing.
But since, O man! thy life and health demand
Not food alone, but labour from thy hand,
First, in the field, beneath the sun's strong rays,
Ask of thy mother earth the needful maize;
She loves the race that courts her yielding soil,
And gives her bounties to the sons of toil.
When now the ox, obedient to thy call,
Repays the loan that fill'd the winter stall,
Pursue his traces o'er the furrow'd plain,
And plant in measured hills the golden grain.
But when the tender germ begins to shoot,
And the green spire declares the sprouting root,
Then guard your nursling from each greedy foe,
The insidious worm, the all-devouring crow.
A little ashes sprinkled round the spire,
Soon steep'd in rain, will bid the worm retire;
The feather'd robber, with his hungry maw
Swift flies the field before your man of straw,
A frightful image, such as schoolboys bring,
When met to burn the pope or hang the king.
Thrice in the season, through each verdant row,
Wield the strong ploughshare and the faithful hoe;
The faithful hoe, a double task that takes,
To till the summer corn and roast the winter cakes.
Slow springs the blade, while check'd by chilling rains,
Ere yet the sun the seat of Cancer gains;
But when his fiercest fires emblaze the land,
Then start the juices, then the roots expand;
Then, like a column of Corinthian mould,
The stalk struts upward and the leaves unfold;
The busy branches all the ridges fill,
Entwine their arms, and kiss from hill to hill.
Here cease to vex them; all your cares are done:
Leave the last labours to the parent sun;
Beneath his genial smiles, the well-dress'd field,
When autumn calls, a plenteous crop shall yield.
Now the strong foliage bears the standards high
And shoots the tall top-gallants to the sky;
The suckling ears the silken fringes bend,
And, pregnant grown, their swelling coats distend;
The loaded stalk, while still the burden grows,
O'erhangs the space that runs between the rows;
High as a hop-field waves the silent grove,
A safe retreat for little thefts of love,
When the pledged roasting-ears invite the maid
To meet her swain beneath the new-form'd shade,
His generous hand unloads the cumbrous hill,
And the green spoils her ready basket fill;
Small compensation for the twofold bliss,
The promised wedding, and the present kiss.
Slight depredations these; but now the moon
Calls from his hollow trees the sly raccoon;
And while by night he bears his prize away,
The bolder squirrel labours through the day.
Both thieves alike, but provident of time,
A virtue rare, that almost hides their crime.
Then let them steal the little stores they can,
And fill their granaries from the toils of man;
We've one advantage where they take no part—
With all their wiles, they ne'er have found the art
To boil the *Hasty Pudding*; nere we shine
Superior far to tenants of the pine;
This envied boon to man shall still belong,
Unshared by them in substance or in song.
At last the closing season browns the plain,
And ripe October gathers in the grain;
Deep-loaded carts the spacious cornhouse fill;
The sack distended marches to the mill;
The labouring mill beneath the burden groans,
And showers the future pudding from the stones;
Till the glad housewife greets the powder'd gold,
And the new crop exterminates the old.

CANTO III.

The days grow short; but though the falling sun
To the glad swain proclaims his day's work done,
Night's pleasing shades his various tasks prolong,
And yield new subjects to my various song.
For now, the corn-house fill'd, the harvest home,
The invited neighbours to the *husking* come;
A frolic scene, where work, and mirth, and play,
Unite their charms to chase the hours away.
Where the huge heap lies center'd in the hall,
The lamp suspended from the cheerful wall,
Brown, corn-fed nymphs, and strong, hard-handed [beaus,
Alternate ranged, extend in circling rows,
Assume their seats, the solid mass attack;
The dry husks rustle, and the corncobs crack;
The song, the laugh, alternate notes resound,
And the sweet cider trips in silence round.
The laws of husking every wight can tell,
And sure no laws he ever keeps so well:
For each red ear a general kiss he gains,
With each smut ear he smuts the luckless swains;

But when to some sweet maid a prize is cast,
Red as her lips and taper as her waist,
She walks the round and culls one favour'd beau,
Who leaps the luscious tribute to bestow.
Various the sport, as are the wits and brains
Of well-pleased lasses and contending swains;
Till the vast mound of corn is swept away,
And he that gets the last ear wins the day.
Meanwhile, the housewife urges all her care,
The well-earn'd feast to hasten and prepare.
The sifted meal already waits her hand,
The milk is strain'd, the bowls in order stand,
The fire flames high; and as a pool (that takes
The headlong stream that o'er the milldam breaks)
Foams, roars, and rages with incessant toils,
So the vex'd caldron rages, roars, and boils.
First with clean salt she seasons well the food,
Then strews the flour, and thickens all the flood.
Long o'er the simmering fire she lets it stand;
To stir it well demands a stronger hand;
The husband takes his turn: and round and round
The ladle flies; at last the toil is crown'd;
When to the board the thronging buskers pour,
And take their seats as at the corn before.
I leave them to their feast. There still belong
More copious matters to my faithful song.
For rules there are, though ne'er unfolded yet,
Nice rules and wise, how pudding should be ate.
Some with molasses line the luscious treat,
And mix, like bards, the useful with the sweet.
A wholesome dish, and well deserving praise;
A great resource in those bleak wintry days,
When the chill'd earth lies buried deep in snow,
And raging Boreas dries the shivering cow.
Bless'd cow! thy praise shall still my notes employ,
Great source of health, the only source of joy;
Mother of Egypt's god—but sure, for me,
Were I to leave my God, I'd worship thee.
How oft thy teats these precious hands have press'd!
How oft thy bounties proved my only feast!
How oft I've fed thee with my favourite grain!
And roar'd, like thee, to find thy children slain!
Yes, swains who know her various worth to prize,
Ah! house her well from winter's angry skies.
Potatoes, pumpkins should her sadness cheer,
Corn from your crib, and mashes from your beer;
When spring returns, she'll well acquit the loan,
And nurse at once your infants and her own.
Milk then with pudding I would always choose;
To this in future I confine my muse,
Till she in haste some further hints unfold,
Well for the young, nor useless to the old.
First in your bowl the milk abundant take,
Then drop with care along the silver lake
Your flakes of pudding; these at first will hide
Their little bulk beneath the swelling tide;
But when their growing mass no more can sink,
When the soft island looms above the brink,
Then check your hand; you've got the portion due:
So taught our sires, and what they taught is true.
There is a choice in spoons. Though small appear
The nice distinction, yet to me 'tis clear.
The deep-bowl'd Gallic spoon, contrived to scoop
In ample draughts the thin, diluted soup,
Performs not well in those substantial things,
Whose mass adhesive to the metal clings;
Where the strong labial muscles must embrace
The gentle curve, and sweep the hollow space.
With ease to enter and discharge the freight,
A bowl less concave, but still more dilate,
Becomes the pudding best. The shape, the size,
A secret rests, unknown to vulgar eyes.
Experienced feeders can alone impart
A rule so much above the lore of art.
These tuneful lips, that thousand spoons have tried,
With just precision could the point decide,
Though not in song; the muse but poorly shines
In cones, and cubes, and geometric lines;
Yet the true form, as near as she can tell,
Is that small section of a goose-egg shell,
Which in two equal portions shall divide
The distance from the centre to the side.
Fear not to slaver; 'tis no deadly sin:
Like the free Frenchman, from your joyous chin
Suspend the ready napkin; or, like me,
Poise with one hand your bowl upon your knee
Just in the zenith your wise head project;
Your full spoon, rising in a line direct,
Bold as a bucket, heeds no drops that fall,—
The wide-mouth'd bowl will surely catch them all!

BURNING OF THE NEW ENGLAND VILLAGES.*

Through solid curls of smoke, the bursting fires
Climb in tall pyramids above the spires,
Concentring all the winds; whose forces, driven
With equal rage from every point of heaven,
Whirl into conflict, round the scantling pour
The twisting flames, and through the rafters roar
Suck up the cinders, send them sailing far,
To warn the nations of the raging war;
Bend high the blazing vortex, swell'd and curl'd,
Careering, brightening o'er the lustred world:
Seas catch the splendour, kindling skies resound,
And falling structures shake the smouldering ground.
Crowds of wild fugitives, with frantic tread,
Flit through the flames that pierce the midnight shade,
Back on the burning domes revert their eyes,
Where some lost friend, some perish'd infant lies.
Their maim'd, their sick, their age-enfeebled sires
Have sunk sad victims to the sateless fires;
They greet with one last look their tottering walls,
See the blaze thicken, as the ruin falls,
Then o'er the country train their dumb despair,
And far behind them leave the dancing glare;
Their own crush'd roofs still lend a trembling light,
Point their long shadows and direct their flight.
Till, wandering wide, they seek some cottage door
Ask the vile pittance due the vagrant poor;
Or, faint and faltering on the devious road,
They sink at last and yield their mortal load.

* This and the following extracts are from the "Columbiad."

TO FREEDOM.

Sun of the moral world! effulgent source
Of man's best wisdom and his steadiest force,
Soul-searching Freedom! here assume thy stand,
And radiate hence to every distant land;
Point out and prove how all the scenes of strife,
The shock of states, the impassion'd-broils of life,
Spring from unequal sway; and how they fly
Before the splendour of thy peaceful eye;
Unfold at last the genuine social plan,
The mind's full scope, the dignity of man,
Bold nature bursting through her long disguise,
And nations daring to be just and wise.
Yes! righteous Freedom, heaven and earth and sea
Yield or withhold their various gifts for thee;
Protected Industry beneath thy reign
Leads all the virtues in her filial train;
Courageous Probity, with brow serene,
And Temperance calm presents her placid mien;
Contentment, Moderation, Labour, Art,
Mould the new man and humanize his heart;
To public plenty private ease dilates,
Domestic peace to harmony of states.
Protected Industry, careering far,
Detects the cause and cures the rage of war,
And sweeps, with forceful arm, to their last graves,
Kings from the earth and pirates from the waves.

MORGAN AND TELL.

Morgan in front of his bold riflers towers,
His host of keen-eyed marksmen, skill'd to pour
Their slugs unerring from the twisted bore.
No sword, no bayonet they learn to wield,
They gall the flank, they skirt the battling field,
Cull out the distant foe in full horse speed,
Couch the long tube, and eye the silver bead,
Turn as he turns, dismiss the whizzing lead,
And lodge the death-ball in his heedless head.
So toil'd the huntsman Tell. His quivering dart,
Press'd by the bended bowstring, fears to part,
Dread the tremendous task, to graze but shun
The tender temples of his infant son;
As the loved youth (the tyrant's victim led)
Bears the poised apple tottering on his head.
The sullen father, with reverted eye,
Now marks the satrap, now the bright-hair'd boy;
His second shaft impatient lies, athirst
To mend the expected error of the first,
To pierce the monster, mid the insulted crowd,
And steep the pangs of nature in his blood.
Deep doubling toward his breast, well poised and slow,
Curve the strain'd horns of his indignant bow;
His left arm straightens as the dexter bends,
And his nerved knuckle with the gripe distends;
Soft slides the reed back with the stiff drawn strand,
Till the steel point has reach'd his steady hand;
Then to his keen fix'd eye the shank he brings,
Twangs the loud cord, the feather'd arrow sings,
Picks off the pippin from the smiling boy,
And Uri's rocks resound with shouts of joy.
Soon by an equal dart the tyrant bleeds;
The cantons league, the work of fate proceeds;
Till Austria's titled hordes, with their own gore,
Fat the fair fields they lorded long before;
On Gothard's height while Freedom first unfurl'd
Her infant banner o'er the modern world.

THE ZONES OF AMERICA.

Where Spring's coy steps in cold Canadia stray,
And joyless seasons hold unequal sway,
He saw the pine its daring mantle rear,
Break the rude blast, and mock the brumal year,
Shag the green zone that bounds the boreal skies,
And bid all southern vegetation rise.
Wild o'er the vast, impenetrable round
The untrod bowers of shadowy nature frown'd;
Millennial cedars wave their honours wide,
The fir's tall boughs, the oak's umbrageous pride,
The branching beach, the aspen's trembling shade
Veil the dim heaven, and brown the dusky glade.
For in dense crowds these sturdy sons of earth,
In frosty regions, claim a stronger birth;
Where heavy beams the sheltering dome requires,
And copious trunks to feed its wintry fires.
But warmer suns, that southern zones emblaze,
A cool, thin umbrage o'er their woodland raise;
Floridia's shores their blooms around him spread,
And Georgian hills erect their shady head;
Whose flowery shrubs regale the passing air
With all the untasted fragrance of the year.
Beneath tall trees, dispersed in loose array,
The rice-grown lawns their humble garb display;
The infant maize, unconscious of its worth,
Points the green spire and bends the foliage forth;
In various forms unbidden harvests rise,
And blooming life repays the genial skies.
Where Mexic hills the breezy gulf defend,
Spontaneous groves with richer burdens bend:
Anana's stalk its shaggy honours yields;
Acassia's flowers perfume a thousand fields;
Their cluster'd dates the mast-like palms unfold
The spreading orange waves a load of gold;
Connubial vines o'ertop the larch they climb;
The long-lived olive mocks the moth of time;
Pomona's pride, that old Grenada claims,
Here smiles and reddens in diviner flames;
Pimento, citron scent the sky serene;
White, woolly clusters fringe the cotton's green
The sturdy fig, the frail, deciduous cane,
And foodful cocoa fan the sultry plain.
Here, in one view, the same glad branches bring
The fruits of autumn and the flowers of spring;
No wintry blasts the unchanging year deform,
Nor beasts unshelter'd fear the pinching storm
But vernal breezes o'er the blossoms rove,
And breathe the ripen'd juices through the grove.

RICHARD ALSOP.

[Born 1759. Died 1815.]

RICHARD ALSOP was a native of Middletown, Connecticut, where he resided during the greater part of his life. He commenced writing for the gazettes at a very early age, but was first known to the public as the author of satires on public characters and events, entitled "The Echo," "The Political Greenhouse," etc., printed in periodicals at New York and Hartford, and afterward collected and published in an octavo volume, in 1807. In these works he was aided by THEODORE DWIGHT, and, in a slight degree, by Dr. HOPKINS, though he was himself their principal author. "The Echo" was at first designed to exhibit the wretched style of the newspaper writers, and the earliest numbers contain extracts from contemporary journals, on a variety of subjects, "done into heroic verse and printed beside the originals." ALSOP and his associates were members of the Federal party, and the "Echo" contained many ludicrous travesties of political speeches and essays made by the opponents of the administration of JOHN ADAMS. The work had much wit and sprightliness, and was very popular in its time; but, with the greater part of the characters and circumstances to which it related, it is now nearly forgotten. In 1800, ALSOP published a "Monody on the Death of Washington," which was much admired; and in the following year a translation of the second canto of BERNI's "Orlando Inamorato," under the title of "The Fairy of the Lake," and another of the Poem of SILIUS ITALICUS on the Second Punic War. In 1807, he translated from the Italian the "History of Chili," by the Abbe MOLINA, to which he added original notes, and others from the French and Spanish versions of the same history. At different periods he translated several less important works from the Greek, Latin, Italian, Spanish, and French languages, and wrote a number of poems and essays for the periodicals. His last publication was "The Adventures of John Jewett," printed in 1815. He died on the twentieth of August, in that year, at Flatbush, Long Island, in the fifty-sixth year of his age. He had, for a considerable period, been writing "The Charms of Fancy," a poem; and besides this, he left manuscript fragments of a poem on the Conquest of Scandinavia by ODIN; "Aristodemus," a tragedy, from the Italian of MONTI; the poem of QUINTUS CALABER on the Trojan war, from the Greek, and a prose translation of a posthumous work by FLORIAN. As a poet ALSOP was often elegant, but his verse was generally without energy. Probably no other American of his time was so well acquainted with the literature of England, France, and Italy, and few were more familiar with the natural sciences. He is said to have been deficient in strength and decision of character, but he was amiable and honourable, and had many friends and few enemies.

FROM "A MONODY ON THE DEATH OF WASHINGTON."

BEFORE the splendours of thy high renown,
How fade the glow-worm lustres of a crown!
How sink, diminish'd, in that radiance lost,
The glare of conquest and of power the boast!
Let Greece her ALEXANDER's deeds proclaim,
Or CÆSAR's triumphs gild the Roman name;
Stript of the dazzling glare around them cast,
Shrinks at their crimes humanity aghast;
With equal claim to honour's glorious meed,
See ATTILA his course of havoc lead;
O'er Asia's realm, in one vast ruin hurl'd,
See furious ZINGES' bloody flag unfurl'd.
On base far different from the conqueror's claim,
Rests the unsullied column of thy fame;
His on the graves of millions proudly based,
With blood cemented and with tears defaced;
Thine on a nation's welfare fixed sublime,
By freedom strengthen'd, and revered by time:
He, as the comet whose portentous light
Spreads baleful splendour o'er the glooms of night,
With dire amazement chills the startled breast,
While storms and earthquakes dread its course attest;
And nature trembles, lost in chaos hurl'd
Should sink the tottering fragment of the world;
Thine, like the sun, whose kind, propitious ray,
Opes the glad morn, and lights the fields of day,
Dispels the wintry storm, the chilling rain,
With rich abundance clothes the fertile plain,
Gives all creation to rejoice around,
And light and life extends, o'er nature's utmost bound.
Though shone thy life a model bright of praise,
Not less the example bright thy death portrays,
When, plunged in deepest wo around thy bed,
Each eye was fix'd, despairing sunk each head,
While nature struggled with extremest pain,
And scarce could life's last lingering powers retain;
In that dread moment, awfully serene,
No trace of suffering marked thy placid mien,
No groan, no murmuring plaint escaped thy tongue;
No longing shadows o'er thy brow were hung;
But, calm in Christian hope, undamp'd with fear,
Thou sawest the high reward of virtue near.
On that bright meed, in surest trust reposed,
As thy firm hand thine eyes expiring closed,
Pleased, to the will of Heaven resign'd thy breath,
And smiled, as nature's struggles closed in death.

ST. JOHN HONEYWOOD.

[Born 1765. Died 1798.]

St John Honeywood was a native of Leicester, Massachusetts, and was educated at Yale College. In 1785, being at that time about twenty years old, he removed to Schenectady, New York, where, during the two succeeding years, he was the principal of a classical school. In 1787 he became a law student in the office of Peter W. Yates, Esquire, of Albany, and on being admitted to the bar removed to Salem, in the same state, where he remained until his death, in September, 1798. He was one of the electors of President of the United States when Mr. Adams became the successor of General Washington, and he held other honourable offices. He was a man of much professional and general learning, rare conversational abilities, and scrupulous integrity; and would probably have been distinguished as a man of letters and a jurist, had he lived to a riper age. The poems embraced in the volume of his writings published in 1801, are generally political, and are distinguished for wit and vigour. The longest in the collection was addressed to M. Adet, on his leaving this country for France.

CRIMES AND PUNISHMENTS.*

Of crimes, empoison'd source of human woes,
Whence the black flood of shame and sorrow flows,
How best to check the venom's deadly force,
To stem its torrent, or direct its course,
To scan the merits of vindictive codes,
Nor pass the faults humanity explodes,
I sing—what theme more worthy to engage
The poet's song, the wisdom of the sage?
Ah! were I equal to the great design,
Were thy bold genius, blest Beccaria! mine,
Then should my work, ennobled as my aim,
Like thine, receive the meed of deathless fame.
O Jay! deserving of a purer age,
Pride of thy country, statesman, patriot, sage,
Beneath whose guardian care our laws assume
A milder form, and lose their Gothic gloom,
Read with indulgent eyes, nor yet refuse
This humble tribute of an artless muse.
Great is the question which the learn'd contest,
What grade, what mode of punishment is best;
In two famed sects the disputants decide,
These ranged on Terror's, those on Reason's side;
Ancient as empire Terror's temple stood,
Capt with black clouds, and founded deep in blood;
Grim despots here their trembling honours paid,
And guilty offerings to their idol made:
The monarch led—a servile crowd ensued,
Their robes distain'd in gore, in gore imbrued;
O'er mangled limbs they held infernal feast,
Moloch the god, and Draco's self the priest.
Mild Reason's fane, in later ages rear'd,
With sunbeams crown'd, in Attic grace appear'd;
In just proportion finish'd every part,
With the fine touches of enlighten'd art.
A thinking few, selected from the crowd,
At the fair shrine with filial rev'rence bow'd;
The sage of Milan led the virtuous choir,
To them sublime he strung the tuneful lyre:

* This poem was found among the author's manuscripts, after his decease; and was, doubtless, unfinished.

Of laws, of crimes, and punishments he sung,
And on his glowing lips persuasion hung:
From Reason's source each inference just he drew,
While truths fresh polish'd struck the mind as new.
Full in the front, in vestal robes array'd,
The holy form of Justice stood display'd:
Firm was her eye, not vengeful, though severe,
And e'er she frown'd she check'd the starting tear.
A sister form, of more benignant face,
Celestial Mercy, held the second place;
Her hands outspread, in suppliant guise she stood,
And oft with eloquence resistless sued;
But where 'twas impious e'en to deprecate,
She sigh'd assent, and wept the wretch's fate.
In savage times, fair Freedom yet unknown,
The despot, clad in vengeance, fill'd the throne;
His gloomy caprice scrawl'd the ambiguous code,
And dyed each page in characters of blood:
The laws transgress'd, the prince in judgment sat,
And Rage decided on the culprit's fate:
Nor stopp'd he here, but, skill'd in murderous art,
The scepter'd brute usurp'd the hangman's part;
With his own hands the trembling victim hew'd,
And basely wallow'd in a subject's blood.
Pleased with the fatal game, the royal mind
On modes of death and cruelty refined:
Hence the dank caverns of the cheerless mine,
Where, shut from light, the famish'd wretches pine;
The face divine, in seams unsightly scar'd,
The eyeballs gouged, the wheel with gore besmear'd,
The Russian knout, the suffocating flame,
And forms of torture wanting yet a name.
Nor was this rage to savage times confined;
It reach'd to later years and courts refined.
Blush, polish'd France, nor let the muse relate
The tragic story of your Damien's fate;
The bed of steel, where long the assassin lay,
In the dark vault, secluded from the day;
The quivering flesh which burning pincers tore,
The pitch, pour'd flaming in the recent sore;
His carcase, warm with life, convulsed with pain,
By steeds dismember'd, dragg'd along the plain.

As daring quacks, unskill'd in medic lore,
Prescribed the nostrums quacks prescribed before;
Careless of age or sex, whate'er befall,
The same dull recipe must serve for all:
Our senates thus, with reverence be it said,
Have been too long by blind tradition led:
Our civil code, from feudal dross refined,
Proclaims the liberal and enlighten'd mind;
But till of late the penal statutes stood
In Gothic rudeness, smear'd with civic blood;
What base memorials of a barbarous age,
What monkish whimsies sullied every page!
The clergy's benefit, a trifling brand,
Jest of the law, a holy sleight of hand:
Beneath this saintly cloak what crimes abhorr'd,
Of sable dye, were shelter'd from the lord;
While the poor starveling, who a cent purloin'd,
No reading saved, no juggling trick essoin'd;
His was the servile lash, a foul disgrace,
Through time transmitted to his hapless race;
The fort and dure, the traitor's motley doom,
Might blot the story of imperial Rome.
What late disgraced our laws yet stand to stain
The splendid annals of a GEORGE's reign.

Say, legislators, for what end design'd
This waste of lives, this havoc of mankind?
Say, by what right (one case exempt alone)
Do ye prescribe, that blood can crimes atone?
If, when our fortunes frown, and dangers press,
To act the Roman's part be to transgress;
For man the use of life alone commands,
The fee residing in the grantor's hands.
Could man, what time the social pact he seal'd,
Cede to the state a right he never held?
For all the powers which in the state reside,
Result from compact, actual or implied.
Too well the savage policy we trace
To times remote, Humanity's disgrace;
E'en while I ask, the trite response recurs,
Example warns, severity deters.
No milder means can keep the vile in awe,
And state necessity compels the law.
But let Experience speak, she claims our trust;
The data false, the inference is unjust.
Ills at a distance, men but slightly fear;
Delusive Fancy never thinks them near:
With stronger force than fear temptations draw,
And Cunning thinks to parry with the law.
"My brother swung, poor novice in his art,
He blindly stumbled on a hangman's cart;
But wiser I, assuming every shape,
As PROTEUS erst, am certain to escape."
The knave, thus jeering, on his skill relies,
For never villain deem'd himself unwise.

When earth convulsive heaved, and, yawning wide,
Engulf'd in darkness Lisbon's spiry pride,
At that dread hour of ruin and dismay,
'Tis famed the harden'd felon prowl'd for prey;
Nor trembling earth, nor thunders could restrain
His daring feet, which trod the sinking fane;
Whence, while the fabric to its centre shook,
By impious stealth the hallow'd vase he took.

What time the gaping vulgar throng to see
Some wretch expire on Tyburn's fatal tree;
Fast by the crowd the luckier villain clings,
And pilfers while the hapless culprit swings.
If then the knave can view, with careless eyes,
The bolt of vengeance darting from the skies,
If Death, with all the pomp of Justice join'd,
Scarce strikes a panic in the guilty mind,
What can we hope, though every penal code,
As DRACO's once, were stamp'd in civic blood?

The blinded wretch, whose mind is bent on ill,
Would laugh at threats, and sport with halters still,
Temptations gain more vigour as they throng,
Crime fosters crime, and wrong engenders wrong;
Fondly he hopes the threaten'd fate to shun,
Nor sees his fatal error till undone.
Wise is the law, and godlike is its aim,
Which frowns to mend, and chastens to reclaim,
Which seeks the storms of passion to control,
And wake the latent virtues of the soul;
For all, perhaps, the vilest of our race,
Bear in their breasts some smother'd sparks of grace:
Nor vain the hope, nor mad the attempt to raise
Those smother'd sparks to Virtue's purer blaze.
When, on the cross accursed, the robber writhed,
The parting prayer of penitence he breathed;
Cheer'd by the Saviour's smile, to grace restored,
He died distinguish'd with his suffering Lord.
As seeds long sterile in a poisonous soil,
If nurs'd by culture and assiduous toil,
May wake to life and vegetative power,
Protrude the germ and yield a fragrant flower:
E'en thus may man, rapacious and unjust,
The slave of sin, the prey of lawless lust,
In the drear prison's gloomy round confined,
To awful solitude and toil consign'd;
Debarr'd from social intercourse, nor less
From the vain world's seductions and caress,
With late and trembling steps he measures back
Life's narrow road, a long abandon'd track;
By Conscience roused, and left to keen Remorse,
The mind at length acquires its pristine force:
Then pardoning Mercy, with cherubic smile,
Dispels the gloom, and smooths the brow of Toil,
Till friendly Death, full oft implored in vain,
Shall burst the ponderous bar and loose the chain,
Fraught with fresh life, an offering meet for God,
The rescued spirit leaves the dread abode.

Nor yet can laws, though SOLON's self should frame,
Each shade of guilt discriminate and name;
For senates well their sacred trust fulfil,
Who general cures provide for general ill.
Much must by his direction be supplied,
In whom the laws the pardoning power confide;
He best can measure every varying grade
Of guilt, and mark the bounds of light and shade:
Weigh each essoin, each incident review,
And yield to Mercy, where she claims her due:
And wise it were so to extend his trust,
With power to mitigate—when 'twere unjust
Full amnesty to give—for though so dear
The name of Mercy to a mortal's ear,
Yet should the chief, to human weakness steel'd
Rarely indeed to suits for pardon yield;
For neither laws nor pardons can efface
The sense of guilt and memory of disgrace

Say, can the man whom Justice doom'd to shame,
With front erect, his country's honours claim?
Can he with cheek unblushing join the crowd,
Claim equal rights, and have his claim allow'd?
What though he mourn, a penitent sincere;
Though every dawn be usher'd with a tear;
The world, more prone to censure than forgive,
Quick to suspect, and tardy to believe,
Will still the hapless penitent despise,
And watch his conduct with invidious eyes:
But the chief end of justice once achieved,
The public weal secured, a soul reprieved,
'T were wise in laws, 't were generous to provide
Some place where blushing penitence might hide;
Yes, 't were humane, 't were godlike to protect
Returning virtue from the world's neglect
And taunting scorn, which pierce with keener pains
The feeling mind, than dungeons, racks, and chains:
Enlarge their bounds; admit a purer air;
Dismiss the servile badge and scanty fare;
The stint of labour lessen or suspend,
Admit at times the sympathizing friend.
Repentance courts the shade; alone she roves
By ruin'd towers and night-embrowning groves;
Or midst dark vaults, by Melancholy led,
She holds ideal converse with the dead:
Lost to the world and each profaner joy,
Her solace tears, and prayer her best employ.

A RADICAL SONG OF 1786.

Huzza, my Jo Bunkers! no taxes we 'll pay;
Here's a pardon for Wheeler, Shays, Parsons, and Day;*
Put green boughs in your hats, and renew the old cause;
Stop the courts in each county, and bully the laws:
Constitutions and oaths, sir, we mind not a rush;
Such trifles must yield to us lads of the bush.
New laws and new charters our books shall display,
Composed by conventions and Counsellor Grey.

Since Boston and Salem so haughty have grown,
We'll make them to know we can let them alone.
Of Glasgow or Pelham we'll make a seaport,
And there we'll assemble our General Court:
Our governor, now, boys, shall turn out to work,
And live, like ourselves, on molasses and pork;
In Adams or Greenwich he'll live like a peer
On three hundred pounds, paper money, a year.

Grand jurors, and sheriffs, and lawyers we'll spurn,
As judges, we'll all take the bench in our turn,
And sit the whole term, without pension or fee,
Nor Cushing or Sewal look graver than we.
Our wigs, though they 're rusty, are decent enough;
Our aprons, though black, are of durable stuff;

* Names of the leaders of the insurrection that arose, in 1786, in the state of Massachusetts, chiefly in the counties of Hampshire, Berkshire, and Worcester; which, after convulsing the state for about a year, was finally quelled by a military force under the command of General Lincoln and General Shepherd. The leaders fled from the state, and were afterwards pardoned. See Minot's History of the Insurrection in Massachusetts.

Array'd in such gear, the laws we 'll explain,
That poor people no more shall have cause to complain.

To Congress and impost we'll plead a release;
The French we can beat half-a-dozen a piece;
We want not their guineas, their arms, or alliance:
And as for the Dutchmen, we bid them defiance.
Then huzza, my Jo Bunkers! no taxes we'll pay;
Here's a pardon for Wheeler, Shays, Parsons, and Day;
Put green boughs in your hats, and renew the old cause;
Stop the courts in each county, and bully the laws.

REFLECTIONS ON SEEING A BULL SLAIN IN THE COUNTRY.

The sottish clown who never knew a charm
Beyond the powers of his nervous arm,
Proud of his might, with self-importance full,
Or climbs the spire, or fights the maddening bull;
The love of praise, impatient of control,
O'erflows the scanty limits of his soul;
In uncouth jargon, turbulently loud,
He bawls his triumphs to the wondering crowd:
"This well-strung arm dispensed the deadly blow,
Fell'd the proud bull and sunk his glories low:"
Not thoughts more towering fill'd Pelides' breast,
When thus to Greece his haughty vaunts express'd:
"I sack'd twelve ample cities on the main,
And six lay smoking on the Trojan plain;"
Thus full and fervid throbb'd the pulse of pride,
When "*Veni, vidi, vici*," Cæsar cried.
Each vain alike, and differing but in names;
These poets flatter—those the mob acclaims;
Impartial Death soon stops the proud career,
And bids Legendre rot with Dumourier.
The God whose sovereign care o'er all extends,
Sees whence their madness springs, and where it ends;
From his blest height, with just contempt, looks down
On thundering heroes and the swaggering clown:
But if our erring reason may presume
The future to divine, more mild his doom
Whose pride was wreck'd on vanquish'd brutes alone,
Than his whose conquests made whole nations groan.
Can Ganges' sacred wave, or Lethe's flood,
Wash clear the garments smear'd with civic blood?
What hand from heaven's dread register shall tear
The page where, stamp'd in blood, the conqueror's crimes appear?

IMPROMPTU ON AN ORDER TO KILL THE DOGS IN ALBANY.

'Tis done! the dreadful sentence is decreed!
The town is mad, and all the dogs must bleed!
Ah me! what boots it that the dogs are slain,
Since the whole race of *puppies* yet remain!

JOHN QUINCY ADAMS.

[Born, 1767. Died, 1848.]

When Mr. Adams took a degree at Harvard College, in 1787, he had already seen much of the world, in foreign schools, or travelling in the suite of his father, or in the official life upon which he had entered, at this early age, as secretary to the American legation at St. Petersburg. In 1790 he was admitted to the bar; in 1791 he wrote a reply to Paine's "Rights of Man;" in 1794 he was appointed minister to the Hague, in 1796 minister to Lisbon, in 1797 minister to Berlin; in 1801 he returned to the United States, in 1803 was chosen to the senate, in 1806 was made professor of rhetoric at Cambridge, in 1809 went to Russia as minister, in 1814 was a member of the peace commission at Ghent, in 1815 became envoy at the court of London, in 1817 was recalled to enter the office of Secretary of State, and in 1824 was elected President. After the close of his administration, in 1829, he was for a short period in private life, but in 1831 he reëntered Congress, as the representative of his native district, and by successive elections held his seat there until he died, on the twenty-third of February, 1848.

The merits of Mr. Adams as a poet are not great, but he wrote much in verse, and frequently with good sense, humour, and scholarly polish. Among his earlier productions are translations of the seventh and thirteenth satires of Juvenal, written for Dennie's "Port Folio," and he once showed me a translation of Wieland's "Oberon," which he made while residing officially at Berlin, in 1798. It would have been printed at the time, had not Wieland informed a friend of Mr. Adams, who exhibited to him the manuscript, of the English version of his poem then just published by Mr. Sotheby, of the existence of which Mr. Adams had not been aware.

The longest of Mr. Adams's original poems is "Dermot Mac Morrogh, or the Conquest of Ireland, an Historical Tale of the Twelfth Century, in Four Cantos," which appeared in 1832. It is a story of various profligacy and brutality, in which it is difficult to see any poetical elements; but Mr. Adams deemed the subject suitable for an historical tale, and to give it "an interest which might invite readers," it appeared "advisable to present it in the garb of poetry." He says, "it is intended also as a moral tale, teaching the citizens of these United States the virtues of conjugal fidelity, of genuine piety, and of devotion to their country, by pointing the finger of scorn at the example six hundred years since exhibited, of a country sold to a foreign invader by the joint agency of violated marriage vows, unprincipled ambition, and religious imposture." It was suspected by shrewd critics that the distinguished bard was thinking of some events nearer home, and that the chronicle of Giraldus Cambrensis, which he refers to as an authority, had not half as much to do with the suggestion of his theme and its treatment as certain scandalous chronicles respecting his own successful competitor for the presidency, and the wife of one of his leading partizans. This suspicion was not lessened by the disclaimer in the opening stanzas of the poem:

"I sing of Dermot, Erin's early pride;
  The pious patriot of the Emerald strand;
The first deliverer, for a stolen bride,
  Who sold to Albion's king his native land.
But, countrymen of mine, let wo betide
  The man who thinks of aught but what's in hand.
What I shall tell you, happen'd, you must know,
Beyond the seas, six hundred years ago.

"'T is strange how often readers will indulge
  Their wits a mystic meaning to discover;
Secrets ne'er dreamt of by the bard divulge,
  And where he shoots a duck will find a plover,
Satiric shafts from every line promulge,—
  Detect a tyrant, when he draws a lover:—
Nay, so intent his hidden thoughts to see,
Cry, if he paint a scoundrel—'That means me.' . . .

"Against all this I enter my protest;
  Dermot Mac Morrogh shows my hero's face;
Nor will I, or in earnest or in jest,
  Permit another to usurp his place;
And give me leave to say that I know best
  My own intentions in the lines I trace;
Let no man therefore draw aside the screen,
And say 't is any other that I mean."

"Dermot Mac Morrogh" added very little to Mr. Adams's literary fame. Reviewers of all parties condemned it as an utter failure in poetry, philosophy, and wit. It is probable that the eminent position of the author was as injurious to him with the critics, as it was advantageous to his booksellers with the public.

A collection of his shorter effusions appeared soon after his death under the title of "Poems of Religion and Society," and the editor expresses an opinion that many of them "are informed with wisdom and various learning," and that some of the illustrious writer's hymns "are among the finest devotional lyrics in our language." This praise is not altogether undeserved, but perhaps it may be discovered that they are more remarkable for the quality of piety than for that of poetry.

Of the intellectual activity of Mr. Adams, his erudition, temper, and general literary character, I have given some account in "The Prose Writers of America." Though one of our most voluminous authors, and possessed of abilities by which he might have been among the most distinguished, he will probably be longer remembered as a statesman than as a man of letters.

THE WANTS OF MAN.

Man wants but little here below,
Nor wants that little long.—GOLDSMITH.

"MAN wants but little here below,
Nor wants that little long."
'T is not with me exactly so,
But 't is so in the song.
My wants are many, and if told
Would muster many a score;
And were each wish a mint of gold,
I still should long for more.

What first I want is daily bread,
And canvas-backs and wine;
And all the realms of nature spread
Before me when I dine;
With four choice cooks from France, beside,
To dress my dinner well;
Four courses scarcely can provide
My appetite to quell.

What next I want, at heavy cost,
Is elegant attire:
Black sable furs for winter's frost,
And silks for summer's fire,
And Cashmere shawls, and Brussels lace
My bosom's front to deck,
And diamond rings my hands to grace,
And rubies for my neck.

And then I want a mansion fair,
A dwelling-house, in style,
Four stories high, for wholesome air—
A massive marble pile;
With halls for banquetings and balls,
All furnished rich and fine;
With high blood studs in fifty stalls,
And cellars for my wine.

I want a garden and a park,
My dwelling to surround—
A thousand acres, (bless the mark!)
With walls encompass'd round—
Where flocks may range and herds may low,
And kids and lambkins play,
And flowers and fruits commingled grow,
All Eden to display.

I want, when summer's foliage falls,
And autumn strips the trees,
A house within the city's walls,
For comfort and for ease;
But here, as space is somewhat scant,
And acres somewhat rare,
My house in town I only want
To occupy—a square.

I want a steward, butler, cooks;
A coachman, footman, grooms;
A library of well-bound books,
And picture-garnished rooms,
CORREGIO's Magdalen, and Night,
The Matron of the Chair;
GUIDO's fleet Coursers, in their flight,
And CLAUDES at least a pair.

I want a cabinet profuse
Of medals, coins, and gems;
A printing-press, for private use,
Of fifty thousand EMS;
And plants, and minerals, and shells;
Worms, insects, fishes, birds;
And every beast on earth that dwells,
In solitude or herds.

I want a board of burnished plate,
Of silver and of gold;
Tureens, of twenty pounds in weight,
And sculpture's richest mould;
Plateaus, with chandeliers and lamps,
Plates, dishes—all the same;
And porcelain vases, with the stamps
Of Sevres and Angouleme.

And maples, of fair glossy stain,
Must form my chamber doors,
And carpets of the Wilton grain
Must cover all my floors;
My walls, with tapestry bedeck'd,
Must never be outdone;
And damask curtains must protect
Their colours from the sun.

And mirrors of the largest pane
From Venice must be brought;
And sandal-wood and bamboo-cane,
For chairs and tables bought;
On all the mantel-pieces, clocks
Of thrice-gilt bronze must stand,
And screens of ebony and box
Invite the stranger's hand.

I want (who does not want?) a wife,
Affectionate and fair,
To solace all the woes of life,
And all its joys to share;
Of temper sweet, of yielding will,
Of firm, yet placid mind,
With all my faults to love me still,
With sentiment refined.

And as Time's car incessant runs,
And Fortune fills my store,
I want of daughters and of sons
From eight to half a score.
I want (alas! can mortal dare
Such bliss on earth to crave?)
That all the girls be chaste and fair—
The boys all wise and brave.

And when my bosom's darling sings,
With melody divine,
A pedal harp of many strings
Must with her voice combine.
A piano, exquisitely wrought,
Must open stand, apart,
That all my daughters may be taught
To win the stranger's heart.

My wife and daughters will desire
Refreshment from perfumes,
Cosmetics for the skin require,
And artificial blooms

The civet fragrance shall dispense,
And treasured sweets return;
Cologne revive the flagging sense,
And smoking amber burn.

And when at night my weary head
Begins to droop and dose,
A chamber south, to hold my bed,
For nature's soft repose;
With blankets, counterpanes, and sheet,
Mattrass, and sack of down,
And comfortables for my feet,
And pillows for my crown.

I want a warm and faithful friend,
To cheer the adverse hour,
Who ne'er to flatter will descend,
Nor bend the knee to power;
A friend to chide me when I 'm wrong,
My inmost soul to see;
And that my friendship prove as strong
For him, as his for me.

I want a kind and tender heart,
For others wants to feel;
A soul secure from Fortune's dart,
And bosom arm'd with steel;
To bear divine chastisement's rod,
And, mingling in my plan,
Submission to the will of God,
With charity to man.

I want a keen, observing eye,
An ever-listening ear,
The truth through all disguise to spy,
And wisdom's voice to hear;
A tongue, to speak at virtue's need,
In Heaven's sublimest strain;
And lips, the cause of man to plead,
And never plead in vain.

I want uninterrupted health,
Throughout my long career,
And streams of never-failing wealth,
To scatter far and near—
The destitute to clothe and feed,
Free bounty to bestow,
Supply the helpless orphan's need,
And soothe the widow's wo.

I want the genius to conceive,
The talents to unfold,
Designs, the vicious to retrieve,
The virtuous to uphold;
Inventive power, combining skill,
A persevering soul,
Of human hearts to mould the will,
And reach from pole to pole.

I want the seals of power and place,
The ensigns of command,
Charged by the people's unbought grace,
To rule my native land;
Nor crown, nor sceptre would I ask,
But from my country's will,
By day, by night, to ply the task
Her cup of bliss to fill.

I want the voice of honest praise
To follow me behind,
And to be thought, in future days,
The friend of human kind;
That after ages, as they rise,
Exulting may proclaim,
In choral union to the skies,
Their blessings on my name.

These are the wants of mortal man;
I cannot need them long,
For life itself is but a span,
And earthly bliss a song.
My last great want, absorbing all,
Is, when beneath the sod,
And summon'd to my final call,—
The mercy of my God.

And oh! while circles in my veins
Of life the purple stream,
And yet a fragment small remains
Of nature's transient dream,
My soul, in humble hope unscared,
Forget not thou to pray,
That this THY WANT may be prepared
To meet the Judgment-Day.

THE PLAGUE IN THE FOREST.

TIME was, when round the lion's den,
A peopled city raised its head;
'T was not inhabited by men,
But by four-footed beasts instead.
The lynx, the leopard, and the bear,
The tiger and the wolf, were there;
The hoof-defended steed;
The bull, prepared with horns to gore
The cat with claws, the tusky boar,
And all the canine breed.

In social compact thus combined,
Together dwelt the beasts of prey;
Their murderous weapons all resigned,
And vowed each other not to slay.
Among them Reynard thrust his phiz;
Not hoof, nor horn, nor tusk was his,
For warfare all unfit;
He whispered to the royal dunce,
And gained a settlement at once;
His weapon was,—his wit.

One summer, by some fatal spell,
(Phœbus was peevish for some scoff,)
The plague upon that city fell,
And swept the beasts by thousands off
The lion, as became his part,
Loved his own people from his heart,
And taking counsel sage,
His peerage summoned to advise
And offer up a sacrifice,
To soothe Apollo's rage.

Quoth Lion, "We are sinners all,
And even it must be confessed,
If among sheep I chance to fall,
I—I am guilty as the rest.

To me the sight of lamb is curst,
It kindles in my throat a thirst,—
I struggle to refrain,—
Poor innocent! his blood so sweet!
His flesh so delicate to eat!
I find resistance vain.

"Now to be candid, I must own
The sheep are weak and I am strong,
But when we find ourselves alone,
The sheep have never done me wrong.
And, since I purpose to reveal
All my offences, nor conceal
One trespass from your view;
My appetite is made so keen,
That with the sheep the time has been
I took,—the shepherd too.

"Then let us all our sins confess,
And whosoe'r the blackest guilt,
To ease my people's deep distress,
Let *his* atoning blood be spilt.
My own confession now you hear,
Should none of deeper dye appear,
Your sentence freely give;
And if on me should fall the lot
Make me the victim on the spot,
And let my people live."

The council with applauses rung,
To hear the Codrus of the wood;
Though still some doubt suspended hung,
If he would make his promise good,—
Quoth Reynard, "Since the world was made,
Was ever love like this displayed!
Let us like subjects true
Swear, as before your feet we fall,
Sooner than you should die for all,
We all will die for you.

"But please your majesty, I deem,
Submissive to your royal grace,
You hold in far too high esteem
That paltry, poltroon, sheepish race;
For oft, reflecting in the shade,
I ask myself why sheep were made
By all-creating power!
And howsoe'er I tax my mind,
This the sole reason I can find—
For lions to devour.

"And as for eating now and then,
As well the shepherd as the sheep,—
How can that braggart breed of men
Expect with you the peace to keep?
'T is time their blustering boast to stem,
That all the world was made for them—
And prove creation's plan;
Teach them by evidence profuse
That man was made for lion's use,
Not lions made for man."

And now the noble peers begin,
And, cheered with such examples bright,
Disclosing each his secret sin,
Some midnight murder brought to light;
Reynard was counsel for them all,
No crime the assembly could appal,
But *he* could botch with paint:
Hark, as his honeyed accents roll;
Each tiger is a gentle soul,
Each blood-hound is a saint.

When each had told his tale in turn,
The long-eared beast of burden came,
And meekly said, "My bowels yearn
To make confession of my shame;
But I remember on a time
I passed, not thinking of a crime,
A haystack on my way:
His lure some tempting devil spread,
I stretched across the fence my head,
And cropped,—a lock of hay."

"Oh, monster! villian!" Reynard cried—
"No longer seek the victim, sire;
Nor why your subjects thus have died,
To expiate Apollo's ire."
The council with one voice decreed;
All joined to execrate the deed,—
"What, steal another's grass!"
The blackest crime *their* lives could show,
Was washed as white as virgin snow;
The victim was,—The Ass.

TO A BEREAVED MOTHER.

Sure, to the mansions of the blest
When *infant* innocence ascends,
Some angel, brighter than the rest,
The spotless spirit's flight attends.
On wings of ecstasy they rise,
Beyond where worlds material roll;
Till some fair sister of the skies
Receives the unpolluted soul.
That inextinguishable beam,
With dust united at our birth,
Sheds a more dim, discolour'd gleam
The more it lingers upon earth. . .

But when the Lord of mortal breath
Decrees his bounty to resume,
And points the silent shaft of death
Which speeds an infant to the tomb—
No passion fierce, nor low desire,
Has quenched the radiance of the flame;
Back, to its God, the living fire
Reverts, unclouded as it came.
Fond mourner! be that solace thine!
Let Hope her healing charm impart,
And soothe, with melodies divine,
The anguish of a mother's heart.

Oh, think! the darlings of thy love,
Divested of this earthly clod,
Amid unnumber'd saints, above,
Bask in the bosom of their God. . . .
O'er thee, with looks of love, they bend:
For thee the Lord of life implore;
And oft, from sainted bliss descend,
Thy wounded quiet to restore.
Then dry, henceforth, the bitter tear;
Their part and thine inverted see.
Thou wert their guardian angel here,
They guardian angels now to thee

JOSEPH HOPKINSON.

[Born, 1770. Died, 1842.]

JOSEPH HOPKINSON, LL.D., son of FRANCIS HOPKINSON, author of "The Battle of the Kegs," &c., was born in Philadelphia in 1770, and educated for the bar in the office of his father. He wrote verses with fluency, but had little claim to be regarded as a poet. His "Hail Columbia!" is, however, one of our very few national songs, and is likely to be looked for in all collections of American poetry. In his old age Judge HOPKINSON wrote me a letter, in which the history of this song is thus given:

..."It was written in the summer of 1798, when war with France was thought to be inevitable. Congress was then in session in Philadelphia, deliberating upon that important subject, and acts of hostility had actually taken place. The contest between England and France was raging, and the people of the United States were divided into parties for the one side or the other, some thinking that policy and duty required us to espouse the cause of republican France, as she was called; while others were for connecting ourselves with England, under the belief that she was the great preservative power of good principles and safe government. The violation of our rights by both belligerents was forcing us from the just and wise policy of President WASHINGTON, which was to do equal justice to both, to take part with neither, but to preserve a strict and honest neutrality between them. The prospect of a rupture with France was exceedingly offensive to the portion of the people who espoused her cause; and the violence of the spirit of party has never risen higher, I think not so high, in our country, as it did at that time, upon that question. The theatre was then open in our city. A young man belonging to it, whose talent was as a singer, was about to take his benefit. I had known him when he was at school. On this acquaintance, he called on me one Saturday afternoon, his benefit being announced for the following Monday. His prospects were very disheartening; but he said that if he could get a patriotic song adapted to the tune of the 'President's March,' he did not doubt of a full house; that the poets of the theatrical corps had been trying to accomplish it, but had not succeeded. I told him I would try what I could do for him. He came the next afternoon; and the song, such as it is, was ready for him.

"The object of the author was to get up an *American spirit*, which should be independent of, and above the interests, passions, and policy of both belligerents; and look and feel exclusively for our own honour and rights. No allusion is made to France or England, or the quarrel between them; or to the question, which was most in fault in their treatment of us: of course the song found favour with both parties, for both were Americans; at least neither could disavow the sentiments and feelings it inculcated. Such is the history of this song, which has endured infinitely beyond the expectation of the author, as it is beyond any merit it can boast of, except that of being truly and exclusively patriotic in its sentiments and spirit."

At the time of his death, which occurred on the fifteenth of January, 1842, the author was President of the Pennsylvania Academy of the Fine Arts, one of the Vice-Presidents of the American Philosophical Society, and a Judge of the District Court of the United States.

HAIL COLUMBIA.

HAIL, Columbia! happy land!
Hail, ye heroes, heaven-born band!
Who fought and bled in Freedom's cause,
Who fought and bled in Freedom's cause,
And when the storm of war was gone,
Enjoy'd the peace your valour won!
Let independence be our boast,
Ever mindful what it cost;
Ever grateful for the prize,
Let its altar reach the skies.
Firm—united—let us be,
Rallying round our liberty;
As a band of brothers join'd,
Peace and safety we shall find.

Immortal patriots! rise once more;
Defend your rights, defend your shore;
Let no rude foe, with impious hand,
Let no rude foe, with impious hand,
Invade the shrine where sacred lies
Of toil and blood the well-earned prize.
While offering peace sincere and just,
In Heaven we place a manly trust,
That truth and justice will prevail,
And every scheme of bondage fail.
Firm—united, &c.

Sound, sound the trump of Fame!
Let WASHINGTON's great name
Ring through the world with loud applause,
Ring through the world with loud applause:
Let every clime to Freedom dear
Listen with a joyful ear.
With equal skill and godlike power,
He governs in the fearful hour
Of horrid war; or guides with ease,
The happier times of honest peace.
Firm—united, &c.

Behold the chief who now commands
Once more to serve his country stands—
The rock on which the storm will beat,
The rock on which the storm will beat:
But, armed in virtue firm and true,
His hopes are fixed on heaven and you.
When Hope was sinking in dismay,
And glooms obscured Columbia's day,
His steady mind, from changes free,
Resolved on death or liberty.
Firm—united, &c.

WILLIAM CLIFFTON.

[Born 1772. Died 1799.]

The father of William Cliffton was a wealthy member of the society of Friends, in Philadelphia. The poet, from his childhood, had little physical strength, and was generally a sufferer from disease; but his mind was vigorous and carefully educated, and had he lived to a mature age, he would probably have won an enduring reputation as an author. His life was marked by few incidents. He made himself acquainted with the classical studies pursued in the universities, and with music, painting, and such field-sports as he supposed he could indulge in with most advantage to his health. He was considered an amiable and accomplished gentleman, and his society was courted alike by the fashionable and the learned. He died in December, 1799, in the twenty-seventh year of his age.

The poetry of Cliffton has more energy of thought and diction, and is generally more correct and harmonious, than any which had been previously written in this country. Much of it is satirical, and relates to persons and events of the period in which he lived; and the small volume of his writings published after his death doubtless contains some pieces which would have been excluded from an edition prepared by himself, for this reason, and because they were unfinished and not originally intended to meet the eye of the world.

TO WILLIAM GIFFORD, ESQ.*

In these cold shades, beneath these shifting skies,
Where Fancy sickens, and where Genius dies;
Where few and feeble are the muse's strains,
And no fine frenzy riots in the veins,
There still are found a few to whom belong
The fire of virtue and the soul of song;
Whose kindling ardour still can wake the strings,
When learning triumphs, and when Gifford sings.
To thee the lowliest bard his tribute pays,
His little wild-flower to thy wreath conveys;
Pleased, if permitted round thy name to bloom,
To boast one effort rescued from the tomb.
While this delirious age enchanted seems
With hectic Fancy's desultory dreams;
While wearing fast away is every trace
Of Grecian vigour, and of Roman grace,
With fond delight, we yet one bard behold,
As Horace polish'd, and as Perseus bold,
Reclaim the art, assert the muse divine,
And drive obtrusive dulness from the shrine.
Since that great day which saw the Tablet rise,
A thinking block, and whisper to the eyes,
No time has been that touch'd the muse so near,
No Age when Learning had so much to fear,
As now, *when love-lorn ladies light verse frame*,
And every rebus-weaver talks of Fame.
When Truth in classic majesty appear'd,
And Greece, on high, the dome of science rear'd,
Patience and perseverance, care and pain
Alone the steep, the rough ascent could gain;
None but the great the sun-clad summit found;
The weak were baffled, and the strong were crown'd.
The tardy transcript's nigh-wrought page confined
To one pursuit the undivided mind.
No venal critic fatten'd on the trade;
Books for delight, and not for sale were made;
Then shone, superior, in the realms of thought,
The chief who govern'd, and the sage who taught:
The drama then with deathless bays was wreath'd
The statue quicken'd, and the canvass breathed.
The poet, then, with unresisted art,
Sway'd every impulse of the captive heart.
Touch'd with a beam of Heaven's creative mind,
His spirit kindled, and his taste refined:
Incessant toil inform'd his rising youth;
Thought grew to thought, and truth attracted truth,
Till, all complete, his perfect soul display'd
Some bloom of genius which could never fade.
So the sage oak, to Nature's mandate true,
Advanced but slow, and strengthen'd as it grew!
But when, at length, (full many a season o'er,)
Its virile head, in pride, aloft it bore;
When steadfast were its roots, and sound its heart,
It bade defiance to the insect's art,
And, storm and time resisting, still remains
The never-dying glory of the plains.
Then, if some thoughtless Bavius dared appear,
Short was his date, and limited his sphere;
He could but please the changeling mob a day,
Then, like his noxious labours, pass away:
So, near a forest tall, some worthless flower
Enjoys the triumph of its gaudy hour,
Scatters its little poison through the skies,
Then droops its empty, hated head, and dies.
Still, as from famed Ilyssus' classic shore,
To Mincius' banks, the muse her laurel bore,
The sacred plant to hands divine was given,
And deathless Maro nursed the boon of Heaven
Exalted bard! to hear thy gentler voice,
The valleys listen, and their swains rejoice;

* Prefixed to William Cobbett's edition of the "Baviad and Mæviad," published in Philadelphia, in 1799.

But when, on some wild mountain's awful form,
We hear thy spirit chanting to the storm,
Of battling chiefs, and armies laid in gore,
We rage, we sigh, we wonder, and adore.
Thus Rome with Greece in rival splendour shone,
But claim'd immortal satire for her own;
While HORACE pierced, full oft, the wanton breast
With sportive censure, and resistless jest;
And that Etrurian, whose indignant lay
Thy kindred genius can so well display,
With many a well-aim'd thought, and pointed line,
Drove the bold villain from his black design.
For, as those mighty masters of the lyre,
With temper'd dignity, or quenchless ire,
Through all the various paths of science trod,
Their school was NATURE and their teacher GOD
Nor did the muse decline till, o'er her head,
The savage tempest of the north was spread;
Till arm'd with desolation's bolt it came,
And wrapp'd her temple in funereal flame.
  But soon the arts once more a dawn diffuse,
And DANTE hail'd it with his morning muse;
PETRARCH and BOCCACE join'd the choral lay,
And Arno glisten'd with returning day.
Thus science rose; and, all her troubles pass'd,
She hoped a steady, tranquil reign at last;
But FAUSTUS came: (indulge the painful thought,)
Were not his countless volumes dearly bought?
For, while to every clime and class they flew,
Their worth diminish'd as their numbers grew.
Some pressman, rich in HOMER's glowing page,
Could give ten epics to one wondering age;
A single thought supplied the great design,
And clouds of Iliads spread from every line.
Nor HOMER's glowing page, nor VIRGIL's fire
Could one lone breast with equal flame inspire,
But, lost in books, irregular and wild,
The poet wonder'd, and the critic smiled:
The friendly smile, a bulkier work repays;
For fools will print, while greater fools will praise.
  Touch'd with the mania, now, what millions rage
To shine the laureat blockheads of the age.
The dire contagion creeps through every grade;
Girls, coxcombs, peers, and patriots drive the trade:
And e'en the hind, his fruitful fields forgot,
For rhyme and misery leaves his wife and cot.
Ere to his breast the wasteful mischief spread,
Content and plenty cheer'd his little shed;
And, while no thoughts of state perplex'd his mind,
His harvests ripening, and Pastora kind,
He laugh'd at toil, with health and vigour bless'd,
For days of labour brought their nights of rest:
But now in rags, ambitious for a name,
The fool of faction, and the dupe of fame,
His conscience haunts him with his guilty life,
His starving children, and his ruin'd wife.
Thus swarming wits, of all materials made,
Their Gothic hands on social quiet laid,
And, as they rave, unmindful of the storm,
Call lust, refinement; anarchy, reform.
  No love to foster, no dear friend to wrong,
Wild as the mountain flood, they drive along:
And sweep, remorseless, every social bloom
To the dark level of an endless tomb.
  By arms assail'd we still can arms oppose,
And rescue learning from her brutal foes;
But when those foes to friendship make pretence,
And tempt the judgment with the baits of sense,
Carouse with passion, laugh at GOD's control,
And sack the little empire of the soul,
What warning voice can save? Alas! 'tis o'er,
The age of virtue will return no more;
The doating world, its manly vigour flown,
Wanders in mind, and dreams on folly's throne.
Come then, sweet bard, again the cause defend,
Be still the muses' and religion's friend;
Again the banner of thy wrath display,
And save the world from DARWIN's tinsel lay.
A soul like thine no listless pause should know;
Truth bids thee strike, and virtue guides the blow
From every conquest still more dreadful come,
Till dulness fly, and folly's self be dumb.

MARY WILL SMILE.

THE morn was fresh, and pure the gale,
  When MARY, from her cot a rover,
Pluck'd many a wild rose of the vale
  To bind the temples of her lover.
As near his little farm she stray'd,
  Where birds of love were ever pairing,
She saw her WILLIAM in the shade,
  The arms of ruthless war preparing.
"Though now," he cried, "I seek the hostile plain,
MARY shall smile, and all be fair again."

She seized his hand, and "Ah!" she cried,
  "Wilt thou, to camps and war a stranger,
Desert thy MARY's faithful side,
  And bare thy life to every danger?
Yet, go, brave youth! to arms away!
  My maiden hands for fight shall dress thee,
And when the drum beats far away,
  I'll drop a silent tear, and bless thee.
Return'd with honour, from the hostile plain,
MARY will smile, and all be fair again.

"The bugles through the forest wind,
  The woodland soldiers call to battle:
Be some protecting angel kind,
  And guard thy life when cannons rattle!"
She sung—and as the rose appears
  In sunshine, when the storm is over,
A smile beam'd sweetly through her tears—
  The blush of promise to her lover.
Return'd in triumph from the hostile plain,
All shall be fair, and MARY smile again.

ROBERT TREAT PAINE.

[Born, 1773. Died, 1811.]

This writer was once ranked by our American critics among the great masters of English verse; and it was believed that his reputation would endure as long as the language in which he wrote. The absurd estimate of his abilities shows the wretched condition of taste in his time, and perhaps caused some of the faults in his later works.

Robert Treat Paine, junior,* was born at Taunton, Massachusetts, on the ninth of December, 1773. His father, an eminent lawyer, held many honourable offices under the state and national governments, and was one of the signers of the Declaration of Independence. The family having removed to Boston, when he was about seven years old, the poet received his early education in that city, and entered Harvard University in 1788. His career here was brilliant and honourable; no member of his class was so familiar with the ancient languages, or with elegant English literature; and his biographer assures us that he was personally popular among his classmates and the officers of the university. When he was graduated, "he was as much distinguished for the opening virtues of his heart, as for the vivacity of his wit, the vigour of his imagination, and the variety of his knowledge. A liberality of sentiment and a contempt of selfishness are usual concomitants, and in him were striking characteristics. Urbanity of manners and a delicacy of feeling imparted a charm to his benignant temper and social disposition."

While in college he had won many praises by his poetical "exercises," and on the completion of his education he was anxious to devote himself to literature as a profession. His father, a man of singular austerity, had marked out for him a different career, and obtained for him a clerkship in a mercantile house in Boston. But he was in no way fitted for the pursuits of business; and after a few months he abandoned the counting-room, to rely upon his pen for the means of living. In 1794 he established the "Federal Orrery," a political and literary gazette, and conducted it two years, but without industry or discretion, and therefore without profit. Soon after leaving the university, he had become a constant visiter of the theatre, then recently established in Boston. His intimacy with persons connected with the stage led to his marriage with an actress; and this to his exclusion from fashionable society, and a disagreement with his father, which lasted until his death.

He was destitute of true courage, and of that kind of pride which arises from a consciousness of integrity and worth. When, therefore, he found himself unpopular with the town, he no longer endeavoured to deserve regard, but neglected his personal appearance, became intemperate, and abandoned himself to indolence. The office of "master of ceremonies" in the theatre, an anomalous station, created for his benefit, still yielded him a moderate income, and, notwithstanding the irregularity of his habits, he never exerted his poetical abilities without success. For his poems and other productions he obtained prices unparalleled in this country, and rarely equalled by the rewards of the most popular European authors. For the "Invention of Letters," written at the request of the President of Harvard University, he received fifteen hundred dollars, or more than five dollars a line. "The Ruling Passion," a poem recited before the Phi Beta Kappa Society, was little less profitable; and he was paid seven hundred and fifty dollars for a song of half a dozen stanzas, entitled "Adams and Liberty."

His habits, in the sunshine, gradually improved, and his friends who adhered to him endeavoured to wean him from dissipation, and to persuade him to study the law, and establish himself in an honourable position in society. They were for a time successful; he entered the office of the Honourable Theophilus Parsons, of Newburyport; applied himself diligently to his studies; was admitted to the bar, and became a popular advocate. No lawyer ever commenced business with more brilliant prospects; but his indolence and recklessness returned; his business was neglected; his reputation decayed; and, broken down and disheartened by poverty, disease, and the neglect of his old associates, the evening of his life presented a melancholy contrast to its morning, when every sign gave promise of a bright career. In his last years, says his biographer, "without a library, wandering from place to place, frequently uncertain whence or whether he could procure a meal, his thirst for knowledge astonishingly increased; neither sickness nor penury abated his love of books and instructive conversation." He died in "an attic chamber of his father's house," on the eleventh of November, 1811, in the thirty-eighth year of his age.

Dr. Johnson said of Dryden, of whom Paine was a servile but unsuccessful imitator, that "his delight was in wild and daring sallies of sentiment, in the irregular and eccentric violence of wit;" that he "delighted to tread upon the brink of meaning where light and darkness begin to mingle; to approach the precipice of absurdity, and hover over the abyss of unideal vacancy." The censure is

* He was originally called Thomas Paine; but on the death of an elder brother, in 1801, his name was changed by an act of the Massachusetts legislature to that of his father.

more applicable to the copy than the original. There was no freshness in PAINE's writings; his subjects, his characters, his thoughts, were all commonplace and familiar. His mind was fashioned by books, and not by converse with the world. He had a brilliant fancy, and a singular command of language; but he was never content to be simple and natural. He endeavoured to be magnificent and striking; he was perpetually searching for conceits and extravagances; and in the multiplicity of his illustrations and ornaments, he was unintelligible and tawdry. From no other writer could so many instances of the false sublime be selected. He never spoke to the heart in its own language.

PAINE wrote with remarkable facility. It is related of him by his biographers, that he had finished "Adams and Liberty," and exhibited it to some gentlemen at the house of a friend. His host pronounced it imperfect, as the name of WASHINGTON was omitted, and declared that he should not approach the sideboard, on which bottles of wine had just been placed, until he had written an additional stanza. The poet mused a moment, called for a pen, and wrote the following lines, which are, perhaps, the best in the song:

Should the tempest of war overshadow our land,
  Its bolts could ne'er rend Freedom's temple asunder;
For, unmoved, at its portal would Washington stand,
  And repulse with his breast the assaults of the thunder!
    His sword from the sleep
    Of its scabbard would leap,
And conduct, with its point, every flash to the deep!
    For ne'er shall the sons, &c.

He had agreed to write the "opening address," on the rebuilding of the Boston Theatre, in 1798. HODGKINSON, the manager, called on him in the evening, before it was to be delivered, and upbraided him for his negligence; the first line of it being yet unwritten. "Pray, do not be angry," said PAINE, who was dining with some literary friends; "sit down and take a glass of wine."—"No, sir," replied the manager; "when you begin to write, I will begin to drink." PAINE took his pen, at a side-table, and in two or three hours finished the address, which is one of the best he ever wrote.

ADAMS AND LIBERTY.

YE sons of Columbia, who bravely have fought
  For those rights, which unstain'd from your sires had descended,
May you long taste the blessings your valour has bought,
  And your sons reap the soil which their fathers defended.
    Mid the reign of mild Peace
    May your nation increase,
With the glory of Rome, and the wisdom of Greece;
  And ne'er shall the sons of Columbia be slaves,
  While the earth bears a plant, or the sea rolls its waves.

In a clime whose rich vales feed the marts of the world,
  Whose shores are unshaken by Europe's commotion,
The trident of commerce should never be hurl'd,
  To incense the legitimate powers of the ocean.
    But should pirates invade,
    Though in thunder array'd,
Let your cannon declare the free charter of trade.
    For ne'er shall the sons, &c.

The fame of our arms, of our laws the mild sway,
  Had justly ennobled our nation in story,
'Till the dark clouds of faction obscured our young day,
  And envelop'd the sun of American glory.
    But let traitors be told,
    Who their country have sold,
And barter'd their God for his image in gold,
    That ne'er will the sons, &c.

While France her huge limbs bathes recumbent in blood,
  And society's base threats with wide dissolution,
May Peace, like the dove who return'd from the flood,
  Find an ark of abode in our mild constitution.
    But though peace is our aim,
    Yet the boon we disclaim,
If bought by our sovereignty, justice, or fame.
    For ne'er shall the sons, &c.

'T is the fire of the flint each American warms:
  Let Rome's haughty victors beware of collision;
Let them bring all the vassals of Europe in arms;
  We're a world by ourselves, and disdain a division.
    While, with patriot pride,
    To our laws we're allied,
No foe can subdue us, no faction divide.
    For ne'er shall the sons, &c.

Our mountains are crowned with imperial oak,
  Whose roots, like our liberties, ages have nourish'd;
But long e'er our nation submits to the yoke,
  Not a tree shall be left on the field where it flourished.
    Should invasion impend,
    Every grove would descend
From the hilltops they shaded our shores to defend.
    For ne'er shall the sons, &c.

Let our patriots destroy Anarch's pestilent worm,
  Lest our liberty's growth should be checked by corrosion;
Then let clouds thicken round us; we heed not the storm;
  Our realm fears no shock, but the earth's own explosion.
    Foes assail us in vain,
    Though their fleets bridge the main,
For our altars and laws with our lives we'll maintain.
    For ne'er shall the sons, &c.

Should the tempest of war overshadow our land,
  Its bolts could ne'er rend Freedom's temple asunder;

For, unmoved, at its portal would Washington
stand,
And repulse, with his breast, the assaults of the
thunder!
His sword from the sleep
Of its scabbard would leap,
And conduct with its point every flash to the deep!
For ne'er shall the sons, &c.

Let Fame to the world sound America's voice;
No intrigues can her sons from their government
sever;
Her pride is her Adams; her laws are his choice,
And shall flourish till Liberty slumbers forever.
Then unite heart and hand,
Like Leonidas' band,
And swear to the God of the ocean and land,
That ne'er shall the sons of Columbia be slaves,
While the earth bears a plant, or the sea rolls
its waves!

FROM A "MONODY ON THE DEATH OF SIR JOHN MOORE."

His heart elate, with modest valour bold,
Beat with fond rage to vie with chiefs of old.
Great by resolve, yet by example warm'd,
Himself the model of his glory form'd.
A glowing trait from every chief he caught:
He paused like Fabius, and like Cesar fought.
His ardent hope survey'd the heights of fame,
Deep on its rocks to grave a soldier's name;
And o'er its cliffs to bid the banner wave,
A Briton fights, to conquer and to save.....
Inspired on fields, with trophied interest graced,
He sigh'd for glory, where he mused from taste.
For high emprise his dazzling helm was plumed,
And all the polish'd patriot-hero bloom'd.
Arm'd as he strode, his glorying country saw
That fame was virtue, and ambition law;
In him beheld, with fond delight, conspire
Her Marlborough's fortune and her Sidney's [fire.
Like Calvi's rock, with clefts abrupt deform'd,
His path to fame toil'd up the breach he storm'd;
Till o'er the clouds the victor chief was seen,
Sublime in terror, and in height serene.
His equal mind so well could triumph greet,
He gave to conquest charms that soothed defeat.
The battle done, his brow, with thought o'ercast,
Benign as Mercy, smiled on perils past.
The death-choked fosse, the batter'd wall, inspired
A sense, that sought him, from the field retired.
Suspiring Pity touch'd that godlike heart,
To which no peril could dismay impart;
And melting pearls in that stern eye could shine,
That lighten'd courage down the thundering line.
So mounts the sea-bird in the boreal sky,
And sits where steeps in beetling ruin lie;
Though warring whirlwinds curl the Norway seas,
And the rocks tremble, and the torrents freeze;
Yet is the fleece, by beauty's bosom press'd,
The down that warms the storm-beat eider's breast;
Mid floods of frost, where Winter smites the deep,
Are fledged the plumes on which the Graces sleep.
In vain thy cliffs, Hispania, lift the sky,
Where Cesar's eagles never dared to fly!
To rude and sudden arms while Freedom springs,
Napoleon's legions mount on bolder wings.
In vain thy sons their steely nerves oppose,
Bare to the rage of tempests and of foes;
In vain, with naked breast, the storm defy
Of furious battle and of piercing sky:
Five waning reigns had marked, in long decay,
The gloomy glory of thy setting day;
While bigot power, with dark and dire disgrace,
Oppress'd the valour of thy gallant race.
No martial phalanx, led by veteran art,
Combined thy vigour, or confirmed thy heart:
Thy bands dispersed, like Rome in wild defeat,
Fled to the mountains, to entrench retreat.....
Illustrious Moore, by foe and famine press'd,
Yet by each soldier's proud affection bless'd,
Unawed by numbers, saw the impending host,
With front extending, lengthen down the coast.
"Charge! Britons, charge!" the exulting chief ex-
claims:
Swift moves the field; the tide of armour flames;
On, on they rush; the solid column flies,
And shouts tremendous, as the foe defies.
While all the battle rung from side to side,
In death to conquer was the warrior's pride.
Where'er the war its unequal tempest pour'd,
The leading meteor was his glittering sword!
Thrice met the fight, and thrice the vanquish'd Gaul
Found the firm line an adamantine wall.
Again repulsed, again the legions drew,
And Fate's dark shafts in volley'd shadows flew.
Now storm'd the scene where soul could soul attest,
Squadron to squadron join'd, and breast to breast,
From rank to rank the intrepid valour glow'd,
From rank to rank the inspiring champion rode
Loud broke the war-cloud, as his charger sped;
Pale the curved lightning quiver'd o'er his head;
Again it bursts; peal, echoing peal, succeeds;
The bolt is launch'd; the peerless soldier bleeds!
Hark! as he falls, Fame's swelling clarion cries,
"Britannia triumphs, though her hero dies!"
The grave he fills is all the realm she yields,
And that proud empire deathless honor shields.
No fabled phœnix from his bier revives;
His ashes perish, but his country lives.
Immortal dead! with musing awe thy foes
Tread not the hillock where thy bones repose!
There, sacring mourner, see, Britannia spreads
A chaplet, glistening with the tears she sheds.
With burning censer glides around thy tomb,
And scatters incense where thy laurels bloom;
With rapt devotion sainted vigil keeps—
Shines with Religion, and with Glory weeps!
Sweet sleep the brave! in solemn chant shall sound
Celestial vespers o'er thy sacred ground!
Long ages hence, in pious twilight seen,
Shall choirs of seraphs sanctify thy green;
At curfew-hour shall dimly hover there,
And charm, with sweetest dirge, the listening air.
With homage tranced, shall every pensive mind
Weep, while the requiem passes on the wind
Till, sadly swelling Sorrow's softest notes,
It dies in distance, while its echo floats!

WILLIAM MUNFORD.

[Born, 1775. Died, 1825.]

WILLIAM MUNFORD, the translator of the "Iliad," was born in the county of Mecklenburg, in Virginia, on the fifteenth of August, 1775. His father, Colonel ROBERT MUNFORD, was honourably distinguished in affairs during the Revolution, and afterward gave much attention to literature. Some of his letters, to be found in collections relating to the time, are written with grace and vigour, and he was the author of several dramatic pieces, of considerable merit, which, with a few minor poems, were published by his son, the subject of the present article, at Petersburg, in 1798. In his best comedy, "The Candidates," in three acts, he exposes to contempt the falsehood and corruption by which it was frequently attempted to influence the elections. In "The Patriots," in five acts, he contrasts, probably with an eye to some instance in Virginia, a real and pretended love of country. He had commenced a translation of OVID's "Metamorphoses" into English verse, and had finished the first book, when death arrested his labours. He was a man of wit and humour, and was respected for many social virtues. His literary activity is referred to thus particularly, because I have not seen that the pursuits and character of the father, have been noticed by any of the writers upon the life of the son, which was undoubtedly in a very large degree influenced by them.

WILLIAM MUNFORD was transferred from an academy at Petersburg, to the college of William and Mary, when only twelve years of age. In a letter written soon after he entered his fourteenth year, we have some information in regard to his situation and prospects. "I received from nature," he says, "a weakly constitution and a sickly body; and I have the unhappiness to know that my poor mother is in want. I am absent from her and my dear sisters. Put this in the scale of evil. I possess the rare and almost inestimable blessing of a friend in Mr. WYTHE and in JOHN RANDOLPH; I have a mother in whose heart I have a large share; two sisters, whose affections I flatter myself are fixed upon me; and fair prospects before me, provided I can complete my education, and am not destitute of the necessaries of life. Put these in the scale of good." This was a brave letter for a boy to write under such circumstances.

Mr. WYTHE here referred to was afterward the celebrated chancellor. He was at this time professor of law in the college, and young MUNFORD lived in his family; and, sharing the fine enthusiasm with which the retired statesman regarded the literatpre of antiquity, he became an object of his warm affection. His design to translate the "Iliad" was formed at an early period, and it was probably encouraged by Mr. WYTHE, who personally instructed him in ancient learning. In 1792, when Mr. WYTHE was made chancellor, and removed to Richmond, Mr. MUNFORD accompanied him, but he afterward returned to the college, where he had graduated with high honours, to attend to the law lectures of Mr. ST. GEORGE TUCKER. In his twentieth year he was called to the bar, in his native county, and his abilities and industry soon secured for him a respectable practice. He rose rapidly in his profession, and in the public confidence, and in 1797 was chosen a member of the House of Delegates, in which he continued until 1802, when he was elected to the senate, which he left after four years, to enter the Privy Council, of which he was a conspicuous member until 1811. He then received the place of clerk of the House of Delegates, which he retained until his death. This occurred at Richmond, where he had resided for nineteen years, on the twenty-first of July, 1825. In addition to his ordinary professional and political labours, he reported the decisions of the Virginia Supreme Court of Appeals, preparing six annual volumes without assistance, and four others, afterward, in connexion with Mr. W. W. HENRY. He possessed in a remarkable degree the affectionate respect of the people of the commonwealth; and the House of Delegates, upon his death, illustrated their regard for his memory by appointing his eldest son to the office which he had so long held, and which has thus for nearly a quarter of a century longer continued in his family.

The only important literary production of Mr. MUNFORD is his HOMER. This was his life-labour. The amazing splendour of the Tale of Troy captivated his boyish admiration, and the cultivation of his own fine mind enabled him but to see more and more its beauty and grandeur. It is not known at what time he commenced his version, but a large portion of it had been written in 1811, and the work was not completed until a short time before he died. In his modest preface he says: "The author of this translation was induced to undertake it by fond admiration of the almost unparalleled sublimity and beauty of the original; neither of which peculiar graces of HOMER's muse has, he conceives, been sufficiently expressed in the smooth and melodious rhymes of POPE. It is true that the fine poem of that elegant writer, which was the delight of my boyish days, and will always be read by me with uncommon pleasure, appears in some parts more beautiful than even the work of HOMER himself; but frequently it is less beautiful; and seldom does it equal the sublimity of the Greek." He had not seen COWPER's "Iliad" until his own was considerably advanced, and it does not appear that he was ever acquainted with CHAPMAN'S or SOTHEBY'S. He wrote, too, before the Homeric poetry had received the attention of those German scholars whose masterly criticisms have given to its literature an entirely new character. But he had studied the "Iliad" until his own mind was thoroughly imbued with its spirit; he approached his task with the fondest enthusiasm; well equipped with the best learning of his day; a style fashioned upon the most approved models: dignified, various, and disciplined into uniform elegance; and a judicial habit of mind, joined with a conscientious determination to present the living HOMER, as he was known in Greece, to the readers of our time and language.

His manuscript remained twenty years in the possession of his family, and was finally published in two large octavo volumes, in Boston, in 1846. It received the attention due from our scholars to such a performance, and the general judgment appears to have assigned it a place near to CHAPMAN'S and COWPER'S in fidelity, and between COWPER'S and POPE'S in elegance, energy, and all the best qualities of an English poem.

EXTRACTS FROM THE "ILIAD."

THE MEETING OF HECTOR AND ANDROMACHE.

To her the mighty HECTOR made reply:
"All thou hast said employs my thoughtful mind.
But from the Trojans much I dread reproach,
And Trojan dames whose garments sweep the
If, like a coward, I should shun the war; [ground,
Nor does my soul to such disgrace incline,
Since to be always bravest I have learn'd,
And with the first of Troy to lead the fight;
Asserting so my father's lofty claim
To glory, and my own renown in arms.
For well I know, in heart and mind convinced,
A day will come when sacred Troy must fall,
And PRIAM, and the people of renown'd
Spear-practised PRIAM! Yet for this, to me
Not such concern arises; not the woes
Of all the Trojans, not my mother's griefs,
Nor royal PRIAM'S nor my brethren's deaths,
Many and brave, who slain by cruel foes
Will be laid low in dust, so wring my heart
As thy distress, when some one of the Greeks
In brazen armour clad, shall drive thee hence,
Thy days of freedom gone, a weeping slave!
Perhaps at Argos thou mayst ply the loom,
For some proud mistress; or mayst water bring,
From Mepsa's or Hyperia's fountain, sad
And much reluctant, stooping to the weight
Of sad necessity: and some one, then,
Seeing thee weep, will say, 'Behold the wife
Of HECTOR, who was first in martial might
Of all the warlike Trojans, when they fought
Around the walls of Ilion!' So will speak
Some heedless passer-by, and grief renew'd
Excite in thee, for such a husband lost,
Whose arm might slavery's evil day avert.
But me may then a heap of earth conceal
Within the silent tomb, before I hear
Thy shrieks of terror and captivity."

This said, illustrious HECTOR stretch'd his arms
To take his child; but to the nurse's breast
The babe clung crying, hiding in her robe
His little face, affrighted to behold
His father's awful aspect; fearing too
The brazen helm, and crest with horse-hair crown'd,
Which, nodding dreadful from its lofty cone,
Alarm'd him. Sweetly then the father smiled,
And sweetly smiled the mother! Soon the chief
Removed the threatening helmet from his head,
And placed it on the ground, all beaming bright;
Then having fondly kiss'd his son beloved
And toss'd him playfully, he thus to Jove
And all the immortals pray'd: "O grant me, Jove,
And other powers divine, that this my son
May be, as I am, of the Trojan race
In glory chief. So! let him be renown'd
For warlike prowess and commanding sway
With power and wisdom join'd, of Ilion king!
And may the people say, 'This chief excels
His father much, when from the field of fame
Triumphant he returns, bearing aloft
The bloody spoils, some hostile hero slain,
And his fond mother's heart expands with joy!'
He said, and placed his child within the arms
Of his belov'd spouse. She him received,
And softly on her fragrant bosom laid,
Smiling with tearful eyes. To pity moved,
Her husband saw: with kind consoling hand
He wiped the tears away, and thus he spake
"My dearest love! grieve not thy mind for me
Excessively. No man can send me hence,
To Pluto's hall, before the appointed time;
And surely none of all the human race,
Base or e'en brave, has ever shunn'd his fate—
His fate foredoom'd, since first he saw the light.
But now, returning home, thy works attend,
The loom and distaff, and direct thy maids
In household duties, while the war shall be
Of men the care; of all, indeed, but most
The care of me, of all in Ilion born."

EMBARKATION OF THE GREEKS.

When with food and drink
All were supplied, the striplings crown'd with wine
The foaming bowls, and handed round to each,
In cups, a portion to libations due.
They, all day long, with hymns the god appeased;
The sons of Greece melodious pæans sang
In praise of great Apollo—he rejoiced
To hear that pleasant song—and when the sun
Descended to the sea, and darkness came,
They near the cables of their vessels slept.
Soon as the rosy-finger'd queen appear'd,
Aurora, lovely daughter of the dawn,
Toward the camp of Greece they took their way,
And friendly Phœbus gave propitious gales.
They raised the mast, and stretch'd the snowy sheet,
To catch the breeze which fill'd the swelling sail.
Around the keel the darken'd waters roar,
As swift the vessel flies. The billows dark
She quickly mounting, stemm'd the watery way.

JOHN SHAW.

[Born, 1778. Died, 1809.]

JOHN SHAW was born in Annapolis, Maryland, on the fourth of May, 1778; graduated at St. John's College, in that city, in 1796; after studying medicine two years, with a private teacher, entered the medical school connected with the University of Pennsylvania, in 1798; in the same year suddenly sailed for Algiers, as surgeon of several vessels built in this country for the Algerine government; became secretary to General Eaton, our consul at Tunis; returned to Annapolis in 1800; the next year went to Edinburgh for the completion of his professional education; in 1803 left Scotland with Lord Selkirk, then about to establish his colony on the north side of Lake St. Clair; in 1805 settled in his native town as a physician; in 1807 was married, and removed to Baltimore, and was busy with efforts to found a medical college there, when his health failed, and died, on a voyage to the Bahama Islands, on the tenth of January, 1809. He had been a writer for "The Port Folio," and other periodicals, and after his death a collection of his poems was published in Baltimore. They have not generally much merit, but among them is a beautiful song, beginning, "Who has robbed the ocean cave!" which will live.

WHO HAS ROBBED THE OCEAN CAVE?

Who has robbed the ocean cave,
To tinge thy lips with coral hue?
Who, from India's distant wave,
For thee those pearly treasures drew?
Who, from yonder orient sky,
Stole the morning of thine eye?

Thousand charms thy form to deck,
From sea, and earth, and air are torn;
Roses bloom upon thy cheek,
On thy breath their fragrance borne:
Guard thy bosom from the day,
Lest thy snows should melt away.

But one charm remains behind,
Which mute earth could ne'er impart;
Nor in ocean wilt thou find,
Nor in the circling air, a heart:
Fairest, wouldst thou perfect be,
Take, oh take that heart from me.

THE LAD FROM TUCKAHOE.

Oh the lad from Tuckahoe,
Is the lad whom I love dearly,
I tell it you sincerely,
That all the truth may know.
From the day that first I knew him
He struck my fancy so,
That my love shall still pursue him,
The lad from Tuckahoe.

He alighted at the door,
Where my aunt and I were spinning,
And his looks they were so winning,
I thought of work no more.
My aunt, her anger hiding,
Ask'd what made me trifle so,
But I never mind her chiding,
When he comes from Tuckahoe.

THE FALSE MAIDEN.

Oh, wert thou hail'd the sole queen
Of all that greets the day-star's view,
And brighter were thy beauty's sheen
Than ever form that fancy drew,
Yet I would never love thee—
No, no, I would not love thee!
Nor ever sigh or tear of mine
Should idly strive to move thee.

As brightly rolls thy dark eye,
And curling falls thy glossy hair,
As soft thy warm cheek's crimson die
They swelling bosom still as fair,
As when I first did love thee,
Most tenderly did love thee;
But now no more my passion lives
Since false as fair I prove thee.

For ah! thy flinty cold heart
Ill suits thy beauty's treacherous glow,
'T is filled alone with woman's art,
And ne'er could love or pity know.
Ah, wo to him who loves thee!—
Not knowing thee he loves thee;
For thou canst trifle with his woes,
While passion never moves thee.

With what fond love I wooed thee,
Each sleepless night sad witness bears,
My breast that heaved with sighs for thee,
My wan cheek wet with bitter tears.
All told how much I loved thee,
And thou didst know I loved thee,
And thou couldst smile to see the pain
Of him who dearly loved thee.

But broken is the fond spell:
My fate no more depends on thee;
And thou, perhaps, one day shalt tell
Thy sorrow and remorse for me;
For none can ever love thee
As dearly as I loved thee,
And I shall court thy chains no more,—
No! no! I will not love thee!

CLEMENT C. MOORE.

[Born 1779. Died 1863.]

CLEMENT C. MOORE, LL. D., a son of the Right Reverend BENJAMIN MOORE, Bishop of the Protestant Episcopal Church in New York, was born at Newtown, on Long Island, about the year 1778, and graduated bachelor of arts at Columbia College in 1799. His early addiction to elegant literature was illustrated in various poetical and prose contributions to the "Port Folio" and the New York "Evening Post;" and his abilities as a critic were shown in a pungent reviewal of contemporary American poetry, especially of Mr. JOSEPH STORY'S "Powers of Solitude," in a letter prefixed to his friend JOHN DUER'S "New Translation of the Third Satire of JUVENAL, with Miscellaneous Poems, Original and Translated," which appeared in 1806. "Anna Matilda," and "Della Crusca,"* were still the fashionable models of our sentimentalists, and Mr. STORY followed Mrs. MORTON, ROBERT TREAT PAINE, WILLIAM LADD, and others of that school, who, to use Mr. MOORE'S language, "if they could procure from the wardrobe of poesy a sufficient supply of dazzling ornaments wherewith to deck their intellectual offspring, were utterly regardless whether the body of sense which these decorations were designed to render attractive were worthy of attention, or mean and distorted and in danger of being overwhelmed by the profusion of its ornaments."

Devoting his attention to biblical learning, Mr. MOORE in 1809 published in two volumes the first American "Lexicon of the Hebrew Language," and he was afterwards many years professor of Hebrew and Greek in the General Theological Seminary, of which he was one of the founders and principal benefactors. His only or most important publications in later years have been a volume of "Poems," in 1844, and "George Castriot, surnamed Scanderbeg, King of Albania," an historical biography, in 1852.

In some touching lines to Mr. SOUTHEY, written in 1832, Dr. MOORE reveals a portion of his private history, which proves that the happiest condition is not exempt from the common ills; but his life appears to have been nearly all passed very quietly, in the cultivation of learning, and in intercourse with a few congenial friends. In his old age, sending a bunch of flowers to the late Mr PHILIP HONE, he wrote to him:

"These new-cull'd blossoms which I send,
With breath so sweet and tints so gay,
I truly know not, my kind friend,
In Flora's language *what* they say;

"Nor which *one* hue I should select,
Nor how they *all* should be combined,
That at a glance you might detect
The true emotions of my mind.

"But, as the rainbow's varied hues,
If mingled in proportions right,
All their distinctive radiance lose,
And only show unspotted white.

"Thus, into one I would combine
These colours that so various gleam,
And bid this offering only shine
With friendship's pure and tranquil beam."

In his answer, Mr. HONE says:

"Filled as thou art with attic fire,
And skilled in classic lore divine,
Not yet content, wouldst thou aspire
In Flora's gorgeous wreath to shine?

"Come as thou wilt, my warm regard,
And welcome, shall thy steps attend;
Scholar, musician, florist, bard—
More dear to me than all, as friend."

In the preface to the collection of his poems, Dr. MOORE remarks that he has printed the melancholy and the lively, the serious, the sportive, and even the trifling, that his children, to whom the book is addressed, might have as true a picture as possible of his mind. They are all marked by good taste and elegance. "I do not pay my readers," he says, "so ill a compliment as to offer the contents of this volume to their view as the mere amusements of my idle hours as though the refuse of my thoughts were good enough for them. On the contrary, some of the pieces have cost me much time and thought, and I have composed them all as carefully and correctly as I could."

* ROBERT MERRY, after being graduated master of arts at Oxford, went to Italy, and by some means was elected into the celebrated Florentine academy of "Della Crusca," the name of which he adopted, with characteristic modesty, as the signature of numerous pieces of verse which he wrote in rapid succession for "The Florence Miscellany," and a periodical in London called "The World." He became the leader of a school of small poets, one of whom was Mrs. PIOZZI, so well known to the readers of BOSWELL, who wrote under the pseudonym of "Anna Matilda," and another, Mrs. ROBINSON, a profligate actress, who announced herself as "Laura Maria." The "nonsense verses" of these people became fashionable; the press teemed for some years with their silly effusions; and men of taste could not refrain from regarding them as an intolerable nuisance. At the same time a base fellow, named JOHN WILLIAMS, was writing lampoons in verse under the name of "Anthony Pasquin." After the publication of GIFFORD'S "Baviad and Mæviad," "Anthony Pasquin" was driven from England by contempt, and "Della Crusca" by derision; and both found an asylum in the United States—the libeller to become the editor of a democratic newspaper, and the sentimentalist to acquire an influence over our fledgeling poets not less apparent than that which TENNYSON has exerted in later years. He resided in our principal cities, and continued to write and publish till he died, in Baltimore, on the twenty-fourth of December, 1798, in the forty-third year of his age. STORY, in his "Powers of Solitude," pays him the following tribute:

"Wild bard of fancy! o'er thy timeless tomb
Shall weep the cypress, and the laurel bloom;
While village nymphs, composed each artless play,
To sing, at evening close, their roundelay,
With Spring's rich flowers shall dress thy sacred grave,
Where sad Patapsco rolls his freighted wave."

A VISIT FROM ST. NICHOLAS.

'T WAS the night before Christmas, when all through the house
Not a creature was stirring, not even a mouse;
The stockings were hung by the chimney with care,
In hopes that St. Nicholas soon would be there;
The children were nestled all snug in their beds,
While visions of sugar-plums danced in their heads;
And mamma in her kerchief, and I in my cap,
Had just settled our brains for a long winter's nap—
When out on the lawn there arose such a clatter,
I sprang from my bed to see what was the matter.
Away to the window I flew like a flash,
Tore open the shutters and threw up the sash.
The moon, on the breast of the new-fallen snow,
Gave the lustre of mid-day to objects below,
When, what to my wondering eyes should appear,
But a miniature sleigh, and eight tiny rein-deer,
With a little old driver, so lively and quick
I knew in a moment it must be St. Nick.
More rapid than eagles his coursers they came,
And he whistled, and shouted, and called them by name;
"Now, Dasher! now, Dancer! now, Prancer and Vixen!
On! Comet, on! Cupid, on! Donder and Blitzen—
To the top of the porch, to the top of the wall!
Now, dash away, dash away, dash away all!"
As dry leaves that before the wild hurricane fly,
When they meet with an obstacle, mount to the sky,
So, up to the house-top the coursers they flew,
With the sleigh full of toys—and St. Nicholas too.
And then in a twinkling I heard on the roof
The prancing and pawing of each little hoof.
As I drew in my head, and was turning around,
Down the chimney St. Nicholas came with a bound.
He was dressed all in fur, from his head to his foot,
And his clothes were all tarnisht with ashes and soot;
A bundle of toys he had flung on his back,
And he looked like a pedlar just opening his pack.
His eyes how they twinkled! his dimples how merry!
His cheeks were like roses, his nose like a cherry;
His droll little mouth was drawn up like a bow,
And the beard on his chin was as white as the snow.
The stump of a pipe he held tight in his teeth,
And the smoke, it encircled his head like a wreath.
He had a broad face and a little round belly
That shook, when he laugh'd, like a bowl full of jelly.
He was chubby and plump; a right jolly old elf;
And I laughed when I saw him, in spite of myself.
A wink of his eye, and a twist of his head,
Soon gave me to know I had nothing to dread.
He spoke not a word, but went straight to his work,
And filled all the stockings; then turned with a jerk,
And laying his finger aside of his nose,
And giving a nod, up the chimney he rose.
He sprang to his sleigh, to his team gave a whistle,
And away they all flew like the down of a thistle;
But I heard him exclaim, ere he drove out of sight,
Happy Christmas to all, and to all a good-night!"

TO MY CHILDREN,

AFTER HAVING MY PORTRAIT TAKEN FOR THEM.

THIS semblance of your parent's time-worn face
Is but a sad bequest, my children dear:
Its youth and freshness gone, and in their place
The lines of care, the track of many a tear!

Amid life's wreck, we struggle to secure
Some floating fragment from oblivion's wave:
We pant for something that may still endure,
And snatch at least a shadow from the grave.

Poor, weak, and transient mortals! why so vain
Of manly vigour, or of beauty's bloom?
An empty shade for ages may remain
When we have mouldered in the silent tomb.

But no! it is not *we* who moulder there,
We, of essential light that ever burns;
We take our way through untried fields of air,
When to the earth this earth-born frame returns.

And 't is the glory of the master's art
Some radiance of this inward light to find,
Some touch that to his canvas may impart
A breath, a sparkle of the immortal mind.

Alas! the pencil's noblest power can show
But some faint shadow of a transient thought,
Some wakened feeling's momentary glow,
Some swift impression in its passage caught.

Oh that the artist's pencil could portray
A father's inward bosom to your eyes,
What hopes, and fears, and doubts perplex his way,
What aspirations for your welfare rise.

Then might this unsubstantial image prove
When I am gone, a guardian of your youth,
A friend forever urging you to move
In paths of honour, holiness, and truth.

Let fond imagination's power supply
The void that baffles all the painter's art;
And when those mimic features meet your eye,
Then fancy that they speak a parent's heart.

Think that you still can trace within those eyes,
The kindling of affection's fervid beam,
The searching glance that every fault espies,
The fond anticipation's pleasing dream.

Fancy those lips still utter sounds of praise,
Or kind reproof that checks each wayward will,
The warning voice, or precepts that may raise
Your thoughts above this treacherous world of ill.

And thus shall art attain her loftiest power;
To noblest purpose shall her efforts tend:
Not the companion of an idle hour,
But Virtue's handmaid, and Religion's friend

JAMES KIRKE PAULDING.

[Born 1779. Died 1860.]

Mr. PAULDING is known by his numerous novels and other prose writings, much better than by his poetry; yet his early contributions to our poetical literature, if they do not bear witness that he possesses, in an eminent degree, "the vision and the faculty divine," are creditable for their patriotic spirit and moral purity.

He was born in the town of Pawling,—the original mode of spelling his name,—in Duchess county, New York, on the 22d of August, 1779, and is descended from an old and honourable family, of Dutch extraction.

His earliest literary productions were the papers entitled "Salmagundi," the first series of which, in two volumes, were written in conjunction with WASHINGTON IRVING, in 1807. These were succeeded, in the next thirty years, by the following works, in the order in which they are named: John Bull and Brother Jonathan, in one volume; The Lay of a Scotch Fiddle, a satirical poem, in one volume; The United States and England, in one volume; Second Series of Salmagundi, in two volumes; Letters from the South, in two volumes The Backwoodsman, a poem, in one volume Koningsmarke, or Old Times in the New World, a novel, in two volumes; John Bull in America, in one volume; Merry Tales of the Wise Men of Gotham, in one volume; The Traveller's Guide, or New Pilgrim's Progress, in one volume; The Dutchman's Fireside, in two volumes; Westward Ho! in two volumes; Slavery in the United States, in one volume; Life of Washington, in two volumes; The Book of St. Nicholas, in one volume; and Tales, Fables, and Allegories, originally published in various periodicals, in three volumes. Beside these, and some less pretensive works, he has written much in the gazettes on political and other questions agitated in his time.

Mr. PAULDING has held various honourable offices in his native state; and in the summer of 1838, he was appointed, by President VAN BUREN, Secretary of the Navy. He continued to be a member of the cabinet until the close of Mr. VAN BUREN's administration, in 1841.

ODE TO JAMESTOWN.

OLD cradle of an infant world,
In which a nestling empire lay,
Struggling a while, ere she unfurl'd
Her gallant wing and soar'd away;
All hail! thou birth-place of the glowing west,
Thou seem'st the towering eagle's ruin'd nest!

What solemn recollections throng,
What touching visions rise,
As, wandering these old stones among,
I backward turn mine eyes,
And see the shadows of the dead flit round,
Like spirits, when the last dread trump shall sound!

The wonders of an age combined,
In one short moment memory supplies
They throng upon my waken'd mind,
As time's dark curtains rise.
The volume of a hundred buried years,
Condensed in one bright sheet, appears.

I hear the angry ocean rave,
I see the lonely little barque
Scudding along the crested wave,
Freighted like old Noah's ark,
As o'er the drowned earth 't was hurl'd,
With the forefathers of another world.

I see a train of exiles stand,
Amid the desert, desolate,
The fathers of my native land,
The daring pioneers of fate,
Who braved the perils of the sea and earth,
And gave a boundless empire birth.

I see the sovereign Indian range
His woodland empire, free as air;
I see the gloomy forest change,
The shadowy earth laid bare;
And, where the red man chased the bounding deer,
The smiling labours of the white appear.

I see the haughty warrior gaze
In wonder or in scorn,
As the pale faces sweat to raise
Their scanty fields of corn,
While he, the monarch of the boundless wood,
By sport, or hair-brain'd rapine, wins his food.

A moment, and the pageant's gone;
The red men are no more;
The pale-faced strangers stand alone
Upon the river's shore;
And the proud wood-king, who their arts disdain'd,
Finds but a bloody grave where once he reign'd.

The forest reels beneath the stroke
Of sturdy woodman's axe;
The earth receives the white man's yoke,
And pays her willing tax
Of fruits, and flowers, and golden harvest fields,
And all that nature to blithe labour yields.

Then growing hamlets rear their heads,
And gathering crowds expand,
Far as my fancy's vision spreads,
O'er many a boundless land,
Till what was once a world of savage strife
Teems with the richest gifts of social life.

Empire to empire swift succeeds,
Each happy, great, and free;
One empires still another breeds,
A giant progeny,
Destined their daring race to run,
Each to the regions of yon setting sun.

Then, as I turn my thoughts to trace
The fount whence these rich waters spring,
I glance towards this lonely place,
And find it, these rude stones among.
Here rest the sires of millions, sleeping round,
The Argonauts, the golden fleece that found.

Their names have been forgotten long;
The stone, but not a word, remains;
They cannot live in deathless song,
Nor breathe in pious strains.
Yet this sublime obscurity, to me
More touching is, than poet's rhapsody.

They live in millions that now breathe;
They live in millions yet unborn,
And pious gratitude shall wreathe
As bright a crown as e'er was worn,
And hang it on the green-leaved bough,
That whispers to the nameless dead below.

No one that inspiration drinks;
No one that loves his native land;
No one that reasons, feels, or thinks,
Can mid these lonely ruins stand,
Without a moisten'd eye, a grateful tear
Of reverent gratitude to those that moulder here.

The mighty shade now hovers round—
Of HIM whose strange, yet bright career,
Is written on this sacred ground
In letters that no time shall sere;
Who in the old world smote the turban'd crew,
And founded Christian empires in the new.

And she! the glorious Indian maid,
The tutelary of this land,
The angel of the woodland shade,
The miracle of God's own hand,
Who join'd man's heart to woman's softest grace,
And thrice redeem'd the scourges of her race

Sister of charity and love,
Whose life-blood was soft Pity's tide,
Dear goddess of the sylvan grove,
Flower of the forest, nature's pride,
He is no man who does not bend the knee,
And she no woman who is not like thee!

Jamestown, and Plymouth's hallow'd rock
To me shall ever sacred be—
I care not who my themes may mock,
Or sneer at them and me.
I envy not the brute who here can stand,
Without a thrill for his own native land.

And if the recreant crawl *her* earth,
Or breathe Virginia's air,
Or, in New England claim his birth,
From the old pilgrims there,
He is a bastard, if he dare to mock
Old Jamestown's shrine, or Plymouth's famous rock

PASSAGE DOWN THE OHIO.*

As down Ohio's ever ebbing tide,
Oarless and sailless, silently they glide,
How still the scene, how lifeless, yet how fair
Was the lone land that met the stranger there!
No smiling villages or curling smoke
The busy haunts of busy men bespoke;
No solitary hut, the banks along,
Sent forth blithe labour's homely, rustic song;
No urchin gamboll'd on the smooth, white sand,
Or hurl'd the skipping-stone with playful hand,
While playmate dog plunged in the clear blue wave,
And swam, in vain, the sinking prize to save.
Where now are seen, along the river side,
Young, busy towns, in buxom, painted pride,
And fleets of gliding boats with riches crown'd,
To distant Orleans or St. Louis bound.
Nothing appear'd but nature unsubdued,
One endless, noiseless woodland solitude,
Or boundless prairie, that aye seem'd to be
As level and as lifeless as the sea;
They seem'd to breathe in this wide world alone,
Heirs of the earth—the land was all their own!
'T was evening now: the hour of toil was o'er,
Yet still they durst not seek the fearful shore,
Lest watchful Indian crew should silent creep,
And spring upon and murder them in sleep;
So through the livelong night they held their way,
And 't was a night might shame the fairest day;
So still, so bright, so tranquil was its reign,
They cared not though the day ne'er came again.
The moon high wheel'd the distant hills above,
Silver'd the fleecy foliage of the grove,
That as the wooing zephyrs on it fell,
Whisper'd it loved the gentle visit well
That fair-faced orb alone to move appear'd,
That zephyr was the only sound they heard.
No deep-mouth'd hound the hunter's haunt betray'd,
No lights upon the shore or waters play'd,
No loud laugh broke upon the silent air,
To tell the wanderers, man was nestling there
All, all was still, on gliding bark and shore,
As if the earth now slept to wake no more.

EVENING.

'T WAS sunset's hallow'd time—and such an eve
Might almost tempt an angel heaven to leave.
Never did brighter glories greet the eye,
Low in the warm and ruddy western sky:
Nor the light clouds at summer eve unfold
More varied tints of purple, red, and gold.
Some in the pure, translucent, liquid breast
Of crystal lake, fast anchor'd seem'd to rest,
Like golden islets scatter'd far and wide,
By elfin skill in fancy's fabled tide,
Where, as wild eastern legends idly feign,
Fairy, or genii, hold despotic reign.

* This, and the two following extracts, are from the "Backwoodsman."

Others, like vessels gilt with burnish'd gold,
Their flitting, airy way are seen to hold,
All gallantly equipp'd with streamers gay,
While hands unseen, or chance directs their way;
Around, athwart, the pure ethereal tide,
With swelling purple sail, they rapid glide,
Gay as the bark where Egypt's wanton queen
Reclining on the shaded deck was seen,
At which as gazed the uxorious Roman fool,
The subject world slipt from his dotard rule.
Anon, the gorgeous scene begins to fade,
And deeper hues the ruddy skies invade;
The haze of gathering twilight nature shrouds,
And pale, and paler wax the changeful clouds.
Then sunk the breeze into a breathless calm;
The silent dews of evening dropp'd like balm;
The hungry night-hawk from his lone haunt hies,
To chase the viewless insect through the skies;
The bat began his lantern-loving flight,
The lonely whip-poor-will, our bird of night,
Ever unseen, yet ever seeming near,
His shrill note quaver'd in the startled ear;
The buzzing beetle forth did gayly hie,
With idle hum, and careless, blundering eye;
The little trusty watchman of pale night,
The firefly, trimm'd anew his lamp so bright,
And took his merry airy circuit round
The sparkling meadow's green and fragrant bound,
Where blossom'd clover, bathed in palmy dew,
In fair luxuriance, sweetly blushing grew.

CROSSING THE ALLEGHANIES.

As look'd the traveller for the world below,
The lively morning breeze began to blow;
The magic curtain roll'd in mists away,
And a gay landscape smiled upon the day.
As light the fleeting vapours upward glide,
Like sheeted spectres on the mountain side,
New objects open to his wondering view
Of various form, and combinations new.
A rocky precipice, a waving wood,
Deep, winding dell, and foaming mountain flood,
Each after each, with coy and sweet delay,
Broke on his sight, as at young dawn of day,
Bounded afar by peak aspiring bold,
Like giant capp'd with helm of burnish'd gold.
So when the wandering grandsire of our race
On Ararat had found a resting-place,
At first a shoreless ocean met his eye,
Mingling on every side with one blue sky;
But as the waters, every passing day,
Sunk in the earth or roll'd in mists away,
Gradual, the lofty hills, like islands, peep
From the rough bosom of the boundless deep,
Then the round hillocks, and the meadows green,
Each after each, in freshen'd bloom are seen,
Till, at the last, a fair and finish'd whole
Combined to win the gazing patriarch's soul.
Yet, oft he look'd, I ween, with anxious eye,
In lingering hope somewhere, perchance, to spy,
Within the silent world, some living thing,
Crawling on earth, or moving on the wing,
Or man, or beast—alas! was neither there
Nothing that breathed of life in earth or air;
'T was a vast, silent, mansion rich and gay,
Whose occupant was drown'd the other day;
A churchyard, where the gayest flowers oft bloom
Amid the melancholy of the tomb;
A charnel-house, where all the human race
Had piled their bones in one wide resting-place;
Sadly he turn'd from such a sight of wo,
And sadly sought the lifeless world below.

THE OLD MAN'S CAROUSAL.

Drink! drink! to whom shall we drink?
To friend or a mistress? Come, let me think!
To those who are absent, or those who are here?
To the dead that we loved, or the living still dear?
Alas! when I look, I find none of the last!
The present is barren—let's drink to the past.

Come! here's to the girl with a voice sweet and low,
The eye all of fire and the bosom of snow,
Who erewhile in the days of my youth that are fled,
Once slept on my bosom, and pillow'd my head!
Would you know where to find such a delicate prize?
Go seek in yon churchyard, for there she lies.

And here's to the friend, the one friend of my youth,
With a head full of genius, a heart full of truth,
Who travell'd with me in the sunshine of life,
And stood by my side in its peace and its strife!
Would you know where to seek a blessing so rare?
Go drag the lone sea, you may find him there.

And here's to a brace of twin cherubs of mine,
With hearts like their mother's, as pure as this wine,
Who came but to see the first act of the play,
Grew tired of the scene, and then both went away.
Would you know where this brace of bright cherubs have hied?
Go seek them in heaven, for there they abide.

A bumper, my boys! to a gray-headed pair,
Who watched o'er my childhood with tenderest care,
God bless them, and keep them, and may they look down,
On the head of their son, without tear, sigh, or frown!
Would you know whom I drink to? go seek mid the dead,
You will find both their names on the stone at their head.

And here's—but, alas! the good wine is no more,
The bottle is emptied of all its bright store;
Like those we have toasted, its spirit is fled,
And nothing is left of the light that it shed.
Then, a bumper of tears, boys! the banquet here ends,
With a health to our dead, since we've no living friends.

WASHINGTON ALLSTON.

[Born, 1779. Died, 1843.]

MR. ALLSTON was born in South Carolina, of a family which has contributed some eminent names to our annals, though none that sheds more lustre upon the parent stock than his own. When very young, by the advice of physicians, he was sent to Newport, Rhode Island, where he remained until he entered Harvard College in 1796. In his boyhood he delighted to listen to the wild tales and traditions of the negroes upon his father's plantation; and while preparing for college, and after his removal to Cambridge, no books gave him so much pleasure as the most marvellous and terrible creations of the imagination. At Newport he became acquainted with MALBONE, the painter, and was thus, perhaps, led to the choice of his profession. He began to paint in oil before he went to Cambridge, and while there divided his attention between his pencil and his books. Upon being graduated he returned to South Carolina, to make arrangements for prosecuting his studies in Europe. He had friends who offered to assist him with money, and one of them, a Scottish gentleman named BOWMAN, who had seen and admired a head which he had painted of Peter hearing the cock crow, pressed him to accept an annuity of one hundred pounds while he should remain abroad; but he declined it, having already sold his paternal estate for a sum sufficient to defray his looked-for expenses; and, with his friend MALBONE, embarked for England in the summer of 1801.

Soon after his arrival in London, he became a student of the Royal Academy, then under the presidency of our countryman, WEST, with whom he contracted an intimate and lasting friendship. His abilities as an artist, brilliant conversation, and gentlemanly manners, made him a welcome guest at the houses of the great painters of the time; and within a year from the beginning of his residence in London, he was a successful exhibitor at Somerset House, and a general favourite with the most distinguished members of his profession.

In 1804, having been three years in England, he accompanied JOHN VANDERLYN to Paris. After passing a few months in that capital, he proceeded to Italy, where he remained four years. Among his fellow-students and intimate associates here, were VANDERLYN, and the Danish sculptor THORWALDSEN. Another friend with whom he now became acquainted, was COLERIDGE. In one of his letters he says: "To no other man do I owe so much, *intellectually*, as to Mr. COLERIDGE, with whom I became acquainted in Rome, and who has honoured me with his friendship for more than five-and-twenty years. He used to call Rome the *silent* city; but I never could think of it as such, while with him; for meet him when or where I would, the fountain of his mind was never dry, but, like the far-reaching aqueducts that once supplied this mistress of the world, its living stream seemed specially to flow for every classic ruin over which we wandered. And when I recall some of our walks under the pines of the villa Borghese, I am almost tempted to dream that I had once listened to PLATO in the groves of the Academy."

In 1809 ALLSTON returned to America, and was soon after married at Boston to a sister of Dr CHANNING. In 1811 he went a second time to England. His reputation as a painter was now well established, and he gained by his picture of the "Dead Man raised by the Bones of Elisha"* a prize of two hundred guineas, at the British Institution, where the first artists in the world were his competitors. A long and dangerous illness succeeded his return to London, and he removed to the village of Clifton, where he wrote "The Sylphs of the Seasons," and some of the other poems included in a volume which he published in 1813. Within two weeks after the renewal of his residence in the metropolis, in the last-mentioned year, his wife died, very suddenly; and the event, inducing the deepest depression and melancholy, caused a temporary suspension of his labours.

In 1818 he accompanied LESLIE to Paris, and in the autumn of the following year came back to America, having been previously elected an associate of the English Royal Academy. In 1830 he married a sister of RICHARD H. DANA, and the remainder of his life was tranquilly passed at Cambridgeport, near Boston, where he was surrounded by warm and genial friends, in assiduous devotion to his art. He died very suddenly, on the night of the eighth of July, 1843.

As a painter ALLSTON had no superior, perhaps not an equal, in his age. He differed from his contemporaries, as he said of MONALDI, "no less in kind than in degree. If he held any thing in common with others, it was with those of ages past, with the mighty dead of the fifteenth century From them he had learned the language of his art, but his thoughts, and their turn of expression, were his own." Among his principal works are "The Dead Man restored to Life by Elisha;" the "Angel liberating Peter from Prison;" "Jacob's Dream;" "Elijah in the Desert;" the "Triumphant Song of Miriam;" "The Angel Uriel in the Sun;" "Saul and the Witch of Endor;" "Spalatro's Vision of the bloody Hand;" "Gabriel setting the Guard of the Heavenly Host;" "Anne Page and Slender;" "Rosalie;" "Donna Marcia in the Robber's Cave;" and "Belshazzar's Feast, or the

* This work he subsequently sold to the Pennsylvania Academy of Fine Arts, for thirty-five hundred dollars.

Handwriting on the Wall." The last work, upon which he had been engaged at intervals for nearly twenty years, he left unfinished.

Besides the volume of poems already mentioned, and many short pieces which have since been given to the public, Mr. Allston was the author of "Monaldi," a story of extraordinary power and interest, in which he displays a deep sensibility to beauty, and philosophic knowledge of human passion. He wrote also a series of discourses on art, which have been printed since his death.

Although Allston owed his chief celebrity to his paintings, which will preserve for his name a place in the list of the greatest artists of all the nations and ages, his literary works alone would have given him a high rank among men of genius. A great painter, indeed, is of necessity a poet, though he may lack the power to express fittingly his conceptions in language. Allston had in remarkable perfection all the faculties required for either art. "The Sylphs of the Seasons," his longest poem, in which he describes the scenery of Spring, Summer, Autumn, and Winter, and the effects of each season on the mind, show that he regarded nature with a curious eye, and had power to exhibit her beauties with wonderful distinctness and fidelity. "The Two Painters" is an admirable satire, intended to ridicule attempts to reach perfection in one excellency in the art of painting, to the neglect of every other; the "Paint King" is a singularly wild, imaginative story; and nearly all his minor poems are strikingly original and beautiful. It was in his paintings, however, that the power and religious grandeur of his imagination were most strongly developed.

When this work was originally published, I dedicated it to Mr. Allston, with whom I had the happiness to be personally acquainted, addressing him as "the eldest of the living poets, and the most illustrious of the painters" of our country. That dedication, which has been retained in previous editions, was an expression of the admiration and reverence in which I, in common with all who knew him, held his genius and character.

THE PAINT KING.

Fair Ellen was long the delight of the young,
No damsel could with her compare;
Her charms were the theme of the heart and the tongue,
And bards without number in ecstasies sung,
The beauties of Ellen the fair.

Yet cold was the maid; and though legions advanced,
All drill'd by Ovidean art,
And languish'd, and ogled, protested and danced,
Like shadows they came, and like shadows they glanced
From the hard polish'd ice of her heart.

Yet still did the heart of fair Ellen implore
A something that could not be found;
Like a sailor she seem'd on a desolate shore,
With nor house, nor a tree, nor a sound but the roar
Of breakers high dashing around.

From object to object still, still would she veer,
Though nothing, alas, could she find;
Like the moon, without atmosphere, brilliant and clear,
Yet doom'd, like the moon, with no being to cheer
The bright barren waste of her mind.

But rather than sit like a statue so still
When the rain made her mansion a *pound*,
Up and down would she go, like the sails of a mill,
And pat every stair, like a woodpecker's bill,
From the tiles of the roof to the ground.

One morn, as the maid from her casement inclined,
Passed a youth, with a frame in his hand.
The casement she closed—not the eye of her mind;
For, do all she could, no, she could not be blind;
Still before her she saw the youth stand.

"Ah, what can he do," said the languishing maid,
"Ah, what with that frame can he do?"
And she knelt to the goddess of secrets and pray'd,
When the youth pass'd again, and again he display'd
The frame and a picture to view.

"Oh, beautiful picture!" the fair Ellen cried,
"I must see thee again or I die."
Then under her white chin her bonnet she tied,
And after the youth and the picture she hied,
When the youth, looking back, met her eye.

"Fair damsel," said he, (and he chuckled the while,)
"This picture I see you admire:
Then take it, I pray you, perhaps 'twill beguile
Some moments of sorrow; (nay, pardon my smile)
Or, at least, keep you home by the fire."

Then Ellen the gift with delight and surprise
From the cunning young stripling received,
But she knew not the poison that enter'd her eyes,
When sparkling with rapture they gazed on her prize—
Thus, alas, are fair maidens deceived!

'T was a youth o'er the form of a statue inclined,
And the sculptor he seem'd of the stone;
Yet he languish'd as though for its beauty he pined,
And gazed as the eyes of the statue so blind
Reflected the beams of his own.

'T was the tale of the sculptor Pygmalion of old,
Fair Ellen remember'd and sigh'd;
"Ah, couldst thou but lift from that marble so cold,
Thine eyes too imploring, thy arms should enfold
And press me this day as thy bride."

She said: when, behold, from the canvas arose
The youth, and he stepp'd from the frame:
With a furious transport his arms did enclose
The love-plighted Ellen: and, clasping, he froze
The blood of the maid with his flame!

She turn'd and beheld on each shoulder a wing.
"Oh, Heaven!" cried she, "who art thou!"
From the roof to the ground did his fierce answer ring,
As, frowning, he thunder'd "I am the Paint King!
And mine, lovely maid, thou art now!"

Then high from the ground did the grim monster lift
The loud-screaming maid like a blast;
And he sped through the air like a meteor swift,
While the clouds, wand'ring by him, did fearfully drift
To the right and the left as he pass'd.

Now suddenly sloping his hurricane flight,
With an eddying whirl he descends;
The air all below him becomes black as night,
And the ground where he treads, as if moved with affright,
Like the surge of the Caspian, bends.

"I am here!" said the fiend, and he thundering knocked
At the gates of a mountainous cave;
The gates open flew, as by magic unlock'd,
While the peaks of the mount, reeling to and fro, rocked
Like an island of ice on the wave.

"Oh, mercy!" cried Ellen, and swoon'd in his arms,
But the PAINT-KING, he scoff'd at her pain.
"Prithee, love," said the monster, "what mean these alarms?"
She hears not, she sees not the terrible charms,
That work her to horror again.

She opens her lids, but no longer her eyes
Behold the fair youth she would woo;
Now appears the PAINT-KING in his natural guise;
His face, like a palette of villanous dyes,
Black and white, red and yellow, and blue.

On the skull of a Titan, that Heaven defied,
Sat the fiend, like the grim giant Gog,
While aloft to his mouth a hugh pipe he applied,
Twice as big as the Eddystone Lighthouse, descried
As it looms through an easterly fog.

And anon, as he puff'd the vast volumes, were seen,
In horrid festoons on the wall,
Legs and arms, heads and bodies emerging between,
Like the drawing-room grim of the Scotch Sawney Beane,
By the Devil dressed out for a ball.

"Ah me!" cried the damsel, and fell at his feet,
"Must I hang on these walls to be dried?"
"Oh, no!" said the fiend, while he sprung from his seat,
"A far nobler fortune thy person shall meet;
Into paint will I grind thee, my bride!"

Then, seizing the maid by her dark auburn hair,
An oil jug he plunged her within;
Seven days, seven nights, with the shrieks of despair,
Did Ellen in torment convulse the dun air,
All covered with oil to the chin.

On the morn of the eighth, on a huge sable stone
Then Ellen, all reeking, he laid;
With a rock for his muller he crushed every bone,
But, though ground to jelly, still, still did she groan;
For life had forsook not the maid.

Now reaching his palette, with masterly care
Each tint on its surface he spread;
The blue of her eyes, and the brown of her hair,
And the pearl and the white of her forehead so fair,
And her lips' and her cheeks' rosy red.

Then, stamping his foot, did the monster exclaim,
"Now I brave, cruel fairy, thy scorn!"
When lo! from a chasm wide-yawning there came
A light tiny chariot of rose-colour'd flame,
By a team of ten glow-worms upborne.

Enthroned in the midst on an emerald bright,
Fair Geraldine sat without peer;
Her robe was a gleam of the first blush of light,
And her mantle the fleece of a noon-cloud white,
And a beam of the moon was her spear.

In an accent that stole on the still charmed air
Like the first gentle language of Eve,
Thus spake from her chariot the fairy so fair:
"I come at the call, but, oh Paint-King, beware,
Beware if again you deceive."

"'T is true," said the monster, "thou queen of my heart,
Thy portrait I oft have essay'd;
Yet ne'er to the canvas could I with my art
The least of thy wonderful beauties impart;
And my failure with scorn you repaid.

"Now I swear by the light of the comet-king's tail!"
And he tower'd with pride as he spoke,
"If again with these magical colours I fail,
The crater of Etna shall hence be my jail,
And my food shall be sulphur and smoke.

"But if I succeed, then, oh, fair Geraldine!
Thy promise with justice I claim,
And thou, queen of fairies, shalt ever be mine,
The bride of my bed; and thy portrait divine
Shall fill all the earth with my fame."

He spake; when, behold, the fair Geraldine's form
On the canvas enchantingly glow'd;
His touches—they flew like the leaves in a storm;
And the pure pearly white and the carnation warm
Contending in harmony flow'd.

And now did the portrait a twin-sister seem
To the figure of Geraldine fair:
With the same sweet expression did faithfully teem
Each muscle, each feature; in short not a gleam
Was lost of her beautiful hair.

'T was the fairy herself! but, alas, her blue eyes
Still a pupil did ruefully lack;
And who shall describe the terrific surprise
That seized the PAINT-KING when, behold, he descries
Not a speck on his palette of black!

"I am lost!" said the fiend, and he shook like a leaf;
When, casting his eyes to the ground,
He saw the lost pupils of Ellen with grief
In the jaws of a mouse, and the sly little thief
Whisk away from his sight with a bound.

"I am lost!" said the fiend, and he fell like a stone;
Then rising the fairy in ire
With a touch of her finger she loosen'd her zone,
(While the limbs on the wall gave a terrible groan,)
And she swell'd to a column of fire.

Her spear, now a thunder-bolt, flash'd in the air,
And sulphur the vault fill'd around:
She smote the grim monster; and now by the hair
High-lifting, she hurl'd him in speechless despair
Down the depths of the chasm profound.

Then over the picture thrice waving her spear,
"Come forth!" said the good Geraldine;
When, behold, from the canvas descending, appear
Fair Ellen, in person more lovely than e'er,
With grace more than ever divine!

THE SYLPHS OF THE SEASONS,

A POET'S DREAM.

Long has it been my fate to hear
The slave of Mammon, with a sneer,
My indolence reprove.
Ah, little knows he of the care,
The toil, the hardship that I bear
While lolling in my elbow-chair,
And seeming scarce to move:

For, mounted on the poet's steed,
I *there* my ceaseless journey speed
O'er mountain, wood, and stream:
And oft, within a little day,
Mid comets fierce, 't is mine to stray,
And wander o'er the milky-way
To catch a poet's dream.

But would the man of lucre know
What riches from my labours flow—
A DREAM is my reply.
And who for wealth has ever pined,
That had a world within his mind,
Where every treasure he may find,
And joys that never die!

One night, my task diurnal done,
(For I had travell'd with the sun
O'er burning sands, o'er snows,)
Fatigued, I sought the couch of rest;
My wonted prayer to Heaven address'd;
But scarce had I my pillow press'd,
When thus a vision rose —

Methought, within a desert cave,
Cold, dark, and solemn as the grave,
I suddenly awoke.
It seem'd of sable night the cell,
Where, save when from the ceiling fell
An oozing drop, her silent spell
No sound had ever broke.

There motionless I stood alone,
Like some strange monument of stone
Upon a barren wild;
Or like (so solid and profound
The darkness seem'd that wall'd me round)
A man that's buried under ground,
Where pyramids are piled.

Thus fix'd, a dreadful hour I pass'd,
And now I heard, as from a blast,
A voice pronounce my name:
Nor long upon my ear it dwelt,
When round me 'gan the air to melt
And motion once again I felt
Quick circling o'er my frame.

Again it call'd; and then a ray,
That seem'd a gushing fount of day,
Across the cavern stream'd.
Half-struck with terror and delight,
I hail'd the little blessed light,
And follow'd till my aching sight
An orb of darkness seem'd.

Nor long I felt the blinding pain;
For soon upon a mountain plain
I gazed with wonder new.
There high a castle rear'd its head;
And far below a region spread,
Where every season seem'd to shed
Its own peculiar hue.

Now, at the castle's massy gate,
Like one that's blindly urged by fate,
A bugle-horn I blew.
The mountain-plain it shook around,
The vales return'd a hollow sound,
And, moving with a sigh profound,
The portals open flew.

Then entering, from a glittering hall
I heard a voice seraphic call,
That bade me "Ever reign!
All hail!" it said in accent wild,
"For thou art Nature's chosen child,
Whom wealth nor blood has e'er defiled,
Hail, lord of this domain!"

And now I paced a bright saloon,
That seem'd illumined by the moon,
So mellow was the light.
The walls with jetty darkness teem'd,
While down them crystal columns stream'd
And each a mountain torrent seem'd,
High-flashing through the night.

Rear'd in the midst, a double throne
Like burnish'd cloud of evening shone;
While, group'd the base around,
Four damsels stood of fairy race;
Who, turning each with heavenly grace
Upon me her immortal face,
Transfix'd me to the ground.

And *thus* the foremost of the train:
"Be thine the throne, and thine to reign
O'er all the varying year!
But ere thou rulest, the Fates command,
That of our chosen rival band
A Sylph shall win thy heart and hand,
Thy sovereignty to share.

"For we, the sisters of a birth,
Do rule by turns the subject earth
To serve ungrateful man;
But since our varied toils impart
No joy to his capricious heart,
'Tis now ordain'd that human art
Shall rectify the plan."

Then spake the Sylph of Spring serene,
"'T is *I* thy joyous heart, I ween,
With sympathy shall move:
For I with living melody
Of birds in choral symphony,
First waked thy soul to poesy,
To piety and love.

"When thou, at call of vernal breeze,
And beckoning bough of budding trees,
Hast left thy sullen fire:

And stretch'd thee in some mossy dell,
And heard the browsing wether's bell,
Blithe echoes rousing from their cell
To swell the tinkling choir:

"Or heard from branch of flowering thorn
The song of friendly cuckoo warn
The tardy-moving swain;
Hast bid the purple swallow hail;
And seen him now through ether sail,
Now sweeping downward o'er the vale,
And skimming now the plain;

"Then, catching with a sudden glance
The bright and silver-clear expanse
Of some broad river's stream,
Beheld the boats adown it glide,
And motion wind again the tide,
Where, chain'd in ice by winter's pride,
Late roll'd the heavy team:

"Or, lured by some fresh-scented gale
That woo'd the moored fisher's sail
To tempt the mighty main,
Hast watch'd the dim, receding shore,
Now faintly seen the ocean o'er,
Like hanging cloud, and now no more
To bound the sapphire plain;

"Then, wrapt in night, the scudding bark,
(That seem'd, self-poised amid the dark,
Through upper air to leap,)
Beheld, from thy most fearful height,
The rapid dolphin's azure light
Cleave, like a living meteor bright,
The darkness of the deep:

"'T was mine the warm, awakening hand
That made thy grateful heart expand,
And feel the high control
Of Him, the mighty Power that moves
Amid the waters and the groves,
And through his vast creation proves
His omnipresent soul.

"Or, brooding o'er some forest rill,
Fringed with the early daffodil,
And quivering maiden-hair,
When thou hast mark'd the dusky bed,
With leaves and water-rust o'erspread,
That seem'd an amber light to shed
On all was shadow'd there;

"And thence, as by its murmur call'd,
The current traced to where it brawl'd
Beneath the noontide ray;
And there beheld the checker'd shade
Of waves, in many a sinuous braid,
That o'er the sunny channel play'd,
With motion ever gay:

"'T was I to these the magic gave,
That made thy heart, a willing slave,
To gentle Nature bend;
And taught thee how with tree and flower,
And whispering gale, and dropping shower,
In converse sweet to pass the hour,
As with an early friend:

"That mid the noontide, sunny haze
Did in thy languid bosom raise
The raptures of the boy;
When, waked as if to second birth,
Thy soul through every pore look'd forth,
And gazed upon the beauteous earth
With myriad eyes of joy:

"That made thy heart, like HIS above,
To flow with universal love
For every living thing.
And, O! if I, with ray divine,
Thus tempering, did thy soul refine,
Then let thy gentle heart be mine,
And bless the Sylph of Spring."

And next the Sylph of Summer fair;
The while her crisped, golden hair
Half-veil'd her sunny eyes:
"Nor less may *I* thy homage claim,
At touch of whose exhaling flame
The fog of Spring, that chill'd thy frame,
In genial vapour flies.

"Oft, by the heat of noon oppress'd
With flowing hair and open vest,
Thy footsteps have I won
To mossy couch of welling grot,
Where thou hast bless'd thy happy lot,
That thou in that delicious spot
Mayst see, not feel, the sun:

"Thence tracing from the body's change,
In curious philosophic range,
The motion of the mind;
And how from thought to thought it flew,
Still hoping in each vision new
The fairy land of bliss to view,
But ne'er that land to find.

"And then, as grew thy languid mood,
To some embowering, silent wood
I led thy careless way;
Where high from tree to tree in air
Thou saw'st the spider swing her snare,
So bright!—as if, entangled there,
The sun had left a ray:

"Or lured thee to some beetling steep,
To mark the deep and quiet sleep
That wrapt the tarn below;
And mountain blue and forest green
Inverted on its plane serene,
Dim gleaming through the filmy sheen
That glazed the painted show;

"Perchance, to mark the fisher's skiff
Swift from beneath some shadowy cliff
Dart, like a gust of wind;
And, as she skimm'd the sunny lake,
In many a playful wreath her wake
Far-trailing, like a silvery snake,
With sinuous length behind.

"Not less, when hill, and dale, and heath
Still Evening wrapt in mimic death.
Thy spirit true I proved:

Around thee as the darkness stole,
Before thy wild, creative soul
I bade each fairy vision roll
Thine infancy had loved.

"Then o'er the silent, sleeping land,
Thy fancy, like a magic wand,
Forth call'd the elfin race:
And now around the fountain's brim
In circling dance they gayly skim;
And now upon its surface swim,
And water-spiders chase;

"Each circumstance of sight or sound
Peopling the vacant air around
With visionary life:
For if amid a thicket stirr'd,
Or flitting bat, or wakeful bird,
Then straight thy eager fancy heard
The din of fairy strife;

"Now, in the passing beetle's hum
The elfin army's goblin drum
To pigmy battle sound;
And now, where dripping dew-drops plash
On waving grass, their bucklers clash,
And now their quivering lances flash,
Wide-dealing death around:

"Or if the moon's effulgent form
The passing clouds of sudden storm
In quick succession veil;
Vast serpents now, their shadows glide,
And, coursing now the mountain's side,
A band of giants huge, they stride
O'er hill, and wood, and dale.

"And still on many a service rare
Could I descant, if need there were,
My firmer claim to bind.
But rest I most my high pretence
On that, my genial influence,
Which made the body's indolence
The vigour of the mind."

And now, in accents deep and low,
Like voice of fondly-cherish'd wo,
The Sylph of Autumn sad:
"Though *I* may not of raptures sing,
That graced the gentle song of Spring,
Like Summer, playful pleasures bring,
Thy youthful heart to glad;

"Yet still may I in hope aspire
Thy heart to touch with chaster fire,
And purifying love:
For I with vision high and holy,
And spell of quickening melancholy,
Thy soul from sublunary folly
First raised to worlds above.

"What though be mine the treasures fair
Of purple grape and yellow pear,
And fruits of various hue,
And harvests rich of golden grain,
That dance in waves along the plain
To merry song of reaping swain,
Beneath the welkin blue;

"With these I may not urge my suit
Of Summer's patient toil the fruit,
For mortal purpose given;
Nor may it fit my sober mood
To sing of sweetly murmuring flood,
Or dyes of many-colour'd wood,
That mock the bow of heaven.

"But, know, 't was mine the secret power
That wak'd thee at the midnight hour
In bleak November's reign:
'T was I the spell around thee cast,
When thou didst hear the hollow blast
In murmurs tell of pleasures past,
That ne'er would come again:

"And led thee, when the storm was o'er,
To hear the sullen ocean roar,
By dreadful calm oppress'd;
Which still, though not a breeze was there,
Its mountain-billows heav'd in air,
As if a living thing it were,
That strove in vain for rest.

"'T was I, when thou, subdued by wo,
Didst watch the leaves descending slow,
To each a moral gave;
And as they moved in mournful train,
With rustling sound, along the plain,
Taught them to sing a seraph's strain
Of peace within the grave.

"And then, upraised thy streaming eye,
I met thee in the western sky
In pomp of evening cloud;
That, while with varying form it roll'd,
Some wizard's castle seem'd of gold,
And now a crimson'd knight of old,
Or king in purple proud.

"And last, as sunk the setting sun,
And Evening with her shadows dun
The gorgeous pageant past,
'T was then of life a mimic show,
Of human grandeur here below,
Which thus beneath the fatal blow
Of Death must fall at last.

"O, then with what aspiring gaze
Didst thou thy tranced vision raise
To yonder orbs on high,
And think how wondrous, how sublime
'T were upwards to their spheres to climb,
And live, beyond the reach of Time,
Child of Eternity!"

And last the Sylph of Winter spake;
The while her piercing voice did shake
The castle-vaults below.
"O, youth, if thou, with soul refin'd,
Hast felt the triumph pure of mind,
And learn'd a secret joy to find
In deepest scenes of wo;

"If e'er with fearful ear at eve
Hast heard the wailing tempests grieve
Through chink of shatter'd wall.

The while it conjured o'er thy brain
Of wandering ghosts a mournful train,
That low in fitful sobs complain
    Of Death's untimely call:

"Or feeling, as the storm increased,
The love of terror nerve thy breast,
    Didst venture to the coast;
To see the mighty war-ship leap
From wave to wave upon the deep,
Like chamois goat from steep to steep,
    Till low in valley lost;

"Then, glancing to the angry sky,
Behold the clouds with fury fly
    The lurid moon athwart;
Like armies huge in battle, throng,
And pour in volleying ranks along,
While piping winds in martial song
    To rushing war exhort:

"O, then to me thy heart be given,
To me, ordain'd by Him in heaven
    Thy nobler powers to wake.
And O! if thou, with poet's soul,
High brooding o'er the frozen pole,
Hast felt beneath my stern control
    The desert region quake;

"Or from old Hecla's cloudy height,
When o'er the dismal, half-year's night
    He pours his sulphurous breath,
Hast known my petrifying wind
Wild ocean's curling billows bind,
Like bending sheaves by harvest hind,
    Erect in icy death;

"Or heard adown the mountain's steep
The northern blast with furious sweep
    Some cliff dissever'd dash;
And seen it spring with dreadful bound
From rock to rock, to gulf profound,
While echoes fierce from caves resound
    The never-ending crash:

"If thus, with terror's mighty spell
Thy soul inspired, was wont to swell,
    Thy heaving frame expand;
O, then to me thy heart incline;
For know, the wondrous charm was mine,
That fear and joy did thus combine
    In magic union bland.

"Nor think confined my native sphere
To horrors gaunt, or ghastly fear,
    Or desolation wild:
For I of pleasures fair could sing,
That steal from life its sharpest sting,
And man have made around it cling,
    Like mother to her child.

"When thou, beneath the clear blue sky,
So calm, no cloud was seen to fly,
    Hast gazed on snowy plain,
Where Nature slept so pure and sweet,
She seem'd a corse in winding-sheet,
Whose happy soul had gone to meet
    The blest, angelic train;

"Or mark'd the sun's declining ray
In thousand varying colours play
    O'er ice-incrusted heath,
In gleams of orange now, and green,
And now in red and azure sheen,
Like hues on dying dolphin seen,
    Most lovely when in death;

"Or seen, at dawn of eastern light
The frosty toil of fays by night
    On pane of casement clear,
Where bright the mimic glaciers shine,
And Alps, with many a mountain pine,
And armed knights from Palestine
    In winding march appear:

"'T was I on each enchanting scene
The charm bestow'd that banished spleen
    Thy bosom pure and light.
But still a *nobler* power I claim;
That power allied to poets' fame,
Which language vain has dared to name—
    The soul's creative might.

"Though Autumn grave, and Summer fair,
And joyous Spring demand a share
    Of Fancy's hallow'd power,
Yet these I hold of humbler kind,
To grosser means of earth confined,
Through mortal *sense* to reach the mind,
    By mountain, stream, or flower.

"But mine, of purer nature still,
Is *that* which to thy secret will
    Did minister unseen,
Unfelt, unheard; when every sense
Did sleep in drowsy indolence,
And silence deep and night intense
    Enshrouded every scene;

"That o'er thy teeming brain did raise
The spirits of departed days
    Through all the varying year;
And images of things remote,
And sounds that long had ceased to float,
With every hue, and every note,
    As living now they were:

"And taught thee from the motley mass
Each harmonizing part to class,
    (Like Nature's self employ'd;)
And then, as work'd thy wayward will,
From these, with rare combining skill,
With new-created worlds to fill
    Of space the mighty void.

"O then to me thy heart incline;
To me, whose plastic powers combine
    The harvest of the mind;
To me, whose magic coffers bear
The spoils of all the toiling year,
That still in mental vision wear
    A lustre more refined."

She ceased—And now, in doubtful mood,
All motionless and mute I stood,
    Like one by charm oppress'd:

By turns from each to each I roved,
And each by turns again I loved;
For ages ne'er could one have proved
More lovely than the rest.

"O blessed band, of birth divine,
What mortal task is like to mine!"—
And further had I spoke,
When, lo! there pour'd a flood of light
So fiercely on my aching sight,
I fell beneath the vision bright,
And with the pain awoke.

AMERICA TO GREAT BRITAIN.*

All hail! thou noble land,
Our fathers' native soil!
O stretch thy mighty hand,
Gigantic grown by toil,
O'er the vast Atlantic wave to our shore;
For thou, with magic might,
Canst reach to where the light
Of Phœbus travels bright
The world o'er!

The genius of our clime,
From his pine-embattled steep,
Shall hail the great sublime;
While the Tritons of the deep
With their conchs the kindred league shall proclaim.
Then let the world combine—
O'er the main our naval line,
Like the milky-way, shall shine
Bright in fame!

Though ages long have pass'd
Since our fathers left their home,
Their pilot in the blast,
O'er untravell'd seas to roam,—
Yet lives the blood of England in our veins!
And shall we not proclaim
That blood of honest fame,
Which no tyranny can tame
By its chains?

While the language free and bold
Which the bard of Avon sung,
In which our Milton told
How the vault of heaven rung,
When Satan, blasted, fell with his host;
While this, with reverence meet,
Ten thousand echoes greet,
From rock to rock repeat
Round our coast;

While the manners, while the arts,
That mould a nation's soul,
Still cling around our hearts,
Between let ocean roll,
Our joint communion breaking with the sun:
Yet, still, from either beach,
The voice of blood shall reach,
More audible than speech,
"We are one!"

* This poem was first published in Coleridge's "Sybilline Leaves," in 1810.

THE SPANISH MAID.

Five weary months sweet Inez number'd
From that unfading bitter day
When last she heard the trumpet bray
That call'd her Isidor away—
That never to her heart has slumber'd;

She hears it now, and sees, far bending
Along the mountain's misty side,
His plumed troop, that, waving wide,
Seems like a rippling, feathery tide,
Now bright, now with the dim shore blending;

She hears the cannon's deadly rattle—
And fancy hurries on to strife,
And hears the drum and screaming fife
Mix with the last sad cry of life.
O, should he—should he fall in battle!

Yet still his *name* would live in story,
And every gallant bard in Spain
Would fight his battles o'er again.
And would not she for such a strain
Resign him to his country's glory!

Thus Inez thought, and pluck'd the flower
That grew upon the very bank
Where first her ear bewilder'd drank
The plighted vow—where last she sank
In that too bitter parting hour.

But now the sun is westward sinking;
And soon amid the purple haze,
That showers from his slanting rays,
A thousand loves there *meet* her gaze,
To change her high heroic thinking.

Then hope, with all its crowd of fancies,
Before her flits and fills the air;
And, deck'd in victory's glorious gear,
In vision Isidor is there.
Then how her heart mid sadness dances!

Yet little thought she, thus forestalling
The coming joy, that in *that* hour
The future, like the colour'd shower
That seems to arch the ocean o'er,
Was in the living present falling.

The foe is slain. His sable charger
All fleck'd with foam comes bounding on:
The wild Morena rings anon,
And on its brow the gallant Don,
And gallant steed grow larger, larger;

And now he nears the mountain-hollow;
The flowery bank and little lake
Now on his startled vision break
And Inez there.—He's not awake—
Ah, what a day this dream will follow!

But no—he surely is not dreaming.
Another minute makes it clear.
A scream, a rush, a burning tear
From Inez' cheek, dispel the fear
That bliss like his is only seeming

ON GREENOUGH'S GROUP OF THE ANGEL AND CHILD.

I stood alone; nor word, nor other sound,
Broke the mute solitude that closed me round;
As when the air doth take her midnight sleep,
Leaving the wintry stars her watch to keep,
So slept she now at noon. But not alone
My spirit then: a light within me shone
That was not mine; and feelings undefined,
And thoughts flow'd in upon me not my own.
'T was that deep mystery—for aye unknown—
The living presence of another's mind.

Another mind was there—the gift of few—
That by its own strong will can all that's *true*
In its own nature unto others give,
And mingling life with life, seem there to live.
I felt it now in mine; and oh! how fair,
How beautiful the thoughts that met me there—
Visions of Love, and Purity, and Truth!
Though form distinct had each, they seem'd, as 'twere,
Imbodied all of one celestial air—
To beam for ever in coequal youth.

And thus I learn'd—as in the mind they moved—
These stranger Thoughts the one the other loved;
That Purity loved Truth, because 't was true,
And Truth, because 't was pure, the first did woo;
While Love, as pure and true, did love the twain;
Then Love was loved of them, for that sweet chain
That bound them all. Thus sure, as passionless,
Their love did grow, till one harmonious strain
Of melting sounds they seem'd; then, changed again,
One angel form they took—Self-Happiness.

This angel form the gifted Artist saw,
That held me in his spell. 'T was his to draw
The veil of sense, and see the immortal race,
The Forms spiritual, that know not place.
He saw it in the quarry, deep in earth,
And stay'd it by his will, and gave it birth
E'en to the world of sense; bidding its cell,
The cold, hard marble, thu in plastic girth
The shape ethereal fix, and body forth
A being of the skies—with man to dwell.

And then another form beside it stood;
'T was one of this our earth—though the warm blood
Had from it pass'd—exhaled as in a breath
Drawn from its lips by the cold kiss of Death.
Its little "dream of human life" had fled;
And yet it seem'd not number'd with the dead,
But one emerging to a life so bright
That, as the wondrous nature o'er it spread,
Its very consciousness did seem to shed
Rays from within, and clothe it all in light.

Now touch'd the Angel Form its little hand,
Turning upon it with a look so bland,
And yet so full of majesty, as less
Than holy natures never may impress—
And more than proudest guilt unmoved may brook.
The Creature of the Earth now felt that look,
And stood in blissful awe—as one above
Who saw his name in the Eternal Book,
And Him that open'd it; e'en Him that took
The Little Child, and bless'd it in his love.

SONNETS.

ON A FALLING GROUP IN THE LAST JUDGMENT OF MICHAEL ANGELO.

How vast, how dread, o'erwhelming is the thought
Of space interminable! to the soul
A circling weight that crushes into naught
Her mighty faculties! a wond'rous whole,
Without or parts, beginning, or an end!
How fearful then on desp'rate wings to send
The fancy e'en amid the waste profound!
Yet, born as if all daring to astound,
Thy giant hand, O Angelo, hath hurl'd
E'en human forms, with all their mortal weight,
Down the dread void—fall endless as their fate!
Already now they seem from world to world
For ages thrown; yet doom'd, another past,
Another still to reach, nor e'er to reach the last!

ON REMBRANT; OCCASIONED BY HIS PICTURE OF JACOB'S DREAM.

As in that twilight, superstitious age,
When all beyond the narrow grasp of mind
Seem'd fraught with meanings of supernal kind,
When e'en the learned philosophic sage,
Wont with the stars thro' boundless space to range,
Listen'd with reverence to the changeling's tale,
E'en so, thou strangest of all beings strange!
E'en so thy visionary scenes I hail;
That like the rambling of an idiot's speech,
No image giving of a thing on earth,
Nor thought significant in reason's reach,
Yet in their random shadowings give birth
To thoughts and things from other worlds that come,
And fill the soul, and strike the reason dumb.

ON THE PICTURES BY RUBENS, IN THE LUXEMBOURG GALLERY.

There is a charm no vulgar mind can reach,
No critic thwart, no mighty master teach;
A charm how mingled of the good and ill!
Yet still so mingled that the mystic whole
Shall captive hold the struggling gazer's wi'
Till vanquish'd reason own its full control
And such, O Rubens, thy mysterious art,
The charm that vexes, yet enslaves the heart!
Thy lawless style, from timid systems free,
Impetuous rolling like a troubled sea,
High o'er the rocks of reason's lofty verge
Impending hangs; yet, ere the foaming surge
Breaks o'er the bound, the refluent ebb of taste
Back from the shore impels the wat'ry waste.

TO MY VENERABLE FRIEND THE PRESIDENT OF THE ROYAL ACADEMY.

From one unused in pomp of words to raise
A courtly monument of empty praise,
Where self, transpiring through the flimsy pile,
Betrays the builder's ostentatious guile,
Accept, O West, these unaffected lays,
Which genius claims and grateful justice pays
Still green in age, thy vig'rous powers impart
The youthful freshness of a blameless heart:
For thine, unaided by another's pain,
The wiles of envy, or the sordid train

Of selfishness, has been the manly race
Of one who felt the purifying grace
Of honest fame; nor found the effort vain
E'en for itself to love thy soul-ennobling art.

ON SEEING THE PICTURE OF ÆOLUS, BY PELIGRINO TIBALDI.

Full well, Tibaldi, did thy kindred mind
The mighty spell of Bonaroti own.
Like one who, reading magic words, receives
The gift of intercourse with worlds unknown,
'T was thine, deciph'ring Nature's mystic leaves,
To hold strange converse with the viewless wind;
To see the spirits, in imbodied forms,
Of gales and whirlwinds, hurricanes and storms.
For, lo! obedient to thy bidding, teems
Fierce into shape their stern, relentless lord:
His form of motion ever-restless seems;
Or, if to rest inclined his turbid soul,
On Hecla's top to stretch, and give the word
To subject winds that sweep the desert pole.

ON THE DEATH OF COLERIDGE.

And thou art gone, most loved, most honour'd Friend!
No—never more thy gentle voice shall blend
With air of earth its pure ideal tones—
Binding in one, as with harmonious zones,
The heart and intellect. And I no more
Shall with thee gaze on that unfathom'd deep,
The human soul; as when, push'd off the shore,
Thy mystic bark would through the darkness sweep,
Itself the while so bright! For oft we seem'd
As on some starless sea—all dark above,
All dark below—yet, onward as we drove,
To plough up light that eve round us stream'd.
But he who mourns is not as one bereft
Of all he loved: thy living truths are left.

THE TUSCAN MAID

How pleasant and how sad the turning tide
Of human life, when side by side
The child and youth begin to glide
Along the vale of years;
The pure twin-being for a little space,
With lightsome heart, and yet a graver face,
Too young for wo, though not for tears.

This turning tide is Ursulina's now;
The time is mark'd upon her brow;
Now every thought and feeling throw
Their shadows on her face;
And so are every thought and feeling join'd,
'T were hard to answer whether heart or mind
Of either were the native place.

The things that once she loved are still the same;
Yet now there needs another name
To give the feeling which they claim,
While she the feeling gives;
She cannot call it gladness or delight;
And yet there seems a richer, lovelier light
On e'en the humblest thing that lives.

She sees the motled moth come twinkling by,
And sees it sip the flowret nigh;
Yet not, as once, with eager cry
She grasps the pretty thing;
Her thoughts now mingle with its tranquil mood—
So poised in air, as if on air it stood
To show its gold and purple wing.

She hears the bird without a wish to snare,
But rather on the azure air
To mount, and with it wander there
To some untrodden land;
As if it told her in its happy song
Of pleasures strange, that never can belong
To aught of sight or touch of hand.

Now the young soul her mighty power shall prove,
And outward things around her move,
Pure ministers of purer love,
And make the heart her home;
Or to the meaner senses sink a slave,
To do their bidding, though they madly crave
Through hateful scenes of vice to roam.

But, Ursulina, thine the better choice;
Thine eyes so speak, as with a voice:
Thy heart may still in earth rejoice
And all its beauty love;
But no, not all this fair, enchanting earth,
With all its spells, can give the rapture birth
That waits thy conscious soul above.

ROSALIE.

O, pour upon my soul again
That sad, unearthly strain,
That seems from other worlds to plain;
Thus falling, falling from afar,
As if some melancholy star
Had mingled with her light her sighs,
And dropped them from the skies.

No—never came from aught below
This melody of wo,
That makes my heart to overflow
As from a thousand gushing springs
Unknown before; that with it brings
This nameless light—if light it be—
That veils the world I see.

For all I see around me wears
The hue of other spheres;
And something blent of smiles and tears
Comes from the very air I breathe.
O, nothing, sure, the stars beneath,
Can mould a sadness like to this—
So like angelic bliss.

So, at that dreamy hour of day,
When the last lingering ray
Stops on the highest cloud to play—
So thought the gentle Rosalie
As on her maiden revery
First fell the strain of him who stole
In music to her soul.

LEVI FRISBIE.

[Born 1784. Died 1822.]

Professor Frisbie was the son of a respectable clergyman at Ipswich, Massachusetts. He entered Harvard University in 1798, and was graduated in 1802. His father, like most of the clergymen of New England, was a poor man, and unable fully to defray the costs of his son's education; and Mr. Frisbie, while an under-graduate, provided in part for his support by teaching a school during vacations, and by writing as a clerk. His friend and biographer, Professor Andrews Norton, alludes to this fact as a proof of the falsity of the opinion that wealth constitutes the only aristocracy in our country. Talents, united with correct morals, and good manners, pass unquestioned all the artificial barriers of society, and their claim to distinction is recognised more willingly than any other.

Soon after leaving the university, Mr. Frisbie commenced the study of the law; but an affection of the eyes depriving him of their use for the purposes of study, he abandoned his professional pursuits, and accepted the place of Latin tutor in Harvard University. In 1811, he was made Professor of the Latin Language, and in 1817, Professor of Moral Philosophy. The last office he held until he died, on the 19th of July, 1822. He was an excellent scholar, an original thinker, and a pure-minded man. An octavo volume, containing a memoir, some of his philosophical lectures, and a few poems, was published in 1823.

A CASTLE IN THE AIR.

I'll tell you, friend, what sort of wife,
Whene'er I scan this scene of life,
  Inspires my waking schemes,
And when I sleep, with form so light,
Dances before my ravish'd sight,
  In sweet aerial dreams.

The rose its blushes need not lend,
Nor yet the lily with them blend,
  To captivate my eyes.
Give me a cheek the heart obeys,
And, sweetly mutable, displays
  Its feelings as they rise;

Features, where, pensive, more than gay,
Save when a rising smile doth play,
  The sober thought you see;
Eyes that all soft and tender seem,
And kind affections round them beam,
  But most of all on me;

A form, though not of finest mould,
Where yet a something you behold
  Unconsciously doth please;
Manners all graceful without art,
That to each look and word impart
  A modesty and ease.

But still her air, her face, each charm
Must speak a heart with feeling warm,
  And mind inform the whole;
With mind her mantling cheek must glow,
Her voice, her beaming eye must show
  An all-inspiring soul.

Ah! could I such a being find,
And were her fate to mine but join'd
  By Hymen's silken tie,
To her myself, my all I'd give,
For her alone delighted live,
  For her consent to die.

Whene'er by anxious care oppress'd,
On the soft pillow of her breast
  My aching head I'd lay;
At her sweet smile each care should cease,
Her kiss infuse a balmy peace,
  And drive my griefs away.

In turn, I'd soften all her care,
Each thought, each wish, each feeling share;
  Should sickness e'er invade,
My voice should soothe each rising sigh,
My hand the cordial should supply;
  I'd watch beside her bed.

Should gathering clouds our sky deform,
My arms should shield her from the storm;
  And, were its fury hurl'd,
My bosom to its bolts I'd bare;
In her defence undaunted dare
  Defy the opposing world.

Together should our prayers ascend;
Together would we humbly bend,
  To praise the Almighty name;
And when I saw her kindling eye
Beam upwards in her native sky,
  My soul should catch the flame.

Thus nothing should our hearts divide,
But on our years serenely glide,
  And all to love be given;
And, when life's little scene was o'er,
We'd part to meet and part no more,
  But live and love in heaven.

JOHN PIERPONT.

[Born 1785.]

The author of the "Airs of Palestine," is a native of Litchfield, Connecticut, and was born on the sixth of April, 1785. His great-grandfather, the Reverend James Pierpont, was the second minister of New Haven, and one of the founders of Yale College; his grandfather and his father were men of intelligence and integrity; and his mother, whose maiden name was Elizabeth Collins, had a mind thoroughly imbued with the religious sentiment, and was distinguished for her devotion to maternal duties. In the following lines, from one of his recent poems, he acknowledges the influence of her example and teachings on his own character:

"She led me first to God;
Her words and prayers were my young spirit's dew.
For, when she used to leave
The fireside, every eve,
I knew it was for prayer that she withdrew.

"That dew, that bless'd my youth,—
Her holy love, her truth,
Her spirit of devotion, and the tears
That she could not suppress,—
Hath never ceased to bless
My soul, nor will it, through eternal years.

"How often has the thought
Of my mourn'd mother brought
Peace to my troubled spirit, and new power
The tempter to repel!
Mother, thou knowest well
That thou hast blessed me since thy mortal hour!"

Mr. Pierpont entered Yale College when fifteen years old, and was graduated in the summer of 1804. During a part of 1805, he assisted the Reverend Doctor Backus, in an academy of which he was principal previous to his election to the presidency of Hamilton College; and in the autumn of the same year, following the example of many young men of New England, he went to the southern states, and was for nearly four years a private tutor in the family of Colonel William Allston, of South Carolina, spending a portion of his time in Charleston, and the remainder on the estate of Colonel Allston, on the Waccamaw, near Georgetown. Here he commenced his legal studies, which he continued after his return to his native state in 1809, in the school of Justices Reeve and Gould; and in 1812, he was admitted to the bar, in Essex county, Massachusetts. Soon after the commencement of the second war with Great Britain, being appointed to address the Washington Benevolent Society of Newburyport, his place of residence, he delivered and afterward published "The Portrait," the earliest of the poems in the recent edition of his works.

In consequence of the general prostration of business in New England during the war, and of his health, which at this time demanded a more active life, he abandoned the profession of law, and became interested in mercantile transactions, first in Boston, and afterward in Baltimore; but these resulting disastrously, in 1816, he sought a solace in literary pursuits, and in the same year published "The Airs of Palestine." The first edition appeared in an octavo volume, at Baltimore; and two other editions were published in Boston, in the following year.

The "Airs of Palestine" is a poem of about eight hundred lines, in the heroic measure, in which the influence of music is shown by examples, principally from sacred history. The religious sublimity of the sentiments, the beauty of the language, and the finish of the versification, placed it at once, in the judgment of all competent to form an opinion on the subject, before any poem at that time produced in America. As a work of art, it would be nearly faultless, but for the occasional introduction of double rhymes, a violation of the simple dignity of the ten-syllable verse, induced by the intention of the author to recite it in a public assembly. He says in the preface to the third edition, that he was "aware how difficult even a good speaker finds it to rehearse heroic poetry, for any length of time, without perceiving in his hearers the somniferous effects of a regular cadence," and "the double rhyme was, therefore, occasionally thrown in, like a ledge of rocks in a smoothly gliding river, to break the current, which, without it, might appear sluggish, and to vary the melody, which might otherwise become monotonous." The following passage, descriptive of a moonlight scene in Italy, will give the reader an idea of its manner:

"On Arno's bosom, as he calmly flows,
And his cool arms round Vallombrosa throws,
Rolling his crystal tide through classic vales,
Alone,—at night,—the Italian boatman sails.
High o'er Mont' Alto walks, in maiden pride,
Night's queen;—he sees her image on that tide,
Now, ride the wave that curls its infant crest
Around his prow, then rippling sinks to rest;
Now, glittering dance around his eddying oar,
Whose every sweep is echo'd from the shore;
Now, far before him, on a liquid bed
Of waveless water, rest her radiant head.
How mild the empire of that virgin queen!
How dark the mountain's shade! how still the scene!
Hush'd by her silver sceptre, zephyrs sleep
On dewy leaves, that overhang the deep,
Nor dare to whisper through the boughs, nor stir
The valley's willow, nor the mountain's fir,
Nor make the pale and breathless aspen quiver,
Nor brush, with ruffling wind, that glassy river.
"Hark!—'tis a convent's bell: its midnight chime
For music measures even the march of time:—
O'er bending trees, that fringe the distant shore,
Gray turrets rise:—the eye can catch no more.
The boatman, listening to the tolling bell,
Suspends his oar:—a low and solemn swell,

From the deep shade, that round the cloister lies,
Rolls through the air, and on the water dies.
What melting song wakes the cold ear of Night?
A funeral dirge, that pale nuns, robed in white,
Chant round a sister's dark and narrow bed,
To charm the parting spirit of the dead.
Triumphant is the spell! with raptured ear,
That uncaged spirit hovering, lingers near;—
Why should she mount? why pant for brighter bliss?
A lovelier scene, a sweeter song, than this!"

Soon after the publication of the "Airs of Palestine," Mr. Pierpont entered seriously upon the study of theology, first by himself, in Baltimore, and afterward as a member of the theological school connected with Harvard College. He left that seminary in October, 1818, and in April, 1819, was ordained as minister of the Hollis Street Unitarian Church, in Boston, as successor to the Reverend Doctor Holley, who had recently been elected to the presidency of the Transylvania University, in Kentucky.

In 1835 and 1836, in consequence of impaired health, he spent a year abroad, passing through the principal cities in England, France, and Italy, and extending his tour into the East, visiting Smyrna, the ruins of Ephesus, in Asia Minor, Constantinople, and Athens, Corinth, and some of the other cities of Greece.

In 1848 he became minister of the Unitarian church in Medford, with which he remained until April, 1856, when he finally retired from the pulpit.

Mr. Pierpont has written in almost every metre, and many of his hymns, odes, and other brief poems, are remarkably spirited and melodious. Several of them, distinguished alike for energy of thought and language, were educed by events connected with the moral and religious enterprises of the time, nearly all of which are indebted to his constant and earnest advocacy for much of their prosperity.

In the preface to the collection of his poems published in 1840, he says, "It gives a true, though an all too feeble expression of the author's feeling and faith,—of his love of right, of freedom, and man, and of his correspondent and most hearty hatred of every thing that is at war with them; and of his faith in the providence and gracious promises of God. Nay, the book is published as an expression of his faith in *man;* his faith that every line, written to rebuke high-handed or under-handed wrong, or to keep alive the fires of civil and religious liberty,—written for solace in affliction, for support under trial, or as an expression, or for the excitement of Christian patriotism or devotion; or even with no higher aim than to throw a little sunshine into the chamber of the spirit, while it is going through some of the wearisome passages of life's history,—will be received as a proof of the writer's interest in the welfare of his fellowmen, of his desire to serve them, and consequently of his claim upon them for a charitable judgment, at least, if not even for a respectful and grateful remembrance."

"PASSING AWAY."

Was it the chime of a tiny bell,
That came so sweet to my dreaming ear,—
Like the silvery tones of a fairy's shell
That he winds on the beach, so mellow and clear,
When the winds and the waves lie together asleep,
And the moon and the fairy are watching the deep,
She dispensing her silvery light,
And he, his notes as silvery quite,
While the boatman listens and ships his oar,
To catch the music that comes from the shore?—
Hark! the notes, on my ear that play,
Are set to words:—as they float, they say,
"Passing away! passing away!"

But no; it was not a fairy's shell,
Blown on the beach, so mellow and clear;
Nor was it the tongue of a silver bell,
Striking the hour, that fill'd my ear,
As I lay in my dream; yet was it a chime
That told of the flow of the stream of time.
For a beautiful clock from the ceiling hung,
And a plump little girl, for a pendulum, swung;
(As you've sometimes seen, in a little ring
That hangs in his cage, a Canary bird swing;)
And she held to her bosom a budding bouquet,
And, as she enjoy'd it, she seem'd to say,
"Passing away! passing away!"

O, how bright were the wheels, that told
Of the lapse of time, as they moved round slow!
And the hands, as they swept o'er the dial of gold,
Seemed to point to the girl below.
And lo! she had changed:—in a few short hours
Her bouquet had become a garland of flowers,
That she held in her outstretched hands, and flung
This way and that, as she, dancing, swung
In the fulness of grace and womanly pride,
That told me she soon was to be a bride;—
Yet then, when expecting her happiest day,
In the same sweet voice I heard her say,
"Passing away! passing away!"

While I gazed at that fair one's cheek, a shade
Of thought, or care, stole softly over,
Like that by a cloud in a summer's day made,
Looking down on a field of blossoming clover.
The rose yet lay on her cheek, but its flush
Had something lost of its brilliant blush;
And the light in her eye, and the light on the wheels,
That marched so calmly round above her,
Was a little dimm'd,—as when evening steals
Upon noon's hot face:—Yet one could n't but love her,
For she look'd like a mother, whose first babe lay
Rock'd on her breast, as she swung all day;—
And she seem'd, in the same silver tone to say
"Passing away! passing away!"

While yet I look'd, what a change there came!
Her eye was quench'd, and her cheek was wan:
Stooping and staff'd was her wither'd frame,
Yet, just as busily, swung she on;
The garland beneath her had fallen to dust;
The wheels above her were eaten with rust;
The hands, that over the dial swept,
Grew crooked and tarnish'd, but on they kept,
And still there came that silver tone
From the shrivell'd lips of the toothless crone,—
(Let me never forget till my dying day
The tone or the burden of her lay,)—
"Passing away! passing away!

FOR THE CHARLESTOWN CENTENNIAL CELEBRATION.

Two hundred years! two hundred years!
How much of human power and pride,
What glorious hopes, what gloomy fears
Have sunk beneath their noiseless tide!

The red man at his horrid rite,
Seen by the stars at night's cold noon,
His bark canoe, its track of light
Left on the wave beneath the moon;

His dance, his yell, his council-fire,
The altar where his victim lay,
His death-song, and his funeral pyre,
That still, strong tide hath borne away.

And that pale pilgrim band is gone,
That on this shore with trembling trod,
Ready to faint, yet bearing on
The ark of freedom and of God.

And war—that since o'er ocean came,
And thunder'd loud from yonder hill,
And wrapp'd its foot in sheets of flame,
To blast that ark—its storm is still.

Chief, sachem, sage, bards, heroes, seers,
That live in story and in song,
Time, for the last two hundred years,
Has raised, and shown, and swept along.

'Tis like a dream when one awakes,
This vision of the scenes of old;
'Tis like the moon when morning breaks,
'Tis like a tale round watchfires told.

Then what are we? then what are we?
Yes, when two hundred years have roll'd
O'er our green graves, our names shall be
A morning dream, a tale that's told.

God of our fathers, in whose sight
The thousand years that sweep away
Man and the traces of his might
Are but the break and close of day—

Grant us that love of truth sublime,
That love of goodness and of thee,
That makes thy children in all time
To share thine own eternity.

MY CHILD.

I cannot make him dead!
His fair sunshiny head
Is ever bounding round my study chair;
Yet, when my eyes, now dim
With tears, I turn to him,
The vision vanishes—he is not there!

I walk my parlour floor,
And, through the open door,
I hear a footfall on the chamber stair;
I'm stepping toward the hall
To give the boy a call;
And then bethink me that—he is not there!

I thread the crowded street;
A satchell'd lad I meet,
With the same beaming eyes and colour'd hair:
And, as he's running by,
Follow him with my eye,
Scarcely believing that—he is not there!

I know his face is hid
Under the coffin lid;
Closed are his eyes; cold is his forehead fair;
My hand that marble felt;
O'er it in prayer I knelt;
Yet my heart whispers that—he is not there!

I cannot *make* him dead!
When passing by the bed,
So long watch'd over with parental care,
My spirit and my eye
Seek it inquiringly,
Before the thought comes that—he is not there!

When, at the cool, gray break
Of day, from sleep I wake,
With my first breathing of the morning air
My soul goes up, with joy,
To Him who gave my boy,
Then comes the sad thought that—he is not there!

When at the day's calm close,
Before we seek repose,
I'm with his mother, offering up our prayer,
Whate'er I may be *saying*,
I am, in spirit, praying
For our boy's spirit, though—he is not there!

Not there!—Where, then, is he?
The form I used to see
Was but the *raiment* that he used to wear.
The grave, that now doth press
Upon that cast-off dress,
Is but his wardrobe lock'd;—*he* is not there!

He lives!—In all the past
He lives; nor, to the last,
Of seeing him again will I despair;
In dreams I see him now;
And, on his angel brow,
I see it written, "Thou shalt see me *there!*"

Yes, we all live to God!
Father, thy chastening rod
So help us, thine afflicted ones, to bear,
That, in the spirit land,
Meeting at thy right hand,
'Twill be our heaven to find that—he is *there*

FOR A CELEBRATION OF THE MASSACHUSETTS MECHANICS' CHARITABLE ASSOCIATION.

Loud o'er thy savage child,
O God, the night-wind roar'd,
As, houseless, in the wild
He bow'd him and adored.
Thou saw'st him there,
As to the sky
He raised his eye
In fear and prayer.

Thine inspiration came!
And, grateful for thine aid,
An altar to thy name
He built beneath the shade:
The limbs of larch
That darken'd round,
He bent and bound
In many an arch;

Till in a sylvan fane
Went up the voice of prayer
And music's simple strain
Arose in worship there.
The arching boughs,
The roof of leaves
That summer weaves,
O'erheard his vows.

Then beam'd a brighter day;
And Salem's holy height
And Greece in glory lay
Beneath the kindling light.
Thy temple rose
On Salem's hill,
While Grecian skill
Adorn'd thy foes.

Along those rocky shores,
Along those olive plains,
Where pilgrim Genius pores
O'er Art's sublime remains
Long colonnades
Of snowy white
Look'd forth in light
Through classic shades.

Forth from the quarry stone
The marble goddess sprung;
And, loosely round her thrown,
Her marble vesture hung;
And forth from cold
And sunless mines
Came silver shrines
And gods of gold.

The Star of Bethlehem burn'd
And where the Stoic trod,
The altar was o'erturn'd,
Rained "to an unknown Go ."
And now there are
No idol fanes
On all the plains
Beneath that star.

To honour thee, dread Power!
Our strength and skill combine,
And temple, tomb, and tower
Attest these gifts divine.
A swelling dome
For pride they gild,
For peace they build
An humbler home.

By these our fathers' host
Was led to victory first,
When on our guardless coast
The cloud of battle burst;
Through storm and spray,
By these controll'd,
Our natives hold
Their thundering way.

Great Source of every art!
Our homes, our pictured halls,
Our throng'd and busy mart,
That lifts its granite walls,
And shoots to heaven
Its glittering spires,
To catch the fires
Of morn and even;

These, and the breathing forms
The brush or chisel gives,
With this when marble warms,
With that when canvass lives;
These all combine
In countless ways
To swell thy praise,
For all are thine.

HER CHOSEN SPOT.

While yet she lived, she walked alone
Among these shades. A voice divine
Whisper'd, "This spot shall be thine own,
Here shall thy wasting form recline,
Beneath the shadow of this pine."

"Thy will be done!" the sufferer said.
This spot was hallow'd from that hour;
And, in her eyes, the evening's shade
And morning's dew this green spot made
More lovely than her bridal bower.

By the pale moon—herself more pale
And spirit-like—these walks she trod;
And, while no voice, from swell or vale,
Was heard, she knelt upon this sod
And gave her spirit back to God.

That spirit, with an angel's wings,
Went up from the young mother's bed:
So, heavenward, soars the lark and sings.
She's lost to earth and earthly things;
But "weep not, for she is not dead,

She sleepeth!" Yea, she sleepeth here,
The first that in these grounds hath slept
This grave, first water'd with the tear
That child or widow'd man hath wept,
Shall be by heavenly watchmen kept.

The babe that lay on her cold breast—
 A rosebud dropp'd on drifted snow—
Its young hand in its father's press'd,
Shall learn that she, who first caress'd
 Its infant cheek, now sleeps below.

And often shall he come alone,
 When not a sound but evening's sigh
Is heard, and, bowing by the stone
That bears his mother's name, with none
 But God and guardian angels nigh,

Shall say, "This was my mother's choice
 For her own grave: O, be it mine!
Even now, methinks, I hear her voice
 Calling me hence, in the divine
 And mournful whisper of this pine."

THE PILGRIM FATHERS.

The Pilgrim Fathers,—where are they?—
 The waves that brought them o'er
Still roll in the bay, and throw their spray
 As they break along the shore:
Still roll in the bay, as they roll'd that day
 When the Mayflower moor'd below,
When the sea around was black with storms,
 And white the shore with snow.

The mists, that wrapp'd the Pilgrim's sleep,
 Still brood upon the tide;
And his rocks yet keep their watch by the deep,
 To stay its waves of pride.
But the snow-white sail, that he gave to the gale
 When the heavens look'd dark, is gone;—
As an angel's wing, through an opening cloud,
 Is seen, and then withdrawn.

The Pilgrim exile,—sainted name!
 The hill, whose icy brow
Rejoiced, when he came, in the morning's flame,
 In the morning's flame burns now.
And the moon's cold light, as it lay that night
 On the hill-side and the sea,
Still lies where he laid his houseless head;—
 But the Pilgrim,—where is he?

The Pilgrim Fathers are at rest;
 When summer's throned on high,
And the world's warm breast is in verdure dress'd,
 Go, stand on the hill where they lie.
The earliest ray of the golden day
 On that hallow'd spot is cast;
And the evening sun, as he leaves the world,
 Looks kindly on that spot last.

The Pilgrim *spirit* has not fled;
 It walks in noon's broad light;
And it watches the bed of the glorious dead,
 With their holy stars, by night.
It watches the bed of the brave who have bled,
 And shall guard this ice-bound shore,
Till the waves of the bay, where the Mayflower lay,
 Shall foam and freeze no more.

PLYMOUTH DEDICATION HYMN.

The winds and waves were roaring;
 The Pilgrims met for prayer;
And here, their God adoring,
 They stood, in open air.
When breaking day they greeted,
 And when its close was calm,
The leafless woods repeated
 The music of their psalm.

Not thus, O God, to praise thee,
 Do we, their children, throng;
The temple's arch we raise thee
 Gives back our choral song.
Yet, on the winds that bore thee
 Their worship and their prayers,
May ours come up before thee
 From hearts as true as theirs!

What have we, Lord, to bind us
 To this, the Pilgrims' shore!—
Their hill of graves behind us,
 Their watery way before,
The wintry surge, that dashes
 Against the rocks they trod,
Their memory, and their ashes,—
 Be thou their guard, O God!

We would not, Holy Father,
 Forsake this hallow'd spot,
Till on that shore we gather
 Where graves and griefs are not;
The shore where true devotion
 Shall rear no pillar'd shrine,
And see no other ocean
 Than that of love divine.

THE EXILE AT REST.

His falchion flash'd along the Nile;
 His hosts he led through Alpine snows;
O'er Moscow's towers, that shook the while,
 His eagle flag unroll'd—and froze.
Here sleeps he now alone: not one
 Of all the kings whose crowns he gave,
Nor sire, nor brother, wife, nor son,
 Hath ever seen or sought his grave.
Here sleeps he now alone; the star
 That led him on from crown to crown
Hath sunk; the nations from afar
 Gazed as it faded and went down.
He sleeps alone: the mountain cloud
 That night hangs round him, and the breath
Of morning scatters, is the shroud
 That wraps his mortal form in death.
High is his couch; the ocean flood
 Far, far below by storms is curl'd,
As round him heaved, while high he stood,
 A stormy and inconstant world.
Hark! Comes there from the Pyramids,
 And from Siberia's wastes of snow,
And Europe's fields, a voice that bids
 The world he awed to mourn him? No:

The only, the perpetual dirge
  That's heard there, is the seabird's cry,
The mournful murmur of the surge,
  The cloud's deep voice, the wind's low sigh.

JERUSALEM.

JERUSALEM, Jerusalem
  How glad should I have been,
Could I, in my lone wanderings,
  Thine aged walls have seen!—
Could I have gazed upon the dome
  Above thy towers that swells,
And heard, as evening's sun went down,
  Thy parting camels' bells:—

Could I have stood on Olivet,
  Where once the Saviour trod,
And, from its height, look'd down upon
  The city of our God;
For is it not, Almighty God,
  Thy holy city still,—
Though there thy prophets walk no more,—
  That crowns Moriah's hill?

Thy prophets walk no more, indeed,
  The streets of Salem now,
Nor are their voices lifted up
  On Zion's sadden'd brow;
Nor are their garnish'd sepulchres
  With pious sorrow kept,
Where once the same Jerusalem,
  That kill'd them, came and wept.

But still the seed of ABRAHAM
  With joy upon it look,
And lay their ashes at its feet,
  That Kedron's feeble brook
Still washes, as its waters creep
  Along their rocky bed,
And Israel's GOD is worshipp'd yet
  Where Zion lifts her head.

Yes; every morning, as the day
  Breaks over Olivet,
The holy name of ALLAH comes
  From every minaret;
At every eve the mellow call
  Floats on the quiet air,
"Lo, GOD is GOD! Before him come,
  Before him come, for prayer!"

I know, when at that solemn call
  The city holds her breath,
That OMAR's mosque hears not the name
  Of Him of Nazareth;
But ABRAHAM's GOD is worshipp'd there
  Alike by age and youth,
And worshipp'd,—hopeth charity,—
  "In spirit and in truth."

Yea, from that day when SALEM knelt
  And bent her queenly neck
To him who was, at once, her priest
  And king,—MELCHISEDEK,
To this, when Egypt's ABRAHAM*
  The sceptre and the sword
Shakes o'er her head, her holy men
  Have bow'd before the Lord.

Jerusalem, I would have seen
  Thy precipices steep,
The trees of palm that overhang
  Thy gorges dark and deep,
The goats that cling along thy cliffs,
  And browse upon thy rocks,
Beneath whose shade lie down, alike,
  Thy shepherds and their flocks.

I would have mused, while night hung out
  Her silver lamp so pale,
Beneath those ancient olive trees
  That grow in Kedron's vale,
Whose foliage from the pilgrim hides
  The city's wall sublime,
Whose twisted arms and gnarled trunks
  Defy the scythe of time.

The garden of Gethsemane
  Those aged olive trees
Are shading yet, and in their shade
  I would have sought the breeze,
That, like an angel, bathed the brow,
  And bore to heaven the prayer
Of Jesus, when in agony,
  He sought the Father there.

I would have gone to Calvary,
  And, where the MARYS stood,
Bewailing loud the Crucified,
  As near him as they could,
I would have stood, till night o'er earth
  Her heavy pall had thrown,
And thought upon my Saviour's cross,
  And learn'd to bear my own.

Jerusalem, Jerusalem,
  Thy cross thou bearest now!
An iron yoke is on thy neck,
  And blood is on thy brow;
Thy golden crown, the crown of truth,
  Thou didst reject as dross,
And now thy cross is on thee laid—
  The crescent is thy cross!

It was not mine, nor will it be,
  To see the bloody rod
That scourgeth thee, and long hath scourged
  Thou city of our GOD!
But round thy hill the spirits throng
  Of all thy murder'd seers,
And voices that went up from it
  Are ringing in my ears,—

Went up that day, when darkness fell
  From all thy firmament,
And shrouded thee at noon; and when
  Thy temple's vail was rent,
And graves of holy men, that touch'd
  Thy feet, gave up their dead:—
Jerusalem, thy prayer is heard,
  HIS BLOOD IS ON THY HEAD!

* This name is now generally written IBRAHIM.

THE POWER OF MUSIC.*

Hear yon poetic pilgrim† of the west
Chant music's praise, and to her power attest;
Who now, in Florida's untrodden woods,
Bedecks, with vines of jessamine, her floods,
And flowery bridges o'er them loosely throws;
Who hangs the canvass where Atala glows,
On the live oak, in floating drapery shrouded,
That like a mountain rises, lightly clouded:
Who, for the son of Outalissi, twines
Beneath the shade of ever-whispering pines
A funeral wreath, to bloom upon the moss
That Time already sprinkles on the cross
Raised o'er the grave where his young virgin sleeps,
And Superstition o'er her victim weeps;
Whom now the silence of the dead surrounds,
Among Scioto's monumental mounds;
Save that, at times, the musing pilgrim hears
A crumbling oak fall with the weight of years,
To swell the mass that Time and Ruin throw
O'er chalky bones that mouldering lie below,
By virtues unembalm'd, unstain'd by crimes,
Lost in those towering tombs of other times;
For, where no bard has cherished virtue's flame,
No ashes sleep in the warm sun of fame.
With sacred lore this traveller beguiles
His weary way, while o'er him fancy smiles.
Whether he kneels in venerable groves,
Or through the wide and green savanna roves,
His heart leaps lightly on each breeze, that bears
The faintest breath of Idumea's airs.
Now he recalls the lamentable wail
That pierced the shades of Rama's palmy vale,
When Murder struck, throned on an infant's bier,
A note for Satan's and for Herod's ear.
Now on a bank, o'erhung with waving wood,
Whose falling leaves flit o'er Ohio's flood,
The pilgrim stands; and o'er his memory rushes
The mingled tide of tears and blood, that gushes
Along the valleys where his childhood stray'd,
And round the temples where his fathers pray'd.
How fondly then, from all but hope exiled,
To Zion's wo recurs religion's child!
He sees the tear of Judah's captive daughters
Mingle, in silent flow, with Babel's waters;
While Salem's harp, by patriot pride unstrung,
Wrapp'd in the mist that o'er the river hung,
Felt but the breeze that wanton'd o'er the billow,
And the long, sweeping fingers of the willow.
And could not music soothe the captive's wo?
But should that harp be strung for Judah's foe?
While thus the enthusiast roams along the stream,
Balanced between a revery and a dream,
Backward he springs; and through his bounding heart
The cold and curdling poison seems to dart.
For, in the leaves, beneath a quivering brake,
Spinning his death-note, lies a coiling snake,
Just in the act, with greenly venom'd fangs,
To strike the foot that heedless o'er him hangs.
Bloated with rage, on spiral folds he rides;
His rough scales shiver on his spreading sides;
Dusky and dim his glossy neck becomes,
And freezing poisons thickens on his gums;
His parch'd and hissing throat breathes hot and dry;
A spark of hell lies burning on his eye:
While, like a vapour o'er his writhing rings,
Whirls his light tail, that threatens while it sings
Soon as dumb fear removes her icy fingers
From off the heart, where gazing wonder lingers,
The pilgrim, shrinking from a doubtful fight,
Aware of danger, too, in sudden flight,
From his soft flute throws music's air around,
And meets his foe upon enchanted ground.
See! as the plaintive melody is flung,
The lightning flash fades on the serpent's tongue;
The uncoiling reptile o'er each shining fold
Throws changeful clouds of azure, green, and gold
A softer lustre twinkles in his eye;
His neck is burnish'd with a glossier dye;
His slippery scales grow smoother to the sight,
And his relaxing circles roll in light.
Slowly the charm retires: with waving sides,
Along its track the graceful listener glides;
While music throws her silver cloud around,
And bears her votary off in magic folds of sound.

* From "Airs of Palestine." † Chateaubriand

OBSEQUIES OF SPURZHEIM.

Stranger, there is bending o'er thee
Many an eye with sorrow wet;
All our stricken hearts deplore thee;
Who, that knew thee, can forget?
Who forgot that thou hast spoken?
Who, thine eye,—that noble frame?
But that golden bowl is broken,
In the greatness of thy fame.

Autumn's leaves shall fall and wither
On the spot where thou shalt rest;
'T is in love we bear thee thither,
To thy mourning mother's breast.
For the stores of science brought us,
For the charm thy goodness gave
To the lessons thou hast taught us,
Can we give thee but a grave?

Nature's priest, how pure and fervent
Was thy worship at her shrine!
Friend of man, of God the servant,
Advocate of truths divine,—
Taught and charm'd as by no other
We have been, and hoped to be;
But, while waiting round thee, brother,
For thy light,—'t is dark with thee.

Dark with thee!—No; thy Creator,
All whose creatures and whose laws
Thou didst love, shall give thee greater
Light than earth's, as earth withdraws
To thy God, thy godlike spirit
Back we give, in filial trust;
Thy cold clay,—we grieve to bear it
To its chamber,—but we must.

THE SEAMAN'S BETHEL.*

Thou, who on the whirlwind ridest,
  At whose word the thunder roars,
Who, in majesty, presidest
  O'er the oceans and their shores;
From those shores, and from the oceans,
  We, the children of the sea,
Come to pay thee our devotions,
  And to give this house to thee.

When, for business on great waters,
  We go down to sea in ships,
And our weeping wives and daughters
  Hang, at parting, on our lips,
This, our Bethel, shall remind us,
  That there's One who heareth prayer,
And that those we leave behind us
  Are a faithful pastor's care.

Visions of our native highlands,
  In our wave-rock'd dreams embalm'd
Winds that come from spicy islands
  When we long have lain becalm'd,
Are not to our souls so pleasant
  As the offerings we shall bring
Hither, to the Omnipresent,
  For the shadow of his wing.

When in port, each day that's holy,
  To this house we'll press in throngs;
When at sea, with spirit lowly,
  We'll repeat its sacred songs.
Outward bound, shall we, in sadness,
  Lose its flag behind the seas;
Homeward bound, we'll greet with gladness
  Its first floating on the breeze.

Homeward bound!—with deep emotion,
  We remember, Lord, that life
Is a voyage upon an ocean,
  Heaved by many a tempest's strife.
Be thy statutes so engraven
  On our hearts and minds, that we,
Anchoring in Death's quiet haven,
  All may make our home with thee.

THE SPARKLING BOWL.

Thou sparkling bowl! thou sparkling bowl!
  Though lips of bards thy brim may press,
And eyes of beauty o'er thee roll,
  And song and dance thy power confess,
I will not touch thee; for there clings
A scorpion to thy side, that stings!

Thou crystal glass! like Eden's tree,
  Thy melted ruby tempts the eye,
And, as from that, there comes from thee
  The voice, "Thou shalt not surely die."
I dare not lift thy liquid gem;—
A snake is twisted round thy stem!

Thou liquid fire! like that which glow'd
  On Melita's surf-beaten shore,
Thou'st been upon my guests bestow'd,
  But thou shalt warm my house no more.
For, wheresoe'er thy radiance falls,
Forth, from thy heat, a viper crawls!

What, though of gold the goblet be,
  Emboss'd with branches of the vine,
Beneath whose burnish'd leaves we see
  Such clusters as pour'd out the wine?
Among those leaves an adder hangs!
I fear him;—for I've felt his fangs.

The Hebrew, who the desert trod,
  And felt the fiery serpent's bite,
Look'd up to that ordain'd of God,
  And found that life was in the sight.
So, the *worm*-bitten's fiery veins
Cool, when he drinks what God ordains.

Ye gracious clouds! ye deep, cold wells!
  Ye gems, from mossy rocks that drip!
Springs, that from earth's mysterious cells
  Gush o'er your granite basin's lip!
To you I look;—your largess give,
And I will drink of you, and live.

FOR THE FOURTH OF JULY.

Day of glory! welcome day!
Freedom's banners greet thy ray;
See! how cheerfully they play
  With thy morning breeze,
On the rocks where pilgrims kneel'd,
On the heights where squadrons wheel'd,
When a tyrant's thunder peal'd
  O'er the trembling seas.

God of armies! did thy "stars
In their courses" smite his cars,
Blast his arm, and wrest his bars
  From the heaving tide?
On our standard, lo! they burn,
And, when days like this return,
Sparkle o'er the soldiers' urn
  Who for freedom died.

God of peace!—whose spirit fills
All the echoes of our hills,
All the murmurs of our rills,
  Now the storm is o'er;—
O, let freemen be our sons;
And let future Washingtons
Rise, to lead their valiant ones,
  Till there's war no more.

By the patriot's hallow'd rest,
By the warrior's gory breast,—
Never let our graves be press'd
  By a despot's throne;
By the Pilgrims' toils and cares,
By their battles and their prayers,
By their ashes,—let our heirs
  Bow to thee alone.

* Written for the dedication of the Seaman's Bethel, under the direction of the Boston Port Society, September fourth, 1833.

SAMUEL WOODWORTH.

[Born, 1785. Died, 1842.]

Mr. Woodworth was a native of Scituate, in Massachusetts. After learning in a country town the art of printing, he went to New York, where he was editor of a newspaper during our second war with England. He subsequently published a weekly miscellany entitled "The Ladies' Literary Gazette," and in 1823, associated with Mr. George P. Morris, he established "The New York Mirror," long the most popular journal of literature and art in this country. For several years before his death he was an invalid, and in this period a large number of the leading gentlemen of New York acted as a committee for a complimentary benefit given for him at the Park Theatre, the proceeds of which made more pleasant his closing days. He died in the month of December, 1842, in the fifty-seventh year of his age, much respected by all who knew him, for his modesty and integrity as well as for his literary abilities.

Mr. Woodworth wrote many pieces for the stage, which had a temporary popularity, and two or three volumes of songs, odes, and other poems, relating chiefly to subjects of rural and domestic life. He dwelt always with delight upon the scenes of his childhood, and lamented that he was compelled to make his home amid the strife and tumult of a city. He was the poet of the "common people," and was happy in the belief that "The Bucket" was read by multitudes who never heard of "Thanatopsis." Some of his pieces have certainly much merit, in their way, and a selection might be made from his voluminous writings that would be very honourable to his talents and his feelings. There has been no recent edition of any of his works.

THE BUCKET.

How dear to this heart are the scenes of my childhood,
When fond recollection presents them to view!
The orchard, the meadow, the deep-tangled wildwood,
And every loved spot which my infancy knew!
The wide-spreading pond, and the mill that stood by it,
The bridge, and the rock where the cataract fell,
The cot of my father, the dairy-house nigh it,
And e'en the rude bucket that hung in the well—
The old oaken bucket, the iron-bound bucket,
The moss-cover'd bucket which hung in the well.

That moss-cover'd vessel I hail'd as a treasure,
For often at noon, when return'd from the field,
I found it the source of an exquisite pleasure,
The purest and sweetest that nature can yield.
How ardent I seized it, with hands that were glowing,
And quick to the white-pebbled bottom it fell;
Then soon, with the emblem of truth overflowing,
And dripping with coolness, it rose from the well—
The old oaken bucket, the iron-bound bucket,
The moss-cover'd bucket, arose from the well.

How sweet from the green mossy brim to receive it,
As poised on the curb it inclined to my lips!
Not a full blushing goblet could tempt me to leave it,
The brightest that beauty or revelry sips.
And now, far removed from the loved habitation,
The tear of regret will intrusively swell,
As fancy reverts to my father's plantation,
And sighs for the bucket that hangs in the well—
The old oaken bucket, the iron-bound bucket,
The moss-cover'd bucket that hangs in the well!

THE NEEDLE.

The gay belles of fashion may boast of excelling
In waltz or cotillion, at whist or quadrille;
And seek admiration by vauntingly telling
Of drawing, and painting, and musical skill;
But give me the fair one, in country or city,
Whose home and its duties are dear to her heart,
Who cheerfully warbles some rustical ditty,
While plying the needle with exquisite art.
The bright little needle—the swift-flying needle,
The needle directed by beauty and art.

If Love have a potent, a magical token,
A talisman, ever resistless and true—
A charm that is never evaded or broken,
A witchery certain the heart to subdue—
'Tis this—and his armoury never has furnish'd
So keen and unerring, or polish'd a dart;
Let Beauty direct it, so pointed and burnish'd,
And Oh! it is certain of touching the heart
The bright little needle—the swift-flying needle,
The needle directed by beauty and art.

Be wise, then, ye maidens, nor seek admiration
By dressing for conquest, and flirting with all,
You never, whate'er be your fortune or station,
Appear half so lovely at rout or at ball,
As gaily convened at a work-cover'd table,
Each cheerfully active and playing her part,
Beguiling the task with a song or a fable,
And plying the needle with exquisite art.
The bright little needle—the swift-flying needle,
The needle directed by beauty and art.

ANDREWS NORTON.

[Born, 1786. Died, 1853.]

THE late eminent scholar, ANDREWS NORTON, descended from the father of the celebrated JOHN NORTON, minister of Ipswich, was born in Hingham, near Boston, on the thirty-first of December, 1786. He was graduated at Harvard College in 1804; studied divinity, and for a short time, in 1809, preached in Augusta, Maine; spent a year as tutor in Bowdoin College; for another year was tutor in mathematics at Cambridge; in 1812 commenced the "General Repository," a religious and literary magazine, which he conducted with remarkable ability two years; in 1813 was chosen librarian of Harvard College, which office he held eight years; about the same time was appointed lecturer on the criticism and interpretation of the Scriptures, in the college, and on the organization of the Divinity School, in 1819, Dexter professor of sacred literature; in 1821 was married to CATHERINE, daughter of SAMUEL ELIOT, of Boston; in 1822 delivered an address before the university on the life and character of his friend Professor FRISBIE, whose literary remains he afterward edited; in 1826, collected the poems of Mrs. HEMANS, and prepared for the press the first American edition of them; in 1828 passed several months in England, and in 1830 resigned his professorship, to reside at Cambridge as a private gentleman.

He now turned his attention to the composition and completion of those important works in criticism and theology which have established his fame as one of the greatest scholars of the last age. His "Statement of Reasons for not Believing the Doctrine of the Trinity" appeared in 1833; the first volume of his "Genuineness of the Gospels," in 1837; a treatise "On the Latest Form of Infidelity," in 1839; the second and third volumes on the "Genuineness of the Gospels," in 1844; "The Internal Evidences of the Gospels," in 1851; and "Tracts on Christianity," in 1852. He died at his summer residence, in Newport, on the evening of the eighteenth of September, 1853; and his last work, a new "Translation of the Gospels," has been published since his death. He was the most able, ingenious, and thoroughly accomplished writer of the Unitarian party in America.

What he was, and what he might have been, in poetry, is evinced by the following highly finished and beautiful productions.

ON THE DEATH OF CHARLES ELIOT.

FAREWELL! before we meet again,
  Perhaps through scenes as yet unknown,
That lie in distant years of pain,
  I have to journey on alone;

To meet with griefs thou wilt not feel,
  Perchance with joys thou canst not share;
And when we both were wont to kneel,
  To breathe alone the silent prayer;

But ne'er a deeper pang to know,
  Than when I watched thy slow decay,
Saw on thy cheeck the hectic glow,
  And felt at last each hope give way.

But who the destined hour may tell,
That bids the loosened spirit fly?
E'en now this pulse's feverish swell
  May warn me of mortality.

But chance what may, thou wilt no more
  With sense and with my hours beguile,
Inform with learning's various lore,
  Or charm with friendship's kindest smile.

Each book I read, each walk I tread,
  Whate'er I feel, whate'er I see,
All speak of hopes forever fled,
  All have some tale to tell of thee.

I shall not, should misfortune lower,
  Should friends desert, and life decline,
I shall not know thy soothing power,
  Nor hear thee say, "My heart is thine."

If thou hadst lived, thy well-earned fame
  Had bade my fading prospect bloom,
Had cast its lustre o'er my name,
  And stood, the guardian of my tomb.

Servant of GOD! thy ardent mind,
  With lengthening years improving still,
Striving, untired, to serve mankind,
  Had thus performed thy Father's will.

Another task to thee was given;
  'T was thine to drink of early wo,
To feel thy hopes, thy friendships riven,
  And bend submissive to the blow;

With patient smile and steady eye,
  To meet each pang that sickness gave,
And see with lingering step draw nigh
  The form that pointed to the grave.

Servant of GOD! thou art not there;
  Thy race of virtue is not run;
What blooms on earth of good and fair,
  Will ripen in another sun.

Dost thou, amid the rapturous glow
  With which the soul her welcome hears,
Dost thou still think of us below,
  Of earthly scenes, of human tears?

Perhaps e'en now thy thoughts return
  To when in summer's moonlight walk,
Of all that now is thine to learn,
  We framed no light nor fruitless talk.

We spake of knowledge, such as soars
  From world to world with ceaseless flight;
And love, that follows and adores,
  As nature spreads before her sight.

How vivid still past scenes appear!
  I feel as though all were not o'er;
As though 't were strange I cannot hear
  Thy voice of friendship yet once more.

But I shall hear it; in that day
  Whose setting sun I may not view,
When earthly voices die away,
  Thine will at last be heard anew.

We meet again; a little while,
  And where thou art I too shall be.
And then, with what an angel smile
  Of gladness, thou wilt welcome me!

A SUMMER SHOWER.

The rain is o'er—How dense and bright
  Yon pearly clouds reposing lie!
Cloud above cloud, a glorious sight,
  Contrasting with the deep-blue sky!

In grateful silence earth receives
  The general blessing; fresh and fair,
Each flower expands its little leaves,
  As glad the common joy to share.

The soften'd sunbeams pour around
  A fairy light, uncertain, pale;
The wind flows cool, the scented ground
  Is breathing odours on the gale.

Mid yon rich clouds' voluptuous pile,
  Methinks some spirit of the air
Might rest to gaze below a while,
  Then turn to bathe and revel there.

The sun breaks forth—from off the scene,
  Its floating veil of mist is flung;
And all the wilderness of green
  With trembling drops of light is hung.

Now gaze on nature—yet the same—
  Glowing with life, by breezes fann'd,
Luxuriant, lovely, as she came,
  Fresh in her youth, from God's own hand.

Hear the rich music of that voice,
  Which sounds from all below, above;
She calls her children to rejoice,
  And round them throws her arms of love.

Drink in her influence—low-born care,
  And all the train of mean desire,
Refuse to breathe this holy air,
  And mid this living light expire.

HYMN.

My God, I thank thee! may no thought
  E'er deem thy chastisements severe;
But may this heart, by sorrow taught,
  Calm each wild wish, each idle fear

Thy mercy bids all nature bloom;
  The sun shines bright, and man is gay;
Thine equal mercy spreads the gloom
  That darkens o'er his little day.

Full many a throb of grief and pain
  Thy frail and erring child must know;
But not one prayer is breathed in vain,
  Nor does one tear unheeded flow.

Thy various messengers employ;
  Thy purposes of love fulfil;
And, mid the wreck of human joy,
  May kneeling faith adore thy will!

TO MRS. ——, ON HER DEPARTURE FOR EUROPE.

Farewell! farewell! for many a day
  Our thoughts far o'er the sea will roam!
Blessings and prayers attend thy way;
  Glad welcomes wait for thee at home.

While gazing upon Alpine snows,
  Or lingering near Italian shores;
Where Nature all her grandeur shows
  Or art unveils her treasured stores;

When mingling with those gifted minds
  That shed their influence on our race,
Thine own its native station finds,
  And takes with them an honour'd place

Forget not, then, how dear thou art
  To many friends not with thee there;
To many a warm and anxious heart,
  Object of love, and hope, and prayer.

When shall we meet again?—some day,
  In a bright morning, when the gale
Sweeps the blue waters as in play;
  Then shall we watch thy coming sail!

When shall we meet again, and where?
  We trust not hope's uncertain voice;
To faith the future all is fair:
  She speaks assured; "Thou shalt rejoice."

Perhaps our meeting may be when,
  Mid new-born life's awakening glow,
The loved and lost appear again,
  Heaven's music sounding sweet and low.

HYMN FOR THE DEDICATION OF A CHURCH.

Where ancient forests round us spread,
Where bends the cataract's ocean-fall,
On the lone mountain's silent head,
There are thy temples, God of all!

Beneath the dark-blue, midnight arch,
Whence myriad suns pour down their rays,
Where planets trace their ceaseless march,
Father! we worship as we gaze.

The tombs thine altars are; for there,
When earthly loves and hopes have fled,
To thee ascends the spirit's prayer,
Thou God of the immortal dead!

All space is holy; for all space
Is fill'd by thee; but human thought
Burns clearer in some chosen place,
Where thy own words of love are taught.

Here be they taught; and may we know
That faith thy servants knew of old;
Which onward bears through weal and wo,
Till Death the gates of heaven unfold!

Nor we alone; may those whose brow
Shows yet no trace of human cares,
Hereafter stand where we do now,
And raise to thee still holier prayers!

FORTITUDE.

Faint not, poor traveller, though thy way
Be rough, like that thy Saviour trod;
Though cold and stormy lower the day,
This path of suffering leads to God.

Nay, sink not; though from every limb
Are starting drops of toil and pain;
Thou dost but share the lot of Him
With whom his followers are to reign.

Thy friends are gone, and thou, alone,
Must bear the sorrows that assail;
Look upward to the eternal throne,
And know a Friend who cannot fail.

Bear firmly; yet a few more days,
And thy hard trial will be past;
Then, wrapt in glory's opening blaze,
Thy feet will rest on heaven at last.

Christian! thy Friend, thy Master pray'd,
When dread and anguish shook his frame;
Then met his sufferings undismay'd;
Wilt thou not strive to do the same?

O! think'st thou that his Father's love
Shone round him then with fainter rays
Than now, when, throned all height above,
Unceasing voices hymn his praise?

Go, sufferer! calmly meet the woes
Which God's own mercy bids thee bear;
Then, rising as thy Saviour rose,
Go! his eternal victory share.

THE CLOSE OF THE YEAR

Another year! another year!
The unceasing rush of time sweeps on
Whelm'd in its surges, disappear
Man's hopes and fears, forever gone!

O, no! forbear that idle tale!
The hour demands another strain,
Demands high thoughts that cannot quail,
And strength to conquer and retain.

'T is midnight—from the dark-blue sky,
The stars, which now look down on earth,
Have seen ten thousand centuries fly,
And given to countless changes birth.

And when the pyramids shall fall,
And, mouldering, mix as dust in air,
The dwellers on this alter'd ball
May still behold them glorious there.

Shine on! shine on! with you I tread
The march of ages, orbs of light!
A last eclipse o'er you may spread,
To me, to me, there comes no night.

O! what concerns it him, whose way
Lies upward to the immortal dead,
That a few hairs are turning gray,
Or one more year of life has fled?

Swift years! but teach me how to bear,
To feel and act with strength and skill,
To reason wisely, nobly dare,
And speed your courses as ye will.

When life's meridian toils are done,
How calm, how rich the twilight glow!
The morning twilight of a sun
Which shines not here on things below.

But sorrow, sickness, death, the pain
To leave, or lose wife, children, friends!
What then—shall we not meet again
Where parting comes not, sorrow ends?

The fondness of a parent's care,
The changeless trust which woman gives
The smile of childhood,—it is there
That all we love in them still lives.

Press onward through each varying hour;
Let no weak fears thy course delay;
Immortal being! feel thy power,
Pursue thy bright and endless way.

ON LISTENING TO A CRICKET.

I love, thou little chirping thing,
To hear thy melancholy noise;
Though thou to Fancy's ear may sing
Of summer past and fading joys.

Thou canst not now drink dew from flowers,
Nor sport along the traveller's path;
But, through the winter's weary hours,
Shalt warm thee at my lonely hearth.

And when my lamp's decaying beam
But dimly shows the lettered page
Rich with some ancient poet's dream,
Or wisdom of a purer age—

Then will I listen to the sound,
And, musing o'er the embers pale
With whitening ashes strewed around,
The forms of memory unveil;

Recall the many-colored dreams
That fancy fondly weaves for youth
When all the bright illusion seems
The pictured promises of Truth;

Perchance observe the fitful light,
And its faint flashes round the room,
And think some pleasures feebly bright
May lighten thus life's varied gloom.

I love the quiet midnight hour,
When Care and Hope and Passion sleep,
And Reason with untroubled power
Can her late vigils duly keep.

I love the night; and sooth to say,
Before the merry birds that sing
In all the glare and noise of day,
Prefer the cricket's grating wing.

A SUMMER NIGHT.

How sweet the summer gales of night,
That blow when all is peaceful round,
As if some spirit's downy flight
Swept silent through the blue profound!

How sweet at midnight to recline
Where flows their cool and fragrant stream!
There half repeat some glowing line,
There court each wild and fairy dream;

Or idly mark the volumed clouds
Their broad deep mass of darkness throw,
When, as the moon her radiance shrouds,
Their changing sides with silver glow;

Or see where, from that depth of shade,
The ceaseless lightning, faintly bright,
In silence plays, as if afraid
To break the deep repose of night;

Or gaze on heaven's unnumbered fires,
While dimly-imaged thoughts arise,
And Fancy, loosed from earth, aspires
To search the secrets of the skies;

What various beings there reside;
What forms of life to man unknown,
Drink the rich flow of bliss, whose tide
Wells from beneath the eternal throne;

Or life's uncertain scenes revolve,
And musing how to act or speak,
Feel some high wish, some proud resolve
Throb in the heart, or flush the cheek.

Meanwhile may reason's light, whose beam
Dimmed by the world's oppressive gloom,
Sheds but a dull unsteady gleam,
In this still hour its rays relume.

Thus oft in this still hour be mine
The light all meaner passions fear,
The wandering thought, the high design,
And soaring dreams to virtue dear.

A WINTER MORNING.

The keen, clear air—the splendid sight—
We waken to a world of ice;
Where all things are enshrined in light,
As by some genii's quaint device.

'T is winter's jubilee: this day
Her stores their countless treasures yield;
See how the diamond glances play,
In ceaseless blaze, from tree and field.

The cold, bare spot, where late we ranged,
The naked woods are seen no more;
This earth to fairy-land is changed,
With glittering silver sheeted o'er.

The morning sun, with cloudless rays,
His powerless splendor round us streams,
From crusted boughs and twinkling sprays
Fly back unloosed the rainbow beams.

With more than summer beauty fair,
The trees in winter's garb are shown:
What a rich halo melts in air,
Around their crystal branches thrown!

And yesterday—how changed the view
From what then charmed us; when the sky
Hung, with its dim and watery hue,
O'er all the soft, still prospect nigh!

The distant groves, arrayed in white,
Might then like things unreal seem,
Just shown awhile in silvery light,
The fictions of a poets' dream.

Like shadowy groves upon that shore,
O'er which Elysium's twilight lay,
By bards and sages feigned of yore,
Ere broke on earth heaven's brighter day

O God of nature! with what might
Of beauty, showered on all below,
Thy guiding power would lead aright
Earth's wanderer all thy love to know.

THE PARTING.

We did not part as others part;
And should we meet on earth no more,
Yet deep and dear within my heart
Some thoughts will rest a treasured store.

How oft, when weary and alone,
Have I recalled each word, each look,
The meaning of each varying tone,
And the last parting glance we took!

Yes, sometimes even here are found
Those who can touch the chords of love,
And wake a glad and holy sound,
Like that which fills the courts above.

It is as when a traveller hears,
In a strange land, his native tongue,
A voice he loved in happier years,
A song which once his mother sung.

We part; the sea may roll between,
While we through different climates roam:
Sad days—a life—may intervene;
But we shall meet again at home.

ON THE DEATH OF A FRIEND.

Oh, stay thy tears! for they are blest
Whose days are past, whose toil is done;
Here midnight care disturbs our rest,
Here sorrow dims the noon-day sun.

For laboring Virtue's anxious toil,
For patient Sorrow's stifled sigh,
For faith that marks the conqueror's spoil,
Heaven grants the recompense,—to die.

How blest are they whose transient years
Pass like an evening meteor's light;
Not dark with guilt, nor dim with tears;
Whose course is short, unclouded, bright!

How cheerless were our lengthened way,
Did Heaven's own light not break the gloom,
Stream downward from eternal day,
And cast a glory round the tomb!

Then stay thy tears: the blest above
Have hailed a spirit's heavenly birth,
Sung a new song of joy and love,
And why should anguish reign on earth?

TO A FRIEND AFTER HER MARRIAGE.

Nay, ask me not now for some proof that my heart
Has learn'd the dear lesson of friendship for thee;
Nay, ask not for words that might feebly impart
The feelings and thoughts which thy glance cannot see.

Whate'er I could wish thee already is thine;
The fair sunshine within sheds its beam through thine eye;
And Pleasure stands near thee, and waits but a sign,
To all whom thou lovest, at thy bidding to fly.

Yet hereafter thy bosom some sorrow may feel,
Some cloud o'er thy heart its chill shadow may throw:
Then ask if thou wilt, and my words shall reveal
The feelings and thoughts which thou now canst not know

FUNERAL HYMN.

He has gone to his God, he has gone to his home;
No more amid peril and error to roam.
His eyes are no longer dim,
His feet no more will falter;
No grief can follow him,
No pang his cheek can alter.

There are paleness and weeping and sighs below
For our faith is faint, and our tears will flow
But the harps of heaven are ringing;
Glad angels come to greet him,
And hymns of joy are singing,
While old friends press to meet him.

Oh! honored, beloved, to earth unconfined,
Thou hast soared on high, thou hast left us behind;
But our parting is not for ever:
We will follow thee by heaven's light,
Where the grave cannot dissever
The souls whom God will unite.

OH! NE'ER UPON MY GRAVE BE SHED.

Oh! ne'er upon my grave be shed
The bitter tears of sinking age,
That mourns its cherished comforts dead,
With grief no human hopes assuage.

When, through the still and gazing street,
My funeral winds its sad array,
Ne'er may a Father's faltering feet
Lead with slow steps the church-yard way

'T is a dread sight,—the sunken eye,
The look of calm and fixed despair,
And the pale lips which breathe no sigh,
But quiver with the unuttered prayer.

Ne'er may a Mother hide her tears,
As the mute circle spreads around;
Or, turning from my grave, she hears
The clods fall fast with heavy sound.

Ne'er may she know the sinking heart,
The dreary loneliness of grief,
When all is o'er,—when all depart,
And cease to yield their sad relief;

Nor, entering in my vacant room,
Feel, in its chill and lifeless air,
As if the dampness of the tomb
And spirits of the dead were there.

Oh! welcome, though with care and pain,
The power to glad a parent's heart;
To bid a parent's joys remain,
And life's approaching ills depart.

Engraved at J. M. Butler's establishment from a Photograph

Richd H Dana

RICHARD H. DANA.

[Born 1787.]

William Dana, Esquire, was sheriff of Middlesex during the reign of Queen Elizabeth. His only descendant at that time living, Richard Dana, came to America about the middle of the seventeenth century, and settled at Cambridge, then called Newtown, near Boston. A grandson of this gentleman, of the same name, was the poet's grandfather. He was an eminent member of the bar of Massachusetts, and an active whig during the troubles in Boston immediately before the Revolution. He married a sister of Edmund Trowbridge, who was one of the king's judges, and the first lawyer in the colony. Francis Dana, the father of Richard H. Dana, after being graduated at Harvard College, studied law with his uncle, Judge Trowbridge, and became equally distinguished for his professional abilities. He was appointed envoy to Russia during the Revolution, was a member of Congress, and of the Massachusetts Convention for adopting the national constitution, and afterward Chief Justice of that Commonwealth. He married a daughter of the Honourable William Ellery, of Rhode Island, one of the signers of the Declaration of Independence, and through her the subject of this sketch is lineally descended from Anne Bradstreet, the wife of Governor Bradstreet, and daughter of Governor Dudley, who was the most celebrated poet of her time in America. Thus, it will be seen, our author has good blood in his veins: an honour which no one pretends to despise who is confident that his grandfather was not a felon or a boor.

Richard Henry Dana was born at Cambridge, on the fifteenth of November, 1787. When about ten years old he went to Newport, Rhode Island, where he remained until a year or two before he entered Harvard College. His health, during his boyhood, was too poor to admit of very constant application to study; and much of his time was passed in rambling along the rock-bound coast, listening to the roar and dashing of the waters, and searching for the wild and picturesque; indicating thus early that love of nature which is evinced in nearly all his subsequent writings, and acquiring that perfect knowledge of the scenery of the sea which is shown in the "Buccaneer," and some of his minor pieces. On leaving college, in 1807, he returned to Newport, and passed nearly two years in studying the Latin language and literature, after which he went to Baltimore, and entered as a student the law office of General Robert Goodloe Harper. The approach of the second war with Great Britain, and the extreme unpopularity of all persons known to belong to the federal party, induced him to return to Cambridge, where he finished his course of study and opened an office. He soon became a member of the legislature, and was for a time a warm partisan.

Feeble health, and great constitutional sensitiveness, the whole current of his mind and feelings, convinced him that he was unfitted for his profession, and he closed his office to assist his relative, Professor Edward T. Channing, in the management of the "North American Review," which had then been established about two years. While connected with this periodical he wrote several articles which (particularly one upon Hazlitt's British Poets) excited much attention among the literary men of Boston and Cambridge. The Pope and Queen Anne school was then triumphant, and the dicta of Jeffrey were law. Dana praised Wordsworth and Coleridge, and saw much to admire in Byron; he thought poetry was something more than a recreation; that it was something superinduced upon the realities of life; he believed the ideal and the spiritual might be as real as the visible and the tangible; thought there were truths beyond the understanding and the senses, and not to be reached by ratiocination; and indeed broached many paradoxes not to be tolerated then, but which now the same community has taken up and carried to an extent at that time unthought of.

A strong party rose against these opinions, and Dana had the whole influence of the university, of the literary and fashionable society of the city, and of the press, to contend against. Being in a minority with the "North American Club," he in 1819 or 1820 gave up all connection with the Review, which passed into the hands of the Everetts and others, and in 1821 began "The Idle Man," for which he found a publisher in Mr. Charles Wiley, of New York. This was read and admired by a class of literary men, but it was of too high a character for the period, and on the publication of the first number of the second volume, Dana received from Mr. Wiley information that he was "writing himself into debt," and gave up the work.

In 1825, he published his first poetical production, "The Dying Raven," in the "New York Review," then edited by Mr. Bryant;* and two

* While Dana was a member of the "North American Club," the poem entitled "Thanatopsis" was offered for publication in the Review. Our critic, with one or two others, read it, and concurred in the belief that it could not have been written by an American. There was a finish and completeness about it, added to the grandeur and beauty of the ideas, to which, it was supposed, none of our own writers had attained. Dana was informed, however, that the author of it was a member of the Massachusetts Senate, then in session, and he walked immediately from Cambridge to the State House in Boston to obtain a view of the remarkable man. A plain, middle-aged gentleman, with a business-like aspect, was pointed

years after gave to the public, in a small volume, "The Buccaneer, and other Poems." This was well received, the popular taste having, in the five years which had clapsed since the publication of the "Idle Man," been considerably improved; but as his publishers failed soon after it was printed, the poet was not made richer by his toil. In 1833 he published his "Poems and Prose Writings," including "The Buccaneer," and other pieces embraced in his previous volume, with some new poems, and the "Idle Man," except the few papers written for it by his friends. For this he received from his bookseller about enough to make up for the loss he had sustained by the "Idle Man." His case illustrates the usual extent of the rewards of exertion in the higher departments of literature in this country. Had his first work been successful, he would probably have been a voluminous writer.

In 1839, he delivered in Boston and New York a series of lectures on English poetry, and the great masters of the art, which were warmly applauded by the educated and judicious. These have not yet been printed.

The longest and most remarkable of DANA's poems is the "Buccaneer," a story in which he has depicted with singular power the stronger and darker passions. It is based on a tradition of a murder committed on an island on the coast of New England, by a pirate, whose guilt in the end meets with strange and terrible retribution. In attempting to compress his language he is sometimes slightly obscure, and his verse is occasionally harsh, but never feeble, never without meaning. The "Buccaneer" is followed by a poem of very different character, entitled "The Changes of Home," in which is related the affection of two young persons, in humble life, whose marriage is deferred until the lover shall have earned the means of subsistence; his departure in search of gain; his return in disappointment; his second departure, and death in absence—a sad history, and one that is too often lived. "Factitious Life," "Thoughts on the Soul," and "The Husband's and Wife's Grave," are the longest of his other poems, and, as well as his shorter pieces, they are distinguished for high religious purpose, profound philosophy, simple sentiment, and pure and vigorous diction.

All the writings of DANA belong to the permanent literature of the country. His prose and poetry will find every year more and more readers. Something resembling poetry "is oftentimes borne into instant and turbulent popularity, while a work of genuine character may be lying neglected by all except the poets. But the tide of time flows on, and the former begins to settle to the bottom, while the latter rises slowly and steadily to the surface, and goes forward, for a spirit is in it."

THE BUCCANEER.

"Boy with thy blac berd,
I rede that thou blin,
And sone set the to shrive,
With sorrow of thi syn;
Ze met with the merchandes
And made tham ful bare:
It es gude reason and right
That ze evill misfare."

LAURENCE MINOT.

THE island lies nine leagues away.
Along its solitary shore,
Of craggy rock and sandy bay,
No sound but ocean's roar,
Save, where the bold, wild sea-bird makes her home,
Her shrill cry coming through the sparkling foam.

But when the light winds lie at rest,
And on the glassy, heaving sea,
The black duck, with her glossy breast,
Sits swinging silently;
How beautiful! no ripples break the reach,
And silvery waves go noiseless up the beach.

And inland rests the green, warm dell;
The brook comes tinkling down its side;
From out the trees the Sabbath bell
Rings cheerful, far and wide,
Mingling its sound with bleatings of the flocks,
That feed about the vale among the rocks.

Nor holy bell nor pastoral bleat
In former days within the vale;
Flapp'd in the bay the pirate's sheet;
Curses were on the gale;
Rich goods lay on the sand, and murder'd men;
Pirate and wrecker kept their revels then.

But calm, low voices, words of grace,
Now slowly fall upon the ear;
A quiet look is in each face,
Subdued and holy fear:
Each motion gentle; all is kindly done—
Come, listen, how from crime this isle was won.

I.

Twelve years are gone since MATTHEW LEE
Held in this isle unquestion'd sway;
A dark, low, brawny man was he;
His law—"It is my way."
Beneath his thick-set brows a sharp light broke
From small gray eyes; his laugh a triumph spoke.

II.

Cruel of heart, and strong of arm,
Loud in his sport, and keen for spoil,
He little reck'd of good or harm,
Fierce both in mirth and toil;
Yet like a dog could fawn, if need there were:
Speak mildly, when he would, or look in fear

one to him; a single glance was sufficient; the legislator could not be the author of Thanatopsis; and he returned without seeking an introduction. A slight and natural mistake of names had misled his informant. The real author being at length discovered, a correspondence ensued; and BRYANT being invited to deliver the Phi Beta Kappa poem at Cambridge, they became personally acquainted, and a friendship sprung up which has lasted until the present time.

III.

Amid the uproar of the storm,
And by the lightning's sharp, red glare,
Were seen LEE's face and sturdy form;
His axe glanced quick in air;
Whose corpse at morn is floating in the sedge?
There's blood and hair, MAT, on thy axe's edge.

IV.

"Nay, ask him yonder; let him tell;
I make the brute, not man, my mark.
Who walks these cliffs, needs heed him well!
Last night was fearful dark.
Think ye the lashing waves will spare or feel?
An ugly gash!—These rocks—they cut like steel."

V.

He wiped his axe; and, turning round,
Said, with a cold and harden'd smile,
"The hemp is saved—the man is drown'd.
Wilt let him float a while?
Or give him Christian burial on the strand?
He'll find his fellows peaceful 'neath the sand."

VI.

LEE's waste was greater than his gain.
"I'll try the merchant's trade," he thought,
"Though less the toil to kill, than feign—
Things sweeter robb'd than bought.—
But, then, to circumvent them at their arts!"
Ship mann'd, and spoils for cargo, LEE departs.

VII.

'T is fearful, on the broad-back'd waves,
To feel them shake, and hear them roar;
Beneath, unsounded, dreadful caves:
Around, no cheerful shore.
Yet mid this solemn world what deeds are done?
The curse goes up, the deadly sea-fight's won;

VIII.

And wanton talk, and laughter heard,
Where speaks GOD's deep and awful voice.
There's awe from that lone ocean-bird;
Pray ye, when ye rejoice!
"Leave prayers to priests," cries LEE; "I'm ruler here!
These fellows know full well whom they should fear!"

IX.

The ship works hard; the seas run high;
Their white tops, flashing through the night,
Give to the eager, straining eye,
A wild and shifting light.
"Hard at the pumps!—The leak is gaining fast!
Lighten the ship!—The devil rode that blast!"

X.

Ocean has swallow'd for its food
Spoils thou didst gain in murderous glee;
MAT, could its waters wash out blood,
It had been well for thee.
Crime fits for crime. And no repentant tear
Hast thou for sin?—Then wait thine hour of fear.

XI.

The sea has like a plaything toss'd
That heavy hull the livelong night.
The man of sin—he is not lost;
Soft breaks the morning light.
Torn spars and sails—her cargo in the deep—
The ship makes port with slow and labouring sweep.

XII.

Within a Spanish port she rides.
Angry and sour'd, LEE walks her deck.
"Then peaceful trade a curse betides?—
And thou, good ship, a wreck!
Ill luck in change!—Ho! cheer ye up, my men!
Rigg'd, and at sea, we'll to old work again!"

XIII.

A sound is in the Pyrenees!
Whirling and dark, comes roaring down
A tide, as of a thousand seas,
Sweeping both cowl and crown.
On field and vineyard, thick and red it stood.
Spain's streets and palaces are wet with blood,

XIV.

And wrath and terror shake the land;
The peaks shine clear in watchfire lights;
Soon comes the tread of that stout band—
Bold ARTHUR and his knights.
Awake ye, MERLIN! Hear the shout from Spain!
The spell is broke!—ARTHUR is come again!

XV.

Too late for thee, thou young fair bride:
The lips are cold, the brow is pale,
That thou didst kiss in love and pride:
He cannot hear thy wail,
Whom thou didst lull with fondly murmur'd sound:
His couch is cold and lonely in the ground.

XVI.

He fell for Spain—her Spain no more;
For he was gone who made it dear;
And she would seek some distant shore,
At rest from strife and fear,
And wait, amid her sorrows, till the day
His voice of love should call her thence away.

XVII.

LEE feign'd him grieved, and bow'd him low
'T would joy his heart could he but aid
So good a lady in her wo,
He meekly, smoothly said.
With wealth and servants she is soon aboard,
And that white steed she rode beside her lord.

XVIII.

The sun goes down upon the sea;
The shadows gather round her home.
"How like a pall are ye to me!
My home, how like a tomb!
O! blow, ye flowers of Spain, above his head
Ye will not blow o'er me when I am dead."

XIX.

And now the stars are burning bright;
Yet still she's looking toward the shore
Beyond the waters black in night.
"I ne'er shall see thee more!
Ye're many, waves, yet lonely seems your flow;
And I'm alone—scarce know I where to go."

XX.

Sleep, sleep, thou sad one, on the sea!
The wash of waters lulls thee now;
His arm no more will pillow thee,
Thy fingers on his brow.
He is not near, to hush thee, or to save.
The ground is his—the sea must be thy grave.

XXI.

The moon comes up; the night goes on.
Why, in the shadow of the mast,
Stands that dark, thoughtful man alone?
Thy pledge, man: keep it fast!
Bethink thee of her youth and sorrows, LEE;
Helpless, alone—and, then, her trust in thee.

XXII.

When told the hardships thou hadst borne,
Her words to thee were like a charm.
With uncheer'd grief her heart is worn;
Thou wilt not do her harm!
He looks out on the sea that sleeps in light,
And growls an oath—"It is too still to-night!"

XXIII.

He sleeps; but dreams of massy gold,
And heaps of pearl. He stretch'd his hands.
He hears a voice—"Ill man, withhold!"
A pale one near him stands.
Her breath comes deathly cold upon his cheek;
Her touch is cold.—He wakes with piercing shriek.

XXIV.

He wakes; but no relentings wake
Within his angry, restless soul.
"What, shall a dream MAT's purpose shake?
The gold will make all whole.
Thy merchant trade had nigh unmann'd thee, lad!
What, balk my chance because a woman's sad!"

XXV.

He cannot look on her mild eye;
Her patient words his spirit quell.
Within that evil heart there lie
The hates and fears of hell.
His speech is short; he wears a surly brow.
There's none will hear her shriek. What fear ye now?

XXVI.

The workings of the soul ye fear;
Ye fear the power that goodness hath;
Ye fear the Unseen One, ever near,
Walking his ocean path.
From out the silent void there comes a cry—
"Vengeance is mine! Thou, murderer, too, shalt die!"

XXVII.

Nor dread of ever-during wo,
Nor the sea's awful solitude,
Can make thee, wretch, thy crime forego.
Then, bloody hand,—to blood!
The scud is driving wildly overhead;
The stars burn dim; the ocean moans its dead.

XXVIII.

Moan for the living; moan our sins,—
The wrath of man, more fierce than thine.
Hark! still thy waves!—The work begins—
LEE makes the deadly sign.
The crew glide down like shadows. Eye and hand
Speak fearful meanings through that silent band.

XXIX.

They're gone.—The helmsman stands alone:
And one leans idly o'er the bow.
Still as a tomb the ship keeps on;
Nor sound nor stirring now.
Hush, hark! as from the centre of the deep—
Shrieks—fiendish yells! They stab them in their sleep!

XXX.

The scream of rage, the groan, the strife,
The blow, the gasp, the horrid cry,
The panting, throttled prayer for life,
The dying's heaving sigh,
The murderer's curse, the dead man's fix'd, still glare,
And fear's and death's cold sweat—they all are there!

XXXI.

On pale, dead men, on burning cheek,
On quick, fierce eyes, brows hot and damp,
On hands that with the warm blood reek,
Shines the dim cabin lamp.
LEE look'd. "They sleep so sound," he, laughing, said,
"They'll scarcely wake for mistress or for maid."

XXXII.

A crash! They've forced the door,—and then
One long, long, shrill, and piercing scream
Comes thrilling through the growl of men.
'T is hers!—O GOD, redeem
From worse than death, thy suffering, helpless child!
That dreadful shriek again—sharp, sharp, and wild!

XXXIII.

It ceased.—With speed o' th' lightning's flash,
A loose-robed form, with streaming hair,
Shoots by.—A leap—a quick, short splash!
'T is gone!—There's nothing there!
The waves have swept away the bubbling tide.
Bright-crested waves, how calmly on they ride!

XXXIV.

She's sleeping in her silent cave.
Nor hears the stern, loud roar above,
Nor strife of man on land or wave.
Young thing! her home of love
She soon has reach'd—Fair, unpolluted thing.
They harm'd her not—Was dying suffering?

XXXV.

O, no!—To live when joy was dead;
To go with one lone, pining thought—
To mournful love her being wed—
Feeling what death had wrought;
To live the child of wo, yet shed no tear,
Bear kindness, and yet share no joy nor fear;

XXXVI.

To look on man, and deem it strange
That he on things of earth should brood,
When all its throng'd and busy range
To her was solitude—
O, this was bitterness! Death came and press'd
Her wearied lids, and brought her sick heart rest.

XXXVII.

Why look ye on each other so,
And speak no word?—Ay, shake the head.
She's gone where ye can never go,
What fear ye from the dead?
They tell no tales; and ye are all true men;
But wash away that blood; then, home again!—

XXXVIII.

'T is on your souls; it will not out!
Lee, why so lost? 'T is not like thee!
Come, where thy revel, oath, and shout?
"That pale one in the sea!—
I mind not blood.—But she—I cannot tell!
A spirit was 't?—it flash'd like fires of hell!—

XXXIX.

"And when it pass'd there was no tread!
It leap'd the deck.—Who heard the sound?
I heard none!—Say, what was it fled?—
Poor girl!—And is she drown'd?—
Went down these depths! How dark they look, and cold!
She's yonder! stop her!—Now!—there!—hold her, hold!"

XL.

They gazed upon his ghastly face.
"What ails thee, Lee; and why that glare?"
"Look! ha, 'tis gone, and not a trace!
No, no, she was not there!—
Who of you said ye heard her when she fell?
'Twas strange—I'll not be fool'd—Will no one tell?"

XLI.

He paused. And soon the wildness pass'd.
Then came the tingling flush of shame.
Remorse and fear are gone as fast.
"The silly thing's to blame
To quit us so. 'Tis plain she loved us not;
Or she'd have stay'd a while, and shared my cot."

XLII.

And then the ribald laugh'd. The jest,
Though old and foul, loud laughter drew;
And fouler yet came from the rest
Of that infernal crew.
Note, heaven, their blasphemy, their broken trust!
Lust panders murder—murder panders lust!

XLIII.

Now slowly up they bring the dead
From out that silent, dim-lit room.
No prayer at their quick burial said;
No friend to weep their doom.
The hungry waves have seized them one by one
And, swallowing down their prey, go roaring on.

XLIV.

Cries Lee, "We must not be betray'd.
'T is but to add another corse!
Strange words, 't is said, an ass once bray'd:
I'll never trust a horse!
Out! throw him on the waves alive! He'll swim
For once a horse shall ride; we all ride him."

XLV.

Such sound to mortal ear ne'er came
As rang far o'er the waters wide.
It shook with fear the stoutest frame:
The horse is on the tide!
As the waves leave, or lift him up, his cry
Comes lower now, and now 't is near and high.

XLVI.

And through the swift wave's yesty crown
His scared eyes shoot a fiendish light,
And fear seems wrath. He now sinks down.
Now heaves again to sight,
Then drifts away; and through the night they hear
Far off that dreadful cry.—But morn is near.

XLVII.

O hadst thou known what deeds were done,
When thou wast shining far away,
Would'st thou let fall, calm-coming sun,
Thy warm and silent ray?
The good are in their graves; thou canst not cheer
Their dark, cold mansions: Sin alone is here.

XLVIII.

"The deed's complete! The gold is ours!
There, wash away that bloody stain!
Pray, who'd refuse what fortune showers?
Now, lads, we'll lot our gain.
Must fairly share, you know, what's fairly got!
A truly good night's work! Who says 't was not?"

XLIX.

There's song, and oath, and gaming deep,
Hot words, and laughter, mad carouse;
There's naught of prayer, and little sleep:
The devil keeps the house!
"Lee cheats!" cried Jack. Lee struck him to the heart.
"That's foul!" one mutter'd.—"Fool! you take your part!—

L.

"The fewer heirs the richer, man!
Hold forth thy palm, and keep thy prate!
Our life, we read, is but a span.
What matters, soon or late?"
And when on shore, and asked, Did many die?
"Near half my crew, poor lads!" he'd say, and sigh

LI.

Within our bay, one stormy night,
The isle-men saw boats make for shore,
With here and there a dancing light,
That flash'd on man and oar.
When hail'd, the rowing stopp'd, and all was dark.
"Ha! lantern-work!—We'll home! They're playing shark!"

LII.

Next day, at noontime, toward the town,
All stared and wonder'd much to see
MAT and his men come strolling down.
The boys shout, "Here comes LEE!"
"Thy ship, good LEE?" "Not many leagues from shore
Our ship by chance took fire."—They learn'd no more.

LIII.

He and his crew were flush of gold.
"You did not lose your cargo, then?"
"Learn, where all's fairly bought and sold,
Heaven prospers those true men.
Forsake your evil ways, as we forsook
Our ways of sin, and honest courses took!

LIV.

"Wouldst see my log-book? Fairly writ
With pen of steel, and ink of blood!
How lightly doth the conscience sit!
Learn, truth's the only good."
And thus, with flout, and cold and impious jeer,
He fled repentance, if he 'scaped not fear.

LV.

Remorse and fear he drowns in drink.
"Come, pass the bowl, my jolly crew!
It thicks the blood to mope and think.
Here's merry days, though few!"
And then he quaffs.—So riot reigns within;
So brawl and laughter shake that house of sin.

LVI.

MAT lords it now throughout the isle.
His hand falls heavier than before.
All dread alike his frown or smile.
None come within his door,
Save those who dipp'd their hands in blood with him;
Save those who laugh'd to see the white horse swim.

LVII.

"To-night's our anniversary;
And, mind me, lads, we'll have it kept
With royal state and special glee!
Better with those who slept
Their sleep that night, had he be now, who slinks
And health and wealth to him who bravely drinks!"

LVIII.

The words they speak, we may not speak.
The tales they tell, we may not tell.
Mere mortal man, forbear to seek
The secrets of that hell!
Their shouts grow loud:—'Tis near mid-hour of night:
What means upon the waters that red light?

LIX.

Not bigger than a star it seems:
And, now, 'tis like the bloody moon:
And, now, it shoots in hairy streams
Its light!—'twill reach us soon!
A ship! and all on fire!—hull, yards, and mast!
Her sheets are sheets of flame!—She's nearing fast.

LX.

And now she rides, upright and still,
Shedding a wild and lurid light
Around the cove, on inland hill,
Waking the gloom of night.
All breathes of terror! men, in dumb amaze,
Gaze on each other 'neath the horrid blaze.

LXI.

It scares the sea-birds from their nests;
They dart and wheel with deafening screams;
Now dark—and now their wings and breasts
Flash back disastrous gleams.
O, sin, what hast thou done on this fair earth?
The world, O man, is wailing o'er thy birth.

LXII.

And what comes up above the wave,
So ghastly white?—A spectral head!—
A horse's head!—(May Heaven save
Those looking on the dead—
The waking dead!) There, on the sea, he stands—
The Spectre-Horse!—He moves; he gains the sands!

LXIII.

Onward he speeds. His ghostly sides
Are streaming with a cold, blue light.
Heaven keep the wits of him who rides
The Spectre-Horse to-night!
His path is shining like a swift ship's wake;
Before LEE's door he gleams like day's gray break.

LXIV.

The revel now is high within;
It breaks upon the midnight air.
They little think, mid mirth and din,
What spirit waits them there.
As if the sky became a voice, there spread
A sound to appal the living, stir the dead.

LXV.

The spirit-steed sent up the neigh.
It seem'd the living trump of hell,
Sounding to call the damn'd away,
To join the host that fell.
It rang along the vaulted sky: the shore
Jarr'd hard, as when the thronging surges roar

LXVI.

It rang in ears that knew the sound;
And hot, flush'd cheeks are blanch'd with fear,
And why does LEE look wildly round?
Thinks he the drown'd horse near?
He drops his cup—his lips are stiff with fright.
Nay, sit thee down! It is thy banquet night.

LXVII.

"I cannot sit. I needs must go:
The spell is on my spirit now.
I go to dread—I go to wo!"
O, who so weak as thou,
Strong man!—His hoof upon the door-stone, see,
The shadow stands!—His eyes are on thee, LEE!—

LXVIII.

Thy hair pricks up!—"O, I must bear
His damp, cold breath! It chills my frame!
His eyes—their near and dreadful glare
Speak that I must not name!"
Thou 'rt mad to mount that horse!—"A power within,
I must obey—cries, 'Mount thee, man of sin!'"

LXIX.

He's now upon the spectre's back,
With rein of silk, and curb of gold.
'Tis fearful speed!—the rein is slack
Within his senseless hold;
Upborne by an unseen power, he onward rides,
Yet touches not the shadow-beast he strides.

LXX.

He goes with speed; he goes with dread!
And now they're on the hanging steep!
And, now! the living and the dead,
They'll make the horrid leap!
The horse stops short:—his feet are on the verge.
He stands, like marble, high above the surge.

LXXI.

And, nigh, the tall ship yet burns on,
With red, hot spars, and crackling flame.
From hull to gallant, nothing's gone.
She burns, and yet's the same!
Her hot, red flame is beating, all the night,
On man and horse, in their cold, phosphor light.

LXXII.

Through that cold light the fearful man
Sits looking on the burning ship.
He ne'er again will curse and ban.
How fast he moves the lip!
And yet he does not speak, or make a sound!
What see you, LEE? the bodies of the drown'd?

LXXIII.

"I look, where mortal man may not—
Into the chambers of the deep.
I see the dead, long, long forgot;
I see them in their sleep.
A dreadful power is mine, which none can know,
Save he who leagues his soul with death and wo."

LXXIV.

Thou mild, sad mother—waning moon,
Thy last, low, melancholy ray
Shines toward him. Quit him not so soon!
Mother, in mercy, stay!
Despair and death are with him; and canst thou,
With that kind, earthward look, go leave him now?

LXXV.

O, thou wast born for things of love;
Making more lovely in thy shine
Whate'er thou look'st on. Hosts above,
In that soft light of thine,
Burn softer:—earth, in silvery veil, seems heaven
Thou 'rt going down!—hast left him unforgiven!

LXXVI.

The far, low west is bright no more.
How still it is! No sound is heard
At sea, or all along the shore,
But cry of passing bird.
Thou living thing—and dar'st thou come so near
These wild and ghastly shapes of death and fear?

LXXVII.

Now long that thick, red light has shone
On stern, dark rocks, and deep, still bay,
On man and horse, that seem of stone,
So motionless are they.
But now its lurid fire less fiercely burns:
The night is going—faint, gray dawn returns.

LXXVIII.

That spectre-steed now slowly pales;
Now changes like the moonlit cloud;
That cold, thin light, now slowly fails.
Which wrapp'd them like a shroud.
Both ship and horse are fading into air.—
Lost, mazed, alone—see, LEE is standing there!

LXXIX.

The morning air blows fresh on him:
The waves dance gladly in his sight;
The sea-birds call, and wheel, and skim—
O, blessed morning light!
He doth not hear their joyous call; he sees
No beauty in the wave; nor feels the breeze.

LXXX.

For he's accursed from all that's good;
He ne'er must know its healing power;
The sinner on his sins must brood,
And wait, alone, his hour.
A stranger to earth's beauty—human love;
There's here no rest for him, no hope above!

LXXXI.

The hot sun beats upon his head;
He stands beneath its broad, fierce blaze,
As stiff and cold as one that's dead:
A troubled, dreamy maze
Of some unearthly horror, all he knows—
Of some wild horror past, and coming woes.

LXXXII.

The gull has found her place on shore;
The sun gone down again to rest;
And all is still but ocean's roar:
There stands the man unbless'd.
But, see, he moves—he turns, as asking where
His mates!—Why looks he with that piteous stare?

LXXXIII.

Go, get thee home, and end thy mirth!
Go, call the revellers again!
They 're fled the isle; and o'er the earth
Are wanderers like Cain.
As he his door-stone pass'd, the air blew chill.
The wine is on the board; Lee, take thy fill!

LXXXIV.

"There's none to meet me, none to cheer;
The seats are empty—lights burnt out;
And I, alone, must sit me here:
Would I could hear their shout!"
He ne'er shall hear it more—more taste his wine!
Silent he sits within the still moonshine.

LXXXV.

Day came again; and up he rose,
A weary man from his lone board;
Nor merry feast, nor sweet repose
Did that long night afford.
No shadowy-coming night, to bring him rest—
No dawn, to chase the darkness of his breast!

LXXXVI.

He walks within the day's full glare
A darken'd man. Where'er he comes,
All shun him. Children peep and stare;
Then, frighten'd, seek their homes.
Through all the crowd a thrilling horror ran.
They point, and say,—"There goes the wicked man!"

LXXXVII.

He turns and curses in his wrath
Both man and child; then hastes away
Shoreward, or takes some gloomy path;
But there he cannot stay:
Terror and madness drive him back to men;
His hate of man to solitude again.

LXXXVIII.

Time passes on, and he grows bold—
His eye is fierce, his oaths are loud;
None dare from Lee the hand withhold;
He rules and scoffs the crowd.
But still at heart there lies a secret fear;
For now the year's dread round is drawing near.

LXXXIX.

He swears, but he is sick at heart;
He laughs, but he turns deadly pale;
His restless eye and sudden start—
These tell the dreadful tale
That will be told: it needs no words from thee,
Thou self-sold slave to fear and misery.

XC.

Bond-slave of sin, see there—that light!
"Ha! take me—take me from its blaze!"
Nay, thou must ride the steed to-night!
But other weary days
And nights must shine and darken o'er thy head,
Ere thou shalt go with him to meet the dead

XCI.

Again the ship lights all the land;
Again Lee strides the spectre-beast;
Again upon the cliff they stand.
This once he 'll be released!—
Gone horse and ship; but Lee's last hope is o'er;
Nor laugh, nor scoff, nor rage can help him more.

XCII.

His spirit heard that spirit say,
"Listen!—I twice have come to thee.
Once more—and then a dreadful way!
And thou must go with me!"
Ay, cling to earth, as sailor to the rock!
Sea-swept, suck'd down in the tremendous shock.

XCIII.

He goes!—So thou must loose thy hold,
And go with Death; nor breathe the balm
Of early air, nor light behold,
Nor sit thee in the calm
Of gentle thoughts, where good men wait their close.
In life, or death, where look'st thou for repose?

XCIV.

Who's sitting on that long, black ledge,
Which makes so far out in the sea;
Feeling the kelp-weed on its edge?
Poor, idle Matthew Lee!
So weak and pale? A year and little more,
And bravely did he lord it round this shore!

XCV.

And on the shingles now he sits,
And rolls the pebbles 'neath his hands,
Now walks the beach; then stops by fits,
And scores the smooth, wet sands;
Then tries each cliff, and cove, and jut, that bounds
The isle; then home from many weary rounds.

XCVI.

They ask him why he wanders so,
From day to day, the uneven strand?
"I wish, I wish that I might go!
But I would go by land;
And there's no way that I can find—I 've tried
All day and night!"—He seaward look'd, and sigh'd.

XCVII.

It brought the tear to many an eye
That, once, his eye had made to quail.
"Lee, go with us; our sloop is nigh;
Come! help us hoist her sail."
He shook. "You know the spirit-horse I ride!
He 'll let me on the sea with none beside!"

XCVIII.

He views the ships that come and go,
Looking so like to living things.
O! 't is a proud and gallant show
Of bright and broad-spread wings,
Making it light around them as they keep
Their course right onward through the unsounded deep.

XCIX.

And where the far-off sand-bars lift
Their backs in long and narrow line,
The breakers shout, and leap, and shift,
And send the sparkling brine
Into the air; then rush to mimic strife—
Glad creatures of the sea, and full of life—

C.

But not to Lee. He sits alone;
No fellowship nor joy for him.
Borne down by wo, he makes no moan,
Though tears will sometimes dim
That asking eye. O, how his worn thoughts crave—
Not joy again, but rest within the grave.

CI.

The rocks are dripping in the mist
That lies so heavy off the shore;
Scarce seen the running breakers;—list
Their dull and smother'd roar!
Lee hearkens to their voice.—"I hear, I hear
Your call.—Not yet!—I know my time is near!"

CII.

And now the mist seems taking shape,
Forming a dim, gigantic ghost,—
Enormous thing!—There 's no escape;
'T is close upon the coast.
Lee kneels, but cannot pray.—Why mock him so?
The ship has clear'd the fog, Lee, see her go!

CIII.

A sweet, low voice, in starry nights,
Chants to his ear a plaining song;
Its tones come winding up the heights,
Telling of wo and wrong;
And he must listen, till the stars grow dim,
The song that gentle voice doth sing to him.

CIV.

O, it is sad that aught so mild
Should bind the soul with bands of fear;
That strains to soothe a little child,
The man should dread to hear!
But sin hath broke the world's sweet peace—unstrung
The harmonious chords to which the angels sung.

CV.

In thick, dark nights he 'd take his seat
High up the cliffs, and feel them shake,
As swung the sea with heavy beat
Below—and hear it break
With savage roar, then pause and gather strength,
And then, come tumbling in its swollen length.

CVI.

But he no more shall haunt the beach,
Nor sit upon the tall cliff's crown,
Nor go the round of all that reach,
Nor feebly sit him down,
Watching the swaying weeds:—another day,
And he 'll have gone far hence that dreadful way.

CVII.

To-night the charmed number 's told.
"Twice have I come for thee," it said.
"Once more, and none shall thee behold.
Come! live one, to the dead!"—
So hears his soul, and fears the coming night;
Yet sick and weary of the soft, calm light.

CVIII.

Again he sits within that room:
All day he leans at that still board;
None to bring comfort to his gloom,
Or speak a friendly word.
Weaken'd with fear, lone, haunted by remorse,
Poor, shatter'd wretch, there waits he that pale horse.

CIX.

Not long he waits. Where now are gone
Peak, citadel, and tower, that stood
Beautiful, while the west sun shone
And bathed them in his flood
Of airy glory?—Sudden darkness fell;
And down they went, peak, tower, citadel.

CX.

The darkness, like a dome of stone,
Ceils up the heavens.—'T is hush as death—
All but the ocean's dull, low moan.
How hard Lee draws his breath!
He shudders as he feels the working Power.
Arouse thee, Lee! up! man thee for thine hour!

CXI.

'T is close at hand; for there, once more,
The burning ship. Wide sheets of flame
And shafts of fire she show'd before;—
Twice thus she hither came;—
But now she rolls a naked hulk, and throws
A wasting light! then, settling, down she goes.

CXII.

And where she sank, up slowly came
The Spectre-Horse from out the sea.
And there he stands! His pale sides flame.
He 'll meet thee shortly, Lee.
He treads the waters as a solid floor;
He 's moving on. Lee waits him at the door.

CXIII.

They 're met.—"I know thou comest for me,
Lee's spirit to the spectre said;
"I know that I must go with thee—
Take me not to the dead.
It was not I alone that did the deed!"
Dreadful the eye of that still, spectral steed.

CXIV.

Lee cannot turn. There is a force
In that fix'd eye, which holds him fast.
How still they stand!—the man and horse.
"Thine hour is almost past."
"O, spare me," cries the wretch, "thou fearful one!"
"My time is full—I must not go alone."

CXV.

"I'm weak and faint. O, let me stay!"
"Nay, murderer, rest nor stay for thee!"
The horse and man are on their way;
He bears him to the sea.
Hark! how the spectre breathes through this still night.
See, from his nostrils streams a deathly light!

CXVI.

He's on the beach; but stops not there;
He's on the sea!—that dreadful horse!
Lee flings and writhes in wild despair!—
In vain! The spirit-corse
Holds him by fearful spell;—he cannot leap.
Within that horrid light he rides the deep.

CXVII.

It lights the sea around their track—
The curling comb, and dark steel wave;
There, yet, sits Lee the spectre's back—
Gone! gone! and none to save!
They're seen no more; the night has shut them in.
May Heaven have pity on thee, man of sin!

CXVIII.

The earth has wash'd away its stain;
The sealed-up sky is breaking forth,
Mustering its glorious hosts again,
From the far south and north;
The climbing moon plays on the rippling sea.
—O, whither on its waters rideth Lee?

THE OCEAN.*

Now stretch your eye off shore, o'er waters made
To cleanse the air and bear the world's great trade,
To rise, and wet the mountains near the sun,
Then back into themselves in rivers run,
Fulfilling mighty uses far and wide,
Through earth, in air, or here, as ocean-tide.
Ho! how the giant heaves himself, and strains
And flings to break his strong and viewless chains;
Foams in his wrath; and at his prison doors,
Hark! hear him! how he beats and tugs and roars,
As if he would break forth again and sweep
Each living thing within his lowest deep.
Type of the Infinite! I look away
Over thy billows, and I cannot stay
My thought upon a resting-place, or make
A shore beyond my vision, where they break;
But on my spirit stretches, till it's pain
To think; then rests, and then puts forth again.
Thou hold'st me by a spell; and on thy beach
I feel all soul; and thoughts unmeasured reach
Far back beyond all date. And, O! how old
Thou art to me. For countless years thou hast roll'd.
Before an ear did hear thee, thou didst mourn,
Prophet of sorrows, o'er a race unborn;
Waiting, thou mighty minister of death,
Lonely thy work, ere man had drawn his breath.
At last thou didst it well! The dread command
Came, and thou swept'st to death the breathing land;
And then once more, unto the silent heaven
Thy lone and melancholy voice was given.
And though the land is throng'd again, O Sea!
Strange sadness touches all that goes with thee.
The small bird's plaining note, the wild, sharp call,
Share thy own spirit: it is sadness all!
How dark and stern upon thy waves looks down
Yonder tall cliff—he with the iron crown.
And see! those sable pines along the steep,
Are come to join thy requiem, gloomy deep!
Like stoled monks they stand and chant the dirge
Over the dead, with thy low beating surge.

* From "Factitious Life."

DAYBREAK.

"The Pilgrim they laid in a large upper chamber, whose window opened towards the sun-rising: the name of the chamber was Peace; where he slept till break of day, and then he awoke and sang."—*The Pilgrim's Progress.*

Now, brighter than the host that all night long,
In fiery armour, far up in the sky
Stood watch, thou comest to wait the morning's song,
Thou comest to tell me day again is nigh,
Star of the dawning! Cheerful is thine eye;
And yet in the broad day it must grow dim.
Thou seem'st to look on me, as asking why
My mourning eyes with silent tears do swim;
Thou bid'st me turn to God, and seek my rest in Him.

Canst thou grow sad, thou say'st, as earth grows bright?
And sigh, when little birds begin discourse
In quick, low voices, ere the streaming light
Pours on their nests, from out the day's fresh source?
With creatures innocent thou must perforce
A sharer be, if that thine heart be pure.
And holy hour like this, save sharp remorse,
Of ills and pains of life must be the cure,
And breathe in kindred calm, and teach thee to endure.

I feel its calm. But there's a sombrous hue,
Edging that eastern cloud, of deep, dull red;
Nor glitters yet the cold and heavy dew;
And all the woods and hill-tops stand outspread
With dusky lights, which warmth nor comfort shed.
Still—save the bird that scarcely lifts its song—
The vast world seems the tomb of all the dead—
The silent city emptied of its throng,
And ended, all alike, grief, mirth, love, hate, and wrong.

But wrong, and hate, and love, and grief, and mirth
Will quicken soon; and hard, hot toil and strife,
With headlong purpose, shake this sleeping earth
With discord strange, and all that man calls life.
With thousand scatter'd beauties nature's rife;

And airs and woods and streams breathe harmonies:
Man weds not these, but taketh art to wife;
Nor binds his heart with soft and kindly ties:—
He, feverish, blinded, lives, and, feverish, sated, dies.

It is because man useth so amiss
Her dearest blessings, Nature seemeth sad;
Else why should she in such fresh hour as this
Not lift the veil, in revelation glad,
From her fair face?—It is that man is mad!
Then chide me not, clear star, that I repine
When nature grieves; nor deem this heart is bad.
Thou look'st toward earth; but yet the heavens are thine;
While I to earth am bound:—When will the heavens be mine?

If man would but his finer nature learn,
And not in life fantastic lose the sense
Of simpler things; could nature's features stern
Teach him be thoughtful, then, with soul intense
I should not yearn for God to take me hence,
But bear my lot, albeit in spirit bow'd,
Remembering humbly why it is, and whence:
But when I see cold man of reason proud,
My solitude is sad—I'm lonely in the crowd.

But not for this alone, the silent tear
Steals to mine eyes, while looking on the morn,
Nor for this solemn hour: fresh life is near;—
But all my joys!—they died when newly born.
Thousands will wake to joy; while I, forlorn,
And like the stricken deer, with sickly eye
Shall see them pass. Breathe calm—my spirit's torn;
Ye holy thoughts, lift up my soul on high!—
Ye hopes of things unseen, the far-off world bring nigh.

And when I grieve, O, rather let it be
That I—whom nature taught to sit with her
On her proud mountains, by her rolling sea—
Who, when the winds are up, with mighty stir
Of woods and waters—feel the quickening spur
To my strong spirit;—who, as my own child,
Do love the flower, and in the ragged bur
A beauty see—that I this mother mild
Should leave, and go with care, and passions fierce and wild!

How suddenly that straight and glittering shaft
Shot 'thwart the earth! In crown of living fire
Up comes the day! As if they conscious quaff'd—
The sunny flood, hill, forest, city spire
Laugh in the wakening light.—Go, vain desire!
The dusky lights are gone; go thou thy way!
And pining discontent, like them, expire!
Be call'd my chamber, PEACE, when ends the day;
And let me with the dawn, like PILGRIM, sing and pray.

INTIMATIONS OF IMMORTALITY.*

O, LISTEN, man!
A voice within us speaks the startling word,
"Man, thou shalt never die!" Celestial voices
Hymn it around our souls: according harps,
By angel fingers touch'd when the mild stars
Of morning sang together, sound forth still
The song of our great immortality!
Thick, clustering orbs, and this our fair domain,
The tall, dark mountains, and the deep-toned seas,
Join in this solemn, universal song.
—O, listen, ye, our spirits! drink it in
From all the air! 'T is in the gentle moonlight;
'T is floating in day's setting glories; night,
Wrapp'd in her sable robe, with silent step
Comes to our bed and breathes it in our ears;
Night and the dawn, bright day and thoughtful eve,
All time, all bounds, the limitless expanse,
As one vast, mystic instrument, are touch'd
By an unseen, living Hand, and conscious chords
Quiver with joy in this great jubilee:
—The dying hear it; and as sounds of earth
Grow dull and distant, wake their passing souls
To mingle in this heavenly harmony.

* From the "Husband's and Wife's Grave."

THE LITTLE BEACH-BIRD.

I.

Thou little bird, thou dweller by the sea,
Why takest thou its melancholy voice?
And with that boding cry
O'er the waves dost thou fly?
O! rather, bird, with me
Through the fair land rejoice!

II.

Thy flitting form comes ghostly dim and pale,
As driven by a beating storm at sea;
Thy cry is weak and scared,
As if thy mates had shared
The doom of us: Thy wail—
What does it bring to me?

III.

Thou call'st along the sand, and haunt'st the surge,
Restless and sad: as if, in strange accord
With the motion and the roar
Of waves that drive to shore,
One spirit did ye urge—
The Mystery—the Word.

IV.

Of thousands, thou both sepulchre and pall,
Old ocean, art! A requiem o'er the dead,
From out thy gloomy cells
A tale of mourning tells—
Tells of man's wo and fall,
His sinless glory fled.

V.

Then turn thee, little bird, and take thy flight
Where the complaining sea shall sadness bring
Thy spirit never more.
Come, quit with me the shore,
For gladness and the light
Where birds of summer sing.

THE MOSS SUPPLICATETH FOR THE POET.

Though I am humble, slight me not,
But love me for the Poet's sake;
Forget me not till he's forgot;
I, care or slight, with him would take.

For oft he pass'd the blossoms by,
And gazed on me with kindly look;
Left flaunting flowers and open sky,
And woo'd me by the shady brook.

And like the brook his voice was low:
So soft, so sad the words he spoke,
That with the stream they seem'd to flow:
They told me that his heart was broke;—

They said, the world he fain would shun,
And seek the still and twilight wood—
His spirit, weary of the sun,
In humblest things found chiefest good;—

That I was of a lowly frame,
And far more constant than the flower,
Which, vain with many a boastful name,
But flutter'd out its idle hour;

That I was kind to old decay,
And wrapt it softly round in green,
On naked root and trunk of gray
Spread out a garniture and screen:—

They said, that he was withering fast,
Without a sheltering friend like me;
That on his manhood fell a blast,
And left him bare, like yonder tree;

That spring would clothe *his* boughs no more,
Nor ring his boughs with song of bird—
Sounds like the melancholy shore
Alone were through his branches heard.

Methought, as then, he stood to trace
The wither'd stems, there stole a tear—
That I could read in his sad face,
Brother, our sorrows make us near.

And then he stretch'd him all along,
And laid his head upon my breast,
Listening the water's peaceful song,—
How glad was I to tend his rest!

Then happier grew his soothed soul.
He turn'd and watch'd the sunlight play
Upon my face, as in it stole,
Whispering, Above is brighter day!

He praised my varied hues—the green,
The silver hoar, the golden, brown;
Said, Lovelier hues were never seen:
Then gently press'd my tender down.

And where I sent up little shoots,
He call'd them trees, in fond conceit:
Like silly lovers in their suits
He talk'd, his care awhile to cheat.

I said, I'd deck me in the dews,
Could I but chase away his care,
And clothe me in a thousand hues,
To bring him joys that I might share.

He answer'd, earth no blessing had
To cure his lone and aching heart—
That I was one, when he was sad,
Oft stole him from his pain, in part.

But e'en from thee, he said, I go,
To meet the world, its care and strife,
No more to watch this quiet flow,
Or spend with thee a gentle life.

And yet the brook is gliding on,
And I, without a care, at rest,
While back to toiling life he's gone,
Where finds his head no faithful breast.

Deal gently with him, world, I pray;
Ye cares, like soften'd shadows come;
His spirit, wellnigh worn away,
Asks with ye but awhile a home.

Oh, may I live, and when he dies
Be at his feet an humble sod;
Oh, may I lay me where he lies,
To die when he awakes in God!

WASHINGTON ALLSTON.

I look through tears on Beauty now;
And Beauty's self, less radiant, looks on me,
Serene, yet touch'd with sadness is the brow
(Once bright with joy) I see.

Joy-waking Beauty, why so sad?
Tell where the radiance of the smile is gone
At which my heart and earth and skies were glad—
That link'd us all in one.

It is not on the mountain's breast;
It comes not to me with the dawning day;
Nor looks it from the glories of the west,
As slow they pass away.

Nor on those gliding roundlets bright
That steal their play among the woody shades,
Nor on thine own dear children doth it light—
The flowers along the glades.

And alter'd to the living mind
(The great high-priestess with her thought-born race
Who round thine altar aye have stood and shined)
The comforts of thy face.

Why shadow'd thus thy forehead fair?
Why on the mind low hangs a mystic gloom?
And spreads away upon the genial air,
Like vapours from the tomb?

Why *should* ye shine, you lights above?
Why, little flowers, open to the heat?
No more within the heart ye filled with love
The living pulses beat.

Well, Beauty, may you mourning stand!
The fine beholding eye whose constant look
Was turn'd on thee is dark—and cold the hand
That gave all vision took.

Nay, heart, be still!—Of heavenly birth
Is Beauty sprung.—Look up! behold the place!
There he who reverent traced her steps on earth
Now sees her face to face.

RICHARD HENRY WILDE.

[Born, 1789. Died, 1847.]

The family of the late Mr. Wilde are of Saxon origin, and their ancient name was De Wilde; but his parents were natives of Dublin, and his father was a wholesale hardware merchant and ironmonger in that city during the American war; near the close of which he emigrated to Maryland, leaving a prosperous business and a large capital in the hands of a partner, by whose bad management they were in a few years both lost.

Richard Henry Wilde was born in the year 1789, and his childhood was passed in Baltimore. He was taught to read by his mother, and received instruction in writing and Latin grammar from a private tutor until he was about seven years old. He afterward attended an academy; but his father's affairs becoming embarrassed, in his eleventh year he was taken home and placed in a store. His constitution was at first tender and delicate. In his infancy he was not expected to live from month to month, and he suffered much from ill health until he was fifteen or sixteen. This induced quiet, retiring, solitary, and studious habits. His mother's example gave him a passion for reading, and all his leisure was devoted to books. The study of poetry was his principal source of pleasure, when he was not more than twelve years old.

About this time his father died; and gathering as much as she could from the wreck of his property, his mother removed to Augusta, Georgia, and commenced there a small business for the support of her family. Here young Wilde, amid the drudgery of trade, taught himself book-keeping, and became familiar with the works in general literature which he could obtain in the meagre libraries of the town, or from his personal friends.

The expenses of a large family, and various other causes, reduced the little wealth of his mother; her business became unprofitable, and he resolved to study law. Unable, however, to pay the usual fee for instruction, he kept his design a secret, as far as possible; borrowed some elementary books from his friends, and studied incessantly, tasking himself to read fifty pages, and write five pages of notes, in the form of questions and answers, each day, besides attending to his duties in the store. And, to overcome a natural diffidence, increased by a slight impediment in his speech, he appeared frequently as an actor at a dramatic society, which he had called into existence for this purpose, and to raise a fund to establish a public library.

All this time his older and graver acquaintances, who knew nothing of his designs, naturally confounded him with his thoughtless companions, who sought only amusement, and argued badly of his future life. He bore the injustice in silence, and pursued his secret studies for a year and a half; at the end of which, pale, emaciated, feeble, and with a consumptive cough, he sought a distant court to be examined, that, if rejected, the news of his defeat might not reach his mother. When he arrived, he found he had been wrongly informed, and that the judges had no power to admit him. He met a friend there, however, who was going to the Greene Superior Court; and, on being invited by him to do so, he determined to proceed immediately to that place. It was the March term, for 1809, Mr. Justice Early presiding; and the young applicant, totally unknown to every one, save the friend who accompanied him, was at intervals, during three days, subjected to a most rigorous examination. Justice Early was well known for his strictness, and the circumstance of a youth leaving his own circuit excited his suspicion; but every question was answered to the satisfaction and even admiration of the examining committee; and he declared that "the young man could not have left his circuit because he was unprepared." His friend certified to the correctness of his moral character; he was admitted without a dissenting voice, and returned in triumph to Augusta. He was at this time under twenty years of age.

His health gradually improved; he applied himself diligently to the study of belles letters, and to his duties as an advocate, and rapidly rose to eminence; being in a few years made attorney-general of the state. He was remarkable for industry in the preparation of his cases, sound logic, and general urbanity. In forensic disputations, he never indulged in personalities,—then too common at the bar,—unless in self-defence; but, having studied the characters of his associates, and stored his memory with appropriate quotations, his ridicule was a formidable weapon against all who attacked him.

In the autumn of 1815, when only a fortnight over the age required by law, Mr. Wilde was elected a member of the national House of Representatives. At the next election, all the representatives from Georgia, but one, were defeated, and Mr. Wilde returned to the bar, where he continued, with the exception of a short service in Congress in 1825, until 1828, when he again became a representative, and so continued until 1835. I have not room to trace his character as a politician very closely. On the occasion of the Force Bill, as it was called, he seceded from a majority of Congress, considering it a measure calculated to produce civil war, and justified himself in a speech of much eloquence. His speeches on the tariff, the relative advantages and disadvantages of a small-note currency, and on the removal of the deposites by General Jackson, show what are his pretensions to industry and sagacity as a politician.

Mr. WILDE's opposition to the Force Bill and the removal of the deposites rendered him as unpopular with the JACKSON party in Georgia, as h's letter from Virginia had made him with the nullifiers. and at the election of 1834 he was left out of Congress. This afforded him the opportunity he had long desired of going abroad, to recruit his health, much impaired by long and arduous public service, and by repeated attacks of the diseases incident to southern climates. He sailed for Europe in June, 1835, spent two years in travelling through England, France, Belgium, Switzerland, and Italy, and settled during three years more in Florence. Here he occupied himself entirely with literature. The romantic love, the madness, and imprisonment of TASSO had become a subject of curious controversy, and he entered into the investigation "with the enthusiasm of a poet, and the patience and accuracy of a case-hunter," and produced a work, published after his return to the United States, in which the questions concerning TASSO are most ably discussed, and lights are thrown upon them by his letters. and by some of his sonnets, which last are rendered into English with rare felicity. Having completed his work on TASSO, he turned his attention to the life of DANTE; and having learned incidentally one day, in conversation with an artist, that an authentic portrait of this great poet, from the pencil of GIOTTO, probably still existed in the *Bargello*, (anciently both the prison and the palace of the republic,) on a wall, which by some strange neglect or inadvertence had been covered with whitewash, he set on foot a project for its discovery and restoration, which after several months, was crowned with complete success. This discovery of a veritable portrait of DANTE, in the prime of his days, says Mr. IRVING, produced throughout Italy some such sensation as in England would follow the sudden discovery of a perfectly well-authenticated likeness of SHAKSPEARE.

Mr. WILDE returned to the United States in 1840, and was engaged in literary studies and in the practice of his profession until his death, on the tenth of September, 1847, at New Orleans, where he held the professorship of law in the University of Louisiana. His life of DANTE, and translated "Specimens of the Italian Poets," were nearly ready for publication, but have not yet been given to the press; nor has the public received any collection of his miscellaneous writings.

Mr. WILDE's name first became familiar in our literature in consequence of a charge of having stolen his beautiful song, "My Life is like the Summer Rose," from an early and obscure Irish bard named KELLY, of whose pretended genius the alleged specimen was printed. The accusation was met with a simple denial, and when it began to be discredited, from a want of proof that such a person as KELLY had existed, to divert attention from this point it was declared that both KELLY and WILDE had translated a fragment of the Greek of ALCÆUS; and some very good Greek verses, which might have been the original of the piece, were produced, and the impeachment generally believed until a gentleman came out with a card acknowledging the Greek to be his own rendition of Mr. WILDE's performance into that language.

Mr. WILDE's original poems and translations are always graceful and correct. Those that have been published were mostly written while he was a member of Congress during moments of relaxation, and they have never been printed collectively. Examples of his translations are excluded, by the plan of this work. His versions from the Italian, Spanish, and French languages, are among the most elegant and scholarly productions of their kind that have been produced in this country.

ODE TO EASE.

I NEVER bent at glory's shrine;
  To wealth I never bow'd the knee;
Beauty has heard no vows of mine;
  I love thee, EASE, and only thee;
Beloved of the gods and men,
  Sister of joy and liberty,
When wilt thou visit me again;
In shady wood, or silent glen,
By falling stream, or rocky den,
Like those where once I found thee, when,
Despite the ills of poverty,
And wisdom's warning prophecy,
I listened to thy siren voice,
And made thee mistress of my choice!

I chose thee, EASE! and glory fled;
For me no more her laurels spread;
Her golden crown shall never shed
Its beams of splendor on my head.
And when within the narrow bed,
To fame and memory ever dead,
  My senseless corpse is thrown,
Nor stately column, sculptured bust,
Nor urn that holds within its trust
The poor remains of mortal dust,
  Nor monumental stone,
Nor willow, waving in the gale,
Nor feeble fence, with whiten'd pale,
Nor rustic cross, memorial frail,
  Shall mark the grave I own.
No lofty deeds in armor wrought;
No hidden truths in science taught;
No undiscover'd regions sought;
No classic page, with learning fraught,
Nor eloquence, nor verse divine,
Nor daring speech, nor high design,
Nor patriotic act of mine
On history's page shall ever shine:
But, all to future ages lost,
Nor even a wreck, tradition toss'd,
Of what I was when valued most
By the few friends whose love I boast,
In after years shall float to shore,
And serve to tell the name I bore.

I chose thee, EASE! and Wealth withdrew,
  Indignant at the choice I made,
And, to her first resentment true,
  My scorn with tenfold scorn repaid.
Now, noble palace, lofty dome,
Or cheerful, hospitable home,
  Are comforts I must never know:
My enemies shall ne'er repine
At pomp or pageantry of mine,
Nor prove, by bowing at my shrine,
  Their souls are abject, base, and low.
No wondering crowd shall ever stand
With gazing eye and waving hand,
  To mark my train, and pomp, and show:
And, worst of all, I shall not live
To taste the pleasures Wealth can give,
  When used to soothe another's wo.
The peasants of my native land
Shall never bless my open hand;
No wandering bard shall celebrate
His patron's hospitable gate:
No war-worn soldier, shatter'd tar,
Nor exile driven from afar,
Nor hapless friend of former years,
Nor widow's prayers, nor orphan's tears,
Nor helpless age relieved from cares,
Nor innocence preserved from snares,
Nor houseless wanderer clothed and fed,
Nor slave from bitter bondage led,
Nor youth to noble actions bred,
Shall call down blessings on my head.

I chose thee, EASE! and yet the while,
So sweet was Beauty's scornful smile,
So fraught with every lovely wile,
Yet seemingly so void of guile,
  It did but heighten all her charms;
And, goddess, had I loved thee then
But with the common love of men,
My fickle heart had changed agen,
Even at the very moment when
  I woo'd thee to my longing arms:
For never may I hope to meet
A smile so sweet, so heavenly sweet.

I chose thee, EASE! and now for me
  No heart shall ever fondly swell,
No voice of rapturous harmony
  Awake the music-breathing shell;
Nor tongue, or witching melody
  Its love in faltering accents tell;
Nor flushing cheek, nor languid eye,
Nor sportive smile, nor artless sigh,
  Confess affection all as well.
No snowy bosom's fall and rise
Shall e'er again enchant my eyes;
No melting lips, profuse of bliss,
Shall ever greet me with a kiss;
Nor balmy breath pour in my ear
The trifles Love delights to hear:
But, living, loveless, hopeless, I
Unmourned and unloved must die.

I chose thee, EASE! and yet to me
Coy and ungrateful thou hast proved;
  Though I have sacrificed to thee
Much that was worthy to be loved.
  But come again, and I will yet
  Thy past ingratitude forget:
  O! come again! thy witching powers
  Shall claim my solitary hours:
  With thee to cheer me, heavenly queen,
  And conscience clear, and health serene,
  And friends, and books, to banish spleen,
  My life should be, as it had been,
    A sweet variety of joys;
  And Glory's crown, and Beauty's smile,
  And treasured hoards should seem the while
    The idlest of all human toys.

SOLOMON AND THE GENIUS.*

SPIRIT OF THOUGHT! Lo! art thou here?
  Lord of the false, fond, ceaseless spell
That mocks the heart, the eye, the ear—
  Art thou, indeed, of heaven or hell?
  In mortal bosoms dost thou dwell,
Self-exiled from thy native sphere?
  Or is the human mind thy cell
Of torment? To inflict and bear
  Thy doom?—the doom of all who fell?

Since thou hast sought to prove my skill,
  Unquestion'd thou shalt not depart,
Be thy behests or good or ill,
  No matter what or whence thou art!
  I will commune with thee apart,
Yea! and compel thee to my will—
  If thou hast power to yield my heart
What earth and Heaven deny it still.

I know thee, Spirit! thou hast been
  Light of my soul by night and day;
All-seeing, though thyself unseen,
  My dreams—my thoughts—and what are they,
  But visions of a calmer ray?
All! all were thine—and thine between
  Each hope that melted fast away,
The throb of anguish, deep and keen!

With thee I've search'd the earth, the sea,
  The air, sun, stars, man, nature, time,
Explored the universe with thee,
  Plunged to the depths of wo and crime,
  Or dared the fearful height to climb,
Where, amid glory none may see
  And live, the ETERNAL reigns sublime,
Who *is*, and *was*, and *is to be!*

And I have sought, with thee have sought,
  Wisdom's celestial path to tread,
Hung o'er each page with learning fraught;
  Question'd the living and the dead:

* The Moslem imagine that SOLOMON acquired dominion over all the orders of the genii—good and evil. It is even believed he sometimes condescended to converse with his new subjects. On this supposition he has been represented interrogating a genius, in the very wise, but very disagreeable mood of mind which led to the conclusion that "All is vanity!" Touching the said genius, the author has not been able to discover whether he or she (even the sex is equivocal) was of Allah or Eblis, and, therefore, left the matter where he found it—in discreet doubt.

The patriarchs of ages fled—
The prophets of the time to come—
All who one ray of light could shed
Beyond the cradle or the tomb.

And I have task'd my busy brain
To learn what haply none may know,
Thy birth, seat, power, thine ample reign
O'er the heart's tides that ebb and flow,
Throb, languish, whirl, rage, freeze, or glow
Like billows of the restless main,
Amid the wrecks of joy and wo
By ocean's caves preserved in vain.

And oft to shadow forth I strove,
To my mind's eye, some form like thine,
And still my soul, like NOAH'S dove,
Return'd, but brought, alas! no sign:
Till, wearying in the mad design,
With fever'd brow and throbbing vein,
I left the *cause* to thread the mine
Of wonderful *effects* again!

But now I see thee face to face,
Thou art indeed, a thing divine;
An eye pervading time and space,
And an angelic look are thine,
Ready to seize, compare, combine
Essence and form—and yet a trace
Of grief and care—a shadowy line
Dims thy bright forehead's heavenly grace.

Yet thou must be of heavenly birth,
Where naught is known of grief and pain;
Though I perceive, alas! where earth
And earthly things have left their stain:
From thine high calling didst thou deign
To prove—in folly or in mirth—
With daughters of the first-born CAIN,
How little HUMAN LOVE is worth?

Ha! dost thou change before mine eyes!
Another form! and yet the same,
But lovelier, and of female guise,
A vision of ethereal flame,
Such as our heart's despair can frame,
Pine for, love, worship, idolize,
Like HERS, who from the sea-foam came,
And lives but in the heart, or skies.

SPIRIT OF CHANGE! I know thee too,
I know thee by thine Iris bow,
By thy cheek's ever-shifting hue,
By all that marks thy steps below;
By sighs that burn, and tears that glow—
False joys—vain hopes—that mock the heart;
From FANCY'S urn these evils flow,
SPIRIT OF LIES! for such thou art!

Saidst thou not once, that all the charms
Of life lay hid in woman's love,
And to be lock'd in Beauty's arms,
Was all men knew of heaven above?
And did I not thy counsels prove,
And all their pleasures, all their pain?
No more! no more my heart they move,
For I, alas! have proved them vain.

Didst thou not then, in evil hour,
Light in my soul ambition's flame?
Didst thou not say the joys of power,
Unbounded sway, undying fame,
A monarch's love alone should claim?
And did I not pursue e'en these?
And are they not, when won, the same?
All VANITY OF VANITIES!

Didst not, to tempt me once again,
Bid new, deceitful visions rise,
And hint, though won with toil and pain,
"Wisdom's the pleasure of the wise?"
And now, when none beneath the skies
Are wiser held by men than me,
What is the value of the prize?
It too, alas! is VANITY!

Then tell me—since I've found on earth
Not one pure stream to slake this thirst,
Which still torments us from our birth,
And in our heart and soul is nursed;
This hopeless wish wherewith we're cursed,
Whence came it, and why was it given?
Thou speak'st not!—Let me know the worst!
Thou pointest!—and it is to HEAVEN!

A FAREWELL TO AMERICA.*

FAREWELL! my more than fatherland!
Home of my heart and friends, adieu!
Lingering beside some foreign strand,
How oft shall I remember you!
How often, o'er the waters blue,
Send back a sigh to those I leave,
The loving and beloved few,
Who grieve for me,—for whom I grieve!

We part!—no matter how we part,
There are some thoughts we utter not,
Deep treasured in our inmost heart,
Never reveal'd, and ne'er forgot!
Why murmur at the common lot?
We part!—I speak not of the pain,—
But when shall I each lovely spot
And each loved face behold again?

It must be months,—it may be years,—
It may—but no!—I will not fill
Fond hearts with gloom,—fond eyes with tears,
"Curious to shape uncertain ill."
Though humble,—few and far,—yet, still
Those hearts and eyes are ever dear;
Theirs is the love no time can chill,
The truth no chance or change can sear!

All I have seen, and all I see,
Only endears them more and more;
Friends cool, hopes fade, and hours flee,
Affection lives when all is o'er!
Farewell, my more than native shore!
I do not seek or hope to find,
Roam where I will, what I deplore
To leave with them and thee behind!

* Written on board ship Westminster, at sea, off the Highlands of Neversink, June 1, 1835.

NAPOLEON'S GRAVE.

FAINT and sad was the moonbeam's smile,
Sullen the moan of the dying wave;
Hoarse the wind in St. Helen's isle.
As I stood by the side of NAPOLEON'S grave.

And is it here that the hero lies,
Whose name has shaken the earth with dread?
And is this all that the earth supplies—
A stone his pillow—the turf his bed?

Is such the moral of human life?
Are these the limits of glory's reign?
Have oceans of blood, and an age of strife,
And a thousand battles been all in vain?

Is nothing left of his victories now
But legions broken—a sword in rust—
A crown that cumbers a dotard's brow—
A name and a requiem—dust to dust?

Of all the chieftains whose thrones he rear'd,
Was there none that kindness or faith could bind?
Of all the monarchs whose crowns he spared,
Had none one spark of his Roman mind?

Did Prussia cast no repentant glance?
Did Austria shed no remorseful tear,
When England's truth, and thine honour, France,
And thy friendship, Russia, were blasted here?

No holy leagues, like the heathen heaven,
Ungodlike shrunk from the giant's shock;
And glorious TITAN, the unforgiven,
Was doom'd to his vulture, and chains, and rock.

And who were the gods that decreed thy doom?
A German CÆSAR—a Prussian sage—
The dandy prince of a counting-room—
And a Russian Greek of earth's darkest age.

Men call'd thee Despot, and call'd thee true;
But the laurel was earn'd that bound thy brow;
And of all who wore it, alas! how few
Were freer from treason and guilt than thou!

Shame to thee, Gaul, and thy faithless horde!
Where was the oath which thy soldiers swore?
Fraud still lurks in the gown, but the sword
Was never so false to its trust before.

Where was thy veteran's boast that day,
"The old Guard dies, but it never yields?"
O! for one heart like the brave DESSAIX,
One phalanx like those of thine early fields!

But, no, no, no!—it was Freedom's charm
Gave them the courage of more than men;
You broke the spell that twice nerved each arm,
Though you were invincible only then.

Yet St. Jean was a deep, not a deadly blow;
One struggle, and France all her faults repairs—
But the wild FAYETTE, and the stern CARNOT
Are dupes, and ruin thy fate and theirs!

STANZAS.

MY life is like the summer rose
That opens to the morning sky,
But ere the shades of evening close,
Is scatter'd on the ground—to die!
Yet on the rose's humble bed
The sweetest dews of night are shed,
As if she wept the waste to see—
But none shall weep a tear for me!

My life is like the autumn leaf
That trembles in the moon's pale ray,
Its hold is frail—its date is brief,
Restless—and soon to pass away!
Yet ere that leaf shall fall and fade,
The parent tree will mourn its shade,
The winds bewail the leafless tree,
But none shall breathe a sigh for me!

My life is like the prints, which feet
Have left on Tampa's desert strand;
Soon as the rising tide shall beat,
All trace will vanish from the sand;
Yet, as if grieving to efface
All vestige of the human race,
On that lone shore loud moans the sea,
But none, alas! shall mourn for me!

TO LORD BYRON.

BYRON! 'tis thine alone, on eagles' pinions,
In solitary strength and grandeur soaring,
To dazzle and delight all eyes; outpouring
The electric blaze on tyrants and their minions
Earth, sea, and air, and powers and dominions,
Nature, man, time, the universe exploring;
And from the wreck of worlds, thrones, creeds, opinions,
Thought, beauty, eloquence, and wisdom storing
O! how I love and envy thee thy glory,
To every age and clime alike belonging;
Link'd by all tongues with every nation's glory.
Thou TACITUS of song! whose echoes, thronging
O'er the Atlantic, fill the mountains hoary
And forests with the name my verse is wronging

TO THE MOCKING-BIRD.

WING'D mimic of the woods! thou motley fool.
Who shall thy gay buffoonery describe?
Thine ever-ready notes of ridicule
Pursue thy fellows still with jest and gibe:
Wit, sophist, songster, YORICK of thy tribe.
Thou sportive satirist of Nature's school;
To thee the palm of scoffing we ascribe,
Arch-mocker and mad Abbot of Misrule!
For such thou art by day—but all night long
Thou pour'st a soft, sweet, pensive, solemn strain,
As if thou didst in this thy moonlight song
Like to the melancholy JAQUES complain,
Musing on falsehood, folly, vice, and wrong,
And sighing for thy motley coat again.

FRANCIS SCOTT KEY.

[Born 1779. Died 1843.]

THE author of the "Star Spangled Banner" was a very able and eloquent lawyer, and one of the most respectable gentlemen whose lives have ever adorned American society. During our second war with England he was residing in Baltimore, and left that city on one occasion for the purpose of procuring the release from the British fleet of a friend who had been captured at Marlborough. He went as far as the mouth of the Patuxent, but was not permitted to return, lest the intended attack on Baltimore should be disclosed by him. Brought up the bay to the mouth of the Petapsco, he was placed on board one of the enemy's ships, from which he was compelled to witness the bombardment of Fort McHenry, which the admiral had boasted that he would carry in a few hours, and the city soon after. Mr. KEY watched the flag over the fort through the whole day, with intense anxiety, and in the night, the bombshells; but he saw at dawn "the star-spangled banner" still waving over its defenders. The following song was partly composed before he was set at liberty. He was a man of much literary cultivation and taste, and his religious poems are not without merit. He died very suddenly at Baltimore on the eleventh of January, 1843.

THE STAR-SPANGLED BANNER.

O! SAY, can you see, by the dawn's early light,
  What so proudly we hail'd at the twilight's last gleaming;
Whose broad stripes and bright stars, through the perilous fight,
  O'er the ramparts we watch'd, were so gallantly streaming?
And the rockets red glare, the bombs bursting in air,
Gave proof thro' the night that our flag was still there;
O! say, does that star-spangled banner yet wave
O'er the land of the free and the home of the brave?

On the shore, dimly seen through the mists of the deep
  Where the foe's haughty host in dread silence reposes,
What is that which the breeze o'er the towering steep
  As it fitfully blows, half-conceals, half discloses!
Now it catches the gleam of the morning's first beam;
Its full glory reflected now shines on the stream:
'T is the star-spangled banner, O! long may it wave
O'er the land of the free and the home of the brave.

And where is the band who so vauntingly swore,
  Mid the havoc of war and the battle's confusion,
A home and a country they'd leave us no more?
  Their blood hath wash'd out their foul footsteps' pollution;
No refuge could save the hireling and slave
From the terror of flight, or the gloom of the grave,
And the star-spangled banner in triumph doth wave
O'er the land of the free and the home of the brave.

O! thus be it ever, when freeman shall stand
  Between our loved home and the war's desolation;
Bless'd with victory and peace, may the heaven-rescued land
  Praise the power that hath made and preserved us a nation!
Then conquer we must, for our cause it is just,
And this be our motto, "In GOD is our trust,"
And the star-spangled banner in triumph shall wave
O'er the land of the free and the home of the brave.

JOHN HOWARD PAYNE.

[Born, 1792. Died, 1852.]

MR. PAYNE was born in New York, on the ninth of June, 1792. His remarkable career as an actor and dramatist belongs to the history of the stage. As a poet he will be known only by a single song He died at Tunis, where he was sometime Consul for the United States.

SWEET HOME.

Mid pleasures and palaces though we may roam,
Be it ever so humble, there's no place like home!
A charm from the skies seems to hallow us there,
Which seek through the world, is ne'er met with elsewhere.
    Home! home, sweet home!
    There's no place like home!

An exile from home, splendor dazzles in vain
Oh, give me my lowly thatched cottage again
The birds singing gayly that come at my call:
Give me these, and the peace of mind, dearer than all.
    Home! sweet sweet home!
    There's no place like home

* From an opera by the author, entitled "Clari, or the Maid of Milan."

JAMES A. HILLHOUSE.

[Born 1789. Died 1841.]

The author of "Hadad" was descended from an ancient and honourable Irish family, in the county of Derry, and his ancestors emigrated to this country and settled in Connecticut in 1720. A high order of intellect seems to have been their right of inheritance, for in every generation we find their name prominent in the political history of the state. The grandfather of the poet, the Honourable William Hillhouse, was for more than fifty years employed in the public service, as a representative, as a member of the council, and in other offices of trust and honour. His father, the Honourable James Hillhouse, who died in 1833, after filling various offices in his native state, and being for three years a member of the House of Representatives, was in 1794 elected to the Senate of the United States, where for sixteen years he acted a leading part in the politics of the country. His wife, the mother of the subject of this sketch, was the daughter of Colonel Melancthon Woolsey, of Dosoris, Long Island. She was a woman distinguished alike for mental superiority, and for feminine softness, purity, and delicacy of character. Although educated in retirement, and nearly self-taught, her son was accustomed to say, when time had given value to his opinions, that she possessed the most elegant mind he had ever met with; and much of the nice discrimination, and the finer and more delicate elements of his own character, were an inheritance from her. Among the little occasional pieces which he wrote entirely for the family circle, was one composed on visiting her birth-place, after her death, which I have been permitted* to make public.

"As yonder frith, round green Dosoris roll'd,
Reflects the parting glories of the skies,
Or quivering glances, like the paly gold,
When on its breast the midnight moonbeam lies;

"Thus, though bedimm'd by many a changeful year,
The hues of feeling varied in her cheek,
That, brightly flush'd, or glittering with a tear,
Seem'd the rapt poet's, or the seraph's meek.

"I have fulfill'd her charge,—dear scenes, adieu!—
The tender charge to see her natal spot;
My tears have flow'd, while busy Fancy drew
The picture of her childhood's happy lot.

"Would I *could* paint the ever-varying grace,
The ethereal glow and lustre of her mind,
Which own'd not time, nor bore of age a trace,
Pure as the sunbeam, gentle and refined!"

* I am indebted for the materials for this biography to the poet's intimate friend, the Reverend William Ingraham Kipp, Rector of St. Paul's Church, in Albany, New York, who kindly consented to write out the character of the poet, as he appeared at home, and as none but his associates could know him, for this work.

Mr. Hillhouse was born in New Haven, on the twenty-sixth of September, 1789. The home of such parents, and the society of the intelligent circle they drew about them, (of which President Dwight was the most distinguished ornament,) was well calculated to cherish and cultivate his peculiar tastes. In boyhood he was remarkable for great activity and excellence in all manly and athletic sports, and for a peculiarly gentlemanly deportment. At the age of fifteen he entered Yale College, and in 1808 he was graduated, with high reputation as a scholar. From his first junior exhibition, he had been distinguished for the elegance and good taste of his compositions. Upon taking his second degree, he delivered an oration on "The Education of a Poet," so full of beauty, that it was long and widely remembered, and induced an appointment by the Phi Beta Kappa Society, (not much in the habit of selecting juvenile writers,) to deliver a poem before them at their next anniversary. It was on this occasion that he wrote "The Judgment," which was pronounced before that society at the commencement of 1812.

A more difficult theme, or one requiring loftier powers, could not have been selected. The reflecting mind regards this subject in accordance with some preconceived views. That Mr. Hillhouse felt this difficulty, is evident from a remark in his preface, that in selecting this theme, "he exposes his work to criticism on account of its theology, as well as its poetry; and they who think the former objectionable, will not easily be pleased with the latter." Other poets, too, had essayed their powers in describing the events of the Last Day. The public voice, however, has decided, that among all the poems on this great subject, that of Mr. Hillhouse stands unequalled. His object was, "to present such a view of the last grand spectacle as seemed the most susceptible of poetical embellishment;" and rarely have we seen grandeur of conception and simplicity of design so admirably united. His representation of the scene is vivid and energetic; while the manner in which he has grouped and contrasted the countless array of characters of every age, displays the highest degree of artistic skill. Each character he summons up appears before us, with historic costume and features faithfully preserved, and we seem to gaze upon him as a reality, and not merely as the bold imagery of the poet.

"For all appear'd
As in their days of earthly pride; the clank
Of steel announced the warrior, and the robe
Of Tyrian lustre spoke the blood of kings."

His description of the last setting of the sun in the west, and the dreamer's farewell to the evening star, as it was fading forever from his sight, are passages of beauty which it would be difficult to find surpassed.

About this period Mr. HILLHOUSE passed three years in Boston, preparing to engage in a mercantile life. During the interruption of business which took place in consequence of the last war with England, he employed a season of leisure passed at home, in the composition of several dramatic pieces, of which "Demetria" and "Percy's Masque" best satisfied his own judgment. When peace was restored, he went to New York, and embarked in commerce, to which, though at variance with his tastes, he devoted himself with fidelity and perseverance. In 1819, he visited Europe, and though the months passed there were a season of great anxiety and business occupations, he still found time to see much to enlarge his mind, and accumulated stores of thought for future use. Among other distinguished literary men, from whom while in London he received attentions, was ZACARY MACAULAY, (father of the Hon. T. BABBINGTON MACAULAY,) who subsequently stated to some American gentlemen, that "he considered Mr. HILLHOUSE the most accomplished young man with whom he was acquainted." It was during his stay in England that "Percy's Masque" was revised and published. The subject of this drama is the successful attempt of one of the Percies, the son of Shakspeare's Hotspur, to recover his ancestral home. The era chosen is a happy one for a poet. He is dealing with the events of an age where every thing to us is clothed with a romantic interest, which invests even the most common every-day occurrences of life.

"They carved at the meal
With gloves of steel,
And they drank the red wine through the helmet barr'd."

Of this opportunity he fully availed himself, in the picture he has here given us of the days of chivalry. As a mere work of art, "Percy's Masque" is one of the most faultless in the language. If subjected to scrutiny, it will bear the strictest criticism by which compositions of this kind can be tried. We cannot detect the violation of a single rule which should be observed in the construction of a tragedy. When, therefore, it was republished in this country, it at once gave its author an elevated rank as a dramatic poet.

In 1822, Mr. HILLHOUSE was united in marriage to CORNELIA, eldest daughter of ISAAC LAWRENCE, of New York. He shortly afterward returned to his native town, and there, at his beautiful place, called *Sachem's Wood*, devoted himself to the pursuits of a country gentleman and practical agriculturist. His taste extended also to the arts with which poetry is allied; and in the embellishment of his residence, there was exhibited evidence of the refinement of its accomplished occupant. Here, with the exception of a few months of the winter, generally spent in New York, he passed the remainder of his life. "And never," remarks his friend, the Reverend Mr. KIPP, "has a domestic circle been anywhere gathered, uniting within itself more of grace, and elegance, and intellect. He who formed its centre and its charm, possessed a character combining most beautifully the high endowments of literary genius with all that is winning and brilliant in social life. They who knew him best in the sacred relations of his own fireside, will never cease to realize, that in him their circle lost its greatest ornament. All who were accustomed to meet his cordial greeting, to listen to his fervid and eloquent conversation, to be delighted with the wit and vivacity of his playful moments; to witness the grace and elegance of his manners, the chivalric spirit, the indomitable energy and high finish of the whole character, can tell how nobly he united the combined attractions of the poet, the scholar, and the perfect gentleman. Never, indeed, have we met with one who could pour forth more eloquently his treasures, drawn from the whole range of English literature, or bring them to bear more admirably upon the passing occurrences of the day. Every syllable, too, which he uttered, conveyed the idea of a high-souled honour, which we associate more naturally with the days of old romance, than with these selfish, prosaic times. His were indeed 'high thoughts, seated in a heart of courtesy.'"

"Hadad" was written in 1824, and printed in the following year. This has generally been esteemed HILLHOUSE's masterpiece. As a sacred drama, it is probably unsurpassed. The scene is in Judea, in the days of David; and as the agency of evil spirits is introduced, an opportunity is afforded to bring forward passages of strange sublimity and wildness. For a work like this, HILLHOUSE was peculiarly qualified. A most intimate acquaintance with the Scriptures enabled him to introduce each minute detail in perfect keeping with historical truth, while from the same study he seems also to have imbibed the lofty thoughts, and the majestic style of the ancient Hebrew prophets.

In 1840, he collected, and published in two volumes, the works which at that time he was willing to give to the world. In addition to those I have already mentioned, was "Demetria," a domestic tragedy, now first revised and printed, after an interval of twenty-six years since its first composition, and several orations, delivered in New Haven, on public occasions, or before literary societies in other parts of the country. The manly eloquence of the latter, is well calculated to add the reputation of an accomplished orator, to that which he already enjoyed as a poet. These volumes contain nearly all that he left us. It is a mistake, however, to suppose that he passed his life merely as a literary man. The early part of it was spent in the anxieties of business, while, through all his days, literature, instead of being his occupation, was merely the solace and delight of his leisure moments.

About this time his friends beheld, with anxiety, the symptoms of failing health. For fifteen months, however, he lingered on, alternately cheering their hearts by the prospect of recovery, and then causing them again to despond, as his weakness increased. In the fall of 1840, he left home for the last time, to visit his friends in Boston. He returned, apparently benefited by the excursion, and no immediate danger was apprehended until the beginning of the following January. On the second of that month his disorder assumed an alarming form, and the next day was passed in intense agony. On Monday, his pain was alleviated; yet his skilful medical attendants beheld in this but the precursor of death; and it became their duty, on the following morning, to impart to him the news that his hours were few and numbered.

"Of the events of this solemn day, when he beheld the sands of life fast running out, and girded up his strength to meet the King of Terrors," says the writer to whom I have before alluded, "I cannot speak. The loss is still too recent to allow us to withdraw the veil and tell of his dying hours. Yet touching was the scene, as the warm affections of that noble heart gathered in close folds around those he was about to leave, or wandered back in remembrance to the opening of life, and the friends of childhood who had already gone. It was also the Christian's death. The mind which had conceived so vividly the scenes of the judgment, must often have looked forward to that hour, which he now could meet in an humble, trusting faith. And thus the day wore on, until, about eight o'clock in the evening, without a struggle, he fell asleep."

As a poet, he possessed qualities seldom found united: a masculine strength of mind, and a most delicate perception of the beautiful. With an imagination of the loftiest order—with "the vision and the faculty divine" in its fullest exercise, the wanderings of his fancy were chastened and controlled by exquisite taste. The grand characteristic of his writings is their classical beauty. Every passage is polished to the utmost, yet there is no exuberance, no sacrifice to false and meretricious taste. He threw aside the gaudy and affected brilliancy with which too many set forth their poems, and left his to stand, like the doric column, charming by its simplicity. Writing not for present popularity, or to catch the senseless applause of the multitude, he was willing to commit his works—as Lord Bacon did his memory—"to the next ages." And the result is proving how wise were his calculations. The "fit audience," which at first hailed his poems with pleasure, from realizing their worth, has been steadily increasing. The scholar studies them as the productions of a kindred spirit, which had drunk deeply at the fountains of ancient lore, until it had itself been moulded into the same form of stern and antique beauty, which marked the old Athenian dramatists. The intellectual and the gifted claim him as one of their own sacred brotherhood; and all who have a sympathy with genius, and are anxious to hold communion with it as they travel on the worn and beaten path of life, turn with ever renewed delight to his pages. They see the evidences of one, who wrote not because he must write, but because he possessed a mind crowded and glowing with images of beauty, and therefore, in the language of poetry, he poured forth its hoarded treasures. Much as we must lament the withdrawal of that bright mind, at an age when it had just ripened into the maturity of its power, and when it seemed ready for greater efforts than it yet had made, we rejoice that the event did not happen until a permanent rank had been gained among the noblest of our poets.

THE JUDGMENT.

I.

The rites were past of that auspicious day
When white-robed altars wreath'd with living green
Adorn the temples;—when unnumber'd tongues
Repeat the glorious anthem sung to harps
Of angels while the star o'er Bethlehem stood;—
When grateful hearts bow low, and deeper joy
Breathes in the Christian than the angel song,
On the great birthday of our Priest and King.
That night, while musing on his wondrous life,
Precepts, and promises to be fulfill'd,
A trance-like sleep fell on me, and a dream
Of dreadful character appall'd my soul.
Wild was the pageant:—face to face with kings,
Heroes, and sages of old note, I stood;
Patriarchs, and prophets, and apostles saw,
And venerable forms, ere round the globe
Shoreless and waste a weltering flood was roll'd,
With angels, compassing the radiant throne
Of Mary's Son, anew descended, crown'd
With glory terrible, to judge the world.

II.

Methought I journey'd o'er a boundless plain,
Unbroke by vale or hill, on all sides stretch'd,
Like circling ocean, to the low-brow'd sky;
Save in the midst a verdant mount, whose sides
Flowers of all hues and fragrant breath adorn'd.
Lightly I trod, as on some joyous quest,
Beneath the azure vault and early sun;
But while my pleased eyes ranged the circuit green,
New light shone round; a murmur came, confused
Like many voices and the rush of wings.
Upward I gazed, and, 'mid the glittering skies,
Begirt by flying myriads, saw a throne
Whose thousand splendours blazed upon the earth
Refulgent as another sun. Through clouds
They came, and vapours colour'd by Aurora,
Mingling in swell sublime, voices, and harps,
And sounding wings, and hallelujahs sweet.
Sudden, a seraph that before them flew,
Pausing upon his wide-unfolded plumes,
Put to his mouth the likeness of a trump,
And toward the four winds four times fiercely breathed.
Doubling along the arch, the mighty peal

To heaven resounded; hell return'd a groan,
And shuddering earth a moment reel'd, confounded,
From her fixed pathway as the staggering ship,
Stunn'd by some mountain billow, reels. The isles,
With heaving ocean, rock'd: the mountains shook
Their ancient coronets: the avalanche
Thunder'd: silence succeeded through the nations.
Earth never listen'd to a sound like this.
It struck the general pulse of nature still,
And broke, forever, the dull sleep of death.

III.

Now, o'er the mount the radiant legions hung,
Like plumy travellers from climes remote
On some sequester'd isle about to stoop.
Gently its flowery head received the throne:
Cherubs and seraphs, by ten thousands, round
Skirting it far and wide, like a bright sea,
Fair forms and faces, crowns, and coronets,
And glistering wings furl'd white and numberless.
About their LORD were those seven glorious spirits
Who in the ALMIGHTY's presence stand. Four lean'd
On golden wands, with folded wings, and eyes
Fix'd on the throne: one bore the dreadful books,
The arbiters of life: another waved
The blazing ensign terrible, of yore,
To rebel angels in the wars of heaven:
What seem'd a trump the other spirit grasp'd,
Of wondrous size, wreathed multiform and strange.
Illustrious stood the seven, above the rest
Towering, like a constellation glowing,
What time the sphere-instructed huntsman, taught
By ATLAS, his star-studded belt displays
Aloft, bright-glittering, in the winter sky.

IV.

Then on the mount, amidst these glorious shapes,
Who reverent stood, with looks of sacred awe,
I saw EMMANUEL seated on his throne.
His robe, methought, was whiter than the light;
Upon his breast the heavenly Urim glow'd
Bright as the sun, and round such lightnings flash'd,
No eye could meet the mystic symbol's blaze.
Irradiant the eternal sceptre shone
Which wont to glitter in his Father's hand:
Resplendent in his face the Godhead beam'd,
Justice and mercy, majesty and grace,
Divinely mingling. Celestial glories play'd
Around with beamy lustre; from his eye
Dominion look'd; upon his brow was stamp'd
Creative power. Yet over all the touch
Of gracious pity dwelt, which, erst, amidst
Dissolving nature's anguish, breathed a prayer
For guilty man. Redundant down his neck
His locks roll'd graceful, as they waved, of old,
Upon the mournful breeze of Calvary.

V.

His throne of heavenly substance seem'd composed,
Whose pearly essence, like the eastern shell,
Or changeful opal, shed a silvery light.
Clear as the moon it look'd through ambient clouds
Of snowy lustre, waving round its base,
That, like a zodiac, thick with emblems set,
Flash'd wondrous beams, of unknown character,
From many a burning stone of lustre rare,
Stain'd like the bow whose mingling splendour stream'd
Confusion bright upon the dazzled eye.
Above him hung a canopy whose skirts
The mount o'ershadow'd like an evening cloud.
Clouds were his curtains: not like their dim types
Of blue and purple round the tabernacle,
That waving vision of the lonely wild,
By pious Israel wrought with cherubim;
Veiling the mysteries of old renown,
Table, and altar, ark, and mercy-seat,
Where, 'twixt the shadow of cherubic wings,
In lustre visible JEHOVAH shone.

VI.

In honour chief, upon the LORD's right hand
His station MICHAEL held: the dreadful sword
That from a starry baldric hung, proclaim'd
The Hierarch. Terrible, on his brow
Blazed the archangel crown, and from his eye
Thick sparkles flash'd. Like regal banners, waved
Back from his giant shoulders his broad vans,
Bedropt with gold, and, turning to the sun,
Shone gorgeous as the multitudinous stars,
Or some illumined city seen by night,
When her wide streets pour noon, and, echoing through
Her thronging thousands, mirth and music ring.
Opposed to him, I saw an angel stand
In sable vesture, with the Books of Life.
Black was his mantle, and his changeful wings
Gloss'd like the raven's; thoughtful seem'd his mien,
Sedate and calm, and deep upon his brow
Had Meditation set her seal; his eyes
Look'd things unearthly, thoughts unutterable,
Or utter'd only with an angel's tongue.
Renown'd was he among the seraphim
For depth of prescience, and sublimest lore;
Skill'd in the mysteries of the ETERNAL,
Profoundly versed in those old records where,
From everlasting ages, live GOD's deeds;
He knew the hour when yonder shining worlds,
That roll around us, into being sprang;
Their system, laws, connexion; all he knew
But the dread moment when they cease to be.
None judged like him the ways of GOD to man,
Or so had ponder'd; his excursive thoughts
Had visited the depths of night and chaos,
Gathering the treasures of the hoary deep.

VII.

Like ocean billows seem'd, ere this, the plain,
Confusedly heaving with a sumless host
From earth's and time's remotest bounds: a roar
Went up before the multitude, whose course
The unfurl'd banner guided, and the bow,
Zone of the universe, athwart the zenith
Sweeping its arch. In one vast conflux roll'd,
Wave following wave, were men of every age,
Nation, and tongue; all heard the warning blast,
And, led by wondr[illegible]s impulse, hither came.

Mingled in wild confusion, now, those met
In distant ages born. Gray forms, that lived
When Time himself was young, whose temples shook
The hoary honours of a thousand years,
Stood side by side with Roman consuls:—here,
Mid prophets old, and heaven-inspired bards,
Were Grecian heroes seen:—there, from a crowd
Of reverend patriarchs, tower'd the nodding plumes,
Tiars, and helms, and sparkling diadems
Of Persia's, Egypt's, or Assyria's kings;
Clad as when forth the hundred gates of Thebes
On sounding cars her hundred princes rush'd;
Or, when, at night, from off the terrace top
Of his aerial garden, touched to soothe
The troubled monarch, came the solemn chime
Of sackbut, psaltery, and harp, adown
The Euphrates, floating in the moonlight wide
O'er sleeping Babylon. For all appear'd
As in their days of earthly pride; the clank
Of steel announced the warrior, and the robe
Of Tyrian lustre spoke the blood of kings.
Though on the angels while I gazed, their names
Appeared not, yet amongst the mortal throng
(Capricious power of dreams!) familiar seem'd
Each countenance, and every name well known.

VIII.

Nearest the mount, of that mix'd phalanx first,
Our general parent stood: not as he look'd
Wandering, at eve, amid the shady bowers
And odorous groves of that delicious garden,
Or flowery banks of some soft-rolling stream,
Pausing to list its lulling murmur, hand
In hand with peerless Eve, the rose too sweet,
Fatal to Paradise. Fled from his cheek
The bloom of Eden; his hyacinthine locks
Were changed to gray; with years and sorrows bow'd
He seem'd, but through his ruined form still shone
The majesty of his Creator: round
Upon his sons a grieved and pitying look
He cast, and in his vesture hid his face.

IX.

Close at his side appear'd a martial form,
Of port majestic, clad in massive arms,
Cowering above whose helm with outspread wings
The Roman eagle flew; around its brim
Was character'd the name at which earth's queen
Bow'd from her seven-fold throne and owned her lord.
In his dilated eye amazement stood;
Terror, surprise, and blank astonishment
Blanch'd his firm cheek, as when, of old, close hemm'd
Within the capitol, amidst the crowd
Of traitors, fearless else, he caught the gleam
Of Brutus' steel. Daunted, yet on the pomp
Of towering seraphim, their wings, their crowns,
Their dazzling faces, and upon the Lord
He fix'd a steadfast look of anxious note,
Like that Pharsalia's hurtling squadrons drew
When all his fortunes hung upon the hour.

X.

Near him, for wisdom famous through the east,
Abraham rested on his staff; in guise
A Chaldee shepherd, simple in his raiment
As when at Mamre in his tent he sat,
The host of angels. Snow-white were his locks
And silvery beard, that to his girdle roll'd.
Fondly his meek eye dwelt upon his Lord,
Like one, that, after long and troubled dreams,
A night of sorrows, dreary, wild, and sad,
Beholds, at last, the dawn of promised joys.
With kindred looks his great descendant gazed
Not in the poor array of shepherds he,
Nor in the many-coloured coat, fond gift
Of doating age, and cause of direful hate;
But, stately, as his native palm, his form
Was, like Egyptian princes', proudly deck'd
In tissued purple sweeping to the ground.
Plumes from the desert waved above his head,
And down his breast the golden collar hung,
Bestow'd by Pharaoh, when through Egypt word
Went forth to bow the knee as to her king.
Graced thus, his chariot with impetuous wheels
Bore him toward Goshen, where the fainting heart
Of Israel waited for his long-lost son,
The son of Rachel. Ah! had she survived
To see him in his glory!—As he rode,
His boyhood, and his mother's tent, arose,
Link'd with a thousand recollections dear,
And Joseph's heart was in the tomb by Ephrath.

XI.

At hand, a group of sages mark'd the scene.
Plato and Socrates together stood,
With him who measured by their shades those piles
Gigantic, 'mid the desert seen, at eve,
By toiling caravans for Memphis bound,
Peering like specks above the horizon's verge,
Whose huge foundations vanish in the mist
Of earliest time. Transfix'd they seem'd with wonder,
Awe-struck,—amazement rapt their inmost souls.
Such glance of deep inquiry and suspense
They threw around, as, in untutor'd ages,
Astronomers upon some dark eclipse,
Close counselling amidst the dubious light
If it portended Nature's death, or spoke
A change in heaven. What thought they, then, of all
Their idle dreams, their proud philosophy,
When on their wilder'd souls redemption, Christ,
And the Almighty broke? But, though they err'd
When all was dark, they reason'd for the truth.
They sought in earth, in ocean, and the stars,
Their maker, arguing from his works toward God;
And from his word had not less nobly argued,
Had they beheld the gospel sending forth
Its pure effulgence o'er the farthest sea,
Lighting the idol mountain-tops, and gilding
The banners of salvation there. These men
Ne'er slighted a Redeemer; of his name
They never heard. Perchance their late-found harps,
Mixing with angel symphonies, may sound
In strains more rapturous things to them so new.

XII.

Nearer the mount stood MOSES; in his hand
The rod which blasted with strange plagues the realm
Of Misraim, and from its time-worn channels
Upturn'd the Arabian sea. Fair was his broad,
High front, and forth from his soul-piercing eye
Did legislation took; which full he fix'd
Upon the blazing panoply, undazzled.
No terrors had the scene for him who, oft,
Upon the thunder-shaken hill-top, veil'd
With smoke and lightnings, with JEHOVAH talk'd,
And from his fiery hand received the law.
Beyond the Jewish ruler, banded close,
A company full glorious, I saw
The twelve apostles stand. O, with what looks
Of ravishment and joy, what rapturous tears,
What hearts of ecstasy, they gazed again
On their beloved Master! what a tide
Of overwhelming thoughts press'd to their souls,
When now, as he so frequent promised, throned,
And circled by the hosts of heaven, they traced
The well-known lineaments of him who shared
Their wants and sufferings here! Full many a day
Of fasting spent with him, and night of prayer,
Rush'd on their swelling hearts. Before the rest,
Close to the angelic spears, had PETER urged,
Tears in his eye, love throbbing at his breast,
As if to touch his vesture, or to catch
The murmur of his voice. On him and them
JESUS beam'd down benignant looks of love.

XIII.

How diverse from the front sublime of PAUL,
Or pale and placid dignity of him
Who in the lonely Isle saw heaven unveil'd,
Was his who in twelve summers won a world!
Not such his countenance nor garb, as when
He foremost breasted the broad Granicus,
Dark-rushing through its steeps from lonely Ida,
His double-tufted plume conspicuous mark
Of every arrow; cheering his bold steed
Through pikes, and spears, and threatening axes, up
The slippery bank through all their chivalry,
Princes and satraps link'd for CYRUS' throne,
With cuirass pierced, cleft helm, and plumeless head,
To youthful conquest: or, when, panic-struck,
DARIUS from his plunging chariot sprang,
Away the bow and mantle cast, and fled.
His robe, all splendid from the silk-worm's loom,
Floated effeminate, and from his neck
Hung chains of gold, and gems from eastern mines.
Bedight with many-colour'd plumage, flamed
His proud tiara, plumage which had spread
Its glittering dyes of scarlet, green, and gold,
To evening suns by Indus' stream: around
Twined careless, glow'd the white and purple band,
The imperial, sacred badge of Persia's kings.
Thus his triumphal car in Babylon
Display'd him, drawn by snow-white elephants,
Whose feet crush'd odours from the flowery wreaths
Boy-Cupids scatter'd, while soft music breathed
And incense fumed around. But dire his hue,
Bloated and bacchanal as on the night
When old Persepolis was wrapp'd in flame!
Fear over all had flung a livid tinge.
A deeper awe subdued him than amazed
PARMENIO and the rest, when they beheld
The white-stoled Levites from Jerusalem,
Thrown open as on some high festival,
With hymns and solemn pomp, come down the hill
To meet the incensed king, and wondering saw,
As on the pontiff's awful form he gazed,
Glistering in purple with his mystic gems,
JOVE's vaunted son, at JADDUA's foot, adore.

XIV.

Turn, now, where stood the spotless Virgin: sweet
Her azure eye, and fair her golden ringlets;
But changeful as the hues of infancy
Her face. As on her son, her GOD, she gazed,
Fix'd was her look,—earnest, and breathless;—now,
Suffused her glowing cheek; now, changed to pale;—
First, round her lip a smile celestial play'd,
Then, fast, fast rain'd the tears.—Who can interpret?—
Perhaps some thought maternal cross'd her heart,
That mused on days long past, when on her breast
He helpless lay, and of his infant smile;
Or, on those nights of terror, when, from worse
Than wolves, she hasted with her babe to Egypt.

XV.

Girt by a crowd of monarchs, of whose fame
Scarce a memorial lives, who fought and reign'd
While the historic lamp shed glimmering light,
Above the rest one regal port aspired,
Crown'd like Assyria's princes; not a crest
O'ertopp'd him, save the giant seraphim.
His countenance, more piercing than the beam
Of the sun-gazing eagle, earthward bent
Its haught, fierce majesty, temper'd with awe.
Seven years with brutish herds had quell'd his pride,
And taught him there's a mightier king in heaven.
His powerful arm founded old Babylon,
Whose bulwarks like the eternal mountains heaved
Their adamantine heads; whose brazen gates
Beleaguering nations foil'd, and bolts of war,
Unshaken, unanswer'd as the pelting hail.
House of the kingdom! glorious Babylon!
Earth's marvel, and of unborn time the theme!
Say where thou stood'st:—or, can the fisherman
Plying his task on the Euphrates, now,
A silent, silver, unpolluted tide,
Point to thy grave, and answer? From a sash
O'er his broad shoulder hung the ponderous sword,
Fatal as sulphurous fires to Nineveh,
That levell'd with her waves the walls of Tyrus,
Queen of the sea; to its foundations shook
Jerusalem, and reap'd the fields of Egypt.

XVI.

Endless the task to name the multitudes
From every land, from isles remote, in seas
Which no adventurous mariner has sail'd:—

From desert-girdled cities, of whose pomp
Some solitary wanderer, by the stars
Conducted o'er the burning wilderness,
Has told a doubted tale: as Europe's sons
Describing Mexic', and, in fair Peru,
The gorgeous Temple of the Sun, its priests,
Its virgin, and its fire, forever bright,
Were fablers deem'd, and, for belief, met scorn.
Around while gazing thus, far in the sky
Appear'd what look'd, at first, a moving star;
But, onward, wheeling through the clouds it came,
With brightening splendour and increasing size,
Till within ken a fiery chariot rush'd,
By flaming horses drawn, whose heads shot forth
A twisted, horn-like beam. O'er its fierce wheels
Two shining forms alighted on the mount,
Of mortal birth, but deathless rapt to heaven.
Adown their breasts their loose beards floated, white
As mist by moonbeams silver'd; fair they seem'd,
And bright as angels; fellowship with heaven
Their mortal grossness so had purified.
Lucent their mantles; other than the seer
By Jordan caught; and in the prophet's face
A mystic lustre, like the Urim's, gleamed.

XVII.

Now for the dread tribunal all prepared:
Before the throne the angel with the books
Ascending kneel'd, and, crossing on his breast
His sable pinions, there the volumes spread.
A second summons echoed from the trump,
Thrice sounded, when the mighty work began.
Waved onward by a seraph's wand, the sea
Of palpitating bosoms toward the mount
In silence roll'd. No sooner had the first
Pale tremblers its mysterious circle touched
Than, instantaneous, swift as fancy's flash,
As lightning darting from the summer cloud,
Its past existence rose before the soul,
With all its deeds, with all its secret store
Of embryo works, and dark imaginings.
Amidst the chaos, thoughts as numberless
As whirling leaves when autumn strips the woods,
Light and disjointed as the sibyl's, thoughts
Scatter'd upon the waste of long, dim years,
Pass'd in a moment through the quicken'd soul.
Not with the glozing eye of earth beheld;
They saw as with the glance of Deity.
Conscience, stern arbiter in every breast,
Decided. Self-acquitted or condemned,
Through two broad, glittering avenues of spears
They cross'd the angelic squadrons, right, or left
The judgment-seat; by power supernal led
To their allotted stations on the plain.
As onward, onward, numberless, they came,
And touch'd, appall'd, the verge of destiny,
The heavenly spirits inly sympathized:—
When youthful saints, or martyrs scarr'd and white,
With streaming faces, hands ecstatic clasp'd,
Sprang to the right, celestial beaming smiles
A ravishing beauty to their radiance gave;
But downcast looks of pity chill'd the left.
What clench'd hands, and frenzied steps were there!
Yet, on my shuddering soul, the stifled groan,
Wrung from some proud blasphemer, as he rush'd,
Constrain'd by conscience, down the path of death,
Knells horrible.—On all the hurrying throng
The unerring pen stamp'd, as they pass'd, their fate.
Thus, in a day, amazing thought! were judged
The millions, since from the ALMIGHTY's hand,
Launch'd on her course, earth roll'd rejoicing. Whose
The doom to penal fires, and whose to joy,
From man's presumption mists and darkness veil.
So pass'd the day; divided stood the world,
An awful line of separation drawn,
And from his labours the MESSIAH ceased.

XVIII.

By this, the sun his westering car drove low;
Round his broad wheel full many a lucid cloud
Floated, like happy isles, in seas of gold:
Along the horizon castled shapes were piled,
Turrets and towers, whose fronts embattled gleam'd
With yellow light: smit by the slanting ray,
A ruddy beam the canopy reflected;
With deeper light the ruby blush'd; and thick
Upon the seraphs' wings the glowing spots
Seem'd drops of fire. Uncoiling from its staff
With fainter wave, the gorgeous ensign hung,
Or, swelling with the swelling breeze, by fits,
Cast off upon the dewy air huge flakes
Of golden lustre. Over all the hill,
The heavenly legions, the assembled world,
Evening her crimson tint forever drew.

XIX.

But while at gaze, in solemn silence, men
And angels stood, and many a quaking heart
With expectation throbb'd; about the throne
And glittering hill-top slowly wreathed the clouds,
Erewhile like curtains for adornment hung,
Involving Shiloh and the seraphim
Beneath a snowy tent. The bands around,
Eyeing the gonfalon that through the smoke
Tower'd into air, resembled hosts who watch
The king's pavilion where, ere battle hour,
A council sits. What their consult might be,
Those seven dread spirits and their LORD, I mused,
I marvell'd. Was it grace and peace?—or death?
Was it of man?—Did pity for the lost
His gentle nature wring, who knew, who felt
How frail is this poor tenement of clay?*
Arose there from the misty tabernacle
A cry like that upon Gethsemane?—
What pass'd in JESUS' bosom none may know,
But close the cloudy dome invested him;
And, weary with conjecture, round I gazed
Where, in the purple west, no more to dawn,
Faded the glories of the dying day.
Mild twinkling through a crimson-skirted cloud,
The solitary star of evening shone.
While gazing wistful on that peerless light,
Thereafter to be seen no more, (as, oft,
In dreams strange images will mix,) sad thoughts
Pass'd o'er my soul. Sorrowing, I cried, "Farewell,
Pale, beauteous planet, that displayest so soft

* For we have not an high priest which cannot be touched with the feeling of our infirmities.—HEB. iv. 15.

Amid yon glowing streak thy transient beam,
A long, a last farewell! Seasons have changed,
Ages and empires roll'd, like smoke, away,
But thou, unalter'd, beamest as silver fair
As on thy birthnight! Bright and watchful eyes,
From palaces and bowers, have hail'd thy gem
With secret transport! Natal star of love,
And souls that love the shadowy hour of fancy,
How much I owe thee, how I bless thy ray!
How oft thy rising o'er the hamlet green,
Signal of rest, and social converse sweet,
Beneath some patriarchal tree, has cheer'd
The peasant's heart, and drawn his benison.
Pride of the west! beneath thy placid light
The tender tale shall never more be told,
Man's soul shall never wake to joy again:
Thou sett'st forever,—lovely orb, farewell!"

XX.

Low warblings, now, and solitary harps
Were heard among the angels, touch'd and tuned
As to an evening hymn, preluding soft
To cherub voices; louder as they swell'd,
Deep strings struck in, and hoarser instruments,
Mix'd with clear, silver sounds, till concord rose
Full as the harmony of winds to heaven;
Yet sweet as nature's springtide melodies
To some worn pilgrim, first with glistening eyes
Greeting his native valley, whence the sounds
Of rural gladness, herds, and bleating flocks,
The chirp of birds, blithe voices, lowing kine,
The dash of waters, reed, or rustic pipe,
Blent with the dulcet, distance-mellow'd bell,
Come, like the echo of his early joys.
In every pause, from spirits in mid air,
Responsive still were golden viols heard,
And heavenly symphonies stole faintly down.

XXI.

Calm, deep, and silent was the tide of joy
That roll'd o'er all the blessed; visions of bliss,
Rapture too mighty, swell'd their hearts to bursting;
Prelude to heaven it seem'd, and in their sight
Celestial glories swam. How fared, alas!
That other band? Sweet to their troubled minds
The solemn scene; ah! doubly sweet the breeze
Refreshing, and the purple light to eyes
But newly oped from that benumbing sleep
Whose dark and drear abode no cheering dream,
No bright-hued vision ever enters, souls
For ages pent, perhaps, in some dim world
Where guilty spectres stalk the twilight gloom.
For, like the spirit's last seraphic smile,
The earth, anticipating now her tomb,
To rise, perhaps, as heaven magnificent,
Appear'd Hesperian: gales of gentlest wing
Came fragrance-laden, and such odours shed
As Yemen never knew, nor those blest isles
In Indian seas, where the voluptuous breeze
The peaceful native breathes, at eventide,
From nutmeg groves and bowers of cinnamon.
How solemn on their ears the choral note
Swell'd of the angel hymn! so late escaped
The cold embraces of the grave, whose damp
Silence no voice or string'd instrument
Has ever broke! Yet with the murmuring breeze
Full sadly chimed the music and the song,
For with them came the memory of joys
Forever past, the stinging thought of what
They once had been, and of their future lot.
To their grieved view the passages of earth
Delightful rise, their tender ligaments
So dear, they heeded not an after state,
Though by a fearful judgment usher'd in.
A bridegroom fond, who lavish'd all his heart
On his beloved, forgetful of the Man
Of many Sorrows, who, for him, resign'd
His meek and spotless spirit on the cross,
Has marked among the blessed bands, array'd
Celestial in a spring of beauty, doom'd
No more to fade, the charmer of his soul,
Her cheek soft blooming like the dawn in heaven.
He recollects the days when on his smile
She lived; when, gently leaning on his breast,
Tears of intense affection dimm'd her eyes,
Of dove-like lustre.—Thoughtless, now, of him
And earthly joys, eternity and heaven
Engross her soul.—What more accursed pang
Can hell inflict? With her, in realms of light,
In never-dying bliss, he might have roll'd
Eternity away; but now, forever
Torn from his bride new-found, with cruel fiends,
Or men like fiends, must waste and weep. Now, now
He mourns with burning, bitter drops his days
Misspent, probation lost, and heaven despised.
Such thoughts from many a bursting heart drew forth
Groans, lamentations, and despairing shrieks,
That on the silent air came from afar.

XXII.

As, when from some proud capital that crowns
Imperial Ganges, the reviving breeze
Sweeps the dank mist, or hoary river fog
Impervious mantled o'er her highest towers,
Bright on the eye rush BRAHMA's temples, capp'd
With spiry tops, gay-trellised minarets,
Pagods of gold, and mosques with burnish'd domes,
Gilded, and glistening in the morning sun,
So from the hill the cloudy curtains roll'd,
And, in the lingering lustre of the eve,
Again the SAVIOUR and his seraphs shone.
Emitted sudden in his rising, flash'd
Intenser light, as toward the right hand host
Mild turning, with a look ineffable,
The invitation he proclaim'd in accents
Which on their ravish'd ears pour'd thrilling, like
The silver sound of many trumpets heard
Afar in sweetest jubilee; then, swift
Stretching his dreadful sceptre to the left,
That shot forth horrid lightnings, in a voice
Clothed but in half its terrors, yet to them
Seem'd like the crush of heaven, pronounced the doom.
The sentence utter'd, as with life instinct,
The throne uprose majestically slow;
Each angel spread his wings; in one dread swell
Of triumph mingling as they mounted, trumpets,
And harps, and golden lyres, and timbrels sweet,
And many a strange and deep-toned instrument

Of heavenly minstrelsy unknown on earth,
And angels' voices, and the loud acclaim
Of all the ransom'd, like a thunder-shout.
Far through the skies melodious echoes roll'd,
And faint hosannas distant climes return'd.

XXIII.

Down from the lessening multitude came faint
And fainter still the trumpet's dying peal,
All else in distance lost; when, to receive
Their new inhabitants, the heavens unfolded.
Up gazing, then, with streaming eyes, a glimpse
The wicked caught of Paradise, whence streaks
Of splendour, golden quivering radiance shone.
As when the showery evening sun takes leave,
Breaking a moment o'er the illumined world.
Seen far within, fair forms moved graceful by,
Slow-turning to the light their snowy wings.
A deep-drawn, agonizing groan escaped
The hapless outcasts, when upon the LORD
The glowing portals closed. Undone, they stood
Wistfully gazing on the cold, gray heaven,
As if to catch, alas! a hope not there.
But shades began to gather; night approach'd
Murky and lowering: round with horror roll'd
On one another, their despairing eyes
That glared with anguish: starless, hopeless gloom
Fell on their souls, never to know an end.
Though in the far horizon linger'd yet
A lurid gleam, black clouds were mustering there;
Red flashes, follow'd by low muttering sounds,
Announced the fiery tempest doom'd to hurl
The fragments of the earth again to chaos.
Wild gusts swept by, upon whose hollow wing
Unearthly voices, yells, and ghastly peals
Of demon laughter came. Infernal shapes
Flitted along the sulphurous wreaths, or plunged
Their dark, impure abyss, as sea-fowl dive
Their watery element.——O'erwhelmed with sights
And sounds appalling, I awoke; and found
For gathering storms, and signs of coming wo,
The midnight moon gleaming upon my bed
Serene and peaceful. Gladly I survey'd her
Walking in brightness through the stars of heaven,
And blessed the respite ere the day of doom.

HADAD'S DESCRIPTION OF THE CITY OF JERUSALEM.

'TIS so;—the hoary harper sings aright;
How beautiful is Zion!—Like a queen,
Arm'd with a helm, in virgin loveliness,
Her heaving bosom in a bossy cuirass,
She sits aloft, begirt with battlements
And bulwarks swelling from the rock, to guard
The sacred courts, pavilions, palaces,
Soft gleaming through the umbrage of the woods
Which tuft her summit, and, like raven tresses,
Waved their dark beauty round the tower of David.
Resplendent with a thousand golden bucklers,
The embrasures of alabaster shine;
Hail'd by the pilgrims of the desert, bound
To Judah's mart with orient merchandise.
But not, for thou art fair and turret-crown'd,
Wet with the choicest dew of heaven, and bless'd
With golden fruits, and gales of frankincense,
Dwell I beneath thine ample curtains. Here,
Where saints and prophets teach, where the stern law
Still speaks in thunder, where chief angels watch,
And where the glory hovers, here I war.

UNTOLD LOVE.*

THE soul, my lord, is fashion'd—like the lyre.
Strike one chord suddenly, and others vibrate.
Your name abruptly mention'd, casual words
Of comment on your deeds, praise from your uncle,
News from the armies, talk of your return,
A word let fall touching your youthful passion,
Suffused her cheek, call'd to her drooping eye
A momentary lustre; made her pulse
Leap headlong, and her bosom palpitate.
I could not long be blind, for love defies
Concealment, making every glance and motion,
Silence, and speech a tell-tale——. . . . .
These things, though trivial of themselves, begat
Suspicion. But long months elapsed,
Ere I knew all. She had, you know, a fever.
One night, when all were weary and at rest,
I, sitting by her couch, tired and o'erwatch'd,
Thinking she slept, suffer'd my lids to close.
Waked by a voice, I found her——never, Signor,
While life endures, will that scene fade from me,—
A dying lamp wink'd in the hearth, that cast,
And snatched the shadows. Something stood before me
In white. My flesh began to creep. I thought
I saw a spirit. It was my lady risen,
And standing in her night-robe with clasp'd hands,
Like one in prayer. Her pallid face display'd
Something, methought, surpassing mortal beauty.
She presently turn'd round, and fix'd her large, wild eyes,
Brimming with tears, upon me, fetched a sigh,
As from a riven heart, and cried: "He's dead!
But, hush!—weep not,—I've bargain'd for his soul,—
That's safe in bliss!"—Demanding who was dead,
Scarce yet aware she raved, she answer'd quick,
Her COSMO, her beloved; for that his ghost,
All pale and gory, thrice had pass'd her bed.
With that, her passion breaking loose, my lord,
She pour'd her lamentation forth in strains
Pathetical beyond the reach of reason.
"Gone, gone, gone to the grave, and never knew
I loved him!"—I'd no power to speak, or move.
I sat stone still,—a horror fell upon me.
At last, her little strength ebb'd out, she sank,
And lay, as in death's arms, till morning.

* From "Demetria."

SCENE FROM HADAD.

The terraced roof of Absalom's *house by night; adorned with vases of flowers and fragrant shrubs; an awning over part of it.* Tamar *and* Hadad.

Tam. No, no, I well remember—proofs, you said,
Unknown to Moses.
Had. Well, my love, thou know'st
I've been a traveller in various climes;
Trod Ethiopia's scorching sands, and scaled
The snow-clad mountains; trusted to the deep;
Traversed the fragrant islands of the sea,
And with the wise conversed of many nations.
Tam. I know thou hast.
Had. Of all mine eyes have seen,
The greatest, wisest, and most wonderful
Is that dread sage, the Ancient of the Mountain.
Tam. Who?
Had. None knows his lineage, age, or name: his locks
Are like the snows of Caucasus; his eyes
Beam with the wisdom of collected ages.
In green, unbroken years he sees, 't is said,
The generations pass, like autumn fruits,
Garner'd, consumed, and springing fresh to life,
Again to perish, while he views the sun,
The seasons roll, in rapt serenity,
And high communion with celestial powers.
Some say 'tis Shem, our father, some say Enoch,
And some Melchisedek.
Tam. I've heard a tale
Like this, but ne'er believed it.
Had. I have proved it.
Through perils dire, dangers most imminent,
Seven days and nights, mid rocks and wildernesses,
And boreal snows, and never-thawing ice,
Where not a bird, a beast, a living thing,
Save the far-soaring vulture comes, I dared
My desperate way, resolved to know or perish.
Tam. Rash, rash adventurer!
Had. On the highest peak
Of stormy Caucasus there blooms a spot
On which perpetual sunbeams play, where flowers
And verdure never die; and there he dwells.
Tam. But didst thou see him?
Had. Never did I view
Such awful majesty: his reverend locks
Hung like a silver mantle to his feet;
His raiment glistered saintly white, his brow
Rose like the gate of Paradise; his mouth
Was musical as its bright guardians' songs.
Tam. What did he tell thee? O! what wisdom fell
From lips so hallow'd?
Had. Whether he possesses
The Tetragrammaton—the powerful name
Inscribed on Moses' rod, by which he wrought
Unheard-of wonders, which constrains the heavens
To shower down blessings, shakes the earth, and rules
The strongest spirits; or if God hath given
A delegated power, I cannot tell.
But 't was from him I learn'd their fate, their fall,
Who erewhile wore resplendent crowns in heaven;
Now scatter'd through the earth, the air, the sea.
Them he compels to answer, and from them
Has drawn what Moses, nor no mortal ear
Has ever heard.
Tam. But did he tell it thee?
Had. He told me much—more than I dare reveal
For with a dreadful oath he seal'd my lips.
Tam. But canst thou tell me nothing? Why unfold
So much, if I must hear no more?
Had. You bade
Explain my words, almost reproach me, sweet,
For what by accident escaped me.
Tam. Ah!
A little—something tell me—sure not all
Were words inhibited.
Had. Then promise never,
Never to utter of this conference
A breath to mortal.
Tam. Solemnly I vow.
Had. Even then, 't is little I can say, compared
With all the marvels he related.
Tam. Come,
I'm breathless. Tell me how they sinn'd, how fell.
Had. Their head, their prince involved them in his ruin.
Tam. What black offence on his devoted head
Drew endless punishment?
Had. The wish to be
Like the All-Perfect.
Tam. Arrogating that
Due only to his Maker! awful crime!
But what their doom? their place of punishment?
Had. Above, about, beneath; earth, sea, and air;
Their habitations various as their minds,
Employments, and desires.
Tam. But are they round us, Hadad? not confined
In penal chains and darkness?
Had. So he said,
And so your holy books infer. What saith
Your prophet? what the prince of Uz?
Tam. I shudder,
Lest some dark minister be near us now.
Had. You wrong them. They are bright intelligences,
Robb'd of some native splendour, and cast down,
'T is true, from heaven; but not deform'd and foul,
Revengeful, malice-working fiends, as fools
Suppose. They dwell, like princes, in the clouds
Sun their bright pinions in the middle sky;
Or arch their palaces beneath the hills,
With stones inestimable studded so,
That sun or stars were useless there.
Tam. Good heavens!
Had. He bade me look on rugged Caucasus.
Crag piled on crag beyond the utmost ken,
Naked and wild, as if creation's ruins
Were heaped in one immeasurable chain
Of barren mountains, beaten by the storms
Of everlasting winter. But within
Are glorious palaces and domes of light,
Irradiate halls and crystal colonnades.

Vaults set with gems the purchase of a crown,
Blazing with lustre past the noontide beam,
Or, with a milder beauty, mimicking
The mystic signs of changeful Mazzaroth.
Tam. Unheard-of splendour!
Had. There they dwell, and muse,
And wander; beings beautiful, immortal,
Minds vast as heaven, capacious as the sky,
Whose thoughts connect past, present, and to come,
And glow with light intense, imperishable.
Thus, in the sparry chambers of the sea
And air-pavilions, rainbow tabernacles,
They study nature's secrets, and enjoy
No poor dominion.
Tam. Are they beautiful,
And powerful far beyond the human race?
Had. Man's feeble heart cannot conceive it. When
The sage described them, fiery eloquence
Flow'd from his lips; his bosom heaved, his eyes
Grew bright and mystical; moved by the theme,
Like one who feels a deity within.
Tam. Wondrous! What intercourse have they with men?
Had. Sometimes they deign to intermix with man,
But oft with woman.
Tam. Ha! with woman?
Had. She
Attracts them with her gentler virtues, soft,
And beautiful, and heavenly, like themselves.
They have been known to love her with a passion
Stronger than human.
Tam. That surpasses all
You yet have told me.
Had. This the sage affirms;
And MOSES, darkly.
Tam. How do they appear?
How manifest their love?
Had. Sometimes 't is spiritual, signified
By beatific dreams, or more distinct
And glorious apparition. They have stoop'd
To animate a human form, and love
Like mortals.
Tam. Frightful to be so beloved!
Who could endure the horrid thought! What makes
Thy cold hand tremble! or is't mine
That feels so deathy?
Had. Dark imaginations haunt me
When I recall the dreadful interview.
Tam. O, tell them not: I would not hear them.
Had. But why contemn a spirit's love? so high,
So glorious, if he haply deign'd!
Tam. Forswear
My Maker! love a demon!
Had. No—O, no—
My thoughts but wander'd. Oft, alas! they wander.
Tam. Why dost thou speak so sadly now! And lo!
Thine eyes are fix'd again upon Arcturus.
Thus ever, when thy drooping spirits ebb,
Thou gazest on that star. Hath it the power
To cause or cure thy melancholy mood?
[*He appears lost in thought.*
Tell me, ascribest thou influence to the stars?
Had. (*starting.*) The stars! What know'st thou of the stars?
Tam. I know that they were made to rule the night.
Had. Like palace lamps! Thou echoest well thy grandsire.
Woman! the stars are living, glorious,
Amazing, infinite!
Tam. Speak not so wildly.
I know them numberless, resplendent, set
As symbols of the countless, countless years
That make eternity.
Had. Eternity!
O! mighty, glorious, miserable thought!
Had ye endured like those great sufferers,
Like them, seen ages, myriad ages roll;
Could ye but look into the void abyss
With eyes experienced, unobscured by torments,
Then mightst thou name it, name it feelingly.
Tam. What ails thee, HADAD? Draw me not so close.
Had. TAMAR! I need thy love—more than thy love—
Tam. Thy cheek is wet with tears—Nay, let us part—
'T is late—I cannot, must not linger.
[*Breaks from him, and exit.*
Had. Loved and abhorr'd! Still, still accursed!
[*He paces twice or thrice up and down, with passionate gestures; then turns his face to the sky, and stands a moment in silence.*]
O! where,
In the illimitable space, in what
Profound of untried misery, when all
His worlds, his rolling orbs of light, that fill
With life and beauty yonder infinite,
Their radiant journey run, forever set,
Where, where, in what abyss shall I be groaning!
[*Exit.*

ARTHUR'S SOLILOQUY.*

HERE let me pause, and breathe a while, and wipe
These servile drops from off my burning brow.
Amidst these venerable trees, the air
Seems hallow'd by the breath of other times.—
Companions of my fathers! ye have mark'd
Their generations pass. Your giant arms
Shadow'd their youth, and proudly canopied
Their silver hairs, when, ripe in years and glory,
These walks they trod to meditate on heaven.
What warlike pageants have ye seen! what trains
Of captives, and what heaps of spoil! what pomp,
When the victorious chief, war's tempest o'er,
In Warkworth's bowers unbound his panoply!
What floods of splendour, bursts of jocund din,
Startled the slumbering tenants of these shades,
When night awoke the tumult of the feast,
The song of damsels, and the sweet-toned lyre!
Then, princely PERCY reigned amidst his halls,
Champion, and judge, and father of the north.
O, days of ancient grandeur! are ye gone?
Forever gone? Do these same scenes behold
His offspring here, the hireling of a foe?
O, that I knew my fate! that I could read
The destiny which Heaven has mark'd for me!

* From "Percy's Masque."

JOHN M. HARNEY.

[Born, 1789. Died, 1825.]

JOHN M. HARNEY, the second of three sons of THOMAS HARNEY, an officer in the continental forces during the revolution, was born in Sussex county, Delaware, on the ninth of March, 1789. In 1791 the family removed to the vicinity of Nashville, Tennessee, and in a few years to Louisiana. The elder brother and our author studied medicine, and the former became a surgeon in the army. The younger brother also entered the army, was commissioned as lieutenant in 1818, and in 1847 was brevetted a brigadier general for gallant conduct in the battle of Cerro Gordo.

Dr. JOHN M. HARNEY settled in Bardstown, Kentucky, where in 1814 he was married to a daughter of Judge JOHN ROWAN. In 1816 he visited the eastern states; and the death of his wife, soon after, caused him to abandon his pursuits at Bardstown and return to Tennessee; and, as soon as he could make suitable preparations, to go abroad. He travelled in Great Britain, Ireland, France, and Spain; spent several years in the naval service of Buenos Ayres; and coming back to the United States, took up his residence at Savannah, Georgia, where he conducted a political newspaper. Excessive exertion and exposure at a fire, in that city, brought on a fever which undermined his constitution, and having removed again to Bardstown, he died there, on the fifteenth of January, 1825.

His "Crystalina, a Fairy Tale," in six cantos, was completed when he was about twenty-three years of age, but in consequence of "the proverbial indifference, and even contempt, with which Americans receive the works of their countrymen," he informs us in a brief preface, was not published until 1816, when it appeared anonymously in New York. It received much attention in the leading literary journals of that day. Its obvious faults were freely censured, but upon the whole it was reviewed with unusual manifestations of kindly interest. The sensitive poet, however, was so deeply wounded by some unfavorable criticisms, that he suppressed nearly all the copies he had caused to be printed, so that it has since been among our rarest books.

The poem is founded chiefly upon superstitions which prevail among the highlands of Scotland. A venerable seer, named ALTAGRAND, is visited by the knight RINALDO, who informs him that the monarch of a distant island had an only daughter, CRYSTALINA, with whom he had fallen in love; that the princess refused to marry him unless he first distinguished himself in battle; that he "plucked laurel wreaths in danger's bloody path," and returned to claim his promised reward, but was informed of the mysterious disappearance of the maid, of whose fate no indications could be discovered, and that he for years had searched for her in vain through every quarter of the world. He implores the aid of the seer, who ascertains from familiar spirits, summoned by his spells, that CRYSTALINA has been stolen by OBERON, and, arming RINALDO with a cross and consecrated weapons, conducts him to a mystic circle, within which, upon the performance of a described ceremony, the earth opens and discloses the way to Fairy Land. In the second, third, and fourth cantos, are related the knight's adventures in that golden subterranean realm; the various stratagems and enchantments by which its sovereign endeavored to seduce or terrify him; his annihilation of all obstacles by exhibiting the cross; the discovery of CRYSTALINA, transformed into a bird, in OBERON's palace; the means by which she was restored to her natural form of beauty; and the triumphant return of the lovers to the upper air. In the fifth and sixth cantos it is revealed that ALTAGRAND is the father of RINALDO, and the early friend of the father of CRYSTALINA, with whom he had fought in the holy wars against the infidel. The king,

> ——"inspired with joy and wine,
> From his loose locks shook off the snows of time,"

and celebrated the restoration of his child and his friend, and the resignation of his crown to RINALDO, in a blissful song:

> . . . "Ye rolling streams, make liquid melody,
> And dance into the sea.
> Let not rude Boreas, on this halcyon day,
>   Forth in his stormy chariot be whirled;
> Let not a cloud its raven wings display,
>   Nor shoot the oak-rending lightnings at the world.
> Let Jove, auspicious, from his red right hand,
> Lay down his thunder brand—
> A child I lost, but two this day have found,
> Let the earth shout, and let the skies resound. . . .
>
> 'Let Atropos forego her dismal trade,
>   And cast her fatal, horrid shears, away,
> While Lachesis spins out a firmer thread;
>   Let hostile armies hold a truce to-day,
> And grim-faced war wash white his gory hand,
> And smile around the land—
> A child I lost, but two this day have found,
> Let the earth shout, and let the skies resound. . .
>
> "Let all the stars of influence benign,
>   This sacred night in heavenly synod meet;
> Let Mars and Venus be in happy trine,
>   And on the wide world look with aspect sweet;
> And let the mystic music of the spheres
> Be audible to mortal ears—
> A child I lost, but two this day have found,
> Then shout, oh earth, and thou, oh sea, resound."

In 1816, Mr. JOHN NEAL was editing "The Portico," a monthly magazine, at Baltimore, and he reviewed this poem in a long and characteristic article. After remarking that it was "the most splendid production" that ever came before him, he says—

"We can produce passages from 'Crystalina' which have not been surpassed in our language. SPENSER himself, who seemed to have condensed all the radiance of fairy-land upon his starry page, never dreamed of more exquisitely fanciful scenery than that which our bard has sometimes painted.... Had this poet written before SHAKSPEARE and SPENSER, he would have been acknowledged 'the child of fancy.'.... Had he dared to think for himself—to blot out some passages, which his judgment, we are sure, could not have approved—the remainder would have done credit to any poet, living or dead.... It is not our intention to run a parallel between the author of 'Crystalina' and the SHAKSPEARE, SPENSER, or MILTON, of another country.... He moves in a different creation, but he moves in as radiant a circle, and at as elevated a point, in his limited sphere, as any whom we have mentioned."

I cannot quite agree with Mr. NEAL. "Crystalina" does not seem to me very much superior to his own "Battle of Niagara." It however evinces decided poetical power, and if carefully revised, by a man of even very inferior talents, if of a more cultivated taste and greater skill in the uses of language, it might be rendered one of the most attractive productions in its class. The precept of HORACE, that a poet should construct his fable from events generally believed to be true, is justified by the fact that so few works in which the characters are impossible, and the incidents altogether incredible, have been successful in modern times. DRAKE'S "Culprit Fay" is undoubtedly a finer poem than MORRIS'S "Woodman, spare that Tree," but it will never be half as popular.

That Dr. HARNEY had an original and poetical fancy will be sufficiently evident from a few examples:

"Thrice had yon moon her pearly chariot driven
Across the starry wilderness of heaven,
In lonely grandeur; thrice the morning star
Danced on the eastern hills before Hyperion's car."
...."Deep silence reigned, so still, so deep, and dread,
That they might hear the fairy's lightest tread,
Might hear the spider as he wove his snare,
From rock to rock."
...."The mountain tops, oak-crowned
Tossed in the storm, and echoed to the sound
Of trees uptorn, and thunders rolling round."
...."The prowlers of the wood
Fled to their caves, or crouching with alarm,
Howled at the passing spirits of the storm;
Eye-blasting spectres and bleached skeletons,
With snow-white raiment, and disjointed bones,
Before them strode, and meteors flickering dire,
Around them trailed their scintillating fire."
...."The fearless songsters sing,
And round me flutter with familiar wing,
Or mid the flowers, like sunbeams glance about,
Sipping, with slender tongues, the dainty nectar out."
...."Morn, ascending from the sparkling main,
Unlocked her golden magazines of light,
And on the sea, and heaven's cerulean plain,
Showered liquid rubies, while retreating Night
In other climes her starred pavilion spread."

After the publication of "Crystalina," Dr. HARNEY commenced an epic poem, of which fragments were found, with numerous shorter compositions, among his papers, after he died. Mr. GALLAGHER, who examined some of his manuscripts, says "they were worthier than 'Crystalina' of his genius and acquirements;" but nearly all of them disappeared, through the negligence or the jealous care of his friends. Among his latest productions was "The Fever Dream," which was written at Savannah, after he had himself been a sufferer from the disease he so vividly describes. In a lighter vein is the ingenious bagatelle entitled "Echo and the Lover," which, as well as "The Fever Dream," was first published after the poet's death.

EXTRACTS FROM "CRYSTALINA."

SYLPHS, BATHING.

THE shores with acclamations rung,
As in the flood the playful damsels sprung:
Upon their beauteous bodies, with delight,
The billows leapt. Oh, 't was a pleasant sight,
To see the waters dimple round, for joy,
Climb their white necks, and on their bosoms toy:
Like snowy swans they vex'd the sparkling tide,
Till little rainbows danced on every side.
Some swam, some floated, some on pearly feet
Stood sidelong, smiling, exquisitely sweet.

TITANIA'S CONCERT.

IN robes of green, fresh youths the concert led,
Measuring the while, with nice, emphatic tread
Of tinkling sandals, the melodious sound
Of smitten timbrels; some, with myrtles crown'd,
Pour the smooth current of sweet melody,
Through ivory tubes; some blow the bugle free,
And some, at happy intervals, around,
With trumps sonorous swell the tide of sound;
Some, bending raptured o'er their golden lyres,
With cunning fingers fret the tuneful wires;
With rosy lips, some press the syren shell,
And, through its crimson labyrinths, impel
Mellifluous breath, with artful sink and swell.
Some blow the mellow, melancholy horn,
Which, save the knight, no man of woman born,
E'er heard and fell not senseless to the ground,
With viewless fetters of enchantment bound.

ON A FRIEND.

DEVOUT, yet cheerful; pious, not austere,
To others lenient, to himself severe;
Though honored, modest; diffident, though praised
The proud he humbled, and the humble raised;
Studious, yet social; though polite, yet plain;
No man more learnéd, yet no man less vain.
His fame would universal envy move,
But envy's lost in universal love.
That he has faults, it may be bold to doubt,
Yet certain 't is we ne'er have found them out.
If faults he has, (as man, 't is said, must have,)
They are the only faults he ne'er forgave.
I flatter not: absurd to flatter where
Just praise is fulsome, and offends the ear.

THE FEVER DREAM.

A FEVER scorched my body, fired my brain;
Like lava in Vesuvius, boiled my blood
Within the glowing caverns of my heart;
I raged with thirst, and begged a cold, clear draught
Of fountain water. 'T was, with tears, denied.
I drank a nauseous febrifuge, and slept,
But rested not—harassed with horrid dreams
Of burning deserts, and of dusty plains,
Mountains disgorging flames, forests on fire,
Steam, sunshine, smoke, and ever-boiling lakes—
Hills of hot sand, and glowing stones, that seemed
Embers and ashes of a burnt-up world.
Thirst raged within me. I sought the deepest vale,
And called on all the rocks and caves for water;—
I climbed a mountain, and from cliff to cliff,
Pursued a flying cloud, howling for water;—
I crushed the withered herbs, and gnawed dry roots,
Still crying, "Water!" while the cliffs and caves,
In horrid mockery, re-echoed "Water!"
Below the mountain gleamed a city, red
With solar flame, upon the sandy bank
Of a broad river. "Soon, oh soon," I cried,
"I'll cool my burning body in that flood,
And quaff my fill!" I ran; I reached the shore;
The river was dried up; its oozy bed
Was dust; and on its arid rocks I saw
The scaly myriads fry beneath the sun;
Where sank the channel deepest, I beheld
A stirring multitude of human forms,
And heard a faint, wild, lamentable wail.
Thither I sped, and joined the general cry
Of "Water!" They had delved a spacious pit
In search of hidden fountains: sad, sad sight!
I saw them rend the rocks up in their rage,
With mad impatience calling on the earth
To open and yield up her cooling springs. [gaze,
Meanwhile the skies, on which they dared not
Stood o'er them like a canopy of brass—
Undimmed by moisture; the red dog-star raged,
And Phœbus from the house of Virgo shot
His scorching shafts. The thirsty multitude
Grew still more frantic. Those who dug the earth
Fell lifeless on the rocks they strained to upheave,
And filled again, with their own carcasses,
The pits they made—undoing their own work.
Despair at length drove out the laborers,
At sight of whom a general groan announced
The death of hope. Ah! now no more was heard
The cry of "Water!" To the city next,
Howling we ran—all hurrying without aim:—
Thence to the woods. The baked plain gaped
for moisture,
And from its arid breast heaved smoke, that seemed
Breath of a furnace—fierce, volcanic fire,
Or hot monsoon, that raises Syrian sands
To clouds. Amid the forests we espied
A faint and bleating herd. Suddenly, shrill
And horrid shouts arose of "Blood! blood! blood!"
We fell upon them with a tiger's thirst,
And drank up all the blood that was not human;
We were all dyed in blood. Despair returned;
The cry was hushed and dumb confusion reigned.
Even then, when hope was dead, and all past hope,
I heard a laugh, and saw a wretched man
Rip madly his own veins, and bleeding drink
With eager joy. The example seized on all;
Each fell upon himself, tearing his veins
Fiercely in search of blood. And some there were,
Who having emptied their own veins, did seize
Their neighbors' arms, and slay them for their blood.
Oh! happy then were mothers who gave suck.
They dashed their little infants from their breasts,
And their shrunk bosoms tortured, to extract
The balmy juice, oh! exquisitely sweet [gone!
To their parched tongues! 'T is done! now all is
Blood, water, and the bosom's nectar!—all!
"Rend, oh, ye lightnings! the sealed firmament,
And flood a burning world. Rain! rain! pour! pour!
Open, ye windows of high heaven! and pour
The mighty deluge! Let us drown and drink
Luxurious death! Ye earthquakes split the globe,
The solid, rock-ribbed globe—and lay all bare
Its subterranean rivers and fresh seas!"
Thus raged the multitude. And many fell
In fierce convulsions; many slew themselves.
And now I saw the city all in flames—
The forest burning—earth itself on fire!
I saw the mountains open with a roar,
Loud as the seven apocalyptic thunders,
And seas of lava rolling headlong down,
Through crackling forests, fierce, and hot as hell—
Down to the plain. I turned to fly—and waked!

ECHO AND THE LOVER.

Lover. ECHO! mysterious nymph, declare
Of what you're made and what you are—
Echo. "Air!"
Lover. 'Mid airy cliffs, and places high,
Sweet Echo! listening, love, you lie—
Echo. "You lie!"
Lover. You but resuscitate dead sounds—
Hark! how my voice revives, resounds!
Echo. "Zounds!"
Lover. I'll question you before I go—
Come, answer me more apropos!
Echo. "Poh! poh!"
Lover. Tell me fair nymph, if e'er you saw
So sweet a girl as Phœbe Shaw!
Echo. "Pshaw!"
Lover. Say, what will win that frisking coney
Into the toils of matrimony?
Echo. "Money!"
Lover. Has Phœbe not a heavenly brow?
Is it not white as pearl—as snow?
Echo. "Ass, no!"
Lover. Her eyes! Was ever such a pair!
Are the stars brighter than they are?
Echo. "They are!"
Lover. Echo, you lie, but can't deceive me;
Her eyes eclipse the stars, believe me—
Echo. "Leave me."
Lover. But come, you saucy, pert romancer,
Who is as fair as Phœbe? answer.
Echo. "Ann, sir."

ALEXANDER H. EVERETT.

(Born, 1790. Died, 1847.)

Alexander Hill Everett, one of the most learned and respectable of our public characters, is best known as a writer by his various, numerous and able productions in prose; but is entitled to notice in a reviewal of American poetry by the volume of original and translated "Poems," which he published in Boston in 1845. He was a son of the Reverend Oliver Everett, of Dorchester, and an elder brother of Edward Everett, and was born on the nineteenth of March, 1790. He was graduated, with the highest honours, at Harvard College, at the early age of sixteen; the following year was a teacher in the Exeter Academy; and afterwards a student in the law office of John Quincy Adams, whom in 1809 he accompanied to Russia, as his private secretary. In St. Petersburgh he passed two years in the assiduous study of languages and politics, and returning to this country was appointed secretary of legation to the Netherlands, in 1813, and in 1818 became *chargé d'affaires* at that post, and in 1825 minister to Spain. He came home in 1829, and in the same year undertook the editorship of "The North American Review." He was subsequently an active but not a very successful politician, several years, and in 1845, after having for a short time been president of the University of Louisiana, was appointed minister plenipotentiary to China, and sailed for Canton in a national ship, but was compelled by ill health to return, after having proceeded as far as Rio Janeiro. The next year, however, he was able to attempt the voyage a second time, and he succeeded in reaching Canton, but to die there just after his arrival, the twenty-ninth of June, 1847.

The principal works of Mr. Everett are described in "The Prose Writers of America." His poems consist of translations from the Greek, Latin, Norse, German, French and Spanish, with a few original pieces, more wise, perhaps, than poetical. Some of the translations are executed with remarkable grace and spirit.

THE PORTRESS.

L'ENVOI, TO M. L.

Fair Saint! who, in thy brightest day
  Of life's meridian joys,
Hast turn'd thy serious thoughts away
  From fashion's fleeting toys,
And fasten'd them with lofty view
Upon the Only Good and True,
Come, listen to me while I tell
A tale of holy miracle.

Come! fly with me on fancy's wing
  To that far, sea-girt strand,
The clime of sunshine, love, and spring,
  Thy favorite Spanish land!
And lo! before our curious eyes
An ancient city's turrets rise,
And circled by its moss-grown wall,
There stands a vast, baronial hall.

And opposite, a convent pile
  Its massy structure rears,
And in the chapel's vaulted aisle
  A holy shrine appears:
And at the shrine devoutly bent,
There kneels a lovely penitent,
In sable vesture, sadly fair,
Come—listen with me to her prayer

BALLAD.

"Blest shrines! from which in evil hour
  My erring footsteps stray'd,
Oh! grant your kind protecting power!
  To a repentant maid!
Sweet Virgin! if in other days
I sang thee hymns of love and praise,
And plaited garlands for thy brow,
Oh! listen to thy votary now!

"The robe, in which thy form is drest,
  These patient fingers wrought;
The flowers that bloom upon thy breast
  With loving zeal I brought;
That holy cross, of diamond clear,
I often wash'd with many a tear,
And dried again in pious bliss.
Sweet Virgin! with a burning kiss

"And when by cruel arts betray'd,
  My wayward course began,
And I forsook thy holy shade,
  With that false-hearted man,
I breathed to thee my parting prayer,
And gave me to thy gentle care;
Sweet Virgin! hear thy votary's vow,
And grant her thy protection now!"

Unhappy Margaret! she had been
  The fairest and the best,
In pious zeal and modest mien
  Outshining all the rest;
And was so diligent withal,
That she had won the trust of all,
And by superior order sate
As Portress at the convent gate.

And well she watch'd that entrance o'er;—
  Ah! had she known the art
To guard as faithfully the door
  Of her own virgin heart.

But when the glozing tempter came
With honied words of sin and shame,
She broke her order's sacred bands,
And follow'd him to distant lands.

And there, in that delicious clime
  Of song, romance, and flowers,
While guilty love was in its prime,
  They dream'd away the hours;
But soon possession's touch of snow
Subdued his passion's fiery glow,
Converting love to scorn and hate,
And he has left her desolate.

And she from Madrid's courtly bowers
  A weary way has gone,
To seek in old Palencia's towers
  False-hearted ALARCON
His hall is vacant: not a beam
Is from the windows seen to gleam,
Nor sound of life is heard to pour
From balcony or open door.

But lo! where in the cool moonlight
  Her home of former years,
The well-known convent opposite
  Its massy structure rears:
And open stands the chapel door,
Saying, with mute language, to the poor,
The heavy-laden, and distrest,
"Come in! and I will give you rest!"

And she has enter'd, and has knelt
  Before the blessed shrine,
And stealing o'er her senses felt
  An influence divine;
And the false world's corrupt control
No more can subjugate her soul,
Where thoughts of innocence again
With undivided empire reign.

Again she sees her quiet cell,
  And the trim garden there;
Again she hears the matin bell,
  That summons her to prayer;
Again she joins, in chorus high,
The strain of midnight minstrelsy,
That lifts her with each thrilling tone,
In transport to the eternal throne.

"Ah! who will give me back?" she said,
  With hotly-gushing tears,
"The blameless heart, the guiltless head
  Of my departed years?
What heavenly power can turn aside
The course of time's unchanging tide,
And make the Penitent again
The Pure one, that she might have been!"

While musing thus, around the dome,
  She casts a vacant glance;
She sees, emerging from the gloom,
  A graceful form advance.
Proceeding forth with noiseless feet,
From a far chapel's dim retreat,
The figure, clad in nun's array,
Along the pavement took her way.

A lantern in her hand she bore,
  The shade upon her face;
And MARGARET vainly scann'd it o'er,
  Familiar lines to trace;
Then murmur'd, fearing to intrude,
"She is not of the sisterhood—
Perhaps a novice, who has come,
Since MARGARET left her convent home."

From shrine to shrine with measured pace,
  The figure went in turn,
And placed the flowers, and trimm'd the dress,
  And made the tapers burn:
Nor ever rested to look back:
And MARGARET follow'd in her track,
Though far behind: a charm unknown
With secret impulse led her on.

Fair sight it was, I ween, but dread
  And strange as well as fair,
To see how as she visited
  Each separate altar there,
A wondrous flame around it play'd,
So soft it scarcely broke the shade,
But glow'd with lustre cold and white,
Like fleecy clouds of boreal light.

Save only where around the nun
  A warmer blaze it threw;
For there the bright suffusion shone
  With tints of various hue;
Pale azure, clear as seraph's eyes,
Mix'd with the rose's blushing dyes,
And gathering to a halo, spread
In rainbow circles round her head.

And every flower her touch beneath
  Renew'd its former bloom,
And from its bell of odorous breath,
  Sent forth a sweet perfume;
And though no voice the silence stirr'd,
A low, sweet melody was heard,
That fell in tones subdued but clear,
Like heavenly music on the ear

Entranced, in ecstacies of awe,
  And joy that none can tell,
The Penitent at distance saw
  The beauteous miracle;
And scarce can trust the evidence
That pours in floods through every sense;
And thinks, so strange the vision seems,
That she is in the land of dreams.

At length, each altar duly dight,
  And all her labors o'er,
The wondrous nun resumed the light,
  And cross'd the minster floor;
Returning to the chapel shade,
From which her entrance she had made,
Along the aisle where MARGARET stood,
And, passing, brush'd the maiden's hood.

Then she the stranger's mantle caught,
  And something she would say,
But on her lips the unutter'd thought
  In silence died away,

"What would'st thou with me, gentle one?"
In sweetest tones inquired the nun.
Poor MARGARET still no language found,
But gazed intently on the ground.

"Say, then, who art thou?" At her side
Pursued the form divine,
"My name is MARGARET." She replied,
"It is the same with mine."
"Thy office, maiden?" "Lady dear!
For years I was a sister here;
And by superior order sate
As Portress at the convent gate."

"I too," the nun replied, "as one
Among the sisters wait,
And am to all the convent known,
As Portress at the gate."
Then first, entranced in wild amaze,
Her downcast eyes did MARGARET raise
And fix them earnestly upon
The stranger's face;—*it was her own!*

Reflected in that glorious nun,
She sees herself appear:
The air, the lineaments, her own,
In form and character:
The dress the same that she has worn;
The keys the same that she has borne;
Herself in person, habit, name,
At once another and the same.

Struck down with speechless ecstasy,
Astonished MARGARET fell:
"Rise!" spake the vision, "I am she,
Whom thou hast served so well;
And when thou forfeitedst thy vows,
To be a perjured traitor's spouse,
And mad'st to me thy parting prayer
For my protecting love and care:

"I heard and granted thy request,
And to conceal thy shame,
I left the mansion of the blest
And took thy humble name,
Thy features, person, office, dress;
And did the duty of thy place,
And daily made report of all
In order to the principal.

"Behold! where still at every shrine
The votive taper stands;
The dress that once thou wor'st is thine,
The keys are in thy hands:
Thy fame is clear, thy trial o'er:
Then, gentle maiden! sin no more!
And think on her, who faithfully
In hours of danger thought on thee!"

A lightning flash!—a thunder peal!—
And parting o'er their heads,
The church's vaulted pinnacle
An ample passage spreads;
And lo! descending angels come
To guard their queen in triumph home,
The while the echoing minster rings
With sweetest notes from heavenly strings.

Then up, on cherub pinions borne,
The Virgin-Mother passed;
And as she rose, on the forlorn
A radiant smile she cast;
And MARGARET saw, with streaming eyes
Of grateful joy, the vision rise,
And watched it till, from earthly view,
It vanished in the depths of blue.

THE YOUNG AMERICAN.

SCION of a mighty stock!
Hands of iron,—hearts of oak,—
Follow with unflinching tread
Where the noble fathers led.

Craft and subtle treachery,
Gallant youth! are not for thee:
Follow thou in word and deeds
Where the God within thee leads.

Honesty with steady eye,
Truth and pure simplicity,
Love that gently winneth hearts,
These shall be thy only arts,—

Prudent in the council train,
Dauntless on the battle plain,
Ready at the country's need
For her glorious cause to bleed.

Where the dews of night distil
Upon Vernon's holy hill;
Where above it, gleaming far,
Freedom lights her guiding star,—

Thither turn the steady eye,
Flashing with a purpose high;
Thither with devotion meet
Often turn the pilgrim feet.

Let thy noble motto be
GOD,—the COUNTRY,—LIBERTY!
Planted on Religion's rock,
Thou shalt stand in every shock.

Laugh at danger far or near;
Spurn at baseness,—spurn at fear;
Still with persevering might,
Speak the truth, and do the right.

So shall peace, a charming guest,
Dove-like in thy bosom rest,
So shall honor's steady blaze
Beam upon thy closing days.

Happy if celestial favor
Smile upon the high endeavor.
Happy if it be thy call
In the holy cause to fall.

SAMUEL GILMAN.

[Born, about 1791.]

Samuel Gilman, D.D. was born in Gloucester, Massachusetts, where his father had been successfully engaged in commerce, until the capture of several vessels in which he was interested, by the French, in 1798, reduced him to bankruptcy, with loss of health perhaps, for he died soon after, leaving a widow with four small children. Among these Samuel was the only son, and his mother, determining to educate him in the best manner possible, placed him in the family of the Reverend Stephen Peabody, of Atkinson, New Hampshire, a remarkable character, of whom Dr. Gilman has given an interesting account in an article in "The Christian Examiner" for 1847, entitled "Reminiscences of a New England Clergyman at the Close of the Last Century." Having been prepared for college by Mr. Peabody, he entered Harvard in 1807, in the same class with N. L. Frothingham and Edward Everett. He was graduated in 1811, and was afterwards, from 1817 to 1819, connected with the college as a tutor; but in the latter year he was married to Miss Caroline Howard, who, as Mrs. Gilman, has been so creditably distinguished in literature, and removed to Charleston, South Carolina, where he has ever since resided, as pastor of the Unitarian church of that city.

Of Dr. Gilman's earlier writings none received more attention than a series of able papers contributed to the "North American Review," while he was a tutor at Cambridge, on the philosophical "Lectures" of Dr. Thomas Brown. About the same time he translated in a very elegant manner several of the satires of Boileau, which he also printed in the "North American Review." After his removal to Charleston he completed his version of Boileau, and sent the MS. to Mr. Murray, of London, for publication, but by some mischance it was lost, and no efforts have since availed for its recovery. In 1829 he gave to the public his "Memoirs of a New England Village Choir," a little book remarkable for quiet and natural humor, presenting a picture, equally truthful and amusing, of village life in New England in the first quarter of this century. He has more recently published elaborate and thoughtful papers in the reviews, on "The Influence of One National Literature upon Another," "The Writings of Edward Everett," and other subjects, besides literary and theological discourses, biographies, essays, and translations, all executed with taste and scholarly finish.

Among the original poems of Dr. Gilman, the most noticeable are the "History of the Ray of Light," which is reprinted in the second volume of Mr. Kettell's "Specimens of American Poetry," and his "Poem read before the Phi Beta Kappa Society" of Harvard College. Some of his minor pieces have been deservedly popular, and may be found in numerous school-books and choice selections of literature.

THE SILENT GIRL.

She seldom spake; yet she imparted
  Far more than language could—
So birdlike, bright, and tender-hearted,
  So natural and good!
Her air, her look, her rest, her actions,
  Were voice enough for her:
Why need a tongue, when those attractions
  Our inmost hearts could stir!

She seldom talked, but, uninvited,
  Would cheer us with a song;
And oft her hands our ears delighted,
  Sweeping the keys along.
And oft when converse round would languish,
  Ask'd or unasked, she read
Some tale of gladness or of anguish,
  And so our evenings sped.

She seldom spake; but she would listen
  With all the signs of soul;
Her cheek would change, her eye would glisten·
  The sigh—the smile—upstole.
Who did not understand and love her,
  With meaning thus o'erfraught!
Though silent as the sky above her,
  Like that, she kindled thought.

Little she spake; but dear attentions
  From her would ceaseless rise;
She checked our wants by kind preventions,
  She hush'd the children's cries;
And, twining, she would give her mother
  A long and loving kiss—
The same to father, sister, brother,
  All round—nor would one miss.

She seldom spake—she speaks no longer;
  She sleeps beneath yon rose;
'T is well for us that ties no stronger
  Awaken memory's woes·
For oh! our hearts would sure be broken,
  Already drained of tears,
If frequent tones, by her outspoken,
  Still lingered in our ears.

CHARLES SPRAGUE.

[Born, 1791.]

CHARLES SPRAGUE was born in Boston, on the twenty-sixth day of October, in 1791. His father, who still survives, was one of that celebrated band who, in 1773, resisted taxation by pouring the tea on board several British ships into the sea.

Mr. SPRAGUE was educated in the schools of his native city, which he left at an early period to acquire in a mercantile house a practical knowledge of trade. When he was about twenty-one years of age, he commenced the business of a merchant on his own account, and continued in it, I believe, until he was elected cashier of the Globe Bank, one of the first establishments of its kind in Massachusetts. This office he now holds, and he has from the time he accepted it discharged its duties in a faultless manner, notwithstanding the venerable opinion that a poet must be incapable of successfully transacting practical affairs. In this period he has found leisure to study the works of the greatest authors, and particularly those of the masters of English poetry, with which, probably, very few contemporary writers are more familiar; and to write the admirable poems on w..ch is based his own reputation.

The first productions of Mr. SPRAGUE which attracted much attention, were a series of brilliant prologues, the first of which was written for the Park Theatre, in New York, in 1821. Prize theatrical addresses are proverbially among the most worthless compositions in the poetic form. Their brevity and peculiar character prevents the development in them of original conceptions and striking ideas, and they are usually made up of commonplace thoughts and images, compounded with little skill. Those by Mr. SPRAGUE are certainly among the best of their kind, and some passages in them are conceived in the true spirit of poetry. The following lines are from the one recited at the opening of a theatre in Philadelphia, in 1822.

"To grace the stage, the bard's careering mind
Seeks other worlds, and leaves his own behind;
He lures from air its bright, unprison'd forms,
Breaks through the tomb, and Death's dull region storms,
O'er ruin'd realms he pours creative day,
And slumbering kings his mighty voice obey.
From its damp shades the long-laid spirit walks,
And round the murderer's bed in vengeance stalks.
Poor, maniac Beauty brings her cypress wreath,—
Her smile a moonbeam on a blasted heath;
Round some cold grave she comes, sweet flowers to strew,
And, lost to Heaven, still to love is true.
Hate shuts his soul when dove-eyed Mercy pleads;
Power lifts his axe, and Truth's bold service bleeds;
Remorse drops anguish from his burning eyes,
Feels hell's eternal worm, and, shuddering, dies;
War's trophied minion, too, forsakes the dust,
Grasps his worn shield, and waves his sword of rust,
Springs to the slaughter at the trumpet's call,
Again to conquer, or again to fall."

The ode recited in the Boston theatre, at a pageant in honour of SHAKSPEARE, in 1823, is one of the most vigorous and beautiful lyrics in the English language. The first poet of the world, the greatness of his genius, the vast variety of his scenes and characters, formed a subject well fitted for the flowing and stately measure chosen by our author, and the universal acquaintance with the writings of the immortal dramatist enables every one to judge of the merits of his composition. Though to some extent but a reproduction of the creations of SHAKSPEARE, it is such a reproduction as none but a man of genius could effect.

The longest of Mr. SPRAGUE's poems is entitled "Curiosity." It was delivered before the Phi Beta Kappa Society, at Cambridge, in August, 1829. It is in the heroic measure, and its diction is faultless. The subject was happily chosen, and admitted of a great variety of illustrations. The descriptions of the miser, the novel-reader, and the father led by curiosity to visit foreign lands, are among the finest passages in Mr. SPRAGUE's writings. "Curiosity" was published in Calcutta a few years ago, as an original work by a British officer, with no other alterations than the omission of a few American names, and the insertion of others in their places, as SCOTT for COOPER, and CHALMERS for CHANNING; and in this form it was reprinted in London, where it was much praised in some of the critical gazettes.

The poem delivered at the centennial celebration of the settlement of Boston, contains many spirited passages, but it is not equal to "Curiosity" or "The Shakspeare Ode." Its versification is easy and various, but it is not so carefully finished as most of Mr. SPRAGUE's productions. "The Winged Worshippers," "Lines on the Death of M. S. C.," "The Family Meeting," "Art," and several other short poems, evidence great skill in the use of language, and show him to be a master of the poetic art. They are all in good taste; they are free from turgidness; and are pervaded by a spirit of good sense, which is unfortunately wanting in much of the verse written in this age.

Mr. SPRAGUE has written, besides his poems, an essay on drunkenness, and an oration, pronounced at Boston on the fiftieth anniversary of the declaration of independence; and I believe he contributed some papers to the "New England Magazine," while it was edited by his friend J. T. BUCKINGHAM. The style of his prose is florid and much less carefully finished than that of his poetry.

He mixes but little in society, and, I have been told, was never thirty miles from his native city. His leisure hours are passed among his books; with the few "old friends, the tried, the true," who travelled with him up the steeps of manhood: or in the quiet of his own fireside. His poems show the strength of his domestic and social affections.

CURIOSITY.*

It came from Heaven—its power archangels knew,
When this fair globe first rounded to their view;
When the young sun reveal'd the glorious scene
Where oceans gather'd and where lands grew green;
When the dead dust in joyful myriads swarm'd,
And man, the clod, with God's own breath was warm'd:
It reign'd in Eden—when that man first woke,
Its kindling influence from his eye-balls spoke;
No roving childhood, no exploring youth
Led him along, till wonder chill'd to truth;
Full-form'd at once, his subject world he trod,
And gazed upon the labours of his God;
On all, by turns, his charter'd glance was cast,
While each pleased best as each appear'd the last;
But when She came, in nature's blameless pride,
Bone of his bone, his heaven-anointed bride,
All meaner objects faded from his sight,
And sense turn'd giddy with the new delight;
Those charm'd his eye, but this entranced his soul,
Another self, queen-wonder of the whole!
Rapt at the view, in ecstasy he stood,
And, like his Maker, saw that all was good.
It reign'd in Eden—in that heavy hour
When the arch-tempter sought our mother's bower,
In thrilling charm her yielding heart assail'd,
And even o'er dread Jehovah's word prevail'd.
There the fair tree in fatal beauty grew,
And hung its mystic apples to her view:
"Eat," breathed the fiend, beneath his serpent guise,
"Ye shall know all things; gather, and be wise!"
Sweet on her ear the wily falsehood stole,
And roused the ruling passion of her soul.
"Ye shall become like God,"—transcendent fate!
That God's command forgot, she pluck'd and ate;
Ate, and her partner lured to share the crime,
Whose wo, the legend saith, must live through time.
For this they shrank before the Avenger's face,
For this He drove them from the sacred place;
For this came down the universal lot,
To weep, to wander, die, and be forgot.
It came from Heaven—it reigned in Eden's shades—
It roves on earth, and every walk invades:
Childhood and age alike its influence own;
It haunts the beggar's nook, the monarch's throne;
Hangs o'er the cradle, leans above the bier,
Gazed on old Babel's tower—and lingers here.
To all that's lofty, all that's low it turns,
With terror curdles and with rapture burns;
Now feels a seraph's throb, now, less than man's,
A reptile tortures and a planet scans;
Now idly joins in life's poor, passing jars,
Now shakes creation off and soars beyond the stars.
'Tis Curiosity—who hath not felt
Its spirit, and before its altar knelt?
In the pleased infant see the power expand,
When first the coral fills his little hand;
Throned in its mother's lap, it dries each tear,
As her sweet legend falls upon his ear;
Next it assails him in his top's strange hum,
Breathes in his whistle, echoes in his drum;
Each gilded toy, that doting love bestows,
He longs to break, and every spring expose.
Placed by your hearth, with what delight he pores
O'er the bright pages of his pictured stores;
How oft he steals upon your graver task,
Of this to tell you, and of that to ask;
And, when the waning hour to-bedward bids,
Though gentle sleep sit waiting on his lids,
How winningly he pleads to gain you o'er
That he may read one little story more!
Nor yet alone to toys and tales confined,
It sits, dark brooding, o'er his embryo mind:
Take him between your knees, peruse his face,
While all you know, or think you know, you trace;
Tell him who spoke creation into birth,
Arch'd the broad heavens, and spread the rolling earth;
Who formed a pathway for the obedient sun,
And bade the seasons in their circles run;
Who fill'd the air, the forest, and the flood,
And gave man all, for comfort, or for food;
Tell him they sprang at God's creating nod—
He stops you short with, "Father, who made God?
Thus through life's stages may we mark the power
That masters man in every changing hour.
It tempts him from the blandishments of home,
Mountains to climb and frozen seas to roam;
By air-blown bubbles buoy'd, it bids him rise,
And hang, an atom in the vaulted skies;
Lured by its charm, he sits and learns to trace
The midnight wanderings of the orbs of space;
Boldly he knocks at wisdom's inmost gate,
With nature counsels, and communes with fate;
Below, above, o'er all he dares to rove,
In all finds God, and finds that God all love.
Turn to the world—its curious dwellers view,
Like Paul's Athenians, seeking something new.
Be it a bonfire's or a city's blaze,
The gibbet's victim, or the nation's gaze,
A female atheist, or a learned dog,
A monstrous pumpkin, or a mammoth hog,
A murder, or a muster, 'tis the same,
Life's follies, glories, griefs, all feed the flame.
Hark, where the martial trumpet fills the air,
How the roused multitude come round to stare;
Sport drops his ball, Toil throws his hammer by,
Thrift breaks a bargain off, to please his eye;
Up fly the windows, even fair mistress cook,
Though dinner burn, must run to take a look.
In the thronged court the ruling passions read,
Where Story dooms, where Wirt and Webster plead;
Yet kindred minds alone their flights shall trace,
The herd press on to see a cut-throat's face.
Around the gallows' foot behold them draw,
When the lost villain answers to the law;
Soft souls, how anxious on his pangs to gloat,
When the vile cord shall tighten round his throat;
And, ah! each hard-bought stand to quit how grieved,
As the sad rumour runs—"The man's reprieved!"
See to the church the pious myriads pour,
Squeeze through the aisles and jostle round the door;

* Delivered before the Phi Beta Kappa Society of Harvard University, in 1829

Does LANGDON preach?—(I veil his quiet name
Who serves his GOD, and cannot stoop to fame;)—
No, 'tis some reverend mime, the latest rage,
Who thumps the desk, that should have trod the stage,
Cant's veriest ranter crams a house, if new,
When PAUL himself, oft heard, would hardly fill a pew.

Lo, where the stage, the poor, degraded stage,
Holds its warp'd mirror to a gaping age;
There, where, to raise the drama's moral tone,
Fool Harlequin usurps Apollo's throne;
There, where grown children gather round, to praise
The new-vamp'd legends of their nursery days;
Where one loose scene shall turn more souls to shame,
Then ten of CHANNING's lectures can reclaim;
There, where in idiot rapture we adore
The herded vagabonds of every shore:
Women unsex'd, who, lost to woman's pride,
The drunkard's stagger ape, the bully's stride;
Pert, lisping girls, who, still in childhood's fetters,
Babble of love, yet barely know their letters;
Neat-jointed mummers, mocking nature's shape,
To prove how nearly man can match an ape;
Vaulters, who, rightly served at home, perchance
Had dangled from the rope on which they dance;
Dwarfs, mimics, jugglers, all that yield content,
Where Sin holds carnival and Wit keeps Lent;
Where, shoals on shoals, the modest million rush,
One sex to laugh, and one to try to blush,
When mincing RAVENOT sports tight pantalettes,
And turns fops' heads while turning pirouettes;
There, at each ribald sally, where we hear
The knowing giggle and the scurrile jeer;
While from the intellectual gallery first
Rolls the base plaudit, loudest at the worst.

Gods! who can grace yon desecrated dome,
When he may turn his SHAKSPEARE o'er at home?
Who there can group the pure ones of his race,
To see and hear what bids him veil his face?
Ask ye who can? why I, and you, and you;
No matter what the nonsense, if 'tis new.
To Doctor Logic's wit our sons give ear;
They have no time for HAMLET, or for LEAR;
Our daughters turn from gentle JULIET's wo,
To count the twirls of ALMAVIVA's toe.

Not theirs the blame who furnish forth the treat,
But ours, who throng the board and grossly eat;
We laud, indeed, the virtue-kindling stage,
And prate of SHAKSPEARE and his deathless page;
But go, announce his best, on COOPER call,
COOPER, "the noblest Roman of them all;"
Where are the crowds, so wont to choke the door?
'T is an old thing, they 've seen it all before.

Pray Heaven, if yet indeed the stage must stand,
With guiltless mirth it may delight the land;
Far better else each scenic temple fall,
And one approving silence curtain all.
Despots to shame may yield their rising youth,
But Freedom dwells with purity and truth;
Then make the effort, ye who rule the stage—
With novel decency surprise the age;
Even Wit, so long forgot, may play its part,
And Nature yet have power to melt the heart;
Perchance the listeners, to their instinct true,
May fancy common sense—'t were surely something new.

Turn to the Press—its teeming sheets survey,
Big with the wonders of each passing day;
Births, deaths, and weddings, forgeries, fires, and wrecks,
Harangues, and hail-storms, brawls, and broken necks;
Where half-fledged bards, on feeble pinions, seek
An immortality of near a week;
Where cruel eulogists the dead restore,
In maudlin praise, to martyr them once more;
Where ruffian slanderers wreak their coward spite,
And need no venom'd dagger while they write:
There, (with a quill so noisy and so vain,
We almost hear the goose it clothed complain,)
Where each hack scribe, as hate or interest burns,
Toad or toad-eater, stains the page by turns;
Enacts virtu, usurps the critic's chair,
Lauds a mock GUIDO, or a mouthing player;
Viceroys it o'er the realms of prose and rhyme,
Now puffs pert "Pelham," now "The Course of Time;"
And, though ere Christmas both may be forgot,
Vows this beats MILTON, and that WALTER SCOTT;
With SAMSON's vigour feels his nerves expand,
To overthrow the nobles of the land;
Soils the green garlands that for OTIS bloom,
And plants a brier even on CABOT's tomb;
As turn the party coppers, heads or tails,
And now this faction and now that prevails;
Applauds to-day what yesterday he cursed,
Lampoons the wisest, and extols the worst;
While, hard to tell, so coarse a daub he lays,
Which sullies most, the slander or the praise.

Yet, sweet or bitter, hence what fountains burst,
While still the more we drink, the more we thirst.
Trade hardly deems the busy day begun,
Till his keen eye along the page has run;
The blooming daughter throws her needle by,
And reads her schoolmate's marriage with a sigh,
While the grave mother puts her glasses on,
And gives a tear to some old crony gone;
The preacher, too, his Sunday theme lays down,
To know what last new folly fills the town;
Lively or sad, life's meanest, mightiest things,
The fate of fighting cocks, or fighting kings;
Naught comes amiss, we take the nauseous stuff,
Verjuice or oil, a libel or a puff.

'T is this sustains that coarse, licentious tribe
Of tenth-rate type-men, gaping for a bribe;
That reptile race, with all that's good at strife,
Who trail their slime through every walk of life;
Stain the white tablet where a great man's name
Stands proudly chisell'd by the hand of Fame;
Nor round the sacred fireside fear to crawl,
But drop their venom there, and poison all.

'T is Curiosity—though, in its round,
No one poor dupe the calumny has found,
Still shall it live, and still new slanders breed;
What though we ne'er believe, we buy and read;
Like Scotland's war-cries, thrown from hand to hand,
To rouse the angry passions of the land.

So the black falsehood flies from ear to ear,
While goodness grieves, but, grieving, still must hear.
All are not such? O no, there are, thank Heaven,
A nobler troop, to whom this trust is given;
Who, all unbribed, on Freedom's ramparts stand,
Faithful and firm, bright warders of the land.
By them still lifts the Press its arm abroad,
To guide all-curious man along life's road;
To cheer young Genius, Pity's tear to start,
In Truth's bold cause to rouse each fearless heart;
O'er male and female quacks to shake the rod,
And scourge the unsex'd thing that scorns her God;
To hunt Corruption from his secret den,
And show the monster up, the gaze of wondering men.
How swells my theme! how vain my power I find,
To track the windings of the curious mind;
Let aught be hid, though useless, nothing boots,
Straightway it must be pluck'd up by the roots.
How oft we lay the volume down to ask
Of him, the victim in the Iron Mask;
The crusted medal rub with painful care,
To spell the legend out—that is not there;
With dubious gaze, o'er mossgrown tombstones bend,
To find a name—the heralds never penn'd;
Dig through the lava-deluged city's breast,
Learn all we can, and wisely guess the rest:
Ancient or modern, sacred or profane,
All must be known, and all obscure made plain;
If 't was a pippin tempted Eve to sin;
If glorious Byron drugg'd his muse with gin;
If Troy e'er stood; if Shakspeare stole a deer;
If Israel's missing tribes found refuge here;
If like a villain Captain Henry lied;
If like a martyr Captain Morgan died.
Its aim oft idle, lovely in its end,
We turn to look, then linger to befriend;
The maid of Egypt thus was led to save
A nation's future leader from the wave;
New things to hear, when erst the Gentiles ran,
Truth closed what Curiosity began.
How many a noble art, now widely known,
Owes its young impulse to this power alone;
Even in its slightest working, we may trace
A deed that changed the fortunes of a race:
Bruce, bann'd and hunted on his native soil,
With curious eye survey'd a spider's toil:
Six times the little climber strove and fail'd;
Six times the chief before his foes had quail'd;
"Once more," he cried, "in thine my doom I read,
Once more I dare the fight, if thou succeed;"
'T was done—the insect's fate he made his own,
Once more the battle waged, and gain'd a throne.
Behold the sick man, in his easy chair,
Barr'd from the busy crowd and bracing air,—
How every passing trifle proves its power
To while away the long, dull, lazy hour.
As down the pane the rival rain-drops chase,
Curious he'll watch to see which wins the race;
And let two dogs beneath his window fight,
He'll shut his Bible to enjoy the sight.
So with each new-born nothing rolls the day,
Till some kind neighbour, stumbling in his way,
Draws up his chair, the sufferer to amuse,
And makes him happy while he tells—the news.
The news! our morning, noon, and evening cry,
Day unto day repeats it till we die.
For this the cit, the critic, and the fop,
Dally the hour away in Tonsor's shop;
For this the gossip takes her daily route,
And wears your threshold and your patience out;
For this we leave the parson in the lurch,
And pause to prattle on the way to church;
Even when some coffin'd friend we gather round,
We ask, "What news?" then lay him in the ground;
To this the breakfast owes its sweetest zest,
For this the dinner cools, the bed remains unpress'd.
What gives each tale of scandal to the street,
The kitchen's wonder, and the parlour's treat!
See the pert housemaid to the keyhole fly,
When husband storms, wife frets, or lovers sigh;
See Tom your pockets ransack for each note,
And read your secrets while he cleans your coat;
See, yes, to listen see even madam deign,
When the smug seamstress pours her ready strain.
This wings that lie that malice breeds in fear,
No tongue so vile but finds a kindred ear;
Swift flies each tale of laughter, shame, or folly,
Caught by Paul Pry and carried home to Polly;
On this each foul calumniator leans,
And nods and hints the villany he means;
Full well he knows what latent wildfire lies
In the close whisper and the dark surmise;
A muffled word, a wordless wink has woke
A warmer throb than if a Dexter spoke;
And he, o'er Everett's periods who would nod,
To track a secret, half the town has trod.
O thou, from whose rank breath nor sex can save,
Nor sacred virtue, nor the powerless grave,—
Felon unwhipp'd! than whom in yonder cells
Full many a groaning wretch less guilty dwells,
Blush—if of honest blood a drop remains,
To steal its lonely way along thy veins,
Blush—if the bronze, long harden'd on thy cheek,
Has left a spot where that poor drop can speak;
Blush to be branded with the slanderer's name,
And, though thou dread'st not sin, at least dread shame.
We hear, indeed, but shudder while we hear
The insidious falsehood and the heartless jeer;
For each dark libel that thou lick'st to shape,
Thou mayest from law, but not from scorn escape.
The pointed finger, cold, averted eye,
Insulted virtue's hiss—thou canst not fly.
The churl, who holds it heresy to *think*,
Who loves no music but the dollar's clink,
Who laughs to scorn the wisdom of the schools,
And deems the first of poets first of fools;
Who never found what good from science grew,
Save the grand truth that one and one are two;
And marvels Bowditch o'er a book should pore
Unless to make those two turn into four;

Who, placed where Catskill's forehead greets the sky,
Grieves that such quarries all unhewn should lie;
Or, gazing where Niagara's torrents thrill,
Exclaims, "A monstrous stream—to turn a mill!"
Who loves to feel the blessed winds of heaven,
But as his freighted barks are portward driven:
Even he, across whose brain scarce dares to creep
Aught but thrift's parent pair—to get, to keep:
Who never learn'd life's real bliss to know—
With Curiosity even he can glow.
Go, seek him out on yon dear Gotham's walk,
Where traffic's venturers meet to trade and talk:
Where Mammon's votaries bend, of each degree,
The hard-eyed lender, and the pale lendee;
Where rogues, insolvent, strut in white-wash'd pride,
And shove the dupes, who trusted them, aside.
How through the buzzing crowd he threads his way,
To catch the flying rumours of the day,—
To learn of changing stocks, of bargains cross'd,
Of breaking merchants, and of cargoes lost;
The thousand ills that traffic's walks invade,
And give the heart-ache to the sons of trade.
How cold he hearkens to some bankrupt's wo,
Nods his wise head, and cries, "I told you so:
The thriftless fellow lived beyond his means,
He must buy brants—I make my folks eat beans;"
What cares he for the knave, the knave's sad wife,
The blighted prospects of an anxious life?
The kindly throbs, that other men control,
Ne'er melt the iron of the miser's soul;
Through life's dark road his sordid way he wends,
An incarnation of fat dividends;
But, when to death he sinks, ungrieved, unsung,
Buoy'd by the blessing of no mortal tongue,—
No worth rewarded, and no want redress'd,
To scatter fragrance round his place of rest, —
What shall that hallow'd epitaph supply—
The universal wo when good men die?
Cold Curiosity shall linger there,
To guess the wealth he leaves his tearless heir;
Perchance to wonder what must be his doom,
In the far land that lies beyond the tomb;—
Alas! for him, if, in its awful plan,
Heaven deal with him as he hath dealt with man.
Child of romance, these work-day scenes you spurn;
For loftier things your finer pulses burn;
Through Nature's walk your curious way you take,
Gaze on her glowing bow, her glittering flake,—
Her spring's first cheerful green, her autumn's last,
Born in the breeze, or dying in the blast;
You climb the mountain's eve lasting wall;
You linger where the thunder-waters fall;
You love to wander by old ocean's side,
And hold communion with its sullen tide;
Wash'd to your foot some fragment of a wreck,
Fancy shall build again the crowded deck
That trod the waves, till, mid the tempest's frown,
The sepulchre of living men went down.
Yet Fancy, with her milder, tenderer glow,
But dreams what Curiosity would know;
Ye would stand listening, as the booming gun
Proclaim'd the work of agony half-done;
There would you drink each drowning seaman's cry,
As wild to heaven he cast his frantic eye;
Though vain all aid, though Pity's blood ran cold,
The mortal havoc ye would dare behold;
Still Curiosity would wait and weep,
Till all sank down to slumber in the deep.
Nor yet appeased the spirit's restless glow:
Ye would explore the gloomy waste below;
There, where the joyful sunbeams never fell,
Where ocean's unrecorded monsters dwell,
Where sleep earth's precious things, her rifled gold,
Bones bleach'd by ages, bodies hardly cold,
Of those who bow'd to fate in every form,
By battle-strife, by pirate, or by storm;
The sailor-chief, who Freedom's foes defied,
Wrapp'd in the sacred flag for which he died;
The wretch, thrown over to the midnight foam,
Stabb'd in his blessed dreams of love and home;
The mother, with her fleshless arms still clasp'd
Round the scared infant, that in death she grasp'd:
On these, and sights like these, ye long to gaze,
The mournful trophies of uncounted days;
All that the miser deep has brooded o'er,
Since its first billow roll'd to find a shore.
Once more the Press,—not that which daily flings
Its fleeting ray across life's fleeting things,—
See tomes on tomes of fancy and of power,
To cheer man's heaviest, warm his holiest hour.
Now Fiction's groves we tread, where young Romance
Laps the glad senses in her sweetest trance;
Now through earth's cold, unpeopled realms we range,
And mark each rolling century's awful change;
Turn back the tide of ages to its head,
And hoard the wisdom of the honour'd dead.
'T was Heaven to lounge upon a couch, said Gray,
And read new novels through a rainy day:
Add but the Spanish weed, the bard was right;
'T is heaven, the upper heaven of calm delight;
The world forgot, to sit at ease reclined,
While round one's head the smoky perfumes wind,
Firm in one hand the ivory folder grasp'd,
Scott's uncut latest by the other clasp'd;
'T is heaven, the glowing, graphic page to turn,
And feel within the ruling passion burn;
Now through the dingles of his own bleak isle,
And now through lands that wear a sunnier smile,
To follow him, that all-creative one,
Who never found a "brother near his throne."
Look, now, directed by yon candle's blaze,
Where the false shutter half its trust betrays,—
Mark that fair girl, reclining in her bed,
Its curtain round her polish'd shoulders spread,
Dark midnight reigns, the storm is up in power,
What keeps her waking in that dreary hour?
See where the volume on her pillow lies—
Claims Radcliffe or Chapone those frequent sighs?
'T is some wild legend,—now her kind eye fills,
And now cold terror every fibre chills:

Still she reads on—in Fiction's labyrinth lost—
Of tyrant fathers, and of true love cross'd;
Of clanking fetters, low, mysterious groans,
Blood-crusted daggers, and uncoffin'd bones,
Pale, gliding ghosts, with fingers dropping gore,
And blue flames dancing round a dungeon door;—
Still she reads on—even though to read she fears,
And in each key-hole moan strange voices hears,
While every shadow that withdraws her look,
Glares in her face, the goblin of the book;
Still o'er the leaves her craving eye is cast;
On all she feasts, yet hungers for the last;
Counts what remain, now sighs there are no more,
And now even those half tempted to skip o'er;
At length, the bad all killed, the good all pleased,
Her thirsting Curiosity appeased,
She shuts the dear, dear book, that made her weep,
Puts out her light, and turns away to sleep.

Her bright, her bloody records to unrol,
See History come, and wake th' inquiring soul:
How bounds the bosom at each wondrous deed
Of those who founded, and of those who freed;
The good, the valiant of our own loved clime,
Whose names shall brighten through the clouds of time.
How rapt we linger o'er the volumed lore
That tracks the glories of each distant shore;
In all their grandeur and in all their gloom,
The throned, the thrall'd rise dimly from the tomb;
Chiefs, sages, bards, the giants of their race,
Earth's monarch men, her greatness and her grace;
Warm'd as we read, the penman's page we spurn,
And to each near, each far arena turn;
Here, where the Pilgrim's altar first was built,
Here, where the patriot's life-blood first was spilt;
There, where new empires spread along each spot
Where old ones fleurish'd but to be forgot,
Or, direr judgment spared to fill a page,
And with their errors warn an after age.

And where is he upon that Rock can stand,
Nor with their firmness feel his heart expand,
Who a new empire planted where they trod,
And gave it to their children and their GOD?
Who yon immortal mountain-shrine hath press'd,
With saintlier relics stored than priest e'er bless'd,
But felt each grateful pulse more warmly glow,
In voiceless reverence for the dead below?
Who, too, by Curiosity led on,
To tread the shores of kingdoms come and gone,
Where Faith her martyrs to the fagot led,
Where Freedom's champions on the scaffold bled,
Where ancient power, though stripp'd of ancient fame,
Curb'd, but not crushed, still lives for guilt and shame,
But prouder, happier, turns on home to gaze,
And thanks his GOD who gave him better days?

Undraw yon curtain; look within that room,
Where all is splendour, yet where all is gloom:
Why weeps that mother? why, in pensive mood,
Group noiseless round, that little, lovely brood?
The battledore is still, laid by each book,
And the harp slumbers in its custom'd nook.
Who hath done this? what cold, unpitying foe
Hath made this house the dwelling-place of wo?
'Tis he, the husband, father, lost in care,
O'er that sweet fellow in his cradle there:
The gallant bark that rides by yonder strand,
Bears him to-morrow from his native land.
Why turns he, half-unwilling, from his home?
To tempt the ocean and the earth to roam?
Wealth he can boast, a miser's sigh would hush,
And health is laughing in that ruddy blush;
Friends spring to greet him, and he has no foe—
So honour'd and so bless'd, what bids him go?—
His eye must see, his foot each spot must tread,
Where sleeps the dust of earth's recorded dead;
Where rise the monuments of ancient time,
Pillar and pyramid in age sublime;
The pagan's temple and the churchman's tower,
War's bloodiest plain and Wisdom's greenest bower;
All that his wonder woke in school-boy themes,
All that his fancy fired in youthful dreams:
Where SOCRATES once taught he thirsts to stray,
Where HOMER pour'd his everlasting lay;
From VIRGIL's tomb he longs to pluck one flower
By Avon's stream to live one moonlight hour;
To pause where England "garners up" her great,
And drop a patriot's tear to MILTON's fate;
Fame's living masters, too, he must behold,
Whose deeds shall blazon with the best of old:
Nations compare, their laws and customs scan,
And read, wherever spread, the book of man;
For these he goes, self-banish'd from his hearth,
And wrings the hearts of all he loves on earth.

Yet say, shall not new joy these hearts inspire
When grouping round the future winter fire,
To hear the wonders of the world they burn,
And lose his absence in his glad return?—
Return! alas! he shall return no more,
To bless his own sweet home, his own proud shore.
Look once again—cold in his cabin now,
Death's finger-mark is on his pallid brow;
No wife stood by, her patient watch to keep,
To smile on him, then turn away to weep;
Kind woman's place rough mariners supplied,
And shared the wanderer's blessing when he died.
Wrapp'd in the raiment that it long must wear,
His body to the deck they slowly bear;
Even there the spirit that I sing is true;
The crew look on with sad, but curious view;
The setting sun flings round his farewell rays;
O'er the broad ocean not a ripple plays;
How eloquent, how awful in its power,
The silent lecture of death's Sabbath-hour:
One voice that silence breaks—the prayer is said,
And the last rite man pays to man is paid;
The plashing waters mark his resting-place,
And fold him round in one long, cold embrace,
Bright bubbles for a moment sparkle o'er,
Then break, to be, like him, beheld no more;
Down, countless fathoms down, he sinks to sleep,
With all the nameless shapes that haunt the deep

"Alps rise on Alps"—in vain my muse essays
To lay the spirit that she dared to raise:
What spreading scenes of rapture and of wo,
With rose and cypress lure me as I go.
In every question and in every glance,
In folly's wonder and in wisdom's trance,

In all of life, nor yet of life alone,
In all beyond, this mighty power we own.
We would unclasp the mystic book of fate,
And trace the paths of all we love and hate;
The father's heart would learn his children's doom,
Even when that heart is crumbling in the tomb;
If they must sink in guilt, or soar to fame,
And leave a hated or a hallow'd name;
By hope elated, or depress'd by doubt,
Even in the death-pang he would find it out.
What boots it to your dust, your son were born
An empire's idol or a rabble's scorn?
Think ye the franchised spirit shall return,
To share his triumph, his disgrace to mourn?
Ah, Curiosity! by thee inspired,
This truth to know how oft has man inquired!
And is it fancy all? can reason say
Earth's loves must moulder with earth's mouldering clay?
That death can chill the father's sacred glow,
And hush the throb that none but mothers know?
Must we believe those tones of dear delight,
The morning welcome and the sweet good-night,
The kind monition and the well-earn'd praise,
That won and warm'd us in our earlier days,
Turn'd, as they fell, to cold and common air!—
Speak, proud Philosophy! the truth declare!
Yet, no, the fond delusion, if no more,
We would not yield for wisdom's cheerless lore;
A tender creed they hold, who dare believe
The dead return, with them to joy or grieve.
How sweet, while lingering slow on shore or hill,
When all the pleasant sounds of earth are still,
When the round moon rolls through the unpillar'd skies,
And stars look down as they were angels' eyes,
How sweet to deem our lost, adored ones nigh,
And hear their voices in the night-winds sigh.
Full many an idle dream that hope had broke,
And the awed heart to holy goodness woke;
Full many a felon's guilt in thought had died,
Fear'd he his father's spirit by his side;—
Then let that fear, that hope, control the mind;
Still let us question, still no answer find;
Let Curiosity of Heaven inquire,
Nor earth's cold dogmas quench the ethereal fire.
Nor even to life, nor death, nor time confined—
The dread hereafter fills the exploring mind;
We burst the grave, profane the coffin's lid,
Unwisely ask of all so wisely hid;
Eternity's dark record we would read,
Mysteries, unravell'd yet by mortal creed;
Of life to come, unending joy and wo,
And all that holy wranglers dream below;
To find their jarring dogmas out we long,
Or which is right, or whether all be wrong;
Things of an hour, we would invade His throne,
And find out Him, the Everlasting One!
Faith we may boast, undarken'd by a doubt,
We thirst to find each awful secret out;
Hope may sustain, and innocence impart
Her sweet specific to the fearless heart;
The inquiring spirit will not be controll'd,
We would make certain all, and all behold.
Unfathom'd well-head of the boundless soul!
Whose living waters lure us as they roll,
From thy pure wave one cheering hope we draw—
Man, man at least shall spurn proud Nature's law.
All that have breath, but he, lie down content,
Life's purpose served, indeed, when life is spent;
All as in Paradise the same are found;
The beast, whose footstep shakes the solid ground,
The insect living on a summer spire,
The bird, whose pinion courts the sunbeam's fire;
In lair and nest, in way and want, the same
As when their sires sought Adam for a name:
Their be-all and their end-all here below,
They nothing need beyond, nor need to know;
Earth and her hoards their every want supply,
They revel, rest, then, fearless, hopeless, die.
But Man, his Maker's likeness, lord of earth,
Who owes to Nature little but his birth,
Shakes down her puny chains, her wants, and woes,
One world subdues, and for another glows.
See him, the feeblest, in his cradle laid;
See him, the mightiest, in his mind array'd!
How wide the gulf he clears, how bold the flight
That bears him upward to the realms of light!
By restless Curiosity inspired,
Through all his subject world he roves untired:
Looks back and scans the infant days of yore,
On to the time when time shall be no more;
Even in life's parting throb its spirit burns,
And, shut from earth, to heaven more warmly turns.
Shall he alone, of mortal dwellers here,
Thus soar aloft to sink in mid-career!
Less favour'd than a worm, shall his stern doom
Lock up these seraph longings in the tomb?—
O Thou, whose fingers raised us from the dust,
Till there we sleep again, be this our trust:
This sacred hunger marks the immortal mind,
By Thee 'twas given, for Thee, for heaven design'd;
There the rapt spirit, from earth's grossness freed,
Shall see, and know, and be like Thee indeed.
Here let me pause—no further I rehearse
What claims a loftier soul, a nobler verse;
The mountain's foot I have but loiter'd round,
Not dared to scale its highest, holiest ground;
But ventured on the pebbly shore to stray,
While the broad ocean all before me lay;—
How bright the boundless prospect there on high!
How rich the pearls that here all hidden lie!
But not for me—to life's coarse service sold,
Where thought lies barren and naught breeds but gold—
'T is yours, ye favour'd ones, at whose command
From the cold world I ventured, here to stand:
Ye who were lapp'd in Wisdom's murmuring bowers,
Who still to bright improvement yield your hours,
To you the privilege and the power belong,
To give my theme the grace of living song;
Yours be the flapping of the eagle's wing,
To dare the loftiest crag, and heavenward spring,
Mine the light task to hop from spray to spray,
Bless'd if I charm one summer hour away.
One summer hour—its golden sands have run,
And the poor labour of the bard is done.—

Yet, ere I fling aside my humble lyre,
Let one fond wish its trembling strings inspire;
Fancy the task to Feeling shall resign,
And the heart prompt the warm, untutor'd line.
Peace to this ancient spot! here, as of old,
May Learning dwell, and all her stores unfold;
Still may her priests around these altars stand,
And train to truth the children of the land;
Bright be their paths, within these shades who rest,
These brother-bands—beneath his guidance bless'd,
Who, with their fathers, here turn'd wisdom's page,
Who comes to them the statesman and the sage.
Praise be his portion in his labours here,
The praise that cheer'd a KIRKLAND's mild career;
The love that finds in every breast a shrine,
When zeal and gentleness with wisdom join.
Here may he sit, while race succeeding race
Go proudly forth his parent care to grace;
In head and heart by him prepared to rise,
To take their stations with the good and wise:
This crowning recompense to him be given,
To see them guard on earth and guide to heaven;
Thus, in their talents, in their virtues bless'd,
O be his ripest years his happiest and his best!

SHAKSPEARE ODE.*

God of the glorious lyre!
Whose notes of old on lofty Pindus rang,
While JOVE's exulting choir
Caught the glad echoes and responsive sang—
Come! bless the service and the shrine
We consecrate to thee and thine.

Fierce from the frozen north,
When Havoc led his legions forth,
O'er Learning's sunny groves the dark destroyer spread:
In dust the sacred statue slept,
Fair Science round her altars wept,
And Wisdom cowl'd his head.

At length, Olympian lord of morn,
The raven veil of night was torn,
When, through golden clouds descending,
Thou didst hold thy radiant flight,
O'er Nature's lovely pageant bending,
Till Avon rolled, all sparkling to thy sight!

There, on its bank, beneath the mulberry's shade,
Wrapp'd in young dreams, a wild-eyed minstrel stray'd.
Lighting there and lingering long,
Thou didst teach the bard his song;
Thy fingers strung his sleeping shell,
And round his brows a garland curl'd;
On his lips thy spirit fell,
And bade him wake and warm the world!

Then SHAKSPEARE rose!
Across the trembling strings
His daring hand he flings,
And, lo! a new creation glows!

There, clustering round, submissive to his will,
Fate's vassal train his high commands fulfil.

Madness, with his frightful scream,
Vengeance, leaning on his lance,
Avarice, with his blade and beam,
Hatred, blasting with a glance;
Remorse, that weeps, and Rage, that roars,
And Jealousy, that dotes, but dooms, and murders, yet adores.

Mirth, his face with sun-beams lit,
Waking laughter's merry swell,
Arm in arm with fresh-eyed Wit,
That waves his tingling lash, while Folly shakes his bell.

Despair, that haunts the gurgling stream,
Kiss'd by the virgin moon's cold beam,
Where some lost maid wild chaplets wreathes,
And, swan-like, there her own dirge breathes,
Then, broken-hearted, sinks to rest,
Beneath the bubbling wave, that shrouds her maniac breast.

Young Love, with eye of tender gloom,
Now drooping o'er the hallow'd tomb
Where his plighted victims lie—
Where they met, but met to die:
And now, when crimson buds are sleeping,
Through the dewy arbour peeping,
Where Beauty's child, the frowning world forgot,
To youth's devoted tale is listening,
Rapture on her dark lash glistening,
While fairies leave their cowslip cells and guard the happy spot.

Thus rise the phantom throng,
Obedient to their master's song,
And lead in willing chain the wandering soul along,
For other worlds war's Great One sigh'd in vain—
O'er other worlds see SHAKSPEARE rove and reign!
The rapt magician of his own wild lay,
Earth and her tribes his mystic wand obey.
Old Ocean trembles, Thunder cracks the skies,
Air teems with shapes, and tell-tale spectres rise:
Night's paltering hags their fearful orgies keep,
And faithless Guilt unseals the lip of Sleep:
Time yields his trophies up, and Death restores
The mouldered victims of his voiceless shores.
The fireside legend, and the faded page,
The crime that cursed, the deed that bless'd an age,
All, all come forth, the good to charm and cheer,
To scourge bold Vice, and start the generous tear;
With pictured Folly gazing fools to shame,
And guide young Glory's foot along the path of Fame.

Lo! hand in hand,
Hell's juggling sisters stand,
To greet their victim from the fight;
Group'd on the blasted heath,
They tempt him to the work of death,
Then melt in air, and mock his wondering sight.

* Delivered in the Boston Theatre, in 1823, at the exhibition of a pageant in honour of SHAKSPEARE.

In midnight's hallow'd hour
He seeks the fatal tower,
Where the lone raven, perch'd on high,
Pours to the sullen gale
Her hoarse, prophetic wail,
And croaks the dreadful moment nigh.
See, by the phantom dagger led,
Pale, guilty thing,
Slowly he steals with silent tread,
And grasps his coward steel to smite his sleeping king.
Hark! 't is the signal bell,
Struck by that bold and unsex'd one,
Whose milk is gall, whose heart is stone;
His ear hath caught the knell—
'T is done! 't is done!
Behold him from the chamber rushing,
Where his dead monarch's blood is gushing:
Look, where he trembling stands,
Sad, gazing there,
Life's smoking crimson on his hands,
And in his felon heart the worm of wild despair.

Mark the sceptred traitor slumbering!
There flit the slaves of conscience round,
With boding tongues foul murderers numbering;
Sleep's leaden portals catch the sound.
In his dream of blood for mercy quaking,
At his own dull scream behold him waking!
Soon that dream to fate shall turn,
For him the living furies burn;
For him the vulture sits on yonder misty peak,
And chides the lagging night, and whets her hungry beak.
Hark! the trumpet's warning breath
Echoes round the vale of death.
Unhorsed, unhelm'd, disdaining shield,
The panting tyrant scours the field.
Vengeance! he meets thy dooming blade!
The scourge of earth, the scorn of heaven,
He falls! unwept and unforgiven,
And all his guilty glories fade.
Like a crush'd reptile in the dust he lies,
And hate's last lightning quivers from his eyes!

Behold yon crownless king—
Yon white-lock'd, weeping sire—
Where heaven's unpillar'd chambers ring,
And burst their streams of flood and fire!
He gave them all—the daughters of his love:
That recreant pair! they drive him forth to rove;
In such a night of wo,
The cubless regent of the wood
Forgets to bathe her fangs in blood,
And caverns with her foe!
Yet one was ever kind:
Why lingers she behind?
O pity!—view him by her dead form kneeling,
Even in wild frenzy holy nature feeling.
His aching eyeballs strain,
To see those curtain'd orbs unfold,
That beauteous bosom heave again:
But all is dark and cold.
In agony the father shakes;
Grief's choking note
Swells in his throat,
Each wither'd heart-string tugs and breaks!
Round her pale neck his dying arms he wreathes,
And on her marble lips his last, his death-kiss breathes.

Down! trembling wing: shall insect weakness keep
The sun-defying eagle's sweep?
A mortal strike celestial strings,
And feebly echo what a seraph sings?
Who now shall grace the glowing throne,
Where, all unrivall'd, all alone,
Bold SHAKSPEARE sat, and look'd creation through,
The minstrel monarch of the worlds he drew?

That throne is cold—that lyre in death unstrung,
On whose proud note delighted Wonder hung.
Yet old Oblivion, as in wrath he sweeps,
One spot shall spare—the grave where SHAKSPEARE sleeps.
Rulers and ruled in common gloom may lie,
But Nature's laureate bards shall never die.
Art's chisell'd boast and Glory's trophied shore
Must live in numbers, or can live no more.
While sculptured Jove some nameless waste may claim,
Still roars the Olympic car in PINDAR's fame:
Troy's doubtful walls, in ashes pass'd away,
Yet frown on Greece in HOMER's deathless lay;
Rome, slowly sinking in her crumbling fanes,
Stands all immortal in her MARO's strains;
So, too, yon giant empress of the isles,
On whose broad sway the sun forever smiles,
To Time's unsparing rage one day must bend,
And all her triumphs in her SHAKSPEARE end!

O thou! to whose creative power
We dedicate the festal hour,
While Grace and Goodness round the altar stand,
Learning's anointed train, and Beauty's rose-lipp'd band—
Realms yet unborn, in accents now unknown,
Thy song shall learn, and bless it for their own
Deep in the west, as Independence roves,
His banners planting round the land he loves,
Where Nature sleeps in Eden's infant grace,
In Time's full hour shall spring a glorious race:
Thy name, thy verse, thy language shall they bear,
And deck for thee the vaulted temple there.
Our Roman-hearted fathers broke
Thy parent empire's galling yoke;
But thou, harmonious monarch of the mind,
Around their sons a gentler chain shall bind;
Still o'er our land shall Albion's sceptre wave,
And what her mighty lion lost, her mightier swan shall save.

THE BROTHERS.

WE are but two—the others sleep
Through death's untroubled night;
We are but two—O, let us keep
The link that binds us bright.

Heart leaps to heart—the sacred flood
That warms us is the same;
That good old man—his honest blood
Alike we fondly claim.

We in one mother's arms were lock'd—
Long be her love repaid;
In the same cradle we were rock'd,
Round the same hearth we play'd.

Our boyish sports were all the same,
Each little joy and wo;—
Let manhood keep alive the flame,
Lit up so long ago.

We are but two—be that the band
To hold us till we die;
Shoulder to shoulder let us stand,
Till side by side we lie.

ART.

When, from the sacred garden driven,
Man fled before his Maker's wrath,
An angel left her place in heaven,
And cross'd the wanderer's sunless path.
'T was Art! sweet Art! new radiance broke
Where her light foot flew o'er the ground,
And thus with seraph voice she spoke:
"The curse a blessing shall be found."

She led him through the trackless wild,
Where noontide sunbeam never blazed;
The thistle shrunk, the harvest smiled,
And Nature gladden'd as she gazed.
Earth's thousand tribes of living things,
At Art's command, to him are given;
The village grows, the city springs,
And point their spires of faith to heaven.

He rends the oak—and bids it ride,
To guard the shores its beauty graced;
He smites the rock—upheaved in pride,
See towers of strength and domes of taste.
Earth's teeming caves their wealth reveal,
Fire bears his banner on the wave,
He bids the mortal poison heal,
And leaps triumphant o'er the grave.

He plucks the pearls that stud the deep,
Admiring beauty's lap to fill;
He breaks the stubborn marble's sleep,
And mocks his own Creator's skill.
With thoughts that fill his glowing soul,
He bids the ore illume the page,
And, proudly scorning Time's control,
Commerces with an unborn age.

In fields of air he writes his name,
And treads the chambers of the sky,
He reads the stars, and grasps the flame
That quivers round the throne on high.
In war renown'd, in peace sublime,
He moves in greatness and in grace;
His power, subduing space and time,
Links realm to realm, and race to race.

"LOOK ON THIS PICTURE."

O, it is life! departed days
Fling back their brightness while I gaze:
'Tis Emma's self—this brow so fair,
Half-curtain'd in this glossy hair,
These eyes, the very home of love,
The dark twin arches traced above,
These red-ripe lips that almost speak,
The fainter blush of this pure cheek,
The rose and lily's beauteous strife—
It is—ah no!—'tis all *but* life.

'Tis all *but* life—art could not save
Thy graces, Emma, from the grave;
Thy cheek is pale, thy smile is past,
Thy love-lit eyes have look'd their last;
Mouldering beneath the coffin's lid,
All we adored of thee is hid;
Thy heart, where goodness loved to dwell,
Is throbless in the narrow cell;
Thy gentle voice shall charm no more;
Its last, last, joyful note is o'er.

Oft, oft, indeed, it hath been sung,
The requiem of the fair and young;
The theme is old, alas! how old,
Of grief that will not be controll'd,
Of sighs that speak a father's wo,
Of pangs that none but mothers know,
Of friendship, with its bursting heart,
Doom'd from the idol-one to part—
Still its sad debt must feeling pay,
Till feeling, too, shall pass away.

O say, why age, and grief, and pain
Shall long to go, but long in vain;
Why vice is left to mock at time,
And, gray in years, grow gray in crime;
While youth, that every eye makes glad,
And beauty, all in radiance clad,
And goodness, cheering every heart,
Come, but come only to depart;
Sunbeams, to cheer life's wintry day,
Sunbeams, to flash, then fade away.

'Tis darkness all! black banners wave
Round the cold borders of the grave;
There, when in agony we bend
O'er the fresh sod that hides a friend,
One only comfort then we know—
We, too, shall quit this world of wo;
We, too, shall find a quiet place
With the dear lost ones of our race;
Our crumbling bones with theirs shall blend,
And life's sad story find an end.

And *is* this all—this mournful doom?
Beams no glad light beyond the tomb?
Mark how yon clouds in darkness ride;
They do not quench the orb they hide;
Still there it wheels—the tempest o'er,
In a bright sky to burn once more;
So, far above the clouds of time,
Faith can behold a world sublime—
There, when the storms of life are past,
The light beyond shall break at last.

CENTENNIAL ODE.*

I.

Not to the pagan's mount I turn
For inspirations now;
Olympus and its gods I spurn—
Pure One, be with me, Thou!
Thou, in whose awful name,
From suffering and from shame
Our fathers fled, and braved a pathless sea;
Thou, in whose holy fear,
They fix'd an empire here,
And gave it to their children and to Thee.

II.

And You! ye bright-ascended Dead,
Who scorn'd the bigot's yoke,
Come, round this place your influence shed;
Your spirits I invoke.
Come, as ye came of yore,
When on an unknown shore
Your daring hands the flag of faith unfurl'd,
To float sublime,
Through future time
The beacon-banner of another world.

III.

Behold! they come—those sainted forms,
Unshaken through the strife of storms;
Heaven's winter cloud hangs coldly down,
And earth puts on its rudest frown;
But colder, ruder was the hand
That drove them from their own fair land;
Their own fair land—refinement's chosen seat,
Art's trophied dwelling, Learning's green retreat;
By valour guarded, and by victory crown'd,
For all, but gentle charity renown'd.
With streaming eye, yet steadfast heart,
Even from that land they dared to part,
And burst each tender tie;
Haunts, where their sunny youth was pass'd,
Homes, where they fondly hoped at last
In peaceful age to die.
Friends, kindred, comfort, all they spurn'd;
Their fathers' hallow'd graves;
And to a world of darkness turn'd,
Beyond a world of waves.

IV.

When Israel's race from bondage fled,
Signs from on high the wanderers led;
But here—Heaven hung no symbol here,
Their steps to guide, *their* souls to cheer;
They saw, through sorrow's lengthening night,
Naught but the fagot's guilty light;
The cloud they gazed at was the smoke
That round their murder'd brethren broke.
Nor power above, nor power below
Sustain'd them in their hour of wo;
A fearful path they trod,
And dared a fearful doom;
To build an altar to their God,
And find a quiet tomb.

* Pronounced at the Centennial Celebration of the Settlement of Boston, September, 1830.

V.

But not alone, not all unbless'd,
The exile sought a place of rest;
One dared with him to burst the knot
That bound her to her native spot;
Her low, sweet voice in comfort spoke,
As round their bark the billows broke;
She through the midnight watch was there,
With him to bend her knees in prayer;
She trod the shore with girded heart,
Through good and ill to claim her part,
In life, in death, with him to seal
Her kindred love, her kindred zeal.

VI.

They come;—that coming who shall tell!
The eye may weep, the heart may swell,
But the poor tongue in vain essays
A fitting note for them to raise.
We hear the after-shout that rings
For them who smote the power of kings;
The swelling triumph all would share,
But who the dark defeat would dare,
And boldly meet the wrath and wo
That wait the unsuccessful blow?
It were an envied fate, we deem,
To live a land's recorded theme,
When we are in the tomb;
We, too, might yield the joys of home,
And waves of winter darkness roam,
And tread a shore of gloom—
Knew we those waves, through coming time,
Should roll our names to every clime;
Felt we that millions on that shore
Should stand, our memory to adore.
But no glad vision burst in light
Upon the Pilgrims' aching sight;
Their hearts no proud hereafter swell'd;
Deep shadows veil'd the way they held;
The yell of vengeance was their trump of fame,
Their monument, a grave without a name.

VII.

Yet, strong in weakness, there they stand,
On yonder ice-bound rock,
Stern and resolved, that faithful band,
To meet fate's rudest shock.
Though anguish rends the father's breast,
For them, his dearest and his best,
With him the waste who trod—
Though tears that freeze, the mother sheds
Upon her children's houseless heads—
The Christian turns to God!

VIII.

In grateful adoration now,
Upon the barren sands they bow.
What tongue of joy e'er woke such prayer
As bursts in desolation there?
What arm of strength e'er wrought such power
As waits to crown that feeble hour?
There into life an infant empire springs!
There falls the iron from the soul;
There Liberty's young accents roll
Up to the King of kings!

To fair creation's farthest bound
That thrilling summons yet shall sound;
The dreaming nations shall awake,
And to their centre earth's old kingdoms shake.
Pontiff and prince, your sway
Must crumble from that day;
Before the loftier throne of Heaven
The hand is raised, the pledge is given—
One monarch to obey, one creed to own,
That monarch, GOD; that creed, His word alone.

IX.

Spread out earth's holiest records here,
Of days and deeds to reverence dear;
A zeal like this what pious legends tell?
On kingdoms built
In blood and guilt,
The worshippers of vulgar triumph dwell—
But what exploits with theirs shall page,
Who rose to bless their kind—
Who left their nation and their age,
Man's spirit to unbind!
Who boundless seas pass'd o'er,
And boldly met, in every path,
Famine, and frost, and heathen wrath,
To dedicate a shore,
Where Piety's meek train might breathe their vow,
And seek their Maker with an unshamed brow;
Where Liberty's glad race might proudly come,
And set up there an everlasting home?

X.

O, many a time it hath been told,
The story of those men of old.
For this fair Poetry hath wreathed
Her sweetest, purest flower;
For this proud Eloquence hath breathed
His strain of loftiest power;
Devotion, too, hath linger'd round
Each spot of consecrated ground,
And hill and valley bless'd;
There, where our banish'd fathers stray'd,
There, where they loved, and wept, and pray'd,
There, where their ashes rest.

XI.

And never may they rest unsung,
While Liberty can find a tongue.
Twine, Gratitude, a wreath for them,
More deathless than the diadem,
Who, to life's noblest end,
Gave up life's noblest powers,
And bade the legacy descend
Down, down to us and ours.

XII.

By centuries now the glorious hour we mark,
When to these shores they steer'd their shatter'd bark;
And still, as other centuries melt away,
Shall other ages come to keep the day.
When we are dust, who gather round this spot,
Our joys, our griefs, our very names forgot,
Here shall the dwellers of the land be seen,
To keep the memory of the Pilgrims green.
Nor here alone their praises shall go round,
Nor here alone their virtues shall abound—
Broad as the empire of the free shall spread,
Far as the foot of man shall dare to tread,
Where oar hath never dipp'd, where human tongue
Hath never through the woods of ages rung,
There, where the eagle's scream and wild wolf's cry
Keep ceaseless day and night through earth and sky,
Even there, in after time, as toil and taste
Go forth in gladness to redeem the waste,
Even there shall rise, as grateful myriads throng,
Faith's holy prayer and Freedom's joyful song;
There shall the flame that flash'd from yonder Rock,
Light up the land, till nature's final shock.

XIII.

Yet while, by life's endearments crown'd,
To mark this day we gather round,
And to our nation's founders raise
The voice of gratitude and praise,
Shall not one line lament that lion race,
For us struck out from sweet creation's face?
Alas! alas! for them—those fated bands,
Whose monarch tread was on these broad, green lands;
Our fathers call'd them savage—them, whose bread
In the dark hour, those famish'd fathers fed;
We call them savage, we,
Who hail the struggling free
Of every clime and hue;
We, who would save
The branded slave,
And give him liberty he never knew;
We, who but now have caught the tale
That turns each listening tyrant pale,
And bless'd the winds and waves that bore
The tidings to our kindred shore;
The triumph-tidings pealing from that land
Where up in arms insulted legions stand;
There, gathering round his bold compeers,
Where He, our own, our welcomed One,
Riper in glory than in years,
Down from his forfeit throne
A craven monarch hurl'd,
And spurn'd him forth, a proverb to the world

XIV.

We call them savage—O, be just!
Their outraged feelings scan;
A voice comes forth, 'tis from the dust—
The savage was a man!
Think ye he loved not? Who stood by,
And in his toils took part?
Woman was there to bless his eye—
The savage had a heart!
Think ye he pray'd not! When on high
He heard the thunders roll,
What bade him look beyond the sky?
The savage had a soul!

XV.

I venerate the Pilgrim's cause,
Yet for the red man dare to plead—
We bow to Heaven's recorded laws,
He turn'd to nature for a creed;

Beneath the pillar'd dome,
We seek our God in prayer;
Through boundless woods he loved to roam,
And the Great Spirit worshipp'd there.
But one, one fellow-throb with us he felt;
To one divinity with us he knelt;
Freedom, the self-same Freedom we adore,
Bade him defend his violated shore.
He saw the cloud, ordain'd to grow,
And burst upon his hills in wo;
He saw his people withering by,
Beneath the invader's evil eye;
Strange feet were trampling on his father's bones
At midnight hour he woke to gaze
Upon his happy cabin's blaze,
And listen to his children's dying groans.
He saw—and, maddening at the sight,
Gave his bold bosom to the fight;
To tiger rage his soul was driven;
Mercy was not—nor sought nor given;
The pale man from his lands must fly;
He would be free—or he would die.

XVI.

And was this savage? say,
Ye ancient few,
Who struggled through
Young Freedom's trial-day—
What first your sleeping wrath awoke?
On your own shores war's larum broke;
What turn'd to gall even kindred blood!
Round your own homes the oppressor stood;
This every warm affection chill'd,
This every heart with vengeance thrill'd,
And strengthen'd every hand;
From mound to mound
The word went round—
"Death for our native land!"

XVII.

Ye mothers, too, breathe ye no sigh
For them who thus could dare to die?
Are all your own dark hours forgot,
Of soul-sick suffering here?
Your pangs, as, from yon mountain spot,
Death spoke in every booming shot
That knell'd upon your ear?
How oft that gloomy, glorious tale ye tell,
As round your knees your children's children hang,
Of them, the gallant ones, ye loved so well,
Who to the conflict for their country sprang!
In pride, in all the pride of wo,
Ye tell of them, the brave laid low,
Who for their birth-place bled;
In pride, the pride of triumph then,
Ye tell of them, the matchless men,
From whom the invaders fled.

XVIII.

And ye, this holy place who throng,
The annual theme to hear,
And bid the exulting song
Sound their great names from year to year;
Ye, who invoke the chisel's breathing grace,
In marble majesty their forms to trace;
Ye, who the sleeping rocks would raise,
To guard their dust and speak their praise;
Ye, who, should some other band
With hostile foot defile the land,
Feel that ye like them would wake,
Like them the yoke of bondage break,
Nor leave a battle-blade undrawn,
Though every hill a sepulchre should yawn—
Say, have not ye one line for those,
One brother-line to spare,
Who rose but as your fathers rose,
And dared as ye would dare?

XIX.

Alas! for them—their day is o'er,
Their fires are out from hill and shore;
No more for them the wild deer bounds;
The plough is on their hunting-grounds;
The pale man's axe rings through their woods
The pale man's sail skims o'er their floods,
Their pleasant springs are dry;
Their children—look, by power oppress'd,
Beyond the mountains of the west,
Their children go—to die.

XX.

O, doubly lost! Oblivion's shadows close
Around their triumphs and their woes.
On other realms, whose suns have set,
Reflected radiance lingers yet;
There sage and bard have shed a light
That never shall go down in night;
There time-crown'd columns stand on high,
To tell of them who cannot die;
Even we, who then were nothing, kneel
In homage there, and join earth's general peal.
But the doom'd Indian leaves behind no trace,
To save his own, or serve another race:
With his frail breath his power has pass'd away,
His deeds, his thoughts are buried with his clay;
Nor lofty pile, nor glowing page
Shall link him to a future age,
Or give him with the past a rank;
His heraldry is but a broken bow,
His history but a tale of wrong and wo,
His very name must be a blank.

XXI.

Cold, with the beast he slew, he sleeps;
O'er him no filial spirit weeps;
No crowds throng round, no anthem-notes ascend,
To bless his coming and embalm his end;
Even that he lived, is for his conqueror's tongue,
By foes alone his death-song must be sung;
No chronicles but theirs shall tell
His mournful doom to future times;
May these upon his virtues dwell,
And in his fate forget his crimes.

XXII.

Peace to the mingling dead:
Beneath the turf we tread,
Chief, pilgrim, patriot sleep.
All gone! how changed! and yet the same
As when Faith's herald bark first came
In sorrow o'er the deep.

Still, from his noonday height,
The sun looks down in light;
Along the trackless realms of space,
The stars still run their midnight race;
The same green valleys smile, the same rough shore
Still echoes to the same wild ocean's roar;—
But where the bristling night-wolf sprang
Upon his startled prey,
Where the fierce Indian's war-cry rang
Through many a bloody fray,
And where the stern old pilgrim pray'd
In solitude and gloom,
Where the bold patriot drew his blade,
And dared a patriot's doom,—
Behold! in Liberty's unclouded blaze
We lift our heads, a race of other days.

XXIII.

All gone! the wild beast's lair is trodden out;
Proud temples stand in beauty there;
Our children raise their merry shout
Where once the death-whoop vex'd the air.
The pilgrim—seek yon ancient mound of graves,
Beneath that chapel's holy shade;
Ask, where the breeze the long grass waves,
Who, who within that spot are laid:
The patriot—go, to Fame's proud mount repair;
The tardy pile, slow rising there,
With tongueless eloquence shall tell
Of them who for their country fell.

XXIV.

All gone! 't is ours, the goodly land—
Look round—the heritage behold;
Go forth—upon the mountains stand;
Then, if ye can, be cold.
See living vales by living waters bless'd;
Their wealth see earth's dark caverns yield;
See ocean roll, in glory dress'd.
For all a treasure, and round all a shield;
Hark to the shouts of praise
Rejoicing millions raise;
Gaze on the spires that rise
To point them to the skies,
Unfearing and unfear'd;
Then, if ye can, O, then forget
To whom ye owe the sacred debt—
The pilgrim race revered!
The men who set Faith's burning lights
Upon these everlasting heights,
To guide their children through the years of time;
The men that glorious law who taught,
Unshrinking liberty of thought,
And roused the nations with the truth sublime.

XXV.

Forget! No, never—ne'er shall die
Those names to memory dear;
I read the promise in each eye
That beams upon me here.
Descendants of a twice-recorded race!
Long may ye here your lofty lineage grace.
'T is not for you home's tender tie
To rend, and brave the waste of waves;
'T is not for you to rouse and die,
Or yield, and live a line of slaves.
The deeds of danger and of death are done:
Upheld by inward power alone,
Unhonour'd by the world's loud tongue,
'T is yours to do unknown,
And then to die unsung.
To other days, to other men belong
The penman's plaudit, and the poet's song;
Enough for glory has been wrought;
By you be humbler praises sought;
In peace and truth life's journey run,
And keep unsullied what your fathers won.

XXVI.

Take then my prayer, ye dwellers of this spot!
Be yours a noiseless and a guiltless lot.
I plead not that ye bask
In the rank beams of vulgar fame;
To light your steps, I ask
A purer and a holier flame.
No bloated growth I supplicate for you,
No pining multitude, no pamper'd few;
'T is not alone to coffer gold,
Nor spreading borders to behold;
'T is not fast-swelling crowds to win,
The refuse-ranks of want and sin.
This be the kind decree:
Be ye by goodness crown'd;
Revered, though not renown'd;
Poor, if Heaven will, but free!
Free from the tyrants of the hour,
The clans of wealth, the clans of power,
The coarse, cold scorners of their God;
Free from the taint of sin,
The leprosy that feeds within,
And free, in mercy, from the bigot's rod.

XXVII.

The sceptre's might, the crosier's pride,
Ye do not fear;
No conquest blade, in life-blood dyed,
Drops terror here,—
Let there not lurk a subtler snare,
For wisdom's footsteps to beware.
The shackle and the stake
Our fathers fled;
Ne'er may their children wake
A fouler wrath, a deeper dread;
Ne'er may the craft that fears the flesh to bind,
Lock its hard fetters on the mind;
Quench'd be the fiercer flame
That kindles with a name;
The pilgrim's faith, the pilgrim's zeal,
Let more than pilgrim kindness seal;
Be purity of life the test,
Leave to the heart, to heaven, the rest.

XXVIII.

So, when our children turn the page,
To ask what triumphs mark'd our age—
What we achieved to challenge praise,
Through the long line of future days—
This let them read, and hence instruction draw:
"Here were the many bless'd,
Here found the virtues rest,
Faith link'd with Love, and Liberty with Law;

Here industry to comfort led;
Her book of light here learning spread;
Here the warm heart of youth
Was woo'd to temperance and to truth;
Here hoary age was found,
By wisdom and by reverence crown'd.
No great but guilty fame
Here kindled pride, that should have kindled shame;
These chose the better, happier part,
That pour'd its sunlight o'er the heart,
That crown'd their homes with peace and health,
And weigh'd Heaven's smile beyond earth's wealth;
Far from the thorny paths of strife
They stood, a living lesson to their race,
Rich in the charities of life,
Man in his strength, and woman in her grace;
In purity and truth their pilgrim path they trod,
And when they served their neighbour, felt they served their God."

XXIX.

This may not wake the poet's verse,
This souls of fire may ne'er rehearse
In crowd-delighting voice;
Yet o'er the record shall the patriot bend,
His quiet praise the moralist shall lend,
And all the good rejoice.

XXX.

This be our story, then, in that far day,
When others come their kindred debt to pay.
In that far day!—O, what shall be,
In this dominion of the free,
When we and ours have render'd up our trust,
And men unborn shall tread above our dust?
O, what shall be?—He, He alone
The dread response can make,
Who sitteth on the only throne
That time shall never shake:
Before whose all-beholding eyes
Ages sweep on, and empires sink and rise.
Then let the song, to Him begun,
To Him in reverence end;
Look down in love, Eternal One,
And Thy good cause defend;
Here, late and long, put forth thy hand,
To guard and guide the Pilgrim's land.

LINES TO A YOUNG MOTHER.

Young mother! what can feeble friendship say,
To soothe the anguish of this mournful day?
They, they alone, whose hearts like thine have bled,
Know how the living sorrow for the dead;
Each tutor'd voice, that seeks such grief to cheer,
Strikes cold upon the weeping parent's ear;
I've felt it all—alas! too well I know
How vain all earthly power to hush thy wo!
God cheer thee, childless mother! 'tis not given
For man to ward the blow that falls from heaven.

I've felt it all—as thou art feeling now;
Like thee, with stricken heart and aching brow.
I've sat and watch'd by dying beauty's bed,
And burning tears of hopeless anguish shed;
I've gazed upon the sweet, but pallid face,
And vainly tried some comfort there to trace;
I've listen'd to the short and struggling breath;
I've seen the cherub eye grow dim in death;
Like thee, I've veil'd my head in speechless gloom,
And laid my first-born in the silent tomb.

I SEE THEE STILL.

"I rock'd her in the cradle,
And laid her in the tomb. She was the *youngest*.
What fireside circle hath not felt the charm
Of that sweet tie? The youngest ne'er grew old.
The fond endearments of our earlier days
We keep alive in them, and when they die,
Our youthful joys we bury with them."

I see thee still:
Remembrance, faithful to her trust,
Calls thee in beauty from the dust;
Thou comest in the morning light,
Thou'rt with me through the gloomy night;
In dreams I meet thee as of old:
Then thy soft arms my neck enfold,
And thy sweet voice is in my ear:
In every scene to memory dear
I see thee still.

I see thee still,
In every hallow'd token round;
This little ring thy finger bound,
This lock of hair thy forehead shaded,
This silken chain by thee was braided,
These flowers, all wither'd now, like thee,
Sweet sister, thou didst cull for me;
This book was thine, here didst thou read,
This picture, ah! yes, here, indeed,
I see thee still.

I see thee still:
Here was thy summer noon's retreat,
Here was thy favourite fireside seat;
This was thy chamber—here, each day,
I sat and watch'd thy sad decay;
Here, on this bed, thou last didst lie,
Here, on this pillow, thou didst die:
Dark hour! once more its woes unfold;
As then I saw thee, pale and cold,
I see thee still.

I see thee still:
Thou art not in the grave confined—
Death cannot claim the immortal mind;
Let earth close o'er its sacred trust,
But goodness dies not in the dust;
Thee, O! my sister, 'tis not thee
Beneath the coffin's lid I see;
Thou to a fairer land art gone;
There, let me hope, my journey done,
To see thee still!

LINES ON THE DEATH OF M. S. C.

I KNEW that we must part—day after day,
I saw the dread Destroyer win his way;
That hollow cough first rang the fatal knell,
As on my ear its prophet-warning fell;
Feeble and slow thy once light footstep grew,
Thy wasting cheek put on death's pallid hue,
Thy thin, hot hand to mine more weakly clung,
Each sweet "Good night" fell fainter from thy tongue;
I knew that we must part—no power could save
Thy quiet goodness from an early grave;
Those eyes so dull, though kind each glance they cast,
Looking a sister's fondness to the last;
Thy lips so pale, that gently press'd my cheek,
Thy voice—alas! thou couldst but try to speak;—
All told thy doom; I felt it at my heart;
The shaft had struck—I knew that we must part.
And we have parted, MARY—thou art gone!
Gone in thine innocence, meek, suffering one.
Thy weary spirit breathed itself to sleep
So peacefully, it seem'd a sin to weep,
In those fond watchers who around thee stood,
And felt, even then, that GOD, even then, was good.
Like stars that struggle through the clouds of night,
Thine eyes one moment caught a glorious light,
As if to thee, in that dread hour, 't were given
To know on earth what faith believes of heaven;
Then like tired breezes didst thou sink to rest,
Nor one, one pang the awful change confess'd.
Death stole in softness o'er that lovely face,
And touch'd each feature with a new-born grace;
On cheek and brow unearthly beauty lay,
And told that life's poor cares had pass'd away.
In my last hour be Heaven so kind to me!
I ask no more than this—to die like thee.
But we have parted, MARY—thou art dead!
On its last resting-place I laid thy head,
Then by thy coffin-side knelt down, and took
A brother's farewell kiss and farewell look;
Those marble lips no kindred kiss return'd;
From those veil'd orbs no glance responsive burn'd;
Ah! then I felt that thou hadst pass'd away,
That the sweet face I gazed on was but clay;
And then came Memory, with her busy throng
Of tender images, forgotten long;
Years hurried back, and as they swiftly roll'd,
I saw thee, heard thee, as in days of old;
Sad and more sad each sacred feeling grew;
Manhood was moved, and Sorrow claim'd her due;
Thick, thick and fast the burning tear-drops started;
I turn'd away—and felt that we had parted.—
But not forever—in the silent tomb,
Where thou art laid, thy kindred shall find room;
A little while, a few short years of pain,
And, one by one, we'll come to thee again;
The kind old father shall seek out the place,
And rest with thee, the youngest of his race;
The dear, dear mother, bent with age and grief,
Shall lay her head by thine, in sweet relief;
Sister and brother, and that faithful friend,
True from the first, and tender to the end,—
All, all, in His good time, who placed us here,
To live, to love, to die, and disappear,
Shall come and make their quiet bed with thee,
Beneath the shadow of that spreading tree;
With thee to sleep through death's long, dreamless night,
With thee rise up and bless the morning light.

THE FAMILY MEETING.*

WE are all here!
Father, mother,
Sister, brother,
All who hold each other dear.
Each chair is fill'd—we're all *at home*;
To-night let no cold stranger come:
It is not often thus around
Our old familiar hearth we're found:
Bless, then, the meeting and the spot;
For once be every care forgot;
Let gentle Peace assert her power,
And kind Affection rule the hour;
We're all—all here.

We're *not* all here!
Some are away—the dead ones dear,
Who throng'd with us this ancient hearth,
And gave the hour to guiltless mirth.
Fate, with a stern, relentless hand,
Look'd in and thinn'd our little band:
Some like a night-flash pass'd away,
And some sank, lingering, day by day;
The quiet graveyard—some lie there—
And cruel Ocean has his share—
We're *not* all here.

We *are* all here!
Even they—the dead—though dead, so dear;
Fond Memory, to her duty true,
Brings back their faded forms to view.
How life-like, through the mist of years,
Each well-remember'd face appears!
We see them as in times long past;
From each to each kind looks are cast;
We hear their words, their smiles behold;
They're round us as they were of old—
We *are* all here.

We are all here!
Father, mother,
Sister, brother,
You that I love with love so dear.
This may not long of us be said;
Soon must we join the gather'd dead;
And by the hearth we now sit round,
Some other circle will be found.
O! then, that wisdom may we know,
Which yields a life of peace below!
So, in the world to follow this,
May each repeat, in words of bliss,
We're all—all *here!*

* Written on the accidental meeting of all the surviving members of a family.

THE WINGED WORSHIPPERS.

Gay, guiltless pair,
What seek ye from the fields of heaven?
Ye have no need of prayer,
Ye have no sins to be forgiven.

Why perch ye here,
Where mortals to their Maker bend?
Can your pure spirits fear
The God ye never could offend?

Ye never knew
The crimes for which we come to weep,
Penance is not for you,
Blessed wanderers of the *upper deep.*

To you 'tis given
To wake sweet nature's untaught lays;
Beneath the arch of heaven
To chirp away a life of praise.

Then spread each wing,
Far, far above, o'er lakes and lands,
And join the choirs that sing
In yon blue dome not rear'd with hands.

Or, if ye stay,
To note the consecrated hour,
Teach me the airy way,
And let me try your envied power.

Above the crowd,
On upward wings could I but fly,
I'd bathe in you bright cloud,
And seek the stars that gem the sky.

'T were heaven indeed
Through fields of trackless light to soar,
On Nature's charms to feed,
And Nature's own great God adore.

DEDICATION HYMN.

God of wisdom, God of might,
Father! dearest name of all,
Bow thy throne and bless our rite;
'T is thy children on thee call.
Glorious One! look down from heaven,
Warm each heart and wake each vow;
Unto Thee this house is given;
With thy presence fill it now.

Fill it now! on every soul
Shed the incense of thy grace,
While our anthem-echoes roll
Round the consecrated place;
While thy holy page we read,
While the prayers Thou lovest ascend,
While thy cause thy servants plead,—
Fill this house, our God, our Friend.

Fill it now—O, fill it long!
So, when death shall call us home,
Still to Thee, in many a throng,
May our children's children come.
Bless them, Father, long and late,
Blot their sins, their sorrows dry;
Make this place to them the gate
Leading to thy courts on high.

There, when time shall be no more,
When the feuds of earth are past,
May the tribes of every shore
Congregate in peace at last!
Then to Thee, thou One all-wise,
Shall the gather'd millions sing,
Till the arches of the skies
With their hallelujahs ring.

TO MY CIGAR.

Yes, social friend, I love thee well,
In learned doctors' spite;
Thy clouds all other clouds dispel,
And lap me in delight.

What though they tell, with phizzes long,
My years are sooner pass'd?
I would reply, with reason strong,
They're sweeter while they last.

And oft, mild friend, to me thou art
A monitor, though still;
Thou speak'st a lesson to my heart,
Beyond the preacher's skill.

Thou'rt like the man of worth, who gives
To goodness every day,
The odour of whose virtues lives
When he has passed away.

When, in the lonely evening hour,
Attended but by thee,
O'er history's varied page I pore,
Man's fate in thine I see.

Oft as thy snowy column grows,
Then breaks and falls away,
I trace how mighty realms thus rose,
Thus tumbled to decay.

A while, like thee, earth's masters burn,
And smoke and fume around,
And then, like thee, to ashes turn,
And mingle with the ground.

Life's but a leaf adroitly roll'd,
And time's the wasting breath,
That late or early, we behold,
Gives all to dusty death.

From beggar's frieze to monarch's robe
One common doom is pass'd:
Sweet nature's works, the swelling globe,
Must all burn out at last.

And what is he who smokes thee now?—
A little moving heap,
That soon like thee to fate must bow,
With thee in dust must sleep.

But though thy ashes downward go,
Thy essence rolls on high;
Thus, when my body must lie low,
My soul shall cleave the sky.

SEBA SMITH.

[Born 1792. Died 1868.]

Seba Smith was born in Buckfield, Maine, on the fourteenth of September, 1792; graduated at Bowdoin College in 1818; and having studied the law, settled in Portland, where his literary tastes led him to a connection with the press, and he edited successively the "Eastern Argus," and the "Portland Courier." It was during his residence in Portland that he originated the popular and natural character of "Major Downing," which has served more frequently and successfully than any other for the illustration of New England peculiarites, in speech and manners. When about thirty years of age, he was married to Elizabeth Oakes Prince, who has since been one of the most conspicuous literary women of this country. In 1842 they removed to New York, where Mr. Smith has published "Letters of Major Jack Downing," "Powhattan, a Metrical Romance," "Way Down East, or Portraitures of Yankee Life," "New Elements of Geometry," &c. One of his earliest attempts in verse was "An Auction Extraordinary," frequently quoted as Lucretia Maria Davidson's. Among his minor poems several are dramatic and picturesque, and noticeable for unusual force of description.

THE BURNING SHIP AT SEA.

The night was clear and mild,
And the breeze went softly by,
And the stars of heaven smiled
As they wandered up the sky;
And there rode a gallant ship on the wave—
But many a hapless wight
Slept the sleep of death that night,
And before the morning light
Found a grave!

All were sunk in soft repose
Save the watch upon the deck;
Not a boding dream arose
Of the horrors of the wreck,
To the mother, or the child, or the sire;
Till a shriek of wo profound,
Like a death-knell echo'd round—
With a wild and dismal sound,
A shriek of "fire!"

Now the flames are spreading fast—
With resistless rage they fly,
Up the shrouds and up the mast,
And are flickering to the sky;
Now the deck is all a blaze; now the rails—
There's no place to rest their feet;
Fore and aft the torches meet,
And a winged lightning sheet
Are the sails.

No one heard the cry of wo
But the sea-bird that flew by;
There was hurrying to and fro,
But no hand to save was nigh;
Still before the burning foe they were driven—
Last farewells were uttered there,
With a wild and phrenzied stare,
And a short and broken prayer
Sent to Heaven.

Some leap over in the flood
To the death that waits them there;
Others quench the flames with blood,
And expire in open air;
Some, a moment to escape from the grave,
On the bowsprit take a stand;
But their death is near at hand—
Soon they hug the burning brand
On the wave.

From his briny ocean-bed,
When the morning sun awoke,
Lo, that gallant ship had fled!
And a sable cloud of smoke
Was the monumental pyre that remained;
But the sea-gulls round it fly,
With a quick and fearful cry,
And the brands that floated by
Blood had stained.

THE SNOW STORM.

The cold winds swept the mountain's height,
And pathless was the dreary wild,
And mid the cheerless hours of night
A mother wander'd with her child:
As through the drifting snow she press'd,
The babe was sleeping on her breast.

And colder still the winds did blow,
And darker hours of night came on,
And deeper grew the drifting snow:
Her limbs were chill'd, her strength was gone.
"Oh, God!" she cried, in accents wild,
"If I must perish, save my child!"

She stripp'd her mantle from her breast,
And bared her bosom to the storm,
And round the child she wrapp'd the vest
And smiled to think her babe was warm.
With one cold kiss, one tear she shed,
And sunk upon her snowy bed.

At dawn a traveller passed by,
And saw her 'neath a snowy veil;
The frost of death was in her eye,
Her cheek was cold, and hard, and pale,
He moved the robe from off the child—
The babe look'd up and sweetly smiled!

N. L. FROTHINGHAM.

[Born, 1793.]

The Reverend Nathaniel Langdon Frothingham, D.D., was born in Boston in the summer of 1793, and was graduated at Cambridge in the class of 1811. While a student there he pronounced the poem at the installation of Dr. Kirkland as president of the university, but his first printed verses of any considerable extent were the "Poem delivered before the Phi Beta Kappa Society" in 1813, which appeared in Mr. Andrews Norton's "General Repository." The year before this he became an instructor in rhetoric and oratory in the college, an office which he was the first to hold, and in which he was succeeded by his friend J. M. Wainwright, afterwards bishop of the Protestant Episcopal Church in New York. He remained in it till the spring of 1815, when he was ordained as pastor of the First Congregational Church in Boston. In this pastorate he continued until ill-health compelled him to resign it, at the same point of the year, in 1850.

Dr. Frothingham has been many years a contributor to the "Christian Examiner," and, less frequently, to some other periodicals. In 1845 he published "Deism or Christianity" in four discourses; in 1852 "Sermons, in the order of a Twelvemonth;" and in other years, about fifty sermons and addresses of various kinds. In 1855 he has gratified his friends, and enriched our literature by printing a collection of his poems, under the title of "Metrical Pieces, Translated and Original."

A singular grace of expression and refinement of sentiment pervade the prose writings of Dr. Frothingham, and his poetry is also marked by exquisite finish and tasteful elegance. His works are among the best models of composition which contemporary New England scholars will present to posterity. The longest of his poems is a masterly version of "The Phenomena or Appearances of the Stars," from the Greek of Aratus. His translations from the German have been very highly esteemed by the most competent critics for fidelity to their first authors, and as English poems. He has exhibited what the Germans accomplished in their own language and what they would have done in ours. His independent productions in verse are what might have been expected from a mind in contemplation and action subordinated so instinctively and sedulously to the laws of beauty.

TO THE OLD FAMILY CLOCK,

SET UP IN A NEW PLACE.

Old things are come to honor. Well they might,
If old like thee, thou reverend monitor!
So gravely bright, so simply decorated;
Thy gold but faded into softer beauty,
While click and hammer-stroke are just the same
As when my cradle heard them. Thou holdst on,
Unwearied, unremitting, constant ever;
The time that thou dost measure leaves no mark
Of age or sorrow on thy gleaming face.
The pulses of thy heart were never stronger;
And thy voice rings as clear as when it told me
How slowly crept the impatient days of childhood.
More than a hundred years of joys and troubles
Have passed and listened to thee; while thy tongue
Still told in its one round the unvaried tale;—
The same to thee, to them how different,
As fears, regrets, or wishes gave it tone!
My mother's childish wonder gazed as mine did
On the raised figures of thy slender door;—
The men, or dames, Chinese, grotesquely human;
The antler'd stag beneath its small round window;
The birds above, of scarce less size than he;
The doubtful house; the tree unknown to nature.
I see thee not in the old-fashioned room,
That first received thee from the mother land,
But yet thou mind'st me of those ancient times
Of homely duties and of plain delights,
Whose love and mirth and sadness sat before thee;—
Their laugh and sigh both over now,—their voices
Sunk and forgotten, and their forms but dust.
Thou, for their sake, stand honored *there* awhile,
Honored wherever standing,—ne'er to leave
The house that calls me master. When there's none
I thus bequeath thee as in trust to those such,
Who shall bear up my name. For each that hears
The music of thy bell, strike on the hours;
Duties between, and heaven's great hope beyond
them!

TO A DEAD TREE,

WITH A VINE TRAINED OVER IT.

The dead tree bears; each dried-up bough
With leaves is overgrown,
And wears a living drapery now
Of verdure not his own.

The worthless stock a use has found,
The unsightly branch a grace;
As climbing first, then dropped around,
The green shoots interlace.

So round that Grecian mystic rod
To Hermes' hand assigned,—
The emblem of a helping god—
First leaves, then serpents, twined.

In thee a holier sign I view
Than in Hebrew rods of power;
Whether they to a serpent grew,
Or budded into flower.

This Vine, but for thy mournful prop,
Would ne'er have learned the way
Thy ruined height to overtop,
And mantle thy decay.

O thou, my soul, thus train thy thought
By Sorrow's barren aid!
Deck with the charms that Faith has brought
The blights that Time has made.

On all that is remediless
Still hang thy gentle vails;
And make thy charities a dress,
When other foliage fails.

The sharp, bare points of mortal lot
With kindly growth o'erspread;—
Some blessing on what pleases not,
Some life on what is dead.

STRENGTH: TO AN INVALID.

"When I am weak, I'm strong,"
The great Apostle cried.
The strength that did not to the earth belong
The might of Heaven supplied.

"When I am weak, I'm strong,"
Blind Milton caught that strain
And flung its victory o'er the ills that throng
Round Age, and Want, and Pain.

"When I am weak, I'm strong,"
Each Christian heart repeats;
These words will tune its feeblest breath to song,
And fire its languid beats.

O Holy Strength! whose ground
Is in the heavenly land;
And whose supporting help alone is found
In God's immortal hand!

O blessed! that appears
When fleshly aids are spent;
And girds the mind when most it faints and fears,
With trust and sweet content!

It bids us cast aside
All thoughts of lesser powers;—
Give up all hopes from changing time and tide,
And all vain will of ours.

We have but to confess
That there's but one retreat;
And meekly lay each need and each distress
Down at the Sovereign feet;—

Then, then it fills the place
Of all we hoped to do;
And sunken Nature triumphs in the Grace
That bears us up and through.

A better glow than health
Flushes the cheek and brow,
The house is stout with store of nameless wealth;—
We can do all things now.

No less sufficience seek;
All counsel less is wrong;
The whole world's force is poor, and mean, and weak;—
"When I am weak, I'm strong."

THE FOUR HALCYON POINTS OF THE YEAR.

Four points divide the skies,
Traced by the Augur's staff in days of old:
"The spongy South," the hard North gleaming cold,
And where days set and rise.

Four seasons span the year:—
The flowering Spring, the Summer's ripening glow,
Autumn with sheaves, and Winter in its snow;
Each brings its separate cheer.

Four halcyon periods part,
With gentle touch, each season into twain,
Spreading o'er all in turn their gentle reign.
O mark them well, my heart!

Janus! the first is thine.
After the freezing solstice locks the ground;—
When the keen blasts, that moan or rave around,
Show not one softening sign;—

It interposes then.
The air relents: the ices thaw to streams;
A mimic Spring shines down with hazy beams,
Ere Winter roars again.

Look thrice four weeks from this.
The vernal days are rough in our stern clime
Yet fickle April wins a mellow time,
Which chilly May shall miss.

Another term is run.
She comes again—the peaceful one—though less
Or needed or perceived in summer dress—
Half lost in the bright sun;

Yet then a place she finds,
And all beneath the sultry calm lies hush;—
Till o'er the chafed and darkening ocean rush
The squally August winds.

Behold her yet once more,
And O how beautiful! Late in the wane
Of the dishevelled year; when hill and plain
Have yielded all their store;—

When the leaves thin and pale—
And they not many—tremble on the bough;
Or, noisy in their crisp decay, e'en now
Roll to the sharpening gale;

In smoky lustre clad,
Its warm breath flowing in a parting hymn,
The "Indian Summer" upon Winter's rim,
Looks on us sweetly sad.

So with the Year of Life.
An Ordering Goodness helps its youth and age,
Posts quiet sentries midway every stage,
And gives it truce in strife.

The Heavenly Providence,
With varying methods, but a steady hold,
Doth trials still with mercies interfold,
For human soul and sense.

The Father that's above,
Remits, assuages; still abating one
Of all the stripes due to the ill that's done,
In his compassionate love.

Help Thou our wayward mind
To own Thee constantly in all our states—
The world of Nature and the world of Fates—
Forbearing, tempering, kind.

HENRY ROWE SCHOOLCRAFT.

[Born 1793. Died 1864.]

The family name of this learned and voluminous author, he informs us in his "Personal Memoirs," was CALCRAFT. The change of the initial syllable was induced by the occupation of his father as a teacher, the usage of the neighborhood being tacitly adopted in the household. He was born in Guilderland, near Albany, on the twenty-eighth of March, 1793. His chief works are a "Treatise on Vitreology," 1817; "View of the Lead Mines of Missouri," 1819; "Journal of a Tour into the Interior of Missouri and Arkansas," 1820; "Narrative of an Expedition to the Head Waters of the Mississippi," 1821; "Travels in the Central Portions of the Mississippi Valley," 1822; "An Expedition to Itasca Lake," 1834; "Algic Researches, comprising Inquiries respecting the Mental Characteristics of the North American Indians," 1839; "Oneota, or Characteristics of the Red Race of America," 1844; "Notes on the Iroquois," 1846; "Personal Memoirs of a Residence of Thirty Years with the Indian Tribes," 1851; "Scenes and Adventures in the Ozark Mountains," 1853; and "Information respecting the History, Condition, and Prospects, of the Indian Tribes of the United States," in five quarto volumes, published by the government.

The poetical compositions of Dr. SCHOOLCRAFT are numerous, frequently ingenious, and have all about them a pleasing air of genuineness. Living many years in remote solitudes, he had "no resort to pass away his time" but the cultivation of his natural taste for verse, and he wisely selected his themes from his own fresh and peculiar experiences. Besides contributions to literary journals, during nearly half a century, he has published, "Transallegania, a Poem," 1820; "The Rise of the West, or a Prospect of the Mississippi Valley," 1830; "The Man of Bronze, a Poem on the Indian Character, in Six Books," read before the Algic Society, at Detroit, 1833; "Alhalla, or the Lord of Talladega, a Tale of the Creek War," 1843; and "Helderbergia," in four cantos, 1855.

FROM "THE WHITE FISH."

OF venison let GOLDSMITH so wittily sing,
A very fine haunch is a very fine thing;
And BURNS, in his tuneful and exquisite way,
The charms of a smoking Scot's haggis display;
But 't is often much harder to eat than descant,
And a poet may praise what a poet may want.
Less question shall be with my muse of my dish,
Whilst her power I invoke in the praise of white fish:
So fine on a platter, so tempting a fry,
So rich in a broil, and so sweet in a pie,
That even before it the red trout must fail,
And that mighty *bonne bouche* of the land, beaver tail!
Its beauty and flavor no person can doubt,
If seen in the water, or tasted without;
And all the dispute that an epicure makes,
Of this king of lake fishes, this deer of the lakes,
Regards not its choiceness, to ponder or sup,
But the best mode of dressing and serving it up.
Now this is a point where good livers may differ,
As tastes become fixed, or opinions are stiffer. ....
The merchant, the lawyer, the cit, and the beau,
The proud and gustative, the poor and the low,
The gay *habitant*, the inquisitive tourist,
The chemic physician, the dinner crost jurist—
To these it is often a casual sweet,
As they dine by appointment, or taste as a treat;
Not so, or as mental or physical joy,
Comes the sight of this fish to the *courier de bois*;
That wild troubadour with his joy-loving crew,
Who sings as he paddles his birchen canoe,
And thinks all the hardships that fall to his lot,
Are richly made up at the platter and pot.
To him there's a charm neither feeble nor vague
In the mighty repast of the *grande Ticameg*;*
And oft as he starves amid Canada's snows,
On dry leather lichens and *bouton de rose*,
He cheers up his spirits to think he shall still
Of *poisson blanc bouillon* once more have his fill. ....
The muse might appeal to the science of books
To picture its ichthyological looks,
Show what is its family likeness or odds,
Compared with its cousins, the salmons and cods;
Tell where it approximates, point where it fails,
By counting its fins, or dissecting its scales;
Or dwell on its habits, migrations, and changes—
The modes of its capture, its cycles and ranges:
But let me forbear—'t is the fault of a song,
A tale, or a book, if too learned or long.
Thus ends my discussion. More would you, I pray
Ask MITCHELL, or HARLAN, LESIEUR, or DE KAY

* A name given the white fish by the Canadians.

FROM "LIKES AND DISLIKES."

WHATE'ER is false, impertinent or dull,
A fop, a meddler, formalist or fool,
O'erbearing consequence, o'ervaunting sense,
The lounger's visit, and the rake's pretence,
The idle man's excuse, the babbler's prate,
These ask for censure, and all these I hate.

I hate the cit, whose tread diurnal brings
Wit's cast off robes, and learning's worn out things,
At home, abroad, in place, or out of place,
With fearful longitude of knowing face.

Who crowds the jest — half hitting and half hit —
The vapid ribaldry, which is not *wit*;
Or where misfortune bows a noble heart,
Wounds the seared bosom with satiric dart.
I hate the tattler, whose bad thirst of fame
Seeks rest in publishing his neighbor's shame,
Whose task it is to catch the latent tale,
The rumored doubt, or inuendo stale,
To fan the darling falsehoods as they rise,
To ponder scandal, and to retail lies.
I hate that ever busy, bustling man,
Whose wink or nod direct the village clan,
Intent not on the public joy or good,
Or e'en his own — a point not understood —
But, armed with little talent, much pretence,
Ten grains of impudence, and one of sense,
A strange compound of villain, fop, and clown,
Struts on, the busy-body of the town.
I hate the sly, insiduous, smirking *"friend,"*
Who, ever driving at some secret end,
Bespeaks your interest for a vote or place,
With smiling sweet amenity of face;
A splendor based upon a neighbor's cash;
Rogues escaped halter, prison, stocks, or lash:
All these, howe'er allied to fortune or to fate,
Demand my censure, and all these I hate.

GEEHALE: AN INDIAN LAMENT.

The blackbird is singing on Michigan's shore
As sweetly and gayly as ever before;
For he knows to his mate he, at pleasure, can hie,
And the dear little brood she is teaching to fly.
The sun looks as ruddy, and rises as bright,
And reflects o'er the mountains as beamy a light
As it ever reflected, or ever express'd, [the best.
When my skies were the bluest, my dreams were
The fox and the panther, both beasts of the night,
Retire to their dens on the gleaming of light,
And they spring with a free and a sorrowless track,
For they know that their mates are expecting
them back.
Each bird and each beast, it is bless'd in degree:
All nature is cheerful, all happy, but me.
I will go to my tent, and lie down in despair;
I will paint me with black, and will sever my hair;
I will sit on the shore, where the hurricane blows,
And reveal to the god of the tempest my woes;
I will weep for a season, on bitterness fed,
For my kindred are gone to the hills of the dead;
But they died not by hunger, or lingering decay:
The steel of the white man hath swept them away.
This snake-skin, that once I so sacredly wore,
I will toss, with disdain, to the storm-beaten shore:
Its charms I no longer obey or invoke,
Its spirit hath left me, its spell is now broke.
I will raise up my voice to the source of the light;
I will dream on the wings of the bluebird at night;
I will speak to the spirits that whisper in leaves,
And that minister balm to the bosom that grieves;
And will take a new Manito — such as shall seem
To be kind and propitious in every dream.
O, then I shall banish these cankering sighs,
And tears shall no longer gush salt from my eyes;
I shall wash from my face every cloud-colored stain,
Red — red shall, alone, on my visage remain!
I will dig up my hatchet, and bend my oak bow;
By night and by day I will follow the foe;
Nor lakes shall impede me, nor mountains, nor
snows;
His blood can, alone, give my spirit repose.
They came to my cabin when heaven was black;
I heard not their coming, I knew not their track;
But I saw, by the light of their blazing fusees,
They were people engender'd beyond the big seas:
My wife and my children,—O, spare me the tale!
For who is there left that is kin to Geehale!

THE BIRCHEN CANOE.

In the region of lakes, where the blue waters sleep,
My beautiful fabric was built;
Light cedars supported its weight on the deep,
And its sides with the sunbeams were gilt.

The bright leafy bark of the betula* tree
A flexible sheathing provides;
And the fir's thready roots drew the parts to agree,
And bound down its high swelling sides.

No compass or gavel was used on the bark,
No art but in simplest degree;
But the structure was finished, and trim to remark,
And as light as a sylph's could be.

Its rim was with tender young roots woven round,
Like a pattern of wicker-work rare;
And it prest on the waves with as lightsome a
As a basket suspended in air. [bound

The builder knew well, in his wild merry mood,
A smile from his sweet-love to win, [wood,
And he sung as he sewed the green bark to the
Leen ata nee saugein.†

The heavens in their brightness and glory below,
Were reflected quite plain to the view,
And it moved like a swan, with as graceful a show,
My beautiful birchen canoe.

The trees on the shore, as I glided along,
Seemed rushing a contrary way:
And my voyagers lightened their toil with a song,
That caused every heart to be gay.

And still as I floated by rock and by shell,
My bark raised a murmur aloud, [fell,
And it danced on the waves as they rose and they
Like a fay on a bright summer cloud.

I thought as I passed o'er the liquid expanse,
With the landscape in smiling array,
How blest I should be, if my life should advance,
Thus tranquil and sweetly away.

The skies were serene, not a cloud was in sight,
Not an angry surge beat on the shore,
And I gazed on the waters, and then on the light,
Till my vision could bear it no more.

Oh! long shall I think of those silver-bright lakes,
And the scenes they exposed to my view;
My friends and the wishes I formed for their sakes,
And my bright yellow birchen canoe.

* Betula papyracæ. † You only I love.

graved by A. W. Graham from a Daguerreotype by Brady

W. C. Bryant.

WILLIAM CULLEN BRYANT.

[Born, 1794.]

Mr. Bryant was born in Cummington, Massachusetts, on the third day of November, 1794. At a very early age he gave indications of superior genius, and his father, an eminent physician, distinguished for erudition and taste as well as for extensive and thorough knowledge of science, watched with deep interest the development of his faculties under the most careful and judicious instruction At ten years of age he made very creditable translations from some of the Latin poets, which were printed in a newspaper at Northampton, and during the vehement controversies between the Federalists and Democrats, which marked the period of Jefferson's administration, he wrote "The Embargo," a political satire, which was printed in Boston in 1808. Tasso when nine years of age wrote some lines to his mother which have been praised, Cowley at ten finished his "Tragical History of Pyramus and Thisbe," Pope when twelve his "Ode to Solitude," and "the wondrous boy Chatterton," at the same age, some verses entitled "A Hymn for Christmas Day;" but none of these pieces are superior to that which gave a title to the volume of our precocious American. The satire was directed against President Jefferson and his party, and has recently been quoted to prove the author an inconsistent politician, the last forty years having furnished no ground, it may be supposed, for such an accusation. The description of a caucus, in the following extract, shows that there has been little change in the character of such assemblies, and it will be confessed that the lines are remarkably spirited and graphic for so young an author:

"E'en while I sing, see Faction urge her claim,
Mislead with falsehood, and with zeal inflame;
Lift her black banner, spread her empire wide,
And stalk triumphant with a Fury's stride.
She blows her brazen trump, and, at the sound,
A motley throng, obedient, flock around;
A mist of changing hue o'er all she flings,
And darkness perches on all her dragon wings!
"Oh, might some patriot rise, the gloom dispel,
Chase Error's mist, and break her magic spell!
But vain the wish, for, hark! the murmuring meed
Of hoarse applause from yonder shed proceed;
Enter, and view the thronging concourse there,
Intent, with gaping mouth and stupid stare;
While, in the midst, their supple leader stands,
Harangues aloud, and flourishes his hands;
To adulation tunes his servile throat,
And sues, successful, for each blockhead's vote."

Some of the democrats affected to believe that Master Bryant was older than was confessed, or that another person had written "The Embargo;" but the book was eagerly read, and in a few months a second edition appeared, with some additional pieces. To this was prefixed the following advertisement:

"A doubt having been intimated in the Monthly Anthology of June last, whether a youth of thirteen years could have been the author of this poem—in justice to his merits the friends of the writer feel obliged to certify the fact from their personal knowledge of himself and his family, as well as his literary improvement and extraordinary talents. They would premise, that they do not come uncalled before the public to bear this testimony. They would prefer that he should be judged by his works, without favour or affection. As the doubt has been suggested, they deem it merely an act of justice to remove it, after which they leave him a candidate for favour in common with other literary adventurers. They therefore assure the public that Mr. Bryant, the author, is a native of Cummington, in the county of Hampshire, and in the month of November last arrived at the age of fourteen years. These facts can be authenticated by many of the inhabitants of that place, as well as by several of his friends, who give this notice; and if it be deemed worthy of further inquiry, the printer is enabled to disclose their names and places of residence."

In the sixteenth year of his age, Bryant entered an advanced class of Williams College, in which he soon became distinguished for his attainments generally, and especially for his proficiency in classical learning. In 1812 he obtained from the faculty an honourable discharge, for the purpose of entering upon the study of the law, and in 1815 he was admitted to the bar, and commenced the practice of his profession in the village of Great Barrington, where he was soon after married.

When but little more than eighteen years of age he had written his noble poem of "Thanatopsis," which was published in the North American Review for 1816.* In 1821 he delivered before the Phi Beta Kappa Society of Harvard College his longest poem, "The Ages," in which, from a survey of the past eras of the world, and of the successive advances of mankind in knowledge, virtue, and happiness, he endeavours to justify and confirm the hopes of the philanthropist for the future destinies of man. It is in the stanza of Spenser, and in its versification is not inferior to "The Faerie Queene." "To a Waterfowl," "Inscription for an entrance to a Wood," and several other pieces of nearly as great merit were likewise written during his residence at Great Barrington.

Having passed ten years in successful practice in the courts, he determined to abandon the uncongenial business of a lawyer, and devote his attention more exclusively to literature. With this view, in 1825, he removed to the city of New York, and

* See note on page 111.

with a friend, established "The New York Review and Atheneum Magazine," in which he published several of his finest poems, and in "The Hymn to Death" paid a touching tribute to the memory of his father, who died in that year. In 1826 he assumed the chief direction of the "Evening Post," one of the oldest and most influential political and commercial gazettes in this country, with which he has ever since been connected. In 1827, 1828, and 1829, he was associated with Mr. VERPLANCK and Mr. SANDS in the production of "The Talisman," an annual; and he wrote two or three of the "Tales of Glauber Spa," to which, besides himself. Miss Sedgwick, Mr. Paulding, Mr. Leggett, and Mr. Sands were contributors. An intimate friendship subsisted between him and Mr. SANDS, and when that brilliant writer died, in 1832, he assisted Mr. VERPLANCK in editing his works.

In the summer of 1834, Mr. BRYANT visited Europe, with his family, intending to devote a few years to literary studies, and to the education of his children. He travelled through France, Germany, and Italy, and resided several months in each of the cities of Florence, Pisa, Munich, and Heidelberg. The dangerous illness of his partner and associate, the late WILLIAM LEGGETT, compelled him to return hastily in the early part of 1836. The summer of 1840 he passed in Florida and the Valley of the Mississippi, and in 1844 he revisited Europe. He resides still in the city of New York, and continues to devote the chief part of his time to the editorship of the Evening Post, which has been for many years the leading journal of the democratic party.

In 1832 a collection of all the poems Mr. BRYANT had then written was published in New York; it was soon after reprinted in Boston, and a copy of it reaching WASHINGTON IRVING, who was then in England, he caused it to be published in London, where it has since passed through several editions. In 1842 he published "The Fountain and other Poems;" in 1844 "The White-Footed Deer and other Poems;" in 1846 an edition of his complete Poetical Works, illustrated with engravings from pictures by Leutze; and in 1855 another edition, containing his later poems, in two volumes. In prose his most recent publication is entitled "Letters of a Traveller;" this appeared in 1852; and he has since revisited Europe and made a journey through Egypt and the Holy Land.

The many and high excellencies of Mr. BRYANT have been almost universally recognised. With men of every variety of tastes he is a favourite. His works abound with passages of profound reflection which the philosopher meditates in his closet, and with others of such simple beauty and obvious intention as please the most illiterate. In his pages are illustrated all the common definitions of poetry, yet they are pervaded by a single purpose and spirit. Of the essential but inferior characteristics of poetry, which make it an art, he has a perfect mastery. Very few equal him in grace and power of expression. Every line has compactness, precision, and elegance, and flows with its fellows in exquisite harmony. His manner is on all occasions fitly chosen for his subject. His verse is solemn and impressive, or airy and playful, as suits his purpose. His beautiful imagery is appropriate, and has that air of freshness which distinguishes the productions of an author writing from his own observations of life and nature rather than from books.

Mr. BRYANT is a translator to the world of the silent language of the universe. He "conforms his life to the beautiful order of God's works." In the meditation of nature he has learned high lessons of philosophy and religion. With no other poet does the subject spring so naturally from the object; the moral, the sentiment, from the contemplation of the things about him. There is nothing forced in his inductions. By a genuine earnestness he wins the sympathy of his reader, and prepares him to anticipate his thought. By an imperceptible influence he carries him from the beginning to the end of a poem, and leaves him infused with the very spirit in which it is conceived.

In his descriptions of nature there is remarkable fidelity. They convey in an extraordinary degree the actual impression of what is grand and beautiful and peculiar in our scenery. The old and shadowy forests stand as they grew up from the seeds God planted, the sea-like prairies stretching in airy undulations beyond the eye's extremest vision, our lakes and mountains and rivers, he brings before us in pictures warmly coloured with the hues of the imagination, and as truthful as those which COLE puts on the canvas.

It has been complained that there is very little sentiment, very little of the blending of passion with philosophy, in BRYANT'S poetry; that his antique and dignified simplicity is never warmed with human sympathy. This is true in a degree, but in many of his poems are passages of touching pathos, and his interest in his race appears, contrary to the general experience, to increase with his age.

It has been denied by some persons, reasoning from our descent, education, language, and manners, identifying us so closely with another people, that we can have a distinctive national literature. But there are very few of BRYANT'S poems that could have been written in any country but our own. They breathe the very spirit of our young and vigorous life. He feels not more sensibly the grandeur and beauty of creation as manifested only in our own land, than he does the elevating influences of that freedom and power which is enjoyed by none but the citizens of this republic. To the thoughtful critic every thing in his verse belongs to America, and is as different from what marks the poetry of England as it is from that which most distinguishes the poetry of Germany or France.

Mr. BRYANT is still in the meridian of his life; among the most recent of his productions are some of the finest he has written; and we may look with confidence to an increase of the bases of his high reputation, second now to that of no contemporary who writes in our language.

THE PRAIRIES.

These are the gardens of the desert, these
The unshorn fields, boundless and beautiful,
For which the speech of England has no name—
The prairies. I behold them for the first,
And my heart swells, while the dilated sight
Takes in the encircling vastness. Lo! they stretch
In airy undulations, far away,
As if the ocean, in his gentlest swell,
Stood still, with all his rounded billows fix'd,
And motionless forever.—Motionless?—
No—they are all unchain'd again. The clouds
Sweep over with their shadows, and, beneath,
The surface rolls and fluctuates to the eye;
Dark hollows seem to glide along and chase
The sunny ridges. Breezes of the south!
Who toss the golden and the flame-like flowers,
And pass the prairie-hawk that, poised on high,
Flaps his broad wings, yet moves not—ye have play'd
Among the palms of Mexico and vines
Of Texas, and have crisp'd the limpid brooks
That from the fountains of Sonora glide
Into the calm Pacific—have ye fann'd
A nobler or a lovelier scene than this?
Man hath no part in all this glorious work:
The hand that built the firmament hath heaved
And smoothed these verdant swells, and sown their slopes
With herbage, planted them with island groves,
And hedged them round with forests. Fitting floor
For this magnificent temple of the sky—
With flowers whose glory and whose multitude
Rival the constellations! The great heavens
Seem to stoop down upon the scene in love,—
A nearer vault, and of a tenderer blue,
Than that which bends above the eastern hills.

As o'er the verdant waste I guide my steed,
Among the high rank grass that sweeps his sides,
The hollow beating of his footstep seems
A sacrilegious sound. I think of those
Upon whose rest he tramples. Are they here—
The dead of other days?—and did the dust
Of these fair solitudes once stir with life
And burn with passion! Let the mighty mounds
That overlook the rivers, or that rise
In the dim forest, crowded with old oaks,
Answer. A race, that long has pass'd away,
Built them;—a disciplined and populous race
Heap'd, with long toil, the earth, while yet the Greek
Was hewing the Pentelicus to forms
Of symmetry, and rearing on its rock
The glittering Parthenon. These ample fields
Nourish'd their harvests; here their herds were fed,
When haply by their stalls the bison low'd,
And bow'd his maned shoulder to the yoke.
All day this desert murmur'd with their toils,
Till twilight blush'd, and lovers walk'd, and woo'd
In a forgotten language, and old tunes,
From instruments of unremember'd form,
Gave the soft winds a voice. The red man came—
The roaming hunter-tribes, warlike and fierce,
And the mound-builders vanish'd from the earth
The solitude of centuries untold
Has settled where they dwelt. The prairie-wolf
Hunts in their meadows, and his fresh-dug den
Yawns by my path. The gopher mines the ground
Where stood their swarming cities. All is gone—
All—save the piles of earth that hold their bones—
The platforms where they worshipp'd unknown gods—
The barriers which they builded from the soil
To keep the foe at bay—till o'er the walls
The wild beleaguerers broke, and, one by one,
The strongholds of the plain were forced, and heap'd
With corpses. The brown vultures of the wood
Flock'd to those vast, uncover'd sepulchres,
And sat, unscared and silent, at their feast.
Haply some solitary fugitive,
Lurking in marsh and forest, till the sense
Of desolation and of fear became
Bitterer than death, yielded himself to die.
Man's better nature triumph'd. Kindly words
Welcomed and soothed him; the rude conquerors
Seated the captive with their chiefs; he chose
A bride among their maidens, and at length
Seem'd to forget,—yet ne'er forgot,—the wife
Of his first love, and her sweet little ones
Butcher'd, amid their shrieks, with all his race.

Thus change the forms of being. Thus arise
Races of living things, glorious in strength,
And perish, as the quickening breath of God
Fills them, or is withdrawn. The red man, too—
Has left the blooming wilds he ranged so long,
And, nearer to the Rocky Mountains, sought
A wider hunting-ground. The beaver builds
No longer by these streams, but far away,
On waters whose blue surface ne'er gave back
The white man's face—among Missouri's springs,
And pools whose issues swell the Oregon,
He rears his little Venice. In these plains
The bison feeds no more. Twice twenty leagues
Beyond remotest smoke of hunter's camp,
Roams the majestic brute, in herds that shake
The earth with thundering steps—yet here I meet
His ancient footprints stamp'd beside the pool.

Still this great solitude is quick with life.
Myriads of insects, gaudy as the flowers
They flutter over, gentle quadrupeds,
And birds, that scarce have learn'd the fear of man,
Are here, and sliding reptiles of the ground,
Startlingly beautiful. The graceful deer
Bounds to the wood at my approach. The bee,
A more adventurous colonist than man,
With whom he came across the eastern deep,
Fills the savannas with his murmurings,
And hides his sweets, as in the golden age,
Within the hollow oak. I listen long
To his domestic hum, and think I hear
The sound of that advancing multitude
Which soon shall fill these deserts. From the ground
Comes up the laugh of children, the soft voice
Of maidens, and the sweet and solemn hymn
Of Sabbath worshippers. The low of herds
Blends with the rustling of the heavy grain
Over the dark-brown furrows. All at once
A fresher wind sweeps by, and breaks my dream
And I am in the wilderness alone.

THANATOPSIS.

To him who in the love of nature holds
Communion with her visible forms, she speaks
A various language; for his gayer hours
She has a voice of gladness, and a smile
And eloquence of beauty; and she glides
Into his darker musings, with a mild
And healing sympathy, that steals away
Their sharpness, ere he is aware. When thoughts
Of the last bitter hour come like a blight
Over thy spirit, and sad images
Of the stern agony, and shroud, and pall,
And breathless darkness, and the narrow house,
Make thee to shudder, and grow sick at heart;—
Go forth, under the open sky, and list
To Nature's teachings, while from all around—
Earth and her waters, and the depths of air—
Comes a still voice—Yet a few days, and thee
The all-beholding sun shall see no more
In all his course; nor yet in the cold ground,
Where thy pale form is laid with many tears,
Nor in the embrace of ocean, shall exist
Thy image. Earth, that nourish'd thee, shall claim
Thy growth, to be resolved to earth again,
And, lost each human trace, surrendering up
Thine individual being, shalt thou go
To mix for ever with the elements,—
To be a brother to the insensible rock,
And to the sluggish clod, which the rude swain
Turns with his share, and treads upon. The oak
Shall send his roots abroad, and pierce thy mould.
Yet not to thine eternal resting-place
Shalt thou retire alone—nor couldst thou wish
Couch more magnificent. Thou shalt lie down
With patriarchs of the infant world—with kings,
The powerful of the earth—the wise, the good,
Fair forms, and hoary seers, of ages past,
All in one mighty sepulchre.—The hills
Rock-ribb'd, and ancient as the sun,—the vales
Stretching in pensive quietness between;
The venerable woods—rivers that move
In majesty, and the complaining brooks
That make the meadows green; and, pour'd round all,
Old ocean's gray and melancholy waste,—
Are but the solemn decorations all
Of the great tomb of man. The golden sun,
The planets, all the infinite host of heaven,
Are shining on the sad abodes of death,
Through the still lapse of ages. All that tread
The globe, are but a handful to the tribes
That slumber in its bosom.—Take the wings
Of morning, and the Barcan desert pierce,
Or lose thyself in the continuous woods
Where rolls the Oregon, and hears no sound
Save his own dashings—yet the dead are there;
And millions in those solitudes, since first
The flight of years began, have laid them down
In their last sleep—the dead there reign alone.
So shalt thou rest,—and what if thou withdraw
Unheeded by the living—and no friend
Take note of thy departure? All that breathe
Will share thy destiny. The gay will laugh
When thou art gone, the solemn brood of care
Plod on, and each one, as before, will chase
His favourite phantom; yet all these shall leave
Their mirth and their employments, and shall come
And make their bed with thee. As the long train
Of ages glide away, the sons of men,
The youth in life's green spring, and he who goes
In the full strength of years, matron, and maid,
And the sweet babe, and the gray-headed man,—
Shall one by one be gather'd to thy side,
By those who, in their turn, shall follow them.
So live, that, when thy summons comes to join
The innumerable caravan, that moves
To that mysterious realm, where each shall take
His chamber in the silent halls of death,
Thou go not, like the quarry-slave, at night,
Scourged to his dungeon, but, sustain'd and soothed
By an unfaltering trust, approach thy grave,
Like one that draws the drapery of his couch
About him, and lies down to pleasant dreams.

FOREST HYMN.

The groves were God's first temples. Ere man learn'd
To hew the shaft, and lay the architrave,
And spread the roof above them,—ere he framed
The lofty vault, to gather and roll back
The sound of anthems; in the darkling wood,
Amid the cool and silence, he knelt down,
And offer'd to the Mightiest solemn thanks,
And supplication. For his simple heart
Might not resist the sacred influences,
Which, from the stilly twilight of the place,
And from the gray old trunks, that high in heaven
Mingled their mossy boughs, and from the sound
Of the invisible breath, that sway'd at once
All their green tops, stole over him, and bow'd
His spirit with the thought of boundless power,
And inaccessible majesty. Ah, why
Should we, in the world's riper years, neglect
God's ancient sanctuaries, and adore
Only among the crowd, and under roofs
That our frail hands have raised? Let me, at least,
Here, in the shadow of this aged wood,
Offer one hymn—thrice happy, if it find
Acceptance in his ear.
Father, thy hand
Hath rear'd these venerable columns, thou
Didst weave this verdant roof. Thou didst look down
Upon the naked earth, and, forthwith, rose
All these fair ranks of trees. They, in thy sun,
Budded, and shook their green leaves in thy breeze,
And shot towards heaven. The century-living crow,
Whose birth was in their tops, grew old and died
Among their branches; till, at last, they stood,
As now they stand, massy, and tall, and dark,
Fit shrine for humble worshipper to hold
Communion with his Maker. These dim vaults,
These winding aisles, of human pomp or pride
Report not. No fantastic carvings show,
The boast of our vain race, to change the form
Of thy fair works. But thou art here—thou fill'st
The solitude. Thou art in the soft winds,
That run along the summit of these trees
In music;—thou art in the cooler breath,

That, from the inmost darkness of the place,
Comes, scarcely felt;—the barky trunks, the ground,
The fresh, moist ground, are all instinct with thee.
Here is continual worship;—nature, here,
In the tranquillity that thou dost love,
Enjoys thy presence. Noiselessly around,
From perch to perch, the solitary bird
Passes; and yon clear spring, that, midst its herbs,
Wells softly forth, and visits the strong roots
Of half the mighty forest, tells no tale
Of all the good it does. Thou hast not left
Thyself without a witness, in these shades,
Of thy perfections. Grandeur, strength, and grace,
Are here to speak of thee. This mighty oak,
By whose immovable stem I stand, and seem
Almost annihilated,—not a prince,
In all that proud old world beyond the deep,
E'er wore his crown as loftily as he
Wears the green coronal of leaves with which
Thy hand has graced him. Nestled at his root
Is beauty, such as blooms not in the glare
Of the broad sun. That delicate forest flower,
With delicate breath, and look so like a smile,
Seems, as it issues from the shapeless mould,
An emanation of the indwelling Life,
A visible token of the upholding Love,
That are the soul of this wide universe.

My heart is awed within me, when I think
Of the great miracle that still goes on
In silence, round me—the perpetual work
Of thy creation, finish'd, yet renew'd
Forever. Written on thy works, I read
The lesson of thy own eternity.
Lo! all grow old and die—but see, again,
How on the faltering footsteps of decay
Youth presses—ever gay and beautiful youth,
In all its beautiful forms. These lofty trees
Wave not less proudly that their ancestors
Moulder beneath them. O, there is not lost
One of earth's charms: upon her bosom yet,
After the flight of untold centuries,
The freshness of her far beginning lies,
And yet shall lie. Life mocks the idle hate
Of his arch-enemy, Death—yea, seats himself
Upon the tyrant's throne—the sepulchre,
And of the triumphs of his ghastly foe
Makes his own nourishment. For he came forth
From thine own bosom, and shall have no end.

There have been holy men who hid themselves
Deep in the woody wilderness, and gave
Their lives to thought and prayer, till they outlived
The generation born with them, nor seem'd
Less aged than the hoary trees and rocks
Around them;—and there have been holy men
Who deem'd it were not well to pass life thus.
But let me often to these solitudes
Retire, and in thy presence reassure
My feeble virtue. Here its enemies,
The passions, at thy plainer footsteps shrink,
And tremble and are still. O, God! when thou
Dost scare the world with tempests, set on fire
The heavens with falling thunderbolts, or fill,
With all the waters of the firmament,
The swift, dark whirlwind that uproots the woods
And drowns the villages; when, at thy call,
Uprises the great deep and throws himself
Upon the continent, and overwhelms
Its cities—who forgets not, at the sight
Of these tremendous tokens of thy power,
His pride, and lays his strifes and follies by?
O, from these sterner aspects of thy face
Spare me and mine, nor let us need the wrath
Of the mad, unchain'd elements to teach
Who rules them. Be it ours to meditate
In these calm shades thy milder majesty,
And to the beautiful order of thy works
Learn to conform the order of our lives.

HYMN TO THE NORTH STAR.

The sad and solemn night
Has yet her multitude of cheerful fires;
The glorious host of light
Walk the dark hemisphere till she retires;
All through her silent watches, gliding slow,
Her constellations come, and climb the heavens, and go.

Day, too, hath many a star
To grace his gorgeous reign, as bright as they:
Through the blue fields afar,
Unseen, they follow in his flaming way:
Many a bright lingerer, as the eve grows dim,
Tells what a radiant troop arose and set with him.

And thou dost see them rise,
Star of the Pole! and thou dost see them set.
Alone, in thy cold skies,
Thou keep'st thy old, unmoving station yet,
Nor join'st the dances of that glittering train,
Nor dipp'st thy virgin orb in the blue western main

There, at morn's rosy birth,
Thou lookest meekly through the kindling air,
And eve, that round the earth
Chases the day, beholds thee watching there;
There noontide finds thee, and the hour that calls
The shapes of polar flame to scale heaven's azure walls.

Alike, beneath thine eye,
The deeds of darkness and of light are done;
High towards the star-lit sky
Towns blaze—the smoke of battle blots the sun—
The night-storm on a thousand hills is loud—
And the strong wind of day doth mingle sea and cloud.

On thy unaltering blaze
The half-wreck'd mariner, his compass lost,
Fixes his steady gaze,
And steers, undoubting, to the friendly coast;
And they who stray in perilous wastes, by night,
Are glad when thou dost shine to guide their footsteps right.

And, therefore, bards of old,
Sages, and hermits of the solemn wood,
Did in thy beams behold
A beauteous type of that unchanging good,
That bright, eternal beacon, by whose ray
The voyager of time should shape his heedful way

THE ANTIQUITY OF FREEDOM.

Here are old trees, tall oaks, and gnarled pines,
That stream with gray-green mosses; here the ground
Was never touch'd by spade, and flowers spring up
Unsown, and die ungather'd. It is sweet
To linger here, among the flitting birds
And leaping squirrels, wandering brooks and winds
That shake the leaves, and scatter as they pass
A fragrance from the cedars thickly set
With pale blue berries. In these peaceful shades—
Peaceful, unpruned, immeasurably old—
My thoughts go up the long dim path of years,
Back to the earliest days of Liberty.
O Freedom! thou art not, as poets dream,
A fair young girl, with light and delicate limbs,
And wavy tresses gushing from the cap
With which the Roman master crown'd his slave,
When he took off the gyves. A bearded man,
Arm'd to the teeth, art thou: one mailed hand
Grasps the broad shield, and one the sword; thy brow,
Glorious in beauty though it be, is scarr'd
With tokens of old wars; thy massive limbs
Are strong and struggling. Power at thee has launch'd
His bolts, and with his lightnings smitten thee;
They could not quench the life thou hast from Heaven.
Merciless Power has dug thy dungeon deep,
And his swart armourers, by a thousand fires,
Have forged thy chain; yet while he deems thee bound,
The links are shiver'd, and the prison walls
Fall outward; terribly thou springest forth,
As springs the flame above a burning pile,
And shoutest to the nations, who return
Thy shoutings, while the pale oppressor flies.
Thy birth-right was not given by human hands:
Thou wert twin-born with man. In pleasant fields,
While yet our race was few, thou sat'st with him,
To tend the quiet flock and watch the stars,
And teach the reed to utter simple airs.
Thou by his side, amid the tangled wood,
Didst war upon the panther and the wolf,
His only foes: and thou with him didst draw
The earliest furrows on the mountain side,
Soft with the Deluge. Tyranny himself,
The enemy, although of reverend look,
Hoary with many years, and far obey'd,
Is later born than thou; and as he meets
The grave defiance of thine elder eye,
The usurper trembles in his fastnesses.
Thou shalt wax stronger with the lapse of years,
But he shall fade into a feebler age;
Feebler, yet subtler; he shall weave his snares,
And spring them on thy careless steps, and clap
His wither'd hands, and from their ambush call
His hordes to fall upon thee. He shall send
Quaint maskers, forms of fair and gallant mien,
To catch thy gaze, and uttering graceful words
To charm thy ear; while his sly imps, by stealth,
Twine round thee threads of steel, light thread on thread,
That grow to fetters; or bind down thy arms
With chains conceal'd in chaplets. Oh! not yet
Mayst thou unbrace thy corslet, nor lay by
Thy sword, nor yet, O Freedom! close thy lids
In slumber; for thine enemy never sleeps.
And thou must watch and combat, till the day
Of the new Earth and Heaven. But wouldst thou rest
Awhile from tumult and the frauds of men,
These old and friendly solitudes invite
Thy visit. They, while yet the forest trees
Were young upon the unviolated earth,
And yet the moss-stains on the rock were new,
Beheld thy glorious childhood, and rejoiced.

THE RETURN OF YOUTH.

My friend, thou sorrowest for thy golden prime,
For thy fair youthful years too swift of flight;
Thou musest, with wet eyes, upon the time
Of cheerful hopes that fill'd the world with light,
Years when thy heart was bold, thy hand was strong,
Thy tongue was prompt the generous thought to speak,
And willing faith was thine, and scorn of wrong
Summon'd the sudden crimson to thy cheek.

Thou lookest forward on the coming days,
Shuddering to feel their shadow o'er thee creep;
A path, thick-set with changes and decays,
Slopes downward to the place of common sleep;
And they who walk'd with thee in life's first stage,
Leave one by one thy side, and, waiting near,
Thou seest the sad companions of thy age—
Dull love of rest, and weariness, and fear.

Yet grieve thou not, nor think thy youth is gone,
Nor deem that glorious season e'er could die.
Thy pleasant youth, a little while withdrawn,
Waits on the horizon of a brighter sky;
Waits, like the morn, that folds her wing and hides,
Till the slow stars bring back her dawning hour;
Waits, like the vanish'd spring, that slumbering bides,
Her own sweet time to waken bud and flower.

There shall he welcome thee, when thou shalt stand
On his bright morning hills, with smiles more sweet
Than when at first he took thee by the hand,
Through the fair earth to lead thy tender feet.
He shall bring back, but brighter, broader still,
Life's early glory to thine eyes again,
Shall clothe thy spirit with new strength, and fill
Thy leaping heart with warmer love than then.

Hast thou not glimpses, in the twilight here,
Of mountains where immortal morn prevails?
Comes there not, through the silence, to thine ear
A gentle rustling of the morning gales;
A murmur, wafted from that glorious shore,
Of streams that water banks for ever fair,
And voices of the loved ones gone before,
More musical in that celestial air?

THE WINDS.

Ye winds, ye unseen currents of the air,
 Softly ye play'd a few brief hours ago;
Ye bore the murmuring bee; ye toss'd the hair
 O'er maiden cheeks, that took a fresher glow;
Ye roll'd the round, white cloud through depths of blue;
Ye shook from shaded flowers the lingering dew;
Before you the catalpa's blossoms flew,
 Light blossoms, dropping on the grass like snow.

How are ye changed! Ye take the cataract's sound,
 Ye take the whirlpool's fury and its might;
The mountain shudders as ye sweep the ground;
 The valley woods lie prone beneath your flight.
The clouds before you sweep like eagles past;
The homes of men are rocking in your blast;
Ye lift the roofs like autumn leaves, and cast,
 Skyward, the whirling fragments out of sight.

The weary fowls of heaven make wing in vain,
 To scape your wrath; ye seize and dash them dead.
Against the earth ye drive the roaring rain;
 The harvest field becomes a river's bed;
And torrents tumble from the hills around,
Plains turn to lakes, and villages are drown'd,
And wailing voices, midst the tempest's sound,
 Rise, as the rushing floods close over head.

Ye dart upon the deep, and straight is heard
 A wilder roar, and men grow pale, and pray;
Ye fling its waters round you, as a bird
 Flings o'er his shivering plumes the fountain's spray.
See! to the breaking mast the sailor clings;
Ye scoop the ocean to its briny springs,
And take the mountain billow on your wings,
 And pile the wreck of navies round the bay.

Why rage ye thus?—no strife for liberty
 Has made you mad; no tyrant, strong through fear,
Has chain'd your pinions, till ye wrench'd them free,
 And rush'd into the unmeasured atmosphere:
For ye were born in freedom where ye blow;
Free o'er the mighty deep to come and go;
Earth's solemn woods were yours, her wastes of snow,
 Her isles where summer blossoms all the year.

O, ye wild winds! a mightier power than yours
 In chains upon the shores of Europe lies;
The sceptred throng, whose fetters he endures,
 Watch his mute throes with terror in their eyes:
And armed warriors all around him stand,
And, as he struggles, tighten every band,
And lift the heavy spear, with threatening hand,
 To pierce the victim, should he strive to rise.

Yet, O, when that wrong'd spirit of our race,
 Shall break, as soon he must, his long-worn chains,
And leap in freedom from his prison-place,
 Lord of his ancient hills and fruitful plains,
Let him not rise, like these mad winds of air,
To waste the loveliness that time could spare,
To fill the earth with wo, and blot her fair
 Unconscious breast with blood from human veins.

But may he, like the spring-time, come abroad,
 Who crumbles winter's gyves with gentle might,
When in the genial breeze, the breath of God,
 Come spouting up the unseal'd springs to light;
Flowers start from their dark prisons at his feet,
The woods, long dumb, awake to hymnings sweet,
And morn and eve, whose glimmerings almost meet,
 Crowd back to narrow bounds the ancient night.

OH MOTHER OF A MIGHTY RACE!

Oh mother of a mighty race,
Yet lovely in thy youthful grace!
The elder dames, thy haughty peers,
Admire and hate thy blooming years.
  With words of shame
And taunts of scorn they join thy name.

For on thy cheeks the glow is spread
That tints the morning hills with red;
Thy step—the wild deer's rustling feet
Within thy woods, are not more fleet;
  Thy hopeful eye
Is bright as thine own sunny sky.

Ay, let them rail—those haughty ones—
While safe thou dwellest with thy sons.
They do not know how loved thou art—
How many a fond and fearless heart
  Would rise to throw
Its life between thee and the foe!

They know not, in their hate and pride,
What virtues with thy children bide;
How true, how good, thy graceful maids
Make bright, like flowers, the valley shades
  What generous men
Spring, like thine oaks, by hill and glen:

What cordial welcomes greet the guest
By the lone rivers of the west;
How faith is kept, and truth revered,
And man is loved, and God is fear'd,
  In woodland homes,
And where the solemn ocean foams!

There's freedom at thy gates, and rest
For earth's down-trodden and oppress'd,
A shelter for the hunted head,
For the starved labourer toil and bread.
  Power, at thy bounds,
Stops and calls back his baffled hounds.

Oh, fair young mother! on thy brow
Shall sit a nobler grace than now.
Deep in the brightness of thy skies
The thronging years in glory rise,
  And, as they fleet,
Drop strength and riches at thy feet.

Thine eye, with every coming hour,
Shall brighten, and thy form shall tower,
And when thy sisters, elder born,
Would brand thy name with words of scorn,
  Before thine eye,
Upon their lips the taunt shall die!

SONG OF MARION'S MEN.

Our band is few, but true and tried,
Our leader frank and bold;
The British soldier trembles
When Marion's name is told.
Our fortress is the good green wood,
Our tent the cypress tree;
We know the forest round us,
As seamen know the sea.
We know its walls of thorny vines,
Its glades of reedy grass,
Its safe and silent islands
Within the dark morass.

Wo to the English soldiery
That little dread us near!
On them shall light at midnight
A strange and sudden fear:
When, waking to their tents on fire,
They grasp their arms in vain,
And they who stand to face us
Are beat to earth again;
And they who fly in terror deem
A mighty host behind,
And hear the tramp of thousands
Upon the hollow wind.

Then sweet the hour that brings release
From danger and from toil:
We talk the battle over,
And share the battle's spoil.
The woodland rings with laugh and shout,
As if a hunt were up,
And woodland flowers are gather'd
To crown the soldier's cup.
With merry songs we mock the wind
That in the pine-top grieves,
And slumber long and sweetly,
On beds of oaken leaves.

Well knows the fair and friendly moon
The band that Marion leads—
The glitter of their rifles,
The scampering of their steeds.
'Tis life to guide the fiery barb
Across the moonlight plain;
'Tis life to feel the night-wind
That lifts his tossing mane.
A moment in the British camp—
A moment—and away
Back to the pathless forest,
Before the peep of day.

Grave men there are by broad Santee,
Grave men with hoary hairs,
Their hearts are all with Marion,
For Marion are their prayers.
And lovely ladies greet our band
With kindliest welcoming,
With smiles like those of summer,
And tears like those of spring.
For them we wear these trusty arms,
And lay them down no more,
Till we have driven the Briton
Forever from our shore.

TO THE PAST.

Thou unrelenting Past!
Strong are the barriers round thy dark domain,
And fetters, sure and fast,
Hold all that enter thy unbreathing reign.

Far in thy realm withdrawn,
Old empires sit in sullenness and gloom;
And glorious ages gone
Lie deep within the shadow of thy womb.

Childhood, with all its mirth,
Youth, manhood, age, that draws us to the ground
And last, man's life on earth,
Glide to thy dim dominions, and are bound.

Thou hast my better years,
Thou hast my earlier friends—the good—the kind,
Yielded to thee with tears—
The venerable form—the exalted mind.

My spirit yearns to bring
The lost ones back—yearns with desire intense,
And struggles hard to wring
Thy bolts apart, and pluck thy captives thence.

In vain—thy gates deny
All passage, save to those who hence depart;
Nor to the streaming eye
Thou givest them back—nor to the broken heart

In thy abysses hide
Beauty and excellence unknown—to thee
Earth's wonder and her pride
Are gather'd, as the waters to the sea.

Labours of good to man,
Unpublish'd charity—unbroken faith—
Love, that midst grief began,
And grew with years, and falter'd not in death.

Full many a mighty name
Lurks in thy depths, unutter'd, unrevered;
With thee are silent fame,
Forgotten arts, and wisdom disappear'd.

Thine, for a space, are they—
Yet shalt thou yield thy treasures up at last;
Thy gates shall yet give way,
Thy bolts shall fall, inexorable Past!

All that of good and fair
Has gone into thy womb, from earliest time,
Shall then come forth, to wear
The glory and the beauty of its prime.

They have not perish'd—no!
Kind words, remember'd voices, once so sweet,
Smiles, radiant long ago,
And features, the great soul's apparent seat;

All shall come back, each tie
Of pure affection shall be knit again;
Alone shall evil die,
And sorrow dwell a prisoner in thy reign.

And then shall I behold
Him, by whose kind paternal side I sprung,
And her, who, still and cold,
Fills the next grave—the beautiful and young.

THE HUNTER OF THE PRAIRIES.

Ay, this is freedom!—these pure skies
  Were never stain'd with village smoke:
The fragrant wind, that through them flies,
  Is breathed from wastes by plough unbroke.
Here, with my rifle and my steed,
  And her who left the world for me,
I plant me, where the red deer feed
  In the green desert—and am free.

For here the fair savannas know
  No barriers in the bloomy grass;
Wherever breeze of heaven may blow,
  Or beam of heaven may glance, I pass.
In pastures, measureless as air,
  The bison is my noble game;
The bounding elk, whose antlers tear
  The branches, falls before my aim.

Mine are the river-fowl that scream
  From the long stripe of waving sedge;
The bear, that marks my weapon's gleam,
  Hides vainly in the forest's edge;
In vain the she-wolf stands at bay;
  The brinded catamount, that lies
High in the boughs to watch his prey,
  Even in the act of springing, dies.

With what free growth the elm and plane
  Fling their huge arms across my way,
Gray, old, and cumber'd with a train
  Of vines, as huge, and old, and gray!
Free stray the lucid streams, and find
  No taint in these fresh lawns and shades;
Free spring the flowers that scent the wind
  Where never scythe has swept the glades.

Alone the fire, when frostwinds sere
  The heavy herbage of the ground,
Gathers his annual harvest here,
  With roaring like the battle's sound,
And hurrying flames that sweep the plain,
  And smoke-streams gushing up the sky:
I meet the flames with flames again,
  And at my door they cower and die.

Here, from dim woods, the aged past
  Speaks solemnly; and I behold
The boundless future in the vast
  And lonely river, seaward roll'd.
Who feeds its founts with rain and dew?
  Who moves, I ask, its gliding mass,
And trains the bordering vines, whose blue,
  Bright clusters tempt me as I pass!

Broad are these streams—my steed obeys,
  Plunges, and bears me through the tide.
Wide are these woods—I thread the maze
  Of giant stems, nor ask a guide.
I hunt, till day's last glimmer dies
  O'er woody vale and grassy height;
And kind the voice, and glad the eyes
  That welcome my return at night.

AFTER A TEMPEST.

The day had been a day of wind and storm;—
  The wind was laid, the storm was overpast,—
And, stooping from the zenith, bright and warm
  Shone the great sun on the wide earth at last.
  I stood upon the upland slope, and cast
My eye upon a broad and beauteous scene,
  Where the vast plain lay girt by mountains vast,
And hills o'er hills lifted their heads of green,
With pleasant vales scoop'd out and villages between.

The rain-drops glisten'd on the trees around,
  Whose shadows on the tall grass were not stirr'd,
Save when a shower of diamonds to the ground
  Was shaken by the flight of startled bird;
  For birds were warbling round, and bees were heard
About the flowers; the cheerful rivulet sung
  And gossip'd, as he hasten'd ocean-ward;
To the gray oak the squirrel, chiding, clung,
And chirping from the ground the grasshopper upsprung.

And from beneath the leaves that kept them dry
  Flew many a glittering insect here and there,
And darted up and down the butterfly,
  That seem'd a living blossom of the air.
  The flocks came scattering from the thicket, where
The violent rain had pent them; in the way
  Stroll'd groups of damsels frolicsome and fair;
The farmer swung the scythe or turn'd the hay,
And 'twixt the heavy swaths his children were at play.

It was a scene of peace—and, like a spell,
  Did that serene and golden sunlight fall
Upon the motionless wood that clothed the fell,
  And precipice upspringing like a wall,
  And glassy river and white waterfall,
And happy living things that trod the bright
  And beauteous scene; while far beyond them all,
On many a lovely valley, out of sight,
Was pour'd from the blue heavens the same soft, golden light.

I look'd, and thought the quiet of the scene
  An emblem of the peace that yet shall be,
When, o'er earth's continents and isles between,
  The noise of war shall cease from sea to sea,
  And married nations dwell in harmony;
When millions, crouching in the dust to one,
  No more shall beg their lives on bended knee,
Nor the black stake be dress'd, nor in the sun
The o'erlabour'd captive toil, and wish his life were done.

Too long, at clash of arms amid her bowers
  And pools of blood, the earth has stood aghast,
The fair earth, that should only blush with flowers
  And ruddy fruits; but not for aye can last
  The storm, and sweet the sunshine when 't is past
Lo, the clouds roll away—they break—they fly,
  And, like the glorious light of summer, cast
O'er the wide landscape from the embracing sky,
On all the peaceful world the smile of heaven shall lie.

THE RIVULET.

This little rill that, from the springs
Of yonder grove, its current brings,
Plays on the slope a while, and then
Goes prattling into groves again,
Oft to its warbling waters drew
My little feet, when life was new.
When woods in early green were dress'd,
And from the chambers of the west
The warmer breezes, travelling out,
Breathed the new scent of flowers about,
My truant steps from home would stray,
Upon its grassy side to play,
List the brown thrasher's vernal hymn,
And crop the violet on its brim,
With blooming cheek and open brow,
As young and gay, sweet rill, as thou.
And when the days of boyhood came,
And I had grown in love with fame,
Duly I sought thy banks, and tried
My first rude numbers by thy side.
Words cannot tell how bright and gay
The scenes of life before me lay.
Then glorious hopes, that now to speak
Would bring the blood into my cheek,
Pass'd o'er me; and I wrote, on high,
A name I deem'd should never die.
Years change thee not. Upon yon hill
The tall old maples, verdant still,
Yet tell, in grandeur of decay,
How swift the years have pass'd away,
Since first, a child, and half-afraid,
I wander'd in the forest shade.
Thou, ever-joyous rivulet,
Dost dimple, leap, and prattle yet;
And sporting with the sands that pave
The windings of thy silver wave,
And dancing to thy own wild chime,
Thou laughest at the lapse of time.
The same sweet sounds are in my ear
My early childhood loved to hear;
As pure thy limpid waters run,
As bright they sparkle to the sun;
As fresh and thick the bending ranks
Of herbs that line thy oozy banks;
The violet there, in soft May dew,
Comes up, as modest and as blue;
As green amid thy current's stress,
Floats the scarce-rooted water-cress;
And the brown ground-bird, in thy glen,
Still chirps as merrily as then.
Thou changest not—but I am changed,
Since first thy pleasant banks I ranged;
And the grave stranger, come to see
The play-place of his infancy,
Has scarce a single trace of him
Who sported once upon thy brim.
The visions of my youth are past—
Too bright, too beautiful to last.
I've tried the world—it wears no more
The colouring of romance it wore.
Yet well has Nature kept the truth
She promised to my earliest youth:
The radiant beauty, shed abroad
On all the glorious works of God,
Shows freshly, to my sober'd eye,
Each charm it wore in days gone by.
A few brief years shall pass away,
And I, all trembling, weak, and gray,
Bow'd to the earth, which waits to fold
My ashes in the embracing mould,
(If haply the dark will of fate
Indulge my life so long a date,)
May come for the last time to look
Upon my childhood's favourite brook.
Then dimly on my eye shall gleam
The sparkle of thy dancing stream;
And faintly on my ear shall fall
Thy prattling current's merry call;
Yet shalt thou flow as glad and bright
As when thou met'st my infant sight.
And I shall sleep—and on thy side,
As ages after ages glide,
Children their early sports shall try,
And pass to hoary age, and die.
But thou, unchanged from year to year,
Gayly shalt play and glitter here;
Amid young flowers and tender grass
Thy endless infancy shalt pass;
And, singing down thy narrow glen,
Shalt mock the fading race of men.

JUNE.

I gazed upon the glorious sky
And the green mountains round:
And thought, that when I came to lie
Within the silent ground,
'T were pleasant, that in flowery June,
When brooks sent up a cheerful tune,
And groves a joyous sound,
The sexton's hand, my grave to make,
The rich, green mountain turf should break

A cell within the frozen mould,
A coffin borne through sleet,
And icy clods above it roll'd,
While fierce the tempests beat—
Away!—I will not think of these—
Blue be the sky and soft the breeze,
Earth green beneath the feet,
And be the damp mould gently press'd
Into my narrow place of rest.

There, through the long, long summer hours,
The golden light should lie,
And thick, young herbs and groups of flowers
Stand in their beauty by.
The oriole should build and tell
His love-tale, close beside my cell;
The idle butterfly
Should rest him there, and there be heard
The housewife-bee and humming bird.

And what, if cheerful shouts, at noon,
Come, from the village sent,
Or songs of maids, beneath the moon,
With fairy laughter blent?

And what if, in the evening light,
Betrothed lovers walk in sight
Of my low monument?
I would the lovely scene around
Might know no sadder sight nor sound.

I know, I know I should not see
The season's glorious show,
Nor would its brightness shine for me,
Nor its wild music flow;
But if, around my place of sleep,
The friends I love should come to weep,
They might not haste to go.
Soft airs, and song, and light, and bloom
Should keep them lingering by my tomb.

These to their soften'd hearts should bear
The thought of what has been,
And speak of one who cannot share
The gladness of the scene;
Whose part, in all the pomp that fills
The circuit of the summer hills,
Is—that his grave is green;
And deeply would their hearts rejoice
To hear, again, his living voice.

TO THE EVENING WIND.

Spirit that breathest through my lattice, thou
That cool'st the twilight of the sultry day!
Gratefully flows thy freshness round my brow;
Thou hast been out upon the deep at play,
Riding all day the wild blue waves till now,
Roughening their crests, and scattering high their spray,
And swelling the white sail. I welcome thee
To the scorch'd land, thou wanderer of the sea!

Nor I alone—a thousand bosoms round
Inhale thee in the fulness of delight;
And languid forms rise up, and pulses bound
Livelier, at coming of the wind of night;
And languishing to hear thy welcome sound,
Lies the vast inland, stretch'd beyond the sight.
Go forth, into the gathering shade; go forth,—
God's blessing breathed upon the fainting earth!

Go, rock the little wood-bird in his nest,
Curl the still waters, bright with stars, and rouse
The wide, old wood from his majestic rest,
Summoning, from the innumerable boughs,
The strange, deep harmonies that haunt his breast:
Pleasant shall be thy way where meekly bows
The shutting flower, and darkling waters pass,
And where the o'ershadowing branches sweep the grass.

Stoop o'er the place of graves, and softly sway
The sighing herbage by the gleaming stone;
That they who near the churchyard willows stray,
And listen in the deepening gloom, alone,
May think of gentle souls that pass'd away,
Like thy pure breath, into the vast unknown,
Sent forth from heaven among the sons of men,
And gone into the boundless heaven again.

The faint old man shall lean his silver head
To feel thee; thou shalt kiss the child asleep,
And dry the moisten'd curls that overspread
His temples, while his breathing grows more deep;
And they who stand about the sick man's bed,
Shall joy to listen to thy distant sweep,
And softly part his curtains to allow
Thy visit, grateful to his burning brow.

Go—but the circle of eternal change,
Which is the life of nature, shall restore,
With sounds and scents from all thy mighty range,
Thee to thy birth-place of the deep once more;
Sweet odours in the sea-air, sweet and strange,
Shall tell the home-sick mariner of the shore;
And, listening to thy murmur, he shall deem
He hears the rustling leaf and running stream.

LINES ON REVISITING THE COUNTRY.

I stand upon my native hills again,
Broad, round, and green, that in the summer sky,
With garniture of waving grass and grain,
Orchards, and beechen forests, basking lie,
While deep the sunless glens are scoop'd between,
Where brawl o'er shallow beds the streams unseen.

A lisping voice and glancing eyes are near,
And ever restless feet of one, who, now,
Gathers the blossoms of her fourth bright year;
There plays a gladness o'er her fair young brow,
As breaks the varied scene upon her sight,
Upheaved and spread in verdure and in light.

For I have taught her, with delighted eye,
To gaze upon the mountains, to behold,
With deep affection, the pure, ample sky,
And clouds along its blue abysses roll'd,
To love the song of waters, and to hear
The melody of winds with charmed ear.

Here, I have 'scaped the city's stifling heat,
Its horrid sounds, and its polluted air;
And where the season's milder fervours beat,
And gales, that sweep the forest borders, bear
The song of bird, and sound of running stream,
Am come a while to wander and to dream.

Ay, flame thy fiercest, sun! thou canst not wake,
In this pure air, the plague that walks unseen.
The maize leaf and the maple bough but take,
From thy strong heats, a deeper, glossier green.
The mountain wind, that faints not in thy ray,
Sweeps the blue streams of pestilence away.

The mountain wind! most spiritual thing of all
The wide earth knows—when, in the sultry time,
He stoops him from his vast, cerulean hall,
He seems the breath of a celestial clime;
As if from heaven's wide-open gates did flow,
Heal[illegible] and refreshment on the world below.

THE OLD MAN'S COUNSEL.

Among our hills and valleys, I have known
Wise and grave men, who, while their diligent hands
Tended or gather'd in the fruits of earth,
Were reverent learners in the solemn school
Of Nature. Not in vain to them were sent
Seed-time and harvest, or the vernal shower
That darken'd the brown tilth, or snow that beat
On the white winter hills. Each brought, in turn,
Some truth; some lesson on the life of man,
Or recognition of the Eternal Mind,
Who veils his glory with the elements.

One such I knew long since, a white-hair'd man,
Pithy of speech, and merry when he would;
A genial optimist, who daily drew
From what he saw his quaint moralities.
Kindly he held communion, though so old,
With me, a dreaming boy, and taught me much,
That books tell not, and I shall ne'er forget.

The sun of May was bright in middle heaven,
And steep'd the sprouting forests, the green hills,
And emerald wheat-fields, in his yellow light.
Upon the apple tree, where rosy buds
Stood cluster'd, ready to burst forth in bloom,
The robin warbled forth his full, clear note
For hours, and wearied not. Within the woods,
Whose young and half-transparent leaves scarce cast
A shade, gay circles of anemones
Danced on their stalks; the shad-bush, white with flowers,
Brighten'd the glens; the new-leaved butternut,
And quivering poplar, to the roving breeze
Gave a balsamic fragrance. In the fields,
I saw the pulses of the gentle wind
On the young grass. My heart was touch'd with joy,
At so much beauty, flushing every hour
Into a fuller beauty; but my friend,
The thoughtful ancient, standing at my side,
Gazed on it mildly sad. I ask'd him why.
"Well may'st thou join in gladness," he replied,
"With the glad earth, her springing plants and flowers,
And this soft wind, the herald of the green,
Luxuriant summer. Thou art young, like them,
And well mayst thou rejoice. But while the flight
Of seasons fills and knits thy spreading frame,
It withers mine, and thins my hair, and dims
These eyes, whose fading light shall soon be quench'd
In utter darkness. Hearest thou that bird?"

I listen'd, and from midst the depth of woods
Heard the low signal of the grouse, that wears
A sable ruff around his mottled neck:
Partridge they call him by our northern streams,
And pheasant by the Delaware. He beat
'Gainst his barr'd sides his speckled wings, and made
A sound like distant thunder; slow the strokes
At first, then fast and faster, till at length
They pass'd into a murmur, and were still.

"There hast thou," said my friend, "a fitting type
Of human life. 'T is an old truth, I know,
But images like these will freshen truth.
Slow pass our days in childhood, every day
Seems like a century; rapidly they glide
In manhood, and in life's decline they fly;
Till days and seasons flit before the mind
As flit the snow-flakes in a winter storm,
Seen rather than distinguish'd. Ah! I seem
As if I sat within a helpless bark,
By swiftly-running waters hurried on
To shoot some mighty cliff. Along the banks
Grove after grove, rock after frowning rock,
Bare sands, and pleasant homesteads; flowery nooks,
And isles and whirlpools in the stream, appear
Each after each; but the devoted skiff
Darts by so swiftly, that their images
Dwell not upon the mind, or only dwell
In dim confusion; faster yet I sweep
By other banks, and the great gulf is near.

"Wisely, my son, while yet thy days are long,
And this fair change of seasons passes slow,
Gather and treasure up the good they yield—
All that they teach of virtue, of pure thoughts,
And kind affections, reverence for thy God,
And for thy brethren; so, when thou shalt come
Into these barren years that fleet away
Before their fruits are ripe, thou mayst not bring
A mind unfurnish'd, and a wither'd heart."

Long since that white-hair'd ancient slept—but still,
When the red flower-buds crowd the orchard bough,
And the ruff'd grouse is drumming far within
The woods, his venerable form again
Is at my side, his voice is in my ear.

AN EVENING REVERIE.*

The summer day has closed—the sun is set:
Well have they done their office, those bright hours,
The latest of whose train goes softly out
In the red west. The green blade of the ground
Has risen, and herds have cropp'd it; the young twig
Has spread its plaited tissues to the sun;
Flowers of the garden and the waste have blown,
And wither'd; seeds have fallen upon the soil
From bursting cells, and in their graves await
Their resurrection. Insects from the pools
Have fill'd the air a while with humming wings,
That now are still forever; painted moths
Have wander'd the blue sky, and died again;
The mother-bird hath broken, for her brood
Their prison-shells, or shoved them from the nest,

* From an unfinished poem.

Plumed for their earliest flight. In bright alcoves,
In woodland cottages with barky walls,
In noisome cells of the tumultuous town,
Mothers have clasp'd with joy the new-born babe.
Graves, by the lonely forest, by the shore
Of rivers and of ocean, by the ways
Of the throng'd city, have been hollow'd out,
And fill'd, and closed. This day hath parted friends,
That ne'er before were parted; it hath knit
New friendships; it hath seen the maiden plight
Her faith, and trust her peace to him who long
Hath woo'd; and it hath heard, from lips which late
Were eloquent of love, the first harsh word,
That told the wedded one her peace was flown.
Farewell to the sweet sunshine! One glad day
Is added now to childhood's merry days,
And one calm day to those of quiet age.
Still the fleet hours run on; and as I lean
Amid the thickening darkness, lamps are lit
By those who watch the dead, and those who twine
Flowers for the bride. The mother from the eyes
Of her sick infant shades the painful light,
And sadly listens to his quick-drawn breath.
O thou great Movement of the universe,
Or Change, or Flight of Time—for ye are one!
That bearest, silently, this visible scene
Into Night's shadow, and the streaming rays
Of starlight, whither art thou bearing me?
I feel the mighty current sweep me on,
Yet know not whither. Man foretells afar
The courses of the stars; the very hour
He knows when they shall darken or grow bright:
Yet doth the eclipse of sorrow and of death
Come unforewarned. Who next, of those I love,
Shall pass from life, or, sadder yet, shall fall
From virtue? Strife with foes, or bitterer strife
With friends, or shame, and general scorn of men—
Which, who can bear?—or the fierce rack of pain,
Lie they within my path? Or shall the years
Push me, with soft and inoffensive pace,
Into the stilly twilight of my age?
Or do the portals of another life,
Even now, while I am glorying in my strength,
Impend around me? O! beyond that bourne,
In the vast cycle of being, which begins
At that broad threshold, with what fairer forms
Shall the great law of change and progress clothe
Its workings? Gently—so have good men taught—
Gently, and without grief, the old shall glide
Into the new, the eternal flow of things,
Like a bright river of the fields of heaven,
Shall journey onward in perpetual peace.

HYMN OF THE CITY.

Not in the solitude
Alone, may man commune with Heaven, or see
Only in savage wood
And sunny vale, the present Deity;
Or only hear his voice
Where the winds whisper and the waves rejoice.

Even here do I behold
Thy steps, Almighty!—here, amidst the crowd
Through the great city roll'd,
With everlasting murmur, deep and loud—
Choking the ways that wind
'Mongst the proud piles, the work of human kind.

Thy golden sunshine comes
From the round heaven, and on their dwellings lies,
And lights their inner homes—
For them thou fill'st with air the unbounded skies,
And givest them the stores
Of ocean, and the harvests of its shores.

Thy spirit is around,
Quickening the restless mass that sweeps along;
And this eternal sound—
Voices and footfalls of the numberless throng—
Like the resounding sea,
Or like the rainy tempest, speaks of thee.

And when the hours of rest
Come, like a calm upon the mid-sea brine,
Hushing its billowy breast—
The quiet of that moment, too, is thine;
It breathes of Him who keeps
The vast and helpless city while it sleeps.

TO A WATERFOWL.

Whither, 'midst falling dew,
While glow the heavens with the last steps of day,
Far, through their rosy depths, dost thou pursue
Thy solitary way!

Vainly the fowler's eye
Might mark thy distant flight to do thee wrong,
As, darkly painted on the crimson sky,
Thy figure floats along.

Seek'st thou the plashy brink
Of weedy lake, or marge of river wide,
Or where the rocking billows rise and sink
On the chafed ocean side?

There is a power whose care
Teaches thy way along that pathless coast,—
The desert and illimitable air,—
Lone wandering, but not lost.

All day thy wings have fann'd,
At that far height, the cold, thin atmosphere,
Yet stoop not, weary, to the welcome land,
Though the dark night is near.

And soon that toil shall end;
Soon shalt thou find a summer home, and rest,
And scream among thy fellows; reeds shall bend,
Soon, o'er thy shelter'd nest.

Thou'rt gone, the abyss of heaven
Hath swallow'd up thy form; yet, on my heart
Deeply hath sunk the lesson thou hast given,
And shall not soon depart.

He who, from zone to zone,
Guides through the boundless sky thy certain flight,
In the long way that I must tread alone,
Will lead my steps aright.

THE BATTLE-FIELD.

Once this soft turf, this rivulet's sands,
Were trampled by a hurrying crowd,
And fiery hearts and armed hands
Encounter'd in the battle-cloud.

Ah! never shall the land forget
How gush'd the life-blood of her brave—
Gush'd, warm with hope and courage yet,
Upon the soil they fought to save.

Now, all is calm, and fresh, and still;
Alone the chirp of flitting bird,
And talk of children on the hill,
And bell of wandering kine are heard.

No solemn host goes trailing by
The black-mouth'd gun and staggering wain;
Men start not at the battle-cry;
O! be it never heard again.

Soon rested those who fought; but thou
Who minglest in the harder strife
For truths which men receive not now,
Thy warfare only ends with life.

A friendless warfare! lingering long
Through weary day and weary year.
A wild and many-weapon'd throng
Hang on thy front, and flank, and rear.

Yet, nerve thy spirit to the proof,
And blench not at thy chosen lot.
The timid good may stand aloof,
The sage may frown—yet faint thou not,

Nor heed the shaft too surely cast,
The hissing, stinging bolt of scorn;
For with thy side shall dwell, at last,
The victory of endurance born.

Truth, crush'd to earth, shall rise again:
The eternal years of God are hers;
But Error, wounded, writhes with pain,
And dies among his worshippers.

Yea, though thou lie upon the dust,
When they who help'd thee flee in fear,
Die full of hope and manly trust,
Like those who fell in battle here.

Another hand thy sword shall wield,
Another hand the standard wave,
Till from the trumpet's mouth is peal'd
The blast of triumph o'er thy grave.

THE DEATH OF THE FLOWERS.

The melancholy days are come,
The saddest of the year,
Of wailing winds, and naked woods,
And meadows brown and sear.
Heap'd in the hollows of the grove,
The wither'd leaves lie dead;
They rustle to the eddying gust,
And to the rabbit's tread.
The robin and the wren are flown,
And from the shrubs the jay,
And from the wood-top calls the crow,
Through all the gloomy day.

Where are the flowers, the fair young flowers,
That lately sprang and stood
In brighter light and softer airs,
A beauteous sisterhood!
Alas! they all are in their graves,
The gentle race of flowers
Are lying in their lowly beds,
With the fair and good of ours.
The rain is falling where they lie,
But the cold November rain
Calls not, from out the gloomy earth,
The lovely ones again.

The wind-flower and the violet,
They perish'd long ago,
And the brier-rose and the orchis died,
Amid the summer glow;
But on the hill the golden-rod,
And the aster in the wood,
And the yellow sun-flower by the brook
In autumn beauty stood,
Till fell the frost from the clear, cold heaven,
As falls the plague on men,
And the brightness of their smile was gone,
From upland, glade, and glen.

And now, when comes the calm, mild day,
As still such days will come,
To call the squirrel and the bee
From out their winter home;
When the sound of dropping nuts is heard,
Though all the trees are still,
And twinkle in the smoky light
The waters of the rill,
The south wind searches for the flowers
Whose fragrance late he bore,
And sighs to find them in the wood
And by the stream no more.

And then I think of one who in
Her youthful beauty died,
The fair, meek blossom that grew up
And faded by my side;
In the cold, moist earth we laid her,
When the forest cast the leaf,
And we wept that one so lovely
Should have a life so brief:
Yet not unmeet it was that one,
Like that young friend of ours,
So gentle and so beautiful,
Should perish with the flowers.

THE FUTURE LIFE.

How shall I know thee in the sphere which keeps
The disembodied spirits of the dead,
When all of thee that time could wither sleeps
And perishes among the dust we tread?

For I shall feel the sting of ceaseless pain
If there I meet thy gentle presence not;
Nor hear the voice I love, nor read again
In thy serenest eyes the tender thought.

Will not thy own meek heart demand me there?
That heart whose fondest throbs to me were given?
My name on earth was ever in thy prayer,
Shall it be banish'd from thy tongue in heaven?

In meadows framed by heaven's life-breathing wind,
In the resplendence of that glorious sphere,
And larger movements of the unfetter'd mind,
Wilt thou forget the love that join'd us here;

The love that lived through all the stormy past,
And meekly with my harsher nature bore,
And deeper grew, and tenderer to the last,—
Shall it expire with life, and be no more?

A happier lot than mine, and larger light,
Await thee there; for thou hast bow'd thy will
In cheerful homage to the rule of right,
And lovest all, and renderest good for ill.

For me, the sordid cares in which I dwell
Shrink and consume the heart, as heat the scroll;
And wrath has left its scar—that fire of hell
Has left its frightful scar upon my soul.

Yet, though thou wear'st the glory of the sky,
Wilt thou not keep the same beloved name,
The same fair thoughtful brow, and gentle eye,
Lovelier in heaven's sweet climate, yet the same?

Shalt thou not teach me in that calmer home
The wisdom that I learn'd so ill in this—
The wisdom which is love—till I become
Thy fit companion in that land of bliss?

TO THE FRINGED GENTIAN.

Thou blossom, bright with autumn dew,
And colour'd with the heaven's own blue,
That openest, when the quiet light
Succeeds the keen and frosty night.

Thou comest not when violets lean
O'er wandering brooks and springs unseen,
Or columbines in purple dress'd,
Nod o'er the ground-bird's hidden nest.

Thou waitest late, and com'st alone,
When woods are bare and birds are flown,
And frosts and shortening days portend
The aged year is near his end.

Then doth thy sweet and quiet eye
Look through its fringes to the sky,
Blue—blue—as if that sky let fall
A flower from its cerulean wall.

I would that thus, when I shall see
The hour of death draw near to me,
Hope, blossoming within my heart,
May look to heaven as I depart.

OH, FAIREST OF THE RURAL MAIDS.

Oh, fairest of the rural maids!
Thy birth was in the forest shades;
Green boughs, and glimpses of the sky,
Were all that met thy infant eye.

Thy sports, thy wanderings, when a child,
Were ever in the sylvan wild;
And all the beauty of the place
Is in thy heart and on thy face.

The twilight of the trees and rocks
Is in the light shade of thy locks;
Thy step is as the wind, that weaves
Its playful way among the leaves.

Thine eyes are springs, in whose serene
And silent waters heaven is seen;
Their lashes are the herbs that look
On their young figures in the brook.

The forest depths, by foot unpress'd,
Are not more sinless than thy breast;
The holy peace that fills the air
Of those calm solitudes, is there.

THE MAIDEN'S SORROW.

Seven long years has the desert rain
Dropp'd on the clods that hide thy face;
Seven long years of sorrow and pain
I have thought of thy burial place.

Thought of thy fate in the distant west,
Dying with none that loved thee near;
They who flung the earth on thy breast
Turn'd from the spot without a tear.

There, I think, on that lonely grave,
Violets spring in the soft May shower;
There in the summer breezes wave
Crimson phlox and moccasin flower.

There the turtles alight, and there
Feeds with her fawn the timid doe;
There, when the winter woods are bare,
Walks the wolf on the crackling snow.

Soon wilt thou wipe my tears away;
All my task upon earth is done;
My poor father, old and gray,
Slumbers beneath the church-yard stone.

In the dreams of my lonely bed,
Ever thy form before me seems;
All night long I talk with the dead,
All day long I think of my dreams.

This deep wound that bleeds and aches,
This long pain, a sleepless pain—
When the Father my spirit takes
I shall feel it no more again.

CARLOS WILCOX.

[Born, 1794. Died, 1827.]

The ancestors of Carlos Wilcox were among the early emigrants to New England. His father was a respectable farmer at Newport, New Hampshire, where the poet was born, on the twenty-second day of October, 1794. When he was about four years old, his parents removed to Orwell, in Vermont; and there, a few years afterward, he accidentally injured himself with an axe; the wound, for want of care or skill, was not healed; it was a cause of suffering for a long period, and of lameness during his life; it made him a minister of religion, and a poet.

Perceiving that this accident and its consequences unfitted him for agricultural pursuits, his parents resolved to give him a liberal education. When, therefore, he was thirteen years old, he was sent to an academy at Castleton; and when fifteen, to the college at Middlebury. Here he became religious, and determined to study theology. He won the respect of the officers, and of his associates, by the mildness of his temper, the gravity of his manners, and the manliness of his conduct; and he was distinguished for his attainments in languages and polite letters.

He was graduated in 1813; and after spending a few months with a maternal uncle, in Georgia, he entered the theological school at Andover, in Massachusetts. He had not been there long when one of his classmates died, and he was chosen by his fellows to pronounce a funeral oration. The departed student was loved by all for his excellent qualities; but by none more than by Wilcox; and the tenderness of feeling, and the purity of diction which characterized his eulogy, established his reputation for genius and eloquence in the seminary.

Wilcox had at this time few associates; he was a melancholy man; "I walk my room," he remarks, in one of his letters, "with my hands clasped in anguish, and my eyes streaming with tears;" he complained that his mind was unstrung, relaxed almost beyond the power of reaction; that he had lost all control of his thoughts and affections, and become a passive slave of circumstances; "I feel borne along," he says, "in despairing listlessness, guided by the current in all its windings, without resolution to raise my head to see where I am, or whither I am going; the roaring of a cataract before me would rather lull me to a deeper sleep than rouse me to an effort to escape destruction." His sufferings were apparent to his friends, among whom there were givings-out concerning an unrequited passion, or the faithlessness of one whose hand had been pledged to him; and he himself mentioned to some who were his confidants, troubles of a different kind: he was indebted to the college faculty, and in other ways embarrassed. Whatever may have been the cause, all perceived that there was something preying on his mind; that he was ever in dejection.

As time wore on, he became more cheerful; he finished the regular course of theological studies, in 1817, and in the following spring returned to Vermont, where he remained a year. In this period he began the poem, in which he has sung

> "Of true Benevolence, its charms divine,
> With other motives to call forth its power,
> And its grand triumphs."

In 1819, Wilcox began to preach; and his professional labours were constant, for a year, at the end of which time his health failed, and he accepted an invitation from a friend at Salisbury, in Connecticut, to reside at his house. Here he remained nearly two years, reading his favourite authors, and composing "The Age of Benevolence." The first book was published at New Haven, in 1822; it was favourably received by the journals and by the public. He intended to complete the poem in five books; the second, third, and fourth, were left by him when he died, ready for the press; but, for some reason, only brief fragments of them have been printed.

During the summer of 1824, Wilcox devoted his leisure hours to the composition of "The Religion of Taste," a poem which he pronounced before the Phi Beta Kappa Society of Yale College; and in the following winter he was ordained as minister of the North Congregational Church, in Hartford. He soon obtained a high reputation for eloquence; his sermons were long, prepared with great care, and delivered with deep feeling. His labours were too arduous; his health rapidly declined; and in the summer of 1825, he sought relief in relaxation and travel. He visited New York, Philadelphia, the springs of Saratoga, and, for the last time, his home in Vermont. In the autumn he returned to his parish, where he remained until the spring, when, finding himself unable to perform the duties of his office, he sent to the government of the church his resignation. It was reluctantly accepted, for he had endeared himself, as a minister and a man, to all who knew him. The summer of 1826 was passed at Newport, Rhode Island, in the hope that the sea-breeze and bathing in the surf would restore his health. He was disappointed; and in September, he visited the White Mountains, in New Hampshire, and afterward went to Boston, where he remained several weeks. Finally, near the end of December, he received an invitation to preach in Danbury, in Connecticut. He went immediately to his new parish, and during the winter discharged the duties of his profession regularly. But as the spring came round, his strength failed; and on the 27th of May, 1827, he died.

There is much merit in some passages of the fragment of the "Age of Benevolence." WILCOX was pious, gentle-hearted, and unaffected and retiring in his manners. The general character of his poetry is religious and sincere. He was a lover of nature, and he described rural sights and sounds with singular clearness and fidelity. In the ethical and narrative parts of his poems, he was less successful than in the descriptive; but an earnestness and simplicity pervaded all that he wrote.

SPRING IN NEW ENGLAND.*

LONG swoln in drenching rain, seeds, germs, and buds
Start at the touch of vivifying beams.
Moved by their secret force, the vital lymph
Diffusive runs, and spreads o'er wood and field
A flood of verdure. Clothed, in one short week,
Is naked Nature in her full attire.
On the first morn, light as an open plain
Is all the woodland, fill'd with sunbeams, pour'd
Through the bare tops, on yellow leaves below,
With strong reflection: on the last, 'tis dark
With full-grown foliage, shading all within.
In one short week the orchard buds and blooms;
And now, when steep'd in dew or gentle showers,
It yields the purest sweetness to the breeze,
Or all the tranquil atmosphere perfumes.
E'en from the juicy leaves of sudden growth,
And the rank grass of steaming ground, the air,
Fill'd with a watery glimmering, receives
A grateful smell, exhaled by warming rays.
Each day are heard, and almost every hour,
New notes to swell the music of the groves.
And soon the latest of the feather'd train
At evening twilight come; the lonely snipe,
O'er marshy fields, high in the dusky air,
Invisible, but with faint, tremulous tones,
Hovering or playing o'er the listener's head;
And, in mid air, the sportive night-hawk, seen
Flying a while at random, uttering oft
A cheerful cry, attended with a shake
Of level pinions, dark, but when upturn'd
Against the brightness of the western sky,
One white plume showing in the midst of each,
Then far down diving with a hollow sound;
And, deep at first within the distant wood,
The whip-poor-will, her name her only song.
She, soon as children from the noisy sport
Of whooping, laughing, talking with all tones,
To hear the echoes of the empty barn,
Are by her voice diverted and held mute,
Comes to the margin of the nearest grove;
And when the twilight, deepen'd into night,
Calls them within, close to the house she comes,
And on its dark side, haply on the step
Of unfrequented door lighting unseen,
Breaks into strains articulate and clear,
The closing sometimes quicken'd, as in sport.
Now, animate throughout, from morn to eve
All harmony, activity, and joy,
Is lovely Nature, as in her bless'd prime.
The robin to the garden or green yard,
Close to the door, repairs to build again
Within her wonted tree; and at her work
Seems doubly busy for her past delay.
Along the surface of the winding stream,
Pursuing every turn, gay swallows skim,
Or round the borders of the spacious lawn
Fly in repeated circles, rising o'er
Hillock and fence with motion serpentine,
Easy, and light. One snatches from the ground
A downy feather, and then upward springs,
Follow'd by others, but oft drops it soon,
In playful mood, or from too slight a hold,
When all at once dart at the falling prize.
The flippant blackbird, with light yellow crown,
Hangs fluttering in the air, and chatters thick
Till her breath fails, when, breaking off, she drops
On the next tree, and on its highest limb
Or some tall flag, and gently rocking, sits,
Her strain repeating. With sonorous notes
Of every tone, mix'd in confusion sweet,
All chanted in the fulness of delight,
The forest rings: where, far around enclosed
With bushy sides, and cover'd high above
With foliage thick, supported by bare trunks,
Like pillars rising to support a roof,
It seems a temple vast, the space within
Rings loud and clear with thrilling melody.
Apart, but near the choir, with voice distinct,
The merry mocking-bird together links
In one continued song their different notes,
Adding new life and sweetness to them all.
Hid under shrubs, the squirrel, that in fields
Frequents the stony wall and briery fence,
Here chirps so shrill, that human feet approach
Unheard till just upon him, when, with cries
Sudden and sharp, he darts to his retreat
Beneath the mossy hillock or aged tree;
But oft a moment after reappears,
First peeping out, then starting forth at once
With a courageous air, yet in his pranks
Keeping a watchful eye, nor venturing far
Till left unheeded. In rank pastures graze,
Singly and mutely, the contented herd;
And on the upland rough the peaceful sheep;
Regardless of the frolic lambs, that, close
Beside them, and before their faces prone,
With many an antic leap and butting feint,
Try to provoke them to unite in sport,
Or grant a look, till tired of vain attempts;
When, gathering in one company apart,
All vigour and delight, away they run,
Straight to the utmost corner of the field,
The fence beside; then, wheeling, disappear
In some small sandy pit, then rise to view;
Or crowd together up the heap of earth
Around some upturn'd root of fallen tree,

* This and the four following extracts are from "The Age of Benevolence."

And on its top a trembling moment stand,
Then to the distant flock at once return.
Exhilarated by the general joy,
And the fair prospect of a fruitful year,
The peasant, with light heart and nimble step,
His work pursues, as it were pastime sweet.
With many a cheering word, his willing team
For labour fresh, he hastens to the field
Ere morning lose its coolness; but at eve,
When loosen'd from the plough, and homeward turn'd,
He follows slow and silent, stopping oft
To mark the daily growth of tender grain
And meadows of deep verdure, or to view
His scatter'd flock and herd, of their own will
Assembling for the night by various paths,
The old now freely sporting with the young,
Or labouring with uncouth attempts at sport.

A SUMMER NOON.

A SULTRY noon, not in the summer's prime,
When all is fresh with life, and youth, and bloom,
But near its close, when vegetation stops,
And fruits mature stand ripening in the sun,
Soothes and enervates with its thousand charms,
Its images of silence and of rest,
The melancholy mind. The fields are still;
The husbandman has gone to his repast,
And, that partaken, on the coolest side
Of his abode, reclines in sweet repose.
Deep in the shaded stream the cattle stand,
The flocks beside the fence, with heads all prone,
And panting quick. The fields, for harvest ripe,
No breezes bend in smooth and graceful waves,
While with their motion, dim and bright by turns,
The sunshine seems to move; nor e'en a breath
Brushes along the surface with a shade
Fleeting and thin, like that of flying smoke.
The slender stalks their heavy bended heads
Support as motionless as oaks their tops.
O'er all the woods the topmost leaves are still;
E'en the wild poplar leaves, that, pendent hung
By stems elastic, quiver at a breath,
Rest in the general calm. The thistle down,
Seen high and thick, by gazing up beside
Some shading object, in a silver shower
Plumb down, and slower than the slowest snow,
Through all the sleepy atmosphere descends;
And where it lights, though on the steepest roof,
Or smallest spire of grass, remains unmoved.
White as a fleece, as dense and as distinct
From the resplendent sky, a single cloud,
On the soft bosom of the air becalm'd,
Drops a lone shadow, as distinct and still,
On the bare plain, or sunny mountain's side;
Or in the polish'd mirror of the lake,
In which the deep reflected sky appears
A calm, sublime immensity below.
No sound nor motion of a living thing
The stillness breaks, but such as serve to soothe,
Or cause the soul to feel the stillness more.
The yellow-hammer by the way-side picks,
Mutely, the thistle's seed; but in her flight,
So smoothly serpentine, her wings outspread
To rise a little, closed to fall as far,
Moving like sea-fowl o'er the heaving waves,
With each new impulse chimes a feeble note.
The russet grasshopper at times is heard,
Snapping his many wings, as half he flies,
Half-hovers in the air. Where strikes the sun
With sultriest beams, upon the sandy plain
Or stony mount, or in the close, deep vale,
The harmless locust of this western clime,
At intervals, amid the leaves unseen,
Is heard to sing with one unbroken sound,
As with a long-drawn breath, beginning low,
And rising to the midst with shriller swell,
Then in low cadence dying all away.
Beside the stream, collected in a flock,
The noiseless butterflies, though on the ground,
Continue still to wave their open fans
Powder'd with gold; while on the jutting twigs
The spindling insects that frequent the banks
Rest, with their thin, transparent wings outspread
As when they fly. Ofttimes, though seldom seen,
The cuckoo, that in summer haunts our groves,
Is heard to moan, as if at every breath
Panting aloud. The hawk, in mid-air high,
On his broad pinions sailing round and round,
With not a flutter, or but now and then,
As if his trembling balance to regain,
Utters a single scream, but faintly heard,
And all again is still.

SEPTEMBER.

THE sultry summer past, September comes,
Soft twilight of the slow-declining year.
All mildness, soothing loneliness, and peace;
The fading season ere the falling come,
More sober than the buxom, blooming May,
And therefore less the favourite of the world,
But dearest month of all to pensive minds.
'T is now far spent; and the meridian sun,
Most sweetly smiling with attemper'd beams,
Sheds gently down a mild and grateful warmth.
Beneath its yellow lustre, groves and woods,
Checker'd by one night's frost with various hues,
While yet no wind has swept a leaf away,
Shine doubly rich. It were a sad delight
Down the smooth stream to glide, and see it tinged
Upon each brink with all the gorgeous hues,
The yellow, red, or purple of the trees
That, singly, or in tufts, or forests thick
Adorn the shores; to see, perhaps, the side
Of some high mount reflected far below,
With its bright colours, intermix'd with spots
Of darker green. Yes, it were sweetly sad
To wander in the open fields, and hear,
E'en at this hour, the noonday hardly past,
The lulling insects of the summer's night;
To hear, where lately buzzing swarms were heard,
A lonely bee long roving here and there
To find a single flower, but all in vain;
Then rising quick, and with a louder hum,
In widening circles round and round his head,

Straight by the listener flying clear away,
As if to bid the fields a last adieu;
To hear, within the woodland's sunny side,
Late full of music, nothing save, perhaps,
The sound of nutshells, by the squirrel dropp'd
From some tall beech, fast falling through the leaves.

SUNSET IN SEPTEMBER.*

THE sun now rests upon the mountain tops—
Begins to sink behind—is half conceal'd—
And now is gone: the last faint, twinkling beam
Is cut in twain by the sharp rising ridge.
Sweet to the pensive is departing day,
When only one small cloud, so still and thin,
So thoroughly imbued with amber light,
And so transparent, that it seems a spot
Of brighter sky, beyond the farthest mount,
Hangs o'er the hidden orb; or where a few
Long, narrow stripes of denser, darker grain,
At each end sharpen'd to a needle's point,
With golden borders,sometimes straight and smooth,
And sometimes crinkling like the lightning stream,
A half-hour's space above the mountain lie;
Or when the whole consolidated mass,
That only threaten'd rain, is broken up
Into a thousand parts, and yet is one,
One as the ocean broken into waves;
And all its spongy parts, imbibing deep
The moist effulgence, seem like fleeces dyed
Deep scarlet, saffron light, or crimson dark,
As they are thick or thin, or near or more remote,
All fading soon as lower sinks the sun,
Till twilight end. But now another scene,
To me most beautiful of all, appears:
The sky, without the shadow of a cloud,
Throughout the west, is kindled to a glow
So bright and broad, it glares upon the eye,
Not dazzling, but dilating with calm force
Its power of vision to admit the whole.
Below, 't is all of richest orange dye,
Midway, the blushing of the mellow peach
Paints not, but tinges the ethereal deep;
And here, in this most lovely region, shines,
With added loveliness, the evening-star.
Above, the fainter purple slowly fades,
Till changed into the azure of mid-heaven.
  Along the level ridge, o'er which the sun
Descended, in a single row arranged,
As if thus planted by the hand of art,
Majestic pines shoot up into the sky,
And in its fluid gold seem half-dissolved.
Upon a nearer peak, a cluster stands
With shafts erect, and tops converged to one,
A stately colonnade, with verdant roof;
Upon a nearer still, a single tree,
With shapely form, looks beautiful alone;
While, farther northward, through a narrow pass
Scoop'd in the hither range, a single mount
Beyond the rest, of finer smoothness seems,
And of a softer, more ethereal blue,
A pyramid of polish'd sapphire built.
  But now the twilight mingles into one
The various mountains; levels to a plain
This nearer, lower landscape, dark with shade,
Where every object to my sight presents
Its shaded side; while here upon these walls,
And in that eastern wood, upon the trunks
Under thick foliage, reflective shows
Its yellow lustre. How distinct the line
Of the horizon, parting heaven and earth!

* Every person, who has witnessed the splendour of the sunset scenery in Andover, will recognise with delight the *local* as well as general truth and beauty of this description. There is not, perhaps, in New England, a spot where the sun goes down, of a clear summer's evening, amidst so much grandeur reflected over earth and sky. In the winter season, too, it is a most magnificent and impressive scene. The great extent of the landscape; the situation of the hill, on the broad, level summit of which stand the buildings of the Theological Institution; the vast amphitheatre of luxuriant forest and field, which rises from its base, and swells away into the heavens; the perfect outline of the horizon; the noble range of blue mountains in the background, that seem to retire one beyond another almost to infinite distance; together with the magnificent expanse of sky visible at once from the elevated spot,—these features constitute at all times a scene on which the lover of nature can never be weary with gazing. When the sun goes down, it is all in a blaze with his descending glory. The sunset is the most perfectly beautiful when an afternoon shower has just preceded it. The gorgeous clouds roll away like masses of amber. The sky, close to the horizon, is a sea of the richest purple. The setting sun shines through the mist, which rises from the wet forest and meadow, and makes the clustered foliage appear invested with a brilliant golden transparency. Nearer to the eye, the trees and shrubs are sparkling with fresh rain-drops, and over the whole scene, the parting rays of sunlight linger with a yellow gleam, as if reluctant to pass entirely away. Then come the varying tints of twilight, "fading, still fading," till the stars are out in their beauty, and a cloudless night reigns, with its silence, shadows, and repose. In the summer, Andover combines almost every thing to charm and elevate the feelings of the student. In winter, the north-western blasts, that sweep fresh from the snow-banks on the Grand Monadnock, make the invalid, at least, sigh for a more congenial climate.—REV. G. B. CHEEVER.

SUMMER EVENING LIGHTNING.

FAR off and low
In the horizon, from a sultry cloud,
Where sleeps in embryo the midnight storm,
The silent lightning gleams in fitful sheets,
Illumes the solid mass, revealing thus
Its darker fragments, and its ragged verge;
Or if the bolder fancy so conceive
Of its fantastic forms, revealing thus
Its gloomy caverns, rugged sides and tops
With beetling cliffs grotesque. But not so bright
The distant flashes gleam as to efface
The window's image, on the floor impress'd
By the dim crescent; or outshines the light
Cast from the room upon the trees hard by,
If haply, to illume a moonless night,
The lighted taper shine; though lit in vain,
To waste away unused, and from abroad
Distinctly through the open window seen,
Lone, pale, and still as a sepulchral lamp.

THE CASTLE OF IMAGINATION.*

Just in the centre of that wood was rear'd
Her castle, all of marble, smooth and white;
Above the thick young trees, its top appear'd
Among the naked trunks of towering height;
And here at morn and eve it glitter'd bright,
As often by the far-off traveller seen
In level sunbeams, or at dead of night,
When the low moon shot in her rays between
That wide-spread roof and floor of solid foliage green.

Through this wide interval the roving eye
From turrets proud might trace the waving line
Where meet the mountains green and azure sky,
And view the deep when sun-gilt billows shine;
Fair bounds to sight, that never thought confine,
But tempt it far beyond, till by the charm
Of some sweet wood-note or some whispering pine
Call'd home again, or by the soft alarm
Of Love's approaching step, and her encircling arm.

Through this wide interval, the mountain side
Show'd many a sylvan slope and rocky steep:
Here roaring torrents in dark forests hide;
There silver streamlets rush to view, and leap
Unheard from lofty cliffs to valleys deep:
Here rugged peaks look smooth in sunset glow,
Along the clear horizon's western sweep;
There from some eastern summit moonbeams flow
Along o'er level wood, far down to plains below.

Now stretch'd a blue, and now a golden zone
Round that horizon; now o'er mountains proud
Dim vapours rest, or bright ones move alone:
An ebon wall, a smooth, portentous cloud,
First muttering low, anon with thunder loud,
Now rises quick, and brings a sweeping wind
O'er all that wood in waves before it bow'd;
And now a rainbow, with its top behind
A spangled veil of leaves, seems heaven and earth to bind.

Above the canopy, so thick and green,
And spread so high o'er that enchanted vale,
Through scatter'd openings oft were glimpses seen
Of fleecy clouds, that, link'd together, sail
In moonlight clear before the gentle gale:
Sometimes a shooting meteor draws a glance;
Sometimes a twinkling star, or planet pale,
Long holds the lighted eye, as in a trance;
And oft the milky-way gleams through the white expanse.

That castle's open windows, though half-hid
With flowering vines, show'd many a vision fair.
A face all bloom, or light young forms, that thrid
Some maze within, or lonely ones that wear
The garb of joy with sorrow's thoughtful air,
Oft caught the eye a moment: and the sound
Of low, sweet music often issued there,
And by its magic held the listener bound,
And seem'd to hold the winds and forests far around.

Within, the queen of all, in pomp or mirth,
While glad attendants at her glance unfold
Their shining wings, and fly through heaven and earth,
Oft took her throne of burning gems and gold,
Adorn'd with emblems that of empire told,
And rising in the midst of trophies bright,
That bring her memory from the days of old,
And help prolong her reign, and with the flight
Of every year increase the wonders of her might.

In all her dwelling, tales of wild romance,
Of terror, love, and mystery dark or gay,
Were scatter'd thick to catch the wandering glance,
And stop the dreamer on his unknown way;
There, too, was every sweet and lofty lay,
The sacred, classic, and romantic, sung
As that enchantress moved in might or play;
And there was many a harp but newly strung,
Yet with its fearless notes the whole wide valley rung.

There, from all lands and ages of her fame,
Were marble forms, array'd in order due,
In groups and single, all of proudest name;
In them the high, the fair, and tender grew
To life intense in love's impassion'd view,
And from each air and feature, bend and swell,
Each shapely neck, and lip, and forehead threw
O'er each enamour'd sense so deep a spell,
The thoughts but with the past or bright ideal dwell.

The walls around told all the pencil's power;
There proud creations of each mighty hand
Shone with their hues and lines, as in the hour
When the last touch was given at the command
Of the same genius that at first had plann'd,
Exulting in its great and glowing thought:
Bright scenes of peace and war, of sea and land,
Of love and glory, to new life were wrought,
From history, from fable, and from nature brought.

With these were others all divine, drawn all
From ground where oft, with signs and accents dread,
The lonely prophet doom'd to sudden fall
Proud kings and cities, and with gentle tread
Bore life's quick triumph to the humble dead,
And where strong angels flew to blast or save,
Where martyr'd hosts of old, and youthful bled,
And where their mighty Lord o'er land and wave
Spread life and peace till death, then spread them through the grave.

From these fix'd visions of the hallow'd eye,
Some kindling gleams of their ethereal glow,
Would ofttimes fall, as from the opening sky,
On eyes delighted, glancing to and fro,
Or fasten'd till their orbs dilated grow;
Then would the proudest seem with joy to learn
Truths they had fear'd or felt ashamed to know;
The skeptic would believe, the lost return;
And all the cold and low would seem to rise and burn.

Theirs was devotion kindled by the vast,
The beautiful, impassion'd, and refined;
And in the deep enchantment o'er them cast,
They look'd from earth, and soar'd above their kind

* This and the two extracts which follow are from "The Religion of Taste."

To the bless'd calm of an abstracted mind,
And its communion with things all its own,
Its forms sublime and lovely; as the blind,
Mid earthly scenes, forgotten, or unknown,
Live in ideal worlds, and wander there alone.

Such were the lone enthusiasts, wont to dwell
With all whom that enchantress held subdued,
As in the holiest circle of her spell,
Where meaner spirits never dare intrude,
They dwelt in calm and silent solitude,
Rapt in the love of all the high and sweet,
In thought, and art, and nature, and imbued
With its devotion to life's inmost seat,
As drawn from all the charms which in that valley meet.

ROUSSEAU AND COWPER.

Rousseau could weep—yes, with a heart of stone
The impious sophist could recline beside
The pure and peaceful lake, and muse alone
On all its loveliness at eventide:
On its small running waves, in purple dyed
Beneath bright clouds, or all the glowing sky,
On the white sails that o'er its bosom glide,
And on surrounding mountains wild and high,
Till tears unbidden gush'd from his enchanted eye.

But his were not the tears of feeling fine,
Of grief or love; at fancy's flash they flow'd,
Like burning drops from some proud, lonely pine,
By lightning fired; his heart with passion glow'd
Till it consumed his life, and yet he show'd
A chilling coldness both to friend and foe,
As Etna, with its centre an abode
Of wasting fire, chills with the icy snow
Of all its desert brow the living world below.

Was he but justly wretched from his crimes?
Then why was Cowper's anguish oft as keen,
With all the heaven-born virtue that sublimes
Genius and feeling, and to things unseen
Lifts the pure heart through clouds that roll between
The earth and skies, to darken human hope?
Or wherefore did those clouds thus intervene
To render vain faith's lifted telescope,
And leave him in thick gloom his weary way to grope?

He, too, could give himself to musing deep;
By the calm lake at evening he could stand,
Lonely and sad, to see the moonlight sleep
On all its breast, by not an insect fann'd,
And hear low voices on the far-off strand,
Or through the still and dewy atmosphere
The pipe's soft tones waked by some gentle hand,
From fronting shore and woody island near
In echoes quick return'd more mellow and more clear.

And he could cherish wild and mournful dreams,
In the pine grove, when low the full moon fair
Shot under lofty tops her level beams,
Stretching the shades of trunks erect and bare,
In stripes drawn parallel with order rare,
As of some temple vast or colonnade,
While on green turf, made smooth without his care,
He wander'd o'er its stripes of light and shade
And heard the dying day-breeze all the boughs pervade.

'Twas thus in nature's bloom and solitude
He nursed his grief till nothing could assuage;
'Twas thus his tender spirit was subdued,
Till in life's toils it could no more engage;
And his had been a useless pilgrimage,
Had he been gifted with no sacred power,
To send his thoughts to every future age;
But he is gone where grief will not devour,
Where beauty will not fade, and skies will never lower.

THE CURE OF MELANCHOLY.

And thou, to whom long worshipp'd nature lends
No strength to fly from grief or bear its weight,
Stop not to rail at foes or fickle friends,
Nor set the world at naught, nor spurn at fate;
None seek thy misery, none thy being hate;
Break from thy former self, thy life begin;
Do thou the good thy thoughts oft meditate,
And thou shalt feel the good man's peace within,
And at thy dying day his wreath of glory win.

With deeds of virtue to embalm his name,
He dies in triumph or serene delight;
Weaker and weaker grows his mortal frame
At every breath, but in immortal might
His spirit grows, preparing for its flight:
The world recedes and fades like clouds of even,
But heaven comes nearer fast, and grows more bright,
All intervening mists far off are driven;
The world will vanish soon, and all will soon be heaven.

Wouldst thou from sorrow find a sweet relief?
Or is thy heart oppress'd with woes untold?
Balm wouldst thou gather for corroding grief?
Pour blessings round thee like a shower of gold:
'Tis when the rose is wrapp'd in many a fold
Close to its heart, the worm is wasting there
Its life and beauty; not when, all unroll'd,
Leaf after leaf, its bosom rich and fair
Breathes freely its perfumes throughout the ambient air.

Wake, thou that sleepest in enchanted bowers,
Lest these lost years should haunt thee on the night
When death is waiting for thy number'd hours
To take their swift and everlasting flight;
Wake ere the earthborn charm unnerve thee quite,
And be thy thoughts to work divine address'd:
Do something—do it soon—with all thy might
An angel's wing would droop if long at rest,
And God himself inactive were no longer bless'd

Some high or humble enterprise of good
Contemplate till it shall possess thy mind,

Become thy study, pastime, rest, and food,
And kindle in thy heart a flame refined;
Pray Heaven with firmness thy whole soul to bind
To this thy purpose—to begin, pursue,
With thoughts all fix'd and feelings purely kind,
Strength to complete, and with delight review,
And grace to give the praise where all is ever due.

No good of worth sublime will Heaven permit
To light on man as from the passing air;
The lamp of genius, though by nature lit,
If not protected, pruned, and fed with care,
Soon dies, or runs to waste with fitful glare;
And learning is a plant that spreads and towers
Slow as Columbia's aloe, proudly rare,
That, mid gay thousands, with the suns and showers
Of half a century, grows alone before it flowers.

Has immortality of name been given
To them that idly worship hills and groves,
And burn sweet incense to the queen of heaven?
Did Newton learn from fancy, as it roves,
To measure worlds, and follow where each moves?
Did Howard gain renown that shall not cease,
By wanderings wild that nature's pilgrim loves?
Or did Paul gain heaven's glory and its peace,
By musing o'er the bright and tranquil isles of Greece?

Beware lest thou, from sloth, that would appear
But lowliness of mind, with joy proclaim
Thy want of worth; a charge thou couldst not hear
From other lips, without a blush of shame,
Or pride indignant; then be thine the blame,
And make thyself of worth; and thus enlist
The smiles of all the good, the dear to fame;
'T is infamy to die and not be miss'd,
Or let all soon forget that thou didst e'er exist.

Rouse to some work of high and holy love,
And thou an angel's happiness shalt know,—
Shalt bless the earth while in the world above;
The good begun by thee shall onward flow
In many a branching stream, and wider grow;
The seed that, in these few and fleeting hours,
Thy hands unsparing and unwearied sow,
Shall deck thy grave with amaranthine flowers,
And yield thee fruits divine in heaven's immortal bowers.

SIGHTS AND SOUNDS OF THE NIGHT.

Ere long the clouds were gone, the moon was set;
When deeply blue without a shade of gray,
The sky was fill'd with stars that almost met,
Their points prolong'd and sharpen'd to one ray;
Through their transparent air the milky-way
Seem'd one broad flame of pure resplendent white,
As if some globe on fire, turn'd far astray,
Had cross'd the wide arch with so swift a flight,
That for a moment shone its whole long track of light.

At length in northern skies, at first but small,
A sheet of light meteorous begun
To spread on either hand, and rise and fall
In waves, that slowly first, then quickly run
Along its edge, set thick but one by one
With spiry beams, that all at once shot high,
Like those through vapours from the setting sun;
Then sidelong as before the wind they fly,
Like streaking rain from clouds that flit along the sky.

Now all the mountain-tops and gulfs between
Seem'd one dark plain; from forests, caves profound,
And rushing waters far below unseen,
Rose a deep roar in one united sound,
Alike pervading all the air around,
And seeming e'en the azure dome to fill,
And from it through soft ether to resound
In low vibrations, sending a sweet thrill
To every finger's end from rapture deep and still.

LIVE FOR ETERNITY.

A bright or dark eternity in view,
With all its fix'd, unutterable things,
What madness in the living to pursue,
As their chief portion, with the speed of wings,
The joys that death-beds always turn to stings!
Infatuated man, on earth's smooth waste
To dance along the path that always brings
Quick to an end, from which with tenfold haste
Back would he gladly fly till all should be retraced!

Our life is like the hurrying on the eve
Before we start, on some long journey bound,
When fit preparing to the last we leave,
Then run to every room the dwelling round,
And sigh that nothing needed can be found;
Yet go we must, and soon as day shall break;
We snatch an hour's repose, when loud the sound
For our departure calls; we rise and take
A quick and sad farewell, and go ere well awake.

Rear'd in the sunshine, blasted by the storms
Of changing time, scarce asking why or whence,
Men come and go like vegetable forms,
Though heaven appoints for them a work immense,
Demanding constant thought and zeal intense,
Awaked by hopes and fears that leave no room
For rest to mortals in the dread suspense,
While yet they know not if beyond the tomb
A long, long life of bliss or wo shall be their doom

What matter whether pain or pleasures fill
The swelling heart one little moment here?
From both alike how vain is every thrill,
While an untried eternity is near!
Think not of rest, fond man, in life's career;
The joys and grief that meet thee, dash aside
Like bubbles, and thy bark right onward steer
Through calm and tempest, till it cross the tide,
Shoot into port in triumph, or serenely glide.

HENRY WARE, JR.

[Born, 1794. Died, 1843.]

Henry Ware, D. D., a son of Henry Ware, D. D., and brother of William Ware, D. D., author of "Probus," etc., was born in Hingham, Massachusetts, on the seventh of April, 1794; was graduated at Cambridge in 1812; completed his theological studies in 1815; was ordained minister of the Second Congregational Church, in Boston, in 1817; received Ralph Waldo Emerson as his colleague, in 1829; for the recovery of his health soon after visited Europe; and on his return, in 1830, resigned his charge and entered upon the office of Professor of Pulpit Eloquence and the Pastoral Care in the Theological School connected with Harvard College, which he held until the summer of 1842, when he gave up his public duties. He died September 22, 1843.

Dr. Ware's writings, theological, critical, and miscellaneous, are numerous and valuable. In 1815 he published "A Poem on Occasion of the Peace;" in 1824 "The Vision of Liberty;" in 1837, "The Feast of the Tabernacles," and at various times many shorter pieces, chiefly devotional.

TO THE URSA MAJOR.

With what a stately and majestic step
That glorious constellation of the north
Treads its eternal circle! going forth
Its princely way among the stars in slow
And silent brightness. Mighty one, all hail!
I joy to see thee on thy glowing path
Walk, like some stout and girded giant; stern,
Unwearied, resolute, whose toiling foot
Disdains to loiter on its destined way.
The other tribes forsake their midnight track,
And rest their weary orbs beneath thy wave;
But thou dost never close thy burning eye,
Nor stay thy steadfast step. But on, still on,
While systems change, and suns retire, and worlds
Slumber and wake, thy ceaseless march proceeds.
The near horizon tempts to rest in vain.
Thou, faithful sentinel, dost never quit
Thy long-appointed watch; but, sleepless still,
Dost guard the fix'd light of the universe,
And bid the north forever know its place.
Ages have witness'd thy devoted trust,
Unchanged, unchanging. When the sons of God
Sent forth that shout of joy which rang through heaven,
And echo'd from the outer spheres that bound
The illimitable universe, thy voice
Join'd the high chorus; from thy radiant orbs
The glad cry sounded, swelling to His praise,
Who thus had cast another sparkling gem,
Little, but beautiful, amid the crowd
Of splendours that enrich his firmament.
As thou art now, so wast thou then the same.
Ages have roll'd their course, and time grown gray;
The earth has gather'd to her womb again,
And yet again, the myriads that were born
Of her uncounted, unremember'd tribes.
The seas have changed their beds; the eternal hills
Have stoop'd with age; the solid continents
Have left their banks; and man's imperial works—
The toil, pride, strength of kingdoms, which had flung
Their haughty honours in the face of heaven,
As if immortal—have been swept away:
Shatter'd and mouldering, buried and forgot.
But time has shed no dimness on thy front,
Nor touch'd the firmness of thy tread; youth, strength,
And beauty still are thine; as clear, as bright,
As when the Almighty Former sent thee forth,
Beautiful offspring of his curious skill,
To watch earth's northern beacon, and proclaim
The eternal chorus of eternal Love.
I wonder as I gaze. That stream of light,
Undimm'd, unquench'd—just as I see it now—
Has issued from those dazzling points through years
That go back far into eternity.
Exhaustless flood! forever spent, renew'd
Forever! Yea, and those refulgent drops,
Which now descend upon my lifted eye,
Left their far fountain twice three years ago.
While those wing'd particles, whose speed outstrips
The flight of thought, were on their way, the earth
Compass'd its tedious circuit round and round,
And, in the extremes of annual change, beheld
Six autumns fade, six springs renew their bloom.
So far from earth those mighty orbs revolve!
So vast the void through which their beams descend!
Yes, glorious lamp of God! He may have quench'd
Your ancient flames, and bid eternal night
Rest on your spheres; and yet no tidings reach
This distant planet. Messengers still come
Laden with your far fire, and we may seem
To see your lights still burning; while their blaze
But hides the black wreck of extinguish'd realms,
Where anarchy and darkness long have reign'd.
Yet what is this, which to the astonish'd mind
Seems measureless, and which the baffled thought
Confounds! A span, a point, in those domains
Which the keen eye can traverse. Seven stars
Dwell in that brilliant cluster, and the sight
Embraces all at once; yet each from each
Recedes as far as each of them from earth.
And every star from every other burns
No less remote. From the profound of heaven

Untravell'd even in thought, keen, piercing rays
Dart through the void, revealing to the sense
Systems and worlds unnumber'd. Take the glass
And search the skies. The opening skies pour down
Upon your gaze thick showers of sparkling fire;
Stars, crowded, throng'd, in regions so remote,
That their swift beams—the swiftest things that be—
Have travell'd centuries on their flight to earth.
Earth, sun, and nearer constellations! what
Are ye amid this infinite extent
And multitude of God's most infinite works!
  And these are suns! vast, central, living fires,
Lords of dependent systems, kings of worlds
That wait as satellites upon their power,
And flourish in their smile. Awake, my soul,
And meditate the wonder! Countless suns
Blaze round thee, leading forth their countless worlds!
Worlds in whose bosoms living things rejoice,
And drink the bliss of being from the fount
Of all-pervading Love. What mind can know,
What tongue can utter all their multitudes!
Thus numberless in numberless abodes!
Known but to thee, bless'd Father! Thine they are,
Thy children, and thy care; and none o'erlook'd
Of thee! No, not the humblest soul that dwells
Upon the humblest globe, which wheels its course
Amid the giant glories of the sky,
Like the mean mote that dances in the beam
Amongst the mirror'd lamps, which fling
Their wasteful splendour from the palace wall,
None, none escape the kindness of thy care;
All compass'd underneath thy spacious wing,
Each fed and guided by thy powerful hand.
  Tell me, ye splendid orbs! as from your throne
Ye mark the rolling provinces that own
Your sway, what beings fill those bright abodes?
How form'd, how gifted? what their powers, their state,
Their happiness, their wisdom? Do they bear
The stamp of human nature? Or has God
Peopled those purer realms with lovelier forms
And more celestial minds? Does Innocence
Still wear her native and untainted bloom?
Or has Sin breathed his deadly blight abroad,
And sow'd corruption in those fairy bowers?
Has War trod o'er them with his foot of fire?
And Slavery forged his chains; and Wrath, and Hate,
And sordid Selfishness, and cruel Lust
Leagued their base bands to tread out light and truth,
And scatter wo where Heaven had planted joy?
Or are they yet all paradise, unfallen
And uncorrupt? existence one long joy,
Without disease upon the frame, or sin
Upon the heart, or weariness of life;
Hope never quench'd, and age unknown,
And death unfear'd; while fresh and fadeless youth
Glows in the light from God's near throne of love?
  Open your lips, ye wonderful and fair!
Speak, speak! the mysteries of those living worlds
Unfold! No language? Everlasting light
And everlasting silence? Yet the eye
May read and understand. The hand of God
Has written legibly what man may know,
THE GLORY OF THE MAKER. There it shines,
Ineffable, unchangeable; and man,
Bound to the surface of this pigmy globe,
May know and ask no more. In other days,
When death shall give the encumber'd spirit wings,
Its range shall be extended; it shall roam,
Perchance, among those vast, mysterious spheres,
Shall pass from orb to orb, and dwell in each,
Familiar with its children; learn their laws,
And share their state, and study and adore
The infinite varieties of bliss
And beauty, by the hand of Power divine
Lavish'd on all its works. Eternity
Shall thus roll on with ever fresh delight;
No pause of pleasure or improvement; world
On world still opening to the instructed mind
An unexhausted universe, and time
But adding to its glories. While the soul,
Advancing ever to the Source of light
And all perfection, lives, adores, and reigns
In cloudless knowledge, purity, and bliss.

SEASONS OF PRAYER.

To prayer, to prayer;—for the morning breaks,
And earth in her Maker's smile awakes.
His light is on all below and above,
The light of gladness, and life, and love.
O, then, on the breath of this early air,
Send up the incense of grateful prayer.

To prayer;—for the glorious sun is gone,
And the gathering darkness of night comes on.
Like a curtain from God's kind hand it flows,
To shade the couch where his children repose.
Then kneel, while the watching stars are bright,
And give your last thoughts to the Guardian of night.

To prayer;—for the day that God has bless'd
Comes tranquilly on with its welcome rest.
It speaks of creation's early bloom;
It speaks of the Prince who burst the tomb.
Then summon the spirit's exalted powers,
And devote to Heaven the hallow'd hours.

There are smiles and tears in the mother's eyes,
For her new-born infant beside her lies.
O, hour of bliss! when the heart o'erflows
With rapture a mother only knows.
Let it gush forth in words of fervent prayer;
Let it swell up to heaven for her precious care.

There are smiles and tears in that gathering band,
Where the heart is pledged with the trembling hand.
What trying thoughts in her bosom swell,
As the bride bids parents and home farewell!
Kneel down by the side of the tearful fair,
And strengthen the perilous hour with prayer.

Kneel down by the dying sinner's side,
And pray for his soul through Him who died.
Large drops of anguish are thick on his brow—
O, what s earth and its pleasures now!

And what shall assuage his dark despair,
But the penitent cry of humble prayer!

Kneel down at the couch of departing faith,
And hear the last words the believer saith.
He has bidden adieu to his earthly friends;
There is peace in his eye that upward bends;
There is peace in his calm, confiding air;
For his last thoughts are God's, his last words prayer

The voice of prayer at the sable bier!
A voice to sustain, to soothe, and to cheer.
It commends the spirit to God who gave;
It lifts the thoughts from the cold, dark grave;
It points to the glory where he shall reign,
Who whisper'd, "Thy brother shall rise again."

The voice of prayer in the world of bliss!
But gladder, purer, than rose from this.
The ransom'd shout to their glorious King,
Where no sorrow shades the soul as they sing;
But a sinless and joyous song they raise;
And their voice of prayer is eternal praise.

Awake, awake, and gird up thy strength
To join that holy band at length.
To him who unceasing love displays,
Whom the powers of nature unceasingly praise,
To Him thy heart and thy hours be given;
For a life of prayer is the life of heaven.

THE VISION OF LIBERTY.*

The evening heavens were calm and bright;
No dimness rested on the glittering light
That sparkled from that wilderness of worlds on high;
Those distant suns burn'd on in quiet ray;
The placid planets held their modest way:
And silence reign'd profound o'er earth, and sea, and sky.

O what an hour for lofty thought!
My spirit burn'd within; I caught
A holy inspiration from the hour.
Around me man and nature slept;
Alone my solemn watch I kept,
Till morning dawn'd, and sleep resumed her power.

A vision pass'd upon my soul.
I still was gazing up to heaven,
As in the early hours of even;
I still beheld the planets roll,
And all those countless sons of light
Flame from the broad blue arch, and guide the moonless night.

When, lo, upon the plain,
Just where it skirts the swelling main,
A massive castle, far and high,
In towering grandeur broke upon my eye.
Proud in its strength and years, the ponderous pile
Flung up its time-defying towers;
Its lofty gates seem'd scornfully to smile
At vain assault of human powers,
And threats and arms deride.
Its gorgeous carvings of heraldric pride
In giant masses graced the walls above,
And dungeons yawn'd below.
Yet ivy there and moss their garlands wove,
Grave, silent chroniclers of time's protracted flow.

Bursting on my steadfast gaze,
See, within, a sudden blaze!
So small at first, the zephyr's slightest swell,
That scarcely stirs the pine-tree top,
Nor makes the wither'd leaf to drop,
The feeble fluttering of that flame would quell.

But soon it spread—
Waving, rushing, fierce, and red—
From wall to wall, from tower to tower,
Raging with resistless power;
Till every fervent pillar glow'd,
And every stone seem'd burning coal,
Instinct with living heat, that flow'd
Like streaming radiance from the kindled pole

Beautiful, fearful, grand,
Silent as death, I saw the fabric stand.
At length a crackling sound began;
From side to side, throughout the pile it ran;
And louder yet and louder grew,
Till now in rattling thunder-peals it grew;
Huge shiver'd fragments from the pillars broke
Like fiery sparkles from the anvil's stroke.
The shatter'd walls were rent and riven,
And piecemeal driven
Like blazing comets through the troubled sky
'Tis done; what centuries had rear'd,
In quick explosion disappear'd,
Nor even its ruins met my wondering eye.

But in their place—
Bright with more than human grace,
Robed in more than mortal seeming,
Radiant glory in her face,
And eyes with heaven's own brightness beaming—
Rose a fair, majestic form,
As the mild rainbow from the storm.
I mark'd her smile, I knew her eye;
And when, with gesture of command,
She waved aloft the cap-crown'd wand,
My slumbers fled mid shouts of "Liberty!"

Read ye the dream? and know ye not
How truly it unlock'd the world of fate!
Went not the flame from this illustrious spot,
And spreads it not, and burns in every state?
And when their old and cumbrous walls,
Fill'd with this spirit, glow intense,
Vainly they rear'd their impotent defence:
The fabric falls!
That fervent energy must spread,
Till despotism's towers be overthrown;
And in their stead,
Liberty stands alone!

Hasten the day, just Heaven!
Accomplish thy design;
And let the blessings thou hast freely given
Freely on all men shine;
Till equal rights be equally enjoy'd
And human power for human good employ'd
Till law, and not the sovereign, rule sustain,
And peace and virtue undisputed reign.—

* From a poem delivered before the Phi Beta Kappa Society, at Cambridge, in 1825.

JOHN NEAL.

[Born about 1794.]

Mr. Neal is a native of Portland. In 1815 he went to Baltimore, and was there associated several years with John Pierpont in mercantile transactions; but these resulting disastrously, he turned his attention to literature, commencing his career by writing for "The Portico," a monthly magazine, a series of critical essays on the works of Byron. In 1818, he published "Keep Cool," a novel, and in the following year "The Battle of Niagara, Goldau the Maniac Harper, and other Poems, by Jehu O'Cataract,"* and "Otho," a tragedy. He also wrote a large portion of Allen's "History of the American Revolution," which appeared early in 1821. In 1822 he published in Philadelphia a second novel, entitled "Logan," which was reprinted soon after in London. This was followed in 1823 by "Seventy-six," the most popular of his fictions; "Randolph,"† a story which attracted considerable attention at the time by the notices it contained of the most prominent politicians, authors, and artists then in the country; and "Errata, or the Works of Will Adams."

Near the close of the last-mentioned year Mr. Neal went abroad. Soon after his arrival in London he became a contributor to various periodicals, for which he wrote, chiefly under the guise of an Englishman, numerous articles to correct erroneous opinions which prevailed in regard to the social and political condition of the United States. He made his first appearance in Blackwood's Magazine, in "Sketches of the Five American Presidents and the Five Candidates for the Presidency," a paper which was widely republished, and, with others, led to his introduction to many eminent persons, among whom was Jeremy Bentham, who continued until his death to be Mr. Neal's warm personal friend.

After passing four years in Great Britain and on the continent, in which time appeared his "Brother Jonathan," a novel, Mr. Neal came back to his native city of Portland, where he now resides. Since his return he has published "Rachel Dyer," "Authorship," "The Down Easters," and "Ruth Elder;" edited "The Yankee," a weekly gazette, two years, and contributed largely to other periodicals.

Mr. Neal's novels contain numerous passages marked by brilliancy of sentiment and expression, and occasional scenes which show that he possesses dramatic ability. They are original; they are written from the impulses of his heart, and are pervaded by the peculiarities of his character; but most of them were produced rapidly and carelessly, and are without unity, aim, or continuous interest.

His poems have the unquestionable stamp of genius. He possesses imagination in a degree of sensibility and energy hardly surpassed in this age. The elements of poetry are poured forth in his verses with a prodigality and power altogether astonishing. But he is deficient in the constructive faculty. He has no just sense of proportion. No one with so rich and abundant materials had ever less skill in using them. Instead of bringing the fancy to adorn the structures of the imagination, he reverses the poetical law, giving to the imagination the secondary office, so that the points illustrated are quite forgotten in the accumulation and splendour of the imagery. The "Battle of Niagara," with its rapid and slow, gay and solemn movement, falls on the ear as if it were composed to martial music. It is marred, however, by his customary faults. The isthmus which bounds the beautiful is as narrow as that upon the borders of the sublime, and he crosses both without hesitation. Passages in it would be very fine but for lines or single words which, if the reader were not confident that he had before him the author's own edition, he would think had been thrown in by some burlesquing enemy.

I have heard an anecdote which illustrates the rapidity with which he writes. When he lived in Baltimore, he went one evening to the rooms of Pierpont, and read to him a poem which he had just completed. The author of "Airs of Palestine" was always a nice critic, and he frankly pointed out the faults of the performance. Neal promised to revise it, and submit it again on the following morning. At the appointed time he repaired to the apartment of his friend, and read to him a new poem, of three or four hundred lines. He had tried to improve his first, but failing to do so, had chosen a new subject, a new measure, and produced an entirely new work, before retiring to sleep.

In the last edition of his Poems, Mr Neal presents some specimens of an intended epic on the conquest of Peru; and he has written many lyrical pieces, not included in his collections, which have been popular.

* "Jehu O'Cataract" was a name given to Neal by the Delphian Club of Baltimore, of which Paul Allen, Gen. Winder, Rev. John Pierpont, Judge Breckenridge, Neal, and other distinguished men, were then members. The second edition of the Battle of Niagara was published in 1819, and for "Jehu O'Cataract" was substituted the real name of the author.

In this edition of "The Poets and Poetry of America" I have quoted from the "Battle of Niagara" as it appeared with the "last additions and corrections." I had seen only the first impression of it when this work was originally prepared for the press.

† In a note in Blackwood's Magazine, Mr. Neal says he wrote "Randolph" in thirty-six days, with an interval of about a week between the two volumes, in which he wrote nothing; "Errata" in less than thirty-nine days; and "Seventy-six" in twenty-seven days. During this time he was engaged in professional business

FROM THE CONQUEST OF PERU.

INVOCATION TO THE DEITY.

O Thou, from whom the rebel angels fled,
When thou didst rend thine everlasting veil,
And show thy countenance in wrath! O Thou,
Before whose brow, unclothed in light—put forth
In awful revelation—they that stood
Erect in heaven, they that walk'd sublime,
E'en in thy presence, Lord! and they that shone
Most glorious 'mid the host of glorious ones,
With Lucifer—the Morning Star, the Terrible,
The chief of old immortals—with the sight
Were suddenly consumed! Almighty! Thou,
Whose face but shone upon the rebel host
Of warring constellations, and their crowns
Were quench'd for ever! and the mightiest fell,
And lo! innumerable wings went up,
And gather'd round about the Eternal's throne,
And all the solitudes of air were fill'd
With thunders and with voices! and the war
Fled from thy presence! And thy wrath was o'er,
And heaven again in peace!......
O Thou—our Inspiration—Thou, O God!
To whom the prophets and the crowned kings,
The bards of many years, who caught from Thee
Their blazing of the spirit! Thou, to whom
The Jewish monarchs, on their ivory thrones,
Flaming with jewelry, have fallen down
And rung their golden harps, age after age!
O Thou, to whom the gifted men of old,
Who stood among the mysteries of heaven,
Read the thick stars, and listened to the wind,
Interpreted the thunder, told the voice
Of Ocean tumbling in his caves, explained
The everlasting characters of flame
That burn upon the firmament, and saw
The face of him that sitteth in the sun,
And read the writing there, that comes and goes,
Revealing to the eyes the fate of men,
Of monarchs, and of empires!—men who stood
Amid the solitudes of heaven and earth, and heard
From the high mountain-top the silent Night
Give out her uninterpreted decrees!—
The venerable men! the old, and mighty,
Prophets and bards and kings, whose souls were fill'd
With immortality, and visions, till
Their hearts have ached with weary supplication;
Till all the Future, rushing o'er their strings,
In tempest and in light, hath drown'd their prayers,
And left their mighty harps all ringing loud
With prophecy and wo! O Thou, to whom
Innumerable suns, and moons, and worlds,
The glorious elevations of the sky,
The choirs of cherubim and seraphim—
Immortal multitudes, that worship round
Thine echoing throne—upon their golden harps
And silver trumps, and organs of the air,
Pour everlasting melody! O Thou, to whom
All this hath been familiar from the hour
When thou didst bow the heavens, and, at the sound
Of many thunders, pealing thy decree,
Creation sprang to light, when time began
And all the boundless sky was full of suns,
Rolling in symphony, and man was made
Sublime and confident, and woman, up
From the sunshine of the Eternal rose,
All intellect and love! and all the hills
And all the vales were green, and all the trees in flower.
—O, bless our trembling harp!

FROM THE BATTLE OF NIAGARA.

A CAVALCADE SEEN AT SUNSET THROUGH A GORGE.

Ah, now let us gaze! what a wonderful sky!
How the robe of the god, in its flame-colored dye,
Goes ruddily, flushingly, sweepingly by!....
Nay, speak! did you ever behold such a night?
While the winds blew about, and the waters were
The sun rolling home in an ocean of light! [bright,
But hush! there is music away in the sky;
Some creatures of magic are charioting by: [wild
Now it comes—what a sound! 't is as cheerful and
As the echo of caves to the laugh of a child;
Ah yes, they are here! See, away to your left,
Where the sun has gone down, where the mountains are cleft,
A troop of tall horsemen! How fearless they ride!
'Tis a perilous path o'er that steep mountain's side;
Careering they come, like a band of young knights
That the trumpet of morn to the tilting invites;
With high-nodding plumes, and with sun-shiny vests;
With wide-tossing manes, and with mail-cover'd breasts;
With arching of necks, and the plunge and the pride
Of their high-mettled steeds, as they galloping ride,
In glitter and pomp; with their housings of gold,
With their scarlet and blue, as their squadrons unfold
Flashing changeable light, like a banner unroll'd!
Now they burst on the eye in their martial array
And now they have gone, like a vision of day.
In a streaming of splendour they came—but they wheel'd;
And instantly all the bright show was conceal'd—
As if 't were a tournament held in the sky,
Betray'd by some light passing suddenly by;
Some band by the flashing of torches reveal'd,
As it fell o'er the boss of an uplifted shield,
Or banners and blades in the darkness conceal'd

APPROACH OF EVENING.

A glow, like enchantment, is seen o'er the lake,
Like the flush of the sky, when the day heralds wake
And o'er its dull bosom their soft plumage shake.
Now the warmth of the heaven is fading away—
Young Evening comes up in pursuit of the Day—
The richness and mist of the tints that were there
Are melting away like the bow of the air—
The blue-bosom'd water heaves darker and bluer,
The cliffs and the trees are seen bolder and truer,
The landscape has less of enchantment and light·
But it lies the more steady and firm in the sight
The lustre-crown'd peaks, while they dazzled the eye
Seem'd loosen'd and passing away in the sky,
And the far-distant hills, in their tremulous blue,
But baffled the eye, as it dwelt on their hue.

The light of the hill, and the wave, and the sky
Grow fainter, and fainter:—The wonders all die!
The visions have gone! they have vanish'd away,
Unobserved in their change, like the bliss of a day.
The rainbows of heaven were bent in our sight,
And fountains were gushing like wine in its light,
And seraphs were wheeling around in their flight—
A moment: and all was enveloped in night!
'Tis thus with the dreams of the high-heaving heart:
They come but to blaze, and they blaze to depart—
Their gossamer wings are too thin to abide
The chilling of sorrow, or burning of pride—
They come, but to brush o'er its young gallant swell,
Like bright birds over ocean—but never to dwell.

MOVEMENTS OF TROOPS AT NIGHT.

Observed ye the cloud on that mountain's dim green
So heavily hanging?—as if it had been
The tent of the Thunderer—the chariot of one
Who dare not appear in the blaze of the sun?
'T is descending to earth! and some horsemen are now,
In a line of dark mist, coming down from its brow.
'T is a helmeted band—from the hills they descend,
Like the monarchs of storm, when the forest trees bend.
No scimitars swing as they gallop along;
No clattering hoof falls sudden and strong,
No trumpet is fill'd, and no bugle is blown
No banners abroad on the wind are thrown,
No shoutings are heard, and no cheerings are given;
No waving of red flowing plumage to heaven;
No flashing of blades, and no loosening of reins;
No neighing of steeds, and no tossing of manes;
No furniture trailing, or warrior helms bowing,
Or crimson and gold-spotted drapery flowing;
But they speed, like coursers whose hoofs are shod
With a silent shoe, from the loosen'd sod;
Like the steeds that career o'er the billowy surf,
Or stretch like the winds o'er the untrodden turf,
Where the willow and yew in their darkness are weeping,
And young, gallant hearts are in sepulchres sleeping;
Like the squadrons, that on the pale light of the moon,
While the night's muffled horn plays a low windy tune,
Are seen to come down from the height of the skies,
By the warrior that on the red battle-field lies,
And wave their cloud-helmets, and charge o'er the field,
And career o'er the tracks where the living had wheel'd,
When the dying half-raise themselves up in a trance,
And gaze on the show, as their thin banners glance,
And wonder to see the dread battle renew'd,
On the turf where themselves and their comrades had stood.
Like these shadows, in swiftness and darkness they ride,
O'er the thunder-reft mount—on its ruggedest side;
From the precipice top, they circle and leap,
Like the warriors of air, that are seen in our sleep;
Like the creatures that pass where a bleeding man lies,
Their heads muffled up to their white filmy eyes,
With gestures more threatening and fierce till he dies:
And away they have gone, with a motionless speed,
Like demons abroad on some terrible deed.
The last one has gone: they have all disappear'd;
Their dull-echoed trampings no longer are heard;
For still, though they pass'd like no steeds of the earth,
The fall of their tread gave some hollow-sounds birth;
Your heart would lie still till it number'd the last;
And your breath would be held till the rear horsemen pass'd,
So swiftly, so mutely, so darkly they went,
Like the spectres of air to the sorcerer sent,
That ye *felt* their approach, and might guess their intent.
Your hero's stern bosom will oftentimes quake,
Your gallant young warrior-plume oftentimes shake,
Before the cool marching that comes in the night,
Passing by, like a cloud in the dim troubled light;
Subduing the heart with a nameless affright,
When *that* would swell strongly, and *this* would appear,
If the sound of one trumpet saluted the ear,
Like some scarlet-wing'd bird, that is nurs'd in the day,
When she shakes her red plumage in wrath o'er her prey.
For be they the horsemen of earth, or of heaven,
No blast that the trumpet of Slaughter hath given,
No roll of the drum, and no cry of the fife,
No neighing of steeds in the bloodiest strife,
Is half so terrific to full swelling hearts,
As the still, pulseless tramp of a band that departs,
With echoless armour, with motionless plume,
With ensigns all furl'd, in the trappings of gloom,
Parading, like those who came up from the tomb,
In silence and darkness—determined and slow,
And dreadfully calm, as the murderer's brow,
When his dagger is forth!—and ye see not the blow,
Till the gleam of the blade shows your heart in its flow!
O, say what ye will! the dull sound that awakes
When the night breeze is down, and the chill spirit aches
With its measureless thought, is more dreadful by far,
Than the burst of the trump, when it peals for the war.
It is the cold summons that comes from the ground,
When a sepulchre answers your light youthful bound,
And loud joyous laugh, with its chill fearful sound,
Compared to the challenge that leaps on the ear,
When the banners of death in their splendors appear,
And the free golden bugle sings freshly and clear!—
The low, sullen moans, that so feebly awake,
At midnight, when one is alone, on some lake,
Compared to the Thunderer's voice, when it rolls
From the bosom of space to the uttermost poles!—
Like something that stirs in the weight of a shroud,
The talking of those who go by in a cloud,
To the cannon's full voice, when it wanders aloud!—
'Tis the light that is seen to burst under the wave,
The pale, fitful omen, that plays o'er a grave,
To the rushing of flame, where the turf is all red,
And farewells are discharged o'er a young soldier's bed,
To the lightnings that blaze o'er the mariner's way,
When the storm is in pomp, and the ocean in spray!

AN INDIAN APOLLO.

Not like the airy god of moulded light,
Just stepping from his chariot on the sight;
Poising his beauties on a rolling cloud,
With outstretch'd arm and bowstring twanging loud
And arrows singing as they pierce the air;
With tinkling sandals, and with flaming hair;
As if he paused upon his bounding way,
And loosen'd his fierce arrows—all in play;
But like that angry god, in blazing light

Bursting from space, and standing in his might—
Reveal'd in his omnipotent array,
Apollo of the skies, and deity of day,
In god-like wrath piercing his myriad-foe
With quenchless shafts, that lighten as they go!
—Not like that god, when up in air he springs,
With brightening mantle and with sunny wings,
When heavenly music murmurs from his strings—
A buoyant vision—an imbodied dream
Of dainty Poesy—and boyishly supreme!
—Not the thin spirit waked by young Desire,
Gazing o'er heaven until her thoughts take fire,
Panting and breathless; in her heart's wild trance,
Bright, shapeless forms, the godlings of Romance!
—Not that Apollo—not resembling him
Of silver bow and woman's nerveless limb—
But man—all man! the monarch of the wild!
—Not the faint spirit that corrupting smiled
On soft, lascivious Greece, but Nature's child,
Arrested in the chase, with piercing eye
Fix'd in its airy lightning on the sky,
Where some red bird goes languid, eddying, drooping,
Pierced by his arrows in her swi test stooping.
Thus springing to the skies, a boy will stand
With arms uplifted and unconscious hand
Tracing his arrow in its loftiest flight,
And watch it kindling, as it cleaves the light
Of worlds unseen but by the Indian's sight—
His robe and hair upon the wind, at length—
A creature of the hills, all grace and strength,
All muscle and all flame—his eager eye
Fix'd on one spot, as if he could descry
His bleeding victim nestling in the sky!
—Not that Apollo!—not the heavenly one,
Voluptuous spirit of a setting sun—
But this, the offspring of young Solitude,
Child of the holy spot, where none intrude
But genii of the torrent, cliff, and wood—
Nurslings of cloud and storm, the desert's fiery brood.

MORNING AFTER A BATTLE.

Who thinks of battle now? The stirring sounds
Spring lightly from the trumpet, yet who bounds
On this sad, still, and melancholy morn,
As he was wont to bound, when the fresh horn
Came dancing on the winds, and peal'd to heaven,
In gone-by hours, before the battle even!
The very horses move with halting pace;
No more they heave their manes with fiery grace,
With plunge, and reach, and step that leaves no trace;
No more they spurn the bit, and sudden fling
Their light hoofs on the air. The bugles sing,
And yet the meteor mane and rolling eye
Lighten no longer at their minstrelsy;
No more their housings blaze, no more the gold
Or purple flashes from the opening fold;
No rich-wrought stars are glittering in their pride
Of changing hues; all, all, is crimson-dyed.
They move with slow, far step; they hear the tread
That measures out the tombing of the dead
The cannon speaks, but now no longer rolls
In heavy thunders to the answering poles;
But bursting suddenly, it calls, and flies,
At breathless intervals, along the skies,
As if some viewless sentinel were there
Whose challenge peals at midnight through the air
Each sullen steed goes on, nor heeds its roar,
Nor pauses when its voice is heard no more;
But snuffs the tainted breeze, and lifts his head,
And slowly wheeling, with a cautious tread,
Shuns, as in reverence, the mighty dead·
Or, rearing suddenly, with flashing eye,
Where some young war-horse lies, he passes by;
Then, with unequal step, he smites the ground,
Utters a startling neigh, and gazes round,
And wonders that he hears no answering sound.
This, while his rider can go by the bier
Of slaughter'd men, and never drop a tear;
And only, when he meets a comrade there,
Stretch'd calmly out, with brow and bosom bare,
And stiffen'd hand uplifted in the air—
With lip still curl'd, and open, glassy eye,
Fix'd on the pageant that is passing by—
And only then—in decency will ride
Less stately in his strength, less lordly in his pride.

MUSIC OF THE NIGHT.

There are harps that complain to the presence of night,
To the presence of night alone—
In a near and unchangeable tone—
Like winds, full of sound, that go whispering by,
As if some immortal had stoop'd from the sky,
And breathed out a blessing—and flown!

Yes! harps that complain to the breezes of night,
To the breezes of night alone;
Growing fainter and fainter, as ruddy and bright
The sun rolls aloft in his drapery of light,
Like a conqueror, shaking his brilliant hair
And flourishing robe, on the edge of the air!
Burning crimson and gold
On the clouds that unfold,
Breaking onward in flame, while an ocean divides
On his right and his left—So the Thunderer rides,
When he cuts a bright path through the heaving tides
Rolling on, and erect, in a charioting throne!

Yes! strings that lie still in the gushing of day,
That awake, all alive, to the breezes of night.
There are hautboys and flutes too, for ever at play
When the evening is near, and the sun is away,
Breathing out the still hymn of delight.
These strings by invisible fingers are play'd—
By spirits, unseen, and unknown,
But thick as the stars, all this music is made;
And these flutes, alone,
In one sweet dreamy tone,
Are ever blown,
For ever and for ever.
The live-long night ye hear the sound,
Like distant waters flowing round
In ringing caves, while heaven is sweet
With crowding tunes, like halls
Where fountain-music falls,
And rival minstrels meet

NIGHT.

'Tis dark abroad. The majesty of Night
Bows down superbly from her utmost height,
Stretches her starless plumes across the world,
And all the banners of the wind are furl'd.
How heavily we breathe amid such gloom,
As if we slumber'd in creation's tomb.
It is the noon of that tremendous hour
When life is helpless, and the dead have power;
When solitudes are peopled; when the sky
Is swept by shady wings that, sailing by,
Proclaim their watch is set; when hidden rills
Are chirping on their course, and all the hills
Are bright with armour; when the starry vests,
And glittering plumes, and fiery twinkling crests
Of moon-light sentinels are sparkling round,
And all the air is one rich floating sound;
When countless voices, in the day unheard,
Are piping from their haunts, and every bird
That loves the leafy wood and blooming bower
And echoing cave, is singing to her flower;
When every lovely, every lonely place,
Is ringing to the light and sandal'd pace
Of twinkling feet; and all about, the flow
Of new-born fountains, murmuring as they go;
When watery tunes are richest, and the call
Of wandering streamlets, as they part and fall
In foaming melody, is all around,
Like fairy harps beneath enchanted ground—
Sweet, drowsy, distant music! like the breath
Of airy flutes that blow before an infant's death.
It is that hour when listening ones will weep
And know not why; when we would gladly sleep
Our last, last sleep, and feel no touch of fear,
Unconscious where we are, or what is near,
Till we are startled by a falling tear,
That unexpected gather'd in our eye,
While we were panting for yon blessed sky;
That hour of gratitude, of whispering prayer,
When we can hear a worship in the air;
When we are lifted from the earth, and feel
Light fanning wings around us faintly wheel,
And o'er our lids and brow a blessing steal;
And then, as if our sins were all forgiven,
And all our tears were wiped, and we in heaven!

ONTARIO.

No sound is on the ear, no boatman's oar
Drops its dull signal to the watchful shore;
But all is listening, as it were to hear
Some seraph harper stooping from her sphere
And calling on the desert to express
Its sense of Silence in her loveliness.
What holy dreaming comes in nights like these,
When, like yon wave, unruffled by a breeze,
The mirrors of the memory all are spread
And fanning pinions sail around your head;
When all that man may love, alive or dead,
Come murmuring sweet, unutterable things,
And nestle on his heart with their young wings,
And all perchance may come, that he may fear,
And mutter doubtful curses in his ear;
Hang on his loaded soul, and fill his brain
With indistinct forebodings, dim, and vain....
The moon goes lightly up her thronging way,
And shadowy things are brightening into day;
And cliff and shrub and bank and tree and stone
Now move upon the eye, and now are gone.
A dazzling tapestry is hung around,
A gorgeous carpeting bestrews the ground;
The willows glitter in the passing beam
And shake their tangling lustres o'er the stream;
And all the full rich foliage of the shore
Seems with a quick enchantment frosted o'er,
And dances at the faintest breath of night,
And trembles like a plume of spangles in the light!...
This dark cool wave is bluer than the deep,
Where sailors, children of the tempest, sleep;
And dropp'd with lights as pure, as still, as those
The wide-drawn hangings of the skies disclose,
Far lovelier than the dim and broken ray,
That Ocean's flashing surges send astray....
This is the mirror of dim Solitude,
On which unholy things may ne'er intrude;
That frowns and ruffles when the clouds appear,
Refusing to reflect their shapes of fear.
Ontario's deeps are spread to multiply
But sunshine, stars, the moon, and clear-blue sky.
No pirate barque was ever seen to ride,
With blood-red streamer, chasing o'er that tide;
Till late, no bugle o'er those waters sang
With aught but huntsman's orisons, that rang
Their clear, exulting, bold, triumphant strain,
Till all the mountain echoes laugh'd again;
Till caverns, depths, and hills, would all reply,
And heaven's blue dome ring out the sprightly melody.

TREES.

The heave, the wave and bend
Of everlasting trees, whose busy leaves
Rustle their songs of praise, while Ruin weaves
A robe of verdure for their yielding bark—
While mossy garlands, full and rich and dark,
Creep slowly round them! Monarchs of the wood,
Whose mighty sceptres sway the mountain brood—
Whose aged bosoms, in their last decay,
Shelter the wing'd idolaters of Day—
Who, mid the desert wild, sublimely stand,
And grapple with the storm-god, hand to hand.
Then drop like weary pyramids away,
Stupendous monuments of calm decay!

INVASION OF THE SETTLER.

Where now fresh streamlets answer to the hues
Of passing seraph-wings; and fiery dews
Hang thick on every bush, when morning wakes,
Like sprinkled flame; and all the green-wood shakes
With liquid jewelry, that Night hath flung
Upon her favourite tresses, while they swung
And wanton'd in the wind—henceforth will be
No lighted dimness, such as you see,
In yonder faint, mysterious scenery,
Where all the woods keep festival, and seem,
Beneath the midnight sky, and mellow beam
Of yonder breathing light, as if they were
Branches and leaves of unimbodied air.

WILLIAM B. TAPPAN.

[Born, 1794. Died, 1849.]

The late Rev. William B. Tappan, the most industrious and voluminous of our religious poets, was born in Beverly, Massachusetts, on the twenty-ninth of October, 1794. His ancestors were among the earliest of the settlers from England, and for one hundred and fifty years had furnished ministers of the gospel in nearly uninterrupted succession. His father was a soldier during the revolution, and afterwards many years a teacher. Upon his death, at Portsmouth, in 1805, William, then in his twelfth year, was apprenticed to a mechanic in Boston. He had already acquired an unusual fondness for reading, though the books to which he had access were comparatively few. "The Bible," "The Pilgrim's Progress," "Robinson Crusoe," and "The Surprising Adventures of Philip Quarles," constituted his library, and of these he was thoroughly master. At nine years of age he commenced rhyming, and he occasionally wrote verses during his apprenticeship, which lasted, by agreement, till he was twenty. There were then none of the lyceums, apprentices' libraries, Lowell lectures, or other means of self-education which are now so abundant in Boston, and he had no resource for intellectual improvement or amusement, except a neighbouring circulating library, the novels, romances, and poems of which he was never weary of reading. What little he had gained, at home, of the common elementary branches of knowledge, he lost during these years; but, master of his business (which however he never fully loved) and with high hopes, he proceeded to Philadelphia, where there seemed to be an opening for him, in 1815, and permanently established himself in that city. He frequently indulged his propensity to write, but was so diffident of his powers, that until he was twenty-three years old he never offered any thing for publication. He then permitted a friend to give several of his pieces to a newspaper, and was subsequently as much surprised as delighted to find that they were widely copied and much praised. Thus encouraged, he began to look for a more congenial occupation, and determining to become a teacher, entered an academy at Somerville, New Jersey, in his twenty-fourth year, to prosecute the necessary preliminary studies. Unfaltering industry and a strong will, with good natural abilities, enabled him to make very rapid advancement, so that in 1821 he was fairly entered upon his new profession, in which he had prospects of abundant success. In 1822 he was married, and four years later he entered the service of the American Sunday School Union, with which society he was connected the rest of his life, a period of more than quarter of a century. For the prosecution of its business, he resided four years in Cincinnati, and in 1837 removed to Boston. He was ordained an evangelist, according to the forms of the Congregational churches, in 1841, and died at West Needham, Massachusetts, on the eighteenth of June, 1849, greatly respected by all who knew him.

Mr. Tappan published his first volume of Poems in Philadelphia, in 1819, encouraged to do so by Mr. Robert Walsh, then editor of the "American Quarterly Review," and Mr. Joseph R. Chandler, the accomplished editor for many years of the "United States Gazette." He subsequently gave to the public more than a dozen volumes, the contents of which are for the most part included in the five comprising his complete Poetical Works, with his final revisions—"The Poetry of Life," "The Sunday-school and other Poems," "The Poetry of the Heart," "Sacred and Miscellaneous Poems," and "Late and Early Poems," which appeared in 1848 and 1849. He wrote with great facility, and many of his pieces are pleasing expressions of natural and pious emotion.

THE TWENTY THOUSAND CHILDREN OF THE SABBATH-SCHOOLS IN NEW YORK, CELEBRATING TOGETHER THE FOURTH OF JULY, 1839.

O, sight sublime, O, sight of fear!
  The shadowing of infinity!
Numbers, whose murmur rises here
  Like whisperings of the mighty sea!

Ye bring strange visions to my gaze;
  Earth's dreamer, heaven before me swims;
The sea of glass, the throne of days,
  Crowns, harps, and the melodious hymns.

Ye rend the air with grateful songs
  For freedom by old warriors won:
O, for the battle which your throngs
  May wage and win through David's Son!

Wealth of young beauty! that now blooms
  Before me like a world of flowers;
High expectation! that assumes
  The hue of life's serenest hours;

Are ye decaying? Must these forms,
  So agile, fair, and brightly gay,
Hidden in dust, be given to worms
  And everlasting night, the prey?

Are ye immortal? Will this mass
  Of life, be life, undying still,
When all these sentient thousands pass
  To where corruption works its will?

Thought! that takes hold of heaven and hell,
  Be in each teacher's heart to-day!
So shall eternity be well
  With these, when time has fled away.

SONG
OF THE THREE HUNDRED THOUSAND DRUNKARDS IN THE UNITED STATES.

We come! we come! with sad array,
And in procession long,
To join the army of the lost,—
Three hundred thousand strong.

Our banners, beckoning on to death,
Abroad we have unrolled;
And Famine, Care, and wan Despair
Are seen on every fold.

Ye heard what music cheers us on,—
The mother's cry, that rang
So wildly, and the babe's that wailed
Above the trumpet's clang.

We've taken spoil; and blighted joys
And ruined homes are here;
We've trampled on the throbbing heart,
And flouted sorrow's tear.

We come! we come! we've searched the land,
The rich and poor are ours—
Enlisted from the shrines of God,
From hovels and from towers.

And who or what shall balk the brave,
Who swear to drink and die?
What boots to such man's muttered curse
Or His that spans the sky?

Our leader! who of all the chiefs,
Who've triumphed from the first,
Can blazon deeds like his? such griefs,
Such wounds, such trophies curst.

We come! Of the world's scourges, who
Like him have overthrown?
What wo had ever earth, like wo
To his stern prowess known?

Onward! though ever on our march,
Hang Misery's countless train;
Onward for hell!—from rank to rank
Pass we the cup again!

We come! we come! to fill our graves,
On which shall shine no star;
To glut the worm that never dies,—
Hurrah! hurrah! hurrah!

HEAVEN.

There is an hour of peaceful rest
To mourning wanderers given:
There is a joy for souls distrest,
A balm for every wounded breast
'T is found alone, in heaven.

There is a home for weary souls,
By sin and sorrow driven:
When toss'd on life's tempestuous shoals,
Where storms arise, and ocean rolls,
And all is drear, but heaven.

There faith lifts up her cheerful eye,
To brighter prospects given,
And views the tempest passing by;—
The evening shadows quickly fly,
And all's serene, in heaven.

There, fragrant flowers immortal bloom,
And joys supreme are given,
There, rays divine disperse the gloom,—
Beyond the confines of the tomb
Appears the dawn of heaven.

TO THE SHIP OF THE LINE PENNSYLVANIA.

"Leap forth to the careering seas,"
O ship of lofty name!
And toss upon thy native breeze
The stars and stripes of fame!
And bear thy thunders o'er the deep
Where vaunting navies ride!
Thou hast a nation's gems to keep—
Her honour and her pride!
Oh! holy is the covenant made
With thee and us to-day;
None from the compact shrinks afraid,
No traitor utters Nay!
We pledge our fervent love, and thou
Thy glorious ribs of oak,
Alive with men who cannot bow
To kings, nor kiss the yoke!

Speed lightnings o'er the Carib sea,
Which deeds of hell deform;
And look! her hands are spread to thee
Where Afric's robbers swarm.
Go! lie upon the Ægean's breast,
Where sparkle emerald isles—
Go! seek the lawless Suliote's nest,
And spoil his cruel wiles.
And keep, where sail the merchant ships,
Stern watch on their highway,
And promptly, through thine iron lips,
When urged, our tribute pay;
Yes, show thy bristling teeth of power,
Wherever tyrants bind,
In pride of their own little hour,
A freeborn, noble mind.

Spread out those ample wings of thine!—
While crime doth govern men,
'T is fit such bulwark of the brine
Should leave the shores of Penn;
For hid within thy giant strength
Are germs of welcome peace,
And such as thou, shalt cause at length
Man's feverish strife to cease.
From every vale, from every crag,
Word of thy beauty's past,
And joy we that our country's flag
Streams from thy towering mast—
Assured that in thy prowess, thou
For her wilt win renown,
Whose sons can die, but know not bow
To strike that pennon down

EDWARD EVERETT.

[Born 1794. Died 1865.]

THIS eminent scholar, orator, statesman, and man of letters, was born in Dorchester, Massachusetts, in 1794; graduated at Harvard College in 1811; appointed professor of Greek literature in 1814; after five years of travel and residence at foreign universities entered upon the duties of his office in 1819; became editor of the North American Review in 1820; was a member of Congress from 1824 to 1834; governor of Massachusetts from 1835 to 1839; minister to England from 1841 to 1845; president of Harvard College from 1845 to 1849; a member of the Senate; Secretary of State; again member of the Senate; and finally retired from public life, in consequence of ill-health, in 1854.

I have given some account of Mr. EVERETT'S principal prose writings in "The Prose Writers of America." In 1822 he contributed to the North American Review an article on the works of Dr. PERCIVAL, in the introductory pages of which he presents an admirable sketch of the condition and promise of our poetical literature at that time. Referring to the great number of those who in this country have published "occasional verses," he remarks that "it happens to almost all men of superior talents to have made an essay at poetry in early life. Whatever direction be finally forced upon them by strong circumstances or strong inclinations, there is a period after the imagination is awakened and the affections are excited, and before the great duties and cares of life begin, when all men of genius write a few lines in the shape of a patriotic song, a sonnet by Julio in a magazine, or stanzas to some fair object. This is the natural outlet."

In these sentences Mr. EVERETT recalls his own poetical effusions, which however are not so few or so unimportant as to be justly described in this manner. His first considerable poem was pronounced before the Phi Beta Kappa Society at Cambridge, in 1812. It is entitled "American Poets," and comprises about four hundred lines, in which some of the most striking themes of American song are suggested, and several of our earlier poets are referred to in phrases of kindly but suitable characterization.

From time to time, in his maturer years, Mr. EVERETT has written poems which evince unquestionable taste and a genuine poetical inspiration. Those which follow are contrasted examples of his abilities in this line, and they are not unworthy the author of some of the noblest orations in defence and illustration of liberty which have appeared in our time.

SANTA CROCE.

NOT chiefly for thy storied towers and halls,
For the bright wonders of thy pictured walls;
Not for the olive's wealth, the vineyard's pride,
That crown thy hills, and teem on Arno's side,
Dost thou delight me, Florence! I can meet
Elsewhere with halls as rich, and vales as sweet;
I prize thy charms of nature and of art,
But yield them not the homage of my heart.
Rather to Santa Croce I repair,
To breathe her peaceful monumental air;
The age, the deeds, the honours to explore,
Of those who sleep beneath her marble floor;
The stern old tribunes of the early time,
The merchant lords of Freedom's stormy prime;
And each great name, in every after age,
The praised, the wise; the artist, bard, and sage.
I feel their awful presence; lo, thy bust,
Thy urn, Oh! DANTE, not alas thy dust.
Florence, that drove thee living from her gate,
Waits for that dust, in vain, and long shall wait.
Ravenna! keep the glorious exile's trust,
And teach remorseless factions to be just,
While the poor Cenotaph, which bears his name,
Proclaims at once his praise,—his country's shame.
Next, in an urn, not void, though cold as thine,
Moulders a godlike spirit's mortal shrine.
Oh! Michael, look not down so still and hard,
Speak to me,* Painter, Builder, Sculptor, Bard!
And shall those cunning fingers, stiff and cold,
Crumble to meaner earth than they did mould?
Art thou, who form and force to clay couldst give,
And teach the quarried adamant to live,
Bid,—in the vaultings of thy mighty dome,—
Pontifical, outvie imperial Rome,
Portray unshrinking, to the dazzled eye,
Creation, Judgment, Time, Eternity,
Art thou so low, and in this narrow cell
Doth that Titanic genius stoop to dwell;
And, while thine arches brave the upper sky,
Art thou content in these dark caves to lie?
And thou, illustrious sage! thine eye is closed,
To which their secret paths new stars exposed.
Haply thy spirit, in some higher sphere,
Soars with the motions which it measured here.
Soft be thy slumbers, Seer, for thanks to thee,
The earth now turns, without a heresy.
Dost thou, whose keen perception pierced the cause
Which gives the pendulum its mystic laws,
Now trace each orb, with telescopic eyes,
And solve the eternal clock-work of the skies,
While thy worn frame enjoys its long repose,
And Santa Croce heals Arcetri's woes?†

* MICHAEL ANGELO, contemplating the statue of St. Mark, by Donatello, used to say, "Marco, perchè non mi parli?"

† GALILEO, toward the close of his life, was imprisoned at Arcetri, near Florence, by order of the Inquisition.

Nor them alone: on her maternal breast
Here MACHIAVELLI'S tortured limbs have rest.
Oh, that the cloud upon his tortured fame
Might pass away, and leave an honest name!
The power of princes o'er thy limbs is stayed,
But thine own "Prince;" that dark spot ne'er shall fade.
Peace to thine ashes; who can have the heart
Above thy grave to play the censor's part.
I read the statesman's fortune in thy doom,—
Toil, greatness, wo; a late and lying tomb;*
Aspiring aims, by grovelling arts pursued,
Faction and self, baptized the public good,
A life traduced, a statue crowned with bays,
And starving service paid with funeral praise.
Here too, at length the indomitable will
And fiery pulse of Asti's bard† are still.
And she,—the Stuart's widow,—rears thy stone,
Seeks the next aisle, and drops beneath her own.
The great, the proud, the fair,—alike they fall;
Thy sickle, Santa Croce, reapeth all!
Yes, reapeth all, or else had spared the bloom
Of that fair bud, now clothed in yonder tomb.
Meek, gentle, pure; and yet to him allied,
Who smote the astonished nations in his pride:
"Worthy his name,"‡ so saith the sculptured line.
Waster of man, would he were worthy thine!
Hosts yet unnamed—the obscure, the known—I leave;
What throngs would rise, could each his marble heave!
But we who muse above the famous dead,
Shall soon be silent, as the dust we tread.
Yet not for me, when I shall fall asleep,
Shall Santa Croce's lamps their vigils keep.
Beyond the main, in Auburn's quiet shade,
With those I loved and love my couch be made;
Spring's pendent branches o'er the hillock wave,
And morning's dew-drops glisten on my grave;
While heaven's great arch shall rise above my bed,
When Santa Croce's crumbles on her dead;
Unknown to erring or to suffering fame,
So I may leave a pure though humble name.

TO A SISTER.

I.

YES, dear one, to the envied train
Of those around, thy homage pay;
But wilt thou never kindly deign
To think of him that's far away?
Thy form, thine eye, thine angel smile,
For many years I may not see;
But wilt thou not sometimes the while,
My sister dear, remember me?

II.

Yet not in Fashion's brilliant hall,
Surrounded by the gay and fair,
And thou, the fairest of them all,—
Oh, think not, think not of me there;
But when the thoughtless crowd is gone,
And hushed the voice of senseless glee,
And all is silent, still and lone,
And thou art sad, remember me.

III.

Remember me—but loveliest, ne'er,
When, in his orbit fair and high,
The morning's glowing charioteer
Rides proudly up the blushing sky;
But when the waning moonbeam sleeps
At midnight on that lonely lea,
And nature's pensive spirit weeps
In all her dews, remember me.

IV.

Remember me, I pray—but not
In Flora's gay and blooming hour,
When every brake hath found its note,
And sunshine smiles in every flower:
But when the falling leaf is sear,
And withers sadly from the tree,
And o'er the ruins of the year
Cold Autumn weeps, remember me.

V.

Remember me—but choose not, dear,
The hour when, on the gentle lake,
The sportive wavelets, blue and clear,
Soft rippling to the margin break;
But when the deafening billows foam
In madness o'er the pathless sea,
Then let thy pilgrim fancy roam
Across them, and remember me.

VI.

Remember me—but not to join
If haply some thy friends should praise;
'T is far too dear, that voice of thine
To echo what the stranger says.
They know us not—but shouldst thou meet
Some faithful friend of me and thee,
Softly, sometimes, to him repeat
My name, and then remember me.

VII.

Remember me—not I entreat,
In scenes of festal week-day joy,
For then it were not kind or meet,
The thought thy pleasure should alloy;
But on the sacred, solemn day,
And, dearest, on thy bended knee,
When thou, for those thou lov'st, dost pray,
Sweet spirit, then, remember me.

VIII.

Remember me—but not as I
On thee forever, ever dwell,
With anxious heart and drooping eye,
And doubts 't would grieve thee should I tell
But in thy calm, unclouded heart,
Whence dark and gloomy visions flee,
Oh, there, my sister, be my part,
And kindly there remember me.

* The monument of Machiavelli in Santa Croce was erected in the latter half of the last century,—The inscription, "tanto nomini nullum par elogium."

† Alfieri.

‡ "Ici repose Charlotte Napoleon Bonaparte, digne de son nom, 1839." The words are translated "worthy *his* name," for an obvious reason.

JOSEPH RODMAN DRAKE.

[Born, 1795. Died, 1820.]

The author of the "Culprit Fay" was born in the city of New York, on the seventh day of August, 1795. His father died while he was very young, and I believe left his family in possession of but little property. Young Drake, therefore, experienced some difficulties in acquiring his education. He entered Columbia College, however, at an early period, and passed through that seminary with a reputation for scholarship, taste, and admirable social qualities. He soon after made choice of the medical profession, and became a student, first, with Doctor Romaine, and subsequently with Doctor Powell, both of whom were at that time popular physicians in New York.

Soon after completing his professional studies he was married to Miss Sarah Eckford, a daughter of the well-known marine architect, Henry Eckford, through whom he inherited a moderate fortune. His health, about the same time, began to decline, and in the winter of 1819 he visited New Orleans, to which city his mother, who had married a second husband, had previously removed with his three sisters. He had anticipated some benefit from the sea-voyage, and the mild climate of Louisiana, but was disappointed, and in the spring of 1820 he returned to New York. His disease—consumption—was now too deeply seated for hope of restoration to be cherished, and he gradually withdrew himself from society, and sought quiet among his books, and in the companionship of his wife and most intimate friends. He lingered through the summer, and died near the close of September, in the twenty-sixth year of his age.

He began to write verses when very young, and was a contributor to several gazettes before he was sixteen years old. He permitted none but his most intimate friends to know his signatures, and sometimes kept the secrets of his authorship entirely to himself. The first four of the once celebrated series of humorous and satirical odes, known as the "Croaker Pieces," were written by him, for the New York "Evening Post," in which they appeared between the tenth and the twentieth of March, 1819. After the publication of the fourth number, Drake made Halleck, then recently arrived in New York, a partner, and the remainder of the pieces were signed "Croaker and Co." The last one written by Drake was "The American Flag," printed on the twenty-ninth of May, and the last of the series, "Curtain Conversations," was contributed by Halleck, on the twenty-fourth of July. These pieces related to persons, events, and scenes, with which most of the readers in New York were familiar, and as they were distinguished alike for playful humour, and an easy and spirited diction, they became very popular, and many efforts were made to find out the authors. Both Drake and Halleck were unknown as poets, and, as they kept the secret from their friends, a considerable period elapsed before they were discovered.

The "Croakers" are now, however, well nigh forgotten, save a few of the least satirical numbers, which Halleck has preserved in the collections of his own and of his friend's writings; and the reputation of either author rests on more elaborate and ingenious productions. The longest poem by Drake is "The Culprit Fay," a story exhibiting the most delicate fancy, and much artistic skill, which was not printed until several years after his death. It was composed hastily among the highlands of the Hudson, in the summer of 1819. The author was walking with some friends, on a warm, moonlit evening, when one of the party remarked, that "it would be difficult to write a fairy poem, purely imaginative, without the aid of human characters." When the friends were reassembled, two or three days afterwards, "The Culprit Fay" was read to them, nearly as it is printed in this volume.

Drake placed a very modest estimate on his own productions, and it is believed that but a small portion of them have been preserved. When on his death-bed, a friend inquired of him what disposition he would have made with his poems? "O, burn them," he replied, "they are quite valueless." Written copies of a number of them were, however, in circulation, and some had been incorrectly printed in the periodicals; and, for this reason, Commodore Dekay, the husband of the daughter and only child of the deceased poet, in 1836 published the single collection of them which has appeared. It includes, beside "The Culprit Fay," eighteen shorter pieces, some of which are very beautiful.

Drake was unassuming and benevolent in his manners and his feelings, and he had an unfailing fountain of fine humour, which made him one of the most pleasant of companions. Halleck closes a tributary poem published soon after his death, in the "Scientific Repository and Critical Review," with the following stanzas—

When hearts, whose truth was proven,
  Like thine, are laid in earth,
There should a wreath be woven
  To tell the world their worth.

And I, who woke each morrow
  To clasp thy hand in mine,
Who shared thy joy and sorrow,
  Whose weal and wo were thine,

It should be mine to braid it
  Around thy faded brow;
But I've in vain essay'd it,
  And feel I cannot now.

While memory bids me weep thee,
  Nor thoughts nor words are free,
The grief is fix'd too deeply
  That mourns a man like thee.

THE CULPRIT FAY.

"My visual orbs are purged from film, and, lo!
Instead of Anster's turnip-bearing vales
I see old fairy land's miraculous show!
Her trees of tinsel kiss'd by freakish gales,
Her Ouphs that, cloak'd in leaf-gold, skim the breeze,
And fairies, swarming ——————"
TENNANT'S ANSTER FAIR.

I.

'Tis the middle watch of a summer's night—
The earth is dark, but the heavens are bright;
Naught is seen in the vault on high
But the moon, and the stars, and the cloudless sky,
And the flood which rolls its milky hue,
A river of light on the welkin blue.
The moon looks down on old Cronest,
She mellows the shades on his shaggy breast,
And seems his huge gray form to throw
In a silver cone on the wave below;
His sides are broken by spots of shade,
By the walnut bough and the cedar made,
And through their clustering branches dark
Glimmers and dies the fire-fly's spark—
Like starry twinkles that momently break
Through the rifts of the gathering tempest's rack.

II.

The stars are on the moving stream,
And fling, as its ripples gently flow,
A burnish'd length of wavy beam
In an eel-like, spiral line below;
The winds are whist, and the owl is still,
The bat in the shelvy rock is hid.
And naught is heard on the lonely hill
But the cricket's chirp, and the answer shrill
Of the gauze-winged katy-did;
And the plaint of the wailing whip-poor-will,
Who moans unseen, and ceaseless sings,
Ever a note of wail and wo,
Till morning spreads her rosy wings,
And earth and sky in her glances glow.

III.

'Tis the hour of fairy ban and spell:
The wood-tick has kept the minutes well;
He has counted them all with click and stroke
Deep in the heart of the mountain-oak,
And he has awaken'd the sentry elve
Who sleeps with him in the haunted tree,
To bid him ring the hour of twelve,
And call the fays to their revelry;
Twelve small strokes on his tinkling bell—
('Twas made of the white snail's pearly shell:—)
"Midnight comes, and all is well!
Hither, hither, wing your way!
'Tis the dawn of the fairy-day."

IV

They come from beds of lichen green,
They creep from the mullen's velvet screen;
Some on the backs of beetles fly
From the silver tops of moon-touched trees,
Where they swung in their cobweb hammocks high,
And rock'd about in the evening breeze;
Some from the hum-bird's downy nest—
They had driven him out by elfin power,
And, pillow'd on plumes of his rainbow breast,
Had slumber'd there till the charmed hour;
Some had lain in the scoop of the rock,
With glittering ising-stars inlaid;
And some had open'd the four-o'clock,
And stole within its purple shade.
And now they throng the moonlight glade,
Above—below—on every side,
Their little minim forms array'd
In the tricksy pomp of fairy pride!

V.

They come not now to print the lea,
In freak and dance around the tree,
Or at the mushroom board to sup,
And drink the dew from the buttercup;—
A scene of sorrow waits them now,
For an Ouphe has broken his vestal vow;
He has loved an earthly maid,
And left for her his woodland shade;
He has lain upon her lip of dew,
And sunn'd him in her eye of blue
Fann'd her cheek with his wing of air,
Play'd in the ringlets of her hair,
And, nestling on her snowy breast,
Forgot the lily-king's behest.
For this the shadowy tribes of air
To the elfin court must haste away:—
And now they stand expectant there,
To hear the doom of the culprit Fay.

VI.

The throne was rear'd upon the grass,
Of spice-wood and of sassafras;
On pillars of mottled tortoise-shell
Hung the burnished canopy—
And o'er it gorgeous curtains fell
Of the tulip's crimson drapery.
The monarch sat on his judgment-seat,
On his brow the crown imperial shone,
The prisoner Fay was at his feet,
And his peers were ranged around the throne
He waved his sceptre in the air,
He look'd around and calmly spoke;
His brow was grave and his eye severe,
But his voice in a soften'd accent broke:

VII.

"Fairy! Fairy! list and mark:
Thou hast broke thine elfin chain;
Thy flame-wood lamp is quench'd and dark,
And thy wings are dyed with a deadly stain—
Thou hast sullied thine elfin purity
In the glance of a mortal maiden's eye,
Thou hast scorn'd our dread decree,
And thou shouldst pay the forfeit high,
But well I know her sinless mind
Is pure as the angel forms above,
Gentle and meek, and chaste and kind,
Such as a spirit well might love;
Fairy! had she spot or taint,
Bitter had been thy punishment.

Tied to the hornet's shardy wings;
Toss'd on the pricks of nettles' stings;
Or seven long ages doom'd to dwell
With the lazy worm in the walnut-shell;
Or every night to writhe and bleed
Beneath the tread of the centipede;
Or bound in a cobweb dungeon dim,
Your jailer a spider huge and grim,
Amid the carrion bodies to lie,
Of the worm, and the bug, and the murder'd fly
These it had been your lot to bear,
Had a stain been found on the earthly fair.
Now list, and mark our mild decree—
Fairy, this your doom must be:

VIII.

"Thou shalt seek the beach of sand
Where the water bounds the elfin land;
Thou shalt watch the oozy brine
Till the sturgeon leaps in the bright moonshine
Then dart the glistening arch below,
And catch a drop from his silver bow.
The water-sprites will wield their arms
And dash around, with roar and rave,
And vain are the woodland spirits' charms,
They are the imps that rule the wave.
Yet trust thee in thy single might:
If thy heart be pure and thy spirit right,
Thou shalt win the warlock fight.

IX.

"If the spray-bead gem be won,
The stain of thy wing is wash'd away:
But another errand must be done
Ere thy crime be lost for aye;
Thy flame-wood lamp is quench'd and dark
Thou must reillume its spark.
Mount thy steed and spur him high
To the heaven's blue canopy;
And when thou seest a shooting star,
Follow it fast, and follow it far—
The last faint spark of its burning train
Shall light the elfin lamp again.
Thou hast heard our sentence, Fay;
Hence! to the water-side, away!"

X.

The goblin mark'd his monarch well;
He spake not, but he bow'd him low,
Then pluck'd a crimson colen-bell,
And turn'd him round in act to go.
The way is long, he cannot fly,
His soiled wing has lost its power,
And he winds adown the mountain high
For many a sore and weary hour.
Through dreary beds of tangled fern,
Through groves of nightshade dark and dern,
Over the grass and through the brake,
Where toils the ant and sleeps the snake;
Now o'er the violet's azure flush
He skips along in lightsome mood;
And now he thrids the bramble-bush,
Till its points are dyed in fairy blood.
He has leap'd the bog, he has pierced the brier
He has swum the brook, and waded the mire,
Till his spirits sank, and his limbs grew weak,
And the red wax'd fainter in his cheek.
He had fallen to the ground outright,
For rugged and dim was his onward track,
But there came a spotted toad in sight,
And he laugh'd as he jump'd upon her back
He bridled her mouth with a silkweed twist,
He lash'd her sides with an osier thong;
And now, through evening's dewy mist,
With leap and spring they bound along,
Till the mountain's magic verge is past,
And the beach of sand is reach'd at last.

XI.

Soft and pale is the moony beam,
Moveless still the glassy stream;
The wave is clear, the beach is bright
With snowy shells and sparkling stones;
The shore-surge comes in ripples light,
In murmurings faint and distant moans;
And ever afar in the silence deep
Is heard the splash of the sturgeon's leap,
And the bend of his graceful bow is seen—
A glittering arch of silver sheen,
Spanning the wave of burnish'd blue,
And dripping with gems of the river-dew.

XII.

The elfin cast a glance around,
As he lighted down from his courser toad
Then round his breast his wings he wound,
And close to the river's brink he strode;
He sprang on a rock, he breathed a prayer,
Above his head his arms he threw,
Then toss'd a tiny curve in air,
And headlong plunged in the waters blue.

XIII.

Up sprung the spirits of the waves,
From the sea-silk beds in their coral caves,
With snail-plate armour snatch'd in haste,
They speed their way through the liquid waste
Some are rapidly borne along
On the mailed shrimp or the prickly prong,
Some on the blood-red leeches glide,
Some on the stony star-fish ride,
Some on the back of the lancing squab,
Some on the sideling soldier-crab;
And some on the jellied quarl, that flings
At once a thousand streamy stings;
They cut the wave with the living oar,
And hurry on to the moonlight shore,
To guard their realms and chase away
The footsteps of the invading Fay.

XIV.

Fearlessly he skims along,
His hope is high, and his limbs are strong,
He spreads his arms like the swallow's wing,
And throws his feet with a frog-like fling,
His locks of gold on the waters shine
At his breast the tiny foam-bees rise.
His back gleams bright above the brine,
And the wake-line foam behind him lies.
But the water-sprites are gathering near
To check his course along the tide

Their warriors come in swift career
  And hem him round on every side;
On his thigh the leech has fix'd his hold,
The quarl's long arms are round him roll'd,
The prickly prong has pierced his skin,
And the squab has thrown his javelin,
The gritty star has rubb'd him raw,
And the crab has struck with his giant claw;
He howls with rage, and he shrieks with pain,
He strikes around, but his blows are vain;
Hopeless is the unequal fight,
Fairy! naught is left but flight.

XV.

He turn'd him round, and fled amain
With hurry and dash to the beach again,
He twisted over from side to side,
And laid his cheek to the cleaving tide;
The strokes of his plunging arms are fleet,
And with all his might he flings his feet,
But the water-sprites are round him still,
To cross his path and work him ill.
They bade the wave before him rise;
They flung the sea-fire in his eyes,
And they stunn'd his ears with the scallop stroke,
With the porpoise heave and the drum-fish croak.
O! but a weary wight was he
When he reach'd the foot of the dogwood tree.
—Gash'd and wounded, and stiff and sore,
He laid him down on the sandy shore;
He bless'd the force of the charmed line,
  And he bann'd the water goblin's spite,
For he saw around in the sweet moonshine
Their little wee faces above the brine,
  Giggling and laughing with all their might
  At the piteous hap of the Fairy wight.

XVI.

Soon he gather'd the balsam dew
  From the sorrel-leaf and the henbane bud;
O'er each wound the balm he drew,
  And with cobweb lint he stanch'd the blood.
The mild west wind was soft and low,
It cool'd the heat of his burning brow,
And he felt new life in his sinews shoot,
As he drank the juice of the calamus root;
And now he treads the fatal shore,
As fresh and vigorous as before.

XVII.

Wrapp'd in musing stands the sprite:
'T is the middle wane of night;
  His task is hard, his way is far,
But he must do his errand right
  Ere dawning mounts her beamy car,
And rolls her chariot wheels of light;
And vain are the spells of fairy-land;
He must work with a human hand.

XVIII.

He cast a sadden'd look around,
  But he felt new joy his bosom swell,
When, glittering on the shadow'd ground,
  He saw a purple muscle-shell;
Thither he ran, and he bent him low,
He heaved at the stern and he heaved at the bow
And he pushed her over the yielding sand,
Till he came to the verge of the haunted land.
She was as lovely a pleasure-boat
  As ever fairy had paddled in,
For she glow'd with purple paint without,
  And shone with silvery pearl within;
A sculler's notch in the stern he made,
An oar he shaped of the bootle blade;
Then sprung to his seat with a lightsome leap,
And launched afar on the calm, blue deep.

XIX.

The imps of the river yell and rave;
They had no power above the wave,
But they heaved the billow before the prow,
  And they dash'd the surge against her side,
And they struck her keel with jerk and blow,
  Till the gunwale bent to the rocking tide.
She wimpled about to the pale moonbeam,
Like a feather that floats on a wind-toss'd stream
And momently athwart her track
The quarl uprear'd his island back,
And the fluttering scallop behind would float,
And patter the water about the boat;
But he bail'd her out with his colen-bell,
  And he kept her trimm'd with a wary tread,
While on every side like lightning fell
  The heavy strokes of his bootle-blade.

XX.

Onward still he held his way,
Till he came where the column of moonshine lay
And saw beneath the surface dim
The brown-back'd sturgeon slowly swim:
Around him were the goblin train—
But he scull'd with all his might and main,
And follow'd wherever the sturgeon led,
Till he saw him upward point his head;
Then he dropp'd his paddle-blade,
And held his colen-goblet up
To catch the drop in its crimson cup.

XXI.

With sweeping tail and quivering fin,
  Through the wave the sturgeon flew,
And, like the heaven-shot javelin,
  He sprung above the waters blue.
Instant as the star-fall light,
  He plunged him in the deep again,
But left an arch of silver bright,
  The rainbow of the moony main.
It was a strange and lovely sight
  To see the puny goblin there;
He seem'd an angel form of light,
  With azure wing and sunny hair,
  Throned on a cloud of purple fair,
Circled with blue and edged with white,
And sitting at the fall of even
Beneath the bow of summer heaven.

XXII.

A moment, and its lustre fell;
  But ere it met the billow blue,

He caught within his crimson bell
A droplet of its sparkling dew—
Joy to thee, Fay! thy task is done,
Thy wings are pure, for the gem is won—
Cheerly ply thy dripping oar,
And haste away to the elfin shore.

XXIII.

He turns, and, lo! on either side
The ripples on his path divide;
And the track o'er which his boat must pass
Is smooth as a sheet of polish'd glass.
Around, their limbs the sea-nymphs lave,
  With snowy arms half-swelling out,
While on the gloss'd and gleamy wave
  Their sea-green ringlets loosely float;
They swim around with smile and song;
  They press the bark with pearly hand,
And gently urge her course along,
  Toward the beach of speckled sand;
  And, as he lightly leap'd to land,
They bade adieu with nod and bow,
  Then gayly kiss'd each little hand,
And dropp'd in the crystal deep below.

XXIV.

A moment stay'd the fairy there;
He kiss'd the beach and breathed a prayer;
Then spread his wings of gilded blue,
And on to the elfin court he flew;
As ever ye saw a bubble rise,
And shine with a thousand changing dyes,
Till, lessening far, through ether driven,
It mingles with the hues of heaven;
As, at the glimpse of morning pale,
The lance-fly spreads his silken sail,
And gleams with blendings soft and bright,
Till lost in the shades of fading night;
So rose from earth the lovely Fay—
So vanish'd, far in heaven away!

. . . . .

Up, Fairy! quit thy chick-weed bower,
The cricket has call'd the second hour,
Twice again, and the lark will rise
To kiss the streaking of the skies—
Up! thy charmed armour don,
Thou'lt need it ere the night be gone.

XXV.

He put his acorn helmet on;
It was plumed of the silk of the thistle-down:
The corslet plate that guarded his breast
Was once the wild bee's golden vest;
His cloak, of a thousand mingled dyes,
Was formed of the wings of butterflies;
His shield was the shell of a lady-bug queen,
Studs of gold on a ground of green;
And the quivering lance which he brandish'd bright,
Was the sting of a wasp he had slain in fight.
Swift he bestrode his fire-fly steed;
  He bared his blade of the bent grass blue;
He drove his spurs of the cockle-seed,
  And away like a glance of thought he flew
To skim the heavens, and follow far
The fiery trail of the rocket-star.

XXVI.

The moth-fly, as he shot in air,
Crept under the leaf, and hid her there;
The katy-did forgot its lay,
The prowling gnat fled fast away,
The fell mosqueto check'd his drone
And folded his wings till the Fay was gone,
And the wily beetle dropp'd his head,
And fell on the ground as if he were dead;
They crouch'd them close in the darksome shade,
  They quaked all o'er with awe and fear,
For they had felt the blue-bent blade,
  And writhed at the prick of the elfin spear;
Many a time, on a summer's night,
When the sky was clear and the moon was bright,
They had been roused from the haunted ground
By the yelp and bay of the fairy hound;
  They had heard the tiny bugle-horn,
They had heard the twang of the maize-silk string,
  When the vine-twig bows were tightly drawn,
  And the needle-shaft through air was borne,
Feather'd with down of the hum-bird's wing.
And now they deem'd the courier ouphe,
  Some hunter-sprite of the elfin ground;
And they watch'd till they saw him mount the roof
  That canopies the world around;
Then glad they left their covert lair,
And freak'd about in the midnight air.

XXVII.

Up to the vaulted firmament
His path the fire-fly courser bent,
And at every gallop on the wind,
He flung a glittering spark behind;
He flies like a feather in the blast
Till the first light cloud in heaven is past.
  But the shapes of air have begun their work,
And a drizzly mist is round him cast,
  He cannot see through the mantle murk,
He shivers with cold, but he urges fast;
  Through storm and darkness, sleet and shade,
He lashes his steed and spurs amain,
For shadowy hands have twitch'd the rein,
  And flame-shot tongues around him play'd,
And near him many a fiendish eye
Glared with a fell malignity,
And yells of rage, and shrieks of fear,
Came screaming on his startled ear.

XXVIII.

His wings are wet around his breast,
The plume hangs dripping from his crest,
His eyes are blurr'd with the lightning's glare,
And his ears are stunn'd with the thunder's blare,
But he gave a shout, and his blade he drew,
  He thrust before and he struck behind,
Till he pierced their cloudy bodies through,
  And gash'd their shadowy limbs of wind;
Howling the misty spectres flew,
  They rend the air with frightful cries,
For he has gain'd the welkin blue,
  And the land of clouds beneath him lies,

XXIX.

Up to the cope careering swift,
In breathless motion fast,
Fleet as the swallow cuts the drift,
Or the sea-roc rides the blast,
The sapphire sheet of eve is shot,
The sphered moon is past,
The earth but seems a tiny blot
On a sheet of azure cast.
O! it was sweet, in the clear moonlight,
To tread the starry plain of even,
To meet the thousand eyes of night,
And feel the cooling breath of heaven!
But the Elfin made no stop or stay
Till he came to the bank of the milky-way,
Then he check'd his courser's foot,
And watch'd for the glimpse of the planet-shoot.

XXX.

Sudden along the snowy tide
That swell'd to meet their footsteps' fall,
The sylphs of heaven were seen to glide,
Attired in sunset's crimson pall;
Around the Fay they weave the dance,
They skip before him on the plain,
And one has taken his wasp-sting lance,
And one upholds his bridle-rein;
With warblings wild they lead him on
To where, through clouds of amber seen,
Studded with stars, resplendent shone
The palace of the sylphid queen.
Its spiral columns, gleaming bright,
Were streamers of the northern light;
Its curtain's light and lovely flush
Was of the morning's rosy blush,
And the ceiling fair that rose aboon
The white and feathery fleece of noon.

XXXI.

But, O! how fair the shape that lay
Beneath a rainbow bending bright;
She seem'd to the entranced Fay
The loveliest of the forms of light;
Her mantle was the purple roll'd
At twilight in the west afar;
'T was tied with threads of dawning gold,
And button'd with a sparkling star.
Her face was like the lily roon
That veils the vestal planet's hue;
Her eyes, two beamlets from the moon,
Set floating in the welkin blue.
Her hair is like the sunny beam,
And the diamond gems which round it gleam
Are the pure drops of dewy even
That ne'er have left their native heaven.

XXXII.

She raised her eyes to the wondering sprite,
And they leap'd with smiles, for well I wee
Never before in the bowers of light
Had the form of an earthly Fay been seen.
Long she look'd in his tiny face;
Long with his butterfly cloak she play'd;
She smooth'd his wings of azure lace,
And handled the tassel of his blade;
And as he told in accents low
The story of his love and wo,
She felt new pains in her bosom rise,
And the tear-drop started in her eyes.
And "O, sweet spirit of earth," she cried,
"Return no more to your woodland height,
But ever here with me abide
In the land of everlasting light!
Within the fleecy drift we'll lie,
We'll hang upon the rainbow's rim;
And all the jewels of the sky
Around thy brow shall brightly beam!
And thou shalt bathe thee in the stream
That rolls its whitening foam aboon,
And ride upon the lightning's gleam,
And dance upon the orbed moon!
We'll sit within the Pleiad ring,
We'll rest on Orion's starry belt,
And I will bid my sylphs to sing
The song that makes the dew-mist melt;
Their harps are of the umber shade,
That hides the blush of waking day,
And every gleamy string is made
Of silvery moonshine's lengthen'd ray;
And thou shalt pillow on my breast,
While heavenly breathings float around,
And, with the sylphs of ether blest,
Forget the joys of fairy ground."

XXXIII.

She was lovely and fair to see
And the elfin's heart beat fitfully;
But lovelier far, and still more fair,
The earthly form imprinted there;
Naught he saw in the heavens above
Was half so dear as his mortal love,
For he thought upon her looks so meek,
And he thought of the light flush on her cheek;
Never again might he bask and lie
On that sweet cheek and moonlight eye,
But in his dreams her form to see,
To clasp her in his revery,
To think upon his virgin bride,
Was worth all heaven, and earth beside.

XXXIV.

"Lady," he cried, "I have sworn to-night,
On the word of a fairy-knight,
To do my sentence-task aright;
My honour scarce is free from stain,
I may not soil its snows again;
Betide me weal, betide me wo,
Its mandate must be answer'd now."
Her bosom heaved with many a sigh,
The tear was in her drooping eye;
But she led him to the palace gate,
And call'd the sylphs who hover'd there,
And bade them fly and bring him straight
Of clouds condensed a sable car.
With charm and spell she bless'd it there,
From all the fiends of upper air;
Then round him cast the shadowy shroud,
And tied his steed behind the cloud;
And press'd his hand as she bade him fly
Far to the verge of the northern sky,

For by its wane and wavering light
There was a star would fall to-night.

XXXV.

Borne afar on the wings of the blast,
Northward away, he speeds him fast,
And his courser follows the cloudy wain
Till the hoof-strokes fall like pattering rain.
The clouds roll backward as he flies,
Each flickering star behind him lies,
And he has reach'd the northern plain,
And back'd his fire-fly steed again,
Ready to follow in its flight
The streaming of the rocket-light.

XXXVI.

The star is yet in the vault of heaven,
But it rocks in the summer gale;
And now 'tis fitful and uneven,
And now 'tis deadly pale;
And now 'tis wrapp'd in sulphur-smoke,
And quench'd is its rayless beam,
And now with a rattling thunder-stroke
It bursts in flash and flame.
As swift as the glance of the arrowy lance
That the storm-spirit flings from high,
The star-shot flew o'er the welkin blue,
As it fell from the sheeted sky.
As swift as the wind in its trail behind
The Elfin gallops along,
The fiends of the clouds are bellowing loud,
But the sylphid charm is strong:
He gallops unhurt in the shower of fire,
While the cloud-fiends fly from the blaze;
He watches each flake till its sparks expire,
And rides in the light of its rays.
But he drove his steed to the lightning's speed,
And caught a glimmering spark;
Then wheel'd around to the fairy ground,
And sped through the midnight dark.

. . . .

Ouphe and Goblin! Imp and Sprite!
Elf of eve! and starry Fay!
Ye that love the moon's soft light,
Hither—hither wend your way;
Twine ye in a jocund ring,
Sing and trip it merrily,
Hand to hand, and wing to wing,
Round the wild witch-hazel tree.

Hail the wanderer again
With dance and song, and lute and lyre,
Pure his wing and strong his chain,
And doubly bright his fairy fire.
Twine ye in an airy round,
Brush the dew and print the lea;
Skip and gambol, hop and bound,
Round the wild witch-hazel tree.

The beetle guards our holy ground,
He flies about the haunted place,
And if mortal there be found,
He hums in his ears and flaps his face;

The leaf harp sounds our roundelay,
The owlet's eyes our lanterns be;
Thus we sing, and dance, and play,
Round the wild witch-hazel tree.

But, hark! from tower on tree-top high,
The sentry-elf his call has made:
A streak is in the eastern sky,
Shapes of moonlight! flit and fade!
The hill-tops gleam in morning's spring,
The sky-lark shakes his dappled wing,
The day-glimpse glimmers on the lawn,
The cock has crow'd, and the Fays are gone.

BRONX.

I sat me down upon a green bank-side,
Skirting the smooth edge of a gentle river,
Whose waters seem'd unwillingly to glide,
Like parting friends, who linger while they sever;
Enforced to go, yet seeming still unready,
Backward they wind their way in many a wistful eddy.

Gray o'er my head the yellow-vested willow
Ruffled its hoary top in the fresh breezes,
Glancing in light, like spray on a green billow,
Or the fine frostwork which young winter freezes;
When first his power in infant pastime trying,
Congeals sad autumn's tears on the dead branches lying.

From rocks around hung the loose ivy dangling,
And in the clefts sumach of liveliest green,
Bright ising-stars the little beech was spangling,
The gold-cup sorrel from his gauzy screen
Shone like a fairy crown, enchased and beaded,
Left on some morn, when light flash'd in their eyes unheeded.

The humbird shook his sun-touch'd wings around,
The bluefinch caroll'd in the still retreat;
The antic squirrel caper'd on the ground
Where lichens made a carpet for his feet;
Through the transparent waves, the ruddy minkle
Shot up in glimmering sparks his red fin's tiny twinkle.

There were dark cedars, with loose, mossy tresses,
White-powder'd dog trees, and stiff hollies flaunting
Gaudy as rustics in their May-day dresses,
Blue pelloret from purple leaves upslanting
A modest gaze, like eyes of a young maiden
Shining beneath dropp'd lids the evening of her wedding.

The breeze fresh springing from the lips of morn,
Kissing the leaves, and sighing so to lose 'em,
The winding of the merry locust's horn,
The glad spring gushing from the rock's bare bosom:
Sweet sights, sweet sounds, all sights, all sound excelling,
O! 'twas a ravishing spot, form'd for a poet's dwelling.

And did I leave thy loveliness, to stand
  Again in the dull world of earthly blindness?
Pain'd with the pressure of unfriendly hands,
  Sick of smooth looks, agued with icy kindness?
Left I for this thy shades, where none intrude,
To prison wandering thought and mar sweet solitude?

Yet I will look upon thy face again,
  My own romantic Bronx, and it will be
A face more pleasant than the face of men.
  Thy waves are old companions, I shall see
A well-remember'd form in each old tree,
And hear a voice long loved in thy wild minstrelsy

THE AMERICAN FLAG.

I.

When Freedom from her mountain height
  Unfurl'd her standard to the air,
She tore the azure robe of night,
  And set the stars of glory there.
She mingled with its gorgeous dyes
The milky baldric of the skies,
And striped its pure, celestial white,
With streakings of the morning light;
Then from his mansion in the sun
She call'd her eagle bearer down,
And gave into his mighty hand
The symbol of her chosen land.

II.

Majestic monarch of the cloud,
  Who rear'st aloft thy regal form,
To hear the tempest trumpings loud
And see the lightning lances driven,
  When strive the warriors of the storm,
And rolls the thunder-drum of heaven,
Child of the sun! to thee 'tis given
  To guard the banner of the free,
To hover in the sulphur smoke,
To ward away the battle-stroke,
And bid its blendings shine afar,
Like rainbows on the cloud of war,
  The harbingers of victory!

III.

Flag of the brave! thy folds shall fly,
  The sign of hope and triumph high,
When speaks the signal trumpet tone,
  And the long line comes gleaming on.
Ere yet the life-blood, warm and wet,
  Has dimm'd the glistening bayonet,
Each soldier eye shall brightly turn
  To where thy sky-born glories burn;
And as his springing steps advance,
Catch war and vengeance from the glance.
And when the cannon-mouthings loud
  Heave in wild wreathes the battle-shroud
And gory sabres rise and fall
Like shoots of flame on midnight's pall;
  Then shall thy meteor glances glow,
And cowering foes shall sink beneath
  Each gallant arm that strikes below
That lovely messenger of death.

IV.

Flag of the seas! on ocean wave
  Thy stars shall glitter o'er the brave;
When death, careering on the gale,
  Sweeps darkly round the bellied sail,
And frighted waves rush wildly back
  Before the broadside's reeling rack,
Each dying wanderer of the sea
  Shall look at once to heaven and thee,
And smile to see thy splendours fly
In triumph o'er his closing eye.

V.

Flag of the free heart's hope and home!
  By angel hands to valour given;
The stars have lit the welkin dome,
  And all thy hues were born in heaven.
Forever float that standard sheet!
  Where breathes the foe but falls before us
With Freedom's soil beneath our feet,
  And Freedom's banner streaming o'er us?

TO SARAH.

I.

One happy year has fled, Sall,
  Since you were all my own;
The leaves have felt the autumn blight,
  The wintry storm has blown.
We heeded not the cold blast,
  Nor the winter's icy air;
For we found our climate in the heart,
  And it was summer there.

II.

The summer sun is bright, Sall,
  The skies are pure in hue;
But clouds will sometimes sadden them,
  And dim their lovely blue;
And clouds may come to us, Sall,
  But sure they will not stay;
For there's a spell in fond hearts
  To chase their gloom away.

III.

In sickness and in sorrow
  Thine eyes were on me still,
And there was comfort in each glance
  To charm the sense of ill:
And were they absent now, Sall,
  I'd seek my bed of pain,
And bless each pang that gave me back
  Those looks of love again.

IV.

O, pleasant is the welcome kiss,
  When day's dull round is o'er,
And sweet the music of the step
  That meets me at the door.
Though worldly cares may visit us,
  I reck not when they fall,
While I have thy kind lips, my Sall,
  To smile away them all.

FITZ-GREENE HALLECK.

[Born 1795. Died 1867.]

THE author of "Red Jacket, and Peter Castaly's "Epistle to Recorder Riker," is a son of ISRAEL HALLECK, of Dutchess county, New York, and MARY ELIOT, his wife, of Guilford, Connecticut, a descendant of JOHN ELIOT, the celebrated "Apostle of the Indians." He was born at Guilford, in August, 1795, and when about eighteen years of age became a clerk in one of the principal banking-houses in New York. He evinced a taste for poetry, and wrote verses, at a very early period, but until he came to New York never published any thing which in the maturity of his years he has deemed worthy of preservation. The "Evening Post," then edited by WILLIAM COLEMAN, was the leading paper of the city, and the only one in which much attention was given to literature. It had a large number of contributors, and youthful wits who gained admission to its columns regarded themselves as fairly started in a career of successful authorship. HALLECK'S first offering to the "Evening Post" was that piece of exquisite versification and refined sentiment of which the first line is—

"There is an evening twilight of the heart."

BRYANT, who was nearly a year older, about the same time published in the "North American Review" his noble poem of "Thanatopsis." COLEMAN gave HALLECK'S lines to the printer as soon as he had read them, which was a great compliment for so fastidious an editor. He did not ascertain who wrote them for several months, and the author in the mean while had become so much of a literary lion that he then reprinted them with a preface asserting their merits.

One evening in the spring of 1819, as HALLECK was on the way home from his place of business, he stopped at a coffee-house then much frequented by young men, in the vicinity of Columbia College. A shower has just fallen, and a brilliant sunset was distinguished by a rainbow of unusual magnificence. In the group about the door, half a dozen had told what they would wish could their wishes be realized, when HALLECK, said, looking at the glorious spectacle above the horizon, "If I could have my wish, it should be to lie in the lap of that rainbow, and read Tom Campbell." A handsome young fellow, standing near, suddenly turned to him and exclaimed, "You and I must be acquainted: my name is DRAKE;" and from that hour till his death JOSEPH RODMAN DRAKE and FITZ-GREENE HALLECK were united in a most fraternal intimacy.

DRAKE had already written the first four of the once-celebrated series of humorous and satirical odes known as the "Croaker Pieces," and they had been published in the "Evening Post." He now made HALLECK a partner, and the remaining numbers were signed "Croaker & Co." The last one written by DRAKE was "The American Flag," printed on the twenty-ninth of May, and the last of the series, "Curtain Conversations," was furnished by HALLECK, on the twenty-fourth of the following July. These pieces related to scenes and events with which most readers in New York were familiar; they were written with great spirit and good-humour, and the curiosity of the town was excited to learn who were their authors; but the young poets kept their secret, and were unsuspected, while their clever performances were from time to time attributed to various well-known literary men. Near the close of the year HALLECK wrote in the same vein his longest poem, "Fanny," a playful satire of the fashions, follies, and public characters of the day. It contains from twelve to fifteen hundred lines, and was completed and printed within three weeks from its commencement.

The next year DRAKE died, of consumption, and HALLECK mourned his loss in those beautiful tributary verses which appeared soon after in the "Scientific Repository and Critical Review," beginning—

"Green be the turf above thee,
Friend of my better days;
None knew thee but to love thee,
None named thee but to praise."

In 1822 and 1823 our author visited Great Britain and the continent of Europe. Among the souvenirs of his travels are two of his finest poems, "Burns," and "Alnwick Castle," which, with a few other pieces, he gave to the public in a small volume in 1827. His fame was now established, and he has ever since been regarded as one of the truest of our poets, and in New York, where his personal qualities, are best known, and his poems, from their local allusions, are read by everybody, he has enjoyed perpetual and almost unexampled popularity.

He was once, as he informs us in one of his witty and graceful epistles, "in the cotton trade and sugar line," but for many years before the death of the late JOHN JACOB ASTOR, he was the principal superintendent of the extensive affairs of that great capitalist. Since then he has resided chiefly in his native town, in Connecticut. He frequently visits New York, however, and the fondness and enthusiasm with which his name is cherished by his old associates was happily illustrated in the beginning of 1854 by a complimentary dinner which was then given him by members of the Century Club.

It was Lord BYRON'S opinion that a poet is always to be ranked according to his execution, and not according to his branch of the art. "The poet who executes best," said he, "is the highest, whatever his department, and will be so rated in the world's esteem." We have no doubt of the justness of that remark; it is the only principle from which sound criticism can proceed, and upon this basis the reputations of the past have been made up. Considered in this light, Mr. HALLECK must be pronounced not merely one of the chief ornaments of a new literature, but one of the great masters in a language classical and immortal for the productions of genius which have illustrated and enlarged its capacities. There is in his compositions an essential pervading grace, a natural brilliancy of wit, a freedom yet refinement of sentiment, a sparkling flow of fancy, and a power of personification, combined with such high and careful finish, and such exquisite nicety of taste, that the larger part of them must be regarded as models almost faultless in the classes to which they belong. They appear to me to show a genuine insight into the principles of art, and a fine use of its resources; and after all that has been written about nature, strength, and originality, the true secret of fame, the real magic of genius, is not force, not passion, not novelty, but art. Look all through MILTON: look at the best passages of SHAKSPEARE; look at the monuments, "all Greek and glorious," which have come down to us from ancient times: what strikes us principally, and it might almost be said only, is the wonderfully artificial character of the composition; it is the principle of their immortality, and without it no poem can be long-lived. It may be easy to acquire popularity, and easy to display art in writing, but he who obtains popularity by the means and employment of careful and elaborate art, may be confident that his reputation is fixed upon a sure basis. This—for his careless playing with the muse by which he once kept the town alive, is scarcely remembered now—this, it seems to me, Mr. HALLECK has done.

EXTRACT FROM "THE RECORDER."

PETER CASTALY COMPARETH THE RECORDER WITH JULIUS CÆSAR AND WITH HIMSELF.

MY dear RECORDER, you and I
  Have floated down life's stream together,
And kept unharmed our friendship's tie
Through every change of Fortune's sky,
  Her pleasant and her rainy weather.
Full sixty times since first we met,
Our birthday suns have risen and set,
And time has worn the baldness now
Of JULIUS CÆSAR on your brow, ...
Whose laurel harvests long have shown
As green and glorious as his own. ....
Both eloquent and learned and brave,
  Born to command and skilled to rule,
One made the citizen a slave,
  The other makes him more—a fool.
The CÆSAR an imperial crown,
  His slaves' mad gift, refused to wear,
The RIKER put his fool's cap on,
  And found it fitted to a hair. ....
The CÆSAR passed the Rubicon
With helm, and shield, and breastplate on,
  Dashing his warhorse through the waters;
The RIKER would have built a barge
Or steamboat at the city's charge,
  And passed it with his wife and daughters.
But let that pass. As I have said,
There's naught, save laurels, on your head,
And time has changed my clustering hair,
And showered snow-flakes thickly there;
And though our lives have ever been,
As different as their different scene;
Mine more renowned for rhymes than riches,
Yours less for scholarship than speeches;
Mine passed in low-roof'd leafy bower,
Yours in high halls of pomp and power,
Yet are we, be the moral told,
Alike in one thing—growing old.

EXTRACT FROM "FANNY."

WEEHAWKEN.

WEHAWKEN! in thy mountain scenery yet,
  All we adore of nature in her wild
And frolic hour of infancy is met;
  And never has a summer's morning smiled
Upon a lovelier scene than the full eye
Of the enthusiast revels on—when high

Amid thy forest solitudes, he climbs
  O'er crags, that proudly tower above the deep,
And knows that sense of danger which sublimes
  The breathless moment—when his daring step
Is on the verge of the cliff, and he can hear
The low dash of the wave, with startled ear,

Like the death music of his coming doom,
  And clings to the green turf with desperate force,
As the heart clings to life; and when resume
  The currents in their veins their wonted course,
There lingers a deep feeling—like the moan
Of wearied ocean, when the storm is gone.

In such an hour he turns, and on his view,
  Ocean, and earth, and heaven, burst before him;
Clouds slumbering at his feet, and the clear blue
  Of summer's sky in beauty bending o'er him—
The city bright below; and far away,
Sparkling in golden light, his own romantic bay

Tall spire, and glittering roof, and battlement,
  And banners floating in the sunny air;
And white sails o'er the calm blue waters bent,
  Green isle, and circling shore, are blended there
In wild reality. When life is old,
And many a scene forgot, the heart will hold

Its memory of this; nor lives there one
  Whose infant breath was drawn, or boyhood's days
Of happiness were passed, beneath that sun,
  That in his manhood's prime can calmly gaze
Upon that bay, or on that mountain stand,
Nor feel the prouder of his native land.

BURNS.

TO A ROSE, BROUGHT FROM NEAR ALLOWAY KIRK, IN AYRSHIRE, IN THE AUTUMN OF 1822.

Wild rose of Alloway! my thanks,
  Thou mindst me of that autumn noon,
When first we met upon "the banks
  And braes o' bonny Doon."

Like thine, beneath the thorn tree's bough,
  My sunny hour was glad and brief,
We've cross'd the winter sea, and thou
  Art wither'd—flower and leaf.

And will not thy death-doom be mine—
  The doom of all things wrought of clay—
And wither'd my life's leaf, like thine,
  Wild rose of Alloway!

Not so his memory, for whose sake
  My bosom bore thee far and long,
His, who an humbler flower could make
  Immortal as his song.

The memory of Burns—a name
  That calls, when brimm'd her festal cup,
A nation's glory, and her shame,
  In silent sadness up.

A nation's glory—be the rest
  Forgot—she's canonized his mind;
And it is joy to speak the best
  We may of human kind.

I've stood beside the cottage-bed
  Where the bard-peasant first drew breath:
A straw-thatch'd roof above his head,
  A straw-wrought couch beneath.

And I have stood beside the pile,
  His monument—that tells to heaven
The homage of earth's proudest isle,
  To that bard-peasant given.

Bid thy thoughts hover o'er that spot,
  Boy-minstrel, in thy dreaming hour;
And know, however low his lot,
  A poet's pride and power.

The pride that lifted Burns from earth,
  The power that gave a child of song
Ascendency o'er rank and birth,
  The rich, the brave, the strong;

And if despondency weigh down
  Thy spirit's fluttering pinions then,
Despair—thy name is written on
  The roll of common men.

There have been loftier themes than his,
  And longer scrolls, and louder lyres,
And lays lit up with Poesy's
  Purer and holier fires:

Yet read the names that know not death;
  Few nobler ones than Burns are there;
And few have won a greener wreath
  Than that which binds his hair.

His is that language of the heart,
  In which the answering heart would speak,
Thought, word, that bids the warm tear start,
  Or the smile light the cheek.

And his that music, to whose tone
  The common pulse of man keeps time,
In cot or castle's mirth or moan,
  In cold or sunny clime.

And who hath heard his song, nor knelt
  Before its spell with willing knee,
And listen'd, and believed, and felt
  The poet's mastery.

O'er the mind's sea, in calm and storm,
  O'er the heart's sunshine and its showers,
O'er Passion's moments, bright and warm,
  O'er Reason's dark, cold hours;

On fields where brave men "die or do,"
  In halls where rings the banquet's mirth,
Where mourners weep, where lovers woo,
  From throne to cottage hearth;

What sweet tears dim the eyes unshed,
  What wild vows falter on the tongue,
When "Scots wha hae wi' Wallace bled,"
  Or "Auld Lang Syne" is sung!

Pure hopes, that lift the soul above,
  Come with his Cotter's hymn of praise,
And dreams of youth, and truth, and love,
  With "Logan's" banks and braes.

And when he breathes his master-lay
  Of Alloway's witch-haunted wall,
All passions in our frames of clay
  Come thronging at his call.

Imagination's world of air,
  And our own world, its gloom and glee,
Wit, pathos, poetry, are there,
  And death's sublimity.

And Burns—though brief the race he ran,
  Though rough and dark the path he trod—
Lived—died—in form and soul a man,
  The image of his God.

Though care, and pain, and want, and wo,
  With wounds that only death could heal,
Tortures—the poor alone can know,
  The proud alone can feel;

He kept his honesty and truth,
  His independent tongue and pen,
And moved, in manhood and in youth,
  Pride of his fellow-men.

Strong sense, deep feeling, passions strong,
  A hate of tyrant and of knave,
A love of right, a scorn of wrong,
  Of coward, and of slave;

A kind, true heart, a spirit high,
  That could not fear and would not bow,
Were written in his manly eye,
  And on his manly brow.

Praise to the bard! his words are driven,
Like flower-seeds by the far winds sown,
Where'er, beneath the sky of heaven,
The birds of fame have flown.

Praise to the man! a nation stood
Beside his coffin with wet eyes,
Her brave, her beautiful, her good,
As when a loved one dies.

And still, as on his funeral day,
Men stand his cold earth-couch around,
With the mute homage that we pay
To consecrated ground.

And consecrated ground it is,
The last, the hallow'd home of one
Who lives upon all memories,
Though with the buried gone.

Such graves as his are pilgrim-shrines,
Shrines to no code or creed confined—
The Delphian vales, the Palestines,
The Meccas of the mind.

Sages, with Wisdom's garland wreathed,
Crown'd kings, and mitred priests of power,
And warriors with their bright swords sheathed,
The mightiest of the hour;

And lowlier names, whose humble home
Is lit by Fortune's dimmer star,
Are there—o'er wave and mountain come,
From countries near and far;

Pilgrims, whose wandering feet have press'd
The Switzer's snow, the Arab's sand,
Or trod the piled leaves of the west,
My own green forest-land;

All ask the cottage of his birth,
Gaze on the scenes he loved and sung,
And gather feelings not of earth
His fields and streams among.

They linger by the Doon's low trees,
And pastoral Nith, and wooded Ayr,
And round thy sepulchres, Dumfries!
The poet's tomb is there.

But what to them the sculptor's art,
His funeral columns, wreaths, and urns?
Wear they not graven on the heart
The name of ROBERT BURNS?

RED JACKET,

A CHIEF OF THE INDIAN TRIBES, THE TUSCARORAS.

COOPER, whose name is with his country's woven,
First in her files, her PIONEER of mind,
A wanderer now in other climes, has proven
His love for the young land he left behind;

And throned her in the senate hall of nations,
Robed like the deluge rainbow, heaven-wrought,
Magnificent as his own mind's creations,
And beautiful as its green world of thought.

And faithful to the act of Congress, quoted
As law-authority—it pass'd nem. con.—
He writes that we are, as ourselves have voted,
The most enlighten'd people ever known.

That all our week is happy as a Sunday
In Paris, full of song, and dance, and laugh;
And that, from Orleans to the bay of Fundy,
There's not a bailiff nor an epitaph.

And, furthermore, in fifty years or sooner,
We shall export our poetry and wine;
And our brave fleet, eight frigates and a schooner
Will sweep the seas from Zembla to the line.

If he were with me, King of Tuscarora,
Gazing as I, upon thy portrait now,
In all its medall'd, fringed, and beaded glory,
Its eyes' dark beauty, and its thoughtful brow—

Its brow, half-martial and half-diplomatic,
Its eye, upsoaring, like an eagle's wings;
Well might he boast that we, the democratic,
Outrival Europe—even in our kings;

For thou wert monarch born. Tradition's pages
Tell not the planting of thy parent tree,
But that the forest-tribes have bent for ages
To thee, and to thy sires, the subject knee.

Thy name is princely. Though no poet's magic
Could make RED JACKET grace an English rhyme,
Unless he had a genius for the tragic,
And introduced it in a pantomime;

Yet it is music in the language spoken
Of thine own land; and on her herald-roll,
As nobly fought for, and as proud a token
As CŒUR DE LION'S, of a warrior's soul.

Thy garb—though Austria's bosom-star would frighten
That medal pale, as diamonds the dark mine,
And GEORGE the FOURTH wore, in the dance at Brighton,
A more becoming evening dress than thine;

Yet 'tis a brave one, scorning wind and weather,
And fitted for thy couch on field and flood,
As ROB ROY'S tartans for the highland heather,
Or forest-green for England's ROBIN HOOD.

Is strength a monarch's merit? (like a whaler's)
Thou art as tall, as sinewy, and as strong
As earth's first kings—the Argo's gallant sailors,
Heroes in history, and gods in song.

Is eloquence? Her spell is thine that reaches
The heart, and makes the wisest head its sport,
And there's one rare, strange virtue in thy speeches,
The secret of their mastery—they are short.

Is beauty? Thine has with thy youth departed,
But the love-legends of thy manhood's years,
And she who perish'd, young and broken-hearted,
Are—but I rhyme for smiles, and not for tears.

The monarch mind—the mystery of commanding,
The godlike power, the art NAPOLEON,
Of winning, fettering, moulding, wielding, banding
The hearts of millions till they move as one;

Thou hast it. At thy bidding men have crowded
The road to death as to a festival;
And minstrel minds, without a blush, have shrouded
With banner-folds of glory their dark pall.

Who will believe—not I—for in deceiving,
Lies the dear charm of life's delightful dream;
I cannot spare the luxury of believing
That all things beautiful are what they seem.

Who will believe that, with a smile whose blessing
Would, like the patriarch's, soothe a dying hour;
With voice as low, as gentle, and caressing
As e'er won maiden's lip in moonlight bower;

With look, like patient Job's, eschewing evil;
With motions graceful as a bird's in air;
Thou art, in sober truth, the veriest devil
That e'er clinch'd fingers in a captive's hair?

That in thy veins there springs a poison fountain,
Deadlier than that which bathes the upas-tree;
And in thy wrath, a nursing cat o' mountain
Is calm as her babe's sleep compared with thee?

And underneath that face like summer's ocean's,
Its lip as moveless, and its cheek as clear,
Slumbers a whirlwind of the heart's emotions,
Love, hatred, pride, hope, sorrow—all, save fear.

Love—for thy land, as if she were thy daughter,
Her pipes in peace, her tomahawk in wars;
Hatred—of missionaries and cold water;
Pride—in thy rifle-trophies and thy scars;

Hope—that thy wrongs will be by the Great Spirit
Remember'd and revenged when thou art gone;
Sorrow—that none are left thee to inherit
Thy name, thy fame, thy passions, and thy throne.

CONNECTICUT.

And still her gray rocks tower above the sea
That murmurs at their feet, a conquer'd wave;
'Tis a rough land of earth, and stone, and tree,
Where breathes no castled lord or cabin'd slave;
Where thoughts, and tongues, and hands are bold and free,
And friends will find a welcome, foes a grave;
And where none kneel, save when to Heaven they pray,
Nor even then, unless in their own way.

Theirs is a pure republic, wild, yet strong,
A "fierce democracie," where all are true
To what themselves have voted—right or wrong—
And to their laws, denominated blue;
(If red, they might to Draco's code belong;)
A vestal state, which power could not subdue,
Nor promise win—like her own eagle's nest,
Sacred—the San Marino of the west.

A justice of the peace, for the time being,
They bow to, but may turn him out next year:
They reverence their priest, but, disagreeing
In price or creed, dismiss him without fear;
They have a natural talent for foreseeing
And knowing all things; and should Park appear
From his long tour in Africa, to show
The Niger's source, they'd meet him with—We know.

They love their land, because it is their own,
And scorn to give aught other reason why;
Would shake hands with a king upon his throne,
And think it kindness to his majesty;
A stubborn race, fearing and flattering none.
Such are they nurtured, such they live and die:
All—but a few apostates, who are meddling
With merchandise, pounds, shillings, pence, and peddling;

Or, wandering through the southern countries, teaching
The A B C from Webster's spelling-book;
Gallant and godly, making love and preaching,
And gaining, by what they call "hook and crook,"
And what the moralists call overreaching,
A decent living. The Virginians look
Upon them with as favourable eyes
As Gabriel on the devil in Paradise.

But these are but their outcasts. View them near
At home, where all their worth and pride is placed;
And there their hospitable fires burn clear,
And there the lowliest farm-house hearth is graced
With manly hearts, in piety sincere,
Faithful in love, in honour stern and chaste,
In friendship warm and true, in danger brave,
Beloved in life, and sainted in the grave.

And minds have there been nurtured, whose control
Is felt even in their nation's destiny;
Men who sway'd senates with a statesman's soul,
And look'd on armies with a leader's eye;
Names that adorn and dignify the scroll
Whose leaves contain their country's history.

. . . .

Hers are not Tempe's nor Arcadia's spring,
Nor the long summer of Cathayan vales,
The vines, the flowers, the air, the skies, that fling
Such wild enchantment o'er Boccaccio's tales
Of Florence and the Arno—yet the wing
Of life's best angel, health, is on her gales
Through sun and snow—and, in the autumn time,
Earth has no purer and no lovelier clime.

Her clear, warm heaven at noon,—the mist that shrouds
Her twilight hills,—her cool and starry eves,
The glorious splendour of her sunset clouds,
The rainbow beauty of her forest leaves,
Come o'er the eye, in solitude and crowds,
Where'er his web of song her poet weaves;
And his mind's brightest vision but displays
The autumn scenery of his boyhood's days.

And when you dream of woman, and her love
Her truth, her tenderness, her gentle power;
The maiden, listening in the moonlight grove;
The mother, smiling in her infant's bower;
Forms, features, worshipp'd while we breathe or move,
Be, by some spirit of your dreaming hour,
Borne, like Loretto's chapel, through the air
To the green land I sing, then wake; you'll find them there.

ALNWICK CASTLE.

Home of the Percy's high-born race,
  Home of their beautiful and brave,
Alike their birth and burial place,
  Their cradle and their grave!
Still sternly o'er the castle gate
Their house's Lion stands in state,
  As in his proud departed hours;
And warriors frown in stone on high,
And feudal banners "flout the sky"
  Above his princely towers.

A gentle hill its side inclines,
  Lovely in England's fadeless green,
To meet the quiet stream which winds
  Through this romantic scene
As silently and sweetly still,
As when, at evening, on that hill,
  While summer's wind blew soft and low,
Seated by gallant Hotspur's side,
His Katharine was a happy bride,
  A thousand years ago.

Gaze on the Abbey's ruin'd pile:
  Does not the succouring ivy, keeping
Her watch around it, seem to smile,
  As o'er a loved one sleeping?

One solitary turret gray
  Still tells, in melancholy glory,
The legend of the Cheviot day,
  The Percy's proudest border story.
That day its roof was triumph's arch;
  Then rang, from aisle to pictured dome,
The light step of the soldier's march,
  The music of the trump and drum;
And babe, and sire, the old, the young,
And the monk's hymn, and minstrel's song,
And woman's pure kiss, sweet and long,
  Welcomed her warrior home.

Wild roses by the abbey towers
  Are gay in their young bud and bloom:
They were born of a race of funeral flowers
That garlanded, in long-gone hours,
  A Templar's knightly tomb.
He died, the sword in his mailed hand,
On the holiest spot of the Blessed Land,
  Where the Cross was damp'd with his dying
    breath,
When blood ran free as festal wine,
And the sainted air of Palestine
  Was thick with the darts of death.

Wise with the lore of centuries,
What tales, if there be "tongues in trees,"
  Those giant oaks could tell,
Of beings born and buried here;
Tales of the peasant and the peer,
Tales of the bridal and the bier,
  The welcome and farewell,
Since on their boughs the startled bird
First, in her twilight slumbers, heard
  The Norman's curfew-bell.

I wander'd through the lofty halls
  Trod by the Percys of old fame,
And traced upon the chapel walls
  Each high, heroic name,
From him who once his standard set
Where now, o'er mosque and minaret,
  Glitter the Sultan's crescent moons;
To him who, when a younger son,
Fought for King George at Lexington,
  A major of dragoons.
* * * * *

That last half stanza—it has dash'd
  From my warm lip the sparkling cup;
The light that o'er my eyebeam flash'd,
  The power that bore my spirit up
Above this bank-note world—is gone;
And Alnwick's but a market town,
And this, alas! its market day,
And beasts and borderers throng the way;
Oxen and bleating lambs in lots,
Northumbrian boors and plaided Scots,
  Men in the coal and cattle line;
From Teviot's bard and hero land,
From royal Berwick's beach of sand,
From Wooler, Morpeth, Hexham, and
  Newcastle-upon-Tyne.

These are not the romantic times
So beautiful in Spenser's rhymes,
  So dazzling to the dreaming boy:
Ours are the days of fact, not fable,
Of knights, but not of the Round Table,
  Of Bailie Jarvie, not Rob Roy:
'Tis what "our President," Monroe,
  Has call'd "the era of good feeling:"
The Highlander, the bitterest foe
To modern laws, has felt their blow,
Consented to be taxed, and vote,
And put on pantaloons and coat,
  And leave off cattle-stealing;
Lord Stafford mines for coal and salt,
The Duke of Norfolk deals in malt,
  The Douglas in red herrings:
And noble name and cultured land,
Palace, and park, and vassal band,
Are powerless to the notes of hand
  Of Rothschild or the Barings.

The age of bargaining, said Burke,
Has come: to-day the turban'd Turk
(Sleep, Richard of the lion heart!
Sleep on, nor from your cerements start)
  Is England's friend and fast ally;
The Moslem tramples on the Greek,
  And on the Cross and altar stone,
  And Christendom looks tamely on,
And hears the Christian maiden shriek,
  And sees the Christian father die:
And not a sabre blow is given
For Greece and fame, for faith and heaven,
  By Europe's craven chivalry.

You'll ask if yet the Percy lives
  In the arm'd pomp of feudal state?
The present representatives
  Of Hotspur and his "gentle Kate,"
Are some half-dozen serving men,
In the drab coat of William Penn;

A chambermaid, whose lip and eye,
And cheek, and brown hair, bright and curling,
Spoke nature's aristocracy;
And one, half groom, half seneschal,
Who bow'd me through court, bower, and hall,
From donjon-keep to turret wall,
For ten-and-sixpence sterling.

MAGDALEN.

A sword, whose olade has ne'er been wet
With blood, except of freedom's foes;
That hope which, though its sun be set,
Still with a starlight beauty glows;
A heart that worshipp'd in Romance
The Spirit of the buried Time,
And dreams of knight, and steed, and lance,
And ladye-love, and minstrel-rhyme;
These had been, and I deemed would 'e
My joy, whate'er my destiny.

Born in a camp, its watch-fires bright
Alone illumed my cradle-bed;
And I had borne with wild delight
My banner where Bolivar led,
Ere manhood's hue was on my cheek,
Or manhood's pride was on my brow.
Its folds are furl'd—the war-bird's beak
Is thirsty on the Andes now;
I long'd, like her, for other skies
Clouded by Glory's sacrifice.

In Greece, the brave heart's Holy Land,
Its soldier-song the bugle sings;
And I had buckled on my brand,
And waited but the sea wind's wings,
To bear me where, or lost or won
Her battle, in its frown or smile,
Men live with those of Marathon,
Or die with those of Scio's isle;
And find in Valour's tent or tomb,
In life or death, a glorious home.

I could have left but yesterday
The scene of my boy-years behind,
And floated on my careless way
Wherever will'd the breathing wind.
I could have bade adieu to aught
I've sought, or met, or welcomed here,
Without an hour of shaded thought,
A sigh, a murmur, or a tear.
Such was I yesterday—but then
I had not known thee, Magdalen.

To-day there is a change within me,
There is a weight upon my brow,
And Fame, whose whispers once could win me
From all I loved, is powerless now.
There ever is a form, a face
Of maiden beauty in my dreams,
Speeding before me, like the race
To ocean of the mot tain streams—
With dancing hair, and laughing eyes,
That seem to mock me as it flies.

My sword—it slumbers in its sheath;
My hopes—their starry light is gone;
My heart—the fabled clock of death,
Beats with the same low, lingering tone:
And this, the land of Magdalen,
Seems now the only spot on earth
Where skies are blue and flowers are green
And here I'd build my household hearth,
And breathe my song of joy, and twine
A lovely being's name with mine.

In vain! in vain! the sail is spread;
To sea! to sea! my task is there;
But when among the unmourned dead
They lay me, and the ocean air
Brings tidings of my day of doom,
Mayst thou be then, as now thou art,
The load-star of a happy home;
In smile and voice, in eye and heart
The same as thou hast ever been,
The loved, the lovely Magdalen.

TWILIGHT.

There is an evening twilight of the heart,
When its wild passion-waves are lull'd to rest,
And the eye sees life's fairy scenes depart,
As fades the day-beam in the rosy west.
'Tis with a nameless feeling of regret
We gaze upon them as they melt away,
And fondly would we bid them linger yet,
But hope is round us with her angel lay,
Hailing afar some happier moonlight hour;
Dear are her whispers still, though lost their early power.

In youth the cheek was crimson'd with her glow;
Her smile was loveliest then; her matin song
Was heaven's own music, and the note of wo
Was all unheard her sunny bowers among.
Life's little world of bliss was newly born;
We knew not, cared not, it was born to die,
Flush'd with the cool breeze and the dews of morn,
With dancing heart we gazed on the pure sky,
And mock'd the passing clouds that dimm'd its blue,
Like our own sorrows then—as fleeting and as few.

And manhood felt her sway too—on the eye,
Half realized, her early dreams burst bright,
Her promised bower of happiness seem'd nigh,
Its days of joy, its vigils of delight;
And though at times might lower the thunder-storm,
And the red lightnings threaten, still the air
Was balmy with her breath, and her loved form,
The rainbow of the heart, was hovering there.
'Tis in life's noontide she is nearest seen, [green.
Her wreath the summer flower, her robe of summer

But though less dazzling in her twilight dress,
There's more of heaven's pure beam about her
That angel-smile of tranquil loveliness, [now;
Which the heart worships, glowing on her brow,
That smile shall brighten the dim evening star
That points our destined tomb, nor e'er depart
Till the faint light of life is fled afar,
And hush'd the last deep beating of the heart
The meteor bearer of our parting breath,
A moonbeam in the midnight cloud of death.

MARCO BOZZARIS.*

At midnight, in his guarded tent,
The Turk was dreaming of the hour
When Greece, her knee in suppliance bent,
Should tremble at his power:
In dreams, through camp and court, he bore
The trophies of a conqueror;
In dreams his song of triumph heard;
Then wore his monarch's signet-ring:
Then press'd that monarch's throne—a king.
As wild his thoughts, and gay of wing,
As Eden's garden-bird.

At midnight, in the forest shades,
Bozzaris ranged his Suliote band,
True as the steel of their tried blades,
Heroes in heart and hand.
There had the Persian's thousands stood,
There had the glad earth drunk their bloo
On old Platæa's day;
And now there breathed that haunted air
The sons of sires who conquer'd there,
With arm to strike, and soul to dare,
As quick, as far as they.

An hour pass'd on—the Turk awoke;
That bright dream was his last;
He awoke—to hear his sentries shriek,
"To arms! they come! the Greek! the Greek
He woke—to die midst flame, and smoke,
And shout, and groan, and sabre-stroke,
And death-shots falling thick and fast
As lightnings from the mountain-cloud;
And heard, with voice as trumpet loud,
Bozzaris cheer his band:
"Strike—till the last arm'd foe expires;
Strike—for your altars and your fires;
Strike—for the green graves of your sires;
God—and your native land!"

They fought—like brave men, long and well;
They piled that ground with Moslem slain;
They conquer'd—but Bozzaris fell,
Bleeding at every vein.
His few surviving comrades saw
His smile when rang their proud hurrah,
And the red field was won:
Then saw in death his eyelids close
Calmly, as to a night's repose,
Like flowers at set of sun.

Come to the bridal chamber, Death!
Come to the mother's, when she feels,
For the first time, her firstborn's breath;
Come when the blessed seals
That close the pestilence are broke,
And crowded cities wail its stroke;
Come in consumption's ghastly form,
The earthquake shock, the ocean-storm,
Come when the heart beats high and warm,
With banquet-song, and dance, and wine:
And thou art terrible—the tear,
The groan, the knell, the pall, the bier;
And all we know, or dream, or fear
Of agony, are thine.

But to the hero, when his sword
Has won the battle for the free,
Thy voice sounds like a prophet's word;
And in its hollow tones are heard
The thanks of millions yet to be.
Come, when his task of fame is wrought—
Come, with her laurel-leaf, blood-bought—
Come in her crowning hour—and then
Thy sunken eye's unearthly light
To him is welcome as the sight
Of sky and stars to prison'd men:
Thy grasp is welcome as the hand
Of brother in a foreign land;
Thy summons welcome as the cry
That told the Indian isles were nigh
To the world-seeking Genoese,
When the land-wind, from woods of palm,
And orange-groves, and fields of balm,
Blew o'er the Haytian seas.

Bozzaris! with the storied brave
Greece nurtured in her glory's time,
Rest thee—there is no prouder grave,
Even in her own proud clime.
She wore no funeral weeds for thee,
Nor bade the dark hearse wave its plume,
Like torn branch from death's leafless tree,
In sorrow's pomp and pageantry,
The heartless luxury of the tomb:
But she remembers thee as one
Long loved, and for a season gone;
For thee her poet's lyre is wreathed,
Her marble wrought, her music breathed;
For thee she rings the birthday bells;
Of thee her babes' first lisping tells:
For thine her evening prayer is said
At palace couch, and cottage bed;
Her soldier, closing with the foe,
Gives for thy sake a deadlier blow;
His plighted maiden, when she fears
For him, the joy of her young years,
Thinks of thy fate, and checks her tears:
And she, the mother of thy boys,
Though in her eye and faded cheek
Is read the grief she will not speak,
The memory of her buried joys,
And even she who gave thee birth,
Will, by their pilgrim-circled hearth,
Talk of thy doom without a sigh:
For thou art Freedom's now, and Fame's,
One of the few, the immortal names,
That were not [illegible] to die.

* He fell in an attack upon the Turkish camp at Laspi, the site of the ancient Platæa, August 20, 1823, and expired in the moment of victory. His last words were: "To die for liberty is a pleasure, not a pain."

James G. Percival

JAMES GATES PERCIVAL.

[Born 1795. Died 1856.]

MR. PERCIVAL was born in Berlin, near Hartford, in Connecticut, on the fifteenth of September, 1795. His father, an intelligent physician, died in 1807, and he was committed to the care of a guardian. His instruction continued to be carefully attended to, however, and when fifteen years of age he entered Yale College. The condition of his health, which had been impaired by too close application to study, rendered necessary a temporary removal from New Haven, but after an absence of about a year he returned, and in 1815 graduated with the reputation of being the first scholar of his class. He subsequently entered the Yale Medical School, and in 1820 received the degree of Doctor of Medicine.

He began to write verses at an early age, and in his fourteenth year is said to have produced a satire in aim and execution not unlike Mr. BRYANT's "Embargo." In the last year of his college life he composed a dramatic piece to be spoken by some of the students at the annual commencement, which was afterwards enlarged and printed under the title of "Zamor, a Tragedy." He did not appear as an author before the public, however, until 1821, when he published at New Haven, with some minor poems, the first part of his "Prometheus," which attracted considerable attention, and was favourably noticed in an article by Mr. EDWARD EVERETT, in the North American Review.

In 1822 he published two volumes of miscellaneous poems and prose writings under the title of "Clio," the first at Charleston, South Carolina, and the second at New Haven. They contain "Consumption," "The Coral Grove," and other pieces which have been regarded as among the finest of his works. In the same year they were followed by an oration, previously delivered before the Phi Beta Kappa Society of Yale College, "On Some of the Moral and Political truths Derivable from History," and the second part of "Prometheus." The whole of this poem contains nearly four hundred stanzas in the Spenserian measure. An edition of his principal poetical writings, embracing a few original pieces, appeared soon after in New York and was reprinted in London.

In 1824 Dr. PERCIVAL was appointed an assistant-surgeon in the army, and stationed at West Point with orders to act as Professor of Chemistry in the Military Academy. He had supposed that the duties of the office were so light as to allow him abundant leisure for the pursuit of his favourite studies, and when undeceived by the experience of a few months, he resigned his commission and went to Boston, where he passed in various literary avocations the greater portion of the year 1825. In this period he wrote his poem on the mind, in which he intimates that its highest office is the creation of beauty, and that there are certain unchanging principles of taste, to which all works of art, all "linked sounds of most elaborate music," must be conformable, to give more than a feeble and transient pleasure.

Early in 1827 he published in New York the third volume of "Clio," and was afterwards engaged nearly two years in superintending the printing of the first quarto edition of Dr. WEBSTER's American Dictionary, a service for which he was eminently qualified by an extensive and critical acquaintance with ancient and modern languages. His next work was a new translation of MALTE-BRUN's Geography, from the French, which was not completed until 1843.

From his boyhood Dr. PERCIVAL has been an earnest and constant student, and there are few branches of learning with which he is not familiar. Perhaps there is not in the country a man of more thorough and comprehensive scholarship. In 1835 he was employed by the government of Connecticut to make a geological survey of that state, which he had already very carefully explored on his own account. His Report on the subject, which is very able and elaborate, was printed in an octavo volume of nearly five hundred pages, in 1842. While engaged in these duties he published poetical translations from the Polish, Russian, Servian, Bohemian, German, Dutch, Danish, Swedish, Italian, Spanish, and Portuguese languages, and wrote a considerable portion of "The Dream of Day and other Poems," which appeared at New Haven in 1843. This is his last volume; it embraces more than one hundred and fifty varieties of measure, and its contents generally show his familiar acquaintance with the poetical art, which in his preface he observes, "requires a mastery of the riches and niceties of a language; a full knowledge of the science of versification, not only in its own peculiar principles of rhythm and melody, but in its relation to elocution and music, with that delicate natural perception and that facile execution which render the composition of verse hardly less easy than that of prose; a deep and quick insight into the nature of man, in all his varied faculties, intellectual and emotive; a clear and full perception of the power and beauty of nature, and of all its various harmonies with our own thoughts and feelings; and, to gain a high rank in the present age, wide and exact attainments in literature and art in general. Nor is the possession of such faculties and attainments all that is necessary; but such a sustained and self-collected state of mind as gives one the mastery of his genius, and at the same time presents to him the ideal as an immediate reality, not as a remote conception."

There are few men who possess these high qualities in a more eminent degree than PERCIVAL; but with the natural qualities of a great poet, and his comprehensive and thorough learning, he lacks the executive skill, or declines the labour, without which few authors gain immortality. He has considerable imagination, remarkable command of language, and writes with a facility rarely equalled; but when his thoughts are once committed to the page, he shrinks from the labour of revising, correcting, and condensing. He remarks in one of his prefaces, that his verse is "very far from bearing the marks of the file and the burnisher," and that he likes to see "poetry in the full ebullition of feeling and fancy, foaming up with the spirit of life, and glowing with the rainbows of a glad inspiration." If by this he means that a poet should reject the slow and laborious process by which a polished excellence is attained, very few who have acquired good reputations will agree with him

CONCLUSION OF THE DREAM OF A DAY.

A SPIRIT stood before me, half unseen,
Majestic and severe; yet o'er him play'd
A genial light—subdued though high his mien,
As by a strong collected spirit sway'd—
In even balance justly poised between
Each wild extreme, proud strength by feeling stay'd—
Dwelling in upper realms serenely bright,
Lifted above the shadowy sphere of night.

He stood before me, and I heard a tone,
Such as from mortal lips had never flow'd,
Soft yet commanding, gentle yet alone,
It bow'd the listener's heart—anon it glow'd
Intensely fervent, then like wood-notes thrown
On the chance winds, in airy lightness rode—
Now swell'd like ocean surge, now pausing fell
Like the last murmur of a muffled bell.

"Lone pilgrim through life's gloom," thus spake the shade,
"Hold on with steady will along thy way:
Thou, by a kindly favouring hand wert made—
Hard though thy lot, yet thine what can repay
Long years of bitter toil—the holy aid
Of spirit aye is thine, be that thy stay:
Thine to behold the true, to feel the pure,
To know the good and lovely—these endure.

Hold on—thou hast in thee thy best reward;
Poor are the largest stores of sordid gain,
If from the heaven of thought thy soul is barr'd,
If the high spirit's bliss is sought in vain:
Think not thy lonely lot is cold or hard,
The world has never bound thee with its chain;
Free as the birds of heaven thy heart can soar,
Thou canst create new worlds—what wouldst thou more?

The future age will know thee—yea, even now
Hearts beat and tremble at thy bidding, tears
Flow as thou movest thy wand, thy word can bow
Even ruder natures, the dull soul uprears
As thou thy trumpet blast attunest—thou
Speakest, and each remotest valley hears:
Thou hast the gift of song—a wealth is thine,
Richer than all the treasures of the mine.

Hold on, glad spirits company thy path—
They minister to thee, though all unseen:
Even when the tempest lifts its voice in wrath,
Thou joyest in its strength; the orient sheen
Gladdens thee with its beauty; winter hath
A holy charm that soothes thee, like the green
Of infant May—all nature is thy friend,
All seasons to thy life enchantment lend.

Man, too, thou know'st and feelest—all the springs
That wake his smile and tear, his joy and sorrow,
All that uplifts him on emotion's wings,
Each longing for a fair and blest to-morrow,
Each tone that soothes or saddens, all that rings
Joyously to him, thou canst fitly borrow
From thy own breast, and blend it in a strain,
To which each human heart beats back again.

Thine the unfetter'd thought, alone controll'd
By nature's truth; thine the wide-seeing eye,
Catching the delicate shades, yet apt to hold
The whole in its embrace—before it lie
Pictured in fairest light, as chart unroll'd,
Fields of the present and of destiny:
The voice of truth amid the senseless throng
May now be lost; 'tis heard and felt ere long.

Hold on—live for the world—live for all time—
Rise in thy conscious power, but gently bear
Thy form among thy fellows; sternly climb
The spirit's alpine peaks; mid snow towers there
Nurse the pure thought, but yet accordant chime
With lowlier hearts in valleys green and fair,—
Sustain thyself—yield to no meaner hand,
Even though he rule awhile thy own dear land.

Brief is his power, oblivion waits the churl
Bound to his own poor self; his form decays,
But sooner fades his name. Thou shalt unfurl
Thy standard to the winds of future days—
Well mayest thou in thy soul defiance hurl
On such who would subdue thee; thou shalt raise
Thy name, when they are dust, and nothing more:
Hold on—in earnest hope still look before.

Nerved to a stern resolve, fulfil thy lot—
Reveal the secrets nature has unveil'd thee;
All higher gifts by toil intense are bought—
Has thy firm will in action ever fail'd thee?
Only on distant summits fame is sought—
Sorrow and gloom thy nature has entail'd thee,
But bright thy present joys, and brighter far
The hope that draws thee like a heavenly star."

The voice was still—its tone in distance dying
Breathed in my ear, like harp faint heard at even,

Soft as the autumn wind through sere leaves sighing
When flaky clouds athwart the moon are driven
Far through the viewless gloom the spirit flying,
Wing'd his high passage to his native heaven,
But o'er me still he seem'd in kindness bending,
Fresh hope and firmer purpose to me lending.

THE POET.

Deep sunk in thought, he sat beside the river—
Its wave in liquid lapses glided by,
Nor watch'd, in crystal depth, his vacant eye
The willow's high o'er-arching foliage quiver.
From dream to shadowy dream returning ever,
He sat, like statue, on the grassy verge;
His thoughts, a phantom train, in airy surge
Stream'd visionary onward, pausing never.
As autumn wind, in mountain forest weaving
Its wondrous tapestry of leaf and bower,
O'ermastering the night's resplendent flower
With tints, like hues of heaven, the eye deceiving—
So, lost in labyrinthine maze, he wove
A wreath of flowers; the golden thread was love.

NIGHT.

Am I not all alone?—The world is still
In passionless slumber—not a tree but feels
The far-pervading hush, and softer steals
The misty river by.—Yon broad bare hill
Looks coldly up to heaven, and all the stars
Seem eyes deep fix'd in silence, as if bound
By some unearthly spell—no other sound
But the owl's unfrequent moan.—Their airy cars
The winds have station'd on the mountain peaks.
Am I not all alone?—A spirit speaks
From the abyss of night, "Not all alone—
Nature is round thee with her banded powers,
And ancient genius haunts thee in these hours—
Mind and its kingdom now are all thy own."

CHORIAMBIC MELODY.

Bear me afar o'er the wave, far to the sacred islands,
Where ever bright blossoms the plain, where no cloud hangs on the highlands—
There be my heart ever at rest, stirr'd by no wild emotion:
There on the earth only repose, halcyon calm on the ocean.

Lay me along, pillow'd on flowers, where steals in silence for ever
Over its sands, still as at noon, far the oblivious river.
Scarce through the grass whispers it by; deep in its wave you may number
Pebble and shell, and image of flower, folded and bent in slumber.

Spirit of life! rather aloft, where on the crest of the mountain,
Clear blow the winds, fresh from the north, sparkles and dashes the fountain,
Lead me along, hot in the chase, still 'mid the storm high glowing—
Only we live—only, when life, like the wild torrent, is flowing.

SAPPHO.

She stands in act to fall—her garland torn,
Its wither'd rose-leaves round the rock are blowing;
Loose to the winds her locks dishevell'd flowing
Tell of the many sorrows she has borne.

Her eye, up-turn'd to heaven, has lost its fire—
One hand is press'd to feel her bosom's beating,
And mark her lingering pulses back retreating—
The other wanders o'er her silent lyre.

Clear rolls the midway sun—she knows it not;
Vainly the winds waft by the flower's perfume;
To her the sky is hung in deepest gloom—
She only feels the noon-beam burning hot.

What to the broken heart the dancing waves,
The air all kindling—what a sounding name?
O! what a mockery, to dream of fame—
It only lures us on to make us slaves.

And Love—O! what art thou with all thy light!
Ineffable joy is round thee, till we know,
Thou art but as a vision of the night—
And then the bursting heart, how deep its wo.

"They tell me I shall live—my name shall rise,
When nature falls—O! blest illusion, stay—"
A moment hopes and joys around her play;
Then darkness hides her—faint she sinks and dies.

THE FESTIVE EVENING.

Cheerful glows the festive chamber;
In the circle pleasure smiles:
Mounts the flame, like wreaths of amber,
Bright as love, its warmth beguiles.
Glad the heart with joy is lighted;
Hand with hand, in faith, is plighted,
As around the goblet flows.
Fill—fill—fill, and quaff the liquid rose!
Bright it glows—
O! how bright the bosom glows.

Pure as light, our social meeting:
Here no passion dares invade.
Joys we know, not light and fleeting:
Flowers we twine, that never fade.
Ours are links, not time can sever:
Brighter still they glow for ever—
Glow in yon eternal day.
No—no—no, ye will not pass away—
Ye will stay—
Social joys, for ever stay!

THE SUN.

Centre of light and energy! thy way
Is through the unknown void; thou hast thy throne,
Morning, and evening, and at noon of day,
Far in the blue, untended and alone:
Ere the first-waken'd airs of earth had blown,
On thou didst march, triumphant in thy light;
Then thou didst send thy glance, which still hath flown
Wide through the never-ending worlds of night,
And yet thy full orb burns with flash as keen and bright.

We call thee Lord of Day, and thou dost give
To earth the fire that animates her crust,
And wakens all the forms that move and live,
From the fine, viewless mould which lurks in dust,
To him who looks to heaven, and on his bust
Bears stamp'd the seal of God, who gathers there
Lines of deep thought, high feeling, daring trust
In his own center'd powers, who aims to share
In all his soul can frame of wide, and great, and fair.

Thy path is high in heaven; we cannot gaze
On the intense of light that girds thy car;
There is a crown of glory in thy rays,
Which bears thy pure divinity afar,
To mingle with the equal light of star,—
For thou, so vast to us, art in the whole
One of the sparks of night that fire the air,
And, as around thy centre planets roll,
So thou, too, hast thy path around the central soul.

I am no fond idolater to thee,
One of the countless multitude, who burn,
As lamps, around the one Eternity,
In whose contending forces systems turn
Their circles round that seat of life, the urn
Where all must sleep, if matter ever dies:
Sight fails me here, but fancy can discern
With the wide glance of her all-seeing eyes,
Where, in the heart of worlds, the ruling Spirit lies.

And thou, too, hast thy world, and unto thee
We are as nothing; thou goest forth alone,
And movest through the wide, aerial sea,
Glad as a conqueror resting on his throne
From a new victory, where he late had shown
Wider his power to nations; so thy light
Comes with new pomp, as if thy strength had grown
With each revolving day, or thou, at night,
Had lit again thy fires, and thus renew'd thy might.

Age o'er thee has no power: thou bring'st the same
Light to renew the morning, as when first,
If not eternal, thou, with front of flame,
On the dark face of earth in glory burst,
And warm'd the seas, and in their bosom nursed
The earliest things of life, the worm and shell;
Till, through the sinking ocean, mountains pierced,
And then came forth the land whereon we dwell,
Rear'd, like a magic fane, above the watery swell.

And there thy searching heat awoke the seeds
Of all that gives a charm to earth, and lends
An energy to nature; all that feeds
On the rich mould, and then, in bearing, bends
Its fruits again to earth, wherein it blends
The last and first of life; of all who bear
Their forms in motion, where the spirit tends,
Instinctive, in their common good to share,
Which lies in things that breathe, or late were living there.

They live in thee: without thee, all were dead
And dark; no beam had lighted on the waste,
But one eternal night around had spread
Funereal gloom, and coldly thus defaced
This Eden, which thy fairy hand hath graced
With such uncounted beauty; all that blows
In the fresh air of spring, and, growing, braced
Its form to manhood, when it stands and glows
In the full-temper'd beam, that gladdens as it goes.

Thou lookest on the earth, and then it smiles;
Thy light is hid, and all things droop and mourn
Laughs the wide sea around her budding isles,
When through their heaven thy changing car is borne;
Thou wheel'st away thy flight, the woods are shorn
Of all their waving locks, and storms awake;
All, that was once so beautiful, is torn
By the wild winds which plough the lonely lake,
And, in their maddening rush, the crested mountains shake.

The earth lies buried in a shroud of snow;
Life lingers, and would die, but thy return
Gives to their gladden'd hearts an overflow
Of all the power that brooded in the urn
Of their chill'd frames, and then they proudly spurn
All bands that would confine, and give to air
Hues, fragrance, shapes of beauty, till they burn,
When, on a dewy morn, thou dartest there
Rich waves of gold to wreathe with fairer light the fair.

The vales are thine; and when the touch of spring
Thrills them, and gives them gladness, in thy light
They glitter, as the glancing swallow's wing
Dashes the water in his winding flight,
And leaves behind a wave that crinkles bright,
And widens outward to the pebbled shore.—
The vales are thine; and when they wake from night,
The dews that bend the grass-tips, twinkling o'er
Their soft and oozy beds, look upward, and adore.

The hills are thine: they catch thy newest beam,
And gladden in thy parting, where the wood
Flames out in every leaf, and drinks the stream,
That flows from out thy fulness, as a flood
Bursts from an unknown land, and rolls the food
Of nations in its waters: so thy rays
Flow and give brighter tints than ever bud,
When a clear sheet of ice reflects a blaze
Of many twinkling gems, as every gloss'd bough plays.

Thine are the mountains, where they purely lift
Snows that have never wasted, in a sky
Which hath no stain; below, the storm may drift
Its darkness, and the thunder-gust roar by;
Aloft in thy eternal smile they lie,
Dazzling, but cold; thy farewell glance looks there;
And when below thy hues of beauty die,
Girt round them, as a rosy belt, they bear,
Into the high, dark vault, a brow that still is fair.

The clouds are thine, and all their magic hues
Are pencill'd by thee; when thou bendest low,
Or comest in thy strength, thy hand imbues
Their waving fold with such a perfect glow
Of all pure tints, the fairy pictures throw
Shame on the proudest art; the tender stain
Hung round the verge of heaven, that as a bow
Girds the wide world, and in their blended chain
All tints to the deep gold that flashes in thy train:

These are thy trophies, and thou bend'st thy arch,
The sign of triumph, in a seven-fold twine,
Where the spent storm is hasting on its march,
And there the glories of thy light combine,
And form with perfect curve a lifted line,
Striding the earth and air; man looks, and tells
How peace and mercy in its beauty shine,
And how the heavenly messenger impels
Her glad wings on the path, that thus in ether swells.

The ocean is thy vassal; thou dost sway
His waves to thy dominion, and they go
Where thou, in heaven, dost guide them on their way,
Rising and falling in eternal flow;
Thou lookest on the waters, and they glow;
They take them wings, and spring aloft in air,
And change to clouds, and then, dissolving, throw
Their treasures back to earth, and, rushing, tear
The mountain and the vale, as proudly on they bear.

I, too, have been upon thy rolling breast,
Widest of waters; I have seen thee lie
Calm, as an infant pillow'd in its rest
On a fond mother's bosom, when the sky,
Not smoother, gave the deep its azure dye,
Till a new heaven was arch'd and glass'd below;
And then the clouds, that, gay in sunset, fly,
Cast on it such a stain, it kindled so,
As in the cheek of youth the living roses grow.

I, too, have seen thee on thy surging path,
When the night-tempest met thee: thou didst dash
Thy white arms high in heaven, as if in wrath,
Threatening the angry sky; thy waves did lash
The labouring vessel, and with deadening crash
Rush madly forth to scourge its groaning sides;
Onward thy billows came, to meet and clash
In a wild warfare, till the lifted tides
Mingled their yesty tops, where the dark storm-cloud rides.

In thee, first light, the bounding ocean smiles,
When the quick winds uprear it in a swell,
That rolls, in glittering green, around the isles,
Where ever-springing fruits and blossoms dwell;
O! with a joy no gifted tongue can tell,
I hurry o'er the waters, when the sail
Swells tensely, and the light keel glances well
Over the curling billow, and the gale
Comes off the spicy groves to tell its winning tale.

The soul is thine: of old thou wert the power
Who gave the poet life; and I in thee
Feel my heart gladden at the holy hour
When thou art sinking in the silent sea;
Or when I climb the height, and wander free
In thy meridian glory, for the air
Sparkles and burns in thy intensity,
I feel thy light within me, and I share
In the full glow of soul thy spirit kindles there.

CONSUMPTION.

There is a sweetness in woman's decay,
When the light of beauty is fading away,
When the bright enchantment of youth is gone.
And the tint that glow'd, and the eye that shone,
And darted around its glance of power,
And the lip that vied with the sweetest flower
That ever in Pæstum's* garden blew,
Or ever was steep'd in fragrant dew,
When all that was bright and fair is fled,
But the loveliness lingering round the dead
O! there is a sweetness in beauty's close,
Like the perfume scenting the wither'd rose;
For a nameless charm around her plays,
And her eyes are kindled with hallow'd rays;
And a veil of spotless purity
Has mantled her cheek with its heavenly dye,
Like a cloud whereon the queen of night
Has pour'd her softest tint of light;
And there is a blending of white and blue,
Where the purple blood is melting through
The snow of her pale and tender cheek;
And there are tones that sweetly speak
Of a spirit who longs for a purer day,
And is ready to wing her flight away.
In the flush of youth, and the spring of feeling,
When life, like a sunny stream, is stealing
Its silent steps through a flowery path,
And all the endearments that pleasure hath
Are pour'd from her full, o'erflowing horn,
When the rose of enjoyment conceals no thorn,
In her lightness of heart, to the cheery song
The maiden may trip in the dance along,
And think of the passing moment, that lies,
Like a fairy dream, in her dazzled eyes,
And yield to the present, that charms around
With all that is lovely in sight and sound;
Where a thousand pleasing phantoms flit,
With the voice of mirth, and the burst of wit
And the music that steals to the bosom's core
And the heart in its fulness flowing o'er
With a few big drops, that are soon repress'd.
For short is the stay of grief in her breast:

* Biferique rosaria Pæsti.—*Virg*

In this enliven'd and gladsome hour
The spirit may burn with a brighter power;
But dearer the calm and quiet day,
When the heaven-sick soul is stealing away.
And when her sun is low declining,
And life wears out with no repining,
And the whisper, that tells of early death,
Is soft as the west wind's balmy breath,
When it comes at the hour of still repose,
To sleep in the breast of the wooing rose:
And the lip, that swell'd with a living glow,
Is pale as a curl of new-fallen snow;
And her cheek, like the Parian stone, is fair,—
But the hectic spot that flushes there
When the tide of life, from its secret dwelling,
In a sudden gush, is deeply swelling,
And giving a tinge to her icy lips,
Like the crimson rose's brightest tips,
As richly red, and as transient too
As the clouds in autumn's sky of blue,
That seem like a host of glory, met
To honour the sun at his golden set;
O! then, when the spirit is taking wing,
How fondly her thoughts to her dear one cling,
As if she would blend her soul with his
In a deep and long-imprinted kiss;
So fondly the panting camel flies,
Where the glassy vapour cheats his eyes;
And the dove from the falcon seeks her nest,
And the infant shrinks to its mother's breast.
And though her dying voice be mute,
Or faint as the tones of an unstrung lute,
And though the glow from her cheek be fled,
And her pale lips cold as the marble dead,
Her eye still beams unwonted fires,
With a woman's love, and a saint's desires,
And her last, fond, lingering look is given
To the love she leaves, and then to heaven,
As if she would bear that love away
To a purer world, and a brighter day.

TO THE EAGLE.

Bird of the broad and sweeping wing,
Thy home is high in heaven,
Where wide the storms their banners fling,
And the tempest clouds are driven.
Thy throne is on the mountain top;
Thy fields, the boundless air;
And hoary peaks, that proudly prop
The skies, thy dwellings are.

Thou sittest like a thing of light,
Amid the noontide blaze:
The midway sun is clear and bright;
It cannot dim thy gaze.
Thy pinions, to the rushing blast,
O'er the bursting billow, spread,
Where the vessel plunges, hurry past,
Like an angel of the dead.

Thou art perch'd aloft on the beetling crag
And the waves are white below,
And on, with a haste that cannot lag,
They rush in an endless flow.

Again thou hast plumed thy wing for flight
To lands beyond the sea,
And away, like a spirit wreathed in light,
Thou hurriest, wild and free.

Thou hurriest over the myriad waves,
And thou leavest them all behind;
Thou sweepest that place of unknown graves,
Fleet as the tempest wind.
When the night-storm gathers dim and dark
With a shrill and boding scream,
Thou rushest by the foundering bark,
Quick as a passing dream.

Lord of the boundless realm of air,
In thy imperial name,
The hearts of the bold and ardent dare
The dangerous path of fame.
Beneath the shade of thy golden wings,
The Roman legions bore,
From the river of Egypt's cloudy springs,
Their pride, to the polar shore.

For thee they fought, for thee they fell,
And their oath was on thee laid;
To thee the clarions raised their swell,
And the dying warrior pray'd.
Thou wert, through an age of death and fears,
The image of pride and power,
Till the gather'd rage of a thousand years
Burst forth in one awful hour.

And then a deluge of wrath it came,
And the nations shook with dread;
And it swept the earth till its fields were flame,
And piled with the mingled dead.
Kings were roll'd in the wasteful flood,
With the low and crouching slave;
And together lay, in a shroud of blood,
The coward and the brave.

And where was then thy fearless flight?
"O'er the dark, mysterious sea,
To the lands that caught the setting light,
The cradle of Liberty.
There, on the silent and lonely shore,
For ages, I watch'd alone,
And the world, in its darkness, ask'd no more
Where the glorious bird had flown.

"But then came a bold and hardy few,
And they breasted the unknown wave;
I caught afar the wandering crew;
And I knew they were high and brave.
I wheel'd around the welcome bark,
As it sought the desolate shore,
And up to heaven, like a joyous lark,
My quivering pinions bore.

"And now that bold and hardy few
Are a nation wide and strong;
And danger and doubt I have led them through,
And they worship me in song;
And over their bright and glancing arms,
On field, and lake, and sea,
With an eye that fires, and a spell that charms,
I guide them to victory."

PREVALENCE OF POETRY.

The world is full of poetry—the air
Is living with its spirit; and the waves
Dance to the music of its melodies,
And sparkle in its brightness. Earth is veil'd,
And mantled with its beauty; and the walls,
That close the universe with crystal in,
Are eloquent with voices, that proclaim
The unseen glories of immensity,
In harmonies, too perfect, and too high,
For aught but beings of celestial mould,
And speak to man in one eternal hymn,
Unfading beauty, and unyielding power.
The year leads round the seasons, in a choir
Forever charming, and forever new,
Blending the grand, the beautiful, the gay,
The mournful, and the tender, in one strain,
Which steals into the heart, like sounds, that rise
Far off, in moonlight evenings, on the shore
Of the wide ocean, resting after storms;
Or tones, that wind around the vaulted roof,
And pointed arches, and retiring aisles
Of some old, lonely minster, where the hand,
Skilful, and moved, with passionate love of art,
Plays o'er the higher keys, and bears aloft
The peal of bursting thunder, and then calls,
By mellow touches, from the softer tubes,
Voices of melting tenderness, that blend
With pure and gentle musings, till the soul,
Commingling with the melody, is borne,
Rapt. and dissolved in ecstasy, to heaven.
'Tis not the chime and flow of words, that move
In measured file, and metrical array;
'Tis not the union of returning sounds,
Nor all the pleasing artifice of rhyme,
And quantity, and accent, that can give
This all-pervading spirit to the ear,
Or blend it with the movings of the soul.
'Tis a mysterious feeling, which combines
Man with the world around him, in a chain
Woven of flowers, and dipp'd in sweetness, till
He taste the high communion of his thoughts,
With all existence, in earth and heaven,
That meet him in the charm of grace and power.
'Tis not the noisy babbler, who displays,
In studied phrase, and ornate epithet,
And rounded period, poor and vapid thoughts,
Which peep from out the cumbrous ornaments
That overload their littleness. Its words
Are few, but deep and solemn; and they break
Fresh from the fount of feeling, and are full
Of all that passion, which, on Carmel, fired
The holy prophet, when his lips were coals,
His language wing'd with terror, as when bolts
Leap from the brooding tempest, arm'd with wrath,
Commission'd to affright us, and destroy.
Passion, when deep, is still: the glaring eye
That reads its enemy with glance of fire,
The lip, that curls and writhes in bitterness,
The brow contracted, till its wrinkles hide
The keen, fix'd orbs, that burn and flash below,
The hand firm clench'd and quivering, and the foot
Planted in attitude to spring, and dart
Its vengeance, are the language it employs.
So the poetic feeling needs no words
To give it utterance; but it swells, and glows,
And revels in the ecstasies of soul,
And sits at banquet with celestial forms,
The beings of its own creation, fair
And lovely, as e'er haunted wood and wave,
When earth was peopled, in its solitudes,
With nymph and naiad—mighty, as the gods,
Whose palace was Olympus, and the clouds,
That hung, in gold and flame, around its brow;
Who bore, upon their features, all that grand
And awful dignity of front, which bows
The eye that gazes on the marble Jove,
Who hurls, in wrath, his thunder, and the god,
The image of a beauty, so divine,
So masculine, so artless, that we seem
To share in his intensity of joy,
When, sure as fate, the bounding arrow sped,
And darted to the scaly monster's heart.
This spirit is the breath of Nature, blown
Over the sleeping forms of clay, who else
Doze on through life in blank stupidity,
Till by its blast, as by a touch of fire,
They rouse to lofty purpose, and send out,
In deeds of energy, the rage within.
Its seat is deeper in the savage breast,
Than in the man of cities; in the child,
Than in the maturer bosoms. Art may prune
Its rank and wild luxuriance, and may train
Its strong out-breakings, and its vehement gusts
To soft refinement, and amenity;
But all its energy has vanish'd, all
Its maddening, and commanding spirit gone,
And all its tender touches, and its tones
Of soul-dissolving pathos, lost and hid
Among the measured notes, that move as dead
And heartless, as the puppets in a show.
Well I remember, in my boyish days,
How deep the feeling, when my eye look'd forth
On Nature, in her loveliness, and storms;
How my heart gladden'd, as the light of spring
Came from the sun, with zephyrs, and with showers,
Waking the earth to beauty, and the woods
To music, and the atmosphere to blow,
Sweetly and calmly, with its breath of balm.
O! how I gazed upon the dazzling blue
Of summer's heaven of glory, and the waves,
That roll'd, in bending gold, o'er hill and plain;
And on the tempest, when it issued forth,
In folds of blackness, from the northern sky,
And stood above the mountains, silent, dark,
Frowning, and terrible; then sent abroad
The lightning, as its herald, and the peal,
That roll'd in deep, deep volleys, round the hills,
The warning of its coming, and the sound,
That usher'd in its elemental war.
And, O! I stood, in breathless longing fix'd,
Trembling, and yet not fearful, as the clouds
Heaved their dark billows on the roaring winds,
That sent, from mountain top, and bending wood
A long, hoarse murmur, like the rush of waves
That burst, in foam and fury, on the shore.

Nor less the swelling of my heart, when high
Rose the blue arch of autumn, cloudless, pure
As nature, at her dawning, when she sprang
Fresh from the hand that wrought her; where the eye
Caught not a speck upon the soft serene,
To stain its deep cerulean, but the cloud,
That floated, like a lonely spirit, there,
White as the snow of Zemla, or the foam
That on the mid-sea tosses, cinctured round,
In easy undulations, with a belt
Woven of bright Apollo's golden hair.
Nor, when that arch, in winter's clearest night,
Mantled in ebon darkness, strew'd with stars
Its canopy, that seem'd to swell, and swell
The higher, as I gazed upon it, till,
Sphere after sphere, evolving, on the height
Of heaven, the everlasting throne shone through,
In glory's effulgence, and a wave,
Intensely bright, roll'd, like a fountain, forth
Beneath its sapphire pedestal, and stream'd
Down the long galaxy, a flood of snow,
Bathing the heavens in light, the spring, that gush'd,
In overflowing richness, from the breast
Of all-maternal nature. These I saw,
And felt to madness; but my full heart gave
No utterance to the ineffable within.
Words were too weak; they were unknown; but still
The feeling was most poignant: it has gone;
And all the deepest flow of sounds, that e'er
Pour'd, in a torrent fulness, from the tongue
Rich with the wealth of ancient bards, and stored
With all the patriarchs of British song
Hallow'd and render'd glorious, cannot tell
Those feelings, which have died, to live no more.

CLOUDS.

Ye Clouds, who are the ornament of heaven;
Who give to it its gayest shadowings,
And its most awful glories; ye who roll
In the dark tempest, or at dewy evening
Hang low in tenderest beauty; ye who, ever
Changing your Protean aspects, now are gather'd,
Like fleecy piles, when the mid-sun is brightest,
Even in the height of heaven, and there repose,
Solemnly calm, without a visible motion,
Hour after hour, looking upon the earth
With a serenest smile:—or ye who rather
Heap'd in those sulphury masses, heavily
Jutting above their bases, like the smoke
Pour'd from a furnace or a roused volcano,
Stand on the dun horizon, threatening
Lightning and storm—who, lifted from the hills,
March onward to the zenith, ever darkening,
And heaving into more gigantic towers
And mountainous piles of blackness—who then roar
With the collected winds within your womb,
Or the far utter'd thunders—who ascend
Swifter and swifter, till wide overhead
Your vanguards curl and toss upon the tempest
Like the stirr'd ocean on a reef of rocks
Just topping o'er its waves, while deep below
The pregnant mass of vapour and of flame
Rolls with an awful pomp, and grimly lowers,
Seeming to the struck eye of fear the car
Of an offended spirit, whose swart features
Glare through the sooty darkness—fired with vengeance,
And ready with uplifted hand to smite
And scourge a guilty nation; ye who lie,
After the storm is over, far away,
Crowning the dripping forests with the arch
Of beauty, such as lives alone in heaven,
Bright daughter of the sun, bending around
From mountain unto mountain, like the wreath
Of victory, or like a banner telling
Of joy and gladness; ye who round the moon
Assemble when she sits in the mid-sky
In perfect brightness, and encircle her
With a fair wreath of all aerial dyes:
Ye who, thus hovering round her, shine like mountains
Whose tops are never darken'd, but remain,
Centuries and countless ages, rear'd for temples
Of purity and light; or ye who crowd
To hail the new-born day, and hang for him,
Above his ocean-couch, a canopy
Of all inimitable hues and colours,
Such as are only pencil'd by the hands
Of the unseen ministers of earth and air,
Seen only in the tinting of the clouds,
And the soft shadowing of plumes and flowers:
Or ye who, following in his funeral train,
Light up your torches at his sepulchre,
And open on us through the clefted hills
Far glances into glittering worlds beyond
The twilight of the grave, where all is light,
Golden and glorious light, too full and high
For mortal eye to gaze on, stretching out
Brighter and ever brighter, till it spread,
Like one wide, radiant ocean, without bounds
One infinite sea of glory:—Thus, ye clouds,
And in innumerable other shapes
Of greatness or of beauty, ye attend us,
To give to the wide arch above us, life
And all its changes. Thus it is to us
A volume full of wisdom, but without ye
One awful uniformity had ever
With too severe a majesty oppress'd us.

MORNING AMONG THE HILLS.

A night had pass'd away among the hills,
And now the first faint tokens of the dawn
Show'd in the east. The bright and dewy star,
Whose mission is to usher in the morn,
Look'd through the cool air, like a blessed thing
In a far purer world. Below there lay,
Wrapp'd round a woody mountain tranquilly,
A misty cloud. Its edges caught the light,
That now came up from out the unseen depth
Of the full fount of day, and they were laced
With colours ever brightening. I had waked
From a long sleep of many changing dreams,
And now in the fresh forest air I stood
Nerved to another day of wandering.

Before me rose a pinnacle of rock,
Lifted above the wood that hemm'd it in,
And now already glowing. There the beams
Came from the far horizon, and they wrapp'd it
In light and glory. Round its vapoury cone
A crown of far-diverging rays shot out,
And gave to it the semblance of an altar
Lit for the worship of the undying flame,
That center'd in the circle of the sun,
Now coming from the ocean's fathomless caves,
Anon would stand in solitary pomp
Above the loftiest peaks, and cover them
With splendour as a garment. Thitherward
I bent my eager steps; and through the grove
Now dark as deepest night, and thickets hung
With a rich harvest of unnumber'd gems,
Waiting a clearer dawn to catch the hues
Shed from the starry fringes of its veil
On cloud, and mist, and dew, and backward thrown
In infinite reflections, on I went,
Mounting with hasty foot, and thence emerging,
I scaled that rocky steep, and there awaited
Silent the full appearing of the sun.

Below there lay a far-extended sea,
Rolling in feathery waves. The wind blew o'er it,
And toss'd it round the high-ascending rocks,
And swept it through the half-hidden forest tops,
Till, like an ocean waking into storm,
It heaved and welter'd. Gloriously the light
Crested its billows, and those craggy islands
Shone on it like to palaces of spar
Built on a sea of pearl. Far overhead,
Thy sky, without a vapour or a stain,
Intensely blue, even deepen'd into purple,
When nearer the horizon it received
A tincture from the mist that there dissolved
Into the viewless air,—the sky bent round,
The awful dome of a most mighty temple,
Built by omnipotent hands for nothing less
Than infinite worship. There I stood in silence—
I had no words to tell the mingled thoughts
Of wonder and of joy that then came o'er me,
Even with a whirlwind's rush. So beautiful,
So bright, so glorious! Such a majesty
In yon pure vault! So many dazzling tints
In yonder waste of waves,—so like the ocean
With its unnumber'd islands there encircled
By foaming surges, that the mounting eagle,
Lifting his fearless pinion through the clouds
To bathe in purest sunbeams, seem'd an ospray
Hovering above his prey, and yon tall pines,
Their tops half-mantled in a snowy veil,
A frigate with full canvass, bearing on
To conquest and to glory. But even these
Had round them something of the lofty air
In which they moved; not like to things of earth
But heighten'd, and made glorious, as became
Such pomp and splendour.
Who can tell the brightness,
That every moment caught a newer glow,
That circle, with its centre like the heart
Of elemental fire, and spreading out
In floods of liquid gold on the blue sky
And on the ophaline waves, crown'd with a rainbow
Bright as the arch that bent above the throne
Seen in a vision by the holy man
In Patmos! who can tell how it ascended,
And flow'd more widely o'er that lifted ocean,
Till instantly the unobstructed sun
Roll'd up his sphere of fire, floating away—
Away in a pure ether, far from earth,
And all its clouds,—and pouring forth unbounded
His arrowy brightness! From that burning centre
At once there ran along the level line
Of that imagined sea, a stream of gold—
Liquid and flowing gold, that seem'd to tremble
Even with a furnace heat, on to the point
Whereon I stood. At once that sea of vapour
Parted away, and melting into air,
Rose round me, and I stood involved in light,
As if a flame had kindled up, and wrapp'd me
In its innocuous blaze. Away it roll'd,
Wave after wave. They climb'd the highest rocks,
Pour'd over them in surges, and then rush'd
Down glens and valleys, like a wintry torrent
Dash'd instant to the plain. It seem'd a moment,
And they were gone, as if the touch of fire
At once dissolved them. Then I found myself
Midway in air; ridge after ridge below,
Descended with their opulence of woods
Even to the dim-seen level, where a lake
Flash'd in the sun, and from it wound a line,
Now silvery bright, even to the farthest verge
Of the encircling hills. A waste of rocks
Was round me—but below how beautiful,
How rich the plain! a wilderness of groves
And ripening harvests; while the sky of June
The soft, blue sky of June, and the cool air,
That makes it then a luxury to live,
Only to breathe it, and the busy echo
Of cascades, and the voice of mountain brooks,
Stole with such gentle meanings to my heart,
That where I stood seem'd heaven.

THE DESERTED WIFE.

He comes not—I have watched the moon go down,
But yet he comes not.—Once it was not so.
He thinks not how these bitter tears do flow,
The while he holds his riot in that town.
Yet he will come, and chide, and I shall weep,
And he will wake my infant from its sleep,
To blend its feeble wailing with my tears.
O! how I love a mother's watch to keep,
Over those sleeping eyes, that smile, which cheers
My heart, though sunk in sorrow, fix'd and deep
I had a husband once, who loved me—now
He ever wears a frown upon his brow,
And feeds his passion on a wanton's lip,
As bees, from laurel flowers, a poison sip;
But yet I cannot hate—O! there were hours.
When I could hang forever on his eye.
And time, who stole with silent swiftness by,
Strew'd, as he hurried on, his path with flowers
I loved him then—he loved me too.—My heart
Still finds its fondness kindle if he smile;
The memory of our loves will ne'er depart,
And though he often sting me with a dart,

Venom'd and barb'd, and waste upon the vile
Caresses, which his babe and mine should share;
Though he should spurn me, I will calmly bear
His madness,—and should sickness come and lay
Its paralyzing hand upon him, then
I would, with kindness, all my wrongs repay,
Until the penitent should weep, and say,
How injured, and how faithful I had been!

THE CORAL GROVE.

Deep in the wave is a coral grove,
Where the purple mullet and gold-fish rove;
Where the sea-flower spreads its leaves of blue,
That never are wet with falling dew,
But in bright and changeful beauty shine,
Far down in the green and glassy brine.
The floor is of sand, like the mountain drift,
And the pearl-shells spangle the flinty snow;
From coral rocks the sea-plants lift
Their boughs, where the tides and billows flow;
The water is calm and still below,
For the winds and waves are absent there,
And the sands are bright as the stars that glow
In the motionless fields of upper air:
There, with its waving blade of green,
The sea-flag streams through the silent water,
And the crimson leaf of the dulse is seen
To blush, like a banner bathed in slaughter:
There, with a light and easy motion,
The fan-coral sweeps through the clear, deep sea;
And the yellow and scarlet tufts of ocean
Are bending like corn on the upland lea:
And life, in rare and beautiful forms,
Is sporting amid those bowers of stone,
And is safe, when the wrathful spirit of storms
Has made the top of the wave his own:
And when the ship from his fury flies,
Where the myriad voices of ocean roar,
When the wind-god frowns in the murky skies,
And demons are waiting the wreck on shore;
Then, far below, in the peaceful sea,
The purple mullet and gold-fish rove,
Where the waters murmur tranquilly,
Through the bending twigs of the coral grove.

DECLINE OF THE IMAGINATION.

Why have ye linger'd on your way so long,
  Bright visions, who were wont to hear my call,
And with the harmony of dance and song
  Keep round my dreaming couch a festival?
Where are ye gone, with all your eyes of light,
  And where the flowery voice I loved to hear,
When, through the silent watches of the night,
  Ye whisper'd like an angel in my ear?
O! fly not with the rapid wing of time,
  But with your ancient votary kindly stay;
And while the loftier dreams, that rose sublime
  In years of higher hope, have flown away:
O! with the colours of a softer clime,
  Give your last touches to the dying day.

GENIUS SLUMBERING.

He sleeps, forgetful of his once bright fame:
  He has no feeling of the glory gone;
He has no eye to catch the mounting flame,
  That once in transport drew his spirit on;
He lies in dull, oblivious dreams, nor cares
Who the wreathed laurel bears.

And yet, not all forgotten, sleeps he there;
  There are who still remember how he bore
Upward his daring pinions, till the air
  Seem'd living with the crown of light he wore:
There are who, now his early sun has set,
Nor can, nor will forget.

He sleeps,—and yet, around the sightless eye
  And the press'd lip, a darken'd glory plays;
Though the high powers in dull oblivion lie,
  There hovers still the light of other days;
Deep in that soul a spirit, not of earth,
Still struggles for its birth.

He will not sleep forever, but will rise
  Fresh to more daring labours; now, even now,
As the close shrouding mist of morning flies,
  The gather'd slumber leaves his lifted brow;
From his half-open'd eye, in fuller beams,
His waken'd spirit streams.

Yes, he will break his sleep; the spell is gone;
  The deadly charm departed; see him fling
Proudly his fetters by, and hurry on,
  Keen as the famish'd eagle darts her wing;
The goal is still before him, and the prize
Still woos his eager eyes.

He rushes forth to conquer: shall they take—
  They, who, with feebler pace, still kept their way,
When he forgot the contest—shall they take,
  Now he renews the race, the victor's bay!
Still let them strive—when he collects his might,
He will assert his right.

The spirit cannot always sleep in dust,
  Whose essence is ethereal; they may try
To darken and degrade it; it may rust
  Dimly a while, but cannot wholly die;
And, when it wakens, it will send its fire
Intenser forth and higher.

GENIUS WAKING.

Slumber's heavy chain hath bound thee—
  Where is now thy fire?
Feebler wings are gathering round thee—
  Shall they hover higher?
Can no power, no spell, recall thee
  From inglorious dreams!
O, could glory so appal thee,
  With his burning beams!

Thine was once the highest pinion
  In the midway air;
With a proud and sure dominion,
  Thou didst upward bear,
Like the herald, wing'd with lightning,
  From the Olympian throne,

Ever mounting, ever brightening,
Thou wert there alone.

Where the pillar'd props of heaven
Glitter with eternal snows,
Where no darkling clouds are driven,
Where no fountain flows—
Far above the rolling thunder,
When the surging storm
Rent its sulphury folds asunder,
We beheld thy form.

O, what rare and heavenly brightness
Flow'd around thy plumes,
As a cascade's foamy whiteness
Lights a cavern's glooms!
Wheeling through the shadowy ocean,
Like a shape of light,
With serene and placid motion,
Thou wert dazzling bright.

From that cloudless region stooping,
Downward thou didst rush,
Not with pinion faint and drooping
But the tempest's gush.
Up again undaunted soaring,
Thou didst pierce the cloud,
When the warring winds were roaring
Fearfully and loud.

Where is now that restless longing
After higher things?
Come they not, like visions, thronging
On their airy wings?
Why should not their glow enchant thee
Upward to their bliss?
Surely danger cannot daunt thee
From a heaven like this?

But thou slumberest; faint and quivering
Hangs thy ruffled wing;
Like a dove in winter shivering,
Or a feebler thing.
Where is now thy might and motion,
Thy imperial flight?
Where is now thy heart's devotion?
Where thy spirit's light?

Hark! his rustling plumage gathers
Closer to his side;
Close, as when the storm-bird weathers
Ocean's hurrying tide.
Now his nodding beak is steady—
Wide his burning eye—
Now his open wings are ready,
And his aim—how high!

Now he curves his neck, and proudly
Now is stretch'd for flight—
Hark! his wings—they thunder loudly,
And their flash—how bright!
Onward—onward over mountains,
Through the rock and storm,
Now, like sunset over fountains,
Flits his glancing form.

Glorious bird, thy dream has left thee—
Thou hast reach'd thy heaven—
Lingering slumber hath not reft thee
Of the glory given.
With a bold, a fearless pinion,
On thy starry road,
None, to fame's supreme dominion,
Mightier ever trode.

NEW ENGLAND.

Hail to the land whereon we tread,
Our fondest boast;
The sepulchre of mighty dead,
The truest hearts that ever bled,
Who sleep on Glory's brightest bed,
A fearless host:
No slave is here; our unchain'd feet
Walk freely as the waves that beat
Our coast.

Our fathers cross'd the ocean's wave
To seek this shore;
They left behind the coward slave
To welter in his living grave;
With hearts unbent, and spirits brave,
They sternly bore
Such toils as meaner souls had quell'd;
But souls like these, such toils impell'd
To soar.

Hail to the morn, when first they stood
On Bunker's height,
And, fearless, stemm'd the invading flood
And wrote our dearest rights in blood,
And mow'd in ranks the hireling brood,
In desperate fight!
O, 'twas a proud, exulting day,
For even our fallen fortunes lay
In light.

There is no other land like thee,
No dearer shore;
Thou art the shelter of the free;
The home, the port of Liberty,
Thou hast been, and shalt ever be,
Till time is o'er.
Ere I forget to think upon
My land, shall mother curse the son
She bore.

Thou art the firm, unshaken rock,
On which we rest;
And, rising from thy hardy stock,
Thy sons the tyrant's frown shall mock,
And slavery's galling chains unlock,
And free the oppress'd:
All, who the wreath of Freedom twine
Beneath the shadow of their vine,
Are bless'd.

We love thy rude and rocky shore,
And here we stand—
Let foreign navies hasten o'er,
And on our heads their fury pour,
And peal their cannon's loudest roar,
And storm our land;
They still shall find our lives are given
To die for home;—and leant on Heaven
Our hand.

MAY.

I feel a newer life in every gale;
The winds, that fan the flowers,
And with their welcome breathings fill the sail,
Tell of serener hours,—
Of hours that glide unfelt away
Beneath the sky of May.

The spirit of the gentle south-wind calls
From his blue throne of air,
And where his whispering voice in music falls,
Beauty is budding there:
The bright ones of the valley break
Their slumbers, and awake.

The waving verdure rolls along the plain,
And the wide forest weaves,
To welcome back its playful mates again,
A canopy of leaves;
And from its darkening shadow floats
A gush of trembling notes.

Fairer and brighter spreads the reign of May;
The tresses of the woods
With the light dallying of the west-wind play;
And the full-brimming floods,
As gladly to their goal they run,
Hail the returning sun.

TO SENECA LAKE.

On thy fair bosom, silver lake,
The wild swan spreads his snowy sail,
And round his breast the ripples break,
As down he bears before the gale.

On thy fair bosom, waveless stream,
The dipping paddle echoes far,
And flashes in the moonlight gleam,
And bright reflects the polar star.

The waves along thy pebbly shore,
As blows the north-wind, heave their foam,
And curl around the dashing oar,
As late the boatman hies him home.

How sweet, at set of sun, to view
Thy golden mirror spreading wide,
And see the mist of mantling blue
Float round the distant mountain's side.

At midnight hour, as shines the moon,
A sheet of silver spreads below,
And swift she cuts, at highest noon,
Light clouds, like wreaths of purest snow.

On thy fair bosom, silver lake,
O! I could ever sweep the oar,
When early birds at morning wake,
And evening tells us toil is o'er.

THE LAST DAYS OF AUTUMN.

Now the growing year is over,
And the shepherd's tinkling bell
Faintly from its winter cover
Rings a low farewell:—
Now the birds of Autumn shiver,
Where the wither'd beech-leaves quiver,
O'er the dark and lazy river,
In the rocky dell.

Now the mist is on the mountains,
Reddening in the rising sun;
Now the flowers around the fountains
Perish one by one:—
Not a spire of grass is growing,
But the leaves that late were glowing,
Now its blighted green are strowing
With a mantle dun.

Now the torrent brook is stealing
Faintly down the furrow'd glade—
Not as when in winter pealing,
Such a din is made,
That the sound of cataracts falling
Gave no echo so appalling,
As its hoarse and heavy brawling
In the pine's black shade.

Darkly blue the mist is hovering
Round the clifted rock's bare height—
All the bordering mountains covering
With a dim, uncertain light:—
Now, a fresher wind prevailing,
Wide its heavy burden sailing,
Deepens as the day is failing,
Fast the gloom of night.

Slow the blood-stain'd moon is riding
Through the still and hazy air,
Like a sheeted spectre gliding
In a torch's glare:—
Few the hours, her light is given—
Mingling clouds of tempest driven
O'er the mourning face of heaven,
All is blackness there.

THE FLIGHT OF TIME.

Faintly flow, thou falling river,
Like a dream that dies away;
Down to ocean gliding ever,
Keep thy calm unruffled way:
Time with such a silent motion,
Floats along, on wings of air,
To eternity's dark ocean,
Burying all its treasures there.

Roses bloom, and then they wither;
Cheeks are bright, then fade and die
Shapes of light are wafted hither—
Then, like visions hurry by:
Quick as clouds at evening driven
O'er the many-colour'd west,
Years are bearing us to heaven,
Home of happiness and rest.

IT IS GREAT FOR OUR COUNTRY TO DIE.

O! IT is great for our country to die, where ranks are contending:
Bright is the wreath of our fame; Glory awaits us for aye—
Glory, that never is dim, shining on with light never ending—
Glory that never shall fade, never, O! never away.

O! it is sweet for our country to die—how softly reposes
Warrior youth on his bier, wet by the tears of his love.
Wet by a mother's warm tears; they crown him with garlands of roses,
Weep, and then joyously turn, bright where he triumphs above.

Not to the shades shall the youth descend, who for country hath perish'd:
HEBE awaits him in heaven, welcomes him there with her smile;
There, at the banquet divine, the patriot spirit is cherish'd;
Gods love the young, who ascend pure from the funeral pile.

Not to Elysian fields, by the still, oblivious river;
Not to the isles of the bless'd, over the blue, rolling sea;
But on Olympian heights, shall dwell the devoted forever;
There shall assemble the good, there the wise, valiant, and free.

O! then, how great for our country to die, in the front rank to perish,
Firm with our breast to the foe, Victory's shout in our ear:
Long they our statues shall crown, in songs our memory cherish;
We shall look forth from our heaven, pleased the sweet music to hear.

EXTRACT FROM PROMETHEUS.

OUR thoughts are boundless, though our frames are frail,
Our souls immortal, though our limbs decay;
Though darken'd in this poor life by a veil
Of suffering, dying matter, we shall play
In truth's eternal sunbeams; on the way
To heaven's high capitol our cars shall roll;
The temple of the Power whom all obey,
That is the mark we tend to, for the soul
Can take no lower flight, and seek no meaner goal.
I feel it—though the flesh is weak, I feel
The spirit has its energies untamed
By all its fatal wanderings; time may heal
The wounds which it has suffer'd; folly claim'd
Too large a portion of its youth; ashamed
Of those low pleasures, it would leap and fly,
And soar on wings of lightning, like the famed
Elijah, when the chariot, rushing by,
Bore him with steeds of fire triumphant to the sky.

We are as barks afloat upon the sea,
Helmless and oarless, when the light has fled,
The spirit, whose strong influence can free
The drowsy soul, that slumbers in the dead
Cold night of mortal darkness; from the bed
Of sloth he rouses at her sacred call,
And, kindling in the blaze around him shed,
Rends with strong effort sin's debasing thrall,
And gives to GOD his strength, his heart, his mind, his all.

Our home is not on earth; although we sleep,
And sink in seeming death a while, yet, then,
The awakening voice speaks loudly, and we leap
To life, and energy, and light, again;
We cannot slumber always in the den
Of sense and selfishness; the day will break,
Ere we forever leave the haunts of men;
Even at the parting hour the soul will wake,
Nor, like a senseless brute, its unknown journey take.

How awful is that hour, when conscience stings
The hoary wretch, who, on his death-bed hears,
Deep in his soul, the thundering voice that rings,
In one dark, damning moment, crimes of years
And, screaming like a vulture in his ears,
Tells, one by one, his thoughts and deeds of shame,
How wild the fury of his soul careers!
His swart eye flashes with intensest flame,
And like the torture's rack the wrestling of his frame.

HOME.

MY place is in the quiet vale,
The chosen haunt of simple thought;
I seek not Fortune's flattering gale,
I better love the peaceful lot.

I leave the world of noise and show,
To wander by my native brook;
I ask, in life's unruffled flow,
No treasure but my friend and book.

These better suit the tranquil home,
Where the clear water murmurs by;
And if I wish a while to roam,
I have an ocean in the sky.

Fancy can charm and feeling bless
With sweeter hours than fashion knows
There is no calmer quietness
Than home around the bosom throws.

SAMUEL G. GOODRICH.

[Born 1796 Died 1860.]

Samuel Griswold Goodrich is a native of Ridgefield, on the western border of Connecticut, and was born about the year 1796. His father was a respectable clergyman, distinguished for his simplicity of character, strong common sense, and eloquence. Our author was educated in the common schools of his native town, and soon after he was twenty-one years old, engaged in the business of publishing, in Hartford, where he resided for several years. In 1824, being in ill health, he visited Europe, and travelled over England, France, Germany, and Holland, devoting his attention particularly to the institutions for education; and on his return, having determined to attempt an improvement in books for the young, established himself in Boston, and commenced the trade of authorship. Since that time he has produced from twenty to thirty volumes, under the signature of "Peter Parley," which have passed through a great number of editions in this country and in England, and been translated into several foreign languages. Of some of these works more than fifty thousand copies are circulated annually. In 1824 Mr. Goodrich commenced "The Token," an annuary, of which he was the editor for fourteen years. In this series he published most of the poems of which he is known to be the author. They were all written while he was actively engaged in business. His "Fireside Education" was composed in sixty days, while he was discharging his duties as a member of the Massachusetts Senate, and superintending his publishing establishment; and his numerous other prose works were produced with equal rapidity. In 1837 he published "The Outcast, and Other Poems;" in 1841 "Sketches from a Student's Window," and in 1852 an edition of his "Poems" with pictorial illustrations.

Under President Fillmore's administration Mr. Goodrich was American consul for Paris, and he now (in the autumn of 1855) resides in New York.

Mr. Goodrich has been a liberal patron of American authors and artists; and it is questionable whether any other person has done as much to improve the style of the book manufacture, or to promote the arts of engraving. It is believed that he has put in circulation more than two millions of volumes of his own productions; all of which inculcate pure morality, and cheerful views of life. His style is simple and unaffected; the flow of his verse melodious; and his subjects generally such as he is capable of treating most successfully.

BIRTHNIGHT OF THE HUMMING-BIRDS.

I.

I'll tell you a fairy tale that's new—
How the merry elves o'er the ocean flew,
From the Emerald isle to this far-off shore,
As they were wont in the days of yore—
And play'd their pranks one moonlit night,
Where the zephyrs alone could see the sight.

II.

Ere the old world yet had found the new,
The fairies oft in their frolics flew,
To the fragrant isles of the Carribee—
Bright bosom-gems of a golden sea.
Too dark was the film of the Indian's eye,
These gossamer sprites to suspect or spy,—
So they danced 'mid the spicy groves unseen,
And gay were their gambolings, I ween;
For the fairies, like other discreet little elves,
Are freest and fondest when all by themselves.
No thought had they that in after time
The muse would echo their deeds in rhyme;
So, gayly doffing light stocking and shoe,
They tripp'd o'er the meadow all dappled in dew.
I could tell, if I would, some right merry tales
Of unslipper'd fairies that danced in the vales-
But the lovers of scandal I leave in the lurch—
And, besides, these elves don't belong to the church.
If they danced—be it known—'twas not in the clime
Of your Mathers and Hookers, where laughter was crime;
Where sentinel virtue kept guard o'er the lip,
Though witchcraft stole into the heart by a slip!
O, no! 'twas the land of the fruit and the flower—
Where summer and spring both dwelt in one bower—
Where one hung the citron, all ripe from the bough,
And the other with blossoms encircled its brow,—
Where the mountains embosom'd rich tissues of gold,
And the rivers o'er rubies and emeralds roll'd.
It was there, where the seasons came only to bless,
And the fashions of Eden still linger'd, in dress,
That these gay little fairies were wont, as I say,
To steal in their merriest gambols away.
But, dropping the curtain o'er frolic and fun,
Too good to be told, or too bad to be done,
I give you a legend from Fancy's own sketch,
Though I warn you he's given to fibbing—the wretch!
But I learn by the legends of breezes and brooks,
'T is as true as the fairy tales told in the books.

III.

One night when the moon shone fair on the main,
Choice spirits were gather'd 'twixt Derry and Spain,
And lightly embarking from Erin's bold cliffs,
They slid o'er the wave in their moonbeam skiffs.
A ray for a rudder—a thought for a sail,
Swift, swift was each bark as the wing of the gale.
Yet long were the tale, should I linger to say
What gambol and frolic enliven'd the way;
How they flirted with bubbles that danced on the wave,
Or listen'd to mermaids that sang from the cave;
Or slid with the moonbeams down deep to the grove
Of coral, "where mullet and gold-fish rove:"
How there, in long vistas of silence and sleep,
They waltzed, as if mocking the death of the deep:
How oft, where the wreck lay scatter'd and torn,
They peep'd in the skull—now ghastly and lorn;
Or deep, mid wild rocks, quizzed the goggling shark,
And mouth'd at the sea-wolf—so solemn and stark—
Each seeming to think that the earth and the sea
Were made but for fairies—for gambol and glee!
Enough, that at last they came to the isle,
Where moonlight and fragrance were rivals the while.
Not yet had those vessels from Palos been here,
To turn the bright gem to the blood-mingled tear.
O, no! still blissful and peaceful the land,
And the merry elves flew from the sea to the strand.
Right happy and joyous seem'd now the bright crew,
As they tripp'd mid the orange groves flashing in dew,
For they were to hold a revel that night,
A gay, fancy ball, and each to be dight
In the gem or the flower that fancy might choose
From mountain or vale, for its fragrance or hues.

IV.

Away sped the maskers like arrows of light,
To gather their gear for the revel bright.
To the dazzling peaks of far-off Peru,
In emulous speed some sportive flew—
And deep in the mine, or mid glaciers on high,
For ruby and sapphire searched heedful and sly.
For diamonds rare that gleam in the bed
Of Brazilian streams, some merrily sped,
While others for topaz and emerald stray,
Mid the cradle cliffs of the Paraguay.
As these are gathering the rarest of gems,
Others are plucking the rarest of stems.
They range wild dells where the zephyr alone
To the blushing blossoms before was known;
Through forests they fly, whose branches are hung
By creeping plants, with fair flowerets strung—
Where temples of nature with arches of bloom,
Are lit by the moonlight, and faint with perfume.
They stray where the mangrove and clematis twine,
Where azalia and laurel in rivalry shine;
Where, tall as the oak, the passion-tree glows,
And jasmine is blent with rhodora and rose.
O'er blooming savannas and meadows of light,
Mid regions of summer they sweep in their flight,
And gathering the fairest they speed to their bower,
Each one with his favourite brilliant or flower.

V.

The hour is come, and the fairies are seen
In their plunder array'd on the moonlit green.
The music is breathed—'tis a soft tone of pleasure,
And the light giddy throng whirl into the measure.
'Twas a joyous dance, and the dresses were bright,
Such as never were known till that famous night;
For the gems and the flowers that shone in the scene,
O'ermatch'd the regalia of princess and queen.
No gaudy slave to a fair one's brow
Was the rose, or the ruby, or emerald now;
But lighted with souls by the playful elves,
The brilliants and blossoms seem'd dancing themselves.

VI.

Of all that did chance, 't were a long tale to tell,
Of the dresses and waltzes, and who was the belle;
But each were so happy, and all were so fair,
That night stole away and the dawn caught them there!
Such a scampering never before was seen
As the fairies' flight on that island green.
They rush'd to the bay with twinkling feet,
But vain was their haste, for the moonlight fleet
Had pass'd with the dawn, and never again
Were those fairies permitted to traverse the main,—
But mid the groves, when the sun was high,
The Indian marked with a worshipping eye
The humming-birds, all unknown before,
Glancing like thoughts from flower to flower,
And seeming as if earth's loveliest things,
The brilliants and blossoms, had taken wings:—
And fancy hath whisper'd in numbers light,
That these are the fairies who danced that night,
And linger yet in the garb they wore,
Content in our clime, and more blest than before

THE RIVER.

O, TELL me, pretty river!
  Whence do thy waters flow?
And whither art thou roaming,
  So pensive and so slow?

"My birthplace was the mountain,
  My nurse, the April showers;
My cradle was a fountain,
  O'ercurtain'd by wild flowers.

"One morn I ran away,
  A madcap, hoyden rill—
And many a prank that day
  I play'd adown the hill!

"And then, mid meadowy banks,
  I flirted with the flowers,
That stoop'd, with glowing lips,
  To woo me to their bowers.

"But these bright scenes are o'er,
  And darkly flows my wave—
I hear the ocean's roar,
  And there must be my grave!"

THE LEAF.

It came with spring's soft sun and showers,
Mid bursting buds and blushing flowers;
It flourish'd on the same light stem,
It drank the same clear dews with them.
The crimson tints of summer morn,
That gilded one, did each adorn.
The breeze, that whisper'd light and brief
To bud or blossom, kiss'd the leaf;
When o'er the leaf the tempest flew,
The bud and blossom trembled too.
But its companions pass'd away,
And left the leaf to lone decay.
The gentle gales of spring went by,
The fruits and flowers of summer die.
The autumn winds swept o'er the hill,
And winter's breath came cold and chill.
The leaf now yielded to the blast,
And on the rushing stream was cast.
Far, far it glided to the sea,
And whirl'd and eddied wearily,
Till suddenly it sank to rest,
And slumber'd in the ocean's breast.
Thus life begins—its morning hours,
Bright as the birth-day of the flowers;
Thus passes like the leaves away,
As wither'd and as lost as they.
Beneath the parent roof we meet
In joyous groups, and gayly greet
The golden beams of love and light,
That kindle to the youthful sight.
But soon we part, and one by one,
Like leaves and flowers, the group is gone
One gentle spirit seeks the tomb,
His brow yet fresh with childhood's bloom.
Another treads the paths of fame,
And barters peace to win a name.
Another still tempts fortune's wave,
And seeking wealth, secures a grave.
The last grasps yet the brittle thread—
Though friends are gone and joy is dead,
Still dares the dark and fretful tide,
And clutches at its power and pride,
Till suddenly the waters sever,
And, like the leaf, he sinks forever.

LAKE SUPERIOR.

"Father of Lakes!" thy waters bend
Beyond the eagle's utmost view,
When, throned in heaven, he sees thee send
Back to the sky its world of blue.

Boundless and deep, the forests weave
Their twilight shade thy borders o'er,
And threatening cliffs, like giants, heave
Their rugged forms along thy shore.

Pale Silence, mid thy hollow caves,
With listening ear, in sadness broods;
Or startled Echo, o'er thy waves,
Sends the hoarse wolf-notes of thy woods.

Nor can the light canoes, that glide
Across thy breast like things of air,
Chase from thy lone and level tide
The spell of stillness reigning there.

Yet round this waste of wood and wave,
Unheard, unseen, a spirit lives,
That, breathing o'er each rock and cave,
To all a wild, strange aspect gives.

The thunder-riven oak, that flings
Its grisly arms athwart the sky,
A sudden, startling image brings
To the lone traveller's kindled eye.

The gnarl'd and braided boughs, that show
Their dim forms in the forest shade,
Like wrestling serpents seem, and throw
Fantastic horrors through the glade.

The very echoes round this shore
Have caught a strange and gibbering tone;
For they have told the war-whoop o'er,
Till the wild chorus is their own.

Wave of the wilderness, adieu!
Adieu, ye rocks, ye wilds and woods!
Roll on, thou element of blue,
And fill these awful solitudes!

Thou hast no tale to tell of man—
God is thy theme. Ye sounding caves
Whisper of Him, whose mighty plan
Deems as a bubble all your waves!

THE SPORTIVE SYLPHS.

The sportive sylphs that course the air,
Unseen on wings that twilight weaves,
Around the opening rose repair,
And breathe sweet incense o'er its leaves.

With sparkling cups of bubbles made,
They catch the ruddy beams of day,
And steal the rainbow's sweetest shade,
Their blushing favourite to array.

They gather gems with sunbeams bright,
From floating clouds and falling showers;
They rob Aurora's locks of light
To grace their own fair queen of flowers.

Thus, thus adorned, the speaking rose
Becames a token fit to tell
Of things that words can ne'er disclose,
And naught but this reveal so well.

Then, take my flower, and let its leaves
Beside thy heart be cherish'd near,
While that confiding heart receives
The thought it whispers to thine ear.

ISAAC CLASON.

[Born about 1796. Died, 1830.]

Isaac Clason wrote the Seventeenth and Eighteenth Cantos of Don Juan—a continuation of the poem of Lord Byron—published in 1825. I have not been able to learn many particulars of his biography. He was born in the city of New York, where his father was a distinguished merchant, and graduated at Columbia College in 1813. He inherited a considerable fortune, but in the pursuit of pleasure he spent it all, and much besides, received from his relatives. He was in turn a gay *roué* in London and Paris, a writer for the public journals, an actor in the theatres, and a private tutor. A mystery hangs over his closing years. It has been stated that he was found dead in an obscure lodging-house in London, under circumstances that led to a belief that he committed suicide, about the year 1830.

Besides his continuation of Don Juan, he wrote but little poetry. The two cantos which he left under that title, have much of the spirit and feeling, in thought and diction, which characterize the work of Byron. He was a man of attractive manners and brilliant conversation. His fate is an unfavourable commentary on his character.

NAPOLEON.*

I love no land so well as that of France—
Land of Napoleon and Charlemagne,
Renown'd for valour, women, wit, and dance,
For racy Burgundy, and bright Champagne,
Whose only word in battle was, Advance;
While that grand genius, who seem'd born to reign,
Greater than Ammon's son, who boasted birth
From heaven, and spurn'd all sons of earth;

Greater than he who wore his buskins high,
A Venus arm'd, impress'd upon his seal;
Who smiled at poor Calphurnia's prophecy,
Nor fear'd the stroke he soon was doom'd to feel;
Who on the ides of March breath'd his last sigh,
As Brutus pluck'd away his "cursed steel,"
Exclaiming, as he expired, "Et tu, Brute,"
But Brutus thought he only did his duty;

Greater than he, who, at nine years of age,
On Carthage' altar swore eternal hate;
Who, with a rancour time could ne'er assuage,
With feelings no reverse could moderate,
With talents such as few would dare engage,
With hopes that no misfortune could abate,
Died like his rival, both with broken hearts,—
Such was their fate, and such was Bonaparte's.

Napoleon Bonaparte! thy name shall live
Till time's last echo shall have ceased to sound;
And if eternity's confines can give
To space reverberation, round and round
The spheres of heaven, the long, deep cry of "Vive
Napoleon!" in thunders shall rebound;
The lightning's flash shall blaze thy name on high,
Monarch of earth now meteor of the sky!

What though on St. Helena's rocky shore
Thy head be pillow'd, and thy form entomb'd,
Perhaps that son, the child thou didst adore,
Fired with a father's fame, may yet be doom'd
To crush the bigot Bourbon, and restore
Thy mouldering ashes ere they be consumed;
Perhaps may run the course thyself didst run,
And light the world, as comets light the sun.

'Tis better thou art gone: 't were sad to see,
Beneath an "imbecile's impotent reign,"
Thine own unvanquish'd legions doom'd to be
Cursed instruments of vengeance on poor Spain,
That land, so glorious once in chivalry,
Now sunk in slavery and shame again;
To see the imperial guard, thy dauntless band,
Made tools for such a wretch as Ferdinand.

Farewell, Napoleon! thine hour is past;
No more earth trembles at thy dreaded name;
But France, unhappy France, shall long contrast
Thy deeds with those of worthless D'Angouleme.
Ye gods! how long shall slavery's thraldom last?
Will France alone remain forever tame!
Say, will no Wallace, will no Washington
Scourge from thy soil the infamous Bourbon?

Is Freedom dead? Is Nero's reign restored?
Frenchmen! remember Jena, Austerlitz:
The first, which made thy emperor the lord
Of Prussia, and which almost threw in fits
Great Frederick William; he who, at the board,
Took all the Prussian uniform to bits;
Frederick, the king of regimental tailors,
As Hudson Lowe, the very prince of jailors.

Farewell, Napoleon! couldst thou have died
The coward scorpion's death, afraid, ashamed
To meet adversity's advancing tide,
The weak had praised thee, but the wise had blamed;
But no! though torn from country, child, and bride
With spirit unsubdued, with soul untamed
Great in misfortune, as in glory high,
Thou daredst to live through life's worst agony.

Pity, for thee, shall weep her fountains dry,
Mercy, for thee, shall bankrupt all her store;
Valour shall pluck a garland from on high,
And Honour twine the wreath thy temples o'er;

* From the Seventeenth Canto of Don Juan.

Beauty shall beckon to thee from the sky,
And smiling seraphs open wide heaven's door;
Around thy head the brightest stars shall meet,
And rolling suns play sportive at thy feet.

Farewell, NAPOLEON! a long farewell,
A stranger's tongue, alas! must hymn thy worth;
No craven Gaul dares wake his harp to tell,
Or sound in song the spot that gave thee birth.
No more thy name, that, with its magic spell,
Aroused the slumbering nations of the earth,
Echoes around thy land; 't is past—at length
France sinks beneath the sway of CHARLES the Tenth.

JEALOUSY.

HE who has seen the red-fork'd lightnings flash
From out some black and tempest-gather'd cloud,
And heard the thunder's simultaneous crash,
Bursting in peals, terrifically loud;
He who has mark'd the madden'd ocean dash
(Robed in its snow-white foam as in a shroud)
Its giant billows on the groaning shore,
While death seem'd echo'd in the deafening roar;

He who has seen the wild tornado sweep
(Its path destruction, and its progress death)
The silent bosom of the smiling deep
With the black besom of its boisterous breath,
Waking to strife the slumbering waves, that leap
In battling surges from their beds beneath,
Yawning and swelling from their liquid caves,
Like buried giants from their restless graves:—

He who has gazed on sights and scenes like these,
Hath look'd on nature in her maddest mood;
But nature's warfare passes by degrees,—
The thunder's voice is hush'd, however rude,
The dying winds unclasp the raging seas,
The scowling sky throws back her cloud-capt hood,
The infant lightnings to their cradles creep,
And the gaunt earthquake rocks herself to sleep.

But there are storms, whose lightnings never glare,
Tempests, whose thunders never cease to roll—
The storms of love, when madden'd to despair,
The furious tempests of the jealous soul.
That kamsin of the heart, which few can bear,
Which owns no limit, and which knows no goal,
Whose blast leaves joy a tomb, and hope a speck,
Reason a blank, and happiness a wreck.

EARLY LOVE.

THE fond caress of beauty, O, that glow!
The first warm glow that mantles round the heart
Of boyhood! when all 's new—the first dear vow
He ever breathed—the tear-drops that first start,
Pure from the unpractised eye—the overflow
Of waken'd passions, that but now impart
A hope, a wish, a feeling yet unfelt,
hat mould to madness, or in mildness melt.

Ah! where's the youth whose stoic heart ne'er knew
The fires of joy, that burst through every vein,
That burn forever bright, forever new,
As passion rises o'er and o'er again!
That, like the phœnix, die but to renew—
Beat in the heart, and throb upon the brain—
Self-kindling, quenchless as the eternal flame
That sports in Etna's base. But I'm to blame

Ignobly thus to yield to raptures past;
To call my buried feelings from their shrouds,
O'er which the deep funereal pall was cast—
Like brightest skies entomb'd in darkest clouds
No matter, these, the latest and the last
That rise, like spectres of the past, in crowds;
The ebullitions of a heart not lost,
But weary, wandering, worn, and tempest-toss'd.

'T is vain, and worse than vain, to think on joys
Which, like the hour that's gone, return no more;
Bubbles of folly, blown by wanton boys—
Billows that swell, to burst upon the shore—
Playthings of passion, manhood's gilded toys,
(Deceitful as the shell that seems to roar,
But proves the mimic mockery of the surge:)
They sink in sorrow's sea, and ne'er emerge.

ALL IS VANITY.

. . . . . I've compass'd every pleasure,
Caught every joy before its *bead* could pass;
I've loved without restriction, without measure—
I've sipp'd enjoyment from each sparkling glass—
I've known what 't is, too, to "repent at leisure"—
I've sat at meeting, and I've served at mass:—
And having roved through half the world's insanities,
Cry, with the Preacher--Vanity of vanities!

What constitutes man's chief enjoyment here?
What forms his greatest antidote to sorrow?
Is 't wealth? Wealth can at last but gild his bier,
Or buy the pall that poverty must borrow.
Is 't love? Alas, love's cradled in a tear;
It smiles to-day, and weeps again to-morrow;
Mere child of passion, that beguiles in youth,
And flies from age, as falsehood flies from truth.

Is 't glory? Pause beneath St. Helen's willow,
Whose weeping branches wave above the spot·
Ask him, whose head now rests upon its pillow,
Its last, low pillow, there to rest, and rot.
Is 't fame? Ask her, who floats upon the billow,
Untomb'd, uncoffin'd, and perchance forgot;
The lovely, lovesick Lesbian, frail as fair,
Victim of love, and emblem of despair.

Is 't honour? Go, ask him whose ashes sleep
Within the crypt of Paul's stupendous dome.
Whose name once thunder'd victory o'er the deep,
Far as his country's navies proudly roam;
Above whose grave no patriot *Dane* shall weep,
No *Frank* deplore the hour he found a home—
A home, whence valour's voice from conquest's car
No more shall rouse the lord—of Trafalgar.

JOHN G. C. BRAINARD.

[Born, 1796. Died, 1828.]

During the present century many persons in this country, whose early productions gave promise of brilliant achievements in maturity, have died young. It has been said that the history of American genius might be written in a series of obituaries of youthful authors. Were Drake, Sands, Griffin, Rockwell, Wilcox, Pinkney, Clarke, the Davidsons, and Brainard now alive, there would be no scarcity of American writers, nor would any of them have passed the ordinary meridian of existence. What they have left us must be regarded as the first-fruits of minds whose full powers were to the last undeveloped, and which were never tasked to their full capacity.

John Gardner Calkins Brainard was a son of the Honourable J. G. Brainard, one of the Justices of the Supreme Court of Connecticut. He was born at New London, in that State, on the twenty-first day of October, 1796. After finishing his preparatory studies, which were pursued under the direction of an elder brother, he entered Yale College, in 1811, being then in the fifteenth year of his age. At this immature period, before the mind is fully awake to the nature and importance of moral and intellectual discipline, severe application to study is unusual. Brainard's books were neglected for communion with his own thoughts and "thick-coming fancies," or for the society of his fellows. His college career was marked by nothing peculiar: he was distinguished for the fine powers he evinced whenever he chose to exert them, for the uniform modesty of his deportment, the kindness which characterized his intercourse with those about him, and a remarkable degree of sensitiveness, which caused him to shrink from every harsh collision, and to court retirement. On leaving college, in 1815, he commenced the study of law, in his native place, and on his admission to the bar, he removed to the city of Middletown, intending to practise there his profession. His success was less than he anticipated; perhaps because of his too great modesty—an unfortunate quality in lawyers—or, it may be, in consequence of his indolence and convivial propensities. One of his biographers remarks that his friends were always welcome, save when they came as clients.

Wearied with the vexations and dry formalities of his profession, he relinquished it in the winter of 1822, to undertake the editorship of the Connecticut Mirror, a weekly political and literary gazette, published in Hartford. But here he found as little to please him as in the business he had deserted. He was too indolent to prepare every week articles of a serious, argumentative character, and gave in their place, graceful or humorous paragraphs, and the occasional pieces of verse on which rests his reputation as a poet. These, at the time, were republished in many periodicals, and much praised. In the departments of poetry and criticism, the Mirror acquired a high reputation; but in others, while under his direction, it hardly rose to mediocrity.*

His first volume of poetry,† containing his contributions to the Mirror, and some other pieces, was published early in 1825. It was favourably received by the public, and its success induced his friends to urge him to undertake the composition of a larger and more important work than he had yet attempted. His constitutional lassitude and aversion to high and continued effort deterred him from beginning the task, until 1827, when his health began to wane, and it was no longer in his power. He then relinquished the editorship of the Mirror, and sought for restoring quiet, and the gentle ministrations of affection, the home of his childhood. His illness soon assumed the character of consumption, and he saw that he had but a brief time to live. A few weeks were passed on the eastern shore of Long Island, in the hope of deriving benefit from a change of air; but nothing could arrest the progress of the fatal malady; and he returned to New London, to prepare for the

* The editor of the last edition of his works, of which I have received a copy since the above was written, and while this volume is passing through the press, speaks as follows of his editorial career:—"We are assured by competent testimony, that laboured and able political articles were withheld from publication, owing to causes over which he had little control. It is not, perhaps, necessary to detail the facts, but they certainly go far to exculpate him from the charge of levity, or weakness, in conducting the editorial department of his paper. Prudential considerations were suffered to have sway, at the expense of his reputation for political tact and foresight. The only substitutes for the articles referred to, were such brief and tame pieces as he could prepare, after the best and almost only hours for composition had passed by. This circumstance, together with the consciousness that the paper was ill sustained in respect to its patronage, was sufficiently discouraging to a person whose sensibilities were as acute as those of Brainard. It accounts, also, for the frequent turns of mental depression which marked his latter years,—heightened, indeed, by that frequent and mortifying concomitant of genius,—slender pecuniary means."

† The volume was introduced by the following characteristic address to the reader:—"The author of the following pieces has been induced to publish them in a book, from considerations which cannot be interesting to the public. Many of these little poems have been printed in the *Connecticut Mirror*: and others are just fit to keep them company. No apologies are made, and no criticisms deprecated. The commonplace story of the importunities of friends, though it had its share in the publication, is not insisted upon; but the vanity of the author, if others choose to call it such, is a natural motive, and the hope of 'making a little something by it,' is an honest acknowledgment, if it is a poor excuse." The motto of the title-page was as quaint:—

"Some said, 'John, print it;' others said 'Not so;'
Some said 'It might do good;' others said, 'No.'"

Bunyan's Apology.

spiritual life upon which he was about to enter. He had always regarded with reverence the Christian character and profession, and he was now united to the visible church,* and received the holiest of the sacraments. He lingered until the twenty-sixth of September, 1828, when he passed peacefully to the rest of those who "know that their Redeemer lives."

The pathway of Brainard was aside from the walks of ambition, and the haunts of worldliness. He lived within himself, holding communion with his own thoughts, and suffering from deep and lasting melancholy. Like Wilcox, it is said, he had met with one of those disappointments in early life, which so frequently impress the soul with sadness; and though there was sometimes gayety in his manner and conversation, it was generally assumed, to conceal painful musings or to beguile sorrow.

His person was small, and well formed; his countenance mild, and indicative of the kindness and gentleness of his nature; and in his eyes there was a look of dreamy listlessness and tenderness. He was fond of society, and his pleasing conversation and amiable character won for him many ardent friends. He was peculiarly sensitive; and Mr. Whittier,* in a sketch of his life, remarks that in his gayest moments a coldly-spoken word, or casual inattention, would check at once the free flow of his thoughts, cause the jest to die on his lips, and "the melancholy which had been lifted from his heart, to fall again with increased heaviness."

Bra nard lacked the mental discipline and strong self-command which alone confer true power. He never could have produced a great work. His poems were nearly all written during the six years in which he edited the Mirror, and they bear marks of haste and carelessness, though some of them are very beautiful. He failed only in his humorous pieces: in all the rest his language is appropriate and pure, his diction free and harmonious, and his sentiments natural and sincere. His serious poems are characterized by deep feeling and delicate fancy; and if we had no records of his history, they would show us that he was a man of great gentleness, simplicity, and purity.

JERUSALEM.†

Four lamps were burning o'er two mighty graves—
 Godfrey's and Baldwin's‡—Salem's Christian kings;
And holy light glanced from Helena's naves,
 Fed with the incense which the pilgrim brings,—
While through the panell'd roof the cedar flings
Its sainted arms o'er choir, and roof, and dome,
 And every porphyry-pillar'd cloister rings
To every kneeler there its "welcome home."
As every lip breathes out, "O Lord, thy kingdom come."

A mosque was garnish'd with its crescent moons,
 And a clear voice call'd Mussulmans to prayer.
There were the splendours of Judea's thrones—
 There were the trophies which its conquerors wear—
 All but the truth, the holy truth, was there:—
For there, with lip profane, the crier stood,
 And him from the tall minaret you might hear,
Singing to all whose steps had thither trod,
That verse misunderstood, "There is no God but God."

Hark! did the pilgrim tremble as he kneel'd?
 And did the turban'd Turk his sins confess?
Those mighty hands the elements that wield,
 That mighty Power that knows to curse or bless,
 Is over all; and in whatever dress
His suppliants crowd around him, He can see
 Their heart, in city or in wilderness,
And probe its core, and make its blindi ess flee,
Owning Him very God, the only Deity.

There was an earthquake once that rent thy fane,
 Proud Julian; when (against the prophecy
Of Him who lived, and died, and rose again,
 "That one stone on another should not lie")
 Thou wouldst rebuild that Jewish masonry
To mock the eternal Word.—The earth below
 Gush'd out in fire; and from the brazen sky,

* On this occasion, says the Reverend Mr. M'Ewen, as he was too feeble to go to the church and remain through the customary services, he arrived at and entered the sanctuary when these were nearly or quite through. Every one present (literally, almost) knew him,—the occasion of his coming was understood,—and when he appeared, pale, feeble, emaciated, and trembling in consequence of his extreme debility, the sensation it produced was at once apparent throughout the whole assembly. There seemed to be an instinctive homage paid to the grace of God in him; or, perhaps, the fact shows how readily a refined Christian community sympathizes with genius and virtue destined to an early tomb.

† The following intelligence from Constantinople was of the eleventh October, 1821: "A severe earthquake is said to have taken place at Jerusalem, which has destroyed great part of that city, shaken down the Mosque of Omar, and reduced the Holy Sepulchre to ruins from top to bottom."

‡ Godfrey and Baldwin were the first Christian kings at Jerusalem. The Empress Helena, mother of Constantine the Great, built the church of the sepulchre on Mount Calvary. The walls are of stone and the roof of cedar. The four lamps which lit it, are very costly. It is kept in repair by the offerings of pilgrims who resort to it. The mosque was originally a Jewish temple. The Emperor Julian undertook to rebuild the temple of Jerusalem at a very great expense, to disprove the prophecy of our Saviour, as it was understood by the Jews; but the work and the workmen were destroyed by an earthquake. The pools of Bethesda and Gihon—the tomb of the Virgin Mary, and of King Jehosaphat—the pillar of Absalom—the tomb of Zachariah—and the *campo santo*, or holy field, which is supposed to have been purchased with the price of Judas's treason, are, or were lately, the most interesting parts of Jerusalem.

* John G. Whittier was one of Brainard's intimate friends, and, soon after his death, he wrote an interesting account of his life, which was prefixed to an edition of his poems, printed in 1832.

And from the boiling seas such wrath did flow,
As saw not Shinar's plain, nor Babel's overthrow.

Another earthquake comes. Dome, roof, and wall
Tremble; and headlong to the grassy bank,
And in the muddied stream the fragments fall,
While the rent chasm spread its jaws, and drank
At one huge draught, the sediment, which sank
In Salem's drained goblet. Mighty Power!
Thou whom we all should worship, praise, and thank,
Where was thy mercy in that awful hour,
When hell moved from beneath, and thine own heaven did lower!

Say, Pilate's palaces—proud Herod's towers—
Say, gate of Bethlehem, did your arches quake?
Thy pool, Bethesda, was it fill'd with showers?
Calm Gihon, did the jar thy waters wake?
Tomb of thee, Mary—Virgin—did it shake?
Glow'd thy bought field, Aceldama, with blood?
Where were the shudderings Calvary might make?
Did sainted Mount Moriah send a flood,
To wash away the spot where once a God had stood?

Lost Salem of the Jews—great sepulchre
Of all profane and of all holy things—
Where Jew, and Turk, and Gentile yet concur
To make thee what thou art! thy history brings
Thoughts mix'd of joy and wo. The whole earth rings
With the sad truth which He has prophesied,
Who would have shelter'd with his holy wings
Thee and thy children. You his power defied:
You scourged him while he lived, and mock'd him as he died!

There is a star in the untroubled sky,
That caught the first light which its Maker made—
It led the hymn of other orbs on high;—
'T will shine when all the fires of heaven shall fade.
Pilgrims at Salem's porch, be that your aid!
For it has kept its watch on Palestine!
Look to its holy light, nor be dismay'd,
Though broken is each consecrated shrine,
Though crush'd and ruin'd all—which men have call'd divine.

ON CONNECTICUT RIVER.

From that lone lake, the sweetest of the chain
That links the mountain to the mighty main,
Fresh from the rock and swelling by the tree,
Rushing to meet, and dare, and breast the sea—
Fair, noble, glorious river! in thy wave
The sunniest slopes and sweetest pastures lave;
The mountain torrent, with its wintry roar,
Springs from its home and leaps upon thy shore:—
The promontories love thee—and for this
Turn their rough cheeks and stay thee for thy kiss.
Stern, at thy source, thy northern guardians stand,
Rude rulers of the solitary land,
Wild dwellers by thy cold, sequester'd springs,
Of earth the feathers and of air the wings;
Their blasts have rock'd thy cradle, and in storm
Cover'd thy couch and swathed in snow thy form—
Yet, bless'd by all the elements that sweep
The clouds above, or the unfathom'd deep,
The purest breezes scent thy blooming hills,
The gentlest dews drop on thy eddying rills,
By the moss'd bank, and by the aged tree,
The silver streamlet smoothest glides to thee.
The young oak greets thee at the water's edge,
Wet by the wave, though anchor'd in the ledge.
—'Tis there the otter dives, the beaver feeds,
Where pensive osiers dip their willowy weeds,
And there the wild-cat purs amid her brood,
And trains them in the sylvan solitude,
To watch the squirrel's leap, or mark the mink
Paddling the water by the quiet brink;—
Or to out-gaze the gray owl in the dark,
Or hear the young fox practising to bark.
Dark as the frost-nipp'd leaves that strew'd the ground,
The Indian hunter here his shelter found;
Here cut his bow and shaped his arrows true,
Here built his wigwam and his bark canoe,
Spear'd the quick salmon leaping up the fall,
And slew the deer without the rifle-ball;
Here his young squaw her cradling tree would choose,
Singing her chant to hush her swart pappoose;
Here stain her quills and string her trinkets rude,
And weave her warrior's wampum in the wood.
—No more shall they thy welcome waters bless,
No more their forms thy moon-lit banks shall press,
No more be heard, from mountain or from grove,
His whoop of slaughter, or her song of love.
Thou didst not shake, thou didst not shrink when, late,
The mountain-top shut down its ponderous gate,
Tumbling its tree-grown ruins to thy side,
An avalanche of acres at a slide.
Nor dost thou say, when winter's coldest breath
Howls through the woods and sweeps along the heath—
One mighty sigh relieves thy icy breast,
And wakes thee from the calmness of thy rest.
Down sweeps the torrent ice—it may not stay
By rock or bridge, in narrow or in bay—
Swift, swifter to the heaving sea it goes,
And leaves thee dimpling in thy sweet repose.
—Yet as the unharm'd swallow skims his way,
And lightly drops his pinions in thy spray,
So the swift sail shall seek thy inland seas,
And swell and whiten in thy purer breeze,
New paddles dip thy waters, and strange oars
Feather thy waves and touch thy noble shores.
Thy noble shores! where the tall steeple shines,
At mid-day, higher than thy mountain pines;
Where the white school-house with its daily drill
Of sunburn'd children, smiles upon the hill;
Where the neat village grows upon the eye,
Deck'd forth in nature's sweet simplicity—
Where hard-won competence, the farmer's wealth,
Gains merit, honour, and gives labour health;
Where Goldsmith's self might send his exiled band
To find a new "Sweet Auburn" in our land
What Art can execute, or Taste devise,
Decks thy fair course and gladdens in thine eyes—

As broader sweep the bendings of thy stream,
To meet the southern sun's more constant beam.
Here cities rise, and sea-wash'd commerce hails
Thy shores and winds with all her flapping sails,
From tropic isles, or from the torrid main—
Where grows the grape, or sprouts the sugar-cane—
Or from the haunts where the striped haddock play,
By each cold, northern bank and frozen bay.
Here, safe return'd from every stormy sea,
Waves the striped flag, the mantle of the free,
—That star-lit flag, by all the breezes curl'd
Of yon vast deep whose waters grasp the world.

In what Arcadian, what Utopian ground
Are warmer hearts or manlier feelings found,
More hospitable welcome, or more zeal
To make the curious "tarrying" stranger feel
That, next to home, here best may he abide,
To rest and cheer him by the chimney-side;
Drink the hale farmer's cider, as he hears
From the gray dame the tales of other years.
Cracking his shag-barks, as the aged crone
—Mixing the true and doubtful into one—
Tells how the Indian scalp'd the helpless child,
And bore its shrieking mother to the wild,
Butcher'd the father hastening to his home,
Seeking his cottage—finding but his tomb.
How drums, and flags, and troops were seen on high,
Wheeling and charging in the northern sky,
And that she knew what these wild tokens meant,
When to the Old French War her husband went.
How, by the thunder-blasted tree, was hid
The golden spoils of far-famed ROBERT KIDD;
And then the chubby grandchild wants to know
About the ghosts and witches long ago,
That haunted the old swamp.
The clock strikes ten—
The prayer is said, nor unforgotten then
The stranger in their gates. A decent rule
Of elders in thy puritanic school.

When the fresh morning wakes him from his dream,
And daylight smiles on rock, and slope, and stream,
Are there not glossy curls and sunny eyes,
As brightly lit and bluer than thy skies;
Voices as gentle as an echo'd call,
And sweeter than the soften'd waterfall
That smiles and dimples in its whispering spray,
Leaping in sportive innocence away:—
And lovely forms, as graceful and as gay
As wild-brier, budding in an April day!
—How like the leaves—the fragrant leaves it bears,
Their sinless purposes and simple cares.

Stream of my sleeping fathers! when the sound
Of coming war echoed thy hills around,
How did thy sons start forth from every glade,
Snatching the musket where they left the spade.
How did their mothers urge them to the fight,
Their sisters tell them to defend the right;—
How bravely did they stand, how nobly fall,
The earth their coffin and the turf their pall;
How did the aged pastor light his eye,
When, to his flock, he read the purpose high
And stern resolve, whate'er the toil may be,
To pledge life, name, fame, all—for liberty.
—Cold is the hand that penn'd that glorious page—
Still in the grave the body of that sage
Whose lip of eloquence and heart of zeal
Made patriots act and listening statesmen feel—
Brought thy green mountains down upon their foes,
And thy white summits melted of their snows,
While every vale to which his voice could come,
Rang with the fife and echoed to the drum.

Bold river! better suited are thy waves
To nurse the laurels clustering round thy graves,
Than many a distant stream, that soaks the mud
Where thy brave sons have shed their gallant blood,
And felt, beyond all other mortal pain,
They ne'er should see their happy home again.

Thou hadst a poet once,—and he could tell,
Most tunefully, whate'er to thee befell;
Could fill each pastoral reed upon thy shore-
But we shall hear his classic lays no more
He loved thee, but he took his aged way,
By Erie's shore, and PERRY's glorious day,
To where Detroit looks out amidst the wood,
Remote beside the dreary solitude.

Yet for his brow thy ivy leaf shall spread,
Thy freshest myrtle lift its berried head,
And our gnarl'd charter-oak put forth a bough,
Whose leaves shall grace thy TRUMBULL's honour'd brow.

ON THE DEATH OF MR. WOODWARD, AT EDINBURGH.

"The spider's most attenuated thread
Is cord—is cable, to man's tender tie
On earthly bliss; it breaks at every breeze."

ANOTHER! 'tis a sad word to the heart,
That one by one has lost its hold on life,
From all it loved or valued, forced to part
In detail. Feeling dies not by the knife
That cuts at once and kills—its tortured strife
Is with distill'd affliction, drop by drop
Oozing its bitterness. Our world is rife
With grief and sorrow! all that we would prop,
Or would be propp'd with, falls—when shall the ruin stop?

The sea has one,* and Palestine has one,
And Scotland has the last. The snooded maid
Shall gaze in wonder on the stranger's stone,
And wipe the dust off with her tartan plaid—
And from the lonely tomb where thou art laid,
Turn to some other monument—nor know
Whose grave she passes, or whose name she read:
Whose loved and honour'd relics lie below;
Whose is immortal joy, and whose is mortal wo.

There is a world of bliss hereafter—else
Why are the bad above, the good beneath
The green grass of the grave? The mower fells
Flowers and briers alike. But man shall breathe
(When he his desolating blade shall sheathe
And rest him from his work) in a pure sky,
Above the smoke of burning worlds;—and Death
On scorched pinions with the dead shall lie,
When time, with all his years and centuries has pass'd by.

* Professor FISHER, lost in the "Albion," and Rev. LEVI PARSONS, missionary to Palestine, who died at Alexandria.

ON A LATE LOSS.*

"He shall not float upon his watery bier
Unwept."

The breath of air that stirs the harp's soft string,
Floats on to join the whirlwind and the storm;
The drops of dew exhaled from flowers of spring,
Rise and assume the tempest's threatening form;
The first mild beam of morning's glorious sun,
Ere night, is sporting in the lightning's flash;
And the smooth stream, that flows in quiet on,
Moves but to aid the overwhelming dash
That wave and wind can muster, when the might
Of earth, and air, and sea, and sky unite.

So science whisper'd in thy charmed ear,
And radiant learning beckon'd thee away.
The breeze was music to thee, and the clear
Beam of thy morning promised a bright lay.
And they have wreck'd thee!—But there is a shore
Where storms are hush'd—where tempests never rage;
Where angry skies and blackening seas no more
With gusty strength their roaring warfare wage.
By thee its peaceful margent shall be trod—
Thy home is heaven, and thy friend is God.

SONNET TO THE SEA-SERPENT.

"Hugest that swims the ocean stream."

Welter upon the waters, mighty one—
And stretch thee in the ocean's trough of brine;
Turn thy wet scales up to the wind and sun,
And toss the billow from thy flashing fin;
Heave thy deep breathings to the ocean's din,
And bound upon its ridges in thy pride:
Or dive down to its lowest depths, and in
The caverns where its unknown monsters hide,
Measure thy length beneath the gulf-stream's tide—
Or rest thee on that navel of the sea
Where, floating on the Maelstrom, abide
The krakens sheltering under Norway's lee;
But go not to Nahant, lest men should swear
You are a great deal bigger than you are.

THE FALL OF NIAGARA.

"Labitur et labetur."

The thoughts are strange that crowd into my brain,
While I look upward to thee. It would seem
As if God pour'd thee from his "hollow hand,"
And hung his bow upon thine awful front;
And spoke in that loud voice, which seem'd to him
Who dwelt in Patmos for his Saviour's sake,
"The sound of many waters;" and had bade
Thy flood to chronicle the ages back,
And notch His centuries in the eternal rocks.
Deep calleth unto deep. And what are we,
That hear the question of that voice sublime?
O! what are all the notes that ever rung
From war's vain trumpet, by thy thundering side!
Yea, what is all the riot man can make
In his short life, to thy unceasing roar!
And yet, bold babbler, what art thou to Him
Who drown'd a world, and heaped the waters far
Above its loftiest mountains!—a light wave,
That breaks, and whispers of its Maker's might.

ON THE DEATH OF A FRIEND.

Who shall weep when the righteous die?
Who shall mourn when the good depart?
When the soul of the godly away shall fly,
Who shall lay the loss to heart?

He has gone into peace—he has laid him down,
To sleep till the dawn of a brighter day;
And he shall wake on that holy morn,
When sorrow and sighing shall flee away.

But ye who worship in sin and shame
Your idol gods, whate'er they be:
Who scoff, in your pride, at your Maker's name,
By the pebbly stream and the shady tree,—

Hope in your mountains, and hope in your streams,
Bow down in their worship, and loudly pray;
Trust in your strength, and believe in your dreams,
But the wind shall carry them all away.

There's one who drank at a purer fountain,
One who was wash'd in a purer flood:
He shall inherit a holier mountain,
He shall worship a holier God.

But the sinner shall utterly fail and die,
Whelm'd in the waves of a troubled sea;
And God, from his throne of light on high,
Shall say, there is no peace for thee.

EPITHALAMIUM.

I saw two clouds at morning,
Tinged by the rising sun,
And in the dawn they floated on,
And mingled into one;
I thought that morning cloud was bless'd,
It moved so sweetly to the west.

I saw two summer currents
Flow smoothly to their meeting,
And join their course, with silent force,
In peace each other greeting;
Calm was their course through banks of green,
While dimpling eddies play'd between.

Such be your gentle motion,
Till life's last pulse shall beat;
Like summer's beam, and summer's stream
Float on, in joy, to meet
A calmer sea, where storms shall cease—
A purer sky, where all is peace.

* Professor Fisher, lost in the Albion, off the coast of Kinsale, Ireland.

TO THE DEAD.

How many now are dead to me
That live to others yet!
How many are alive to me
Who crumble in their graves, nor see
That sickening, sinking look, which we
Till dead can ne'er forget.

Beyond the blue seas, far away,
Most wretchedly alone,
One died in prison, far away,
Where stone on stone shut out the day,
And never hope or comfort's ray
In his lone dungeon shone.

Dead to the world, alive to me,
Though months and years have pass'd;
In a lone hour, his sigh to me
Comes like the hum of some wild bee,
And then his form and face I see,
As when I saw him last.

And one with a bright lip, and check,
And eye, is dead to me.
How pale the bloom of his smooth cheek!
His lip was cold—it would not speak:
His heart was dead, for it did not break:
And his eye, for it did not see.

Then for the living be the tomb,
And for the dead the smile;
Engrave oblivion on the tomb
Of pulseless life and deadly bloom,—
Dim is such glare: but bright the gloom
Around the funeral pile.

THE DEEP.

There's beauty in the deep:
The wave is bluer than the sky;
And, though the lights shine bright on high,
More softly do the sea-gems glow,
That sparkle in the depths below;
The rainbow's tints are only made
When on the waters they are laid;
And sun and moon most sweetly shine
Upon the ocean's level brine.
There's beauty in the deep.

There's music in the deep:—
It is not in the surf's rough roar,
Nor in the whispering, shelly shore,—
They are but earthly sounds, that tell
How little of the sea-nymph's shell,
That sends its loud, clear note abroad,
Or winds its softness through the flood,
Echoes through groves, with coral gay,
And dies, on spongy banks, away.
There's music in the deep.

There's quiet in the deep:—
Above, let tides and tempests rave,
And earth-born whirlwinds wake the wave;
Above, let care and fear contend
With sin and sorrow, to the end:
Here, far beneath the tainted foam
That frets above our peaceful home;
We dream in joy, and wake in love,
Nor know the rage that yells above.
There's quiet in the deep.

MR. MERRY'S LAMENT FOR "LONG TOM."

"Let us think of them that sleep,
Full many a fathom deep,
By thy wild and stormy steep,
Elsinore."

Thy cruise is over now,
Thou art anchor'd by the shore,
And never more shalt thou
Hear the storm around thee roar;
Death has shaken out the sands of thy glass
Now around thee sports the whale,
And the porpoise snuffs the gale,
And the night-winds wake their wail,
As they pass.

Thy sea-grass round thy bier
Shall bend beneath the tide,
Nor tell the breakers near
Where thy manly limbs abide;
But the granite rock thy tombstone shall be.
Though the edges of thy grave
Are the combings of the wave—
Yet unheeded they shall rave
Over thee.

At the piping of all hands,
When the judgment signal's spread—
When the islands, and the lands,
And the seas give up their dead,
And the south and the north shall come;
When the sinner is dismay'd,
And the just man is afraid,
Then heaven be thy aid,
Poor Tom.

THE INDIAN SUMMER.

What is there saddening in the autumn leaves?
Have they that "green and yellow melancholy"
That the sweet poet spake of?—Had he seen
Our variegated woods, when first the frost
Turns into beauty all October's charms—
When the dread fever quits us—when the storms
Of the wild equinox, with all its wet,
Has left the land, as the first deluge left it,
With a bright bow of many colours hung
Upon the forest tops—he had not sighed.
The moon stays longest for the hunter now:
The trees cast down their fruitage, and the blithe
And busy squirrel hoards his winter store:
While man enjoys the breeze that sweeps along
The bright, blue sky above him, and that bends
Magnificently all the forest's pride,
Or whispers through the evergreens, and asks,
"What is there saddening in the autumn leaves?"

STANZAS.

The dead leaves strew the forest walk,
  And wither'd are the pale wild flowers;
The frost hangs blackening on the stalk,
  The dew-drops fall in frozen showers.
  Gone are the spring's green sprouting bowers,
Gone summer's rich and mantling vines,
  And autumn, with her yellow hours,
On hill and plain no longer shines.

I learn'd a clear and wild-toned note,
  That rose and swell'd from yonder tree—
A gay bird, with too sweet a throat,
  There perch'd, and raised her song for me.
  The winter comes, and where is she?
Away—where summer wings will rove,
  Where buds are fresh, and every tree
Is vocal with the notes of love.

Too mild the breath of southern sky,
  Too fresh the flower that blushes there,
The northern breeze that rustles by
  Finds leaves too green, and buds too fair;
  No forest tree stands stripp'd and bare,
No stream beneath the ice is dead,
  No mountain top, with sleety hair,
Bends o'er the snows its reverend head.

Go there, with all the birds, and seek
  A happier clime, with livelier flight,
Kiss, with the sun, the evening's cheek,
  And leave me lonely with the night.
  I'll gaze upon the cold north light,
And mark where all its glories shone,—
  See—that it all is fair and bright,
Feel—that it all is cold and gone.

THE STORM OF WAR.

O! once was felt the storm of war!
  It had an earthquake's roar;
It flash'd upon the mountain height,
  And smoked along the shore.
It thunder'd in a dreaming ear,
  And up the farmer sprang;
It mutter'd in a bold, true heart,
  And a warrior's harness rang.

It rumbled by a widow's door,—
  All but her hope did fail;
It trembled through a leafy grove,
  And a maiden's cheek was pale.
It steps upon the sleeping sea,
  And waves around it howl;
It strides from top to foaming top,
  Out-frowning ocean's scowl.

And yonder sail'd the merchant ship,
  There was peace upon her deck;
Her friendly flag from the mast was torn,
  And the waters whelm'd the wreck.
But the same blast that bore her down
  Fill'd a gallant daring sail,
That loved the might of the blackening storm,
  And laugh'd in the roaring gale.

The stream, that was a torrent once,
  Is rippled to a brook,
The sword is broken, and the spear
  Is but a pruning-hook.
The mother chides her truant boy,
  And keeps him well from harm;
While in the grove the happy maid
  Hangs on her lover's arm.

Another breeze is on the sea,
  Another wave is there,
And floats abroad triumphantly
  A banner bright and fair.
And peaceful hands, and happy hearts,
  And gallant spirits keep
Each star that decks it pure and bright,
  Above the rolling deep.

THE GUERILLA.

Though friends are false, and leaders fail,
  And rulers quake with fear;
Though tamed the shepherd in the vale,
  Though slain the mountaineer;
Though Spanish beauty fill their arms,
  And Spanish gold their purse—
Sterner than wealth's or war's alarms
  Is the wild Guerilla's curse.

No trumpets range us to the fight
  No signal sound of drum
Tells to the foe, that, in their might,
  The hostile squadrons come.
No sunbeam glitters on our spears,
  No warlike tramp of steeds
Gives warning—for the first that hears
  Shall be the first that bleeds.

The night-breeze calls us from our bed
  At dew-fall forms the line,
And darkness gives the signal dread
  That makes our ranks combine:
Or should some straggling moonbeam lie
  On copse or lurking hedge,
'T would flash but from a Spaniard's eye,
  Or from a dagger's edge.

'T is clear in the sweet vale below,
  And misty on the hill;
The skies shine mildly on the foe,
  But lour upon us still.
This gathering storm shall quickly burst,
  And spread its terrors far,
And at its front we'll be the first,
  And with it go to war.

O! the mountain peak shall safe remain—
  'T is the vale shall be despoil'd,
And the tame hamlets of the plain
  With ruin shall run wild;
But liberty shall breathe our air
  Upon the mountain head,
And freedom's breezes wander here,
  Here all their fragrance shed.

THE SEA-BIRD'S SONG.

On the deep is the mariner's danger,
On the deep is the mariner's death,
Who, to fear of the tempest a stranger,
Sees the last bubble burst of his breath?
'T is the sea-bird, sea-bird, sea-bird,
Lone looker on despair,
The sea-bird, sea-bird, sea-bird,
The only witness there.

Who watches their course, who so mildly
Careen to the kiss of the breeze?
Who lists to their shrieks, who so wildly
Are clasp'd in the arms of the seas?
'T is the sea-bird, &c.

Who hovers on high o'er the lover,
And her who has clung to his neck?
Whose wing is the wing that can cover,
With its shadow, the foundering wreck?
'T is the sea-bird, &c.

My eye in the light of the billow,
My wing on the wake of the wave,
I shall take to my breast, for a pillow,
The shroud of the fair and the brave.
I'm a sea-bird, &c.

My foot on the iceberg has lighted,
When hoarse the wild winds veer about,
My eye, when the bark is benighted,
Sees the lamp of the light-house go out.
I'm the sea-bird, sea-bird, sea-bird,
Lone looker on despair;
The sea-bird, sea-bird, sea-bird,
The only witness there.

TO THE DAUGHTER OF A FRIEND.

I pray thee, by thy mother's face,
And by her look, and by her eye,
By every decent matron grace
That hover'd round the resting-place
Where thy young head did lie;
And by the voice that soothed thine ear,
The hymn, the smile, the sigh, the tear,
That match'd thy changeful mood;
By every prayer thy mother taught,
By every blessing that she sought,
I pray thee to be good.

Is not the nestling, when it wakes,
Its eye upon the wood around,
And on its new-fledged pinions takes
Its taste of leaves, and boughs, and brakes—
Of motion, sight, and sound,—
Is it not like the parent? Then
Be like thy mother, child, and when
Thy wing is bold and strong,—
As pure and steady be thy light,
As high and heavenly be thy flight,
As holy be thy song.

SALMON RIVER.*

Hic viridis tenera prætexit arundine ripas
Mincius.—Virgil.

'T is a sweet stream—and so, 't is true, are all
That, undisturb'd, save by the harmless brawl
Of mimic rapid or slight waterfall,
Pursue their way
By mossy bank, and darkly waving wood,
By rock, that since the deluge fix'd has stood,
Showing to sun and moon their crisping flood
By night and day.

But yet there's something in its humble rank,
Something in its pure wave and sloping bank,
Where the deer sported, and the young fawn drank
With unscared look;
There 's much in its wild history, that teems
With all that's superstitious—and that seems
To match our fancy and eke out our dreams
In that small brook.

Havoc has been upon its peaceful plain,
And blood has dropp'd there, like the drops of rain;
The corn grows o'er the still graves of the slain—
And many a quiver,
Fill'd from the reeds that grew on yonder hill,
Has spent itself in carnage. Now 't is still,
And whistling ploughboys oft their runlets fill
From Salmon river.

Here, say old men, the Indian magi made
Their spells by moonlight; or beneath the shade
That shrouds sequester'd rock, or darkening glade,
Or tangled dell.
Here Philip came, and Miantonimo,
And ask'd about their fortunes long ago,
As Saul to Endor, that her witch might show
Old Samuel.

And here the black fox roved, that howl'd and shook
His thick tail to the hunters, by the brook
Where they pursued their game, and him mistook
For earthly fox;
Thinking to shoot him like a shaggy bear,
And his soft peltry, stripp'd and dress'd, to wear,
Or lay a trap, and from his quiet lair
Transfer him to a box.

Such are the tales they tell. 'T is hard to rhym
About a little and unnoticed stream,
That few have heard of—but it is a theme
I chance to love;
And one day I may tune my rye-straw reed,
And whistle to the note of many a deed
Done on this river—which, if there be need,
I'll try to prove.

* This river enters into the Connecticut at East Haddam

WALTER COLTON.

[Born, 1797. Died, 1851.]

WALTER COLTON was born in Rutland county, Vermont, on the ninth of May, 1797. When about seventeen years of age he determined to acquire a liberal education, and commenced with industrious energy his preparatory studies. In 1818 he entered Yale College, where he received the Berkleyan prize in Latin and Greek, and delivered the valedictory poem, when he graduated, in 1822. He soon afterward went to the Theological Seminary at Andover, where he remained three years, giving much of his time to literature, and writing, besides various moral and critical dissertations, a "Sacred Drama," which was acted by the students at one of their rhetorical exhibitions, and an elaborate poem pronounced when his class received their diplomas. On being ordained an evangelist, according to the usage of the Congregational church, he became Professor of Moral Philosophy and Belles-Lettres in the Scientific and Military Academy at Middletown, then under the presidency of Captain ALDEN PARTRIDGE. While occupying this position, he wrote a prize "Essay on Duelling;" a "Discussion of the Genius of Coleridge;" "The Moral Power of the Poet, Painter, and Sculptor, contrasted," and many contributions in verse and prose to the public journals, under the signature of "Bertram." In 1828 he resigned his professorship, and settled in Washington, as editor of the "American Spectator," a weekly gazette, which he conducted with industry, and such tact and temper as to preserve the most intimate relations with the leaders of the political party to which it was opposed. He was especially a favourite with President JACKSON, who was accustomed to send for him two or three times in a week to sit with him in his private chamber; and when Mr. COLTON's health declined, so that a sea voyage was recommended by his physicians, the President offered him, without solicitation, a consulship or a chaplaincy in the Navy. The latter was accepted, and he held the office from 1830 till the end of his life.

His first appointment was to the West India squadron, in which he continued but seven or eight months. He next sailed for the Mediterranean, in the flag-ship Constellation, Commodore READ, and in the three years of his connection with this station he travelled through Spain, Italy, Greece, and Asia Minor, visited Constantinople, and made his way to Paris and London. The results of his observations are partially given to the public in volumes entitled "Ship and Shore," and "A Visit to Constantinople and Athens." Soon after the publication of these works, he was appointed historiographer to the South Sea Surveying and Exploring Expedition; but the ultimate reduction of the force designed for the Pacific squadron, and the resignation of his associates induced him to forego the advantages of this office, for which he had made very careful preparations in ethnographical studies.

He was now stationed at Philadelphia, where he was chaplain successively of the Navy Yard and the Naval Asylum. In this city I became acquainted with him, and for several years enjoyed his frequent society and intimate friendship. In 1841 and 1842, with the consent of the Government, he added to his official duties the editorship of the Philadelphia "North American," and in these and the following years he wrote much on religious and literary subjects for other journals. In 1844 he delivered before the literary societies of the University of Vermont a poem entitled "The Sailor." In the summer of 1846 he was married, and in the following autumn was ordered to the Congress, the flag-ship of the Pacific squadron, in which he arrived off the western coast of America soon after the commencement of the war with Mexico. The incidents of the voyage round Cape Horn are detailed with more than his usual felicity in the book called "Deck and Port," which he published in 1850.

Soon after the arrival of the squadron at Monterey, he was appointed alcalde, or chief magistrate, of that city, an office demanding untiring industry, zeal, and fortitude. He displayed in it eminent faithfulness and ability, and won as much the regard of the conquered inhabitants of the country, as the respect of his more immediate associates. Besides performing his ordinary duties he established the first newspaper printed in California, "The Californian;" built the first school-house in the territory; and also a large hall for public meetings, which the citizens called "Colton Hall," in honour of his public spirit and enterprise. It was during his administration of affairs at Monterey that the discovery of gold in the Sacramento Valley was first made; and the honour of first making it publicly known in the Atlantic states, whether by accident or otherwise, belongs properly to him. It was first announced in a letter bearing his initials, in the Philadelphia "North American," and the next day in a letter also written by him, in the New York "Journal of Commerce."

Mr. COLTON returned to his home early in the summer of 1850, anticipating years of undisturbed happiness. With an attached family, a large circle of friends, good reputation, and a fortune equal to his desires, he applied himself leisurely to the preparation of his manuscript journals for the press, and the revision of his earlier publications. He had completed, besides "Deck and Port," already mentioned, "Three Years in California," and had nearly ready for the printer a much enlarged and improved edition of "Ship and

Shore," which was to be followed by "A Visit to Constantinople, Athens, and the Ægean," a collection of his "Poems," and a volume of "Miscellanies of Literature and Religion." His health however, began to decline, and a cold, induced by exposure during a visit to Washington, ended in disease which his physician soon discovered to be incurable. Being in Philadelphia on the twenty-second of January, I left my hotel to pay him an early visit, and found the death signs upon his door; he had died at two o'clock that morning, surrounded by his relations, and in the presence of his friends the Rev. ALBERT BARNES and the Rev. Dr. HERMAN HOOKER—died very calmly, without mortal enemies and at peace with God.

Mr. COLTON was of an eminently genial nature, fond of society, and with such qualities as made him always a welcome associate. His extensive and various travel had left upon his memory a thousand delightful pictures, which were reflected in his conversation so distinctly and with such skilful preparation of the mind, that his companions lived over his life with him as often as he chose to summon its scenes before them.

It cannot be said that there are in the poems of Mr. COLTON indications of genius, but many of his pieces display a quiet humour and refinement of feeling, and they have generally the merit of being apparently fruits of his own experience.

THE SAILOR.

A SAILOR ever loves to be in motion,
Roaming about he scarce knows where or why;
He looks upon the dim and shadowy ocean
As home, abhors the land; and e'en the sky,
Boundless and beautiful, has naught to please,
Except some clouds, which promise him a breeze.

He is a child of mere impulse and passion,
Loving his friends, and generous to his foes,
And fickle as the most ephemeral fashion,
Save in the cut and colour of his clothes,
And in a set of phrases which, on land,
The wisest head could never understand.

He thinks his dialect the very best
That ever flow'd from any human lip,
And whether in his prayers, or at a jest,
Uses the terms for managing a ship;
And even in death would order up the helm,
In hope to clear the "undiscover'd realm."

He makes a friend where'er he meets a shore,
One whom he cherishes with some affection;
But leaving port, he thinks of her no more,
Unless it be, perchance, in some reflection
Upon his wicked ways, then, with a sigh,
Resolves on reformation—ere he die.

In calms, he gazes at the sleeping sea,
Or seeks his lines, and sets himself to angling,
Or takes to politics, and, being free
Of facts and full of feeling, falls to wrangling:
Then recollects a distant eye and lip,
And rues the day on which he saw a ship:

Then looks up to the sky to watch each cloud,
As it displays its faint and fleeting form;
Then o'er the calm begins to mutter loud,
And swears he would exchange it for a storm,
Tornado, any thing—to put a close
To this most dead, monotonous repose.

An order given, and he obeys, of course,
Though 'twere to run his ship upon the rocks—
Capture a squadron with a boat's-crew force—
Or batter down the massive granite blocks
Of some huge fortress with a swivel, pike,
Pistol, aught that will throw a ball, or strike.

He never shrinks, whatever may betide;
His weapon may be shiver'd in his hand,
His last companion shot down at his side,
Still he maintains his firm and desperate stand—
Bleeding and battling—with his colours fast
As nail can bind them to his shatter'd mast....

I love the sailor—his eventful life—
His generous spirit—his contempt of danger—
His firmness in the gale, the wreck, and strife;
And though a wild and reckless ocean-ranger,
GOD grant he make that port, when life is o'er,
Where storms are hush'd, and billows break no more.

MY FIRST LOVE, AND MY LAST.

CATHARA, when the many silent tears
Of beauty, bending o'er thy bed,
Bespoke the change familiar to our fears,
I could not think thy spirit yet had fled—
So like to life the slumber death had cast
On thy sweet face, my first love and my last.

I watch'd to see those lids their light unfold,
For still thy forehead rose serene and fair,
As when those raven ringlets richly roll'd
O'er life, which dwelt in thought and beauty there
Thy cheek the while was rosy with the theme
That flush'd along the spirit's mystic dream.

Thy lips were circled with that silent smile
Which oft around their dewy freshness woke,
When some more happy thought or harmless wile
Upon thy warm and wandering fancy broke:
For thou wert Nature's child, and took the tone
Of every pulse, as if it were thine own.

I watch'd, and still believed that thou wouldst wake,
When others came to place thee in the shroud:
I thought to see this seeming slumber break,
As I have seen a light, transparent cloud
Disperse, which o'er a star's sweet face had thrown
A shadow like to that which veil'd thine own.

But, no: there was no token, look, or breath:
The tears of those around, the tolling bell
And hearse told us at last that this was death!
I know not if I breathed a last farewell;
But since that day my sweetest hours have pass'd
In thought of thee, my first love and my last.

WILLIAM B. WALTER.

[Born, about 1796. Died, 1823.]

The first American ancestor of William B. Walter was "the good old puritan," as Whitfield styles him, the Reverend Nehemiah Walter, who was graduated at Harvard College in 1681, and was soon after ordained as colleague of the apostle Eliot. He was a great grandson of the Reverend Increase Mather, one of the most celebrated characters in the ecclesiastical and civil history of New England; a grandson of the Reverend Nathaniel Walter, many years a distinguished minister of Roxbury; and a son of the Reverend William Walter, D.D., sometime rector of Trinity Church, in Boston. He was educated at Bowdoin College, where he took his bachelor's degree in 1818. In 1821 he published in Boston two volumes, entitled "Sukey," and "Poems." Of "Sukey" a third edition was printed the same year in Baltimore. He confesses an anxiety for fame, and informs us that these works are the measure of his best abilities.

WHERE IS HE!

His way was on the waters deep,
For lands, far distant and unknown;
His heart could feel, his eye could weep,
For sufferings other than his own;
And he could seem what others be,
Yet only seem: but where is he?

I wander through this grove of love—
The valley lone—and climb the hill,
Where he was wont in life to rove;
And all looks calm and pleasant still;
And there, his bower and cypress tree—
That tree of gloom—but where is he?

The sun above shines now as bright
Through heaven's blue depths, as once it shone;
The clouds roll beautiful in light,
Sweeping around the Eternal's throne;
The singing birds are full of glee,
Their songs are sweet: but where is he?

The mirror of the moon on high—
That bright lake—seems as softly calm;
The stars as richly throng the sky;
The night winds breathe their fragrant balm;
Rolls on as bright that deep blue sea
Its mighty waves: but where is he?

Here is the wreath he twined; but now
This rosy wreath is twined in vain;
Tears, nor the bosom's warmest glow,
Will ever give it life again!—
All this is dark and strange to me,
And still I ask: oh, where is he?

I touch his harp; the magic strings,
The loveliest sounds of music pour—
But sadly wild, as if the wings
Of Death's dark angel swept them o'er;
The chords are lulled! It may not be!
And spirits whisper: Where is he?

His way was on the waters deep;
His corse is on an unknown shore;
He sleeps a long and dreamless sleep,
And we shall see his face no more.
'T is a sad tale! he died for me!
Oh, God! enough!—but where is he?

EXTRACT FROM A POEM "TO AN INFANT."

Ah! little deemest thou, my child,
The way of life is dark and wild—
Its sunshine, but a light whose play
Serves but to dazzle and betray—
Weary and long; its end, the tomb,
Where darkness spreads her wings of gloom,
That resting-place of things which live,
The goal of all that earth can give.

It may be that the dreams of fame,
Proud Glory's plume, the warrior's name,
Shall lure thee to the field of blood,
Where, like a god, war's fiery flood
May bear thee on; while, far above,
Thy crimson banners proudly move,
Like the red clouds which skirt the sun,
When the fierce tempest-day is done!

Or lead thee to a cloister'd cell,
Where Learning's votaries lonely dwell—
The midnight lamp and brow of care,
The frozen heart that mocks despair,
Consumption's fires that burn the cheek,
The brain that throbs, but will not break,
The travail of the soul, to gain
A name, and die—alas! in vain.

Thou reckest not, sweet slumberer, there,
Of this world's crimes; of many a snare
To catch the soul; of pleasures wild,
Friends false, foes dark, and hearts beguiled;
Of Passion's ministers who sway,
With iron sceptre, all who stray;
Of broken hearts still loving on,
When all is lost, and changed, and gone!

Thy tears will flow, and thou wilt weep
As he has wept who eyes thy sleep,
But weeps no more: His heart is cold,
Warp'd, sicken'd, sear'd, with woes untold
And be it so! the clouds which roll
Dark, heavy, o'er my troubled soul,
Bring with them lightnings, which illume,
To shroud the mind in deeper gloom!

JAMES WALLIS EASTBURN.

[Born, 1797. Died, 1819.]

The literary career of JAMES WALLIS EASTBURN was so intimately connected with that of ROBERT C. SANDS, that its most interesting features will necessarily be stated in the biography of that author. He was a son of JAMES EASTBURN, a well-known New York bookseller, and a brother of MANTON EASTBURN, now bishop of the Protestant Episcopal Church in Massachusetts. He was graduated at Columbia College, in New York, studied theology under Bishop GRISWOLD, at Bristol, Rhode Island, and, being admitted to orders, was settled in Virginia. Declining health soon compelled him to relinquish his professional occupations, however, and on the twenty-eighth of November, 1819, he sailed from New York for Santa Cruz, as a last resource for recruiting his exhausted constitution, and died at sea, four days after, at the early age of twenty-two years.

"Yamoyden" was planned by young EASTBURN during his residence amid the scenes of King PHILIP'S wars, in Rhode Island, and he undoubtedly wrote a considerable portion of the first and second cantos; but the genius of SANDS is apparent in the more remarkable passages of the poem, and he must have been the author of much the greater part of it, though he modestly withheld his name from the title page, on its publication, after EASTBURN'S death. Besides an unfinished metrical version of the Psalms, EASTBURN left a volume of manuscript poems, from which a considerable number of specimens were published in the "United States Literary Gazette" for 1824.

TO PNEUMA.

TEMPESTS their furious course may sweep
Swiftly o'er the troubled deep,
Darkness may lend her gloomy aid,
And wrap the groaning world in shade;
But man can show a darker hour,
And bend beneath a stronger power:
There is a tempest of the soul,
A gloom where wilder billows roll!

The howling wilderness may spread
Its pathless deserts, parched and dread,
Where not a blade of herbage blooms,
Nor yields the breeze its soft perfumes;
Where silence, death, and horror reign,
Uncheck'd, across the wide domain:
There is a desert of the mind
More hopeless, dreary, undefined.

There sorrow, moody discontent,
And gnawing care are wildly blent;
There horror hangs her darkest clouds,
And the whole scene in gloom enshrouds;
A sickly ray is cast around,
Where naught but dreariness is found;
A feeling that may not be told,
Dark, rending, lonely, drear, and cold.

The wildest ills that darken life
Are rapture, to the bosom's strife;
The tempest, in its blackest form,
Is beauty, to the bosom's storm;
The ocean, lashed to fury loud,
Its high wave mingling with the cloud,
Is peaceful, sweet serenity,
To passion's dark and boundless sea.

There sleeps no calm, there smiles no rest,
When storms are warring in the breast;
There is no moment of repose
In bosoms lashed by hidden woes;
The scorpion stings, the fury rears
And every trembling fibre tears,
The vulture preys, with bloody beak,
Upon—the heart that can but break!

SONG OF AN INDIAN MOTHER.

SLEEP, child of my love! be thy slumber as light
As the redbird's that nestles secure on the spray;
Be the visions that visit thee fairy and bright
As the dewdrops that sparkle around with the ray!

Oh, soft flows the breath from thine innocent breast;
In the wild wood sleep cradles, in roses, thy head;
But her who protects thee, a wanderer unbless'd,
He forsakes, or surrounds with his phantoms of dread.

I fear for thy father! why stays he so long
On the shores where the wife of the giant was thrown,
And the sailor oft lingered to hearken her song,
So sad o'er the wave, ere she hardened to stone!

He skims the blue tide in his birchen canoe,
Where the foe in the moonbeams his path may descry;
The ball to its scope may speed rapid and true,
And lost in the wave be thy father's death cry!

The POWER that is round us, whose presence is near,
In the gloom and the solitude felt by the soul,
Protect that frail bark in its lonely career,
And shield *thee* when roughly life's billows shall roll.

ROBERT C. SANDS.

[Born, 1799. Died, 1832.]

The history of American literature, for the period which has already passed, will contain the names of few men of greater genius, or more general learning, than Robert C. Sands. His life has been written so well by his intimate friend, Gulian C. Verplanck, LL. D., that I shall attempt only to present an abstract of the narrative of that accomplished scholar and critic.

Sands was born in the city of New York, (where his father, who had been distinguished for his patriotism during the revolutionary struggle, was an eminent merchant,) on the eleventh of May, 1799. At a very early age he was remarkable for great quickness of apprehension, and facility of acquiring knowledge. When seven years old, he began to study the Latin language, and at thirteen he was admitted to the sophomore class of Columbia College. He had already, under Mr. Findlay, of Newark, and the Reverend Mr. Whelpley, of New York, made great progress in classical knowledge; and while in the college, which had long been distinguished for sound and accurate instruction in the dead languages, he excelled all his classmates in ancient learning, and was equally successful in the mathematics and other branches of study. In his second collegiate year, in conjunction with his friend Eastburn, and some other students, he established a periodical entitled "The Moralist," and afterward another, called "Academic Recreations," of both of which he wrote the principal contents. He was graduated in 1815, and soon after became a student in the law-office of David B. Ogden, one of the most distinguished advocates of the time. He pursued his legal studies with great ardour; his course of reading was very extensive; and he became not only familiar with the more practical part of professional knowledge, but acquired a relish for the abstruse doctrines and subtle reasonings of the ancient common law.

Still he found time for the study of the classics; and, in company with two or three friends, read several of the most difficult of the Greek authors, exactly and critically. His love of composition continued to grow upon him. He wrote on all subjects, and for all purposes; and, in addition to essays and verses, on topics of his own choice, volunteered to write orations for the commencement displays of young graduates, verses for young lovers, and even sermons for young divines. Several of the latter, written in an animated style, were much admired, when delivered in the pulpit with good emphasis and discretion, to congregations who little suspected to whom they were indebted for their edification. One of them, at least, has been printed under the name of the clergyman by whom it was delivered. In 1817 he published a poem, which he had begun and in great part written four years before. It was called "The Bridal of Vaumond," and was a metrical romance, founded on the same legend of the transformation of a decrepit and miserable wretch into a youthful hero, by compact with the infernal powers, which forms the groundwork of Byron's "Deformed Transformed."

It was during the period of these studies, that he and three of his friends, of as many different professions, formed an association, of a somewhat remarkable character, under the name of the Literary Confederacy. The number was limited to four; and they bound themselves to preserve a friendly communication in all the vicissitudes of life, and to endeavour, by all proper means, to advance their mutual and individual interest, to advise each other on every subject, and to receive with good temper the rebuke or admonition which might thus be given. They proposed to unite, from time to time, in literary publications, covenanting solemnly that no matter hostile to the great principles of religion or morals should be published by any member. This compact was most faithfully kept to the time of Sands's death, though the primary objects of it were gradually given up, as other duties engrossed the attention of its members. In the first year of its existence, the confederacy contributed largely to several literary and critical gazettes, besides publishing in one of the daily papers of the city a series of essays, under the title of the "Amphilogist," and a second under that of the "Neologist," which attracted much attention, and were very widely circulated and republished in the newspapers of the day. Sands wrote a large portion of these, both in prose and verse.

His friend Eastburn had now removed to Bristol, Rhode Island, where, after studying divinity for some time under the direction of Bishop Griswold, he took orders, and soon after settled in Virginia. A regular correspondence was kept up between the friends; and the letters that have been preserved are filled with the evidence of their literary industry. Eastburn had undertaken a new metrical version of the Psalms, which the pressure of his clerical duties and his untimely death prevented him from ever completing. Sands was led by curiosity, as well as by his intimacy with Eastburn, to acquire some knowledge of the Hebrew. It was not very profound, but it enabled him to try his skill at the same translation; and he from time to time sent his friend a Psalm paraphrased in verse.

But amid their severer studies and their literary amusements, they were engaged in a bolder poetical enterprise. This was a romantic poem, founded on the history of Philip, the celebrated sachem of the Pequods, and leader of the great Indian wars against the New England colonists in 1665 and 1676. It was planned by EASTBURN, during his residence in the vicinity of Mount Hope, in Rhode Island, the ancient capital of the Pequod race, where the scene is laid. In the year following, when he visited New York, the plan of the story was drawn up in conjunction with his friend. "We had then," said SANDS, "read nothing on the subject; and our plot was formed from a hasty glance into a few pages of HUBBARD's Narrative. After EASTBURN's return to Bristol, the poem was written, according to the parts severally assigned, and transmitted, reciprocally, in the course of correspondence. It was commenced in November, 1817, and finished before the summer of 1818, except the concluding stanzas of the sixth canto, which were added after Mr. EASTBURN left Bristol. As the fable was defective, from our ignorance of the subject, the execution was also, from the same cause, and the hasty mode of composition, in every respect imperfect. Mr. EASTBURN was then preparing to take orders; and his studies, with that view, engrossed his attention. He was ordained in October, 1818. Between that time and the period of his going to Accomack county, Virginia, whence he had received an invitation to take charge of a congregation, he transcribed the first two cantos of this poem, with but few material variations, from the first collating copy. The labours of his ministry left him no time even for his most delightful amusement. He had made no further progress in the correction of the work when he returned to New York, in July, 1819. His health was then so much impaired, that writing of any kind was too great a labour. He had packed up the manuscripts, intending to finish his second copy in Santa Cruz, whither it was recommended to him to go, as the last resource to recruit his exhausted constitution." He died on the fourth day of his passage, on the second of December, 1819. The work, thus left imperfect, was revised, arranged, and completed, with many additions, by SANDS. It was introduced by a proem, in which the surviving poet mourned, in noble and touching strains, the accomplished friend of his youth.

The work was published under the title of "Yamoyden," at New York, in 1820. It unquestionably shows some marks of the youth of its authors, besides other imperfections arising from the mode of its composition, which could not fail to prove a serious impediment to a clear connection of the plot, and a vivid and congruous conception of all the characters. Yet it has high merit in various ways. Its descriptions of natural scenery are alike accurate and beautiful. Its style is flexible, flowing, and poetical. It is rich throughout with historical and antiquarian knowledge of Indian history and tradition; and every thing in the customs, manners, superstitions, and story of the aborigines of New England, that could be applied to poetical purposes, is used with skill, judgment, and taste.

In 1820, SANDS was admitted to the bar, and opened an office in the city of New York. He entered upon his professional career with high hopes and an ardent love of the learning of the law. His first attempt as an advocate was, however, unsuccessful, and he was disheartened by the result. Though he continued the business of an attorney, he made no second attempt of consequence before a jury, and after a few years he gradually withdrew himself from the profession. During this period he persevered in his law reading, and renewed and extended his acquaintance with the Latin poets, and the "grave, lofty tragedians" of Greece; acquiring an intimacy such as professors might have envied, with the ancient languages and learning. He had early learned French, and was familiar with its copious and elegant literature; but he never much admired it, and in his multifarious literary conversation and authorship, rarely quoted or alluded to a French author, except for facts. He now acquired the Italian, and read carefully and with great admiration all its great writers, from DANTE to ALFIERI. His versions and imitations of POLITIAN, MONTI, and METASTASIO, attest how fully he entered into their spirit. Some time after he acquired the Spanish language very critically, and, after studying its more celebrated writers, read very largely all the Spanish historians and documents he could find touching American history. In order to complete his acquaintance with the cognate modern languages of Latin origin, he some years later acquired the Portuguese, and read such of its authors as he could procure.

In 1822 and 1823 he wrote many articles for "The Literary Review," a monthly periodical then published in New York, which received great increase of reputation from his contributions. In the winter of 1823-4, he and some friends published seven numbers of a sort of mock-magazine, entitled "The St. Tammany Magazine." Here he gave the reins to his most extravagant and happiest humour, indulging in parody, burlesque, and grotesque satire, thrown off in the gayest mood and with the greatest rapidity, but as good-natured as satire and parody could well be. In May, 1824, "The Atlantic Magazine" was established in New York, and placed under his charge. At the end of six months he gave up this work; but when it changed its name, and in part its character, and became the New York Review, he was reëngaged as an editor, and assisted in conducting it until 1827. During this same period he assisted in preparing and publishing a digest of equity cases, and also in editing some other legal compilations, enriching them with notes of the American decisions. These publications were, it is true, not of a high class of legal authorship; but they show professional reading and knowledge, as well as the ready versatility of his mind. He had now become an author by profession, and looked to his pen for support, as heretofore for fame or for amusement. When, therefore, an offer of a liberal salary was made him as an assistant editor of the "New York Commercial Advertiser," a long-established and well-known daily evening paper, he accepted it, and continued his connection with that journal until his death.

His daily task of political or literary discussion was far from giving him sufficient literary employment. His mind overflowed in all directions into other journals, even some of different political opinions from those which he supported. He had a propensity for innocent and playful literary mischief. It was his sport to excite public curiosity by giving extracts, highly spiced with fashionable allusions and satire, "*from the forthcoming novel;*" which novel, in truth, was, and is yet to be written; or else to entice some unhappy wight into a literary or historical newspaper discussion, then to combat him anonymously, or, under the mask of a brother editor, to overwhelm him with history, facts, quotations, and authorities, all, if necessary, manufactured for the occasion; in short, like SHAKSPEARE's "merry wanderer of the night," to lead his unsuspecting victim around "through bog, through bush, through brier." One instance of this sportive propensity occurred in relation to a controversy about the material of the Grecian crown of victory, which arose during the excitement in favour of Grecian liberty some years ago. Several ingenious young men, fresh from their college studies, had exhausted all the learning they could procure on this grave question, either from their own acquaintance with antiquity, or at second hand from the writers upon Grecian antiquities, LEMPRIERE, POTTER, BARTHELEMI, or the more erudite *Paschalis de Corona;* till SANDS grew tired of seeing so much scholarship wasted, and ended the controversy by an essay filled with excellent learning, chiefly fabricated by himself for the occasion, and resting mainly on a passage of PAUSANIAS, quoted in the original Greek, for which it is in vain to look in any edition of that author, ancient or modern. He had also other and graver employments. In 1828, some enterprising printers proposed to supply South America with Spanish books suited to that market, and printed in New York. Among the works selected for this purpose were the original letters of CORTES, the conqueror of Mexico. No good life of CORTES then existing in the English or Spanish language, SANDS was employed by the publishers to prepare one, which was to be translated into Spanish, and prefixed to the edition. He was fortunately relieved from any difficulty arising from the want of materials, by finding in the library of the New York Historical Society a choice collection of original Spanish authorities, which afforded him all that he desired. His manuscript was translated into Spanish, and prefixed to the letters of the Conquistador, of which a large edition was printed, while the original remained in manuscript until SANDS's writings were collected, after his death, by Mr. VERPLANCK. Thus his work had the singular fortune of being read throughout Spanish America, in another language, while it was totally unknown in its own country and native tongue. Soon after completing this piece of literary labour, he became accidentally engaged in another undertaking which afforded him much amusement and gratification. The fashion of decorated literary annuals, which the English and French had borrowed some years before from the literary almanacs, so long the favourites of Germany, had reached the United States, and the booksellers in the principal cities were ambitiously vieing with each other in the "Souvenirs," "Tokens," and other annual volumes. Mr. BLISS, a bookseller of New York, desirous to try his fortune in the same way, pressed Mr. SANDS to undertake the editorship of a work of this sort. This he at first declined; but it happened that, in conversation with his two friends, Mr. VERPLANCK and Mr. BRYANT, a regret was expressed that the old fashion of Queen ANNE's time, of publishing volumes of miscellanies by two or three authors together, had gone out of date. They had the advantage, it was said, over our ordinary magazines, of being more select and distinctive in the characters and subjects, and yet did not impose upon the authors the toil or responsibility of a regular and separate work. In this way POPE and SWIFT had published their minor pieces, as had other writers of that day, of no small merit and fame. One of the party proposed to publish a little volume of their own miscellanies, in humble imitation of the English wits of the last century. It occurred to SANDS to combine this idea with the form and decorations of the annual. The materials of a volume were hastily prepared, amid other occupations of the several authors, without any view to profit, and more for amusement than reputation; the kindness of several artists, with whom SANDS was in habits of intimacy, furnished some respectable embellishments; and thus a miscellany which, with the exception of two short poetical contributions, was wholly written by Mr. SANDS and his two friends above named, was published with the title of "The Talisman," and under the name and character of an imaginary author, FRANCIS HERBERT, Esq. It was favourably received, and, on the solicitation of the publisher, a second volume was as hastily prepared in the following year, by the same persons. Of this publication about one-fourth was entirely from SANDS's pen, and about as much more was his joint work with one or another of his friends. This, as the reader must have remarked, was a favourite mode of authorship with him. He composed with ease and rapidity, and, delighting in the work of composition, it gave him additional pleasure to make it a social enjoyment. He had this peculiarity, that the presence of others, in which most authors find a restraint upon the free course of their thoughts and fancies, was to him a source of inspiration and excitement. This was peculiarly visible in gay or humorous writing. In social compositions of this nature, his talent for ludicrous description and character and incident rioted and revelled, so that it generally became more the business of his coadjutor to chasten and sober his thick-coming fancies, than to furnish any thing like an equal contingent of thought or invention. For the purpose of such joint-stock authorship it is necessary that one of the associates should possess SANDS's unhesitating and rapid fluency of written style, and his singular power of seizing the ideas and images of his friends, and assimilating them perfectly to his own.

His "Dream of PAPANTZIN,"* a poem, one of the fruits of his researches into Mexican history, is remarkable for the religious solemnity of the thoughts, the magnificence of the imagery, and the flow of the versification. It was first published in "The Talisman," for the year 1839.

His next literary employment was the publication of a new "Life of PAUL JONES," from original letters and printed and manuscript materials furnished him by a niece of the commodore. He at first meditated an entirely original work, as attractive and discursive as he could make it; but various circumstances limited him in great part to compilation and correction of the materials furnished him, or, as he termed it in one of his letters, in his accustomed quaintness of phrase, "upsetting some English duodecimos, together with all the manuscripts, into an American octavo, withou worrying his brains much about the matter." This biography was printed in 1831, in a closely-printed octavo, and is doubtless the best and most authentic narrative of the life of this gallant, chivalrous, and erratic father of the American navy.

In the close of the year 1832, a work, entitled "Tales of the Glauber Spa," was published in New York. This was a series of original tales by different authors—BRYANT, PAULDING, LEGGETT, and Miss SEDGWICK. To this collection SANDS contributed the introduction, which is tinged with his peculiar humour, and two of the tales, both of which are written in his happiest vein.

The last finished composition of SANDS was a little poem entitled "The Dead of 1832," which appeared anonymously in "The Commercial Advertiser," about a week before his own death. He was destined to join those whom he mourned within the few remaining days of the same year. CHARLES F. HOFFMAN had then just established "The Knickerbocker Magazine," and SANDS, on the seventeenth of December, about four o'clock in the afternoon, sat down to finish an article on "Esquimaux Literature," which he had engaged to furnish for that periodical. After writing with a pencil the following line, suggested, probably, by some topic in the Greenland mythology,

"O, think not my spirit among you abides,"

he was suddenly struck with the disease which removed his own spirit from its material dwelling. Below this line, on the original manuscript, were observed, after his death, several irregular pencil-marks, extending nearly across the page, as if traced by a hand that moved in darkness, or no longer obeyed the impulse of the will. He rose, opened the door, and attempted to pass out of the room, but fell on the threshold. On being assisted to his chamber, and placed on the bed, he was observed to raise his powerless right arm with the other, and looking at it, to shed tears. He shortly after relapsed into a lethargy, from which he never awoke, and in less than four hours from the attack, expired without a struggle. He died in his thirty-fourth year, when his talents, enriched by study and the experience of life, and invigorated by constant exercise, were fully matured for greater and bolder literary enterprise than any he had yet essayed. His death was deeply mourned by many friends, and most deeply by those who knew him best.

* "PAPANTZIN, a Mexican princess, sister of MOTEUCZOMA, and widow of the governor of Tlatelolco, died, as was supposed, in the palace of the latter, in 1509. Her funeral rites were celebrated with the usual pomp; her brother and all the nobility attending. She was buried in a cave, or subterranean grotto, in the gardens of the same palace, near a reservoir in which she usually bathed. The entrance of the cave was closed with a stone of no great size. On the day after the funeral, a little girl, five or six years old, who lived in the palace, was going from her mother's house to the residence of the princess's major-domo, in a farther part of the garden; and passing by, she heard the princess calling to her *cocoton*, a phrase used to call and coax children, &c. &c. The princess sent the little girl to call her mother, and much alarm was of course excited. At length the King of Tezcuco was notified of her resurrection; and, on his representation, MOTEUCZOMA himself, full of terror, visited her with his chief nobility. He asked her if she was his sister. 'I am,' said she, 'the same whom you buried yesterday. I am alive, and desire to tell you what I have seen, as it imports to know it.' Then the kings sat down, and the others remained standing, marvelling at what they heard.

"Then the princess, resuming her discourse, said:—'After my life, or, if that is possible, after sense and the power of motion departed, incontinently I found myself in a vast plain, to which there was no bound in any direction. In the midst I discerned a road, which divided into various paths, and on one side was a great river, whose waters made a frightful rushing noise. Being minded to leap into it to cross to the opposite side, a fair youth stood before my eyes, of noble presence, clad in long robes, white as snow, and resplendent as the sun. He had two wings of beautiful plumage, and bore this sign on his forehead, (so saying, the princess made with her fingers the sign of the cross;) and taking me by the hand, said, 'Stay, it is not yet time to pass this river. God loves thee, although thou dost not know it.' Thence he led me along the shores of the river, where I saw many skulls and human bones, and heard such doleful groans, that they moved me to compassion. Then, turning my eyes to the river, I saw in it divers great barks, and in them many men, different from those of these regions in dress and complexion. They were white and bearded, having standards in their hands, and helmets on their heads. Then the young man said to me, 'GOD wills that you should live, that you may bear testimony of the revolutions which are to occur in these countries. The clamours thou hast heard on these banks are those of the souls of thine ancestors, which are and ever will be tormented in punishment of their sins. The men whom thou seest passing in the barks, are those who with arms will make themselves masters of this country; and with them will come also an annunciation of the true GOD, Creator of heaven and earth. When the war is finished, and the ablution promulgated which washes away sin, thou shalt be first to receive it, and guide by thine example all the inhabitants of this land.' Thus having said, the young man disappeared; and I found myself restored to life—rose from the place on which I lay—lifted the stone from the sepulchre, and issued forth from the garden, where the servants found me.'

"MOTEUCZOMA went to his house of mourning, full of heavy thoughts, saying nothing to his sister, (whom he would never see again,) nor to the King of Tezcuco, nor to his courtiers, who tried to persuade him that it was a feverish fantasy of the princess. She lived many years afterward, and in 1524 was baptized."

This incident, says CLAVIGERO, was universally known, and made a great noise at the time. It is described in several Mexican pictures, and affidavits of its truth were sent to the court of Spain.—*The Talisman.*

PROEM TO YAMOYDEN.

Go forth, sad fragments of a broken strain,
The last that either bard shall e'er essay!
The hand can ne'er attempt the chords again,
That first awoke them, in a happier day:
Where sweeps the ocean breeze its desert way,
His requiem murmurs o'er the moaning wave;
And he who feebly now prolongs the lay,
Shall ne'er the minstrel's hallow'd honours crave;
His harp lies buried deep, in that untimely grave!

Friend of my youth, with thee began the love
Of sacred song; the wont, in golden dreams,
Mid classic realms of splendours past to rove,
O'er haunted steep, and by immortal streams;
Where the blue wave, with sparkling bosom, gleams
Round shores, the mind's eternal heritage,
Forever lit by memory's twilight beams;
Where the proud dead, that live in storied page,
Beckon, with awful port, to glory's earlier age.

There would we linger oft, entranced, to hear,
O'er battle fields, the epic thunders roll;
Or list, where tragic wail upon the ear,
Through Argive palaces shrill echoing, stole;
There would we mark, uncurb'd by all control,
In central heaven, the Theban eagle's flight;
Or hold communion with the musing soul
Of sage or bard, who sought, mid pagan night,
In loved Athenian groves, for truth's eternal light.

Homeward we turn'd, to that fair land, but late
Redeem'd from the strong spell that bound it fast,
Where mystery, brooding o'er the waters, sate
And kept the key, till three millenniums pass'd;
When, as creation's noblest work was last;
Latest, to man it was vouchsafed, to see
Nature's great wonder, long by clouds o'ercast,
And veiled in sacred awe, that it might be
An empire and a home, most worthy for the free.

And here, forerunners strange and meet were found,
Of that bless'd freedom, only dream'd before;—
Dark were the morning mists, that linger'd round
Their birth and story, as the hue they bore.
"Earth was their mother;"—or they knew no more,
Or would not that their secret should be told;
For they were grave and silent; and such lore,
To stranger ears, they loved not to unfold,
The long-transmitted tales their sires were taught of old.

Kind nature's commoners, from her they drew
Their needful wants, and learn'd not how to hoard;
And him whom strength and wisdom crown'd they knew,
But with no servile reverence, as their lord.
And on their mountain summits they adored
One great, good Spirit, in his high abode,
And thence their incense and orisons pour'd
To his pervading presence, that abroad
They felt through all his works,—their Father, King, and God.

And in the mountain mist, the torrent's spray,
The quivering forest, or the glassy flood,
Soft-falling showers, or hues of orient day,
They imaged spirits beautiful and good;
But when the tempest roar'd, with voices rude,
Or fierce red lightning fired the forest pine,
Or withering heats untimely sear'd the wood,
The angry forms they saw of powers malign;
These they besought to spare, those bless'd for aid divine.

As the fresh sense of life, through every vein,
With the pure air they drank, inspiring came,
Comely they grew, patient of toil and pain,
And as the fleet deer's, agile was their frame;
Of meaner vices scarce they knew the name;
These simple truths went down from sire to son,—
To reverence age,—the sluggish hunter's shame
And craven warrior's infamy to shun,—
And still avenge each wrong, to friends or kindred done.

From forest shades they peer'd, with awful dread,
When, uttering flame and thunder from its side,
The ocean-monster, with broad wings outspread,
Came ploughing gallantly the virgin tide.
Few years have pass'd, and all their forests' pride
From shores and hills has vanish'd, with the race,
Their tenants erst, from memory who have died,
Like airy shapes, which eld was wont to trace,
In each green thicket's depths, and lone, sequester'd place.

And many a gloomy tale, tradition yet
Saves from oblivion, of their struggles vain,
Their prowess and their wrongs, for rhymer meet,
To people scenes where still their names remain;
And so began our young, delighted strain,
That would evoke the plumed chieftains brave,
And bid their martial hosts arise again,
Where Narraganset's tides roll by their grave,
And Haup's romantic steeps are piled above the wave.

Friend of my youth! with thee began my song,
And o'er thy bier its latest accents die;
Misled in phantom-peopled realms too long,—
Though not to me the muse adverse deny,
Sometimes, perhaps, her visions to descry,
Such thriftless pastime should with youth be o'er;
And he who loved with thee his notes to try,
But for thy sake, such idlesse would deplore,
And swears to meditate the thankless muse no more.

But, no! the freshness of the past shall still
Sacred to memory's holiest musings be;
When through the ideal fields of song, at will,
He roved and gather'd chaplets wild with thee;
When, reckless of the world, alone and free,
Like two proud barks, we kept our careless way
That sail by moonlight o'er the tranquil sea;
Their white apparel and their streamers gay
Bright gleaming o'er the main, beneath the ghostly ray;—

And downward, far, reflected in the clear
Blue depths, the eye their fairy tackling sees;
So buoyant, they do seem to float in air,
And silently obey the noiseless breeze:

Till, all too soon, as the rude winds may please,
They part for distant ports: the gales benign
Swift wafting, bore, by Heaven's all-wise decrees,
To its own harbour sure, where each divine
And joyous vision, seen before in dreams, is thine.

Muses of Helicon! melodious race
Of Jove and golden-hair'd Mnemosyne;
Whose art from memory blots each sadder trace,
And drives each scowling form of grief away!
Who, round the violet fount, your measures gay
Once trod, and round the altar of great Jove:
Whence, wrapt in silvery clouds, your nightly way
Ye held, and ravishing strains of music wove,
That soothed the Thunderer's soul, and fill'd his courts above.

Bright choir! with lips untempted, and with zone
Sparkling, and unapproach'd by touch profane;
Ye, to whose gladsome bosoms ne'er was known
The blight of sorrow, or the throb of pain;
Rightly invoked,—if right the elected swain,
On your own mountain's side ye taught of yore,
Whose honour'd hand took not your gift in vain,
Worthy the budding laurel-bough it bore,—
Farewell! a long farewell! I worship you no more.

DREAM OF THE PRINCESS PAPANTZIN.

Mexitlis' power was at its topmost pride;
The name was terrible from sea to sea;
From mountains, where the tameless Ottomite
Maintain'd his savage freedom, to the shores
Of wild Higueras. Through the nations pass'd,
As stalks the angel of the pestilence,
The great king's messengers. They marked the young,
The brave and beautiful, and bore them on
For their foul sacrifices. Terror went
Before the tyrant's heralds. Grief and wrath
Remain'd behind their steps: but they were dumb.
He was as God. Yet in his capital
Sat Moteuczoma, second of that name,
Trembling with fear of dangers long foretold
In ancient prophecies, and now announced
By signs in heaven and portents upon earth;
By the reluctant voices of pale priests;
By the grave looks of solemn counsellors;
But chief, by sickening heaviness of heart
That told of evil, dimly understood,
But evil which must come. With face obscured,
And robed in night, the giant phantom rose,
Of his great empire's ruin, and his own.
Happier, though guiltier, he, before whose glance
Of reckless triumph, moved the spectral hand
That traced the unearthly characters of fate.
'T was then, one eve, when o'er the imperial lake
And all its cities, glittering in their pomp,
The lord of glory threw his parting smiles,
In Tlatelolco's palace, in her bower,
Papantzin lay reclined; sister of him
At whose name monarchs trembled. Yielding there
To musings various, o'er her senses crept
Or sleep, or kindred death. It seem'd she stood
In an illimitable plain, that stretch'd
Its desert continuity around,
Upon the o'erwearied sight; in contrast strange
With that rich vale, where only she had dwelt,
Whose everlasting mountains, girdling it,
As in a chalice held a kingdom's wealth;
Their summits freezing, where the eagle tired,
But found no resting-place. Papantzin look'd
On endless barrenness, and walk'd perplex'd
Through the dull haze, along the boundless heath,
Like some lone ghost in Mictlan's cheerless gloom
Debarred from light and glory. Wandering thus,
She came where a great sullen river pour'd
Its turbid waters with a rushing sound
Of painful moans; as if the inky waves
Were hastening still on their complaining course
To escape the horrid solitudes. Beyond
What seem'd a highway ran, with branching paths
Innumerous. This to gain, she sought to plunge
Straight in the troubled stream. For well she knew
To shun with agile limbs the current's force,
Nor fear'd the noise of waters. She had play'd
From infancy in her fair native lake,
Amid the gay plumed creatures floating round,
Wheeling or diving, with their changeful hues
As fearless and as innocent as they.
A vision stay'd her purpose. By her side
Stood a bright youth; and startling, as she gazed
On his effulgence, every sense was bound
In pleasing awe and in fond reverence.
For not Tezcatlipoca, as he shone
Upon her priest-led fancy, when from heaven
By filmy thread sustain'd he came to earth,
In his resplendent mail reflecting all
Its images, with dazzling portraiture,
Was, in his radiance and immortal youth,
A peer to this new god.—His stature was
Like that of men; but match'd with his, the port
Of kings all dreaded was the crouching mien
Of suppliants at their feet. Serene the light
That floated round him, as the lineaments
It cased with its mild glory. Gravely sweet
The impression of his features, which to scan
Their lofty loveliness forbade: His eyes
She felt, but saw not: only, on his brow—
From over which, encircled by what seem'd
A ring of liquid diamond, in pure light
Revolving ever, backward flow'd his locks
In buoyant, waving clusters—on his brow
She mark'd a cross described; and lowly bent,
She knew not wherefore, to the sacred sign.
From either shoulder mantled o'er his front
Wings dropping feathery silver; and his robe,
Snow-white, in the still air was motionless,
As that of chisell'd god, or the pale shroud
Of some fear-conjured ghost. Her hand he took
And led her passive o'er the naked banks
Of that black stream, still murmuring angrily.
But, as he spoke, she heard its moans no more;
His voice seem'd sweeter than the hymnings raised
By brave and gentle souls in Paradise,
To celebrate the outgoing of the sun,
On his majestic progress over heaven.
"Stay, princess," thus he spoke, "thou mayst not yet
O'erpass these waters. Though thou know'st it not,
Nor him, God loves thee." So he led her on,

Unfainting, amid hideous sights and sounds:
For now, o'er scatter'd skulls and grisly bones
They walk'd; while underneath, before, behind,
Rise dolorous wails and groans protracted long,
Sobs of deep anguish, screams of agony,
And melancholy sighs, and the fierce yell
Of hopeless and intolerable pain.
  Shuddering, as, in the gloomy whirlwind's pause,
Through the malign, distemper'd atmosphere,
The second circle's purple blackness, pass'd
The pitying Florentine, who saw the shades
Of poor Francesca and her paramour,—
The princess o'er the ghastly relics stepp'd,
Listening the frightful clamour; till a gleam,
Whose sickly and phosphoric lustre seem'd
Kindled from these decaying bones, lit up
The sable river. Then a pageant came
Over its obscure tides, of stately barks,
Gigantic, with their prows of quaint device,
Tall masts, and ghostly canvass, huge and high,
Hung in the unnatural light and lifeless air.
Grim, bearded men, with stern and angry looks,
Strange robes, and uncouth armour, stood behind
Their galleries and bulwarks. One ship bore
A broad sheet-pendant, where, inwrought with gold,
She mark'd the symbol that adorned the brow
Of her mysterious guide. Down the dark stream
Swept on the spectral fleet, in the false light
Flickering and fading. Louder then uprose
The roar of voices from the accursed strand,
Until in tones, solemn and sweet, again
Her angel-leader spoke. "Princess, God wills
That thou shouldst live, to testify on earth
What changes are to come: and in the world
Where change comes never, live, when earth and all
Its changes shall have pass'd like earth away.
The cries that pierced thy soul and chill'd thy veins
Are those of thy tormented ancestors.
Nor shall their torment cease; for God is just.
Foredoom'd,—since first from Aztlan led to rove,
Following, in quest of change, their kindred tribes—
Where'er they rested, with foul sacrifice
They stain'd the shuddering earth. Their monu-
By blood cemented, after ages pass'd, [ments,
With idle wonder of fantastic guess
The traveller shall behold. For, broken, then,
Like their own ugly idols, buried, burn'd,
Their fragments spurn'd for every servile use,
Trampled and scatter'd to the reckless winds,
The records of their origin shall be.
Still in their cruelty and untamed pride,
They lived and died condemn'd; whether they
Outcasts, upon a soil that was not theirs, [dwelt
All sterile as it was, and won by stealth
Food from the slimy margent of the lake,
And digg'd the earth for roots and unclean worms;
Or served in bondage to another race,
Who loved them not. Driven forth, they wander'd
In miserable want, until they came [then
Where from the thriftless rock the nopal grew,
On which the hungry eagle perch'd and scream'd,
And founded Tenochtitlan; rearing first,
With impious care, a cabin for their god
Huitzilopochtli, and with murderous rites
Devoting to his guardianship themselves
And all their issue. Quick the nopal climb'd,
Its harsh and bristly growth towering o'er all
The vale of Anahuac. Far for his prey,
And farther still the ravenous eagle flew;
And still with dripping beak, but thirst unslaked,
With savage cries wheel'd home. Nine kings have
            reign'd,
Their records blotted and besmear'd with blood
So thick that none may read them. Down the stairs
And o'er the courts and winding corridors
Of their abominable piles, uprear'd
In the face of heaven, and naked to the sun,
More blood has flow'd than would have fill'd the lakes
O'er which, enthron'd midst carnage, they have sat,
Heaping their treasures for the stranger's spoil.
Prodigious cruelty and waste of life,
Unnatural riot and blaspheming pride,—
All that God hates,—and all that tumbles down
Great kingdoms and luxurious commonwealths,
After long centuries waxing all corrupt,—
In their brief annals aggregated, forced,
And monstrous, are compress'd. And now the cup
Of wrath is full; and now the hour has come.
Nor yet unwarn'd shall judgment overtake
The tribes of Aztlan, and in chief their lords,
Mexitlis' blind adorers. As to one
Who feels his inward malady remain,
Howe'er health's seeming mocks his destiny,
In gay or serious mood the thought of death
Still comes obtrusive; so old prophecy,
From age to age preserved, has told thy race
How strangers, from beyond the rising sun,
Should come with thunder arm'd, to overturn
Their idols, to possess their lands, and hold
Them and their children in long servitude.
  "Thou shalt bear record that the hour is nigh
The white and bearded men whose grim array
Swept o'er thy sight, are those who are to come,
And with strong arms, and wisdom stronger far,
Strange beasts, obedient to their masters' touch,
And engines hurling death, with Fate to aid,
Shall wrest the sceptre from the Azteques' line,
And lay their temples flat. Horrible war,
Rapine, and murder, and destruction wild
Shall hurry like the whirlwind o'er the land.
Yet with the avengers come the word of peace;
With the destroyers comes the bread of life;
And, as the wind-god, in thine idle creed,
Opens a passage with his boisterous breath
Through which the genial waters over earth
Shed their reviving showers; so, when the storm
Of war has pass'd, rich dews of heavenly grace
Shall fall on flinty hearts. And thou, the flower,—
Which, when huge cedars and most ancient pines,
Coeval with the mountains, are uptorn,
The hurricane shall leave unharm'd,—thou, then,
Shalt be the first to lift thy drooping head
Renew'd, and cleansed from every former stain.
  "The fables of thy people teach, that when
The deluge drown'd mankind, and one sole pair
In fragile bark preserved, escaped and climb'd
The steeps of Colhuacan, daughters and sons
Were born to them, who knew not how to frame
Their simplest thoughts in speech; till from the
A dove pour'd forth, in regulated sounds, [grove

Each varied form of language. Then they spake,
Though neither by another understood.
But thou shalt then hear of that holiest Dove,
Which is the Spirit of the eternal God.
When all was void and dark, he moved above
Infinity; and from beneath his wings
Earth and the waters and the islands rose;
The air was quicken'd, and the world had life.
Then all the lamps of heaven began to shine,
And man was made to gaze upon their fires.
"Among thy fathers' visionary tales,
Thou'st heard, how once near ancient Tula dwelt
A woman, holy and devout, who kept
The temple pure, and to its platform saw
A globe of emerald plumes descend from heaven.
Placing it in her bosom to adorn
Her idol's sanctuary, (so the tale
Runs,) she conceived, and bore MEXITLI. He,
When other children had assail'd her life,
Sprang into being, all equipp'd for war;
His green plumes dancing in their circlet bright,
Like sheaf of sun-lit spray cresting the bed
Of angry torrents. Round, as Tonatiuh
Flames in mid-heaven, his golden buckler shone;
Like nimble lightning flash'd his dreadful lance;
And unrelenting vengeance in his eyes
Blazed with its swarthy lustre. He, they tell,
Led on their ancestors; and him the god
Of wrath and terror, with the quivering hearts
And mangled limbs of myriads, and the stench
Of blood-wash'd shrines and altars they appease.
But then shall be reveal'd to thee the name
And vision of a virgin undefiled,
Embalm'd in holy beauty, in whose eyes,
Downcast and chaste, such sacred influence lived,
That none might gaze in their pure spheres and feel
One earth-born longing. Over her the Dove
Hung, and the Almighty power came down. She
In lowliness, and as a helpless babe, [bore
Heir to man's sorrows and calamities,
His great Deliverer, Conqueror of Death;
And thou shalt learn, how when in years he grew
Perfect, and fairer than the sons of men,
And in that purifying rite partook
Which thou shalt share, as from his sacred locks
The glittering waters dropp'd, high over head
The azure vault was open'd, and that Dove
Swiftly, serenely floating downwards, stretch'd
His silvery pinions o'er the anointed LORD,
Sprinkling celestial dews. And thou shalt hear
How, when the sacrifice for man had gone
In glory home, as his chief messengers
Were met in council, on a mighty wind
The Dove was borne among them; on each brow
A forked tongue of fire unquenchable lit;
And, as the lambent points shot up and waved,
Strange speech came to them; thence to every land,
In every tongue, they, with untiring steps,
Bore the glad tidings of a world redeem'd."
Much more, which now it suits not to rehearse,
The princess heard. The historic prophet told
Past, present, future,—things that since have been,
And things that are to come. And, as he ceased,
O'er the black river, and the desert plain,
As o'er the close of counterfeited scenes,
Shown by the buskin'd muse, a veil came down,
Impervious; and his figure faded swift
In the dense gloom. But then, in starlike light,
That awful symbol which adorn'd his brow
In size dilating show'd: and up, still up,
In its clear splendour still the same, though still
Lessening, it mounted; and PAPANTZIN woke.
She woke in darkness and in solitude.
Slow pass'd her lethargy away, and long
To her half-dreaming eye that brilliant sign
Distinct appear'd. Then damp and close she felt
The air around, and knew the poignant smell
Of spicy herbs collected and confined.
As those awakening from a troubled trance
Are wont, she would have learn'd by touch if yet
The spirit to the body was allied,
Strange hindrances prevented. O'er her face
A mask thick-plated lay: and round her swathed
Was many a costly and encumbering robe,
Such as she wore on some high festival,
O'erspread with precious gems, rayless and cold,
That now press'd hard and sharp against her touch
The cumbrous collar round her slender neck,
Of gold, thick studded with each valued stone
Earth and the sea-depths yield for human pride—
The bracelets and the many twisted rings
That girt her taper limbs, coil upon coil—
What were they in this dungeon's solitude?
The plumy coronal that would have sprung
Light from her fillet in the purer air,
Waving in mockery of the rainbow tints,
Now drooping low, and steep'd in clogging dews,
Oppressive hung. Groping in dubious search,
She found the household goods, the spindle, broom,
GICALLI quaintly sculptured, and the jar
That held the useless beverage for the dead.
By these, and by the jewel to her lip
Attach'd, the emerald symbol of the soul,
In its green life immortal, soon she knew
Her dwelling was a sepulchre. She loosed
The mask, and from her feathery bier uprose,
Casting away the robe, which like long alb
Wrapp'd her; and with it many an aloe leaf,
Inscribed with Azteck characters and signs,
To guide the spirit where the serpent hiss'd,
Hills tower'd, and deserts spread, and keen winds blew,
And many a "Flower of Death;" though their frail leaves
Were yet unwither'd. For the living warmth
Which in her dwelt, their freshness had preserved;
Else, if corruption had begun its work,
The emblems of quick change would have survived
Her beauty's semblance. What is beauty worth,
If the cropp'd flower retains its tender bloom
When foul decay has stolen the latest lines
Of loveliness in death! Yet even now
PAPANTZIN knew that her exuberant locks—
Which, unconfined, had round her flow'd to earth,
Like a stream rushing down some rocky steep,
Threading ten thousand channels—had been shorn
Of half their waving length,—and liked it not.
But through a crevice soon she mark'd a gleam
Of rays uncertain; and, with staggering steps,
But strong in reckless dreaminess, while still

Presided o'er the chaos of her thoughts
The revelation that upon her soul
Dwelt with its power, she gain'd the cavern's throat,
And push'd the quarried stone aside, and stood
In the free air, and in her own domain.
  But now, obscurely o'er her vision swam
The beauteous landscape, with its thousand tints
And changeful views; long alleys of bright trees
Bending beneath their fruits; espaliers gay
With tropic flowers and shrubs that fill'd the breeze
With odorous incense, basins vast, where birds
With shining plumage sported, smooth canals
Leading the glassy wave, or towering grove
Of forest veterans. On a rising bank,
Her seat accustom'd, near a well hewn out
From ancient rocks, into which waters gush'd
From living springs, where she was wont to bathe,
She threw herself to muse. Dim on her sight
The imperial city and its causeways rose,
With the broad lake and all its floating isles
And glancing shallops, and the gilded pomp
Of princely barges, canopied with plumes
Spread fanlike, or with tufted pageantry
Waving magnificent. Unmark'd around
The frequent huitzilin, with murmuring hum
Of ever-restless wing, and shrill, sweet note,
Shot twinkling, with the ruby star that glow'd
Over his tiny bosom, and all hues
That loveliest seem in heaven, with ceaseless change,
Flashing from his fine films. And all in vain
Untiring, from the rustling branches near,
Pour'd the centzontli all his hundred strains
Of imitative melody. Not now
She heeded them. Yet pleasant was the shade
Of palms and cedars; and through twining boughs
And fluttering leaves, the subtle god of air,
The serpent arm'd with plumes, most welcome crept,
And fann'd her cheek with kindest ministry.
  A dull and dismal sound came booming on;
A solemn, wild, and melancholy noise,
Shaking the tranquil air; and afterward
A clash and jangling, barbarously prolonged,
Torturing the unwilling ear, rang dissonant.
Again the unnatural thunder roll'd along,
Again the crash and clamour follow'd it.
Shuddering she heard, who knew that every peal
From the dread gong announced a victim's heart
Torn from his breast, and each triumphant clang,
A mangled corse, down the great temple's stairs
Hurl'd headlong; and she knew, as lately taught,
How vengeance was ordain'd for cruelty;
How pride would end; and uncouth soldiers tread
Through bloody furrows o'er her pleasant groves
And gardens; and would make themselves a road
Over the dead, choking the silver lake,
And cast the batter'd idols down the steps
That climb'd their execrable towers, and raze
Sheer from the ground Ahuitzol's mighty pile.
  There had been wail for her in Mexico,
And with due rites and royal obsequies,
Not without blood at devilish altars shed,
She had been number'd with her ancestry.
Here when beheld, revisiting the light,
Great marvel rose, and greater terror grew,
Until the kings came trembling, to receive
The foreshown tidings. To his house of wo
Silent and mournful, Moteuczoma went.
  Few years had pass'd, when by the rabble bands
Of his own subjects, in ignoble bonds
He fell; and on a hasty gibbet rear'd
By the road-side, with scorn and obloquy
The brave and gracious Guatemotzin hung;
While to Honduras, thirsting for revenge,
And gloomier after all his victories,
Stern Cortes stalked. Such was the will of God.
  And then, with holier rites and sacred pomp,
Again committed to the peaceful grave,
Papantzin slept in consecrated earth.

MONODY ON SAMUEL PATCH.*

By water shall he die, and take his end.—Shakspeare.

Toll for Sam Patch! Sam Patch, who jumps no more,
  This or the world to come. Sam Patch is dead!
The vulgar pathway to the unknown shore
  Of dark futurity, he would not tread.
  No friends stood sorrowing round his dying bed
Nor with decorous wo, sedately stepp'd
  Behind his corpse, and tears by retail shed;—
The mighty river, as it onward swept,
In one great, wholesale sob, his body drown'd and kept.

Toll for Sam Patch! he scorn'd the common way
  That leads to fame, up heights of rough ascent,
And having heard Pope and Longinus say,
  That some great men had risen to falls, he went
  And jump'd, where wild Passaic's waves had rent
The antique rocks;—the air free passage gave,—
  And graciously the liquid element
Upbore him, like some sea-god on its wave;
And all the people said that Sam was very brave.

Fame, the clear spirit that doth to heaven upraise,
  Led Sam to dive into what Byron calls
The hell of waters. For the sake of praise,
  He woo'd the bathos down great waterfalls;
  The dizzy precipice, which the eye appals
Of travellers for pleasure, Samuel found
  Pleasant, as are to women lighted halls,
Cramm'd full of fools and fiddles; to the sound
Of the eternal roar, he timed his desperate bound.

Sam was a fool. But the large world of such
  Has thousands—better taught, alike absurd,
And less sublime. Of fame he soon got much,
  Where distant cataracts spout, of him men heard.

* Samuel Patch was a boatman on the Erie Canal, in New York. He made himself notorious by leaping from the masts of ships, from the Falls of Niagara, and from the Falls in the Genesee River, at Rochester. His last feat was in the summer of 1831, when, in the presence of many thousands, he jumped from above the highest rock over which the water falls in the Genesee, and was lost. He had become intoxicated, before going upon the scaffold, and lost his balance in descending. The above verses were written a few days after this event.

Alas for SAM! Had he aright preferr'd
The kindly element, to which he gave
Himself so fearlessly, we had not heard
That it was now his winding-sheet and grave,
Nor sung, 'twixt tears and smiles, our requiem for the brave.

He soon got drunk, with rum and with renown,
As many others in high places do;—
Whose fall is like SAM's last—for down and down,
By one mad impulse driven, they flounder through
The gulf that keeps the future from our view,
And then are found not. May they rest in peace!
We heave the sigh to human frailty due—
And shall not SAM have his? The muse shall cease
To keep the heroic roll, which she began in Greece—

With demigods, who went to the Black Sea
For wool, (and, if the best accounts be straight,
Came back, in negro phraseology,
With the same wool each upon his pate,)
In which she chronicled the deathless fate
Of him who jump'd into the perilous ditch
Left by Rome's street commissioners, in a state
Which made it dangerous, and by jumping which
He made himself renown'd, and the contractors rich—

I say, the muse shall quite forget to sound
The chord whose music is undying, if
She do not strike it when SAM PATCH is drown'd.
LEANDER dived for love. Leucadia's cliff
The Lesbian SAPPHO leap'd from in a miff,
To punish PHAON; ICARUS went dead,
Because the wax did not continue stiff;
And, had he minded what his father said,
He had not given a name unto his watery bed.

And HELLE's case was all an accident,
As everybody knows. Why sing of these?
Nor would I rank with SAM that man who went
Down into Ætna's womb—EMPEDOCLES,
I think he call'd himself. Themselves to please,
Or else unwillingly, they made their springs;
For glory in the abstract, SAM made his,
To prove to all men, commons, lords, and kings,
That "some things may be done, as well as other things."

I will not be fatigued, by citing more
Who jump'd of old, by hazard or design,
Nor plague the weary ghosts of boyish lore,
VULCAN, APOLLO, PHAETON—in fine,
All TOOKE's Pantheon. Yet they grew divine
By their long tumbles; and if we can match
Their hierarchy, shall we not entwine
One wreath? Who ever came "up to the scratch,"
And, for so little, jump'd so bravely as SAM PATCH?

To long conclusions many men have jump'd
In logic, and the safer course they took;
By any other, they would have been stump'd,
Unable to argue, or to quote a book,
And quite dumb-founded, which they cannot brook;
They break no bones, and suffer no contusion,
Hiding their woful fall, by hook and crook,
In slang and gibberish, sputtering and confusion;
But that was not the way SAM came to his conclusion.

He jump'd in person. Death or Victory
Was his device, "and there was no mistake,"
Except his last; and then he did but die,
A blunder which the wisest men will make.
Aloft, where mighty floods the mountains break
To stand, the target of ten thousand eyes,
And down into the coil and water-quake
To leap, like MAIA's offspring, from the skies—
For this, all vulgar flights he ventured to despise.

And while Niagara prolongs its thunder,
Though still the rock primeval disappears,
And nations change their bounds—the theme of wonder
Shall SAM go down the cataract of long years
And if there be sublimity in tears,
Those shall be precious which the adventurer shed
When his frail star gave way, and waked his fears
Lest by the ungenerous crowd it might be said,
That he was all a hoax, or that his pluck had fled.

Who would compare the maudlin ALEXANDER,
Blubbering, because he had no job in hand,
Acting the hypocrite, or else the gander,
With SAM, whose grief we all can understand?
His crying was not womanish, nor plann'd
For exhibition; but his heart o'erswell'd
With its own agony, when he the grand
Natural arrangements for a jump beheld,
And, measuring the cascade, found not his courage quell'd.

His last great failure set the final seal
Unto the record Time shall never tear,
While bravery has its honour,—while men feel
The holy, natural sympathies which are
First, last, and mightiest in the bosom. Where
The tortured tides of Genessee descend,
He came—his only intimate a bear,—
(We know not that he had another friend,)
The martyr of renown, his wayward course to end.

The fiend that from the infernal rivers stole
Hell-draughts for man, too much tormented him,
With nerves unstrung, but steadfast in his soul,
He stood upon the salient current's brim;
His head was giddy, and his sight was dim;
And then he knew this leap would be his last,—
Saw air, and earth, and water wildly swim,
With eyes of many multitudes, dense and vast,
That stared in mockery; none a look of kindness cast.

Beat down, in the huge amphitheatre
"I see before me the gladiator lie,"
And tier on tier, the myriads waiting there
The bow of grace, without one pitying eye—
He was a slave—a captive hired to die;—
SAM was born free as CÆSAR; and he might
The hopeless issue have refused to try;
No! with true leap, but soon with faltering flight,—
"Deep in the roaring gulf, he plunged to endless night."

But, ere he leap'd, he begg'd of those who made
Money by his dread venture, that if he
Should perish, such collection should be paid
As might be pick'd up from the "company"

To his mother. This, his last request, shall be,—
Though she who bore him ne'er his fate should
An iris, glittering o'er his memory, [know—
When all the streams have worn their barriers low,
And, by the sea drunk up, forever cease to flow.

On him who chooses to jump down cataracts,
Why should the sternest moralist be severe?
Judge not the dead by prejudice—but facts,
Such as in strictest evidence appear;
Else were the laurels of all ages sere.
Give to the brave, who have pass'd the final goal,—
The gates that ope not back,—the generous tear;
And let the muse's clerk upon her scroll, [roll.
In coarse, but honest verse, make up the judgment-

Therefore it is consider'd, that Sam Patch
Shall never be forgot in prose or rhyme;
His name shall be a portion in the batch
Of the heroic dough, which baking Time
Kneads for consuming ages—and the chime
Of Fame's old bells, long as they truly ring,
Shall tell of him; he dived for the sublime,
And found it. Thou, who with the eagle's wing,
Being a goose, wouldst fly,—dream not of such a thing!

EVENING.*

Hail! sober evening! thee the harass'd brain
And aching heart with fond orisons greet;
The respite thou of toil; the balm of pain;
To thoughtful mind the hour for musing meet:
'T is then the sage, from forth his lone retreat,
The rolling universe around espies;
'T is then the bard may hold communion sweet
With lovely shapes, unkenn'd by grosser eyes,
And quick perception comes of finer mysteries.

The silent hour of bliss! when in the west
Her argent cresset lights the star of love:—
The spiritual hour! when creatures bless'd
Unseen return o'er former haunts to rove;
While sleep his shadowy mantle spreads above,
Sleep, brother of forgetfulness and death,
Round well-known couch, with noiseless tread they rove,
In tones of heavenly music comfort breathe,
And tell what weal or bale shall chance the moon beneath.

Hour of devotion! like a distant sea,
The world's loud voices faintly murmuring die;
Responsive to the spheral harmony,
While grateful hymns are borne from earth on high.
O! who can gaze on yon unsullied sky,
And not grow purer from the heavenward view?
As those, the Virgin Mother's meek, full eye,
Who met, if uninspired lore be true,
Felt a new birth within, and sin no longer knew.

Let others hail the oriflamme of morn,
O'er kindling hills unfurl'd with gorgeous dyes.
O, mild, blue Evening! still to thee I turn,
With holier thought, and with undazzled eyes;—
Where wealth and power with glare and splendour rise,
Let fools and slaves disgustful incense burn!
Still Memory's moonlight lustre let me prize;
The great, the good, whose course is o'er, discern,
And, from their glories past, time's mighty lessons learn!

* From "Yamoyden."

WEEHAWKEN.

Eve o'er our path is stealing fast;
Yon quivering splendours are the last
The sun will fling, to tremble o'er
The waves that kiss the opposing shore;
His latest glories fringe the height
Behind us, with their golden light.

The mountain's mirror'd outline fades
Amid the fast-extending shades;
Its shaggy bulk, in sterner pride,
Towers, as the gloom steals o'er the tide;
For the great stream a bulwark meet
That leaves its rock-encumber'd feet.

River and mountain! though to song
Not yet, perchance, your names belong;
Those who have loved your evening hues
Will ask not the recording muse
What antique tales she can relate,
Your banks and steeps to consecrate.

Yet, should the stranger ask, what lore
Of by-gone days, this winding shore,
Yon cliffs and fir-clad steeps could tell,
If vocal made by Fancy's spell,—
The varying legend might rehearse
Fit themes for high, romantic verse.

O'er yon rough heights and moss-clad sod
Oft hath the stalworth warrior trod;
Or peer'd, with hunter's gaze, to mark
The progress of the glancing bark.
Spoils, strangely won on distant waves,
Have lurk'd in yon obstructed caves.

When the great strife for Freedom rose,
Here scouted oft her friends and foes,
Alternate, through the changeful war,
And beacon-fires flash'd bright and far;
And here, when Freedom's strife was won,
Fell, in sad feud, her favour'd son:—

Her son,—the second of the band,
The Romans of the rescued land.
Where round yon capes the banks ascend,
Long shall the pilgrim's footsteps bend;
There, mirthful hearts shall pause to sigh,
There, tears shall dim the patriot's eye.

There last he stood. Before his sight
Flow'd the fair river, free and bright;
The rising mart, and isles, and bay,
Before him in their glory lay,—
Scenes of his love and of his fame,—
The instant ere the death-shot came.

THE GREEN ISLE OF LOVERS.

They say that, afar in the land of the west,
Where the bright golden sun sinks in glory to rest,
Mid fens where the hunter ne'er ventured to tread,
A fair lake unruffled and sparkling is spread;
Where, lost in his course, the rapt Indian discovers,
In distance seen dimly, the green Isle of Lovers.

There verdure fades never; immortal in bloom,
Soft waves the magnolia its groves of perfume;
And low bends the branch with rich fruitage depress'd,
All glowing like gems in the crowns of the east;
There the bright eye of nature, in mild glory hovers:
'T is the land of the sunbeam,—the green Isle of Lovers!

Sweet strains wildly float on the breezes that kiss
The calm-flowing lake round that region of bliss
Where, wreathing their garlands of amaranth, fair choirs
Glad measures still weave to the sound that inspires
The dance and the revel, mid forests that cover
On high with their shade the green Isle of the Lover.

But fierce as the snake, with his eyeballs of fire,
When his scales are all brilliant and glowing with ire,
Are the warriors to all, save the maids of their isle,
Whose law is their will, and whose life is their smile;
From beauty there valour and strength are not rovers,
And peace reigns supreme in the green Isle of Lovers.

And he who has sought to set foot on its shore,
In mazes perplex'd, has beheld it no more;
It fleets on the vision, deluding the view,
Its banks still retire as the hunters pursue;
O! who in this vain world of wo shall discover
The home undisturb'd, the green Isle of the Lover!

THE DEAD OF 1832.

O, Time and Death! with certain pace,
Though still unequal, hurrying on,
O'erturning, in your awful race,
The cot, the palace, and the throne!

Not always in the storm of war,
Nor by the pestilence that sweeps
From the plague-smitten realms afar,
Beyond the old and solemn deeps:

In crowds the good and mighty go,
And to those vast, dim chambers hie:
Where, mingled with the high and low,
Dead Cæsars and dead Shakspeares lie!

Dread ministers of God! sometimes
Ye smite at once to do his will,
In all earth's ocean-sever'd climes,
Those —whose renown ye cannot kill!

When all the brightest stars that burn
At once are banish'd from their spheres,
Men sadly ask, when shall return
Such lustre to the coming years!

For where is he*—who lived so long—
Who raised the modern Titan's ghost,
And show'd his fate in powerful song,
Whose soul for learning's sake was lost?

Where he—who backward to the birth
Of Time itself, adventurous trod,
And in the mingled mass of earth
Found out the handiwork of God?†

Where he—who in the mortal head,‡
Ordain'd to gaze on heaven, could trace
The soul's vast features, that shall tread
The stars, when earth is nothingness?

Where he—who struck old Albyn's lyre,§
Till round the world its echoes roll,
And swept, with all a prophet's fire,
The diapason of the soul?

Where he—who read the mystic lore‖
Buried where buried Pharaohs sleep;
And dared presumptuous to explore
Secrets four thousand years could keep?

Where he—who, with a poet's eye¶
Of truth, on lowly nature gazed,
And made even sordid Poverty
Classic, when in his numbers glazed?

Where—that old sage so hale and staid,**
The "greatest good" who sought to find
Who in his garden mused, and made
All forms of rule for all mankind?

And thou—whom millions far removed††
Revered—the hierarch meek and wise,
Thy ashes sleep, adored, beloved,
Near where thy Wesley's coffin lies.

He, too—the heir of glory—where‡‡
Hath great Napoleon's scion fled?
Ah! glory goes not to an heir!
Take him, ye noble, vulgar dead!

But hark! a nation sighs! for he,§§
Last of the brave who perill'd all
To make an infant empire free,
Obeys the inevitable call!

They go—and with them is a crowd,
For human rights who thought and did:
We rear to them no temples proud,
Each hath his mental pyramid.

All earth is now their sepulchre,
The mind, their monument sublime—
Young in eternal fame they are—
Such are your triumphs, Death and Time.

* Goethe and his Faust. † Cuvier.
‡ Spurzheim. § Scott.
‖ Champollion. ¶ Crabbe.
** Jeremy Bentham. †† Adam Clarke
‡‡ The Duke of Reichstadt. §§ Charles Carroll

PARTING.

Say, when afar from mine thy home shall be,
Still will thy soul unchanging turn to me?
When other scenes in beauty round thee lie,
Will these be present to thy mental eye?
Thy form, thy mind, when others fondly praise,
Wilt thou forget thy poet's humbler lays?
Ah me! what is there, in earth's various range,
That time and absence may not sadly change!
And can the heart, that still demands new ties,
New thoughts, for all its thousand sympathies—
The waxen heart, where every seal may set,
In turn, its stamp—remain unalter'd yet,
While nature changes with each fleeting day,
And seasons dance their varying course away?
Ah! shouldst thou swerve from truth, all else must part,
That yet can feed with life this wither'd heart!
Whate'er its doubts, its hopes, its fears may be,
'T were, even in madness, faithful still to thee;
And shouldst thou snap that silver chord in twain,
The golden bowl no other links sustain;
Crush'd in the dust, its fragments then must sink,
And the cold earth its latest life-drops drink.
Blame not, if oft, in melancholy mood,
This theme, too far, sick fancy hath pursued;
And if the soul, which high with hope should beat,
Turns to the gloomy grave's unbless'd retreat.
  Majestic nature! since thy course began,
Thy features wear no sympathy for man;
The sun smiles loveliest on our darkest hours;
O'er the cold grave fresh spring the sweetest flowers,
And man himself, in selfish sorrows bound,
Heeds not the melancholy ruin round.
The crowd's vain roar still fills the passing breeze
That bends above the tomb the cypress-trees.
One only heart, still true in joy or wo,
Is all the kindest fates can e'er bestow.
If frowning Heaven that heart refuse to give,
O, who would ask the ungracious boon—to live?
Then better 'twere, if longer doom'd to prove
The listless load of life, unbless'd with love,
To seek midst ocean's waste some island fair,—
And dwell, the anchorite of nature, there;—
Some lonely isle, upon whose rocky shore
No sound, save curlew's scream, or billow's roar,
Hath echoed ever; in whose central woods,
With the quick spirit of its solitudes,
In converse deep, strange sympathies untried,
The soul might find, which this vain world denied.
  But I will trust that heart, where truth alone,
In loveliest guise, sits radiant on her throne;
And thus believing, fear not all the power
Of absence drear, or time's most tedious hour.
If e'er I sigh to win the wreaths of fame,
And write on memory's scroll a deathless name,
'T is but thy loved, approving smile to meet,
And lay the budding laurels at thy feet.
If e'er for worldly wealth I heave a sigh,
And glittering visions float on fancy's eye,
'T is but with rosy wreaths thy path to spread,
And place the diadem on beauty's head.
Queen of my thoughts, each subject to thy sway,
Thy ruling presence lives but to obey;
And shouldst thou e'er their bless'd allegiance slight,
The mind must wander, lost in endless night.
  Farewell! forget me not, when others gaze
Enamour'd on thee, with the looks of praise;
When weary leagues before my view are cast,
And each dull hour seems heavier than the last,
Forget me not. May joy thy steps attend,
And mayst thou find in every form a friend;
With care unsullied be thy every thought;
And in thy dreams of home, forget me not!

CONCLUSION TO YAMOYDEN.

Sad was the theme, which yet to try we chose,
In pleasant moments of communion sweet:
When least we thought of earth's unvarnish'd woes,
And least we dream'd, in fancy's fond deceit,
That either the cold grasp of death should meet,
Till after many years, in ripe old age;
Three little summers flew on pinions fleet,
And thou art living but in memory's page,
And earth seems all to me a worthless pilgrimage.

Sad was our theme; but well the wise man sung,
"Better than festal halls, the house of wo;"
'T is good to stand destruction's spoils among,
And muse on that sad bourne to which we go.
The heart grows better when tears freely flow;
And, in the many-colour'd dream of earth,
One stolen hour, wherein ourselves we know,
Our weakness and our vanity,—is worth
Years of unmeaning smiles, and lewd, obstreperous mirth.

'T is good to muse on nations pass'd away,
Forever, from the land we call our own;
Nations, as proud and mighty in their day,
Who deem'd that everlasting was their throne.
An age went by, and they no more were known
Sublimer sadness will the mind control,
Listening time's deep and melancholy moan;
And meaner griefs will less disturb the soul;
And human pride falls low, at human grandeur's goal.

Philip! farewell! thee King, in idle jest,
Thy persecutors named; and if indeed,
The jewell'd diadem thy front had press'd,
It had become *thee* better, than the breed
Of palaces, to sceptres that succeed,
To be of courtier or of priest the tool,
Satiate dull sense, or count the frequent bead,
Or pamper gormand hunger; thou wouldst rule
Better than the worn rake, the glutton, or the fool!

I would not wrong thy warrior shade, could I
Aught in my verse or make or mar thy fame;
As the light carol of a bird flown by
Will pass the youthful strain that breathed thy name:
But in that land whence thy destroyers came,
A sacred bard thy champion shall be found;
He of the laureate wreath for thee shall claim
The hero's honours, to earth's farthest bound.
Where Albion's tongue is heard, or Albion's songs resound.

INVOCATION.

Oh quick for me the goblet fill,
From bright Castalia's sparkling rill;
Pluck the young laurel's flexile bough,
And let its foliage wreathe my brow;
And bring the lyre with sounding shell,
The four-string'd lyre I loved so well!

Lo! as I gaze, the picture flies
Of weary life's realities;
Behold the shade, the wild wood shade,
The mountain steeps, the checker'd glade;
And hoary rocks and bubbling rills,
And painted waves and distant hills.

Oh! for an hour, let me forget
How much of life is left me yet;
Recall the visions of the past,
Fair as these tints that cannot last,
That all the heavens and waters o'er
Their gorgeous, transient glories pour.

Ye pastoral scenes, by fancy wrought!
Ye pageants of the loftier thought!
Creations proud! majestic things!
Heroes, and demigods, and kings!
Return, with all of shepherds' lore,
Or old romance that pleased before!

Ye forms that are not of the earth,
Of grace, of valour, and of worth!
Ye bright abstractions, by the thought
Like the great master's pictures, wrought
To the ideal's shadowy mien,
From beauties fancied, dreamt or seen!

Ye speaking sounds, that poet's ear
Alone in nature's voice can hear!
Thou full conception, vast and wide,
Hour of the lonely minstrel's pride,
As when projection gave of old
Alchymy's visionary gold!

Return! return! oblivion bring
Of cares that vex, and thoughts that sting!
The hour of gloom is o'er my soul;
Disperse the shades, the fiends control,
As David's harp had power to do,
If sacred chronicles be true.

Oh come! by every classic spell,
By old Pieria's haunted well;
By revels on the Olmeian height
Held in the moon's religious light;
By virgin forms that wont to lave,
Permessus! in thy lucid wave!

In vain! in vain! the strain has pass'd;
The laurel leaves upon the blast
Float, wither'd, ne'er again to bloom,
The cup is drain'd—the song is dumb—
And spell and rhyme alike in vain
Would woo the genial muse again.

GOOD-NIGHT.

Good night to all the world! there's none,
Beneath the "over-going" sun,
To whom I feel or hate or spite,
And so to all a fair good-night.

Would I could say good night to pain,
Good night to conscience and her train,
To cheerless poverty, and shame
That I am yet unknown to fame!

Would I could say good night to dreams
That haunt me with delusive gleams,
That through the sable future's veil
Like meteors glimmer, but to fail.

Would I could say a long good-night
To halting between wrong and right,
And, like a giant with new force,
Awake prepared to run my course!

But time o'er good and ill sweeps on,
And when few years have come and gone,
The past will be to me as naught,
Whether remember'd or forgot.

Yet let me hope one faithful friend,
O'er my last couch shall tearful bend;
And, though no day for me was bright,
Shall bid me then a long good-night.

FROM A MONODY ON J. W. EASTBURN

But now, that cherish'd voice was near;
  And all around yet breathes of him;—
We look, and we can only hear
  The parting wings of cherubim!
Mourn ye, whom haply nature taught
  To share the bard's communion high;
To scan the ideal world of thought,
  That floats before the poet's eye;—
Ye, who with ears o'ersated long,
  From native bards disgusted fly,
Expecting only, in their song,
  The ribald strains of calumny;—
Mourn ye a minstrel chaste as sweet,
  Who caught from heaven no doubtful fire,
But chose immortal themes as meet
  Alone for an immortal lyre.
O silent shell! thy chords are riven!
  That heart lies cold before its prime!
Mute are those lips, that might have given
  One deathless descant to our clime!
No laurel chaplet twines he now;
  He sweeps a harp of heavenly tone,
And plucks the amaranth for his brow
  That springs beside the eternal throne.
Mourn ye, whom friendship's silver chain
  Link'd with his soul in bonds refined;
That earth had striven to burst in vain,—
  The sacred sympathy of mind.
Still long that sympathy shall last:
  Still shall each object, like a spell,
Recall from fate the buried past,
  Present the mind beloved so well.
That pure intelligence—Oh where
  Now is its onward progress won?
Through what new regions does it dare
  Push the bold quest on earth begun?
In realms with boundless glory fraught,
  Where fancy can no trophies raise—
In blissful vision, where the thought
  Is whelm'd in wonder and in praise!

Till life's last pulse, O triply dear,
  A loftier strain is due to thee;
But constant memory's votive tear
  Thy sacred epitaph must be.

TO THE MANITTO OF DREAMS.

SPIRIT! THOU SPIRIT of subtlest air,
  Whose power is upon the brain,
When wondrous shapes, and dread and fair,
  As the film from the eyes
  At thy bidding flies,
To sight and sense are plain!

Thy whisper creeps where leaves are stirr'd;
  Thou sighest in woodland gale;
Where waters are gushing thy voice is heard;
  And when stars are bright,
  At still midnight,
Thy symphonies prevail!

Where the forest ocean, in quick commotion,
  Is waving to and fro,
Thy form is seen, in the masses green,
  Dimly to come and go.
From thy covert peeping, where thou layest sleeping
  Beside the brawling brook,
Thou art seen to wake, and thy flight to take
  Fleet from thy lonely nook.

  Where the moonbeam has kiss'd
  The sparkling tide,
  In thy mantle of mist
  Thou art seen to glide.
  Far o'er the blue waters
  Melting away,
  On the distant billow,
  As on a pillow,
  Thy form to lay.

  Where the small clouds of even
  Are wreathing in heaven
  Their garland of roses,
  O'er the purple and gold,
  Whose hangings enfold
  The hall that encloses
  The couch of the sun,
  Whose empire is done,—
  There thou art smiling,
  For thy sway is begun;
  Thy shadowy sway,
  The senses beguiling,
  When the light fades away,
And thy vapour of mystery o'er nature ascending,
  The heaven and the earth,
  The things that have birth,
And the embryos that float in the future are blending.

From the land, on whose shores the billows break
The sounding waves of the mighty lake;
From the land where boundless meadows be,
Where the buffalo ranges wild and free;
With silvery coat in his little isle,
Where the beaver plies his ceaseless toil;
The land where pigmy forms abide,
Thou leadest thy train at the eventide;
And the wings of the wind are left behind,
So swift through the pathless air they glide.

Then to the chief who has fasted long,
When the chains of his slumber are heavy and strong
SPIRIT! thou comest; he lies as dead,
His weary lids are with heaviness weigh'd;
But his soul is abroad on the hurricane's pinion,
Where foes are met in the rush of fight,
In the shadowy world of thy dominion
Conquering and slaying, till morning light

Then shall the hunter who waits for thee,
The land of the game rejoicing see;
Through the leafless wood,
O'er the frozen flood,
And the trackless snows his spirit goes,
Along the sheeted plain,
Where the hermit bear, in his sullen lair,
Keeps his long fast, till the winter hath pass'd
And the boughs have budded again.
SPIRIT OF DREAMS! all thy visions are true,
Who the shadow hath seen, he the substance shall
    view!

Thine the riddle, strange and dark,
Woven in the dreamy brain:—
Thine to yield the power to mark
Wandering by, the dusky train;
Warrior ghosts for vengeance crying,
Scalped on the lost battle's plain,
Or who died their foes defying,
Slow by lingering tortures slain.

Thou, the war-chief hovering near,
Breathest language on his ear;
When his winged words depart,
Swift as arrows to the heart;
When his eye the lightning leaves;
When each valiant bosom heaves;
Through the veins when hot and glowing
Rage like liquid fire is flowing;
Round and round the war pole whirling,
Furious when the dancers grow;
When the maces swift are hurling
Promised vengeance on the foe·
Thine assurance, SPIRIT true!
Glorious victory gives to view!

When of thought and strength despoil'd,
Lies the brave man like a child;
When discolour'd visions fly,
Painful o'er his glazing eye,
And wishes wild through his darkness rove,
Like flitting wings through the tangled grove,—
Thine is the wish; the vision thine,
And thy visits, SPIRIT! are all divine!

When the dizzy senses spin,
And the brain is madly reeling,
Like the Pów-wah, when first within
The present spirit feeling;
When rays are flashing athwart the gloom,
Like the dancing lights of the northern heaven.
When voices strange of tumult come
On the ear, like the roar of battle driven,—
The Initiate then shall thy wonders see,
And thy priest, O SPIRIT! is full of thee!

WILLIAM B. O. PEABODY.

[Born, 1799. Died, 1847.]

William B. O. Peabody was born at Exeter, New Hampshire, on the ninth of July, 1799; was graduated at Cambridge in 1816; and in 1820 became pastor of a Unitarian Society in Springfield, Massachusetts, where he resided until his death, on the twenty-eighth of May, 1847. He was a voluminous and elegant writer in theology, natural history, literary and historical criticism, and poetry.

HYMN OF NATURE.

God of the earth's extended plains!
  The dark, green fields contented lie;
The mountains rise like holy towers,
  Where man might commune with the sky;
The tall cliff challenges the storm
  That lowers upon the vale below,
Where shaded fountains send their streams,
  With joyous music in their flow.

God of the dark and heavy deep!
  The waves lie sleeping on the sands,
Till the fierce trumpet of the storm
  Hath summon'd up their thundering bands;
Then the white sails are dash'd like foam,
  Or hurry, trembling, o'er the seas,
Till, calm'd by thee, the sinking gale
  Serenely breathes, Depart in peace.

God of the forest's solemn shade!
  The grandeur of the lonely tree,
That wrestles singly with the gale,
  Lifts up admiring eyes to thee;
But more majestic far they stand,
  When, side by side, their ranks they form,
To wave on high their plumes of green,
  And fight their battles with the storm.

God of the light and viewless air!
  Where summer breezes sweetly flow,
Or, gathering in their angry might,
  The fierce and wintry tempests blow;
All—from the evening's plaintive sigh,
  That hardly lifts the drooping flower,
To the wild whirlwind's midnight cry,
  Breathe forth the language of thy power.

God of the fair and open sky!
  How gloriously above us springs
The tented dome, of heavenly blue,
  Suspended on the rainbow's rings!
Each brilliant star, that sparkles through,
  Each gilded cloud, that wanders free
In evening's purple radiance, gives
  The beauty of its praise to thee.

God of the rolling orbs above!
  Thy name is written clearly bright
In the warm day's unvarying blaze,
  Or evening's golden shower of light.

For every fire that fronts the sun,
  And every spark that walks alone
Around the utmost verge of heaven,
  Were kindled at thy burning throne.

God of the world! the hour must come,
  And nature's self to dust return;
Her crumbling altars must decay;
  Her incense fires shall cease to burn;
But still her grand and lovely scenes
  Have made man's warmest praises flow;
For hearts grow holier as they trace
  The beauty of the world below.

TO WILLIAM.

WRITTEN BY A BEREAVED FATHER.

It seems but yesterday, my love,
  Thy little heart beat high;
And I had almost scorn'd the voice
  That told me thou must die.
I saw thee move with active bound,
  With spirits wild and free;
And infant grace and beauty gave
  Their glorious charm to thee.

Far on the sunny plains, I saw
  Thy sparkling footsteps fly,
Firm, light, and graceful, as the bird
  That cleaves the morning sky;
And often, as the playful breeze
  Waved back thy shining hair,
Thy cheek display'd the red rose-tint
  That health had painted there.

And then, in all my thoughtfulness,
  I could not but rejoice
To hear, upon the morning wind,
  The music of thy voice,—
Now, echoing in the rapturous laugh,
  Now sad, almost to tears,
'Twas like the sounds I used to hear
  In old and happier years.

Thanks for that memory to thee,
  My little, lovely boy,—
That memory of my youthful bliss,
  Which time would fain destroy.

I listen'd, as the mariner
  Suspends the out-bound oar,
To taste the farewell gale that breathes
  From off his native shore.

So gentle in thy loveliness!—
  Alas! how could it be,
That death would not forbear to lay
  His icy hand on thee;
Nor spare thee yet a little while,
  In childhood's opening bloom,
While many a sad and weary soul
  Was longing for the tomb!

Was mine a happiness too pure
  For erring man to know?
Or why did Heaven so soon destroy
  My paradise below!
Enchanting as the vision was,
  It sunk away as soon
As when, in quick and cold eclipse,
  The sun grows dark at noon.

I loved thee, and my heart was bless'd;
  But, ere the day was spent,
I saw thy light and graceful form
  In drooping illness bent,
And shudder'd as I cast a look
  Upon thy fainting head;
The mournful cloud was gathering there,
  And life was almost fled.

Days pass'd; and soon the seal of death
  Made known that hope was vain;
I knew the swiftly-wasting lamp
  Would never burn again;
The cheek was pale; the snowy lips
  Were gently thrown apart;
And life, in every passing breath,
  Seem'd gushing from the heart.

I knew those marble lips to mine
  Should never more be press'd,
And floods of feeling, undefined,
  Roll'd wildly o'er my breast;
Low, stifled sounds, and dusky forms
  Seem'd moving in the gloom,
As if death's dark array were come,
  To bear thee to the tomb.

And when I could not keep the tear
  From gathering in my eye,
Thy little hand press'd gently mine,
  In token of reply;
To ask one more exchange of love,
  Thy look was upward cast,
And in that long and burning kiss
  Thy happy spirit pass'd.

I never trusted to have lived
  To bid farewell to thee,
And almost said, in agony,
  It ought not so to be;
I hoped that thou within the grave
  My weary head shouldst lay,
And live, beloved, when I was gone,
  For many a happy day.

With trembling hand, I vainly tried
  Thy dying eyes to close;
And almost envied, in that hour,
  Thy calm and deep repose;
For I was left in loneliness,
  With pain and grief oppress'd,
And thou wast with the sainted,
  Where the weary are at rest.

Yes, I am sad and weary now,
  But let me not repine,
Because a spirit, loved so well,
  Is earlier bless'd than mine;
My faith may darken as it will,
  I shall not much deplore,
Since thou art where the ills of life
  Can never reach thee more.

MONADNOCK.

Upon the far-off mountain's brow
  The angry storm has ceased to beat;
And broken clouds are gathering now
  In sullen reverence round his feet;
I saw their dark and crowded bands
  In thunder on his breast descending;
But there once more redeem'd he stands,
  And heaven's clear arch is o'er him bending,

I've seen him when the morning sun
  Burn'd like a bale-fire on the height;
I've seen him when the day was done,
  Bathed in the evening's crimson light.
I've seen him at the midnight hour,
  When all the world were calmly sleeping
Like some stern sentry in his tower,
  His weary watch in silence keeping.

And there, forever firm and clear,
  His lofty turret upward springs;
He owns no rival summit near,
  No sovereign but the King of kings.
Thousands of nations have pass'd by,
  Thousands of years unknown to story,
And still his aged walls on high
  He rears, in melancholy glory.

The proudest works of human hands
  Live but an age before they fall;
While that severe and hoary tower
  Outlasts the mightiest of them all.
And man himself, more frail, by far,
  Than even the works his hand is raising,
Sinks downward, like the falling star
  That flashes, and expires in blazing.

And all the treasures of the heart,
  Its loves and sorrows, joys and fears,
Its hopes and memories, must depart
  To sleep with unremember'd years.
But still that ancient rampart stands
  Unchanged, though years are passing o'er him;
And time withdraws his powerless hands,
  While ages melt away before him.

So should it be—for no heart beats
  Within his cold and silent breast;
To him no gentle voice repeats
  The soothing words that make us blest.
And more than this—his deep repose
  Is troubled by no thoughts of sorrow;
He hath no weary eyes to close,
  No cause to hope or fear to-morrow.

Farewell! I go my distant way;
  Perchance, in some succeeding years,
The eyes that know no cloud to-day,
  May gaze upon thee dim with tears.
Then may thy calm, unaltering form
  Inspire in me the firm endeavour—
Like thee, to meet each lowering storm,
  Till life and sorrow end forever.

THE WINTER NIGHT.

'Tis the high festival of night!
The earth is radiant with delight;
And, fast as weary day retires,
The heaven unfolds its secret fires,
Bright, as when first the firmament
Around the new-made world was bent,
And infant seraphs pierced the blue,
Till rays of heaven came shining through.

And mark the heaven's reflected glow
On many an icy plain below;
And where the streams, with tinkling clash,
Against their frozen barriers dash,
Like fairy lances fleetly cast,
The glittering ripples hurry past;
And floating sparkles glance afar,
Like rivals of some upper star.

And see, beyond, how sweetly still
The snowy moonlight wraps the hill,
And many an aged pine receives
The steady brightness on its leaves,
Contrasting with those giant forms,
Which, rifled by the winter storms,
With naked branches, broad and high,
Are darkly painted on the sky.

From every mountain's towering head
A white and glistening robe is spread,
As if a melted silver tide
Were gushing down its lofty side;
The clear, cold lustre of the moon
Is purer than the burning noon;
And day hath never known the charm
That dwells amid this evening calm.

The idler, on his silken bed,
May talk of nature, cold and dead;
But we will gaze upon this scene,
Where some transcendent power hath been,
And made these streams of beauty flow
In gladness on the world below,
Till nature breathes from every part
The rapture of her mighty heart.

DEATH.

Lift high the curtain's drooping fold,
  And let the evening sunlight in;
I would not that my heart grew cold
  Before its better years begin.
'T is well; at such an early hour,
  So calm and pure, a sinking ray
Should shine into the heart, with power
  To drive its darker thoughts away.

The bright, young thoughts of early days
  Shall gather in my memory now,
And not the later cares, whose trace
  Is stamp'd so deeply on my brow.
What though those days return no more?
  The sweet remembrance is not vain,
For Heaven is waiting to restore
  The childhood of my soul again.

Let no impatient mourner stand
  In hollow sadness near my bed,
But let me rest upon the hand,
  And let me hear that gentle tread
Of her, whose kindness long ago,
  And still, unworn away by years,
Has made my weary eyelids flow
  With grateful and admiring tears.

I go, but let no plaintive tone
  The moment's grief of friendship tell:
And let no proud and graven stone
  Say where the weary slumbers well.
A few short hours, and then for heaven!
  Let sorrow all its tears dismiss;
For who would mourn the warning given
  Which calls us from a world like this?

AUTUMN EVENING.

Behold the western evening light!
  It melts in deepening gloom;
So calmly Christians sink away,
  Descending to the tomb.

The wind breathes low; the withering leaf
  Scarce whispers from the tree;
So gently flows the parting breath,
  When good men cease to be.

How beautiful on all the hills
  The crimson light is shed!
'T is like the peace the Christian gives
  To mourners round his bed.

How mildly on the wandering cloud
  The sunset beam is cast!
'T is like the memory left behind
  When loved ones breathe their last.

And now, above the dews of night,
  The yellow star appears;
So faith springs in the heart of those
  Whose eyes are bathed in tears.

But soon the morning's happier light
  Its glory shall restore;
And eyelids that are seal'd in death
  Shall wake, to close no more.

GRENVILLE MELLEN.

[Born, 1799. Died, 1841.]

GRENVILLE MELLEN was the third son of the late Chief Justice PRENTISS MELLEN, LL. D., of Maine, and was born in the town of Biddeford, in that state, on the nineteenth day of June, 1799. He was educated at Harvard College, and after leaving that seminary became a law-student in the office of his father, who had before that time removed to Portland. Soon after being admitted to the bar, he was married, and commenced the practice of his profession at North Yarmouth, a pleasant village near his native town. Within three years—in October, 1828—his wife, to whom he was devotedly attached, died, and his only child followed her to the grave in the succeeding spring. From this time his character was changed. He had before been an ambitious and a happy man. The remainder of his life was clouded with melancholy.

I believe Mr. MELLEN did not become known as a writer until he was about twenty-five years old. He was then one of thé contributors to the Cambridge "United States Literary Gazette." In the early part of 1827, he published a satire entitled "Our Chronicle of Twenty-six," and two years afterward, "Glad Tales and Sad Tales," a collection of prose sketches, which had previously been printed in the periodicals. "The Martyr's Triumph, Buried Valley, and other Poems," appeared in 1834. The principal poem in this volume is founded on the history of Saint Alban, the first Christian martyr in England. It is in the measure of the "Faery Queene," and has some creditable passages; but, as a whole, it hardly rises above mediocrity. In the "Buried Valley" he describes the remarkable avalanche near the Notch in the White Mountains, by which the Willey family were destroyed, many years ago. In a poem entitled "The Rest of Empires," in the same collection, he laments the custom of the elder bards to immortalize the deeds of conquerors alone, and contrasts their prostitution of the influence of poetry with the nobler uses to which it is applied in later days, in the following lines, which are characteristic of his best manner:—

"We have been taught, in oracles of old,
Of the enskied divinity of song;
That Poetry and Music, hand in hand,
Came in the light of inspiration forth,
And claim'd alliance with the rolling heavens.
And were those peerless bards, whose strains have come
In an undying echo to the world,
Whose numbers floated round the Grecian isles,
And made melodious all the hills of Rome,—
Were they inspired?—Alas, for Poetry!
That her great ministers, in early time,
Sung for the brave alone—and bade the soul
Battle for heaven in the ranks of war!
It was the treason of the godlike art
That pointed glory to the sword and spear,
And left the heart to moulder in its mail!
It was the menial service of the bard—
It was the basest bondage of his powers,
In later times to consecrate a feast,
And sing of gallantry in hall and bower,
To courtly knights and ladies. . . . . .
"But other times have strung new lyres again,
And other music greets us. Poetry
Comes robed in smiles, and, in low breathing sounds,
Takes counsel, like a friend, in our still hours,
And points us to the stars—the waneless stars—
That whisper an hereafter to our souls.
It breathes upon our spirits a rich balm,
And, with its tender tones and melody,
Draws mercy from the warrior—and proclaims
A morn of bright and universal love
To those who journey with us through the vale;
It points to moral greatness—deeds of mind,
And the high struggles, worthy of a man.
Have we no minstrels in our echoing halls,
No wild CADWALLON, with his wilder strain,
Pouring his war-songs upon helmed ears?
We have sounds stealing from the far retreats
Of the bright company of gifted men,
Who pour their mellow music round our age,
And point us to our duties and our hearts;
The poet's constellation beams around—
A pensive COWPER lives in all his lines,
And MILTON hymns us on to hope and heaven!"

After spending five or six years in Boston, Mr. MELLEN removed to New York, where he resided nearly all the remainder of his life. He wrote much for the literary magazines, and edited several works for his friend, Mr. COLMAN, the publisher. In 1839, he established a Monthly Miscellany, but it was abandoned after the publication of a few numbers. His health had been declining for several years; his disease finally assumed the form of consumption, and he made a voyage to Cuba, in the summer of 1840, in the hope that he would derive advantage from a change of climate, and the sea air. He was disappointed; and learning of the death of his father, in the following spring, he returned to New York, where he died, on the fifth of September, 1841.

Mr. MELLEN was a gentle-hearted, amiable man, social in his feelings, and patient and resigned in the long period of physical suffering which preceded his death. As a poet, he enjoyed a higher reputation in his lifetime than his works will preserve. They are without vigour of thought or language, and are often dreamy, mystic, and unintelligible. In his writings there is no evidence of creative genius; no original, clear, and manly thought; no spirited and natural descriptions of life or nature; no humour, no pathos, no passion; nothing that appeals to the common sympathies of mankind. The little poem entitled "The Bugle," although "it whispers whence it stole its spoils," is probably superior to any thing else he wrote. It is free from the affectations and unmeaning epithets which distinguish nearly all his works.

ENGLISH SCENERY.

The woods and vales of England!—is there not
A magic and a marvel in their names?
Is there not music in the memory
Of their old glory?—is there not a sound,
As of some watchword, that recalls at night
All that gave light and wonder to the day?
In these soft words, that breathe of loveliness,
And summon to the spirit scenes that rose
Rich on its raptured vision, as the eye
Hung like a tranced thing above the page
That genius had made golden with its glow—
The page of noble story—of high towers,
And castled halls, envista'd like the line
Of heroes and great hearts, that centuries
Had led before their hearths in dim array—
Of lake and lawn, and gray and cloudy tree,
That rock'd with banner'd foliage to the storm
Above the walls it shadow'd, and whose leaves,
Rustling in gather'd music to the winds,
Seem'd voiced as with the sound of many seas!
The woods and vales of England! O, the founts,
The living founts of memory! how they break
And gush upon my stirr'd heart as I gaze!
I hear the shout of reapers, the far low
Of herds upon the banks, the distant bark
Of the tired dog, stretch'd at some cottage door,
The echo of the axe, mid forest swung,
And the loud laugh, drowning the faint halloo.
Land of our fathers! though 'tis ours to roam
A land upon whose bosom thou mightst lie,
Like infant on its mother's—though 'tis ours
To gaze upon a nobler heritage
Than thou couldst e'er unshadow to thy sons,—
Though ours to linger upon fount and sky,
Wilder, and peopled with great spirits, who
Walk with a deeper majesty than thine,—
Yet, as our father-land, O, who shall tell
The lone, mysterious energy which calls
Upon our sinking spirits to walk forth
Amid thy wood and mount, where every hill
Is eloquent with beauty, and the tale
And song of centuries, the cloudless years
When fairies walk'd thy valleys, and the turf
Rung to their tiny footsteps, and quick flowers
Sprang with the lifting grass on which they trod—
When all the landscape murmur'd to its rills,
And joy with hope slept in its leafy bowers!

MOUNT WASHINGTON.

Mount of the clouds, on whose Olympian height
The tall rocks brighten in the ether air,
And spirits from the skies come down at night,
To chant immortal songs to Freedom there!
Thine is the rock of other regions, where
The world of life, which blooms so far below,
Sweeps a wide waste: no gladdening scenes appear,
Save where, with silvery flash, the waters flow
Beneath the far-off mountain, distant, calm, and slow.

Thine is the summit where the clouds repose,
Or, eddying wildly, round thy cliffs are borne;
When Tempest mounts his rushing car, and throws
His billowy mist amid the thunder's home!
Far down the deep ravine the whirlwinds come,
And bow the forests as they sweep along;
While, roaring deeply from their rocky womb,
The storms come forth, and, hurrying darkly on,
Amid the echoing peaks the revelry prolong!

And when the tumult of the air is fled,
And quench'd in silence all the tempest flame,
There come the dim forms of the mighty dead,
Around the steep which bears the hero's name:
The stars look down upon them; and the same
Pale orb that glistens o'er his distant grave
Gleams on the summit that enshrines his fame,
And lights the cold tear of the glorious brave,
The richest, purest tear that memory ever gave!

Mount of the clouds! when winter round thee throws
The hoary mantle of the dying year,
Sublime amid thy canopy of snows,
Thy towers in bright magnificence appear!
'T is then we view thee with a chilling fear,
Till summer robes thee in her tints of blue;
When, lo! in soften'd grandeur, far, yet clear,
Thy battlements stand clothed in heaven's own hue,
To swell as Freedom's home on man's unbounded view!

THE BUGLE.

O! wild, enchanting horn!
Whose music up the deep and dewy air
Swells to the clouds, and calls on Echo there,
Till a new melody is born—

Wake, wake again, the night
Is bending from her throne of beauty down,
With still stars burning on her azure crown,
Intense and eloquently bright.

Night, at its pulseless noon!
When the far voice of waters mourns in song,
And some tired watch-dog, lazily and long
Barks at the melancholy moon.

Hark! how it sweeps away,
Soaring and dying on the silent sky,
As if some sprite of sound went wandering by,
With lone halloo and roundelay!

Swell, swell in glory out!
Thy tones come pouring on my leaping heart,
And my stirr'd spirit hears thee with a start
As boyhood's old remember'd shout.

O! have ye heard that peal,
From sleeping city's moon-bathed battlements,
Or from the guarded field and warrior tents,
Like some near breath around you steal?

Or have ye in the roar
Of sea, or storm, or battle, heard it rise,
Shriller than eagle's clamour, to the skies,
Where wings and tempests never soar?

Go, go—no other sound,
No music that of air or earth is born,
Can match the mighty music of that horn,
On midnight's fathomless profound!

ON SEEING AN EAGLE PASS NEAR ME IN AUTUMN TWILIGHT.

Sail on, thou lone, imperial bird,
  Of quenchless eye and tireless wing;
How is thy distant coming heard,
  As the night's breezes round thee ring!
Thy course was 'gainst the burning sun
  In his extremest glory. How!
Is thy unequall'd daring done,
  Thou stoop'st to earth so lowly now?

Or hast thou left thy rocking dome,
  Thy roaring crag, thy lightning pine,
To find some secret, meaner home,
  Less stormy and unsafe than thine?
Else why thy dusky pinions bend
  So closely to this shadowy world,
And round thy searching glances send,
  As wishing thy broad pens were furl'd?

Yet lonely is thy shatter'd nest,
  Thy eyry desolate, though high;
And lonely thou, alike at rest,
  Or soaring in the upper sky.
The golden light that bathes thy plumes
  On thine interminable flight,
Falls cheerless on earth's desert tombs,
  And makes the north's ice-mountains bright.

So come the eagle-hearted down,
  So come the high and proud to earth,
When life's night-gathering tempests frown
  Over their glory and their mirth·
So quails the mind's undying eye,
  That bore, unveil'd, fame's noontide sun;
So man seeks solitude, to die,
  His high place left, his triumphs done.

So, round the residence of power,
  A cold and joyless lustre shines,
And on life's pinnacles will lower
  Clouds, dark as bathe the eagle's pines.
But, O, the mellow light that pours
  From God's pure throne—the light that saves!
It warms the spirit as it soars,
  And sheds deep radiance round our graves.

THE TRUE GLORY OF AMERICA.

Italia's vales and fountains,
  Though beautiful ye be,
I love my soaring mountains
  And forests more than ye;
And though a dreamy greatness rise
  From out your cloudy years,
Like hills on distant stormy skies,
  Seem dim through Nature's tears,
Still, tell me not of years of old,
  Or ancient heart and clime;
Ours is the land and age of gold,
  And ours the hallow'd time!

The jewell'd crown and sceptre
  Of Greece have pass'd away;
And none, of all who wept her,
  Could bid her splendour stay.
The world has shaken with the tread
  Of iron-sandall'd crime—
And, lo! o'ershadowing all the dead,
  The conqueror stalks sublime!
Then ask I not for crown and plume
  To nod above my land;
The victor's footsteps point to doom,
  Graves open round his hand!

Rome! with thy pillar'd palaces,
  And sculptured heroes all,
Snatch'd, in their warm, triumphal days,
  To Art's high festival;
Rome! with thy giant sons of power,
  Whose pathway was on thrones,
Who built their kingdoms of an hour
  On yet unburied bones,—
I would not have my land like thee,
  So lofty—yet so cold!
Be hers a lowlier majesty,
  In yet a nobler mould.

Thy marbles—works of wonder!
  In thy victorious days,
Whose lips did seem to sunder
  Before the astonish'd gaze;
When statue glared on statue there,
  The living on the dead,—
And men as silent pilgrims were
  Before some sainted head!
O, not for faultless marbles yet
  Would I the light forego
That beams when other lights have set,
  And Art herself lies low!

O, ours a holier hope shall be
  Than consecrated bust,
Some loftier mean of memory
  To snatch us from the dust.
And ours a sterner art than this,
  Shall fix our image here,—
The spirit's mould of loveliness—
  A nobler Belvidere!

Then let them bind with bloomless flowers
  The busts and urns of old,—
A fairer heritage be ours,
  A sacrifice less cold!
Give honour to the great and good,
  And wreathe the living brow,
Kindling with Virtue's mantling blood,
  And pay the tribute now!

So, when the good and great go down,
  Their statues shall arise,
To crowd those temples of our own,
  Our fadeless memories!
And when the sculptured marble falls,
  And Art goes in to die,
Our forms shall live in holier halls,
  The Pantheon of the sky!

GEORGE W. DOANE.

[Born 1799. Died 1859.]

THE Right Reverend GEORGE W. DOANE, D.D., LL.D., was born in Trenton, New Jersey, in 1799. He was graduated at Union College, Schenectady, when nineteen years of age, and immediately after commenced the study of theology. He was ordained deacon by Bishop HOBART, in 1821, and priest by the same prelate in 1823. He officiated in Trinity Church, New York, three years, and, in 1824, was appointed professor of belles lettres and Oratory in Washington College, Connecticut. He resigned that office in 1828, and soon after was elected rector of Trinity Church, in Boston. He was consecrated Bishop of the Diocese of New Jersey, on the thirty-first of October, 1832.

Bishop DOANE's "Songs by the Way," a collection of poems, chiefly devotional, were published in 1824, and appear to have been mostly produced during his college life. He has since, from time to time, written poetry for festival-days and other occasions, but has published no second volume. His published sermons, charges, conventional addresses, literary and historical discourses, and other publications in prose, amount to more than one hundred, and fill more than three thousand octavo pages. His writings generally are marked by refinement and elegance, and evince a profound devotion to the interests of the Protestant Episcopal Church.

ON A VERY OLD WEDDING-RING.

THE DEVICE—Two hearts united.
THE MOTTO—"Dear love of mine, my heart is thine."

I LIKE that ring—that ancient ring,
Of massive form, and virgin gold,
As firm, as free from base alloy,
As were the sterling hearts of old.
I like it—for it wafts me back,
Far, far along the stream of time,
To other men, and other days,
The men and days of deeds sublime.

But most I like it, as it tells
The tale of well-requited love;
How youthful fondness persevered,
And youthful faith disdain'd to rove—
How warmly *he* his suit preferr'd,
Though *she*, unpitying, long denied,
Till, soften'd and subdued, at last,
He won his "fair and blooming bride."—

How, till the appointed day arrived,
They blamed the lazy-footed hours—
How, then, the white-robed maiden train
Strew'd their glad way with freshest flowers—
And how, before the holy man,
They stood, in all their youthful pride,
And spoke those words, and vow'd those vows,
Which bind the husband to his bride:

All this it tells; the plighted troth—
The gift of every earthly thing—
The hand in hand—the heart in heart—
For this I like that ancient ring.
I like its old and quaint device;
"Two blended hearts"—though time may wear them,
No mortal change, no mortal chance,
"Till death," shall e'er in sunder tear them.

Year after year, 'neath sun and storm,
Their hopes in heaven, their trust in GOD,
In changeless, heartfelt, holy love,
These two the world's rough pathway trod.
Age might impair their youthful fires,
Their strength might fail, mid life's bleak weather
Still, hand in hand, they travell'd on—
Kind souls! they slumber now together.

I like its simple poesy too:
"Mine own dear love, this heart is thine!"
Thine, when the dark storm howls along,
As when the cloudless sunbeams shine.
"This heart is thine, mine own dear love!"
Thine, and thine only, and forever;
Thine, till the springs of life shall fail,
Thine, till the cords of life shall sever.

Remnant of days departed long,
Emblem of plighted troth unbroken,
Pledge of devoted faithfulness,
Of heartfelt, holy love the token:
What varied feelings round it cling!
For these I like that ancient ring.

MALLEUS DOMINI.

JEREMIAH xxiii. 29.

SLEDGE of the Lord, beneath whose stroke
The rocks are rent—the heart is broke—
I hear thy pond'rous echoes ring,
And fall, a crushed and crumbled thing.

Meekly, these mercies I implore,
Through HIM whose cross our sorrow bore:
On earth, thy new-creating grace;
In heaven, the very lowest place.

Oh, might I be a living stone,
Set in the pavement of thy throne!
For sinner saved, what place so meet,
As at the SAVIOUR's bleeding feet!

"STAND AS AN ANVIL, WHEN IT IS BEATEN UPON."

"Stand, like an anvil," when the stroke
Of stalwart men falls fierce and fast:
Storms but more deeply root the oak,
Whose brawny arms embrace the blast.

"Stand like an anvil," when the sparks
Fly, far and wide a fiery shower;
Virtue and truth must still be marks,
Where malice proves its want of power.

"Stand, like an anvil," when the bar
Lies, red and glowing, on its breast:
Duty shall be life's leading star,
And conscious innocence its rest.

"Stand like an anvil," when the sound
Of ponderous hammers pains the ear:
Thine, but the still and stern rebound
Of the great heart that cannot fear.

"Stand, like an anvil;" noise and heat
Are born of earth, and die with time:
The soul, like God, its source and seat,
Is solemn, still, serene, sublime.

THAT SILENT MOON.

That silent moon, that silent moon,
Careering now through cloudless sky,
O! who shall tell what varied scenes
Have pass'd beneath her placid eye,
Since first, to light this wayward earth,
She walk'd in tranquil beauty forth!

How oft has guilt's unhallow'd hand,
And superstition's senseless rite,
And loud, licentious revelry
Profaned her pure and holy light:
Small sympathy is hers, I ween,
With sights like these, that virgin queen!

But dear to her, in summer eve,
By rippling wave, or tufted grove,
When hand in hand is purely clasp'd,
And heart meets heart in holy love,
To smile in quiet loneliness,
And hear each whisper'd vow, and bless.

Dispersed along the world's wide way,
When friends are far, and fond ones rove,
How powerful she to wake the thought,
And start the tear for those we love,
Who watch with us at night's pale noon,
And gaze upon that silent moon.

How powerful, too, to hearts that mourn,
The magic of that moonlight sky,
To bring again the vanish'd scenes—
The happy eves of days gone by;
Again to bring, mid bursting tears,
The loved, the lost of other years.

And oft she looks, that silent moon,
On lonely eyes that wake to weep
In dungeon dark, or sacred cell,
Or couch, whence pain has banish'd sleep:
O! softly beams her gentle eye
On those who mourn, and those who die!

But, beam on whomsoe'er she will,
And fall where'er her splendours may,
There's pureness in her chasten'd light,
There's comfort in her tranquil ray:
What power is hers to soothe the heart—
What power, the trembling tear to start!

The dewy morn let others love,
Or bask them in the noontide ray;
There's not an hour but has its charm,
From dawning light to dying day:—
But, O! be mine a fairer boon—
That silent moon, that silent moon!

THERMOPYLÆ.

'T was an hour of fearful issues,
When the bold three hundred stood,
For their love of holy freedom,
By that old Thessalian flood;
When, lifting high each sword of flame,
They call'd on every sacred name,
And swore, beside those dashing waves,
They never, never would be slaves!

And, O! that oath was nobly kept:
From morn to setting sun
Did desperation urge the fight
Which valour had begun;
Till, torrent-like, the stream of blood
Ran down and mingled with the flood,
And all, from mountain-cliff to wave,
Was Freedom's, Valour's, Glory's grave.

O, yes, that oath was nobly kept,
Which nobly had been sworn,
And proudly did each gallant heart
The foeman's fetters spurn;
And firmly was the fight maintain'd,
And amply was the triumph gain'd;
They fought, fair Liberty, for thee:
They fell—TO DIE IS TO BE FREE.

ROBIN REDBREAST.*

Sweet Robin, I have heard them say,
That thou wert there, upon the day,
The Christ was crown'd in cruel scorn;
And bore away one bleeding thorn,
That, so, the blush upon thy breast,
In shameful sorrow, was impressed;
And thence thy genial sympathy,
With our redeemed humanity.

Sweet Robin, would that I might be,
Bathed in my Saviour's blood, like thee;
Bear in my breast, whate'er the loss,
The bleeding blazon of the cross;
Live, ever, with thy loving mind,
In fellowship with human kind;
And take my pattern still from thee,
In gentleness and constancy.

* I have somewhere met with an old legend, that a robin hovering about the Cross, bore off a thorn, from our dear Saviour's crown, and dyed his bosom with the blood; and that from that time robins have been the friends of man

"WHAT IS THAT, MOTHER?"

What is that, Mother?—The lark, my child!—
The morn has but just look'd out, and smiled,
When he starts from his humble grassy nest,
And is up and away, with the dew on his breast,
And a hymn in his heart, to yon pure, bright sphere,
To warble it out in his Maker's ear.
Ever, my child, be thy morn's first lays
Tuned, like the lark's, to thy Maker's praise.

What is that, Mother?—The dove, my son!—
And that low, sweet voice, like a widow's moan,
Is flowing out from her gentle breast,
Constant and pure, by that lonely nest,
As the wave is pour'd from some crystal urn,
For her distant dear one's quick return:
Ever, my son, be thou like the dove,
In friendship as faithful, as constant in love.

What is that, Mother?—The eagle, boy!—
Proudly careering his course of joy;
Firm, on his own mountain vigour relying,
Breasting the dark storm, the red bolt defying,
His wing on the wind, and his eye on the sun,
He swerves not a hair, but bears onward, right on.
Boy, may the eagle's flight ever be thine,
Onward, and upward, and true to the line.

What is that, Mother?—The swan, my love!—
He is floating down from his native grove,
No loved one now, no nestling nigh,
He is floating down, by himself to die;
Death darkens his eye, and unplumes his wings,
Yet his sweetest song is the last he sings.
Live so, my love, that when death shall come,
Swan-like and sweet, it may waft thee home.

A CHERUB.

"Dear Sir, I am in some little disorder by reason of the death of a little child of mine, a boy that lately made us very glad; but now he rejoices in his little orbe, while we thinke, and sigh, and long to be as safe as he is."—Jeremy Taylor to Evelyn, 1656.

Beautiful thing, with thine eye of light,
And thy brow of cloudless beauty bright,
Gazing for aye on the sapphire throne
Of Him who dwelleth in light alone—
Art thou hasting now, on that golden wing,
With the burning seraph choir to sing?
Or stooping to earth, in thy gentleness,
Our darkling path to cheer and bless?

Beautiful thing! thou art come in love,
With gentle gales from the world above,
Breathing of pureness, breathing of bliss,
Bearing our spirits away from this,
To the better thoughts, to the brighter skies,
Where heaven's eternal sunshine lies;
Winning our hearts, by a blessed guile,
With that infant look and angel smile.

Beautiful thing! thou art come in joy,
With the look and the voice of our darling boy—
Him that was torn from the bleeding hearts
He had twined about with his infant arts,
To dwell, from sin and sorrow far,
In the golden orb of his little star:
There he rejoiceth in light, while we
Long to be happy and safe as he.

Beautiful thing! thou art come in peace,
Bidding our doubts and our fears to cease;
Wiping the tears which unbidden start
From that bitter fount in the broken heart,
Cheering us still on our lonely way,
Lest our spirits should faint, or our feet should stray
Till, risen with Christ, we come to be,
Beautiful thing, with our boy and thee.

LINES BY THE LAKE SIDE.

This placid lake, my gentle girl,
Be emblem of thy life,
As full of peace and purity,
As free from care and strife;
No ripple on its tranquil breast
That dies not with the day,
No pebble in its darkest depths,
But quivers in its ray.

And see, how every glorious form
And pageant of the skies,
Reflected from its glassy face,
A mirror'd image lies;
So be thy spirit ever pure,
To God and virtue given,
And thought, and word, and action bear
The imagery of heaven.

THE CHRISTIAN'S DEATH.

Lift not thou the wailing voice,
Weep not, 'tis a Christian dieth,—
Up, where blessed saints rejoice,
Ransom'd now, the spirit flieth;
High, in heaven's own light, she dwelleth,
Full the song of triumph swelleth;
Freed from earth, and earthly failing,
Lift for her no voice of wailing!

Pour not thou the bitter tear;
Heaven its book of comfort opeth;
Bids thee sorrow not, nor fear,
But, as one who alway hopeth,
Humbly here in faith relying,
Peacefully in Jesus dying,
Heavenly joy her eye is flushing,—
Why should thine with tears be gushing!

They who die in Christ are bless'd,-
Ours be, then, no thought of grieving!
Sweetly with their God they rest,
All their toils and troubles leaving:
So be ours the faith that saveth,
Hope that every trial braveth,
Love that to the end endureth,
And, through Christ, the crown secureth!

GEORGE BANCROFT.

[Born, 1800.]

MR. BANCROFT is more distinguished as a politician and a historian than as a poet; but his earliest aspirations were for the wreath of the bard; the first flowerings of his genius were in a volume of poems; and whatever the ambitions of his later years, he has continued to find in the divinest of the arts a recreation for himself and a means of conferring happiness on others. He was born in Worcester, Massachusetts, where his father was many years honourably distinguished as a pious and learned clergyman, and at the early age of seventeen was graduated bachelor of arts at Harvard College. The next year he went to Europe, and for four years studied at Gottingen and Berlin, and travelled in Germany, Italy, Switzerland, and England. On his return, in 1823, he published a volume of "Poems," most of which were written while he was abroad. He soon after established the academy of Round Hill, at Northampton, but in a few years became too deeply interested in politics for a teacher, and about the same period began the composition of that great work on the history of this country, which is destined to be the best measure of his literary abilities. In 1838 he was appointed collector of Boston; in 1844 was the candidate of the democratic party for the office of Governor of Massachusetts; in 1845 was made secretary of the Navy; in 1846 was sent as minister-plenipotentiary to England; and on his return, in 1849, became a resident of New York, where he has since devoted himself principally to the composition of his "History of the United States," of which the fifth volume appeared in 1854. He has recently published a volume of "Literary and Historical Miscellanies," embracing essays; studies in German literature, including poetical translations from GOETHE, SCHILLER, RUECKERT, and others; studies in history; and occasional addresses. Of his History I have printed some observations in "The Prose Writers of America." To what rank he might have attained as a poet, the judicious reader may see from the specimens of his verse which are here quoted.

MIDNIGHT, AT MEYRINGEN.

Is there no slumber for the hearts that mourn?
  Vainly I long my weary eyes to close;
Sleep does but mock me with unfeeling scorn,
  And only to the careless sends repose.

Nor night, nor silence lends my bosom rest;
  My visionary spirit wanders far;
With heart and hopes I follow to the West
  In its calm motion Hesper's flaming star.

Ah! there the fates spin sorrow's blackest thread,
  And restless weave misfortune's broadest woof;
There Destiny, with threatening wings outspread,
  Broods in still darkness o'er my home's dear roof.

I dread his power; and still my heart must sigh
  In anguish; down the midnight stars are gone;
The moon has set; the hours are hurrying by;
  And I am wakeful, sorrowing, and alone.

THE SIMPLON.

FAREWELL TO SWITZERLAND.

Land of the brave! land of the free! farewell!
  Thee nature moulded in her wildest mood,
Scoop'd the deep glen and bade the mountains swell
  O'er the dark belt of arrowy tannen wood.

The hills I roamed in gladness; pure and white
  Beams their broad mantle of eternal snows
In sparkling splendour; and with crimson light
  Tinged are its curling folds when sunset glows

With my own hands 't was sweet to climb the crag,
  Upborne and nourished by the mountain air;
While the lean mules would far behind me lag,
  The fainting sons of indolence that bear.

'T was sweet at noonday, stretched in idle ease,
  To watch the stream, that hurries o'er the steep:
At one bold bound the precipice he frees,
  Pours from the rocks, and hastes through vales to sweep;

There in still nook he forms the smiling lake
  Of glassy clearness, where the boatman glides;
And thence a gentler course his torrents take,
  And white-walled towns like lillies deck his sides.

And as I lay in Nature's soothing arms,
  On Memory's leaf she drew in colours bright
The mountain landscape's ever varying charms,
  And bade Remembrance guard each haughty height,

I dared to tread, each vale I wander'd through,
  And every tree that cooled me with its shade,
Each glacier whence the air refreshing blew,
  Each limpid fountain that my thirst allayed.

O Earth! I cried, thou kindest nurse, still turns
  To thee the heart, that withered like the leaf
In autumn's blast, and bruised by anguish, mourns
  Departed happiness. There is relief

Upon thy bosom; from the fountains gush
To cool the heated brow with purest wave;
And when distress the struggling soul would crush,
Thy tranquil mien hath power to heal, and save

From wasting grief. My spirit too was sear,
As is the last gray leaf, that lingers yet
On oaken branch, although my twentieth year
Upon my youthful head no mark had set.

To thee in hope and confidence I came,
And thou didst lend thine air a soothing balm;
Didst teach me sorrow's fearful power to tame,
And be, though pensive, cheerful, pleased, and calm.

My heart was chilled; age stole upon my mind,
In hour untimely, Spring from life to wrest;
I wandered far, my long-lost youth to find,
And I regain it, Nature, on thy breast!

AN ADDRESS TO THE DEITY.

AT KANDERSTEG.

FATHER in heaven! while friendless and alone
I gaze on nature's face in Alpine wild,
I would approach thee nearer. Wilt thou own
The solitary pilgrim for thy child!

When on the hill's majestic height I trod,
And thy creation smiling round me lay,
The soul reclaimed its likeness unto GOD,
And spurned its union with the baser clay.

The stream of thought flowed purely, like the air
That from untrodden snows passed coolly by;
Base passion died within me; low-born care
Fled, and reflection raised my soul on high.

Then wast thou with me, and didst sweetly pour
Serene delight into my wounded breast;
The mantle of thy love hung gently o'er
The lonely wanderer, and my heart had rest.

I gazed on thy creation. O! 't is fair;
The vales are clothed in beauty, and the hills
In their deep bosom icy oceans bear,
To feed the mighty floods and bubbling rills.

I marvel not at nature. She is thine;
Thy cherished daughter, whom thou lov'st to bless;
Through thee her hills in glistening whiteness shine;
Through thee her valleys laugh in loveliness.

'T is thou, when o'er my path beams cheerful day,
That smiling guid'st me through the stranger's land;
And when mild winds around my temples play,
On my hot brow I feel thy lenient hand.

And shall I fear thee?—wherefore fear thy wrath,
When life and hope and youth from thee descend?
O! be my guide in life's uncertain path,
The pilgrim's guardian, counsellor, and friend.

MY GODDESS.

A FREE VERSION FROM GOETHE.

WHO, of heaven's immortal train,
Shall the highest prize obtain?
Strife I would with all give o'er,
But there's one I'll aye adore,
Ever new and ever changing,
Through the paths of marvel raging,
Dearest in her father's eye,
Jove's own darling, Fantasy.
For to her, and her alone,
All his secret whims are known;
And in all her faults' despite
Is the maid her sire's delight.
Oft, with aspect mild, she goes,
Decked with lilies and the rose,
Walks among the flowery bands,
Summer's insect swarm commands,
And for food with honeyed lips
Dew-drops from the blossom sips;—
Or, with darker mein, and hair
Streaming loose in murky air,
With the storm she rushes by,
Whistling where the crags are high,
And, with hues of thousand dyes,
Like the late and early skies,
Changes and is changed again,
Fast as moons that wax and wane.
Him, the ancient sire, we'll praise
Who, as partner of our days,
Hath to mortal man allied
Such a fair, unfading bride.
For to us alone she's given,
And is bound by bonds of heaven
Still to be our faithful bride,
And, though joy or wo betide,
Ne'er to wander from our side.
Other tribes, that have their birth
In the fruitful teeming earth,
All, through narrow life, remain
In dark pleasures, gloomy pain,
Live their being's narrow round,
To the passing moment bound,
And, unconscious, roam and feed,
Bent beneath the yoke of need.
But to us, with kind intent,
He his frolic daughter sent,
Nursed with fondest tenderness.
Welcome her with love's caress,
And take heed, that none but she
Mistress of the mansion be.
And of wisdom's power beware,
Lest the old step-mother dare
Rudely harm the tender fair.
Yet I know Jove's elder child,
Graver and serenely mild,
My beloved, my tranquil friend.
From me never may she wend,—
She, that knows with ill to cope,
And to action urges—Hope.

GEORGE HILL.

[Born, 1800.]

George Hill is a native of Guilford, on Long Island Sound, near New Haven. He was admitted to Yale College in his fifteenth year, and, when he graduated, took the Berkeleian prize, as the best classic. He was subsequently attached to the navy, as Professor of Mathematics; and visited in this capacity the Mediterranean, its storied islands, and classic shores. After his return, he was appointed librarian to the State Department, at Washington: a situation which he at length resigned on account of ill health, and was appointed Consul of the United States for the south-western portion of Asia Minor. The climate disagreeing with him, he returned to Washington; and he is now attached again to one of the bureaus in the Department of State.

The style of Mr. Hill's poetry is severe, and sometimes so elliptical as to embarrass his meaning; this is especially true of his more elaborate production, "The Ruins of Athens," written in the Spenserian stanza. He is most successful in his lyrics, where he has more freedom, without a loss of energy His "Titania," a dramatic piece, is perhaps the most original of his productions. It is wild and fanciful, and graced with images of much beauty and freshness.

FROM "THE RUINS OF ATHENS."

The daylight fades o'er old Cyllene's hill,
And broad and dun the mountain shadows fall;
The stars are up and sparkling, as if still
Smiling upon their altars; but the tall,
Dark cypress, gently, as a mourner, bends—
Wet with the drops of evening as with tears—
Alike o'er shrine and worshipper, and blends,
All dim and lonely, with the wrecks of years,
As of a world gone by no coming morning cheers.

There sits the queen of temples—gray and lone.
She, like the last of an imperial line,
Has seen her sister structures, one by one,
To Time their gods and worshippers resign;
And the stars twinkle through the weeds that twine
Their roofless capitals; and, through the night,
Heard the hoarse drum and the exploding mine,
The clash of arms and hymns of uncouth rite,
From their dismantled shrines the guardian powers affright.

Go! thou from whose forsaken heart are reft
The ties of home; and, where a dwelling-place
Not Jove himself the elements have left,
The grass-grown, undefined arena pace! [hear
Look on its rent, though tower-like shafts, and
The loud winds thunder in their aged face;
Then slowly turn thine eye, where moulders near
A Cæsar's arch, and the blue depth of space
Vaults like a sepulchre the wrecks of a past race.

Is it not better with the Eremite,
Where the weeds rustle o'er his airy cave,
Perch'd on their summit, through the long, still night
To sit and watch their shadows slowly wave—
While oft some fragment, sapp'd by dull decay.
In thunder breaks the silence, and the fowl
Of Ruin hoots—and turn in scorn away
Of all man builds, time levels, and the cowl
Awards her moping sage in common with the owl?

Or, where the palm, at twilight's holy hour,
By Theseus' fane her lonely vigil keeps:
Gone are her sisters of the leaf and flower,
With them the living crop earth sows and reaps,
But these revive not: the weed with them sleeps,
But clothes herself in beauty from their clay,
And leaves them to their slumber; o'er them weeps
Vainly the Spring her quickening dews away,
And Love as vainly mourns, and mourns, alas! for aye.

Or, more remote, on Nature's haunts intrude,
Where, since creation, she has slept on flowers,
Wet with the noonday forest-dew, and woo'd
By untamed choristers in unpruned bowers:
By pathless thicket, rock that time-worn towers
O'er dells untrodden by the hunter, piled
Ere by its shadow measured were the hours
To human eye, the rampart of the wild,
Whose banner is the cloud, by carnage undefiled.

The weary spirit that forsaken plods
The world's wide wilderness, a home may find
Here, mid the dwellings of long-banish'd gods,
And thoughts they bring, the mourners of the mind;
The spectres that no spell has power to bind.
The loved, but lost, whose soul's life is in ours,
As incense in sepulchral urns, enshrined,
The sense of blighted or of wasted powers,
The hopes whose promised fruits have perish'd with their flowers.

There is a small, low cape—there, where the moon
Breaks o'er the shatter'd and now shapeless stone;
The waters, as a rude but fitting boon,
Weeds and small shells have, like a garland, thrown
Upon it, and the wind's and wave's low moan,
And sighing grass, and cricket's plaint, are heard
To steal upon the stillness, like a tone
Remember'd. Here, by human foot unstirr'd,
Its seed the thistle sheds, and builds the ocean-bird.

Lurks the foul toad, the lizard basks secure
Within the sepulchre of him whose name
Had scatter'd navies like the whirlwind. Sure,
If aught ambition's fiery wing may tame,
'Tis here; the web the spider weaves where Fame
Planted her proud but sunken shaft, should be
To it a fetter, still it springs the same,
Glory's fool-worshipper! here bend thy knee!
The tomb thine altar-stone, thine idol Mockery:

A small, gray elf, all sprinkled o'er with dust
Of crumbling catacomb, and mouldering shred
Of banner and embroider'd pall, and rust
Of arms, time-worn monuments, that shed
A canker'd gleam on dim escutcheons, where
The groping antiquary pores to spy—
A what? a name—perchance ne'er graven there;
At whom the urchin, with his mimic eye,
Sits peering through a skull, and laughs continually.

THE MOUNTAIN-GIRL.

The clouds, that upward curling from
Nevada's summit fly,
Melt into air: gone are the showers,
And, deck'd, as 't were with bridal flowers,
Earth seems to wed the sky.

All hearts are by the spirit that
Breathes in the sunshine stirr'd;
And there's a girl that, up and down,
A merry vagrant, through the town,
Goes singing like a bird.

A thing all lightness, life, and glee;
One of the shapes we seem
To meet in visions of the night;
And, should they greet our waking sight,
Imagine that we dream.

With glossy ringlet, brow that is
As falling snow-flake white,
Half-hidden by its jetty braid,
And eye like dewdrop in the shade,
At once both dark and bright;

And cheek whereon the sunny clime
Its brown tint gently throws,
Gently, as it reluctant were
To leave its print on thing so fair—
A shadow on a rose

She stops, looks up—what does she see?
A flower of crimson dye,
Whose vase, the work of Moorish hands,
A lady sprinkles, as it stands
Upon a balcony:

High, leaning from a window forth,
From curtains that half-shroud
Her maiden form with tress of gold,
And brow that mocks their snow-white fold,
Like Dian from a cloud.

Nor flower, nor lady fair she sees—
That mountain-girl—but dumb
And motionless she stands, with eye
That seems communing with the sky:
Her visions are of home.

That flower to her is as a tone
Of some forgotten song,
One of a slumbering thousand, struck
From an old harp-string; but, once woke,
It brings the rest along.

She sees beside the mountain-brook,
Beneath the old cork tree
And toppling crag, a vine-thatch'd shed,
Perch'd, like the eagle, high o'erhead,
The home of liberty;

The rivulet, the olive shade,
The grassy plot, the flock;
Nor does her simple thought forget,
Haply, the little violet,
That springs beneath the rock.

Sister and mate, they may not from
Her dreaming eye depart;
And one, the source of gentler fears,
More dear than all, for whom she wears
The token at her heart.

And hence her eye is dim, her cheek
Has lost its livelier glow;
Her song has ceased, and motionless
She stands, an image of distress:—
Strange, what a flower can do!

THE MIGHT OF GREECE.*

The might of Greece! whose story has gone forth,
Like the eternal echo of a lyre
Struck by an angel, to the bounds of earth,
A marvel and a melody; a fire
Unquench'd, unquenchable. Castalia's choir
Mourn o'er their altars worshipless or gone;
But the free mountain-air they did respire
Has borne their music onward, with a tone
Shaking earth's tyrant race through every distant zone!

A never-dying music, borne along [fraught
The stream of years, that else were mute, and
—A boundless echo, thunder peal'd in song—
With the unconquerable might of thought:
The Titan that shall rive the fetters wrought
By the world's god, Opinion, and set free
The powers of mind, giants from darkness brought;
The trophies of whose triumph-march shall be
Thrones, dungeons swept away, as rampires by the sea.

* From "The Ruins of Athens."

THE FALL OF THE OAK.

A glorious tree is the old gray oak:
He has stood for a thousand years,
Has stood and frown'd
On the trees around,
Like a king among his peers;
As round their king they stand, so now,
When the flowers their pale leaves fold,
The tall trees round him stand, array'd
In their robes of purple and gold.

He has stood like a tower
Through sun and shower,
And dared the winds to battle;
He has heard the hail,
As from plates of mail,
From his own limbs shaken, rattle;
He has toss'd them about, and shorn the tops
(When the storm had roused his might)
Of the forest trees, as a strong man doth
The heads of his foes in fight.

The autumn sun looks kindly down,
But the frost is on the lea,
And sprinkles the horn
Of the owl at morn,
As she hies to the old oak tree.
Not a leaf is stirr'd;
Not a sound is heard
But the thump of the thresher's flail,
The low wind's sigh,
Or the distant cry
Of the hound on the fox's trail.

The forester he has whistling plunged
With his axe, in the deep wood's gloom,
That shrouds the hill,
Where few and chill
The sunbeams struggling come:
His brawny arm he has bared, and laid
His axe at the root of the tree,
The gray old oak,
And, with lusty stroke,
He wields it merrily:—

With lusty stroke,—
And the old gray oak,
Through the folds of his gorgeous vest
You may see him shake,
And the night-owl break
From her perch in his leafy crest.
She will come but to find him gone from where
He stood at the break of day;
Like a cloud that peals as it melts to air,
He has pass'd, with a crash, away.

Though the spring in the bloom and the frost in gold
No more his limbs attire,
On the stormy wave
He shall float, and brave
The blast and the battle-fire!
Shall spread his white wings to the wind,
And thunder on the deep,
As he thunder'd when
His bough was green,
On the high and st·rmy steep.

LIBERTY.

There is a spirit working in the world,
Like to a silent subterranean fire;
Yet, ever and anon, some monarch hurl'd
Aghast and pale, attests its fearful ire.
The dungeon'd nations now once more respire
The keen and stirring air of Liberty.
The struggling giant wakes, and feels he's free.
By Delphi's fountain-cave, that ancient choir
Resume their song; the Greek astonish'd hears,
And the old altar of his worship rears.
Sound on, fair sisters! sound your boldest lyre,—
Peal your old harmonies as from the spheres.
Unto strange gods too long we've bent the knee,
The trembling mind, too long and patiently.

TO A YOUNG MOTHER.

What things of thee may yield a semblance meet,
And him, thy fairy portraiture? a flower
And bud, moon and attending star, a sweet
Voice and its sweeter echo. Time has small power
O'er features the mind moulds; and such are thine,
Imperishably lovely. Roses, where
They once have bloom'd, a fragrance leave behind;
And harmony will linger on the wind;
And suns continue to light up the air,
When set; and music from the broken shrine
Breathes, it is said, around whose altar-stone
His flower the votary has ceased to twine:—
Types of the beauty that, when youth is gone,
Beams from the soul whose brightness mocks decline.

SPRING.

Now Heaven seems one bright, rejoicing eye,
And Earth her sleeping vesture flings aside,
And with a blush awakes as does a bride;
And Nature speaks, like thee, in melody.
The forest, sunward, glistens, green and high;
The ground each moment, as some blossom springs,
Puts forth, as does thy cheek, a lovelier dye,
And each new morning some new songster brings.
And, hark! the brooks their rocky prisons break,
And echo calls on echo to awake,
Like nymph to nymph. The air is rife with wings,
Rustling through wood or dripping over lake.
Herb, bud, and bird return—but not to me
With song or beauty, since they bring not thee.

NOBILITY.

Go, then, to heroes, sages if allied,
Go! trace the scroll, but not with eye of pride,
Where Truth depicts their glories as they shone,
And leaves a blank where should have been your own.

Mark the pure beam on yon dark wave impress'd;
So shines the star on that degenerate breast—
Each twinkling orb, that burns with borrow'd fires,—
So ye reflect the glory of your sires.

JAMES G. BROOKS.

[Born, 1801. Died, 1841.]

The late James Gordon Brooks was born at Red Hook, near the city of New York, on the third day of September, 1801. His father was an officer in the revolutionary army, and, after the achievement of our independence, a member of the national House of Representatives. Our author was educated at Union College, in Schenectady, and was graduated in 1819. In the following year he commenced studying the law with Mr. Justice Emott, of Poughkeepsie; but, though he devoted six or seven years to the acquisition of legal knowledge, he never sought admission to the bar. In 1823, he removed to New York, where he was for several years an editor of the Morning Courier, one of the most able and influential journals in this country.

Mr. Brooks began to write for the press in 1817. Two years afterward he adopted the signature of "Florio," by which his contributions to the periodicals were from that time known. In 1828, he was married. His wife, under the signature of "Norma," had been for several years a writer for the literary journals, and, in 1829, a collection of the poetry of both was published, entitled "The Rivals of Este, and other Poems, by James G. and Mary E. Brooks." The poem which gave its title to the volume was by Mrs. Brooks. The longest of the pieces by her husband was one entitled "Genius," which he had delivered before the Phi Beta Kappa Society of Yale College, in 1827. He wrote but little poetry after the appearance of this work.

In 1830 or 1831, he removed to Winchester, in Virginia, where, for four or five years, he edited a political and literary gazette. He returned to the state of New York, in 1838, and established himself in Albany, where he remained until the 20th day of February, 1841, when he died.

The poems of Mr. Brooks are spirited and smoothly versified, but diffuse and carelessly written. He was imaginative, and composed with remarkable ease and rapidity; but was too indifferent in regard to his reputation ever to rewrite or revise his productions.

GREECE—1832.

Land of the brave! where lie inurn'd
  The shrouded forms of mortal clay,
In whom the fire of valour burn'd,
  And blazed upon the battle's fray:
Land, where the gallant Spartan few
  Bled at Thermopylæ of yore,
When death his purple garment threw
  On Helle's consecrated shore!

Land of the Muse! within thy bowers
  Her soul-entrancing echoes rung,
While on their course the rapid hours
  Paused at the melody she sung—
Till every grove and every hill,
  And every stream that flow'd along,
From morn to night repeated still
  The winning harmony of song.

Land of dead heroes! living slaves!
  Shall glory gild thy clime no more?
Her banner float above thy waves
  Where proudly it hath swept before?
Hath not remembrance then a charm
  To break the fetters and the chain,
To bid thy children nerve the arm,
  And strike for freedom once again?

No! coward souls, the light which shone
  On Leuctra's war-empurpled day,
The light which beam'd on Marathon
  Hath lost its splendour, ceased to play;
And thou art but a shadow now,
  With helmet shatter'd—spear in rust—
Thy honour but a dream—and thou
  Despised—degraded in the dust!

Where sleeps the spirit, that of old
  Dash'd down to earth the Persian plume,
When the loud chant of triumph told
  How fatal was the despot's doom?—
The bold three hundred—where are they,
  Who died on battle's gory breast?
Tyrants have trampled on the clay
  Where death hath hush'd them into rest.

Yet, Ida, yet upon thy hill
  A glory shines of ages fled;
And fame her light is pouring still,
  Not on the living, but the dead!
But 'tis the dim, sepulchral light,
  Which sheds a faint and feeble ray,
As moonbeams on the brow of night,
  When tempests sweep upon their way

Greece! yet awake thee from thy trance,
  Behold, thy banner waves afar;
Behold, the glittering weapons glance
  Along the gleaming front of war!
A gallant chief, of high emprize,
  Is urging foremost in the field,
Who calls upon thee to arise
  In might—in majesty reveal'd.

In vain, in vain the hero calls—
  In vain he sounds the trumpet loud!
His banner totters—see! it falls
  In ruin, Freedom's battle-shroud:
Thy children have no soul to dare
  Such deeds as glorified their sires;
Their valour's but a meteor's glare,
  Which gleams a moment, and expires.

Lost land! where Genius made his reign,
  And rear'd his golden arch on high;
Where Science raised her sacred fane,
  Its summits peering to the sky;
Upon thy clime the midnight deep
  Of ignorance hath brooded long,
And in the tomb, forgotten, sleep
  The sons of science and of song.

Thy sun hath set—the evening storm
  Hath pass'd in giant fury by,
To blast the beauty of thy form,
  And spread its pall upon the sky!
Gone is thy glory's diadem,
  And freedom never more shall cease
To pour her mournful requiem
  O'er blighted, lost, degraded Greece!

TO THE DYING YEAR.

Thou desolate and dying year!
  Emblem of transitory man,
Whose wearisome and wild career,
  Like thine, is bounded to a span;
It seems but as a little day
  Since nature smiled upon thy birth,
And Spring came forth in fair array,
  To dance upon the joyous earth.

Sad alteration! now how lone,
  How verdureless is nature's breast,
Where ruin makes his empire known,
  In autumn's yellow vesture dress'd;
The sprightly bird, whose carol sweet
  Broke on the breath of early day,
The summer flowers she loved to greet;
  The bird, the flowers, O! where are they?

Thou desolate and dying year!
  Yet lovely in thy lifelessness
As beauty stretch'd upon the bier,
  In death's clay-cold and dark caress;
There's loveliness in thy decay,
  Which breathes, which lingers on thee still,
Like memory's mild and cheering ray
  Beaming upon the night of ill.

Yet, yet the radiance is not gone,
  Which shed a richness o'er the scene,
Which smiled upon the golden dawn,
  When skies were brilliant and serene;
O! still a melancholy smile
  Gleams upon Nature's aspect fair,
To charm the eye a little while,
  Ere ruin spreads his mantle there!

Thou desolate and dying year!
  Since time entwined thy vernal wreath,
How often love hath shed the tear,
  And knelt beside the bed of death;
How many hearts, that lightly sprung
  When joy was blooming but to die,
Their finest chords by death unstrung,
  Have yielded life's expiring sigh,

And, pillow'd low beneath the clay,
  Have ceased to melt, to breathe, to burn;
The proud, the gentle, and the gay,
  Gather'd unto the mouldering urn;
While freshly flow'd the frequent tear
  For love bereft, affection fled;
For all that were our blessings here,
  The loved, the lost, the sainted dead!

Thou desolate and dying year!
  The musing spirit finds in thee
Lessons, impressive and serene,
  Of deep and stern morality;
Thou teachest how the germ of youth,
  Which blooms in being's dawning day,
Planted by nature, rear'd by truth,
  Withers, like thee, in dark decay.

Promise of youth! fair as the form
  Of Heaven's benign and golden bow,
Thy smiling arch begirds the storm,
  And sheds a light on every wo;
Hope wakes for thee, and to her tongue
  A tone of melody is given,
As if her magic voice were strung
  With the empyreal fire of heaven.

And love which never can expire,
  Whose origin is from on high,
Throws o'er thy morn a ray of fire,
  From the pure fountains of the sky;
That ray which glows and brightens still
  Unchanged, eternal and divine;
Where seraphs own its holy thrill,
  And bow before its gleaming shrine.

Thou desolate and dying year!
  Prophetic of our final fall;
Thy buds are gone, thy leaves are sear,
  Thy beauties shrouded in the pall;
And all the garniture that shed
  A brilliancy upon thy prime,
Hath like a morning vision fled
  Unto the expanded grave of time.

Time! Time! in thy triumphal flight,
  How all life's phantoms fleet away;
Thy smile of hope, and young delight,
  Fame's meteor-beam, and Fancy's ray
They fade; and on the heaving tide,
  Rolling its stormy waves afar,
Are borne the wreck of human pride,
  The broken wreck of Fortune's war.

There, in disorder, dark and wild,
  Are seen the fabrics once so high;
Which mortal vanity had piled
  As emblems of eternity!

And deem'd the stately piles, whose forms
  Frown'd in their majesty sublime,
Would stand unshaken by the storms
  That gather'd round the brow of Time.

Thou desolate and dying year!
  Earth's brightest pleasures fade like thine;
Like evening shadows disappear,
  And leave the spirit to repine.
The stream of life, that used to pour
  Its fresh and sparkling waters on,
While Fate stood watching on the shore,
  And number'd all the moments gone—

Where hath the morning splendour flown,
  Which danced upon the crystal stream.
Where are the joys to childhood known,
  When life was an enchanted dream?
Enveloped in the starless night
  Which destiny hath overspread;
Enroll'd upon that trackless flight
  Where the death-wing of time hath sped!

O! thus hath life its even-tide
  Of sorrow, loneliness, and grief;
And thus, divested of its pride,
  It withers like the yellow leaf:
O! such is life's autumnal bower,
  When plunder'd of its summer bloom;
And such is life's autumnal hour,
  Which heralds man unto the tomb!

TO THE AUTUMN LEAF.

Thou faded leaf! it seems to be
    But as of yesterday,
When thou didst flourish on the tree
    In all the pride of May:
Then t'was the merry hour of spring,
Of nature's fairest blossoming,
    On field, on flower, and spray;
It promised fair; how changed the scene
To what is now, from what hath been!

So fares it with life's early spring;
    Hope gilds each coming day.
And sweetly doth the syren sing
    Her fond, delusive lay:
Then the young, fervent heart beats high,
While passion kindles in the eye,
    With bright, unceasing play;
Fair are thy tints, thou genial hour,
Yet transient as the autumn flower.

Thou faded leaf! how like to thee
    Is beauty in her morning pride,
When life is but a summer sea,
    And hope illumes its placid tide:
Alas! for beauty's autumn hour,
Alas! for beauty's blighted flower,
    When hope and bliss have died!
Her pallid brow, her cheek of grief,
Have thy sad hue, thou faded leaf!

Autumnal leaf! thus honour's plume,
    And valour's laurel wreath must fade;
Must lose the freshness, and the bloom
    On which the beam of glory play'd;
The banner waving o'er the crowd,
Far streaming like a silver cloud,
    Must sink within the shade,
Where dark oblivion's waters flow
O'er human weal and human wo.

Autumnal leaf! there is a stern
    And warning tone in thy decay
Like thee must man to death return
    With his frail tenement of clay
Thy warning is of death and doom,
Of genius blighted in its bloom,
    Of joy's beclouded ray;
Life, rapture, hope, ye are as brief
And fleeting as the autumn leaf!

THE LAST SONG.

Strike the wild harp yet once again!
  Again its lonely numbers pour;
Then let the melancholy strain
  Be hush'd in death for evermore.
For evermore, for evermore,
  Creative fancy, be thou still;
And let oblivious Lethe pour
  Upon my lyre its waters chill.

Strike the wild harp yet once again!
  Then be its fitful chords unstrung,
Silent as is the grave's domain,
  And mute as the death-moulder'd tongue.
Let not a thought of memory dwell
  One moment on its former song;
Forgotten, too, be this farewell,
  Which plays its pensive strings along!

Strike the wild harp yet once again!
  The saddest and the latest lay;
Then break at once its strings in twain,
  And they shall sound no more for aye:
And hang it on the cypress tree:
  The hours of youth and song have pass'd,
Have gone, with all their witchery;
  Lost lyre! these numbers are thy last.

JOY AND SORROW.

Joy kneels, at morning's rosy prime,
  In worship to the rising sun;
But Sorrow loves the calmer time,
  When the day-god his course hath run:
When Night is on her shadowy car,
  Pale sorrow wakes while Joy doth sleep;
And, guided by the evening star,
  She wanders forth to muse and weep.

Joy loves to cull the summer-flower,
  And wreathe it round his happy brow;
But when the dark autumnal hour
  Hath laid the leaf and blossoms low;
When the frail bud hath lost its worth,
  And Joy hath dash'd it from his crest,
Then Sorrow takes it from the earth,
  To wit.ar on her wither'd breast.

GEORGE P. MORRIS.

[Born 1801. Died 1864.]

This popular song-writer is a native of Philadelphia. In common with many prominent authors of the present time, he commenced his literary career by contributions to the journals. When about fifteen years of age he wrote verses for the "New York Gazette," and he subsequently filled occasionally "the poet's corner" in the "American," at that time under the direction of Mr. Johnson Verplanck. In 1823, with the late Mr. Woodworth, he established the "New York Mirror," a weekly miscellany which for nearly nineteen years was conducted with much taste and ability. In 1827 his play, in five acts, entitled "Brier Cliff, a tale of the American Revolution," was brought out at the Chatham Theatre by Mr. Wallack, and acted forty nights successively. I have been informed that its popularity was so great that it was played at four theatres in New York, to full houses, on the same evening, and that it yielded the author a profit of three thousand five hundred dollars, a larger sum, probably, than was ever paid for any other dramatic composition in the United States.

In 1836 General Morris published a volume of amusing prose writings under the title of "The Little Frenchman and his Water Lots;" in 1838 "The Deserted Bride and other Poems," of which an enlarged edition, illustrated by Wier and Chapman, appeared in 1843; and in 1852 a complete collection of his "Poetical Works." The composition which is understood to rank highest in his own estimation is the poetry of "The Maid of Saxony," an opera with music by Mr. Charles Horn, produced at the Park Theatre in 1842. In 1843, in conjunction with Mr. Willis, he reëstablished "The Mirror," and he is now associated with that popular author in conducting "The Home Journal."

If there is any literary work which calls for a special gift of nature, perhaps it is the song. In terms of a sounder theory, I may say, that its successful accomplishment, beyond almost any other composition, demands an intelligent insight into the principles upon which its effect depends, and a capacity, if not to combine with imposing strength, yet to select with the nicest judgment. Other productions often gratify long and highly, in spite of considerable defects, while the song, to succeed at all, must be nearly perfect. It implies a taste delicately skilled in the fine influences of language. It has often shunned the diligence of men who have done greater things. Starting from some common perception, by almost a crystalline process of accretion, it should grow up into a poem. Its first note should find the hearer in sympathy with it, and its last should leave him moved and wondering. Throughout, it must have an affinity to some one fixed idea. Its propriety is, not so much to give expression to a feeling existing in the bosom of the author, as to reproduce that feeling in the heart of the listener. The tone of the composition ought therefore to be, as much as is possible, *below* the force of the feeling which it would inspire. It should be simple, entire, and glowing.

The distinction and difficulty of the song are illustrated by the genius of Jonson, Marlowe, and Dryden; by the fame of Moore, and the failure of Byron. Several of the songs of Morris, whether judged of by their success, or by the application of any rules of criticism, are nearly faultless. They are in a very chaste style of art. They have the simplicity which is the characteristic of the classic models, and the purity which was once deemed an indispensable quality in the lyric poet. They are marked by neatness of language, free from every thing affected or finical; a natural elegance of sentiment, and a correct moral purpose. His best effusions have few marks of imitation; they are like each other, but no English song can be named from which, in character and tone, they are not different. "The Chieftain's Daughter" is an example of the narrative song, in which the whole story is told, in a few lines, without omission and without redundancy; "When other friends are round thee," is a beautiful expression of affection; "Land, Ho!" is an exceedingly spirited and joyous nautical piece; and in "Near the Lake," the very delicate effect which the author has contemplated is attained with remarkable precision. In sentiment, as in sound, there are certain natural melodies, which seem to be discovered rather than contrived, and which, as they are evolved from time to time by the felicity or skill of successive artists, are sure to be received with unbounded popularity. The higher and more elaborate productions of genius are best appreciated by the thoughtful analysis of a single critic; but the appropriate test of the merit of these simple, apparently almost spontaneous effusions, is the response which they meet with from the common heart of man. The melodies of Mozart and Auber, doubtless, enchanted their ears who first heard them played by the composers, but we know them to be founded in the enduring truth of art, only because they have made themselves a home in the streets of every city of Europe and America, and after long experience have been found to be among the natural formulas by which gaiety and melancholy express themselves in every rank and in every land. The song of "Woodman, spare that Tree," has touched one of those cords of pervading nature which fraternize multitudes of different nations.

Mr. N. P. Willis, who has been for twenty years associated with General Morris in various literary labors, in one of his letters gives characteristically the following estimate of his literary and personal qualities:

"Morris is the best-known poet of the country, by acclamation, not by criticism. He is just what poets would be if they sang, like birds, without criticism; and it is a peculiarity of his fame, that it seems as regardless of criticism as a bird in the air. Nothing can stop a song of his. It is very easy to say that they are easy to do. They have a momentum, somehow, that it is difficult for others to give, and that speeds them to the far goal of popularity—the best proof consisting in the fact that he can, at any moment, get fifty dollars for a song unread, when the whole remainder of the American Parnassus could not sell one to the same buyer for a shilling. It may, or may not, be one secret of his popularity, but it is the truth—that Morris's heart is at the level of most other people's, and his poetry flows out by that door. He stands breast-high in the common stream of sympathy, and the fine oil of his poetic feeling goes from him upon an element it is its nature to float upon, and which carries it safe to other bosoms, with little need of deep-diving or high-flying. His sentiments are simple, honest, truthful, and familiar; his language is pure and eminently musical, and he is prodigally full of the poetry of everyday feeling. These are days when poets try experiments; and while others succeed by taking the world's breath away with flights and plunges, Morris uses his feet to walk quietly with nature. Ninety-nine people in a hundred, taken as they come in the census, would find more to admire in Morris's songs, than in the writings of any other American poet; and that is a parish in the poetical episcopate well worthy a wise man's nurture and prizing.

"As to the man—Morris, my friend—I can hardly venture to 'burn incense on his moustache,' as the French say—write his praises under his very nose—but as far off as Philadelphia, you may pay the proper tribute to his loyal nature and manly excellencies. His personal qualities have made him universally popular, but this overflow upon the world does not impoverish him for his friends. I have outlined a true poet, and a fine fellow—fill up the picture to your liking."

I NEVER HAVE BEEN FALSE TO THEE.

I never have been false to thee!
The heart I gave thee still is thine;
Though thou hast been untrue to me,
And I no more may call thee mine!
I've loved as woman ever loves,
With constant soul in good or ill;
Thou 'st proved, as man too often proves,
A rover—but I love thee still!

Yet think not that my spirit stoops
To bind thee captive in my train!
Love's not a flower, at sunset droops,
But smiles when comes her god again!
Thy words, which fall unheeded now,
Could once my heart-strings madly thrill!
Love's golden chain and burning vow
Are broken—but I love thee still.

Once what a heaven of bliss was ours,
When love dispelled the clouds of care,
And time went by with birds and flowers,
While song and incense filled the air!
The past is mine—the present thine—
Should thoughts of me thy future fill,
Think what a destiny is mine,
To lose—but love thee, false one, still.

WOMAN.

Ah, woman! in this world of ours,
What boon can be compared to thee?
How slow would drag life's weary hours,
Though man's proud brow were bound with flowers,
And his the wealth of land and sea,
If destined to exist alone,
And ne'er call woman's heart his own

My mother! at that holy name
Within my bosom there's a gush
Of feeling, which no time can tame—
A feeling, which, for years of fame,
I would not, could not, crush;
And sisters! ye are dear as life;
But when I look upon my wife,
My heart blood gives a sudden rush,
And all my fond affections blend
In mother, sister, wife, and friend.

Yes, woman's love is free from guile,
And pure as bright Aurora's ray;
The heart will melt before her smile,
And base-born passions fade away;
Were I the monarch of the earth,
Or master of the swelling sea,
I would not estimate their worth,
Dear woman! half the price of thee!

WE WERE BOYS TOGETHER.

We were boys together,
And never can forget
The school-house near the heather,
In childhood where we met;
The humble home to memory dear,
Its sorrows and its joys;
Where woke the transient smile or tear,
When you and I were boys.

We were youths together,
And castles built in air,
Your heart was like a feather,
And mine weighed down with care;
To you came wealth with manhood's prime,
To me it brought alloys—
Foreshadowed in the primrose time,
When you and I were boys.

We're old men together—
The friends we loved of yore,
With leaves of autumn weather,
Are gone for evermore.
How blest to age the impulse given,
The hope time ne'er destroys—
Which led our thoughts from earth to heaven,
When you and I were boys.

THE WEST.

Ho! brothers—come hither and list to my story—
Merry and brief will the narrative be:
Here, like a monarch, I reign in my glory—
Master am I, boys, of all that I see.
Where once frown'd a forest a garden is smiling—
The meadow and moorland are marshes no more;
And there curls the smoke of my cottage, beguiling
The children who cluster like grapes at the door,
Then enter, boys; cheerly, boys, enter and rest;
The land of the heart is the land of the west.
Oho, boys!—oho, boys!—oho!

Talk not of the town, boys,—give me the broad prairie,
Where man like the wind roams impulsive and free;
Behold how its beautiful colours all vary,
Like those of the clouds, or the deep-rolling sea.
A life in the woods, boys, is even as changing;
With proud independence we season our cheer,
And those who the world are for happiness ranging,
Won't find it at all, if they don't find it here.
Then enter, boys; cheerly, boys, enter and rest;
I'll show you the life, boys, we live in the west.
Oho, boys!—oho, boys!—oho!

Here, brothers, secure from all turmoil and danger,
We reap what we sow, for the soil is our own;
We spread hospitality's board for the stranger,
And care not a fig for the king on his throne;
We never know want, for we live by our labour,
And in it contentment and happiness find;
We do what we can for a friend or a neighbour,
And die, boys, in peace and good-will to mankind.
Then enter, boys; cheerly, boys, enter and rest;
You know how we live, boys, and die in the west!
Oho, boys!—oho, boys!—oho!

"LAND-HO!"

Up, up, with the signal! The land is in sight!
We'll be happy, if never again, boys, to-night!
The cold, cheerless ocean in safety we've pass'd,
And the warm genial earth glads our vision at last.
In the land of the stranger true hearts we shall find,
To soothe us in absence of those left behind.
Land!—land-ho! All hearts glow with joy at the sight!
We'll be happy, if never again, boys, to-night!

The signal is waving! Till morn we'll remain,
Then part in the hope to meet one day again
Round the hearth-stone of home in the land of our birth,
The holiest spot on the face of the earth!
Dear country! our thoughts are as constant to thee,
As the steel to the star, or the stream to the sea.
Ho!—land-ho! We near it—we bound at the sight!
Then be happy, if never again, boys, to-night!

The signal is answer'd! The foam-sparkles rise
Like tears from the fountain of joy to the eyes!
May rain-drops that fall from the storm-clouds of care,
Melt away in the sun-beaming smiles of the fair!
One health, as chime gayly the nautical bells,
To woman—God bless her!—wherever she dwells!
THE PILOT'S ON BOARD!—and, thank Heaven, all's right!
So be happy, if never again, boys, to-night!

THE CHIEFTAIN'S DAUGHTER.

UPON the barren sand
A single captive stood,
Around him came, with bow and brand,
The red men of the wood.
Like him of old, his doom he hears,
Rock-bound on ocean's rim:—
The chieftain's daughter knelt in tears,
And breathed a prayer for him.

Above his head in air,
The savage war-club swung,
The frantic girl, in wild despair,
Her arms about him flung.
Then shook the warriors of the shade,
Like leaves on aspen limb,
Subdued by that heroic maid
Who breathed a prayer for him.

"Unbind him?" gasp'd the chief,
"Obey your king's decree!"
He kiss'd away her tears of grief,
And set the captive free.
'Tis ever thus, when in life's storm,
Hope's star to man grows dim,
An angel kneels in woman's form,
And breathes a prayer for him.

NEAR THE LAKE.

NEAR the lake where droop'd the willow,
Long time ago!
Where the rock threw back the billow,
Brighter than snow;
Dwelt a maid, beloved and cherish'd,
By high and low;
But with autumn's leaf she perished,
Long time ago!

Rock and tree and flowing water,
Long time ago!
Bee and bird and blossom taught her
Love's spell to know!
While to my fond words she listened,
Murmuring low,
Tenderly her dove-eyes glistened
Long time ago!

Mingled were our hearts for ever!
Long time ago!
Can I now forget her?—Never!
No, lost one, no!
To her grave these tears are given,
Ever to flow;
She's the star I miss'd from heaven,
Long time ago!

"WHEN OTHER FRIENDS ARE ROUND THEE."

When other friends are round thee,
And other hearts are thine,
When other bays have crown'd thee,
More fresh and green than mine,
Then think how sad and lonely
This doating heart will be,
Which, while it throbs, throbs only,
Beloved one, for thee!

Yet do not think I doubt thee,
I know thy truth remains;
I would not live without thee,
For all the world contains.
Thou art the star that guides me
Along life's changing sea;
And whate'er fate betides me,
This heart still turns to thee.

WOODMAN, SPARE THAT TREE.*

Woodman, spare that tree!
Touch not a single bough!
In youth it shelter'd me,
And I'll protect it now.
'Twas my forefather's hand
That placed it near his cot;
There, woodman, let it stand,
Thy axe shall harm it not!

That old familiar tree,
Whose glory and renown
Are spread o'er land and sea,
And wouldst thou hew it down?
Woodman, forbear thy stroke!
Cut not its earth-bound ties;
Oh spare that aged oak,
Now towering to the skies!

When but an idle boy
I sought its grateful shade;
In all their gushing joy
Here too my sisters play'd.
My mother kiss'd me here;
My father press'd my hand—
Forgive this foolish tear,
But let that old oak stand!

My heart-strings round thee cling,
Close as thy bark, old friend!
Here shall the wild-bird sing,
And still thy branches bend.
Old tree! the storm still brave!
And, woodman, leave the spot;
While I've a hand to save,
Thy axe shall harm it not.

*After I had sung the noble ballad of *Woodman, spare that tree*, at Boulogne, says Mr. Henry Russell, the vocalist, an old gentleman, among the audience, who was greatly moved by the simple and touching beauty of the words, rose and said, "I beg your pardon, Mr. Russell, but was the tree really spared?" "It was," said I. "I am very glad to hear it," said he, as he took his seat amidst the unanimous applause of the whole assembly. I never saw such excitement in a concert-room.

"WHERE HUDSON'S WAVE."

Where Hudson's wave o'er silvery sands
Winds through the hills afar,
Old Cronest like a monarch stands,
Crown'd with a single star!
And there, amid the billowy swells
Of rock-ribb'd, cloud-capp'd earth,
My fair and gentle Ida dwells,
A nymph of mountain birth.

The snow-flake that the cliff receives,
The diamonds of the showers,
Spring's tender blossoms, buds, and leaves,
The sisterhood of flowers,
Morn's early beam, eve's balmy breeze,
Her purity define;
But Ida's dearer far than these
To this fond breast of mine

My heart is on the hills. The shades
Of night are on my brow:
Ye pleasant haunts and quiet glades,
My soul is with you now!
I bless the star-crown'd highlands where
My Ida's footsteps roam—
Oh! for a falcon's wing to bear
Me onward to my home.

THE PASTOR'S DAUGHTER.

An ivy-mantled cottage smiled,
Deep-wooded near a streamlet's side,
Where dwelt the village pastor's child,
In all her maiden bloom and pride.
Proud suitors paid their court and duty
To this romantic sylvan beauty:
Yet none of all the swains who sought her,
Was worthy of the pastor's daughter.

The town-gallants cross'd hill and plain,
To seek the groves of her retreat,
And many follow'd in her train,
To lay their riches at her feet.
But still, for all their arts so wary,
From home they could not lure the fairy.
A maid without a heart, they thought her,
And so they left the pastor's daughter.

One balmy eve in dewy spring
A bard became her father's guest;
He struck his harp, and every string
To love vibrated in her breast.
With that true faith which cannot falter,
Her hand was given at the altar,
And faithful was the heart he brought her
To wedlock and the pastor's daughter.

How seldom learn the worldly gay,
With all their sophistry and art,
The sweet and gentle primrose-way
To woman's fond, devoted heart:
They seek, but never find the treasure,
Although reveal'd in jet and azure.
To them, like truth in wells of water,
A fable is the pastor's daughter.

WILLIAM LEGGETT.

[Born, 1802. Died, 1840.]

This distinguished political and miscellaneous writer was born in the city of New York, in the summer of 1802, and was educated at the Georgetown College, in the District of Columbia. In 1822 he entered the navy of the United States as a midshipman; but in consequence of the arbitrary conduct of his commander, Captain John Orde Creighton, he retired from the service in 1826, after which time he devoted himself mainly to literary pursuits. His first publication was entitled "Leisure Hours at Sea," and was composed of various short poems written while he was in the navy. In 1828 he established, in New York, "The Critic," a weekly literary gazette, which he conducted with much ability for seven or eight months, at the end of which time it was united with the "Mirror," to which he became a regular contributor. In "The Critic" and "The Mirror," he first published "The Rifle," "The Main Truck, or the Leap for Life," "White Hands, or Not Quite in Character," and other stories, afterward embraced in the volumes entitled "Tales by a Country Schoolmaster," and "Sketches of the Sea." These tales and sketches are probably the most spirited and ingenious productions of their kind ever written in this country.

In 1829 Mr. Leggett became associated with Mr. Bryant, in the editorship of the "Evening Post," and on the departure of that gentleman for Europe, in 1834, the entire direction of that able journal was devolved to him. A severe illness, which commenced near the close of the succeeding year, induced him to relinquish his connexion with the "Post;" and on his recovery, in 1836, he commenced "The Plaindealer," a weekly periodical devoted to politics and literature, for which he obtained great reputation by his independent and fearless assertion of doctrines, and the vigorous eloquence and powerful reasoning by which he maintained them. It was discontinued, in consequence of the failure of his publisher, before the close of the year; and his health, after that period, prevented his connexion with any other journal. In 1828 he had been married to Miss Elmira Waring, daughter of Mr. Jona. Waring, of New Rochelle; and to that pleasant village he now retired, with his family. He occasionally visited his friends in the city, and a large portion of the democratic party there proposed to nominate him for a seat in Congress; but as he had acted independently of a majority of the party in regard to certain important political questions, his formal nomination was prevented. In April, 1840, he was appointed by Mr. Van Buren, then President of the United States, a diplomatic agent* from our government to the Republic of Guatemala. He was preparing to depart for that country, when he suddenly expired, on the twenty-ninth day of following month, in the thirty-eighth year of his age.

A few months after his death, a collection of his political writings, in two large duodecimo volumes, was published, under the direction of his friend, Mr. Theodore Sedgwick. Besides the works already mentioned, he wrote much in various periodicals, and was one of the authors of "The Tales of Glauber Spa," published in 1832. In the maturity of his powers, his time and energies were devoted to political writing. His poems are the poorest of his productions, and were written while he was in the naval service, or during his editorship of "The Critic." In addition to his Melodies—which are generally ingenious and well versified—he wrote one or two prize addresses for the theatres, and some other pieces, which have considerable merit.

His death was deeply and generally deplored, especially by the members of the democratic party, who regarded him as one of the ablest champions of their principles. Mr. Bryant, with whom he was for several years intimately associated, published in the "Democratic Review" the following tribute to his character:—

"The earth may ring from shore to shore,
With echoes of a glorious name;
But he whose loss our hearts deplore
Has left behind him more than fame.

"For when the death-frost came to lie
Upon that warm and mighty heart,
And quench that bold and friendly eye,
His spirit did not all depart.

"The words of fire that from his pen
Were flung upon the lucid page,
Still move, still shake the hearts of men,
Amid a cold and coward age.

"His love of Truth, too warm—too strong
For Hope or Fear to chain or chill,
His hate of Tyranny and Wrong,
Burn in the breasts he kindled still."

Mr. Sedgwick, in the preface to his political writings, remarks that "every year was softening his prejudices, and calming his passions; enlarging his charities, and widening the bounds of his liberality. Had a more genial clime invigorated his constitution, and enabled him to return to his labours, a brilliant and honourable future might have been predicted of him. It is not the suggestion of a too fond affection, but the voice of a calm judgment, which declares that, whatever public career he had pursued, he must have raised to his memory an imperishable monument, and that as no name is now dearer to his friends, so few could have been more honourably associated with the history of his country, than that of William Leggett."

* Soon after the death of Mr. Leggett, Mr. John L. Stephens, whose "Travels in Central America" have been since published, was appointed his successor as diplomatic agent to that country.

A SACRED MELODY.

If yon bright stars which gem the night
  Be each a blissful dwelling sphere,
Where kindred spirits reunite,
  Whom death has torn asunder here;
How sweet it were at once to die,
  And leave this blighted orb afar—
Mixed soul with soul, to cleave the sky,
  And soar away from star to star.

But, O! how dark, how drear, how lone
  Would seem the brightest world of bliss,
If, wandering through each radiant one,
  We fail'd to find the loved of this!
If there no more the ties should twine,
  Which death's cold hand alone can sever,
Ah! then these stars in mockery shine,
  More hateful, as they shine forever.

It cannot be! each hope and fear
  That lights the eye or clouds the brow,
Proclaims there is a happier sphere
  Than this bleak world that holds us now!
There is a voice which sorrow hears,
  When heaviest weighs life's galling chain;
'Tis heaven that whispers, "Dry thy tears:
  The pure in heart shall meet again!"

LOVE AND FRIENDSHIP.

The birds, when winter shades the sky,
  Fly o'er the seas away,
Where laughing isles in sunshine lie,
  And summer breezes play;

And thus the friends that flutter near
  While fortune's sun is warm,
Are startled if a cloud appear,
  And fly before the storm.

But when from winter's howling plains
  Each other warbler's past,
The little snow-bird still remains,
  And chirrups midst the blast.

Love, like that bird, when friendship's throng
  With fortune's sun depart,
Still lingers with its cheerful song,
  And nestles on the heart.

SONG.

I trust the frown thy features wear
  Ere long into a smile will turn;
I would not that a face so fair
  As thine, beloved, should look so stern.
The chain of ice that winter twines,
  Holds not for aye the sparkling rill,
It melts away when summer shines,
  And leave the waters sparkling still.
Thus let thy cheek resume the smile
  That shed such sunny light before;
And though I left thee for a while,
  I'll swear to leave thee, love, no more.

As he who, doomed o'er waves to roam,
  Or wander on a foreign strand,
Will sigh whene'er he thinks of home,
  And better love his native land;
So I, though lured a time away,
  Like bees by varied sweets, to rove,
Return, like bees, by close of day,
  And leave them all for thee, my love.
Then let thy cheek resume the smile
  That shed such sunny light before,
And though I left thee for a while,
  I swear to leave thee, love, no more.

LIFE'S GUIDING STAR.

The youth whose bark is guided o'er
  A summer stream by zephyr's breath,
With idle gaze delights to pore
  On imaged skies that glow beneath.
But should a fleeting storm arise
  To shade a while the watery way,
Quick lifts to heaven his anxious eyes,
  And speeds to reach some sheltering bay,

'Tis thus, down time's eventful tide,
  While prosperous breezes gently blow,
In life's frail bark we gayly glide,
  Our hopes, our thoughts all fix'd below.
But let one cloud the prospect dim,
  The wind its quiet stillness mar,
At once we raise our prayer to Him
  Whose light is life's best guiding star.

TO ELMIRA.

WRITTEN WITH FRENCH CHALK* ON A PANE OF GLASS IN THE HOUSE OF A FRIEND.

On this frail glass, to others' view,
  No written words appear;
They see the prospect smiling through,
  Nor deem what secret's here.
But shouldst thou on the tablet bright
  A single breath bestow,
At once the record starts to sight
  Which only thou must know.

Thus, like this glass, to strangers' gaze
  My heart seemed unimpress'd;
In vain did beauty round me blaze,
  It could not warm my breast.
But as one breath of thine can make
  These letters plain to see,
So in my heart did love awake
  When breathed upon by thee.

* The substance usually called French chalk has this singular property, that what is written on glass, though easily rubbed out again, so that no trace remains visible, by being breathed on becomes immediately distinctly legible.

EDWARD C. PINKNEY.

[Born 1802. Died 1828.]

EDWARD COATE PINKNEY was born in London, in October, 1802, while his father, the Honourable WILLIAM PINKNEY, was the American Minister at the court of St. James'. Soon after the return of his family to Baltimore, in 1811, he entered St. Mary's College, in that city, and remained there until he was fourteen years old, when he was appointed a midshipman in the navy. He continued in the service nine years, and in that period visited the Mediterranean and several other foreign stations, and acquired much general knowledge and acquaintance with mankind.

The death of his father, and other circumstances, induced him, in 1824, to resign his place in the navy; and in the same year he was married, and admitted to the Maryland bar. His career as a lawyer was brief and unfortunate. He opened an office in Baltimore, and applied himself earnestly to his profession; but though his legal acquirements and forensic abilities were respectable, his rooms were seldom visited by a client; and after two years had passed, disheartened by neglect, and with a prospect of poverty before him, he suddenly determined to enter the naval service of Mexico, in which a number of our officers had already won distinction and fortune. When, however, he presented himself before Commodore PORTER, then commanding the sea-forces of that country, the situation he solicited was refused,* and he was compelled reluctantly to return to the United States.

He reappeared in Baltimore, poor and dejected. He turned his attention again to the law, but in his vigorous days he had been unable to support himself by his profession; and now, when he was suffering from disease and a settled melancholy, it was not reasonable to anticipate success. The erroneous idea that a man of a poetical mind cannot transact business requiring patience and habits of careful investigation, was undoubtedly one of the principal causes of his failure as a lawyer; for that he was respected, and that his fellow-citizens were willing to confer upon him honours, is evident from the fact that, in 1826, he was appointed one of the professors in the University of Maryland. This office, however, was one of honour only: it yielded no profit.

PINKNEY now became sensible that his constitution was broken, and that he could not long survive; but he had no wish to live. His feelings at this period are described in one of his poems:—

"A sense it was, that I could see
 The angel leave my side—
That thenceforth my prosperity
 Must be a falling tide;
A strange and ominous belief,
That in spring-time the yellow leaf
 Had fallen on my hours;
And that all hope must be most vain,
Of finding on my path again
 Its former vanish'd flowers."

Near the close of the year 1827, a political gazette, entitled "The Marylander," was established in Baltimore, and, in compliance with the general wish of the proprietors, Mr. PINKNEY undertook to conduct it. He displayed much sagacity and candour, and in a few weeks won a high reputation in his new vocation; but his increasing illness compelled him to leave it, and he died on the eleventh of April, 1828, at the early age of twenty-five years and six months. He was a man of genius, and had all the qualities of mind and heart that win regard and usually lead to greatness, except HOPE and ENERGY.

A small volume containing "Rodolph," and other poems, was published by PINKNEY in 1825. "Rodolph" is his longest work. It was first published, anonymously, soon after he left the navy, and was probably written while he was in the Mediterranean. It is in two cantos. The first begins,—

"The summer's heir on land and sea
 Had thrown his parting glance
And winter taken angrily
 His waste inheritance.
The winds in stormy revelry
Sported beneath a frowning sky;
The chafing waves, with hollow roar,
Tumbled upon the shaken shore,
And sent their spray in upward showers
To Rodolph's proud ancestral towers,
Whose bastion, from its mural crown,
A regal look cast sternly down."

There is no novelty in the story, and not much can be said for its morality. The hero, in the season described in the above lines, arrives at his own domain, after many years of wandering in foreign lands, during which he had "grown old in heart, and infirm of frame." In his youth he had loved—the wife of another—and his passion had been returned. "At an untimely tide," he had met the husband, and, in encounter, slain him. The wife goes into a convent, and her paramour seeks refuge from remorse in distant countries. In the beginning of the second canto, he is once more in his own castle; but, feeling some dark presentiment, he wanders to a cemetery, where, in the morning, he is found by his vassals, "senseless

* It has been said that Commodore PORTER refused to give PINKNEY a commission, because he was known to be a warm adherent of an administration to which he was himself opposed; but it is more reasonable to believe, as was alleged at the time, that the navy of Mexico was full, and that the citizens of that republic had begun to regard with jealousy the too frequent admission of foreigners into the service.

beside his lady's urn." In the delirium which follows, he raves of many crimes, but most

> . . . "Of one too dearly loved,
> And one untimely slain,
> Of an affection hardly proved
> By murder done in vain."

He dies in madness, and the story ends abruptly and coldly. It has more faults than PINKNEY's other works; in many passages it is obscure; its beauty is marred by the use of obsolete words; and the author seems to delight in drawing his comparisons from the least known portions of ancient literature.

Some of his lighter pieces are very beautiful. "A Health," "The Picture-Song," and "A Serenade," have not often been equalled; and "Italy,"—an imitation of GOETHE's *Kennst du das Land*—has some noble lines. Where is there a finer passage than this:

> "The winds are awed, nor dare to breathe aloud;
> The air seems never to have borne a cloud,
> Save where volcanoes send to heaven their curl'd
> And solemn smokes, like altars of the world!"

PINKNEY's is the first instance in this country in which we have to lament the prostitution of true poetical genius to unworthy purposes. Pervading much that he wrote there is a selfish melancholy and sullen pride; dissatisfaction with the present, and doubts in regard to the future life. The great distinguishing characteristic of American poetry is its pure and high morality. May i ever be so!

ITALY.

KNOW'ST thou the land which lovers ought to choose!
Like blessings there descend the sparkling dews;
In gleaming streams the crystal rivers run,
The purple vintage clusters in the sun;
Odours of flowers haunt the balmy breeze,
Rich fruits hang high upon the verdant trees;
And vivid blossoms gem the shady groves,
Where bright-plumed birds discourse their careless loves.
Beloved!—speed we from this sullen strand,
Until thy light feet press that green shore's yellow sand.

Look seaward thence, and naught shall meet thine eye
But fairy isles, like paintings on the sky;
And, flying fast and free before the gale,
The gaudy vessel with its glancing sail;
And waters glittering in the glare of noon,
Or touch'd with silver by the stars and moon,
Or fleck'd with broken lines of crimson light,
When the far fisher's fire affronts the night.
Lovely as loved! toward that smiling shore
Bear we our household gods, to fix forever more.

It looks a dimple on the face of earth,
The seal of beauty, and the shrine of mirth;
Nature is delicate and graceful there,
The place's genius, feminine and fair;
The winds are awed, nor dare to breathe aloud;
The air seems never to have borne a cloud,
Save where volcanoes send to heaven their curl'd
And solemn smokes, like altars of the world.
Thrice beautiful!—to that delightful spot
Carry our married hearts, and be all pain forgot.

There Art, too, shows, when Nature's beauty palls,
Her sculptured marbles, and her pictured walls;
And there are forms in which they both conspire
To whisper themes that know not how to tire;
The speaking ruins in that gentle clime
Have but been hallow'd by the hand of Time,
And each can mutely prompt some thought of flame:
The meanest stone is not without a name.
Then come, beloved!—hasten o'er the sea,
To build our happy hearth in blooming Italy.

THE INDIAN'S BRIDE.

I.

Why is that graceful female here
With yon red hunter of the deer?
Of gentle mien and shape, she seems
For civil halls design'd,
Yet with the stately savage walks,
As she were of his kind.
Look on her leafy diadem,
Enrich'd with many a floral gem.
Those simple ornaments about
Her candid brow, disclose
The loitering spring's last violet,
And summer's earliest rose;
But not a flower lies breathing there
Sweet as herself, or half so fair.
Exchanging lustre with the sun,
A part of day she strays—
A glancing, living, human smile
On Nature's face she plays.
Can none instruct me what are these
Companions of the lofty trees?

II.

Intent to blend her with his lot,
Fate form'd her all that he was not;
And, as by mere unlikeness, thoughts
Associate we see,
Their hearts, from very difference, caught
A perfect sympathy.
The household goddess here to be
Of that one dusky votary,
She left her pallid countrymen,
An earthling most divine,
And sought in this sequester'd wood
A solitary shrine.
Behold them roaming hand in hand,
Like night and sleep, along the land;
Observe their movements:—he for her
Restrains his active stride,
While she assumes a bolder gait
To ramble at his side;
Thus, even as the steps they frame,
Their souls fast alter to the same.

The one forsakes ferocity,
And momently grows mild;
The other tempers more and more
The artful with the wild.
She humanizes him, and he
Educates him to liberty.

III.

O, say not they must soon be old,—
Their limbs prove faint, their breasts feel cold!
Yet envy I that sylvan pair
More than my words express,—
The singular beauty of their lot,
And seeming happiness.
They have not been reduced to share
The painful pleasures of despair;
Their sun declines not in the sky,
Nor are their wishes cast,
Like shadows of the afternoon,
Repining towards the past:
With nought to dread or to repent,
The present yields them full content.
In solitude there is no crime;
Their actions all are free,
And passion lends their way of life
The only dignity;
And how can they have any cares?—
Whose interest contends with theirs?

IV.

The world, for all they know of it,
Is theirs:—for them the stars are lit;
For them the earth beneath is green,
The heavens above are bright;
For them the moon doth wax and wane,
And decorate the night;
For them the branches of those trees
Wave music in the vernal breeze;
For them, upon that dancing spray,
The free bird sits and sings,
And glittering insects flit about
Upon delighted wings;
For them that brook, the brakes among,
Murmurs its small and drowsy song;
For them the many-colour'd clouds
Their shapes diversify,
And change at once, like smiles and frowns,
The expression of the sky.
For them, and by them, all is gay,
And fresh and beautiful as they:
The images their minds receive,
Their minds assimilate
To outward forms, imparting thus
The glory of their state.

V.

Could aught be painted otherwise
Than fair, seen through her star-bright eyes?
He, too, because she fills his sight,
Each object falsely sees;
The pleasure that he has in her
Makes all things seem to please.
And this is love;—and it is life
They lead,—that Indian and his wife.

SONG.

We break the glass, whose sacred wine,
To some beloved health we drain,
Lest future pledges, less divine,
Should e'er the hallow'd toy profane;
And thus I broke a heart that pour'd
Its tide of feelings out for thee,
In draughts, by after-times deplored,
Yet dear to memory.

But still the old, impassion'd ways
And habits of my mind remain,
And still unhappy light displays
Thine image chamber'd in my brain,
And still it looks as when the hours
Went by like flights of singing birds,
Or that soft chain of spoken flowers,
And airy gems—thy words.

A HEALTH.

I fill this cup to one made up
Of loveliness alone,
A woman, of her gentle sex
The seeming paragon;
To whom the better elements
And kindly stars have given
A form so fair, that, like the air,
'Tis less of earth than heaven.

Her every tone is music's own,
Like those of morning birds,
And something more than melody
Dwells ever in her words;
The coinage of her heart are they,
And from her lips each flows
As one may see the burden'd bee
Forth issue from the rose.

Affections are as thoughts to her,
The measures of her hours;
Her feelings have the fragrancy,
The freshness of young flowers;
And lovely passions, changing oft,
So fill her, she appears
The image of themselves by turns,—
The idol of past years!

Of her bright face one glance will trace
A picture on the brain,
And of her voice in echoing hearts
A sound must long remain;
But memory, such as mine of her,
So very much endears,
When death is nigh my latest sigh
Will not be life's, but hers.

I fill'd this cup to one made up
Of loveliness alone,
A woman, of her gentle sex
The seeming paragon—
Her health! and would on earth there stood
Some more of such a frame,
That life might be all poetry,
And weariness a name.

THE VOYAGER'S SONG.*

Sound trumpets, ho!—weigh anchor—loosen sail—
The seaward flying banners chide delay;
As if 't were heaven that breathes this kindly gale,
Our life-like bark beneath it speeds away.
Flit we, a gliding dream, with troublous motion,
Across the slumbers of uneasy ocean;
And furl our canvass by a happier land,
So fraught with emanations from the sun,
That potable gold streams through the sand
Where element should run.

Onward, my friends, to that bright, florid isle,
The jewel of a smoothe and silver sea,
With springs on which perennial summers smile
A power of causing immortality.
For Bimini;—in its enchanted ground,
The hallow'd fountains we would seek, are found;
Bathed in the waters of those mystic wells,
The frame starts up in renovated truth,
And, freed from Time's deforming spells,
Resumes its proper youth.

Hail, bitter birth!—once more my feelings all
A graven image to themselves shall make,
And, placed upon my heart for pedestal,
That glorious idol long will keep awake
Their natural religion, nor be cast
To earth by Age, the great Iconoclast.
As from Gadara's founts they once could come,
Charm-call'd, from these Love's genii shall arise,
And build their perdurable home,
Miranda, in thine eyes.

By Nature wisely gifted, not destroy'd
With golden presents, like the Roman maid,—
A sublunary paradise enjoy'd,
Shall teach thee bliss incapable of shade;—
An Eden ours, nor angry gods, nor men,
Nor star-clad Fates, can take from us again.
Superior to animal decay,
Sun of that perfect heaven, thou'lt calmly see
Stag, raven, phenix, drop away
With *human* transiency.

Thus rich in being,—beautiful,—adored,
Fear not exhausting pleasure's precious mine;
The wondrous waters we approach, when pour'd
On passion's lees, supply the wasted wine:
Then be thy bosom's tenant prodigal,
And confident of termless carnival.
Like idle yellow leaves afloat on time,
Let others lapse to death's pacific sea,—
We'll fade nor fall, but sport sublime
In green eternity.

* "A tradition prevailed among the natives of Puerto Rico, that in the Isle of Bimini, one of the Lucayos, there was a fountain of such wonderful virtue, as to renew the youth and recall the vigour of every person who bathed in its salutary waters. In hopes of finding this grand restorative, Ponce de Leon and his followers, ranged through the islands, searching with fruitless solicitude for the fountain, which was the chief object of the expedition."—Robertson's *America.*

The envious years, which steal our pleasures, thou
Mayst call at once, like magic memory, back,
And, as they pass o'er thine unwithering brow,
Efface their footsteps ere they form a track.
Thy bloom with wilful weeping never stain,
Perpetual life must not belong to pain.
For me,—this world has not yet been a place
Conscious of joys so great as will be mine,
Because the light has kiss'd no face
Forever fair as thine.

A PICTURE-SONG.

How may this little tablet feign
The features of a face,
Which o'er informs with loveliness
Its proper share of space;
Or human hands on ivory,
Enable us to see
The charms, that all must wonder at,
Thou work of gods in thee!

But yet, methinks, that sunny smile
Familiar stories tells,
And I should know those placid eyes,
Two shaded crystal wells;
Nor can my soul, the limner's art
Attesting with a sigh,
Forget the blood that deck'd thy cheek,
As rosy clouds the sky.

They could not semble what thou art,
More excellent than fair,
As soft as sleep or pity is,
And pure as mountain-air;
But here are common, earthly hues,
To such an aspect wrought,
That none, save thine, can seem so like
The beautiful of thought.

The song I sing, thy likeness like,
Is painful mimicry
Of something better, which is now
A memory to me,
Who have upon life's frozen sea
Arrived the icy spot,
Where man's magnetic feelings show
Their guiding task forgot.

The sportive hopes, that used to chase
Their shifting shadows on,
Like children playing in the sun,
Are gone—forever gone;
And on a careless, sullen peace,
My double-fronted mind,
Like Janus when his gates were shut,
Looks forward and behind.

Apollo placed his harp, of old,
A while upon a stone,
Which has resounded since, when struck,
A breaking harp-string's tone;
And thus my heart, though wholly now,
From early softness free,
If touch'd, will yield the music yet,
It first received of thee.

THE OLD TREE.

And is it gone, that venerable tree,
The old spectator of my infancy?—
It used to stand upon this very spot,
And now almost its absence is forgot.
I knew its mighty strength had known decay,
Its heart, like every old one, shrunk away,
But dreamt not that its frame would fall, ere mine
At all partook my weary soul's decline.
The great reformist, that each day removes
The old, yet never on the old improves,
The dotard, Time, that like a child destroys,
As sport or spleen may prompt, his ancient toys,
And shapes their ruins into something new—
Has planted other playthings where it grew.
The wind pursues an unobstructed course,
Which once among its leaves delay'd perforce;
The harmless Hamadryad, that of yore
Inhabited its bole, subsists no more;
Its roots have long since felt the ruthless plough—
There is no vestige of its glories now!
But in my mind, which doth not soon forget,
That venerable tree is growing yet;
Nourish'd, like those wild plants that feed on air,
By thoughts of years unconversant with care,
And visions such as pass ere man grows wholly
A fiendish thing, or mischief adds to folly.
I still behold it with my fancy's eye,
A vernant record of the days gone by:
I see not the sweet form and face more plain,
Whose memory *was* a weight upon my brain.
—Dear to my song, and dearer to my soul,
Who knew but half my heart, yet had the whole
Sun of my life, whose presence and whose flight
Its brief day caused, and never-ending night!
Must this delightless verse, which is indeed
The mere wild product of a worthless weed,
(But which, like sunflowers, turns a loving face
Towards the lost light, and scorns its birth and place,)
End with such cold allusion unto you,
To whom, in youth, my very dreams were true?
It must; I have no more of that soft kind,
My age is not the same, nor is my mind.

TO ———.

'Twas eve; the broadly shining sun
Its long, celestial course had run;
The twilight heaven, so soft and blue,
Met earth in tender interview,
E'en as the angel met of yore
His gifted mortal paramour,
Woman, a child of morning then,—
A spirit still,—compared with men.
Like happy islands of the sky,
The gleaming clouds reposed on high,
Each fix'd sublime, deprived of motion,
A Delos to the airy ocean.
Upon the stirless shore no breeze
Shook the green drapery of the trees,
Or, rebel to tranquillity,
Awoke a ripple on the sea.
Nor, in a more tumultuous sound,
Were the world's audible breath'ngs drown'd;
The low, strange hum of herbage growing,
The voice of hidden waters flowing,
Made songs of nature, which the ear
Could scarcely be pronounced to hear;
But noise had furl'd its subtle wings,
And moved not through material things,
All which lay calm as they had been
Parts of the painter's mimic scene.
'Twas eve; my thoughts belong to thee,
Thou shape of separate memory!
When, like a stream to lands of flame,
Unto my mind a vision came.
Methought, from human haunts and strife
Remote, we lived a loving life;
Our wedded spirits seem'd to blend
In harmony too sweet to end,
Such concord as the echoes cherish
Fondly, but leave at length to perish.
Wet rain-stars are thy lucid eyes,
The Hyades of earthly skies,
But then upon my heart they shone,
As shines on snow the fervid sun.
And fast went by those moments bright,
Like meteors shooting through the night;
But faster fleeted the wild dream
That clothed them with their transient beam
Yet love can years to days condense,
And long appear'd that life intense;
It was,—to give a better measure
Than time,—a century of pleasure.

ELYSIUM.

She dwelleth in Elysium; there,
Like Echo, floating in the air;
Feeding on light as feed the flowers,
She fleets away uncounted hours,
Where halcyon Peace, among the bless'd,
Sits brooding o'er her tranquil nest.

She needs no impulse; one she is,
Whom thought supplies with ample bliss:
The fancies fashion'd in her mind
By Heaven, are after its own kind;
Like sky-reflections in a lake,
Whose calm no winds occur to break.

Her memory is purified,
And she seems never to have sigh'd:
She hath forgot the way to weep;
Her being is a joyous sleep;
The mere imagining of pain,
Hath pass'd, and cannot come again.

Except of pleasure most intense
And constant, she hath lost all sense
Her life is day without a night,
An endless, innocent delight;
No chance her happiness now mars,
Howe'er Fate twine *her* wreaths of stars,

And palpable and pure, the part
Which pleasure playeth with her heart;
For every joy that seeks the maid,
Foregoes its common painful shade
Like shapes that issue from the grove
Arcadian, dedicate to Jove

TO H——.

THE firstlings of my simple song
  Were offer'd to thy name;
Again the altar, idle long,
  In worship rears its flame.
My sacrifice of sullen years,
My many hecatombs of tears,
  No happier hours recall—
Yet may thy wandering thoughts restore
To one who ever loved thee more
  Than fickle Fortune's all.

And now, farewell!—and although here
  Men hate the source of pain,
I hold thee and thy follies dear,
  Nor of thy faults complain.
For my misused and blighted powers,
My waste of miserable hours,
  I will accuse thee not:—
The fool who could from self depart,
And take for fate one human heart,
  Deserved no better lot.

I reck of mine the less, because
  In wiser moods I feel
A doubtful question of its cause
  And nature, on me steal—
An ancient notion, that time flings
Our pains and pleasures from his wings
  With much equality—
And that, in reason, happiness
Both of accession and decrease
  Incapable must be.

UNWISE, or most unfortunate,
  My way was; let the sign,
The proof of it, be simply this—
  Thou art not, wert not mine!
For 'tis the wont of chance to bless
Pursuit, if patient, with success;
  And envy may repine,
That, commonly, some triumph must
Be won by every lasting lust.

How I have lived imports not now;
  I am about to die,
Else I might chide thee that my life
  Has been a stifled sigh;
Yes, life; for times beyond the line
Our parting traced, appear not mine,
  Or of a world gone by;
And often almost would evince,
My soul had transmigrated since.

Pass wasted flowers; alike the grave,
  To which I fast go down,
Will give the joy of nothingness
  To me, and to renown:
Unto its careless tenants, fame
Is idle as that gilded name,
  Of vanity the crown,
Helvetian hands inscribe upon
The forehead of a skeleton.

List the last cadence of a lay,
  That, closing as begun,
 s govern'd by a note of pain,
  O, lost and worshipp'd one!
None shall attend a sadder strain,
Till MEMNON'S statue stand again
  To mourn the setting sun,—
Nor sweeter, if my numbers seem
To share the na ure of their theme.

SERENADE.

LOOK out upon the stars, my love,
  And shame them with thine eyes,
On which, than on the lights above,
  There hang more destinies.
Night's beauty is the harmony
  Of blending shades and light;
Then, lady, up,—look out, and be
  A sister to the night!—

Sleep not!—thine image wakes for aye
  Within my watching breast:
Sleep not!—from her soft sleep should fly,
  Who robs all hearts of rest.
Nay, lady, from thy slumbers break,
  And make this darkness gay
With looks, whose brightness well might make
  Of darker nights a day.

THE WIDOW'S SONG.

I BURN no incense, hang no wreath
  O'er this, thine early tomb:
Such cannot cheer the place of death,
  But only mock its gloom.
Here odorous smoke and breathing flower
  No grateful influence shed;
They lose their perfume and their power,
  When offer'd to the dead.

And if, as is the Afghaun's creed,
  The spirit may return,
A disembodied sense, to feed
  On fragrance, near its urn—
It is enough, that she, whom thou
  Didst love in living years,
Sits desolate beside it now,
  And falls these heavy tears.

SONG.

I NEED not name thy thrilling name,
  Though now I drink to thee, my dear,
Since all sounds shape that magic word,
  That fall upon my ear,—MARY;
And silence, with a wakeful voice,
  Speaks it in accents loudly free,
As darkness hath a light that shows
  Thy gentle face to me,—MARY.

I pledge thee in the grape's pure soul,
  With scarce one hope, and many fears,
Mix'd, were I of a melting mood,
  With many bitter tears.—MARY—
I pledge thee, and the empty cup
  Emblems this hollow life of mine,
To which, a gone enchantment, thou
  No more wilt be the wine,—MARY.

FORTUNATUS COSBY.

[Born 1802.]

FORTUNATUS COSBY, a son of Mr. Justice COSBY, for many years one of the most eminent lawyers of Louisville, Kentucky, was born at Harrod's Creek, Jefferson county, in that state, on the second of May, 1802; graduated at Yale College in 1819; married a young lady of New England in 1825; and has since been known as a lover of literature, and a poet, though too careless of his fame as an author to collect the many waifs he has from time to time contributed to the periodicals, some of which have been widely published under the names of other writers. In his later years he has resided in Washington.

Mr. COSBY has sung with natural grace and genuine feeling of domestic life, and of the charms of nature, as seen in the luxuriant west, where, in his own time, forests of a thousand years have disappeared before the axe of the settler, and cities, with all the institutions of cultivated society, have taken the places of wigwams and hunting-camps. Among the longer effusions which he has printed anonymously, besides the following fine ode "To the Mocking Bird," (written about the year 1826,) may be mentioned "The Traveler in the Desert," "A Dream of Long Ago," "Fireside Fancies," and "The Solitary Fountain."

TO THE MOCKING BIRD.*

BIRD of the wild and wondrous song,
I hear thy rich and varied voice
Swelling the greenwood depths among,
Till hill and vale the while rejoice.
Spell-bound, entranced, in rapture's chain,
I list to that inspiring strain;
I thread the forest's tangled maze
The thousand choristers to see,
Who, mingled thus, their voices raise
In that delicious minstrelsy;
I search in vain each pause between—
The choral band is still unseen.

'T is but the music of a dream,
An airy sound that mocks the ear;
But hark again! the eagle's scream—
It rose and fell, distinct and clear!
And list! in yonder hawthorn bush,
The red bird, robin, and the thrush!
Lost in amaze I look around,
Nor thrush nor eagle there behold:
But still that rich ærial sound,
Like some forgotten song of old
That o'er the heart has held control,
Falls sweetly on the ravished soul.

And yet the woods are vocal still,
The air is musical with song;
O'er the near stream, above the hill,
The wildering notes are borne along;
But whence that gush of rare delight?
And what art thou, or bird, or sprite?—
Perched on yon maple's topmost bough,
With glancing wings and restless feet,
Bird of untiring throat, art thou
Sole songster in this concert sweet!

So perfect, full, and rich, each part,
It mocks the highest reach of art.

Once more, once more, that thrilling strain!—
Ill-omened owl, be mute, be mute!—
Thy native tones I hear again,
More sweet than harp or lover's lute;
Compared with thy impassioned tale,
How cold, how tame the nightingale.
Alas! capricious in thy power,
Thy "wood-note wild" again is fled:
The mimic rules the changeful hour,
And all the "soul of song" is dead!
But no—to every borrowed tone
He lends a sweetness all his own!

On glittering wing, erect and bright,
With arrowy speed he darts aloft,
As though his soul had ta'en its flight,
In that last strain, so sad and soft,
And he would call it back to life,
To mingle in the mimic strife!
And ever, to each fitful lay,
His frame in restless motion wheels,
As though he would indeed essay
To act the ecstacy he feels—
As though his very feet kept time
To that inimitable chime!

And ever, as the rising moon
Climbs with full orb the trees above,
He sings his most enchanting tune,
While echo wakes through all the grove;
His descant soothes, in care's despite,
The weary watches of the night;
The sleeper from his couch starts up,
To listen to that lay forlorn;
And he who quaffs the midnight cup
Looks out to see the purple morn!
Oh, ever in the merry spring,
Sweet mimic, let me hear thee sing!

* In earlier editions of this volume erroneously attributed to Mr. ALFRED B. MEEK.

JAMES WILLIAM MILLER.

[Born about 1802. Died 1829.]

James William Miller was a young man of singular refinement, and most honorable character, "with the single defect of indecision," which, according to his biographer, "attended almost every action in his chequered existence," so that, young as he was when he died, "he had been engaged in as many as eight different pursuits, none of which was prosecuted with sufficient perseverance to command success." In 1828, after having passed some time in the desultory study of the law, at Middleborough, near Boston, he suddenly determined to make a desperate effort* to acquire fortune, or at least a competence, in the West Indies; and after visiting several of the islands, finally settled upon one of those which are subject to Spain, and though his health was feeble and precarious, was prosecuting his plans with great energy, and prospects of abundant success, when he died—his brain and heart and body overtasked—in 1829, at the age of twenty-seven years. Mr. N. P. Willis describes him, in his "American Monthly Magazine," for October, 1830, as having been "a man of exceeding sensitiveness, and great delicacy, both of native disposition and culture;" and "of the kind of genius which is out of place in common life, and which, at the same time that it interests and attracts you, excites your fear and pity."

Mr. Miller was for a short time associated with John Neal in the editorship of "The Yankee," and he wrote for this and other periodicals, many poems, simple and touching in sentiment, for the most part, but with indications of his constitutional carelessness, which after his death were collected and published, with a graceful and appreciative memoir.

A SHOWER.

The pleasant rain!—the pleasant rain!
  By fits it plashing falls
On twangling leaf and dimpling pool—
  How sweet its warning calls!
They know it—all the bosomy vales,
  High slopes, and verdant meads;
The queenly elms and princely oaks
  Bow down their grateful heads.

The withering grass, and fading flowers,
  And drooping shrubs look gay;
The bubbly brook, with gladlier song,
  Hies on its endless way!
All things of earth, all grateful things!
  Put on their robes of cheer;
They hear the sound of the warning burst,
  And know the rain is near.

It comes! it comes! the pleasant rain!
  I drink its cooler breath;
It is rich with sighs of fainting flowers,
  And roses' fragrant death;
It hath kiss'd the tomb of the lilly pale,
  The beds where violets die,
And it bears its life on its living wings—
  I feel it wandering by.

And yet it comes! the lightning's flash
  Hath torn the lowering cloud;
With a distant roar, and a nearer crash,
  Out bursts the thunder loud;
It comes with the rush of a god's descent
  On the hush'd and trembling earth,
To visit the shrines of the hallow'd groves
  Where a poet's soul had birth.

With a rush as of a thousand steeds,
  Is the mighty god's descent;
Beneath the weight of his passing tread,
  The conscious groves are bent.
His heavy tread—it is lighter now—
  And yet it passeth on;
And now it is up, with a sudden lift—
  The pleasant rain hath gone.

The pleasant rain!—the pleasant rain!
  It hath passed above the earth,
I see the smile of the opening cloud,
  Like the parted lips of mirth.
The golden joy is spreading wide
  Along the blushing west,
And the happy earth gives back her smiles,
  Like the glow of a grateful breast.

As a blessing sinks in a grateful heart,
  That knoweth all its need,
So came the good of the pleasant rain,
  O'er hill and verdant mead.
It shall breathe this truth on the human ear,
  In hall and cotter's home,
That to bring the gift of a bounteous Heaven
  The pleasant rain hath come.

---

* "He left this country abruptly, to run a wild hazard of life for which his delicate habits unfitted him—for a reward most distant and visionary. . . . The country he was going to was rude and sickly; the pursuits he was to engage in were coarse and repulsive; the language, the people, new to him; the prospects of success too distant for anything but *desperation*."—*Notice by N. P. Willis.*

ALBERT G. GREENE.

[Born, 1802.]

Mr Greene was born in Providence, Rhode Island, on the tenth day of February, 1802. He was educated at Brown University, in that city, at which he was graduated in 1820. He was soon after admitted to the bar, and followed his profession until 1834, when he was elected to an office under the city government, in which he has since remained. One of his earliest metrical compositions was the familiar piece entitled "Old Grimes," which was written in the year in which he entered the university.

His poems, except one delivered before a literary society, at Providence, were written for periodicals, and have never been published in a collected form.

THE BARON'S LAST BANQUET.

O'er a low couch the setting sun
  Had thrown its latest ray,
Where in his last strong agony
  A dying warrior lay,
The stern, old Baron Rudiger,
  Whose fame had ne'er been bent
By wasting pain, till time and toil
  Its iron strength had spent.

"They come around me here, and say
  My days of life are o'er,
That I shall mount my noble steed
  And lead my band no more;
They come, and to my beard they dare
  To tell me now, that I,
Their own liege lord and master born,—
  That I—ha! ha!—must die.

"And what is death? I've dared him oft
  Before the Paynim spear,—
Think ye he's entered at my gate,
  Has come to seek me here?
I've met him, faced him, scorn'd him,
  When the fight was raging hot,—
I'll try his might—I'll brave his power;
  Defy, and fear him not.

"Ho! sound the tocsin from my tower,—
  And fire the culverin,—
Bid each retainer arm with speed,—
  Call every vassal in;
Up with my banner on the wall,—
  The banquet board prepare,—
Throw wide the portal of my hall,
  And bring my armour there!"

A hundred hands were busy then,—
  The banquet forth was spread,—
And rung the heavy oaken floor
  With many a martial tread,
While from the rich, dark tracery
  Along the vaulted wall,
Lights gleam'd on harness, plume, and spear,
  O'er the proud, old Gothic hall.

Fast hurrying through the outer gate,
  The mail'd retainers pour'd,
On through the portal's frowning arch,
  And throng'd around the board.
While at its head, within his dark,
  Carved oaken chair of state,
Arm'd cap-a-pie, stern Rudiger,
  With girded falchion, sate.

"Fill every beaker up, my men,
  Pour forth the cheering wine;
There's life and strength in every drop,—
  Thanksgiving to the vine!
Are ye all there, my vassals true?—
  Mine eyes are waxing dim;—
Fill round, my tried and fearless ones,
  Each goblet to the brim.

"Ye're there, but yet I see ye not.
  Draw forth each trusty sword,—
And let me hear your faithful steel
  Clash once around my board:
I hear it faintly:—Louder yet!—
  What clogs my heavy breath?
Up all,—and shout for Rudiger,
  'Defiance unto Death!'"

Bowl rang to bowl,—steel clang'd to steel,
  —And rose a deafening cry
That made the torches flare around,
  And shook the flags on high:—
"Ho! cravens, do ye fear him?—
  Slaves, traitors! have ye flown?
Ho! cowards, have ye left me
  To meet him here alone!

But *I* defy him:—let him come!"
  Down rang the massy cup,
While from its sheath the ready blade
  Came flashing halfway up;
And, with the black and heavy plumes
  Scarce trembling on his head,
There, in his dark, carved, oaken chair,
  Old Rudiger sat, *dead*.

TO THE WEATHERCOCK ON OUR STEEPLE.

The dawn has broke, the morn is up,
  Another day begun;
And there thy poised and gilded spear
  Is flashing in the sun,
Upon that steep and lofty tower
  Where thou thy watch hast kept,
A true and faithful sentinel,
  While all around thee slept.

For years, upon thee, there has pour'd
  The summer's noon-day heat,
And through the long, dark, starless night,
  The winter storms have beat;
But yet thy duty has been done,
  By day and night the same,
Still thou hast met and faced the storm,
  Whichever way it came.

No chilling blast in wrath has swept
  Along the distant heaven,
But thou hast watch'd its onward course,
  And distant warning given;
And when mid-summer's sultry beams
  Oppress all living things,
Thou dost foretell each breeze that comes
  With health upon its wings.

How oft I've seen, at early dawn,
  Or twilight's quiet hour,
The swallows, in their joyous glee,
  Come darting round thy tower,
As if, with thee, to hail the sun
  And catch his earliest light,
And offer ye the morn's salute,
  Or bid ye both,—good-night.

And when, around thee or above,
  No breath of air has stirr'd,
Thou seem'st to watch the circling flight
  Of each free, happy bird,
Till, after twittering round thy head
  In many a mazy track,
The whole delighted company
  Have settled on thy back.

Then, if, perchance, amidst their mirth,
  A gentle breeze has sprung,
And, prompt to mark its first approach,
  Thy eager form hath swung,
I've thought I almost heard thee say,
  As far aloft they flew,—
"Now all away!—here ends our play,
  For I have work to do!"

Men slander thee, my honest friend,
  And call thee, in their pride,
An emblem of their fickleness,
  Thou ever-faithful guide.
Each weak, unstable human mind
  A "weathercock" they call;
And thus, unthinkingly, mankind
  Abuse thee, one and all.

They have no right to make thy name
  A by-word for their deeds:—
They change their friends, their principles,
  Their fashions, and their creeds;
Whilst thou hast ne'er, like them, been known
  Thus causelessly to range;
But when thou *changest sides*, canst give
  Good reason for the change.

Thou, like some lofty soul, whose course
  The thoughtless oft condemn,
Art touch'd by many airs from heaven
  Which never breathe on them,—
And moved by many impulses
  Which they do never know,
Who, round their earth-bound circles, plod
  The dusty paths below.

Through one more dark and cheerless night
  Thou well hast kept thy trust,
And now in glory o'er thy head
  The morning light has burst.
And unto earth's true watcher, thus,
  When his dark hours have pass'd,
Will come "the day-spring from on high,"
  To cheer his path at last.

Bright symbol of *fidelity*,
  Still may I think of thee:
And may the lesson thou dost teach
  Be never lost on me;—
But still, in sunshine or in storm,
  Whatever task is mine,
May I be faithful to *my* trust,
  As thou hast been to *thine*.

ADELHEID.

Why droop the sorrowing trees,
Swayed by the autumn breeze,
  Heavy with rain?
    Drearily, wearily,
    Move as in pain?
  Weeping and sighing,
  They ever seem crying,
"Adelheid! Adelheid!" evening and morn:
"Adelheid! Adelheid! where has she gone?"

With their arms bending there,
In the cold winter air,
    Icy and chill,
  Trembling and glistening,
  Watching and listening,
    Awaiting her still,
With the snow round their feet,
Still they the name repeat—
"Adelheid! Adelheid! here is her home:
Adelheid! Adelheid! when will she come?"

With the warm breath of Spring
    Now the foliage is stirr'd;
On the pathway below them
    A footstep is heard.

Now bent gently o'er her,
How joyous the greeting.
Now waving before her
Each sound seems repeating—
"Adelheid! Adelheid! welcome again."
Their branches upspringing,
The breeze through them ringing,
The birds through them singing,
Unite in the strain—
"Adelheid! Adelheid! welcome again!"

OLD GRIMES.

Old Grimes is dead; that good old man
We never shall see more:
He used to wear a long, black coat,
All button'd down before.

His heart was open as the day,
His feelings all were true;
His hair was some inclined to gray—
He wore it in a queue.

Whene'er he heard the voice of pain,
His breast with pity burn'd;
The large, round head upon his cane
From ivory was turn'd.

Kind words he ever had for all;
He knew no base design:
His eyes were dark and rather small,
His nose was aquiline.

He lived at peace with all mankind,
In friendship he was true:
His coat had pocket-holes behind,
His pantaloons were blue.

Unharm'd, the sin which earth pollutes
He pass'd securely o'er,
And never wore a pair of boots
For thirty years or more.

But good old Grimes is now at rest,
Nor fears misfortune's frown:
He wore a double-breasted vest—
The stripes ran up and down.

He modest merit sought to find,
And pay it its desert:
He had no malice in his mind,
No ruffles on his shirt.

His neighbours he did not abuse—
Was sociable and gay:
He wore large buckles on his shoes,
And changed them every day.

His knowledge, hid from public gaze,
He did not bring to view,
Nor make a noise, town-meeting days,
As many people do.

His worldly goods he never threw
In trust to fortune's chances,
But lived (as all his brothers do)
In easy circumstances.

Thus undisturb'd by anxious cares
His peaceful moments ran;
And everybody said he was
A fine old gentleman.

OH, THINK NOT THAT THE BOSOM'S LIGHT.

Oh think not that the bosom's light
Must dimly shine, its fire be low,
Because it doth not all invite
To feel its warmth and share its glow.
The altar's strong and steady blaze
On all around may coldly shine,
But only genial warmth conveys
To those who gather near the shrine.
The lamp within the festal hall
Doth not more clear and brightly burn
Than that, which shrouded by the pall,
Lights but the cold funereal urn.

The fire which lives through one brief hour,
More sudden heat perchance reveals
Than that whose tenfold strength and power
Its own unmeasured depth conceals.
Brightly the summer cloud may glide
But bear no heat within its breast,
Though all its gorgeous folds are dyed
In the full glories of the west:
'Tis that which through the darken'd sky,
Surrounded by no radiance, sweeps—
In which, conceal'd from every eye,
The wild and vivid lightning sleeps.

Do the dull flint, the rigid steel,
Which thou within thy hand mayst hold,
Unto thy sight or touch reveal
The hidden power which they enfold?
But take those cold, unyielding things,
And beat their edges till you tire,
And every atom forth that springs
Is a bright spark of living fire:
Each particle, so dull and cold
Until the blow that woke it came,
Did still within it slumbering hold
A power to wrap the world in flame.

What is there, when thy sight is turn'd
To the volcano's icy crest,
By which the fire can be discern'd
That rages in its silent breast;
Which hidden deep, but quenchless still,
Is at its work of sure decay,
And will not cease to burn until
It wears its giant heart away.
The mountain's side upholds in pride
Its head amid the realms of snow,
And gives its bosom depth to hide
The burning mass which lies below.

While thus in things of sense alone
Such truths from sense lie still conceal'd,
How can the living heart be known,
Its secret, inmost depths reveal'd?
Oh, many an overburden'd soul
Has been at last to madness wrought,
While proudly struggling to control
Its burning and consuming thought—
When it had sought communion long,
And had been doom'd in vain to seek
For feelings far too deep and strong
For heart to bear or tongue to speak!

RALPH WALDO EMERSON.

[Born, about 1803.]

RALPH WALDO EMERSON, a son of the Reverend WILLIAM EMERSON, one of the associates of Chief Justice PARSONS, ALEXANDER H. EVERETT, J. S. BUCKMINSTER, WILLIAM TUDOR, JOHN T. KIRKLAND, GEORGE TICKNOR, and others, in the "Anthology Society," was born in Boston about the year 1803, and after taking his degree of bachelor of arts at Harvard College, in 1821, studied theology, and, in 1829, was ordained as the colleague of the late Reverend HENRY WARE, Jr., over the second Unitarian church of his native city; but subsequently abandoned the pulpit on account of having adopted certain heterodox opinions in regard to the supernatural character of Christianity, and has since, except during two excursions in Europe, lived in retirement at Concord, devoting his attention to literature and philosophy. He has been a contributor to "The North American Review" and "The Christian Examiner," and was two years editor of "The Dial," established in Boston by Mr. RIPLEY, in 1840. He published several orations and addresses in 1837, 1838, 1839, and 1840, and in 1841 the first series of his "Essays," in 1844 the second series of his "Essays," in 1846 a collection of his "Poems," in 1851 "Representative Men," and in 1852, in connection with W. H. CHANNING and JAMES FREEMAN CLARKE, "Memoirs of MARGARET FULLER OSSOLI."

In a notice of Mr. EMERSON'S essays and orations in "The Prose Writers of America," I have attempted a speculation and characterization of his genius; but that genius, in whatever forms it may be exhibited, is essentially poetical; and though he defies classification as a philosopher, few will doubt that he is eminently a poet, even in his poetry. As a thinker he disdains the trammels of systems and methods; his utterances are the free developments of himself: all his thoughts appearing and claiming record in the order of their suggestion and growth, so that they have, if a more limited, also a more just efficiency. In poetry he is as impatient of the laws of verbal harmony, as in discussion of the processes of logic; and if his essential ideas are made to appear, so as not to seem altogether obscure to himself, he cares little whether they move to any music which was not made for them. In his degree, he holds it to be his prerogative to say, I am: let the herd who have no individuality of their own, accommodate themselves to me, and those who are my peers have respect for me. If you cannot sing his songs to the melodies of MILTON, or SPENSER, or POPE, or TENNYSON, study till you discover the key and scale of EMERSON; then all will be harmonious, and no doubt you will find your compensation.

Mr. EMERSON'S sympathy with nature is evinced in every thing he has written; beauty, in external objects, whether it be grandeur, sublimity, splendor, or simple grace, is not with him an illustration merely; it is an instructing presence, to be questioned and heard as one of the forms or manifestations of divinity. The old prayer of AJAX is translated in his verse:

"Give me of the true,—
Whose ample leaves and tendrils, curled
Among the silver hills of heaven,
Draw everlasting dew;
Wine of wine,
Blood of the world,
Form of forms, and mould of statures,
That I, intoxicated,
And by the draught assimilated,
May float at pleasure through all natures;
The bird-language rightly spell,
And that which roses say so well."

What to others who have repeated the words has been an unmeaning fable, has to him been a truth: he has found

"Tongues in trees, books in the running brooks,
Sermons in stones, and good in every thing;"

and this he says for himself, in a little poem called

"THE APOLOGY.

"Think me not unkind and rude
That I walk alone in grove and glen;
I go to the god of the wood
To fetch his word to men.

"Tax not my sloth that I
Fold my arms beside the brook
Each cloud that floated in the sky
Writes a letter in my book.

"Chide me not, laborious band,
For the idle flowers I brought;
Every aster in my hand
Goes home loaded with a thought.

"There was never mystery
But 't is figured in the flowers;
Was never secret history
But birds tell it in the bowers.

"One harvest from thy field
Homeward brought the oxen strong;
A second crop thy acres yield,
Which I gather in a song."

Consistency is perhaps not to be expected of one who defies all formula and method; and the following lines are here quoted from the poem entitled "Woodnotes," not so much because they seem to discredit this "Apology," therefore, as for their exquisite beauty:

"As sunbeams stream through liberal space,
And nothing jostle or displace,
So waved the pine-tree through my thought,
And fanned the dreams it never brought."

The metaphysician laboriously educes an inference, which he announces more or less doubtfully; the poet speaks face to face familiarly with the sphinx, and sweetly or bravely sings his revelation. Hence EMERSON disclaims the title and function of reasoner: it is more honorable to be in the confidence of the gods. In a characteristic letter to HENRY WARE, in 1838, he says:

"IT strikes me very oddly, that good and wise men at Cambridge and Boston should think of raising me into an object of criticism. I have always been, from my very incapacity of methodical writing, a 'chartered libertine,' free to worship and free to rail—lucky when I could make myself understood, but never esteemed near enough to the institutions and mind of society to deserve the notice of the masters of literature and religion. I have appreciated fully the advantages of my position; for well I know that there is no scholar less willing or less able to be a polemic. I could not give an account of myself, if challenged. I could not possibly give you one of the 'arguments' on which any doctrine of mine stands; for I do not know what arguments mean in reference to any expression of a thought. I delight in telling what I think; but, if you ask me how I dare say so, or why it is so, I am the most helpless of mortal men. I do not even see that either of these questions admits of an answer. . . . I shall go on, just as before, seeing whatever I can, and telling what I see; and I suppose, with the same fortune that has hitherto attended me: the joy of finding that my older and better brothers, who work with the sympathy of society, loving and beloved, do now and then unexpectedly confirm my perceptions, and find my nonsense is only their own thought in motley."

For myself I am not of his school altogether; I doubt the correctness of his short-hand translations sometimes; the poet may misunderstand nature, or there may be lying sphinxes, as the fools are apt to say of rapping spirits. Nevertheless the higher class of intelligences have in the poetical faculty an inspiration which resembles, in a degree, that purer influence or energy which in a more strict sense is a special gift of heaven.

EACH IN ALL.

LITTLE thinks in the field yon red-cloak'd clown
Of thee from the hill-top looking down;
And the heifer that lows in the upland farm
Far heard, lows not thine ear to charm;
The sexton tolling his bell at noon
Dreams not that great NAPOLEON
Stops his horse, and lists with delight,
Whilst his files sweep round yon Alpine height;
Nor knowest thou what argument
Thy life to thy neighbour's creed hath lent,
All are needed by each one;
Nothing is fair or good alone.

I thought the sparrow's note from heaven,
Singing at dawn on the alder bough;
I brought him home in his nest at even,—
He sings the song, but it pleases not now,
For I did not bring home the river and sky,
He sang to my ear, these sang to my eye.
The delicate shells lay on the shore—
The bubbles of the latest wave
Fresh pearls to their enamel gave,
And the bellowing of the savage sea
Greeted their safe escape to me.
I wiped away the weeds and foam,
I fetch'd my sea-born treasures home,
But the poor, unsightly, noisome things
Had left their beauty on the shore,
With the sun, and the sand, and the wild uproar.
Nor rose, nor stream, nor bird is fair,
Their concord is beyond compare.

The lover watch'd his graceful maid
As mid the virgin train she stray'd,
Nor knew her beauty's best attire
Was woven still by that snow-white quire.
At last, she came to his hermitage,
Like the bird from the woodlands to the cage,—
The gay enchantment was undone,—
A gentle wife, but fairy none.

Then, I said, "I covet truth;
Beauty is unripe childhood's cheat;
I leave 't behind with the games of youth;"
——As I spoke, beneath my feet
The ground-pine curl'd its pretty wreath,
Running over the hair-cap burs:
I inhaled the violet's breath:
Around me stood the oaks and firs:
Pine-cones and acorns lay on the ground.
Over me soar'd the eternal sky
Full of light and of deity;
Again I saw—again I heard,
The rolling river, the morning bird:
Beauty through my senses stole,—
I yielded myself to the perfect whole.

"GOOD-BYE, PROUD WORLD!"

GOOD-BYE, proud world! I'm going home;
Thou art not my friend; I am not thine:
Too long through weary crowds I roam:—
A river ark on the ocean brine,
Too long I am toss'd like the driven foam;
But now, proud world, I'm going home

Good-bye to Flattery's fawning face;
To Grandeur with his wise grimace:
To upstart Wealth's averted eye;
To supple office, low and high;
To crowded halls, to court and street,
To frozen hearts, and hasting feet,
To those who go, and those who come,
Good-bye, proud world, Im going home.

I go to seek my own hearth-stone
Bosom'd in yon green hills alone;
A secret lodge in a pleasant land,
Whose groves the frolic fairies plann'd,
Where arches green, the livelong day
Echo the blackbird's roundelay,
And evil men have never trod
A spot that is sacred to thought and GOD.

O, when I am safe in my sylvan home,
I mock at the pride of Greece and Rome;
And when I am stretch'd beneath the pines
Where the evening star so holy shines,
I laugh at the lore and pride of man,
At the sophist schools, and the learned clan;
For what are they all in their high conceit,
When man in the bush with God may meet?

TO THE HUMBLE-BEE.

Fine humble-bee! fine humble-bee!
Where thou art is clime for me,
Let them sail for Porto Rique,
Far-off heats through seas to seek,—
I will follow thee alone,
Thou animated torrid zone!
Zig-zag steerer, desert cheerer,
Let me chase thy waving lines,
Keep me nearer, me thy hearer,
Singing over shrubs and vines.

Flower-bells,
Honey'd cells,—
These the tents
Which he frequents.

Insect lover of the sun,
Joy of thy dominion!
Sailor of the atmosphere,
Swimmer through the waves of air,
Voyager of light and noon,
Epicurean of June,
Wait, I prithee, till I come
Within earshot of thy hum,—
All without is martyrdom.

When the south wind, in May days,
With a net of shining haze,
Silvers the horizon wall,
And with softness touching all,
Tints the human countenance
With a colour of romance,
And infusing subtle heats
Turns the sod to violets,—
Thou in sunny solitudes,
Rover of the underwoods,
The green silence dost displace
With thy mellow breezy bass.

Hot midsummer's petted crone,
Sweet to me thy drowsy tune,
Telling of countless sunny hours,
Long days, and solid banks of flowers,
Of gulfs of sweetness without bound
In Indian wildernesses found,
Of Syrian peace, immortal leisure.
Firmest cheer, and bird-like pleasure.

Aught unsavoury or unclean
Hath my insect never seen,
But violets, and bilberry bells,
Maple sap, and daffodels,
Clover, catchfly, adders-tongue,
And brier-roses dwelt among.
All beside was unknown waste,
All was picture as he pass'd.

Wiser far than human seer,
Yellow-breech'd philosopher,
Seeing only what is fair,
Sipping only what is sweet
Thou dost mock at fate and care,
Leave the chaff and take the wheat.
When the fierce north-western blast
Cools sea and land so far and fast,—
Thou already slumberest deep,
Wo and want thou canst outsleep;
Want and wo which torture us,
Thy sleep makes ridiculous.

THE RHODORA.

LINES ON BEING ASKED, WHENCE IS THE FLOWER?

In May, when sea-winds pierced our solitudes,
I found the fresh Rhodora in the woods,
Spreading its leafless blooms in a damp nook,
To please the desert and the sluggish brook;
The purple petals fallen in the pool
Made the black waters with their beauty gay;
Young Raphael might covet such a school;
The lively show beguiled me from my way.
Rhodora! if the sages ask thee why
This charm is wasted on the marsh and sky,
Dear, tell them, that if eyes were made for seeing,
Then beauty is its own excuse for being.
Why, thou wert there, O, rival of the rose!
I never thought to ask, I never knew,
But in my simple ignorance suppose
The selfsame Power that brought me there, brought you.

THE SNOW-STORM.

Announced by all the trumpets of the sky
Arrives the snow, and driving o'er the fields,
Seems nowhere to alight: the whited air
Hides hills and woods, the river, and the heaven,
And veils the farm-house at the garden's end.
The sled and traveller stopp'd, the courier's feet
Delay'd, all friends shut out, the housemates sit
Around the radiant fire-place, enclosed
In a tumultuous privacy of storm.
Come see the north-wind's masonry.
Out of an unseen quarry evermore
Furnish'd with tile, the fierce artificer
Curves his white bastions with projected roof
Round every windward stake, or tree, or door.
Speeding, the myriad-handed, his wild work
So fanciful, so savage, nought cares he
For number or proportion. Mockingly
On coop or kennel he hangs Parian wreaths;
A swan-like form invests the hidden thorn;
Fills up the farmer's lane from wall to wall,
Maugre the farmer's sighs, and at the gate
A tapering turret overtops the work.
And when his hours are number'd, and the world
Is all his own, retiring, as he were not,
Leaves, when the sun appears, astonish'd Art
To mimic in slow structures, stone by stone,
Built in an age, the mad wind's night-work,
The frolic architecture of the snow.

THE SPHINX.

The Sphinx is drowsy,
  Her wings are furl'd,
Her ear is heavy,
  She broods on the world.
"Who'll tell me my secret
  The ages have kept!
I awaited the seer
  While they slumber'd and slept.

"The fate of the manchild,—
  The meaning of man,—
Known fruit of the unknown,
  Dædalian plan.
Out of sleeping a waking,
  Out of waking a sleep,
Life death overtaking,
  Deep underneath deep.

"Erect as a sunbeam
  Upspringeth the palm;
The elephant browses
  Undaunted and calm;
In beautiful motion
  The thrush plies his wings,
Kind leaves of his covert!
  Your silence he sings.

"The waves unashamed
  In difference sweet,
Play glad with the breezes,
  Old playfellows meet.
The journeying atoms,
  Primordial wholes,
Firmly draw, firmly drive,
  By their animate poles.

"Sea, earth, air, sound, silence,
  Plant, quadruped, bird,
By one music enchanted,
  One deity stirr'd,
Each the other adorning,
  Accompany still,
Night veileth the morning,
  The vapour the hill.

"The babe, by its mother
  Lies bathed in joy,
Glide its hours uncounted,
  The sun is its toy;
Shines the peace of all being
  Without cloud in its eyes,
And the sum of the world
  In soft miniature lies.

"But man crouches and blushes,
  Absconds and conceals;
He creepeth and peepeth,
  He palters and steals;
Infirm, melancholy,
  Jealous glancing around,
An oaf, an accomplice,
  He poisons the ground.

"Outspoke the great mother
  Beholding his fear;—
At the sound of her accents
  Cold shudder'd the sphere;—
'Who has drugg'd my boy's cup,
  Who has mix'd my boy's bread?
Who, with sadness and madness,
  Has turn'd the manchild's head?'"

I heard a poet answer
  Aloud and cheerfully,
"Say on, sweet Sphinx!—thy dirges
  Are pleasant songs to me.
Deep love lieth under
  These pictures of time,
They fade in the light of
  Their meaning sublime.

"The fiend that man harries
  Is love of the Best,
Yawns the Pit of the Dragon
  Lit by rays from the Blest;
The Lethe of Nature
  Can't trance him again,
Whose soul sees the Perfect
  Which his eyes seek in vain.

"Profounder, profounder
  Man's spirit must dive:
To his aye-rolling orbit
  No goal will arrive.
The heavens that now draw him
  With sweetness untold,
Once found,—for new heavens
  He spurneth the old.

"Pride ruin'd the angels,
  Their shame them restores
And the joy that is sweetest
  Lurks in stings of remorse
Have I a lover
  Who is noble and free,—
I would he were nobler
  Than to love me.

"Eterne alternation
  Now follows, now flies,
And under pain, pleasure,—
  Under pleasure, pain lies.
Love works at the centre
  Heart heaving alway,
Forth speed the strong pulses
  To the borders of day.

"Dull Sphinx, Jove keep thy five wits,
  Thy sight is growing blear;
Hemlock and vitriol for the Sphinx
  Her muddy eyes to clear."
The old Sphinx bit her thick lip,—
  Said, "Who taught thee me to name?
Manchild! I am thy spirit;
  Of thine eye I am eyebeam.

"Thou art the unanswer'd question;—
  Couldst see thy proper eye,
Alway it asketh, asketh,
  And each answer is a lie.
So take thy quest through nature,
  It through thousand natures ply,
Ask on, thou clothed eternity,
  Time is the false reply."

Uprose the merry Sphinx,
And crouch'd no more in stone,
She hopp'd into the baby's eyes,
She hopp'd into the moon,
She spired into a yellow flame,
She flower'd in blossoms red,
She flow'd into a foaming wave,
She stood Monadnoc's head.

Thorough a thousand voices
Spoke the universal dame,
"Who telleth one of my meanings
Is master of all I am."

THE PROBLEM.

I LIKE a church, I like a cowl,
I love a prophet of the soul,
And on my heart monastic aisles
Fall like sweet strains or pensive smiles,
Yet not for all his faith can see
Would I that cowled churchman be.
Why should the vest on him allure,
Which I could not on me endure?
Not from a vain or shallow thought
His awful Jove young Phidias brought;
Never from lips of cunning fell
The thrilling Delphic oracle;
Out from the heart of nature roll'd
The burdens of the Bible old;
The litanies of nations came,
Like the volcano's tongue of flame,
Up from the burning core below,—
The canticles of love and wo.
The hand that rounded Peter's dome,
And groin'd the aisles of Christian Rome,
Wrought in a sad sincerity.
Himself from God he could not free;
He builded better than he knew,
The conscious stone to beauty grew.
Know'st thou what wove yon wood-bird's nest
Of leaves, and feathers from her breast;
Or how the fish outbuilt her shell,
Painting with morn each annual cell;
Or how the sacred pine tree adds
To her old leaves new myriads?
Such and so grew these holy piles,
Whilst love and terror laid the tiles.
Earth proudly wears the Parthenon
As the best gem upon her zone;
And morning opes with haste her lids
To gaze upon the Pyramids;
O'er England's Abbeys bends the sky
As on its friends with kindred eye;
For, out of Thought's interior sphere
These wonders rose to upper air,
And nature gladly gave them place,
Adopted them into her race,
And granted them an equal date
With Andes and with Ararat.
These temples grew as grows the grass,
Art might obey but not surpass.
The passive Master lent his hand
To the vast Soul that o'er him plann'd,
And the same power that rear'd the shrine,
Bestrode the tribes that knelt within.
Ever the fiery Pentacost
Girds with one flame the countless host,
Trances the heart through chanting quires,
And through the priest the mind inspires.
The word unto the prophet spoken,
Was writ on tables yet unbroken;
The word by seers or sybils told
In groves of oak or fanes of gold,
Still floats upon the morning wind,
Still whispers to the willing mind.
One accent of the Holy Ghost
The heedless world hath never lost.
I know what say the Fathers wise,—
The book itself before me lies,—
Old *Chrysos'om*, best Augustine,
And he who blent both in his line,
The younger *Golden Lips* or mines,
Taylor, the Shakspeare of divines;
His words are music in my ear,
I see his cowled portrait dear,
And yet, for all his faith could see,
I would not the good bishop be.

THE FORE-RUNNERS.

LONG I follow'd happy guides:
I could never reach their sides.
Their step is forth and, ere the day,
Breaks up their leaguer and away.
Keen my sense, my heart was young,
Right good will my sinews strung,
But no speed of mine avails
To hunt upon their shining trails.
On and away, their hasting feet
Make the morning proud and sweet.
Flowers they strew, I catch the scent,
Or tone of silver instrument
Leaves on the wind melodious trace,
Yet I could never see their face.
On eastern hills I see their smokes
Mix'd with mist by distant lochs.
I met many travellers
Who the road had surely kept,
They saw not my fine revellers,
These had cross'd them while they slept.
Some had heard their fair report,
In the country or the court.
Fleetest couriers alive
Never yet could once arrive,
As they went or they return'd,
At the house where these sojourn'd.
Sometimes their strong speed they slacken,
Though they are not overtaken:
In sleep their jubilant troop is near,
I tuneful voices overhear,
It may be in wood or waste,—
At unawares 'tis come and pass'd.
Their near camp my spirit knows
By signs gracious as rainbows
I thenceforward and long after,
Listen for their harp-like laughter,
And carry in my heart for days
Peace that hallows rudest ways.

THE POET.

For this present, hard
Is the fortune of the bard
  Born out of time;
All his accomplishment
From nature's utmost treasure spent
  Booteth not him.
When the pine tosses its cones
To the song of its waterfall tones,
He speeds to the woodland walks,
To birds and trees he talks:
Cæsar of his leafy Rome,
There the poet is at home.
He goes to the river side,—
  Not hook nor line hath he:
He stands in the meadows wide,—
  Nor gun nor scythe to see;
With none has he to do,
  And none to seek him,
Nor men below,
  Nor spirits dim.
What he knows nobody wants;
What he knows, he hides, not vaunts.
Knowledge this man prizes best
Seems fantastic to the rest;
Pondering shadows, colours, clouds,
Grass buds, and caterpillars' shrouds.
Boughs on which the wild bees settle,
Tints that spot the violets' petal,
Why nature loves the number five,
  And why the star-form she repeats;—
Lover of all things alive,
  Wonderer at all he meets,
Wonderer chiefly at himself,—
  Who can tell him what he is;
Or how meet in human elf
  Coming and past eternities? ....
And such I knew, a forest seer,
A minstrel of the natural year,
Foreteller of the vernal ides,
Wise harbinger of spheres and tides,
A lover true, who knew by heart
Each joy the mountain dales impart;
It seem'd that nature could not raise
A plant in any secret place,
In quaking bog, on snowy hill,
Beneath the grass that shades the rill,
Under the snow, between the rocks,
In damp fields known to bird and fox,
But he would come in the very hour
It open'd in its virgin bower,
As if a sunbeam show'd the place,
And tell its long descended race.
It seem'd as if the breezes brought him,
It seem'd as if the sparrows taught him,
As if by secret sight he knew
Where in far fields the orchis grew.
There are many events in the field,
  Which are not shown to common eyes,
But all her shows did nature yield
  To please and win this pilgrim wise.
He saw the partridge drum in the woods,
  He heard the woodcock's evening hymn,
He found the tawny thrush's broods,
  And the shy hawk did wait for him
What others did at distance hear,
  And guess'd within the thicket's gloom,
Was show'd to this philosopher,
  And at his bidding seem'd to come.

DIRGE.

Knows he who tills this lonely field
  To reap its scanty corn,
What mystic fruit his acres yield
  At midnight and at morn?

In the long sunny afternoon
  The plain was full of ghosts,
I wander'd up, I wander'd down,
  Beset by pensive hosts.

The winding Concord gleam'd below,
  Pouring as wide a flood
As when my brothers, long ago,
  Came with me to the wood.

But they are gone—the holy ones
  Who trod with me this lonely vale,
The strong, star-bright companions
  Are silent, low, and pale.

My good, my noble, in their prime,
  Who made this world the feast it was,
Who learn'd with me the lore of Time,
  Who loved this dwelling-place;

They took this valley for their toy,
  They play'd with it in every mood,
A cell for prayer, a hall for joy,
  They treated Nature as they would.

They colour'd the whole horizon round,
  Stars flamed and faded as they bade,
All echoes hearken'd for their sound,
  They made the woodlands glad or mad.

I touch this flower of silken leaf
  Which once our childhood knew,
Its soft leaves wound me with a grief
  Whose balsam never grew.

Hearken to yon pine warbler,
  Singing aloft in the tree;
Hearest thou, O traveller!
  What he singeth to me?

Not unless God made sharp thine ear
  With sorrow such as mine,
Out of that delicate lay couldst thou
  Its heavy tale divine.

"Go, lonely man," it saith,
  "They loved thee from their birth,
Their hands were pure, and pure their faith,
  There are no such hearts on earth.

"Ye drew one mother's milk,
  One chamber held ye all,
A very tender history
  Did in your childhood fall.

"Ye cannot unlock your heart,
  The key is gone with them;
The silent organ loudest chants
  The master's requiem."

TO RHEA.

Thee, dear friend, a brother soothes,
Not with flatteries, but truths,
Which tarnish not, but purify
To light which dims the morning's eye.
I have come from the spring-woods,
From the fragrant solitudes:
Listen what the poplar tree
And murmuring waters counsell'd me.
If with love thy heart has burn'd,
If thy love is unreturn'd,
Hide thy grief within thy breast,
Though it tear thee unexpress'd;
For when love has once departed
From the eyes of the false-hearted,
And one by one has torn off quite
The bandages of purple light,
Though thou wert the loveliest
Form the soul had ever dress'd,
Thou shalt seem, in each reply,
A vixen to his altered eye;
Thy softest pleadings seem too bold,
Thy praying lute will seem to scold;
Though thou kept the straightest road,
Yet thou errest far and broad.
But thou shalt do as do the gods
In their cloudless periods;
For of this lore be thou sure—
Though thou forget, the gods, secure,
Forget never their command,
But make the statute of this land.
As they lead, so follow all,
Ever have done, ever shall.
Warning to the blind and deaf,
'T is written on the iron leaf—
Who drinks of Cupid's nectar cup,
Loveth downward, and not up;
Therefore, who loves, of gods or men,
Shall not by the same be loved again;
His sweetheart's idolatry
Falls, in turn, a new degree.
When a god is once beguiled
By beauty of a mortal child,
And by her radiant youth delighted,
He is not fool'd, but warily knoweth
His love shall never be requited.
And thus the wise Immortal doeth.—
'T is his study and delight
To bless that creature day and night—
From all evils to defend her,
In her lap to pour all splendour,
To ransack earth for riches rare,
And fetch her stars to deck her hair;
He mixes music with her thoughts,
And saddens her with heavenly doubts:
All grace, all good, his great heart knows,
Profuse in love, the king bestows:
Saying, "Hearken! earth, sea, air!
This monument of my despair
Build I to the All-Good, All-Fair.
Not for a private good,
But I, from my beatitude,
Albeit scorn'd as none was scorn'd,
Adorn her as was none adorn'd.
I make this maiden an ensample
To Nature, through her kingdoms ample,
Whereby to model newer races,
Statelier forms, and fairer faces;
To carry man to new degrees
Of power and of comeliness.
These presents be the hostages
Which I pawn for my release.
See to thyself, O Universe!
Thou art better, and not worse."—
And the god, having given all,
Is freed forever from his thrall.

TO EVA.

Oh fair and stately maid, whose eyes
Were kindled in the upper skies
At the same torch that lighted mine;
For so I must interpret still
Thy sweet dominion o'er my will,
A sympathy divine.

Ah, let me blameless gaze upon
Features that seem at heart my own;
Nor fear those watchful sentinels,
Who charm the more their glance forbids,
Chaste-glowing, underneath their lids,
With fire that draws while it repels.

THE AMULET.

Your picture smiles as first it smiled;
The ring you gave is still the same;
Your letter tells, oh changing child!
No tidings since it came.

Give me an amulet
That keeps intelligence with you—
Red when you love, and rosier red,
And when you love not, pale and blue.

Alas! that neither bonds nor vows
Can certify possession:
Torments me still the fear that love
Died in its last expression.

THINE EYES STILL SHINED.

Thine eyes still shined for me, though far
I lonely roved the land or sea:
As I behold yon evening star,
Which yet beholds not me.

This morn I climb'd the misty hill,
And roamed the pastures through;
How danced thy form before my path,
Amidst the deep-eyed dew!

When the red-bird spread his sable wing,
And show'd his side of flame—
When the rosebud ripen'd to the rose—
In both I read thy name.

SUMNER LINCOLN FAIRFIELD.

[Born 1803. Died 1844.]

The author of "The Last Night of Pompeii" was born in Warwick, near the western border of Massachusetts, in the autumn of 1803. His father, a respectable physician, died in 1806, and his mother, on becoming a widow, returned with two children to her paternal home in Worcester.

Mr. Fairfield entered Harvard College when thirteen years of age; but, after spending two years in that seminary, was compelled to leave it, to aid his mother in teaching a school in a neighbouring village. He subsequently passed two or three years in Georgia and South Carolina, and in 1824 went to Europe. He returned in 1826, was soon afterwards married, and from that period resided in Philadelphia, where for several years he conducted the "North American Magazine," a monthly miscellany in which appeared most of his prose writings and poems.

He commenced the business of authorship at a very early period, and perhaps produced more in the form of poetry than any of his American contemporaries. "The Cities of the Plain," one of his earliest poems, was originally published in England. It was founded on the history of the destruction of Sodom and Gomorrah, in the eighteenth and nineteenth chapters of Genesis. The "Heir of the World," which followed in 1828, is a poetical version of the life of Abraham. It is in the Spenserian measure, and contains some fine passages, descriptive of scenery and feeling. His next considerable work, "The Spirit of Destruction," appeared in 1830. Its subject is the deluge. Like the "Cities of the Plain," it is in the heroic verse, in which he wrote with great facility. His "Last Night of Pompeii"* was published in 1832. It is the result of two years' industrious labour, and was written amid the cares and vexations of poverty. The destruction of the cities of Herculaneum, Pompeii, Retina and Stabiæ, by an eruption of Vesuvius, in the summer of the year seventy-nine, is perhaps one of the finest subjects for poetry in modern history. Mr. Fairfield in this poem exhibits a familiar acquaintance with the manners and events of the period, and his style is stately and sustained. His shorter pieces, though in some cases turgid and unpolished, are generally distinguished for vigour of thought and depth of feeling. An edition of his principal writings was published in a closely-printed octavo volume, in Philadelphia, in 1841.

The first and last time I ever saw Fairfield was in the summer of 1842, when he called at my hotel to thank me for some kind notice of him in one of the journals, of which he supposed me to be the author. In a note sent to my apartment he described himself as "an outcast from all human affections" except those of his mother and his children, with whom he should remain but a little while, for he "felt the weight of the arm of Death." He complained that every man's hand had been against him, that exaggerated accounts had been published of his infirmities, and uncharitable views given of his misfortunes. He said his mother, who had "been abused as an annoying old crone," in the newspapers, for endeavouring to obtain subscribers for his works, was attending him from his birth to his burial, and would never grow weary till the end. This prediction was verified About a year afterwards I read in a published letter from New Orleans that Fairfield had wandered to that city, lived there a few months in solitude and destitution, and after a painful illness died. While he lingered on his pallet, between the angel of death and his mother, she counted the hours of day and night, never slumbering by his side, nor leaving him, until as his only mourner she had followed him to a grave.

Not wishing to enter into any particular examination of his claims to personal respect, I must still express an opinion that Fairfield was harshly treated, and that even if the specific charges against him were true, it was wrong to permit the private character of the author to have any influence upon critical judgments of his works. He wrote much, and generally with commendable aims. His knowledge of books was extensive and accurate. He had considerable fancy, which at one period was under the dominion of cultivated taste and chastened feeling; but troubles, mostly resulting from a want of skill in pecuniary affairs, induced recklessness, misanthropy, intemperance, and a general derangement and decay of his intellectual and moral nature. I see not much to admire in his poems, but they are by no means contemptible; and "the poet Fairfield" had during a long period too much notoriety not to deserve some notice in a work of this sort, even though his verses had been still less poetical.

Persons of an ardent temperament and refined sensibilities have too frequently an aversion to the practical and necessary duties of common life, to the indulgence of which they owe their chief misfortunes and unhappiness. The mind of the true poet, however, is well ordered and comprehensive, and shrinks not from the humblest of duties. Fairfield had the weakness or madness, absurdly thought to belong to the poetical character, which unfitted him for an honourable and distinguished life. He needed, besides his "some learning and more feeling," a strong will and good sense, to be either great or useful.

* Mr. Fairfield accused Sir Edward Bulwer Lytton of founding on this poem his romance of the "Last Days of Pompeii."

DESTRUCTION OF POMPEII.*

A roar, as if a myriad thunders burst,
Now hurtled o'er the heavens, and the deep earth
Shudder'd, and a thick storm of lava hail
Rush'd into air, to fall upon the world.
And low the lion cower'd, with fearful moans
And upturn'd eyes, and quivering limbs, and clutch'd
The gory sand instinctively in fear.
The very soul of silence died, and breath
Through the ten thousand pallid lips, unfelt,
Stole from the stricken bosoms; and there stood,
With face uplifted, and eyes fix'd on air,
(Which unto him was throng'd with angel forms,)
The Christian—waiting the high will of Heaven.
A wandering sound of wailing agony,
A cry of coming horror, o'er the street
Of tombs arose, and all the lurid air
Echo'd the shrieks of hopelessness and death.
"Hear ye not now?" said Pansa. Death is here!
Ye saw the avalanche of fire descend
Vesuvian steeps, and, in its giant strength
Sweep on to Herculaneum; and ye cried,
'It threats not us: why should we lose the sport?
Though thousands perish, why should we refrain?'
Your sister city—the most beautiful—
Gasps in the burning ocean—from her domes
Fly the survivors of her people, driven
Before the torrent-floods of molten earth,
With desolation red—and o'er her grave
Unearthly voices raise the heart's last cries—
'Fly, fly! O, horror! O, my son! my sire!'
The hoarse shouts multiply; without the mount
Are agony and death—within, such rage
Of fossil fire as man may not behold!
Hark! the destroyer slumbers not—and now,
Be your theologies but true, your Jove,
Mid all his thunders, would shrink back aghast,
Listening the horrors of the Titan's strife.
The lion trembles; will ye have my blood,
Or flee, ere Herculaneum's fate is yours?"
Vesuvius answer'd: from its pinnacles
Clouds of far-flashing cinders, lava showers,
And seas, drank up by the abyss of fire,
To be hurl'd forth in boiling cataracts,
Like midnight mountains, wrapp'd in lightnings, fell.
O, then, the love of life! the struggling rush,
The crushing conflict of escape! few, brief,
And dire the words delirious fear spake now,—
One thought, one action sway'd the tossing crowd.
All through the vomitories madly sprung,
And mass on mass of trembling beings press'd,
Gasping and goading, with the savageness
That is the child of danger, like the waves
Charybdis from his jagged rocks throws down,
Mingled in madness—warring in their wrath.
Some swoon'd, and were trod down by legion feet;
Some cried for mercy to the unanswering gods;
Some shriek'd for parted friends, forever lost;
And some, in passion's chaos, with the yells
Of desperation, did blaspheme the heavens;
And some were still in utterness of wo.
Yet all toil'd on in trembling waves of life
Along the subterranean corridors.
Moments were centuries of doubt and dread;
Each breathing obstacle a hated thing;
Each trampled wretch a footstool to o'erlook
The foremost multitudes; and terror, now,
Begat in all a maniac ruthlessness,—
For, in the madness of their agonies,
Strong men cast down the feeble, who delay'd
Their flight; and maidens on the stones were crush'd,
And mothers madden'd when the warrior's heel
Pass'd o'er the faces of their sons! The throng
Press'd on, and in the ampler arcades now
Beheld, as floods of human life roll'd by,
The uttermost terrors of the destined hour.
In gory vapours the great sun went down;
The broad, dark sea heaved like the dying heart,
'Tween earth and heaven hovering o'er the grave
And moan'd through all its waters; every dome
And temple, charr'd and choked with ceaseless showers
Of suffocating cinders, seem'd the home
Of the triumphant desolator, Death.
One dreadful glance sufficed,—and to the sea,
Like Lybian winds, breathing despair, they fled.
Nature's quick instinct, in most savage beasts,
Prophesies danger ere man's thought awakes,
And shrinks in fear from common savageness,
Made gentle by its terror; thus, o'erawed,
E'en in his famine's fury, by a Power
Brute beings more than human oft adore,
The lion lay, his quivering paws outspread,
His white teeth gnashing, till the crushing throngs
Had pass'd the corridors; then, glaring up,
His eyes imbued with samiel light, he saw
The crags and forests of the Apennines
Gleaming far off, and, with the exulting sense
Of home and lone dominion, at a bound
He leap'd the lofty palisades, and sprung
Along the spiral passages, with howls
Of horror, through the flying multitudes,
Flying to seek his lonely mountain-lair.
From every cell shrieks burst; hyenas cried,
Like lost child, wandering o'er the wilderness,
That, in deep loneliness, mingles its voice
With wailing winds and stunning waterfalls;
The giant elephant, with matchless strength,
Struggled against the portal of his tomb,
And groan'd and panted; and the leopard's yell,
And tiger's growl, with all surrounding cries
Of human horror mingled; and in air,
Spotting the lurid heavens and waiting prey,
The evil birds of carnage hung and watch'd,
As ravening heirs watch o'er the miser's couch.
All awful sounds of heaven and earth met now;
Darkness behind the sun-god's chariot roll'd,
Shrouding destruction, save when volcan fires
Lifted the folds, to glare on agony;
And, when a moment's terrible repose
Fell on the deep convulsions, all could hear
The toppling cliffs explode and crash below,—
While multitudinous waters from the sea
In whirlpools through the channel'd mountain rocks
Rush'd, and, with hisses like the damned's speech,
Fell in the mighty furnace of the mount.

* From "The Last Night of Pompeii." This scene follows the destruction of Herculaneum. Pansa, a Christian, condemned by Diomede, is brought into the gladiatorial arena, when a new eruption from Vesuvius causes a suspension of the proceedings.

VISIONS OF ROMANCE.

When dark-brow'd midnight o'er the slumbering world
Mysterious shadows and bewildering throws,
And the tired wings of human thought are furl'd,
And sleep descends, like dew upon the rose,—
How full of bliss the poet's vigil hour,
When o'er him elder time hath magic power!

Before his eye past ages stand reveal'd,
When feudal chiefs held lordly banquettings,
In the spoils revelling of flood and field,
Among their vassals proud, unquestion'd kings:
While honour'd minstrels round the ample board
The lays of love or songs of battle pour'd.

The dinted helmet, with its broken crest,
The serried sabre, and the shatter'd shield
Hung round the wainscot, dark, and well express'd
That wild, fierce pride, which scorn'd, unscathed, to yield;
The pictures there, with dusky glory rife,
From age to age bore down stern characters of strife.

Amid long lines of glorious ancestry,
Whose eyes flash'd o'er them from the gray, old walls,
What craven quails at Danger's lightning eye?
What warrior blenches when his brother falls?
Bear witness Cressy and red Agincourt!
Bosworth, and Bannockburn, and Marston Moor!

The long, lone corridors, the antler'd hall,
The massive walls, the all-commanding towers—
Where revel reign'd, and masquerading ball,
And beauty won stern warriors to her bowers—
In ancient grandeur o'er the spirit move,
With all their forms of chivalry and love.

The voice of centuries bursts upon the soul;
Long-buried ages wake and live again;
Past feats of fame and deeds of glory roll,
Achieved for ladye-love in knighthood's reign;
And all the simple state of olden time
Assumes a garb majestic and sublime.

The steel-clad champion on his vaulting steed,
The mitred primate, and the Norman lord,
The peerless maid, awarding valour's meed,
And the meek vestal, who her God adored—
The pride, the pomp, the power and charm of earth
From fancy's dome of living thought come forth.

The feast is o'er, the huntsman's course is done,
The trump of war, the shrill horn sounds no more;
The heroic revellers from the hall have gone,
The lone blast moans the ruin'd castle o'er!
The spell of beauty, and the pride of power
Have pass'd forever from the feudal tower.

No more the drawbridge echoes to the tread
Of visor'd knights, o'ercanopied with gold;
O'er mouldering gates and crumbling archways spread,
Dark ivy waves in many a mazy fold,
Where chiefs flash'd vengeance from their lightning glance,
And grasp'd the brand, and couch'd the conquering lance.

The gorgeous pageantry of times gone by,
The tilt, the tournament, the vaulted hall,
Fades in its glory on the spirit's eye,
And fancy's bright and gay creations—all
Sink into dust, when reason's searching glance
Unmasks the age of knighthood and romance.

Like lightning hurtled o'er the lurid skies,
Their glories flash along the gloom of years;
The beacon-lights of time, to wisdom's eyes,
O'er the deep-rolling stream of human tears.
Fade! fade! ye visions of antique romance!
Tower, casque, and mace, and helm, and banner'd lance!

AN EVENING SONG OF PIEDMONT.

Ave Maria! 't is the midnight hour,
The starlight wedding of the earth and heaven,
When music breathes its perfume from the flower,
And high revealings to the heart are given;
Soft o'er the meadows steals the dewy air—
Like dreams of bliss; the deep-blue ether glows,
And the stream murmurs round its islets fair
The tender night-song of a charm'd repose.

Ave Maria! 't is the hour of love,
The kiss of rapture, and the link'd embrace,
The hallow'd converse in the dim, still grove,
The elysium of a heart-revealing face,
When all is beautiful—for we are bless'd,
When all is lovely—for we are beloved,
When all is silent—for our passions rest,
When all is faithful—for our hopes are proved.

Ave Maria! 't is the hour of prayer,
Of hush'd communion with ourselves and Heaven,
When our waked hearts their inmost thoughts declare,
High, pure, far-searching, like the light of even;
When hope becomes fruition, and we feel
The holy earnest of eternal peace,
That bids our pride before the Omniscient kneel,
That bids our wild and warring passions cease.

Ave Maria! soft the vesper hymn
Floats through the cloisters of yon holy pile,
And, mid the stillness of the night-watch dim,
Attendant spirits seem to hear and smile!
Hark! hath it ceased? The vestal seeks her cell,
And reads her heart—a melancholy tale!
A song of happier years, whose echoes swell
O'er her lost love, like pale bereavement's wail.

Ave Maria! let our prayers ascend
From them whose holy offices afford
No joy in heaven—on earth without a friend
That true, though faded image of the Lord!
For them in vain the face of nature glows,
For them in vain the sun in glory burns,
The hollow breast consumes in fiery woes,
And meets despair and death where'er it turns.

Ave Maria! in the deep pine wood,
On the clear stream, and o'er the azure sky
Bland midnight smiles, and starry solitude
Breathes hope in every breeze that wanders by.
Ave Maria! may our last hour come
As bright, as pure, as gentle, Heaven! as this!
Let faith attend us smiling to the tomb,
And life and death are both the heirs of bliss!

RUFUS DAWES.

[Born 1803. Died 1859.]

The family of the author of "Geraldine" is one of the most ancient and respectable in Massachusetts. His ancestors were among the earliest settlers of Boston; and his grandfather, as president of the Council, was for a time acting governor of the state, on the death of the elected chief magistrate. His father, Thomas Dawes, was for ten years one of the associate judges of the Supreme Court of Massachusetts, and was distinguished among the advocates of the Federal Constitution, in the state convention called for its consideration. He was a sound lawyer, a man of great independence of character, and was distinguished for the brilliancy of his wit, and for many useful qualities.*

Rufus Dawes was born in Boston, on the twenty-sixth of January, 1803, and was the youngest but one of sixteen children. He entered Harvard College in 1820; but in consequence of class disturbances, and insubordination, of which it was afterward shown he was falsely accused, he was compelled to leave that institution without a degree. This indignity he retaliated by a severe satire on the most prominent members of the faculty—the first poem he ever published. He then entered the office of General William Sullivan, as a law-student, and was subsequently admitted a member of the Suffolk county bar. He has howewer never pursued the practice of the legal profession, having been attracted by other pursuits more congenial with his feelings.

In 1829 he was married to the third daughter of Chief Justice Cranch, of Washington. In 1830 he published "The Valley of the Nashaway, and other Poems," some of which had appeared originally in the Cambridge "United States Literary Gazette;" and in 1839, "Athenia of Damascus," "Geraldine," and his miscellaneous poetical writings. His last work, "Nix's Mate," an historical romance, appeared in the following year.

With Mr. Dawes poetry seems to have been a passion, which is fast subsiding and giving place to a love of philosophy. He has been said to be a disciple of Coleridge, but in reality is a devoted follower of Swedenborg; and to this influence must be ascribed the air of mysticism which pervades his later productions. He has from time to time edited several legal, literary, and political works, and in the last has shown himself to be an adherent to the principles of the old Federal party. As a poet, his standing is yet unsettled, there being a wide difference of opinion respecting his writings. His versification is generally easy and correct, and in some pieces he exhibits considerable imagination.

In the winter of 1840–41, he delivered a course of lectures in the city of New York, before the American Institute, in which he combated the principles of the French eclectics and the Transcendentalists, contending that their philosophy is only a sublimated natural one, and very far removed from the true system of causes, and genuine spirituality.

LANCASTER.

The Queen of May has bound her virgin brow,
And hung with blossoms every fruit-tree bough;
The sweet Southwest, among the early flowers,
Whispers the coming of delighted hours,
While birds within the heaping foliage, sing
Their music-welcome to returning Spring.
O, Nature! loveliest in thy green attire—
Dear mother of the passion-kindling lyre;
Thou who, in early days, upled'st me where
The mountains freeze above the summer air;
Or luredst my wandering way beside the streams,
To watch the bubbles as they mock'd my dreams,
Lead me again thy flowery paths among,
To sing of native scenes as yet unsung!
Dear Lancaster! thy fond remembrance brings
Thoughts, like the music of Æolian strings,
When the hush'd wind breathes only as it sleeps,
While tearful Love his anxious vigil keeps:—
When press'd with grief, or sated with the show
That Pleasure's pageant offers here below,
Midst scenes of heartless mirth or joyless glee,
How oft my aching heart has turn'd to thee,
And lived again, in memory's sweet recess,
The innocence of youthful happiness!
In life's dull dream, when want of sordid gain
Clings to our being with its cankering chain,
When lofty thoughts are cramp'd to stoop below
The vile, rank weeds that in their pathway grow,
Who would not turn amidst the darken'd scene,
To memoried spots where sunbeams intervene;
And dwell with fondness on the joyous hours,
When youth built up his pleasure-dome of flowers?
Now, while the music of the feather'd choir
Rings where the sheltering blossoms wake desire,
When dew-eyed Love looks tenderness, and speaks
A silent language with his mantling cheeks;
I think of those delicious moments past,
Which joyless age shall dream of to the last

* He is classed by Mr. Kettell among the American poets; and in the Book of "Specimens" published by him are given some passages of his "Law given on Sinai," published in Boston in 1777.

As now, though far removed, the Muse would tell,
Though few may listen, what she loved so well.
Dear hours of childhood, youth's propitious spring,
When Time fann'd only roses with his wing,
When dreams, that mock reality, could move
To yield an endless holiday to Love,
How do ye crowd upon my fever'd brain,
And, in imagination, live again!
Lo! I am with you now, the sloping green,
Of many a sunny hill is freshly seen;
Once more the purple clover bends to meet,
And shower their dew-drops on the pilgrim's feet;
Once more he breathes the fragrance of your fields,
Once more the orchard tree its harvest yields,
Again he hails the morning from your hills,
And drinks the cooling water of your rills,
While, with a heart subdued, he feels the power
Of every humble shrub and modest flower.
O thou who journeyest through that Eden-clime,
Winding thy devious way to cheat the time,
Delightful Nashaway! beside thy stream,
Fain would I paint thy beauties as they gleam.
Eccentric river! poet of the woods!
Where, in thy far secluded solitudes,
The wood-nymphs sport and naiads plash thy wave,
With charms more sweet than ever Fancy gave;
How oft with Mantua's bard, from school let free,
I've conn'd the silver lines that flow like thee,
Couch'd on thy emerald banks, at full length laid,
Where classic elms grew lavish of their shade,
Or indolently listen'd, while the throng
Of idler beings woke their summer song;
Or, with rude angling gear, outwatched the sun,
Comparing mine to deeds by WALTON done,
Far down the silent stream, where arching trees
Bend their green boughs so gently to the breeze,
One live, broad mass of molten crystal lies,
Clasping the mirror'd beauties of the skies!
Look, how the sunshine breaks upon the plains!
So the deep blush their flatter'd glory stains.
Romantic river! on thy quiet breast,
While flash'd the salmon with his lightning crest,
Not long ago, the Indian's thin canoe
Skimm'd lightly as the shadow which it threw;
Not long ago, beside thy banks of green,
The night-fire blazed and spread its dismal sheen.
Thou peaceful valley! when I think how fair
Thy various beauty shines, beyond compare,
I cannot choose but own the Power that gave
Amidst thy woes a helping hand to save,
When o'er thy hills the savage war-whoop came,
And desolation raised its funeral flame!
'Tis night! the stars are kindled in the sky,
And hunger wakes the famished she-wolf's cry,
While, o'er the crusted snow, the careful tread
Betrays the heart whose pulses throb with dread;
Yon flickering light, kind beacon of repose!
The weary wanderer's homely dwelling shows,
Where, by the blazing fire, his bosom's joy
Holds to her heart a slumbering infant boy;
While every sound her anxious bosom moves,
She starts and listens for the one she loves;—
Hark! was't the night-bird's cry that met her ear,
Curdling the blood that thickens with cold fear?—
"Again, O God! that voice,—'tis his! 'tis his!"
She hears the death-shriek and the arrow's whiz,
When, as she turns, she sees the bursting door
Roll her dead husband bleeding on the floor.
Loud as the burst of sudden thunder, rose
The maddening war-cry of the ambush'd foes;
Startling in sleep, the dreamless infant wakes,
Like morning's smile when daylight's slumber breaks;
"For mercy! spare my child, forbear the blow!"
In vain;—the warm blood crimsons on the snow.
O'er the cold earth the captive mother sighs,
Her ears still tortured by her infant's cries;
She cannot weep, but deep resolve, unmoved,
Plots vengeance for the victims so beloved;
Lo! by their fire the glutted warriors lie,
Locked in the death-sleep of ebriety,
When from her bed of snow, whence slumber flew,
The frenzied woman rose the deed to do;—
Firmly beside the senseless men of blood,
With vengeful arm, the wretched mother stood;
She hears her groaning, dying lord expire,
Her woman's heart nerves up with maddening fire,
She sees her infant dashed against the tree,—
'Tis done!—the red men sleep eternally.
Such were thy wrongs, sweet Lancaster! but now,
No spot so peaceful and serene as thou;
Thy hills and fields in checker'd richness stand,
The glory and the beauty of the land.
From calm repose, while glow'd the eastern sky,
And the fresh breeze went fraught with fragrance by,
Waked by the noisy woodbird, free from care,
What joy was mine to drink the morning air!
Not all the bliss maturer life can bring,
When ripen'd manhood soars with strengthen'd wing,—
Not all the rapture Fancy ever wove,
Nor less than that which springs from mutual love,
Could challenge mine, when to the ravish'd sense
The sunrise painted GOD's magnificence!
George-hill, thou pride of Nashaway, for thee,—
Thyself the garden of fertility,—
Nature has hung a picture to the eye,
Where Beauty smiles at sombre Majesty.
The river winding in its course below,
Through fertile fields where yellowing harvests grow,
The bowering elms that so majestic grew,
A green arcade for waves to wander through;
The deep, broad valley, where the new-mown hay
Loads the fresh breezes of the rising day,
And, distant far, Wachusett's towering height,
Blue in the lingering shadows of the night,
Have power to move the sternest heart to love,
That Nature's loveliness could ever move.
Ye who can slumber when the starlight fades,
And clouds break purpling through the eastern shades,
Whose care-worn spirits cannot wake at morn,
To lead your buoyant footsteps o'er the lawn,
Can never know what joy the ravish'd sense
Feels in that moment's sacred influence.
I will not ask the meed of fortune's smile,
The flatterer's praise, that masks his heart of guile,
So I can walk beneath the ample sky,
And hear the birds' discordant melody,

And see reviving Spring, and Summer's gloom,
And Autumn bending o'er his icy tomb,
And hoary Winter pile his snowy drifts;
For these to me are Fortune's highest gifts;
And I have found in poor, neglected flowers,
Companionship for many weary hours;
And high above the mountain's crest of snow,
Communed with storm-clouds in their wrath below;
And where the vault of heaven, from some vast height
Grew black, as fell the shadows of the night,
Where the stars seem to come to you, I've woo'd
The grandeur of the fearful solitude.
From such communion, feelings often rise,
To guard the heart midst life's perplexities,
Lighting a heaven within, whose deep-felt joy
Compensates well for Sorrow's dark alloy.
Then, though the worldly chide, and wealth deny,
And passion conquer where it fain would fly,
Though friends you love betray, while these are left,
The heart can never wholly be bereft.
Hard by yon giant elm, whose branches spread
A rustling robe of leaves above your head;
Where weary travellers, from noonday heat,
Beneath the hospitable shade retreat,
The school-house met the stranger's busy eye,
Who turned to gaze again, he knew not why.
Thrice lovely spot! where, in the classic spring,
My young ambition dipp'd her fever'd wing,
And drank unseen the vision and the fire
That break with quenchless glory from the lyre!
Amidst thy wealth of art, fair Italy!
While Genius warms beneath thy cloudless sky,
As o'er the waking marble's polished mould
The sculptor breathes PYGMALION's prayer of old,
His heart shall send a frequent sigh to rove,
A pilgrim to the birth-place of his love!
And can I e'er forget that hallowed spot,
Whence springs a charm that may not be forgot;
Where, in a grove of elm and sycamore,
The pastor show'd his hospitable door,
And kindness shone so constantly to bless
That sweet abode of peace and happiness?
The oaken bucket—where I stoop'd to drink
The crystal water, trembling at the brink,
Which through the solid rock in coldness flow'd,
While creaked the ponderous lever with its load;
The dairy—where so many moments flew,
With half the dainties of the soil in view; [care,
Where the broad pans spread out the milkmaid's
To feed the busy churn that labour'd there;
The garden—where such neatness met the eye,
A stranger could not pass unheeding by;
The orchard—and the yellow-mantled fields,
Each in its turn some dear remembrance yields.
Ye who can mingle with the glittering crowd,
Where Mammon struts in rival splendour proud;
Who pass your days in heartless fashion's round,
And bow with hatred, where ye fear to wound;
Away! no flatterer's voice, nor coward's sneer,
Can find a welcome, or an altar here.
But ye who look beyond the common ken,
Self-unexalted when ye judge of men,
Who, conscious of defects, can hurry by
Faults that lay claim upon your charity;
Who feel that thrilling vision of the soul
Which looks through faith beyond an earthly goal,
And will not yet refuse the homely care
Which every being shares, or ought to share;
Approach! the home of Goodness is your own,
And such as ye are worthy, such alone.
When silence hung upon the Sabbath's smile,
And noiseless footsteps paced the sacred aisle,
When hearts united woke the suppliant lay,
And happy faces bless'd the holy day;
O, Nature! could thy worshipper have own'd
Such joy, as then upon his bosom throned;
When feelings, even as the printless snow,
Were harmless, guileless as a child can know;
Or, if they swerved from right, were pliant still,
To follow Virtue from the path of ill?
No! when the morning's old, the mist will rise
To cloud the fairest vision of our eyes;
As hopes too brightly formed in rainbow dyes,
A moment charm—then vanish in the skies!
Sweet hour of holy rest, to mortals given,
To paint with love the fairest way to heaven;
When from the sacred book instruction came
With fervid eloquence and kindling flame.
No mystic rites were there; to GOD alone
Went up the grateful heart before his throne,
While solemn anthems from the organ pour'd
Thanksgiving to the high and only LORD.
Lo! where yon cottage whitens through the green.
The loveliest feature of a matchless scene;
Beneath its shading elm, with pious fear,
An aged mother draws her children near;
While from the Holy Word, with earnest air,
She teaches them the privilege of prayer.
Look! how their infant eyes with rapture speak;
Mark the flush'd lily on the dimpled cheek;
Their hearts are filled with gratitude and love,
Their hopes are center'd in a world above,
Where, in a choir of angels, faith portrays
The loved, departed father of their days.
Beside yon grassless mound, a mourner kneels,
There gush no tears to soothe the pang he feels;
His loved, his lost, lies coffin'd in the sod,
Whose soul has found a dwelling-place with GOD!
Though press'd with anguish, mild religion shows
His aching heart a balm for all its woes;
And hope smiles upward, where his love shall find
A union in eternity of mind!
Turn there your eyes, ye cold, malignant crew,
Whose vile ambition dims your reason's view,
Ye faithless ones, who preach religion vain,
And, childlike, chase the phantoms of your brain;
Think not to crush the heart whose truth has
Its confidence in heavenly love reveal'd. [seal'd
Let not the atheist deem that Fate decrees
The lot of man to misery or ease,
While to the contrite spirit faith is given,
To find a hope on earth, a rest in heaven.
Unrivall'd Nashaway! where the willows throw
Their frosted beauty on thy path below,
Beneath the verdant drapery of the trees,
Luxuriant Fancy woos the sighing breeze.
The redbreast singing where the fruit-tree weaves
Its silken canopy of mulb'ry leaves;

Enamell'd fields of green, where herding kine
Crop the wet grass, or in the shade recline;
The tapping woodbird, and the minstrel bee,
The squirrel racing on his moss-grown tree,
With clouds of pleasant dreams, demand in vain
Creative thought to give them life again.
I turn where, glancing down, the eye surveys
Art building up the wreck of other days;
For graves of silent tribes upheave the sod,
And Science smiles where savage Philip trod;
Where wing'd the poison'd shaft along the skies,
The hammer rings, the noisy shuttle flies;
Impervious forests bow before the blade,
And fields rise up in yellow robes array'd.
No lordly palace nor imperial seat
Grasps the glad soil where freemen plant their feet;
No ruin'd castle here with ivy waves,
To make us blush for ancestry of slaves;
But, lo! unnumber'd dwellings meet the eye,
Where men lie down in native majesty:
The morning birds spring from their leafy bed,
As the stern ploughman quits his happy shed;
His arm is steel'd to toil—his heart to bear
The robe of pain, that mortals always wear;
Though wealth may never come, a plenteous board
Smiles at the pamper'd rich man's joyless hoard;
True, when among his sires, no gilded heir
Shall play the fool, and damn himself to care,
But Industry and Knowledge lead the way,
Where Independence braves the roughest day.
Nurse of my country's infancy, her stay
In youthful trials and in danger's day;
Diffusive Education! 'tis to thee
She owes her mountain-breath of Liberty;
To thee she looks, through time's illusive gloom,
To light her path, and shield her from the tomb;
Beneath thine Ægis tyranny shall fail,
Before thy frown the traitor's heart shall quail;
Ambitious foes to liberty may wear
A patriot mask, to compass what they dare,
And sting the thoughtless nation, while they smile
Benignantly and modestly the while;
But thou shalt rend the virtuous-seeming guise,
And guard her from the worst of enemies.
Eternal Power! whose tempted thunder sleeps,
While heaven-eyed Mercy turns away and weeps;
Thou who didst lead our fathers where to send
Their free devotions to their God and friend;
Thou who hast swept a wilderness away,
That men may walk in freedom's cloudless day;
Guard well their trust, lest impious faction dare
Unlock the chain that binds our birthright fair;
That private views to public good may yield,
And honest men stand fearless in the field!
Once more I turn to thee, fair Nashaway!
The farewell tribute of my humble lay;
The time may come, when lofty notes shall bear
Thy peerless beauty to the gladden'd air;
Now to the lyre no daring hand aspires,
And rust grows cankering on its tuneless wires.
Our lays are like the fitful streams that flow
From careless birds, that carol as they go;
Content, beneath the mountain-top to sing,
And only touch Castalia with a wing.

ANNE BOLEYN.

I weep while gazing on thy modest face,
Thou pictured history of woman's love!
Joy spreads his burning pinions on thy cheek,
Shaming its whiteness; and thine eyes are full
Of conscious beauty, as they undulate.
Yet all thy beauty, poor, deluded girl!
Served but to light thy ruin.—Is there not,
Kind Heaven! some secret talisman of hearts,
Whereby to find a resting-place for love?
Unhappy maiden! let thy story teach
The beautiful and young, that while their path
Softens with roses,—danger may be there;
That Love may watch the bubbles of the stream,
But never trust his image on the wave.

SUNRISE,

FROM MOUNT WASHINGTON.

The laughing hours have chased away the night,
Plucking the stars out from her diadem:—
And now the blue-eyed Morn, with modest grace,
Looks through her half-drawn curtains in the east,
Blushing in smiles and glad as infancy.
And see, the foolish Moon, but now so vain
Of borrow'd beauty, how she yields her charms,
And, pale with envy, steals herself away!
The clouds have put their gorgeous livery on,
Attendant on the day—the mountain-tops
Have lit their beacons, and the vales below
Send up a welcoming;—no song of birds,
Warbling to charm the air with melody,
Floats on the frosty breeze; yet Nature hath
The very soul of music in her looks!
The sunshine and the shade of poetry.
I stand upon thy lofty pinnacle,
Temple of Nature! and look down with awe
On the wide world beneath me, dimly seen;
Around me crowd the giant sons of earth,
Fixed on their old foundations, unsubdued;
Firm as when first rebellion bade them rise
Unrifted to the Thunderer—now they seem
A family of mountains, clustering round
Their hoary patriarch, emulously watching
To meet the partial glances of the day.
Far in the glowing east the flickering light,
Mellow'd by distance, with the blue sky blending
Questions the eye with ever-varying forms.
The sun comes up! away the shadows fling
From the broad hills—and, hurrying to the west
Sport in the sunshine, till they die away.
The many beauteous mountain-streams leap down,
Out-welling from the clouds, and sparkling light
Dances along with their perennial flow.
And there is beauty in yon river's path,
The glad Connecticut! I know her well,
By the white veil she mantles o'er her charms:
At times, she loiters by a ridge of hills,
Sportfully hiding—then again with glee
Out-rushes from her wild-wood lurking-place.
Far as the eye can bound, the ocean-waves,
And hills and rivers, mountains, lakes and woods,
And all that hold the faculty entranced,

Bathed in a flood of glory, float in air,
And sleep in the deep quietude of joy.
There is an awful stillness in this place,
A Presence, that forbids to break the spell,
Till the heart pour its agony in tears.
But I must drink the vision while it lasts;
For even now the curling vapours rise,
Wreathing their cloudy coronals to grace
These towering summits—bidding me away;—
But often shall my heart turn back again,
Thou glorious eminence! and when oppress'd,
And aching with the coldness of the world,
Find a sweet resting-place and home with thee.

SPIRIT OF BEAUTY.

The Spirit of Beauty unfurls her light,
And wheels her course in a joyous flight;
I know her track through the balmy air,
By the blossoms that cluster and whiten there;
She leaves the tops of the mountains green,
And gems the valley with crystal sheen.

At morn, I know where she rested at night,
For the roses are gushing with dewy delight;
Then she mounts again, and round her flings
A shower of light from her crimson wings;
Till the spirit is drunk with the music on high,
That silently fills it with ecstasy.

At noon she hies to a cool retreat,
Where bowering elms over waters meet;
She dimples the wave where the green leaves dip,
As it smilingly curls like a maiden's lip,
When her tremulous bosom would hide, in vain,
From her lover, the hope that she loves again.

At eve she hangs o'er the western sky
Dark clouds for a glorious canopy,
And round the skirts of their deepen'd fold
She paints a border of purple and gold,
Where the lingering sunbeams love to stay,
When their god in his glory has passed away.

She hovers around us at twilight hour,
When her presence is felt with the deepest power;
She silvers the landscape, and crowds the stream
With shadows that flit like a fairy dream;
Then wheeling her flight through the gladden'd air,
The Spirit of Beauty is everywhere

LOVE UNCHANGEABLE.

Yes! still I love thee:—Time, who sets
His signet on my brow,
And dims my sunken eye, forgets
The heart he could not bow;—
Where love, that cannot perish, grows
For one, alas! that little knows
How love may sometimes last;
Like sunshine wasting in the skies,
When clouds are overcast.

The dew-drop hanging o'er the rose,
Within its robe of light,
Can never touch a leaf that blows,
Though *seeming* to the sight;
And yet it still will linger there,
Like hopeless love without despair,—
A snow-drop in the sun!
A moment finely exquisite,
Alas! but only one.

I would not have thy married heart
Think momently of me,—
Nor would I tear the cords apart,
That bind me so to thee;
No! while my thoughts seem pure and mild,
Like dew upon the roses wild,
I would not have thee know,
The stream that seems to thee so still,
Has such a tide below!

Enough! that in delicious dreams
I see thee and forget—
Enough, that when the morning beams,
I feel my eyelids wet!
Yet, could I hope, when Time shall fall
The darkness, for creation's pall,
To meet thee,—and to love,—
I would not shrink from aught below,
Nor ask for more above.

EXTRACT FROM "GERALDINE."

I know a spot where poets fain would dwell,
To gather flowers and food for afterthought,
As bees draw honey from the rose's cell,
To hive among the treasures they have wrought;
And there a cottage from a sylvan screen
Sent up its curling smoke amidst the green.

Around that hermit-home of quietude,
The elm trees whisper'd with the summer air,
And nothing ever ventured to intrude,
But happy birds, that caroll'd wildly there,
Or honey-laden harvesters, that flew
Humming away to drink the morning dew.

Around the door the honeysuckle climbed,
And Multa-flora spread her countless roses,
And never minstrel sang nor poet rhymed
Romantic scene where happiness reposes,
Sweeter to sense than that enchanting dell,
Where home-sick memory fondly loves to dwell

Beneath a mountain's brow the cottage stood,
Hard by a shelving lake, whose pebbled bed
Was skirted by the drapery of a wood,
That hung its festoon foliage over head,
Where wild deer came at eve, unharm'd, to drink,
While moonlight threw their shadows from the brink.

The green earth heaved her giant waves around,
Where through the mountain vista one vast height
Tower'd heavenward without peer, his forehead bound
With gorgeous clouds, at times of changeful light,
While far below, the lake, in bridal rest,
Slept with his glorious picture on her breast.

EDMUND D. GRIFFIN.

[Born, 1804. Died, 1830.]

Edmund Dorr Griffin was born in the celebrated valley of Wyoming, in Pennsylvania, on the tenth day of September, 1804. During his infancy his parents removed to New York, but on account of the delicacy of his constitution, he was educated, until he was twelve years old, at various schools in the country. He entered Columbia College, in New York, in 1819, and until he was graduated, four years afterwards, maintained the highest rank in the successive classes. During this period most of his Latin and English poems were composed. He was admitted to deacon's orders, in the Episcopal Church, in 1826, and after spending two years in the active discharge of the duties of his profession, set out on his travels. He passed through France, Italy, Switzerland, England, and Scotland, and returned to New York in the spring of 1830. He was then appointed an associate professor in Columbia College, but resigned the office after a few months, in consequence of ill health, and closed a life of successful devotion to learning, and remarkable moral purity, on the first day of September, in the same year. His travels in Europe, sermons, and miscellaneous writings were published in two large octavo volumes, in 1831.

LINES WRITTEN ON LEAVING ITALY.

"Deh! fossi tu men bella, o almen piu forte."—Filicaja.

Would that thou wert more strong, at least less fair,
Land of the orange grove and myrtle bower!
To hail whose strand, to breathe whose genial air,
Is bliss to all who feel of bliss the power;
To look upon whose mountains in the hour
When thy sun sinks in glory, and a veil
Of purple flows around them, would restore
The sense of beauty when all else might fail.

Would that thou wert more strong, at least less fair,
Parent of fruits, alas! no more of men!
Where springs the olive e'en from mountains bare,
The yellow harvests loads the scarce till'd plain.
Spontaneous shoots the vine, in rich festoon
From tree to tree depending, and the flowers
Wreathe with their chaplets, sweet though fading soon,
E'en fallen columns and decaying towers.

Would that thou wert more strong, at least less fair,
Home of the beautiful, but not the brave!
Where noble form, bold outline, princely air,
Distinguish e'en the peasant and the slave:
Where, like the goddess sprung from ocean's wave,
Her mortal sisters boast immortal grace,
Nor spoil those charms which partial Nature gave,
By art's weak aids or fashion's vain grimace.

Would that thou wert more strong, at least less fair,
Thou nurse of every art, save one alone,
The art of self-defence! Thy fostering care
Brings out a nobler life from senseless stone,
And bids e'en canvass speak; thy magic tone,
Infused in music, now constrains the soul
With tears the power of melody to own,
And now with passionate throbs that spurn control.

Would that thou wert less fair, at least more strong,
Grave of the mighty dead, the living mean!
Can nothing rouse ye both? no tyrant's wrong,
No memory of the brave, of what has been!
Yon broken arch once spoke of triumph, then
That mouldering wall too spoke of brave defence:
Shades of departed heroes, rise again!
Italians, rise, and thrust the oppressors hence!

O, Italy! my country, fare thee well!
For art thou not my country, at whose breast
Were nurtured those whose thoughts within me dwell,
The fathers of my mind? whose fame impress'd
E'en on my infant fancy, bade it rest
With patriot fondness on thy hills and streams,
E'er yet thou didst receive me as a guest,
Lovelier than I had seen thee in my dreams?

Then fare thee well, my country, loved and lost:
Too early lost, alas! when once so dear;
I turn in sorrow from thy glorious coast,
And urge the feet forbid to linger here.
But must I rove by Arno's current clear,
And hear the rush of Tiber's yellow flood,
And wander on the mount, now waste and drear,
Where Cæsar's palace in its glory stood;

And see again Parthenope's loved bay,
And Paestum's shrines, and Baiae's classic shore,
And mount the bark, and listen to the lay
That floats by night through Venice—never more?
Far off I seem to hear the Atlantic roar—
It washes not thy feet, that envious sea,
But waits, with outstretch'd arms, to waft me o'er
To other lands, far, far, alas, from thee.

Fare—fare thee well once more. I love thee not
As other things inanimate. Thou art
The cherish'd mistress of my youth; forgot
Thou never canst be while I have a heart.
Launch'd on those waters, wild with storm and wind,
I know not, ask not, what may be my lot;
For, torn from thee, no fear can touch my mind,
Brooding in gloom on that one bitter thought.

DESCRIPTION OF LOVE, BY VENUS.

Though old in cunning, as in years,
He is so small, that like a child
In face and form, the god appears,
And sportive like a boy, and wild;
Lightly he moves from place to place,
In none at rest, in none content;
Delighted some new toy to chase—
On childish purpose ever bent.
Beware! to childhood's spirit gay
Is added more than childhood's power
And you perchance may rue the hour
That saw you join his seeming play.

He quick is anger'd, and as quick
His short-lived passion's over past,
Like summer lightnings, flashing thick,
But flying ere a bolt is cast.
I've seen, myself, as 'twere together,
Now joy, now grief assume its place,
Shedding a sort of April weather,
Sunshine and rain upon his face.
His curling hair floats on the wind,
Like Fortune's, long and thick before,
And rich and bright as golden ore:
Like hers, his head is bald behind.

His ruddy face is strangely bright,
It is the very hue of fire,
The inward spirit's quenchless light,
The glow of many a soft desire.
He hides his eye that keenly flashes,
But sometimes steals a thrilling glance
From 'neath his drooping silken lashes,
And sometimes looks with eye askance;
But seldom ventures he to gaze
With looks direct and open eye;
For well he knows—the urchin sly—
But one such look his guile betrays.

His tongue, that seems to have left just then
His mother's breast, discourses sweet,
And forms his lisping infant strain
In words scarce utter'd, half-complete;
Yet, wafted on a winged sigh,
And led by Flattery, gentle guide,
Unseen into the heart they fly,
Its coldness melt, and tame its pride.
In smiles that hide intended wo,
His ruddy lips are always dress'd,
As flowers conceal the listening crest
Of the coil'd snake that lurks below.

In carriage courteous, meek, and mild,
Humble in speech, and soft in look,
He seems a wandering orphan child,
And asks a shelter in some nook
Or corner left unoccupied:
But, once admitted as a guest,
By slow degrees he lays aside
That lowly port and look distress'd—
Then insolent assumes his reign,
Displays his captious, high-bred airs,
His causeless pets and jealous fears,
His fickle fancy and unquiet brain.

EMBLEMS.

Yon rose, that bows her graceful head to hail
The welcome visitant that brings the morn,
And spreads her leaves to gather from the gale
The coolness on its early pinions borne,
Listing the music of its whisper'd tale,
And giving stores of perfume in return—
Though fair she seem, full many a thorn doth hide;
Perhaps a worm pollutes her bosom's pride.

Yon oak, that proudly throws his arms on high,
Threshing the air that flies their frequent strokes,
And lifts his haughty crest towards the sky,
Daring the thunder that its height provokes,
And spreads his foliage wide, a shelter nigh,
From noonday heats to guard the weary flocks—
Though strong he seem, must dread the bursting storm,
And e'en the malice of the feeble worm.

The moon, that sits so lightly on her throne,
Gliding majestic on her silent way,
And sends her silvery beam serenely down,
'Mong waving boughs and frolic leaves to play,
To sleep upon the bank with moss o'ergrown,
Or on the clear waves, clearer far than they—
Seems purity itself; but if again
We look, and closely, we perceive a stain.

Fit emblems all, of those unworthy joys
On which our passions and our hopes dilate:
We wound ourselves to seize on Pleasure's toys,
Nor see their worthlessness until too late;
And Power, with all its pomp and all its noise,
Meets oft a sudden and a hapless fate;
And Fame of gentle deeds and daring high,
Is often stain'd by blots of foulest dye.

Where then shall man, by his Creator's hand
Gifted with feelings that must have an aim,
Aspiring thoughts and hopes, a countless band;
Affections glowing with a quenchless flame,
And passions, too, in dread array that stand,
To aid his virtue or to stamp his shame:
Where shall he fix a soul thus form'd and given?
Fix it on God, and it shall rise to Heaven.

TO A LADY.

Like target for the arrow's aim,
Like snow beneath the sunny heats,
Like wax before the glowing flame,
Like cloud before the wind that fleets,
I am—'tis love that made me so,
And, lady, still thou sayst me no.

The wound's inflicted by thine eyes,
The mortal wound to hope and me,
Which naught, alas, can cicatrize,
Nor time, nor absence, far from thee.
Thou art the sun, the fire, the wind,
That make me such; ah, then be kind!

My thoughts are darts, my soul to smite;
Thy charms the sun, to blind my sense,
My wishes—ne'er did passion light
A flame more pure or more intense.
Love all these arms at once employs,
And wounds, and dazzles, and destroys.

J. H. BRIGHT.

[Born, 1804. Died, 1837.]

Jonathan Huntington Bright was born in Salem, Massachusetts, in 1804. At an early age he went to New York, where he resided several years, after which he removed to Albany, and subsequently to Richmond, in Virginia, where he was married. In the autumn of 1836 he sailed for New Orleans, and soon after his arrival in that city was induced to ascend the Mississippi, to take part in a mercantile interest at Manchester, where he died, very suddenly, in the thirty-third year of his age. He was for several years a writer for the public journals and literary magazines, under the signature of "Viator." His poetry has never been published collectively.

THE VISION OF DEATH.

The moon was high in the autumn sky,
The stars waned cold and dim,
Where hoarsely the mighty Oregon
Peals his eternal hymn;
And the prairie-grass bent its seedy heads
Far over the river's brim.

An impulse I might not defy,
Constrain'd my footsteps there,
When through the gloom a red eye burn'd
With fix'd and steady glare;
And a huge, misshapen form of mist
Loom'd in the midnight air.

Then out it spake: "My name is Death!"
Thick grew my blood, and chill—
A sense of fear weigh'd down my breath,
And held my pulses still;
And a voice from that unnatural shade
Compell'd me to its will.

"Dig me a grave! dig me a grave!"
The gloomy monster said,
"And make it deep, and long, and wide,
And bury me my dead."
A corpse without sheet or shroud, at my feet,
And rusted mattock laid.

With trembling hand the tool I spann'd,
'T was wet with blood, and cold,
And from its slimy handle hung
The gray and ropy mould;
And I sought to detach my stiffen'd grasp,
But could not loose my hold.

"Now cautiously turn up the sod;
God's image once it bore,
And time shall be when each small blade
To life He will restore,
And the separate particles shall take
The shape which first they wore."

Deeply my spade the soft earth pierced,
It touch'd the festering dead;
Tier above tier the corpses lay,
As leaves in autumn shed;
The vulture circled, and flapp'd his wings,
And scream'd, above my head.

O, then I sought to rest my brow,
The spade I held, its prop;
"Toil on! toil on!" scream'd the ugly fiend,
"My servants never stop!
Toil on! toil on! at the judgment-day
Ye'll have a glorious crop!"

Now, wheresoe'er I turn'd my eyes,
'T was horrible to see
How the grave made bare her secret work,
And disclosed her depths to me;
While the ground beneath me heaved and roll'd
Like the billows of the sea.

The spectre skinn'd his yellow teeth—
"Ye like not this, I trow:
Six thousand years your fellow-man
Has counted me his foe,
And ever when he cursed I laugh'd,
And drew my fatal bow.

"And generations all untold
In this dark spot I've laid—
The forest ruler and the young
And tender Indian maid;
And moulders with their carcasses
Behemoth of the glade.

"Yet here they may no more remain;
I fain would have this room:
And they must seek another rest,
Of deeper, lonelier gloom;
Long ages since I mark'd this spot
To be the white man's tomb.

"Already his coming steps I hear,
From the east's remotest line,
While over his advancing hosts
The forward banners shine:
And where he builds his cities and towns,
I ever must build mine."

Anon a pale and silvery mist
Was girdled round the moon:
Slowly the dead unclosed their eyes,
On midnight's solemn noon.
"Ha!" mutter'd the mocking sprite, "I fear
We've waken'd them too soon!

"Now marshal all the numerous host
In one concentred band,

And hurry them to the west," said he,
"Where ocean meets the land:
They shall regard thy bidding voice,
And move at thy command."

Then first I spake—the sullen corpse
Stood on the gloomy sod,
Like the dry bones the prophet raised,
When bidden by his GOD;
A might company, so vast,
Each on the other trod.

They stalk'd erect as if alive,
Yet not to life allied,
But like the pestilence that walks,
And wasteth at noontide,
Corruption animated, or
The grave personified.

The earth-worm drew his slimy trail
Across the bloodless cheek,
And the carrion bird in hot haste came
To gorge his thirsty beak;
But, scared by the living banquet, fled,
Another prey to seek.

While ever as on their way they moved,
No voice they gave, nor sound,
And before and behind, and about their sides,
Their wither'd arms they bound;
As the beggar clasps his skinny hands
His tatter'd garments round.

On, on we went through the livelong night,
Death and his troop, and I;
We turn'd not aside for forest or stream
Or mountain towering high,
But straight and swift as the hurricane sweeps
Athwart the stormy sky.

Once, once I stopp'd, where something gleam'd,
With a bright and star-like ray,
And I stoop'd to take the diamond up
From the grass in which it lay;
'T was an eye that from its socket fell,
As some wretch toil'd on his way.

At length our army reach'd the verge
Of the far-off western shore;
Death drove them into the sea, and said,
"Ye shall remove no more."
The ocean hymn'd their solemn dirge,
And his waters swept them o'er.

The stars went out, the morning smiled
With rosy tints of light,
The bird began his early hymn,
And plumed his wings for flight:
And the vision of death was broken with
The breaking up of night.

HE WEDDED AGAIN.

ERE death had quite stricken the bloom from her cheek,
Or worn off the smoothness and gloss of her brow,
When our quivering lips her dear name could not speak,
And our hearts vainly strove to GOD's judgment to bow,
He estranged himself from us, and cheerfully then
Sought out a new object, and wedded again.

The dust had scarce settled itself on her lyre,
And its soft, melting tones still held captive the ear,
While we look'd for her fingers to glide o'er the wire,
And waited in fancy her sweet voice to hear;
He turn'd from her harp and its melody then,
Sought out a new minstrel and wedded again.

The turf had not yet by a stranger been trod,
Nor the pansy a single leaf shed on her grave,
The cypress had not taken root in the sod,
Nor the stone lost the freshness the sculptor first gave;
He turn'd from these mournful remembrances then,
Wove a new bridal chaplet, and wedded again.

His dwelling to us, O, how lonely and sad!
When we thought of the light death had stolen away,
Of the warm hearts which once in its keeping it had,
And that one was now widow'd and both in decay;
But its deep desolation had fled even then—
He sought a new idol, and wedded again.

But can *she* be quite blest who presides at his board?
Will no troublesome vision her happy home shade,
Of a future love luring and charming her lord,
When she with our lost one forgotten is laid?
She must know he will worship some other star then,
Seek out a new love, and be wedded again.

SONG.

SHOULD sorrow o'er thy brow
Its darken'd shadows fling,
And hopes that cheer thee now,
Die in their early spring;
Should pleasure at its birth
Fade like the hues of even,
Turn thou away from earth,—
There's rest for thee in heaven!

If ever life shall seem
To thee a toilsome way,
And gladness cease to beam
Upon its clouded day;
If, like the wearied dove,
O'er shoreless ocean driven,
Raise thou thine eye above,—
There's rest for thee in heaven!

But, O! if always flowers
Throughout thy pathway bloom,
And gayly pass the hours,
Undimm'd by earthly gloom;
Still let not every thought
To this poor world be given,
Not always be forgot
Thy better rest in heaven!

When sickness pales thy cheek,
And dims thy lustrous eye,
And pulses low and weak
Tell of a time to die—
Sweet hope shall whisper then
"Though thou from earth be riven,
There's bliss beyond thy ken,—
There's rest for thee in heaven!"

OTWAY CURRY.

(Born 1804. Died 1855.)

COLONEL JAMES CURRY of Virginia served in the continental army during the greater part of the revolutionary war, and was taken prisoner with the forces surrendered by General LINCOLN at Charleston in 1780. After the peace he emigrated to Ohio, distinguished himself in civil affairs, rose to be a judge, and was one of the electors of President who gave the vote of that state for JAMES MONROE. His son, OTWAY CURRY, was born in what is now Greenfield, Highland county, on the twenty-sixth of March, 1804, and having received such instruction as was offered in the common school, and declining an opportunity to study the law, he proceeded to Chilicothe, and there worked several years as a carpenter, improving his mind meanwhile by industrious but discursive reading during his leisure hours, so that at the end of his apprenticeship he had a familiar knowledge of the most popular contemporary literature, and a capacity for writing which was creditably illustrated from time to time in essays for the press.

He now removed to Cincinnati, where he found more profitable employment, and in 1827 published in the journals of that city, under the signature of "Abdallah," several poems which attracted considerable attention, and led to his acquaintance with WILLIAM D. GALLAGHER and other young men of congenial tastes. At this period he was a frequent player on the flute; his music, as well as his poetry, was pensive and dreamy; and his personal manners were singularly modest and engaging. On the seventeenth of December, 1828, the young carpenter was married, and setting out on his travels, he worked at various places in the lower part of the valley of the Mississippi, sending back occasional literary performances to his friends in Cincinnati, which kept alive their friendly interest, and greatly increased his good reputation.

Dissatisfied with his experiences in the South, he returned to Ohio, and for some time turned his attention to farming, in his native town. In 1836 and 1837 he was elected to the legislature, and while attending to his duties at Columbus engaged with Mr. GALLAGHER in the publication of "The Hesperian," a monthly magazine, of which the first number was issued in May, 1838. In 1839 he removed to Maysville, the seat of justice for Union county, where he was admitted to the bar. In 1842 he was again elected to the legislature, and during the session of the following winter, "The Hesperian" having been discontinued, purchased the "Torch Light," a newspaper printed at Xenia, Green county, which he edited two years, on the expiration of which he retired to Maysville, and entered upon the practice of the law. In 1850 he was chosen a member of the State Convention for forming a new Constitution, in 1851 he bought the "Scioto Gazette," a journal published at Chilicothe; and in the spring of 1854 returned again to Maysville, was made District Attorney, and in what seemed to be an opening career of success, died suddenly, on the fifteenth of February, 1855.

Mr. CURRY wrote much, in prose as well as in verse, and always with apparent sincerity and earnestness. He was many years an active member of the Methodist church, and his poems are frequently marked by a fine religious enthusiasm, which appears to have been as characteristic of his temper as their more strictly poetical qualities were of his intellect. In dying he remarked to a friend that one of his earliest compositions, entitled "Kingdom Come," embodied the belief and hope of his life and death.

THE GREAT HEREAFTER.*

'T IS sweet to think when struggling
The goal of life to win,
That just beyond the shores of time
The better years begin.

When through the nameless ages
I cast my longing eyes,
Before me, like a boundless sea,
The Great Hereafter lies.

Along its brimming bosom
Perpetual summer smiles;
And gathers, like a golden robe,
Around the emerald isles.

There in the blue long distance,
By lulling breezes fanned,
I seem to see the flowering groves
Of old Beulah's land.

And far beyond the islands
That gem the wave serene,
The image of the cloudless shore
Of holy Heaven is seen.

Unto the Great Hereafter—
Aforetime dim and dark—
I freely now and gladly give
Of life the wandering bark.

And in the far-off haven,
When shadowy seas are passed,
By angel hands its quivering sails
Shall all be furled at last!

* "IN the great hereafter I see the fulfilment of my desires. Yea, amid all this turmoil and humiliation I enter already upon its rest and glory."—*The Huguenot.*

KINGDOM COME.

I do not believe the sad story
  Of ages of sleep in the tomb;
I shall pass far away to the glory
  And grandeur of Kingdom Come.
The paleness of death, and its stillness,
  May rest on my brow for awhile;
And my spirit may lose in its chillness
  The splendour of hope's happy smile;

But the gloom of the grave will be transient,
  And light as the slumbers of worth;
And then I shall blend with the ancient
  And beautiful forms of the earth.
Through the climes of the sky, and the bowers
  Of bliss, evermore I shall roam,
Wearing crowns of the stars and the flowers
  That glitter in Kingdom Come.

The friends who have parted before me
  From life's gloomy passion and pain,
When the shadow of death passes o'er me
  Will smile on me fondly again.
Their voices are lost in the soundless
  Retreats of their endless home,
But soon we shall meet in the boundless
  Effulgence of Kingdom Come.

THE ARMIES OF THE EVE.

Not in the golden morning
  Shall faded forms return,
For languidly and dimly then
  The lights of memory burn:

Nor when the noon unfoldeth
  Its sunny light and smile,
For these unto their bright repose
  The wondering spirit wile:

But when the stars are wending
  Their radiant way on high,
And gentle winds are whispering back
  The music of the sky;

O, then those starry millions
  Their streaming banners weave,
To marshal on their wildering way
  The Armies of the Eve:

The dim and shadowy armies
  Of our unquiet dreams,
Whose footsteps brush the feathery fern
  And print the sleeping streams.

We meet them in the calmness
  Of high and holier climes;
We greet them with the blessed names
  Of old and happier times.

And, marching in the starlight
  Above the sleeping dust,
They freshen all the fountain-springs
  Of our undying trust.

Around our every pathway
  In beauteous ranks they roam,
To guide us to the dreamy rest
  Of our eternal home.

TO A MIDNIGHT PHANTOM.

Pale, melancholy one!
  Why art thou lingering here?
Memorial of dark ages gone,
  Herald of darkness near:
Thou stand'st immortal, undefiled—
Even thou, the unknown, the strange, the wild,
  Spell-word of mortal fear.

Thou art a shadowy form,
  A dreamlike thing of air;
My very sighs thy robes deform,
  So frail, so passing fair—
Thy crown is of the fabled gems,
The bright ephemeral diadems
  That unseen spirits wear.

Thou hast revealed to me
  The lore of phantom song,
With thy wild, fearful melody,
  Chiming the whole night long
Forebodings of untimely doom,
Of sorrowing years and dying gloom,
  And unrequited wrong.

Through all the dreary night,
  Thine icy hands, that now
Send to the brain their maddening blight,
  Have pressed upon my brow—
My phrenzied thoughts all wildly blend
With spell-wrought shapes that round me wend,
  Or down in mockery bow.

Away, pale form, away—
  The break of morn is nigh,
And far and dim, beyond the day
  The eternal night-glooms lie:
Art thou a dweller in the dread
Assembly of the mouldering dead,
  Or in the worlds on high?

Art thou of the blue waves,
  Or of yon starry clime—
An inmate of the ocean graves,
  Or of the heavens sublime?
Is thy mysterious place of rest
The eternal mansions of the blest,
  Or the dim shores of time?

Hast thou forever won
  A high and glorious name,
And proudly grasped and girdled on
  The panoply of fame—
Or wanderest thou on weary wing
A lonely and a nameless thing,
  Unchangingly the same?

Thou answerest not. The sealed
  And hidden things that lie
Beyond the grave, are unrevealed,
  Unseen by mortal eye—
Thy dreamy home is all unknown,
For spirits freed by death alone
  May win the viewless sky.

WILLIAM CROSWELL.

[Born, 1804. Died, 1851.]

WILLIAM CROSWELL was born at Hudson, in New York, on the seventh of November, 1804. His father, then editor of a literary and political journal, in a few years became a clergyman of the Episcopal church, and removed to New Haven, Connecticut, where the son was prepared for college by Mr. JOEL JONES, since well known as one of the justices of the Superior Court of Pennsylvania. He was graduated at New Haven, in 1822, and, with his brother SHERMAN, soon after opened a select school in that city, which was surrendered at the end of the second quarter, after which he passed nearly four years in desultory reading in the house of his father. An invitation to study medicine, with an uncle, was declined, partly from an unconquerable aversion to surgical exhibitions; and a short experience of the editorial profession, in the office of his cousin, Mr. EDWIN CROSWELL, of the Albany Argus, discouraged all thoughts of devotion to the press and to politics. In the summer before his twentieth birth-day, his reputation for talents was such that the public authorities of Hartford requested him to deliver an oration on the anniversary of the declaration of independence, and he accepted the invitation, substituting a poem of several hundred lines for a discourse in prose. In 1826, after much hesitation, arising from the modesty of his nature, and his sense of the dignity of the priestly office, he entered the General Theological Seminary of the Episcopal Church, in New York, and there, and subsequently under Bishop BROWNELL, in Hartford, pursued the usual course of professional studies, conducting meanwhile for two years, with Mr. DOANE, now Bishop of the Episcopal Church in New Jersey, a religious newspaper called "The Episcopal Watchman." An intimate friendship thus commenced between Mr. CROSWELL and Mr. DOANE, ended only with Mr. CROSWELL's life. "Man has never been in closer bonds with man," says the Bishop, in a discourse on his death, "than he with me, for five and twenty years."

Mr. DOANE having resigned his professorship in Washington College, Hartford, to become rector of Trinity church, in Boston, the editorship of the "Episcopal Watchman" was relinquished; and soon after Mr. CROSWELL received priest's orders, in 1829, he too went to Boston, where for eleven years he was settled as minister of Christ church. In this period he was a bachelor, and passing most of his time in "the cloister," a room fitted up in the rear of the church for his study, and at the Athenæum, attended with singular faithfulness to the duties of his calling, while he kept up a loving acquaintance with literature and art, and with a few men of congenial tastes and pursuits.

When Mr. DOANE became bishop of the Episcopal church in New Jersey, Boston no longer possessed its most agreeable charm for his friend, and he wrote:

"TO G. W. D.

"I miss thee at the morning tide,
The glorious hour of prime;
I miss thee more, when day has died,
At blessèd evening time.
As slide the aching hours away,
Still art thou unforgot;
Sleeping or waking, night and day,
When do I miss thee not?

"How can I pass that gladsome door,
Where every favorite room
Thy presence made so bright before
Is loneliness and gloom?—
Each place where most thou lov'dst to be,
Thy home, thy house of prayer,
Seem yearning for thy company:
I miss thee everywhere."

He also addressed the youthful bishop the following sonnet, which seems now to have had a sort of prophetic significance.

"AD AMICUM.

"Let no gainsaying lips despise thy youth;
Like his, the great Apostle's favorite son,
Whose early rule at Ephesus begun:
Thy Urim and thy Thummim—Light and Truth—
Be thy protection from the Holy One:
And for thy fiery trials, be there shed
A sevenfold grace on thine anointed head,
Till thy 'right onward' course shall all be run.
And when thy earthly championship is through,
Thy warfare fought, thy battle won,
And heaven's own palms of triumph bright in view,
May this thy thrilling welcome be: 'Well done!
Because thou hast been faithful over few,
A mightier rule be thine, O servant good and true.'"

In 1840 Mr. CROSWELL resigned the rectorship of Christ church in Boston, to accept that of St. Peter's, in Auburn, New York, where he remained four years, during which period he was married to an estimable woman of Boston; and this last circumstance was perhaps one of the causes of his return to that city, in 1844, though the chief cause was doubtless his sympathy with several of his old friends there as to those views which are known in the Episcopal church as "Tractarian." A new parish was organized, the church of the Advent was erected, and he became its rector, with a congregation in which were the venerable poet DANA, his son, the author of "Two Years before the Mast," and other persons of social and intellectual eminence. Of the unhappy controversy which ensued between the rector of the Advent and his bishop this is not the place to speak; nor, were it otherwise, am I sufficiently familiar with its merits to attempt to do justice to either party in a statement of it. This controversy was a continual pain to Dr. CROSWELL, and his more intimate friends, until his death, which occurred under the most impressive circumstances, on Sunday, the ninth of November, 1851, just seven years after his return to Boston. He had preached in the morning and during the afternoon service, which was appointed for the children of the congregation, his strength suddenly failed, he gave out a hymn, repeated with touching pathos a prayer, and in a feeble voice, while still kneeling, pronounced the apostolic benediction, and in a little while was dead.

Since the death of Dr. CROSWELL, his aged father, who had previously been occupied with the arrangement of materials for his own memoirs that they might be written by his son, has published a most interesting biography of that son and in this is the only collection of his poems which has appeared, except a small one which Bishop DOANE many years ago added to an edition of KEBLE'S "Christian Year."

Dr. CROSWELL had a fine taste in literature, and among his poems are many of remarkable grace and sweetness. They are for the most part souvenirs of his friendships, or of the vicissitudes of his religious life, and seem to have been natural and unstudied expressions of his feelings. Bishop DOANE well describes him by saying "he had more unwritten poetry in him" than any man he ever knew.

THE SYNAGOGUE.

"But even unto this day, when Moses is read, the veil is upon their heart. Nevertheless, when it shall turn to the Lord, the veil shall be taken away."—ST. PAUL.

I SAW them in their synagogue,
As in their ancient day,
And never from my memory
The scene will fade away,
For, dazzling on my vision, still
The latticed galleries shine
With Israel's loveliest daughters,
In their beauty half-divine!

It is the holy Sabbath eve,—
The solitary light
Sheds, mingled with the hues of day,
A lustre nothing bright;
On swarthy brow and piercing glance
It falls with saddening tinge,
And dimly gilds the Pharisee's
Phylacteries and fringe.

The two-leaved doors slide slow apart
Before the eastern screen,
As rise the Hebrew harmonies,
With chanted prayers between,
And mid the tissued vails disclosed,
Of many a gorgeous dye,
Enveloped in their jewell'd scarfs,
The sacred records lie.

Robed in his sacerdotal vest,
A silvery-headed man
With voice of solemn cadence o'er
The backward letters ran,
And often yet methinks I see
The glow and power that sate
Upon his face, as forth he spread
The roll immaculate.

And fervently that hour I pray'd,
That from the mighty scroll
Its light, in burning characters,
Might break on every soul,
That on their harden'd hearts the veil
Might be no longer dark,
But be forever rent in twain
Like that before the ark.

For yet the tenfold film shall fall,
O, Judah! from thy sight,
And every eye be purged to read
Thy testimonies right,
When thou, with all MESSIAH'S signs
In CHRIST distinctly seen,
Shall, by JEHOVAH'S nameless name,
Invoke the Nazarene.

THE CLOUDS.

"Cloud land! Gorgeous land!"—COLERIDGE.

I CANNOT look above and see
Yon high-piled, pillowy mass
Of evening clouds, so swimmingly
In gold and purple pass,
And think not, LORD, how thou wast seen
On Israel's desert way,
Before them, in thy shadowy screen,
Pavilion'd all the day!

Or, of those robes of gorgeous hue
Which the Redeemer wore,
When, ravish'd from his followers' view,
Aloft his flight he bore,
When lifted, as on mighty wing,
He curtained his ascent,
And, wrapt in clouds, went triumphing
Above the firmament.

Is it a trail of that same pall
Of many-colour'd dyes,
That high above, o'ermantling all,
Hangs midway down the skies—
Or borders of those sweeping folds
Which shall be all unfurl'd
About the Saviour, when he holds
His judgment on the world!

For in like manner as he went,—
My soul, hast thou forgot?—
Shall be his terrible descent,
When man expecteth not!
Strength, Son of man, against that hour,
Be to our spirits given,
When thou shalt come again with power,
Upon the clouds of heaven!

THE ORDINAL.

Alas for me if I forget
 The memory of that day
Which fills my waking thoughts, nor yet
 E'en sleep can take away!
In dreams I still renew the rites
 Whose strong but mystic chain
The spirit to its God unites,
 And none can part again.

How oft the bishop's form I see,
 And hear that thrilling tone
Demanding with authority
 The heart for God alone;
Again I kneel as then I knelt,
 While he above me stands,
And seem to feel, as then I felt,
 The pressure of his hands.

Again the priests in meet array,
 As my weak spirit fails,
Beside me bend them down to pray
 Before the chancel-rails;
As then, the sacramental host
 Of God's elect are by,
When many a voice its utterance lost,
 And tears dimm'd many an eye.

As then they on my vision rose,
 The vaulted aisles I see,
And desk and cushion'd book repose
 In solemn sanctity,—
The mitre o'er the marble niche,
 The broken crook and key,
That from a bishop's tomb shone rich
 With polished tracery;

The hangings, the baptismal font,
 All, all, save me unchanged,
The holy table, as was wont,
 With decency arranged;
The linen cloth, the plate, the cup,
 Beneath their covering shine,
Ere priestly hands are lifted up
 To bless the bread and wine.

The solemn ceremonial past,
 And I am set apart
To serve the Lord, from first to last,
 With undivided heart;
And I have sworn, with pledges dire,
 Which God and man have heard,
To speak the holy truth entire,
 In action and in word.

O Thou, who in thy holy place
 Hast set thine orders three,
Grant me, thy meanest servant, grace
 To win a good degree;
That so, replenish'd from above,
 And in my office tried,
Thou mayst be honoured, and in love
 Thy church be edified!

CHRISTMAS EVE.

The thickly-woven boughs they wreathe
 Through every hallow'd fane
A soft, reviving odour breathe
 Of summer's gentle reign;
And rich the ray of mild green light
 Which, like an emerald's glow,
Comes struggling through the latticed height
 Upon the crowds below.

O, let the streams of solemn thought
 Which in those temples rise,
From deeper sources spring than aught
 Dependent on the skies:
Then, though the summer's pride departs,
 And winter's withering chill
Rests on the cheerless woods, our hearts
 Shall be unchanging still.

THE DEATH OF STEPHEN.

With awful dread his murderers shook,
 As, radiant and serene,
The lustre of his dying look
 Was like an angel's seen;
Or Moses' face of paly light,
 When down the mount he trod,
All glowing from the glorious sight
 And presence of his God.

To us, with all his constancy,
 Be his rapt vision given,
To look above by faith, and see
 Revealments bright of heaven.
And power to speak our triumphs out,
 As our last hour draws near,
While neither clouds of fear nor doubt
 Before our view appear.

THE CHRISTMAS OFFERING.

We come not with a costly store,
 O Lord, like them of old,
The masters of the starry lore,
 From Ophir's shore of gold:
No weepings of the incense tree
 Are with the gifts we bring,
No odorous myrrh of Araby
 Blends with our offering.

But still our love would bring its best,
 A spirit keenly tried
By fierce affliction's fiery test,
 And seven times purified:
The fragrant graces of the mind,
 The virtues that delight
To give their perfume out, will find
 Acceptance in thy sight.

GEORGE D. PRENTICE.

[Born, 1804.]

Mr. Prentice is a native of Preston, in Connecticut, and was educated at Brown University, in Providence, where he was graduated in 1823. He edited for several years, at Hartford, "The New England Weekly Review," in connection, I believe, with John G. Whittier; and in 1831 he removed to Louisville, Kentucky, where he has since conducted the "Journal," of that city, one of the most popular gazettes ever published in this country. Nearly all his poems were written while he was in the university. They have never been published collectively.

THE CLOSING YEAR.

'T is midnight's holy hour—and silence now
Is brooding, like a gentle spirit, o'er
The still and pulseless world. Hark! on the winds
The bell's deep tones are swelling; 'tis the knell
Of the departed year. No funeral train
Is sweeping past; yet, on the stream and wood,
With melancholy light, the moonbeams rest,
Like a pale, spotless shroud; the air is stirr'd,
As by a mourner's sigh; and on yon cloud,
That floats so still and placidly through heaven,
The spirits of the seasons seem to stand, [form,
Young Spring, bright Summer, Autumn's solemn
And Winter with his aged locks, and breathe
In mournful cadences, that come abroad
Like the far wind-harp's wild and touching wail,
A melancholy dirge o'er the dead year,
Gone from the earth forever. 'T is a time
For memory and for tears. Within the deep,
Still chambers of the heart, a spectre dim,
Whose tones are like the wizard voice of Time,
Heard from the tomb of ages, points its cold
And solemn finger to the beautiful
And holy visions that have pass'd away,
And left no shadow of their loveliness
On the dead waste of life. That spectre lifts
The coffin-lid of hope, and joy, and love,
And, bending mournfully above the pale
Sweet forms that slumber there, scatters dead flowers
O'er what has pass'd to nothingness. The year
Has gone, and, with it, many a glorious throng
Of happy dreams. Its mark is on each brow,
Its shadow in each heart. In its swift course,
It waved its sceptre o'er the beautiful,
And they are not. It laid its pallid hand
Upon the strong man, and the haughty form
Is fallen, and the flashing eye is dim.
It trod the hall of revelry, where throng'd
The bright and joyous, and the tearful wail
Of stricken ones is heard, where erst the song
And reckless shout resounded. It pass'd o'er
The battle-plain, where sword and spear and shield
Flash'd in the light of midday—and the strength
Of serried hosts is shiver'd, and the grass,
Green from the soil of carnage, waves above
The crush'd and mouldering skeleton. It came
And faded like a wreath of mist at eve;
Yet, ere it melted in the viewless air,
It heralded its millions to their home
In the dim land of dreams. Remorseless Time—
Fierce spirit of the glass and scythe—what power
Can stay him in his silent course, or melt
His iron heart to pity? On, still on
He presses, and forever. The proud bird,
The condor of the Andes, that can soar
Through heaven's unfathomable depths, or brave
The fury of the northern hurricane,
And bathe his plumage in the thunder's home,
Furls his broad wings at nightfall, and sinks down
To rest upon his mountain-crag,—but Time
Knows not the weight of sleep or weariness,
And night's deep darkness has no chain to bind
His rushing pinion. Revolutions sweep
O'er earth, like troubled visions o'er the breast
Of dreaming sorrow; cities rise and sink,
Like bubbles on the water; fiery isles
Spring, blazing, from the ocean, and go back
To their mysterious caverns; mountains rear
To heaven their bald and blacken'd cliffs, and bow
Their tall heads to the plain; new empires rise,
Gathering the strength of hoary centuries,
And rush down like the Alpine avalanche,
Startling the nations; and the very stars,
Yon bright and burning blazonry of God,
Glitter a while in their eternal depths,
And, like the Pleiad, loveliest of their train,
Shoot from their glorious spheres, and pass away,
To darkle in the trackless void:—yet Time—
Time, the tomb-builder, holds his fierce career,
Dark, stern, all-pitiless, and pauses not
Amid the mighty wrecks that strew his path,
To sit and muse, like other conquerors,
Upon the fearful ruin he has wrought.

LINES TO A LADY.

Lady, I love, at eventide,
  When stars, as now, are on the wave,
To stray in loneliness, and muse
  Upon the one dear form that gave
Its sunlight to my boyhood; oft
That same sweet look sinks, still and soft,
Upon my spirit, and appears
As lovely as in by-gone years.

Eve's low, faint wind is breathing now,
  With deep and soul-like murmuring,
Through the dark pines; and thy sweet words
  Seem borne on its mysterious wing;

And oft, mid musings sad and lone,
At night's deep noon, that thrilling tone
Swells in the wind, low, wild, and clear,
Like music in the dreaming air.

When sleep's calm wing is on my brow,
And dreams of peace my spirit lull,
Before me, like a misty star,
That form floats dim and beautiful;
And, when the gentle moonbeam smiles
On the blue streams and dark-green isles,
In every ray pour'd down the sky,
That same light form seems stealing by.

It is a blessed picture, shrined
In memory's urn; the wing of years
Can change it not, for there it glows,
Undimm'd by "weaknesses and tears;"
Deep-hidden in its still recess,
It beams with love and holiness,
O'er hours of being, dark and dull,
Till life seems almost beautiful.

The vision cannot fade away;
'T is in the stillness of my heart,
And o'er its brightness I have mused
In solitude; it is a part
Of my existence; a dear flower
Breathed on by Heaven: morn's earliest hour
That flower bedews, and its blue eye
At eve still rests upon the sky.

Lady, like thine, my visions cling
To the dear shrine of buried years;
The past, the past! it is too bright,
Too deeply beautiful for tears;
We have been bless'd; though life is made
A tear, a silence, and a shade,
And years have left the vacant breast
To loneliness—we have been bless'd!

Those still, those soft, those summer eyes,
When by our favourite stream we stood,
And watch'd our mingling shadows there,
Soft-pictured in the deep-blue flood,
Seem'd one enchantment. O! we felt,
As there, at love's pure shrine, we knelt,
That life was sweet, and all its hours
A glorious dream of love and flowers.

And still 'tis sweet. Our hopes went by
Like sounds upon the unbroken sea;
Yet memory wings the spirit back
To deep, undying melody;
And still, around her early shrine,
Fresh flowers their dewy chaplets twine,
Young Love his brightest garland wreathes,
And Eden's richest incense breathes.

Our hopes are flown—yet parted hours
Still in the depths of memory lie,
Like night-gems in the silent blue
Of summer's deep and brilliant sky;
And Love's bright flashes seem again
To fall upon the glowing chain
Of our existence. Can it be
That all is but a mockery?

Lady, adieu! to other climes
I go, from joy, and hope, and thee;
A weed on Time's dark waters thrown,
A wreck on life's wild-heaving sea;
I go; but O, the past, the past!
Its spell is o'er my being cast,—
And still, to Love's remember'd eves,
With all but hope, my spirit cleaves.

Adieu! adieu! My farewell words
Are on my lyre, and their wild flow
Is faintly dying on the chords,
Broken and tuneless. Be it so!
Thy name—O, may it never swell
My strain again—yet long 'twill dwell
Shrined in my heart, unbreathed, unspoken—
A treasured word—a cherish'd token.

THE DEAD MARINER.

Sleep on, sleep on! above thy corse
The winds their Sabbath keep;
The waves are round thee, and thy breast
Heaves with the heaving deep.
O'er thee mild eve her beauty flings,
And there the white gull lifts her wings,
And the blue halcyon loves to lave
Her plumage in the deep blue wave.

Sleep on; no willow o'er thee bends
With melancholy air,
No violet springs, nor dewy rose
Its soul of love lays bare;
But there the sea-flower, bright and young,
Is sweetly o'er thy slumbers flung,
And, like a weeping mourner fair,
The pale flag hangs its tresses there.

Sleep on, sleep on; the glittering depths
Of ocean's coral caves
Are thy bright urn—thy requiem
The music of its waves;
The purple gems forever burn
In fadeless beauty round thy urn,
And, pure and deep as infant love,
The blue sea rolls its waves above.

Sleep on, sleep on; the fearful wrath
Of mingling cloud and deep
May leave its wild and stormy track
Above thy place of sleep;
But, when the wave has sunk to rest,
As now, 'twill murmur o'er thy breast,
And the bright victims of the sea
Perchance will make their home with thee.

Sleep on; thy corse is far away,
But love bewails thee yet;
For thee the heart-wrung sigh is breathed,
And lovely eyes are wet:
And she, thy young and beauteous bride,
Her thoughts are hovering by thy side,
As oft she turns to view, with tears,
The Eden of departed years.

SABBATH EVENING.

How calmly sinks the parting sun!
Yet twilight lingers still;
And beautiful as dream of Heaven
It slumbers on the hill;
Earth sleeps, with all her glorious things,
Beneath the Holy Spirit's wings,
And, rendering back the hues above,
Seems resting in a trance of love.

Round yonder rocks the forest-trees
In shadowy groups recline,
Like saints at evening bow'd in prayer
Around their holy shrine;
And through their leaves the night-winds blow
So calm and still, their music low
Seems the mysterious voice of prayer,
Soft echo'd on the evening air.

And yonder western throng of clouds,
Retiring from the sky,
So calmly move, so softly glow,
They seem to fancy's eye
Bright creatures of a better sphere,
Come down at noon to worship here,
And, from their sacrifice of love,
Returning to their home above.

The blue isles of the golden sea,
The night-arch floating by,
The flowers that gaze upon the heavens,
The bright streams leaping by,
Are living with religion—deep
On earth and sea its glories sleep,
And mingle with the starlight rays,
Like the soft light of parted days.

The spirit of the holy eve
Comes through the silent air
To feeling's hidden spring, and wakes
A gush of music there!
And the far depths of ether beam
So passing fair, we almost dream
That we can rise, and wander through
Their open paths of trackless blue.

Each soul is fill'd with glorious dreams,
Each pulse is beating wild;
And thought is soaring to the shrine
Of glory undefiled!
And holy aspirations start,
Like blessed angels, from the heart,
And bind—for earth's dark ties are riven—
Our spirits to the gates of heaven.

TO A LADY.

I THINK of thee when morning springs
From sleep, with plumage bathed in dew,
And, like a young bird, lifts her wings
Of gladness on the welkin blue.

And when, at noon, the breath of love
O'er flower and stream is wandering free,
And sent in music from the grove,
I think of thee—I think of thee.

I think of thee, when, soft and wide,
The evening spreads her robes of light,
And, like a young and timid bride,
Sits blushing in the arms of night.

And when the moon's sweet crescent springs
In light o'er heaven's deep, waveless sea,
And stars are forth, like blessed things,
I think of thee—I think of thee.

I think of thee;—that eye of flame,
Those tresses, falling bright and free,
That brow, where "Beauty writes her name,"
I think of thee—I think of thee.

WRITTEN AT MY MOTHER'S GRAVE

THE trembling dew-drops fall
Upon the shutting flowers; like souls at rest
The stars shine gloriously: and all
Save me, are blest.

Mother, I love thy grave!
The violet, with its blossoms blue and mild,
Waves o'er thy head; when shall it wave
Above thy child?

'T is a sweet flower, yet must
Its bright leaves to the coming tempest bow;
Dear mother, 't is thine emblem; dust
Is on thy brow.

And I could love to die:
To leave untasted life's dark, bitter streams—
By thee, as erst in childhood, lie,
And share thy dreams.

And I must linger here,
To stain the plumage of my sinless years,
And mourn the hopes to childhood dear
With bitter tears.

Ay, I must linger here,
A lonely branch upon a wither'd tree,
Whose last frail leaf, untimely sere,
Went down with thee!

Oft, from life's wither'd bower,
In still communion with the past, I turn,
And muse on thee, the only flower
In memory's urn.

And, when the evening pale
Bows, like a mourner, on the dim, blue wave,
I stray to hear the night-winds wail
Around thy grave.

Where is thy spirit flown?
I gaze above—thy look is imaged there;
I listen—and thy gentle tone
Is on the air.

O, come, while here I press
My brow upon thy grave; and, in those mild
And thrilling tones of tenderness,
Bless, bless thy child!

Yes, bless your weeping child;
And o'er thine urn—religion's holiest shrine—
O, give his spirit, undefiled,
To blend with thine.

WILLIAM PITT PALMER.

[Born, 1805.]

Mr. Palmer is descended from a Puritan ancestor who came to America in the next ship after the May Flower. His father was a youthful soldier in the Revolution, and one of the latest, if not the last, of the survivors of the Jersey prison ship. Having acquired a competency as the captain of a New York merchantman, he retired from the sea early in the present century, to Stockbridge, Berkshire county, Massachusetts, where he spent the remainder of his days, in that sunshine of love and respect which has gilded the declining years of so many men of our heroic age. There, on the twenty-second of February, 1805, our poet was born, and named in honour of the great orator whose claims to gratitude are recognised among us in a thousand living monuments which bear the name of William Pitt.

In his native county, Mr. Palmer has told me, the first and happiest half of his life was spent on the farm, in the desultory acquisition of such knowledge as could then be obtained from a New England common school, and a "college" with a single professor. The other half has been chiefly passed in New York, as a medical student, teacher, writer for the gazettes, and, for several years, clerk in a public office.

Mr. Palmer is a man of warm affections, who finds a heaven in a quiet home. He is a lover of nature, too, and like most inhabitants of the pent-up city, whose early days have been passed in the country, he delights in recollections of rural life. Some of his poems have much tenderness and delicacy, and they are generally very complete and pol shed.

LIGHT.

From the quicken'd womb of the primal gloom
The sun roll'd black and bare,
Till I wove him a vest for his Ethiop breast,
Of the threads of my golden hair;
And when the broad tent of the firmament
Arose on its airy spars,
I pencill'd the hue of its matchless blue,
And spangled it round with stars.

I painted the flowers of the Eden bowers,
And their leaves of living green,
And mine were the dyes in the sinless eyes
Of Eden's virgin queen:
And when the fiend's art, on her trustful heart,
Had fasten'd its mortal spell,
In the silvery sphere of the first-born tear
To the trembling earth I fell.

When the waves that burst o'er a world accursed
Their work of wrath hath sped,
And the Ark's lone few, the tried and true,
Came forth among the dead;
With the wondrous gleams of my braided beams
I bade their terrors cease;
As I wrote on the roll of the storm's dark scroll
God's covenant of peace.

Like a pall at rest on a pulseless breast,
Night's funeral shadow slept,
Where shepherd swains on the Bethlehem plains
Their lonely vigils kept;
When I flash'd on their sight the heralds bright
Of heaven's redeeming plan,
As they chanted the morn of a Saviou born—
Joy, joy to the outcast man!

Equal favour I show to the lofty and low,
On the just and unjust I descend;
E'en the blind, whose vain spheres roll in darkness and tears,
Feel my smile the best smile of a friend:
Nay, the flower of the waste by my love is embraced,
As the rose in the garden of kings;
As the chrysalis bier of the worm I appear,
And lo! the gay butterfly's wings!

The desolate Morn, like a mourner forlorn,
Conceals all the pride of her charms,
Till I bid the bright Hours chase the Night from her bowers,
And lead the young Day to her arms;
And when the gay rover seeks Eve for his lover,
And sinks to her balmy repose,
I wrap their soft rest by the zephyr-fann'd west,
In curtains of amber and rose.

From my sentinel steep, by the night-brooded deep,
I gaze with unslumbering eye,
When the cynosure star of the mariner
Is blotted from the sky;
And guided by me through the merciless sea,
Though sped by the hurricane's wings,
His compassless bark, lone, weltering, dark,
To the haven-home safely he brings.

I waken the flowers in their dew-spangled bowers,
The birds in their chambers of green,
And mountain and plain glow with beauty again,
As they bask in my matinal sheen.
O, if such the glad worth of my presence to earth
Though fitful and fleeting the while,
What glories must rest on the home of the bless'd,
Ever bright with the Deity's smile!

LINES TO A CHRYSALIS.

Musing long I asked me this,
Chrysalis,
Lying helpless in my path,
Obvious to mortal scath
From a careless passer by,
What thy life may signify?
Why, from hope and joy apart,
Thus thou art?

Nature surely did amiss,
Chrysalis,
When she lavish'd fins and wings
Nerved with nicest moving-springs,
On the mote and madripore,
Wherewithal to swim or soar;
And dispensed so niggardly
Unto thee.

E'en the very worm may kiss,
Chrysalis,
Roses on their topmost stems
Blazon'd with their dewy gems,
And may rock him to and fro
As the zephyrs softly blow;
Whilst thou lyest dark and cold
On the mould.

Quoth the Chrysalis, Sir Bard,
Not so hard
Is my rounded destiny
In the great Economy:
Nay, by humble reason view'd,
There is much for gratitude
In the shaping and upshot
Of my lot.

Though I seem of all things born
Most forlorn,
Most obtuse of soul and sense,
Next of kin to Impotence,
Nay, to Death himself; yet ne'er
Priest or prophet, sage or seer,
May sublimer wisdom teach
Than I preach.

From my pulpit of the sod,
Like a god,
I proclaim this wondrous truth,
Farthest age is nearest youth,
Nearest glory's natal porch,
Where with pale, inverted torch,
Death lights downward to the rest
Of the blest.

Mark yon airy butterfly's
Rainbow-dyes!
Yesterday that shape divine
Was as darkly hearsed as mine;
But to-morrow I shall be
Free and beautiful as she,
And sweep forth on wings of light,
Like a sprite.

Soul of man in crypt of clay!
Bide the day
When thy latent wings shall be
Plumed for immortality,
And with transport marvellous
Cleave their dark sarcophagus,
O'er Elysian fields to soar
Evermore!

THE HOME VALENTINE.

Still fond and true, though wedded long
The bard, at eve retired,
Sat smiling o'er the annual song
His home's dear Muse inspired:
And as he traced her virtues now
With all love's vernal glow,
A gray hair from his bended brow,
Like faded leaf from autumn bough,
Fell to the page below.

He paused, and with a mournful mien
The sad memento raised,
And long upon its silvery sheen
In pensive silence gazed:
And if a sigh escaped him then,
It were not strange to say;
For fancy's favourites are but men;
And who e'er felt the stoic when
First conscious of decay?

Just then a soft cheek press'd his own
With beauty's fondest tear,
And sweet words breathed in sweeter tone
Thus murmur'd in his ear:
Ah, sigh not, love to mark the trace
Of time's unsparing wand!
It was not manhood's outward grace,
No charm of faultless form or face,
That won my heart and hand.

Lo! dearest, mid these matron locks,
Twin-fated with thine own,
A dawn of silvery lustre mocks
The midnight they have known:
But time to blighted cheek and tress
May all his snows impart;
Yet shalt thou feel in my caress
No chill of waning tenderness,
No winter of the heart!

Forgive me, dearest Beatrice!
The grateful bard replied,
As nearer and with tenderer kiss
He pressed her to his side:
Forgive the momentary tear
To manhood's faded prime;
I should have felt, hadst thou been near,
Our hearts indeed have nought to fear
From all the frosts of time!

GEORGE W. BETHUNE.

[Born 1805 Died 1862.]

The Reverend George W. Bethune, D.D. is a native of New York. When twenty one years of age he entered the ministry of the Presbyterian church, from which, in the following year, he passed to that of the Dutch Reformed church. After residing at Rhinebeck, and Utica, in New York, he in 1834 removed to Philadelphia, where he remained until 1849, in which year he became pas-tor of a church in Brooklyn. There are in the American pulpit few better scholars or more elo-quent preachers. He has published several volumes of literary and religious discourses, and in 1847 gave to the public a volume of graceful and elegant poems, entitled "Lays of Love and Faith."

TO MY MOTHER.

My mother!—Manhood's anxious brow
  And sterner cares have long been mine;
Yet turn I to thee fondly now,
  As when upon thy bosom's shrine
My infant griefs were gently hush'd to rest,
And thy low-whisper'd prayers my slumber bless'd.

I never call that gentle name,
  My mother! but I am again
E'en as a child; the very same
  That prattled at thy knee; and fain
Would I forget, in momentary joy,
That I no more can be thy happy boy;—

The artless boy, to whom thy smile
  Was sunshine, and thy frown sad night,
(Though rare that frown, and brief the while
  It veil'd from me thy loving light;)
For well-conn'd task, ambition's highest bliss,
To win from thine approving lips a kiss.

I've loved through foreign lands to roam,
  And gazed o'er many a classic scene;
Yet would the thought of that dear home,
  Which once was ours, oft intervene,
And bid me close again my weary eye
To think of thee, and those sweet days gone by.

That pleasant home of fruits and flowers,
  Where, by the Hudson's verdant side
My sisters wove their jasmine bowers,
  And he, we loved, at eventide
Would hastening come from distant toil to bless
Thine, and his children's radiant happiness.

Alas, the change! the rattling car
  On flint-paved streets profanes the spot,
Where o'er the sod, we sow'd the Star
  Of Bethlehem, and Forget-me-not.
Oh, wo to Mammon's desolating reign!
We ne'er shall find on earth a home again!

I've pored o'er many a yellow page
  Of ancient wisdom, and have won,
Perchance, a scholar's name—but sage
  Or bard have never taught thy son
Lessons so dear, so fraught with holy truth,
As those his mother's faith shed on his youth.

If, by the Saviour's grace made meet,
  My God will own my life and love,
Methinks, when singing at His feet,
  Amid the ransom'd throng above,
Thy name upon my glowing lips shall be,
And I will bless that grace for heaven and thee.

For thee and heaven; for thou didst tread
  The way that leads me heavenward, and
My often wayward footsteps led
  In the same path with patient hand;
And when I wander'd far, thy earnest call
Restored my soul from sin's deceitful thrall.

I have been bless'd with other ties,
  Fond ties and true, yet never deem
That I the less thy fondness prize;
  No, mother! in my warmest dream
Of answer'd passion, through this heart of mine
One chord will vibrate to no name but thine.

Mother! thy name is widow—well
  I know no love of mine can fill
The waste place of thy heart, or dwell
  Within one sacred recess: still
Lean on the faithful bosom of thy son,
My parent, thou art mine, my *only* one!

NIGHT STUDY.

    I am alone; and yet
In the still solitude there is a rush
    Around me, as were met
A crowd of viewless wings; I hear a gush
Of utter'd harmonies—heaven meeting earth,
Making it to rejoice with holy mirth.

    Ye winged Mysteries,
Sweeping before my spirit's conscious eye,
    Beckoning me to arise,
And go forth from my very self, and fly
With you far in the unknown, unseen immense
Of worlds beyond our sphere—What are ye!
      Whence?

    Ye eloquent voices,
Now soft as breathings of a distant flute,
    Now strong as when rejoices,
The trumpet in the victory and pursuit;
Strange are ye, yet familiar, as ye call
My soul to wake from earth's sense and its thrall

    I know you now—I see
With more than natural light—ye are the good
    The wise *departed*—ye

Are come from heaven to claim your brotherhood
With mortal brother, struggling in the strife
And chains, which once were yours in this sad life.

Ye hover o'er the page
Ye traced in ancient days with glorious thought
For many a distant age;
Ye love to watch the inspiration caught,
From your sublime examples, and so cheer
The fainting student to your high career.

Ye come to nerve the soul
Like him who near the ATONER stood, when HE,
Trembling, saw round him roll
The wrathful potents of Gethsemane,
With courage strong: the promise ye have known
And proved, rapt for me from the Eternal throne.

Still keep! O, keep me near you,
Compass me round with your immortal wings:
Still let my glad soul hear you
Striking your triumphs from your golden strings,
Until with you I mount, and join the song,
An angel, like you, 'mid the white-robed throng.

LINES
WRITTEN ON SEEING THORWALDSEN'S BAS-RELIEF REPRESENTING NIGHT.

YES! bear them to their rest;
The rosy babe, tired with the glare of day,
The prattler fallen asleep e'en in his play,
Clasp them to thy soft breast,
O Night,
Bless them in dreams with a deep hush'd delight.

Yet must they wake again,
Wake soon to all the bitterness of life.
The pang of sorrow, the temptation strife,
Aye, to the conscience-pain—
O Night,
Canst thou not take with them a longer flight?

Canst thou not bear them far—
E'en now all innocent—before they know
The taint of sin, its consequence of wo,
The world's distracting jar,
O Night,
To some ethereal, holier, happier height?

Canst thou not bear them up
Through starlit skies, far from this planet dim
And sorrowful, e'en while they sleep, to Him
Who drank for us the cup,
O Night,
The cup of wrath for hearts in faith contrite?

To Him, for them who slept
A babe all lowly on His mother's knee,
And from that hour to cross-crown'd Calvary,
In all our sorrows wept,
O Night,
That on our souls might dawn Heaven's cheering light.

So, lay their little heads
Close to that human breast, with love divine
Deep beating, while his arms immortal twine
Around them as he sheds,
O Night,
On them a brother's grace of GOD's own boundless might.

Let them immortal wake
Among the breathless flowers of Paradise,
Where angel-songs of welcome with surprise
This their last sleep may break,
O Night,
And to celestial joy their kindred souls invite.

There can come no sorrow,
The brow shall know no shade, the eye no tears,
For ever young through heaven's eternal years,
In one unfading morrow,
O Night,
Nor sin, nor age, nor pain their cherub-beauty blight.

Would we could sleep as they,
So stainless and so calm, at rest with thee,
And only wake in immortality!
Bear us with them away,
O Night,
To that ethereal, holier, happier height.

TO MY WIFE.

AFAR from thee! the morning breaks,
But morning brings no joy to me;
Alas! my spirit only wakes
To know I am afar from thee.
In dreams I saw thy blessed face,
And thou wert nestled on my breast;
In dreams I felt thy fond embrace,
And to mine own thy heart was press'd.

Afar from thee! 'tis solitude!
Though smiling crowds around me be,
The kind, the beautiful, the good,
For I can only think of thee;
Of thee, the kindest, loveliest, best,
My earliest and my only one!
Without thee I am all unbless'd,
And wholly bless'd with thee alone.

Afar from thee! the words of praise
My listless ear unheeded greet;
What sweetest seem'd, in better days,
Without thee seems no longer sweet.
The dearest joy fame can bestow
Is in thy moisten'd eye to see,
And in thy cheek's unusual glow,
Thou deem'st me not unworthy thee.

Afar from thee! the night is come,
But slumbers from my pillow flee;
Oh, who can rest so far from home?
And my heart's home is, love, with thee.
I kneel me down in silent prayer,
And then I know that thou art nigh:
For GOD, who seeth everywhere,
Bends on us both his watchful eye.

Together, in his loved embrace,
No distance can our hearts divide;
Forgotten quite the mediate space,
I kneel thy kneeling form beside.
My tranquil frame then sinks to sleep,
But soars the spirit far and free;
Oh, welcome be night's slumbers deep,
For then, sweet love, I am with thee.

CHARLES FENNO HOFFMAN.

[Born, 1806.]

The author of "Greyslaer," "Wild Scenes in the Forest and the Prairie," etc., is a brother of the Honourable Ogden Hoffman, and a son of the late eminent lawyer of the same name.* He is the child of a second marriage. His maternal grandfather was John Fenno, of Philadelphia, one of the ablest political writers of the old Federal party, during the administration of Washington. The family, which is a numerous one in the state of New York, planted themselves, at an early day, in the valley of the Hudson, as appears from the Dutch records of Peter Stuyvesant's storied reign.

Mr. Hoffman was born in New York, in the year 1806. He was sent to a Latin grammar-school in that city, when six years old, from which, at the age of nine, he was transferred to the Poughkeepsie academy, a seminary upon the Hudson, about eighty miles from New York, which at that time enjoyed great reputation. The harsh treatment he received here induced him to run away, and his father, finding that he had not improved under a course of severity, did not insist upon his return, but placed him under the care of an accomplished Scottish gentleman in one of the rural villages of New Jersey. During a visit home from this place, and when about twelve years of age, he met with an injury which involved the necessity of the immediate amputation of the right leg, above the knee. The painful circumstances are minutely detailed in the New York "Evening Post," of the twenty-fifth of October, 1817, from which it appears, that while, with other lads, attempting the dangerous feat of leaping aboard a steamer as she passed a pier, under full way, he was caught between the vessel and the wharf. The steamer swept by, and left him clinging by his hands to the pier, crushed in a manner too frightful for description. This deprivation, instead of acting as a disqualification for the manly sports of youth, and thus turning the subject of it into a retired student, seems rather to have given young Hoffman an especial ambition to excel in swimming, riding, etc., to the still further neglect of perhaps more useful acquirements.

When fifteen years old, he entered Columbia College, and here, as at preparatory schools, was noted rather for success in gymnastic exercises than in those of a more intellectual character His reputation, judging from his low position in his class, contrasted with the honours that were awarded him by the college-societies at their anniversary exhibitions, was greater with the students than with the faculty, though the honorary degree of Master of Arts, conferred upon him under peculiarly gratifying circumstances, after leaving the institution in his third or junior year, without having graduated, clearly implies that he was still a favourite with his *alma mater*.*

Immediately after leaving college—being then eighteen years old—he commenced the study of the law with the Honourable Harmanus Bleecker, of Albany, now *Chargé d'Affaires* of the United States at the Hague. When twenty-one, he was admitted to the bar, and in the succeeding three years he practised in the courts of the city of New York. During this period he wrote anonymously for the New York American—having made his first essay as a writer for the gazettes while in Albany—and I believe finally became associated with Mr. Charles King in the editorship of that paper. Certainly he gave up the legal profession, for the successful prosecution of which he appears to have been unfitted by his love of books, society, and the rod and gun. His feelings at this period are described in some rhymes, entitled "Forest Musings," from which the following stanzas are quoted, to show the fine relish for forest-life and scenery which has thrown a peculiar charm around every production from his pen:—

> The hunt is up—
> The merry woodland shout,
> That rung these echoing glades about
> An hour agone,
> Hath swept beyond the eastern hills,
> Where, pale and lone,
> The moon her mystic circle fills;
> A while across the setting sun's broad disc
> The dusky larch,
> As if to pierce the blue o'erhanging arch,
> Lifts its tall obelisk.
> And now from thicket dark,
> Where, by the mist-wreathed river,
> The fire-fly's spark
> Will fitful quiver,
> And bubbles round the lily's cup
> From lurking trout come coursing up,
> The doe hath led her fawn to drink;
> While, scared by step so near,
> Uprising from the sedgy brink
> The lonely bittern's cry will sink
> Upon the startled ear.
> And thus upon my dreaming youth,
> When boyhood's gambols pleased no more,
> And young Romance, in guise of Truth,
> Usurp'd the heart all theirs before;

* Judge Hoffman was, in early life, one of the most distinguished advocates at the American bar. He won his first cause in New Jersey at the age of seventeen; the illness of counsel or the indulgence of the court giving him the opportunity to speak. At twenty-one he succeeded his father as representative, from New York, in the state legislature. At twenty-six he filled the office of attorney-general; and thenceforth the still youthful pleader was often the successful competitor of Hamilton, Burr, Pinkney, and other professional gian s, for the highest honours of the legal forum.

* At the first semi-centennial anniversary of the incorporation of Columbia College, the honorary degree Master of Arts was conferred upon Fitz-Greene Halleck, William Cullen Bryant, and Charles Fenno Hoffman.

Thus broke ambition's trumpet-note
On Visions wild,
Yet blithesome as this river
On which the smiling moon-beams float,
That thus have there for ages smiled,
And will thus smile forever.
And now no more the fresh green-wood,
The forest's fretted aisles
And leafy domes above them bent,
And solitude
So eloquent!
Mocking the varied skill that's blent
In art's most gorgeous piles—
No more can soothe my soul to sleep
Than they can awe the sounds that sweep
To hunter's horn and merriment
Their verdant passes through,
When fresh the dun-deer leaves his scent
Upon the morning dew.
The game's afoot!—and let the chase
Lead on, whate'er my destiny—
Though fate her funeral drum may brace
Full soon for me!
And wave death's pageant o'er me—
Yet now the new and untried world
Like maiden banner first unfurl'd,
Is glancing bright before me!
The quarry soars! and mine is now the sky,
Where, "at what bird I please, my hawk shall fly!"
Yet something whispers through the wood
A voice like that perchance
Which taught the haunter of EGERIA's grove
To tame the Roman's dominating mood
And lower, for awhile, his conquering lance
Before the Images of Law and Love—
Some mystic voice that ever since hath dwelt
Along with Echo in her dim retreat,
A voice whose influence all, at times, have felt
By wood, or glen, or where on silver strand
The clasping waves of Ocean's belt
Do clashing meet
Around the land:
It whispers me that soon—too soon
The pulses which now beat so high
Impatient with the world to cope
Will, like the hues of autumn sky,
Be changed and fallen ere life's noon
Should tame its morning hope.
It tells me not of heart betray'd
Of health impair'd,
Of fruitless toil,
And ills alike by thousands shared,
Of which each year some link is made
To add to "mortal coil:"
And yet its strange prophetic tone
So faintly murmurs to my soul
The fate to be my own,
That all of these may be
Reserved for me
Ere manhood's early years can o'er me roll.
Yet why,
While Hope so jocund singeth
And with her plumes the gray-beard's arrow wingeth,
Should I
Think only of the barb it bringeth?
Though every dream deceive
That to my youth is dearest,
Until my heart they leave
Like forest leaf when searest—
Yet still, mid forest leaves,
Where now
Its tissue thus my idle fancy weaves,
Still with heart new-blossoming
While leaves, and buds, and wild flowers spring
At Nature's shrine I'll bow;
Nor seek in vain that truth in her
She keeps for her idolater.

From this period Mr. HOFFMAN devoted his attention almost constantly to literature. While connected with the "American," he published a series of brilliant articles in that paper, under the signature of a *star* (*), which attracted much attention. In 1833, for the benefit of his health, he left New York on a travelling tour for the "far west," and his letters, written during his absence, were also first published in that popular journal. They were afterward included in his "Winter in the West," of which the first impression appeared in New York, in 1834, and the second, soon after, in London. This work has passed through many editions, and it will continue to be popular so long as graphic descriptions of scenery and character, and richness and purity of style, are admired. His next work, entitled "Wild Scenes in the Forest and the Prairie," was first printed in 1837, and, like its predecessor, it contains many admirable pictures of scenery, inwoven with legends of the western country, and descriptive poetry. This was followed by a romance, entitled "Greyslaer," founded upon the famous criminal trial of BEAUCHAMP, for the murder of Colonel SHARPE, the Solicitor-General of Kentucky,—the particulars of which, softened away in the novel, are minutely detailed in the appendix to his "Winter in the West." "Greyslaer" was a successful novel—two editions having appeared in the author's native city, one in Philadelphia, and a fourth in London, in the same year. It placed him in the front rank of American novelists. He describes in it, with remarkable felicity, American forest-life, and savage warfare, and gives a truer idea of the border contests of the Revolution than any formal history of the period that has been published.

The Knickerbocker magazine was first issued under the editorial auspices of Mr. HOFFMAN. He subsequently became the proprietor of the American Monthly Magazine, (one of the ablest literary periodicals ever published in this country.) and during the long term of which he was the chief editor of this journal, he also, for one year, conducted the New York Mirror, for its proprietor, and wrote a series of zealous papers in favour of international copyright, for the New Yorker, the Corsair, and other journals.

Mr. HOFFMAN published in 1843 "The Vigil of Faith, a Legend of the Andirondack Mountains, and other Poems;" in 1844, "The Echo, or Borrowed Notes for Home Circulation;" and in 1848, a more complete collection of his various lyrical compositions, under the title of "Love's Calendar."

When the first edition of "The Poets and Poetry of America" appeared there had been printed no volume of Mr. HOFFMAN's songs, and few except his intimate friends knew what he had written. He was more largely quoted by me because it was not then probable that his pieces would be accessible in another form. In a reviewal of my book in the London "Foreign Quarterly Review" it was remarked that "American poetry is little better than a far off echo of the father-land," and Mr. HOFFMAN was particularly attacked as a plagiarist, much stress being laid upon "the magnitude of his obligations to Mr. MOORE." This led to the publication of "The Echo, or Borrowed Notes," which was addressed to me in the following letter:

"TO RUFUS W. GRISWOLD.

"MY DEAR SIR:—You may remember some three or four years since having asked me for a list of the various signatures under which my anonymous verses had appeared in different American periodicals during the last twenty years. You are perhaps aware, also, of the disparaging remarks which your free and flattering use, in 'The Poetry of America,' of the verses thus patiently collected by you, has called out in some quarters. I have often regretted that I permitted those effusions (most of which had long since answered the casual purpose for which they were written) to be thus exhumed: regretted it, not from any particular sensibility to the critical dicta by which they have been assailed; but simply because, like many a sanguine yet indolent person originally conscious of rather vivid poetic aspirations, I had, from my boyhood upward, from early manhood onward, 'lived along in hope of doing something or other' in the way of a poem that my countrymen would not unwillingly let live: and because (while thus probably much overrating poetic powers in reserve) I was unwilling that these fugitive pieces should fix a character upon my writings it might be difficult to supersede by any subsequent effort in a higher order of composition. That fanciful regret, if not abated, has, with the considerations from which it sprung, been swallowed up lately by a reality which I deem of more imperious moment than any thing affecting mere *literary* reputation.

"One of those British reviews, which, in the absence of an international copyright, do the thinking of this country upon literary matters, and which, you know, are circulated so widely and are of such authority here that it is idle for an American author to refuse to plead to any indictment they may prefer, has recently done me the honor, amid a confused mass of indiscriminate accusations against my countrymen at large, to select me specially and individually for the odious charge of gross and hitherto unheard-of literary dishonesty.*

"Now, my dear sir, while it is due to you to relieve you from all responsibility as god-father of these questionable effusions, by publishing them under my own name,—this is likewise the only way by which so sweeping and damnatory a charge can be fully met, without involving myself in egotistical explanations far worse than those I am furnishing here, because they would be endless. I have, therefore, as the question is one of *character*, and not of mere literary taste, collected all the pieces by which I have attempted 'to hocus the Americans,' that I could lay my hands upon: and though the unconscious imposition has been running on so long that many may have escaped me, yet there are enough of all kinds for the present purpose, which is to give that portion of the abused public who feel any interest in the matter, an opportunity of deciding (not whether it is good poetry, for that is not the question—but) whether they have really been taken in so much after all: whether or not the affecting predicament of the amiable Parisian who spoke *prose* for so many years without knowing it, has found a whimsical counterpart in the unconscious use of the *poetry* of others by the writer of these effusions: or whether, finally, they do sometimes—however rarely—(to borrow the language of my friendly reviewer) 'possess the property described in the mocking birds—a solitary note of their own.' I am, dear sir, your friend and servant, C. F. HOFFMAN."

NEW YORK, *February 22d*, 1844."

Mr. HOFFMAN had already published "The Vigil of Faith," the longest of his poems, and perhaps the best long poem in our literature upon a subject connected with the Indians. Two chiefs are rivals in love, and the accepted lover is about to be made happy, when his betrothed is murdered by the chief who has been discarded. Revenge is sought in the careful preservation of the life of the assassin, lest he should be the first to meet the maiden in the other world.

On the first of May, 1847, Mr. HOFFMAN became connected with the "Literary World," which had then reached only its seventh number, and he conducted this periodical until the beginning of October, 1848, when he resigned it to the brothers DUYCKINCK, the eldest of whom had been its first editor. In this paper he wrote much and well; in his relations with the authors of the country he was always courteous, and though invariably disposed to kindness, was in the main candid and just. After retiring from its management he contributed to it a series of essays on American society, which are among the happiest and most characteristic of his productions, though written after the commencement of that sad malady which since 1850 has quite withdrawn him from the public.

In what I have written of General MORRIS, I have endeavored to define the sphere and dignity of the song: but whatever may be thought of it as an order of writing, I am satisfied that Mr. HOFFMAN has come as near to the highest standard or idea of excellence which belongs to this species of composition, as any American poet has done in his own department, whatever that department may be. Many of his productions have received whatever testimony of merit is afforded by great and continued popular favor; and though there are undoubtedly some sorts of composition respecting which the applause or silence of the multitude is right or wrong only by accident, yet, as regards a song, popularity appears to me to be the only test, and lasting popularity to be an infallible test of excellence.

---

* "*It is reserved for Charles Fenno Hoffman to distance all plagiarists of ancient and modern times in the enormity and magnitude of his thefts.* 'No American,' says Mr. Griswold, 'is comparable to him as a song-writer.' We are not surprised at the fact, considering the magnitude of his obligations to Moore. Hoffman is Moore hocused for the American market. His songs are *rifaciamenties*. The turns of the melody, the flooding of the images, the scintillating conceits—all are Moore. Sometimes he steals the very words. One song begins, 'Blame not the bowl'—a hint taken from 'Blame not the bard;' another, 'One bumper yet, gallants, at parting.' Hoffman is like a hand-organ—a single touch sets him off—he wants only the key-note, and he plays away as long as his wind lasts. The resemblance, when it runs into whole lines and verses, is more like a parody than a simple plagiarism. One specimen will be ample:—

'Tis in moments like this, when each bosom
  With its highest-toned feeling is warm,
Like the music that's said from the ocean
  To rise in the gathering storm,
That her image around us should hover,
  Whose name, though our lips ne'er reveal,
We may breathe through the foam of a bumper,
  As we drink to the myrtle and steel.'

"He had Moore's measure ringing in his ear, and demanding a simile in the middle of the first quatrain—hence the music from the ocean. The third and fourth lines are an echo of a sound, without the smallest particle of meaning or application in them. They constitute the means, nevertheless, by which Hoffman hocuses the Americans. Drop them out altogether, and, so far as the sense is concerned, the song would be materially improved."—*Foreign Quarterly Review, for January*, 1844.

["The examples given by the reviewer to prove his charge, *perhaps* shake his position, and *possibly* they do not. He is certainly mistaken about the similarity of 'measure,' as any one may verify by counting the feet in the different songs mentioned. As for their identity of thought with those delicious things of Moore's upon which the ingenious reviewer insists they are modelled, any 'American' who feels a curiosity to ascertain how far he has been 'hocused,' may determine for himself by referring to 'Moore's Melodies'—a work not wholly unknown in this country.—H."]

MOONLIGHT ON THE HUDSON.

WRITTEN AT WEST POINT.

I'm not romantic, but, upon my word,
There are some moments when one can't help feeling
As if his heart's chords were so strongly stirr'd
By things around him, that 'tis vain concealing
A little music in his soul still lingers,
Whene'er its keys are touch'd by Nature's fingers:

And even here, upon this settee lying,
With many a sleepy traveller near me snoozing,
Thoughts warm and wild are through my bosom flying,
Like founts when first into the sunshine oozing:
For who can look on mountain, sky, and river,
Like these, and then be cold and calm as ever?

Bright Dian, who, Camilla-like, dost skim yon
Azure fields—thou who, once earthward bending,
Didst loose thy virgin zone to young Endymion
On dewy Latmos to his arms descending—
Thou whom the world of old on every shore,
Type of thy sex, Triformis, did adore:

Tell me—where'er thy silver bark be steering,
By bright Italian or soft Persian lands,
Or o'er those island-studded seas careering,
Whose pearl-charged waves dissolve on coral strands;
Tell if thou visitest, thou heavenly rover,
A lovelier stream than this the wide world over?

Doth Achelöus or Araxes, flowing
Twin-born from Pindus, but ne'er-meeting brothers—
Doth Tagus, o'er his golden pavement glowing,
Or cradle-freighted Ganges, the reproach of mothers,
The storied Rhine, or far-famed Guadalquiver—
Match they in beauty my own glorious river?

What though no cloister gray nor ivied column
Along these cliffs their sombre ruins rear?
What though no frowning tower nor temple solemn
Of despots tell and superstition here—
What though that mouldering fort's fast-crumbling walls
Did ne'er enclose a baron's banner'd halls—

Its sinking arches once gave back as proud
An echo to the war-blown clarion's peal—
As gallant hearts its battlements did crowd
As ever beat beneath a vest of steel,
When herald's trump on knighthood's haughtiest day
Call'd forth chivalric host to battle-fray:

For here amid these woods did he keep court,
Before whose mighty soul the common crowd
Of heroes, who alone for fame have fought,
Are like the patriarch's sheaves to Heaven's chosen bow'd—
He who his country's eagle taught to soar,
And fired those stars which shine o'er every shore.

And sights and sounds at which the world have wonder'd
Within these wild ravines have had their birth;
Young Freedom's cannon from these glens have thunder'd,
And sent their startling echoes o'er the earth;
And not a verdant glade nor mountain hoary
But treasures up within the glorious story.

And yet not rich in high-soul'd memories only,
Is every moon-kiss'd headland round me gleaming,
Each cavern'd glen and leafy valley lonely,
And silver torrent o'er the bald rock streaming:
But such soft fancies here may breathe around,
As make Vaucluse and Clarens hallow'd ground.

Where, tell me where, pale watcher of the night—
Thou that to love so oft has lent its soul,
Since the lorn Lesbian languish'd 'neath thy light,
Or fiery Romeo to his Juliet stole—
Where dost thou find a fitter place on earth
To nurse young love in hearts like theirs to birth?

O, loiter not upon that fairy shore,
To watch the lazy barks in distance glide,
When sunset brightens on their sails no more,
And stern-lights twinkle in the dusky tide—
Loiter not there, young heart, at that soft hour,
What time the bird of night proclaims love's power.

Even as I gaze upon my memory's track,
Bright as that coil of light along the deep,
A scene of early youth comes dream-like back,
Where two stand gazing from yon tide-wash'd steep—
A sanguine stripling, just toward manhood flushing,
A girl scarce yet in ripen'd beauty blushing.

The hour is his—and, while his hopes are soaring,
Doubts he that maiden will become his bride?
Can she resist that gush of wild adoring,
Fresh from a heart full-volumed as the tide?
Tremulous, but radiant is that peerless daughter
Of loveliness—as is the star-paved water!

The moist leaves glimmer as they glimmer'd then—
Alas! how oft have they been since renew'd!
How oft the whip-poor-will from yonder glen
Each year has whistled to her callow brood!
How oft have lovers by yon star's same beam
Dream'd here of bliss—and waken'd from their dream!

But now, bright Peri of the skies, descending,
Thy pearly car hangs o'er yon mountain's crest,
And Night, more nearly now each step attending,
As if to hide thy envied place of rest,
Closes at last thy very couch beside,
A matron curtaining a virgin bride.

Farewell! Though tears on every leaf are starting:
While through the shadowy boughs thy glances quiver,
As of the good when heavenward hence departing,
Shines thy last smile upon the placid river.
So—could I fling o'er glory's tide one ray—
Would I too steal from this dark world away.

THE FOREST CEMETERY.

WILD TAWASENTHA!* in thy brook-laced glen
The doe no longer lists her lost fawn's bleating,
As panting there, escaped from hunter's ken,
She hears the chase o'er distant hills retreating;
No more, uprising from the fern around her,
The Indian archer, from his "still-hunt" lair,
Wings the death-shaft which hath that moment found her
When Fate seem'd foil'd upon her footsteps there:

Wild Tawasentha! on thy cone-strew'd sod,
O'er which yon Pine his giant arm is bending,
No more the Mohawk marks its dark crown nod
Against the sun's broad disk toward night descending,
Then crouching down beside the brands that redden
The column'd trunks which rear thy leafy dome,
Forgets his toils in hunter's slumbers leaden,
Or visions of the red man's spirit home:

But where his calumet by that lone fire,
At night beneath these cloister'd boughs was lighted,
The Christian orphan will in prayer aspire,
The Christian parent mourn his proud hope blighted;
And in thy shade the mother's heart will listen
The spirit-cry of babe she clasps no more,
And where thy rills through hemlock-branches glisten,
There many a maid her lover will deplore.

Here children link'd in love and sport together,
Who check their mirth as creaks the slow hearse by,
Will totter lonely in life's autumn weather,
To ponder where life's spring-time blossoms lie;
And where the virgin soil was never dinted
By the rude ploughshare since creation's birth,
Year after year fresh furrows will be printed
Upon the sad cheek of the grieving Earth.

Yon sun returning in unwearied stages,
Will gild the cenotaph's ascending spire,
O'er names on history's yet unwritten pages
That unborn crowds will, worshipping, admire;
Names that shall brighten through my country's story
Like meteor hues that fire her autumn woods,
Encircling high her onward course of glory
Like the bright bow which spans her mountain-floods.

Here where the flowers have bloom'd and died for ages—
Bloom'd all unseen and perish'd all unsung—
On youth's green grave, traced out beside the sage's,
Will garlands now by votive hearts be flung;
And sculptur'd marble and funereal urn,
O'er which gray birches to the night air wave,
Will whiten through thy glades at every turn,
And woo the moonbeam to some poet's grave!

Thus back to Nature, faithful, do we come,
When Art hath taught us all her best beguiling,
Thus blend their ministry around the tomb
Where, pointing upward, still sits Nature smiling!
And never, Nature's hallow'd spots adorning,
Hath Art, with her a sombre garden dress'd,
Wild Tawasentha! in this vale of mourning
With more to consecrate their children's rest.

And still that stream will hold its winsome way,
Sparkling as now upon the frosty air,
When all in turn shall troop in pale array
To that dim land for which so few prepare.
Still will yon oak, which now a sapling waves,
Each year renew'd, with hardy vigour grow,
Expanding still to shade the nameless graves
Of nameless men that haply sleep below.

Nameless as they—in one dear memory blest,
How tranquil in these phantom-peopled bowers
Could I here wait the partner of my rest
In some green nook that should be only ours;
Under old boughs, where moist the livelong summer
The moss is green and springy to the tread,
When thou, my friend, shouldst be an often comer
To pierce the thicket, seeking for my bed:

For thickets heavy all around should screen it
From careless gazer that might wander near;
Nor e'en to him who by some chance had seen it,
Would I have aught to catch his eye, appear:
One lonely stem—a trunk those old boughs lifting,
Should mark the spot; and, haply, new thrift owe
To that which upward through its sap was drifting
From what lay mouldering round its roots below.

The wood-duck there her glossy-throated brood
Should unmolested gather to her wings;
The schoolboy, awed, as near that mound he stood,
Should spare the redstart's nest that o'er it swings,
And thrill when there, to hear the cadenced winding
Of boatman's horn upon the distant river,
Dell unto dell in long-link'd echoes binding—
Like far-off requiem, floating on for ever.

There my freed spirit with the dawn's first beaming
Would come to revel round the dancing spray;
There would it linger with the day's last gleaming,
To watch thy footsteps thither track their way.
The quivering leaf should whisper in that hour
Things that for thee alone would have a sound,
And parting boughs my spirit-glances shower
In gleams of light upon the mossy ground.

There, when long years and all thy journeyings over—
Loosed from this world thyself to join the free,
Thou too wouldst come to rest beside thy lover
In that sweet cell beneath our trysting-tree;
Where earliest birds above our narrow dwelling
Should pipe their matins as the morning rose,
And woodland symphonies majestic swelling,
In midnight anthem, hallow our repose.

* Tawasentha—meaning, in Mohawk, "The place of the many dead"—is the finely-appropriate name of the new Forest Cemetery on the banks of the Hudson, between Albany and Troy.

THE BOB-O-LINKUM.

Thou vocal sprite—thou feather'd troubadour!
In pilgrim weeds through many a clime a ranger,
Com'st thou to doff thy russet suit once more,
And play in foppish trim the masquing stranger?
Philosophers may teach thy whereabouts and nature,
But wise, as all of us, perforce, must think 'em,
The school-boy best hath fix'd thy nomenclature,
And poets, too, must call thee Bob-O-Linkum.

Say! art thou, long mid forest glooms benighted,
So glad to skim our laughing meadows over—
With our gay orchards here so much delighted,
It makes thee musical, thou airy rover?
Or are those buoyant notes the pilfer'd treasure
Of fairy isles, which thou hast learn'd to ravish
Of all their sweetest minstrelsy at pleasure,
And, Ariel-like, again on men to lavish?

They tell sad stories of thy mad-cap freaks
Wherever o'er the land thy pathway ranges;
And even in a brace of wandering weeks,
They say, alike thy song and plumage changes;
Here both are gay; and when the buds put forth,
And leafy June is shading rock and river,
Thou art unmatch'd, blithe warbler of the North,
While through the balmy air thy clear notes
quiver.

Joyous, yet tender—was that gush of song
Caught from the brooks, where mid its wild flowers
The silent prairie listens all day long, [smiling
The only captive to such sweet beguiling;
Or didst thou, flitting through the verdurous halls
And column'd isles of western groves symphoni-
Learn from the tuneful woods, rare madrigals, [ous,
To make our flowering pastures here harmonious?

Caught'st thou thy carol from Otawa maid, [ing,
Where, through the liquid fields of wild rice plash-
Brushing the ears from off the burden'd blade,
Her birch canoe o'er some lone lake is flashing?
Or did the reeds of some savannah South,
Detain thee while thy northern flight pursuing,
To place those melodies in thy sweet mouth,
The spice-fed winds had taught them in their
wooing?

Unthrifty prodigal!—is no thought of ill
Thy ceaseless roundelay disturbing ever?
Or doth each pulse in choiring cadence still
Throb on in music till at rest for ever?
Yet now in wilder'd maze of concord floating,
'T would seem that glorious hymning to prolong,
Old Time in hearing thee might fall a-doating
And pause to listen to thy rapturous song!

THE REMONSTRANCE.

You give up the world! why, as well might the sun,
When tired of drinking the dew from the flowers,
While his rays, like young hopes, stealing off one
by one,
Die away with the muezzin's last note from the
towers,
Declare that he never would gladden again,
With one rosy smile, the young morn in its birth;
But leave weeping Day, with her sorrowful train
Of hours, to grope o'er a pall-cover'd earth.

The light of that soul once so brilliant and steady,
So far can the incense of flattery smother,
That, at thought of the world of hearts conquer'd
already,
Like Macedon's madman, you weep for another?
O! if sated with this, you would seek worlds untried,
And fresh as was ours, when first we began it,
Let me know but the sphere where you next will
abide,
And that instant, for one, I am off for that planet

PRIMEVAL WOODS.

Yes! even here, not less than in the crowd,
Here, where yon vault in formal sweep seems piled
Upon the pines, monotonously proud,
Fit dome for fane, within whose hoary veil
No ribald voice an echo hath defiled—
Where *Silence* seems articulate; up-stealing
Like a low anthem's heavenward wail:—
Oppressive on my bosom weighs the feeling
Of thoughts that language cannot shape aloud;
For song too solemn, and for prayer too wild,—
Thoughts, which beneath no human power could
quail,
For lack of utterance, in abasement bow'd,—
The cavern'd waves that struggle for revealing,
Upon whose idle foam alone God's light hath smiled.

Ere long thine every stream shall find a tongue,
Land of the Many Waters! But the sound
Of human music, these wild hills among,
Hath no one save the Indian mother flung
Its spell of tenderness? Oh, o'er this ground
So redolent of *beauty*, hath there play'd no breath
Of human poesy—none beside the word
Of Love, as, murmur'd these old boughs beneath,
Some fierce and savage suitor it hath stirr'd
To gentle issues—none but these been heard?
No mind, no soul here kindled but my own?
Doth not one hollow trunk about resound
With the faint echoes of a song long flown,
By shadows like itself now haply heard alone?

And Ye, with all this primal growth must go!
And loiterers beneath some lowly spreading shade,
Where pasture-kissing breezes shall, ere then, have
play'd,
A century hence, will doubt that there could grow
From that meek land such Titans of the glade!
Yet wherefore *primal?* when beneath my tread
Are roots whose thrifty growth, perchance, hath
arm'd
The Anak spearman when his trump alarm'd!
Roots that the Deluge wave hath plunged below;
Seeds that the Deluge wind hath scattered;
Berries that Eden's warblers may have fed,
Safe in the slime of earlier worlds embalm'd:
Again to quicken, germinate and blow, [charm'd
Again to charm the land as erst the land the

RIO BRAVO.

A MEXICAN LAMENT.—*Air*—Roncesvalles.

Rio Bravo! Rio Bravo!—saw men ever such a sight
Since the field of Roncesvalles seal'd the fate of many a knight!
Dark is Palo Alto's story—sad Resaca Palma's rout—
Ah me! upon those fields so gory how many a gallant life went out.
There our best and bravest lances shiver'd 'gainst the Northern steel,
Left the valiant hearts that couch'd them 'neath the Northern charger's heel.
Rio Bravo! Rio Bravo! brave hearts ne'er mourn'd such a sight,
Since the noblest lost their life-blood in the Roncesvalles fight.

There Arista, best and bravest—there Raguena, tried and true,
On the fatal field thou lavest, nobly did all men could do;
Vainly there those heroes rally, Castile on Montezuma's shore,
Vainly there shone Aztec valour brightly as it shone of yore.
Rio Bravo! Rio Bravo! saw men ever such a sight,
Since the dews of Roncesvalles wept for paladin and knight?

Heard ye not the wounded coursers shrieking on yon trampled banks,
As the Northern wing'd artillery thunder'd on our shatter'd ranks?
On they came—those Northern horsemen—on like eagles toward the sun;
Follow'd then the Northern bayonet, and the field was lost and won.
Rio Bravo! Rio Bravo! minstrel ne'er sung such a fight,
Since the lay of Roncesvalles sang the fame of martyr'd knight.

Rio Bravo! fatal river! saw ye not, while red with gore,
One cavalier all headless quiver, a nameless trunk upon thy shore?
Other champions not less noted sleep beneath thy sullen wave:
Sullen water, thou hast floated armies to an ocean grave.
Rio Bravo! Rio Bravo! lady ne'er wept such a sight,
Since the moon of Roncesvalles kiss'd in death her own loved knight.

Weepest thou, lorn Lady Inez, for thy lover mid the slain?
Brave La Vega's trenchant sabre cleft his slayer to the brain—
Brave La Vega, who, all lonely, by a host of foes beset,
Yielded up his falchion only when his equal there he met.
Oh, for Roland's horn to rally his paladins by the sad shore!
Rio Bravo, Roncesvalles, ye are names link'd evermore.

Sullen river! sullen river! vultures drink thy gory wave,
But they blur not those loved features, which not Love himself could save.
Rio Bravo, thou wilt name not that lone corse upon thy shore,
But in prayer sad Inez names him—names him praying evermore.
Rio Bravo! Rio Bravo! lady ne'er mourn'd such a knight,
Since the fondest hearts were broken by the Roncesvalles fight.

LOVE'S MEMORIES.

To-night! to-night! what memories to-night
Came thronging o'er me as I stood near thee!
Thy form of loveliness, thy brow of light,
Thy voice's thrilling flow—
All, all were there; to me—to me as bright
As when they claim'd my soul's idolatry
Years, long years ago.

That gulf of years! Oh, God! hadst thou been mine,
Would all that's precious have been swallow'd there?
Youth's meteor hope, and manhood's high design,
Lost, lost, forever lost—
Lost with the love that with them all would twine,
The love that left no harvest but despair—
Unwon at such a cost.

Was it *ideal*, that wild, wild love I bore thee?
Or thou thyself—didst thou my soul enthrall?
Such as thou art to-night did I adore thee,
Ay, idolize—in vain!
Such as thou art to-night—could time restore me
That wealth of loving—shouldst thou have it all,
To waste perchance again?

No! Thou didst break the coffers of my heart,
And set so lightly by the hoard within,
That I too learn'd at last the squanderer's art—
Went idly here and there,
Filing my soul, and lavishing a part
On each, less cold than thou, who cared to win
And seem'd to prize a share.

No! Thou didst wither up my flowering youth,
If blameless, still the bearer of a blight;
The unconscious agent of the deadliest ruth
That human heart hath riven;
Teaching me scorn of my own spirit's truth,
Holding, not me, but that fond worship light
Which link'd my soul to Heaven.

No, no!—For me the weakest heart before
One so untouch'd by tenderness as thine;
Angels have enter'd through the frail tent door
That pass the palace now—
And He who spake the words, "Go, sin no more,"
Mid human passions saw the spark divine,
But not in such as thou!

ROSALIE CLARE.

Who owns not she's peerless, who calls her not fair,
Who questions the beauty of Rosalie Clare?
Let him saddle his courser and spur to the field,
And, though harness'd in proof, he must perish or yield;
For no gallant can splinter, no charger may dare
The lance that is couch'd for young Rosalie Clare.

When goblets are flowing, and wit at the board
Sparkles high, while the blood of the red grape is pour'd,
And fond wishes for fair ones around offer'd up
From each lip that is wet with the dew of the cup,
What name on the brimmer floats oftener there,
Or is whisper'd more warmly, than Rosalie Clare?

They may talk of the land of the olive and vine,
Of the maids of the Ebro, the Arno, or Rhine;
Of the houris that gladden the East with their smiles,
Where the sea's studded over with green summer isles;
But what flower of far-away clime can compare
With the blossom of ours—bright Rosalie Clare?

Who owns not she's peerless, who calls her not fair?
Let him meet but the glances of Rosalie Clare!
Let him list to her voice, let him gaze on her form,
And if, seeing and hearing, his soul do not warm,
Let him go breathe it out in some less happy air
Than that which is bless'd by sweet Rosalie Clare.

THINK OF ME, DEAREST.

Think of me, dearest, when day is breaking
Away from the sable chains of night,
When the sun, his ocean-couch forsaking,
Like a giant first in his strength awaking,
Is flinging abroad his limbs of light;
As the breeze that first travels with morning forth,
Giving life to her steps o'er the quickening earth—
As the dream that has cheated my soul through the night,
Let me in thy thoughts come fresh with the light.

Think of me, dearest, when day is sinking
In the soft embrace of twilight gray,
When the starry eyes of heaven are winking,
And the weary flowers their tears are drinking,
As they start like gems on the moon-touch'd spray.
Let me come warm in thy thoughts at eve,
As the glowing track which the sunbeams leave,
When they, blushing, tremble along the deep,
While stealing away to their place of sleep.

Think of me, dearest, when round thee smiling
Are eyes that melt while they gaze on thee;
When words are winning and looks are wiling,
And those words and looks, of *others*, beguiling
Thy fluttering heart from love and me.
Let me come true in thy thoughts in that hour;
Let my trust and my faith—my devotion—have power,
When all that can lure to thy young soul is nearest,
To summon each truant thought back to me, dearest.

WE PARTED IN SADNESS.

We parted in sadness, but spoke not of parting;
We talk'd not of hopes that we both must resign,
I saw not her eyes, and but one tear-drop starting,
Fell down on her hand as it trembled in mine
Each felt that the past we could never recover,
Each felt that the future no hope could restore·
She shudder'd at wringing the heart of her lover,
I dared not to say I must meet her no more.

Long years have gone by, and the spring-time smiles ever
As o'er our young loves it first smiled in their birth.
Long years have gone by, yet that parting, O! never
Can it be forgotten by either on earth.
The note of each wild bird that carols toward heaven,
Must tell her of swift-winged hopes that were mine,
And the dew that steals over each blossom at even,
Tells me of the tear-drop that wept their decline.

THE ORIGIN OF MINT JULEPS.

And first behold this cordial Julep here,
That flames and dances in its crystal bounds,
With spirits of balm and fragrant syrups mixed;
Not that Nepenthes which the wife of Thome
In Egypt gave to Jove-born Helena,
Is of such power to stir up Joy as this,
To life so friendly, or so cool to thirst.

Milton—*Comus.*

'Tis said that the gods, on Olympus of old,
(And who the bright legend profanes with a doubt?)
One night, 'mid their revels, by Bacchus were told
That his last butt of nectar had somehow run out!

But, determined to send round the goblet once more,
They sued to the fairer immortals for aid
In composing a draught, which, till drinking were o'er,
Should cast every wine ever drank in the shade.

Grave Ceres herself blithely yielded her corn,
And the spirit that lives in each amber hued grain,
And which first had its birth from the dews of the morn,
Was taught to steal out in bright dew-drops again.

Pomona, whose choicest of fruits on the board
Were scatter'd profusely in every one's reach,
When called on a tribute to cull from the hoard,
Express'd the mild juice of the delicate peach.

The liquids were mingled, while Venus looked on,
With glances so fraught with sweet magical power,
That the honey of Hybla, e'en when they were gone.
Has never been missed in the draught from that hour

Flora then, from her bosom of fragrancy, shook,
And with roseate fingers press'd down in the bowl,
All dripping and fresh as it came from the brook,
The herb whose aroma should flavour the whole.

The draught was delicious, each god did exclaim,
Though something yet wanting they all did bewail;
But juleps the drink of immortals became,
When Jove himself added a handful of hail.

LE FAINEANT.

"Now arouse thee, Sir Knight, from thine indolent ease,
Fling boldly thy banner abroad in the breeze,
Strike home for thy lady—strive hard for the prize,
And thy guerdon shall beam from her love-lighted eyes!"

"I shrink not the trial," that bluff knight replied—
"But I battle—not *I*—for an unwilling bride;
Where the boldest may venture to do and to dare,
My pennon shall flutter—my bugle peal there!

"I quail not at aught in the struggle of life,
I'm not all unproved even now in the strife,
But the wreath that I win, all unaided—alone,
Round a faltering brow it shall never be thrown!"

"Now fie on thy manhood, to deem it a sin
That she loveth the glory thy falchion might win;
Let them doubt of thy prowess and fortune no more;
Up! Sir Knight, for thy lady—and do thy devoir!"

"She hath shrunk from my side, she hath fail'd in her *trust*,
Not relied on my blade, but remember'd its rust;
It shall brighten once more in the field of its fame,
But it is not for her I would now win a name."

The knight rode away, and the lady she sigh'd,
When he featly as ever his steed would bestride,
While the mould from the banner he shook to the wind
Seem'd to fall on the breast he left aching behind.

But the rust on his glaive and the rust in his heart
Had corroded too long and too deep to depart,
And the brand only brighten'd in honour once more,
When the heart ceased to beat on the fray-trampled shore.

TO AN AUTUMN ROSE.

Tell her I love her—love her for those eyes
Now soft with feeling, radiant now with mirth
Which, like a lake reflecting autumn skies,
Reveal two heavens here to us on Earth—
The one in which their soulful beauty lies,
And that wherein such soulfulness has birth:
Go to my lady ere the season flies,
And the rude winter comes thy bloom to blast—
Go! and with all of eloquence thou hast,
The burning story of my love discover,
And if the theme should fail, alas! to move her,
Tell her when youth's gay budding-time is past,
And summer's gaudy flowering is over,
Like thee, my love will blossom to the last!

SYMPATHY.

Well! call it *Friendship!* have I ask'd for more,
Even in those moments, when I gave thee most?
'Twas but for thee, I look'd so far before!
I saw our bark was hurrying blindly on,
A guideless thing upon a dangerous coast—
With thee—with thee, where would I not have gone?
But could I see thee *drift* upon the shore,
Unknowing drift upon a shore, unknown?
Yes, call it Friendship, and let no revealing
If love be there, e'er make love's wild name heard,
It will not die, if it be worth concealing!
Call it then Friendship—but oh, let that word
Speak but for me—for me, a deeper feeling
Than ever yet a lover's bosom stirr'd!

A PORTRAIT.

Not hers the charms which Laura's lover drew,
Or Titian's pencil on the canvas threw;
No soul enkindled beneath southern skies
Glow'd on her cheek and sparkled in her eyes;
No prurient charms set off her slender form
With swell voluptuous and with contour warm;
While each proportion was by Nature told
In maiden beauty's most bewitching mould.
High on her peerless brow—a radiant throne
Unmix'd with aught of earth—pale genius sat alone.
And yet, at times, within her eye there dwelt
Softness that would the sternest bosom melt;
A depth of tenderness which show'd, when woke,
That woman there as well as angel spoke.
Yet well that eye could flash resentment's rays,
Or, proudly scornful, check the boldest gaze;
Chill burning passion with a calm disdain,
Or with one glance rekindle it again.
Her mouth—Oh! never fascination met
Near woman's lips half so alluring yet:
For round her mouth there play'd, at times, a smile,
Such as did man from Paradise beguile;
Such, could it light him through this world of pain,
As he'd not barter Eden to regain.
What though that smile might beam alike on all;
What though that glance on each as kindly fall;
What though you knew, while worshipping their power,
Your homage but the pastime of the hour,
Still they, however guarded were the heart,
Could every feeling from its fastness start—
Deceive one still, howe'er deceived before,
And make him wish thus to be cheated more,
Till, grown at last in such illusions gray,
Faith follow'd Hope and stole with Love away.
Such was Alinda; such in her combined
Those charms which round our very nature wind,
Which, when together they in one conspire,
He who admires must love—who sees, admire.
Variably perilous; upon the sight
Now beam'd her beauty in resistless light,
And subtly now into the heart it stole,
And, ere it startled, occupied the whole.
'Twas well for her, that lovely mischief, well
That she could not the pangs it waken'd tell;
That, like the princess in the fairy tale,
No soft emotions could her soul assail;
For Nature,—that Alinda should not feel
For wounds her eyes might make, but never heal,
In mercy, while she did each gift impart
Of rarest excellence, *withheld a heart!*

INDIAN SUMMER, 1828.

Light as love's smiles, the silvery mist at morn
Floats in loose flakes along the limpid river;
The blue bird's notes upon the soft breeze borne,
As high in air he carols, faintly quiver;
The weeping birch, like banners idly waving,
Bends to the stream, its spicy branches laving;
Beaded with dew, the witch-elm's tassels shiver;
The timid rabbit from the furze is peeping,
And from the springy spray the squirrel's gayly leaping.

I love thee, Autumn, for thy scenery ere
The blasts of winter chase the varied dyes
That richly deck the slow-declining year;
I love the splendour of thy sunset skies,
The gorgeous hues that tinge each failing leaf,
Lovely as beauty's cheek, as woman's love too, brief;
I love the note of each wild bird that flies,
As on the wind he pours his parting lay,
And wings his loitering flight to summer climes away.

O, Nature! still I fondly turn to thee,
With feelings fresh as e'er my childhood's were;—
Though wild and passion-toss'd my youth may be,
Toward thee I still the same devotion bear;
To thee—to thee—though health and hope no more
Life's wasted verdure may to me restore—
I still can, child-like, come as when in prayer
I bow'd my head upon a mother's knee,
And deem'd the world, like her, all truth and purity.

TOWN REPININGS.

River! O, river! thou rovest free,
From the mountain height to the fresh blue sea!
Free thyself, but with silver chain,
Linking each charm of land and main,
From the splinter'd crag thou leap'st below,
Through leafy glades at will to flow—
Lingering now, by the steep's moss'd edge—
Loitering now mid the dallying sedge:
And pausing ever, to call thy waves
From grassy meadows and fern-clad caves—
And then, with a prouder tide to break
From wooded valley, to breezy lake:
Yet all of these scenes, though fair they be,
River! O, river! are bann'd to me.

River! O, river! upon thy tide
Full many a freighted bark doth glide;
Would that thou thus couldst bear away
The thoughts that burthen my weary day!
Or that I, from all save them made free,
Though laden still, might rove with thee!
True that thy waves brief lifetime find,
And live at the will of the wanton wind—
True that thou seekest the ocean's flow,
To be lost therein for evermoe.
Yet the slave who worships at Glory's shrine,
But toils for a bubble as frail as thine:
But loses his freedom here, to be
Forgotten as soon as in death set free.

THE WESTERN HUNTER TO HIS MISTRESS.

Wend, love, with me, to the deep woods, wend.
Where far in the forest the wild flowers keep,
Where no watching eye shall over us bend,
Save the blossoms that into thy bower peep.
Thou shalt gather from buds of the oriole's hue,
Whose flaming wings round our pathway flit,
From the saffron orchis and lupin blue,
And those like the foam on my courser's bit.

One steed and one saddle us both shall bear,
One hand of each on the bridle meet;
And beneath the wrist that entwines me there,
An answering pulse from my heart shall beat.
I will sing thee many a joyous lay,
As we chase the deer by the blue lake-side,
While the winds that over the prairie play
Shall fan the cheek of my woodland bride.

Our home shall be by the cool, bright streams,
Where the beaver chooses her safe retreat,
And our hearth shall smile like the sun's warm gleams
Through the branches around our lodge that meet.
Then wend with me, to the deep woods wend,
Where far in the forest the wild flowers keep,
Where no watching eye shall over us bend,
Save the blossoms that into thy bower peep.

THY NAME.

It comes to me when healths go round,
And o'er the wine their garlands wreathing
The flowers of wit, with music wound,
Are freshly from the goblet breathing;
From sparkling song and sally gay
It comes to steal my heart away,
And fill my soul, mid festal glee,
With sad, sweet, silent thoughts of thee.

It comes to me upon the mart,
Where care in jostling crowds is rife;
Where Avarice goads the sordid heart,
Or cold Ambition prompts the strife;
It comes to whisper, if I'm there,
'T is but with thee each prize to share,
For Fame were not success to me,
Nor riches wealth unshared with thee.

It comes to me when smiles are bright
On gentle lips that murmur round me,
And kindling glances flash delight
In eyes whose spell would once have bound me
It comes—but comes to bring alone
Remembrance of some look or tone,
Dearer than aught I hear or see,
Because 't was born or breathed by thee

It comes to me where cloister'd boughs
Their shadows cast upon the sod;
A while in Nature's fane my vows
Are lifted from her shrine to God;
It comes to tell that all of worth
I dream in heaven or know on earth,
However bright or dear it be,
Is blended with my thought of thee.

THE MYRTLE AND STEEL.

One bumper yet, gallants, at parting,
One toast ere we arm for the fight;
Fill round, each to her he loves dearest—
'T is the last he may pledge her, to-night.
Think of those who of old at the banquet
Did their weapons in garlands conceal,
The patriot heroes who hallowed
The entwining of myrtle and steel!
Then hey for the myrtle and steel,
Then ho for the myrtle and steel,
Let every true blade that e'er loved a fair maid,
Fill round to the myrtle and steel!

'T is in moments like this, when each bosom
With its highest-toned feeling is warm,
Like the music that's said from the ocean
To rise ere the gathering storm,
That her image around us should hover,
Whose name, though our lips ne'er reveal,
We may breathe mid the foam of a bumper,
As we drink to the myrtle and steel.
Then hey for the myrtle and steel,
Then ho for the myrtle and steel,
Let every true blade that e'er loved a fair maid,
Fill round to the myrtle and steel!

Now mount, for our bugle is ringing
To marshal the host for the fray,
Where proudly our banner is flinging
Its folds o'er the battle-array;
Yet gallants—one moment—remember,
When your sabres the death-blow would deal,
That Mercy wears *her* shape who's cherish'd
By lads of the myrtle and steel.
Then hey for the myrtle and steel,
Then ho for the myrtle and steel,
Let every true blade that e'er loved a fair maid,
Fill round to the myrtle and steel!

EPITAPH UPON A DOG.

An ear that caught my slightest tone,
In kindness or in anger spoken;
An eye that ever watch'd my own,
In vigils death alone has broken;
Its changeless, ceaseless, and unbought
Affection to the last revealing;
Beaming almost with human thought,
And more—far more than human feeling!

Can such in endless sleep be chill'd,
And mortal pride disdain to sorrow,
Because the pulse that here was still'd
May wake to no immortal morrow?
Can faith, devotedness, and love,
That seem to humbler creatures given
To tell us what we owe above,—
The types of what is due to Heaven,—

Can these be with the things that *were*,
Things cherish'd—but no more returning,
And leave behind no trace of care,
No shade that speaks a moment's mourning?

Alas! my friend, of all of worth
That years have stolen or years yet leave me,
I've never known so much on earth,
But that the loss of thine must grieve me

ANACREONTIC.

Blame not the bowl—the fruitful bowl,
Whence wit, and mirth, and music spring,
And amber drops elysian roll,
To bathe young Love's delighted wing.
What like the grape Osiris gave
Makes rigid age so lithe of limb?
Illumines memory's tearful wave,
And teaches drowning hope to swim?
Did ocean from his radiant arms
To earth another Venus give,
He ne'er could match the mellow charms
That in the breathing beaker live.

Like burning thoughts which lovers hoard,
In characters that mock the sight,
Till some kind liquid, o'er them pour'd,
Brings all their hidden warmth to light—
Are feelings bright, which, in the cup,
Though graven deep, appear but dim,
Till, fill'd with glowing Bacchus up,
They sparkle on the foaming brim.
Each drop upon the first you pour
Brings some new tender thought to life,
And, as you fill it more and more,
The last with fervid soul is rife.

The island fount, that kept of old
Its fabled path beneath the sea,
And fresh, as first from earth it roll'd,
From earth again rose joyously:
Bore not beneath the bitter brine
Each flower upon its limpid tide,
More faithfully than in the wine
Our hearts toward each other glide
Then drain the cup, and let thy soul
Learn, as the draught delicious flies,
Like pearls in the Egyptian's bowl,
Truth beaming at the bottom lies.

A HUNTER'S MATIN.

Up, comrades, up! the morn's awake
Upon the mountain side,
The curlew's wing hath swept the lake,
And the deer has left the tangled brake,
To drink from the limpid tide
Up, comrades, up! the mead-lark's note
And the plover's cry o'er the prairie float;
The squirrel, he springs from his covert now,
To prank it away on the chestnut bough,
Where the oriole's pendant nest, high up,
Is rock'd on the swaying trees,
While the humbird sips from the harebell's cup,
As it bends to the morning breeze.
Up, comrades, up! our shallops grate
Upon the pebbly strand,
And our stalwart hounds impatient wait
To spring from the huntsman's hand.

SPARKLING AND BRIGHT.

Sparkling and bright in liquid light
Does the wine our goblets gleam in,
With hue as red as the rosy bed
Which a bee would choose to dream in.
Then fill to-night with hearts as light,
To loves as gay and fleeting
As bubbles that swim on the beaker's brim,
And break on the lips while meeting.

O! if Mirth might arrest the flight
Of Time through Life's dominions,
We here a while would now beguile
The graybeard of his pinions,
To drink to-night with hearts as light,
To loves as gay and fleeting
As bubbles that swim on the beaker's brim,
And break on the lips while meeting.

But since delight can't tempt the wight,
Nor fond regret delay him,
Nor Love himself can hold the elf,
Nor sober Friendship stay him,
We'll drink to-night with hearts as light,
To loves as gay and fleeting
As bubbles that swim on the beaker's brim,
And break on the lips while meeting.

SEEK NOT TO UNDERSTAND HER.

Why seek her heart to understand,
If but enough thou knowest
To prove that all thy love, like sand,
Upon the wind thou throwest?
The ill thou makest out at last
Doth but reflect the bitter past,
While all the good thou learnest yet,
But makes her harder to forget.

What matters all the nobleness
Which in her breast resideth,
And what the warmth and tenderness
Her mien of coldness hideth,
If but ungenerous thoughts prevail
When thou her bosom wouldst assail,
While tenderness and warmth doth ne'er,
By any chance, toward thee appear.

Sum up each token thou hast won
Of kindred feeling there—
How few for Hope, to build upon,
How many for Despair!
And if e'er word or look declareth
Love or aversion, which she beareth,
While of the first, no proof thou hast,
How many are there of the last!

Then strive no more to understand
Her heart, of whom thou knowest
Enough to prove thy love like sand
Upon the wind thou throwest:
The ill thou makest out at last
Doth but reflect the bitter past,
While all the good thou learnest yet
But makes her harder to forget.

ASK NOT WHY I SHOULD LOVE HER.

Ask me not why I should love her:
Look upon those soul-full eyes!
Look while mirth or feeling move her,
And see there how sweetly rise
Thoughts gay and gentle from a breast,
Which is of innocence the nest—
Which, though each joy were from it shred,
By truth would still be tenanted!

See, from those sweet windows peeping,
Emotions tender, bright, and pure,
And wonder not the faith I'm keeping
Every trial can endure!
Wonder not that looks so winning
Still for me new ties are spinning;
Wonder not that heart so true
Keeps mine from ever changing too.

SHE LOVES, BUT 'T IS NOT ME.

She loves, but 't is not me she loves:
Not me on whom she ponders,
When, in some dream of tenderness,
Her truant fancy wanders.
The forms that flit her visions through
Are like the shapes of old,
Where tales of prince and paladin
On tapestry are told.
Man may not hope her heart to win,
Be his of common mould.

But I—though spurs are won no more
Where herald's trump is pealing,
Nor thrones carved out for lady fair
Where steel-clad ranks are wheeling—
I loose the falcon of my hopes
Upon as proud a flight
As those who hawk'd at high renown,
In song-ennobled fight.
If *daring*, then, true love may crown,
My love she must requite.

THY SMILES.

'T is hard to share her smiles with many!
And while she is so dear to me,
To fear that I, far less than any,
Call out her spirit's witchery!
To find my inmost heart when near her
Trembling at every glance and tone,
And feel the while each charm grow dearer
That will not beam for me alone.

How can she thus, sweet spendthrift, squander
The treasures one alone can prize!
How can her eyes to all thus wander,
When I but live in those sweet eyes!
Those syren tones so lightly spoken
Cause many a heart I know to thrill;
But mine, and only mine, till broken,
In every pulse must answer still.

LOVE AND POLITICS.

A BIRTH-DAY MEDITATION.

Another year! alas, how swift,
 Alinda, do these years flit by,
Like shadows thrown by clouds that drift
 In flakes along a wintry sky.
Another year! another leaf
Is turn'd within life's volume brief,
And yet not one bright page appears
Of mine within that book of years.

There are some moments when I feel
 As if it should not yet be so;
As if the years that from me steal
 Had not a right alike to go,
And lose themselves in Time's dark sea,
Unbuoy'd up by aught from me;
Aught that the future yet might claim
To rescue from their wreck a name.

But it was love that taught me rhyme,
 And it was thou that taught me love;
And if I in this idle chime
 Of words a useless sluggard prove,
It was thine eyes the habit nurs'd,
And in their light I learn'd it first.
It is thine eyes which, day by day,
Consume my time and heart away.

And often bitter thoughts arise
 Of what I've lost in loving thee,
And in my breast my spirit dies,
 The gloomy cloud around to see,
Of baffled hopes and ruined powers
Of mind, and miserable hours—
Of self-upbraiding, and despair—
Of heart, too strong and fierce to bear.

"Why, what a peasant slave am I,"
 To bow my mind and bend my knee
To woman in idolatry,
 Who takes no thought of mine or me.
O, God! that I could breathe my life
On battle-plain in charging strife—
In one mad impulse pour my soul
Far beyond passion's base control.

Thus do my jarring thoughts revolve
 Their gather'd causes of offence,
Until I in my heart resolve
 To dash thine angel image thence;
When some bright look, some accent kind,
Comes freshly in my heated mind,
And scares, like newly-flushing day,
These brooding thoughts like owls away.

And then for hours and hours I muse
 On things that might, yet will not be,
Till, one by one, my feelings lose
 Their passionate intensity,
And steal away in visions soft,
Which on wild wing those feelings waft
Far, far beyond the drear domain
Of Reason and her freezing reign.

And now again from their gay track
 I call, as I despondent sit,
Once more these truant fancies back,
 Which round my brain so idly flit;
And some I treasure, some I blush
To own—and these I try to crush—
And some, too wild for reason's reign,
I loose in idle rhyme again.

And even thus my moments fly,
 And even thus my hours decay,
And even thus my years slip by,
 My life itself is wiled away;
But distant still the mounting hope,
The burning wish with men to cope
In aught that minds of iron mould
May do or dare for fame or gold.

Another year! another year,
 Alinda, it shall not be so;
Both love and lays forswear I here,
 As I've forsworn thee long ago.
That name, which thou wouldst never share,
Proudly shall Fame emblazon where
On pumps and corners posters stick it,
The highest on the Jackson ticket.

WHAT IS SOLITUDE?

Not in the shadowy wood,
 Not in the crag-hung glen,
Not where the echoes brood
 In caves untrod by men;
Not by the bleak sea-shore,
 Where loitering surges break,
Not on the mountain hoar,
 Not by the breezeless lake,
Not on the desert plain,
 Where man hath never stood,
Whether on isle or main—
 Not there is solitude!

Birds are in woodland bowers,
 Voices in lonely dells,
Streams to the listening hours
 Talk in earth's secret cells;
Over the gray-ribb'd sand
 Breathe ocean's frothing lips,
Over the still lake's strand
 The flower toward it dips;
Pluming the mountain's crest,
 Life tosses in its pines;
Coursing the desert's breast,
 Life in the steed's mane shines.

Leave—if thou wouldst be lonely-
 Leave Nature for the crowd;
Seek there for one—one only—
 With kindred mind endow'd!
There—as with Nature erst
 Closely thou wouldst commune
The deep soul-music, nursed
 In either heart, attune!
Heart-wearied, thou wilt own.
 Vainly that phantom woo'd,
That thou at last hast known
 What is true solitude!

JAMES NACK.

[Born, about 1807.]

There are few more interesting characters in our literary annals than James Nack. He is a native of New York, and when between nine and ten years of age, by a fall, while descending a flight of stairs with a little playmate in his arms, received such injury in his head as deprived him irrecoverably of the sense of hearing, and, gradually, in consequence, of the faculty of speech. He was placed in the Institution for the Education of the Deaf and Dumb, where he acquired knowledge in all departments with singular exactness and rapidity. He was subsequently for many years an assistant in the office of the Clerk of the City and County, and in 1838 was married.

In 1827 Mr. Nack published "The Legend of the Rocks, and other Poems;" in 1839, "Earl Rupert, and other Tales and Poems," with an interesting memoir of his life, by General Wetmore; and in 1852 a third volume of "Poems," with an introduction by his friend General Morris. What is most remarkable in these works is their excellent versification. In other respects they deserve a great deal of praise; but that a person deaf and dumb from so early a period of childhood should possess such a mastery of the harmonies of language is marvellous. The various productions of Mr. Nack illustrate a genial temper, and a refined and richly cultivated taste. The range and completeness of his accomplishments as a linguist is illustrated in spirited and elegant translations from Dutch, German, French, and other literatures.

MIGNONNE.

She calls me "father!" though my ear
That thrilling name shall never hear,
Yet to my heart affection brings
The sound in sweet imaginings;
I feel its gushing music roll
The stream of rapture on my soul;
And when she starts to welcome me,
And when she totters to my knee,
And when she climbs it, to embrace
My bosom for her hiding-place,
And when she nestling there reclines,
And with her arms my neck entwines,
And when her lips of roses seek
To press their sweetness on my cheek,
And when upon my careful breast
I lull her to her cherub rest,
I whisper o'er the sinless dove—
"I love thee with a father's love!"

SPRING IS COMING.

Spring is coming! spring is coming!
Birds are chirping, insects humming,
Flowers are peeping from their sleeping,
Streams escaped from winter's keeping,
In delighted freedom rushing,
Dance along in music gushing;
Scenes of late in deadness sadden'd
Smile in animation gladden'd;
All is beauty, all is mirth,
All is glory upon earth.
Shout we then, with Nature's voice—
Welcome Spring! rejoice! rejoice!

Spring is coming! come, my brother,
Let us rove with one another,

To our well-remember'd wild-wood,
Flourishing in nature's childhood,
Where a thousand flowers are springing,
And a thousand birds are singing;
Where the golden sunbeams quiver
On the verdure bordered river;
Let our youth of feeling out
To the youth of nature shout,
While the waves repeat our voice—
Welcome Spring! rejoice! rejoice!

MARY'S BEE.

As Mary with her lip of roses
Is tripping o'er the flowery mead,
A foolish little bee supposes
The rosy lip a rose indeed,
And so, astonish'd at his bliss,
He steals the honey of her kiss.

A moment there he wantons; lightly
He sports away on careless wing;
But ah! why swells that wound unsightly?
The rascal! he has left a sting!
She runs to me with weeping eyes,
Sweet images of April skies.

"Be this," said I, "to heedless misses,
A warning they should bear in mind;
Too oft a lover steals their kisses,
Then flies, and leaves a sting behind."
"This may be wisdom to be sure,"
Said Mary, "but I want a cure."

What could I do? To ease the swelling
My lips with hers impassion'd meet—
And trust me, from so sweet a dwelling,
I found the very poison sweet!
Fond boy! unconscious of the smart,
I sucked the poison to my heart!

WILLIAM GILMORE SIMMS.

[Born, 1806.]

The author of "Guy Rivers," "Southern Passages and Pictures," etc., was born in Charleston, South Carolina, in the spring of 1806. His mother died during his infancy, and his father soon after emigrated to one of the western territories, leaving him under the guardianship of a grandmother, who superintended his early education. When not more than nine or ten years old, he began to write verses; at fifteen he was a contributor to the poetical department of the gazettes printed near his home; and at eighteen he published his first volume, entitled "Lyrical and other Poems," which was followed in the next two years by "Early Lays," and "The Vision of Cortez and other Pieces," and in 1830, by "The Tricolor, or Three Days of Blood in Paris." In each of these four volumes there were poetical ideas, and occasionally well-finished verses; but they are worthy of little regard, except as indications of the early tendency of the author's mind.

When twenty-one years old, Mr. Simms was admitted to the bar, and began to practise his profession in his native district; but feeling a deep interest in the political questions which then agitated the country, he soon abandoned the courts, and purchased a daily gazette at Charleston, which he edited for several years, with industry, integrity, and ability.* It was, however, unsuccessful, and he lost by it all his property, as well as the prospective earnings of several years. His ardour was not lessened by this failure, and, confident of success, he determined to retrieve his fortune by authorship. He had been married at an early age; his wife, as well as his father, was now dead; and no domestic ties binding him to Charleston, he in the spring of 1832 visited for the first time the northern states. After travelling over the most interesting portions of the country, he paused at the rural village of Hingham, in Massachusetts, and there prepared for the press his principal poetical work, "Atalantis, a Story of the Sea," which was published at New York in the following winter. This is an imaginative story, in the dramatic form; its plot is exceedingly simple, but effectively managed, and it contains much beautiful imagery, and fine description. While a vessel glides over a summer sea, Leon, one of the principal characters, and his sister Isabel, hear a benevolent spirit of the air warning them of the designs of a sea-god to lure them into peril.

Leo. Didst hear the strain it utter'd, Isabel?
Isa. All, all! It spoke, methought, of peril near,
From rocks and wiles of the ocean; did it not?
Leon. It did, but idly! Here can lurk no rocks;
For, by the chart which now before me lies,
Thy own unpractised eye may well discern
The wide extent of the ocean—shoreless all.
The land, for many a league, to the eastward hangs
And not a point beside it.
Isa. Wherefore, then,
Should come this voice of warning?
Leon. From the deep:
It hath its demons as the earth and air,
All tributaries to the master-fiend
That sets their springs in motion. This is one,
That, doubting to mislead us, plants this wile,
So to divert our course, that we may strike
The very rocks he fain would warn us from.
Isa. A subtle sprite: and, now I think of it,
Dost thou remember the old story told
By Diaz Ortis, the lame mariner,
Of an adventure in the Indian Seas,
Where he made one with John of Portugal,
Touching a woman of the ocean wave,
That swam beside the barque, and sang strange songs
Of riches in the waters; with a speech
So winning on the senses, that the crew
Grew all infected with the melody;
And, but for a good father of the church,
Who made the sign of the cross, and offer'd up
Befitting prayers, which drove the fiend away,
They had been tempted by her cunning voice
To leap into the ocean.
Leon. I do, I do!
And, at the time, I do remember me,
I made much mirth of the extravagant tale,
As a deceit of the reason: the old man
Being in his second childhood, and at fits
Wild, as you know, on other themes than this.
Isa. I never more shall mock at marvellous things.
Such strange conceits hath after-time found true,
That once were themes for jest. I shall not smile
At the most monstrous legend.
Leon. Nor will I:
To any tale of mighty wonderment
I shall bestow my ear, nor wonder more;
And every fancy that my childhood bred,
In vagrant dreams of frolic, I shall look
To have, without rebuke, my sense approve.
Thus, like a little island in the sea,
Girt in by perilous waters, and unknown
To all adventure, may be yon same cloud,
Specking, with fleecy bosom, the blue sky,
Lit by the rising moon. There we may dream,
And find no censure in an after day—
Throng the assembled fairies, perched on beams,
And riding on their way triumphantly.
There gather the coy spirits. Many a fay,
Roving the silver sands of that same isle,
Floating in azure ether, plumes her wing
Of ever-frolicsome fancy, and pursues—
While myriads, like herself, do watch the chase—
Some truant sylph, through the infinitude
Of their uncircumscribed and rich domain.
There sport they through the night, with mimicry
Of strife and battle; striking their tiny shields
And gathering into combat; meeting fierce,
With lip compress'd and spear aloft, and eye
Glaring with fight and desperate circumstance;
Then sudden—in a moment all their wrath
Mellow'd to friendly terms of courtesy—
Throwing aside the dread array, and link'd
Each in his foe's embrace. Then comes the dance,
The grateful route, the wild and musical pomp,

* The Charleston City Gazette, conducted by Mr. Simms, was, I believe, the first journal in South Carolina that took ground against the principle of nullification

The long procession o'er fantastic realms
Of cloud and moonbeam, through the enamour'd night,
Making it all one revel. Thus the eye,
Breathed on by fancy, with enlarged scope,
Through the protracted and deep hush of night
May note the fairies, coursing the lazy hours
In various changes, and without fatigue.
A fickle race, who tell their time by flowers,
And live on zephyrs, and have stars for lamps,
And night-dews for ambrosia; perch'd on beams,
Speeding through space, even with the scattering light
On which they feed and frolic.

Isa. A sweet dream:
And yet, since this same tale we laugh'd at once,
The story of old OBTIS, is made sooth—
Perchance not all a dream. I would not doubt.

Leon. And yet there may be, dress'd in subtle guise
Of unsuspected art, some gay deceit
Of human conjuration mix'd with this.
Some cunning seaman having natural skill—
As, from the books, we learn may yet be done—
Hath 'yond our vessel's figure pitch'd his voice,
Leading us wantonly.

Isa. It is not so,
Or does my sense deceive? Look there: the wave
A perch beyond our barque. What dost thou see?

Leon. A marvellous shape, that with the billow curls,
In gambols of the deep, and yet is not
Its wonted burden; for beneath the waves
I mark a gracious form, though nothing clear
Of visage I discern. Again it speaks.

The ship is wrecked, and ATALANTIS, a fairy, wandering along the beach with an attendant, NEA, discovers the inanimate form of LEON clinging to a spar.

But what is here,
Grasping a shaft, and lifelessly stretch'd out?

Nea. One of the creatures of that goodly barque—
Perchance the only one of many men,
That, from their distant homes, went forth in her,
And here have perish'd.

Atal. There is life in him—
And his heart swells beneath my hand, with pulse
Fitful and faint, returning now, now gone,
That much I fear it may not come again.
How very young he is—how beautiful!
Made, with a matchless sense of what is true,
In manly grace and chisell'd elegance;
And features, rounded in as nice a mould
As our own, NEA. There, his eye unfolds—
Stand away, girl, and let me look on him!
It cannot be, that such a form as this,
So lovely and compelling, ranks below
The creatures of our kingdom. He is one,
That, 'mongst them all, might well defy compare—
Outshining all that shine!

Nea. He looks as well,
In outward seeming, as our own, methinks—
And yet, he may be but a shaped thing,
Wanting in every show of that high sense
Which makes the standard of true excellence.

Atal. O, I am sure there is no want in him—
The spirit must be true, the sense be high,
The soul as far ascending, strong and bright,
As is the form he wears, and they should be
Pleased to inhabit—'t were a fitting home!
Breathe on him, NEA. Fan him with thy wing,
And so arouse him. I would have him speak,
And satisfy my doubt. Stay, yet a while—
Now, while his senses sleep, I'll place my lip
Upon his own—it is so beautiful!
Such lips should give forth music—such a sweet
Should have been got in heaven—the produce there
Of never-blighted gardens. [*Kisses him.*

Leon. [*starts.*] Cling to me—
Am I not with thee now, my ISABEL? [*Swoons again.*

Atal. O, gentle sounds—how sweetly did they fall
In broken murmurs, like a melody,
From lips that waiting long on loving hearts,
Had learned to murmur like them. Wake again,
Sweet stranger! If my lips have wrought this spell,
And won thee back to life, though but to sigh,
And sleep again in death, they shall, once more,
Wake and restore thee.

MR. SIMMS now commenced that career of intellectual activity of which the results are as voluminous and as various, perhaps, as can be exhibited by any author of his age. His first romance was "Martin Faber, the Story of a Criminal," published in New York in 1833. The most important of his subsequent productions in this department, as classified in the edition lately issued by Mr. REDFIELD, are, the revolutionary series, "The Partisan," "Mellichampe," "Katherine Walton," "The Scout," "Woodcraft," "The Foragers," and "Eutaw;" border tales, "Guy Rivers," "Richard Hurdis," "Border Beagles," "Charlemont," "Beauchampe," and "Confession;" historical, "The Yemassee," "Vasconcellos," "The Lily and the Totem," "Pelayo," and "Count Julian." Besides his more extended romantic fictions, he has produced a great number of shorter stories, some of which may be ranked as the best exhibitions of his powers. He has also given to the public a "History of South Carolina," a "Life of Captain JOHN SMITH, the Founder of Virginia," a "Life of NATHANIEL GREENE," a "Life of FRANCIS MARION," a "Life of the Chevalier BAYARD," "Views and Reviews of American History, Literature, and Art," and other performances in biography, description, and speculation.

In poetry, since the appearance of "Atalantis," he has published "Southern Passages and Pictures," 1839; "Donna Florida, in Five Cantos," 1843; "Grouped Thoughts and Scattered Fancies, a collection of Sonnets," 1845; "Areytos, or Songs of the South," 1846; "Lays of the Palmetto, a Tribute to the South Carolina Regiment, in the War with Mexico," 1846; "The Cacique of Accube, and other Poems," 1848; "Norman Maurice," 1850; and a collection of his principal poetical works, under the title of "Poems, Descriptive, Legendary, and Contemplative," in two volumes, 1854.

A more particular account of the novels of Dr. SIMMS, (he has received the degree of LL.D. from the University of Alabama,) is given in "The Prose Writers of America." His poems, like his other productions, are noticeable for warmth of feeling and coloring, and vivid and just displays of the temper and sentiments of the southern people, the characteristics of southern life, and the rivers, forests, savannas, and all else that is peculiar in southern nature. He has sung the physical and moral aspects and the traditions of the south, with the appreciation of a poet, and the feeling of a son. His verse is free and musical, his language copious and well-selected, and his fancy fertile and apposite. The best of his dramatic pieces is "Norman Maurice," a play of singular originality in design and execution, which strikes me as the best composition of its kind on an American subject.

He resides at "Woodlands," a pleasant plantation in the vicinity of Charleston.

THE SLAIN EAGLE.

The eye that mark'd thy flight with deadly aim,
Had less of warmth and splendour than thine own;
The form that did thee wrong could never claim
The matchless vigour which thy wing hath shown;
Yet art thou in thy pride of flight o'erthrown;
And the far hills that echoed back thy scream,
As from storm-gathering clouds thou sent'st it down,
Shall see no more thy red-eyed glances stream
For their far summits round, with strong and terrible gleam.

Lone and majestic monarch of the cloud!
No more I see thee on the tall cliff's brow,
When tempests meet, and from their watery shroud
Pour their wild torrents on the plains below,
Lifting thy fearless wing, still free to go,
True in thy aim, undaunted in thy flight,
As seeking still, yet scorning, every foe—
Shrieking the while in consciousness of might,
To thy own realm of high and undisputed light.

Thy thought was not of danger then—thy pride
Left thee no fear. Thou hadst gone forth in storms,
And thy strong pinions had been bravely tried
Against their rush. Vainly their gathering forms
Had striven against thy wing. Such conflict warms
The nobler spirit; and thy joyful shriek
Gave token that the strife itself had charms
For the born warrior of the mountain peak,
He of the giant brood, sharp fang, and bloody beak.

How didst thou then, in very mirth, spread far
Thy pinions' strength!—with freedom that became
Audacious license, with the winds at war,
Striding the yielding clouds that girt thy frame,
And, with a fearless rush that naught could tame,
Defying earth—defying all that mars
The flight of other wings of humbler name;
For thee, the storm had impulse, but no bars
To stop thy upward flight, thou pilgrim of the stars!

Morning above the hills, and from the ocean,
Ne'er leap'd abroad into the fetterless blue
With such a free and unrestrained motion,
Nor shook from her ethereal wing the dew
That else had clogg'd her flight and dimm'd her view,
With such calm effort as 'twas thine to wear—
Bending with sunward course erect and true,
When winds were piping high and lightnings near,
By day-guide all withdrawn, through fathomless fields of air.

The moral of a chosen race wert thou,
In such proud fight. From out the ranks of men—
The million moilers, with earth-cumber'd brow,
That slink, like coward tigers to their den,
Each to his hiding-place and corner then—
One mighty spirit watch'd thee in that hour,
Nor turn'd his lifted heart to earth again;
Within his soul there sprang a holy power,
And he grew strong to sway, whom tempests made not cower.

Watching, he saw thy rising wing. In vain,
From his superior dwelling, the fierce sun
Shot forth his brazen arrows, to restrain
The audacious pilgrim, who would gaze upon
The secret splendours of his central throne;
Proudly, he saw thee to that presence fly,
And, Eblis-like, unaided and alone,
His dazzling glories seek, his power defy,
Raised to thy god's own face, meanwhile, thy rebel eye.

And thence he drew a hope, a hope to soar,
Even with a wing like thine. His daring glance
Sought, with as bold a vision, to explore
The secret of his own deliverance—
The secret of his wing—and to advance
To sovereign sway like thine—to rule, to rise
Above his race, and nobly to enhance
Their empire as his own—to make the skies,
The extended earth, far seas, and solemn stars, his prize.

He triumphs—and he perishes like thee!
Scales the sun's heights, and mounts above the winds,
Breaks down the gloomy barrier, and is free!
The worm receives his winglet: he unbinds
The captive thought, and in its centre finds
New barriers, and a glory in his gaze;
He mocks, as thou, the sun!—but scaly blinds
Grow o'er his vision, till, beneath the daze,
From his proud height he falls, amid the world's amaze.

And thou, brave bird! thy wing hath pierced the cloud,
The storm had not a battlement for thee;
But, with a spirit fetterless and proud,
Thou hast soar'd on, majestically free,
To worlds, perchance, which men shall never see!
Where is thy spirit now? the wing that bore?
Thou hast lost wing and all, save liberty!
Death only could subdue—and that is o'er:
Alas! the very form that slew thee should deplore!

A proud exemplar hath been lost the proud,
And he who struck thee from thy fearless flight—
Thy noble loneliness, that left the crowd,
To seek, uncurb'd, that singleness of height
Which glory aims at with unswerving sight—
Had learn'd a nobler toil. No longer base
With lowliest comrades, he had given his might,
His life—that had been cast in vilest place—
To raise his hopes and homes—to teach and lift his race.

'Tis he should mourn thy fate, for he hath lost
The model of dominion. Not for him
The mighty eminence, the gathering host
That worships, the high glittering pomps that dim
The bursting homage and the hailing hymn:
He dies—he hath no life, that, to a star,
Rises from dust and sheds a holy gleam
To light the struggling nations from afar,
And show, to kindred souls, where fruits of glory are.

Exulting now, he clamours o'er his prey;
His secret shaft hath not been idly sped;
He lurk'd within the rocky cleft all day,
Till the proud bird rose sweeping o'er his head,
And thus he slew him! He should weep him dead,
Whom, living, he could love not—weep that he,
The noble lesson taught him, never read—
Exulting o'er the victim much more free
Than, in his lowly soul, he e'er can hope to be.

'T is triumph for the base to overthrow
That which they reach not—the ignoble mind
Loves ever to assail with secret blow
The loftier, purer beings of their kind:
In this their petty villany is blind;
They hate their benefactors—men who keep
Their names from degradation—men design'd
Their guides and guardians: well, if late they weep
The cruel shaft that struck such noble hearts so deep.

Around thy mountain dwelling the winds lie—
Thy wing is gone, thy eyry desolate;
O, who shall teach thy young ones when to fly,—
Who fill the absence of thy watchful mate?
Thou type of genius! bitter is thy fate,
A boor has sent the shaft that leaves them lone,
Thy clustering fellows, guardians of thy state—
Shaft from the reedy fen whence thou hast flown,
And feather from the bird thy own wing hath struck down!

THE BROOKLET.

A LITTLE farther on, there is a brook
Where the breeze lingers idly. The high trees
Have roof'd it with their crowding limbs and leaves,
So that the sun drinks not from its sweet fount,
And the shade cools it. You may hear it now,
A low, faint beating, as, upon the leaves
That lie beneath its rapids, it descends
In a fine, showery rain, that keeps one tune,
And 't is a sweet one, still of constancy.
Beside its banks, through the whole livelong day,
Ere yet I noted much the speed of time,
And knew him but in songs and ballad-books,
Nor cared to know him better, I have lain;
With thought unchid by harsher din than came
From the thick thrush, that, gliding through the copse,
Hurried above me; or the timid fawn
That came down to the brooklet's edge to drink,
And saunter'd through its shade, cropping the grass,
Even where I lay,—having a quiet mood,
And not disturbing, while surveying mine.
Thou smilest—and on thy lip a straying thought
Says I have trifled—calls my hours misspent,
And looks a solemn warning! A true thought,—
And so my errant mood were well rebuked!—
Yet there was pleasant sadness that became
Meetly the gentle heart and pliant sense,
In that same idlesse—gazing on that brook
So pebbly and so clear,—prattling away,
Like a young child, all thoughtless, till it goes
From shadow into sunlight, and is lost.

THE SHADED WATER.

WHEN that my mood is sad, and in the noise
And bustle of the crowd, I feel rebuke,
I turn my footsteps from its hollow joys,
And sit me down beside this little brook:
The waters have a music to mine ear
It glads me much to hear.

It is a quiet glen as you may see,
Shut in from all intrusion by the trees,
That spread their giant branches, broad and free
The silent growth of many centuries;
And make a hallow'd time for hapless moods,
A Sabbath of the woods.

Few know its quiet shelter,—none, like me,
Do seek it out with such a fond desire,
Poring, in idlesse mood, on flower and tree,
And listening, as the voiceless leaves respire,—
When the far-travelling breeze, done wandering,
Rests here his weary wing.

And all the day, with fancies ever new,
And sweet companions from their boundless store
Of merry elves, bespangled all with dew,
Fantastic creatures of the old time lore,—
Watching their wild but unobtrusive play,
I fling the hours away.

A gracious couch,—the root of an old oak,
Whose branches yield it moss and canopy,—
Is mine—and so it be from woodman's stroke
Secure, shall never be resigned by me;
It hangs above the stream that idly plies,
Heedless of any eyes.

There, with eye sometimes shut, but upward bent,
Sweetly I muse through many a quiet hour,
While every sense, on earnest mission sent,
Returns, thought-laden, back with bloom and flower;
Pursuing though rebuked by those who moil,
A profitable toil.

And still the waters, trickling at my feet,
Wind on their way with gentlest melody,
Yielding sweet music, which the leaves repeat,
Above them, to the gay breeze gliding by,—
Yet not so rudely as to send one sound
Through the thick copse around.

Sometimes a brighter cloud than all the rest
Hangs o'er the archway opening through the trees,
Breaking the spell that, like a slumber, press'd
On my worn spirit its sweet luxuries,—
And, with awaken'd vision upward bent,
I watch the firmament.

How like—its sure and undisturb'd retreat,
Life's sanctuary at last, secure from storm—
To the pure waters trickling at my feet,
The bending trees that overshade my form;
So far as sweetest things of earth may seem
Like those of which we dream.

Thus, to my mind, is the philosophy
The young bird teaches, who, with sudden flight,
Sails far into the blue that spreads on high,
Until I lose him from my straining sight,—
With a most lofty discontent, to fly
Upward, from earth to sky.

TO THE BREEZE:
AFTER A PROTRACTED CALM AT SEA.

Thou hast been slow to bless us, gentle breeze;
Where hast thou been a lingerer, welcome friend?
Where, when the midnight gather'd to her brow
Her pale and crescent minister, wert thou?
On what far, sullen, solitary seas,
Piping the mariner's requiem, didst thou tend
The home-returning bark,
Curling the white foam o'er her lifted prow, [dark?
White, when the rolling waves around her all were

Gently, and with a breath
Of spicy odour from Sabæan vales,
Where subtle life defies and conquers death,
Fill'dst thou her yellow sails!
On, like some pleasant bird,
With glittering plumage and light-loving eye,
While the long pennant lay aloft unstirr'd,
And sails hung droopingly,
Camest thou with tidings of the land to cheer
The weary mariner.

How, when the ocean slept.
Making no sign;
And his dumb waters, of all life bereft,
Lay 'neath the sun-girt line;
His drapery of storm-clouds lifted high
In some far, foreign sky,
While a faint moaning o'er his bosom crept,
As the deep breathings of eternity,
Above the grave of the unburied time,
Claiming its clime—
How did the weary tar,
His form reclined along the burning deck,
Stretch his dim eye afar,
To hail the finger, and delusive speck,
Thy bending shadow, from some rocky steep,
Down-darting o'er the deep!

Born in the solemn night,
When the deep skies were bright,
With all their thousand watchers on the sight—
Thine was the music through the firmament
By the fond nature sent,
To hail the blessed birth,
To guide to lowly earth
The glorious glance, the holy wing of light!

Music to us no less,
Thou comest in our distress,
To cheer our pathway. It is clear, through thee,
O'er the broad wastes of sea.
How soothing to the heart that glides alone,
Unwatch'd and unremember'd, on the wave,
Perchance his grave!—
Should he there perish, to thy deeper moan
What lip shall add one tone?

I bless thee, gentle breeze!
Sweet minister to many a fond desire,
Thou bear'st me to my sire,
Thou, and these rolling seas!
What—O, thou God of this strong element!—
Are we, that it is sent,
Obedient to our fond and fervent hope?
But that its pinion on our path is bent,
We had been doom'd beyond desire to grope,
Where plummet's cast is vain, and human art,
Lacking all chart.

THE LOST PLEIAD

Not in the sky,
Where it was seen,
Nor on the white tops of the glistering wave,
Nor in the mansions of the hidden deep,—
Though green,
And beautiful, its caves of mystery,—
Shall the bright watcher have
A place—and, as of old, high station keep.

Gone, gone!
O, never more to cheer
The mariner who holds his course alone
On the Atlantic, through the weary night,
When the stars turn to watchers and do sleep,
Shall it appear,
With the sweet fixedness of certain light,
Down-shining on the shut eyes of the deep.

Vain, vain!
Hopeful most idly then, shall he look forth,
That mariner from his bark—
Howe'er the north
Doth raise his certain lamp when tempests lower—
He sees no more that perish'd light again!
And gloomier grows the hour [dark.
Which may not, through the thick and crowding
Restore that lost and loved one to her tower.

He looks,—the shepherd on Chaldea's hills,
Tending his flocks,—
And wonders the rich beacon doth not blaze,
Gladdening his gaze;
And, from his dreary watch along the rocks,
Guiding him safely home through perilous ways!
How stands he in amaze,
Still wondering, as the drowsy silence fills
The sorrowful scene, and every hour distils
Its leaden dews—how chafes he at the night,
Still slow to bring the expected and sweet light,
So natural to his sight!

And lone,
Where its first splendours shone,
Shall be that pleasant company of stars:
How should they know that death
Such perfect beauty mars;
And, like the earth, its common bloom and breath,
Fallen from on high,
Their lights grow blasted by its touch, and die—
All their concerted springs of harmony,
Snapp'd rudely, and the generous music gone.

A strain—a mellow strain—
Of wailing sweetness, fill'd the earth and sky;
The stars lamenting in unborrow'd pain
That one of the selectest ones must die;
Must vanish, when most lovely, from the rest!
Alas! 'tis ever more the destiny,
The hope, heart-cherish'd, is the soonest lost;
The flower first budded soonest feels the frost:
Are not the shortest-lived still loveliest?
And, like the pale star shooting down the sky,
Look they not ever brightest when they fly
The desolate home they bless'd?

THE EDGE OF THE SWAMP.

'Tis a wild spot, and hath a gloomy look;
The bird sings never merrily in the trees,
And the young leaves seem blighted. A rank growth
Spreads poisonously round, with power to taint
With blistering dews the thoughtless hand that dares
To penetrate the covert. Cypresses
Crowd on the dank, wet earth; and, stretch'd at [length,
The cayman—a fit dweller in such home—
Slumbers, half-buried in the sedgy grass.
Beside the green ooze where he shelters him,
A whooping crane erects his skeleton form,
And shrieks in flight. Two summer ducks, aroused
To apprehension, as they hear his cry,
Dash up from the lagoon, with marvellous haste,
Following his guidance. Meetly taught by these,
And startled at our rapid, near approach,
The steel-jaw'd monster, from his grassy bed,
Crawls slowly to his slimy, green abode,
Which straight receives him. You behold him now,
His ridgy back uprising as he speeds,
In silence, to the centre of the stream,
Whence his head peers alone. A butterfly,
That, travelling all the day, has counted climes
Only by flowers, to rest himself a while,
Lights on the monster's brow. The surly mute
Straightway goes down, so suddenly, that he,
The dandy of the summer flowers and woods,
Dips his light wings, and spoils his golden coat,
With the rank water of that turbid pond.
Wondering and vex'd, the plumed citizen
Flies, with a hurried effort, to the shore,
Seeking his kindred flowers:—but seeks in vain—
Nothing of genial growth may there be seen,
Nothing of beautiful! Wild, ragged trees,
That look like felon spectres—fetid shrubs,
That taint the gloomy atmosphere—dusk shades,
That gather, half a cloud, and half a fiend
In aspect, lurking on the swamp's wild edge,—
Gloom with their sternness and forbidding frowns
The general prospect. The sad butterfly,
Waving his lacker'd wings, darts quickly on,
And, by his free flight, counsels us to speed
For better lodgings, and a scene more sweet,
Than these drear borders offer us to-night.

CHANGES OF HOME.

Well may we sing her beauties,
This pleasant land of ours,
Her sunny smiles, her golden fruits,
And all her world of flowers;
The young birds of her forest-groves
The blue folds of her sky,
And all those airs of gentleness,
That never seem to fly;
They wind about our forms at noon,
They woo us in the shade,
When panting, from the summer's heats,
The woodman seeks the glade;
They win us with a song of love,
They cheer us with a dream,
That gilds our passing thoughts of life,
As sunlight does the stream;
And well would they persuade us now,
In moments all too dear,
That, sinful though our hearts may be,
We have our Eden here.

Ah, well has lavish nature,
From out her boundless store,
Spread wealth and loveliness around,
On river, rock, and shore:
No sweeter stream than Ashley glides—
And, what of southern France?—
She boasts no brighter fields than ours,
Within her matron glance;
Our skies look down in tenderness
From out their realms of blue,
The fairest of Italian climes
May claim no softer hue;
And let them sing of fruits of Spain,
And let them boast the flowers,
The Moors' own culture they may claim,
No dearer sweet than ours—
Perchance the dark-hair'd maiden
Is a glory in your eye,
But the blue-eyed Carolinian rules,
When all the rest are nigh.

And none may say, it is not true,
The burden of my lay,
'T is written, in the sight of all,
In flower and fruit and ray;
Look on the scene around us now,
And say if sung amiss,
The song that pictures to your eye
A spot so fair as this:
Gay springs the merry mocking-bird
Around the cottage pale,—
And, scarcely taught by hunter's aim,
The rabbit down the vale;
Each boon of kindly nature,
Her buds, her blooms, her flowers,
And, more than all, the maidens fair
That fill this land of ours,
Are still in rich perfection,
As our fathers found them first,
But our sons are gentle now no more,
And all the land is cursed.

Wild thoughts are in our bosoms
And a savage discontent;
We love no more the life we led,
The music, nor the scent;
The merry dance delights us not,
As in that better time,
When, glad, in happy bands we met,
With spirits like our clime.
And all the social loveliness,
And all the smile is gone,
That link'd the spirits of our youth,
And made our people one.
They smile no more together,
As in that earlier day,
Our maidens sigh in loneliness,
Who once were always gay;
And though our skies are bright,
And our sun looks down as then—
Ah, me! the thought is sad I feel,
We shall never smile again.

JONATHAN LAWRENCE.

[Born, 1807. Died, 1833.]

Few persons in private life, who have died so young, have been mourned by so many warm friends as was Jonathan Lawrence. Devoted to a profession which engaged nearly all his time, and regardless of literary distinction, his productions would have been known only to his associates, had not a wiser appreciation of their merits withdrawn them from the obscurity to which his own low estimate had consigned them.

He was born in New York, in November, 1807, and, after the usual preparatory studies, entered Columbia College, at which he was graduated before he was fifteen years of age. He soon after became a student in the office of Mr. W. Slosson, an eminent lawyer, where he gained much regard by the assiduity with which he prosecuted his studies, the premature ripeness of his judgment, and the undeviating purity and honourableness of his life. On being admitted to the bar, he entered into a partnership with Mr. Slosson, and daily added confirmation to the promise of his probational career, until he was suddenly called to a better life, in April, 1833.

The industry with which he attended to his professional duties did not prevent him from giving considerable attention to general literature; and in moments—to use his own language—

> "Stolen from hours I should have tied
> To musty volumes at my side,
> Given to hours that sweetly woo'd
> My heart from study's solitude,"—

he produced many poems and prose sketches of considerable merit. These, with one or two exceptions, were intended not for publication, but as tributes of private friendship, or as contributions to the exercises of a literary society—still in existence—of which he was for several years an active member. After his death, in compliance with a request by this society, his brother made a collection of his writings, of which a very small edition was printed, for private circulation. Their character is essentially meditative. Many of them are devotional, and all are distinguished for the purity of thought which guided the life of the man.

THOUGHTS OF A STUDENT.

Many a sad, sweet thought have I,
  Many a passing, sunny gleam,
Many a bright tear in mine eye,
  Many a wild and wandering dream,
Stolen from hours I should have tied
To musty volumes by my side,
Given to hours that sweetly woo'd
My heart from study's solitude.

Oft, when the south wind's dancing free
  Over the earth and in the sky,
And the flowers peep softly out to see
  The frolic Spring as she wantons by;
When the breeze and beam like thieves come in,
To steal me away, I deem it sin
To slight their voice, and away I'm straying
Over the hills and vales a-Maying.

Then can I hear the earth rejoice,
  Happier than man may ever be;
Every fountain hath then a voice,
  That sings of its glad festivity;
For it hath burst the chains that bound
Its currents dead in the frozen ground,
And, flashing away in the sun, has gone
Singing, and singing, and singing on.

Autumn hath sunset hours, and then
  Many a musing mood I cherish;
Many a hue of fancy, when
  The hues of earth are about to perish;
Clouds are there, and brighter, I ween,
Hath real sunset never seen,
Sad as the faces of friends that die,
And beautiful as their memory.

Love hath its thoughts, we cannot keep,
  Visions the mind may not control,
Waking, as fancy does in sleep,
  The secret transports of the soul;
Faces and forms are strangely mingled,
Till one by one they're slowly singled,
To the voice, and lip, and eye of her
I worship like an idolater.

Many a big, proud tear have I,
  When from my sweet and roaming track,
From the green earth and misty sky,
  And spring, and love, I hurry back;
Then what a dismal, dreary gloom
Settles upon my loathed room,
Darker to every thought and sense
Than if they had never travell'd thence.

Yet, I have other thoughts, that cheer
  The toilsome day and lonely night,
And many a scene and hope appear,
  And almost make me gay and bright.
Honour and fame that I would win,
Though every toil that yet hath been
Were doubly borne, and not an hour
Were brightly hued by Fancy's power

And, though I sometimes sigh to think
Of earth and heaven, and wind and sea,
And know that the cup which others drink
Shall never be brimm'd by me;
That many a joy must be untasted,
And many a glorious breeze be wasted,
Yet would not, if I dared, repine,
That toil, and study, and care are mine.

SEA-SONG.

Over the far blue ocean-wave,
On the wild winds I flee,
Yet every thought of my constant heart
Is winging, love, to thee;
For each foaming leap of our gallant ship
Had barb'd a pang for me,
Had not thy form, through sun and storm,
Been my only memory.

O, the sea-mew's wings are fleet and fast,
As he dips in the dancing spray;
But fleeter and faster the thoughts, I ween,
Of dear ones far away!
And lovelier, too, than yon rainbow's hue,
As it lights the tinted sea,
Are the daylight dreams and sunny gleams
Of the heart that throbs for thee.

And when moon and stars are asleep on the waves,
Their dancing tops among,
And the sailor is guiling the long watch-hour
By the music of his song;
When our sail is white in the dark midnight,
And its shadow is on the sea,
O, never knew hall such festival
As my fond heart holds with thee!

LOOK ALOFT.

In the tempest of life, when the wave and the gale
Are around and above, if thy footing should fail,
If thine eye should grow dim, and thy caution depart,
"Look aloft," and be firm, and be fearless of heart.

If the friend, who embraced in prosperity's glow,
With a smile for each joy and a tear for each wo,
Should betray thee when sorrows like clouds are array'd,
"Look aloft" to the friendship which never shall fade.

Should the visions which hope spreads in light to thine eye,
Like the tints of the rainbow, but brighten to fly,
Then turn, and, through tears of repentant regret,
"Look aloft" to the sun that is never to set.

Should they who are dearest, the son of thy heart,
The wife of thy bosom, in sorrow depart,
"Look aloft" from the darkness and dust of the tomb,
To that soil where "affection is ever in bloom."

And, O! when death comes in his terrors, to cast
His fears on the future, his pall on the past,
In that moment of darkness, with hope in thy heart,
And a smile in thine eye, "look aloft," and depart!

TO MAY.

Come, gentle May!
Come with thy robe of flowers,
Come with thy sun and sky, thy clouds and showers;
Come, and bring forth unto the eye of day,
From their imprisoning and mysterious night,
The buds of many hues, the children of thy light.

Come, wondrous May!
For, at the bidding of thy magic wand,
Quick from the caverns of the breathing land,
In all their green and glorious array
They spring, as spring the Persian maids to hail
Thy flushing footsteps in Cashmerian vale.

Come, vocal May!
Come with thy train, that high
On some fresh branch pour out their melody;
Or, carolling thy praise the livelong day,
Sit perch'd in some lone glen, on echo calling,
Mid murmuring woods and musical waters falling.

Come, sunny May!
Come with thy laughing beam,
What time the lazy mist melts on the stream,
Or seeks the mountain-top to meet thy ray,
Ere yet the dew-drop on thine own soft flower
Hath lost its light, or died beneath his power.

Come, holy May!
When, sunk behind the cold and western hill,
His light hath ceased to play on leaf and rill,
And twilight's footsteps hasten his decay;
Come with thy musings, and my heart shall be
Like a pure temple consecrate to thee.

Come, beautiful May!
Like youth and loveliness,
Like her I love; O, come in thy full dress,
The drapery of dark winter cast away;
To the bright eye and the glad heart appear
Queen of the spring, and mistress of the year.

Yet, lovely May!
Teach her whose eyes shall rest upon this rhyme
To spurn the gilded mockeries of time,
The heartless pomp that beckons to betray,
And keep, as thou wilt find, that heart each year,
Pure as thy dawn, and as thy sunset clear.

And let me too, sweet May!
Let thy fond votary see,
As fade thy beauties, all the vanity
Of this world's pomp; then teach, that though decay
In his short winter bury beauty's frame,
In fairer worlds the soul shall break his sway,
Another spring shall bloom, eternal and the same.

J. O. ROCKWELL.

(Born, 1807. Died, 1831.)

James Otis Rockwell was born in Lebanon, an agricultural town in Connecticut, in 1807. At an early age he was apprenticed to a printer, in Utica, and in his sixteenth year he began to write verses for the newspapers. Two years afterward he went to New York, and subsequently to Boston, in each of which cities he laboured as a journeyman compositor. He had now acquired considerable reputation by his poetical writings, and was engaged as associate editor of the "Statesman," an old and influential journal published in Boston, with which, I believe, he continued until 1829, when he became the conductor of the Providence "Patriot," with which he was connected at the time of his death.

He was poor, and in his youth he had been left nearly to his own direction. He chose to learn the business of printing, because he thought it would afford him opportunities to improve his mind; and his education was acquired by diligent study during the leisure hours of his apprenticeship. When he removed to Providence, it became necessary for him to take an active part in the discussion of political questions. He felt but little interest in public affairs, and shrank instinctively from the strife of partisanship; but it seemed the only avenue to competence and reputation, and he embarked in it with apparent ardour. Journalism, in the hands of able and honourable men, is the noblest of callings; in the hands of the ignorant and mercenary, it is among the meanest. There are at all times connected with the press, persons of the baser sort, who derive their support and chief enjoyment from ministering to the worst passions; and by some of this class Rockwell's private character was assailed, and he was taunted with his obscure parentage, defective education, and former vocation, as if to have elevated his position in society, by perseverance and the force of mind, were a ground of accusation. He had too little energy in his nature to regard such assaults with the indifference they merited; and complained in some of his letters that they "robbed him of rest and of all pleasure." With constantly increasing reputation, however, he continued his editorial labours until the summer of 1831, when, at the early age of twenty-four years, he was suddenly called to a better world. He felt unwell, one morning, and, in a brief paragraph, apologized for the apparent neglect of his gazette. The next number of it wore the signs of mourning for his death. A friend of Rockwell's,* in a notice of him published in the "Southern Literary Messenger," mentions as the immediate cause of his death, that he "was troubled at the thought of some obligation which, from not receiving money then due to him, he was unable to meet, and shrank from the prospect of a *debtor's prison*." That it was in some way a result of his extreme sensitiveness, was generally believed among his friends at the time. Whittier, who was then editor of the "New England Weekly Review," soon after wrote the following lines to his memory:

"The turf is smooth above him! and this rain
Will moisten the rent roots, and summon back
The perishing life of its green-bladed grass,
And the crush'd flower will lift its head again
Smilingly unto heaven, as if it kept
No vigil with the dead. Well—it is meet
That the green grass should tremble, and the flowers
Blow wild about his resting-place. His mind
Was in itself a flower but half-disclosed—
A bud of blessed promise which the storm
Visited rudely, and the passer by
Smote down in wantonness. But we may trust
That it hath found a dwelling, where the sun
Of a more holy clime will visit it,
And the pure dews of mercy will descend,
Through Heaven's own atmosphere, upon its head.

"His form is now before me, with no trace
Of death in its fine lineaments, and there
Is a faint crimson on his youthful cheek,
And his free lip is softening with the smile
Which in his eye is kindling. I can feel
The parting pressure of his hand, and hear
His last 'God bless you!' Strange—that he is there
Distinct before me like a breathing thing,
Even when I know that he is with the dead,
And that the damp earth hides him. I would not
Think of him otherwise—his image lives
Within my memory as he seem'd before
The curse of blighted feeling, and the toil
And fever of an uncongenial strife, had left
Their traces on his aspect. Peace to him!
He wrestled nobly with the weariness
And trials of our being—smiling on,
While poison mingled with his springs of life,
And wearing a calm brow, while on his heart
Anguish was resting like a hand of fire—
Until at last the agony of thought
Grew insupportable, and madness came
Darkly upon him,—and the sufferer died!

"Nor died he unlamented! To his grave
The beautiful and gifted shall go up,
And muse upon the sleeper. And young lips
Shall murmur in the broken tones of grief—
His own sweet melodies—and if the ear
Of the freed spirit heedeth aught beneath
The brightness of its new inheritance,
It may be joyful to the parted one
To feel that earth remembers him in love!"

The specimens of Rockwell's poetry which have fallen under my notice show him to have possessed considerable fancy and deep feeling His imagery is not always well chosen, and his versification is sometimes defective; but his thoughts are often original, and the general effect of his pieces is striking. His later poems are his best, and probably he would have produced works of much merit had he lived to a maturer age.

* Reverend Charles W. Everest, of Meriden Connecticut.

THE SUM OF LIFE.

Searcher of gold, whose days and nights
  All waste away in anxious care,
Estranged from all of life's delights,
  Unlearn'd in all that is most fair—
Who sailest not with easy glide,
But delvest in the depths of tide,
    And strugglest in the foam;
O! come and view this land of graves,
Death's northern sea of frozen waves,
    And mark thee out thy home.

Lover of woman, whose sad heart
  Wastes like a fountain in the sun,
Clings most, where most its pain does start,
  Dies by the light it lives upon;
Come to the land of graves; for here
Are beauty's smile, and beauty's tear,
    Gather'd in holy trust;
Here slumber forms as fair as those
Whose cheeks, now living, shame the rose,
    Their glory turn'd to dust.

Lover of fame, whose foolish thought
  Steals onward o'er the wave of time,
Tell me, what goodness hath it brought,
  Atoning for that restless crime?
The spirit-mansion desolate,
And open to the storms of fate,
    The absent soul in fear;
Bring home thy thoughts and come with me,
And see where all thy pride must be:
    Searcher of fame, look here!

And, warrior, thou with snowy plume,
  That goest to the bugle's call,
Come and look down; this lonely tomb
  Shall hold thee and thy glories all:
The haughty brow, the manly frame,
The daring deeds, the sounding fame,
    Are trophies but for death!
And millions who have toil'd like thee,
Are stay'd, and here they sleep; and see,
    Does glory lend them breath?

TO ANN.

Thou wert as a lake that lieth
  In a bright and sunny way;
I was as a bird that flieth
  O'er it on a pleasant day;
When I look'd upon thy features
  Presence then some feeling lent;
But thou knowest, most false of creatures,
  With thy form thy image went.

With a kiss my vow was greeted,
  As I knelt before thy shrine;
But I saw that kiss repeated
  On another lip than mine;
And a solemn vow was spoken
  That thy heart should not be changed;
But that binding vow was broken,
  And thy spirit was estranged.

I could blame thee for awaking
  Thoughts the world will but deride;
Calling out, and then forsaking
  Flowers the winter wind will chide;
Guiling to the midway ocean
  Barks that tremble by the shore.
But I hush the sad emotion,
  And will punish thee no more.

THE LOST AT SEA.

Wife, who in thy deep devotion
  Puttest up a prayer for one
Sailing on the stormy ocean,
  Hope no more—his course is done.
Dream not, when upon thy pillow,
  That he slumbers by thy side;
For his corse beneath the billow
  Heaveth with the restless tide.

Children, who, as sweet flowers growing
  Laugh amid the sorrowing rains,
Know ye many clouds are throwing
  Shadows on your sire's remains?
Where the hoarse, gray surge is rolling
  With a mountain's motion on,
Dream ye that its voice is tolling
  For your father lost and gone?

When the sun look'd on the water,
  As a hero on his grave,
Tinging with the hue of slaughter
  Every blue and leaping wave,
Under the majestic ocean,
  Where the giant current roll'd,
Slept thy sire, without emotion,
  Sweetly by a beam of gold;

And the silent sunbeams slanted,
  Wavering through the crystal deep,
Till their wonted splendours haunted
  Those shut eyelids in their sleep.
Sands, like crumbled silver gleaming,
  Sparkled through his raven hair;
But the sleep that knows no dreaming
  Bound him in its silence there.

So we left him; and to tell thee
  Of our sorrow and thine own,
Of the wo that then befell thee,
  Come we weary and alone.
That thine eye is quickly shaded,
  That thy heart-blood wildly flows,
That thy cheek's clear hue is faded,
  Are the fruits of these new woes.

Children, whose meek eyes, inquiring
  Linger on your mother's face—
Know ye that she is expiring,
  That ye are an orphan race?
God be with you on the morrow,
  Father, mother,—both no more;
One within a grave of sorrow,
  One upon the ocean's floor!

THE DEATH-BED OF BEAUTY.

She sleeps in beauty, like the dying rose
By the warm skies and winds of June forsaken;
Or like the sun, when dimm'd with clouds it goes
To its clear ocean-bed, by light winds shaken:
Or like the moon, when through its robes of snow
It smiles with angel meekness—or like sorrow
When it is soothed by resignation's glow,
Or like herself,—she will be dead to-morrow.

How still she sleeps! The young and sinless girl!
And the faint breath upon her red lips trembles!
Waving, almost in death, the raven curl
That floats around her; and she most resembles
The fall of night upon the ocean foam,
Wherefrom the sun-light hath not yet departed;
And where the winds are faint. She stealeth home,
Unsullied girl! an angel broken-hearted!

O, bitter world! that hadst so cold an eye
To look upon so fair a type of heaven;
She could not dwell beneath a winter sky,
And her heart-strings were frozen here and riven,
And now she lies in ruins—look and weep!
How lightly leans her cheek upon the pillow!
And how the bloom of her fair face doth keep
Changed, like a stricken dolphin on the billow.

TO THE ICE-MOUNTAIN.

Grave of waters gone to rest!
Jewel, dazzling all the main!
Father of the silver crest!
Wandering on the trackless plain,
Sleeping mid the wavy roar,
Sailing mid the angry storm,
Ploughing ocean's oozy floor,
Piling to the clouds thy form!

Wandering monument of rain,
Prison'd by the sullen north!
But to melt thy hated chain,
Is it that thou comest forth?
Wend thee to the sunny south,
To the glassy summer sea,
And the breathings of her mouth
Shall unchain and gladden thee!

Roamer in the hidden path,
'Neath the green and clouded wave!
Trampling in thy reckless wrath,
On the lost, but cherish'd brave;
Parting love's death-link'd embrace—
Crushing beauty's skeleton—
Tell us what the hidden race
With our mourned lost have done!

Floating isle, which in the sun
Art an icy coronal;
And beneath the viewless dun,
Throw'st o'er barks a wavy pall;
Shining death upon the sea!
Wend thee to the southern main;
Warm skies wait to welcome thee!
Mingle with the wave again!

THE PRISONER FOR DEBT.

When the summer sun was in the west,
Its crimson radiance fell,
Some on the blue and changeful sea,
And some in the prisoner's cell.
And then his eye with a smile would beam,
And the blood would leave his brain,
And the verdure of his soul return,
Like sere grass after rain!

But when the tempest wreathed and spread
A mantle o'er the sun,
He gather'd back his woes again,
And brooded thereupon;
And thus he lived, till Time one day
Led Death to break his chain:
And then the prisoner went away,
And he was free again!

TO A WAVE.

List! thou child of wind and sea,
Tell me of the far-off deep,
Where the tempest's breath is free,
And the waters never sleep!
Thou perchance the storm hast aided,
In its work of stern despair,
Or perchance thy hand hath braided,
In deep caves, the mermaid's hair.

Wave! now on the golden sands,
Silent as thou art, and broken,
Bear'st thou not from distant strands
To my heart some pleasant token?
Tales of mountains of the south,
Spangles of the ore of silver;
Which, with playful singing mouth,
Thou hast leap'd on high to pilfer?

Mournful wave! I deem'd thy song
Was telling of a floating prison,
Which, when tempests swept along,
And the mighty winds were risen,
Founder'd in the ocean's grasp,
While the brave and fair were dying,
Wave! didst mark a white hand clasp
In thy folds, as thou wert flying?

Hast thou seen the hallow'd rock
Where the pride of kings reposes,
Crown'd with many a misty lock,
Wreathed with sapphire, green, and rose?
Or with joyous, playful leap,
Hast thou been a tribute flinging,
Up that bold and jutty steep,
Pearls upon the south wind stringing?

Faded Wave! a joy to thee,
Now thy flight and toil are over!
O, may my departure be
Calm as thine, thou ocean-rover!
When this soul's last pain or mirth
On the shore of time is driven,
Be its lot like thine on earth,
To be lost away in heaven!

MICAH P. FLINT.

[Born about 1807. Died 1830.]

MICAH P. FLINT, a son of the Reverend TIMOTHY FLINT, the well-known author of "Francis Berrian," was born in Lunenburg, Massachusetts; at an early age accompanied his father to the valley of the Mississippi; studied the law, and was admitted to the bar at Alexandria; and had hopes of a successful professional career, when arrested by the illness which ended in his early death. He published in Boston, in 1826, "The Hunter, and other Poems," which are described in the preface as the productions of a very young man, and results of lonely meditations in the southwestern forests, during intervals of professional studies "The Hunter" is a narrative, in three cantos, of "adventures in the pathless woods." The situations and incidents are poetical, but the work is, upon the whole, feebly executed. "Sorotaphian," an argument for urn-burial, subsequently reprinted with some improvements in "The Western Monthly Magazine," lines "On Passing the Grave of My Sister," and several other poems, illustrated the growth of the author's mind, and justified the sanguine hopes of his father that he would "become the pride of his family."

ON PASSING THE GRAVE OF MY SISTER.

ON yonder shore, on yonder shore,
Now verdant with the depths of shade,
Beneath the white-arm'd sycamore,
There is a little infant laid.
Forgive this tear.—A brother weeps.—
'T is there the faded floweret sleeps.

She sleeps alone, she sleeps alone,
And summer's forests o'er her wave;
And sighing winds at autumn moan
Around the little stranger's grave,
As though they murmur'd at the fate
Of one so lone and desolate.

In sounds that seems like sorrow's own,
Their funeral dirges faintly creep;
Then deepening to an organ tone,
In all their solemn cadence sweep,
And pour, unheard, along the wild,
Their desert anthem o'er a child.

She came, and pass'd. Can I forget,
How we whose hearts had hailed her birth,
Ere three autumnal suns had set,
Consign'd her to her mother earth!
Joys and their memories pass away;
But griefs are deeper plough'd than they.

We laid her in her narrow cell,
We heap'd the soft mould on her breast;
And parting tears, like rain-drops, fell
Upon her lonely place of rest.
May angels guard it; may they bless
Her slumbers in the wilderness.

She sleeps alone, she sleeps alone;
For all unheard, on yonder shore,
The sweeping flood, with torrent moan,
At evening lifts its solemn roar,
As in one broad, eternal tide,
The rolling waters onward glide.

There is no marble monument,
There is no stone with graven lie,
To tell of love and virtue blent
In one almost too good to die.
We needed no such useless trace
To point us to her resting-place.

She sleeps alone, she sleeps alone;
But midst the tears of April showers,
The genius of the wild hath strown
His germs of fruits, his fairest flowers,
And cast his robes of vernal bloom
In guardian fondness o'er her tomb.

She sleeps alone, she sleeps alone;
Yet yearly is her grave-turf dress'd,
And still the summer vines are thrown,
In annual wreaths across her breast,
And still the sighing autumn grieves,
And strews the hallow'd spot with leaves.

AFTER A STORM.

THERE was a milder azure spread
Around the distant mountain's head;
And every hue of that fair bow,
Whose beauteous arch had risen there
Now sank beneath a brighter glow,
And melted into ambient air.
The tempest which had just gone by,
Still hung along the eastern sky,
And threatened, as it rolled away.
The birds, from every dripping spray,
Were pouring forth their joyous mirth;
The torrent, with its waters brown,
From rock to rock came rushing down,
While, from among the smoky hills,
The voices of a thousand rills
Were heard exulting at its birth.
A breeze came whispering through the wood
And, from its thousand tresses, shook
The big round drops that trembling stood,
Like pearls, in every leafy nook.

Engraved at J. M. Butler's establishment from a Painting by Lawrence

Henry W. Longfellow

HENRY WADSWORTH LONGFELLOW.

(Born, 1807.)

MR. LONGFELLOW, son of Mr. STEPHEN LONGFELLOW, an eminent lawyer of that city, was born in Portland, Maine, on the twenty-seventh of February, 1807. When fourteen years of age he entered Bowdoin College, where he graduated in 1825. He soon after commenced the study of the law, but being appointed Professor of Modern Languages in the college in which he was educated, he in 1826 sailed for Europe to prepare himself for the duties of his office, and passed three years and a half visiting or residing in France, Spain, Italy, Germany, Holland, and England. When he returned he entered upon the labours of instruction, and in 1831 was married. The professorship of Modern Languages and Literatures in Harvard College was made vacant, in 1835, by the resignation of Mr. TICKNOR. Mr. LONGFELLOW, being elected his successor, gave up his place in Brunswick, and went a second time to Europe, to make himself more thoroughly acquainted with the subjects of his studies in the northern nations. He passed the summer in Denmark and Sweden; the autumn and winter in Germany—losing in that period his wife, who died suddenly at Heidelberg; and the following spring and summer in the Tyrol and Switzerland. Returning to the United States in October, 1836, he entered upon his duties at Cambridge, where he has since resided.

The earliest of LONGFELLOW's metrical compositions were written for "The United States Literary Gazette," printed in Boston, while he was an undergraduate; and from that period he has been known as a poet, and his effusions, improving as each year added to his scholarship and taste, have been extensively read and admired. While a professor in Brunswick, he wrote several elegant and judicious papers for the "North American Review;" made a translation of *Coplas de Manrique;* and published "Outre Mer, or a Pilgrimage beyond the Sea," a collection of agreeable tales and sketches, chiefly written during his first residence abroad. In 1839 appeared his "Hyperion," a romance, and in 1848 "Kavanagh," his last work in prose. In the summer of 1845 he gave to the press "The Poets and Poetry of Europe," the most comprehensive, complete and accurate review of the poetry of the continental nations that has ever appeared in any language.

The first collection of his own poems was published in 1839, under the title of "Voices of the Night." His "Ballads and other Poems" followed in 1841; "The Spanish Student, a Play," in 1843; "Poems on Slavery," in 1844; "The Belfry of Bruges and other Poems," in 1845; "Evangeline, a Tale of Acadie," in 1847; "The Seaside and the Fireside," in 1849; "The Golden Legend," in 1851; and "The Song of Hiawatha," in 1855. Editions of his collected poetical works appeared in 1845, 1848, and subsequent years.

A considerable portion of Mr. LONGFELLOW's volumes consists of translations. One of the longest and most elaborate of these is the "Children of the Lord's Supper," from the Swedish of ESAIAS TEGNER, a venerable bishop of the Lutheran church, and the most illustrious poet of northern Europe. The genius of TEGNER had already been made known in this country by a learned and elaborate criticism, illustrated by translated passages of great beauty, from his "Frithiof's Saga," contributed by LONGFELLOW to the "North American Review" soon after he came home from his second visit to Europe. The "Children of the Lord's Supper" is little less celebrated than the author's great epic, and the English version of it was among the most difficult tasks to be undertaken, as spondaic words, necessary in the construction of hexameters, and common in the Greek, Latin, and Swedish, are so rare in the English language. Unquestionably the most charming production of LONGFELLOW's genius is "Evangeline," founded on one of the most remarkable and poetical episodes in American history. In this he has admirably displayed not only his finest vein of sentiment, but an exquisite sensibility to the beauties of nature, and a nice observation of the changes wrought by the seasons in those latitudes near which he passed his youth. "The Golden Legend," a dramatic poem, recalling the miracle plays of the Middle Ages, was upon the whole an unsuccessful performance. His last work, "The Song of Hiawatha," has surpassed all the rest in popularity, and has probably been more widely read than any other poem of its length within so short a period from its publication. In three months twenty thousand copies were sold in the United States alone. It is an attempt to invest with the attractions of poetry the traditions and superstitions of American savage life.

Of all our poets LONGFELLOW best deserves the title of artist. He has studied the principles of verbal melody, and rendered himself master of the mysterious affinities which exist between sound and sense, word and thought, feeling and expression. His tact in the use of language is probably the chief cause of his success. There is an aptitude, a gracefulness, and vivid beauty, in many of his stanzas, which at once impress the memory and win the ear and heart. There is in the tone of his poetry little passion, but much quiet earnestness. It is not so much the power of the instrument, as the skill with which it is managed, that excites our sympathy. His acquaintance with foreign literature has been of great advantage, by rendering him familiar with all the delicate capacities of language, from the grand symphonic roll of Northern tongue to the "soft, bastard Latin" of the South. His ideas and metaphors are often very striking and poetical; but there is no affluence of imagery, or wonderful glow of emotion, such as take us captive in BYRON or SHELLEY: the claim of LONGFELLOW consists rather in the wise and tasteful use of his materials than in their richness or originality. He has done much for the Art of Poetry in this country by his example, and in this respect may claim the praise which all good critics of English Poetry have bestowed on GRAY and COLLINS. The spirit of LONGFELLOW's muse is altogether unexceptionable in a moral point of view. He illustrates the gentler themes of song, and pleads for justice, humanity, and particularly the beautiful, with a poet's deep conviction of their eternal claims upon the instinctive recognition of the man.

NUREMBERG.

In the valley of the Pegnitz, where across broad meadow-lands
Rise the blue Franconian mountains, Nuremberg, the ancient, stands.

Quaint old town of toil and traffic, quaint old town of art and song,
Memories haunt thy pointed gables, like the rooks that round them throng;

Memories of the Middle Ages, when the emperors, rough and bold,
Had their dwelling in thy castle, time-defying, centuries old;

And thy brave and thrifty burghers boasted, in their uncouth rhyme,
That their great imperial city stretch'd its hand through every clime.

In the court-yard of the castle, bound with many an iron band,
Stands the mighty linden planted by Queen CUNIGUNDE's hand;

On the square the oriel window, where in old heroic days
Sat the poet MELCHIOR singing Kaiser MAXIMILIAN's praise.

Everywhere I see around me rise the wondrous world of Art,—
Fountains wrought with richest sculpture standing in the common mart;

And above cathedral doorways saints and bishops carved in stone,
By a former age commission'd as apostles to our own.

In the church of sainted SEBALD sleeps enshrined his holy dust,
And in bronze the Twelve Apostles guard from age to age their trust;

In the church of sainted LAWRENCE stands a pix of sculpture rare,
Like the foamy sheaf of fountains, rising through the painted air.

Here, when art was still religion, with a simple, reverent heart,
Lived and labour'd ALBRECHT DURER, the Evangelist of Art;

Hence in silence and in sorrow, toiling still with busy hand,
Like an emigrant he wander'd, seeking for the Better Land.

Emigravit is the inscription on the tombstone where he lies;
Dead he is not,—but departed,—for the artist never dies.

Fairer seems the ancient city, and the sunshine seems more fair,
That he once has trod its pavement, that he once has breathed its air!

Through these streets so broad and stately, these obscure and dismal lanes,
Walked of yore the Mastersingers, chanting rude poetic strains.

From remote and sunless suburbs, came they to the friendly guild,
Building nests in Fame's great temple, as in spouts the swallows build.

As the weaver plied the shuttle, wove he too the mystic rhyme,
And the smith his iron measures hammer'd to the anvil's chime;

Thanking God, whose boundless wisdom makes the flowers of poesy bloom
In the forge's dust and cinders, in the tissues of the loom.

Here HANS SACHS, the cobbler-poet, laureate of the gentle craft,
Wisest of the Twelve Wise Masters, in huge folios sang and laugh'd.

But his house is now an ale-house, with a nicely sanded floor,
And a garland in the window, and his face above the door,

Painted by some humble artist, as in ADAM PUSCHMAN's song,
As the old man gray and dove-like, with his great beard white and long.

And at night the swart mechanic comes to drown his cark and care,
Quaffing ale from pewter tankards, in the master's antique chair.

Vanish'd is the ancient splendour, and before my dreamy eye
Wave these mingling shapes and figures, like a faded tapestry.

Not thy Councils, not thy Kaisers, win for thee the world's regard;
But thy painter, ALBRECHT DURER, and HANS SACHS, thy cobbler-bard.

Thus, O Nuremberg, a wanderer from a region far away,
As he paced thy streets and court-yards, sang in thought his careless lay:

Gathering from the pavement's crevice, as a floweret of the soil,
The nobility of labour,—the long pedigree of toil.

THE ARSENAL AT SPRINGFIELD.

This is the Arsenal. From floor to ceiling,
Like a huge organ, rise the burnish'd arms,
But from their silent pipes no anthem pealing,
Startles the villages with strange alarms.

Ah! what a sound will rise, how wild and dreary,
When the death-angel touches those swift keys!
What loud lament and dismal Miserere
Will mingle with their awful symphonies!

I hear even now the infinite fierce chorus,
The cries of agony, the endless groan,
Which, through the ages that have gone before us,
In long reverberations reach our own.

On helm and harness rings the Saxon hammer,
Through Cimbric forest roars the Norsemen's song,
And loud, amid the universal clamor,
O'er distant deserts sounds the Tartar gong.

I hear the Florentine, who from his palace
Wheels out his battle bell with dreadful din,
And Aztec priests upon their teocallis
Beat the wild war-drums made of serpent's skin;

The tumult of each sacked and burning village;
The shout that every prayer for mercy drowns;
The soldiers revels in the midst of pillage;
The wail of famine in beleaguered towns;

The bursting shell, the gateway wrench'd asunder,
The rattling musketry, the clashing blade;
And ever and anon, in tones of thunder,
The diapason of the cannonade.

Is it, O man, with such discordant noises,
With such accursed instruments as these,
Thou drownest Nature's sweet and kindly voices,
And jarrest the celestial harmonies?

Were half the power, that fills the world with terror,
Were half the wealth, bestow'd on camps and courts,
Given to redeem the human mind from error,
There were no need of arsenals nor forts:

The warrior's name would be a name abhorred!
And every nation, that should lift again
Its hand against a brother, on its forehead
Would wear for evermore the curse of Cain!

Down the dark future, through long generations,
The echoing sounds grow fainter and then cease;
And like a bell, with solemn, sweet vibrations,
I hear once more the voice of Christ say "Peace!"

Peace! and no longer from its brazen portals
The blast of war's great organ shakes the skies!
But beautiful as songs of the immortals,
The holy melodies of love arise.

THE SKELETON IN ARMOUR

"Speak! speak! thou fearful guest!
Who, with thy hollow breast
Still in rude armour drest,
Comest to daunt me!
Wrapt not in Eastern balms,
But with thy fleshless palms
Stretch'd, as if asking alms,
Why dost thou haunt me?"

Then, from those cavernous eyes
Pale flashes seemed to rise,
As when the Northern skies
Gleam in December;
And, like the water's flow
Under December's snow,
Came a dull voice of wo
From the heart's chamber.

"I was a Viking old!
My deeds, though manifold,
No Skald in song has told,
No Saga taught thee!
Take heed, that in thy verse
Thou dost the tale rehearse,
Else dread a dead man's curse!
For this I sought thee.

"Far in the Northern Land,
By the wild Baltic's strand,
I, with my childish hand,
Tamed the ger-falcon;
And, with my skates fast-bound,
Skimm'd the half-frozen Sound,
That the poor whimpering hound
Trembled to walk on.

"Oft to his frozen lair
Track'd I the grizzly bear,
While from my path the hare
Fled like a shadow;
Oft through the forest dark
Followed the were-wolf's bark,
Until the soaring lark
Sang from the meadow.

"But when I older grew,
Joining a corsair's crew,
O'er the dark sea I flew
With the marauders.
Wild was the life we led;
Many the souls that sped,
Many the hearts that bled,
By our stern orders.

"Many a wassail-bout
Wore the long winter out;
Often our midnight shout
Set the cocks crowing,
As we the Berserk's tale
Measured in cups of ale,
Draining the oaken pail,
Fill'd to o'erflowing.

"Once as I told in glee
Tales of the stormy sea,
Soft eyes did gaze on me,
Burning out tender;

And as the white stars shine
On the dark Norway pine,
On that dark heart of mine
Fell their soft splendour.

"I woo'd the blue-eyed maid,
Yielding, yet half afraid,
And in the forest's shade
Our vows were plighted.
Under its loosen'd vest
Flutter'd her little breast,
Like birds within their nest
By the hawk frighted.

"Bright in her father's hall
Shields gleam'd upon the wall,
Loud sang the minstrels all,
Chanting his glory;
When of old Hildebrand
I ask'd his daughter's hand,
Mute did the minstrel stand
To hear my story.

"While the brown ale he quaff'd
Loud then the champion laugh'd,
And as the wind-gusts waft
The sea-foam brightly,
So the loud laugh of scorn,
Out of those lips unshorn,
From the deep drinking-horn
Blew the foam lightly.

"She was a Prince's child,
I but a Viking wild,
And though she blush'd and smiled,
I was discarded!
Should not the dove so white
Follow the sea-mew's flight,
Why did they leave that night
Her nest unguarded?

"Scarce had I put to sea,
Bearing the maid with me,—
Fairest of all was she
Among the Norsemen!—
When on the white sea-strand,
Waving his armed hand,
Saw we old Hildebrand,
With twenty horsemen.

"Then launch'd they to the blast,
Bent like a reed each mast,
Yet we were gaining fast,
When the wind fail'd us;
And with a sudden flaw
Came round the gusty Skaw,
So that our foe we saw
Laugh as he hail'd us.

"And as to catch the gale
Round veer'd the flapping sail,
Death! was the helmsman's hail,
Death without quarter!
Mid-ships with iron keel
Struck we her ribs of steel;
Down her black hulk did reel
Through the black water.

"As with his wings aslant,
Sails the fierce cormorant,
Seeking some rocky haunt,
With his prey laden,
So toward the open main,
Beating to sea again,
Through the wild hurricane,
Bore I the maiden.

"Three weeks we westward bore,
And when the storm was o'er,
Cloud-like we saw the shore
Stretching to lee-ward;
There for my lady's bower
Built I the lofty tower,
Which, to this very hour,
Stands looking sea-ward.

"There lived we many years;
Time dried the maiden's tears;
She had forgot her fears,
She was a mother;
Death closed her mild blue eyes,
Under that tower she lies:
Ne'er shall the sun arise
On such another!

"Still grew my bosom then,
Still as a stagnant fen!
Hateful to me were men,
The sun-light hateful!
In the vast forest here,
Clad in my warlike gear,
Fell I upon my spear,
O, death was grateful!

"Thus, seam'd with many scars
Bursting these prison bars,
Up to its native stars
My soul ascended!
There from the flowing bowl
Deep drinks the warrior's soul,
Skoal! to the Northland! *skoal!*"*
—Thus the tale ended.

* In Scandinavia this is the customary salutation when drinking a health. The orthography of the word is slightly changed, to preserve the correct pronunciation.

NOTE.—This poem was suggested by the Round Tower at Newport, now claimed by the Danes, as a work of their ancestors. Mr. Longfellow remarks, On this ancient structure, there are no ornaments remaining which might possibly have served to guide us in assigning the probable date of its erection. That no vestige whatever is found of the pointed arch, nor any approximation to it, is indicative of an earlier rather than of a later period. From such characteristics as remain, however, we can scarcely form any other inference than one, in which I am persuaded that all, who are familiar with Old-Northern architecture, will concur, THAT THIS BUILDING WAS ERECTED AT A PERIOD DECIDEDLY NOT LATER THAN THE TWELFTH CENTURY. This remark applies, of course, to the original building only, and not to the alterations that it subsequently received; for there are several such alterations in the upper part of the building, which cannot be mistaken, and which were most likely occasioned by its being adapted in modern times to various uses, for example as the substructure of a wind-mill, and latterly, as a hay magazine. To the same times may be referred the windows, the fire-place, and the apertures made above the columns. That this building could not have been erected for a wind-mill, is what an architect will easily discern.—PROFESSOR RAFN, in the *Mémoires de la Société Royale des Antiquaires du Nord*, for 1838–1839.

A PSALM OF LIFE.

WHAT THE HEART OF THE YOUNG MAN SAID TO THE PSALMIST.

Tell me not, in mournful numbers,
Life is but an empty dream!
For the soul is dead that slumbers,
And things are not what they seem.

Life is real! Life is earnest!
And the grave is not its goal;
Dust thou art, to dust returnest,
Was not spoken of the soul.

Not enjoyment, and not sorrow,
Is our destined end or way;
But to act, that each to-morrow
Find us farther than to-day.

Art is long, and Time is fleeting,
And our hearts, though stout and brave,
Still, like muffled drums, are beating
Funeral marches to the grave.

In the world's broad field of battle,
In the bivouac of Life,
Be not like dumb, driven cattle!
Be a hero in the strife!

Trust no Future, howe'er pleasant!
Let the dead Past bury its dead!
Act,—act in the living Present!
Heart within, and God o'erhead!

Lives of great men all remind us
We can make our lives sublime,
And, departing, leave behind us
Footprints on the sands of time;

Footprints, that perhaps another,
Sailing o'er life's solemn main,
A forlorn and shipwreck'd brother,
Seeing, shall take heart again.

Let us, then, be up and doing,
With a heart for any fate;
Still achieving, still pursuing,
Learn to labour and to wait.

THE LIGHT OF STARS.

The night is come, but not too soon;
And sinking silently,
All silently, the little moon
Drops down behind the sky.

There is no light in earth or heaven,
But the cold light of stars;
And the first watch of night is given
To the red planet Mars.

Is it the tender star of love?
The star of love and dreams?
O no! from that blue tent above
A hero's armour gleams.

And earnest thoughts within me rise,
When I behold afar,
Suspended in the evening skies,
The shield of that red star

O star of strength! I see thee stand
And smile upon my pain;
Thou beckonest with thy mailed hand,
And I am strong again.

Within my breast there is no light,
But the cold light of stars:
I give the first watch of the night
To the red planet Mars.

The star of the unconquer'd will,
He rises in my breast,
Serene, and resolute, and still,
And calm, and self-possess'd.

And thou, too, whosoe'er thou art,
That readest this brief psalm,
As one by one thy hopes depart,
Be resolute and calm.

O fear not in a world like this,
And thou shalt know ere long,
Know how sublime a thing it is
To suffer and be strong.

ENDYMION.

The rising moon has hid the stars,
Her level rays, like golden bars,
Lie on the landscape green,
With shadows brown between.

And silver white the river gleams,
As if Diana, in her dreams,
Had dropt her silver bow
Upon the meadows low.

On such a tranquil night as this,
She woke Endymion with a kiss,
When, sleeping in the grove,
He dream'd not of her love.

Like Dian's kiss, unask'd, unsought,
Love gives itself, but is not bought;
Nor voice, nor sound betrays
Its deep, impassion'd gaze.

It comes—the beautiful, the free,
The crown of all humanity—
In silence and alone
To seek the elected one.

It lifts the bows, whose shadows deep
Are Life's oblivion, the soul's sleep,
And kisses the closed eyes
Of him, who slumbering lies.

O, weary hearts! O, slumbering eyes!
O, drooping souls, whose destinies
Are fraught with fear and pain,
Ye shall be loved again!

No one is so accursed by fate,
No one so utterly desolate,
But some heart, though unknown,
Responds unto its own.

Responds—as if, with unseen wings,
A breath from heaven had touch'd its strings;
And whispers, in its song,
"Where hast thou stay'd so long?"

FOOTSTEPS OF ANGELS.

When the hours of day are number'd,
And the voices of the Night
Wake the better soul that slumber'd
To a holy, calm delight;

Ere the evening lamps are lighted,
And, like phantoms grim and tall,
Shadows from the fitful fire-light
Dance upon the parlour-wall;

Then the forms of the departed
Enter at the open door;
The beloved ones, the true-hearted,
Come to visit me once more;

He, the young and strong, who cherish'd
Noble longings for the strife,—
By the road-side fell and perish'd,
Weary with the march of life!

They, the holy ones and weakly,
Who the cross of suffering bore,—
Folded their pale hands so meekly,—
Spake with us on earth no more!

And with them the Being Beauteous,
Who unto my youth was given,
More than all things else to love me,
And is now a saint in heaven.

With a slow and noiseless footstep,
Comes that messenger divine,
Takes the vacant chair beside me,
Lays her gentle hand in mine.

And she sits and gazes at me,
With those deep and tender eyes,
Like the stars, so still and saintlike,
Looking downward from the skies.

Utter'd not, yet comprehended,
Is the spirit's voiceless prayer,
Soft rebukes, in blessings ended,
Breathing from her lips of air.

O, though oft depress'd and lonely,
All my fears are laid aside,
If I but remember only
Such as these have lived and died!

THE BELEAGURED CITY.

I have read in some old marvellous tale
Some legend strange and vague,
That a midnight host of spectres pale
Beleagured the walls of Prague.

Beside the Moldau's rushing stream,
With the wan moon overhead,
There stood, as in an awful dream,
The army of the dead.

White as a sea-fog, landward bound,
The spectral camp was seen,
And, with a sorrowful, deep sound,
The river flow'd between.

No other voice nor sound was there,
No drum, nor sentry's pace;
The mist-like banners clasp'd the air,
As clouds with clouds embrace.

But, when the old cathedral bell
Proclaim'd the morning prayer,
The white pavilions rose and fell
On the alarmed air.

Down the broad valley fast and far
The troubled army fled;
Up rose the glorious morning star,
The ghastly host was dead.

I have read in the marvellous heart of man,
That strange and mystic scroll,
That an army of phantoms vast and wan
Beleaguer the human soul.

Encamp'd beside Life's rushing stream,
In Fancy's misty light,
Gigantic shapes and shadows gleam
Portentous through the night.

Upon its midnight battle-ground
The spectral camp is seen
And with a sorrowful, deep sound,
Flows the River of Life between.

No other voice, nor sound is there,
In the army of the grave;
No other challenge breaks the air,
But the rushing of Life's wave.

And, when the solemn and deep church-bell
Entreats the soul to pray,
The midnight phantoms feel the spell,
The shadows sweep away.

Down the broad Vale of Tears afar
The spectral camp is fled;
Faith shineth as a morning star,
Our ghastly fears are dead.

IT IS NOT ALWAYS MAY.

The sun is bright, the air is clear,
The darting swallows soar and sing,
And from the stately elms I hear
The blue-bird prophesying Spring.

So blue yon winding river flows,
It seems an outlet from the sky,
Where, waiting till the west wind blows,
The freighted clouds at anchor lie.

All things are new—the buds, the leaves,
That gild the elm-tree's nodding crest,
And even the nest beneath the eaves—
There are no birds in last year's nest.

All things rejoice in youth and love,
The fulness of their first delight,
And learn from the soft heavens above
The melting tenderness of night.

Maiden! that read'st this simple rhyme,
Enjoy thy youth—it will not stay;
Enjoy the fragrance of thy prime,
For, O! it is not always May!

Enjoy the spring of Love and Youth,
To some good angel leave the rest,
For Time will teach thee soon the truth—
There are no birds in last year's nest.

MIDNIGHT MASS FOR THE DYING YEAR.

Yes, the year is growing old,
And his eye is pale and blear'd!
Death, with frosty hand and cold,
Plucks the old man by the beard,
Sorely,—sorely!

The leaves are falling, falling,
Solemnly and slow;
Caw! caw! the rooks are calling,
It is a sound of wo,
A sound of wo!

Through woods and mountain-passes
The winds, like anthems, roll;
They are chanting solemn masses,
Singing; Pray for this poor soul,
Pray,—pray!

The hooded clouds, like friars,
Tell their beads in drops of rain,
And patter their doleful prayers;—
But their prayers are all in vain,
All in vain!

There he stands, in the foul weather,
The foolish, fond Old Year,
Crown'd with wild flowers and with heather,
Like weak, despised Lear,
A king,—a king!

Then comes the summer-like day,
Bids the old man rejoice!
His joy! his last! O, the old man gray
Loveth her ever-soft voice,
Gentle and low.

To the crimson woods he saith,
And the voice gentle and low
Of the soft air, like a daughter's breath,
Pray do not mock me so!
Do not laugh at me!

And now the sweet day is dead;
Cold in his arms it lies,
No stain from its breath is spread
Over the glassy skies,
No mist nor stain!

Then, too, the Old Year dieth,
And the forests utter a moan,
Like the voice of one who crieth
In the wilderness alone,
Vex not his ghost!

Then comes, with an awful roar,
Gathering and sounding on,
The storm-wind from Labrador,
The wind Euroclydon,
The storm-wind!

Howl! howl! and from the forest
Sweep the red leaves away!
Would, the sins that thou abhorrest,
O soul! could thus decay,
And be swept away!

For there shall come a mightier blast,
There shall be a darker day;
And the stars, from heaven down-cast,
Like red leaves be swept away!
Kyrie Eleyson!
Christe Eleyson!

THE VILLAGE BLACKSMITH.

Under a spreading chestnut tree
The village smithy stands;
The smith, a mighty man is he,
With large and sinewy hands;
And the muscles of his brawny arms
Are strong as iron bands.

His hair is crisp, and black, and long;
His face is like the tan;
His brow is wet with honest sweat;
He earns whate'er he can,
And looks the whole world in the face,
For he owes not any man.

Week in, week out, from morn till night,
You can hear his bellows blow;
You can hear him swing his heavy sledge,
With measured beat and slow,
Like a sexton ringing the village bell
When the evening sun is low.

And children coming home from school
Look in at the open door;
They love to see the flaming forge,
And hear the bellows roar,
And catch the burning sparks that fly
Like chaff from a threshing-floor.

He goes on Sunday to the church,
And sits among his boys;
He hears the parson pray and preach,
He hears his daughter's voice,
Singing in the village choir,
And it makes his heart rejoice.

It sounds to him like her mother's voice,
Singing in Paradise!
He needs must think of her once more,
How in the grave she lies;
And with his hard, rough hand he wipes
A tear out of his eyes.

Toiling—rejoicing—sorrowing—
Onward through life he goes:
Each morning sees some task begin,
Each evening sees it close;
Something attempted—something done,
Has earned a night's repose.

Thanks, thanks to thee, my worthy friend
For the lesson thou hast taught!
Thus at the flaming forge of Life
Our fortunes must be wrought,
Thus on its sounding anvil shaped
Each burning deed and thought

EXCELSIOR.

The shades of night were falling fast,
As through an Alpine village pass'd
A youth, who bore, mid snow and ice,
A banner with the strange device,
Excelsior!

His brow was sad; his eye beneath
Flash'd like a faulchion from its sheath,
And like a silver clarion rung
The accents of that unknown tongue,
Excelsior!

In happy homes he saw the light
Of household fires gleam warm and bright:
Above, the spectral glaciers shone,
And from his lips escaped a groan,
Excelsior!

"Try not the pass!" the old man said;
"Dark lowers the tempest overhead,
The roaring torrent is deep and wide!"
And loud that clarion voice replied,
Excelsior!

"O stay," the maiden said, "and rest
Thy weary head upon this breast!"
A tear stood in his bright blue eye,
But still he answer'd, with a sigh,
Excelsior!

"Beware the pine tree's wither'd branch!
Beware the awful avalanche!"
This was the peasant's last good-night;
A voice replied, far up the height,
Excelsior!

At break of day, as heavenward
The pious monks of Saint Bernard
Utter'd the oft-repeated prayer,
A voice cried through the startled air,
Excelsior!

A traveller, by the faithful hound,
Half-buried in the snow was found,
Still grasping in his hand of ice
That banner with the strange device,
Excelsior!

There, in the twilight cold and gray,
Lifeless, but beautiful, he lay,
And from the sky, serene and far,
A voice fell, like a falling star!
Excelsior!

THE RAINY DAY.

The day is cold, and dark, and dreary;
It rains, and the wind is never weary;
The vine still clings to the mouldering wall,
But at every gust the dead leaves fall,
And the day is dark and dreary.

My life is cold, and dark, and dreary;
It rains, and the wind is never weary;
My thoughts still cling to the mouldering past,
But the hopes of youth fall thick in the blast,
And the days are dark and dreary.

Be still, sad heart, and cease repining;
Behind the clouds is the sun still shining;
Thy fate is the common fate of all.
Into each life some rain must fall,
Some days must be dark and dreary.

MAIDENHOOD.

Maiden! with the meek, brown eyes,
In whose orbs a shadow lies,
Like the dusk in evening skies!

Thou, whose locks outshine the sun,
Golden tresses, wreathed in one,
As the braided streamlets run!

Standing, with reluctant feet,
Where the brook and river meet!
Womanhood and childhood fleet!

Gazing, with a timid glance,
On the brooklet's swift advance,
On the river's broad expanse!

Deep and still, that gliding stream
Beautiful to thee must seem,
As the river of a dream.

Then, why pause with indecision,
When bright angels in thy vision
Beckon thee to fields Elysian?

Seest thou shadows sailing by,
As the dove, with startled eye,
Sees the falcon's shadow fly?

Hearest thou voices on the shore,
That our ears perceive no more,
Deafen'd by the cataract's roar?

O, thou child of many prayers!
Life hath quicksands,—Life hath snares!
Care and age come unawares!

Like the swell of some sweet tune,
Morning rises into noon,
May glides onward into June.

Childhood is the bough where slumber'd
Birds and blossoms many-number'd;—
Age, that bough with snows encumber'd

Gather, then, each flower that grows,
When the young heart overflows,
To embalm that tent of snows.

Bear a lily in thy hand;
Gates of brass cannot withstand
One touch of that magic wand.

Bear, through sorrow, wrong, and ruth,
In thy heart the dew of youth,
On thy lips the smile of truth.

O, that dew, like balm, shall steal
Into wounds, that cannot heal,
Even as sleep our eyes doth seal;

And that smile, like sunshine, dart
Into many a sunless heart,
For a smile of God thou art.

GEORGE LUNT.

[Born about 1807.]

MR. LUNT is a native of the pleasant town of Newburyport, near Boston, from which, for a long period, his ancestors and relatives "followed the sea." He was educated at Cambridge, and soon after leaving the university entered upon the study of the law, and, being admitted to the bar, practised his profession in Newburyport until 1849, when, being appointed by President Taylor United States Attorney for Massachusetts, he removed to Boston. He has been a representative of the people in the state Senate and House of Assembly, and has held various other offices.

When he was about nineteen years of age, he wrote "The Grave of Byron," a poem in the Spenserian measure, which has considerable merit; and, in 1839, appeared a collection of his later productions, of which the largest is a metrical essay entitled "Life," in which he has attempted to show, by reference to the condition of society in different ages, that Christianity is necessary to the development of man's moral nature. More recently he has published "The Age of Gold and other Poems;" "Lyric Poems, Sonnets, and Miscellanies;" and two or three other small volumes, besides "Julia," a satire, and a novel in prose, entitled "Eastford," under the pseudonym of WESLEY BROOKE.

AUTUMN MUSINGS.

COME thou with me! If thou hast worn away
All this most glorious summer in the crowd,
Amid the dust of cities, and the din,
While birds were carolling on every spray;
If, from gray dawn to solemn night's approach,
Thy soul hath wasted all its better thoughts,
Toiling and panting for a little gold;
Drudging amid the very lees of life
For this accursed slave that makes men slaves;
Come thou with me into the pleasant fields:
Let Nature breathe on us and make us free!
For thou shalt hold communion, pure and high,
With the great Spirit of the Universe;
It shall pervade thy soul; it shall renew
The fancies of thy boyhood; thou shalt know
Tears, most unwonted tears dimming thine eyes;
Thou shalt forget, under the old brown oak,
That the good south wind and the liberal west
Have other tidings than the songs of birds,
Or the soft news wafted from fragrant flowers.
Look out on Nature's face, and what hath she
In common with thy feelings? That brown hill,
Upon whose sides, from the gray mountain-ash,
We gather'd crimson berries, look'd as brown
When the leaves fell twelve autumn suns ago;
This pleasant stream, with the well-shaded verge,
On whose fair surface have our buoyant limbs
So often play'd, caressing and caress'd;
Its verdant banks are green as then they were;
So went its bubbling murmur down the tide.
Yes, and the very trees, those ancient oaks,
The crimson-crested maple, feathery elm,
And fair, smooth ash, with leaves of graceful gold,
Look like familiar faces of old friends.
From their broad branches drop the wither'd leaves,
Drop, one by one, without a single breath,
Save when some eddying curl round the old roots
Twirls them about in merry sport a while.
They are not changed; their office is not done;
The first soft breeze of spring shall see them fresh
With sprouting twigs bursting from every branch,
As should fresh feelings from our wither'd hearts.
Scorn not the moral; for, while these have warm'd
To annual beauty, gladdening the fields
With new and ever-glorious garniture,
Thou hast grown worn and wasted, almost gray
Even in thy very summer. 'T is for this
We have neglected nature! Wearing out
Our hearts and all our life's dearest charities
In the perpetual turmoil, when we need
To strengthen and to purify our minds
Amid the venerable woods; to hold
Chaste converse with the fountains and the winds!
So should we elevate our souls; so be
Ready to stand and act a nobler part
In the hard, heartless struggles of the world.
Day wanes; 't is autumn eventide again;
And, sinking on the blue hills' breast, the sun
Spreads the large bounty of his level blaze,
Lengthening the shades of mountains and tall trees,
And throwing blacker shadows o'er the sheet
Of this dark stream, in whose unruffled tide
Waver the bank-shrub and the graceful elm,
As the gay branches and their trembling leaves
Catch the soft whisper of the coming air:
So doth it mirror every passing cloud,
And those which fill the chambers of the west
With such strange beauty, fairer than all thrones,
Blazon'd with orient gems and barbarous gold.
I see thy full heart gathering in thine eyes;
I see those eyes swelling with precious tears;
But, if thou couldst have look'd upon this scene
With a cold brow, and then turn'd back to thoughts
Of traffic in thy fellow's wretchedness,
Thou wert not fit to gaze upon the face
Of Nature's naked beauty; most unfit
To look on fairer things, the loveliness
Of earth's most lovely daughters, whose glad forms
And glancing eyes do kindle the great souls
Of better men to emulate pure thoughts,
And, in high action, all ennobling deeds

But lo! the harvest moon! She climbs as fair
Among the cluster'd jewels of the sky,
As, mid the rosy bowers of paradise,
Her soft light, trembling upon leaf and flower,
Smiled o'er the slumbers of the first-born man.
And, while her beauty is upon our hearts,
Now let us seek our quiet home, that sleep
May come without bad dreams; may come as light
As to that yellow-headed cottage-boy,
Whose serious musings, as he homeward drives
His sober herd, are of the frosty dawn,
And the ripe nuts which his own hand shall pluck.
Then, when the bird, high-courier of the morn,
Looks from his airy vantage over the world,
And, by the music of his mounting flight,
Tells many blessed things of gushing gold,
Coming in floods o'er the eastern wave,
Will we arise, and our pure orisons
Shall keep us in the trials of the day.

JEWISH BATTLE-SONG.

Ho! Princes of Jacob! the strength and the stay
Of the daughter of Zion,—now up, and array;
Lo, the hunters have struck her, and bleeding alone
Like a pard in the desert she maketh her moan:
Up, with war-horse and banner, with spear and with sword,
On the spoiler go down in the might of the Lord!

She lay sleeping in beauty, more fair than the moon,
With her children about her, like stars in night's noon,
When they came to her covert, these spoilers of Rome,
And are trampling her children and rifling her home:
O, up, noble chiefs! would you leave her forlorn,
To be crush'd by the Gentile, a mock and a scorn?

Their legions and cohorts are fair to behold,
With their iron-clad bosoms, and helmets of gold;
But, gorgeous and glorious in pride though they be,
Their avarice is broad as the grasp of the sea;
They talk not of pity; the mercies they feel
Are cruel and fierce as their death-doing steel.

Will they laugh at the hind they have struck to the earth,
When the bold stag of Naphtali bursts on their mirth?
Will they dare to deride and insult, when in wrath
The lion of Judah glares wild in their path?
O, say, will they mock us, when down on the plain
The hoofs of our steeds thunder over their slain?

They come with their plumes tossing haughty and free,
And white as the crest of the old hoary sea;
Yet they float not so fierce as the wild lion's mane,
To whose lair ye have track'd him, whose whelps ye have slain;
But, dark mountain-archer! your sinews to-day
Must be strong as the spear-shaft to drive in the prey.

And the tribes are all gathering; the valleys ring out
To the peal of the trumpet—the timbrel—the shout·
Lo, Zebulon comes; he remembers the day
When they perill'd their lives to the death in the fray;
And the riders of Naphtali burst from the hills
Like a mountain-swollen stream in the pride of its rills.

Like Sisera's rolls the foe's chariot-wheel,
And he comes, like the Philistine, girded in steel;
Like both shall he perish, if ye are but men,
If your javelins and hearts are as mighty as then;
He trusts in his buckler, his spear, and his sword;
His strength is but weakness;—we trust in the Lord!

"PASS ON, RELENTLESS WORLD."

Swifter and swifter, day by day,
Down Time's unquiet current hurl'd,
Thou passest on thy restless way,
Tumultuous and unstable world!
Thou passest on! Time hath not seen
Delay upon thy hurried path;
And prayers and tears alike have been
In vain to stay thy course of wrath!

Thou passest on, and with thee go
The loves of youth, the cares of age;
And smiles and tears, and joy and wo,
Are on thy history's troubled page!
There, every day, like yesterday,
Writes hopes that end in mockery;
But who shall tear the veil away
Before the abyss of things to be!

Thou passest on, and at thy side,
Even as a shade, Oblivion treads,
And o'er the dreams of human pride
His misty shroud forever spreads;
Where all thine iron hand hath traced
Upon that gloomy scroll to-day,
With records ages since effaced,—
Like them shall live, like them decay.

Thou passest on, with thee the vain,
Who sport upon thy flaunting blaze,
Pride, framed of dust and folly's train,
Who court thy love, and run thy ways:
But thou and I,—and be it so,—
Press onward to eternity;
Yet not together let us go
To that deep-voiced but shoreless sea.

Thou hast thy friends,—I would have mine;
Thou hast thy thoughts,—leave me my own;
I kneel not at thy gilded shrine,
I bow not at thy slavish throne;
I see them pass without a sigh,—
They wake no swelling raptures now,
The fierce delights that fire thine eye,
The triumphs of thy haughty brow.

Pass on, relentless world! I grieve
No more for all that thou hast riven,
Pass on, in God's name,—only leave
The things thou never yet hast given—
A heart at ease, a mind at home,
Affections fixed above thy sway,
Faith set upon a world to come,
And patience through life's little day.

HAMPTON BEACH.

Again upon the sounding shore,
And, O how bless'd, again alone!
I could not bear to hear thy roar,
Thy deep, thy long, majestic tone;
I could not bear to think that one
Could view with me thy swelling might,
And, like a very stock or stone,
Turn coldly from the glorious sight,
And seek the idle world, to hate and fear and fight.

Thou art the same, eternal sea!
The earth hath many shapes and forms,
Of hill and valley, flower and tree;
Fields that the fervid noontide warms,
Or winter's rugged grasp deforms,
Or bright with autumn's golden store;
Thou coverest up thy face with storms,
Or smilest serene,—but still thy roar
And dashing foam go up to vex the sea-beat shore.

I see thy heaving waters roll,
I hear thy stern, uplifted voice,
And trumpet-like upon my soul
Falls the deep music of that noise
Wherewith thou dost thyself rejoice;
The ships, that on thy bosom play,
Thou dashest them about like toys,
And stranded navies are thy prey,
Strown on thy rock-bound coast, torn by the whirling spray.

As summer twilight, soft and calm,
Or when in stormy grandeur drest,
Peals up to heaven the eternal psalm,
That swells within thy boundless breast;
Thy curling waters have no rest;
But day and night the ceaseless throng
Of waves that wait thy high behest,
Speak out in utterance deep and strong,
And loud the craggy beach howls back their savage song.

Terrible art thou in thy wrath,—
Terrible in thine hour of glee,
When the strong winds, upon their path,
Bound o'er thy breast tumultuously,
And shout their chorus loud and free
To the sad sea-bird's mournful wail,
As, heaving with the heaving sea,
The broken mast and shatter'd sail
Tell of thy cruel strength the lamentable tale.

Ay, 'tis indeed a glorious sight
To gaze upon thine ample face;
An awful joy,—a deep delight!
I see thy laughing waves embrace
Each other in their frolic race;
I sit above the flashing spray,
That foams around this rocky base,
And, as the bright blue waters play,
Feel that my thoughts, my life, perchance, are vain [as they.

This is thy lesson, mighty sea!
Man calls the dimpled earth his own,
The flowery vale, the golden lea;
And on the wild, gray mountain-stone
Claims nature's temple for his throne!
But where thy many voices sing
Their endless song, the deep, deep tone
Calls back his spirit's airy wing,
He shrinks into himself, where God alone is king!

PILGRIM SONG.

Over the mountain wave, see where they come;
Storm-cloud and wintry wind welcome them home
Yet, where the sounding gale howls to the sea,
There their song peals along, deep-toned and free.
"Pilgrims and wanderers, hither we come;
Where the free dare to be—this is our home."

England hath sunny dales, dearly they bloom;
Scotia hath heather-hills, sweet their perfume:
Yet through the wilderness cheerful we stray,
Native land, native land—home far away!
"Pilgrims and wanderers, hither we come;
Where the free dare to be—this is our home!

Dim grew the forest-path: onward they trod;
Firm beat their noble hearts, trusting in God!
Gray men and blooming maids, high rose their song
Hear it sweep, clear and deep, ever along:
"Pilgrims and wanderers, hither we come;
Where the free dare to be—this is our home!

Not theirs the glory-wreath, torn by the blast;
Heavenward their holy steps, heavenward they past
Green be their mossy graves! ours be their fame
While their song peals along, ever the same:
"Pilgrims and wanderers, hither we come;
Where the free dare to be—this is our home!"

THE LYRE AND SWORD.

The freeman's glittering sword be blest,—
Forever blest the freeman's lyre,—
That rings upon the tyrant's crest;
This stirs the heart like living fire:
Well can he wield the shining brand,
Who battles for his native land;
But when his fingers sweep the chords,
That summon heroes to the fray,
They gather at the feast of swords,
Like mountain-eagles to their prey!

And mid the vales and swelling hills,
That sweetly bloom in Freedom's land,
A living spirit breathes and fills
The freeman's heart and nerves his hand;
For the bright soil that gave him birth,
The home of all he loves on earth,—
For *this*, when Freedom's trumpet calls,
He waves on high his sword of fire,—
For *this*, amidst his country's halls
Forever strikes the freeman's lyre!

His burning heart he may not lend
To serve a doting despot's sway,—
A suppliant knee he will not bend,
Before these things of "brass and clay:"
When wrong and ruin call to war,
He knows the summons from afar;
On high his glittering sword he waves,
And myriads feel the freeman's fire,
While he, around their fathers' graves,
Strikes to old strains the freeman's lyre!

ROBERT H. MESSINGER.

[Born about 1807.]

Our cleverest writers of verse, in many cases, have never collected the waifs they have given to magazines and newspapers, and some of the best fugitive pieces thus published have a periodical currency without the endorsement of a name, or their authors, having written for the love of writing, rather than for reputation, have permitted whoever would to run away with the literary honors to which they were entitled. Mr. Messinger is an example of this class.

Robert Hinckley Messinger is a native of Boston, and comes from an old puritan and pilgrim stock, being a descendant in the seventh generation from Henry Messinger, who was made a freeman of Boston in the year 1630, and a great grandson of the Reverend Henry Messinger, who was graduated at Harvard College in 1719, and elected the first minister of Wrentham, Massachusetts, in 1720.

With a view to his education at Cambridge he was placed at the Boston Latin School, then under the administration of Benjamin A. Gould; but after three years' attendance there, preferring mercantile pursuits, he left for the city of New York, where he resided many years. The poems we have from his pen were mostly written at about the age of twenty to twenty-five years, and appeared in the New York "American." The lines, "Give me the Old," suggested by a famous saying of Alphonso of Castile, were first published in that paper for the twenty-sixth of April, 1838, and were reprinted in an early edition of the "Poets and Poetry of America," under an impression that they were from the hand of the ingenious and elegant essayist, Mr. Henry Cary; but that gentleman, on discovering my error, took the first opportunity to deny their authorship to me.

Mr. Messinger's residence at present (1855) is in New London, one of the mountain villages of New Hampshire.

GIVE ME THE OLD.

OLD WINE TO DRINK, OLD WOOD TO BURN, OLD BOOKS TO READ, AND OLD FRIENDS TO CONVERSE WITH.

I.

Old wine to drink!—
Ay, give the slippery juice,
That drippeth from the grape thrown loose,
Within the tun;
Pluck'd from beneath the cliff
Of sunny-sided Teneriffe,
And ripened 'neath the blink
Of India's sun!
Peat whiskey hot,
Tempered with well-boiled water!
These make the long night shorter,—
Forgetting not
Good stout old English porter.

II.

Old wood to burn!—
Ay, bring the hill-side beech
From where the owlets meet and screech,
And ravens croak;
The crackling pine, and cedar sweet;
Bring too a clump of fragrant peat,
Dug 'neath the fern;
The knotted oak,
A faggot too, perhap,
Whose bright flame, dancing, winking,
Shall light us at our drinking;
While the oozing sap
Shall make sweet music to our thinking.

III.

Old books to read!—
Ay, bring those nodes of wit,
The brazen-clasp'd, the vellum writ,
Time-honour'd tomes!
The same my sire scanned before,
The same my grandsire thumbed o'er,
The same his sire from college bore,
The well-earn'd meed
Of Oxford's domes:
Old Homer blind,
Old Horace, rake Anacreon, by
Old Tully, Plautus, Terence lie;
Mort Arthur's olden minstrelsie,
Quaint Burton, quainter Spenser, ay,
And Gervase Markham's venerie—
Nor leave behind
The Holye Book by which we live and die.

IV.

Old friends to talk!—
Ay, bring those chosen few,
The wise, the courtly and the true,
So rarely found;
Him for my wine, him for my stud,
Him for my easel, distich, bud
In mountain walk!
Bring Walter good:
With soulful Fred; and learned Will,
And thee, my *alter ego*, (dearer still
For every mood.)*

* "It is rather a sad commentary on the last verse, to know that the 'Walter good,' the 'soulful Fred,' and the 'learned Will,' are in their graves."—*Note from the author, dated March 9, 1855, in the "Home Journal."*

JOHN H. BRYANT.

[Born, 1807.]

John Howard Bryant was born in Cummington, Massachusetts, on the twenty-second day of July, 1807. His youth was passed principally in rural occupations, and in attending the district and other schools, until he was nineteen years of age, when he began to study the Latin language, with a view of entering one of the colleges. In 1826, he wrote the first poem of which he retained any copy. This was entitled "My Native Village," and first appeared in the "United States Review and Literary Gazette," a periodical published simultaneously at New York and Boston, of which his brother, William Cullen Bryant, was one of the editors. It is included in the present collection. After this he gave up the idea of a university education, and placed himself for a while at the Rensselaer School at Troy, under the superintendance of Professor Eaton. He subsequently applied himself to the study of the mathematical and natural sciences, under different instructors, and in his intervals of leisure produced several poems, which were published in the gazettes.

In April, 1831, he went to Jacksonville, in Illinois; and in September of the next year went to Princeton, in the same state, where he sat himself down as a *squatter*, or inhabitant of the public lands not yet ordered to be sold by the government. When the lands came into the market, he purchased a farm, bordering on one of the fine groves of that country. He was married in 1833. He accepted soon afterward two or three public offices, one of which was that of Recorder of Bureau county; but afterward resigned them, and devoted himself to agricultural pursuits. Of his poems, part were written in Massachusetts, and part in Illinois. They have the same general characteristics as those of his brother. He is a lover of nature, and describes minutely and effectively. To him the wind and the streams are ever musical, and the forests and the prairies clothed in beauty. His versification is easy and correct, and his writings show him to be a man of refined taste and kindly feelings, and to have a mind stored with the best learning.

THE NEW ENGLAND PILGRIM'S FUNERAL.

It was a wintry scene,
The hills were whiten'd o'er,
And the chill north winds were blowing keen
Along the rocky shore.

Gone was the wood-bird's lay,
That the summer forest fills,
And the voice of the stream has pass'd away
From its path among the hills.

And the low sun coldly smiled
Through the boughs of the ancient wood,
Where a hundred souls, sire, wife, and child,
Around a coffin stood.

They raised it gently up,
And, through the untrodden snow,
They bore it away, with a solemn step,
To a woody vale below.

And grief was in each eye,
As they moved towards the spot,
And brief, low speech, and tear and sigh
Told that a friend was not.

When they laid his cold corpse low
In its dark and narrow cell,
Heavy the mingled earth and snow
Upon his coffin fell.

Weeping, they pass'd away,
And left him there alone,
With no mark to tell where their dead friend lay,
But the mossy forest-stone.

When the winter storms were gone
And the strange birds sung around,
Green grass and violets sprung upon
That spot of holy ground.

And o'er him giant trees
Their proud arms toss'd on high,
And rustled music in the breeze
That wander'd through the sky.

When these were overspread
With the hues that Autumn gave,
They bow'd them in the wind, and shed
Their leaves upon his grave.

These woods are perish'd now,
And that humble grave forgot,
And the yeoman sings, as he drives his plough
O'er that once sacred spot.

Two centuries are flown
Since they laid his cold corpse low,
And his bones are moulder'd to dust, and strown
To the breezes long ago.

And they who laid him there,
That sad and suffering train,
Now sleep in dust,—to tell us where
No letter'd stones remain.

Their memory remains,
And ever shall remain,
More lasting than the aged fanes
Of Egypt's storied plain.

A RECOLLECTION.

Here tread aside, where the descending brook
Pays a scant tribute to the mightier stream,
And all the summer long, on silver feet,
Glides lightly o'er the pebbles, sending out
A mellow murmur on the quiet air.
Just up this narrow glen, in yonder glade
Set, like a nest amid embowering trees,
Where the green grass, fresh as in early spring,
Spreads a bright carpet o'er the hidden soil,
Lived, in my early days, an humble pair,
A mother and her daughter. She, the dame,
Had well nigh seen her threescore years and ten.
Her step was tremulous; slight was her frame,
And bow'd with time and toil; the lines of care
Were deep upon her brow. At shut of day
I've met her by the skirt of this old wood,
Alone, and faintly murmuring to herself,
Haply, the history of her better days.
I knew that history once, from youth to age:—
It was a sad one; he who wedded her
Had wrong'd her love, and thick the darts of death
Had fallen among her children and her friends.
One solace for her age remained,—a fair
And gentle daughter, with blue, pensive eyes,
And cheeks like summer roses. Her sweet songs
Rang like the thrasher's warble in these woods,
And up the rocky dells. At noon and eve,
Her walk was o'er the hills, and by the founts
Of the deep forest. Oft she gather'd flowers
In lone and desolate places, where the foot
Of other wanderers but seldom trod.
Once, in my boyhood, when my truant steps
Had led me forth among the pleasant hills,
I met her in a shaded path, that winds
Far through the spreading groves. The sun was low,
The shadow of the hills stretch'd o'er the vale,
And the still waters of the river lay
Black in the early twilight. As we met,
She stoop'd and press'd her friendly lips to mine,
And, though I then was but a simple child,
Who ne'er had dream'd of love, nor knew its power,
I wonder'd at her beauty. Soon a sound
Of thunder, muttering low, along the west,
Foretold a coming storm; my homeward path
Lay through the woods, tangled with undergrowth.
A timid urchin then, I fear'd to go,
Which she observing, kindly led the way,
And left me when my dwelling was in sight.
I hasten'd on; but, ere I reach'd the gate,
The rain fell fast, and the drench'd fields around
Were glittering in the lightning's frequent flash.
But where was now Eliza? When the morn
Blush'd on the summer hills, they found her dead,
Beneath an oak, rent by the thunderbolt.
Thick lay the splinters round, and one sharp shaft
Had pierced hersnow-white brow. And here she lies,
Where the green hill slopes toward the southern sky.
'Tis thirty summers since they laid her here;
The cottage where she dwelt is razed and gone;
Her kindred all are perish'd from the earth,
And this rude stone, that simply bears her name,
Is mouldering fast; and soon this quiet spot,
Held sacred now, will be like common ground.

Fit place is this for so much loveliness
To find its rest. It is a hallow'd shrine,
Where nature pays her tribute. Dewy spring
Sets the gay wild flowers thick around her grave;
The green boughs o'er her, in the summer-time,
Sigh to the winds; the robin takes his perch
Hard by, and warbles to his sitting mate;
The brier-rose blossoms to the sky of June,
And hangs above her in the winter days
Its scarlet fruit. No rude foot ventures near;
The noisy schoolboy keeps aloof, and he
Who hunts the fox, when all the hills are white,
Here treads aside. Not seldom have I found,
Around the head-stone carefully entwined,
Garlands of flowers, I never knew by whom.
For two years past I've miss'd them; doubtless one
Who held this dust most precious, placed them there,
And, sorrowing in secret many a year,
At last hath left the earth to be with her.

MY NATIVE VILLAGE.

There lies a village in a peaceful vale,
With sloping hills and waving woods around,
Fenced from the blasts. There never ruder gale
Bows the tall grass that covers all the ground;
And planted shrubs are there, and cherish'd flowers,
And a bright verdure, born of gentler showers.

'Twas there my young existence was begun,
My earliest sports were on its flowery green,
And often, when my schoolboy task was done,
I climb'd its hills to view the pleasant scene,
And stood and gazed till the sun's setting ray
Shone on the height, the sweetest of the day.

There, when that hour of mellow light was come,
And mountain shadows cool'd the ripen'd grain,
I watch'd the weary yeoman plodding home,
In the lone path that winds across the plain,
To rest his limbs, and watch his child at play,
And tell him o'er the labours of the day

And when the woods put on their autumn glow,
And the bright sun came in among the trees,
And leaves were gathering in the glen below,
Swept softly from the mountains by the breeze,
I wander'd till the starlight on the stream
At length awoke me from my fairy dream.

Ah! happy days, too happy to return,
Fled on the wings of youth's departed years,
A bitter lesson has been mine to learn,
The truth of life, its labours, pains, and fears;
Yet does the memory of my boyhood stay,
A twilight of the brightness pass'd away.

My thoughts steal back to that sweet village still,
Its flowers and peaceful shades before me rise,
The play-place, and the prospect from the hill,
Its summer verdure, and autumnal dyes;
The present brings its storms; but, while they last,
I shelter me in the delightful past.

FROM A POEM ENTITLED "A DAY IN AUTUMN."

One ramble through the woods with me,
 Thou dear companion of my days,—
These mighty woods! how quietly
 They sleep in Autumn's golden haze

The gay leaves, twinkling in the breeze,
 Still to the forest branches cling;
They lie like blossoms on the trees—
 The brightest blossoms of the spring.

Flowers linger in each sheltered nook,
 And still the cheerful song of bird,
And murmur of the bee and brook,
 Through all the quiet groves are heard.

And bell of kine, that, sauntering, browse,
 And squirrel chirping as he hides
Where gorgeously, with crimson boughs,
 The creeper clothes the oak's gray sides.

How mild the light in all the skies!
 How balmily the south wind blows!
The smile of God around us lies,
 His rest is in this deep repose.

These whispers of the flowing air,
 These waters that in music fall,
These sounds of peaceful life declare
 The Love that keeps and hushes all.

ON FINDING A FOUNTAIN IN A SECLUDED PART OF A FOREST.

Three hundred years are scarcely gone
 Since, to the New World's virgin shore,
Crowds of rude men were pressing on
 To range its boundless regions o'er.

Some bore the sword in bloody hands,
 And sacked its helpless towns for spoil;
Some searched for gold the rivers' sands,
 Or trenched the mountains' stubborn soil.

And some with higher purpose sought
 Through forests wild and wastes uncouth—
Sought with long toil, yet found it not—
 The fountain of eternal youth.

They said in some green valley, where
 The foot of man had never trod,
There gushed a fountain bright and fair,
 Up from the ever-verdant sod.

They there who drank should never know
 Age with its weakness, pain, and gloom;
And from its brink the old should go
 With youth's light step and radiant bloom.

Is not this fount so pure and sweet
 Whose stainless current ripples o'er
The fringe of blossoms at my feet
 The same those pilgrims sought of yore?

How brightly leap mid glittering sands
 The living waters from below;
Oh, let me dip these lean brown hands,
 Drink deep, and bathe my wrinkled brow;

And feel through every shrunken vein
 The warm red blood flow swift and free,
Feel waking in my heart again
 Youth's brightest hopes, youth's wildest glee

'T is vain, for still the life-blood plays
 With sluggish course through all my frame,
The mirror of the pool betrays
 My wrinkled visage still the same.

And the sad spirit questions still—
 Must this warm frame, these limbs that yield
To each light motion of the will,
 Lie with the dull clods of the field?

Has nature no renewing power
 To drive the frost of age away?
Has earth no fount, or herb, or flower,
 Which man may taste and live for aye?

Alas! for that unchanging state
 Of youth and strength in vain we yearn
And only after death's dark gate
 Is reached and passed, can youth return.

THE TRAVELLER'S RETURN.

It was the glorious summer-time,
 As on a hill I stood,
Amid a group of towering trees,
 The patriarchs of the wood;
A lovely vale before me lay,
 And on the golden air,
Crept the blue smoke in quiet trains
 From roofs that clustered there.

I saw where, in my early years,
 I passed the pleasant hours,
Beside the winding brook that still
 Went prattling to its flowers;
And still, around my parent's home,
 The slender poplars grew,
Whose glossy leaves were swayed and turned
 By every wind that blew.

The clover, with its heavy bloom
 Was tossing in the gale,
And the tall crowfoot's golden stars
 Still sprinkled all the vale;
Young orchards on the sunny slope,
 Tall woodlands on the height,
All in their freshest beauty rose
 To my delighted sight.

The wild vine in the woody glen,
 Swung o'er the sounding brook;
The clear-voiced wood-thrush sang all unseen
 Within his leafy nook:
And as the evening sunlight fell,
 Where beechen forests lie;
I watched the clouds on crimson wings,
 Float softly through the sky.

All these are what they were when first
 These pleasant hills I ranged;
But the faces that I knew before,
 By time and toil are changed:
Where youth and bloom were on the cheek
 And gladness on the brow,
I only meet the marks of care,
 And pain, and sorrow now.

THE INDIAN SUMMER.

THAT soft autumnal time
Is come, that sheds, upon the naked scene,
Charms only known in this our northern clime—
Bright seasons, far between.

The woodland foliage now
Is gather'd by the wild November blast;
E'en the thick leaves upon the poplar's bough
Are fallen, to the last.

The mighty vines, that round
The forest trunks their slender branches bind,
Their crimson foliage shaken to the ground,
Swing naked in the wind.

Some living green remains
By the clear brook that shines along the lawn;
But the sear grass stands white o'er all the plains,
And the bright flowers are gone.

But these, these are thy charms—
Mild airs and temper'd light upon the lea;
And the year holds no time within its arms
That doth resemble thee.

The sunny noon is thine,
Soft, golden, noiseless as the dead of night;
And hues that in the flush'd horizon shine
At eve and early light.

The year's last, loveliest smile,
Thou comest to fill with hope the human heart,
And strengthen it to bear the storms a while,
Till winter days depart.

O'er the wide plains, that lie
A desolate scene, the fires of autumn spread,
And nightly on the dark walls of the sky
A ruddy brightness shed.

Far in a shelter'd nook
I've met, in these calm days, a smiling flower,
A lonely aster, trembling by a brook,
At the quiet noontides' hour:

And something told my mind,
That, should old age to childhood call me back,
Some sunny days and flowers I still might find
Along life's weary track.

THE BLIND RESTORED TO SIGHT.

"And I went and washed, and I received sight."—JOHN ix. 11.

WHEN the great Master spoke,
He touch'd his wither'd eyes,
And at one gleam upon him broke
The glad earth and the skies.

And he saw the city's walls,
And kings' and prophets' tomb,
And mighty arches, and vaulted halls,
And the temple's lofty dome.

He look'd on the river's flood,
And the flash of mountain rills,
And the gentle wave of the palms that stood
Upon Judea's hills.

He saw on heights and plains
Creatures of every race:
But a mighty thrill ran through his veins
When he met the human face;

And his virgin sight beheld
The ruddy glow of even,
And the thousand shining orbs that fill'd
The azure depths of heaven.

And woman's voice before
Had cheer'd his gloomy night,
But to see the angel form she wore
Made deeper the delight.

And his heart, at daylight's close,
For the bright world where he trod,
And when the yellow morning rose,
Gave speechless thanks to GOD.

SONNET.

THERE is a magic in the moon's mild ray,—
What time she softly climbs the evening sky,
And sitteth with the silent stars on high,—
That charms the pang of earth-born grief away
I raise my eye to the blue depths above,
And worship Him whose power, pervading space,
Holds those bright orbs at peace in his embrace,
Yet comprehends earth's lowliest things in love.
Oft, when that silent moon was sailing high,
I've left my youthful sports to gaze, and now,
When time with graver lines has mark'd my brow
Sweetly she shines upon my sober'd eye.
O, may the light of truth, my steps to guide,
Shine on my eve of life—shine soft, and long abide

SONNET.

'TIS Autumn, and my steps have led me far
To a wild hill, that overlooks a land
Wide-spread and beautiful. A single star
Sparkles new-set in heaven. O'er its bright sand
The streamlet slides with mellow tones away;
The west is crimson with retiring day;
And the north gleams with its own native light.
Below, in autumn green, the meadows lie,
And through green banks the river wanders by,
And the wide woods with autumn hues are bright
Bright—but of fading brightness!—soon is past
That dream-like glory of the painted wood;
And pitiless decay o'ertakes, as fast,
The pride of men, the beauteous, great, and good.

N. P. Willis.

N. P. WILLIS.

[Born 1807. Died 1867.]

Nathaniel P. Willis was born at Portland, in Maine, on the twentieth day of January, 1807. During his childhood his parents removed to Boston; and at the Latin school in that city, and at the Philips Academy in Andover, he pursued his studies until he entered Yale College, in 1823. While he resided at New Haven, as a student, he won a high reputation, for so young an author, by a series of "Scripture Sketches," and a few other brief poems; and it is supposed that the warm and too indiscriminate praises bestowed upon these productions, influenced unfavourably his subsequent progress in the poetic art. He was graduated in 1827, and in the following year he published a "Poem delivered before the Society of United Brothers of Brown University," which, as well as his "Sketches," issued soon after he left college, was very favourably noticed in the best periodicals of the time. He also edited "The Token," a well-known annuary, for 1828; and about the same period published, in several volumes, "The Legendary," and established "The American Monthly Magazine." To this periodical several young writers, who afterward became distinguished, were contributors; but the articles by its editor, constituting a large portion of each number, gave to the work its character, and were of all its contents the most popular. In 1830 it was united to the "New York Mirror," of which Mr. Willis became one of the conductors; and he soon after sailed for Europe, to be absent several years.

He travelled over Great Britain, and the most interesting portions of the continent, mixing largely in society, and visiting every thing worthy of his regard as a man of taste, or as an American; and his "First Impressions" were given in his letters to the "Mirror," in which he described, with remarkable spirit and fidelity, and in a style peculiarly graceful and elegant, scenery and incidents, and social life among the polite classes in Europe. His letters were collected and republished in London under the title of "Pencillings by the Way," and violently attacked in several of the leading periodicals, ostensibly on account of their too great freedom of personal detail. Captain Marryat, who was at the time editing a monthly magazine, wrote an article, characteristically gross and malignant, which led to a hostile meeting at Chatham, and Mr. Lockhart, in the "Quarterly Review," published a "criticism" alike illiberal and unfair. Mr. Willis perhaps erred in giving to the public dinner-table conversations, and some of his descriptions of manners; but Captain Marryat himself is not undeserving of censure on account of the "personalities" in his writings; and for other reasons he could not have been the most suitable person in England to avenge the wrong it was alleged Mr. Willis had offered to society. That the author of "Peter's Letters to his Kinsfolk," a work which is filled with far more reprehensible personal allusions than are to be found in the "Pencillings," should have ventured to attack the work on this ground, may excite surprise among those who have not observed that the "Quarterly Review" is spoken of with little reverence in the letters of the American traveller.

In 1835 Mr. Willis was married in England. He soon after published his "Inklings of Adventure," a collection of tales and sketches originally written for a London magazine, under the signature of "Philip Slingsby;" and in 1837 he returned to the United States, and retired to his beautiful estate on the Susquehanna, named "Glenmary," in compliment to one of the most admirable wives that ever gladdened a poet's solitude. In the early part of 1839, he became one of the editors of "The Corsair," a literary gazette, and in the autumn of that year went again to London, where, in the following winter, he published his "Loiterings of Travel," in three volumes, and "Two Ways of Dying for a Husband," comprising the plays "Bianca Visconti," and "Tortesa the Usurer." In 1840 appeared the illustrated edition of his poems, and his "Letters from Under a Bridge," and he retired a second time to his seat in western New York. The death of Mrs. Willis, in 1843, caused him to revisit England, where he published a collection of his magazine papers, under the title of "Dashes at Life, with a Free Pencil." In October, 1846, he married a daughter of Mr. Grinnell, a distinguished citizen of Massachusetts, and has since resided at Idlewild, near Newburgh, on the Hudson, a romantic place, which he has cultivated and embellished until it is one of the most charming homes which illustrate the rural life of our country. Here, except during a "Health Trip to the Tropics," in the winter of 1851 and 1852, he has passed his time, in the preparation of new editions of his earlier works, and in writing every week more or less for the "Home Journal," in which he is again successfully engaged with his old friend General Morris as an editor.

Although Mr. Willis is one of the most popular of our poets, the fame he has acquired in other works has so eclipsed that won by his poems that the most appropriate place for a consideration of his genius seemed to be in "The Prose Writers of America," and in that volume I have therefore attempted his proper characterization. A man of wit, kindly temper, and elegant tastes—somewhat artificial in their more striking displays—with a vocabulary of unusual richness in all the elements which are most essential for the picturesque and dramatic treatment of a peculiar vein of sentiment, and a corresponding observation of society and nature, it must be admitted that he is a word-painter of extraordinary skill and marked individuality.

MELANIE.

I.

I STOOD on yonder rocky brow,*
And marvell'd at the Sybil's fane,
When I was not what I am now.
My life was then untouch'd of pain;
And, as the breeze that stirr'd my hair,
My spirit freshen'd in the sky,
And all things that were true and fair
Lay closely to my loving eye,
With nothing shadowy between
I was a boy of seventeen.
Yon wondrous temple crests the rock,
As light upon its giddy base,
As stirless with the torrent's shock,
As pure in its proportion'd grace,
And seems a thing of air, as then,
Afloat above this fairy glen;
But though mine eye will kindle still
In looking on the shapes of art,
The link is lost that sent the thrill,
Like lightning, instant to my heart.
And thus may break, before we die,
The electric chain 'twixt soul and eye!

Ten years—like yon bright valley, sown
Alternately with weeds and flowers—
Had swiftly, if not gayly, flown,
And still I loved the rosy hours;
And if there lurk'd within my breast
Some nerve that had been overstrung
And quiver'd in my hours of rest,
Like bells by their own echo rung,
I was with Hope a masker yet,
And well could hide the look of sadness,
And, if my heart would not forget,
I knew, at least, the trick of gladness,
And when another sang the strain
I mingled in the old refrain.

'T were idle to remember now,
Had I the heart, my thwarted schemes.
I bear beneath this alter'd brow
The ashes of a thousand dreams:
Some wrought of wild Ambition's fingers,
Some colour'd of Love's pencil well,
But none of which a shadow lingers,
And none whose story I could tell.
Enough, that when I climb'd again
To Tivoli's romantic steep,
Life had no joy, and scarce a pain,
Whose wells I had not tasted deep;
And from my lips the thirst had pass'd
For every fount save one—the sweetest—and the last.
The last—the last! My friends were dead,
Or false; my mother in her grave;
Above my father's honour'd head
The sea had lock'd its hiding wave;
Ambition had but foil'd my grasp,
And Love had perish'd in my clasp;
And still, I say, I did not slack
My love of life, and hope of pleasure,
But gather'd my affections back;
And, as the miser hugs his treasure,
When plague and ruin bid him flee,
I closer clung to mine—my loved, lost MELANIE!

The last of the DE BREVERN race,
My sister claim'd no kinsman's care;
And, looking from each other's face,
The eye stole upward unaware—
For there was naught whereon to lean
Each other's heart and heaven between—
Yet that was world enough for me,
And, for a brief, but blessed while,
There seem'd no care for MELANIE,
If she could see her brother smile;
But life, with her, was at the flow,
And every wave went sparkling higher,
While mine was ebbing, fast and low,
From the same shore of vain desire,
And knew I, with prophetic heart,
That we were wearing aye insensibly apart.

II.

We came to Italy. I felt
A yearning for its sunny sky·
My very spirit seem'd to melt
As swept its first warm breezes by.
From lip and cheek a chilling mist,
From life and soul a frozen rime
By every breath seem'd softly kiss'd:
GOD's blessing on its radiant clime!
It was an endless joy to me
To see my sister's new delight;
From Venice, in its golden sea,
To Pæstum, in its purple light,
By sweet Val d'Arno's tinted hills,
In Vallombrosa's convent gloom,
Mid Terni's vale of singing rills,
By deathless lairs in solemn Rome,
In gay Palermo's "Golden Shell,"
At Arethusa's hidden well,
We loiter'd like the impassion'd sun,
That slept so lovingly on all,
And made a home of every one—
Ruin, and fane, and waterfall—
And crown'd the dying day with glory,
If we had seen, since morn, but one old haunt of story.

We came, with spring, to Tivoli.
My sister loved its laughing air
And merry waters, though, for me,
My heart was in another key;
And sometimes I could scarcely bear
The mirth of their eternal play,
And, like a child that longs for home,
When weary of its holiday,
I sigh'd for melancholy Rome.
Perhaps—the fancy haunts me still—
'Twas but a boding sense of ill.

It was a morn, of such a day
As might have dawn'd on Eden first,
Early in the Italian May.
Vine-leaf and flower had newly burst,

* The story is told during a walk around the Cascatelles of Tivoli.

And, on the burden of the air,
The breath of buds came faint and rare;
And, far in the transparent sky,
The small, earth-keeping birds were seen,
Soaring deliriously high;
And through the clefts of newer green
Yon waters dash'd their living pearls;
And, with a gayer smile and bow,
Troop'd on the merry village-girls;
And, from the Contadina's brow,
The low-slouch'd hat was backward thrown,
With air that scarcely seem'd his own;
And MELANIE, with lips apart,
And clasped hands upon my arm,
Flung open her impassion'd heart,
And bless'd life's mere and breathing charm,
And sang old songs, and gather'd flowers,
And passionately bless'd once more life's thrilling hours.

In happiness and idleness
We wander'd down yon sunny vale,—
O, mocking eyes! a golden tress
Floats back upon this summer gale!
A foot is tripping on the grass!
A laugh rings merry in mine ear!
I see a bounding shadow pass!—
O, GOD! my sister *once* was here!
Come with me, friend;—we rested yon;
There grew a flower she pluck'd and wore;
She sat upon this mossy stone!
That broken fountain, running o'er
With the same ring, like silver bells;
She listen'd to its babbling flow,
And said, "Perhaps the gossip tells
Some fountain nymph's love-story now!"
And, as her laugh rang clear and wild,
A youth—a painter—pass'd and smiled.

He gave the greeting of the morn
With voice that linger'd in mine ear.
I knew him sad and gentle born
By those two words, so calm and clear.
His frame was slight, his forehead high,
And swept by threads of raven hair;
The fire of thought was in his eye,
And he was pale and marble fair;
And Grecian chisel never caught
The soul in those slight features wrought.
I watch'd his graceful step of pride,
Till hidden by yon leaning tree,
And loved him e'er the echo died:
And so, alas! did MELANIE!

We sat and watch'd the fount a while
In silence, but our thoughts were one;
And then arose, and, with a smile
Of sympathy, we saunter'd on;
And she by sudden fits was gay,
And then her laughter died away;
And, in this changefulness of mood,
Forgotten now those May-day spells,
We turn'd where VARRO's villa stood,
And, gazing on the Cascatelles,
(Whose hurrying waters, wild and white,
Seem'd madden'd as they burst to light,)
I chanced to turn my eyes away,
And, lo! upon a bank alone,
The youthful painter, sleeping, lay!
His pencils on the grass were thrown,
And by his side a sketch was flung,
And near him as I lightly crept,
To see the picture as he slept,
Upon his feet he lightly sprung
And, gazing with a wild surprise
Upon the face of MELANIE,
He said—and dropp'd his earnest eyes—
"Forgive me! but I dream'd of thee!"
His sketch, the while, was in my hand,
And, for the lines I look'd to trace—
A torrent by a palace spann'd,
Half-classic and half-fairy-land—
I only found—my sister's face!

III.

Our life was changed. Another love
In its lone woof began to twine;
But, ah! the golden thread was wove
Between my sister's heart and mine!
She who had lived for me before—
She who had smiled for me alone—
Would live and smile for me no more!
The echo to my heart was gone!
It seem'd to me the very skies
Had shone through those averted eyes;
The air had breathed of balm—the flower
Of radiant beauty seem'd to be
But as *she* loved them, hour by hour,
And murmur'd of that love to *me!*
O, though it be so heavenly high
The selfishness of earth above,
That, of the watchers in the sky,
He sleeps who guards a brother's love—
Though to a sister's present weal—
The deep devotion far transcends
The utmost that the soul can feel
For even its own higher ends—
Though next to GOD, and more than heaven
For his own sake, he loves her, even—
'T is difficult to see another,
A passing stranger of a day,
Who never hath been friend or brother,
Pluck with a look her heart away,—
To see the fair, unsullied brow,
Ne'er kiss'd before without a prayer,
Upon a stranger's bosom now,
Who for the boon took little care,
Who is enrich'd, he knows not why;
Who suddenly hath found a treasure
Golconda were too poor to buy;
And he, perhaps, too cold to measure,
(Albeit, in her forgetful dream,
The unconscious idol happier seem,)
'T is difficult at once to crush
The rebel mourner in the breast,
To press the heart to earth, and hush
Its bitter jealousy to rest,—
And difficult—the eye gets dim—
The lip wants power to smile on him!

I thank sweet MARY Mother now,
Who gave me strength those pangs to hide,

And touch'd mine eyes and lit my brow
  With sunshine that my heart belied.
I never spoke of wealth or race,
  To one who ask'd so much of me,—
I look'd but in my sister's face,
  And mused if she would happier be;
And, hour by hour, and day by day,
  I loved the gentle painter more,
  And in the same soft measure wore
My selfish jealousy away;
  And I began to watch his mood,
And feel, with her, love's trembling care,
  And bade God bless him as he woo'd
That loving girl, so fond and fair,
  And on my mind would sometimes press
  A fear that she might love him less.

But Melanie—I little dream'd
  What spells the stirring heart may move—
Pygmalion's statue never seem'd
  More changed with life, than she with love.
The pearl-tint of the early dawn
  Flush'd into day-spring's rosy hue;
The meek, moss-folded bud of morn
  Flung open to the light and dew;
The first and half-seen star of even
Wax'd clear amid the deepening heaven—
  Similitudes perchance may be;
But these are changes oftener seen,
  And do not image half to me
My sister's change of face and mien.
  'T was written in her very air,
  That love had pass'd and enter'd there.

IV.

A calm and lovely paradise
  Is Italy, for minds at ease.
The sadness of its sunny skies
  Weighs not upon the lives of these.
The ruin'd aisle, the crumbling fane,
  The broken column, vast and prone—
It may be joy, it may be pain,
  Amid such wrecks to walk alone;
The saddest man will sadder be,
  The gentlest lover gentler there,
As if, whate'er the spirit's key,
  It strengthen'd in that solemn air.

The heart soon grows to mournful things;
  And Italy has not a breeze
But comes on melancholy wings;
  And even her majestic trees
Stand ghost-like in the Cæsar's home,
  As if their conscious roots were set
In the old graves of giant Rome,
  And drew their sap all kingly yet!
And every stone your feet beneath
  Is broken from some mighty thought,
And sculptures in the dust still breathe
  The fire with which their lines were wrought,
And sunder'd arch, and plunder'd tomb
Still thunder back the echo, "Rome!"

Yet gayly o'er Egeria's fount
  The ivy flings its emerald veil,
And flowers grow fair on Numa's mount,
  And light-sprung arches span the dale,
And soft, from Caracalla's Baths,
  The herdsman's song comes down the breeze,
While climb his goats the giddy paths
  To grass-grown architrave and frieze;
And gracefully Albano's hill
  Curves into the horizon's line,
And sweetly sings that classic rill,
  And fairly stands that nameless shrine;
And here, O, many a sultry noon
And starry eve, that happy June,
  Came Angelo and Melanie,
And earth for us was all in tune—
For while Love talk'd with them, Hope walk'd
  apart with me!

V.

I shrink from the embitter'd close
  Of my own melancholy tale.
'T is long since I have waked my woes—
  And nerve and voice together fail!
The throb beats faster at my brow,
  My brain feels warm with starting tears,
And I shall weep—but heed not thou!
  'T will soothe a while the ache of years.
The heart transfix'd—worn out with grief—
Will turn the arrow for relief.
The painter was a child of shame!
  It stirr'd my pride to know it first,
For I had question'd but his name,
  And thought, alas! I knew the worst,
Believing him unknown and poor.
His blood, indeed, was not obscure;
  A high-born Conti was his mother,
But, though he knew one parent's face,
  He never had beheld the other,
Nor knew his country or his race.
  The Roman hid his daughter's shame
Within St. Mona's convent wall,
  And gave the boy a painter's name—
And little else to live withal!
  And, with a noble's high desires
Forever mounting in his heart,
  The boy consumed with hidden fires,
But wrought in silence at his art;
  And sometimes at St. Mona's shrine,
Worn thin with penance harsh and long,
  He saw his mother's form divine,
And loved her for their mutual wrong.
I said my pride was stirr'd—but no!
  The voice that told its bitter tale
Was touch'd so mournfully with wo,
  And, as he ceased, all deathly pale,
He loosed the hand of Melanie,
And gazed so gaspingly on me—
  The demon in my bosom died!
"Not thine," I said, "another's guilt;
  I break no hearts for silly pride;
So, kiss yon weeper if thou wilt!"

VI.

St. Mona's morning mass was done;
  The shrine-lamps struggled with the day;
And, rising slowly, one by one,
  Stole the last worshippers away.
The organist play'd out the hymn,
  The incense, to St. Mary swung,

Had mounted to the cherubim,
  Or to the pillars thinly clung;
And boyish chorister replaced
  The missal that was read no more,
And closed, with half-irreverent haste,
  Confessional and chancel-door;
And as, through aisle and oriel pane,
  The sun wore round his slanting beam,
The dying martyr stirr'd again,
  And warriors battled in its gleam;
And costly tomb and sculptured knight
Show'd warm and wondrous in the light.
  I have not said that Melanie
    Was radiantly fair—
  This earth again may never see
    A loveliness so rare!
  She glided up St. Mona's aisle
    That morning as a bride,
  And, full as was my heart the while,
    I bless'd her in my pride!
The fountain may not fail the less
  Whose sands are golden ore,
And a sister for her loveliness
  May not be loved the more;
But as, the fount's full heart beneath,
  Those golden sparkles shine,
My sister's beauty seem'd to breathe
  Its brightness over mine!

St. Mona has a chapel dim
  Within the altar's fretted pale,
Where faintly comes the swelling hymn,
  And dies, half-lost, the anthem's wail.
And here, in twilight meet for prayer,
  A single lamp hangs o'er the shrine,
And Raphael's Mary, soft and fair,
  Looks down with sweetness half-divine,
And here St. Mona's nuns alway
Through latticed bars are seen to pray.

Ave and sacrament were o'er,
  And Angelo and Melanie
Still knelt the holy shrine before;
  But prayer, that morn, was not for me!
My heart was lock'd! The lip might stir,
  The frame might agonize—and yet,
O God! I could not pray for *her!*
  A seal upon my soul was set—
My brow was hot—my brain opprest—
And fiends seem'd muttering round, "Your bridal is unblest!"

With forehead to the lattice laid,
  And thin, white fingers straining through,
A nun the while had softly pray'd.
  O, e'en in prayer that voice I knew!
Each faltering word, each mournful tone,
  Each pleading cadence, half-suppress'd—
Such music had its like alone
  On lips that stole it at her breast!
And ere the orison was done
I loved the mother as the son!

And now, the marriage-vow to hear,
  The nun unveil'd her brow;
When, sudden, to my startled ear,
There crept a whisper, hoarse, like fear,
  "De Brevern! *is it thou!*"

The priest let fall the golden ring,
  The bridegroom stood aghast;
While, like some wierd and frantic thing,
  The nun was muttering fast;
And as, in dread, I nearer drew,
She thrust her arms the lattice through,
And held me to her straining view;
  But suddenly begun
To steal upon her brain a light,
That stagger'd soul, and sense, and sight,
And, with a mouth all ashy white,
  She shriek'd, "*It is his son!*
The bridegroom is thy blood—thy brother!
Rodolph de Brevern *wrong'd his mother!*"
  And, as that doom of love was heard,
My sister sunk, and died, without a sign or word!

* * * * * * * *

I shed no tear for her. She died
  With her last sunshine in her eyes.
Earth held for her no joy beside
  The hope just shatter'd,—and she lies
In a green nook of yonder dell;
  And near her, in a newer bed,
Her lover—brother—sleeps as well!
  Peace to the broken-hearted dead!

THE CONFESSIONAL.

I thought of thee—I thought of thee
  On ocean many a weary night,
When heaved the long and sullen sea,
  With only waves and stars in sight.
We stole along by isles of balm,
  We furl'd before the coming gale,
We slept amid the breathless calm,
  We flew beneath the straining sail,—
But thou wert lost for years to me,
And day and night I thought of thee!

I thought of thee—I thought of thee
  In France, amid the gay saloon,
Where eyes as dark as eyes may be
  Are many as the leaves in June:
Where life is love, and e'en the air
  Is pregnant with impassion'd thought,
And song, and dance, and music are
  With one warm meaning only fraught.
My half-snared heart broke lightly free,
And, with a blush, I thought of thee!

I thought of thee—I thought of thee
  In Florence, where the fiery hearts
Of Italy are breathed away
  In wonders of the deathless arts;
Where strays the Contadina, down
  Val d' Arno, with song of old;
Where clime and women seldom frown,
  And life runs over sands of gold;
I stray'd to lonely Fiesole,
On many an eve, and thought of thee

I thought of thee—I thought of thee
  In Rome, when, on the Palatine,
Night left the Cesar's palace free
  To Time's forgetful foot and mine

Or, on the Coliseum's wall,
When moonlight touch'd the ivied stone,
Reclining, with a thought of all
That o'er this scene hath come and gone,
The shades of Rome would start and flee
Unconsciously—I thought of thee.

I thought of thee—I thought of thee
In Vallombrosa's holy shade,
Where nobles born the friars be,
By life's rude changes humbler made.
Here MILTON framed his Paradise;
I slept within his very cell;
And, as I closed my weary eyes,
I thought the cowl would fit me well;
The cloisters breathed, it seem'd to me,
Of heart's-ease—but I thought of thee.

I thought of thee—I thought of thee
In Venice, on a night in June;
When, through the city of the sea,
Like dust of silver, slept the moon.
Slow turn'd his oar the gondolier,
And, as the black barks glided by,
The water, to my leaning ear,
Bore back the lover's passing sigh;
It was no place alone to be,
I thought of thee—I thought of thee.

I thought of thee—I thought of thee
In the Ionian isles, when straying
With wise ULYSSES by the sea,
Old HOMER's songs around me playing;
Or, watching the bewitch'd caique,
That o'er the star-lit waters flew,
I listen'd to the helmsman Greek,
Who sung the song that SAPPHO knew:
The poet's spell, the bark, the sea,
All vanish'd as I thought of thee.

I thought of thee—I thought of thee
In Greece, when rose the Parthenon
Majestic o'er the Egean sea,
And heroes with it, one by one;
When, in the grove of Academe,
Where LAIS and LEONTIUM stray'd
Discussing PLATO's mystic theme,
I lay at noontide in the shade—
The Egean wind, the whispering tree
Had voices—and I thought of thee.

I thought of thee—I thought of thee
In Asia, on the Dardanelles,
Where, swiftly as the waters flee,
Each wave some sweet old story tells;
And, seated by the marble tank
Which sleeps by Ilium's ruins old,
(The fount where peerless HELEN drank,
And VENUS laved her locks of gold,)
I thrill'd such classic haunts to see,
Yet even here I thought of thee.

thought of thee—I thought of thee
Where glide the Bosphor's lovely waters,
All palace-lined from sea to sea:
And ever on its shores the daughters
Of the delicious east are seen,
Printing the brink with slipper'd feet,
And, O, the snowy folds between,
What eyes of heaven your glances meet!
Peris of light no fairer be.
Yet, in Stamboul, I thought of thee.

I've thought of thee—I've thought of thee,
Through change that teaches to forget;
Thy face looks up from every sea,
In every star thine eyes are set.
Though roving beneath orient skies,
Whose golden beauty breathes of rest,
I envy every bird that flies
Into the far and clouded west;
I think of thee—I think of thee!
O, dearest! hast thou thought of me!

LINES ON LEAVING EUROPE.

BRIGHT flag at yonder tapering mast,
Fling out your field of azure blue;
Let star and stripe be westward cast,
And point as Freedom's eagle flew!
Strain home! O lithe and quivering spars!
Point home, my country's flag of stars!

The wind blows fair, the vessel feels
The pressure of the rising breeze,
And, swiftest of a thousand keels,
She leaps to the careering seas!
O, fair, fair cloud of snowy sail,
In whose white breast I seem to lie,
How oft, when blew this eastern gale,
I've seen your semblance in the sky,
And long'd, with breaking heart, to flee
On such white pinions o'er the sea!

Adieu, O lands of fame and eld!
I turn to watch our foamy track,
And thoughts with which I first beheld
Yon clouded line, come hurrying back;
My lips are dry with vague desire,
My cheek once more is hot with joy;
My pulse, my brain, my soul on fire!
O, what has changed that traveller-boy!
As leaves the ship this dying foam,
His visions fade behind—his weary heart speeds home!

Adieu, O soft and southern shore,
Where dwelt the stars long miss'd in heaven;
Those forms of beauty, seen no more,
Yet once to Art's rapt vision given!
O, still the enamour'd sun delays,
And pries through fount and crumbling fane,
To win to his adoring gaze
Those children of the sky again!
Irradiate beauty, such as never
That light on other earth hath shone,
Hath made this land her home forever;
And, could I live for this alone,
Were not my birthright brighter far
Than such voluptuous slave's can be;
Held not the west one glorious star,
New-born and blazing for the free,
Soar'd not to heaven our eagle yet,
Rome, with her helot sons, should teach me to forget

Adieu, O, fatherland! I see
  Your white cliffs on the horizon's rim,
And, though to freer skies I flee,
  My heart swells, and my eyes are dim!
As knows the dove the task you give her,
  When loosed upon a foreign shore;
As spreads the rain-drop in the river
  In which it may have flow'd before—
To England, over vale and mountain,
  My fancy flew from climes more fair,
My blood, that knew its parent fountain,
  Ran warm and fast in England's air.

My mother! in thy prayer to-night
  There come new words and warmer tears!
On long, long darkness breaks the light,
  Comes home the loved, the lost for years!
Sleep safe, O wave-worn mariner,
  Fear not, to-night, or storm or sea!
The ear of Heaven bends low to *her!*
  He comes to shore who sails with me!
The wind-toss'd spider needs no token
  How stands the tree when lightnings blaze:
And, by a thread from heaven unbroken,
  I know my mother lives and prays!

Dear mother! when our lips can speak,
  When first our tears will let us see,
When I can gaze upon thy cheek,
  And thou, with thy dear eyes, on me—
'T will be a pastime little sad
  To trace what weight Time's heavy fingers
Upon each other's forms have had;
  For all may flee, so feeling lingers!
But there's a change, beloved mother,
  To stir far deeper thoughts of thine;
I come—but with me comes another,
  To share the heart once only mine!
Thou, on whose thoughts, when sad and lonely,
  One star arose in memory's heaven;
Thou, who hast watch'd *one* treasure only,
  Water'd *one* flower with tears at even:
Room in thy heart! The hearth she left,
  Is darken'd to make light to ours!
There are bright flowers of care bereft,
  And hearts that languish more than flowers;
She was their light, their very air— [prayer!
Room, mother, in thy heart! place for her in thy

SPRING.

The Spring is here, the delicate-footed May,
  With its slight fingers full of leaves and flowers;
And with it comes a thirst to be away,
  Wasting in wood-paths its voluptuous hours;
A feeling that is like a sense of wings,
Restless to soar above these perishing things.

We pass out from the city's feverish hum,
  To find refreshment in the silent woods;
And nature, that is beautiful and dumb,
  Like a cool sleep upon the pulses broods;
Yet, even there, a restless thought will steal,
To teach the indolent heart it still must *feel.*

Strange, that the audible stillness of the noon,
  The waters tripping with their silver feet,
The turning to the light of leaves in June,
  And the light whisper as their edges meet:
Strange, that they fill not, with their tranquil tone,
The spirit, walking in their midst alone.

There's no contentment in a world like this,
  Save in forgetting the immortal dream;
We may not gaze upon the stars of bliss,
  That through the cloud-rifts radiantly stream;
Bird-like, the prison'd soul *will* lift its eye
And pine till it is hooded from the sky.

TO ERMENGARDE.

I know not if the sunshine waste,
  The world is dark since thou art gone!
The hours are, O! so leaden-paced!
  The birds sing, and the stars float on,
But sing not well, and look not fair;
A weight is in the summer air,
  And sadness in the sight of flowers;
And if I go where others smile,
  Their love but makes me think of ours,
And Heaven gets my heart the while.
Like one upon a desert isle,
  I languish of the dreary hours;
I never thought a life could be
So flung upon one hope, as mine, dear love, on thee!

I sit and watch the summer sky:
  There comes a cloud through heaven alone;
A thousand stars are shining nigh,
  It feels no light, but darkles on!
Yet now it nears the lovelier moon,
  And, flashing through its fringe of snow,
There steals a rosier dye, and soon
  Its bosom is one fiery glow!
The queen of life within it lies,
  Yet mark how lovers meet to part:
The cloud already onward flies,
  And shadows sink into its heart;
And (dost thou see them where thou art?)
  Fade fast, fade all those glorious dyes!
Its light, like mine, is seen no more,
And, like my own, its heart seems darker than
  before.

Where press, this hour, those fairy feet?
  Where look, this hour, those eyes of blue?
What music in thine ear is sweet?
  What odour breathes thy lattice through?
What word is on thy lip? What tone,
What look, replying to thine own?
Thy steps along the Danube stray,
  Alas, it seeks an orient sea!
Thou wouldst not seem so far away,
  Flow'd but its waters back to me!
I bless the slowly-coming moon,
  Because its eye look'd late in thine;
I envy the west wind of June,
  Whose wings will bear it up the Rhine;
The flower I press upon my brow
Were sweeter if its like perfumed thy chamber now

HAGAR IN THE WILDERNESS.

The morning broke. Light stole upon the clouds
With a strange beauty. Earth received again
Its garment of a thousand dyes; and leaves,
And delicate blossoms, and the painted flowers,
And every thing that bendeth to the dew,
And stirreth with the daylight, lifted up
Its beauty to the breath of that sweet morn.

All things are dark to sorrow; and the light,
And loveliness, and fragrant air, were sad
To the dejected Hagar. The moist earth
Was pouring odours from its spicy pores,
And the young birds were singing, as if life
Were a new thing to them; but, O! it came
Upon her heart like discord, and she felt
How cruelly it tries a broken heart,
To see a mirth in any thing it loves.
She stood at Abraham's tent. Her lips were press'd
Till the blood started; and the wandering veins
Of her transparent forehead were swell'd out,
As if her pride would burst them. Her dark eye
Was clear and tearless, and the light of heaven,
Which made its language legible, shot back
From her long lashes, as it had been flame.
Her noble boy stood by her, with his hand
Clasp'd in her own, and his round, delicate feet,
Scarce train'd to balance on the tented floor,
Sandall'd for journeying. He had look'd up
Into his mother's face, until he caught
The spirit there, and his young heart was swelling
Beneath his dimpled bosom, and his form
Straighten'd up proudly in his tiny wrath,
As if his light proportions would have swell'd,
Had they but match'd his spirit, to the man.

Why bends the patriarch as he cometh now
Upon his staff so wearily? His beard
Is low upon his breast, and on his high brow,
So written with the converse of his God,
Beareth the swollen vein of agony.
His lip is quivering, and his wonted step
Of vigour is not there; and, though the morn
Is passing fair and beautiful, he breathes
Its freshness as it were a pestilence.
O, man may bear with suffering: his heart
Is a strong thing, and godlike in the grasp
Of pain, that wrings mortality; but tear
One chord affection clings to, part one tie
That binds him to a woman's delicate love,
And his great spirit yieldeth like a reed.

He gave to her the water and the bread,
But spoke no word, and trusted not himself
To look upon her face, but laid his hand
In silent blessing on the fair-hair'd boy,
And left her to her lot of loneliness.

Should Hagar weep? May slighted woman turn,
And, as a vine the oak hath shaken off,
Bend lightly to her leaning trust again?
O, no! by all her loveliness, by all
That makes life poetry and beauty, no!
Make her a slave; steal from her rosy cheek
By needless jealousies; let the last star
Leave her a watcher by your couch of pain;
Wrong her by petulance, suspicion, all
That makes her cup a bitterness,—yet give
One evidence of love, and earth has not
An emblem of devotedness like hers.
But, O! estrange her once—it boots not how—
By wrong or silence, any thing that tells
A change has come upon your tenderness—
And there is not a high thing out of heaven
Her pride o'ermastereth not.

She went her way with a strong step and slow;
Her press'd lip arch'd, and her clear eye undimm'd,
As it had been a diamond, and her form
Borne proudly up, as if her heart breathed through.
Her child kept on in silence, though she press'd
His hand till it was pain'd: for he had caught,
As I have said, her spirit, and the seed
Of a stern nation had been breathed upon.

The morning pass'd, and Asia's sun rode up
In the clear heaven, and every beam was heat.
The cattle of the hills were in the shade,
And the bright plumage of the Orient lay
On beating bosoms in her spicy trees.
It was an hour of rest; but Hagar found
No shelter in the wilderness, and on
She kept her weary way, until the boy
Hung down his head, and open'd his parch'd lips
For water; but she could not give it him.
She laid him down beneath the sultry sky,—
For it was better than the close, hot breath
Of the thick pines,—and tried to comfort him;
But he was sore athirst, and his blue eyes
Were dim and bloodshot, and he could not know
Why God denied him water in the wild.
She sat a little longer, and he grew
Ghastly and faint, as if he would have died.
It was too much for her. She lifted him,
And bore him further on, and laid his head
Beneath the shadow of a desert shrub;
And, shrouding up her face, she went away,
And sat to watch, where he could see her not,
Till he should die; and, watching him, she mourn'd:

"God stay thee in thine agony, my boy!
I cannot see thee die; I cannot brook
Upon thy brow to look,
And see death settle on my cradle-joy.
How have I drunk the light of thy blue eye!
And could I see thee die?

"I did not dream of this when thou wert straying,
Like an unbound gazelle, among the flowers;
Or wearing rosy hours,
By the rich gush of water-sources playing,
Then sinking weary to thy smiling sleep,
So beautiful and deep.

"O, no! and when I watch'd by thee the while,
And saw thy bright lip curling in thy dream,
And thought of the dark stream
In my own land of Egypt, the far Nile,
How pray'd I that my father's land might be
An heritage for thee!

"And now the grave for its cold breast hath won thee,
And thy white, delicate limbs the earth will press
And, O! my last caress
Must feel thee cold, for a chill hand is on thee.
How can I leave my boy, so pillow'd there
Upon his clustering hair!"

She stood beside the well her GOD had given
To gush in that deep wilderness, and bathed
The forehead of her child until he laugh'd
In his reviving happiness, and lisp'd
His infant thought of gladness at the sight
Of the cool plashing of his mother's hand.

THOUGHTS

WHILE MAKING A GRAVE FOR A FIRST CHILD, BORN DEAD.

ROOM, gentle flowers! my child would pass to heaven!
Ye look'd not for her yet with your soft eyes,
O, watchful ushers at Death's narrow door!
But, lo! while you delay to let her forth,
Angels, beyond, stay for her! One long kiss
From lips all pale with agony, and tears,
Wrung after anguish had dried up with fire
The eyes that wept them, were the cup of life
Held as a welcome to her. Weep, O, mother!
But not that from this cup of bitterness
A cherub of the sky has turn'd away.
One look upon her face ere she depart!
My daughter! it is soon to let thee go!
My daughter! with thy birth has gush'd a spring
I knew not of: filling my heart with tears,
And turning with strange tenderness to thee!
A love—O, GOD, it seems so—which must flow
Far as thou fleest, and 'twixt Heaven and me,
Henceforward, be a sweet and yearning chain,
Drawing me after thee! And so farewell!
'T is a harsh world in which affection knows
No place to treasure up its loved and lost
But the lone grave! Thou, who so late was sleeping
Warm in the close fold of a mother's heart,
Scarce from her breast a single pulse receiving,
But it was sent thee with some tender thought—
How can I leave thee *here!* Alas, for man!
The herb in its humility may fall,
And waste into the bright and genial air,
While we, by hands that minister'd in life
Nothing but love to us, are thrust away,
The earth thrown in upon our just cold bosoms,
And the warm sunshine trodden out forever!
Yet have I chosen for thy grave, my child,
A bank where I have lain in summer hours,
And thought how little it would seem like death
To sleep amid such loveliness. The brook
Tripping with laughter down the rocky steps
That lead us to thy bed, would still trip on,
Breaking the dread hush of the mourners gone;
The birds are never silent that build here,
Trying to sing down the more vocal waters;
The slope is beautiful with moss and flowers;
And, far below, seen under arching leaves,
Glitters the warm sun on the village spire,
Pointing the living after thee. And this
Seems like a comfort, and, replacing now
The flowers that have made room for thee, I go
To whisper the same peace to her who lies
Robb'd of her child, and lonely. 'T is the work
Of many a dark hour, and of many a prayer,
To bring the heart back from an infant gone!
Hope must give o'er, and busy fancy blot
Its images from all the silent rooms,
And every sight and sound familiar to her
Undo its sweetest link; and so, at last,
The fountain that, once loosed, must flow forever,
Will hide and waste in silence. When the smile
Steals to her pallid lip again, and spring
Wakens its buds above thee, we will come,
And, standing by thy music-haunted grave,
Look on each other cheerfully, and say,
A child that we have loved is gone to heaven,
And by this gate of flowers she pass'd away!

THE BELFRY PIGEON.

ON the cross-beam under the Old South bell
The nest of a pigeon is builded well.
In summer and winter that bird is there,
Out and in with the morning air;
I love to see him track the street,
With his wary eye and active feet;
And I often watch him as he springs,
Circling the steeple with easy wings,
Till across the dial his shade has pass'd,
And the belfry edge is gain'd at last.
'T is a bird I love, with its brooding note,
And the trembling throb in its mottled throat
There's a human look in its swelling breast,
And the gentle curve of its lowly crest;
And I often stop with the fear I feel,
He runs so close to the rapid wheel.
Whatever is rung on that noisy bell—
Chime of the hour, or funeral knell—
The dove in the belfry must hear it well.
When the tongue swings out to the midnight moon,
When the sexton cheerly rings for noon,
When the clock strikes clear at morning light,
When the child is waked with "nine at night,"
When the chimes play soft in the Sabbath air,
Filling the spirit with tones of prayer,—
Whatever tale in the bell is heard,
He broods on his folded feet unstirr'd,
Or, rising half in his rounded nest,
He takes the time to smoothe his breast,
Then drops again, with filmed eyes,
And sleeps as the last vibration dies.
Sweet bird! I would that I could be
A hermit in the crowd like thee!
With wings to fly to wood and glen!
Thy lot, like mine, is cast with men;
And daily, with unwilling feet,
I tread, like thee the crowded street;
But, unlike me, when day is o'er,
Thou canst dismiss the world, and soar,
Or, at a half-felt wish for rest,
Canst smoothe thy feathers on thy breast,
And drop, forgetful, to thy nest.
I would that, in such wings of gold,
I could my weary heart upfold;
I would I could look down unmoved,
(Unloving as I am unloved,)
And, while the world throngs on beneath,
Smoothe down my cares and calmly breathe;
And never sad with others' sadness,
And never glad with others' gladness,
Listen, unstirr'd, to knell or chime,
And, lapp'd in quiet, bide my time

APRIL.

"A violet by a mossy stone,
Half-hidden from the eye,
Fair as a star, when only one
Is shining in the sky."
WORDSWORTH.

I HAVE found violets. April hath come on,
And the cool winds feel softer, and the rain
Falls in the beaded drops of summer-time.
You may hear birds at morning, and at eve
The tame dove lingers till the twilight falls,
Cooing upon the eaves, and drawing in
His beautiful, bright neck; and, from the hills,
A murmur like the hoarseness of the sea,
Tells the release of waters, and the earth
Sends up a pleasant smell, and the dry leaves
Are lifted by the grass; and so I know
That Nature, with her delicate ear, hath heard
The dropping of the velvet foot of Spring.
Take of my violets! I found them where
The liquid south stole o'er them, on a bank
That lean'd to running water. There's to me
A daintiness about these early flowers,
That touches me like poetry. They blow
With such a simple loveliness among
The common herbs of pasture, and breathe out
Their lives so unobtrusively, like hearts
Whose beatings are too gentle for the world.
I love to go in the capricious days
Of April and hunt violets, when the rain
Is in the blue cups trembling, and they nod
So gracefully to the kisses of the wind.
It may be deem'd too idle, but the young
Read nature like the manuscript of Heaven,
And call the flowers its poetry. Go out!
Ye spirits of habitual unrest,
And read it, when the "fever of the world"
Hath made your hearts impatient, and, if life
Hath yet one spring unpoison'd, it will be
Like a beguiling music to its flow,
And you will no more wonder that I love
To hunt for violets in the April-time.

THE ANNOYER.

LOVE knoweth every form of air,
And every shape of earth,
And comes, unbidden, everywhere,
Like thought's mysterious birth.
The moonlit sea and the sunset sky
Are written with Love's words,
And you hear his voice unceasingly,
Like song, in the time of birds.

He peeps into the warrior's heart
From the tip of a stooping plume,
And the serried spears, and the many men,
May not deny him room.
He'll come to his tent in the weary night,
And be busy in his dream,
And he'll float to his eye in morning light,
Like a fay on a silver beam.

He hears the sound of the hunter's gun,
And rides on the echo back,
And sighs in his ear like a stirring leaf,
And flits in his woodland track.
The shade of the wood, and the sheen of the river,
The cloud, and the open sky,—
He will haunt them all with his subtle quiver,
Like the light of your very eye.

The fisher hangs over the leaning boat,
And ponders the silver sea,
For Love is under the surface hid,
And a spell of thought has he:
He heaves the wave like a bosom sweet,
And speaks in the ripple low,
Till the bait is gone from the crafty line,
And the hook hangs bare below.

He blurs the print of the scholar's book,
And intrudes in the maiden's prayer,
And profanes the cell of the holy man
In the shape of a lady fair.
In the darkest night, and the bright daylight,
In earth, and sea, and sky,
In every home of human thought
Will Love be lurking nigh.

TO A FACE BELOVED.

THE music of the waken'd lyre
Dies not upon the quivering strings,
Nor burns alone the minstrel's fire
Upon the lip that trembling sings;
Nor shines the moon in heaven unseen,
Nor shuts the flower its fragrant cells,
Nor sleeps the fountain's wealth, I ween,
Forever in its sparry wells;
The spells of the enchanter lie
Not on his own lone heart, his own rapt ear and eye.

I look upon a face as fair
As ever made a lip of heaven
Falter amid its music-prayer!
The first-lit star of summer even
Springs not so softly on the eye,
Nor grows, with watching, half so bright,
Nor, mid its sisters of the sky,
So seems of heaven the dearest light;
Men murmur where that face is seen—
My youth's angelic dream was of that look and mien

Yet, though we deem the stars are blest,
And envy, in our grief, the flower
That bears but sweetness in its breast,
And fear'd the enchanter for his power,
And love the minstrel for his spell
He winds out of his lyre so well;
The stars are almoners of light,
The lyrist of melodious air,
The fountain of its waters bright,
And every thing most sweet and fair
Of that by which it charms the ear,
The eye of him that passes near;
A lamp is lit in woman's eye
That souls, else lost on earth, remember angels by.

THEODORE S. FAY.

[Born, 1807.]

The author of "Dreams and Reveries," "Norman Leslie," and "The Countess Ida," was born in the city of New York on the tenth of February, 1807. His father was a lawyer of unusual professional and literary abilities, which were honorably displayed in an earnest and persistent advocacy of the abolition of imprisonment for debt, in numerous contributions to the public journals under the signature of "Howard." After his death, in 1825, Mr. Fay continued the study of the law with Mr. Sylvanus Miller, and was admitted to the bar in 1829. He acquired his earliest distinction as a writer by completing a series of papers entitled "The Little Genius," commenced by his father, in the "New York Mirror," of which he became one of the editors. In 1833 he was married, and soon after went to Europe, where he has nearly ever since resided. He was appointed secretary of the United States legation at the court of Berlin in 1837, and in 1853 became the first resident minister from this country in Switzerland. An account of his essays and novels may be found in "The Prose Writers of America." In poetry he has published, besides a considerable number of fugitive pieces, "Ulric, or the Voices," of which nineteen cantos appeared in one volume in 1851, and an additional canto in "The Knickerbocker Gallery," in 1855. The scene of the poem is laid in Germany during the great reformation in the fifteenth century. The hero, Ulric Von Rosenberg, a young rittmaster, or captain of cavalry, is converted to the doctrines of Luther, and makes a public profession of his faith, after which he is exposed to extraordinary temptations, to struggles between conscience and inclination, which Mr. Fay describes as "supernatural solicitings," and "voices," from heaven and hell. The work has not been very popular. Mr. Fay is more successful in prose fiction.

MY NATIVE LAND.

Columbia, was thy continent stretch'd wild,
In later ages, the huge seas above?
And art thou Nature's youngest, fairest child,
Most favoured by thy gentle mother's love?
Where now we stand, did ocean monsters rove,
Tumbling uncouth, in those dim, vanished years,
When through the Red Sea Pharaoh's thousands drove,
When struggling Joseph dropp'd fraternal tears,
When God came down from heaven, and mortal men were seers?

Or, have thy forests waved, thy rivers run,
Elysian solitudes, untrod by man,
Silent and lonely, since, around the sun,
Her ever-wheeling circle earth began?
Thy unseen flowers did here the breezes fan,
With wasted perfume ever on them flung?
And o'er thy showers neglected rainbows span,
When Alexander fought, when Homer sung,
And the old populous world with thundering battle rung?

Yet, what to me, or when, or how thy birth,—
No musty tomes are here to tell of thee;
None know, if cast when nature first the earth
Shaped round, and clothed with grass, and flower, and tree,
Or whether since, by changes, silently,
Of sand, and shell, and wave, thy wonders grew;
Or if, before man's little memory,
Some shock stupendous rent the globe in two,
And thee, a fragment, far in western oceans threw.

I know but that I love thee. On my heart,
Like a dear friend's are stamp'd thy features now;
Though there the Roman or the Grecian art
Hath lent, to deck thy plain and mountain brow,
No broken temples, fain at length to bow,
Moss-grown and crumbling, with the weight of time.
Not these o'er thee their mystic splendours throw,
Themes eloquent for pencil or for rhyme,
As many a soul can tell that pours its thoughts sublime,

But thou art sternly artless, wildly free.
We worship thee for beauties all thine own:
Like damsel, young and sweet, and sure to be
Admired, but only for herself alone.
With richer foliage ne'er was land o'ergrown,
No mightier rivers run, nor mountains rise,
Nor ever lakes with lovelier graces shone,
Nor wealthier harvests waved in human eyes,
Nor lay more liquid stars along more heavenly skies.

I dream of thee, fairest of fairy streams,
Sweet Hudson! Float we on thy summer breast:
Who views thy enchanted windings ever deems
Thy banks, of mortal shores the loveliest!
Hail to thy shelving slopes, with verdure dress'd,
Bright break thy waves the varied beach upon;
Soft rise thy hills, by amorous clouds caress'd:
Clear flow thy waters, laughing in the sun—
Would through such peaceful scenes, my life might gently run!

And, lo! the Catskills print the distant sky,
And o'er their airy tops the faint clouds driven,
So softly blending, that the cheated eye
Forgets or which is earth, or which is heaven,—
Sometimes, like thunder-clouds, they shade the even,
Till, as you nearer draw, each wooded height
Puts off the azure hues by distance given:
And slowly break upon the enamour'd sight,
Ravine, crag, field, and wood, in colours true and bright.

Mount to the cloud-kissed summit. Far below
Spreads the vast champaign like a shoreless sea.
Mark yonder narrow streamlet feebly flow,
Like idle brook that creeps ingloriously;
Can that the lovely, lordly Hudson be,
Stealing by town and mountain? Who beholds,
At break of day this scene, when, silently,
Its map of field, wood, hamlet, is unrolled,
While, in the east, the sun uprears his locks of gold,

Till earth receive him never can forget.
Even when returned amid the city's roar,
The fairy vision haunts his memory yet,
As in the sailor's fancy shines the shore.
Imagination cons the moment o'er,
When first discover'd, awe-struck and amazed,
Scarce loftier Jove—whom men and gods adore—
On the extended earth beneath him gazed,
Temple, and tower, and town, by human insect raised.

Blow, scented gale, the snowy canvass swell,
And flow, thou silver, eddying current on.
Grieve we to bid each lovely point farewell,
That, ere its graces half are seen, is gone.
By woody bluff we steal, by leaning lawn,
By palace, village, cot, a sweet surprise,
At every turn the vision breaks upon;
Till to our wondering and uplifted eyes
The Highland rocks and hills in solemn grandeur rise.

Nor clouds in heaven, nor billows in the deep,
More graceful shapes did ever heave or roll,
Nor came such pictures to a painter's sleep,
Nor beamed such visions on a poet's soul!
The pent-up flood, impatient of control,
In ages past here broke its granite bound,
Then to the sea in broad meanders stole,
While ponderous ruins strew'd the broken ground,
And these gigantic hills forever closed around.

And ever-wakeful echo here doth dwell,
The nymph of sportive mockery, that still
Hides behind every rock, in every dell,
And softly glides, unseen, from hill to hill.
No sound doth rise but mimic it she will,—
The sturgeon's splash repeating from the shore,
Aping the boy's voice with a voice as shrill,
The bird's low warble, and the thunder's roar,
Always she watches there, each murmur telling o'er.

Awake my lyre, with other themes inspired,
Where you bold point repels the crystal tide,
The Briton youth, lamented and admired,
His country's hope, her ornament and pride,
A traitor's death ingloriously died—
On freedom's altar offered, in the sight
Of God, by men who will their act abide,
On the great day, and hold their deed aright—
To stop the breath would quench young freedom's holy light.

But see! the broadening river deeper flows,
Its tribute floods intent to reach the sea,
While, from the west, the fading sunlight throws
Its softening hues on stream, and field, and tree;
All silent nature bathing, wondrously,
In charms that soothe the heart with sweet desires,
And thoughts of friends we ne'er again may see,
Till lo! ahead, Manhatta's bristling spires,
Above her thousand roofs red with day's dying fires,

May greet the wanderer of Columbia's shore,
Proud Venice of the west! no lovelier scene.
Of thy vast throngs now faintly comes the roar,
Though late like beating ocean surf I ween,—
And everywhere thy various barks are seen,
Cleaving the limpid floods that round thee flow,
Encircled by thy banks of sunny green,—
The panting steamer plying to and fro,
Or the tall sea-bound ship abroad on wings of snow.

And radiantly upon the glittering mass
The god of day his parting glances sends,
As some warm soul, from earth about to pass,
Back on its fading scenes and mourning friends
Deep words of love and looks of rapture bends,
More bright and bright, as near their end they be.
On, on, great orb! to earth's remotest ends,
Each land irradiate, and every sea—
But oh, my native land, not one, not one like thee!

SONG.

A careless, simple bird, one day
Fluttering in Flora's bowers,
Fell in a cruel trap which lay
All hid among the flowers,
Forsooth, the pretty, harmless flowers

The spring was closed; poor, silly soul,
He knew not what to do,
Till, pressing through a tiny hole,
At length away he flew,
Unhurt—at length away he flew.

And now from every fond regret
And idle anguish free,
He, singing, says, "You need not set
Another trap for me,
False girl! another trap for me."

EDWARD SANFORD.

[Born, 1807.]

Edward Sanford, a son of the late Chancellor Sanford, is a native of the city of New York. He was graduated at the Union College in 1824, and in the following year became a law student in the office of Benjamin F. Butler, afterward Attorney-General of the United States. He subsequently practised several years in the courts of New York, but finally abandoned his profession to conduct the "Standard," an able democratic journal, with which he was connected during the political contest which resulted in the election of Mr. Van Buren to the Presidency, after which he was for a time one of the editors of "The Globe," at Washington. He now resides in New York.

ADDRESS TO BLACK HAWK.

There's beauty on thy brow, old chief! the high
  And manly beauty of the Roman mould,
And the keen flashing of thy full, dark eye
  Speaks of a heart that years have not made cold;
Of passions scathed not by the blight of time;
  Ambition, that survives the battle-rout.
The man within thee scorns to play the mime
  To gaping crowds, that compass thee about.
Thou walkest, with thy warriors by thy side,
Wrapp'd in fierce hate, and high, unconquer'd pride.

Chief of a hundred warriors! dost thou yet—
  Vanquish'd and captive—dost thou deem that here
The glowing day-star of thy glory set—
  Dull night has closed upon thy bright career?
Old forest-lion, caught and caged at last,
  Dost pant to roam again thy native wild?
To gloat upon the lifeblood flowing fast
  Of thy crush'd victims; and to slay the child,
To dabble in the gore of wives and mothers, [thers!
And kill, old Turk! thy harmless, pale-faced bro-

For it was cruel, Black Hawk, thus to flutter
  The dove-cotes of the peaceful pioneers,
To let thy tribe commit such fierce and utter
  Slaughter among the folks of the frontiers.
Though thine be old, hereditary hate,
  Begot in wrongs, and nursed in blood, until
It had become a madness, 'tis too late [will
  To crush the hordes who have the power and
To rob thee of thy hunting-grounds and fountains,
And drive thee backward to the Rocky Mountains.

Spite of thy looks of cold indifference, [wonder;
  There's much thou'st seen that must excite thy
Wakes not upon thy quick and startled sense
  The cannon's harsh and pealing voice of thunder?
Our big canoes, with white and widespread wings,
  That sweep the waters as birds sweep the sky;
Our steamboats, with their iron lungs, like things
  Of breathing life, that dash and hurry by?
Or, if thou scorn'st the wonders of the ocean,
What think'st thou of our railroad locomotion?

Thou'st seen our museums, beheld the dummies
  That grin in darkness in their coffin cases;
What think'st thou of the art of making mummies,
  So that the worms shrink from their dry embraces?

Thou'st seen the mimic tyrants of the stage
  Strutting, in paint and feathers, for an hour;
Thou'st heard the bellowing of their tragic rage,
  Seen their eyes glisten, and their dark brows lower.
Anon, thou'st seen them, when their wrath cool'd
      down,
Pass in a moment from a king—to clown.

Thou seest these things unmoved! sayst so, old
      fellow?
  Then tell us, have the white man's glowing
      daughters
Set thy cold blood in motion? Has't been mellow
  By a sly cup or so of our fire-waters?
They are thy people's deadliest poison. They
  First make them cowards, and then white men's
      slaves;
And sloth, and penury, and passion's prey,
  And lives of misery, and early graves.
For, by their power, believe me, not a day goes
But kills some Foxes, Sacs, and Winnebagoes.

Say, does thy wandering heart stray far away,
  To the deep bosom of thy forest-home?
The hill-side, where thy young pappooses play,
  And ask, amid their sports, when thou wilt come?
Come not the wailings of thy gentle squaws
  For their lost warrior loud upon thine ear,
Piercing athwart the thunder of huzzas,
  That, yell'd at every corner, meet thee here?
The wife who made that shell-deck'd wampum belt,
Thy rugged heart must think of her—and melt.

Chafes not thy heart, as chafes the panting breast
  Of the caged bird against his prison-bars,
That thou, the crowned warrior of the West,
  The victor of a hundred forest-wars,
Shouldst in thy age become a raree-show,
  Led, like a walking bear, about the town,
A new-caught monster, who is all the go,
  And stared at, gratis, by the gaping clown?
Boils not thy blood, while thus thou'rt led about,
The sport and mockery of the rabble rout?

Whence came thy cold philosophy? whence came,
  Thou tearless, stern, and uncomplaining one,
The power that taught thee thus to veil the flame
  Of thy fierce passions? Thou despisest fun,

And thy proud spirit scorns the white men's glee,
Save thy fierce sport, when at the funeral-pile
Of a bound warrior in his agony,
Who meets thy horrid laugh with dying smile.
Thy face, in length, reminds one of a Quaker's;
Thy dances, too, are solemn as a Shaker's.

Proud scion of a noble stem! thy tree
Is blanch'd, and bare, and sear'd, and leafless now.
I'll not insult its fallen majesty,
Nor drive, with careless hand, the ruthless plough
Over its roots. Torn from its parent mould,
Rich, warm, and deep, its fresh, free, balmy air,
No second verdure quickens in our cold,
New, barren earth; no life sustains it there,
But, even though prostrate, 'tis a noble thing,
Though crownless, powerless, "every inch a king."

Give us thy hand, old nobleman of nature,
Proud ruler of the forest aristocracy;
The best of blood glows in thy every feature,
And thy curl'd lip speaks scorn for our democracy.
Thou wear'st thy titles on that godlike brow;
Let him who doubts them meet thine eagle-eye,
He'll quail beneath its glance, and disavow
All question of thy noble family;
For thou mayst here become, with strict propriety,
A leader in our city good society.

TO A MUSQUITO.

His voice was ever soft, gentle, and low.—King Lear.

Thou sweet musician, that around my bed
Dost nightly come and wind thy little horn,
By what unseen and secret influence led,
Feed'st thou my ear with music till 'tis morn?
The wind-harp's tones are not more soft than thine,
The hum of falling waters not more sweet:
I own, *indeed*, I own thy song divine,
And when next year's warm summer nights we meet,
(Till then, farewell!) I promise thee to be
A patient listener to thy minstrelsy.

Thou tiny minstrel, who bid thee discourse
Such eloquent music? was't thy tuneful sire?
Some old musician? or didst take a course
Of lessons from some master of the lyre?
Who bid thee twang so sweetly thy small trump?
Did Norton form thy notes so clear and full?
Art a phrenologist, and is the bump
Of song developed in thy little skull?
At Niblo's hast thou been when crowds stood mute,
Drinking the birdlike tones of Cuddy's flute?

Tell me the burden of thy ceaseless song.
Is it thy evening hymn of grateful prayer,
Or lay of love, thou pipest through the long,
Still night? With song dost drive away dull care?
Art thou a vieux garçon, a gay deceiver,
A wandering blade, roaming in search of sweets,
Pledging thy faith to every fond believer,
Who thy advance with halfway shyness meets?
Or art o' the softer sex, and sing'st in glee,
"In maiden meditation, fancy free!"

Thou little siren, when the nymphs of yore
Charm'd with their songs till men forgot to dine,
And starved, though music-fed, upon their shore,
Their voices breathed no softer lays than thine.
They sang but to entice, and thou dost sing
As if to lull our senses to repose,
That thou mayst use, unharm'd, thy little sting,
The very moment we begin to doze;
Thou worse than siren, thirsty, fierce blood-sipper
Thou living vampire, and thou gallinipper!

Nature is full of music, sweetly sings
The bard, (and thou dost sing most sweetly too,)
Through the wide circuit of created things,
Thou art the living proof the bard sings true.
Nature is full of thee; on every shore,
'Neath the hot sky of Congo's dusky child,
From warm Peru to icy Labrador,
The world's free citizen, thou roamest wild.
Wherever "mountains rise or oceans roll,"
Thy voice is heard, from "Indus to the Pole."

The incarnation of Queen Mab art thou,
"The fairies' midwife;"—thou dost nightly sip,
With amorous proboscis bending low,
The honey-dew from many a lady's lip—
(Though that they "straight on kisses dream," I doubt—)
On smiling faces, and on eyes that weep,
Thou lightest, and oft with "sympathetic snout"
"Ticklest men's noses as they lie asleep;
And sometimes dwellest, if I rightly scan,
"On the forefinger of an alderman."

Yet thou canst glory in a noble birth.
As rose the sea-born Venus from the wave,
So didst thou rise to life; the teeming earth,
The living water and the fresh air gave
A portion of their elements to create
Thy little form, though beauty dwells not there
So lean and gaunt, that economic fate
Meant thee to feed on music or on air.
Our vein's pure juices were not made for thee,
Thou living, singing, stinging atomy.

The hues of dying sunset are most fair,
And twilight's tints just fading into night,
Most dusky soft, and so thy soft notes are
By far the sweetest when thou takest thy flight.
The swan's last note is sweetest, so is thine;
Sweet are the wind-harp's tones at distance heard;
'Tis sweet at distance, at the day's decline,
To hear the opening song of evening's bird.
But notes of harp or bird at distance float
Less sweetly on the ear than thy last note.

The autumn-winds are wailing: 'tis thy dirge;
Its leaves are sear, prophetic of thy doom.
Soon the cold rain will whelm thee, as the surge
Whelms the toss'd mariner in its watery tomb
Then soar, and sing thy little life away!
Albeit thy voice is somewhat husky now.
'Tis well to end in music life's last day,
Of one so gleeful and so blithe as thou:
For thou wilt soon live through its joyous hours,
And pass away with autumn's dying flowers.

THOMAS WARD.

[Born, 1807.]

Doctor Ward was born at Newark, in New Jersey, on the eighth of June, 1807. His father, General Thomas Ward, is one of the oldest, wealthiest, and most respectable citizens of that town; and has held various offices of public trust in his native state, and represented his district in the national Congress.

Doctor Ward received his classical education at the academies in Bloomfield and Newark, and the college at Princeton. He chose the profession of physic, and, after the usual preparation, obtained his degree of Doctor of Medicine in the spring of 1829, at the Rutgers Medical College, in New York. In the autumn of the same year he went to Paris, to avail himself of the facilities afforded in that capital for the prosecution of every branch of medical inquiry; and, after two years' absence, during which he accomplished the usual tour through Italy, Switzerland, Holland, and Great Britain, he returned to New York, and commenced the practice of medicine in that city. In the course of two or three years, however, he gradually withdrew from business, his circumstances permitting him to exchange devotion to his profession for the more congenial pursuits of literature and general knowledge. He is married, and still resides in New York; spending his summers, however, in his native city, and among the more romantic and beautiful scenes of New Jersey. His first literary efforts were brief satirical pieces, in verse and prose, published in a country gazette, in 1825 and 1826. It was not until after his return from Europe, when he adopted the signature of "Flaccus," and began to write for the "New York American," that he attracted much attention. His principal work, "Passaic, a Group of Poems touching that River," appeared in 1841. It contains some fine descriptive passages, and its versification is generally correct and musical. "The Monomania of Money-getting," a satire, and many of his minor pieces, are more distinguished for vigour and sprightliness, than for mere poetical qualities.

MUSINGS ON RIVERS.

Beautiful rivers! that adown the vale
With graceful passage journey to the deep,
Let me along your grassy marge recline
At ease, and musing, meditate the strange
Bright history of your life; yes, from your birth,
Has beauty's shadow chased your every step;
The blue sea was your mother, and the sun
Your glorious sire: clouds your voluptuous cradle,
Roof'd with o'erarching rainbows; and your fall
To earth was cheer'd with shout of happy birds,
With brighten'd faces of reviving flowers
And meadows, while the sympathising west
Took holiday, and donn'd her richest robes.
From deep, mysterious wanderings your springs
Break bubbling into beauty; where they lie
In infant helplessness a while, but soon
Gathering in tiny brooks, they gambol down
The steep sides of the mountain, laughing, shouting,
Teasing the wild flowers, and at every turn
Meeting new playmates still to swell their ranks;
Which, with the rich increase resistless grown,
Shed foam and thunder, that the echoing wood
Rings with the boisterous glee; while o'er their heads,
Catching their spirit blithe, young rainbows sport,
The frolic children of the wanton sun.

Nor is your swelling prime, or green old age,
Though calm, unlovely; still, where'er ye move,
Your train is beauty; trees stand grouping by
To mark your graceful progress: giddy flowers,
And vain, as beauties wont, stoop o'er the verge
To greet their faces in your flattering glass;
The thirsty herd are following at your side;
And water-birds, in clustering fleets, convoy
Your sea-bound tides; and jaded man, released
From worldly thraldom, here his dwelling plants,
Here pauses in your pleasant neighbourhood,
Sure of repose along your tranquil shores.
And when your end approaches, and ye blend
With the eternal ocean, ye shall fade
As placidly as when an infant dies;
And the death-angel shall your powers withdraw
Gently as twilight takes the parting day,
And, with a soft and gradual decline
That cheats the senses, lets it down to night.

Bountiful rivers! not upon the earth
Is record traced of God's exuberant grace
So deeply graven as the channels worn
By ever-flowing streams: arteries of earth,
That, widely branching, circulate its blood:
Whose ever-throbbing pulses are the tides.
The whole vast enginery of Nature, all
The roused and labouring elements combine
In their production; for the mighty end
Is growth, is life to every living thing.
The sun himself is charter'd for the work:
His arm uplifts the main, and at his smile
The fluttering vapours take their flight for heaven,
Shaking the briny sea-dregs from their wings;
Here, wrought by unseen fingers, soon is wove
The cloudy tissue, till a mighty fleet,
Freighted with treasures bound for distant shores,
Floats waiting for the breeze; loosed on the sky
Rush the strong tempests, that, with sweeping breath,
Impel the vast flotilla to its port;
Where, overhanging wide the arid plain,
Drops the rich mercy down; and oft, when summer
Withers the harvest, and the lazy clouds
Drag idly at the bidding of the breeze.

New riders spur them, and enraged they rush,
Bestrode by thunders, that, with hideous shouts
And crackling thongs of fire, urge them along.
As falls the blessing, how the satiate earth
And all her race shed grateful smiles!—not here
The bounty ceases: when the drenching streams
Have, inly sinking, quench'd the greedy thirst
Of plants, of woods, some kind, invisible hand
In bright, perennial springs draws up again
For needy man and beast; and, as the brooks
Grow strong, apprenticed to the use of man,
The ponderous wheel they turn, the web to weave,
The stubborn metal forge; and, when advanced
To sober age at last, ye seek the sea.
Bearing the wealth of commerce on your backs,
Ye seem the unpaid carriers of the sky
Vouchsaf'd to earth for burden; and your host
Of shining branches, linking land to land.
Seem bands of friendship—silver chains of love,
To bind the world in brotherhood and peace.
Back to the primal chaos fancy sweeps
To trace your dim beginning; when dull earth
Lay sunken low, one level, plashy marsh,
Girdled with mists; while saurian reptiles, strange,
Measureless monsters, through the cloggy plain
Paddled and flounder'd; and the Almighty voice,
Like silver trumpet, from their hidden dens
Summon'd the central and resistless fires,
That with a groan from pole to pole upheave
The mountain-masses, and, with dreadful rent,
Fracture the rocky crust; then Andes rose,
And Alps their granite pyramids shot up,
Barren of soil; but gathering vapours round
Their stony scalps, condensed to drops, from drops
To brooks, from brooks to rivers, which set out
Over that rugged and untravell'd land,
The first exploring pilgrims, to the sea.
Tedious their route, precipitous and vague,
Seeking with humbleness the lowliest paths:
Oft shut in valleys deep, forlorn they turn
And find no vent; till, gather'd into lakes,
Topping the basin's brimming lip, they plunge
Headlong, and hurry to the level main,
Rejoicing: misty ages did they run,
And, with unceasing friction, all the while
Fritter'd to granular atoms the dense rock,
And ground it into soil—then dropp'd (O! sure
From heaven) the precious seed: first mosses, lichens
Seized on the sterile flint, and from their dust
Sprang herbs and flowers: last from the deepening mould
Uprose to heaven in pride the princely tree,
And earth was fitted for her coming lord.

TO THE MAGNOLIA.

When roaming o'er the marshy field,
Through tangled brake and treacherous slough,
We start, that spot so foul should yield,
Chaste blossom! such a balm as thou.
Such lavish fragrance there we meet,
That all the dismal waste is sweet.

So, in the dreary path of life,
Through clogging toil and thorny care,
Love rears his blossom o'er the strife,
Like thine, to cheer the wanderer there:
Which pours such incense round the spot,
His pains, his cares, are all forgot.

TO AN INFANT IN HEAVEN.

Thou bright and star-like spirit!
That, in my visions wild,
I see mid heaven's seraphic host—
O! canst thou be my child!

My grief is quench'd in wonder,
And pride arrests my sighs;
A branch from this unworthy stock
Now blossoms in the skies.

Our hopes of thee were lofty,
But have we cause to grieve?
O! could our fondest, proudest wish
A nobler fate conceive?

The little weeper, tearless,
The sinner, snatch'd from sin;
The babe, to more than manhood grown,
Ere childhood did begin.

And I, thy earthly teacher,
Would blush thy powers to see;
Thou art to me a parent now,
And I, a child to thee!

Thy brain, so uninstructed
While in this lowly state,
Now threads the mazy track of spheres,
Or reads the book of fate.

Thine eyes, so curb'd in vision,
Now range the realms of space—
Look down upon the rolling stars,
Look up to God's own face.

Thy little hand, so helpless,
That scarce its toys could hold,
Now clasps its mate in holy prayer,
Or twangs a harp of gold.

Thy feeble feet, unsteady,
That totter'd as they trod,
With angels walk the heavenly paths
Or stand before their God.

Nor is thy tongue less skilful,
Before the throne divine
'T is pleading for a mother's weal,
As once she pray'd for thine.

What bliss is born of sorrow!
'T is never sent in vain—
The heavenly surgeon maims to save,
He gives no useless pain.

Our God, to call us homeward,
His only Son sent down:
And now, still more to tempt our hearts,
Has taken up our own.

EPHRAIM PEABODY.

[Born 1807, Died 1856.]

THE year in which EPHRAIM PEABODY was born, is remarkable in our annals for having produced an extraordinary number of literary characters. HENRY W. LONGFELLOW, NATHANIEL P. WILLIS, THEODORE S. FAY, GEORGE B. CHEEVER, GEORGE LUNT, THOMAS WARD, EDWARD SANDFORD, and some dozen other makers of American books, were born in that year. The native place of Mr. PEABODY is Wilton, in New Hampshire, where he passed his boyhood. He entered Bowdoin College, in Maine, when about sixteen years of age, and was graduated bachelor of arts in 1827. He studied theology at Cambridge, and in 1831 became pastor of a Unitarian church in Cincinnati; whence he removed in 1838 to New Bedford, Massachusetts, where he remained until 1846, since which time he has been minister of King's Chapel, in Boston.

Mr. PEABODY's writings, in prose and verse, are marked by a charming freshness, and some of his descriptions have a truthfulness and picturesqueness which can have been derived only from a loving study of nature. Several of his best poems were produced while he was in college, and others, as their subjects indicate, while he was residing or travelling in the valley of the Mississippi. Mr. GALLAGHER, in his "Selections from the Poetical Literature of the West," published in Cincinnati in 1841, claims him as a western writer, and quotes him largely. Few western poets have written so frequently or so well of western themes.

THE SKATER'S SONG.

AWAY! away! our fires stream bright
  Along the frozen river;
And their arrowy sparkles of frosty light,
  On the forest branches quiver.
Away! away! for the stars are forth,
  And on the pure snows of the valley,
In a giddy trance, the moonbeams dance—
  Come, let us our comrades rally!

Away! away! o'er the sheeted ice,
  Away, away we go;
On our steel-bound feet we move as fleet
  As deer o'er the Lapland snow.
What though the sharp north winds are out,
  The skater heeds them not—
Midst the laugh and shout of the jocund rout,
  Gray winter is forgot.

'T is a pleasant sight, the joyous throng,
  In the light of the reddening flame,
While with many a wheel on the ringing steel,
  They wage their riotous game;
And though the night-air cutteth keen,
  And the white moon shineth coldly,
Their homes, I ween, on the hills have been—
  They should breast the strong blast boldly.

Let others choose more gentle sports,
  By the side of the winter hearth;
Or 'neath the lamps of the festal hall,
  Seek for their share of mirth;
But as for me, away! away!
  Where the merry skaters be—
Where the fresh wind blows and the smooth
      ice glows,
  There is the place for me!

LAKE ERIE.

THESE lovely shores! how lone and still,
  A hundred years ago,
The unbroken forest stood above,
  The waters dash'd below—
The waters of a lonely sea,
  Where never sail was furl'd,
Embosom'd in a wilderness,
  Which was itself a world.

A hundred years! go back, and lo!
  Where, closing in the view,
Juts out the shore, with rapid oar
  Darts round a frail canoe—
'T is a white voyager, and see,
  His prow is westward set
O'er the calm wave: Hail to thy bold,
  World-seeking barque, MARQUETTE!

The lonely bird, that picks his food
  Where rise the waves and sink,
At their strange coming, with shrill
    scream,
  Starts from the sandy brink;
The fishhawk, hanging in mid sky,
  Floats o'er on level wing,
And the savage from his covert looks,
  With arrow on the string.

A hundred years are past and gone
  And all the rocky coast
Is turreted with shining towns,
  An empire's noble boast;
And the old wilderness is changed
  To cultured vale and hill;
And the circuit of its mountains
  An empire's numbers fill!

THE BACKWOODSMAN.

The silent wilderness for me!
  Where never sound is heard,
Save the rustling of the squirrel's foot,
  And the flitting wing of bird,
Or its low and interrupted note,
  And the deer's quick, crackling tread,
And the swaying of the forest boughs,
  As the wind moves overhead.

Alone, (how glorious to be free!)
  My good dog at my side,
My rifle hanging in my arm,
  I range the forest wide.
And now the regal buffalo
  Across the plains I chase;
Now track the mountain stream to find
  The beaver's lurking-place

I stand upon the mountain's top,
  And (solitude profound!)
Not even a woodman's smoke curls up
  Within the horizon's bound.
Below, as o'er its ocean breadth
  The air's light currents run,
The wilderness of moving leaves
  Is glancing in the sun.

I look around to where the sky
  Meets the far forest line,
And this imperial domain—
  This kingdom—all is mine.
This bending heaven, these floating clouds,
  Waters that ever roll,
And wilderness of glory, bring
  Their offerings to my soul.

My palace, built by God's own hand,
  The world's fresh prime hath seen;
Wide stretch its living halls away,
  Pillar'd and roof'd with green
My music is the wind that now
  Pours loud its swelling bars,
Now lulls in dying cadences,
  My festal lamps are stars.

Though when in this my lonely home,
  My star-watch'd couch I press,
I hear no fond "good-night"—think not
  I am companionless.
O, no! I see my father's house,
  The hill, the tree, the stream,
And the looks and voices of my home
  Come gently to my dream.

And in these solitary haunts,
  While slumbers every tree
In night and silence, God himself
  Seems nearer unto me.
I feel His presence in these shades,
  Like the embracing air;
And as my eyelids close in sleep,
  My heart is hush'd in prayer.

RAFTING.

An August night was shutting down,
  The first stars faintly glowed,
And deep and wide the river's tide,
  Through the mountain gorges flowed
The woods swelled up from either side,
  The clear night-sky bent o'er,
And the gliding waters darkly gleamed
  In the shadows of the shore.

A moving mass swept round the hills,
  In the midst a broad, bright flame;
And flitting forms passed to and fro
  Around it, as it came
The raft-fire with its flying light,
  Fill'd the thin river haze;
And rock and tree and darkling cliff,
  Stooped forward in the blaze.

And while it floated down the stream,
  Yet nearer and more near,
A bugle blast on the still night air,
  Rose loftily and clear.
From cliff to cliff, from hill to hill,
  Through the ancient woods and wide,
The sound swelled on, and far away
  In their silent arches died.

    And ever and anon they sung,
      Yo, heave ho!
    And loud and long the echo rung,
      Yo, heave ho!

And now the tones burst sharp and fast,
  As if the heavens to climb;
Now their soft fall made musical,
  The waters ceaseless chime.
Then all was hushed, till might be heard
  The plashing of the oar;
Or the speech and laugh, half audible,
  Upon the silent shore.

We flung to them some words of cheer,
  And loud jests flung they back;
Good night! they cried, and drifted on,
  Upon their lonely track.
We watched them till a sudden bend
  Received them from our sight;
Yet still we heard the bugle blast
  In the stillness of the night.

    But soon its loud notes on the ear,
      Fell faint and low;
    And we ceased to hear the hearty cheer
      Of Yo, heave ho!

Thus quickly did the river pass,
  Forth issuing from the dark—
A moment, lighting up the scene
  Drifted the phantom ark.
And thus our life. From the unknown,
  To the unknown, we sweep;
Like mariners who cross and hail
  Each other o'er the deep.

JOHN GREENLEAF WHITTIER.

(Born, 1808.)

THE ancestors of MR. WHITTIER settled at an early period in the town of Haverhill, on the banks of the Merrimack River, in Massachusetts. They were Quakers, and some of them suffered from the "sharp laws" which the fierce Independents enacted against those "devil-driven heretics," as they are styled in the "Magnalia" of COTTON MATHER. The poet was born in the year 1808, on a spot inhabited by his family during four or five generations; and until he was eighteen years of age, his time was chiefly passed in the district schools, and in aiding his father on the farm. His nineteenth year was spent in a Latin school, and in 1828 he went to Boston to conduct "The American Manufacturer," a gazette established to advocate a protective tariff. He had previously won some reputation as a writer by various contributions, in prose and verse, to the newspapers printed in his native town and in Newburyport, and the ability with which he managed the "Manufacturer," now made his name familiar throughout the country. In 1830 he went to Hartford, in Connecticut, to take charge of the "New England Weekly Review." He remained here about two years, during which he was an ardent politician, of what was then called the National Republican party, and devoted but little attention to literature. He published, however, in this period his "Legends of New England," a collection of poems and prose sketches, founded on events in the early history of the country; wrote the memoir of his friend BRAINARD, prefixed to the collection of that author's works printed in 1830; and several poems which appeared in the "Weekly Review."

In 1831 Mr. WHITTIER returned to Haverhill, where he was five or six years engaged in agricultural pursuits. He represented that town in the legislature, in its sessions for 1835 and 1836, and declined a reëlection in 1837. His longest poem, "Mogg Megone," was first published in 1836. He regarded the story of the hero only as a framework for sketches of the scenery and of the primitive settlers of Massachusetts and the adjacent states. In portraying the Indian character, he followed as closely as was practicable the rough but natural delineations of CHURCH, MATHEW, CHARLEVOIX, and ROGER WILLIAMS, discarding much of the romance which more modern writers have thrown around the red-man's life. In this, as in the fine ballad of "Cassandra Southwick," and in some of his prose writings, he has exhibited in a very striking manner the intolerant spirit of the Puritans. It can excite no surprise that a New England Quaker refuses to join in the applause which it is the custom to bestow upon the persecutors of his ancestors. But our poet, by a very natural exaggeration, may have done them even less than justice.

Impelled by that hatred of every species of oppression which perhaps is the most marked of his characteristics, Mr. WHITTIER entered at an early period upon the discussion of the abolition question, and since the year 1836, when he was elected one of the secretaries of the American Anti-Slavery Society, he has been among the most prominent and influential advocates of immediate emancipation. His poems on this subject are full of indignant and nervous remonstrance, invective and denunciation. Very few in this country express themselves with uniform freedom and sincerity. Nowhere else is there so common and degrading a servility. We have therefore comparatively little individuality, and of course less than we otherwise should have that is original. Mr. WHITTIER rates this tyranny of public opinion at its true value. Whatever may be its power he despises it. He gives to his mind and heart their true voice. His simple, direct and earnest appeals have produced deep and lasting impressions. Their reception has happily shown that plain and unprejudiced speech is not less likely to be heard than the vapid self-praise and wearisome iteration of inoffensive commonplaces with which the great mass of those who address the public ply the drowsy ears of the hydra.

Mr. WHITTIER published a volume of "Ballads" in 1838; "Lays of my Home, and other Poems," in 1845; a full collection of his "Poems" in 1849; "Songs of Labor," in 1851; and "The Chapel of the Hermits, and other Poems," in 1852. His prose works, besides "Legends of New England," before-mentioned, are "The Stranger in Lowell," a collection of prose essays, 1845; "Supernaturalism in New England," 1847; "Leaves from MARGARET SMITH'S Journal," illustrating the age of the Puritans, 1849; "Old Portraits and Modern Sketches," 1850; and "Literary Recreations and Miscellanies," in 1854.

Although boldness and energy are WHITTIER'S leading characteristics, his works are not without passages scarcely less distinguished for tenderness and grace. He may reasonably be styled a national poet. His works breathe affection for and faith in our republican polity and unshackled religion, but an affection and a faith that do not blind him to our weakness or wickedness. He is of that class of authors whom we most need in America to build up a literature that shall elevate with itself the national feeling and character.

He resides at Amesburg, and has been for several years a "corresponding editor of the "National Era," published in Washington.

THE BALLAD OF CASSANDRA SOUTHWICK.*

To the God of all sure mercies let my blessing rise to-day,
From the scoffer and the cruel he hath pluck'd the spoil away,—
Yea, He who cool'd the furnace around the faithful three,
And tamed the Chaldean lions, hath set his handmaid free!

Last night I saw the sunset melt through my prison bars,
Last night across my damp earth-floor fell the pale gleam of stars;
In the coldness and the darkness all through the long night time,
My grated casement whitened with Autumn's early rime.

Alone, in that dark sorrow, hour after hour crept by;
Star after star looked palely in and sank adown the sky;
No sound amid night's stillness, save that which seem'd to be
The dull and heavy beating of the pulses of the sea;

All night I sat unsleeping, for I knew that on the morrow
The ruler and the cruel priest would mock me in my sorrow,
Dragg'd to their place of market, and bargain'd for and sold,
Like a lamb before the shambles, like a heifer from the fold!

Oh, the weakness of the flesh was there—the shrinking and the shame;
And the low voice of the Tempter like whispers to me came:
"Why sit'st thou thus forlornly?" the wicked murmur said,
"Damp walls thy bower of beauty, cold earth thy maiden bed?

"Where be the smiling faces, and voices soft and sweet,
Seen in thy father's dwelling, heard in the pleasant street?
Where be the youths, whose glances the summer Sabbath through
Turn'd tenderly and timidly unto thy father's pew?

"Why sit'st thou here, Cassandra?—Bethink thee with what mirth
Thy happy schoolmates gather around the warm bright hearth;
How the crimson shadows tremble, on foreheads white and fair,
On eyes of merry girlhood, half hid in golden hair.

"Not for thee the hearth-fire brightens, not for thee kind words are spoken,
Not for thee the nuts of Wenham woods by laughing boys are broken;
No first-fruits of the orchard within thy lap are laid,
For thee no flowers of Autumn the youthful hunters braid.

"Oh! weak, deluded maiden!—by crazy fancies led,
With wild and raving railers an evil path to tread;
To leave a wholesome worship, and teaching pure and sound;
And mate with maniac women, loose-hair'd and sackcloth-bound.

"Mad scoffers of the priesthood, who mock at things divine,
Who rail against the pulpit, and holy bread and wine;
Sore from their cart-tail scourgings, and from the pillory lame,
Rejoicing in their wretchedness, and glorying in their shame.

"And what a fate awaits thee!—a sadly toiling slave,
Dragging the slowly length'ning chain of bondage to the grave!
Think of thy woman's nature, subdued in hopeless thrall,
The easy prey of any, the scoff and scorn of all!"

Oh!—ever as the Tempter spoke, and feeble Nature's fears
Wrung drop by drop the scalding flow of unavailing tears,
I wrestled down the evil thoughts, and strove in silent prayer
To feel, oh, Helper of the weak!—that Thou indeed wert there!

I thought of Paul and Silas, within Philippi's cell,
And how from Peter's sleeping limbs the prison-shackles fell,
Till I seem'd to hear the trailing of an angel's robe of white,
And to feel a blessed presence invisible to sight.

Bless the Lord for all His mercies!—for the peace and love I felt,
Like dew of Hermon's holy hill, upon my spirit melt;
When, "Get behind me, Satan!" was the language of my heart,
And I felt the Evil Tempter with all his doubts depart.

Slow broke the gray cold morning; again the sunshine fell,
Fleck'd with the shade of bar and grate within my lonely cell;

* This ballad has its foundation upon a somewhat remarkable event in the history of Puritan intolerance. Two young persons, son and daughter of Lawrence Southwick, of Salem, who had himself been imprisoned and deprived of all his property for having entertained two Quakers at his house, were fined ten pounds each for non-attendance at church, which they were unable to pay. The case being represented to the General Court, at Boston, that body issued an order which may still be seen on the court records, bearing the signature of Edward Rawson, Secretary, by which the treasurer of the County was "fully empowered to *sell the said persons* to any of the English nation *at Virginia or Barbadoes*, to answer said fines." An attempt was made to carry this barbarous order into execution, but no shipmaster was found willing to convey them to the West Indies. Vide SEWALL's History, pp. 225–6, G. BISHOP.

The hoarfrost melted on the wall, and upward from the street
Came careless laugh and idle word, and tread of passing feet.

At length the heavy bolts fell back, my door was open cast,
And slowly at the sheriff's side, up the long street I pass'd;
I heard the murmur round me, and felt, but dared not see,
How, from every door and window, the people gazed on me.

And doubt and fear fell on me, shame burn'd upon my cheek,
Swam earth and sky around me, my trembling limbs grew weak;
"O Lord! support thy handmaid; and from her soul cast out
The fear of man, which brings a snare—the weakness and the doubt."

Then the dreary shadows scatter'd like a cloud in morning's breeze,
And a low deep voice within me seem'd whispering words like these:
"Though thy earth be as the iron, and thy heaven a brazen wall,
Trust still His loving-kindness whose power is over all."

We paused at length, where at my feet the sunlit waters broke
On glaring reach of shining beach, and shingly wall of rock;
The merchants-ships lay idly there, in hard clear lines on high,
Tracing with rope and slender spar their net-work on the sky.

And there were ancient citizens, cloak-wrapp'd and grave and cold,
And grim and stout sea-captains with faces bronzed and old,
And on his horse, with Rawson, his cruel clerk at hand,
Sat dark and haughty Endicott, the ruler of the land.

'nd poisoning with his evil words the ruler's ready ear,
The priest lean'd o'er his saddle, with laugh and scoff and jeer;
It stirr'd my soul, and from my lips the seal of silence broke,
As if through woman's weakness a warning spirit spoke.

I cried, "The Lord rebuke thee, thou smiter of the meek,
Thou robber of the righteous, thou trampler of the weak!
Go light the dark, cold hearth-stones—go turn the prison lock
Of the poor hearts thou hast hunted, thou wolf amid the flock!"

Dark lower'd the brows of Endicott, and with a deeper red
O'er Rawson's wine-empurpled cheek the flush of anger spread;
"Good people," quoth the white-lipp'd priest, "heed not her words so wild,
Her master speaks within her—the Devil owns his child!"

But gray heads shook, and young brows knit, the while the sheriff read
That law the wicked rulers against the poor have made,
Who to their house of Rimmon and idol priesthood bring
No bended knee of worship, nor gainful offering.

Then to the stout sea-captains the sheriff turning said:
"Which of ye, worthy seamen, will take this Quaker maid?
In the Isle of fair Barbadoes, or on Virginia's shore,
You may hold her at a higher price than Indian girl or Moor."

Grim and silent stood the captains; and when again he cried,
"Speak out, my worthy seamen!"—no voice or sign replied;
But I felt a hard hand press my own, and kind words met my ear:
"God bless thee, and preserve thee, my gentle girl and dear!"

A weight seem'd lifted from my heart,—a pitying friend was nigh,
I felt it in his hard, rough hand, and saw it in his eye;
And when again the sheriff spoke, that voice, so kind to me,
Growl'd back its stormy answer like the roaring of the sea:

"Pile my ship with bars of silver—pack with coins of Spanish gold,
From keel-piece up to deck-plank, the roomage of her hold,
By the living God who made me!—I would sooner in your bay
Sink ship and crew and cargo, than bear this child away!"

"Well answer'd, worthy captain, shame on their cruel laws!"
Ran through the crowd in murmurs loud the people's just applause.
"Like the herdsman of Tekoa, in Israel of old,
Shall we see the poor and righteous again for silver sold?"

I look'd on haughty Endicott; with weapon half way drawn,
Swept round the throng his lion glare of bitter hate and scorn;
Fiercely he drew his bridle rein, and turn'd in silence back,
And sneering priest and baffled clerk rode murmuring in his track.

Hard after them the sheriff look'd in bitterness of soul;
Thrice smote his staff upon the ground, and crush'd his parchment roll.

"Good friends," he said, "since both have fled, the ruler and the priest,
Judge ye, if from their further work I be not well released."

Loud was the cheer which, full and clear, swept round the silent bay,
As, with kind words and kinder looks, he bade me go my way;
For He who turns the courses of the streamlet of the glen,
And the river of great waters, had turn'd the hearts of men.

Oh, at that hour the very earth seem'd changed beneath my eye,
A holier wonder round me rose the blue walls of the sky,
A lovelier light on rock and hill, and stream and woodland lay,
And softer lapsed on sunnier sands the waters of the bay.

Thanksgiving to the Lord of life!—to Him all praises be,
Who from the hands of evil men hath set his handmaid free;
All praise to Him before whose power the mighty are afraid,
Who takes the crafty in the snare, which for the poor is laid!

Sing, oh, my soul, rejoicingly; on evening's twilight calm
Uplift the loud thanksgiving—pour forth the grateful psalm;
Let all dear hearts with me rejoice, as did the saints of old,
When of the Lord's good angel the rescued Peter told.

And weep and howl, ye evil priests and mighty men of wrong,
The Lord shall smite the proud and lay His hand upon the strong.
Wo to the wicked rulers in His avenging hour!
Wo to the wolves who seek the flocks to raven and devour:

But let the humble ones arise,—the poor in heart be glad,
And let the mourning ones again with robes of praise be clad,
For He who cool'd the furnace, and smoothed the stormy wave,
And tamed the Chaldean lions, is mighty still to save!

NEW ENGLAND.

Land of the forest and the rock—
  Of dark-blue lake and mighty river—
Of mountains rear'd aloft to mock
The storm's career, the lightning's shock—
  My own green land for ever!
Land of the beautiful and brave—
The freeman's home—the martyr's grave—
The nursery of giant men,
Whose deeds have link'd with every glen,
And every hill, and every stream,
The romance of some warrior-dream!
Oh! never may a son of thine,
Where'er his wandering steps incline,
Forget the sky which bent above
His childhood like a dream of love,
The stream beneath the green hill flowing,
The broad-arm'd trees above it growing,
The clear breeze through the foliage blowing;
Or hear, unmoved, the taunt of scorn
Breathed o'er the brave New England born,
Or mark the stranger's jaguar-hand
  Disturb the ashes of thy dead,
The buried glory of a land
  Whose soil with noble blood is red,
And sanctified in every part,—
  Nor feel resentment, like a brand,
Unsheathing from his fiery heart!

Oh! greener hills may catch the sun
  Beneath the glorious heaven of France;
And streams, rejoicing as they run
  Like life beneath the day-beam's glance,
May wander where the orange-bough
With golden fruit is bending low;
And there may bend a brighter sky
O'er green and classic Italy—
And pillar'd fane and ancient grave
  Bear record of another time,
And over shaft and architrave
  The green, luxuriant ivy climb;
And far toward the rising sun
  The palm may shake its leaves on high,
Where flowers are opening, one by one,
  Like stars upon the twilight sky;
And breezes soft as sighs of love
  Above the broad banana stray,
And through the Brahmin's sacred grove
  A thousand bright-hued pinions play!
Yet unto thee, New England, still
  Thy wandering sons shall stretch their arms,
And thy rude chart of rock and hill
  Seem dearer than the land of palms;
Thy massy oak and mountain-pine
  More welcome than the banyan's shade
And every free, blue stream of thine
  Seem richer than the golden bed
Of oriental waves, which glow
And sparkle with the wealth below!

TO JOHN PIERPONT.

Not to the poet, but the man, I bring
In friendship's fearless trust my offering:
How much it lacks I feel, and thou wilt see,
Yet well I know that thou hast deem'ed with me
Life all too earnest, and its time too short,
For dreamy ease and Fancy's graceful sport;
  And girded for thy constant strife with wrong,
Like Nehemiah, fighting while he wrought
  The broken walls of Zion, even thy song
Hath a rude martial tone, a blow in every thought!

PALESTINE.

Blest land of Judea! thrice hallow'd of song,
Where the holiest of memories pilgrim-like throng;
In the shade of thy palms, by the shores of thy sea,
On the hills of thy beauty, my heart is with thee.

With the eye of a spirit I look on that shore,
Where pilgrim and prophet have linger'd before;
With the glide of a spirit I traverse the sod
Made bright by the steps of the angels of God.

Blue sea of the hills!—in my spirit I hear
Thy waters, Gennesaret, chime on my ear;
Where the Lowly and Just with the people sat down,
And thy spray on the dust of His sandals was thrown.

Beyond are Bethulia's mountains of green,
And the desolate hills of the wild Gadarene:
And I pause on the goat-crags of Tabor to see
The gleam of thy waters, O, dark Galilee!

Hark, a sound in the valley! where, swollen and strong,
Thy river, O, Kishon, is sweeping along;
Where the Canaanite strove with Jehovah in vain,
And thy torrent grew dark with the blood of the slain.

There, down from his mountains stern Zebulon came,
And Naphtali's stag, with his eyeballs of flame,
And the chariots of Jabin roll'd harmlessly on,
For the arm of the Lord was Abinoam's son!

There sleep the still rocks and the caverns which rang
To the song which the beautiful prophetess sang,
When the princes of Issachar stood by her side,
And the shout of a host in its triumph replied.

Lo, Bethlehem's hill-site before me is seen,
With the mountains around and the valleys between;
There rested the shepherds of Judah, and there
The song of the angels rose sweet on the air.

And Bethany's palm trees in beauty still throw
Their shadows at noon on the ruins below;
But where are the sisters who hasten'd to greet
The lowly Redeemer, and sit at His feet?

I tread where the twelve in their wayfaring trod;
I stand where they stood with the chosen of God—
Where His blessings was heard and his lessons were taught,
Where the blind were restored and the healing was wrought.

O, here with His flock the sad Wanderer came—
These hills He toil'd over in grief, are the same—
The founts where He drank by the way-side still flow,
And the same airs are blowing which breath'd on his brow!

And throned on her hills sits Jerusalem yet,
But with dust on her forehead, and chains on her feet;
For the crown of her pride to the mocker hath gone,
And the holy Shechinah is dark where it shone

But wherefore this dream of the earthly abode
Of humanity clothed in the brightness of God?
Were my spirit but tuned from the outward and dim,
It could gaze, even now, on the presence of Him!

Not in clouds and in terrors, but gentle as when,
In love and in meekness, He moved among men;
And the voice which breathed peace to the waves of the sea,
In the hush of my spirit would whisper to me!

And what if my feet may not tread where He stood,
Nor my ears hear the dashing of Galilee's flood,
Nor my eyes see the cross which he bow'd him to bear,
Nor my knees press Gethsemane's garden of prayer.

Yet, Loved of the Father, Thy Spirit is near
To the meek, and the lowly, and penitent here;
And the voice of thy love is the same even now,
As at Bethany's tomb, or on Olivet's brow.

O, the outward hath gone!—but, in glory and power,
The Spirit surviveth the things of an hour;
Unchanged, undecaying, its Pentecost flame
On the heart's secret altar is burning the same!

PENTUCKET.*

How sweetly on the wood-girt town
The mellow light of sunset shone!
Each small, bright lake, whose waters still
Mirror the forest and the hill,
Reflected from its waveless breast
The beauty of a cloudless west,
Glorious as if a glimpse were given
Within the western gates of Heaven,
Left, by the spirit of the star
Of sunset's holy hour, ajar!

Beside the river's tranquil flood
The dark and low-wall'd dwellings stood,
Where many a rood of open land
Stretch'd up and down on either hand,
With corn-leaves waving freshly green
The thick and blacken'd stumps between;
Behind, unbroken, deep and dread,
The wild, untravell'd forest spread,
Back to those mountains, white and cold,
Of which the Indian trapper told,
Upon whose summits never yet
Was mortal foot in safety set.

Quiet and calm, without a fear
Of danger darkly lurking near,
The weary labourer left his plough
The milk-maid caroll'd by her cow—

* The village of Haverhill, on the Merrimack, called by the Indians Pentucket, was for nearly seventy years a frontier town, and during thirty years endured all the horrors of savage warfare. In the year 1708, a combined body of French and Indians, under the command of De Challions, and Hertel de Rouville, the infamous and bloody sacker of Deerfield, made an attack upon the village, which, at that time, contained only thirty houses. Sixteen of the villagers were massacred, and a still larger number made prisoners. About thirty, of the enemy also fell, and among them Hertel de Rouville. The minister of the place, Benjamin Rolfe, was killed by a shot through his own door

From cottage door and household hearth
Rose songs of praise, or tones of mirth.
At length the murmur died away,
And silence on that village lay.—
So slept Pompeii, tower and hall,
Ere the quick earthquake swallow'd all,
Undreaming of the fiery fate
Which made its dwellings desolate!

Hours pass'd away. By moonlight sped
The Merrimack along his bed.
Bathed in the pallid lustre, stood
Dark cottage-wall and rock and wood,
Silent, beneath that tranquil beam,
As the hush'd grouping of a dream.
Yet on the still air crept a sound—
No bark of fox—no rabbit's bound—
No stir of wings—nor waters flowing—
Nor leaves in midnight breezes blowing.

Was that the tread of many feet,
Which downward from the hill-side beat?
What forms were those which darkly stood
Just on the margin of the wood?—
Charr'd tree-stumps in the moonlight dim,
Or paling rude, or leafless limb?
No—through the trees fierce eyeballs glow'd,
Dark human forms in moonshine show'd,
Wild from their native wilderness,
With painted limbs and battle-dress!

A yell, the dead might wake to hear,
Swell'd on the night air, far and clear—
Then smote the Indian tomahawk
On crashing door and shattering lock—
Then rang the rifle-shot—and then
The shrill death-scream of stricken men—
Sunk the red axe in woman's brain,
And childhood's cry arose in vain—
Bursting through roof and window came,
Red, fast, and fierce, the kindled flame;
And blended fire and moonlight glared
Over dead corse and weapons bared.

The morning sun look'd brightly through
The river-willows, wet with dew.
No sound of combat fill'd the air,
No shout was heard,—nor gun-shot there:
Yet still the thick and sullen smoke
From smouldering ruins slowly broke;
And on the green sward many a stain,
And, here and there, the mangled slain,
Told how that midnight bolt had sped,
Pentucket, on thy fated head!

Even now, the villager can tell
Where Rolfe beside his hearth-stone fell,
Still show the door of wasting oak
Through which the fatal death-shot broke,
And point the curious stranger where
De Rouville's corse lay grim and bare—
Whose hideous head, in death still fear'd,
Bore not a trace of hair or beard—
And still, within the churchyard ground,
Heaves darkly up the ancient mound,
Whose grass-grown surface overlies
The victims of that sacrifice.

LINES ON THE DEATH OF S. OLIVER TORREY, OF BOSTON.

Gone before us, O, our brother,
  To the spirit-land!
Vainly look we for another
  In thy place to stand.
Who shall offer youth and beauty
  On the wasting shrine
Of a stern and lofty duty,
  With a faith like thine?

O! thy gentle smile of greeting
  Who again shall see?
Who, amidst the solemn meeting,
  Gaze again on thee?—
Who, when peril gathers o'er us,
  Wear so calm a brow?
Who, with evil men before us,
  So serene as thou?

Early hath the spoiler found thee,
  Brother of our love!
Autumn's faded earth around thee,
  And its storms above!
Evermore that turf lie lightly,
  And, with future showers,
O'er thy slumbers fresh and brightly
  Blow the summer-flowers!

In the locks thy forehead gracing,
  Not a silvery streak;
Nor a line of sorrow's tracing
  On thy fair, young cheek;
Eyes of light and lips of roses,
  Such as Hylas wore—
Over all that curtain closes,
  Which shall rise no more!

Will the vigil Love is keeping
  Round that grave of thine,
Mournfully, like Jazer weeping
  Over Sibmah's vine*—
Will the pleasant memories, swelling
  Gentle hearts, of thee,
In the spirit's distant dwelling
  All unheeded be?

If the spirit ever gazes,
  From its journeyings, back;
If the immortal ever traces
  O'er its mortal track;
Wilt thou not, O brother, meet us
  Sometimes on our way,
And, in hours of sadness, greet us
  As a spirit may?

Peace be with thee, O our brother,
  In the spirit-land!
Vainly look we for another
  In thy place to stand.
Unto Truth and Freedom giving
  All thy early powers,
Be thy virtues with the living,
  And thy spirit ours!

* "O, vine of Sibmah! I will weep for thee with the weeping of Jazer!"—*Jeremiah* xlviii. 32.

RANDOLPH OF ROANOKE.

Oh, Mother Earth! upon thy lap
  Thy weary ones receiving,
And o'er them, silent as a dream,
  Thy grassy mantle weaving—
Fold softly in thy long embrace
  That heart so worn and broken,
And cool its pulse of fire beneath
  Thy shadows old and oaken.

Shut out from him the bitter word
  And serpent hiss of scorning;
Nor let the storms of yesterday
  Disturb his quiet morning.
Breathe over him forgetfulness
  Of all save deeds of kindness,
And, save to smiles of grateful eyes,
  Press down his lids in blindness.

There, where with living ear and eye
  He heard Potomac's flowing,
And, through his tall ancestral trees
  Saw Autumn's sunset glowing,
He sleeps—still looking to the west,
  Beneath the dark wood shadow,
As if he still would see the sun
  Sink down on wave and meadow.

Bard, sage, and tribune!—in himself
  All moods of mind contrasting—
The tenderest wail of human wo,
  The scorn like lightning blasting;
The pathos which from rival eyes
  Unwilling tears could summon,
The stinging taunt, the fiery burst
  Of hatred scarcely human!

Mirth, sparkling like a diamond-shower,
  From lips of life-long sadness;
Clear picturings of majestic thought
  Upon a ground of madness;
And over all, romance and song
  A classic beauty throwing,
And laurell'd Clio at his side
  Her storied pages showing.

All parties fear'd him: each in turn
  Beheld its schemes disjointed,
As right or left his fatal glance
  And spectral finger pointed.
Sworn foe of Cant, he smote it down
  With trenchant wit unsparing,
And, mocking, rent with ruthless hand
  The robe Pretence was wearing.

Too honest or too proud to feign
  A love he never cherish'd,
Beyond Virginia's border line
  His patriotism perish'd.
While others hail'd in distant skies
  Our eagle's dusky pinion,
He only saw the mountain bird
  Stoop o'er his Old Dominion!

Still through each change of fortune strange,
  Rack'd nerve, and brain all burning,
His loving faith in mother-land
  Knew never shade of turning:
By Britain's lakes, by Neva's wave,
  Whatever sky was o'er him,
He heard her rivers' rushing sound,
  Her blue peaks rose before him.

He held his slaves, yet made withal
  No false and vain pretences,
Nor paid a lying priest to seek
  For scriptural defences.
His harshest words of proud rebuke,
  His bitterest taunt and scorning,
Fell firelike on the northern brow
  That bent to him in fawning.

He held his slaves: yet kept the while
  His reverence for the human;
In the dark vassals of his will
  He saw but man and woman!
No hunter of God's outraged poor
  His Roanoke valley enter'd;
No trader in the souls of men
  Across his threshold ventured.

And when the old and wearied man
  Laid down for his last sleeping,
And at his side, a slave no more,
  His brother man stood weeping,
His latest thought, his latest breath,
  To freedom's duty giving,
With failing tongue and trembling hand
  The dying bless'd the living.

Oh! never bore his ancient state
  A truer son or braver;
None trampling with a calmer scorn
  On foreign hate or favor.
He knew her faults, yet never stoop'd
  His proud and manly feeling
To poor excuses of the wrong,
  Or meanness of concealing.

But none beheld with clearer eye
  The plague-spot o'er her spreading,
None heard more sure the steps of Doom
  Along her future treading.
For her as for himself he spake,
  When, his gaunt frame upbracing,
He traced with dying hand, "Remorse!" *
  And perished in the tracing.

As from the grave where Henry sleeps,
  From Vernon's weeping willow,
And from the grassy pall which hides
  The sage of Monticello,
So from the leaf-strewn burial-stone
  Of Randolph's lowly dwelling,
Virginia! o'er thy land of slaves
  A warning voice is swelling.

And hark! from thy deserted fields
  Are sadder warnings spoken,
From quench'd hearths, where thine exiled sons
  Their household gods have broken.
The curse is on thee—wolves for men,
  And briers for corn-sheaves giving!
Oh! more than all thy dead renown
  Were now one hero living!

* See the remarkable statement of Dr. Parrish, his medical attendant.

THE PRISONER FOR DEBT.

Look on him—through his dungeon-grate,
  Feebly and cold, the morning light
Comes stealing round him, dim and late,
  As if it loathed the sight.
Reclining on his strawy bed,
His hand upholds his drooping head—
His bloodless cheek is seam'd and hard,
Unshorn his gray, neglected beard;
And o'er his bony fingers flow
His long, dishevell'd locks of snow.

No grateful fire before him glows,—
  And yet the winter's breath is chill:
And o'er his half-clad person goes
  The frequent ague-thrill!
Silent—save ever and anon,
A sound, half-murmur and half-groan,
Forces apart the painful grip
Of the old sufferer's bearded lip:
O, sad and crushing is the fate
Of old age chain'd and desolate!

Just God! why lies that old man there?
  A murderer shares his prison-bed,
Whose eyeballs, through his horrid hair,
  Gleam on him fierce and red;
And the rude oath and heartless jeer
Fall ever on his loathing ear,
And, or in wakefulness or sleep,
Nerve, flesh, and fibre thrill and creep,
Whene'er that ruffian's tossing limb,
Crimson'd with murder, touches him!

What has the gray-hair'd prisoner done?
  Has murder stain'd his hands with gore?
Not so: his crime's a fouler one:
  God made the old man poor!
For this he shares a felon's cell—
The fittest earthly type of hell!
For this—the boon for which he pour'd
His young blood on the invader's sword,
And counted light the fearful cost—
His blood-gain'd liberty is lost!

And so, for such a place of rest,
  Old prisoner, pour'd thy blood as rain
On Concord's field, and Bunker's crest,
  And Saratoga's plain?
Look forth, thou man of many scars,
Through thy dim dungeon's iron bars!
It must be joy, in sooth, to see
Yon monument* uprear'd to thee—
Piled granite and a prison-cell—
The land repays thy service well!

Go, ring the bells and fire the guns,
  And fling the starry banner out;
Shout "Freedom!" till your lisping ones
  Give back their cradle-shout:
Let boasted eloquence declaim
Of honour, liberty, and fame;
Still let the poet's strain be heard,
With "glory" for each second word,
And every thing with breath agree
To praise "our glorious liberty!"

And when the patriot cannon jars
  That prison's cold and gloomy wall,
And through its grates the stripes and stars
  Rise on the wind, and fall—
Think ye that prisoner's aged ear
Rejoices in the general cheer?
Think ye his dim and failing eye
Is kindled at your pageantry?
Sorrowing of soul, and chain'd of limb,
What is your carnival to him?

Down with the law that binds him thus!
  Unworthy freemen, let it find
No refuge from the withering curse
  Of God and human kind!
Open the prisoner's living tomb,
And usher from its brooding gloom
The victims of your savage code,
To the free sun and air of God!
No longer dare as crime to brand
The chastening of the Almighty's hand!

* Bunker Hill Monument.

THE MERRIMACK.

Stream of my fathers! sweetly still
The sunset rays thy valley fill;
Pour'd slantwise down the long defile,
Wave, wood, and spire beneath them smile.
I see the winding Powow fold
The green hill in its belt of gold,
And, following down its wavy line,
Its sparkling waters blend with thine.
There's not a tree upon thy side,
Nor rock, which thy returning tide
As yet hath left abrupt and stark
Above thy evening water-mark;
No calm cove with its rocky hem,
No isle whose emerald swells begem
Thy broad, smooth current; not a sail
Bow'd to the freshening ocean-gale;
No small boat with its busy oars,
Nor gray wall sloping to thy shores;
Nor farm-house with its maple shade,
Or rigid poplar colonnade,
But lies distinct and full in sight,
Beneath this gush of sunset light.
Centuries ago, that harbour-bar,
Stretching its length of foam afar,
And Salisbury's beach of shining sand,
And yonder island's wave-smoothed strand,
Saw the adventurer's tiny sail
Flit, stooping from the eastern gale;
And o'er these woods and waters broke
The cheer from Britain's hearts of oak,
As brightly on the voyager's eye,
Weary of forest, sea, and sky,
Breaking the dull, continuous wood,
The Merrimack roll'd down his flood;
Mingling that clear, pellucid brook
Which channels vast Agioochook—
When spring-time's sun and shower unlock
The frozen fountains of the rock,

And more abundant waters given
From that pure lake, 'The Smile of Heaven,'
Tributes from vale and mountain side—
With ocean's dark, eternal tide!

On yonder rocky cape which braves
The stormy challenge of the waves,
Midst tangled vine and dwarfish wood,
The hardy Anglo-Saxon stood,
Planting upon the topmost crag
The staff of England's battle-flag;
And, while from out its heavy fold
St. George's crimson cross unroll'd.
Midst roll of drum and trumpet blare,
And weapons brandishing in air,
He gave to that lone promontory
The sweetest name in all his story;
Of her—the flower of Islam's daughters,
Whose harems look on Stamboul's waters—
Who, when the chance of war had bound
The Moslem chain his limbs around,
Wreathed o'er with silk that iron chain,
Soothed with her smiles his hours of pain,
And fondly to her youthful slave
A dearer gift than freedom gave.

But look! the yellow light no more
Streams down on wave and verdant shore;
And clearly on the calm air swells
The distant voice of twilight bells.
From ocean's bosom, white and thin
The mist comes slowly rolling in;
Hills, woods, the river's rocky rim,
Amidst the sea-like vapour swim,
While yonder lonely coast-light set
Within its wave-wash'd minaret,
Half-quench'd, a beamless star and pale,
Shines dimly through its cloudy veil!
Vale of my fathers!—I have stood
Where Hudson roll'd his lordly flood;
Seen sunrise rest and sunset fade
Along his frowning palisade;
Look'd down the Appalachian peak
On Juniata's silver streak;
Have seen along his valley gleam
The Mohawk's softly winding stream;
The setting sun, his axle red
Quench darkly in Potomac's bed;
The autumn's rainbow-tinted banner
Hang lightly o'er the Susquehanna;
Yet, wheresoe'er his step might be,
Thy wandering child look'd back to thee!
Heard in his dreams thy river's sound
Of murmuring on its pebbly bound,
The unforgotten swell and roar
Of waves on thy familiar shore;
And seen amidst the curtain'd gloom
And quiet of my lonely room,
Thy sunset scenes before me pass;
As, in Agrippa's magic glass,
The loved and lost arose to view,
Remember'd groves in greenness grew;
And while the gazer lean'd to trace,
More near, some old familiar face,
He wept to find the vision flown—
A phantom and a dream alone!

GONE.

Another hand is beckoning us,
Another call is given;
And glows once more with angel-steps
The path which reaches Heaven.

Our young and gentle friend whose smile
Made brighter summer hours,
Amid the frosts of autumn time
Has left us, with the flowers.

No paling of the cheek of bloom
Forewarned us of decay,
No shadow from the silent land
Fell around our sister's way.

The light of her young life went down,
As sinks behind the hill
The glory of a setting star—
Clear, suddenly, and still.

As pure and sweet her fair brow seemed—
Eternal as the sky;
And like the brook's low song, her voice—
A sound which could not die.

And half we deemed she needed not
The changing of her sphere,
To give to heaven a shining one,
Who walked an angel here.

The blessing of her quiet life
Fell on us like the dew;
And good thoughts, where her footsteps press'd,
Like fairy blossoms grew.

Sweet promptings unto kindest deeds
Were in her very look;
We read her face, as one who reads
A true and holy book:

The measure of a blessed hymn,
To which our hearts could move;
The breathing of an inward psalm—
A canticle of love.

We miss her in the place of prayer,
And by the hearth-fire's light;
We pause beside her door to hear
Once more her sweet "Good night!"

There seems a shadow on the day,
Her smile no longer cheers;
A dimness on the stars of night,
Like eyes that look through tears.

Alone unto our Father's will
One thought hath reconciled—
That He whose love exceedeth ours
Hath taken home his child.

Fold her, oh Father! in thine arms,
And let her henceforth be
A messenger of love between
Our human hearts and thee.

Still let her mild rebuking stand
Between us and the wrong,
And her dear memory serve to make
Our faith in goodness strong.

And grant that she who, trembling, here
Distrusted all her powers,
May welcome to her holier home
The well belov'd of ours.

LINES

WRITTEN IN THE BOOK OF A FRIEND.

On page of thine I cannot trace
The cold and heartless commonplace—
A statue's fix'd and marble grace.

For ever as these lines are penn'd,
Still with the thought of thee will blend
That of some loved and common friend,

Who, in life's desert track has made
His pilgrim tent with mine, or laid
Beneath the same remember'd shade.

And hence my pen unfetter'd moves
In freedom which the heart approves—
The negligence which friendship loves.

And wilt thou prize my poor gift less
For simple air and rustic dress,
And sign of haste and carelessness!—

O! more than specious counterfeit
Of sentiment, or studied wit,
A heart like thine should value it.

Yet half I fear my gift will be
Unto thy book, if not to thee,
Of more than doubtful courtesy.

A banish'd name from fashion's sphere—
A lay unheard of Beauty's ear,
Forbid, disown'd,—what do they here?

Upon my ear not all in vain
Came the sad captive's clanking chain—
The groaning from his bed of pain.

And sadder still, I saw the wo
Which only wounded spirits know
When pride's strong footsteps o'er them go.

Spurn'd not alone in walks abroad,
But in the "temples of the Lord,"
Thrust out apart like things abhorr'd.

Deep as I felt, and stern and strong
In words which prudence smother'd long
My soul spoke out against the wrong.

Not mine alone the task to speak
Of comfort to the poor and weak,
And dry the tear on sorrow's cheek;

But, mingled in the conflict warm,
To pour the fiery breath of storm
Through the harsh trumpet of reform;

To brave opinion's settled frown,
From ermined robe and saintly gown,
While wrestling hoary error down.

Founts gush'd beside my pilgrim way,
Cool shadows on the green sward lay,
Flowers swung upon the bending spray,

And, broad and bright on either hand
Stretch'd the green slopes of fairy land,
With hope's eternal sunbow spann'd;

Whence voices call'd me like the flow,
Which on the listener's ear will grow,
Of forest streamlets soft and low.

And gentle eyes, which still retain
Their picture on the heart and brain,
Smiled, beckoning from that path of pain.

In vain!—nor dream, nor rest, nor pause,
Remain for him who round him draws
The batter'd mail of freedom's cause.

From youthful hopes—from each green spot
Of young romance, and gentle thought,
Where storm and tumult enter not.

From each fair altar, where belong
The offerings love requires of song
In homage to her bright-eyed throng,

With soul and strength, with heart and hand,
I turn'd to freedom's struggling band—
To the sad helots of our land.

What marvel then that Fame should turn
Her notes of praise to those of scorn—
Her gifts reclaim'd—her smiles withdrawn.

What matters it!—a few years more,
Life's surge so restless heretofore
Shall break upon the unknown shore!

In that far land shall disappear
The shadows which we follow here—
The mist-wreaths of our atmosphere!

Before no work of mortal hand
Of human will or strength expand
The pearl gates of the "better land;"

Alone in that pure love which gave
Life to the sleeper of the grave,
Resteth the power to "seek and save."

Yet, if the spirit gazing through
The vista of the past can view
One deed to heaven and virtue true;

If through the wreck of wasted powers,
Of garlands wreathed from folly's bowers,
Of idle aims and misspent hours,

The eye can note one sacred spot
By pride and self profaned not—
A green place in the waste of thought,

Where deed or word hath render'd less
"The sum of human wretchedness,"
And gratitude looks forth to bless—

The simple burst of tenderest feeling
From sad hearts won by evil-dealing,
For blessing on the hand of healing,—

Better than glory's pomp will be
That green and blessed spot to me—
A landmark in eternity!—

Something of time which may invite
The purified and spiritual sight
To rest on with a calm delight.

And when the summer winds shall sweep
With their light wings my place of sleep,
And mosses round my head-stone creep,

If still, as freedom's rallying sign,
Upon the young heart's altars shine
The very fires they caught from mine,

If words my lips once utter'd still
In the calm faith and steadfast will
Of other hearts, their work fulfil,

Perchance with joy the soul may learn
These tokens, and its eye discern
The fires which on those altars burn,—

A marvellous joy that even then
The spirit hath its life again,
In the strong hearts of mortal men.

Take, lady, then, the gift I bring,
No gay and graceful offering—
No flower-smile of the laughing spring.

Midst the green buds of youth's fresh May,
With fancy's leaf-enwoven bay,
My sad and sombre gift I lay.

And if it deepens in thy mind
A sense of suffering human kind—
The outcast and the spirit-blind:

Oppress'd and spoil'd on every side,
By prejudice, and scorn, and pride;
Life's common courtesies denied:

Sad mothers mourning o'er their trust,
Children by want and misery nursed,
Tasting life's bitter cup at first.

If to their strong appeals which come
From fireless hearth, and crowded room,
And the dark alley's noisome gloom,—

Though dark the hands upraised to thee
In mute, beseeching agony,
Thou lend'st thy woman's sympathy,

Not vainly on thy gentle shrine
Where love, and mirth, and friendship twine
Their varied gifts, I offer mine.

DEMOCRACY.

Oh, fairest born of love and light,
  Yet bending brow and eye severe
On all which pains the holy sight
  Or wounds the pure and perfect ear!

Beautiful yet thy temples rise,
  Though there profaning gifts are thrown;
And fires unkindled of the skies
  Are glaring round thy altar-stone

Still sacred—though thy name be breathed
  By those whose hearts thy truth deride;
And garlands, pluck'd from thee, are wreathed
  Around the haughty brows of pride.

O, ideal of my boyhood's time!
  The faith in which my father stood,
Even when the sons of lust and crime
  Had stain'd thy peaceful courts with blood!

Still to those courts my footsteps turn,
  For, through the mists that darken there,
I see the flame of freedom burn—
  The Kebla of the patriot's prayer!

The generous feeling, pure and warm,
  Which owns the right of *all* divine—
The pitying heart—the helping arm—
  The prompt self-sacrifice—are thine.

Beneath thy broad, impartial eye,
  How fade the lines of caste and birth!
How equal in their suffering lie
  The groaning multitudes of earth!

Still to a stricken brother true,
  Whatever clime hath nurtured him;
As stoop'd to heal the wounded Jew
  The worshipper of Gerizim.

By misery unrepell'd, unawed
  By pomp or power, thou see'st a MAN
In prince or peasant—slave or lord—
  Pale priest, or swarthy artisan.

Through all disguise, form, place or name,
  Beneath the flaunting robes of sin,
Through poverty and squalid shame,
  Thou lookest on the *man* within.

On man, as man, retaining yet,
  Howe'er debased, and soil'd, and dim,
The crown upon his forehead set—
  The immortal gift of God to him.

And there is reverence in thy look;
  For that frail form which mortals wear
The Spirit of the Holiest took,
  And veil'd His perfect brightness there.

Not from the cold and shallow fount
  Of vain philosophy thou art,
He who of old on Syria's mount
  Thrill'd, warm'd by turns the listener's heart

In holy words which cannot die,
  In thoughts which angels lean'd to know,
Proclaim'd thy message from on high—
  Thy mission to a world of wo.

That voice's echo hath not died!
  From the blue lake of Galilee,
And Tabor's lonely mountain side,
  It calls a struggling world to thee.

Thy name and watchword o'er this land
  I hear in every breeze that stirs,
And round a thousand altars stand
  Thy banded party worshippers.

Not to these altars of a day,
  At party's call, my gift I bring;
But on thy olden shrine I lay
  A freeman's dearest offering:

The voiceless utterance of his will—
  His pledge to freedom and to truth.
That manhood's heart remembers still
  The homage of its generous youth

THE CYPRESS TREE OF CEYLON.*

They sat in silent watchfulness
The sacred cypress tree about,
And from the wrinkled brows of age
Their failing eyes look'd out.

Gray age and sickness waiting there,
Through weary night and lingering day,
Grim as the idols at their side,
And motionless as they.

Unheeded, in the boughs above,
The song of Ceylon's birds was sweet;
Unseen of them the island's flowers
Bloom'd brightly at their feet.

O'er them the tropic night-storm swept,
The thunder crash'd on rock and hill,
The lightning wrapp'd them like a cloud,—
Yet there they waited still!

What was the world without to them?
The Moslem's sunset call—the dance
Of Ceylon's maids—the passing gleam
Of battle-flag and lance!

They waited for that falling leaf
Of which the wandering Jogees sing,
Which lends once more to wintry age
The greenness of its spring.

O! if these poor and blinded ones
In trustful patience wait to feel
O'er torpid pulse and failing limb
A youthful freshness steal:

Shall we, who sit beneath that tree
Whose healing leaves of life are shed
In answer to the breath of prayer,
Upon the waiting head:

Not to restore our failing forms,
Nor build the spirit's broken shrine,
But on the fainting soul to shed
A light and life divine:

Shall we grow weary at our watch,
And murmur at the long delay,—
Impatient of our Father's time,
And his appointed way?

Or shall the stir of outward things
Allure and claim the Christian's eye,
When on the heathen watcher's ear
Their powerless murmurs die?

Alas! a deeper test of faith
Than prison-cell or martyr's stake,
The self-abasing watchfulness
Of silent prayer may make.

We gird us bravely to rebuke
Our erring brother in the wrong;
And in the ear of pride and power
Our warning voice is strong.

Easier to smite with Peter's sword,
Than "watch one hour" in humbling prayer
Life's "great things," like the Syrian lord,
Our souls can do and dare.

But, O, we shrink from Jordan's side,
From waters which alone can save;
And murmur for Abana's banks,
And Pharpar's brighter wave.

O! Thou who in the garden's shade
Didst wake thy weary ones again,
Who slumber'd in that fearful hour,
Forgetful of thy pain:

Bend o'er us now, as over them
And set our sleep-bound spirits free,
Nor leave us slumbering in the watch
Our souls should keep with thee!

* Ibn Batuta, the celebrated Mussulman traveller of the fourteenth century, speaks of a cypress tree in Ceylon, universally held sacred by the inhabitants, the leaves of which were said to fall only at long and uncertain periods; and he who had the happiness to find and eat one of them was restored at once to youth and vigour. The traveller saw several venerable Jogees, or saints, sitting silent under the tree, patiently waiting the fall of a leaf.

THE WORSHIP OF NATURE.*

The ocean looketh up to heaven,
As 't were a living thing;
The homage of its waves is given
In ceaseless worshipping.

They kneel upon the sloping sand,
As bends the human knee,
A beautiful and tireless band,
The priesthood of the sea!

They pour the glittering treasures out
Which in the deep have birth,
And chant their awful hymns about
The watching hills of earth.

The green earth sends its incense up
From every mountain-shrine,
From every flower and dewy cup
That greeteth the sunshine.

The mists are lifted from the rills,
Like the white wing of prayer;
They lean above the ancient hills,
As doing homage there.

The forest-tops are lowly cast
O'er breezy hill and glen,
As if a prayerful spirit pass'd
On nature as on men.

The clouds weep o'er the fallen world,
E'en as repentant love;
Ere, to the blessed breeze unfurl'd,
They fade in light above.

The sky is as a temple's arch,
The blue and wavy air
Is glorious with the spirit-march
Of messengers at prayer.

The gentle moon, the kindling sun,
The many stars are given,
As shrines to burn earth's incense on,
The altar-fires of Heaven!

* "It hath beene as it were especially rendered unto mee, and made plaine and legible to my understandynge, that a great worshipp is going on among the thyngs of God."—Grahame.

THE FUNERAL TREE OF THE SOKOKIS.*

AROUND Sebago's lonely lake
There lingers not a breeze to break
The mirror which its waters make.

The solemn pines along its shore,
The firs which hang its gray rocks o'er,
Are painted on its glassy floor.

The sun looks o'er, with hazy eye,
The snowy mountain-tops which lie
Piled coldly up against the sky.

Dazzling and white! save where the bleak,
Wild winds have bared some splintering peak,
Or snow-slide left its dusky streak.

Yet green are Saco's banks below,
And belts of spruce and cedar show,
Dark fringing round those cones of snow.

The earth hath felt the breath of spring,
Though yet upon her tardy wing
The lingering frosts of winter cling.

Fresh grasses fringe the meadow-brooks,
And mildly from its sunny nooks
The blue eye of the violet looks.

And odours from the springing grass,
The sweet birch, and the sassafras,
Upon the scarce-felt breezes pass.

Her tokens of renewing care
Hath Nature scatter'd everywhere,
In bud and flower, and warmer air.

But in their hour of bitterness,
What reck the broken Sokokis,
Beside their slaughter'd chief, of this?

The turf's red stain is yet undried—
Scarce have the death-shot echoes died
Along Sebago's wooded side:

And silent now the hunters stand,
Group'd darkly, where a swell of land
Slopes upward from the lake's white sand.

Fire and the axe have swept it bare,
Save one lone beech, unclosing there
Its light leaves in the April air.

With grave, cold looks, all sternly mute,
They break the damp turf at its foot,
And bare its coil'd and twisted root.

They heave the stubborn trunk aside,
The firm roots from the earth divide—
The rent beneath yawns dark and wide.

And there the fallen chief is laid,
In tassell'd garb of skins array'd,
And girdled with his wampum-braid.

The silver cross he loved is press'd
Beneath the heavy arms, which rest
Upon his scarr'd and naked breast.*

'Tis done: the roots are backward sent,
The beechen tree stands up unbent—
The Indian's fitting monument!

When of that sleeper's broken race
Their green and pleasant dwelling-place
Which knew them once, retains no trace;

O! long may sunset's light be shed
As now upon that beech's head—
A green memorial of the dead!

There shall his fitting requiem be,
In northern winds, that, cold and free,
Howl nightly in that funeral tree.

To their wild wail the waves which break
Forever round that lonely lake
A solemn under-tone shall make!

And who shall deem the spot unblest,
Where Nature's younger children rest,
Lull'd on their sorrowing mother's breast?

Deem ye that mother loveth less
These bronzed forms of the wilderness
She foldeth in her long caress?

As sweet o'er them her wild flowers flow,
As if with fairer hair and brow
The blue-eyed Saxon slept below.

What though the places of their rest
No priestly knee hath ever press'd—
No funeral rite nor prayer hath bless'd?

What though the bigot's ban be there,
And thoughts of wailing and despair,
And cursing in the place of prayer!†

Yet Heaven hath angels watching round
The Indian's lowliest forest-mound—
And *they* have made it holy ground.

There ceases man's frail judgment; all
His powerless bolts of cursing fall
Unheeded on that grassy pall.

O, peel'd, and hunted, and reviled!
Sleep on, dark tenant of the wild!
Great Nature owns her simple child!

And Nature's GOD, to whom alone
The secret of the heart is known—
The hidden language traced thereon;

Who, from its many cumberings
Of form and creed, and outward things,
To light the naked spirit brings;

Not with our partial eye shall scan—
Not with our pride and scorn shall ban
The spirit of our brother man!

---

* POLAN, a chief of the Sokokis Indians, the original inhabitants of the country lying between Agamenticus and Casco bay, was killed in a skirmish at Windham, on the Sebago lake, in the spring of 1756. He claimed all the lands on both sides of the Presumpscot river to its mouth at Casco, as his own. He was shrewd, subtle, and brave. After the white men had retired, the surviving Indians "swayed" or bent down a young tree until its roots were turned up, placed the body of their chief beneath them, and then released the tree to spring back to its former position.

* The Sokokis were early converts to the Catholic faith. Most of them, prior to the year 1756, had removed to the French settlements on the St. Francois.

† The brutal and unchristian spirit of the early settlers of New England toward the red man is strikingly illustrated in the conduct of the man who shot down the Sokokis chief. He used to say he always noticed the anniversary of that exploit, as "the day on which he sent the devil a present."—WILLIAMSON'S *History of Maine.*

RAPHAEL.

I SHALL not soon forget that sight:
The glow of autumn's westering day,
A hazy warmth, a dreamy light,
On Raphael's picture lay.

It was a simple print I saw,
The fair face of a musing boy;
Yet while I gazed a sense of awe
Seem'd blending with my joy.

A simple print:—the graceful flow
Of boyhood's soft and wavy hair,
And fresh young lip and cheek, and brow
Unmark'd and clear, were there.

Yet through its sweet and calm repose
I saw the inward spirit shine;
It was as if before me rose
The white veil of a shrine.

As if, as Gothland's sage has told,
The hidden life, the man within,
Dissever'd from its frame and mould,
By mortal eye were seen.

Was it the lifting of that eye,
The waving of that pictured hand?
Loose as a cloud-wreath on the sky
I saw the walls expand.

The narrow room had vanish'd—space
Broad, luminous, remain'd alone,
Through which all hues and shapes of grace
And beauty look'd or shone.

Around the mighty master came
The marvels which his pencil wrought,
Those miracles of power whose fame
Is wide as human thought.

There droop'd thy more than mortal face,
O Mother, beautiful and mild!
Enfolding in one dear embrace
Thy Saviour and thy child!

The rapt brow of the Desert John;
The awful glory of that day
When all the Father's brightness shone
Through manhood's veil of clay.

And, midst gray prophet forms, and wild
Dark visions of the days of old,
How sweetly woman's beauty smiled
Through locks of brown and gold!

There Fornarina's fair young face
Once more upon her lover shone,
Whose model of an angel's grace
He borrow'd from her own.

Slow pass'd that vision from my view,
But not the lesson which it taught;
The soft, calm shadows which it threw
Still rested on my thought:

The truth, that painter, bard and sage,
Even in earth's cold and changeful clime,
Plant for their deathless heritage
The fruits and flowers of time.

We shape ourselves the joy or fear
Of which the coming life is made,
And fill our future's atmosphere
With sunshine or with shade.

The tissue of the life to be
We weave with colours all our own,
And in the field of destiny
We reap as we have sown.

Still shall the soul around it call
The shadows which it gather'd here,
And painted on the eternal wall
The past shall reappear.

Think ye the notes of holy song
On Milton's tuneful ear have died?
Think ye that Raphael's angel throng
Has vanish'd from his side?

Oh no!—we live our life again:
Or warmly touch'd or coldly dim
The pictures of the past remain,—
Man's works shall follow him!

MEMORIES.

A BEAUTIFUL and happy girl
With step as soft as summer air,
And fresh young lip and brow of pearl
Shadow'd by many a careless curl
Of unconfined and flowing hair:
A seeming child in every thing
Save thoughtful brow, and ripening charms,
As nature wears the smile of spring
When sinking into summer's arms.

A mind rejoicing in the light
Which melted through its graceful bower,
Leaf after leaf serenely bright
And stainless in its holy white
Unfolding like a morning flower:
A heart, which, like a fine-toned lute
With every breath of feeling woke,
And, even when the tongue was mute,
From eye and lip in music spoke.

How thrills once more the lengthening chain
Of memory at the thought of thee!—
Old hopes which long in dust have lain,
Old dreams come thronging back again,
And boyhood lives again in me;
I feel its glow upon my cheek,
Its fulness of the heart is mine,
As when I lean'd to hear thee speak,
Or raised my doubtful eye to thine.

I hear again thy low replies,
I feel thy arm within my own,
And timidly again uprise
The fringed lids of hazel eyes
With soft brown tresses overblown.
Ah! memories of sweet summer eves,
Of moonlit wave and willowy way,
Of stars and flowers and dewy leaves,
And smiles and tones more dear than they!

Ere this thy quiet eye hath smiled
  My picture of thy youth to see,
When half a woman, half a child,
Thy very artlessness beguiled,
  And folly's self seem'd wise in thee.
I too can smile, when o'er that hour
  The lights of memory backward stream,
Yet feel the while that manhood's power
  Is vainer than my boyhood's dream.

Years have pass'd on, and left their trace
  Of graver care and deeper thought;
And unto me the calm, cold face
Of manhood, and to thee the grace
  Of woman's pensive beauty brought,
On life's rough blasts for blame or praise
  The schoolboy's name has widely flown;
Thine in the green and quiet ways
  Of unobtrusive goodness known.

And wider yet in thought and deed
  Our still diverging thoughts incline,
Thine the Genevan's sternest creed,
While answers to my spirit's need
  The Yorkshire peasant's simple line.
For thee the priestly rite and prayer,
  And holy day and solemn psalm,
For me the silent reverence where
  My brethren gather, slow and calm.

Yet hath thy spirit left on me
  An impress time has not worn out,
And something of myself in thee,
A shadow from the past, I see
  Lingering even yet thy way about.
Not wholly can the heart unlearn
  That lesson of its better hours,
Not yet has Time's dull footstep worn
  To common dust that path of flowers.

Thus, while at times before our eye
  The clouds about the present part,
And, smiling through them, round us lie
Soft hues of memory's morning sky—
  The Indian summer of the heart,
In secret sympathies of mind,
  In founts of feeling which retain
Their pure, fresh flow, we yet may find
  Our early dreams not wholly vain!

TO A FRIEND,

ON HER RETURN FROM EUROPE.

How smiled the land of France
Under thy blue eye's glance,
    Light-hearted rover!
Old walls of chateaux gray,
Towers of an early day
Which the three colours play
    Flauntingly over.

Now midst the brilliant train
Thronging the banks of Seine:
    Now midst the splendour
Of the wild Alpine range,
Waking with change on change
Thoughts in thy young heart strange,
    Lovely and tender.

Vales, soft, Elysian,
Like those in the vision
    Of Mirza, when, dreaming
He saw the long hollow dell
Touch'd by the prophet's spell
Into an ocean's swell
    With its isles teeming.

Cliffs wrapt in snows of years,
Splintering with icy spears
    Autumn's blue heaven:
Loose rock and frozen slide,
Hung on the mountain side,
Waiting their hour to glide
    Downward, storm-driven!

Rhine stream, by castle old
Baron's and robber's hold,
    Peacefully flowing;
Sweeping through vineyards green,
Or where the cliffs are seen
O'er the broad wave between
    Grim shadows throwing.

Or, where St. Peter's dome
Swells o'er eternal Rome
    Vast, dim, and solemn,—
Hymns ever chanting low—
Censers swung to and fro—
Sable stoles sweeping slow
    Cornice and column!

Oh, as from each and all
Will there not voices call
    Evermore back again?
In the mind's gallery
Wilt thou not ever see
Dim phantoms beckon thee
    O'er that old track again!

New forms thy presence haunt—
New voices softly chant—
    New faces greet thee!—
Pilgrims from many a shrine
Hallow'd by poet's line
At memory's magic sign
    Rising to meet thee.

And when such visions come
Unto thy olden home,
    Will they not waken
Deep thoughts of Him whose hand
Led thee o'er sea and land
Back to the household band
    Whence thou wast taken!

While at the sunset time,
Swells the cathedral's chime,
    Yet, in thy dreaming,
While to thy spirit's eye
Yet the vast mountain's lie
Piled in the Switzer's sky,
    Icy and gleaming:

Prompter of silent prayer,
Be the wild picture there
In the mind's chamber,
And, through each coming day
Him, who, as staff and stay,
Watch'd o'er thy wandering way,
Freshly remember.

So, when the call shall be
Soon or late unto thee,
As to all given,
Still may that picture live,
And its fair forms survive,
And to thy spirit give
Gladness in heaven!

THE REFORMER.

All grim, and soil'd, and brown with tan,
I saw a strong one, in his wrath,
Smiting the godless shrines of man
Along his path.

The Church beneath her trembling dome
Essay'd in vain her ghostly charm:
Wealth shook within his gilded home
With strange alarm.

Fraud from his secret chambers fled
Before the sunlight bursting in:
Sloth drew her pillow o'er her head
To drown the din.

"Spare," Art implored, "yon holy pile;
That grand, old, time-worn turret spare!"
Meek Reverence, kneeling in the aisle,
Cried out, "Forbear!"

Gray-bearded Use, who, deaf and blind,
Groped for his old, accustom'd stone,
Lean'd on his staff, and wept, to find
His seat o'erthrown.

Young Romance raised his dreamy eyes,
O'erhung with paly locks of gold:
"Why smite," he asked in sad surprise,
"The fair, the old!"

Yet louder rang the strong one's stroke,
Yet nearer flash'd his axe's gleam!
Shuddering and sick of heart I woke,
As from a dream.

I look'd: aside the dust-cloud roll'd—
The waster seem'd the builder too;
Upspringing from the ruin'd old,
I saw the new.

'Twas but the ruin of the bad—
The wasting of the wrong and ill;
Whate'er of good the old time had,
Was living still.

Calm grew the brows of him I fear'd;
The frown which awed me pass'd away,
And left behind a smile which cheer'd
Like breaking day.

The grain grew green on battle-plains,
O'er swarded war-mounds grazed the cow;
The slave stood forging from his chains
The spade and plough.

Where frown'd the fort, pavilions gay
And cottage windows, flower-entwined,
Look'd out upon the peaceful bay
And hills behind.

Through vine-wreath'd cups with wine once red,
The lights on brimming crystal fell,
Drawn, sparkling, from the rivulet head
And mossy well.

Through prison walls, like Heaven-sent hope,
Fresh breezes blew, and sunbeams stray'd,
And with the idle gallows-rope
The young child play'd.

Where the doom'd victim in his cell
Had counted o'er the weary hours,
Glad school-girls, answering to the bell,
Came crown'd with flowers.

Grown wiser for the lesson given,
I fear no longer, for I know
That, where the share is deepest driven,
The best fruits grow.

The outworn rite, the old abuse,
The pious fraud transparent grown,
The good held captive in the use
Of wrong alone—

These wait their doom, from that great law
Which makes the past time serve to-day,
And fresher life the world shall draw
From their decay.

Oh! backward-looking son of Time!—
The new is old, the old is new—
The cycle of a change sublime
Still sweeping through.

So wisely taught the Indian seer;
Destroying Seva, forming Brahm,
Who wake by turns Earth's love and fear,
Are one, the same.

As idly as, in that old day,
Thou mournest, did thy sires repine:
So, in his time, thy child grown gray,
Shall sigh for thine.

Yet, not the less for them or thou
The eternal step of Progress beats
To that great anthem, calm and slow,
Which God repeats!

Take heart!—the waster builds again—
A charmed life old Goodness hath;
The tares may perish—but the grain
Is not for death.

God works in all things; all obey
His first propulsion from the night:
Ho, wake and watch!—the world is gray
With morning light!

MY SOUL AND I.

Stand still, my soul: in the silent dark
I would question thee,
Alone in the shadow drear and stark
With God and me!

What, my soul, was thine errand here?
Was it mirth or ease,
Or heaping up dust from year to year?
"Nay, none of these."

Speak, soul, aright in His holy sight
Whose eye looks still
And steadily on thee through the night:
"To do his will!"

What hast thou done, oh, soul of mine,
That thou tremblest so?—
Hast thou wrought His task, and kept the line
He bade thee go?

What, silent all!—art sad of cheer?
Art fearful now?
When God seem'd far, and men were near,
How brave wert thou!

Aha! thou tremblest!—well I see
Thou'rt craven grown.
Is it so hard with God and me
To stand alone?

Summon thy sunshine bravery back,
Oh, wretched sprite!
Let me hear thy voice through this deep and black
Abysmal night.

What hast thou wrought for Right and Truth,
For God and man,
From the golden hours of bright-eyed youth
To life's mid span?

Ah, soul of mine, thy tones I hear,
But weak and low;
Like far, sad murmurs on my ear
They come and go.

"I have wrestled stoutly with the Wrong,
And borne the Right
From beneath the footfall of the throng
To life and light.

"Wherever Freedom shiver'd a chain,
'God speed,' quoth I;
To Error amidst her shouting train
I gave the lie."

Ah, soul of mine! ah, soul of mine!
Thy deeds are well:
Were they wrought for Truth's sake or for thine?
My soul, pray tell.

"Of all the work my hand hath wrought
Beneath the sky,
Save a place in kindly human thought,
No gain have I."

Go to, go to!—for thy very self
Thy deeds were done:
Thou for fame, the miser for pelf,
Your end is one.

And where art thou going, soul of mine?
Canst see the end?
And whither this troubled life of thine
Evermore doth tend?

What daunts thee now?—what shakes thee so?
My sad soul, say.
"I see a cloud like a curtain low
Hang o'er my way.

"Whither I go I cannot tell:
That cloud hangs black,
High as the heaven and deep as hell,
Across my track.

"I see its shadow coldly enwrap
The souls before.
Sadly they enter it, step by step,
To return no more!

"They shrink, they shudder, dear God! they kneel
To thee in prayer.
They shut their eyes on the cloud, but feel
That it still is there.

"In vain they turn from the dread Before
To the Known and Gone;
For while gazing behind them evermore,
Their feet glide on.

"Yet, at times, I see upon sweet, pale faces
A light begin
To tremble, as if from holy places
And shrines within.

"And at times methinks their cold lips move
With hymn and prayer,
As if somewhat of awe, but more of love
And hope were there.

"I call on the souls who have left the light,
To reveal their lot;
I bend mine ear to that wall of night,
And they answer not.

"But I hear around me sighs of pain
And the cry of fear,
And a sound like the slow, sad dropping of rain,
Each drop a tear!

"Ah, the cloud is dark, and, day by day,
I am moving thither:
I must pass beneath it on my way—
God pity me!—whither?"

Ah, soul of mine, so brave and wise
In the life-storm loud,
Fronting so calmly all human eyes
In the sunlit crowd!

Now standing apart with God and me,
Thou art weakness all,
Gazing vainly after the things to be
Through Death's dread wall.

But never for this, never for this
Was thy being lent;
For the craven's fear is but selfishness,
Like his merriment.

Folly and Fear are sisters twain:
One closing her eyes,
The other peopling the dark inane
With spectral lies.

Know well, my soul, God's hand controls
Whate'er thou fearest:

Round him in calmest music rolls
    Whate'er thou hearest.

What to thee is shadow, to him is day,
    And the end he knoweth,
And not on a blind and aimless way
    The spirit goeth.

Man sees no future—a phantom show
    Is alone before him;
Past Time is dead, and the grasses grow,
    And flowers bloom o'er him.

Nothing before, nothing behind:
    The steps of Faith
Fall on the seeming void, and find
    The rock beneath.

The Present, the Present is all thou hast
    For thy sure possessing;
Like the patriarch's angel, hold it fast
    Till it gives its blessing.

Why fear the night? why shrink from Death,
    That phantom wan?
There is nothing in heaven, or earth beneath,
    Save God and man.

Peopling the shadows, we turn from Him
    And from one another;
All is spectral, and vague, and dim,
    Save God and our brother!

Like warp and woof, all destinies
    Are woven fast,
Linked in sympathy like the keys
    Of an organ vast.

Pluck one thread, and the web ye mar;
    Break but one
Of a thousand keys, and the paining jar
    Through all will run.

Oh, restless spirit! wherefore strain
    Beyond thy sphere?—
Heaven and hell, with their joy and pain,
    Are now and here.

Back to thyself is measured well
    All thou hast given;
Thy neighbor's wrong is thy present hell,
    His bliss thy heaven.

And in life, in death, in dark and light,
    All are in God's care;
Sound the black abyss, pierce the deep of night,
    And he is there!

All which is real now remaineth,
    And fadeth never:
The hand which upholds it now, sustaineth
    The soul for ever.

Leaning on Him, make with reverent meekness
    His own thy will,
And with strength from him shall thy utter weakness
    Life's task fulfil:

And that cloud itself, which now before thee
    Lies dark in view,
Shall with beams of light from the inner glory
    Be stricken through.

And like meadow-mist through Autumn's dawn
    Uprolling thin,
Its thickest folds when about thee drawn
    Let sunlight in.

Then of what is to be, and of what is done,
    Why queriest thou?—
The past and the time to be are one,
    And both are NOW!

TO A FRIEND, ON THE DEATH OF HIS SISTER.

THINE is a grief, the depth of which another
        May never know;
Yet, o'er the waters, oh, my stricken brother!
        To thee I go.

I lean my heart unto thee, sadly folding
        Thy hand in mine;
With even the weakness of my soul upholding
        The strength of thine.

I never knew, like thee, the dear departed,
        I stood not by
When, in calm trust, the pure and tranquil-hearted
        Lay down to die.

And on thine ears my words of weak condoling
        Must vainly fall:
The funeral-bell which in thy heart is tolling,
        Sounds over all!

I will not mock thee with the poor world's common
        And heartless phrase,
Nor wrong the memory of a sainted woman
        With idle praise.

With silence only as their benediction,
        God's angels come
Where, in the shadow of a great affliction,
        The soul sits dumb!

Yet, would I say what thine own heart approveth:
        Our Father's will,
Calling to him the dear one whom he loveth,
        Is mercy still.

Not upon thee or thine the solemn angel
        Hath evil wrought:
Her funeral-anthem is a glad evangel—
        The good die not!

God calls our loved ones, but we lose not wholly
        What he hath given;
They live on earth, in thought and deed, as truly
        As in his heaven.

And she is with thee: in thy path of trial
        She walketh yet;
Still with the baptism of thy self-denial
        Her locks are wet.

Up, then, my brother! Lo, the fields of harvest
        Lie white in view!
She lives and loves thee, and the God thou servest
        To both is true.

Thrust in thy sickle! England's toil-worn peasants
        Thy call abide;
And she thou mourn'st, a pure and holy presence,
        Shall glean beside!

GEORGE W. PATTEN.

[Born, 1808.]

MAJOR PATTEN was born in Newport, Rhode Island, on the twenty-sixth of December, 1808. He was the third son of WILLIAM PATTEN, D.D., who was minister of the second Congregational church in that city for half a century. When only twelve years of age he entered Brown University, where he was distinguished rather for abilities than for application, being naturally averse to systematic study, and addicted to poetry and music. He was, however, preëminent in chemistry, as subsequently at West Point in mathematics. At fourteen he wrote a class poem, entitled "Logan," and when he was graduated, in 1825, recited a lyrical story called "The Maid of Scio." Both these pieces were warmly praised, as illustrations of an unfolding genius of a very high order. After leaving the university he remained a year in his father's house, at Newport, before deciding on the choice of a profession. Dr. PATTEN hoped this son at least would follow in the long line of his ancestors, who, since the landing of the Mayflower, had furnished an almost uninterrupted succession of pastors; but the young man felt no predilection for the pulpit, and rejected the profession of the law because his two elder brothers had already chosen it, and for want of *nerve*, that of medicine, to become a soldier. When he disclosed his wishes on this subject, Dr. PATTEN expressed regret that the son of a minister should think of a career so incompatible with the principles of the gospel, and declined aiding him to a cadet's appointment. To his inquiry, however, whether he would consent to his entering the Military Academy if he could himself obtain one, he answered in the affirmative, willing that his son should learn by experience the futility of such an attempt; and he was as much surprised as pained when, after a few weeks, the credentials of a cadet were exhibited to him. JOHN C. CALHOUN, ASHER ROBBINS, WILLIAM HUNTER, and other powerful friends, had willingly and successfully exerted their influence with the President in behalf of a member of the family of Dr. PATTEN. The excellent clergyman could not help saying now, "I give you my consent, my son, because I promised it: my approbation I cannot give." Young PATTEN, nevertheless, proceeded to West Point, and soon acquired there the same brilliant reputation for talents which he had enjoyed at the university. He received his commission as lieutenant in the second regiment of infantry in 1830, was made a captain in 1846, and in 1848 was brevetted major, for his gallantry in the action of Cerro Gordo, where he lost his left hand. His reputation as an officer has always been very high; he is one of the best disciplinarians and bravest soldiers in the army.

Major PATTEN writes in verse with a rarely equalled fluency, and has probably been one of the most prolific of American poets. Led by the exigencies of the service into almost every part of our vast empire, his singularly impressible faculties have been kindled by the various charms of its scenery, by never-ending diversities of character, and by the always fresh and frequently romantic experiences of his profession. His writings display a fine vein of sentiment, and considerable fancy, but have the faults of evident haste and carelessness.

TO S. T. P.

SHADOWS and clouds are o'er me;
  Thou art not here, my bride!
The billows dash before me
  Which bear me from thy side;
On lowering waves benighted,
  Dim sets the weary day;
Thou art not here, my plighted,
  To smile the storm away.

When nymphs of ocean slumber,
  I strike the measured stave
With wild and mournful number,
  To charm the wandering wave.
Hark to the words of sorrow
  Along the fading main!
"'Tis night—but will the morrow
  Restore that smile again?"

Mid curtain'd dreams descending,
  Thy gentle form I trace;
Dimly with shadows blending,
  I gaze upon thy face;
Thy voice comes o'er me gladly,
  Thy hand is on my brow;
I wake—the wave rolls madly
  Beneath the ploughing prow!

Speed on, thou surging billow!
  O'er ocean speed away!
And bear unto her pillow
  The burden of my lay:
Invest her visions brightly
  With passion's murmur'd word,
And bid her bless him nightly—
  Him of the lute and sword.

And *her*, of dreams unclouded,
  With tongue of lisping tale,
Whose eye I left soft shrouded
  'Neath slumber's misty veil,—
When morn at length discloses
  The smile I may not see,
Bear to her cheek of roses
  A father's kiss for me.

FREDERICK W. THOMAS.

[Born 1808. Died 1864.]

The family of the author of "Clinton Bradshaw," by the father's side, were among the early settlers of New England. Isaiah Thomas, founder of the American Antiquarian Society, of Worcester, Massachusetts, and author of the "History of Printing," was his father's uncle. During the revolutionary war Mr. Isaiah Thomas conducted the "Massachusetts Spy," and was a warm and sagacious whig. With him Mr. E. S. Thomas, the father of Frederick William, learned the printing business, and he afterward emigrated to Charleston, South Carolina, where he established himself as a bookseller. Here he met and married Miss Ann Fornerden, of Baltimore, who was then on a visit to the South. Shortly after this marriage Mr. Thomas removed to Providence, where our author was born, on the twenty-fifth of October, 1808. He considers himself a Southerner, however, as he left Rhode island for Charleston when a child in the nurse's arms, and never returned. When about four years of age he slipped from a furniture box on which he was playing, and injured his left leg. Little notice was taken of the accident at the time, and in a few weeks the limb became very painful, his health gradually declined, and it was thought advisable to send him to a more bracing climate. He was accordingly placed in charge of an aunt in Baltimore, where he grew robust, and had recovered from his lameness, with the exception of an occasional weakness in the limb, when a second fall, in his eighth or ninth year, had such an effect upon it that he was confined to the house for many months, and was compelled to resort to crutches, which he used until he grew up to manhood, when they were superseded by a more convenient support. In consequence of these accidents, and his general debility, he went to school but seldom, and never long at a time; but his ardent mind busied itself in study at home, and he was noted for his contemplative habits. At seventeen he commenced reading in the law, and about the same period began his literary career by inditing a poetical satire on some fops about town, the result of which was that the office of the paper in which it was printed was mobbed and demolished.

Soon after he was admitted to the bar, the family removed to Cincinnati, where, in the winter of 1834–5, Mr. Thomas wrote his first novel, "Clinton Bradshaw," which was published in Philadelphia in the following autumn. It was followed in 1836 by "East and West," and in 1840 by "Howard Pinckney." His last work was "Sketches of John Randolph, and other Public Characters," which appeared in Philadelphia in 1853.

Mr. Thomas has published two volumes of poems: "The Emigrant," descriptive of a wanderer's feelings while descending the Ohio, in Cincinnati, in 1833, and "The Beechen Tree and other Poems," in New York, in 1844. He has also written largely in verse as well as in prose for the periodicals.

He has a nice discrimination of the peculiarities of character which give light and shade to the surface of society, and a hearty relish for that peculiar humor which abounds in that portion of our country which undoubtedly embraces most that is original and striking in manners and unrestrained in conduct. He must rank with the first illustrators of manners in the valley of the Mississippi, and deserves praise for many excellencies in general authorship.

SONG.

'T is said that absence conquers love!
  But, O! believe it not;
I 've tried, alas! its power to prove,
  But thou art not forgot.
Lady, though fate has bid us part,
  Yet still thou art as dear,
As fix'd in this devoted heart
  As when I clasp'd thee here.

I plunge into the busy crowd,
  And smile to hear thy name;
And yet, as if I thought aloud,
  They know me still the same.
And when the wine-cup passes round,
  I toast some other fair,—
But when I ask my heart the sound,
  Thy name is echoed there.

And when some other name I learn,
  And try to whisper love,
Still will my heart to thee return,
  Like the returning dove.
In vain! I never can forget,
  And would not be forgot;
For I must bear the same regret,
  Whate'er may be my lot.

E'en as the wounded bird will seek
  Its favorite bower to die,
So, lady, I would hear thee speak,
  And yield my parting sigh.
'T is said that absence conquers love!
  But, O! believe it not;
I've tried, alas! its power to prove,
  But thou art not forgot.

Cincinnati, 1838.

W. D. Gallagher.

WILLIAM D. GALLAGHER.

[Born, 1808.]

William D. Gallagher, the third of four sons of an Irishman who came to this country soon after the rebellion, near the close of the last century, and married a native of New Jersey, was born in Philadelphia, in 1808, and in 1816 migrated with his widowed mother to Cincinnati, which was then a filthy and unhealthy village. For three years he lived with a farmer in the neighborhood, attending a district school in the winters, and in 1825 was apprenticed to the printer of one of the Cincinnati newspapers. From the beginning of his life in the printing office he wrote occasionally for the press, but preserved the secret of his literary habits until 1828, when the late Mr. Benjamin Drake made it known that he was the author of a series of letters from Kentucky and Missouri, which were attracting considerable attention in his "Saturday Evening Chronicle." This led in 1830 to Mr. Gallagher's connection with "The Backwoodsman," a political journal published at Xenia, where he resided about a year. In 1831 he was married, and became editor of "The Cincinnati Mirror," the first literary gazette conducted with much tact or taste in the western states. At the end of two years, the late Mr. Thomas H. Shreve joined him in its management, and it remained under their direction, through varying fortunes, until 1836. In that year Mr. Gallagher edited "The Western Literary Journal and Monthly Review," of which but one volume was published, and in 1837 "The Western Monthly Magazine and Literary Journal," which had a similarly brief existence. In 1838 he was associated with a younger brother in a political newspaper at Columbus, the capital of the state, and there established "The Hesperian, a Monthly Miscellany of General Literature," in which, during its first half year, he was assisted by the late Mr. Otway Curry. "The Hesperian" shared the fate of all previous literary magazines in the west,* and was discontinued on the completion of the third semi-annual volume.

Mr. Gallagher had now been for ten years the most industrious literary man in the valley of the Mississippi, and had done much for the extension and refinement of literary culture, but his labors were neither justly appreciated nor adequately rewarded, and he therefore gladly accepted, near the close of 1839, an offer by the late Mr. Charles Hammond, to share with him the editorship of the "Cincinnati Gazette." With this important journal he retained his connection until the whigs came into power in 1849, when his friend Mr. Corwin, on being appointed Secretary of the Treasury, conferred on him the post of confidential clerk in that department, and he took up his residence in Washington. On the breaking up of the whig administration, in 1853, he removed to Louisville, Kentucky, where he was for several months one of the editors of the "Daily Courier;" but the manly earnestness with which he denounced the crime of the jurors who acquitted the notorious murderer, Matthew Ward, led to some disagreement between him and his partner, and he has since resided on a plantation a few miles from that city.

The poems of Mr. Gallagher are numerous, various, and of very unequal merit. Some are exquisitely modulated and in every respect finished with excellent judgment, while others are inharmonious, inelegant, and betray unmistakeable signs of carelessness. His most unstudied performances, however, are apt to be forcible and picturesque, fragrant with the freshness of western woods and fields, and instinct with the aspiring and determined life of the race of western men. The poet of a new country is naturally of the party of progress; his noblest theme is man, and his highest law liberty. The key-note of Mr. Gallagher's social speculation is in his poem of "The Laborer." Ohio is without a past and without traditions; populous and rich as are her broad domains, in her villages still walk the actors in her earliest civilized history; and our author never strikes a more popular chord than when he celebrates

> "The mothers of our forest land,"

or sings of

> "The free and manly lives we led,
> Mid verdure or mid snow,
> In the days when we were pioneers,
> Fifty years ago."

But his best pieces, of which "August" is a spe-

---

* "The Western Review and Miscellaneous Magazine," by William Gibbes Hunt, was commenced in Lexington, Kentucky, in 1829, and published two years. "The Western Monthly Review," by the Rev. Timothy Flint, was commenced in Cincinnati, in 1827, and published three years. "The Illinois Monthly Magazine," was commenced by Judge James Hall, at Vandalia, Illinois, in 1829, and having been published there two years, was removed to Cincinnati, where it appeared under the title of "The Western Monthly Magazine," until 1836, when it was discontinued. "The Western Quarterly Review," from which the facts in this article are mainly derived, was another illustration of the indifference with which the western people regard western literature. The first number appeared in January, 1849, and the second and last in the following April. The only successful literary periodical yet published in the valley of the Mississippi has been "The Ladies' Repository," a monthly magazine issued under the patronage of the Methodist Episcopal Church, for a considerable number of years, and edited with much taste and knowledge, by gentlemen appointed by the Conferences of that denomination.

cimen, are descriptive of external nature. He delights in painting the phenomena of the changing seasons, the sights and sounds of the forest, and the more poetical aspects of rural and humble life, and in all his pictures there is, with a happy freedom of outline and coloring, the utmost fidelity in detail and general effect.

Mr. GALLAGHER published many years ago three small volumes of poems under the title of "Erato;" they contained his juvenile pieces, his songs and romances of love, and other exhibitions of youthful enthusiasm; and in 1846 a collection of the pieces he had then written which met the approval of his maturer judgment, under the simple title of "Poems." Two or three of his longer productions have since appeared in pamphlets; and a few of his best poems are quoted in "Selections from the Poetical Literature of the West," which appeared in Cincinnati, under his editorial supervision, in 1841; but there has not been published any complete or satisfactory collection of his works.

In prose he has written orations and addresses and numerous and various magazine papers.

CONSERVATISM.

THE owl, he fareth well
In the shadows of the night,
And it puzzleth him to tell
Why the eagle loves the light.

Away he floats—away,
From the forest dim and old,
Where he pass'd the garish day—
The night doth make him bold!

The wave of his downy wing,
As he courses round about,
Disturbs no sleeping thing,
That he findeth in his route.

The moon looks o'er the hill,
And the vale grows softly light;
And the cock, with greeting shrill,
Wakes the echoes of the night.

But the moon—he knoweth well
Its old familiar face;
And the cock—it doth but tell,
Poor fool! its resting-place.

And as still as the spirit of Death
On the air his pinions play;
There 's not the noise of a breath
As he grapples with his prey.

Oh, the shadowy night for him!
It bringeth him fare and glee:
And what cares he how dim
For the eagle it may be?

It clothes him from the cold,
It keeps his larders full;
And he loves the darkness old,
To the eagle all so dull.

But the dawn is in the east,
And the shadows disappear;
And at once his timid breast
Feels the presence of a fear.

He resists—but all in vain!
The clear light is not for him;
So he hastens back again
To the forest old and dim.

Through his head strange fancies run:
For he cannot comprehend
Why the moon, and then the sun,
Up the heavens should ascend—

When the old and quiet night,
With its shadows dark and deep,
And the half-revealing light
Of its stars, he 'd ever keep.

And he hooteth loud and long:
But the eagle greets the day—
And on pinions bold and strong,
Like a roused thought, sweeps away!

THE INVALID.

SHE came in Spring, when leaves were green,
And birds sang blithe in bower and tree—
A stranger, but her gentle mien
It was a calm delight to see.

In every motion, grace was hers;
On every feature, sweetness dwelt;
Thoughts soon became her worshippers—
Affections soon before her knelt.

She bloom'd through all the summer days
As sweetly as the fairest flowers,
And till October's softening haze
Came with its still and dreamy hours.

So calm the current of her life,
So lovely and serene its flow,
We hardly mark'd the deadly strife
Disease forever kept below.

But autumn winds grew wild and chill,
And pierced her with their icy breath;
And when the snow on plain and hill
Lay white, she pass'd, and slept in death.

Tones only of immortal birth
Our memory of her voice can stir;
With things too beautiful for earth
Alone do we remember her.

She came in Spring, when leaves were green,
And birds sang blithe in bower and tree,
And flowers sprang up and bloom'd between
Low branches and the quickening lea.

The greenness of the leaf is gone,
The beauty of the flower is riven,
The birds to other climes have flown,
And there's an angel more in heaven!

THE EARLY LOST.

When the soft airs and quickening showers
Of spring-time make the meadows green,
And clothe the sunny hills with flowers,
And the cool hollows scoop'd between—
Ye go, and fondly bending where
The bloom is brighter than the day,
Ye pluck the loveliest blossom there
Of all that gem the rich array.
The stem, thus robb'd and rudely press'd,
Stands desolate in the purple even;
The flower has wither'd on your breast,
But given its perfume up to heaven.
When, mid our hopes that waken fears,
And mid our joys that end in gloom,
The children of our earthly years
Around us spring, and bud, and bloom—
An angel from the blest above
Comes down among them at their play,
And takes the one that most we love,
And bears it silently away.
Bereft, we feel the spirit's strife;
But while the inmost soul is riven,
Our dear and beauteous bud of life
Receives immortal bloom in heaven.

FIFTY YEARS AGO.

A song for the early times out west,
And our green old forest-home,
Whose pleasant memories freshly yet
Across the bosom come:
A song for the free and gladsome life
In those early days we led,
With a teeming soil beneath our feet,
And a smiling heaven o'erhead!
Oh, the waves of life danced merrily,
And had a joyous flow,
In the days when we were pioneers,
Fifty years ago!

The hunt, the shot, the glorious chase,
The captured elk or deer;
The camp, the big, bright fire, and then
The rich and wholesome cheer;
The sweet, sound sleep, at dead of night,
By our camp-fire blazing high—
Unbroken by the wolf's long howl,
And the panther springing by.
Oh, merrily pass'd the time, despite
Our wily Indian foe,
In the days when we were pioneers,
Fifty years ago!

We shunn'd not labour; when 't was due
We wrought with right good will;
And for the home we won for them,
Our children bless us still.
We lived not hermit lives, but oft
In social converse met;
And fires of love were kindled then,
That burn on warmly yet.
Oh, pleasantly the stream of life
Pursued its constant flow,
In the days when we were pioneers,
Fifty years ago!

We felt that we were fellow-men;
We felt we were a band
Sustain'd here in the wilderness
By Heaven's upholding hand.
And when the solemn sabbath came,
We gather'd in the wood,
And lifted up our hearts in prayer
To God, the only good.
Our temples then were earth and sky;
None others did we know
In the days when we were pioneers,
Fifty years ago!

Our forest life was rough and rude,
And dangers closed us round,
But here, amid the green old trees,
Freedom we sought and found.
Oft through our dwellings wintry blasts
Would rush with shriek and moan:
We cared not—though they were but frail,
We felt they were our own!
Oh, free and manly lives we led,
Mid verdure or mid snow,
In the days when we were pioneers,
Fifty years ago!

But now our course of life is short;
And as, from day to day,
We're walking on with halting step,
And fainting by the way,
Another land, more bright than this,
To our dim sight appears,
And on our way to it we'll soon
Again be pioneers!
Yet while we linger, we may all
A backward glance still throw
To the days when we were pioneers,
Fifty years ago!

TRUTH AND FREEDOM.

On the page that is immortal,
We the brilliant promise see:
"Ye shall know the truth, my people,
And its might shall make you free!"

For the truth, then, let us battle,
Whatsoever fate betide;
Long the boast that we are freemen,
We have made and publish'd wide.

He who has the truth, and keeps it,
Keeps what not to him belongs—
But performs a selfish action,
That his fellow-mortal wrongs.

He who seeks the truth, and trembles
At the dangers he must brave,
Is not fit to be a freeman—
He at best is but a slave.

He who hears the truth, and places
Its high promptings under ban,
Loud may boast of all that's manly,
But can never be a man!

Friend, this simple lay who readest,
Be not thou like either them—
But to truth give utmost freedom,
And the tide it raises stem.

Bold in speech and bold in action
  Be forever!—Time will test,
Of the free-soul'd and the slavish,
  Which fulfils life's mission best.

Be thou like the noble ancient—
  Scorn the threat that bids thee fear:
Speak!—no matter what betide thee;
  Let them strike, but make them hear!

Be thou like the first apostles—
  Be thou like heroic PAUL:
If a free thought seek expression,
  Speak it boldly—speak it all!

Face thine enemies—accusers;
  Scorn the prison, rack, or rod;
And, if thou hast truth to utter,
  Speak, and leave the rest to GOD!

AUGUST.

Dust on thy mantle! dust,
Bright Summer, on thy livery of green!
A tarnish, as of rust,
Dims thy late-brilliant sheen:
And thy young glories—leaf, and bud, and flower—
Change cometh over them with every hour.

Thee hath the August sun
Look'd on with hot, and fierce, and brassy face;
And still and lazily run,
Scarce whispering in their pace,
The half-dried rivulets, that lately sent
A shout of gladness up, as on they went.

Flame-like, the long midday,
With not so much of sweet air as hath stirr'd
The down upon the spray,
Where rests the panting bird,
Dozing away the hot and tedious noon,
With fitful twitter, sadly out of tune.

Seeds in the sultry air,
And gossamer web-work on the sleeping trees;
E'en the tall pines, that rear
Their plumes to catch the breeze,
The slightest breeze from the unfreshening west,
Partake the general languor, and deep rest.

Happy, as man may be,
Stretch'd on his back, in homely bean-vine bower,
While the voluptuous bee
Robs each surrounding flower,
And prattling childhood clambers o'er his breast,
The husbandman enjoys his noonday rest.

Against the hazy sky
The thin and fleecy clouds, unmoving, rest.
Beneath them far, yet high
In the dim, distant west,
The vulture, scenting thence its carrion-fare,
Sails, slowly circling in the sunny air.

Soberly, in the shade,
Repose the patient cow, and toil-worn ox;
Or in the shoal stream wade,
Shelter'd by jutting rocks:
The fleecy flock, fly-scourged and restless, rush
Madly from fence to fence, from bush to bush.

Tediously pass the hours,
And vegetation wilts, with blister'd root,
And droop the thirsting flowers,
Where the slant sunbeams shoot:
But of each tall, old tree, the lengthening line,
Slow-creeping eastward, marks the day's decline.

Faster, along the plain,
Moves now the shade, and on the meadow's edge:
The kine are forth again,
The bird flits in the hedge.
Now in the molten west sinks the hot sun.
Welcome, mild eve!—the sultry day is done.

Pleasantly comest thou,
Dew of the evening, to the crisp'd-up grass;
And the curl'd corn-blades bow,
As the light breezes pass,
That their parch'd lips may feel thee, and expand.
Thou sweet reviver of the fever'd land.

So, to the thirsting soul,
Cometh the dew of the Almighty's love;
And the scathed heart, made whole,
Turneth in joy above,
To where the spirit freely may expand,
And rove, untrammel'd, in that "better land."

SPRING VERSES.

How with the song of every bird,
  And with the scent of every flower,
Some recollection dear is stirr'd
  Of many a long-departed hour,
Whose course, though shrouded now in night,
Was traced in lines of golden light!

I know not if, when years have cast
  Their shadows on life's early dreams,
'Tis wise to touch the hope that's past,
  And re-illume its fading beams:
But, though the future hath its star,
That olden hope is dearer far.

Of all the present, much is bright;
  And in the coming years, I see
A brilliant and a cheering light,
  Which burns before me constantly;
Guiding my steps, through haze and gloom,
To where Fame's turrets proudly loom.

Yet coldly shines it on my brow;
  And in my breast it wakes to life
None of the holy feelings now,
  With which my boyhood's heart was rife:
It cannot touch that secret spring
Which erst made life so bless'd a thing.

Give me, then give me birds and flowers,
  Which are the voice and breath of Spring!
For those the songs of life's young hours
  With thrilling touch recall and sing:
And these, with their sweet breath, impart
Old tales, whose memory warms the heart

MAY.

Would that thou couldst last for aye,
Merry, ever-merry May!
Made of sun-gleams, shade, and showers,
Bursting buds, and breathing flowers;
Dripping-lock'd, and rosy-vested,
Violet-slipper'd, rainbow-crested;
Girdled with the eglantine,
Festoon'd with the dewy vine:
Merry, ever-merry May,
Would that thou couldst last for aye!

Out beneath thy morning sky
Dian's bow still hangs on high;
And in the blue depths afar
Glimmers, here and there, a star.
Diamonds robe the bending grass,
Glistening, early flowers among—
Monad's world, and fairy's glass,—
Bathing-fount for wandering sprite—
By mysterious fingers hung,
In the lone and quiet night.
Now the freshening breezes pass—
Gathering, as they steal along,
Rich perfume, and matin-song;
And quickly to destruction hurl'd
Is fairy's diamond glass, and monad's dew-drop world.
Lo! yon cloud, which hung but now
Black upon the mountain's brow,
Threatening the green earth with storm;
See! it heaves its giant form,
And, ever changing shape and hue,
Each time presenting something new,
Moves slowly up, and spreading rolls away
Towards the rich purple streaks that usher in the day;
Brightening, as it onward goes,
Until its very centre glows
With the warm, cheering light, the coming sun bestows:
As the passing Christian's soul,
Nearing the celestial goal,
Brighter and brighter grows, till God illumes the whole.

Out beneath thy noontide sky,
On a shady slope I lie,
Giving fancy ample play;
And there's not more blest than I,
One of Adam's race to-day.
Out beneath thy noontide sky!
Earth, how beautiful! how clear
Of cloud or mist the atmosphere!
What a glory greets the eye!
What a calm, or quiet stir,
Steals o'er Nature's worshipper—
Silent, yet so eloquent,
That we feel 'tis heaven-sent!
Waking thoughts, that long have slumber'd,
Passion-dimm'd and earth-encumber'd—
Bearing soul and sense away,
To revel in the perfect day
Which 'waits us, when we shall for aye
Discard this darksome dust—this prison-house of clay!

Out beneath thy evening sky,
Not a breeze that wanders by
But hath swept the green earth's bosom;
Rifling the rich grape-vine blossom,
Dallying with the simplest flower
In mossy nook and rosy bower;
To the perfumed green-house straying,
And with rich exotics playing;
Then, unsated, sweeping over
Banks of thyme, and fields of clover!
Out beneath thy evening sky,
Groups of children caper by,
Crown'd with flowers, and rush along
With joyous laugh, and shout, and song.
Flashing eye, and radiant cheek,
Spirits all unsunn'd bespeak.
They are in life's May-month hours,
And those wild bursts of joy, what are they but life's flowers?

Would that thou couldst last for aye,
Merry, ever-merry May!
Made of sun-gleams, shade, and showers,
Bursting buds, and breathing flowers;
Dripping-lock'd, and rosy-vested,
Violet-slipper'd, rainbow-crested;
Girdled with the eglantine,
Festoon'd with the dewy vine:
Merry, ever-merry May,
Would that thou couldst last for aye!

OUR EARLY DAYS.

Our early days!—How often back
We turn on life's bewildering track,
To where, o'er hill and valley, plays
The sunlight of our early days!

A boy—my truant steps were seen
Where streams were bright, and meadows green
Where flowers, in beauty and perfume,
Breathed ever of the Eden-bloom;
And birds, abroad in the free wind,
Sang, as they left the earth behind
And wing'd their joyous way above,
Of Eden-peace, and Eden-love.
That life was of the soul, as well
As of the outward visible;
And now, its streams are dry; and sere
And brown its meadows all appear;
Gone are its flowers; its bird's glad voice
But seldom bids my heart rejoice;
And, like the mist as comes the day,
Its Eden-glories roll away.

A youth—the mountain-torrent made
The music which my soul obey'd.
To shun the crowded ways of men,
And seek the old tradition'd glen,
Where, through the dim, uncertain light,
Moved many an ever-changing sprite,
Alone the splinter'd crag to dare,
While trooping shadows fill'd the air,
And quicken'd fancy many a form
Traced vaguely in the gathering storm,
To tread the forest's lone arcades,
And dream of Sherwood's peopled shades,

And Windsor's haunted "alleys green"
"Dingle" and "bosky bourn" between,
Till burst upon my raptured glance
The whole wide realm of Old Romance:
Such was the life I lived—a youth!
But vanish'd, at the touch of Truth,
And never to be known agen,
Is all that made my being then.

A man—the thirst for fame was mine,
And bow'd me at Ambition's shrine,
Among the votaries who have given
Time, health, hope, peace—and madly striven,
Ay, madly! for that which, when found,
Is oftenest but an empty sound.
And I have worshipp'd!—even yet
Mine eye is on the idol set;
But it hath found so much to be
But hollowness and mockery,
That from its worship oft it turns
To where a light intenser burns,
Before whose radiance, pure and warm,
Ambition's star must cease to charm.

Our early days!—They haunt us ever—
Bright star-gleams on life's silent river,
Which pierce the shadows, deep and dun,
That bar e'en manhood's noonday sun.

THE LABOURER.

Stand up—erect! Thou hast the form,
And likeness of thy God!—who more?
A soul as dauntless mid the storm
Of daily life, a heart as warm
And pure, as breast e'er wore.

What then?—Thou art as true a man
As moves the human mass among;
As much a part of the great plan
That with Creation's dawn began,
As any of the throng.

Who is thine enemy? the high
In station, or in wealth the chief?
The great, who coldly pass thee by,
With proud step and averted eye?
Nay! nurse not such belief.

If true unto thyself thou wast,
What were the proud one's scorn to thee?
A feather, which thou mightest cast
Aside, as idly as the blast
The light leaf from the tree.

No:—uncurb'd passions, low desires,
Absence of noble self-respect,
Death, in the breast's consuming fires,
To that high nature which aspires
Forever, till thus check'd;

These are thine enemies—thy worst;
They chain thee to thy lowly lot:
Thy labour and thy life accursed.
O, stand erect! and from them burst!
And longer suffer not!

Thou art thyself thine enemy!
The great!—what better they than thou?
As theirs, is not thy will as free?
Has God with equal favours thee
Neglected to endow?

True, wealth thou hast not—'tis but dust!
Nor place—uncertain as the wind!
But that thou hast, which, with thy crust
And water, may despise the lust
Of both—a noble mind.

With this, and passions under ban,
True faith, and holy trust in God,
Thou art the peer of any man.
Look up, then: that thy little span
Of life may be well trod!

THE MOTHERS OF THE WEST.

The mothers of our forest-land!
Stout-hearted dames were they
With nerve to wield the battle-brand,
And join the border-fray.
Our rough land had no braver,
In its days of blood and strife—
Aye ready for severest toil,
Aye free to peril life.

The mothers of our forest-land!
On old Kentucky's soil
How shared they, with each dauntless band,
War's tempest and life's toil!
They shrank not from the foeman—
They quail'd not in the fight—
But cheer'd their husbands through the day,
And soothed them through the night.

The mothers of our forest-land!
Their bosoms pillow'd men!
And proud were they by such to stand,
In hammock, fort, or glen,
To load the sure, old rifle—
To run the leaden ball—
To watch a battling husband's place,
And fill it, should he fall:

The mothers of our forest-land!
Such were their daily deeds.
Their monument!—where does it stand?
Their epitaph!—who reads?
No braver dames had Sparta,
No nobler matrons Rome—
Yet who or lauds or honours them,
E'en in their own green home?

The mothers of our forest-land!
They sleep in unknown graves:
And had they borne and nursed a band
Of ingrates, or of slaves,
They had not been more neglected!
But their graves shall yet be found,
And their monuments dot here and there
"The Dark and Bloody Ground."

Oliver Wendell Holmes

OLIVER WENDELL HOLMES.

[Born, 1809.]

Oliver Wendell Holmes is a son of the late Abiel Holmes, D. D., and was born at Cambridge, Massachusetts, on the twenty-ninth day of August, 1809. He received his early education at the Phillips Exeter Academy, and entered Harvard University in 1825. On being graduated he commenced the study of the law, but relinquished it, after one year's application, for the more congenial pursuit of medicine, to which he devoted himself with ardour and industry. For the more successful prosecution of his studies, he visited Europe in the spring of 1833, passing the principal portion of his residence abroad at Paris, where he attended the hospitals, acquired an intimate knowledge of the language, and became personally acquainted with many of the most eminent physicians of France.

He returned to Boston near the close of 1835, and in the following spring commenced the practice of medicine in that city. In the autumn of the same year he delivered a poem before the Phi Beta Kappa Society of Harvard University, which was received with extraordinary and merited applause. In 1838 he was elected Professor of Anatomy and Physiology in the medical institution connected with Dartmouth College, but resigned the place on his marriage, two years afterward. Devoting all his attention to his profession, he soon acquired a large and lucrative practice, and in 1847 he succeeded Dr. Warren as Professor of Anatomy in the medical department of Harvard University. His principal medical writings are comprised in his "Boylston Prize Essays," "Lectures on Popular Delusions in Medicine," and the "Theory and Practice," by himself and Dr. Bigelow. His other compositions in prose consist of occasional addresses, and papers in the North American Review.

The earlier poems of Dr. Holmes appeared in "The Collegian."* They were little less distinguished for correct and melodious versification than his more recent and most elaborate productions. They attracted attention by their humour and originality, and were widely republished in the periodicals. But a small portion of them have been printed under his proper signature.

In 1831 a small volume appeared in Boston, entitled "Illustrations of the Athenæum Gallery of Paintings," and composed of metrical pieces, chiefly satirical, written by Dr. Holmes and Epes Sargent. It embraced many of our author's best humorous verses, afterward printed among his acknowledged works. His "Poetry, a Metrical Essay," was delivered before a literary society at Cambridge. It is in the heroic measure, and in its versification it is not surpassed by any poem written in this country. It relates to the nature and offices of poetry, and is itself a series of brilliant illustrations of the ideas of which it is an expression. Of the universality of the poetical feeling he says:—

> There breathes no being but has some pretence
> To that fine instinct call'd poetic sense;
> The rudest savage, roaming through the wild,
> The simplest rustic, bending o'er his child,
> The infant, listening to the warbling bird,
> The mother, smiling at its half-formed word;
> The freeman, casting with unpurchased hand
> The vote that shakes the turrets of the land;
> The slave, who, slumbering on his rusted chain,
> Dreams of the palm-trees on his burning plain;
> The hot-cheek'd reveller, tossing down the wine,
> To join the chorus pealing "Auld lang syne;"
> The gentle maid, whose azure eye grows dim,
> While Heaven is listening to her evening hymn;
> The jewell'd beauty, when her steps draw near
> The circling dance and dazzling chandelier;
> E'en trembling age, when spring's renewing air
> Waves the thin ringlets of his silver'd hair—
> All, all are glowing with the inward flame,
> Whose wider halo wreathes the poet's name,
> While, unembalm'd, the silent dreamer dies,
> His memory passing with his smiles and sighs!

The poet, he contends, is

> He, whose thoughts differing not in shape, but dress
> What others feel, more fitly can express.

In another part of the essay is the following fine description of the different English measures:

> Poets, like painters, their machinery claim.
> And verse bestows the varnish and the frame;
> Our grating English, whose Teutonic jar
> Shakes the rack'd axle of Art's rattling car,
> Fits like Mosaic in the lines that gird
> Fast in its place each many-angled word;
> From Saxon lips Anacreon's numbers glide,
> As once they melted on the Teian tide,
> And, fresh transfused, the Iliad thrills again
> From Albion's cliffs as o'er Achaia's plain;
> The proud heroic, with its pulse-like beat,
> Rings like the cymbals, clashing as they meet;
> The sweet Spenserian, gathering as it flows,
> Sweeps gently onward to its dying close,
> Where waves on waves in long succession pour,
> Till the ninth billow melts along the shore;
> The lonely spirit of the mournful lay,
> Which lives immortal in the verse of Gray,
> In sable plumage slowly drifts along,
> On eagle pinion, through the air of song;
> The glittering lyric bounds elastic by,
> With flashing ringlets and exulting eye,
> While every image, in her airy whirl,
> Gleams like a diamond on a dancing girl!

In 1843 Dr. Holmes published "Terpsichore," a poem read at the annual dinner of the Phi Beta Kappa Society in that year; and in 1846, "Urania, a Rhymed Lesson," pronounced before the

* "The Collegian" was a monthly miscellany published in 1830, by the undergraduates at Cambridge. Among the editors were Holmes, the late William H. Simmons, who will be remembered for his admirable lectures on the poets and orators of England, and John O Sargent, who has distinguished himself as a lawyer and as a political writer.

Mercantile Library Association. The last is a collection of brilliant thoughts, with many local allusions, in compact but flowing and harmonious versification, and is the longest poem Dr. HOLMES has published since the appearance of his "Metrical Essay" in 1835.

Dr. HOLMES is a poet of wit and humour and genial sentiment, with a style remarkable for its purity, terseness, and point, and for an exquisite finish and grace. His lyrics ring and sparkle like cataracts of silver, and his serious pieces—as successful in their way as those mirthful frolics of his muse for which he is best known—arrest the attention by touches of the most genuine pathos and tenderness. All his poems illustrate a manly feeling, and have in them a current of good sense the more charming because somewhat out of fashion now in works of imagination and fancy.

ON LENDING A PUNCH-BOWL.

THIS ancient silver bowl of mine—it tells of good old times—
Of joyous days, and jolly nights, and merry Christmas chimes;
They were a free and jovial race, but honest, brave, and true,
That dipp'd their ladle in the punch when this old bowl was new.

A Spanish galleon brought the bar—so runs the ancient tale;
'T was hammer'd by an Antwerp smith, whose arm was like a flail;
And now and then between the strokes, for fear his strength should fail,
He wiped his brow, and quaff'd a cup of good old Flemish ale.

'T was purchased by an English squire to please his loving dame,
Who saw the cherubs, and conceived a longing for the same;
And oft, as on the ancient stock another twig was found,
'T was fill'd with caudle spiced and hot, and handed smoking round.

But, changing hands, it reach'd at length a Puritan divine,
Who used to follow Timothy, and take a little wine,
But hated punch and prelacy; and so it was, perhaps,
He went to Leyden, where he found conventicles and schnaps.

And then, of course, you know what's next: it left the Dutchman's shore
With those that in the May-Flower came—a hundred souls and more—
Along with all the furniture, to fill their new abodes—
To judge by what is still on hand, at least a hundred loads.

'T was on a dreary winter's eve, the night was closing dim,
When old MILES STANDISH took the bowl, and fill'd it to the brim;
The little captain stood and stirr'd the posset with his sword,
And all his sturdy men-at-arms were ranged about the board.

He pour'd the fiery Hollands in—the man that never fear'd—
He took a long and solemn draught, and wiped his yellow beard:
And one by one the musketeers—the men that fought and pray'd—
All drank as 't were their mother's milk, and not a man afraid.

That night, affrighted from his nest, the screaming eagle flew:
He heard the Pequot's ringing whoop, the soldier's wild halloo;
And there the sachem learn'd the rule he taught to kith and kin:
"Run from the white man when you find he smells of Hollands gin!"

A hundred years, and fifty more, had spread their leaves and snows,
A thousand rubs had flatten'd down each little cherub's nose;
When once again the bowl was fill'd, but not in mirth or joy—
'T was mingled by a mother's hand to cheer her parting boy.

"Drink, JOHN," she said, "'t will do you good; poor child, you'll never bear
This working in the dismal trench, out in the midnight air;
And if—God bless me—you were hurt, 't would keep away the chill."
So JOHN *did* drink—and well he wrought that night at Bunker's hill!

I tell you, there was generous warmth in good old English cheer;
I tell you, 't was a pleasant thought to drink its symbol here.
'T is but the fool that loves excess: hast thou a drunken soul?
Thy bane is in thy shallow skull—not in my silver bowl!

I love the memory of the past—its press'd yet fragrant flowers—
The moss that clothes its broken walls, the ivy on its towers—
Nay, this poor bauble it bequeath'd: my eyes grow moist and dim,
To think of all the vanish'd joys that danced around its brim.

Then fill a fair and honest cup, and bear it straight to me;
The goblet hallows all it holds, whate'er the liquid be;
And may the cherubs on its face protect me from the sin
That dooms one to those dreadful words—"My dear, where *have* you been?"

LEXINGTON.

SLOWLY the mist o'er the meadow was creeping,
Bright on the dewy buds glisten'd the sun,
When from his couch—while his children were sleeping—
Rose the bold rebel and shoulder'd his gun.
Waving her golden veil
Over the silent dale,
Blithe look'd the morning on cottage and spire;
Hush'd was his parting sigh,
While from his noble eye
Flash'd the last sparkle of Liberty's fire.

On the smooth green where the fresh leaf is springing
Calmly the first-born of glory have met:
Hark! the death-volley around them is ringing—
Look! with their life-blood the young grass is wet.
Faint is the feeble breath,
Murmuring low in death—
"Tell to our sons how their fathers have died;"
Nerveless the iron hand,
Raised for its native land,
Lies by the weapon that gleams at its side.

Over the hillsides the wild knell is tolling,
From their far hamlets the yeomanry come;
As thro' the storm-clouds the thunder-burst rolling,
Circles the beat of the mustering drum.
Fast on the soldier's path
Darken the waves of wrath;
Long have they gather'd, and loud shall they fall:
Red glares the musket's flash,
Sharp rings the rifle's crash,
Blazing and clanging from thicket and wall.

Gayly the plume of the horseman was dancing,
Never to shadow his cold brow again;
Proudly at morning the war-steed was prancing,
Reeking and panting he droops on the rein;
Pale is the lip of scorn,
Voiceless the trumpet-horn
Torn is the silken-fring'd red cross on high;
Many a belted breast
Low on the turf shall rest,
Ere the dark hunters the herd have pass'd by.

Snow-girdled crags where the hoarse wind is raving,
Rocks where the weary floods murmur and wail,
Wilds where the fern by the furrow is waving,
Reel'd with the echoes that rode on the gale;
Far as the tempest thrills
Over the darken'd hills,
Far as the sunshine streams over the plain,
Roused by the tyrant band,
Woke all the mighty land,
Girded for battle, from mountain to main.

Green be the graves where her martyrs are lying!
Shroudless and tombless they sunk to their rest;
While o'er their ashes the starry fold flying,
Wraps the proud eagle they roused from his nest.
Borne on her northern pine,
Long o'er the foaming brine
Spread her broad banner to storm and to sun;
Heaven keep her ever free
Wide as o'er land and sea
Floats the fair emblem her heroes have won!

A SONG OF OTHER DAYS.

As o'er the glacier's frozen sheet
Breathes soft the Alpine rose,
So, through life's desert springing sweet,
The flower of friendship grows;
And as, where'er the roses grow,
Some rain or dew descends,
'T is Nature's law that wine should flow
To wet the lips of friends.
Then once again, before we part,
My empty glass shall ring;
And he that has the warmest heart
Shall loudest laugh and sing.

They say we were not born to eat,
But gray-haired sages think
It means—"Be moderate in your meat,
And partly live to drink."
For baser tribes the rivers flow
That know not wine or song;
Man wants but little drink below,
But wants that little strong.
Then once again, &c.

If one bright drop is like the gem
That decks a monarch's crown,
One goblet holds a diadem
Of rubies melted down!
A fig for CÆSAR's blazing brow,
But, like the Egyptian queen,
Bid each dissolving jewel glow
My thirsty lips between.
Then once again, &c.

The Grecian's mound, the Roman's urn,
Are silent when we call,
Yet still the purple grapes return
To cluster on the wall;
It was a bright Immortal's head
They circled with the vine,
And o'er their best and bravest dead
They pour'd the dark-red wine.
Then once again, &c.

Methinks o'er every sparkling glass
Young EROS waves his wings,
And echoes o'er its dimples pass
From dead ANACREON's strings;
And, tossing round its beaded brim
Their locks of floating gold,
With bacchant dance and choral hymn
Return the nymphs of old.
Then once again, &c.

A welcome, then, to joy and mirth,
From hearts as fresh as ours,
To scatter o'er the dust of earth
Their sweetly mingled flowers;
'T is Wisdom self the cup that fills,
In spite of Folly's frown;
And Nature, from her vine-clad hills,
That rains her life-blood down!
Then once again, before we part,
My empty glass shall ring;
And he that has the warmest heart
Shall loudest laugh and sing.

THE CAMBRIDGE CHURCHYARD.

Our ancient church! its lowly tower,
Beneath the loftier spire,
Is shadow'd when the sunset hour
Clothes the tall shaft in fire;
It sinks beyond the distant eye,
Long ere the glittering vane,
High wheeling in the western sky,
Has faded o'er the plain.

Like sentinel and nun, they keep
Their vigil on the green;
One seems to guard, and one to weep,
The dead that lie between;
And both roll out, so full and near,
Their music's mingling waves,
They shake the grass, whose pennon'd spear
Leans on the narrow graves.

The stranger parts the flaunting weeds,
Whose seeds the winds have strown
So thick beneath the line he reads,
They shade the sculptured stone;
The child unveils his cluster'd brow,
And ponders for a while
The graven willow's pendent bough,
Or rudest cherub's smile.

But what to them the dirge, the knell?
These were the mourner's share;
The sullen clang, whose heavy swell
Throbb'd through the beating air;
The rattling cord,—the rolling stone,—
The shelving sand that slid,
And, far beneath, with hollow tone
Rung on the coffin's lid.

The slumberer's mound grows fresh and green,
Then slowly disappears;
The mosses creep, the gray stones lean,
Earth hides his date and years;
But, long before the once-loved name
Is sunk or worn away,
No lip the silent dust may claim,
That press'd the breathing clay.

Go where the ancient pathway guides,
See where our sires laid down
Their smiling babes, their cherish'd brides,
The patriarchs of the town;
Hast thou a tear for buried love?
A sigh for transient power?
All that a century left above,
Go, read it in an hour!

The Indian's shaft, the Briton's ball,
The sabre's thirsting edge,
The hot shell, shattering in its fall,
The bayonet's rending wedge,—
Here scatter'd death; yet seek the spot,
No trace thine eye can see,
No altar,—and they need it not
Who leave their children free!

Look where the turbid rain-drops stand
In many a chisell'd square,
The knightly crest, the shield, the brand
Of honour'd names were there;
Alas! for every tear is dried
Those blazon'd tablets knew,
Save when the icy marble's side
Drips with the evening dew.

Or gaze upon yon pillar'd stone,*
The empty urn of pride;
There stands the goblet and the sun,—
What need of more beside?
Where lives the memory of the dead?
Who made their tomb a toy?
Whose ashes press that nameless bed?
Go, ask the village boy!

Lean o'er the slender western wall,
Ye ever-roaming girls;
The breath that bids the blossom fall
May lift your floating curls,
To sweep the simple lines that tell
An exile's† date and doom;
And sigh, for where his daughters dwell,
They wreathe the stranger's tomb.

And one amid these shades was born,
Beneath this turf who lies,
Once beaming as the summer's morn,
That closed her gentle eyes;
If sinless angels love as we,
Who stood thy grave beside,
Three seraph welcomes waited thee,
The daughter, sister, bride!

I wander'd to thy buried mound,
When earth was hid, below
The level of the glaring ground,
Choked to its gates with snow,
And when with summer's flowery waves
The lake of verdure roll'd,
As if a sultan's white-robed slaves
Had scatter'd pearls and gold.

Nay, the soft pinions of the air,
That lifts this trembling tone,
Its breath of love may almost bear,
To kiss thy funeral-stone;
And, now thy smiles have pass'd away,
For all the joy they gave,
May sweetest dews and warmest ray
Lie on thine early grave!

When damps beneath, and storms above,
Have bow'd these fragile towers,
Still o'er the graves yon locust-grove
Shall swing its orient flowers;
And I would ask no mouldering bust,
If o'er this humble line,
Which breathed a sigh o'er other's dust,
Might call a tear on mine.

---

* The tomb of the VASSALL family is marked by a free stone tablet, supported by five pillars, and bearing nothing but the sculptured reliefs of the goblet and the sun,—*Vas-Sol*,—which designated a powerful family, now almost forgotten.

† The exile referred to in this stanza was a native of Honfleur, in Normandy.

AN EVENING THOUGHT.

WRITTEN AT SEA.

If sometimes in the dark-blue eye,
Or in the deep-red wine,
Or soothed by gentlest melody,
Still warms this heart of mine,
Yet something colder in the blood,
And calmer in the brain,
Have whisper'd that my youth's bright flood
Ebbs, not to flow again.

If by Helvetia's azure lake,
Or Arno's yellow stream,
Each star of memory could awake,
As in my first young dream,
I know that when mine eye shall greet
The hill-sides bleak and bare,
That gird my home, it will not meet
My childhood's sunsets there.

O, when love's first, sweet, stolen kiss
Burn'd on my boyish brow,
Was that young forehead worn as this?
Was that flush'd cheek as now?
Where that wild pulse and throbbing heart
Like these, which vainly strive,
In thankless strains of soulless art,
To dream themselves alive?

Alas! the morning dew is gone,
Gone ere the full of day;
Life's iron fetter still is on,
Its wreaths all torn away;
Happy if still some casual hour
Can warm the fading shrine,
Too soon to chill beyond the power
Of love, or song, or wine!

LA GRISETTE.

Ah, Clemence! when I saw thee last
Trip down the Rue de Seine,
And turning, when thy form had pass'd
I said, "We meet again,"—
I dream'd not in that idle glance
Thy latest image came,
And only left to memory's trance
A shadow and a name.

The few strange words my lips had taught
Thy timid voice to speak;
Their gentler sighs, which often brought
Fresh roses to thy cheek;
The trailing of thy long, loose hair
Bent o'er my couch of pain,
All, all return'd, more sweet, more fair;
O, had we met again!

I walk'd where saint and virgin keep
The vigil lights of Heaven,
I knew that thou hadst woes to weep,
And sins to be forgiven;
I watch'd where Genevieve was laid,
I knelt by Mary's shrine,
Beside me low, soft voices pray'd;
Alas! but where was thine?

And when the morning sun was bright,
When wind and wave were calm,
And flamed, in thousand-tinted light,
The rose* of Notre Dame,
I wander'd through the haunts of men,
From Boulevard to Quai,
Till, frowning o'er Saint Etienne,
The Pantheon's shadow lay.

In vain, in vain; we meet no more,
Nor dream what fates befall;
And long upon the stranger's shore
My voice on thee may call,
When years have clothed the line in moss
That tells thy name and days,
And wither'd, on thy simple cross,
The wreaths of Pere-la-Chaise!

THE TREADMILL SONG.

The stars are rolling in the sky,
The earth rolls on below,
And we can feel the rattling wheel
Revolving as we go.
Then tread away, my gallant boys,
And make the axle fly;
Why should not wheels go round about
Like planets in the sky?

Wake up, wake up, my duck-legg'd man,
And stir your solid pegs;
Arouse, arouse, my gawky friend,
And shake your spider-legs;
What though you're awkward at the trade!
There's time enough to learn,—
So lean upon the rail, my lad,
And take another turn.

They've built us up a noble wall,
To keep the vulgar out;
We've nothing in the world to do,
But just to walk about;
So faster, now, you middle men,
And try to beat the ends:—
It's pleasant work to ramble round
Among one's honest friends.

Here, tread upon the long man's toes,
He sha'n't be lazy here;
And punch the little fellow's ribs,
And tweak that lubber's ear;
He's lost them both; don't pull his hair,
Because he wears a scratch,
But poke him in the farther eye,
That isn't in the patch.

Hark! fellows, there's the supper-bell,
And so our work is done;
It's pretty sport,—suppose we take
A round or two for fun!
If ever they should turn me out,
When I have better grown,
Now, hang me, but I mean to have
A treadmill of my own!

* Circular-stained windows are called roses

DEPARTED DAYS.

Yes, dear, departed, cherish'd days,
Could Memory's hand restore
Your morning light, your evening rays,
From Time's gray urn once more,—
Then might this restless heart be still,
This straining eye might close,
And Hope her fainting pinions fold,
While the fair phantoms rose.

But, like a child in ocean's arms,
We strive against the stream,
Each moment farther from the shore,
Where life's young fountains gleam —
Each moment fainter wave the fields,
And wilder rolls the sea;
The mist grows dark—the sun goes down—
Day breaks—and where are we!

THE DILEMMA.

Now, by the bless'd Paphian queen,
Who heaves the breast of sweet sixteen;
By every name I cut on bark
Before my morning-star grew dark;
By Hymen's torch, by Cupid's dart,
By all that thrills the beating heart;
The bright, black eye, the melting blue,—
I cannot choose between the two.

I had a vision in my dreams;
I saw a row of twenty beams;
From every beam a rope was hung,
In every rope a lover swung.
I ask'd the hue of every eye
That bade each luckless lover die;
Ten livid lips said, heavenly blue,
And ten accused the darker hue.

I ask'd a matron, which she deem'd
With fairest light of beauty beam'd;
She answer'd, some thought both were fair—
Give her blue eyes and golden hair.
I might have liked her judgment well,
But as she spoke, she rung the bell,
And all her girls, nor small nor few,
Came marching in—their eyes were blue.

I ask'd a maiden; back she flung
The locks that round her forehead hung,
And turn'd her eye, a glorious one,
Bright as a diamond in the sun,
On me, until, beneath its rays,
I felt as if my hair would blaze;
She liked all eyes but eyes of green;
She look'd at me; what could she mean?

Ah! many lids Love lurks between,
Nor heeds the colouring of his screen;
And when his random arrows fly,
The victim falls, but knows not why.
Gaze not upon his shield of jet,
The shaft upon the string is set;
Look not beneath his azure veil,
Though every limb were cased in mail.

Well, both might make a martyr break
The chain that bound him to the stake,
And both, with but a single ray,
Can melt our very hearts away;
And both, when balanced, hardly seem
To stir the scales, or rock the beam;
But that is dearest, all the while,
That wears for us the sweetest smile.

THE STAR AND THE WATER-LILY.

The Sun stepp'd down from his golden throne,
And lay in the silent sea,
And the Lily had folded her satin leaves
For a sleepy thing was she;
What is the Lily dreaming of?
Why crisp the waters blue?
See, see, she is lifting her varnish'd lid!
Her white leaves are glistening through!

The Rose is cooling his burning cheek
In the lap of the breathless tide;
The Lily hath sisters fresh and fair,
That would lie by the Rose's side;
He would love her better than all the rest,
And he would be fond and true;
But the Lily unfolded her weary lids,
And look'd at the sky so blue.

Remember, remember, thou silly one,
How fast will thy summer glide,
And wilt thou wither a virgin pale,
Or flourish a blooming bride?
"O, the Rose is old, and thorny, and cold,
And he lives on earth," said she;
"But the Star is fair and he lives in the air,
And he shall my bridegroom be."

But what if the stormy cloud should come,
And ruffle the silver sea?
Would he turn his eye from the distant sky,
To smile on a thing like thee?
O, no! fair Lily, he will not send
One ray from his far-off throne;
The winds shall blow and the waves shall flow
And thou wilt be left alone.

There is not a leaf on the mountain-top,
Nor a drop of evening dew,
Nor a golden sand on the sparkling shore,
Nor a pearl in the waters blue,
That he has not cheer'd with his fickle smile,
And warm'd with his faithless beam,—
And will he be true to a pallid flower,
That floats on the quiet stream?

Alas, for the Lily! she would not heed,
But turn'd to the skies afar,
And bared her breast to the trembling ray
That shot from the rising star;
The cloud came over the darken'd sky,
And over the waters wide,
She look'd in vain through the beating rain
And sank in the stormy tide.

THE MUSIC-GRINDERS.

There are three ways in which men take
One's money from his purse,
And very hard it is to tell
Which of the three is worse;
But all of them are bad enough
To make a body curse.

You're riding out some pleasant day,
And counting up your gains;
A fellow jumps from out a bush
And takes your horse's reins,
Another hints some words about
A bullet in your brains.

It's hard to meet such pressing friends
In such a lonely spot;
It's very hard to lose your cash,
But harder to be shot;
And so you take your wallet out,
Though you would rather not.

Perhaps you're going out to dine,—
Some filthy creature begs
You'll hear about the cannon-ball
That carried off his pegs,
And says it is a dreadful thing
For men to lose their legs.

He tells you of his starving wife,
His children to be fed,
Poor, little, lovely innocents,
All clamorous for bread,—
And so you kindly help to put
A bachelor to bed.

You're sitting on your window-seat
Beneath a cloudless moon;
You hear a sound, that seems to wear
The semblance of a tune,
As if a broken fife should strive
To drown a crack'd bassoon.

And nearer, nearer still, the tide
Of music seems to come,
There's something like a human voice,
And something like a drum;
You sit, in speechless agony,
Until your ear is numb.

Poor "Home, sweet home" should seem to be
A very dismal place;
Your "Auld acquaintance," all at once,
Is alter'd in the face;
Their discords sting through Burns and Moore,
Like hedgehogs dress'd in lace.

You think they are crusaders, sent
From some infernal clime,
To pluck the eyes of Sentiment,
And dock the tail of Rhyme,
To crack the voice of Melody,
And break the legs of Time.

But, hark! the air again is still,
The music all is ground,
And silence, like a poultice, comes
To heal the blows of sound;
It cannot be,—it is,—it is,—
A hat is going round!

No! Pay the dentist when he leaves
A fracture in your jaw,
And pay the owner of the bear,
That stunn'd you with his paw,
And buy the lobster, that has had
Your knuckles in his claw;

But if you are a portly man,
Put on your fiercest frown,
And talk about a constable
To turn them out of town;
Then close your sentence with an oath,
And shut the window down!

And if you are a slender man,
Not big enough for that,
Or, if you cannot make a speech,
Because you are a flat,
Go very quietly and drop
A button in the hat!

THE PHILOSOPHER TO HIS LOVE

Dearest, a look is but a ray
Reflected in a certain way;
A word, whatever tone it wear,
Is but a trembling wave of air;
A touch, obedience to a clause
In nature's pure material laws.

The very flowers that bend and meet,
In sweetening others, grow more sweet;
The clouds by day, the stars by night,
Inweave their floating locks of light;
The rainbow, Heaven's own forehead's braid,
Is but the embrace of sun and shade.

How few that love us have we found!
How wide the world that girds them round!
Like mountain-streams we meet and part,
Each living in the other's heart,
Our course unknown, our hope to be
Yet mingled in the distant sea.

But ocean coils and heaves in vain,
Bound in the subtle moonbeam's chain;
And love and hope do but obey
Some cold, capricious planet's ray,
Which lights and leads the tide it charms,
To Death's dark caves and icy arms.

Alas! one narrow line is drawn,
That links our sunset with our dawn;
In mist and shade life's morning rose,
And clouds are round it at its close;
But, ah! no twilight beam ascends
To whisper where that evening ends.

O! in the hour when I shall feel
Those shadows round my senses steal,
When gentle eyes are weeping o'er
The clay that feels their tears no more
Then let thy spirit with me be,
Or some sweet angel, likest thee!

L'INCONNUE.

Is thy name MARY, maiden fair?
  Such should, methinks, its music be;
The sweetest name that mortals bear,
  Were best befitting thee;
And she to whom it once was given,
Was half of earth and half of heaven.

I hear thy voice, I see thy smile,
  I look upon thy folded hair;
Ah! while we dream not they beguile,
  Our hearts are in the snare;
And she, who chains a wild bird's wing,
Must start not if her captive sing.

So, lady, take the leaf that falls,
  To all but thee unseen, unknown;
When evening shades thy silent walls,
  Then read it all alone;
In stillness read, in darkness seal,
Forget, despise, but not reveal!

THE LAST READER.

I SOMETIMES sit beneath a tree,
  And read my own sweet songs;
Though naught they may to others be,
  Each humble line prolongs
A tone that might have pass'd away,
But for that scarce-remember'd lay.

I keep them like a lock or leaf,
  That some dear girl has given;
Frail record of an hour, as brief
  As sunset clouds in heaven,
But spreading purple twilight still
High over memory's shadow'd hill.

They lie upon my pathway bleak,
  Those flowers that once ran wild,
As on a father's care-worn cheek
  The ringlets of his child;
The golden mingling with the gray,
And stealing half its snows away.

What care I though the dust is spread
  Around these yellow leaves,
Or o'er them his sarcastic thread
  Oblivion's insect weaves;
Though weeds are tangled on the stream,
It still reflects my morning's beam.

And therefore love I such as smile
  On these neglected songs,
Nor deem that flattery's needless wile
  My opening bosom wrongs;
For who would trample, at my side,
A few pale buds, my garden's pride?

It may be that my scanty ore
  Long years have wash'd away,
And where were golden sands before,
  Is naught but common clay;
Still something sparkles in the sun,
For Memory to look back upon.

And when my name no more is heard,
  My lyre no more is known,
Still let me, like a winter's bird,
  In silence and alone,
Fold over them the weary wing
Once flashing through the dews of spring.

Yes, let my fancy fondly wrap
  My youth in its decline,
And riot in the rosy lap
  Of thoughts that once were mine,
And give the worm my little store,
When the last reader reads no more!

THE LAST LEAF.

I SAW him once before,
As he pass'd by the door,
    And again
The pavement-stones resound
As he totters o'er the ground
    With his cane.

They say that in his prime,
Ere the pruning-knife of Time
    Cut him down,
Not a better man was found
By the crier on his round
    Through the town.

But now he walks the streets,
And he looks at all he meets
    So forlorn;
And he shakes his feeble head,
That it seems as if he said,
    "They are gone."

The mossy marbles rest
On the lips that he has press'd
    In their bloom,
And the names he loved to hear
Have been carved for many a year
    On the tomb.

My grandmamma has said—
Poor old lady! she is dead
    Long ago—
That he had a Roman nose,
And his cheek was like a rose
    In the snow.

And now his nose is thin,
And it rests upon his chin
    Like a staff,
And a crook is in his back,
And a melancholy crack
    In his laugh.

I know it is a sin
For me to sit and grin
    At him here,
But the old three-corner'd hat,
And the breeches—and all that
    Are so queer!

And if I should live to be
The last leaf upon the tree
    In the spring—
Let them smile as I do now
At the old forsaken bough
    Where I cling.

OLD IRONSIDES.*

Ay, tear her tatter'd ensign down!
Long has it waved on high,
And many an eye has danced to see
That banner in the sky;
Beneath it rung the battle-shout,
And burst the cannon's roar;
The meteor of the ocean air
Shall sweep the clouds no more!

Her deck, once red with heroes' blood,
Where knelt the vanquish'd foe,
When winds were hurrying o'er the flood,
And waves were white below,
No more shall feel the victor's tread,
Or know the conquer'd knee;
The harpies of the shore shall pluck
The eagle of the sea!

O, better that her shatter'd hulk
Should sink beneath the wave;
Her thunders shook the mighty deep,
And there should be her grave;
Nail to the mast her holy flag,
Set every threadbare sail,
And give her to the god of storms,—
The lightning and the gale!

STANZAS.

Strange! that one lightly-whisper'd tone
Is far, far sweeter unto me,
Than all the sounds that kiss the earth,
Or breathe along the sea;
But, lady, when thy voice I greet,
Not heavenly music seems so sweet.

I look upon the fair, blue skies,
And naught but empty air I see;
But when I turn me to thine eyes,
It seemeth unto me
Ten thousand angels spread their wings
Within those little azure rings.

The lily hath the softest leaf
That ever western breeze hath fann'd,
But thou shalt have the tender flower,
So I may take thy hand;
That little hand to me doth yield
More joy than all the broider'd field.

O, lady! there be many things
That seem right fair, below, above;
But sure not one among them all
Is half so sweet as love;—
Let us not pay our vows alone,
But join two altars both in one.

* Written when it was proposed to break up the frigate Constitution, as unfit for service.

THE STEAMBOAT.

See how yon flaming herald treads
The ridged and rolling waves,
As, crashing o'er their crested heads,
She bows her surly slaves!
With foam before and fire behind,
She rends the clinging sea,
That flies before the roaring wind,
Beneath her hissing lee.

The morning spray, like sea-born flowers
With heap'd and glistening bells,
Falls round her fast in ringing showers,
With every wave that swells;
And, flaming o'er the midnight deep,
In lurid fringes thrown,
The living gems of ocean sweep
Along her flashing zone.

With clashing wheel, and lifting keel,
And smoking torch on high,
When winds are loud, and billows reel,
She thunders foaming by!
When seas are silent and serene,
With even beam she glides,
The sunshine glimmering through the green
That skirts her gleaming sides.

Now, like a wild nymph, far apart
She veils her shadowy form,
The beating of her restless heart
Still sounding through the storm;
Now answers, like a courtly dame,
The reddening surges o'er,
With flying scarf of spangled flame,
The Pharos of the shore.

To-night yon pilot shall not sleep,
Who trims his narrow'd sail;
To-night yon frigate scarce shall keep
Her broad breast to the gale;
And many a foresail, scoop'd and strain'd,
Shall break from yard and stay,
Before this smoky wreath has stain'd
The rising mist of day.

Hark! hark! I hear yon whistling shroud,
I see yon quivering mast;
The black throat of the hunted cloud
Is panting forth the blast!
An hour, and, whirl'd like winnowing chaff,
The giant surge shall fling
His tresses o'er yon pennon-staff,
White as the sea-bird's wing!

Yet rest, ye wanderers of the deep;
Nor wind nor wave shall tire
Those fleshless arms, whose pulses leap
With floods of living fire;
Sleep on—and when the morning light
Streams o'er the shining bay,
O, think of those for whom the night
Shall never wake in day!

B. B. THATCHER.

(Born, 1809. Died, 1840.)

Benjamin Bussey Thatcher was born in Warren, Maine, on the eighth of October, 1809; entered Bowdoin College, two years in advance, at the age of fifteen, and was graduated bachelor of arts, in 1826. He afterward studied the law, but on being admitted to the bar, finding the duties of the profession too arduous for his delicate constitution, devoted himself to literature, and besides writing much and ably for several periodicals, produced two works on the aborigines of this country, "Indian Biography," and "Indian Traits," which had a wide and well-deserved popularity. In 1836 he went to England, where he remained about two years, writing industriously meanwhile for British and American reviews, and for two or three journals in Boston and New York as a correspondent. He returned in 1838, still struggling with disease, but with a spirit unbroken, and labored with unfaltering assiduity until near th time of his death, which occurred on the fourteenth of July, 1840, when he was in the thirty-first year of his age. He left an account of his residence abroad, which has not been published; nor has there been any collection of his numerous reviews, essays, and poems, many of which are creditable to his abilities, taste, and character.

THE BIRD OF THE BASTILE.*

Come to my breast, thou lone
And weary bird!—one tone,
Of the rare music of my childhood! Dear
Is that strange sound to me;
Dear is the memory
It brings my soul of many a parted year!

Again, yet once again,
O minstrel of the main!
Lo! festal face, and form familiar, throng
Unto my waking eye;
And voices of the sky
Sing, from these walls of death, unwonted song.

Nay, cease not: I would call
Thus, from the silent hall
Of the unlighted grave, the joys of old:
Beam on me yet once more,
Ye blessed eyes of yore,
Starting life blood through all my being cold.

Ah! cease not; phantoms fair
Fill thick the dungeon's air;
They wave me from its gloom; I fly—I stand
Again upon that spot,
Which ne'er hath been forgot
In all time's tears, my own green, glorious land!

There, on each noon-bright hill,
By fount and flashing rill,
Slowly the faint flocks sought the breezy shade;
There gleamed the sunset's fire,
On the tall tapering spire,
And windows low, along the upland glade.

Sing, sing!—I do not dream—
It is my own blue stream,
I see far down where white walls fleck the vale;—
I know it by the hedge
Of rose-trees at its edge,
Vaunting their crimson beauty to the gale:

There, there, 'mid clustering leaves,
Glimmer my father's eaves,
And the worn threshold of my youth beneath;—
I know them by the moss,
And the old elms that toss
Their lithe arms up where winds the smoke's gray wreath.

Sing, sing!—I am not mad—
Sing! that the visions glad
May smile that smiled, and speak that spake but now;
Sing, sing!—I might have knelt
And prayed; I might have felt
Their breath upon my bosom and my brow.

I might have pressed to this
Cold bosom, in my bliss,
Each long-lost form that ancient hearth beside;
O heaven! I might have heard,
From living lips, one word,
Thou mother of my childhood! and have died.

Nay, nay, 'tis sweet to weep,
Ere yet in death I sleep;
It minds me I have been, and am again,—
And the world wakes around
It breaks the madness, bound,
While I have dreamed, these ages on my brain.

And sweet it is to love
Even this gentle dove,
This breathing thing from all life else apart:—
Ah! leave me not the gloom
Of my eternal tomb
To bear alone—alone! Come to my heart,

My bird!—*Thou* shalt go free
And come, oh come to me
Again, when from the hills the spring-gale blows;
So shall I learn, at least,
One other year hath ceased—
That the long wo throbs lingering to its close.

* One prisoner I saw there, who had been imprisoned from his youth, and was said to be occasionally insane in consequence. He enjoyed no companionship (the keeper told me) but that of a beautiful tamed bird. Of what name or clime it was, I know not—only that he called it fondly, *his dove*, and seemed never happy but when it sang to him.—*MS. of a Tour through France.*

ALBERT PIKE.

[Born, 1809.]

Albert Pike was born in Boston, on the twenty-ninth day of December, 1809. When he was about four years old, his parents removed to Newburyport. His father, he informs me, "was a journeyman shoemaker, who worked hard, paid his taxes, and gave all his children the benefit of an education." The youth of the poet was passed principally in attending the district-schools at Newburyport, and an academy at Framingham, until he was sixteen years of age, when, after a rigid and triumphant examination, he was admitted to Harvard College. Not being able to pay the expenses of a residence at Cambridge, however, he soon after became an assistant teacher in the grammar-school at Newburyport, and, at the end of a year, its principal. He was induced to resign this office after a short time, and in the winter which followed was the preceptor of an academy at Fairhaven. He returned to Newburyport in the spring, on foot, and for one year taught there a private school. During all this time he had been a diligent student, intending to enter the university, *in advance;* but in the spring of 1831 he changed his plans, and started on his travels to the west and south.

He went first to Niagara, and then, through Cleveland, Cincinnati, Nashville, and Paducah, much of the way on foot, to Saint Louis. He left that city in August, with a company of forty persons, among whom were two young men besides himself from Newburyport, for Mexico; and after much fatigue and privation, arrived at Santa Fe on the twenty-eighth of November. Here he remained nearly a year, passing a part of the time as a clerk in a store, and the residue in selling merchandise through the country. Near the close of September, 1832, he left Taos, with a trapping-party; travelled around the sources of Red River to the head waters of the Brazos; separated from the company, with four others, and came into Arkansas,—travelling the last five hundred miles on foot, and reaching Fort Smith, in November, "without a rag of clothing, a dollar in money, or knowing a person in the territory."

Near this place he spent the winter in teaching a few children, and in the following July he went further down the country, and opened a school under more favourable auspices; but after a few weeks, being attacked by a fever, was compelled to abandon it. He had in the mean time written several poems for a newspaper printed at Little Rock, which pleased the editor so much that he sent for him to go there and become his partner. The proposition was gladly accepted, and in October he crossed the Arkansas and landed at Little Rock, paying his last cent for the ferriage of a poor old soldier, who had known his father in New England.

Here commenced a new era in the life of Pike. From this time his efforts appear to have been crowned with success. The "Arkansas Advocate" was edited by him until the autumn of 1834, when it became his property. Soon after his arrival at his new home he began to devote his leisure to the study of the law, and he was now admitted to the bar. He continued both to write for his paper and to practise in the courts, until the summer of 1836, when he sold his printing establishment; and since then he has successfully pursued his profession. He was married at Little Rock, in November, 1834.

About this time he published at Boston a volume of prose sketches and poems, among which are an interesting account of his journeys over the prairies, and some fine poetry, written at Santa Fe and among the mountains and forests of Mexico. In the preface to it, he says: "What I have written has been a transcript of my own feelings—too much so, perhaps, for the purposes of fame. Writing has always been to me a communion with my own soul. These poems were composed in desertion and loneliness, and sometimes in places of fear and danger. My only sources of thought and imagery have been my own mind, and Nature, who has appeared to me generally in desolate guise and utter dreariness, and not unfrequently in sublimity."

His "Hymns to the Gods," published afterward, were composed at an early age, in Fairhaven, and principally while he was surrounded by pupils, in the school-room. They are bold, spirited, scholarly and imaginative, and their diction is appropriate and poetical, though in some instances marred by imperfect and double rhymes. Of his minor pieces, "Spring" and "To the Mocking-bird," are the best. I have heard praise bestowed on "Ariel," a poem much longer than these, published in 1835, but as it appeared in a periodical which had but a brief existence, I have not been able to obtain a copy of it. In "Fantasma," in which, I suppose, he intended to shadow forth his own "eventful history," he speaks of one who

"Was young,
And had not known the bent of his own mind,
Until the mighty spell of Coleridge woke
Its hidden powers,"

and in some of his poems there is a cast of thought similar to that which pervades many of the works of this poet, though nothing that amounts to imitation. His early struggles, and subsequent wanderings and observations furnished him with the subjects, thoughts, and imagery of many of his pieces, and they therefore leave on the mind an impression of nature and truth.

In 1854 Mr. Pike printed in Philadelphia a collection of his poems, under the title of "Nugæ," for his friends. It was not published.

HYMNS TO THE GODS.

NO. I.—TO NEPTUNE.

God of the mighty deep! wherever now
The waves beneath thy brazen axles bow—
Whether thy strong, proud steeds, wind-wing'd
and wild,
Trample the storm-vex'd waters round them piled,
Swift as the lightning-flashes, that reveal
The quick gyrations of each brazen wheel;
While round and under thee, with hideous roar,
The broad Atlantic, with thy scourging sore,
Thundering, like antique Chaos in his spasms,
In heaving mountains and deep-yawning chasms,
Fluctuates endlessly; while, through the gloom,
Their glossy sides and thick manes fleck'd with foam,
Career thy steeds, neighing with frantic glee
In fierce response to the tumultuous sea,—
Whether thy coursers now career below,
Where, amid storm-wrecks, hoary sea-plants grow,
Broad-leaved, and fanning with a ceaseless motion
The pale, cold tenants of the abysmal ocean—
O, come! our altars waiting for thee stand,
Smoking with incense on the level strand!

Perhaps thou lettest now thy horses roam
Upon some quiet plain; no wind-toss'd foam
Is now upon their limbs, but leisurely
They tread with silver feet the sleeping sea,
Fanning the waves with slowly-floating manes,
Like mist in sunlight; haply, silver strains
From clamorous trumpets round thy chariot ring,
And green-robed sea-gods unto thee, their king,
Chant, loud in praise: APOLLO now doth gaze
With loving looks upon thee, and his rays
Light up thy steeds' wild eyes: a pleasant warmth
Is felt upon the sea, where fierce, cold storm
Has just been rushing, and the noisy winds,
That ÆOLUS now within their prison binds,
Flying with misty wings: perhaps, below
Thou liest in green caves, where bright things glow
With myriad colours—many a monster cumbers
The sand a-near thee, while old TRITON slumbers
As idly as his wont, and bright eyes peep
Upon thee every way, as thou dost sleep.

Perhaps thou liest on some Indian isle,
Under a waving tree, where many a mile
Stretches a sunny shore, with golden sands
Heap'd up in many shapes by naiads' hands,
And, blushing as the waves come rippling on,
Shaking the sunlight from them as they run
And curl upon the beach—like molten gold
Thick-set with jewellery most rare and old—
And sea-nymphs sit, and, with small, delicate shells,
Make thee sweet melody: as in deep dells
We hear, of summer nights, by fairies made,
The while they dance within some quiet shade,
Sounding their silver flutes most low and sweet,
In strange but beautiful tunes, that their light feet
May dance upon the bright and misty dew
In better time: all wanton airs that blew
But lately over spice trees, now are here,
Waving their wings, all odour-laden, near
The bright and laughing sea. O, wilt thou rise,
And come with them to our new sacrifice!

NO. II.—TO APOLLO.

Bright-hair'd APOLLO!—thou who ever art
A blessing to the world—whose mighty heart
Forever pours out love, and light, and life:
Thou, at whose glance all things of earth are rife
With happiness; to whom, in early spring,
Bright flowers raise up their heads, where'er they [cling
On the steep mountain-side, or in the vale
Are nestled calmly. Thou at whom the pale
And weary earth looks up, when winter flees,
With patient gaze: thou for whom wind-stripp'd trees
Put on fresh leaves, and drink deep of the light
That glitters in thine eye: thou in whose bright
And hottest rays the eagle fills his eye
With quenchless fire, and far, far up on high
Screams out his joy to thee: by all the names
That thou dost bear—whether thy godhead claims
PHŒBUS, or SOL, or golden-hair'd APOLLO,
Cynthian or Pythian—if thou dost follow
The fleeing night, O, hear
Our hymn to thee, and smilingly draw near!

O, most high poet! thou whose great heart's swell
Pours itself out on mountain and deep dell:
Thou who dost touch them with thy golden feet,
And make them for a poet's theme most meet:
Thou who dost make the poet's eye perceive
Great beauty everywhere—in the slow heave
Of the unquiet sea, or in the war
Of its unnumber'd waters; on the shore
Of pleasant streams, upon the jagged cliff
Of savage mountain, where the black clouds drift
Full of strange lightning; or upon the brow
Of silent night, that solemnly and slow
Comes on the earth; O, thou! whose influence
Touches all things with beauty, makes each sense
Double delight, tinges with thine own heart
Each thing thou meetest; thou who ever art
Living in beauty—nay, who art, in truth,
Beauty imbodied—hear, while all our youth
With earnest calling cry!
Answer our hymn, and come to us, most high!

O, thou! who strikest oft thy golden lyre
In strange disguise, and with a wondrous fire
Sweepest its strings upon the sunny glade,
While dances to thee many a village maid,
Decking her hair with wild flowers, or a wreath
Of thine own laurel, while, reclined beneath
Some ancient oak, with smiles at thy good heart,
As though thou wert of this our world a part.
Thou lookest on them in the darkening wood,
While fauns come forth, and, with their dances rude
Flit round among the trees with merry leap,
Like their god, PAN; and from fir thickets deep
Come up the satyrs, joining the wild crew,
And capering for thy pleasure: from each yew,
And oak, and beech, the wood-nymphs oft peep out
To see the revelry, while merry shout
And noisy laughter rings about the wood,
And thy lyre cheers the darken'd solitude—
O, come! while we do sound
Our flutes and pleasant-pealing lyres around!

O, most high prophet!—thou that showest men
Deep-hidden knowledge: thou that from its den

Bringest futurity, that it comes by
In visible shape, passing before the eye
Shrouded in visions: thou in whose high power
Are health and sickness: thou who oft dost shower
Great plagues upon the nations, with hot breath
Scorching away their souls, and sending death
Like fiery mist amid them; or again,
Like the sweet breeze that comes with summer rain,
Touching the soul with joy, thou sendest out
Bright health among the people, who about
With dewy feet and fanning wings doth step,
And touch each poor, pale cheek with startling lip,
Filling it with rich blood, that leaps anew
Out from the shrivell'd heart, and courses through
The long-forsaken veins!—O, thou, whose name
Is sung by all, let us, too, dare to claim
Thy holy presence here!
Hear us, bright god, and come in beauty near!

O, thou, the lover of the springing bow!
Who ever in the gloomy woods dost throw
Thine arrows to the mark, like the keen flight
Of those thine arrows that with midday light
Thou proudly pointest; thou from whom grim bears
And lordly lions flee, with strange, wild fears,
And hide among the mountains: thou whose cry
Sounds often in the woods, where whirl and fly
The time-worn leaves—when, with a merry train,
BACCHUS is on the hills, and on the plain
The full-arm'd CERES—when upon the sea
The brine-gods sound their horns, and merrily
The whole earth rings with pleasure: then thy voice
Stills into silence every stirring noise,
With utmost sweetness pealing on the hills,
And in the echo of the dancing rills,
And o'er the sea, and on the busy plain,
And on the air, until all voices wane
Before its influence—
O, come, great god, be ever our defence!

By that most gloomy day, when with a cry
Young HYACINTH fell down, and his dark eye
Was fill'd with dimming blood—when on a bed
Of his own flowers he laid his wounded head,
Breathing deep sighs; by those heart-cherish'd eyes
Of long-loved HYACINTH—by all the sighs
That thou, O, young APOLLO, then didst pour
On every gloomy hill and desolate shore,
Weeping at thy great soul, and making dull
Thy ever-quenchless eye, till men were full
Of strange forebodings for thy lustre dimm'd,
And many a chant in many a fane was hymn'd
Unto the pale-eyed sun; the satyrs stay'd
Long time in the dull woods, then on the glade
They came and look'd for thee; and all in vain
Poor DIAN sought thy love, and did complain
For want of light and life;—by all thy grief,
O, bright APOLLO! hear, and give relief
To us who cry to thee—
O, come, and let us now thy glory see!

NO. III.—TO VENUS.

O, thou, most lovely and most beautiful!
Whether thy doves now lovingly do lull
Thy bright eyes to soft slumbering upon
Some dreamy south wind: whether thou hast gone
Upon the heaven now, or if thou art
Within some floating cloud, and on its heart
Pourest rich-tinted joy; whether thy wheels
Are touching on the sun-forsaken fields,
And brushing off the dew from bending grass,
Leaving the poor green blades to look, alas!
With dim eyes at the moon—(ah! so dost thou
Full oft quench brightness!)—VENUS, whether now
Thou passest o'er the sea, while each light wing
Of thy fair doves is wet, while sea-maids bring
Sweet odours for thee—(ah! how foolish they!
They have not felt thy smart!)—
They know not, while in ocean-caves they play,
How strong thou art.

Where'er thou art, O, VENUS! hear our song—
Kind goddess, hear! for unto thee belong
All pleasant offerings: bright doves coo to thee,
The while they twine their necks with quiet glee
Among the morning leaves; thine are all sounds
Of pleasure on the earth; and where abounds
Most happiness, for thee we ever look;
Among the leaves, in dimly-lighted nook,
Most often hidest thou, where winds may wave
Thy sunny curls, and cool airs fondly lave
Thy beaming brow, and ruffle the white wings
Of thy tired doves; and where his love-song sings,
With lightsome eyes, some little, strange, sweet bird,
With notes that never but by thee are heard—
O, in such scene, most bright, thou liest now
And, with half-open eye,
Drinkest in beauty—O, most fair, that thou
Wouldst hear our cry!

O, thou, through whom all things upon the earth
Grow brighter: thou for whom even laughing mirth
Lengthens his note; thou whom the joyous bird
Singeth continuously; whose name is heard
In every pleasant sound: at whose warm glance
All things look brighter: for whom wine doth dance
More merrily within the brimming vase,
To meet thy lip: thou, at whose quiet pace
Joy leaps on faster, with a louder laugh,
And Sorrow tosses to the sea his staff,
And pushes back the hair from his dim eyes,
To look again upon forgotten skies;
While Avarice forgets to count his gold,
Yea, unto thee his wither'd hand doth hold,
Fill'd with that heart-blood: thou, to whose high might
All things are made to bow,
Come thou to us, and turn thy looks of light
Upon us now!

O, hear, great goddess! thou whom all obey;
At whose desire rough satyrs leave their play,
And gather wild-flowers, decking the bright hair
Of her they love, and oft blackberries bear
To shame them at her eyes: O, thou! to whom,
They leap in awkward mood, within the gloom
Of darkening oak trees, or at lightsome noon
Sing unto thee, upon their pipes, a tune
Of wondrous languishment: thou whose great power
Brings up the sea-maids from each ocean-bower,
With many an idle song, to sing to thee,
And bright locks flowing half above the sea,

And gleaming eyes, as if in distant caves
They spied their lovers—(so among the waves
Small bubbles flit, mocking the kindly sun,
With little, laughing brightness)—
O, come, and ere our festival be done,
Our new loves bless!

O, thou who once didst weep, and with sad tears
Bedew the pitying woods!—by those great fears
That haunted thee when thy beloved lay
With dark eyes drown'd in death—by that dull day
When poor ADONIS fell, with many a moan,
Among the leaves, and sadly and alone
Breathed out his spirit—O, do thou look on
All maidens who, for too great love, grow wan,
And pity them: come to us when night brings
Her first faint stars, and let us hear the wings
Of thy most beauteous and bright-eyed doves
Stirring the breathless air; let all thy loves
Be flying round thy car, with pleasant songs
Moving upon their lips: come! each maid longs
For thy fair presence—goddess of rich love!
Come on the odorous air;
And, as thy light wheels roll, from us remove
All love-sick care!

Lo, we have many kinds of incense here
To offer thee, and sunny wine and clear,
Fit for young BACCHUS: flowers we have here too,
That we have gather'd when the morning dew
Was moist upon them; myrtle-wreaths we bear,
To place upon thy bright, luxuriant hair,
And shade thy temples too; 'tis now the time
Of all fair beauty: thou who lovest the clime
Of our dear Cyprus, where sweet flowers blow
With honey in their cups, and with a glow
Like thine own cheek, raising their modest heads
To be refresh'd with the transparent beads
Of silver dew: behold, this April night,
Our altars burn for thee; lo, on the light
We pour out incense from each golden vase;
O, goddess, hear our words!
And hither turn, with thine own matchless grace,
Thy white-wing'd birds.

NO. IV.—TO DIANA.

Most graceful goddess!—whether now thou art
Hunting the dun deer in the silent heart
Of some old, quiet wood, or on the side
Of some high mountain, and, most eager-eyed,
Dashing upon the chase, with bended bow
And arrow at the string, and with a glow
Of wondrous beauty on thy cheek, and feet
Like thine own silver moon—yea, and as fleet
As her best beams—and quiver at the back,
Rattling to all thy steppings; if some track
In distant Thessaly thou followest up,
Brushing the dews from many a flower-cup
And quiet leaf, and listening to the bay
Of thy good hounds, while in the deep woods they,
Strong-limb'd and swift, leap on with eager bounds,
And with their long, deep note each hill resounds,
Making thee music:—goddess, hear our cry,
And let us worship thee, while far and high
Goes up thy brother—while his light is full
Upon the earth, for, when the night-winds lull
The world to sleep, then to the lightless sky
DIAN must go, with silver robes of dew,
And sunward eye.

Perhaps thou liest on some shady spot
Among the trees, while frighten'd beasts hear not
The deep bay of thy hounds; but, dropping down
Upon green grass, and leaves all sere and brown,
Thou pillowest thy delicate head upon
Some ancient mossy root, where wood-winds run
Wildly about thee, and thy fair nymphs point
Thy death-wing'd arrows, or thy hair anoint
With Lydian odours, and thy strong hounds lie
Lazily on the earth, and watch thine eye,
And watch thine arrows, while thou hast a dream.
Perchance, in some deep-bosom'd, shaded stream
Thou bathest now, where even thy brother sun
Cannot look on thee—where dark shades and dun
Fall on the water, making it most cool,
Like winds from the broad sea, or like some pool
In deep, dark cavern: hanging branches dip
Their locks into the stream, or slowly drip
With tear-drops of rich dew: before no eyes
But those of flitting wind-gods, each nymph hies
Into the deep, cool, running stream, and there
Thou pillowest thyself upon its breast,
O queen, most fair!

By all thine hours of pleasure—when thou wast
Upon tall Latmos, moveless, still, and lost
In boundless pleasure, ever gazing on
Thy bright-eyed youth, whether the unseen sun
Was lighting the deep sea, or at mid-noon
Careering through the sky—by every tune
And voice of joy that thrill'd about the chords
Of thy deep heart, when thou didst hear his words
In that cool, shady grot, where thou hadst brought
And placed ENDYMION; where fair hands had taught
All beauty to shine forth; where thy fair maids
Had brought up shells for thee, and from the glades
All sunny flowers, with precious stones and gems
Of utmost beauty, pearly diadems
Of many sea-gods; birds were there, that sang
Ever most sweetly; living waters rang
Their changes to all time, to soothe the soul
Of thy ENDYMION; pleasant breezes stole
With light feet through the cave, that they might
His dewy lips;—O, by those hours of bliss [kiss
That thou didst then enjoy, come to us, fair
And beautiful DIANA—take us now
Under thy care!

NO. IV.—TO MERCURY.

O, winged messenger! if thy light feet
Are in the star-paved halls where high gods meet,
Where the rich nectar thou dost take and sip
At idly-pleasant leisure, while thy lip
Utters rich eloquence, until thy foe,
JUNO herself, doth her long hate forego,
And hangs upon thine accents; VENUS smiles,
And aims her looks at thee with winning wiles;
And wise MINERVA's cup stands idly by
The while thou speakest! Whether up on high
Thou wing'st thy way—or dost but now unfurl
Thy pinions like the eagle, while a whirl

Of air takes place about thee—if thy wings
Are over the broad sea, where Afric flings
His hot breath on the waters; by the shore
Of Araby the blest, or in the roar
Of crashing northern ice—O, turn, and urge
Thy winged course to us! Leave the rough surge,
Or icy mountain-height, or city proud,
Or haughty temple, or dim wood down bow'd
With weaken'd age,
And come to us, thou young and mighty sage!

Thou who invisibly dost ever stand
Nea. each high orator; and, hand in hand
With the gold-robed Apollo, touch the tongue
Of every poet; on whom men have hung
With strange enchantment, when in dark disguise
Thou hast descended from cloud-curtain'd skies,
And lifted up thy voice, to teach bold men
Thy world-arousing art: O, thou! that, when
The ocean was untrack'd, didst teach them send
Great ships upon it: thou who dost extend
In storm a calm protection to the hopes
Of the fair merchant: thou who on the slopes
Of Mount Cyllene first madest sound the lyre
And many-toned harp with childish fire,
And thine own beauty sounding in the caves
A strange, new tune, unlike the ruder staves
That PAN had utter'd—while each wondering nymph
Came out from tree and mountain, and pure lymph
Of mountain-stream, to drink each rolling note
That o'er the listening woods did run and float
With fine, clear tone,
Like silver trumpets o'er still waters blown:

O, matchless artist! thou of wondrous skill,
Who didst in ages past the wide earth fill
With every usefulness: thou who dost teach
Quick-witted thieves the miser's gold to reach,
And rob him of his sleep for many a night,
Getting thee curses: O, mischievous sprite!
Thou Rogue-god MERCURY! ever glad to cheat
All gods and men; with mute and noiseless feet
Going in search of mischief; now to steal
The fiery spear of MARS, now clog the wheel
Of bright APOLLO's car, that it may crawl
Most slowly upward: thou whom wrestlers call,
Whether they strive upon the level green
At dewy nightfall, under the dim screen
Of ancient oak, or at the sacred games
In fierce contest: thou whom each then names
In half-thought prayer, when the quick breath is drawn
For the last struggle: thou whom on the lawn
The victor praises, making unto thee
Offering for his proud honours—let us be
Under thy care:
O, winged messenger, hear, hear our prayer!

NO. VI.—TO BACCHUS.

Where art thou, BACCHUS? On the vine-spread hills
Of some rich country, where the red wine fills
The cluster'd grapes—staining thy lips all red
With generous liquor—pouring on thy head
The odorous wine, and ever holding up
Unto the smiling sun thy brimming cup,
And filling it with light? Or doth thy car,
Under the blaze of the far northern star,
Roll over Thracia's hills, while all around
Are shouting Bacchanals, and every sound
Of merry revelry, while distant men
Start at thy noisings? Or in shady glen
Reclinest thou, beneath green ivy leaves,
And idlest off the day, while each Faun weaves
Green garlands for thee, sipping the rich bowl
That thou hast given him—while the loud roll
Of thy all-conquering wheels is heard no more,
And thy strong tigers have lain down before
Thy grape-stain'd feet!
O, BACCHUS! come and meet
Thy worshippers, the while, with merry lore
Of ancient song, thy godhead they do greet!

O, thou who lovest pleasure! at whose heart
Rich wine is always felt; who hast a part
In all air-swelling mirth; who in the dance
Of merry maidens join'st, where the glance
Of bright black eyes, or white and twinkling feet
Of joyous fair ones, doth thy quick eyes greet
Upon some summer-green: Maker of joy
To all care-troubled men! who dost destroy
The piercing pangs of grief; for whom the maids
Weave ivy garlands, and in pleasant glades
Hang up thy image, and with beaming looks
Go dancing round, while shepherds with their crooks
Join the glad company, and pass about,
With merry laugh and many a gleesome shout,
Staining with rich, dark grapes each little cheek
They most do love; and then, with sudden freak,
Taking the willing hand, and dancing on
About the green mound: O, thou merry son
Of lofty JOVE!
Where thou dost rove
Among the grape-vines, come, ere day is done,
And let us too thy sunny influence prove!

Where art thou, conqueror? before whom fell
The jewell'd kings of Ind, when the strong swell
Of thy great multitudes came on them, and
Thou hadst thy thyrsus in thy red, right hand,
Shaking it over them, till every soul
Grew faint as with wild lightning; when the roll
Of thy great chariot-wheels was on the neck
Of many a conqueror, when thou didst check
Thy tigers and thy lynxes at the shore
Of the broad ocean, and didst still the roar,
Pouring a sparkling and most pleasant wine
Into its waters; when the dashing brine
Toss'd up new odours, and a pleasant scent
Upon its breath, and many who were spent
With weary sickness, breathed of life anew,
When wine-inspired breezes on them blew;—
BACCHUS! who bringest all men to thy feet!
Wine-god! with brow of light, and smiles most sweet!
Make this our earth
A sharer in thy mirth—
Let us rejoice thy wine-dew'd hair to greet.
And chant to thee, who gavest young loy his birth.

Come to our ceremony! lo, we rear
An altar of bright turf unto thee here.

And crown it with the vine and pleasant leaf
Of clinging ivy: Come, and drive sad Grief
Far from us! lo, we pour thy turf upon
Full cups of wine, bidding the westering sun
Fill the good air with odour; see, a mist
Is rising from the sun-touch'd wine!—(ah! hist!—
Alas! 't was not his cry!)—with all thy train
Of laughing Satyrs, pouring out a strain
Of utmost shrillness on the noisy pipe—
O, come!—with eye and lip of beauty, ripe
And wondrous rare—O! let us hear thy wheels
Coming upon the hills, while twilight steals
Upon us quietly—while the dark night
Is hinder'd from her course by the fierce light
Of thy wild tigers' eyes;—O! let us see
The revelry of thy wild company,
With all thy train;
And, ere night comes again,
We'll pass o'er many a hill and vale with thee,
Raising to thee a loudly-joyous strain.

NO. VII.—TO SOMNUS.

O, thou, the leaden-eyed! with drooping lid
Hanging upon thy sight, and eye half-hid
By matted hair: that, with a constant train
Of empty dreams, all shadowless and vain
As the dim wind, dost sleep in thy dark cave
With poppies at the mouth, which night-winds wave,
Sending their breathings downward—on thy bed,
Thine only throne, with darkness overspread,
And curtains black as are the eyes of night:
Thou, who dost come at time of waning light
And sleep among the woods, where night doth hide
And tremble at the sun, and shadows glide
Among the waving tree-tops; if now there
Thou sleepest in a current of cool air,
Within some nook, amid thick flowers and moss,
Gray-colour'd as thine eyes, while thy dreams toss
Their fantasies about the silent earth,
In waywardness of mirth—
O, come! and hear the hymn that we are chanting
Amid the star-light through the thick leaves slanting.

Thou lover of the banks of idle streams
O'ershaded by broad oaks, with scatter'd gleams
From the few stars upon them; of the shore
Of the broad sea, with silence hovering o'er;
The great moon hanging out her lamps to gild
The murmuring waves with hues all pure and mild,
Where thou dost lie upon the sounding sands,
While winds come dancing on from southern lands
With dreams upon their backs, and unseen waves
Of odours in their hands: thou, in the caves
Of the star-lighted clouds, on summer eves
Reclining lazily, while Silence leaves
Her influence about thee: in the sea
That liest, hearing the monotony
Of waves far-off above thee, like the wings
Of passing dreams, while the great ocean swings
His bulk above thy sand-supported head—
(As chain'd upon his bed
Some giant, with an idleness of motion
So swings the still and sleep-enthrall'd ocean.)

Thou who dost bless the weary with thy touch,
And makest Agony relax his clutch
Upon the bleeding fibres of the heart;
Pale Disappointment lose her constant smart,
And Sorrow dry her tears, and cease to weep
Her life away, and gain new cheer in sleep·
Thou who dost bless the birds, in every place
Where they have sung their songs with wondrous grace
Throughout the day, and now, with drooping wing,
Amid the leaves receive thy welcoming:—
Come with thy crowd of dreams, O, thou! to whom
All noise is most abhorr'd, and in this gloom,
Beneath the shaded brightness of the sky,
Where are no sounds but as the winds go by,—
Here touch our eyes, great SOMNUS! with thy wand;
Ah! here thou art, with touch most mild and bland,
And we forget our hymn, and sink away
And here, until broad day
Come up into the sky, with fire-steeds leaping,
Will we recline, beneath the vine-leaves sleeping.

NO. VIII.—TO CERES.

Goddess of bounty! at whose spring-time call,
When on the dewy earth thy first tones fall,
Pierces the ground each young and tender blade,
And wonders at the sun; each dull, gray glade
Is shining with new grass; from each chill hole,
Where they had lain enchain'd and dull of soul,
The birds come forth, and sing for joy to thee
Among the springing leaves; and, fast and free,
The rivers toss their chains up to the sun,
And through their grassy banks leapingly run,
When thou hast touch'd them: thou who ever art
The goddess of all beauty: thou whose heart
Is ever in the sunny meads and fields;
To whom the laughing earth looks up and yields
Her waving treasures: thou that in thy car,
With winged dragons, when the morning star
Sheds his cold light, touchest the morning trees
Until they spread their blossoms to the breeze;—
O, pour thy light
Of truth and joy upon our souls this night,
And grant to us all plenty and good ease!

O, thou, the goddess of the rustling corn!
Thou to whom reapers sing, and on the lawn
Pile up their baskets with the full-ear'd wheat;
While maidens come, with little dancing feet,
And bring thee poppies, weaving thee a crown
Of simple beauty, bending their heads down
To garland thy full baskets: at whose side,
Among the sheaves of wheat, doth BACCHUS ride
With bright and sparkling eyes, and feet and mouth
All wine-stain'd from the warm and sunny south:
Perhaps one arm about thy neck he twines,
While in his car ye ride among the vines,
And with the other hand he gathers up
The rich, full grapes, and holds the glowing cup
Unto thy lips—and then he throws it by,
And crowns thee with bright leaves to shade thine eye,
So it may gaze with richer love and light
Upon his beaming brow: If thy swift flight
Be on some hill
Of vine-hung Thrace—O, come, while night is still,
And greet with heaping arms our gladden'd sight!

Lo! the small stars, above the silver wave,
Come wandering up the sky, and kindly lave
The thin clouds with their light, like floating sparks
Of diamonds in the air; or spirit barks,
With unseen riders, wheeling in the sky.
Lo! a soft mist of light is rising high,
Like silver shining through a tint of red,
And soon the queened moon her love will shed,
Like pearl-mist, on the earth and on the sea,
Where thou shalt cross to view our mystery.
Lo! we have torches here for thee, and urns,
Where incense with a floating odour burns,
And altars piled with various fruits and flowers,
And ears of corn, gather'd at early hours,
And odours fresh from India, with a heap
Of many-colour'd poppies:—Lo! we keep
Our silent watch for thee, sitting before
Thy ready altars, till to our lone shore
  Thy chariot wheels
Shall come, while ocean to the burden reels,
And utters to the sky a stifled roar.

TO THE PLANET JUPITER.

Thou art, in truth, a fair and kingly star,
Planet! whose silver crest now gleams afar
Upon the edge of yonder eastern hill,
That, night-like, seems a third of heaven to fill.
Thou art most worthy of a poet's lore,
His worship—as a thing to bend before;
And yet thou smilest as if I might sing,
Weak as I am—my lyre unused to ring
Among the thousand harps which fill the world.
The sun's last fire upon the sky has curl'd,
And on the clouds, and now thou hast arisen,
And in the east thine eye of love doth glisten—
Thou, whom the ancients took to be a king,
And that of gods; and, as thou wert a spring
Of inspiration, I would soar and drink,
While yet thou art upon the mountain's brink.
Who bid men say that thou, O silver peer,
Wast to the moon a servitor, anear
To sit, and watch her eye for messages,
Like to the other fair and silver bees
That swarm around her when she sits her throne?
What of the moon? She bringeth storm alone,
At new, and full, and every other time: [rhyme,
She turns men's brains, and so she makes them
And rave, and sigh away their weary life;
And shall she be of young adorers rife,
And thou have none? Nay, one will sing to thee,
And turn his eye to thee, and bend the knee.
Lo! on the marge of the dim western plain,
The star of love doth even yet remain—
She of the ocean-foam—and watch thy look,
As one might gaze upon an antique book,
When he doth sit and read, at deep, dead night,
Stealing from Time his hours. Ah, sweet delay!
And now she sinks to follow fleeting day,
Contented with thy glance of answering love:
And where she worships can I thoughtless prove?
Now as thou risest higher into sight,
Marking the water with a line of light,
On wave and ripple quietly aslant,
Thy influences steal upon the heart,
With a sweet force and unresisted art,
Like the still growth of some unceasing plant.
The mother, watching by her sleeping child,
Blesses thee, when thy light, so still and mild,
Falls through the casement on her babe's pale face,
And tinges it with a benignant grace,
Like the white shadow of an angel's wing.
The sick man, who has lain for many a day,
And wasted like a lightless flower away,
He blesses thee, O JOVE! when thou dost shine
Upon his face, with influence divine,
Soothing his thin, blue eyelids into sleep.
The child its constant murmuring will keep,
Within the nurse's arms, till thou dost glad
His eyes, and then he sleeps. The thin, and sad,
And patient student closes up his books
A space or so, to gain from thy kind looks
Refreshment. Men, in dungeons pent,
Climb to the window, and, with head upbent,
Gaze they at thee. The timid deer awake,
And, 'neath thine eye, their nightly rambles make,
Whistling their joy to thee. The speckled trout
From underneath his rock comes shooting out,
And turns his eye to thee, and loves thy light,
And sleeps within it. The gray water plant
Looks up to thee beseechingly aslant,
And thou dost feed it there, beneath the wave.
Even the tortoise crawls from out his cave,
And feeds wherever, on the dewy grass,
Thy light hath linger'd. Thou canst even pass
To water-depths, and make the coral-fly
Work happier, when flatter'd by thine eye.
Thou touchest not the roughest heart in vain;
Even the sturdy sailor, and the swain,
Bless thee, whene'er they see thy lustrous eye
Open amid the clouds, stilling the sky.
The lover praises thee, and to thy light
Compares his love, thus tender and thus bright;
And tells his mistress thou dost kindly mock
Her gentle eye. Thou dost the heart unlock
Which Care and Wo have render'd comfortless
And teachest it thy influence to bless,
And even for a time its grief to brave.
The madman, that beneath the moon doth rave,
Looks to thy orb, and is again himself.
The miser stops from counting out his pelf,
When through the barred windows comes thy lull—
And even he, he thinks thee beautiful.
O! while thy silver arrows pierce the air,
And while beneath thee, the dim forests, where
The wind sleeps, and the snowy mountains tall
Are still as death—O! bring me back again
The bold and happy heart that bless'd me, when
My youth was green; ere home and hope were veil'd
In desolation! Then my cheek was paled,
But not with care. For, late at night, and long,
I toil'd, that I might gain myself among
Old tomes, a knowledge; and in truth I did:
I studied long, and things the wise had hid
In their quaint books, I learn'd; and then I thought
The poet's art was mine; and so I wrought
My boyish feelings into words, and spread
Them out before the world—and I was fed
With praise, and with a name. Alas! to him,

Whose eye and heart must soon or late grow dim,
Toiling with poverty, or evils worse,
This gift of poetry is but a curse,
Unfitting it amid the world to brood,
And toil and jostle for a livelihood.
The feverish passion of the soul hath been
My bane. O JOVE! couldst thou but wean
Me back to boyhood for a space, it were
Indeed a gift. There was a sudden stir,
Thousands of years ago, upon the sea;
The waters foam'd, and parted hastily,
As though a giant left his azure home,
And Delos woke, and did to light up come
Within that Grecian sea. LATONA had,
Till then, been wandering, listlessly and sad,
About the earth, and through the hollow vast
Of water, follow'd by the angry haste
Of furious JUNO. Many a weary day,
Above the shaggy hills where, groaning, lay
ENCELADUS and TYPHON, she had roam'd,
And over volcanoes, where fire upfoam'd;
And sometimes in the forests she had lurk'd,
Where the fierce serpent through the herbage work'd,
Over gray weeds, and tiger-trampled flowers,
And where the lion hid in tangled bowers,
And where the panther, with his dappled skin,
Made day like night with his deep moaning din:
All things were there to fright the gentle soul—
The hedgehog, that across the path did roll,
Gray eagles, fang'd like cats, old vultures, bald,
Wild hawks and restless owls, whose cry appall'd,
Black bats and speckled tortoises, that snap,
And scorpions, hiding underneath gray stones,
With here and there old piles of human bones
Of the first men that found out what was war,
Brass heads of arrows, rusted scimetar,
Old crescent, shield, and edgeless battle-axe,
And near them skulls, with wide and gaping cracks,
Too old and dry for worms to dwell within;
Only the restless spider there did spin,
And made his house. And then she down would lay
Her restless head, among dry leaves, and faint,
And close her eyes till thou wouldst come and paint
Her visage with thy light; and then the blood
Would stir again about her heart, endued,
By thy kind look, with life again, and speed;
And then wouldst thou her gentle spirit feed
With new-wing'd hopes, and sunny fantasies,
And, looking piercingly amid the trees,
Drive from her path all those unwelcome sights.
Then would she rise, and o'er the flower-blights,
And through the tiger-peopled solitudes,
And odorous brakes, and panther-guarded woods,
Would keep her way until she reach'd the edge
Of the blue sea, and then, on some high ledge
Of thunder-blacken'd rocks, would sit and look
Into thine eye, nor fear lest from some nook
Should rise the hideous shapes that JUNO ruled,
And persecute her. Once her feet she cool'd
Upon a long and narrow beach. The brine
Had mark'd, as with an endless serpent-spine,
The sanded shore with a long line of shells,
Like those the Nereids weave, within the cells
Of their queen THETIS—such they pile around
The feet of cross old NEREUS, having found
That this will gain his grace, and such they bring
To the quaint PROTEUS, as an offering,
When they would have him tell their fate, and who
Shall first embrace them with a lover's glow.
And there LATONA stepp'd along the marge
Of the slow waves, and when one came more large,
And wet her feet, she tingled, as when JOVE
Gave her the first, all-burning kiss of love.
Still on she kept, pacing along the sand,
And on the shells, and now and then would stand,
And let her long and golden hair outfloat
Upon the waves—when, lo! the sudden note
Of the fierce, hissing dragon met her ear.
She shudder'd then, and, all-possess'd with fear,
Rush'd wildly through the hollow-sounding vast
Into the deep, deep sea; and then she pass'd
Through many wonders—coral-rafter'd caves,
Deep, far below the noise of upper waves—
Sea-flowers, that floated into golden hair
Like misty silk—fishes, whose eyes did glare,
And some surpassing lovely—fleshless spine
Of old behemoths—flasks of hoarded wine
Among the timbers of old, shatter'd ships—
Goblets of gold, that had not touch'd the lips
Of men a thousand years. And then she lay
Her down, amid the ever-changing spray,
And wish'd, and begg'd to die; and then it was
That voice of thine the deities that awes,
Lifted to light beneath the Grecian skies
That rich and lustrous Delian paradise,
And placed LATONA there, while yet asleep,
With parted lip, and respiration deep,
And open palm; and when at length she woke,
She found herself beneath a shadowy oak,
Huge and majestic; from its boughs look'd out
All birds, whose timid nature 't is to doubt
And fear mankind. The dove, with patient eyes
Earnestly did his artful nest devise,
And was most busy under sheltering leaves;
The thrush, that loves to sit upon gray eaves
Amid old ivy, she, too, sang and built; [spilt
And mock-bird songs rang out like hail-showers
Among the leaves, or on the velvet grass;
The bees did all around their store amass,
Or down depended from a swinging bough,
In tangled swarms. Above her dazzling brow
The lustrous humming-bird was whirling; and,
So near, that she might reach it with her hand,
Lay a gray lizard—such do notice give
When a foul serpent comes, and they do live
By the permission of the roughest hind;
Just at her feet, with mild eyes up-inclined,
A snowy antelope cropp'd off the buds
From hanging limbs; and in the solitudes
No noise disturb'd the birds, except the dim
Voice of a fount, that, from the grassy brim,
Rain'd upon violets its liquid light,
And visible love; also, the murmur slight
Of waves, that softly sang their anthem, and
Trode gently on the soft and noiseless sand,
As gentle children in sick-chambers grieve,
And go on tiptoe. Here, at call of eve,
When thou didst rise above the barred east,
Touching with light LATONA's snowy breast
And gentler eyes, and when the happy earth

Sent up its dews to thee—then she gave birth
Unto Apollo and the lustrous Dian;
And when the wings of morn commenced to fan
The darkness from the east, afar there rose,
Within the thick and odour-dropping forests, [est,
Where moss was grayest and dim caves were hoar-
Afar there rose the known and dreadful hiss
Of the pursuing dragon. Agonies
Grew on Latona's soul; and she had fled,
And tried again the ocean's pervious bed,
Had not Apollo, young and bright Apollo,
Restrained from the dim and perilous hollow,
And ask'd what meant the noise. "It is, O child!
The hideous dragon that hath aye defiled
My peace and quiet, sent by heaven's queen
To slay her rival, me." Upon the green
And mossy grass there lay a nervous bow,
And heavy arrows, eagle-wing'd, which thou,
O Jove! hadst placed within Apollo's reach.
These grasping, the young god stood in the breach
Of circling trees, with eye that fiercely glanced,
Nostril expanded, lip press'd, foot advanced,
And arrow at the string; when, lo! the coil
Of the fierce snake came on with winding toil,
And vast gyrations, crushing down the branches,
With noise as when a hungry tiger cranches
Huge bones: and then Apollo drew his bow
Full at the eye—nor ended with one blow:
Dart after dart he hurl'd from off the string—
All at the eye—until a lifeless thing
The dragon lay. Thus the young sun-god slew
Old Juno's scaly snake: and then he threw
(So strong was he) the monster in the sea;
And sharks came round and ate voraciously,
Lashing the waters into bloody foam,
By their fierce fights. Latona, then, might roam
In earth, air, sea, or heaven, void of dread;
For even Juno badly might have sped
With her bright children, whom thou soon didst set
To rule the sun and moon, as they do yet.
Thou! who didst then their destiny control,
I here would woo thee, till into my soul
Thy light might sink. O Jove! I am full sure
None bear unto thy star a love more pure
Than I; thou hast been, everywhere, to me
A source of inspiration. I should be
Sleepless, could I not first behold thine orb
Rise in the west; then doth my heart absorb,
Like other withering flowers, thy light and life;
For that neglect, which cutteth like a knife,
I never have from thee, unless the lake
Of heaven be clouded. Planet! thou wouldst make
Me, as thou didst thine ancient worshippers,
A poet; but, alas! whatever stirs
My tongue and pen, they both are faint and weak:
Apollo hath not, in some gracious freak,
Given to me the spirit of his lyre,
Or touch'd my heart with his ethereal fire
And glorious essence: thus, whate'er I sing
Is weak and poor, and may but humbly ring
Above the waves of Time's far-booming sea.
All I can give is small; thou wilt not scorn
A heart: I give no golden sheaves of corn;
I burn to thee no rich and odorous gums;
I offer up to thee no hecatombs,
And build no altars: 't is a heart alone;
Such as it is, I give it—'t is thy own.

TO THE MOCKING-BIRD.

Thou glorious mocker of the world! I hear
Thy many voices ringing through the glooms
Of these green solitudes—and all the clear,
Bright joyance of their song enthralls the ear
And floods the heart. Over the sphered tombs
Of vanish'd nations rolls thy music tide.
No light from history's starlike page illumes
The memory of those nations—they have died.
None cares for them but thou, and thou mayst sing,
Perhaps, o'er me—as now thy song doth ring
Over their bones by whom thou once wast deified.

Thou scorner of all cities! Thou dost leave
The world's turmoil and never-ceasing din,
Where one from others no existence weaves,
Where the old sighs, the young turns gray and grieves,
Where misery gnaws the maiden's heart within:
And thou dost flee into the broad, green woods,
And with thy soul of music thou dost win
Their heart to harmony—no jar intrudes
Upon thy sounding melody. O, where,
Amid the sweet musicians of the air,
Is one so dear as thee to these old solitudes?

Ha! what a burst was that! the Æolian strain
Goes floating through the tangled passages
Of the lone woods—and now it comes again—
A multitudinous melody—like a rain
Of glossy music under echoing trees,
Over a ringing lake; it wraps the soul
With a bright harmony of happiness—
Even as a gem is wrapt, when round it roll
Their waves of brilliant flame—till we become,
E'en with the excess of our deep pleasure, dumb,
And pant like some swift runner clinging to the goal.

I would, sweet bird, that I might live with thee,
Amid the eloquent grandeur of the shades,
Alone with nature—but it may not be;
I have to struggle with the tumbling sea
Of human life, until existence fades
Into death's darkness. Thou wilt sing and soar
Through the thick woods and shadow-checker'd glades,
While naught of sorrow casts a dimness o'er
The brilliance of thy heart—but I must wear
As now, my garmenting of pain and care—
As penitents of old their galling sackcloth wore.

Yet why complain?—What though fond hopes deferr'd
Have overshadow'd Youth's green paths with gloom!
Still, joy's rich music is not all unheard,—
There is a voice sweeter than thine, sweet bird,
To welcome me, within my humble home;—
There is an eye with love's devotion bright,
The darkness of existence to illume!
Then why complain?—When death shall cast his blight
Over the spirit, then my bones shall rest
Beneath these trees—and from thy swelling breast,
O'er them thy song shall pour like a rich flood of light.

TO SPRING.

O thou delicious Spring!
Nursed in the lap of thin and subtle showers,
Which fall from clouds that lift their snowy wing
From odorous beds of light-enfolded flowers,
And from enmassed bowers,
That over grassy walks their greenness fling,
Come, gentle Spring!

Thou lover of young wind,
That cometh from the invisible upper sea
Beneath the sky, which clouds, its white foam, bind,
And, settling in the trees deliciously,
Makes young leaves dance with glee,
Even in the teeth of that old, sober hind,
Winter unkind,

Come to us; for thou art
Like the fine love of children, gentle Spring!
Touching the sacred feeling of the heart,
Or like a virgin's pleasant welcoming;
And thou dost ever bring
A tide of gentle but resistless art
Upon the heart.

Red Autumn from the south
Contends with thee; alas! what may he show?
What are his purple-stain'd and rosy mouth,
And browned cheeks, to thy soft feet of snow,
And timid, pleasant glow,
Giving earth-piercing flowers their primal growth,
And greenest youth?

Gay Summer conquers thee;
And yet he has no beauty such as thine;
What is his ever-streaming, fiery sea,
To the pure glory that with thee doth shine?
Thou season most divine,
What may his dull and lifeless minstrelsy
Compare with thee?

Come, sit upon the hills,
And bid the waking streams leap down their side,
And green the vales with their slight-sounding rills;
And when the stars upon the sky shall glide,
And crescent Dian ride,
I too will breathe of thy delicious thrills,
On grassy hills.

Alas! bright Spring, not long
Shall I enjoy thy pleasant influence;
For thou shalt die the summer heat among,
Sublimed to vapour in his fire intense,
And, gone forever hence,
Exist no more: no more to earth belong,
Except in song.

So I who sing shall die:
Worn unto death, perchance, by care and sorrow;
And, fainting thus with an unconscious sigh,
Bid unto this poor body a good-morrow,
Which now sometimes I borrow,
And breathe of joyance keener and more high,
Ceasing to sigh!

LINES WRITTEN ON THE ROCKY MOUNTAINS.

The deep, transparent sky is full
Of many thousand glittering lights—
Unnumber'd stars that calmly rule
The dark dominions of the night.
The mild, bright moon has upward risen,
Out of the gray and boundless plain,
And all around the white snows glisten,
Where frost, and ice, and silence reign,—
While ages roll away, and they unchanged remain.

These mountains, piercing the blue sky
With their eternal cones of ice;
The torrents dashing from on high,
O'er rock and crag and precipice;
Change not, but still remain as ever,
Unwasting, deathless, and sublime,
And will remain while lightnings quiver,
Or stars the hoary summits climb,
Or rolls the thunder-chariot of eternal Time.

It is not so with all—I change,
And waste as with a living death,
Like one that hath become a strange,
Unwelcome guest, and lingereth
Among the memories of the past,
Where he is a forgotten name;
For Time hath greater power to blast
The hopes, the feelings, and the fame,
To make the passions fierce, or their first strength to tame.

The wind comes rushing swift by me,
Pouring its coolness on my brow;
Such was I once—as proudly free,
And yet, alas! how alter'd now!
Yet, while I gaze upon yon plain,
These mountains, this eternal sky,
The scenes of boyhood come again,
And pass before the vacant eye,
Still wearing something of their ancient brilliancy.

Yet why complain?—for what is wrong,
False friends, cold-heartedness, deceit,
And life already made too long,
To one who walks with bleeding feet
Over its paths?—it will but make
Death sweeter when it comes at last—
And though the trampled heart may ache,
Its agony of pain is past,
And calmness gathers there, while life is ebbing fast.

Perhaps, when I have pass'd away,
Like the sad echo of a dream,
There may be some one found to say
A word that might like sorrow seem.
That I would have—one sadden'd tear,
One kindly and regretting thought—
Grant me but that!—and even here,
Here, in this lone, unpeopled spot,
To breathe away this life of pain, I murmur not

PARK BENJAMIN.

[Born 1809. Died 1864.]

The paternal ancestors of Mr. Benjamin came to New England at an early period from Wales. His father, who was a merchant, resided many years at Demerara, in British Guiana, where he acquired a large fortune. There the subject of this notice was born in the year 1809. When he was about three years old, in consequence of a severe illness he was brought to this country, under the care of a faithful female guardian, and here, except during a few brief periods, he has since resided. The improper medical treatment to which he had been subjected in Demerara prevented his complete restoration under the more skilful physicians of New England, and he has been lame from his childhood; but I believe his general health has been uniformly good for many years.

While a boy he was sent to an excellent school in the rural village of Colchester, in Connecticut. At twelve he was removed to New Haven, where he resided three years in his father's family, after which he was sent to a private boarding school near Boston, in which he remained until he entered Harvard College, in 1825. He left this venerable institution before the close of his second academic year, in consequence of a protracted and painful illness, and on his recovery entered Washington College, at Hartford, then under the presidency of the Right Reverend Thomas C. Brownell, now Bishop of Connecticut. He was graduated in 1829, with the highest honours of his class.

In 1830, Mr. Benjamin entered the Law School at Cambridge, at that time conducted by Mr. Justice Story and Professor Ashmun. He pursued his legal studies with much industry for a considerable period at this seminary, but finished the acquirement of his profession at New Haven, under Chief Justice Daggett and Professor Hitchcock. He was admitted to the Connecticut bar in 1833, and removing soon after to Boston, the residence of his relatives and friends, he was admitted to the courts of Massachusetts, as attorney and counsellor at law and solicitor in chancery.

His disposition to devote his time to literature prevented his entering upon the practice of his profession, and on the death of Edwin Buckingham, one of its original editors, I believe he became connected with the "New England Magazine." In 1836 that periodical was joined to the "American Monthly Magazine," published in New York, and edited by Charles F. Hoffman, and Mr. Benjamin was soon after induced to go to reside permanently in that city. By unfortunate investments, and the calamities in which so many were involved in that period, he had lost most of his patrimonial property, and the remainder of it he now invested in a publishing establishment; but the commercial distress of the time, by which many of the wealthiest houses were overthrown, prevented the realization of his expectations, and the business was abandoned. He purchased, I believe, near the close of the year 1837, the "American Monthly Magazine," and for about two years conducted it with much ability, but by giving to some of the later numbers of it a political character, its prosperity was destroyed, and he relinquished it to become associated with Mr. Horace Greeley in the editorship of the "New Yorker," a popular weekly periodical, devoted to literature and politics. In 1840 several weekly gazettes of unprecedented size were established in New York, and rapidly attained a great circulation. With the most prominent of these he was connected, and his writings contributed largely to its success.

In both prose and verse Mr. Benjamin has been a very prolific author. His rhythmical compositions would fill many volumes. They are generally short. "A Poem on the Contemplation of Nature," read before the classes of Washington College, on the day of his graduation; "Poetry, a Satire," published in 1843, and "Infatuation, a Satire," published in 1845, are the longest of his printed works. He has written several dramatic pieces, of which only fragments have been given to the public.

There have not been many successful American satires. Trumbull's "Progress of Dulness" and "McFingal," are the best that had been produced at the close of the Revolution. Freneau, Hopkins, Dwight, Alsop, Cliffton, and others, attempted this kind of writing with various success, but none of them equalled Trumbull. More recently Fessenden, Verplanck, Pierpont, Halleck, Holmes, Ward, Osborn, and Benjamin, have essayed it. Halleck's "Fanny" and "Epistles" are witty, spirited and playful, but local in their application. The "Vision of Rubeta" has felicitous passages, and shows that its author is a scholar, but it is cumbrous and occasionally coarse. Mr. Benjamin's satires are lively, pointed, and free from malignity or licentiousness.

In some of his shorter poems, Mr. Benjamin has shown a quick perception of the ridiculous; in others, warm affections and a meditative spirit; and in more, gayety. His poems are adorned with apposite and pretty fancies, and seem generally to be expressive of actual feelings. Some of his humourous pieces, as the sonnet entitled "Sport," which is quoted in the following pages, are happily expressed, but his style is generally more like that of an improvisator than an artist. He rarely makes use of the burnisher.

GOLD.

"Gold is, in its last analysis, the sweat of the poor and the blood of the brave."—Joseph Napoleon.

Waste treasure like water, ye noble and great!
Spend the wealth of the world to increase your es-
Pile up your temples of marble, and raise [tate;
Columns and domes, that the people may gaze
And wonder at beauty, so gorgeously shown
By subjects more rich than the king on his throne.
Lavish and squander—for why should ye save
"The sweat of the poor and the blood of the brave?"

Pour wine into goblets, all crusted with gems—
Wear pearls on your collars and pearls on your
Let diamonds in splendid profusion outvie [hems;
The myriad stars of a tropical sky!
Though from the night of the fathomless mine
These may be dug at your banquet to shine,
Little care ye for the chains of the slave,
"The sweat of the poor and the blood of the brave."

Behold, at your gates stand the feeble and old,
Let them burn in the sunshine and freeze in the cold;
Let them starve: though a morsel, a drop will impart
New vigour and warmth to the limb and the heart:
You taste not their anguish, you feel not their pain,
Your heads are not bare to the wind and the rain—
Must wretches like these of your charity crave
"The sweat of the poor and the blood of the brave?"

An army goes out in the morn's early light,
Ten thousand gay soldiers equipp'd for the fight;
An army comes home at the closing of day;
O, where are their banners, their goodly array?
Ye widows and orphans, bewail not so loud—
Your groans may imbitter the feast of the proud;
To win for their store, did the wild battle rave,
"The sweat of the poor and the blood of the brave."

Gold! gold! in all ages the curse of mankind,
Thy fetters are forged for the soul and the mind:
The limbs may be free as the wings of a bird,
And the mind be the slave of a look and a word.
To gain thee, men barter eternity's crown,
Yield honour, affection, and lasting renown,
And mingle like foam with life's swift-rushing wave
"The sweat of the poor and the blood of the brave."

UPON SEEING A PORTRAIT

OF A LADY, PAINTED BY GIOVANNI C. THOMPSON.

There is a sweetness in those upturn'd eyes,
A tearful lustre—such as fancy lends
To the Madonna—and a soft surprise,
As if they saw strange beauty in the air;
Perchance a bird, whose little pinion bends
To the same breeze that lifts that flowing hair.
And, O, that lip, and cheek, and forehead fair,
Reposing on the canvass!—that bright smile,
Casting a mellow radiance over all!
Say, didst thou strive, young artist, to beguile
The gazer of his reason, and to thrall
His every sense in meshes of delight—
When thou, unconscious, mad'st this phantom bright?
Sure nothing real lives, which thus can charm the sight!

THE STORMY PETREL.

This is the bird that sweeps o'er the sea—
Fearless and rapid and strong is he;
He never forsakes the billowy roar,
To dwell in calm on the tranquil shore,
Save when his mate from the tempest's shocks
Protects her young in the splinter'd rocks.

Birds of the sea, they rejoice in storms;
On the top of the wave you may see their forms
They run and dive, and they whirl and fly,
Where the glittering foam spray breaks on high;
And against the force of the strongest gale,
Like phantom ships they soar and sail

All over the ocean, far from land,
When the storm-king rises dark and grand,
The mariner sees the petrel meet
The fathomless waves with steady feet,
And a tireless wing and a dauntless breast,
Without a home or a hope of rest.

So, mid the contest and toil of life,
My soul! when the billows of rage and strife
Are tossing high, and the heavenly blue
Is shrouded by vapours of sombre hue—
Like the petrel wheeling o'er foam and spray,
Onward and upward pursue thy way!

THE NAUTILUS.

The Nautilus ever loves to glide
Upon the crest of the radiant tide.
When the sky is clear and the wave is bright,
Look over the sea for a lovely sight!
You may watch, and watch for many a mile,
And never see Nautilus all the while.
Till, just as your patience is nearly lost,
Lo! there is a bark in the sunlight toss'd!

"Sail ho! and whither away so fast?"
What a curious thing she has rigg'd for a mast!
"Ahoy! ahoy! don't you hear our hail?"
How the breeze is swelling her gossamer sail!
The good ship Nautilus—yes, 'tis she!
Sailing over the gold of the placid sea;
And though she will never deign reply,
I could tell her hull with the glance of an eye.

Now, I wonder where Nautilus can be bound;
Or does she always sail round and round,
With the fairy queen and her court on board,
And mariner-sprites, a glittering horde?
Does she roam and roam till the evening light?
And where does she go in the deep midnight?
So crazy a vessel could hardly sail,
Or weather the blow of "a fine, stiff gale."

O, the selfsame hand that holds the chain
Which the ocean binds to the rocky main—
Which guards from the wreck when the tempest raves,
And the stout ship reels on the surging waves—
Directs the course of thy little bark,
And in the light or the shadow dark,
And near the shore or far at sea,
Makes safe a billowy path for thee!

TO ONE BELOVED.

I.

Years, years have pass'd,
My sweetest, since I heard thy voice's tone,
Saying thou wouldst be mine and mine alone;
Dark years have cast
Their shadows on me, and my brow no more
Smiles with the happy light that once it wore.

My heart is sere,
As a leaf toss'd upon the autumnal gale;
The early rose-hues of my life are pale,
Its garden drear,
Its bower deserted, for my singing bird
Among its dim retreats no more is heard.

O, trust them not
Who say that I have long forgotten thee,
Or even now thou art not dear to me!
Though far my lot
From thine, and though Time's onward rolling tide
May never bear me, dearest, to thy side.

I would forget,
Alas! I strive in vain—in dreams, in dreams
The radiance of thy glance upon me beams:—
No star has met
My gaze for years whose beauty doth not shine,
Whose look of speechless love is not like thine!

The evening air—
Soft witness of the floweret's fragrant death—
Strays not so sweetly to me as thy breath;
The moonlight fair
On snowy waste sleeps not with sweeter ray,
Than thy clear memory on my heart's decay.

I love thee still—
And I shall love thee ever, and above
All earthly objects with undying love.
The mountain-rill
Seeks, with no surer flow, the far, bright sea,
Than my unchanged affection flows to thee.

II.

A year has flown,
My heart's best angel, since to thee I strung
My frail, poetic lyre—since last I sung,
In faltering tone,
My love undying: though in all my dreams
Thy smiles have linger'd, like the stars in streams.

On ruffled wing,
Like storm-toss'd bird, that year has sped away
Into the shadow'd past, and not a day
To me could bring
Familiar joys like those I knew of yore,
But morn, and noon, and night, a sorrow bore.

Alas, for Time!
For me his sickle reaps the harvest fair
Of hopes that blossom'd in the summer air
Of youth's sweet clime;
But leaves to bloom the deeply-rooted tree
Which thou hast planted, deathless Memory!

Beneath its shade
I muse, and muse alone—while daylight dies,
Changing its dolphin hues in western skies,
And when they fade,
And when the moon, of fairy stars the queen,
Waves her transparent wand o'er all the scene;

I seek the vale,
And, while inhaling the moss-rose's breath,—
(Less sweet than thine, unmatch'd Elizabeth!)
A vision, pale
As the far robes of seraphs in the night,
Rises before me with supernal light.

I seek the mount,
And there, in closest commune with the blue,
Thy spiritual glances meet my view.
I seek the fount:
And thou art my Egeria, and the glade
Encircling it around is holier made.

I seek the brook:
And, in the silver shout of waters, hear
Thy merry, melting tones salute mine ear:
And, in the look
Of lilies floating from the flowery land,
See something soft and stainless as thy hand.

All things convey
A likeness of my early, only love—
All fairest things around, below, above:
The foamy spray
Over the billow, and the bedded pearls,
And the light flag the lighter breeze unfurls.

For, in the grace
As well as in the beauty of the sea,
I find a true similitude to thee;
And I can trace
Thine image in the loveliness that dwells
Mid inland forests and sequester'd dells.

I am thine own,
My dearest, though thou never mayst be mine;
I would not if I could the band untwine
Around me thrown—
Since first I breathed to thee that word of fire—
Re-echo'd now, how feebly! by my lyre.

Love, constant love!
Age cannot quench it—like the primal ray
From the vast fountain that supplies the day,
Far, far above
Our cloud-encircled region, it will flow
As pure and as eternal in its glow.

O, when I die
(If until then thou mayst not drop a tear)
Weep then for one to whom thou wert most dear,
To whom thy sigh,
Denied in life, in death, if fondly given,
Will seem the sweetest incense-air of heaven!

III.

Dost thou not turn,
Fairest and sweetest, from the flowery way
On which thy feet are treading every day,
And seek to learn
Tidings, sometimes, of him who loved thee well—
More than his pen can write or tongue can tell?

Gaze not thine eyes
(O, wild and lustrous eyes, ye were my fate!)
Upon the lines he fashion'd not of late,
But when the skies

Of joy were over him, and he was bless'd
That he could sing of treasures he possess'd?

Treasures more dear
Than gold in ingots, or barbaric piles
Of pearls and diamonds, thy most precious smiles!
Bring, bring me here,
O, ruthless Time, some of those treasures now,
And print a hundred wrinkles on my brow.

Make me grow old
Before my years are many—take away
Health, youth, ambition—let my strength decay,
My mind be sold
To be the slave of some strange, barren lore—
Only those treasures to my heart restore!

Ah! I implore
A boon that cannot be, a blessing flown
Unto a realm so distant from my own,
That, could I soar
On eagle's wings, it still would be afar,
As if I strove by flight to reach a star!

The future vast
Before me lifts majestic steeps on high,
Which I must stand upon before I die!
For, in the past
Love buried lies; and nothing lives but fame
To speak unto the coming age my race and name.

THE TIRED HUNTER.

Rest thee, old hunter! the evening cool
Will sweetly breathe on thy heated brow,
Thy dogs will lap of the shady pool;
Thou art very weary—O, rest thee now!
Thou hast wander'd far through mazy woods,
Thou hast trodden the bright-plumed birds' retreat,
Thou hast broken in on their solitudes,—
O, give some rest to thy tired feet!

There's not a nook in the forest wide
Nor a leafy dell unknown to thee,
Thy step has been where no sounds, beside
The rustle of wings in the sheltering tree,
The sharp, clear cry of the startled game,
The wind's low murmur, the tempest's roar,
The bay that follow'd thy gun's sure aim,
Or thy whistle shrill, were heard before.

Then rest thee!—thy wife in her cottage-door,
Shading her eyes from the sun's keen ray,
Peers into the forest beyond the moor,
To hail thy coming ere fall of day;—
But thou art a score of miles from home,
And the hues of the kindling autumn leaves
Grow brown in the shadow of evening's dome,
And swing to the rush of the freshening breeze.

Thou must even rest! for thou canst not tread
Till yon star in the zenith of midnight glows,
And a sapphire light over earth is spread,
The place where thy wife and babes repose.
Rest thee a while—and then journey on
Through the wide forest, and over the moor:
Then call to thy dogs, and fire thy gun,
And a taper will gleam from thy cottage-door!

THE DEPARTED.

The departed! the departed!
They visit us in dreams,
And they glide above our memories
Like shadows over streams;
But where the cheerful lights of home
In constant lustre burn,
The departed, the departed
Can never more return!

The good, the brave, the beautiful,
How dreamless is their sleep,
Where rolls the dirge-like music
Of the ever-tossing deep!
Or where the hurrying night-winds
Pale winter's robes have spread
Above their narrow palaces,
In the cities of the dead!

I look around and feel the awe
Of one who walks alone
Among the wrecks of former days,
In mournful ruin strown;
I start to hear the stirring sounds
Among the cypress trees,
For the voice of the departed
Is borne upon the breeze.

That solemn voice! it mingles with
Each free and careless strain;
I scarce can think earth's minstrelsy
Will cheer my heart again.
The melody of summer waves,
The thrilling notes of birds,
Can never be so dear to me
As their remember'd words.

I sometimes dream their pleasant smiles
Still on me sweetly fall,
Their tones of love I faintly hear
My name in sadness call.
I know that they are happy,
With their angel-plumage on,
But my heart is very desolate
To think that they are gone.

I AM NOT OLD.

I am not old—though years have cast
Their shadows on my way;
I am not old—though youth has pass'd
On rapid wings away.
For in my heart a fountain flows,
And round it pleasant thoughts repose,
And sympathies and feelings high,
Spring like the stars on evening's sky.

I am not old—Time may have set
"His signet on my brow,"
And some faint furrows there have met,
Which care may deepen now:
Yet love, fond love, a chaplet weaves
Of fresh, young buds and verdant leaves;
And still in fancy I can twine
Thoughts, sweet as flowers, that once were mine.

THE DOVE'S ERRAND.

Under cover of the night,
Feather'd darling, take your flight!
Lest some cruel archer fling
Arrow at your tender wing,
And your white, unspotted side
Be with crimson colour died:—
For with men who know not love
You and I are living, Dove.

Now I bind a perfumed letter
Round your neck with silken fetter;
Bear it safely, bear it well,
Over mountain, lake, and dell.
While the darkness is profound
You may fly along the ground,
But when morning's herald sings,
Mount ye on sublimer wings;
High in heaven pursue your way
Till the fading light of day,
From the palace of the west,
Tints with fleckering gold your breast,
Shielded from the gaze of men,
You may stoop to earth again.

Stay, then, feather'd darling, stay,
Pause, and look along your way:
Well I know how fast you fly,
And the keenness of your eye.
By the time the second eve
Comes, your journey you'll achieve,
And above a gentle vale
Will on easy pinion sail.
In that vale, with dwellings strown,
One is standing all alone:
White it rises mid the leaves,
Woodbines clamber o'er its eaves,
And the honeysuckle falls
Pendant on its silent walls.
'T is a cottage, small and fair
As a cloud in summer air.

By a lattice, wreathed with flowers
Such as link the dancing hours,
Sitting in the twilight shade,
Envied dove, behold a maid!
Locks escaped from sunny band,
Cheeks reclined on snowy hand,
Looking sadly to the sky,
She will meet your searching eye.
Fear not, doubt not, timid dove,
You have found the home of love!
She will fold you to her breast—
Seraphs have not purer rest;
She your weary plumes will kiss—
Seraphs have not sweeter bliss!
Tremble not, my dove, nor start,
Should you feel her throbbing heart;
Joy has made her bright eye dim—
Well she knows you came from *him*,
Him she loves. O, luckless star!
He from her must dwell afar.

From your neck her fingers fine
Will the silken string untwine;
Reading then the words I trace,
Blushes will suffuse her face:
To her lips the lines she'll press,
And again *my* dove caress.
Mine, yes, mine—O, would that I
Could on rapid pinions fly!
Then I should not send you, dove,
On an errand to my love:
For I'd brave the sharpest gale,
And along the tempest sail;
Caring not for danger near,
Hurrying heedless, void of fear,
But to hear one tender word,
Breathed for me, my happy bird!

At the early dawn of day,
She will send you on your way,
Twining with another fetter
Round your neck another letter.
Speed ye, then, O, swiftly speed,
Like a prisoner newly freed:
O'er the mountain, o'er the vale,
Homeward, homeward, swiftly sail!
Never, never poise a plume,
Though beneath you Edens bloom:
Never, never think of rest,
Till night's shadow turns your breast
From pure white to mottled gray,
And the stars are round your way,—
Love's bright beacons, they will shine,
Dove, to show your home and mine!

"HOW CHEERY ARE THE MARINERS!"

How cheery are the mariners—
  Those lovers of the sea!
Their hearts are like its yesty waves,
  As bounding and as free.
They whistle when the storm-bird wheels
  In circles round the mast;
And sing when deep in foam the ship
  Ploughs onward to the blast.

What care the mariners for gales?
  There's music in their roar,
When wide the berth along the lee,
  And leagues of room before.
Let billows toss to mountain heights,
  Or sink to chasms low,
The vessel stout will ride it out,
  Nor reel beneath the blow.

With streamers down and canvass furl'd,
  The gallant hull will float
Securely, as on inland lake
  A silken-tassell'd boat;
And sound asleep some mariners,
  And some with watchful eyes,
Will fearless be of dangers dark
  That roll along the skies.

God keep those cheery mariners!
  And temper all the gales
That sweep against the rocky coast
  To their storm-shatter'd sails;
And men on shore will bless the ship
  That could so guided be,
Safe in the hollow of His hand,
  To brave the mighty sea!

LINES SPOKEN BY A BLIND BOY.

The bird, that never tried his wing,
Can blithely hop and sweetly sing,
Though prison'd in a narrow cage,
Till his bright feathers droop with age.
So I, while never bless'd with sight,
Shut out from heaven's surrounding light,
Life's hours, and days, and years enjoy,—
Though blind, a merry-hearted boy.

That captive bird may never float
Through heaven, or pour his thrilling note
Mid shady groves, by pleasant streams
That sparkle in the soft moonbeams;
But he may gayly flutter round
Within his prison's scanty bound,
And give his soul to song, for he
Ne'er longs to taste sweet liberty.

O! may I not as happy dwell
Within my unillumined cell?
May I not leap, and sing, and play,
And turn my constant night to day?
I never saw the sky, the sea,
The earth was never green to me:
Then why, O, why should I repine
For blessings that were never mine!

Think not that blindness makes me sad,
My thoughts, like yours, are often glad.
Parents I have, who love me well,
Their different voices I can tell.
Though far away from them, I hear,
In dreams, their music meet my ear.
Is there a star so dear above
As the low voice of one you love?

I never saw my father's face,
Yet on his forehead when I place
My hand, and feel the wrinkles there,
Left less by time than anxious care,
I fear the world has sights of wo,
To knit the brows of manhood so,—
I sit upon my father's knee:
He'd love me less if I could see.

I never saw my mother smile:
Her gentle tones my heart beguile.
They fall like distant melody,
They are so mild and sweet to me.
She murmurs not—my mother dear!
Though sometimes I have kiss'd the tear
From her soft cheek, to tell the joy
One smiling word would give her boy.

Right merry was I every day!
Fearless to run about and play
With sisters, brothers, friends, and all,—
To answer to their sudden call,
To join the ring, to speed the chase,
To find each playmate's hiding-place,
And pass my hand across his brow,
To tell him I could do it now!

Yet though delightful flew the hours,
So pass'd in childhood's peaceful bowers,
When all were gone to school but I,
I used to sit at home and sigh;
And though I never long'd to view
The earth so green, the sky so blue,
I thought I'd give the world to look
Along the pages of a book.

Now, since I've learn'd to read and write,
My heart is fill'd with new delight;
And music too,—can there be found
A sight so beautiful as sound?
Tell me, kind friends, in one short word,
Am I not like a captive bird!
I live in song, and peace, and joy,—
Though blind, a merry-hearted boy.

THE ELYSIAN ISLE.

"It arose before them, the most beautiful island in the world."—IRVING'S *Columbus*.

It was a sweet and pleasant isle—
  As fair as isle could be;
And the wave that kiss'd its sandy shore
  Was the wave of the Indian sea

It seem'd an emerald set by Heaven
  On the ocean's dazzling brow—
And where it glow'd long ages past,
  It glows as greenly now.

I've wander'd oft in its valleys bright,
  Through the gloom of its leafy bowers,
And breathed the breath of its spicy gales
  And the scent of its countless flowers.

I've seen its bird with the crimson wing
  Float under the clear, blue sky;
I've heard the notes of its mocking-bird
  On the evening waters die.

In the starry noon of its brilliant night,
  When the world was hush'd in sleep—
I dream'd of the shipwreck'd gems that lie
  On the floor of the soundless deep.

And I gather'd the shells that buried were
  In the heart of its silver sands,
And toss'd them back on the running wave,
  To be caught by viewless hands.

There are sister-spirits that dwell in the sea,
  Of the spirits that dwell in the air;
And they never visit our northern clime,
  Where the coast is bleak and bare:

But around the shores of the Indian isles
  They revel and sing alone—
Though I saw them not, I heard by night
  Their low, mysterious tone.

Elysian isle! I may never view
  Thy birds and roses more,
Nor meet the kiss of thy loving breeze
  As it seeks thy jewell'd shore.

Yet thou art treasured in my heart
  As in thine own deep sea;
And, in all my dreams of the spirits' home,
  Dear isle, I picture thee!

A GREAT NAME.

TIME! thou destroyest the relics of the past,
And hidest all the footprints of thy march
On shatter'd column and on crumbled arch,
By moss and ivy growing green and fast.
Hurl'd into fragments by the tempest-blast,
The Rhodian monster lies; the obelisk,
That with sharp line divided the broad disc
Of Egypt's sun, down to the sands was cast:
And where these stood, no remnant-trophy stands,
And even the art is lost by which they rose:
Thus, with the monuments of other lands,
The place that knew them now no longer knows.
Yet triumph not, O, Time; strong towers decay,
But a great name shall never pass away!

INDOLENCE.

THERE is no type of indolence like this:—
A ship in harbour, not a signal flying,
The wave unstirr'd about her huge sides lying,
No breeze her drooping pennant-flag to kiss,
Or move the smallest rope that hangs aloft:
Sailors recumbent, listless, stretch'd around
Upon the polish'd deck or canvass—soft
To his tough limbs that scarce have ever found
A bed more tender, since his mother's knee
The stripling left to tempt the changeful sea.
Some are asleep, some whistle, try to sing,
Some gape, and wonder when the ship will sail,
Some 'damn' the calm and wish it was a gale;
But every lubber there is lazy as a king.

SPORT.

To see a fellow of a summer's morning,
With a large foxhound of a slumberous eye
And a slim gun, go slowly lounging by,
About to give the feather'd bipeds warning,
That probably they may be shot hereafter,
Excites in me a quiet kind of laughter;
For, though I am no lover of the sport
Of harmless murder, yet it is to me
Almost the funniest thing on earth to see
A corpulent person, breathing with a snort,
Go on a shooting frolic all alone;
For well I know that when he's out of town,
He and his dog and gun will all lie down,
And undestructive sleep till game and light are flown.

M. I.

BORN in the north, and rear'd in tropic lands:
Her mind has all the vigour of a tree,
Sprung from a rocky soil beside the sea,
And all the sweetness of a rose that stands
In the soft sunshine on some shelter'd lea.
She seems all life, and light, and love to me!
No winter lingers in her glowing smile,
No coldness in her deep, melodious words,
But all the warmth of her dear Indian isle,
And all the music of its tuneful birds.
With her conversing of my native bowers,
In the far south, I feel the genial air
Of some delicious morn, and taste those flowers,
Which, like herself, are bright above compare.

TO MY SISTER.

SISTER! dear sister, I am getting old:
My hair is thinner, and the cheerful light
That glisten'd in mine eyes is not as bright,
Though while on thee I look, 'tis never cold.
My hand is not so steady while I pen
These simple words to tell how warm and clear
Flows my heart's fountain toward thee, sister dear!
For years I've lived among my fellow-men,
Shared their deep passions, known their griefs and joys,
And found Pride, Power, and Fame but gilded toys;
And, sailing far upon Ambition's waves,
Beheld brave mariners on a troubled sea,
Meet, what they fear'd not—shipwreck and their graves.
My spirit seeks its haven, dear, with thee!

TO ——.

'T IS Winter now—but Spring will blossom soon,
And flowers will lean to the embracing air
And the young buds will vie with them to snare
Each zephyr's soft caress; and when the Moon
Bends her new silver bow, as if to fling
Her arrowy lustre through some vapour's wing,
The streamlets will return the glance of night
From their pure, gliding mirrors, set by Spring
Deep in rich frames of clustering chrysolite,
Instead of Winter's crumbled sparks of white.
So, dearest! shall our loves, though frozen now
By cold unkindness, bloom like buds and flowers,
Like fountain's flash, for Hope with smiling brow
Tells of a Spring, whose sweets shall all be ours!

TO ——.

LADY, farewell! my heart no more to thee
Bends like the Parsee to the dawning sun;
No more thy beauty lights the world for me,
Or tints with gold the moments as they run.
A cloud is on the landscape, and the beams
That made the valleys so divinely fair,
And scatter'd diamonds on the gliding streams,
And crown'd the mountains in their azure air—
Are veil'd forever!—Lady, fare thee well!
Sadly as one who longeth for a sound
To break the stillness of a deep profound,
I turn and strike my frail, poetic shell:—
Listen! it is the last; for thee alone
My heart no more shall wake its sorrowing tone.

TO A LADY WITH A BOUQUET.

FLOWERS are love's truest language; they betray,
Like the divining rods of Magi old,
Where priceless wealth lies buried, not of gold,
But love—strong love, that never can decay!
I send thee flowers, O dearest! and I deem
That from their petals thou wilt hear sweet words,
Whose music, clearer than the voice of birds,
When breathed to thee alone, perchance, may seem
All eloquent of feelings unexpress'd.
O, wreathe them in those tresses of dark hair!
Let them repose upon thy forehead fair,
And on thy bosom's yielding snow be press'd!
Thus shall thy fondness for my flowers reveal
The love that maiden coyness would conceal!

RALPH HOYT.

[Born about 1810.]

Rev. Ralph Hoyt was born in the city of New York, of which he is a resident, in the second lustrum of the present century. After passing several years as a teacher, and as a writer for the gazettes, he studied theology, and was ordained a presbyter of the Protestant Episcopal church in 1842. Verse is but an episode, though a natural one, in the life of a clergyman devoted to the active pursuit of good. Mr. Hoyt may have written much, but he has acknowledged little. He is known chiefly by "The Chaunt of Life and other Poems," published in 1844, and by the second portion of "The Chaunt of Life," etc., which appeared in the summer of 1845. The "Chaunt of Life" is chiefly occupied with passages of personal sentiment and reflection. The pieces entitled "Snow" and "The World for Sale," in his first volume, attracted more attention, and the author was led to pursue the vein, in "New" and "Old," which were subsequently written. A simple, natural current of feeling runs through them; the versification grows out of the subject, and the whole clings to us as something written from the heart of the author. A few such pieces have often prolonged a reputation, while writers of greater effort have been forgotten.

OLD.

By the wayside, on a mossy stone,
  Sat a hoary pilgrim sadly musing;
Oft I marked him sitting there alone,
  All the landscape like a page perusing;
    Poor, unknown—
By the wayside, on a mossy stone.

Buckled knee and shoe, and broad-rimm'd hat,
  Coat as ancient as the form 'twas folding,
Silver buttons, queue, and crimpt cravat,
  Oaken staff, his feeble hand upholding,
    There he sat!
Buckled knee and shoe, and broad-rimm'd hat.

Seem'd it pitiful he should sit there,
  No one sympathising, no one heeding,
None to love him for his thin gray hair,
  And the furrows all so mutely pleading,
    Age, and care:
Seem'd it pitiful he should sit there.

It was summer, and we went to school,
  Dapper country lads, and little maidens,
Taught the motto of the "Dunce's Stool,"
  Its grave import still my fancy ladens,
    "Here's a fool!"
It was summer, and we went to school.

When the stranger seem'd to mark our play,
  Some of us were joyous, some sad-hearted,
I remember well,—too well, that day!
  Oftentimes the tears unbidden started,
    Would not stay!
When the stranger seemed to mark our play.

One sweet spirit broke the silent spell,
  Ah! to me her name was always heaven!
She besought him all his grief to tell,
  (I was then thirteen, and she eleven,)
    Isabel!
One sweet spirit broke the silent spell.

Angel, said he sadly, I am old;
  Earthly hope no longer hath a morrow,
Yet, why I sit here thou shalt be told,
  Then his eye betray'd a pearl of sorrow,
    Down it roll'd!
Angel, said he sadly, I am old!

I have totter'd here to look once more
  On the pleasant scene where I delighted
In the careless, happy days of yore,
  Ere the garden of my heart was blighted
    To the core!
I have totter'd here to look once more!

All the picture now to me how dear!
  E'en this gray old rock where I am seated,
Is a jewel worth my journey here;
  Ah, that such a scene must be completed
    With a tear!
All the picture now to me how dear!

Old stone school-house!—it is still the same!
  There's the very step I so oft' mounted;
There's the window creaking in its frame,
  And the notches that I cut and counted
    For the game;
Old stone school-house!—it is still the same!

In the cottage, yonder, I was born;
  Long my happy home—that humble dwelling;
There the fields of clover, wheat, and corn,
  There the spring, with limpid nectar swelling;
    Ah, forlorn!
In the cottage, yonder, I was born.

Those two gate-way sycamores you see,
  Then were planted, just so far asunder
That long well-pole from the path to free,
  And the wagon to pass safely under;
    Ninety-three!
Those two gate-way sycamores you see!

There's the orchard where we used to climb
When my mates and I were boys together,
Thinking nothing of the flight of time,
Fearing naught but work and rainy weather;
Past its prime!
There's the orchard where we used to climb!

There, the rude, three-corner'd chestnut rails,
Round the pasture where the flocks were grazing,
Where, so sly, I used to watch for quails
In the crops of buckwheat we were raising,
Traps and trails,—
There, the rude, three-corner'd chestnut rails.

There's the mill that ground our yellow grain;
Pond, and river still serenely flowing;
Cot, there nestling in the shaded lane,
Where the lily of my heart was blowing,
Mary Jane!
There's the mill that ground our yellow grain!

There's the gate on which I used to swing,
Brook, and bridge, and barn, and old red stable;
But alas! no more the morn shall bring
That dear group around my father's table;
Taken wing!
There's the gate on which I used to swing!

I am fleeing!—all I loved are fled!
Yon green meadow was our place for playing;
That old tree can tell of sweet things said,
When around it Jane and I were straying:
She is dead!
I am fleeing!—all I loved are fled!

Yon white spire, a pencil on the sky,
Tracing silently life's changeful story,
So familiar to my dim old eye,
Points me to seven that are now in glory
There on high!
Yon white spire, a pencil on the sky!

Oft the aisle of that old church we trod,
Guided thither by an angel mother;
Now she sleeps beneath its sacred sod,
Sire and sisters, and my little brother;
Gone to God!
Oft the aisle of that old church we trod!

There I heard of wisdom's pleasant ways,
Bless the holy lesson!—but, ah, never
Shall I hear again those songs of praise,
Those sweet voices,—silent now for ever!
Peaceful days!
There I heard of wisdom's pleasant ways!

There my Mary blest me with her hand,
When our souls drank in the nuptial blessing,
Ere she hasten'd to the spirit-land;
Yonder turf her gentle bosom pressing;
Broken band!
There my Mary blest me with her hand!

I have come to see that grave once more,
And the sacred place where we delighted,
Where we worshipp'd in the days of yore,
Ere the garden of my heart was blighted
To the core!
I have come to see that grave once more.

Angel, said he sadly, I am old!
Earthly hope no longer hath a morrow;
Now, why I sit here thou hast been told·
In his eye another pearl of sorrow,
Down it rolled!
Angel, said he sadly, I am old!

By the wayside, on a mossy stone,
Sat the hoary pilgrim, sadly musing;
Still I marked him, sitting there alone,
All the landscape, like a page, perusing
Poor, unknown,
By the wayside, on a mossy stone!

NEW.

Still sighs the world for something new,
For something new;
Imploring me, imploring you,
Some Will-o'-wisp to help pursue
Ah, hapless world, what will it do!
Imploring me, imploring you,
For something new!

Each pleasure, tasted, fades away,
It fades away;
Nor you, nor I can bid it stay,
A dew-drop trembling on a spray;
A rainbow at the close of day;
Nor you, nor I can bid it stay;
It fades away.

Fill up life's chalice to the brim;
Up to the brim;
'Tis only a capricious whim;
A dreamy phantom, flitting dim,
Inconstant still for Her, or Him;
'Tis only a capricious whim,
Up to the brim!

SHE.

She, young and fair, expects delight;
Expects delight;
Forsooth, because the morn is bright,
She deems it never will be night,
That youth hath not a wing for flight,
Forsooth, because the morn is bright,
Expects delight!

The rose, once gather'd, cannot please,
It cannot please;
Ah, simple maid, a rose to seize,
That only blooms to tempt and tease
With thorns to rob the heart of ease,
Ah, simple maid, a rose to seize;
It cannot please!

'Tis winter, but she pines for spring·
She pines for spring;
No bliss its frost and follies bring;
A bird of passage on the wing,

Unhappy, discontented thing;
  No bliss its frost and follies bring;
    She pines for spring!

Delicious May, and azure skies;
    And azure skies;
With flowers of paradisial dyes;
  Now, maiden, happy be and wise:
Ah, June can only charm her eyes
  With flowers of paradisial dyes,
    And azure skies!

The glowing, tranquil summertime;
    The summertime;
Too listless in a maiden's prime,
  Dull, melancholy pantomime;
Oh, for a gay autumnal clime:
  Too listless in a maiden's prime,
    The summertime!

October! with earth's richest store;
    Earth's richest store;
Alas! insipid as before;
  Days, months, and seasons, o'er and o'er,
Remotest lands their treasures pour;
  Alas, insipid as before,
    Earth's richest store!

Love nestles in that gentle breast;
    That gentle breast;
Ah, love will never let it rest;
  The cruel, sly, ungrateful guest;
A viper in a linnet's nest,
  Ah, love will never let it rest;
    That gentle breast!

Could she embark on Fashion's tide;
    On fashion's tide;
How gaily might a maiden glide;—
  Contentment, innocence, and pride,
All stranded upon either side;—
  How gaily might a maiden glide,
    On fashion's tide!

Ah, maiden, time will make thee smart:
    Will make thee smart;
Some new, and keen, and poison'd dart,
  Will pierce at last that restless heart;
Youth, friends, and beauty will depart;
  Some new, and keen, and poisoned dart,
    Will make thee smart!

So pants for change the fickle fair;
    The fickle fair;
A feather, floating in the air,
  Still wafted here, and wafted there,
No charm, no hazard worth her care;
  A feather floating in the air,
    The fickle fair!

HE.

How sad his lot, the hapless swain;
    The hapless swain;
With care, and toil, in heat and rain,
  To speed the plough or harvest-wain;
Still reaping only fields of grain,
  With care, and toil, in heat and rain;
    The hapless swain!

Youth, weary youth, 'twill soon be past;
  'Twill soon be past;
His MANHOOD'S happiness shall last;
  Renown, and riches, far and fast.
Their potent charms shall round him cast,
  His Manhood's happiness shall last:—
    'Twill soon be past!

Now toiling up ambition's steep;
    Ambition's steep;
The rugged path is hard to keep;
  The spring how far! the well how deep!
Ah me! in folly's bower asleep!
  The rugged path is hard to keep;
    Ambition's steep!

The dream fulfilled! rank, fortune, fame;
    Rank, fortune, fame;
Vain fuel for celestial flame!
  He wins and wears a glittering name,
Yet sighs his longing soul the same;
  Vain fuel for celestial flame,
    Rank, fortune, fame!

Sweet beauty aims with Cupid's bow;
  With Cupid's bow;
Can she transfix him now?—ah, no!
  Amid the fairest flowers that blow,
The torment but alights—to go:
  Can she transfix him now?—ah, no,
    With Cupid's bow!

Indulgent heav'n, O grant but this,
    O grant but this,
The boon shall be enough of bliss,
  A HOME, with true affection's kiss,
To mend whate'er may hap amiss,
    O grant but this!

The Eden won:—insatiate still;
    Insatiate still;—
A wider, fairer range, he will;
  Some mountain higher than his hill;
Some prospect fancy's map to fill;
  A wider, fairer range, he will;
    Insatiate still!

From maid to matron, son to sire:
    From son to sire,
Each bosom burns with quenchless fire,
  Where life's vain phantasies expire
In some new phœnix of desire;
  Each bosom burns with quenchless fire,
    From son to sire!

Still sighs the world for something new;
    For something new;
Imploring me, imploring you
  Some Will-o'-wisp to help pursue.
Ah hapless world, what will it do;
  Imploring me, imploring you,
    FOR SOMETHING NEW!

SALE.

THE WORLD FOR SALE!—Hang out the sign;
Call every traveller here to me;
Who'll buy this brave estate of mine,
And set me from earth's bondage free:—
'Tis going!—Yes, I mean to fling
The bauble from my soul away;
I'll sell it, whatsoe'r it bring;—
The World at Auction here to-day!

It is a glorious thing to see,—
Ah, it has cheated me so sore!
It is not what it seems to be:
For sale! It shall be mine no more.
Come, turn it o'er and view it well;—
I would not have you purchase dear;
'Tis going—going!—I must sell!
Who bids?—Who'll buy the Splendid Tear?

Here's WEALTH in glittering heaps of gold,—
Who bids!—But let me tell you fair,
A baser lot was never sold:—
Who'll buy the heavy heaps of care?
And here, spread out in broad domain,
A goodly landscape all may trace;
Hall—cottage—tree—field—hill and plain;
Who'll buy himself a burial place!

Here's LOVE, the dreamy potent spell
That beauty flings around the heart;
I know its power, alas! too well;—
'Tis going—Love and I must part!
Must part!—What can I more with Love!
All over the enchanter's reign;
Who'll buy the plumeless, dying dove,—
An hour of bliss,—an age of pain!

And FRIENDSHIP,—rarest gem of earth,—
(Who e'er hath found the jewel his?)
Frail, fickle, false and little worth,—
Who bids for Friendship—as it is!
'Tis going—going!—Hear the call:
Once, twice, and thrice!—'Tis very low!
'Twas once my hope, my stay, my all,—
But now the broken staff must go!

FAME! hold the brilliant meteor high;
How dazzling every gilded name!
Ye millions, now's the time to buy!—
How much for Fame! How much for Fame!
Hear how it thunders!—Would you stand
On high Olympus, far renown'd,—
Now purchase, and a world command!—
And be with a world's curses crown'd!

Sweet star of HOPE! with ray to shine
In every sad foreboding breast,
Save this desponding one of mine,—
Who bids for man's last friend and best!
Ah, were not mine a bankrupt life,
This treasure should my soul sustain;
But Hope and I are now at strife,
Nor ever may unite again.

And SONG!—For sale my tuneless lute;
Sweet solace, mine no more to hold;
The chords that charmed my soul are mute,
I cannot wake the notes of old!

Or e'en were mine a wizard shell,
Could chain a world in raptures high;
Yet now a sad farewell!—farewell!—
Must on its last faint echoes die.

Ambition, fashion, show, and pride,—
I part from all for ever now;
Grief, in an overwhelming tide,
Has taught my haughty heart to bow.
Poor heart! distracted, ah, so long,—
And still its aching throb to bear;—
How broken, that was once so strong;
How heavy, once so free from care.

No more for me life's fitful dream;—
Bright vision, vanishing away!
My bark requires a deeper stream;
My sinking soul a surer stay.
By Death, stern sheriff! all bereft,
I weep, yet humbly kiss the rod,
The best of all I still have left—
My Faith, my Bible, and my God.

SNOW.

THE blessed morn is come again;
The early gray
Taps at the slumberer's window-pane,
And seems to say
"Break, break from the enchanter's chain,
Away,—away!"

'Tis winter, yet there is no sound
Along the air,
Of winds upon their battle-ground,
But gently there,
The snow is falling,—all around
How fair—how fair!

The jocund fields would masquerade;
Fantastic scene!
Tree, shrub, and lawn, and lonely glade
Have cast their green,
And join'd the revel, all array'd
So white and clean.

E'en the old posts, that hold the bars
And the old gate,
Forgetful of their wintry wars
And age sedate,
High-capp'd, and plumed, like white hussars,
Stand there in state.

The drifts are hanging by the sill,
The eaves, the door;
The hay-stack has become a hill;
All cover'd o'er
The wagon, loaded for the mill
The eve before.

Maria brings the water-pail,—
But where's the well!
Like magic of a fairy tale,
Most strange to tell,
All vanish'd,—curb, and crank, and rail;—
How deep it fell!

The wood-pile too is playing hide;
    The axe—the log—
The kennel of that friend so tried—
    (The old watch-dog.)
The grindstone standing by its side,
    All now *incog.*

The bustling cock looks out aghast
    From his high shed;
No spot to scratch him a repast,
    Up curves his head,
Starts the dull hamlet with a blast,
    And back to bed.

The barn-yard gentry, musing, chime
    Their morning moan;
Like Memnon's music of old time—
    That voice of stone!
So marbled they—and so sublime
    Their solemn tone.

Good Ruth has called the younker folk
    To dress below;
Full welcome was the word she spoke,
    Down, down they go,
The cottage quietude is broke,—
    The snow!—the snow!

Now rises from around the fire
    A pleasant strain;
Ye giddy sons of mirth, retire!
    And ye profane!—
A hymn to the Eternal Sire
    Goes up again.

The patriarchal Book divine,
    Upon the knee,
Opes where the gems of Judah shine,—
    (Sweet minstrelsie!)
How soars each heart with each fair line,
    O God! to Thee!

Around the altar low they bend,
    Devout in prayer;
As snows upon the roof descend,
    So angels there
Guard o'er that household, to defend
    With gentle care.

Now sings the kettle o'er the blaze;
    The buckwheat heaps;
Rare Mocha, worth an Arab's praise,
    Sweet Susan steeps;
The old round stand her nod obeys,
    And out it leaps.

Unerring presages declare
    The banquet near;
Soon, busy appetites are there;
    And disappear
The glories of the ample fare,
    With thanks sincere.

Now let the busy day begin:—
    Out rolls the churn;
Forth hastes the farm-boy, and brings in
    The brush to burn:—
Sweep, shovel, scour, sew, knit, and spin,
    Till night's return

To delve his threshing John must hie;
    His sturdy shoe
Can all the subtle damp defy:
    How wades he through!
While dainty milkmaids, slow and shy,
    His track pursue.

Each to the hour's allotted care:
    To shell the corn;
The broken harness to repair;
    The sleigh t'adorn:
So cheerful—tranquil—snowy—fair
    The WINTER MORN.

EXTRACT FROM "THE BLACKSMITH'S NIGHT."

PRIMEVAL Night! infinitude of gloom!
    My prayer fulfilled, yet brings it no release:
O for the deeper shadow of the tomb,
        Its dreamless peace,
Where the last throb of my sad heart may cease!

Yet thrills that voice again the murky air,
    Never a midnight but there came a morn!
Up from the dungeon now of thy despair,
        For thou wert born
To conquer sorrow, and all fear to scorn!

To thee is granted to behold how Truth
    Links the strong worker with the happy skies,
In Care's deep furrows plants immortal youth,
        And gives the prize
Of endless glory to the bravely wise!

Centre thou art and Soul of a domain
    Vast as thy utmost wish could e'er desire;
Struggle! the Spirit never strives in vain;
        Can ne'er expire;
Up for thy sceptre, take thy throne of fire!

For man is regal when his strength is tried;
    When spirit wills, all matter must obey;
Sweeps the resistless mandate like a tide
        Away, away,
Till earth and heaven feel the potent sway!

Now as this rayless gloom aside I fling,
    Thy realm of action spreading on the view,
Calls to the sooty Blacksmith—be a king!
        Thy reign renew;
Grasping thy mace again, arise and DO!

And as the massive hammer thunders down,
    Shaping the stubborn iron to the plan,
Know that each stroke adds lustre to the crown,
        And yon wide span
Of gazing planets shout—behold a MAN!

A glorious Man! and thy renown shall be
    Borne by the winds and waters through all time
While there's a keel to carve it on the sea
        From clime to clime,
Or GOD ordains that idleness is crime!

WILLIS GAYLORD CLARK.

[Born, 1810. Died, 1841.]

Willis Gaylord Clark was born at Otisco, an agricultural town in central New York, in the year 1810. His father had been a soldier in the revolutionary army, and his services had won for him tributes of acknowledgment from the government. He had read much, and was fond of philosophical speculations; and in his son he found an earnest and ready pupil. The teachings of the father, and the classical inculcations of the Reverend George Colton, a maternal relative, laid a firm foundation for the acquirements which afterward gave grace and vigour to his writings.

At an early age, stimulated by the splendid scenery outspread on every side around him, Clark began to feel the poetic impulse. He painted the beauties of Nature with singular fidelity, and in numbers most musical; and as he grew older, a solemnity and gentle sadness of thought pervaded his verse, and evidenced his desire to gather from the scenes and images it reflected, lessons of morality.

When he was about twenty years of age he repaired to Philadelphia, where his reputation as a poet had already preceded him, and under the auspices of his friend, the Reverend Doctor Ely, commenced a weekly miscellany similar in design to the "Mirror," then and now published in New York. This work was abandoned after a brief period, and Clark assumed, with the Reverend Doctor Brantley, an eminent Baptist clergyman, now President of the College of South Carolina, the charge of the "Columbian Star," a religious and literary periodical, of high character, in which he printed many brief poems of considerable merit, a few of which were afterward included in a small volume with a more elaborate work entitled "The Spirit of Life," originally prepared as an exercise at a collegiate exhibition, and distinguished for the melody of its versification and the rare felicity of its illustrations.

After a long association with the reverend editor of the "Columbian Star," Clark was solicited to take charge of the "Philadelphia Gazette," one of the oldest and most respectable journals in Pennsylvania. He ultimately became its proprietor, and from that time until his death continued to conduct it. In 1836 he was married to Anne Poyntell Caldcleugh, the daughter of one of the wealthiest citizens of Philadelphia, and a woman of great personal beauty, rare accomplishments, and an affectionate disposition, who fell a victim to that most terrible disease of our climate, consumption, in the meridian of her youth and happiness, leaving her husband a prey to the deepest melancholy. In the following verses, written soon after this bereavement, his emotions are depicted with unaffected feeling:

'T is an autumnal eve—the low winds, sighing
 To wet leaves rustling as they hasten by;
The eddying gusts to tossing boughs replying,
 And ebon darkness filling all the sky,—
The moon, pale mistress, pall'd in solemn vapour,
 The rack, swift-wandering through the void above,
As I, a mourner by my lonely taper,
 Send back to faded hours the plaint of love.

Blossoms of peace, once in my pathway springing,
 Where have your brightness and your splendour gone
And thou, whose voice to me came sweet as singing,
 What region holds thee, in the vast unknown?
What star far brighter than the rest contains thee,
 Beloved, departed—empress of my heart?
What bond of full beatitude enchains thee,—
 In realms unveil'd by pen, or prophet's art?

Ah! loved and lost! in these autumnal hours,
 When fairy colours deck the painted tree,
When the vast woodlands seem a sea of flowers,
 O! then my soul, exulting, bounds to thee!
Springs, as to clasp thee yet in this existence,
 Yet to behold thee at my lonely side;
But the fond vision melts at once to distance,
 And my sad heart gives echo—she has died!

Yes! when the morning of her years was brightest,
 That angel-presence into dust went down,—
While yet with rosy dreams her rest was lightest,
 Death for the olive wove the cypress-crown,—
Sleep, which no waking knows, o'ercame her bosom,
 O'ercame her large, bright, spiritual eyes;
Spared in her bower connubial one fair blossom—
 Then bore her spirit to the upper skies.

There let me meet her, when, life's struggles over,
 The pure in love and thought their faith renew,—
Where man's forgiving and redeeming Lover
 Spreads out his paradise to every view.
Let the dim Autumn, with its leaves descending,
 Howl on the winter's verge!—yet spring will come:
So my freed soul, no more 'gainst fate contending,
 With all it loveth shall regain its home!

From this time his health gradually declined, and his friends perceived that the same disease which had robbed him of the "light of his existence," would soon deprive them also of his fellowship. Though his illness was of long duration, he was himself unaware of its character, and when I last saw him, a few weeks before his death, he was rejoicing at the return of spring, and confident that he would soon be well enough to walk about the town or to go into the country. He continued to write for his paper until the last day of his life, the twelfth of June, 1841.

His metrical writings are all distinguished for a graceful and elegant diction, thoughts morally and poetically beautiful, and chaste and appropriate imagery. The sadness which pervades them is not the gloom of misanthropy, but a gentle religious melancholy; and while they portray the changes of life and nature, they point to another and a purer world, for which our affections are chastened, and our desires made perfect by suffering in this.

The qualities of his prose are essentially different from those of his poetry. Occasionally he poured forth grave thoughts in eloquent and fervent language, but far more often delighted his readers by passages of irresistible humour and wit. His perception of the ludicrous was acute, and his jests and "cranks and wanton wiles" evinced the fulness of his powers and the benevolence of his feelings. The tales and essays which he found leisure to write for the New York "Knickerbocker Magazine,"—a monthly miscellany of high reputation edited by his only and twin brother, Mr. Lewis Gaylord Clark—and especially a series of amusing papers under the quaint title of "Ollapodiana," will long be remembered as affording abundant evidence of the qualities I have enumerated.

In person Mr. Clark was of the middle height, his form was erect and manly, and his countenance pleasing and expressive. In ordinary intercourse he was cheerful and animated, and he was studious to conform to the conventional usages of society. Warm-hearted, confiding, and generous, he was a true friend, and by those who knew him intimately he was much loved.

A LAMENT.

There is a voice I shall hear no more—
There are tones whose music for me is o'er,
Sweet as the odours of spring were they,—
Precious and rich—but they died away;
They came like peace to my heart and ear—
Never again will they murmur here;
They have gone like the blush of a summer morn,
Like a crimson cloud through the sunset borne.

There were eyes, that late were lit up for me,
Whose kindly glance was a joy to see;
They reveal'd the thoughts of a trusting heart,
Untouch'd by sorrow, untaught by art;
Whose affections were fresh as a stream of spring,
When birds in the vernal branches sing;
They were fill'd with love that hath pass'd with them,
And my lyre is breathing their requiem.

I remember a brow, whose serene repose
Seem'd to lend a beauty to cheeks of rose,
And lips, I remember, whose dewy smile,
As I mused on their eloquent power the while,
Sent a thrill to my bosom, and bless'd my brain
With raptures that never may dawn again;
Amidst musical accents, those smiles were shed—
Alas! for the doom of the early dead!

Alas! for the clod that is resting now
On those slumbering eyes—on that fated brow,
Wo for the cheek that hath ceased to bloom—
For the lips that are dumb, in the noisome tomb;
Their melody broken, their fragrance gone,
Their aspect cold as the Parian stone;
Alas, for the hopes that with thee have died—
O, loved one!—would I were by thy side!

Yet the joy of grief it is mine to bear;
I hear thy voice in the twilight air;
Thy smile, of sweetness untold, I see
When the visions of evening are borne to me;
Thy kiss on my dreaming lip is warm—
My arm embraceth thy graceful form;
I wake in a world that is sad and drear,
To feel in my bosom—thou art not here.

O! once the summer with thee was bright;
The day, like thine eyes, wore a holy light.
There was bliss in existence when thou wert nigh,
There was balm in the evening's rosy sigh;
Then earth was an Eden, and thou its guest—
A Sabbath of blessings was in my breast;
My heart was full of a sense of love,
Likest of all things to heaven above.

Now, thou art gone to that voiceless hall,
Where my budding raptures have perish'd all;
To that tranquil and solemn place of rest,
Where the earth lies damp on the sinless breast:
Thy bright locks all in the vault are hid—
Thy brow is conceal'd by the coffin lid;—
All that was lovely to me is there—
Mournful is life, and a load to bear!

MEMORY.

'T is sweet to remember! I would not forego
The charm which the past o'er the present can throw,
For all the gay visions that Fancy may weave
In her web of illusion, that shines to deceive.
We know not the future—the past we have *felt*—
Its cherish'd enjoyments the bosom can melt;
Its raptures anew o'er our pulses may roll,
When thoughts of the morrow fall cold on the soul.

'T is sweet to remember! when storms are abroad,
To see in the rainbow the promise of God:
The day may be darken'd, but far in the west,
In vermilion and gold, sinks the sun to his rest;
With smiles like the morning he passeth away:
Thus the beams of delight on the spirit can play,
When in calm reminiscence we gather the flowers
Which love scatter'd round us in happier hours.

'T is sweet to remember! When friends are unkind,
When their coldness and carelessness shadow the mind:
Then, to draw back the veil which envelopes a land
Where delectable prospects in beauty expand;
To smell the green fields, the fresh waters to hear
Whose once fairy music enchanted the ear;
To drink in the smiles that delighted us then,
To list the fond voices of childhood again,—
O, this the sad heart, like a reed that is bruised,
Binds up, when the banquet of hope is refused.

'T is sweet to remember! And naught can destroy
The balm-breathing comfort, the glory, the joy,
Which spring from that fountain, to gladden our way,
When the changeful and faithless desert or betray.
I would not forget!—though my thoughts should be dark,
O'er the ocean of life I look back from my bark,
And I see the lost Eden, where once I was blest,
A type and a promise of heavenly rest.

SONG OF MAY.

The spring's scented buds all around me are swelling:
There are songs in the stream—there is health in the gale;
A sense of delight in each bosom is dwelling,
As float the pure daybeams o'er mountain and vale;
The desolate reign of old winter is broken—
The verdure is fresh upon every tree;
Of Nature's revival the charm, and a token
Of love, O thou Spirit of Beauty, to thee!

The sun looketh forth from the halls of the morning,
And flushes the clouds that begirt his career;
He welcomes the gladness and glory, returning
To rest on the promise and hope of the year:
He fills with delight all the balm-breathing flowers;
He mounts to the zenith and laughs on the wave;
He wakes into music the green forest-bowers,
And gilds the gay plains which the broad rivers lave.

The young bird is out on his delicate pinion—
He timidly sails in the infinite sky;
A greeting to May, and her fairy dominion,
He pours on the west-winds that fragrantly sigh;
Around and above, there are quiet and pleasure—
The woodlands are singing, the heaven is bright;
The fields are unfolding their emerald treasure,
And man's genial spirit is soaring in light.

Alas! for my weary and care-haunted bosom!
The spells of the spring-time arouse it no more;
The song in the wildwood, the sheen in the blossom,
The fresh-swelling fountain—their magic is o'er!
When I list to the stream, when I look on the flowers,
They tell of the Past with so mournful a tone,
That I call up the throngs of my long vanish'd hours,
And sigh that their transports are over and gone.

From the far-spreading earth and the limitless heaven
There have vanish'd an eloquent glory and gleam;
To my sad mind no more is the influence given,
Which coloureth life with the hues of a dream;
The bloom-purpled landscape its loveliness keepeth;
I deem that a light as of old gilds the wave;
But the eye of my spirit in weariness sleepeth,
Or sees but my youth, and the visions it gave.

Yet it is not that age on my years hath descended—
'T is not that its snow-wreaths encircle my brow;
But the newness and sweetness of being are ended:
I feel not their love-kindling witchery now;
The shadows of death o'er my path have been sweeping—
There are those who have loved me debarr'd from the day;
The green turf is bright where in peace they are sleeping,
And on wings of remembrance my soul is away.

It is shut to the glow of this present existence—
It hears, from the Past, a funereal strain;
And it eagerly turns to the high-seeming distance,
Where the last blooms of earth will be garner'd again:

Where no mildew the soft damask-rose cheek shall nourish,
Where grief bears no longer the poisonous sting;
Where pitiless Death no dark sceptre can flourish,
Or stain with his blight the luxuriant spring.

It is thus that the hopes which to others are given
Fall cold on my heart in this rich month of May;
I hear the clear anthems that ring through the heaven—
I drink the bland airs that enliven the day;
And if gentle Nature, her festival keeping,
Delights not my bosom, ah! do not condemn;
O'er the lost and the lovely my spirit is weeping,
For my heart's fondest raptures are buried with them.

DEATH OF THE FIRST-BORN.

Young mother, he is gone!
His dimpled cheek no more will touch thy breast
No more the music-tone
Float from his lips, to thine all fondly press'd;
His smile and happy laugh are lost to thee:
Earth must his mother and his pillow be.

His was the morning hour,
And he hath pass'd in beauty from the day,
A bud, not yet a flower,
Torn, in its sweetness, from the parent spray;
The death-wind swept him to his soft repose,
As frost, in spring-time, blights the early rose.

Never on earth again
Will his rich accents charm thy listening ear,
Like some Æolian strain,
Breathing at eventide serene and clear;
His voice is choked in dust, and on his eyes
The unbroken seal of peace and silence lies.

And from thy yearning heart,
Whose inmost core was warm with love for him,
A gladness must depart,
And those kind eyes with many tears be dim·
While lonely memories, an unceasing train,
Will turn the raptures of the past to pain.

Yet, mourner, while the day
Rolls like the darkness of a funeral by,
And hope forbids one ray
To stream athwart the grief-discolour'd sky;
There breaks upón thy sorrow's evening gloom
A trembling lustre from beyond the tomb.

'T is from the better land!
There, bathed in radiance that around them springs,
Thy loved one's wings expand;
As with the choiring cherubim he sings,
And all the glory of that God can see,
Who said, on earth, to children, "Come to me

Mother, thy child is bless d:
And though his presence may be lost to thee,
And vacant leave thy breast,
And miss'd, a sweet load from thy parent knee
Though tones familiar from thine ear have pass'd
Thou 'lt meet thy first-born with his Lord at last

SUMMER.

The Spring's gay promise melted into thee,
Fair Summer! and thy gentle reign is here;
The emerald robes are on each leafy tree;
In the blue sky thy voice is rich and clear;
And the free brooks have songs to bless thy reign—
They leap in music midst thy bright domain.

The gales, that wander from the unclouded west,
Are burden'd with the breath of countless fields;
They teem with incense from the green earth's breast
That up to heaven its grateful odour yields;
Bearing sweet hymns of praise from many a bird,
By nature's aspect into rapture stirr'd.

In such a scene the sun-illumined heart
Bounds like a prisoner in his narrow cell,
When through its bars the morning glories dart,
And forest-anthems in his hearing swell—
And, like the heaving of the voiceful sea,
His panting bosom labours to be free.

Thus, gazing on thy void and sapphire sky,
O, Summer! in my inmost soul arise
Uplifted thoughts, to which the woods reply,
And the bland air with its soft melodies;—
Till basking in some vision's glorious ray,
I long for eagle's plumes to flee away.

I long to cast this cumbrous clay aside,
And the impure, unholy thoughts that cling
To the sad bosom, torn with care and pride:
I would soar upward, on unfetter'd wing,
Far through the chambers of the peaceful skies,
Where the high fount of Summer's brightness lies!

THE EARLY DEAD.

If it be sad to mark the bow'd with age
Sink in the halls of the remorseless tomb,
Closing the changes of life's pilgrimage
In the still darkness of its mouldering gloom:
O! what a shadow o'er the heart is flung,
When peals the requiem of the loved and young.

They to whose bosoms, like the dawn of spring
To the unfolding bud and scented rose,
Comes the pure freshness age can never bring,
And fills the spirit with a rich repose,
How shall we lay them in their final rest,
How pile the clods upon their wasting breast?

Life openeth brightly to their ardent gaze;
A glorious pomp sits on the gorgeous sky;
O'er the broad world hope's smile incessant plays,
And scenes of beauty win the enchanted eye:
How sad to break the vision, and to fold
Each lifeless form in earth's embracing mould!

Yet this is life! To mark from day to day,
Youth, in the freshness of its morning prime,
Pass, like the anthem of a breeze away,
Sinking in waves of death ere chill'd by time!
Ere yet dark years on the warm cheek had shed
Autumnal mildew o'er the rose-like red!

And yet what mourner, though the pensive eye
Be dimly thoughtful in its burning tears,
But should with rapture gaze upon the sky,
Through whose far depths the spirit's wing careers!
There gleams eternal o'er their ways are flung,
Who fade from earth while yet their years are young!

THE SIGNS OF GOD

I mark'd the Spring as she pass'd along,
With her eye of light, and her lip of song;
While she stole in peace o'er the green earth's breast,
While the streams sprang out from their icy rest.
The buds bent low to the breeze's sigh,
And their breath went forth in the scented sky;
When the fields look'd fresh in their sweet repose,
And the young dews slept on the new-born rose.

The scene was changed. It was Autumn's hour:
A frost had discolour'd the summer bower;
The blast wail'd sad mid the wither'd leaves,
The reaper stood musing by gather'd sheaves;
The mellow pomp of the rainbow woods
Was stirr'd by the sound of the rising floods;
And I knew by the cloud—by the wild wind's strain
That Winter drew near with his storms again!

I stood by the ocean; its waters roll'd
In their changeful beauty of sapphire and gold;
And day look'd down with its radiant smiles,
Where the blue waves danced round a thousand isles:
The ships went forth on the trackless seas,
Their white wings play'd in the joyous breeze;
Their prows rushed on mid the parted foam,
While the wanderer was wrapp'd in a dream of home!

The mountain arose with its lofty brow,
While its shadow was sleeping in vales below;
The mist like a garland of glory lay,
Where its proud heights soar'd in the air away;
The eagle was there on his tireless wing,
And his shriek went up like an offering:
And he seem'd, in his sunward flight, to raise
A chant of thanksgiving—a hymn of praise!

I look'd on the arch of the midnight skies,
With its deep and unsearchable mysteries:
The moon, mid an eloquent multitude
Of unnumber'd stars, her career pursued:
A charm of sleep on the city fell,
All sounds lay hush'd in that brooding spell;
By babbling brooks were the buds at rest,
And the wild-bird dream'd on his downy nest.

I stood where the deepening tempest pass'd,
The strong trees groan'd in the sounding blast
The murmuring deep with its wrecks roll'd on,
The clouds o'ershadow'd the mighty sun;
The low reeds bent by the streamlet's side,
And hills to the thunder-peal replied;
The lightning burst forth on its fearful way,
While the heavens were lit in its red array!

And hath man the power, with his pride and his skill,
To arouse all nature with storms at will?
Hath he power to colour the summer-cloud—
To allay the tempest when the hills are bow'd?
Can he waken the spring with her festal wreath?
Can the sun grow dim by his lightest breath?
Will he come again when death's vale is trod?
Who then shall dare murmur "*There is no God!*"

EUTHANASIA.

Methinks, when on the languid eye
 Life's autumn scenes grow dim;
When evening's shadows veil the sky,
 And Pleasure's syren hymn
Grows fainter on the tuneless ear,
Like echoes from another sphere,
 Or dream of seraphim,
It were not sad to cast away
This dull and cumbrous load of clay.

It were not sad to feel the heart
 Grow passionless and cold;
To feel those longings to depart
 That cheer'd the good of old;
To clasp the faith which looks on high,
Which fires the Christian's dying eye,
 And makes the curtain-fold
That falls upon his wasting breast
The door that leads to endless rest.

It were not lonely thus to lie
 On that triumphant bed,
Till the pure spirit mounts on high,
 By white-wing'd seraphs led:
Where glories earth may never know
O'er "many mansions" lingering glow,
 In peerless lustre shed;
It were not lonely thus to soar,
Where sin and grief can sting no more.

And, though the way to such a goal
 Lies through the clouded tomb,
If on the free, unfetter'd soul
 There rest no stains of gloom,
How should its aspirations rise
Far through the blue, unpillar'd skies,
 Up, to its final home!
Beyond the journeyings of the sun,
Where streams of living waters run.

AN INVITATION.

"They that seek me early shall find me."

Come, while the blossoms of thy years are brightest,
 Thou youthful wanderer in a flowery maze,
Come, while the restless heart is bounding lightest,
 And joy's pure sunbeams tremble in thy ways;
Come, while sweet thoughts, like summer-buds unfolding,
 Waken rich feelings in the careless breast,
While yet thy hand the ephemeral wreath is holding—
 Come—and secure interminable rest!

Soon will the freshness of thy days be over,
 And thy free buoyancy of soul be flown;
Pleasure will fold her wing, and friend and lover
 Will to the embraces of the worm have gone;
Those who now love thee will have pass'd forever,
 Their looks of kindness will be lost to thee;
Thou wilt need balm to heal thy spirit's fever,
 As thy sick heart broods over years to be!

Come, while the morning of thy life is glowing,
 Ere the dim phantoms thou art chasing die;
Ere the gay spell which earth is round thee throwing
 Fades, like the crimson from a sunset sky;
Life hath but shadows, save a promise given,
 Which lights the future with a fadeless ray;
O, touch the sceptre!—win a hope in Heaven—
 Come, turn thy spirit from the world away!

Then will the crosses of this brief existence
 Seem airy nothings to thine ardent soul;—
And, shining brightly in the forward distance,
 Will of thy patient race appear the goal:
Home of the weary!—where, in peace reposing,
 The spirit lingers in unclouded bliss,
Though o'er its dust the curtain'd grave is closing,
 Who would not, *early*, choose a lot like this?

THE BURIAL-PLACE AT LAUREL HILL.*

Here the lamented dead in dust shall lie,
 Life's lingering languors o'er, its labours done,
Where waving boughs, betwixt the earth and sky,
 Admit the farewell radiance of the sun.

Here the long concourse from the murmuring town,
 With funeral pace and slow, shall enter in,
To lay the loved in tranquil silence down,
 No more to suffer, and no more to sin.

And in this hallow'd spot, where Nature showers
 Her summer smiles from fair and stainless skies,
Affection's hand may strew her dewy flowers,
 Whose fragrant incense from the grave shall rise.

And here the impressive stone, engraved with words
 Which grief sententious gives to marble pale,
Shall teach the heart; while waters, leaves, and birds
 Make cheerful music in the passing gale.

Say, wherefore should we weep, and wherefore pour
 On scented airs the unavailing sigh—
While sun-bright waves are quivering to the shore,
 And landscapes blooming—that the loved must die?

There is an emblem in this peaceful scene;
 Soon rainbow colours on the woods will fall,
And autumn gusts bereave the hills of green,
 As sinks the year to meet its cloudy pall.

Then, cold and pale, in distant vistas round,
 Disrobed and tuneless, all the woods will stand.
While the chain'd streams are silent as the ground,
 As Death had numb'd them with his icy hand.

Yet, when the warm, soft winds shall rise in spring,
 Like struggling daybeams o'er a blasted heath,
The bird return'd shall poise her golden wing,
 And liberal Nature break the spell of Death.

So, when the tomb's dull silence finds an end,
 The blessed dead to endless youth shall rise,
And hear the archangel's thrilling summons blend
 Its tone with anthems from the upper skies.

There shall the good of earth be found at last,
 Where dazzling streams and vernal fields expand,
Where Love her crown attains—her trials past—
 And, fill'd with rapture, hails the "better land!"

* Near the city of Philadelphia.

A CONTRAST.

It was the morning of a day in spring;
The sun look'd gladness from the eastern sky;
Birds were upon the trees and on the wing,
And all the air was rich with melody; [high;
The heaven—the calm, pure heaven, was bright on
Earth laugh'd beneath in all its freshening green,
The free blue streams sang as they wandered by,
And many a sunny glade and flowery scene
Gleam'd out, like thoughts of youth, life's troubled years between.

The rose's breath upon the south wind came,
Oft as its whisperings the young branches stirr'd,
And flowers for which the poet hath no name;
While, mid the blossoms of the grove, were heard
The restless murmurs of the humming-bird;
Waters were dancing in the mellow light;
And joyous notes and many a cheerful word
Stole on the charmed ear with such delight
As waits on soft, sweet tones of music heard at night.

The night-dews lay in the half-open'd flower,
Like hopes that nestle in the youthful breast;
And ruffled by the light airs of the hour,
Awoke the pure lake from its glassy rest:
Slow blending with the blue and distant west,
Lay the dim woodlands, and the quiet gleam
Of amber-clouds, like islands of the blest—
Glorious and bright, and changing like a dream,
And lessening fast away beneath the intenser beam.

Songs were amid the valleys far and wide,
And on the green slopes and the mountains high:
While, from the springing flowers on every side,
Upon his painted wings, the butterfly
Roam'd, a gay blossom of the sunny sky;
The visible smile of joy was on the scene;
'T was a bright vision, but too soon to die!
Spring may not linger in her robes of green—
Autumn, in storm and shade shall quench the summer sheen.

I came again. 'T was Autumn's stormy hour:
The voice of winds was in the faded wood;
The sere leaves, rustling in deserted bower,
Were hurl'd in eddies to the moaning flood:
Dark clouds were in the west—and red as blood,
The sun shone through the hazy atmosphere;
While torrent voices broke the solitude,
Where, straying lonely, as with steps of fear,
I mark'd the deepening gloom which shrouds the dying year.

The ruffled lake heaved wildly; near the shore
It bore the red leaves of the shaken tree,
Shed in the violent north wind's restless roar,
Emblems of man upon life's stormy sea!
Pale autumn leaves! once to the breezes free
They waved in spring and summer's golden prime;
Now, even as clouds or dew how fast they flee;
Weak, changing like the flowers in autumn's clime,
As man sinks down in death, chill'd by the touch of time!

I mark'd the picture—'t was the changeful scene
Which life holds up to the observant eye:
Its spring, and summer, and its bowers of green,
The streaming sunlight of its morning sky,
And the dark clouds of death, which linger by;
For oft, when life is fresh and hope is strong,
Shall early sorrow breathe the unbidden sigh,
While age to death moves peacefully along,
As on the singer's lip expires the finish'd song

THE FADED ONE.

Gone to the slumber which may know no waking
Till the loud requiem of the world shall swell;
Gone! where no sound thy still repose is breaking,
In a lone mansion through long years to dwell,
Where the sweet gales that herald bud and blossom
Pour not their music nor their fragrant breath:
A seal is set upon thy budding bosom,
A bond of loneliness—a spell of death!

Yet 't was but yesterday that all before thee
Shone in the freshness of life's morning hours;
Joy's radiant smile was playing briefly o'er thee,
And thy light feet impress'd but vernal flowers.
The restless spirit charm'd thy sweet existence,
Making all beauteous in youth's pleasant maze,
While gladsome hope illumed the onward distance,
And lit with sunbeams thy expectant days.

How have the garlands of thy childhood wither'd,
And hope's false anthem died upon the air!
Death's cloudy tempests o'er thy way have gather'd,
And his stern bolts have burst in fury there.
On thy pale forehead sleeps the shade of even,
Youth's braided wreath lies stain'd in sprinkled
Yet looking upward in its grief to Heaven, [dust,
Love should not mourn thee, save in hope and trust.

A REMEMBRANCE.

I see thee still! thou art not dead,
Though dust is mingling with thy form,
The broken sunbeam hath not shed
The final rainbow on the storm:
In visions of the midnight deep,
Thine accents through my bosom thrill,
Till joy's fond impulse bids me weep,—
For, wrapt in thought I see thee still!

I see thee still,—that cheek of rose,—
Those lips, with dewy fragrance wet,
That forehead in serene repose,—
Those soul-lit eyes—I see them yet!
Sweet seraph! Sure thou art not dead,—
Thou gracest still this earthly sphere,
An influence still is round me shed,
Like thine,—and yet thou art not here!

Farewell, beloved! To mortal sight,
Thy vermeil cheek no more may bloom,
No more thy smiles inspire delight,
For thou art garner'd in the tomb.
Rich harvest for that ruthless power
Which hath no bound to mar his will:—
Yet, as in hope's unclouded hour,
Throne! in my heart, I see thee still.

JAMES ALDRICH.

[Born, 1810.]

JAMES ALDRICH was born near the Hudson, in the county of Suffolk, on the tenth of July, 1810 He received his education partly in Orange county, and partly in the city of New York, where, early in life, he became actively engaged in mercantile business. In 1836 he was married to MATILDA, daughter of Mr. JOHN B. LYON, of Newport, Rhode Island, and in the same year relinquished the occupation of a merchant. He for some time gave his attention to literature, edited two or three periodicals, and contributed to others, but has not recently published any thing. He resides in New York.

MORN AT SEA.

CLEARLY, with mental eye,
Where the first slanted ray of sunlight springs,
I see the morn with golden-fringed wings
Up-pointed to the sky.

In youth's divinest glow,
She stands upon a wandering cloud of dew,
Whose skirts are sun-illumed with every hue
Worn by GOD's covenant bow!

The child of light and air!
O'er land or wave, where'er her pinions move,
The shapes of earth are clothed in hues of love
And truth, divinely fair.

Athwart this wide abyss,
On homeward way impatiently I drift;
O, might she bear me now where sweet flowers lift
Their eyelids to her kiss!

Her smile hath overspread
The heaven-reflecting sea, that evermore
Is tolling solemn knells from shore to shore
For its uncoffin'd dead.

Most like an angel-friend,
With noiseless footsteps, which no impress leave,
She comes in gentleness to those who grieve,
Bidding the long night end.

How joyfully will hail,
With reënliven'd hearts, her presence fair,
The hapless shipwreck'd, patient in despair,
Watching a far-off sail.

Vain all affection's arts
To cheer the sick man through the night have been:
She to his casement goes, and, looking in,
Death's shadow thence departs.

How many, far from home,
Wearied, like me, beneath unfriendly skies,
And mourning o'er affection's broken ties,
Have pray'd for her to come.

Lone voyager on time's sea!
When my dull night of being shall be past,
O, may I waken to a morn, at last,
Welcome as this to me.

A DEATH-BED.

HER suffering ended with the day,
Yet lived she at its close,
And breathed the long, long night away,
In statue-like repose.

But when the sun, in all his state,
Illumed the eastern skies,
She pass'd through Glory's morning-gate,
And walk'd in Paradise!

MY MOTHER'S GRAVE.

IN beauty lingers on the hills
The death-smile of the dying day;
And twilight in my heart instils
The softness of its rosy ray.
I watch the river's peaceful flow,
Here, standing by my mother's grave,
And feel my dreams of glory go,
Like weeds upon its sluggish wave.

GOD gives us ministers of love,
Which we regard not, being near;
Death takes them from us—then we feel
That angels have been with us here!
As mother, sister, friend, or wife,
They guide us, cheer us, soothe our pain;
And when the grave has closed between
Our hearts and theirs, we love—in vain!

Would, mother! thou couldst hear me tell
How oft, amid my brief career,
For sins and follies loved too well,
Hath fallen the free, repentant tear.
And, in the waywardness of youth,
How better thoughts have given to me
Contempt for error, love for truth,
Mid sweet remembrances of thee.

The harvest of my youth is done,
And manhood, come with all its cares,
Finds, garner'd up within my heart,
For every flower a thousand tares.
Dear mother! couldst thou know my thoughts,
Whilst bending o'er this holy shrine,
The depth of feeling in my breast,
Thou wouldst not blush to call me thine!

A SPRING-DAY WALK.

ADIEU, the city's ceaseless hum,
  The haunts of sensual life, adieu!
Green fields, and silent glens! we come,
  To spend this bright spring-day with you.
Whether the hills and vales shall gleam
  With beauty, is for us to choose;
For leaf and blossom, rock and stream,
  Are colour'd with the spirit's hues.

Here, to the seeking soul, is brought
  A nobler view of human fate,
And higher feeling, higher thought,
  And glimpses of a higher state.
Through change of time, on sea and shore,
  Serenely nature smiles away;
Yon infinite blue sky bends o'er
  Our world, as at the primal day.

The self-renewing earth is moved
  With youthful life each circling year;
And flowers that CERES' daughter loved
  At Enna, now are blooming here.
Glad nature will this truth reveal,
  That GOD is ours and we are HIS;
O, friends, my friends! what joy to feel
  That HE our loving father is!

TO ONE FAR AWAY.

SWIFTER far than swallow's flight,
  Homeward o'er the twilight lea;
Swifter than the morning light,
  Flashing o'er the pathless sea,
Dearest! in the lonely night
  Memory flies away to thee!
Stronger far than is desire;
  Firm as truth itself can be;
Deeper than earth's central fire;
  Boundless as the circling sea;
Yet as mute as broken lyre,
  Is my love, dear wife, for thee!
Sweeter far than miser's gain,
  Or than note of fame can be
Unto one who long in vain
  Treads the paths of chivalry—
Are my dreams, in which again
  My fond arms encircle thee!

BEATRICE.

UNTOUCH'D by mortal passion,
  Thou seem'st of heavenly birth,
Pure as the effluence of a star
  Just reach'd our distant earth!
Gave Fancy's pencil never
  To an ideal fair
Such spiritual expression
  As thy sweet features wear.
An inward light to guide thee
  Unto thy soul is given,
Pure and serene as its divine
  Original in heaven.
Type of the ransom'd PSYCHE;
  How gladly, hand in hand,
To some new world I'd fly with thee
  From off this mortal strand.

LINES.

UNDERNEATH this marble cold,
Lies a fair girl turn'd to mould;
One whose life was like a star,
Without toil or rest to mar
Its divinest harmony,
Its GOD-given serenity.
One, whose form of youthful grace,
One, whose eloquence of face
Match'd the rarest gem of thought
By the antique sculptors wrought:
Yet her outward charms were less
Than her winning gentleness,
Her maiden purity of heart,
Which, without the aid of art,
Did in coldest hearts inspire
Love, that was not all desire.
Spirit forms with starry eyes,
That seem to come from Paradise,
Beings of ethereal birth,
Near us glide sometimes on earth,
Like glimmering moonbeams dimly seen
Glancing down through alleys green;
Of such was she who lies beneath
This silent effigy of grief.
Wo is me! when I recall
One sweet word by her let fall—
One sweet word but half-express'd—
Downcast eyes told all the rest,
To think beneath this marble cold,
Lies that fair girl turn'd to mould.

THE DREAMING GIRL.

SHE floats upon a sea of mist,
In fancy's boat of amethyst!
A dreaming girl, with her fair cheek
  Supported by a snow-white arm,
In the calm joy of innocence,
  Subdued by some unearthly charm.

The clusters of her dusky hair
Are floating on her bosom fair,
Like early darkness stealing o'er
  The amber tints that daylight gave,
Or, like the shadow of a cloud
  Upon a fainting summer-wave.

Is it a spirit of joy or pain
Sails on the river of her brain?
For, lo! the crimson on her cheek
  Faints and glows like a dying flame;
Her heart is beating loud and quick-
  Is not love that spirit's name?

Up-waking from her blissful sleep,
She starts with fear too wild to weep;
Through the trailing honeysuckle,
  All night breathing odorous sighs,
Which her lattice dimly curtains,
  The morn peeps in with his bright eyes.

Perfume loved when it is vanish'd,
Pleasure hardly felt ere banish'd,
Is the happy maiden's vision,
  That doth on her memory gleam,
And her heart leaps up with gladness—
  That bliss was nothing but a dream!

ISAAC McLELLAN, JR.

[Born about 1810.]

Mr. McLellan is a native of the city of Portland. He was educated at Bowdoin College, in Maine, where he was graduated in 1826. He subsequently studied the law, and for a few years practised his profession in Boston. He has recently resided in the country, and devoted his attention principally to agricultural pursuits. In the spring of 1830 he published "The Fall of the Indian;" in 1832, "The Year, and other Poems;" and in 1844 a third volume, comprising his later miscellaneous pieces in verse. His best compositions are lyrical.

NEW ENGLAND'S DEAD.

New England's dead! New England's dead!
 On every hill they lie;
On every field of strife, made red
 By bloody victory.
Each valley, where the battle pour'd
 Its red and awful tide,
Beheld the brave New England sword
 With slaughter deeply dyed.
Their bones are on the northern hill,
 And on the southern plain,
By brook and river, lake and rill,
 And by the roaring main.

The land is holy where they fought,
 And holy where they fell;
For by their blood that land was bought,
 The land they loved so well.
Then glory to that valiant band,
The honour'd saviours of the land!

O, few and weak their numbers were—
 A handful of brave men;
But to their God they gave their prayer,
 And rush'd to battle then.
The God of battles heard their cry,
And sent to them the victory.

They left the ploughshare in the mould,
Their flocks and herds without a fold,
The sickle in the unshorn grain,
The corn, half-garner'd, on the plain,
And muster'd, in their simple dress,
For wrongs to seek a stern redress,
To right those wrongs, come weal, come wo,
To perish, or o'ercome their foe.

And where are ye, O fearless men?
 And where are ye to-day?
I call:—the hills reply again
 That ye have pass'd away;
That on old Bunker's lonely height,
 In Trenton, and in Monmouth ground,
The grass grows green, the harvest bright
 Above each soldier's mound.
The bugle's wild and warlike blast
 Shall muster them no more;
An army now might thunder past,
 And they heed not its roar.
The starry flag, 'neath which they fought,
 In many a bloody day,
From their old graves shall rouse them not,
 For they have pass'd away

THE DEATH OF NAPOLEON.*

Wild was the night; yet a wilder night
 Hung round the soldier's pillow;
In his bosom there waged a fiercer fight
 Than the fight on the wrathful billow.

A few fond mourners were kneeling by,
 The few that his stern heart cherish'd;
They knew, by his glazed and unearthly eye,
 That life had nearly perish'd.

They knew by his awful and kingly look,
 By the order hastily spoken,
That he dream'd of days when the nations shook,
 And the nations' hosts were broken.

He dream'd that the Frenchman's sword still slew,
 And triumph'd the Frenchman's "eagle;"
And the struggling Austrian fled anew,
 Like the hare before the beagle.

The bearded Russian he scourged again,
 The Prussian's camp was routed,
And again, on the hills of haughty Spain,
 His mighty armies shouted.

Over Egypt's sands, over Alpine snows,
 At the pyramids, at the mountain,
Where the wave of the lordly Danube flows,
 And by the Italian fountain,

On the snowy cliffs, where mountain-streams
 Dash by the Switzer's dwelling,
He led again, in his dying dreams,
 His hosts, the broad earth quelling.

Again Marengo's field was won,
 And Jena's bloody battle;
Again the world was overrun,
 Made pale at his cannons' rattle.

He died at the close of that darksome day,
 A day that shall live in story:
In the rocky land they placed his clay,
 "And left him alone with his glory."

* "The 5th of May came amid wind and rain. Napoleon's passing spirit was deliriously engaged in a strife more terrible than the elements around. The words '*tête d'armée*,' (head of the army,) the last which escaped from his lips, intimated that his thoughts were watching the current of a heady fight. About eleven minutes before six in the evening, Napoleon expired."—Scott's *Life of Napoleon*.

THE NOTES OF THE BIRDS.

Well do I love those various harmonies
That ring so gayly in spring's budding woods,
And in the thickets, and green, quiet haunts,
And lonely copses of the summer-time,
And in red autumn's ancient solitudes.
If thou art pain'd with the world's noisy stir,
Or crazed with its mad tumults, and weigh'd down
With any of the ills of human life;
If thou art sick and weak, or mournest at the loss
Of brethren gone to that far distant land
To which we all do pass, gentle and poor,
The gayest and the gravest, all alike;—
Then turn into the peaceful woods, and hear
The thrilling music of the forest-birds.
How rich the varied choir! The unquiet finch
Calls from the distant hollows, and the wren
Uttereth her sweet and mellow plaint at times,
And the thrush mourneth where the kalmia hangs
Its crimson-spotted cups, or chirps half-hid
Amid the lowly dogwood's snowy flowers,
And the blue jay flits by, from tree to tree,
And, spreading its rich pinions, fills the ear
With its shrill-sounding and unsteady cry.
With the sweet airs of spring, the robin comes;
And in her simple song there seems to gush
A strain of sorrow when she visiteth
Her last year's wither'd nest. But when the gloom
Of the deep twilight falls, she takes her perch
Upon the red-stemm'd hazel's slender twig,
That overhangs the brook, and suits her song
To the slow rivulet's inconstant chime.
In the last days of autumn, when the corn
Lies sweet and yellow in the harvest-field,
And the gay company of reapers bind
The bearded wheat in sheaves,—then peals abroad
The blackbird's merry chant. I love to hear,
Bold plunderer, thy mellow burst of song
Float from thy watch-place on the mossy tree
Close at the corn-field edge.
Lone whip-poor-will,
There is much sweetness in thy fitful hymn,
Heard in the drowsy watches of the night.
Ofttimes, when all the village lights are out,
And the wide air is still, I hear thee chant
Thy hollow dirge, like some recluse who takes
His lodging in the wilderness of woods,
And lifts his anthem when the world is still:
And the dim, solemn night, that brings to man
And to the herds, deep slumbers, and sweet dews
To the red roses and the herbs, doth find
No eye, save thine, a watcher in her halls.
I hear thee oft at midnight, when the thrush
And the green, roving linnet are at rest,
And the blithe, twittering swallows have long ceased
Their noisy note, and folded up their wings.
Far up some brook's still course, whose current mines
The forest's blacken'd roots, and whose green marge
Is seldom visited by human foot,
The lonely heron sits, and harshly breaks
The Sabbath-silence of the wilderness:
And you may find her by some reedy pool,
Or brooding gloomily on the time-stain'd rock,
Beside some misty and far-reaching lake.
Most awful is thy deep and heavy boom,
Gray watcher of the waters! Thou art king
Of the blue lake; and all the winged kind
Do fear the echo of thine angry cry.
How bright thy savage eye! Thou lookest down
And seest the shining fishes as they glide;
And, poising thy gray wing, thy glossy beak
Swift as an arrow strikes its roving prey.
Ofttimes I see thee, through the curling mist,
Dart, like a spectre of the night, and hear
Thy strange, bewildering call, like the wild scream
Of one whose life is perishing in the sea.
And now, wouldst thou, O man, delight the ear
With earth's delicious sounds, or charm the eye
With beautiful creations! Then pass forth,
And find them midst those many-colour'd birds
That fill the glowing woods. The richest hues
Lie in their splendid plumage, and their tones
Are sweeter than the music of the lute,
Or the harp's melody, or the notes that gush
So thrillingly from Beauty's ruby lip.

LINES,

SUGGESTED BY A PICTURE BY WASHINGTON ALLSTON.

The tender Twilight with a crimson cheek
Leans on the breast of Eve. The wayward Wind
Hath folded her fleet pinions, and gone down
To slumber by the darken'd woods—the herds
Have left their pastures, where the sward grows green
And lofty by the river's sedgy brink,
And slow are winding home. Hark, from afar
Their tinkling bells sound through the dusky glade
And forest-openings, with a pleasant sound;
While answering Echo, from the distant hill,
Sends back the music of the herdsman's horn.
How tenderly the trembling light yet plays
O'er the far-waving foliage! Day's last blush
Still lingers on the billowy waste of leaves,
With a strange beauty—like the yellow flush
That haunts the ocean, when the day goes by.
Methinks, whene'er earth's wearying troubles pass
Like winter shadows o'er the peaceful mind,
'T were sweet to turn from life, and pass abroad,
With solemn footsteps, into Nature's vast
And happy palaces, and lead a life
Of peace in some green paradise like this.
The brazen trumpet and the loud war-drum
Ne'er startled these green woods:—the raging sword
Hath never gather'd its red harvest here!
The peaceful summer-day hath never closed
Around this quiet spot, and caught the gleam
Of War's rude pomp:—the humble dweller here
Hath never left his sickle in the field,
To slay his fellow with unholy hand;
The maddening voice of battle, the wild groan,
The thrilling murmuring of the dying man,
And the shrill shriek of mortal agony,
Have never broke its Sabbath-solitude

JONES VERY.

[Born about 1810.]

Jones Very is a native of the city of Salem. In his youth he accompanied his father, who was a sea-captain, on several voyages to Europe; and he wrote his "Essay on Hamlet" with the more interest from having twice seen Elsineur. After his father's death, he prepared himself to enter college, and in 1832 became a student at Cambridge. He was graduated in 1836, and in the same year was appointed Greek tutor in the university. While he held this office, a religious enthusiasm took possession of his mind, which gradually produced so great a change in him, that his friends withdrew him from Cambridge, and he returned to Salem, where he wrote most of the poems in the small collection of his writings published in 1839. His essays entitled "Epic Poetry," "Shakspeare," and "Hamlet," are fine specimens of learned and sympathetic criticism; and his sonnets, and other pieces of verse, are chaste, simple, and poetical, though they have little range of subjects and illustration. They are religious, and some of them are mystical, but they will be recognised by the true poet as the overflowings of a brother's soul.

TO THE PAINTED COLUMBINE.

Bright image of the early years
When glow'd my cheek as red as thou,
And life's dark throng of cares and fears
Were swift-wing'd shadows o'er my sunny brow!

Thou blushest from the painter's page,
Robed in the mimic tints of art;
But Nature's hand in youth's green age
With fairer hues first traced thee on my heart.

The morning's blush, she made it thine,
The morn's sweet breath, she gave it thee;
And in thy look, my Columbine!
Each fond-remember'd spot she bade me see.

I see the hill's far-gazing head,
Where gay thou noddest in the gale;
I hear light-bounding footsteps tread
The grassy path that winds along the vale.

I hear the voice of woodland song
Break from each bush and well-known tree,
And, on light pinions borne along,
Comes back the laugh from childhood's heart of glee.

O'er the dark rock the dashing brook,
With look of anger, leaps again,
And, hastening to each flowery nook,
ts distant voice is heard far down the glen.

Fair child of art! thy charms decay,
Touch'd by the wither'd hand of Time;
And hush'd the music of that day,
When my voice mingled with the streamlet's chime;

But on my heart thy cheek of bloom
Shall live when Nature's smile has fled;
And, rich with memory's sweet perfume,
Shall o'er her grave thy tribute incense shed.

There shalt thou live and wake the glee
That echoed on thy native hill;
And when, loved flower! I think of thee,
My infant feet will seem to seek thee still.

LINES TO A WITHERED LEAF SEEN ON A POET'S TABLE.

Poet's hand has placed thee there,
Autumn's brown and wither'd scroll!
Though to outward eye not fair,
Thou hast beauty for the soul;

Though no human pen has traced
On that leaf its learned lore,
Love divine the page has graced,—
What can words discover more?

Not alone dim autumn's blast
Echoes from yon tablet sear,—
Distant music of the past
Steals upon the poet's ear.

Voices sweet of summer-hours,
Spring's soft whispers murmur by;
Feather'd songs from leafy bowers
Draw his listening soul on high.

THE HEART.

There is a cup of sweet or bitter drink,
Whose waters ever o'er the brim must well,
Whence flow pure thoughts of love as angels think,
Or of its demon depths the tongue will tell;
That cup can ne'er be cleansed from outward stains
While from within the tide forever flows;
And soon it wearies out the fruitless pains
The treacherous hand on such a task bestows.
But ever bright its crystal sides appear,
While runs the current from its outlet pure;
And pilgrims hail its sparkling waters near,
And stoop to drink the healing fountain sure
And bless the cup that cheers their fainting soul
While through this parchi g waste they seek their heavenly goal.

TO THE CANARY-BIRD.

I cannot hear thy voice with others' ears,
Who make of thy lost liberty a gain;
And in thy tale of blighted hopes and fears
Feel not that every note is born with pain.
Alas! that with thy music's gentle swell
Past days of joy should through thy memory [throng,
And each to thee their words of sorrow tell,
While ravish'd sense forgets thee in thy song.
The heart that on the past and future feeds,
And pours in human words its thoughts divine,
Though at each birth the spirit inly bleeds,
Its song may charm the listening ear like thine,
And men with gilded cage and praise will try
To make the bard, like thee, forget his native sky.

THY BEAUTY FADES.

Thy beauty fades, and with it too my love,
For 't was the selfsame stalk that bore its flower;
Soft fell the rain, and breaking from above
The sun look'd out upon our nuptial hour;
And I had thought forever by thy side
With bursting buds of hope in youth to dwell;
But one by one Time strew'd thy petals wide,
And every hope's wan look a grief can tell:
For I had thoughtless lived beneath his sway,
Who like a tyrant dealeth with us all,
Crowning each rose, though rooted on decay,
With charms that shall the spirit's love enthrall,
And for a season turn the soul's pure eyes
From virtue's changeless bloom, that time and death [defies.

THE WIND-FLOWER.

Thou lookest up with meek, confiding eye
Upon the clouded smile of April's face,
Unharm'd though Winter stands uncertain by,
Eyeing with jealous glance each opening grace.
Thou trustest wisely! in thy faith array'd,
More glorious thou than Israel's wisest king;
Such faith was His whom men to death betray'd,
As thine who hearest the timid voice of Spring,
While other flowers still hide them from her call
Along the river's brink and meadow bare.
Thee will I seek beside the stony wall,
And in thy trust with childlike heart would share,
O'erjoy'd that in thy early leaves I find
A lesson taught by Him who loved all human kind.

ENOCH.

I look'd to find a man who walk'd with God,
Like the translated patriarch of old;—
Though gladden'd millions on his footstool trod,
Yet none with him did such sweet converse hold;
I heard the wind in low complaint go by,
That none its melodies like him could hear;
Day unto day spoke wisdom from on high,
Yet none like David turn'd a willing ear;
God walk'd alone unhonour'd through the earth;
For him no heart-built temple open stood,
The soul, forgetful of her nobler birth,
Had hewn him lofty shrines of stone and wood,
And left unfinish'd and in ruins still
The only temple he delights to fill.

MORNING.

The light will never open sightless eyes,
It comes to those who willingly would see;
And every object,—hill, and stream, and skies,
Rejoice within the encircling line to be;
'T is day,—the field is fill'd with busy hands,
The shop resounds with noisy workmen's din,
The traveller with his staff already stands
His yet unmeasured journey to begin;
The light breaks gently too within the breast,—
Yet there no eye awaits the crimson morn,
The forge and noisy anvil are at rest,
Nor men nor oxen tread the fields of corn,
Nor pilgrim lifts his staff,—it is no day
To those who find on earth their place to stay.

NIGHT.

I thank thee, Father, that the night is near
When I this conscious being may resign;
Whose only task thy words of love to hear,
And in thy acts to find each act of mine;
A task too great to give a child like me,
The myriad-handed labours of the day,
Too many for my closing eyes to see,
Thy words too frequent for my tongue to say;
Yet when thou seest me burden'd by thy love,
Each other gift more lovely then appears,
For dark-robed night comes hovering from above,
And all thine other gifts to me endears;
And while within her darken'd couch I sleep,
Thine eyes untired above will constant vigils keep

THE SPIRIT-LAND.

Father! thy wonders do not singly stand,
Nor far removed where feet have seldom stray'd,
Around us ever lies the enchanted land,
In marvels rich to thine own sons display'd;
In finding thee are all things round us found;
In losing thee are all things lost beside;
Ears have we, but in vain strange voices sound,
And to our eyes the vision is denied;
We wander in the country far remote,
Mid tombs and ruin'd piles in death to dwell;
Or on the records of past greatness dote,
And for a buried soul the living sell;
While on our path bewilder'd falls the night
That ne'er returns us to the fields of light.

THE TREES OF LIFE.

For those who worship Thee there is no death,
For all they do is but with Thee to dwell;
Now, while I take from Thee this passing breath,
It is but of Thy glorious name to tell;
Nor words nor measured sounds have I to find,
But in them both my soul doth ever flow;
They come as viewless as the unseen wind,
And tell thy noiseless steps where'er I go;
The trees that grow along thy living stream,
And from its springs refreshment ever drink,
Forever glittering in thy morning beam,
They bend them o'er the river's grassy brink;
And as more high and wide their branches grow
They look more fa r within the depths below.

THE ARK.

There is no change of time and place with Thee;
Where'er I go, with me 'tis still the same;
Within thy presence I rejoice to be,
And always hallow thy most holy name;
The world doth ever change; there is no peace
Among the shadows of its storm-vex'd breast;
With every breath the frothy waves increase,
They toss up mire and dirt, they cannot rest;
I thank Thee that within thy strong-built ark
My soul across the uncertain sea can sail,
And, though the night of death be long and dark,
My hopes in Christ shall reach within the veil;
And to the promised haven steady steer,
Whose rest to those who love is ever near.

NATURE.

The bubbling brook doth leap when I come by,
Because my feet find measure with its call;
The birds know when the friend they love is nigh,
For I am known to them, both great and small;
The flower that on the lovely hill-side grows
Expects me there when spring its bloom has given;
And many a tree and bush my wanderings knows,
And e'en the clouds and silent stars of heaven;
For he who with his Maker walks aright,
Shall be their lord as Adam was before;
His ear shall catch each sound with new delight,
Each object wear the dress that then it wore;
And he, as when erect in soul he stood,
Hear from his Father's lips that all is good.

THE TREE.

I love thee when thy swelling buds appear,
And one by one their tender leaves unfold,
As if they knew that warmer suns were near,
Nor longer sought to hide from winter's cold;
And when with darker growth thy leaves are seen
To veil from view the early robin's nest,
I love to lie beneath thy waving screen,
With limbs by summer's heat and toil oppress'd;
And when the autumn winds have stript thee bare,
And round thee lies the smooth, untrodden snow,
When naught is thine that made thee once so fair,
I love to watch thy shadowy form below,
And through thy leafless arms to look above
On stars that brighter beam when most we need
their love.

THE SON.

Father, I wait thy word. The sun doth stand
Beneath the mingling line of night and day,
A listening servant, waiting thy command
To roll rejoicing on its silent way;
The tongue of time abides the appointed hour,
Till on our ear its solemn warnings fall;
The heavy cloud withholds the pelting shower,
Then every drop speeds onward at thy call;
The bird reposes on the yielding bough,
With breast unswollen by the tide of song;
So does my spirit wait thy presence now
To pour thy praise in quickening life along,
Chiding with voice divine man's lengthen'd sleep,
While round the unutter'd word and love their
vigils keep.

THE ROBIN.

Thou need'st not flutter from thy half-built nest,
Whene'er thou hear'st man's hurrying feet go by,
Fearing his eye for harm may on thee rest,
Or he thy young unfinish'd cottage spy;
All will not heed thee on that swinging bough,
Nor care that round thy shelter spring the leaves,
Nor watch thee on the pool's wet margin now,
For clay to plaster straws thy cunning weaves;
All will not hear thy sweet out-pouring joy,
That with morn's stillness blends the voice of song,
For over-anxious cares their souls employ,
That else upon thy music borne along
And the light wings of heart-ascending prayer
Had learn'd that Heaven is pleased thy simple joys
to share.

THE RAIL-ROAD.

Thou great proclaimer to the outward eye
Of what the spirit too would seek to tell,
Onward thou goest, appointed from on high
The other warnings of the Lord to swell;
Thou art the voice of one that through the world
Proclaims in startling tones, "Prepare the way;"
The lofty mountain from its seat is hurl'd,
The flinty rocks thine onward march obey;
The valleys, lifted from their lowly bed,
O'ertop the hills that on them frown'd before,
Thou passest where the living seldom tread,
Through forests dark, where tides beneath thee roar,
And bidd'st man's dwelling from thy track remove,
And would with warning voice his crooked paths
reprove.

THE LATTER RAIN.

The latter rain,—it falls in anxious haste
Upon the sun-dried fields and branches bare,
Loosening with searching drops the rigid waste,
As if it would each root's lost strength repair;
But not a blade grows green as in the spring,
No swelling twig puts forth its thickening leaves;
The robins only mid the harvests sing,
Pecking the grain that scatters from the sheaves
The rain falls still,—the fruit all ripen'd drops,
It pierces chestnut-burr and walnut-shell,
The furrow'd fields disclose the yellow crops,
Each bursting pod of talents used can tell,
And all that once received the early rain
Declare to man it was not sent in vain.

JAMES FREEMAN CLARKE.

[Born, 1810.]

The Rev. James Freeman Clarke, whose ancestors, on the mother's side, have lived in Newton, near Boston, since the first settlement of the country, was born in Hanover, New Hampshire, on the fourth of April, 1810. He was prepared for college by his grandfather, the Rev. James Freeman, D.D., and in the Boston Latin school, and graduated at Cambridge, in 1829. Becoming a Unitarian minister, he went to Louisville, Kentucky, in 1833, and there edited for several years "The Western Messenger," a monthly magazine of religion and literature. In 1839 he married Anna, daughter of H. J. Heidekoper, of Meadville, Pennsylvania. In 1840 he returned to Boston, and established a church, on the principles of free seats, congregational worship, and social intercourse, called the Church of the Disciples, of which he is still the pastor. In 1849, and again in 1852, he visited Europe. He published a very entertaining and instructive account of his first visit, under the title of "Eleven Weeks in Europe." He has also published two small books on "Forgiveness," and "Prayer;" some anti-slavery tracts, and articles in periodicals, besides taking part in a "Memoir of General William Hull," and with Mr. Emerson and Mr. Channing, in the "Memoirs of Margaret Fuller Ossoli."

In poetry, his longest production is "A Poem delivered before the Phi Beta Kappa Society, of Harvard College," in 1846. It is a spirited satire of the social phenomena of the day, in heroic couplets. A characteristic paragraph is the following, of our intellectual condition:

"And if our land's heroic day is fled,
Have we romance, art, poetry, instead?
There have been ages when the soul of Art
Was poured abroad upon a nation's heart;
When genius filled the waters, woods, and skies,
With forms of life and fair divinities,
There, through the leaves which shade the haunted stream,
The naiad's limbs in pearly lustre gleam;
And in green forest-depths the Grecian ear
The dryad's gentle voice was used to hear.
But modern bards expect no rights like these,
Nor watch for meanings in the streams and trees.
Our only dryads now are lumberers stout,
Our naiads, gentlemen who fish for trout.
We in our studies build the lofty verse,
Nor find our books in brooks—but the reverse;
Copy each other's copies in our songs,
Each stealing what to nobody belongs—
As in the story to our childhood taught,
Thieves came to rob a man—and he had nought."

He has contributed to volumes edited by his friends some fine translations from the German poets, and has printed in magazines occasional poems, some of which have much sweetness, directness, and force.

TRIFORMIS DIANA.

I.

So pure her forehead's dazzling white,
So swift and clear her radiant eyes,
Within the treasure of whose light
Lay undeveloped destinies,—
Of thoughts repressed such hidden store
Was hinted by each flitting smile,
I could but wonder and adore,
Far off, in awe, I gazed the while.

I gazed at her, as at the moon,
Hanging in lustrous twilight skies,
Whose virgin crescent, sinking soon,
Peeps through the leaves before it flies:
Untouched Diana, flitting dim,
While sings the wood its evening hymn.

II.

Again we met. O, joyful meeting!
Her radiance now was all for me,
Like kindly airs her kindly greeting,
So full, so musical, so free;
Within Kentucky forest aisles,
Within romantic paths, we walked,
I bathed me in her sister smiles,
I breathed her beauty as we talked.

So full-orbed Cynthia walks the skies,
Filling the earth with melodies;
Even so she condescends to kiss
Drowsy Endymion, coarse and dull,
Or fills our waking souls with bliss,
Making long nights too beautiful.

III.

O fair, but fickle, lady-moon,
Why must thy full form ever wane?
O love! O friendship! why so soon
Must your sweet light recede again?
I wake me in the dead of night,
And start—for through the misty gloom
Red Hecate stares—a boding sight!-
Looks in—but never fills my room.

Thou music of my boyhood's hour!
Thou shining light on manhood's way!
No more dost thou fair influence shower,
To move my soul by night or day.
O strange! that while in hall and street
Thy hand I touch, thy grace I meet,
Such miles of polar ice should part
The slightest touch of mind and heart!—
But all thy love has waned, and so,
I gladly let thy beauty go.

CANA.

Dear Friend! whose presence in the house,
  Whose gracious word benign
Could once, at Cana's wedding feast,
  Change water into wine;

Come, visit us! and when dull work
  Grows weary, line on line,
Revive our souls, and let us see
  Life's water turned to wine.

Gay mirth shall deepen into joy,
  Earth's hopes grow half divine,
When Jesus visits us, to make
  Life's water glow as wine.

The social talk, the evening fire,
  The homely household shrine,
Grow bright with angel visits, when
  The Lord pours out the wine

For when self-seeking turns to love,
  Not knowing mine nor thine,
The miracle again is wrought,
  And water turned to wine.

THE GENUINE PORTRAIT.

Ask you why this portrait bears not
  The romance of those lips and lashes?
Why that bosom's blush it shares not,
  Mirrors not her eyes' quick flashes?
Is it false in not revealing
  Her girlish consciousness of beauty—
The graceful, half-developed feeling,
  Desire—opposing fancied duty?

For on the canvas, shadowy hair
  Floats backward from an earnest face;
The features one expression bear,
  The various lines one story trace.
And what is their expression? Love.
  Not wildfire passion—bright but damp,—
A purer flame, which points above,
  Though kindled at an earthly lamp.

Call it devotion—call it joy;
  'T is the true love of woman's heart,
Emotion, pure from alloy,
  Action, complete in every part.
Blame not the artist, then, who leaves
  The circumstances of the hour—
Within the husk the fruit perceives,
  Within the husk the future flower.

He took the one pervading grace
  Which charms in all, and fixed it there,
The deepest secret of her face—
  The key to her locked character—
The spirit of her life, which beats
  In every pulse of thought and feeling—
The central fire which lights and heats,
  Explaining earth, and heaven revealing

WHITE-CAPT WAVES.

White-capt waves far round the Ocean,
  Leaping in thanks or leaping in play,
All your bright faces, in happy commotion,
  Make glad matins this summer day.

The rosy light through the morning's portals
  Tinges your crest with an August hue;
Calling on us, thought-prisoned mortals,
  Thus to live in the moment too.

For, graceful creatures, you live by dying,
  Save your life when you fling it away,
Flow through all forms, all form defying,
  And in wildest freedom strict rule obey.

Show us your art, O genial daughters
  Of solemn Ocean, thus to combine
Freedom and force of rolling waters
  With sharp observance of law divine.

THE POET.

He touch'd the earth, a soul of flame,
  His bearing proud, his spirit high;
Fill'd with the heavens whence he came,
  He smiled upon man's destiny;
Yet smiled as one who knows no fear,
  And felt a secret strength within;
Who wonder'd at the pitying tear
  Shed over human loss and sin.
Lit by an inward, brighter light,
  Than aught that round about him shone,
He walk'd erect through shades of night;
  Clear was his pathway—but how lone!

Men gaze in wonder and in awe
  Upon a form so like to theirs,
Worship the presence, yet withdraw
  And carry elsewhere warmer prayers.

Yet when the glorious pilgrim-guest,
  Forgetting once his strange estate,
Unloosed the lyre from off his breast,
  And strung its chords to human fate;
And, gayly snatching some rude air,
  Caroll'd by idle, passing tongue,
Gave back the notes that linger'd there,
  And in Heaven's tones earth's low lay sung
Then warmly grasp'd the hand that sought
  To thank him with a brother's soul,
And when the generous wine was brought,
  Shared in the feast, and quaff'd the bowl;
Men laid their hearts low at his feet,
  And sunn'd their being in his light,
Press'd on his way his steps to greet,
  And in his love forgot his might.

And when, a wanderer long on earth,
  On him its shadow also fell,
And dimm'd the lustre of a birth
  Whose day-spring was from Heaven's own well
They cherish'd e'en the tears he shed,
  Their woes were hallow'd by his wo,
Humanity, half cold and dead,
  Had been revived in genius' glow

JACOB'S WELL.*

Here, after Jacob parted from his brother,
His daughters linger'd round this well, new-made;
Here, seventeen centuries after, came another,
And talk'd with Jesus, wondering and afraid.
Here, other centuries past, the emperor's mother
Shelter'd its waters with a temple's shade.
Here, mid the fallen fragments, as of old,
The girl her pitcher dips within its waters cold.

And Jacob's race grew strong for many an hour,
Then torn beneath the Roman eagle lay;
The Roman's vast and earth-controlling power
Has crumbled like these shafts and stones away;
But still the waters, fed by dew and shower,
Come up, as ever, to the light of day,
And still the maid bends downward with her urn,
Well pleased to see its glass her lovely face return.

And those few words of truth, first utter'd here,
Have sunk into the human soul and heart;
A spiritual faith dawns bright and clear,
Dark creeds and ancient mysteries depart;
The hour for God's true worshippers draws near;
Then mourn not o'er the wrecks of earthly art:
Kingdoms may fall, and human works decay,
Nature moves on unchanged—*Truths* never pass away.

THE VIOLET.†

When April's warmth unlocks the clod,
Soften'd by gentle showers,
The violet pierces through the sod,
And blossoms, first of flowers;
So may I give my heart to God
In childhood's early hours.

Some plants, in gardens only found,
Are raised with pains and care:
God scatters *violets* all around,
They blossom everywhere;
Thus may my love to *all* abound,
And all my fragrance share.

Some scentless flowers stand straight and high,
With pride and haughtiness:
But violets perfume land and sky,
Although they promise less.
Let me, with all humility,
Do more than I profess.

Sweet flower, be thou a type to me
Of blameless joy and mirth,
Of widely-scatter'd sympathy,
Embracing all God's earth—
Of early-blooming piety,
And unpretending worth.

* Suggested by a sketch of Jacob's Well, and Mount Gerizim.

† Written for a little girl to speak on May-day, in the character of the Violet.

TO A BUNCH OF FLOWERS.

Little firstlings of the year!
Have you come my room to cheer?
You are dry and parch'd, I think;
Stand within this glass and drink;
Stand beside me on the table,
'Mong my books—if I am able,
I will find a vacant space
For your bashfulness and grace;
Learned tasks and serious duty
Shall be lighten'd by your beauty.
Pure affection's sweetest token,
Choicest hint of love unspoken,
Friendship in your help rejoices,
Uttering her mysterious voices.
You are gifts the poor may offer—
Wealth can find no better proffer:
For you tell of tastes refined,
Thoughtful heart and spirit kind.
Gift of gold or jewel-dresses
Ostentatious thought confesses;
Simplest mind this boon may give,
Modesty herself receive.
For lovely woman you were meant
The just and natural ornament,
Sleeping on her bosom fair,
Hiding in her raven hair,
Or, peeping out mid golden curls,
You outshine barbaric pearls;
Yet you lead no thought astray,
Feed not pride nor vain display,
Nor disturb her sisters' rest,
Waking envy in their breast.
Let the rich, with heart elate,
Pile their board with costly plate;
Richer ornaments are ours,
We will dress our homes with flowers,
Yet no terror need we feel
Lest the thief break through to steal.
Ye are playthings for the child,
Gifts of love for maiden mild,
Comfort for the aged eye,
For the poor, cheap luxury.
Though your life is but a day,
Precious things, dear flowers, you say,
Telling that the Being good
Who supplies our daily food,
Deems it needful to supply
Daily food for heart and eye.
So, though your life is but a day,
We grieve not at your swift decay:
He, who smiles in your bright faces,
Sends us more to take your places;
'Tis for this ye fade so soon,
That He may renew the boon;
That kindness often may repeat
These mute messages so sweet:
That Love to plainer speech may get,
Conning oft his alphabet;
That beauty may be rain'd from heaven,
New with every morn and even,
With freshest fragrance sunrise greeting:
Therefore are ye, flowers, so fleeting.

GEORGE W. CUTTER.

[Born, 18 – .]

Mr. Cutter published at Cincinnati, in 1848, a volume entitled "Buena Vista, and other Poems," in the preface of which he says to the "gentle reader," "I desire that you will not for a moment suppose me insensible to their many and great imperfections, or deem me so vain as to expect that you will be startled by any sudden display of genius, or charmed by any imposing array of erudition. They were written, for the most part, amid the turmoil and excitement incident to the discharge of the duties of an arduous profession, in hours that were clouded by no ordinary toils, with no other object or end in view but to lighten the burden of existence, to dissipate the gloom of the moment."

In the previous year, Mr. Cutter had joined the army for the invasion of Mexico, as a captain of volunteers, and he participated in the victory of Buena Vista, and wrote upon the field his poem descriptive of that battle. The finest of his compositions is "The Song of Steam," which is worthy of the praise it has received, of being one of the best lyrics of the century. "The Song of Lightning," written more recently, is perhaps next to it in merit

THE SONG OF STEAM.

Harness me down with your iron bands;
  Be sure of your curb and rein:
For I scorn the power of your puny hands,
  As the tempest scorns a chain!
How I laugh'd, as I lay conceal'd from sight,
  For many a countless hour,
At the childish boast of human might,
  And the pride of human power!

When I saw an army upon the land,
  A navy upon the seas,
Creeping along, a snail-like band,
  Or waiting the wayward breeze;
When I mark'd the peasant fairly reel
  With the toil which he faintly bore,
As he feebly turn'd the tardy wheel,
  Or tugg'd at the weary oar:

When I measured the panting courser's speed,
  The flight of the courier-dove,
As they bore the law a king decreed,
  Or the lines of impatient love—
I could not but think how the world would feel,
  As these were outstripp'd afar,
When I should be bound to the rushing keel,
  Or chain'd to the flying car!

Ha, ha, ha! they found me at last;
  They invited me forth at length,
And I rushed to my throne with a thunder-blast,
  And laugh'd in my iron strength!
Oh! then ye saw a wondrous change
  On the earth and ocean wide,
Where now my fiery armies range,
  Nor wait for wind and tide.

Hurrah! hurrah! the water's o'er,
  The mountains steep decline;
Time—space—have yielded to my power;
  The world—the world is mine!
The rivers the sun hath earliest blest,
  Or those where his beams decline;
The giant streams of the queenly West,
  And the Orient floods divine.

The ocean pales where'er I sweep,
  To hear my strength rejoice,
And the monsters of the briny deep
  Cower, trembling at my voice.
I carry the wealth and the lord of earth,
  The thoughts of his godlike mind;
The wind lags after my flying forth,
  The lightning is left behind.

In the darksome depths of the fathomless mine
  My tireless arm doth play,
Where the rocks never saw the sun's decline,
  Or the dawn of the glorious day.
I bring earth's glittering jewels up
  From the hidden cave below,
And I make the fountain's granite cup
  With a crystal gush o'erflow.

I blow the bellows, I forge the steel,
  In all the shops of trade;
I hammer the ore and turn the wheel
  Where my arms of strength are made.
I manage the furnace, the mill, the mint—
  I carry, I spin, I weave;
And all my doings I put into print
  On every Saturday eve.

I've no muscles to weary, no breast to decay,
  No bones to be "laid on the shelf,"
And soon I intend you may "go and play,'
  While I manage this world myself.
But harness me down with your iron bands,
  Be sure of your curb and rein:
For I scorn the strength of your puny hands,
  As the tempest scorns a chain!

THE SONG OF LIGHTNING.

Away, away through the sightless air—
Stretch forth your iron thread;
For I would not dim my sandals fair
With the dust ye tamely tread;
Ay, rear it up on its million piers—
Let it reach the world around,
And the journey ye make in a hundred years
I'll clear at a single bound!

Though I cannot toil like the groaning slave
Ye have fetter'd with iron skill,
To ferry you over the boundless wave,
Or grind in the noisy mill;
Let him sing his giant strength and speed:
Why, a single shaft of mine
Would give that monster a flight, indeed
To the depths of the ocean brine.

No, no! I'm the spirit of light and love
To my unseen hand 't is given
To pencil the ambient clouds above,
And polish the stars of heaven.
I scatter the golden rays of fire
On the horizon far below,
And deck the skies where storms expire
With my red and dazzling glow.

The deepest recesses of earth are mine—
I traverse its silent core;
Around me the starry diamonds shine,
And the sparkling fields of ore;
And oft I leap from my throne on high
To the depths of the ocean's caves,
Where the fadeless forests of coral lie,
Far under the world of waves.

My being is like a lovely thought
That dwells in a sinless breast;
A tone of music that ne'er was caught—
A word that was ne'er expressed.
I burn in the bright and burnish'd halls,
Where the fountains of sunlight play—
Where the curtain of gold and opal falls
O'er the scenes of the dying day.

With a glance I cleave the sky in twain,
I light it with a glare,
When fall the boding drops of rain
Through the darkly-curtain'd air;
The rock-built towers, the turrets gray,
The piles of a thousand years,
Have not the strength of potters' clay
Before my glittering spears.

From the Alps' or the highest Andes' crag,
From the peaks of eternal snow,
The dazzling folds of my fiery flag
Gleam o'er the world below;
The earthquake heralds my coming power,
The avalanche bounds away,
And howling storms at midnight hour
Proclaim my kingly sway.

Ye tremble when my legions come—
When my quivering sword leaps out
O'er the hills that echo my thunder-drum,
And rend with my joyous shout:
Ye quail on the land or upon the seas,
Ye stand in your fear aghast,
To see me burn the stalwart trees,
Or shiver the stately mast.

The hieroglyphs on the Persian wall,
The letters of high command,
Where the prophet read the tyrant's fall,
Were traced with my burning hand;
And oft in fire have I wrote since then,
What angry Heaven decreed—
But the sealéd eyes of sinful men
Were all too blind to read.

At last the hour of light is here,
And kings no more shall blind,
Nor the bigots crush with craven fear
The forward march of mind;
The words of Truth, and Freedom's rays
Are from my pinions hurl'd,
And soon the sun of better days
Shall rise upon the world.

But away, away, through the sightless air
Stretch forth your iron thread;
For I would not soil my sandals fair
With the dust ye tamely tread.
Ay, rear it upon its million piers—
Let it circle the world around,
And the journey ye make in a hundred years
I'll clear at a single bound!

ON THE DEATH OF GENERAL WORTH

Now let the solemn minute gun
Arouse the morning ray,
And only with the setting sun
In echoes die away......
The muffled drum, the wailing fife,
Ah! let them murmur low,
O'er him who was their breath of life,
The solemn notes of wo!......

At Chippewa and Lundy's Lane,
On Palaklaba's field,
Around him fell the crimson rain,
The battle-thunder peal'd;
But proudly did the soldier gaze
Upon his daring form,
When charging o'er the cannon's blaze
Amid the sulphur storm.

Upon the heights of Monterey
Again his flag unroll'd,
And when the grape-shot rent away
Its latest starry fold,
His plumèd cap above his head
He waved upon the air,
And cheer'd the gallant troops he led
To glorious victory there.

But ah! the dreadful seal is broke—
In darkness walks abroad
The pestilence, whose silent stroke
Is like the doom of God!
And the hero by its fell decree
In death is sleeping now,
With the laurel wreath of victory
Still green upon his brow!

ROBERT T. CONRAD.

[Born 1810. Died 1858.]

Robert T. Conrad was born in Philadelphia on the tenth of June, 1810. His first American ancestor was Dennis Conrad, an enlightened German pastor, who withdrew his flock from the religious intolerance of the father-land and settled with them in the neighborhood of Philadelphia during the residence of William Penn in the colony. The family remained in the vicinity, and has furnished a succession of good citizens. The grandfather of our author, Mr. Michael Conrad, an eminent teacher of mathematics, discharged his class, on the breaking out of the revolution, and with his musket joined the army of Washington. His father, John Conrad, was from 1798 for many years the most extensive publisher and bookseller in this country, his main establishment being in Philadelphia, with branches in the principal cities of the South and West. He represented the city in the legislature, filled other offices of trust and honor here, and for several years before his death was mayor of the Northern Liberties, next to the city proper the most important of those municipalities which now constitute the consolidated town. He possessed a vigorous and finely cultivated understanding, gentle affections, and in all respects a perfect integrity of character. Mr. Conrad's poems are in his best sonnet dedicated to his father. His maternal grandfather, John Wilkes Kittera, was a learned lawyer, long at the head of the bar of Lancaster, which county he represented in Congress, and an intimate friend of the elder President Adams, who appointed him the federal attorney-general for the state.

Mr. Conrad studied law with his uncle, Mr. Thomas Kittera, a distinguished jurist who represented Philadelphia several years in the national legislature, and was admitted to practice in 1830. While a student he wrote his first tragedy, "Conrad of Naples," which was successfully produced in the principal theatres of the country, and has been regarded by his friends as the best of his poems. He withdrew it from the stage, and with characteristic carelessness as to his literary productions, has suffered it to be lost. About the time of his early admission to the bar, being married, he connected himself with the press, and after having shared in the editorial duties of several journals, commenced in 1832 the publication of the "Daily Intelligencer," some years afterwards united with the ancient "Philadelphia Gazette," in the management of which he was associated with Condy Raguet, the able œconomist, subsequently well known as our chivalric minister, during a stormy crisis, at Rio Janeiro. The arduous labors of the editor's room enfeebled his health, and in 1834 he resumed the practice of his profession, and in the following year was called to the bench. He was the youngest man, with, perhaps, the exception of Judge Wilson, ever dignified with the ermine in Pennsylvania. In March, 1838, he was elected to a court of higher and more extended jurisdiction, and in 1840, by an executive of conflicting politics, and against the protests of the administration party, on the unanimous recommendation of the bar was appointed to a still more elevated judicial position. It became his duty to try many of the most important cases ever adjudicated in the commonwealth, arising from those mercantile convulsions which a few years ago crushed the most powerful corporations and threw their officers and dependants before the bar of justice. A change occurred in the judicial system of which he had been a minister, and declining a place in the newly constituted court, he resumed the place of a counsellor and advocate.

His interest in public affairs soon led him to undertake the leading articles of the "North American," and the editorial charge of "Graham's Magazine." More recently he has been president of one of the more important western railroad companies, and on the union of the various municipalities of Philadelphia into one great city, was elected by an extraordinary majority its first chief magistrate. To the duties of this office, involving the establishment of a new and complicated system of administration, he has since devoted himself.

The literary labors of Judge Conrad have for the most part been but relaxations from more arduous and less congenial pursuits; yet in a career singularly various, and always laborious, he has probably written as much for the press as any man so young. Most of his productions, in prose or verse, have been occasional, and have not diverted him from what he may have conceived to be the paramount obligations of practical life. His "Aylmere" was written in intervals of leisure during a period in which he was not absent for a day from the bench. It was intended for Mr. Forrest, and has proved the most successful American drama yet written. After deriving a large amount of money from its popularity on the American stage, Mr. Forrest presented it with equal good fortune in the theatres of Great Britain and Ireland. Mr. Davenport also played in it nearly every night for an entire season in London. At the request of Mr. Forrest the author wrote another tragedy for him; it is entitled "The Heretic," and is founded on the massacre of St. Bartholomew; but though accepted by the actor, and paid for with his usual liberality, it has not been produced on the stage.

In 1852 Judge Conrad published in one volume "Aylmere or the Bondman of Kent, and other Poems," and he has prepared for the press a work under the title of "Bible Breathings," some portions of which have appeared in the periodicals. "Aylmere" is his principal production, and its merits as a poem are not less remarkable than those it possesses as an acting play. The hero, known in history as JACK CADE, AYLMERE, MENDALL, or MORTIMER, leader of the English peasantry in the insurrection of 1450, is a noble subject for a republican dramatist, and Judge CONRAD has presented him in the splendid colors of a patriot, sharing the extremest sufferings of the oppressed masses, knowing their rights, and braving all dangers for their vindication. The influence of institutions upon literature is strikingly illustrated in the different treatment which "Mr. JOHN AYLMERE, physician," as he is styled in contemporary records — a man of talents and discretion, according to the best authorities—receives from SHAKSPEARE, who pleases a court by contemptuous portrayal of his own peer in social elevation, and from Judge CONRAD, who, "in the audience of the people," delineates a man of the people as possessed of that respectability which justifies his eminence. The vehement, daring, and aspiring character of AYLMERE, softened and harmonized by a fine enthusiasm, is happily contrasted with the gentle nature of his wife, which is delineated with much delicacy, and presents frequent occasions for the author to show that conspicuous as are his powers as a rhetorician, displayed appropriately in the passionate declamation of the master in the play's movement, he is not less at home in passages of repose and tender grace.

The other principal poems of Judge CONRAD, are "The Sons of the Wilderness," and a series of "Sonnets on the Lord's Prayer," marked alike by earnestness, vigor, and pathos; and in his volume are a considerable number of shorter pieces, of which some of the most characteristic are here copied. The finest examples of his imagination, passion, and skill in the details of art, are undoubtedly to be found in his dramatic poems, but from these it is extremely difficult to make satisfactory extracts, so dependent for its effect is every sentence upon the lines to which it is in relation, or the character or situation of the person speaking.

ON A BLIND BOY,

SOLICITING CHARITY BY PLAYING ON HIS FLUTE.

"Had not God, for some wise purpose, steeled
The hearts of men, they must perforce have melted,
And barbarism itself have pitied him."

'T is vain! They heed thee not! Thy flute's meek tone
Thrills thine own breast alone. As streams that glide
Over the desert rock, whose sterile frown
Melts not beneath the soft and crystal tide,
So passes thy sweet strain o'er hearts of stone.
Thine outstretched hands, thy lips unuttered moan,
Thine orbs upturning to the darkened sky,
(Darkened, alas! poor boy, to thee alone!)
Are all unheeded here. They pass thee by:—
Away! Those tears unmarked, fall from thy sightless eye!

Ay, get thee gone, benighted one! Away!
This is no place for thee. The buzzing mart
Of selfish trade, the glad and garish day,
Are not for strains like thine. There is no heart
To echo to their soft appeal:—depart!
Go seek the noiseless glen, where shadows reign,
Spreading a kindred gloom; and there, apart
From the cold world, breathe out thy pensive strain;
Better to trees and rocks, than heartless man, complain!

I pity thee! thy life a live-long night;
No friend to greet thee, and no voice to cheer;
No hand to guide thy darkling steps aright,
Or from thy pale face wipe th' unbidden tear.
I pity thee! thus dark and lone and drear!
Yet haply it is well. The world from thee
Hath veiled its wintry frown, its withering sneer,
Th' oppressor's triumph, and the mocker's glee:
Why, then, rejoice, poor boy—rejoice thou can'st not see!

THE STRICKEN.*

HEAVY! heavy! Oh, my heart
Seems a cavern deep and drear,
From whose dark recesses start,
Flutteringly, like birds of night,
Throes of passion, thoughts of fear,
Screaming in their flight;
Wildly o'er the gloom they sweep,
Spreading a horror dim—a woe that cannot weep!

Weary! weary! What is life
But a spectre-crowded tomb?
Startled with unearthly strife—
Spirits fierce in conflict met,
In the lightning and the gloom,
The agony and sweat;
Passions wild and powers insane,
And thoughts with vulture beak, and quick Promethean pain!

Gloomy—gloomy is the day;
Tortured, tempest-tost the night;
Fevers that no founts allay—
Wild and wildering unrest—
Blessings festering into blight—
A gored and gasping breast!
From their lairs what terrors start,
At that deep earthquake voice—the earthquake of the heart!

Hopeless! hopeless! Every path
Is with ruins thick bestrown;
Hurtling bolts have fallen to scathe
All the greenness of my heart
And I now am Misery's own—
We never more shall part!
My spirit's deepest, darkest wave
Writhes with the wrestling storm. Sleep! sleep! the grave! the grave!

* "Turn thou unto me, and have mercy upon me; for I am desolate and in misery."—PSALMS

MY BROTHER.*

Forever gone! I am alone—alone!
Yet my heart doubts; to me thou livest yet:
Love's lingering twilight o'er my soul is thrown,
E'en when the orb that lent that light is set.
Thou minglest with my hopes—does Hope forget?
I think of thee, as thou wert at my side;
I grieve, a whisper—"he too will regret;"
I doubt and ponder—"how will he decide?"
I strive, but 'tis to win thy praises and thy pride.

For I thy praise could win—thy praise sincere.
How lovedst thou me—with more than woman's love!
And thou to me wert e'en as honor dear!
Nature in one fond woof our spirits wove:
Like wedded vines enclasping in the grove,
We grew. Ah! withered now the fairer vine!
But from the living who the dead can move?
Blending their sere and green leaves, there they twine,
And will, till dust to dust shall mingle mine with thine.

The sunshine of our boyhood! I bethink
How we were wont to beat the briery wood;
Or clamber, boastful, up the craggy brink,
Where the rent mountain frowns upon the flood
That thrids that vale of beauty and of blood,
Sad Wyoming! The whispering past will tell,
How by the silver-browed cascade we stood,
And watched the sunlit waters as they fell
(So youth drops in the grave) down in the shadowy dell.

And how we plunged in Lackawana's wave;
The wild-fowl startled, when to echo gay,
In that hushed dell, glad laugh and shout we gave.
Or on the shaded hill-side how we lay,
And watched the bright rack on its beamy way,
Dreaming high dreams of glory and of pride;
What heroes we, in freedom's deadliest fray!
How poured we gladly forth life's ruddy tide,
Looked to our skyey flag, and shouted, smiled, and died!

Bright dreams—forever past! I dream no more!
Memory is now my being: her sweet tone
Can, like a spirit-spell, the lost restore—
My tried, my true, my brave, bright-thoughted one!
Few have a friend—and such a friend! But none
Have, in this bleak world, more than one; and he,
Ever mine own, mine only—he is gone?
He fell—as hope had promised—for the free:
Our early dream,—alas! it was no dream to thee!

We were not near thee! Oh! I would have given,
To pillow in my arms thy aching head,
All that I love of earth or hope of heaven!
But strangers laid thee in thy prairie-bed;
And though the drum was rolled, and tears were shed,
'T was not by those who loved thee first and best.
Now waves the billowy grass above the dead;
The prairie-herd tread on thy throbless breast;
Woe's me! I may not weep above thy place of rest.

Now must I turn to stone! Fair virtue, truth,
Faith, love, were living things when thou wert here;
We shared a world, bright with the dew of youth,
And spanned by rainbow thoughts. Our souls sincere
Knew, in their love, nor selfish taint, nor fear:
We would have smiled, and for each other died!
All this to us how real and how dear!
But now my bosom's welling founts are dried,
Or pour, like ice-bound streams, a chilled and voiceless tide.

Must it be ever thus? The festive hour
Is festive now no more; for dimpling joy
Smiles with thy smile; and music's melting power
Speaks to my soul of thee! The struggling sigh
Chokes the faint laugh; and from my swimming eye,
The tear-drop trickling, turns my cup to gall;
E'en as the hour that bade thee, brother, die,
Mingles with all my days and poisons all,
Mantling my life with gloom, as with a dead man's pall.

Oh, may not men, like strings that chord in tone,
Mingle their spirits, and hereafter be
One in their nature, in their being one?
And may I not be blended thus with thee!
Parted in body, brother, bore not we
The self-same soul! Ah me! with restless pain,
My halvéd spirit yearneth to be free,
And clasp its other self: for I would fain,
Brother, be with the dead, to be with thee again!

* "He was asked whom he loved most, and he answered, 'His brother;' the person who put the question then asked him, whom he loved next, and again he said 'his brother.' 'Whom in the third place?' and still it was 'My brother,' and so on till he put no more questions to him about it."—Plutarch's Cato.

THE PRIDE OF WORTH.

There is a joy in worth,
A high, mysterious, soul-pervading charm;
Which, never daunted, ever bright and warm,
Mocks at the idle, shadowy ills of earth;
Amid the gloom is bright, and tranquil in the storm.

It asks, it needs no aid;
It makes the proud and lofty soul its throne:
There, in its self-created heaven, alone,
No fear to shake, no memory to upbraid,
It sits a lesser God;—life, life is all its own!

The stoic was not wrong:
There is no evil to the virtuous brave;
Or in the battle's rift, or on the wave,
Worshipped or scorned, alone or 'mid the throng,
He is himself—a man! not life's nor fortune's slave

Power and wealth and fame
Are but as weeds upon life's troubled tide:
Give me but these, a spirit tempest-tried,
A brow unshrinking and a soul of flame,
The joy of conscious worth, its courage and its pride!

HENRY R. JACKSON.

[Born 1810.]

HENRY R. JACKSON is a native of Savannah, Georgia, and was educated at the Franklin College, in Athens. He was several years one of the editors of the "Savannah Georgian," but on the invasion of Mexico, in 1846, joined the Georgia volunteers, as a colonel, and continued in the army until the close of the war. In 1849 he was elected by the legislature one of the judges of the Georgia eastern circuit, for four years, and in 1853 received the appointment of Minister Resident of the United States at the court of Austria. Mr JACKSON is the author of "Tallulah and other Poems," published in Savannah in 1850. In this volume are several pieces of uncommon merit. That entitled "My Father," and one addressed from the battle-field of Camargo, "To My Wife and Child," are marked by simplicity and genuine feeling, as others are by an enthusiastic affection for his native state, her scenery, traditions, and institutions.

MY FATHER.

As die the embers on the hearth,
  And o'er the floor the shadows fall,
And creeps the chirping cricket forth,
  And ticks the deathwatch in the wall,
I see a form in yonder chair,
  That grows beneath the waning light;
There are the wan, sad features—there
  The pallid brow, and locks of white!

My father! when they laid thee down,
  And heap'd the clay upon thy breast,
And left thee sleeping all alone
  Upon thy narrow couch of rest—
I know not why, I could not weep,
  The soothing drops refused to roll—
And oh, that grief is wild and deep
  Which settles tearless on the soul!

But when I saw thy vacant chair—
  Thine idle hat upon the wall—
Thy book—the pencilled passage where
  Thine eye had rested last of all—
The tree beneath whose friendly shade
  Thy trembling feet had wandered forth—
The very prints those feet had made,
  When last they feebly trod the earth—

And thought, while countless ages fled,
  Thy vacant seat would vacant stand,
Unworn thy hat, thy book unread,
  Effaced thy footsteps from the sand—
And widowed in this cheerless world,
  The heart that gave its love to thee—
Torn, like a vine whose tendrils curled
  More closely round the fallen tree!—

Oh, father! then for her and thee
  Gushed madly forth the scorching tears;
And oft, and long, and bitterly,
  Those tears have gush'd in later years;
For as the world grows cold around,
  And things take on their real hue,
'Tis sad to learn that love is found
  Alone above the stars, with you!

MY WIFE AND CHILD,

THE tattoo beats; the lights are gone;
  The camp around in slumber lies;
The night with solemn pace moves on;
  The shadows thicken o'er the skies;
But sleep my weary eyes hath flown,
  And sad, uneasy thoughts arise.
I think of thee, oh, dearest one!
  Whose love mine early life hath blest;
Of thee and him—our baby son—
  Who slumbers on thy gentle breast:—
God of the tender, frail and lone,
  Oh, guard that little sleeper's rest!
And hover, gently hover near
  To her, whose watchful eye is wet—
The mother, wife—the doubly dear,
  In whose young heart have freshly met
Two streams of love, so deep and clear—
  And cheer her drooping spirit yet!
Now, as she kneels before thy throne,
  Oh, teach her, Ruler of the skies!
That while by thy behest alone
  Earth's mightiest powers fall or rise,
No tear is wept to thee unknown,
  Nor hair is lost, nor sparrow dies;
That thou canst stay the ruthless hand
  Of dark disease, and soothe its pain—
That only by thy stern command
  The battle's lost, the soldier slain;
That from the distant sea or land
  Thou bring'st the wanderer home again.
And when, upon her pillow lone,
  Her tear-wet cheek is sadly pressed,
May happier visions beam upon
  The brightening currents of her breast,—
Nor frowning look, nor angry tone
  Disturb the sabbath of her rest!
Wherever fate those forms may throw,
  Loved with a passion almost wild—
By day, by night—in joy or wo—
  By fears oppressed, or hopes beguiled—
From every danger, every foe,
  Oh, God! protect my wife and child!

Engraved by A. W. Graham from a Painting [illegible]

Edgar A. Poe.

EDGAR ALLAN POE.

[Born, 1811. Died, 1849.]

The family of Mr Poe is one of the oldest and most respectable in Baltimore. David Poe, his paternal grandfather, was a quartermaster-general in the Maryland line during the Revolution, and the intimate friend of Lafayette, who, during his last visit to the United States, called personally upon the general's widow, and tendered her his acknowledgments for the services rendered to him by her husband. His great-grandfather, John Poe, married, in England, Jane, a daughter of Admiral James McBride, noted in British naval history, and claiming kindred with some of the most illustrious English families. His father and mother died within a few weeks of each other, of consumption, leaving him an orphan, at two years of age. Mr. John Allan, a wealthy gentleman of Richmond, Virginia, took a fancy to him, and persuaded General Poe, his grandfather, to suffer him to adopt him. He was brought up in Mr. Allan's family; and as that gentleman had no other children, he was regarded as his son and heir. In 1816 he accompanied Mr. and Mrs. Allan to Great Britain, visited every portion of it, and afterward passed four or five years in a school kept at Stoke Newington, near London, by the Reverend Doctor Bransby. He returned to America in 1822, and in 1825 went to the Jefferson University, at Charlottesville, in Virginia, where he led a very dissipated life, the manners of the college being at that time extremely dissolute. He took the first honours, however, and went home greatly in debt. Mr. Allan refused to pay some of his debts of *honour*, and he hastily quitted the country on a Quixotic expedition to join the Greeks, then struggling for liberty. He did not reach his original destination, however, but made his way to St. Petersburg, in Russia, where he became involved in difficulties, from which he was extricated by the late Mr. Henry Middleton, the American minister at that capital. He returned home in 1829, and immediately afterward entered the military academy at West Point. In about eighteen months from that time, Mr. Allan, who had lost his first wife while Mr Poe was in Russia, married again. He was sixty-five years of age, and the lady was young: Poe quarrelled with her, and the veteran husband, taking the part of his wife, addressed him an angry letter, which was answered in the same spirit. He died soon after, leaving an infant son the heir to his property, and bequeathed Poe nothing.

The army, in the opinion of the young cadet, was not a place for a poor man; so he left West Point abruptly, and determined to maintain himself by authorship. He had printed, while in the military academy, a small volume of poems, most of which were written in early youth. They illustrated the character of his abilities, and justified his anticipations of success. For a considerable time, however, his writings attracted but little attention. At length, in 1831, the proprietor of a weekly literary gazette in Baltimore offered two premiums, one for the best story in prose, and the other for the best poem. In due time our author sent in two articles, both of which were successful with the examining committee, and popular upon their appearance before the public. The late Mr. Thomas W. White had then recently established "The Southern Literary Messenger," at Richmond, and upon the warm recommendation of Mr. John P. Kennedy, who was a member of the committee that has been referred to, Mr. Poe was engaged by him to be its editor. He continued in this situation about a year and a half, in which he wrote many brilliant articles, and raised the "Messenger" to the first rank of literary periodicals.

He next removed to Philadelphia, to assist Mr. W. E. Burton in the editorship of the "Gentleman's Magazine," a miscellany that in 1840 was merged in "Graham's Magazine," of which Mr. Poe became one of the principal writers, particularly in criticism, in which his papers attracted much attention, by their careful and skilful analysis, and generally caustic severity. At this period, however, he appears to have been more ambitious of securing distinction in romantic fiction, and a collection of his compositions in this department, published in 1841, under the title of "Tales of the Grotesque and the Arabesque," established his reputation for ingenuity, imagination, and extraordinary power in tragical narration.

Near the end of 1844 Mr. Poe removed to New York, where he conducted for several months a literary miscellany called "The Broadway Journal." In 1845 he published a volume of "Tales," and a collection of his "Poems;" in 1846 wrote a series of literary and personal sketches entitled "The Literati of New York City," which commanded much attention; in 1848 gave to the public, first as a lecture, and afterwards in print, "Eureka, a Prose Poem;" and in the summer of 1849 delivered several lectures, in Richmond and other cities, and on the seventh of October, while on his way to New York, died, suddenly, at Baltimore.

After his death a collection of his works, in three volumes, was published in New York, edited by me, in fulfilment of wishes he had expressed on the subject. It embraced nearly all his writings, except "Arthur Gordon Pym," a nautical romance, originally printed in the "Southern Literary Messenger," and a few pieces of humorous prose, in which he was less successful than in other kinds of literature. In a memoir which is contained in these volumes I have endeavored to present, with as much kindly reserve in regard to his life as was consistent with justice, a view of his extraordinary intellectual and moral character. Unquestionably he was a man of genius, and those who are familiar with his melancholy history will not doubt that his genius was in a singular degree wasted or misapplied.

In poetry, as in prose, he was most successful in the metaphysical treatment of the passions. His poems are constructed with wonderful ingenuity and finished with consummate art. They illustrate a morbid sensitiveness of feeling, a shadowy and gloomy imagination, and a taste almost faultless in the apprehension of that sort of beauty most agreeable to his temper. His rank as a poet is with the first class of his times. "The Raven," "Ulalume." "The Bells," and several of his other pieces, will be remembered as among the finest monuments of the capacities of the English language.

THE CITY IN THE SEA.

Lo! Death has rear'd himself a throne
In a strange city lying alone
Far down within the dim west,
Where the good and the bad and the worst and the best
Have gone to their eternal rest.
There shrines, and palaces, and towers,
(Time-eaten towers that tremble not!)
Resemble nothing that is ours.
Around, by lifting winds forgot,
Resignedly beneath the sky
The melancholy waters lie.
No rays from the holy heaven come down
On the long night-time of that town;
But light from out the lurid sea
Streams up the turrets silently—
Gleams up the pinnacles far and free—
Up domes—up spires—up kingly halls—
Up fanes—up Babylon-like walls—
Up shadowy, long-forgotten bowers
Of sculptured ivy and stone flowers—
Up many and many a marvellous shrine
Whose wreathéd friezes intertwine
The viol, the violet, and the vine.
Resignedly beneath the sky
The melancholy waters lie.
So blend the turrets and shadows there
That all seem pendulous in air,
While from a proud tower in the town
Death looks gigantically down.
There open fanes and gaping graves
Yawn level with the luminous waves;
But not the riches there that lie
In each idol's diamond eye—
Not the gayly-jewell'd dead
Tempt the waters from their bed;
For no ripples curl, alas!
Along that wilderness of glass—
No swellings tell that winds may be
Upon some far-off happier sea—
No heavings hint that winds have been
On seas less hideously serene.
But lo, a stir is in the air!
The wave—there is a movement there!
As if the towers had thrust aside,
In slightly sinking, the dull tide—
As if their tops had feebly given
A void within the filmy heaven.
The waves have now a redder glow—
The hours are breathing faint and low—
And when, amid no earthly moans,
Down, down that town shall settle hence,
Hell, rising from a thousand thrones,
Shall do it reverence.

ANNABEL LEE.

It was many and many a year ago,
In a kingdom by the sea,
That a maiden there lived whom you may know
By the name of Annabel Lee;
And this maiden she lived with no other thought
Than to love and be loved by me.

I was a child and *she* was a child,
In this kingdom by the sea;
But we loved with a love that was more than love—
I and my Annabel Lee—
With a love that the wingéd seraphs of heaven
Coveted her and me.

And this was the reason that, long ago,
In this kingdom by the sea,
A wind blew out of a cloud, chilling
My beautiful Annabel Lee;
So that her highborn kinsmen came
And bore her away from me,
To shut her up in a sepulchre,
In this kingdom by the sea.

The angels, not half so happy in heaven,
Went envying her and me—
Yes!—that was the reason (as all men know,
In this kingdom by the sea),
That the wind came out of the cloud by night,
Chilling and killing my Annabel Lee.

But our love it was stronger by far than the love
Of those who were older than we—
Of many far wiser than we—
And neither the angels in heaven above,
Nor the demons down under the sea,
Can ever dissever my soul from the soul
Of the beautiful Annabel Lee:

For the moon never beams, without bringing me dreams
Of the beautiful Annabel Lee;
And the stars never rise, but I feel the bright eyes
Of the beautiful Annabel Lee:
And so, all the night-tide, I lie down by the side
Of my darling—my darling—my life and my bride,
In her sepulchre there by the sea—
In her tomb by the sounding sea.

ULALUME: A BALLAD.

THE skies they were ashen and sober;
  The leaves they were crispéd and sere—
  The leaves they were withering and sere;
It was night in the lonesome October
  Of my most immemorial year;
It was hard by the dim lake of Auber,
  In the misty mid region of Weir—
It was down by the dank tarn of Auber,
  In the ghoul-haunted woodland of Weir.

Here once, through an alley Titanic,
  Of cypress, I roamed with my soul—
  Of cypress, with Psyché, my soul.
These were days when my heart was volcanic
  As the scoriac rivers that roll—
  As the lavas that restlessly roll
Their sulphurous currents down Yaanek
  In the ultimate climes of the pole—
That groan as they roll down Mount Yaanek
  In the realms of the boreal pole.

Our talk had been serious and sober,
  But our thoughts they were palsied and sere—
  Our memories were treacherous and sere—
For we knew not the month was October,
  And we marked not the night of the year—
  (Ah, night of all nights in the year!)
We noted not the dim lake of Auber,
  (Though once we had journeyed down here)—
Remember'd not the dank tarn of Auber,
  Nor the ghoul-haunted woodland of Weir.

And now, as the night was senescent,
  And star-dials pointed to morn—
  As the star-dials hinted of morn—
At the end of our path a liquescent
  And nebulous lustre was born,
Out of which a miraculous crescent
  Arose with a duplicate horn—
Astarte's bediamonded crescent
  Distinct with its duplicate horn.

And I said—"She is warmer than Dian:
  She rolls through an ether of sighs—
  She revels in a region of sighs:
She has seen that the tears are not dry on
  These cheeks, where the worm never dies,
And has come past the stars of the Lion
  To point us the path to the skies—
  To the Lethean peace of the skies—
Come up, in despite of the Lion,
  To shine on us with her bright eyes—
Come up through the lair of the Lion,
  With love in her luminous eyes."

But Psyché, uplifting her finger,
  Said—"Sadly this star I mistrust—
  Her pallor I strangely mistrust:
Oh, hasten!—oh, let us not linger!
  Oh, fly!—let us fly!—for we must."
In terror she spoke, letting sink her
  Wings til they trai ed in the dust—
In agony sobbed letting sink her
  Plumes till they trailed in the dust—
  Till they sorrowfully tra'led in the dust.

I replied—"This is nothing but dreaming:
  Let us on by this tremulous light—
  Let us bathe in this crystalline light!
Its sybilic splendor is beaming
  With hope and in beauty to-night:
  See, it flickers up the sky through the night.
Ah, we safely may trust to its gleaming,
  And be sure it will lead us aright—
We safely may trust to a gleaming
  That cannot but guide us aright,
  Since it flickers up to heaven through the night."

Thus I pacified Psyché and kissed her,
  And tempted her out of her gloom—
  And conquered her scruples and gloom;
And we passed to the end of the vista,
  But were stopped by the door of a tomb—
  By the door of a legended tomb;
And I said, "What is written, sweet sister,
  On the door of this legended tomb?"
She replied, "Ulalume—Ulalume—
'T is the vault of thy lost Ulalume!"

Then my heart it grew ashen and sober
  As the leaves that were crispéd and sere—
  As the leaves that were withering and sere,
And I cried, "It was surely October
  On *this* very night of last year,
  That I journeyed—I journeyed down here—
  That I brought a dread burden down here—
  On this night of all nights in the year
  Oh, what demon has tempted me here!
Well I know, now, this dim lake of Auber,
  This misty mid region of Weir—
Well I know, now, this dank tarn of Auber,
  In the ghoul-haunted woodland of Weir."

Said *we* then—the two, then—"Ah, can it
  Have been that the woodlandish ghouls—
  The pitiful, the merciful ghouls—
To bar up our way and to ban it
  From the secret that lies in these wolds—
  From the thing that lies hidden in these wolds—
Have drawn up the spectre of a planet
  From the limbo of lunary souls—
This sinfully scintillant planet
  From the hell of the planetary souls?"

TO ZANTE.

FAIR isle, that from the fairest of all flowers
  Thy gentlest of all gentle names dost take!
How many memories of what radiant hours
  At sight of thee and thine at once awake!
How many scenes of what departed bliss!
  How many thoughts of what entombéd hopes!
How many visions of a maiden that is
  No more—no more upon thy verdant slopes!
No more! alas, that magical sad sound
Transforming all! Thy charms shall please *no more*—
Thy memory *no more!* Accursed ground
Henceforth I hold thy flower-enamelled shore,
O hyacinthine isle! O purple Zante!
  "Isola d'oro! Fior di Levante!"

TO —— —— ——.

I saw thee once—once only—years ago:
I must not say how many—but not many.
It was a July midnight; and from out
A full-orbed moon that, like thine own soul, soaring,
Sought a precipitant pathway up through heaven,
There fell a silvery-silken veil of light,
With quietude, and sultriness, and slumber,
Upon the upturned faces of a thousand
Roses that grew in an enchanted garden,
Where no wind dared to stir, unless on tiptoe—
Fell on the upturned faces of these roses
That gave out, in return for the love-light,
Their odorous souls in an ecstatic death—
Fell on the upturned faces of these roses
That smiled and died in this parterre, enchanted
By thee and by the poetry of thy presence.

Clad all in white, upon a violet bank
I saw thee half reclining; while the moon
Fell on the upturned faces of the roses,
And on thine own, upturned—alas! in sorrow.

Was it not Fate that, on this July midnight—
Was it not Fate (whose name is also Sorrow)
That bade me pause before that garden-gate
To breathe the incense of those slumbering roses?
No footstep stirred: the hated world all slept,
Save only thee and me. I paused—I looked—
And in an instant all things disappeared.
(Ah, bear in mind this garden was enchanted!)
The pearly lustre of the moon went out:
The mossy banks and the meandering paths,
The happy flowers and the repining trees,
Were seen no more: the very roses' odors
Died in the arms of the adoring airs.
All, all expired save thee—save less than thou:
Save only the divine light in thine eyes—
Save but the soul in thine uplifted eyes.
I saw but them—they were the world to me.
I saw but them—saw only them for hours—
Saw only them until the moon went down.
What wild heart-histories seemed to lie enwritten
Upon those crystalline, celestial spheres!
How dark a wo, yet how sublime a hope!
How silently serene a sea of pride!
How daring an ambition! yet how deep—
How fathomless a capacity for love!

But now, at length, dear Dian sank from sight
Into a western couch of thunder-cloud,
And thou, a ghost, amid the entombing trees
Didst glide away. Only thine eyes remained.
They would not go—they never yet have gone.
Lighting my lonely pathway home that night,
They have not left me (as my hopes have) since.
They follow me, they lead me through the years;
They are my ministers—yet I their slave.
Their office is to illumine and enkindle—
My duty, to be saved by their bright light,
And purified in their electric fire—
And sanctified in their elysian fire.
They fill my soul with beauty (which is hope),
And are far up in heaven, the stars I kneel to
In the sad, silent watches of my night;
While even in the meridian glare of day
I see them still—two sweetly scintillant
Venuses, unextinguished by the sun!

DREAM-LAND.

By a route obscure and lonely,
Haunted by ill angels only,
Where an Eidolon, named Night,
On a black throne reigns upright,
I have reached these lands but newly
From an ultimate dim Thulé—
From a wild, weird clime that lieth, sublime,
Out of space—out of time.

Bottomless vales and boundless floods,
And chasms, and caves, and Titan woods
With forms that no man can discover
For the dews that drip all over;
Mountains toppling evermore
Into seas without a shore;
Seas that restlessly aspire,
Surging, unto skies of fire;
Lakes that endlessly outspread
Their lone waters—lone and dead—
Their still waters—still and chilly
With the snows of the lolling lily.

By the lakes that thus outspread
Their lone waters, lone and dead—
Their sad waters, sad and chilly
With the snows of the lolling lily—
By the mountains, near the river
Murmuring lowly, murmuring ever—
By the gray woods—by the swamp
Where the toad and the newt encamp—
By the dismal tarns and pools
Where dwell the ghouls—
By each spot the most unholy,
In each nook most melancholy—
There the traveller meets aghast
Sheeted memories of the past;
Shrouded forms that start and sigh
As they pass the wanderer by;
White-robed forms of friends long given,
In agony, to earth—and heaven!

For the heart whose woes are legion
'T is a peaceful, soothing region;
For the spirit that walks in shadow
'T is—oh, 't is an Eldorado!
But the traveller, travelling through it,
May not, dare not openly view it;
Never its mysteries are exposed
To the weak human eye unclosed;
So wills its King, who hath forbid
The uplifting of the fringed lid;
And thus the sad soul that here passes
Beholds it but through darken'd glasses.

By a route obscure and lonely,
Haunted by ill angels only,
Where an Eidolon, named Night,
On a black throne reigns upright,
I have wander'd home but newly
From this ultimate dim Thulé.

LENORE.

AH, broken is the golden bowl,
The spirit flown forever!
Let the bell toll!
A saintly soul
Floats on the Stygian river
And, GUY DE VERE,
Hast *thou* no tear!
Weep now or never more!
See, on yon drear
And rigid bier
Low lies thy love, LENORE!
Come, let the burial-rite be read—
The funeral-song be sung!—
An anthem for the queenliest dead
That ever died so young—
A dirge for her the doubly dead,
In that she died so young!

"Wretches! ye loved her for her wealth,
And hated her for her pride;
And when she fell in feeble health,
Ye bless'd her—that she died!
How *shall* the ritual, then, be read?
The requiem how be sung
By you—by yours, the evil eye—
By yours, the slanderous tongue
That did to death the innocence
That died, and died so young!"

Peccavimus;
But rave not thus!
And let a sabbath song
Go up to God so solemnly, the dead may feel no wrong!
The sweet LENORE
Hath "gone before,"
With Hope, that flew beside,
Leaving thee wild
For the dear child
That should have been thy bride—
For her, the fair
And *debonair*,
That now so lowly lies,
The life upon her yellow hair
But not within her eyes—
The life still there,
Upon her hair—
The death upon her eyes.

"Avaunt! to-night
My heart is light.
No dirge will I upraise,
But waft the angel on her flight
With a pæan of old days!
Let *no* bell toll!—
Lest her sweet soul,
Amid its hallow'd mirth,
Should catch the note,
As it doth float—
Up from the damnéd earth.
To friends above, from fiends below,
The indignant ghost is riven—
From hell unto a high estate
Far up within the heaven—
From grief and groan,
To a golden throne,
Beside the King of Heaven."

ISRAFEL.*

IN heaven a spirit doth dwell
"Whose heart-strings are a lute;"
None sing so wildly well
As the angel ISRAFEL,
And the giddy stars (so legends tell)
Ceasing their hymns, attend the spell
Of his voice, all mute.

Tottering above
In her highest noon,
The enamour'd moon
Blushes with love,
While, to listen, the red levin
(With the rapid Pleiads, even,
Which were seven)
Pauses in heaven.

And they say (the starry choir
And the other listening things)
That ISRAFELI's fire
Is owing to that lyre
By which he sits and sings—
The trembling living wire
Of those unusual strings.

But the skies that angel trod,
Where deep thoughts are a duty—
Where Love's a grown-up god—
Where the Houri glances are
Imbued with all the beauty
Which we worship in a star.

Therefore, thou art not wrong,
ISRAFELI, who despisest
An unimpassion'd song;
To thee the laurels belong,
Best bard, because the wisest!
Merrily live, and long!

The ecstasies above
With thy burning measures suit—
Thy grief, thy joy, thy hate, thy love,
With the fervour of thy lute—
Well may the stars be mute!
Yes, heaven is thine; but this
Is a world of sweets and sours;
Our flowers are merely—flowers,
And the shadow of thy perfect bliss
Is the sunshine of ours.

If I could dwell
Where ISRAFEL
Hath dwelt, and he where I,
He might not sing so wildly well
A mortal melody,
While a bolder note than this might swell
From my lyre within the sky.

* "And the angel ISRAFEL, whose heart-strings are a lute, and who has the sweetest voice of all God's creatures." KORAN.

THE BELLS.

I.

Hear the sledges with the bells—
Silver bells—
What a world of merriment their melody foretells!
How they tinkle, tinkle, tinkle,
In the icy air of night!
While the stars that oversprinkle
All the heavens, seem to twinkle
With a crystalline delight;
Keeping time, time, time,
In a sort of Runic rhyme,
To the tintinabulation that so musically wells
From the bells, bells, bells, bells,
Bells, bells, bells—
From the jingling and the tinkling of the bells.

II.

Hear the mellow wedding bells,
Golden bells!
What a world of happiness their harmony foretells!
Through the balmy air of night
How they ring out their delight!
From the molten-golden notes,
And all in tune,
What a liquid ditty floats
To the turtle-dove that listens, while she gloats
On the moon!
Oh, from out the sounding cells,
What a gush of euphony voluminously wells!
How it swells!
How it dwells
On the Future! how it tells
Of the rapture that impels
To the swinging and the ringing
Of the bells, bells, bells,
Of the bells, bells, bells, bells,
Bells, bells, bells—
To the rhyming and the chiming of the bells!

III.

Hear the loud alarum bells—
Brazen bells!
What a tale of terror, now, their turbulency tells!
In the startled ear of night
How they scream out their affright!
Too much horrified to speak,
They can only shriek, shriek,
Out of tune,
In a clamorous appealing to the mercy of the fire,
In a mad expostulation with the deaf and frantic fire
Leaping higher, higher, higher,
With a desperate desire,
And a resolute endeavour
Now—now to sit or never,
By the side of the pale-faced moon.
Oh, the bells, bells, bells!
What a tale their terror tells
Of Despair!
How they clang, and clash, and roar!
What a horror they outpour
On the bosom of the palpitating air!
Yet the ear it fully knows,
By the twanging,
And the clanging,
How the danger ebbs and flows;
Yet the ear distinctly tells,
In the jangling,
And the wrangling,
How the danger sinks and swells,
By the sinking or the swelling in the anger of the bells—
Of the bells—
Of the bells, bells, bells, bells,
Bells, bells, bells—
In the clamour and the clangour of the bells!

IV.

Hear the tolling of the bells—
Iron bells!
What a world of solemn thought their monody compels!
In the silence of the night,
How we shiver with affright
At the melancholy menace of their tone!
For every sound that floats
From the rust within their throats
Is a groan.
And the people—ah, the people—
They that dwell up in the steeple,
All alone,
And who tolling, tolling, tolling,
In that muffled monotone,
Feel a glory in so rolling
On the human heart a stone—
They are neither man nor woman—
They are neither brute nor human—
They are Ghouls:
And their king it is who tolls;
And he rolls, rolls, rolls,
Rolls,
A pæan from the bells!
And his merry bosom swells
With the pæan of the bells!
And he dances and he yells;
Keeping time, time, time,
In a sort of Runic rhyme,
To the pæan of the bells—
Of the bells:
Keeping time, time, time,
In a sort of Runic rhyme,
To the throbbing of the bells—
Of the bells, bells, bells—
To the sobbing of the bells;
Keeping time, time, time,
As he knells, knells, knells,
In a happy Runic rhyme,
To the rolling of the bells—
Of the bells, bells, bells—
To the tolling of the bells,
Of the bells, bells, bells, bells—
Bells, bells, bells—
To the moaning and the groaning of the bells.

TO F. S. O.

Thou wouldst be loved?—then let thy heart
From its present pathway part not!
Being every thing which now thou art,
Be nothing which thou art not.
So with the world thy gentle ways,
Thy grace, thy more than beauty,
Shall be an endless theme of praise,
And love—a simple duty.

FOR ANNIE.

Thank Heaven! the crisis—
  The danger, is past,
And the lingering illness
  Is over at last—
And the fever called "Living"
  Is conquer'd at last.

Sadly, I know
  I am shorn of my strength,
And no muscle I move
  As I lie at full length;
But no matter!—I feel
  I am better at length.

And I rest so composedly,
  Now, in my bed,
That any beholder
  Might fancy me dead—
Might start at beholding me,
  Thinking me dead.

The moaning and groaning,
  The sighing and sobbing,
Are quieted now,
  With that horrible throbbing
At heart:—ah that horrible,
  Horrible throbbing!

The sickness—the nausea—
  The pitiless pain—
Have ceased, with the fever
  That madden'd my brain—
With the fever called "Living"
  That burn'd in my brain.

And oh! of all tortures,
  That torture the worst
Has abated—the terrible
  Torture of thirst
For the napthaline river
  Of Passion accurst:
I have drank of a water
  That quenches all thirst:—

Of a water that flows,
  With a lullaby sound,
From a spring but a very few
  Feet under ground—
From a cavern not very far
  Down under ground.

And ah! let it never
  Be foolishly said
That my room it is gloomy
  And narrow my bed;
For man never slept
  In a different bed—
And, *to sleep*, you must slumber
  In just such a bed.

My tantalized spirit
  Here blandly reposes,
Forgetting, or never
  Regretting, its roses—
Its old agitations
  Of myrtles and roses:

For now, while so quietl
  Lying, it fancies
A holier odour
  About it, of pansies—
A rosemary odour,
  Commingled with pansies—
With rue and the beautiful
  Puritan pansies.

And so it lies happily,
  Bathing in many
A dream of the truth
  And the beauty of Annie—
Drown'd in a bath
  Of the tresses of Annie.

She tenderly kiss'd me
  She fondly caress'd,
And then I fell gently
  To sleep on her breast—
Deeply to sleep
  From the heaven of her breast.

When the light was extinguish d,
  She cover'd me warm,
And she pray'd to the angels
  To keep me from harm—
To the queen of the angels
  To shield me from harm.

And I lie so composedly,
  Now, in my bed,
(Knowing her love,)
  That you fancy me dead—
And I rest so contentedly,
  Now, in my bed,
(With her love at my breast,)
  That you fancy me dead—
That you shudder to look at me,
  Thinking me dead:—

But my heart it is brighter
  Than all of the many
Stars of the sky,
  For it sparkles with Annie—
It glows with the light
  Of the love of my Annie—
With the thought of the light
  Of the eyes of my Annie.

TO ONE IN PARADISE.

Thou wast all that to me, love,
  For which my soul did pine—
A green isle in the sea, love,
  A fountain and a shrine,
All wreath'd with fairy fruits and flowers
  And all the flowers were mine.

Ah, dream too bright to last!
  Ah, starry Hope! that didst arise
But to be overcast!
  A voice from out the Future cries,
"On! on!"—but o'er the Past
  (Dim gulf!) my spirit hovering lies
Mute, motionless, aghast!

For, alas! alas! with me
  The light of life is o'er!
  No more—no more—no more—
(Such language holds the solemn sea
  To the sands upon the shore)

Shall bloom the thunder-blasted tree,
Or the stricken eagle soar!

And all my days are trances,
And all my nightly dreams
Are where thy dark eye glances,
And where thy footstep gleams—
In what ethereal dances,
By what eternal streams.

THE RAVEN.

Once upon a midnight dreary,
While I ponder'd, weak and weary,
Over many a quaint and curious
Volume of forgotten lore,
While I nodded, nearly napping,
Suddenly there came a tapping,
As of some one gently rapping,
Rapping at my chamber door.
"'Tis some visiter," I mutter'd,
"Tapping at my chamber door—
Only this, and nothing more."

Ah, distinctly I remember,
It was in the bleak December,
And each separate dying ember
Wrought its ghost upon the floor.
Eagerly I wish'd the morrow;
Vainly I had tried to borrow
From my books surcease of sorrow—
Sorrow for the lost Lenore—
For the rare and radiant maiden
Whom the angels name Lenore—
Nameless here for evermore.

And the silken, sad, uncertain
Rustling of each purple curtain
Thrill'd me—fill'd me with fantastic
Terrors never felt before;
So that now, to still the beating
Of my heart, I stood repeating
"'Tis some visiter entreating
Entrance at my chamber door—
Some late visiter entreating
Entrance at my chamber door;—
This it is, and nothing more."

Presently my soul grew stronger;
Hesitating then no longer,
"Sir," said I, "or Madam, truly
Your forgiveness I implore;
But the fact is I was napping,
And so gently you came rapping,
And so faintly you came tapping,
Tapping at my chamber door,
That I scarce was sure I heard you,"—
Here I open'd wide the door:
Darkness there, and nothing more!

Deep into that darkness peering,
Long I stood there wondering, fearing,
Doubting, dreaming dreams no mortal
Ever dared to dream before;
But the silence was unbroken,
And the darkness gave no token,
And the only word there spoken
Was the whisper'd word, "Lenore!"
This *I* whisper'd, and an echo
Murmur'd back the word, "Lenore!"
Merely this, and nothing more.

Then into the chamber turning,
All my soul within me burning,
Soon I heard again a tapping
Somewhat louder than before.
"Surely," said I, "surely that is
Something at my window lattice;
Let me see, then, what thereat is,
And this mystery explore—
Let my heart be still a moment,
And this mystery explore;—
'Tis the wind, and nothing more!"

Open here I flung the shutter,
When, with many a flirt and flutter,
In there stepp'd a stately raven
Of the saintly days of yore;
Not the least obeisance made he;
Not an instant stopp'd or stay'd he;
But, with mien of lord or lady,
Perch'd above my chamber door—
Perch'd upon a bust of Pallas
Just above my chamber door—
Perch'd, and sat, and nothing more.

Then this ebony bird beguiling
My sad fancy into smiling,
By the grave and stern decorum
Of the countenance it wore,
"Though thy crest be shorn and shaven,
Thou," I said, "art sure no craven,
Ghastly grim and ancient raven,
Wandering from the Nightly shore—
Tell me what thy lordly name is
On the Night's Plutonian shore!"
Quoth the raven "Nevermore."

Much I marvell'd this ungainly
Fowl to hear discourse so plainly,
Though its answer little meaning—
Little relevancy bore;
For we cannot help agreeing
That no living human being
Ever yet was bless'd with seeing
Bird above his chamber door—
Bird or beast upon the sculptured
Bust above his chamber door,
With such name as "Nevermore.

But the raven sitting lonely
On the placid bust, spoke only
That one word, as if his soul in
That one word he did outpour.
Nothing farther then he utter'd—
Not a feather then he flutter'd—
Till I scarcely more than mutter'd
"Other friends have flown before—
On the morrow *he* will leave me,
As my hopes have flown before."
Then the bird said "Nevermore."

Startled at the stillness broken
By reply so aptly spoken,
"Doubtless," said I, "what it utters
Is its only stock and store
Caught from some unhappy master
Whom unmerciful Disaster
Follow'd fast and follow'd faster,
Till his songs one burden bore—
Till the dirges of his Hope the
Melancholy burden bore
Of 'Nevermore,'—of 'Nevermore.'"

But the raven still beguiling
All my sad soul into smiling,
Straight I wheel'd a cushion'd seat in
Front of bird, and bust and door;
Then upon the velvet sinking,
I betook myself to linking
Fancy unto fancy, thinking
What this ominous bird of yore—
What this grim, ungainly, ghastly,
Gaunt and ominous bird of yore
Meant in croaking "Nevermore."

This I sat engaged in guessing,
But no syllable expressing
To the fowl whose fiery eyes now
Burn'd into my bosom's core;
This and more I sat divining,
With my head at ease reclining
On the cushion's velvet lining
That the lamplight gloated o'er
But whose velvet violet lining
With the lamplight gloating o'er,
She shall press, ah, never more!

Then, methought, the air grew denser,
Perfum'd from an unseen censer,
Swung by angels whose faint foot-falls
Tinkled on the tufted floor.
"Wretch," I cried, "thy God hath lent thee
By these angels he hath sent thee
Respite—respite and nepenthe
From thy memories of Lenore!
Quaff, oh quaff this kind nepenthe,
And forget this lost Lenore!"
Quoth the raven "Nevermore."

"Prophet!" said I, "thing of evil!—
Prophet still, if bird or devil!
Whether tempter sent, or whether
Tempest toss'd thee here ashore,
Desolate yet all undaunted,
On this desert land enchanted—
On this home by Horror haunted—
Tell me truly, I implore—
Is there—is there balm in Gilead?
Tell me—tell me, I implore!"
Quoth the raven "Nevermore."

"Prophet!" said I, "thing of evil—
Prophet still, if bird or devil!
By that heaven that bends above us—
By that God we both adore—
Tell this soul with sorrow laden
If, within the distant Aidenn,
It shall clasp a sainted maiden
Whom the angels name Lenore—
Clasp a rare and radiant maiden
Whom the angels name Lenore."
Quoth the raven "Nevermore."

"Be that word our sign of parting,
Bird or fiend!" I shriek'd, upstarting—
"Get thee back into the tempest
And the Night's Plutonian shore!
Leave no black plume as a token
Of that lie thy soul hath spoken!
Leave my loneliness unbroken!—
Quit the bust above my door!
Take thy beak from out my heart,
And take thy form from off my door!"
Quoth the raven "Nevermore."

And the raven, never flitting,
Still is sitting, still is sitting
On the pallid bust of Pallas
Just above my chamber door;
And his eyes have all the seeming
Of a demon that is dreaming,
And the lamplight o'er him streaming
Throws his shadow on the floor;
And my soul from out that shadow
That lies floating on the floor
Shall be lifted—nevermore!

THE CONQUEROR WORM.

Lo! 'tis a gala night
Within the lonesome latter years!
An angel throng, bewing'd, bedight
In veils, and drown'd in tears,
Sit in a theatre, to see
A play of hopes and fears,
While the orchestra breathes fitfully
The music of the spheres.

Mimes, in the form of God on high,
Mutter and mumble low,
And hither and thither fly—
Mere puppets they, who come and go
At bidding of vast formless things
That shift the scenery to and fro,
Flapping from out their Condor wings
Invisible Wo!

That motley drama!—oh, be sure
It shall not be forgot!
With its Phantom chased for evermore,
By a crowd that seize it not,
Through a circle that ever returneth in
To the self-same spot,
And much of Madness, and more of Sin,
And Horror the soul of the plot.

But see, amid the mimic rout,
A crawling shape intrude!
A blood-red thing that writhes from out
The scenic solitude!
It writhes!—it writhes!—with mortal pangs,
The mimes become its food,
And the angels sob at vermin fangs
In human gore imbued.

Out—out are the lights—out all!
  And, over each quivering form,
The curtain, a funeral pall,
  Comes down with the rush of a storm,
And the angels, all pallid and wan,
  Uprising, unveiling, affirm
That the play is the tragedy, "Man,"
  Its hero the Conqueror Worm.

THE HAUNTED PALACE.

In the greenest of our valleys,
  By good angels tenanted,
Once a fair and stately palace
  (Snow-white palace) rear'd its head.
In the monarch Thought's dominion
  It stood there!
Never seraph spread a pinion
  Over fabric half so fair.

Banners, yellow, glorious, golden,
  On its roof did float and flow;
(This, all this, was in the olden
  Time, long ago.)
And every gentle air that dallied,
  In that sweet day,
Along the ramparts plumed and pallid,
  A winged odour went away.

Wanderers in that happy valley
  Through two luminous windows saw
Spirits moving musically,
  To a lute's well-tunéd law;
Round about a throne, where, sitting
  (Porphyrogene!)
In state his glory well-befitting,
  The ruler of the realm was seen.

And all with pearl and ruby glowing
  Was the fair palace-door,
Through which came flowing, flowing, flowing,
  And sparkling evermore,
A troop of echoes, whose sweet duty
  Was but to sing,
In voices of surpassing beauty,
  The wit and wisdom of their king.

But evil things, in robes of sorrow,
  Assail'd the monarch's high estate;
(Ah! let us mourn, for never morrow
  Shall dawn upon him, desolate!)
And round about his home the glory
  That blush'd and bloom'd,
Is but a dim-remember'd story
  Of the old time entomb'd.

And travellers now within that valley,
  Through the red-litten windows see
Vast forms, that move fantastically
  To a discordant melody;
While, like a rapid, ghastly river,
  Through the pale door,
A hideous throng rush out for ever,
  And laugh—but smile no more.

THE SLEEPER.

At midnight, in the month of June,
I stand beneath the mystic moon.
An opiate vapour, dewy, dim,
Exhales from out her golden rim,
And, softly dripping, drop by drop,
Upon the quiet mountain-top,
Steals drowsily and musically
Into the universal valley.
The rosemary nods upon the grave;
The lily lolls upon the wave;
Wrapping the mist about its breast,
The ruin moulders into rest;
Looking like Lethe, see, the lake
A conscious slumber seems to take,
And would not for the world awake.
All beauty sleeps!—and, lo! where lies,
With casement open to the skies,
Irene and her destinies!

O, lady bright, can it be right,
This lattice open to the night?
The bodiless airs, a wizard rout,
Flit through thy chamber, in and out,
And wave the curtain-canopy
So fitfully, so fearfully,
Above the closed and fringéd lid
'Neath which thy slumbering soul lies hid.
That o'er the floor and down the wall,
Like ghosts, the shadows rise and fall.
O, lady dear, hast thou no fear?
Why and what art thou dreaming here?
Sure thou art come o'er far-off seas,
A wonder to our garden-trees!
Strange is thy pallor—strange thy dress—
Stranger thy glorious length of tress,
And this all-solemn silentness!

The lady sleeps. O, may her sleep,
Which is enduring, so be deep!
Soft may the worms about her creep!
This bed, being changed for one more holy,
This room for one more melancholy,
I pray to God that she may lie
Forever with uncloséd eye!
My love she sleeps. O, may her sleep,
As it is lasting, so be deep!
Heaven have her in its sacred keep!
Far in the forest, dim and old,
For her may some tall tomb unfold—
Some tomb that oft hath flung its black
And wing-like pannels, fluttering back,
Triumphant o'er the crested palls
Of her grand family funerals,—
Some sepulchre, remote, alone,
Against whose portal she hath thrown,
In childhood, many an idle stone,—
Some vault from out whose sounding door
She ne'er shall force an echo more,
Nor thrill to think, poor child of sin,
It was the dead who groan'd within.

ALFRED B. STREET.

[B. c. 1811.]

Mr. Street was born in Poughkeepsie, one of the most beautiful of the many large towns upon the Hudson, on the eighteenth of December, 1811. General Randall S. Street, his father, was an officer in active service during our second war with England, and subsequently several years a representative in Congress; and his paternal grandfather was a direct and lineal descendant of the Reverend Nicholas Street, who came to this country soon after the landing of John Carver, and was ordained minister of the first church in New Haven, in 1659. His mother's father was Major Andrew Billings, of the revolutionary army, who was connected by marriage with the influential and wealthy family of the Livingstons, which has furnished for some two centuries so many eminent citizens of the State of New York.

When the poet was about fourteen years of age his father removed to Monticello, in the county of Sullivan. Up to this period he had been in an academy at Poughkeepsie, and had already written verses in which is exhibited some of that peculiar taste, and talent for description, for which his later works are so much distinguished. Sullivan is what is called a "wild county," though it is extremely fertile where well cultivated. Its scenery is magnificent, and its deep forests, streams as clear as dew-drops, gorges of piled rock and black shade, mountains and valleys, could hardly fail to waken into life all the faculties that slumbered in the brain of a youthful poet.

Mr. Street studied law in the office of his father, and, in the first years after his admission to the bar, attended the courts of Sullivan county; but in the winter of 1839 he removed to Albany, and has since successfully practised his profession in that city.

His "Nature," a poem read before the literary societies of the college at Geneva, appeared in 1840; "The Burning of Schenectady and other Poems," in 1843, and "Drawings and Tintings," a collection of pieces chiefly descriptive, in 1844. The last and most complete edition of his poems was published by Clark and Austin, of New York, in 1845.

Mr. Street, as has been intimated above, is a descriptive poet, and in his particular department he has, perhaps, no superior in this country. He has a hearty love of rural sports and pastimes, a quick perception of the grand and beautiful, and he writes with apparent ease and freedom, from the impulses of his own heart, and from actual observations of life and nature.

The greatest merits of any style of writing are clearness, directness and condensation. Diffuseness is even more objectionable in verse than in prose, and in either is avoided by men of taste. A needless word is worse than one ill chosen, and scarcely any thing is more offensive than a line, though never was other one so musical, which could be omitted without affecting the transparency or force of the attempted expression. The beauty of Mr. Street's poems would sometimes be greater but for the use of epithets which serve no other purpose than to fill his lines, and his singular minuteness, though the most extreme particularity is a fault in description only when it lessens the distinctness and fidelity of the general impression. Occasionally his pictures of still nature remind us of the daguerreotype, and quite as often of the masterly landscapes of our Cole and Doughty. Some of his exhibitions of the ordinary phenomena of the seasons have rarely been equalled. What, for example, could be finer than these lines on a rain in June?—

> Wafted up,
> The stealing cloud with soft gray blinds the sky,
> And, in its vapoury mantle, onward steps
> The summer shower; over the shivering grass
> It merrily dances, rings its tinkling bells
> Upon the dimpling stream, and moving on,
> It treads upon the leaves with pattering feet
> And softly murmur'd music. Off it glides,
> And as its misty robe lifts up, and melts,
> The sunshine, darting, with a sudden burst,
> Strikes o'er the scene a magic brilliancy.

His works are full of passages not less picturesque and truthful. The remarkable fidelity of Mr. Street's description and narrative is best appreciated by persons who are familiar with new settlements in our northern latitudes. To others he may seem always lashing himself into excitement, to be extravagant, and to exaggerate beyond the requirements of art. But within a rifle-shot of the little village where nearly all his life has been passed, are centurial woods, from which the howlings of wolves have disturbed his sleep, and in which he has tracked the bear and the deer, and roused from their nests their winged inhabitants. In the spring time he has looked from his window upon fallow fires, and in the summer upon fields of waving grain, spotted by undecayed stumps of forest giants, and on trees that stand, charred and black, in mournful observation of the settler's invasion. Scenes and incidents which the inhabitant of the city might regard as extraordinary have been to him common and familiar, and his writings are valuable as the fruits of a genuine American experience, to which the repose, of which it is complained that they are deficient, does not belong. They are on some accounts among the most peculiarly *national* works in our literature.

THE GRAY FOREST-EAGLE.

WITH storm-daring pinion and sun-gazing eye,
The gray forest-eagle is king of the sky!
O, little he loves the green valley of flowers,
Where sunshine and song cheer the bright summer hours,
For he hears in those haunts only music, and sees
Only rippling of waters and waving of trees;
There the red robin warbles, the honey-bee hums,
The timid quail whistles, the sly partridge drums;
And if those proud pinions, perchance, sweep along,
There's a shrouding of plumage, a hushing of song;
The sunlight falls stilly on leaf and on moss,
And there's naught but his shadow black gliding across;
But the dark, gloomy gorge, where down plunges the foam
Of the fierce, rock-lash'd torrent, he claims as his home:
There he blends his keen shriek with the roar of the flood,
And the many-voiced sounds of he blast-smitten wood;
From the crag-grasping fir-top, where morn hangs its wreath,
He views the mad waters white writhing beneath:
On a limb of that moss-bearded hemlock far down,
With bright azure mantle and gay mottled crown,
The kingfisher watches, where o'er him his foe,
The fierce hawk, sails circling, each moment more low:
Now poised are those pinions and pointed that beak,
His dread swoop is ready, when, hark! with a shriek,
His eye-balls red-blazing, high bristling his crest,
His snake-like neck arch'd, talons drawn to his breast,
With the rush of the wind-gust, the glancing of light,
The gray forest-eagle shoots down in his flight;
One blow of those talons, one plunge of that neck,
The strong hawk hangs lifeless, a blood-dripping wreck;
And as dives the free kingfisher, dart-like on high
With his prey soars the eagle, and melts in the sky.

A fitful red glaring, a low, rumbling jar,
Proclaim the storm demon yet raging afar:
The black cloud strides upward, the lightning more red,
And the roll of the thunder more deep and more dread;
A thick pall of darkness is cast o'er the air,
And on bounds the blast with a howl from its lair:
The lightning darts zig-zag and fork'd through the gloom,
And the bolt launches o'er with crash, rattle, and boom;
The gray forest-eagle, where, where has he sped?
Does he shrink to his eyrie, and shiver with dread?
Does the glare blind his eye? Has the terrible blast
On the wing of the sky-king a fear-fetter cast?
No, no, the brave eagle! he thinks not of fright;
The wrath of the tempest but rouses delight;
To the flash of the lightning his eye casts a gleam,
To the shriek of the wild blast he echoes his scream,
And with front like a warrior that speeds to the fray,
And a clapping of pinions, he's up and away!
Away, O, away, soars the fearless and free!
What recks he the sky's strife?—its monarch is he!
The lightning darts round him, undaunted his sight;
The blast sweeps against him, unwaver'd his flight;
High upward, still upward, he wheels, till his form
Is lost in the black, scowling gloom of the storm.

The tempest sweeps o'er with its terrible train,
And the splendour of sunshine is glowing again;
Again smiles the soft, tender blue of the sky,
Waked bird-voices warble, fann'd leaf-voices sigh;
On the green grass dance shadows, streams sparkle and run,
The breeze bears the odour its flower-kiss has won,
And full on the form of the demon in flight
The rainbow's magnificence gladdens the sight!
The gray forest-eagle! O, where is he now,
While the sky wears the smile of its GOD on its brow?
There's a dark, floating spot by yon cloud's pearly wreath,
With the speed of the arrow 't is shooting beneath!
Down, nearer and nearer it draws to the gaze,
Now over the rainbow, now blent with its blaze,
To a shape it expands, still it plunges through air,
A proud crest, a fierce eye, a broad wing are there;
'T is the eagle—the gray forest-eagle—once more
He sweeps to his eyrie: his journey is o'er!

Time whirls round his circle, his years roll away,
But the gray forest-eagle minds little his sway;
The child spurns its buds for youth's thorn-hidden bloom,
Seeks manhood's bright phantoms, finds age and a tomb;
But the eagle's eye dims not, his wing is unbow'd,
Still drinks he the sunshine, still scales he the cloud!
The green, tiny pine-shrub points up from the moss,
The wren's foot would cover it, tripping across;
The beech-nut down dropping would crush it beneath,
But 't is warm'd with heaven's sunshine, and fann'd by its breath;
The seasons fly past it, its head is on high,
Its thick branches challenge each mood of the sky;
On its rough bark the moss a green mantle creates,
And the deer from his antlers the velvet-down grates;
Time withers its roots, it lifts sadly in air
A trunk dry and wasted, a top jagg'd and bare,
Till it rocks in the soft breeze, and crashes to earth,
Its blown fragments strewing the place of its birth.
The eagle has seen it up-struggling to sight,
He has seen it defying the storm in its might,
Then prostrate, soil-blended, with plants sprouting o'er,
But the gray forest-eagle is still as of yore.
His flaming eye dims not, his wing is unbow'd,
Still drinks he the sunshine, still scales he the cloud!
He has seen from his eyrie the forest below
In bud and in leaf, robed with crimson and snow.
The thickets, deep wolf-lairs, the high crag his throne,
And the shriek of the panther has answer'd his own.
He has seen the wild red man the lord of the shades,
And the smoke of his wigwams curl thick in the glades;
He has seen the proud forest melt breath-like away,
And the breast of the earth lying bare to the day;

He sees the green meadow-grass hiding the lair,
And his crag-throne spread naked to sun and to air;
And his shriek is now answer'd, while sweeping along,
By the low of the herd and the husbandman's song;
He has seen the wild red man off-swept by his foes,
And he sees dome and roof where those smokes once arose;
But his flaming eye dims not, his wing is unbow'd,
Still drinks he the sunshine, still scales he the cloud!

An emblem of Freedom, stern, haughty, and high,
Is the gray forest-eagle, that king of the sky!
It scorns the bright scenes, the gay places of earth—
By the mountain and torrent it springs into birth;
There rock'd by the wild wind, baptized in the foam,
It is guarded and cherish'd, and there is its home!
When its shadow steals black o'er the empires of kings,
Deep terror, deep heart-shaking terror it brings;
Where wicked Oppression is arm'd for the weak,
Then rustles its pinion, then echoes its shriek;
Its eye flames with vengeance, it sweeps on its way,
And its talons are bathed in the blood of its prey.
O, that eagle of Freedom! when cloud upon cloud
Swathed the sky of my own native land with a shroud,
When lightnings gleam'd fiercely, and thunder-bolts rung,
How proud to the tempest those pinions were flung!
Though the wild blast of battle swept fierce through the air
With darkness and dread, still the eagle was there;
Unquailing, still speeding, his swift flight was on,
Till the rainbow of Peace crown'd the victory won.
O, that eagle of Freedom! age dims not his eye,
He has seen Earth's mortality spring, bloom, and die!
He has seen the strong nations rise, flourish, and fall,
He mocks at Time's changes, he triumphs o'er all:
He has seen our own land with wild forests o'erspread,
He sees it with sunshine and joy on its head;
And his presence will bless this, his own, chosen clime,
Till the archangel's fiat is set upon time.

FOWLING.

A MORN in September, the east is yet gray;
Come, Carlo! come, Jupe! we'll try fowling to-day:
The fresh sky is bright as the bright face of one,
A sweeter than whom the sun shines not upon;
And those wreathed clouds that melt to the breath of the south,
Are white as the pearls of her beautiful mouth:
My hunting-piece glitters, and quick is my task
In slinging around me my pouch and my flask;
Cease, dogs, your loud yelpings, you'll deafen my brain!
Desist from your rambles, and follow my train.

Here, leave the geese, Carlo, to nibble their grass,
Though they do stretch their long necks, and hiss as we pass·
And the fierce litte bantam, that flies your attack,
Then struts, flaps, and crows, with such airs, at your back;
And the turkey, too, smoothing his plumes in your face,
Then ruffling so proud, as you bound from the place;
Ha! ha! that old hen, bristling up mid her brood,
Has taught you a lesson, I hope, for your good;
By the wink of your eye, and the droop of your crest,
I see your maraudings are now put at rest.

The rail-fence is leap'd, and the wood-boughs are round,
And a moss-couch is spread for my foot on the ground:
A shadow has dimm'd the leaves' amethyst glow,
The first glance of Autumn, his presence to show.
The beech-nut is ripening above in its sheath,
Which will burst with the black frost, and drop it beneath.
The hickory hardens, snow-white, in its burr,
And the cones are full grown on the hemlock and fir;
The hopple's red berries are tinging with brown,
And the tips of the sumach have darken'd their down;
The white, brittle Indian-pipe lifts up its bowl,
And the wild turnip's leaf curls out broad like a scroll;
The cohosh displays its white balls and red stems,
And the braid of the mullen is yellow with gems;
While its rich, spangled plumage the golden-rod shows,
And the thistle yields stars to each air-breath that blows.

A quick, startling whirr now bursts loud on my ear,
The partridge! the partridge! swift pinion'd by fear,
Low onward he whizzes, Jupe yelps as he sees,
And we dash through the brushwood, to note where he trees;
I see him! his brown, speckled breast is display'd
On the branch of yon maple, that edges the glade;
My fowling-piece rings, Jupe darts forward so fleet,
While loading, he drops the dead bird at my feet:
I pass by the scaurberries' drops of deep red,
In their green, creeping leaves, where he daintily fed,
And his couch near the root, in the warm forest-mould,
Where he wallow'd, till sounds his close danger foretold.

On yon spray, the bright oriole dances and sings,
With his rich, crimson bosom, and glossy black wings;
And the robin comes warbling, then flutters away,
For I harm not GOD's creatures so tiny as they;
But the quail, whose quick whistle has lured me along,
No more will recall his stray'd mate with his song,
And the hawk that is circling so proud in the blue,
Let him keep a look-out, or he'll tumble down too
He stoops—the gun echoes—he flutters beneath,
His yellow claws curl'd, and fierce eyes glazed in death:
Lie there, cruel Arab! the mocking-bird now
Can rear her young brood, without fear of thy blow
And the brown wren can warble his sweet little lay,
Nor dread more thy talons to rend and to slay:
And, with luck, an example I'll make of that crow,
For my green, sprouting wheat knew no hungrier foe;
But the rascal seems down from his summit to scoff,
And as I creep near him, he croaks, and is off.

The woods shrink away, and wide spreads the morass,
With junipers cluster'd, and matted with grass;
Trees, standing like ghosts, their arms jagged and bare,
And hung with gray lichens, like age-whiten'd hair.
The tamarack here and there rising between,
Its boughs clothed with rich, star-like fringes of green,
And clumps of dense laurels, and brown-headed flags,
And thick, slimy basins, black dotted with snags:
Tread softly now, Carlo! the woodcock is here,
He rises—his long bill thrust out like a spear;
The gun ranges on him—his journey is sped;
Quick scamper, my spaniel! and bring in the dead!

We plunge in the swamp—the tough laurels are round;
No matter; our shy prey not lightly is found;
Another up-darts, but unharm'd is his flight;
Confound it! the sunshine then dazzled my sight;
But the other my shot overtakes as he flies:
Come, Carlo! come, Carlo! I wait for my prize;
One more—still another—till, proofs of my sway,
From my pouch dangle heads, in a ghastly array.

From this scene of exploits, now made birdless, I pass;
Pleasant Pond gleams before me, a mirror of glass:
The boat's by the marge, with green branches supplied,
From the keen-sighted duck my approaches to hide;
A flock spots the lake; now crouch, Carlo, below!
And I move with light paddle, on softly and slow,
By that wide lily-island, its meshes that weaves
Of rich yellow globules, and green oval leaves.
I watch them; how bright and superb is the sheen
Of their plumage, gold blended with purple and green;
How graceful their dipping—how gliding their way!
Are they not all too lovely to mark as a prey?
One flutters, enchain'd, in those brown, speckled stems,
His yellow foot striking up bubbles, like gems,
While another, with stretch'd neck, darts swiftly across
To the grass, whose green points dot the mirror-like gloss.
But I pause in my toil; their wise leader, the drake,
Eyes keen the queer thicket afloat on the lake;
Now they group close together—both barrels!—O, dear!
What a diving, and screaming, and splashing are here!
The smoke-curls melt off, as the echoes rebound,
Hurrah! five dead victims are floating around!

But "cloud-land" is tinged now with sunset, and bright
On the water's smooth polish stretch long lines of light;
The headlands their masses of shade, too, have lain,
And I pull with my spoil to the margin again.

A FOREST WALK.

A lovely sky, a cloudless sun,
  A wind that breathes of leaves and flowers
O'er hill, through dale, my steps have won,
  To the cool forest's shadowy bowers;
One of the paths all round that wind,
  Traced by the browsing herds, I choose,
And sights and sounds of human kind
  In nature's lone recesses lose;
The beech displays its marbled bark,
  The spruce its green tent stretches wide
While scowls the hemlock, grim and dark,
  The maple's scallop'd dome beside:
All weave on high a verdant roof,
That keeps the very sun aloof,
Making a twilight soft and green,
Within the column'd, vaulted scene.

Sweet forest-odours have their birth
From the clothed boughs and teeming earth:
  Where pine-cones dropp'd, leaves piled and dead,
Long tufts of grass, and stars of fern,
With many a wild flower's fairy urn,
  A thick, elastic carpet spread;
Here, with its mossy pall, the trunk,
Resolving into soil, is sunk;
There, wrench'd but lately from its throne,
  By some fierce whirlwind circling past,
Its huge roots mass'd with earth and stone,
  One of the woodland kings is cast.

Above, the forest-tops are bright
With the broad blaze of sunny light:
But now a fitful air-gust parts
  The screening branches, and a glow
Of dazzling, startling radiance darts
  Down the dark stems, and breaks below;
The mingled shadows off are roll'd,
The sylvan floor is bathed in gold:
Low sprouts and herbs, before unseen,
Display their shades of brown and green:
Tints brighten o'er the velvet moss,
Gleams twinkle on the laurel's gloss;
The robin, brooding in her nest,
Chirps as the quick ray strikes her breast;
And, as my shadow prints the ground,
I see the rabbit upward bound,
With pointed ears an instant look,
Then scamper to the darkest nook,
Where, with crouch'd limb, and staring eye.
He watches while I saunter by.

A narrow vista, carpeted
With rich green grass, invites my tread;
Here showers the light in golden dots,
There sleeps the shade in ebon spots,
So blended, that the very air
Seems network as I enter there.
The partridge, whose deep-rolling drum
  Afar has sounded on my ear,
Ceasing his beatings as I come,
  Whirrs to the sheltering branches near;
The little milk-snake glides away,
The brindled marmot dives from day;
And now, between the boughs, a space
Of the blu . laughing sky I trace:

On each side shrinks the bowery shade;
Before me spreads an emerald glade;
The sunshine steeps its grass and moss,
That couch my footsteps as I cross;
Merrily hums the tawny bee,
The glittering humming-bird I see;
Floats the bright butterfly along,
The insect choir is loud in song:
A spot of light and life, it seems
A fairy haunt for fancy dreams.

Here stretch'd, the pleasant turf I press,
In luxury of idleness;
Sun-streaks, and glancing wings, and sky,
Spotted with cloud-shapes, charm my eye·
While murmuring grass, and waving trees
Their leaf-harps sounding to the breeze,
And water-tones that tinkle near,
Blend their sweet music to my ear;
And by the changing shades alone
The passage of the hours is known.

WINTER.

A SABLE pall of sky—the billowy hills,
Swathed in the snowy robe that winter throws
So kindly over nature—skeleton trees,
Fringed with rich silver drapery, and the stream
Numb in its frosty chains. Yon rustic bridge
Bristles with icicles; beneath it stand
The cattle-group, long pausing while they drink
From the ice-hollow'd pools, that skim in sheets
Of delicate glass, and shivering as the air [trunks,
Cuts with keen, stinging edge; and those gaunt
Bending with ragged branches o'er the bank,
Seem, with their mocking scarfs of chilling white,
Mourning for the green grass and fragrant flowers,
That summer mirrors in the rippling flow
Of the bright stream beneath them. Shrub and rock
Are carved in pearl, and the dense thicket shows
Clusters of purest ivory. Comfortless
The frozen scene, yet not all desolate.
Where slopes, by tree and bush, the beaten track,
The sleigh glides merrily with prancing steeds,
And the low homestead, nestling by its grove,
Clings to the leaning hill. The drenching rain
Had fallen, and then the large, loose flakes had shower'd,
Quick freezing where they lit; and thus the scene,
By winter's alchymy, from gleaming steel
Was changed to sparkling silver. Yet, though bright
And rich, the landscape smiles with lovelier look
When summer gladdens it. The fresh, blue sky
Bends like God's blessing o'er; the scented air
Echoes with bird-songs, and the emerald grass
Is dappled with quick shadows; the light wing
Of the soft west makes music in the leaves;
The ripples murmur as they dance along;
The thicket by the road-side casts its cool
Black breadth of shade across the heated dust.
The cattle seek the pools beneath the banks,
Where sport the gnat-swarms, glancing in the sun,
Gray, whirling specks, and darts the dragon-fly,
A gold-green arrow; and the wandering flock
Nibble the short, thick sward that clothes the brink,
Down sloping to the waters. Kindly tones
And happy faces make the homestead walls
A paradise. Upon the mossy roof
The tame dove coos and bows; beneath the eaves
The swallow frames her nest; the social wren
Lights on the flower-lined paling, and trills through
Its noisy gamut; the humming-bird
Shoots, with that flying harp, the honey-bee,
Mid the trail'd honeysuckle's trumpet-bloom;
Sunset wreathes gorgeous shapes within the west,
To eyes that love the splendour; morning wakes
Light hearts to joyous tasks; and when deep night
Breathes o'er the earth a solemn solitude,
With stars for watchers, or the holy moon,
A sentinel upon the steeps of heaven,
Smooth pillows yield their balm to prayer and trust,
And slumber, that sweet medicine of toil,
Sheds her soft dews and weaves her golden dreams.

THE SETTLER.

HIS echoing axe the settler swung
  Amid the sea-like solitude,
And, rushing, thundering, down were flung
  The Titans of the wood;
Loud shriek'd the eagle, as he dash'd
From out his mossy nest, which crash'd
  With its supporting bough,
And the first sunlight, leaping, flash'd
  On the wolf's haunt below.

Rude was the garb, and strong the frame
  Of him who plied his ceaseless toil:
To form that garb the wild-wood game
  Contributed their spoil;
The soul that warm'd that frame disdain'd
The tinsel, gaud, and glare, that reign'd
  Where men their crowds collect;
The simple fur, untrimm'd, unstain'd,
  This forest-tamer deck'd.

The paths which wound mid gorgeous trees,
  The stream whose bright lips kiss'd their flowers,
The winds that swell'd their harmonies
  Through those sun-hiding bowers,
The temple vast, the green arcade,
The nestling vale, the grassy glade,
  Dark cave, and swampy lair:
These scenes and sounds majestic, made
  His world, his pleasures, there.

His roof adorn'd a pleasant spot,
  Mid the black logs green glow'd the grain,
And herbs and plants the woods knew not,
  Throve in the sun and rain.
The smoke-wreath curling o'er the dell,
The low, the bleat, the tinkling bell,
  All made a landscape strange,
Which was the living chronicle
  Of deeds that wrought the change.

The violet sprung at spring's first tinge,
  The rose of summer spread its glow,
The maize hung out its autumn fringe,
  Rude winter brought his snow;
And still the lone one labour'd there,
His shout and whistle broke the air,
  As cheerily he plied
His garden-spade, or drove his share
  Along the hillock's side.

He mark'd the fire-storm's blazing flood
  Roaring and crackling on its path,
And scorching earth, and melting wood,
  Beneath its greedy wrath;
He mark'd the rapid whirlwind shoot,
Trampling the pine tree with its foot,
  And darkening thick the day
With streaming bough and sever'd root,
  Hurl'd whizzing on its way.

His gaunt hound yell'd, his rifle flash'd,
  The grim bear hush'd his savage growl;
In blood and foam the panther gnash'd
  His fangs, with dying howl;
The fleet deer ceased its flying bound,
Its snarling wolf-foe bit the ground,
  And, with its moaning cry,
The beaver sank beneath the wound
  Its pond-built Venice by.

Humble the lot, yet his the race,
  When Liberty sent forth her cry,
Who throng'd in conflict's deadliest place,
  To fight—to bleed—to die!
Who cumber'd Bunker's height of red,
By hope through weary years were led,
  And witness'd York Town's sun
Blaze on a nation's banner spread,
  A nation's freedom won.

AN AMERICAN FOREST IN SPRING.

Now fluttering breeze, now stormy blast,
  Mild rain, then blustering snow:
Winter's stern, fettering cold is past,
  But, sweet Spring! where art thou?
The white cloud floats mid smiling blue,
The broad, bright sunshine's golden hue
  Bathes the still frozen earth:
'T is changed! above, black vapours roll:
We turn from our expected stroll,
  And seek the blazing hearth.

Hark! that sweet carol! with delight
  We leave the stifling room!
The little blue-bird greets our sight,
  Spring, glorious Spring, has come!
The south wind's balm is in the air,
The melting snow-wreaths everywhere
  Are leaping off in showers;
And Nature, in her brightening looks,
Tells that her flowers, and leaves, and brooks,
  And birds, will soon be ours.

A few soft, sunny days have shone,
  The air has lost its chill,
A bright-green tinge succeeds the brown,
  Upon the southern hill.
Off to the woods! a pleasant scene!
Here sprouts the fresh young wintergreen,
  There swells a mossy mound;
Though in the hollows drifts are piled,
The wandering wind is sweet and mild,
  And buds are bursting round.

Where its long rings uncurls the fern,
  The violet, nestling low,
Casts back the white lid of its urn,
  Its purple streaks to show
Beautiful blossom! first to rise
And smile beneath Spring's wakening skies;
  The courier of the band
Of coming flowers, what feelings sweet
Gush, as the silvery gem we meet
  Upon its slender wand.

A sudden roar—a shade is cast—
  We look up with a start,
And, sounding like a transient blast,
  O'erhead the pigeons dart;
Scarce their blue glancing shapes the eye
Can trace, ere dotted on the sky,
  They wheel in distant flight
A chirp! and swift the squirrel scours
Along the prostrate trunk, and cowers
  Within its clefts from sight.

Amid the creeping pine, which spreads
  Its thick and verdant wreath,
The scaurberry's downy spangle sheds
  Its rich, delicious breath.
The bee-swarm murmurs by, and now
It clusters black on yonder bough:
  The robin's mottled breast
Glances that sunny spot across,
As round it seeks the twig and moss
  To frame its summer nest.

Warmer is each successive sky,
  More soft the breezes pass,
The maple's gems of crimson lie
  Upon the thick, green grass.
The dogwood sheds its clusters white,
The birch has dropp'd its tassels slight,
  Cowslips are by the rill;
The thresher whistles in the glen,
Flutters around the warbling wren,
  And swamps have voices shrill.

A simultaneous burst of leaves
  Has clothed the forest now,
A single day's bright sunshine weaves
  This vivid, gorgeous show.
Masses of shade are cast beneath,
The flowers are spread in varied wreath,
  Night brings her soft, sweet moon;
Morn wakes in mist, and twilight gray
Weeps its bright dew, and smiling May
  Melts blooming into June!

THE LOST HUNTER.

Numb'd by the piercing, freezing air,
  And burden'd by his game,
The hunter, struggling with despair,
  Dragg'd on his shivering frame;
The rifle he had shoulder'd late
Was trail'd along, a weary weight;
  His pouch was void of food;
The hours were speeding in their flight,
And soon the long, keen, winter night
  Would wrap the solitude.

Oft did he stoop a listening ear,
  Sweep round an anxious eye,—
No bark or axe-blow could he hear,
  No human trace descry.

His sinuous path, by blazes, wound
Among trunks group'd in myriads round;
  Through naked boughs, between
Whose tangled architecture, fraught
With many a shape grotesquely wrought,
  The hemlock's spire was seen.

An antler'd dweller of the wild
  Had met his eager gaze,
And far his wandering steps beguiled
  Within an unknown maze;
Stream, rock, and run-way he had cross'd,
Unheeding, till the marks were lost
  By which he used to roam;
And now, deep swamp and wild ravine
And rugged mountain were between
  The hunter and his home.

A dusky haze, which slow had crept
  On high, now darken'd there,
And a few snow-flakes fluttering swept
  Athwart the thick, gray air,
Faster and faster, till between
The trunks and boughs, a mottled screen
  Of glimmering motes was spread,
That tick'd against each object round
With gentle and continuous sound,
  Like brook o'er pebbled bed.

The laurel tufts, that drooping hung
  Close roll'd around their stems,
And the sear beech-leaves still that clung,
  Were white with powdering gems.
But, hark! afar a sullen moan
Swell'd out to louder, deeper tone,
  As surging near it pass'd,
And, bursting with a roar, and shock
That made the groaning forest rock,
  On rush'd the winter blast.

As o'er it whistled, shriek'd, and hiss'd,
  Caught by its swooping wings,
The snow was whirl'd to eddying mist,
  Barb'd, as it seem'd, with stings;
And now 'twas swept with lightning flight
Above the loftiest hemlock's height,
  Like drifting smoke, and now
It hid the air with shooting clouds,
And robed the trees with circling shrouds,
  Then dash'd in heaps below.

Here, plunging in a billowy wreath,
  There, clinging to a limb,
The suffering hunter gasp'd for breath,
  Brain reel'd, and eye grew dim;
As though to whelm him in despair,
Rapidly changed the blackening air
  To murkiest gloom of night,
Till naught was seen around, below,
But falling flakes and mantled snow,
  That gleam'd in ghastly white.

At every blast an icy dart
  Seem'd through his nerves to fly,
The blood was freezing to his heart—
  Thought whisper'd he must die.
The thundering tempest echo'd death,
He felt it in his tighten'd breath;
  Spoil, rifle dropp'd, and slow
As the dread torpor crawling came
Along his staggering, stiffening frame,
  He sunk upon the snow.

Reason forsook her shatter'd throne,—
  He deem'd that summer-hours
Again around him brightly shone
  In sunshine, leaves, and flowers;
Again the fresh, green, forest-sod,
Rifle in hand, he lightly trod,—
  He heard the deer's low bleat;
Or, couch'd within the shadowy nook,
He drank the crystal of the brook
  That murmur'd at his feet.

It changed;—his cabin roof o'erspread,
  Rafter, and wall, and chair,
Gleam'd in the crackling fire, that shed
  Its warmth, and he was there;
His wife had clasp'd his hand, and now
Her gentle kiss was on his brow,
  His child was prattling by,
The hound crouch'd, dozing, near the blaze,
And through the pane's frost-pictured haze
  He saw the white drifts fly.

That pass'd;—before his swimming sight
  Does not a figure bound,
And a soft voice, with wild delight,
  Proclaim the lost is found!
No, hunter, no! 'tis but the streak
Of whirling snow—the tempest's shriek
  No human aid is near!
Never again that form will meet
Thy clasp'd embrace—those accents sweet
  Speak music to thine ear.

Morn broke;—away the clouds were chased,
  The sky was pure and bright,
And on its blue the branches traced
  Their webs of glittering white.
Its ivory roof the hemlock stoop'd,
The pine its silvery tassel droop'd,
  Down bent the burden'd wood,
And, scatter'd round, low points of green,
Peering above the snowy scene,
  Told where the thickets stood.

In a deep hollow, drifted high,
  A wave-like heap was thrown,
Dazzlingly in the sunny sky
  A diamond blaze it shone;
The little snow-bird, chirping sweet,
Dotted it o'er with tripping feet;
  Unsullied, smooth, and fair,
It seem'd, like other mounds, where trunk
And rock amid the wreaths were sunk,
  But, O! the dead was there.

Spring came with wakening breezes bland,
  Soft suns and melting rains,
And, touch'd by her Ithuriel wand,
  Earth bursts its winter-chains.
In a deep nook, where moss and grass
And fern-leaves wove a verdant mass
  Some scatter'd bones beside,
A mother, kneeling with her child,
Told by her tears and wailings wild
  That there the lost had died.

WILLIAM H. BURLEIGH.

[Born, 1812.]

William H. Burleigh was born in the town oi Woodstock, in Connecticut, on the second day of February, 1812. His paternal ancestors came to this country from Wales; and on both sides he is descended from the stern old Puritan stock, being on the mother's a lineal descendant of Governor Bradford, whose name appears conspicuously and honourably in the early annals of Massachusetts. An intermediate descendant, the grandfather of Mr. Burleigh, served with credit under Washington, in the war of the Revolution. Such ancestral recollections are treasured, with just pride, in many an humble but happy home in New England.

In his infancy, Mr. Burleigh's parents removed to Plainfield, in his native state, where his father was for many years the principal of a popular academy, until the loss of sight induced him to abandon his charge, before his son had attained an age to derive much benefit from his instructions. He retired to a farm, and the boy's time was mainly devoted to its culture, varied by the customary attendance in a district-school through the winter-months, until he was sixteen, when he proposed to become an apprentice to a neighbouring clothier, but abandoned the idea after two weeks' trial, from an inveterate loathing of the coarseness and brutality of those among whom he was set to labour. Here, however, while engaged in the repulsive cares of his employment, he composed his first sonnet, which was published in a gazette printed in the vicinity. Returning to his father's house, he in the following summer became an apprentice to a village printer, whom he left after eight months' tedious endurance, leaving in his "stick" a farewell couplet to his master, which is probably remembered unforgivingly to this day. He did not, however, desert the business, of which he had thus obtained some slight knowledge, but continued to labour as half-apprentice, journeyman, sub-editor, etc., through the next seven years, during which he assisted in the conduct of perhaps as many periodicals, deriving thereby little fame and less profit. In December, 1834, while editor of "The Literary Journal," in the city of Schenectady, he married an estimable woman, who has since "divided his sorrows and doubled his joys." In July, 1836, abandoning the printing business for a season, he commenced a new career as a public lecturer, under the auspices of a philanthropic society, and in his new employment he continued for two years. At the close of that period he assumed the editorship of "The Christian Witness," at Pittsburg, Pennsylvania, which he held two years and a half, when he resigned it, to take charge of "The Washington Banner," a gazette published at Allegheny, on the opposite side of the Ohio. Between this duty, and the study of the law, his time is now divided.

His contributions to the periodical literature of the country commenced at an early age, and have been continued at intervals to the present day. "The New Yorker" was for years his favourite medium of communication with the public. A collection of his poems appeared in Philadelphia, early in 1840.

ELEGIAC STANZAS.

She hath gone in the spring-time of life,
Ere her sky had been dimm'd by a cloud,
While her heart with the rapture of love was yet rife,
And the hopes of her youth were unbow'd—
From the lovely, who loved her too well;
From the heart that had grown to her own;
From the sorrow which late o'er her young spirit fell,
Like a dream of the night she hath flown;
And the earth hath received to its bosom its trust—
Ashes to ashes, and dust unto dust.

The spring, in its loveliness dress'd,
Will return with its music-wing'd hours,
And, kiss'd by the breath of the sweet south-west,
The buds shall burst out in flowers;
And the flowers her grave-sod above,
Though the sleeper beneath recks it not,
Shall thickly be strown by the hand of Love,
To cover with beauty the spot—
Meet emblems are they of the pure one and bright,
Who faded and fell with so early a blight.

Ay, the spring will return—but the blossom
That bloom'd in our presence the sweetest,
By the spoiler is borne from the cherishing bosom,
The loveliest of all and the fleetest!
The music of stream and of bird
Shall come back when the winter is o'er;
But the voice that was dearest to us shall be heard
In our desolate chambers no more!
The sunlight of May on the waters shall quiver—
The light of her eye hath departed forever!

As the bird to its sheltering nest,
When the storm on the hills is abroad,
So her spirit hath flown from this world of unrest
To repose on the bosom of God!
Where the sorrows of earth never more
May fling o'er its brightness a stain;
Where, in rapture and love, it shall ever adore,
With a gladness unmingled with pain;
And its thirst shall be slaked by the waters which spring,
Like a river of light, from the throne of the King.

There is weeping on earth for the lost!
 There is bowing in grief to the ground!
But rejoicing and praise mid the sanctified host,
 For a spirit in Paradise found!
Though brightness hath pass'd from the earth,
 Yet a star is new-born in the sky,
And a soul hath gone home to the land of its birth,
 Where are pleasures and fulness of joy!
And a new harp is strung, and a new song is given
To the breezes that float o'er the gardens of heaven.

"LET THERE BE LIGHT."

Night, stern, eternal, and alone,
 Girded with solemn silence round,
Majestic on his starless throne,
 Sat brooding o'er the vast profound—
And there unbroken darkness lay,
 Deeper than that which veils the tomb,
While circling ages wheel'd away
 Unnoted mid the voiceless gloom.

Then moved upon the waveless deep
 The quickening Spirit of the Lord,
And broken was its pulseless sleep
 Before the Everlasting Word!
"Let there be light!" and listening earth,
 With tree, and plant, and flowery sod,
"In the beginning" sprang to birth,
 Obedient to the voice of God.

Then, in his burning track, the sun
 Trod onward to his joyous noon,
And in the heavens, one by one,
 Cluster'd the stars around the moon—
In glory bathed, the radiant day
 Wore like a king his crown of light—
And, girdled by the "Milky Way,"
 How queenly look'd the star-gemm'd night!

Bursting from choirs celestial, rang
 Triumphantly the notes of song;
The morning-stars together sang
 In concert with the heavenly throng;
And earth, enraptured, caught the strain
 That thrill'd along her fields of air,
Till every mountain-top and plain
 Flung back an answering echo there!

Creator! let thy Spirit shine
 The darkness of our souls within,
And lead us by thy grace divine
 From the forbidden paths of sin;
And may that voice which bade the earth
 From Chaos and the realms of Night,
From doubt and darkness call us forth
 To God's own liberty and light!

Thus, made partakers of Thy love,
 The baptism of the Spirit ours,
Our grateful hearts shall rise above,
 Renew'd in purposes and powers;
And songs of joy again shall ring
 Triumphant through the arch of heaven—
The glorious songs which angels sing,
 Exulting over souls forgiven!

JUNE.

 June, with its roses—June!
The gladdest month of our capricious year,
With its thick foliage and its sunlight clear;
 And with the drowsy tune
Of the bright leaping waters, as they pass
Laughingly on amid the springing grass!

 Earth, at her joyous coming,
Smiles as she puts her gayest mantle on;
And Nature greets her with a benison;
 While myriad voices, humming
Their welcome song, breathe dreamy music round,
Till seems the air an element of sound.

 The overarching sky
Weareth a softer tint, a lovelier blue,
As if the light of heaven were melting through
 Its sapphire home on high;
Hiding the sunshine in their vapoury breast,
The clouds float on like spirits to their rest.

 A deeper melody,
Pour'd by the birds, as o'er their callow young
Watchful they hover, to the breeze is flung—
 Gladsome, yet not of glee—
Music heart-born, like that which mothers sing
Above their cradled infants slumbering.

 On the warm hill-side, where
The sunlight lingers latest, through the grass
Peepeth the luscious strawberry! As they pass,
 Young children gambol there,
Crushing the gather'd fruit in playful mood,
And staining their bright faces with its blood.

 A deeper blush is given
To the half-ripen'd cherry, as the sun
Day after day pours warmth the trees upon,
 Till the rich pulp is riven;
The truant schoolboy looks with longing eyes,
And perils limb and neck to win the prize.

 The farmer, in his field,
Draws the rich mould around the tender maize;
While Hope, bright-pinion'd, points to coming days,
 When all his toil shall yield
An ample harvest, and around his hearth
There shall be laughing eyes and tones of mirth.

 Poised on his rainbow-wing,
The butterfly, whose life is but an hour,
Hovers coquettishly from flower to flower,
 A gay and happy thing;
Born for the sunshine and the summer-day,
Soon passing, like the beautiful, away!

 These are thy pictures, June!
Brightest of summer-months—thou month of flowers!
First-born of beauty, whose swift-footed hours
 Dance to the merry tune
Of birds, and waters, and the pleasant shout
Of childhood on the sunny hills peal'd out.

 I feel it were not wrong
To deem thou art a type of heaven's clime,
Only that there the clouds and storms of time
 Sweep not the sky along;
The flowers—air—beauty—music—all are thine,
But brighter—purer—lovelier—more divine!

SPRING.

THE sweet south wind, so long
Sleeping in other climes, on sunny seas,
Or dallying gayly with the orange-trees
In the bright land of song,
Wakes unto us, and laughingly sweeps by,
Like a glad spirit of the sunlit sky.

The labourer at his toil
Feels on his cheek its dewy kiss, and lifts
His open brow to catch its fragrant gifts—
The aromatic spoil
Borne from the blossoming gardens of the south—
While its faint sweetness lingers round his mouth.

The bursting buds look up
To greet the sunlight, while it lingers yet
On the warm hill-side,—and the violet
Opens its azure cup
Meekly, and countless wild flowers wake to fling
Their earliest incense on the gales of spring.

The reptile that hath lain
Torpid so long within his wintry tomb,
Pierces the mould, ascending from its gloom
Up to the light again—
And the lithe snake crawls forth from caverns chill,
To bask as erst upon the sunny hill.

Continual songs arise
From universal nature—birds and streams
Mingle their voices, and the glad earth seems
A second Paradise!
Thrice blessed Spring!—thou bearest gifts divine!
Sunshine, and song, and fragrance—all are thine.

Nor unto earth alone—
Thou hast a blessing for the human heart,
Balm for its wounds and healing for its smart,
Telling of Winter flown,
And bringing hope upon thy rainbow wing,
Type of eternal life—thrice-blessed Spring!

REQUIEM.

THE strife is o'er—Death's seal is set
On ashy lip and marble brow;
'Tis o'er, though faintly lingers yet
Upon the cheek a life-like glow:
The feeble pulse hath throbb'd its last,
The aching head is laid at rest—
Another from our ranks hath pass'd,
The dearest and the loveliest!

Press down the eyelids—for the light,
Erewhile so radiant underneath,
Is gone forever from our sight,
And darken'd by the spoiler, Death:
Press down the eyelids—who can bear
To look beneath their fringed fold?
And softly part the silken hair
Upon the brow so deathly cold.

The strife is o'er! The loved of years,
To whom our yearning hearts had grown,
Hath left us, with life's gathering fears
To struggle darkly and alone;
Gone, with the wealth of love which dwelt,
Heart-kept, with holy thoughts and high—
Gone, as the clouds of evening melt
Beyond the dark and solemn sky.

Yet mourn her not—the voice of wo
Befits not this, her triumph-hour;
Let Sorrow's tears no longer flow,
For life eternal is her dower!
Freed from the earth's corrupt control,
The trials of a world like this,
Joy! for her disembodied soul
Drinks at the fount of perfect bliss!

STANZAS,

WRITTEN ON VISITING MY BIRTH-PLACE.

WE are scatter'd—we are scatter'd—
Though a jolly band were we!
Some sleep beneath the grave-sod,
And some are o'er the sea;
And Time hath wrought his changes
On the few who yet remain;
The joyous band that once we were
We cannot be again!

We are scatter'd—we are scatter'd!—
Upon the village-green,
Where we play'd in boyish recklessness,
How few of us are seen!
And the hearts that beat so lightly
In the joyousness of youth—
Some are crumbled in the sepulchre,
And some have lost their truth.

The beautiful—the beautiful
Are faded from our track!
We miss them and we mourn them,
But we cannot lure them back;
For an iron sleep hath bound them
In its passionless embrace—
We may weep—but cannot win them
From their dreary resting-place.

How mournfully—how mournfully
The memory doth come
Of the thousand scenes of happiness
Around our childhood's home!
A salutary sadness
Is brooding o'er the heart,
As it dwells upon remembrances
From which it will not part.

In memory—in memory—
How fondly do we gaze
Upon the magic loveliness
Of childhood's fleeting days!
The sparkling eye—the thrilling tone—
The smile upon its lips:
They all have gone!—but left a light
Which time cannot eclipse.

The happiness—the happiness
Of boyhood must depart;
Then comes the sense of loneliness
Upon the stricken heart!

We will not, or we cannot fling
Its sadness from our breast,
We cling to it instinctively,
We pant for its unrest!

We are scatter'd—we are scatter'd!
Yet may we meet again
In a brighter and a purer sphere,
Beyond the reach of pain!
Where the shadows of this lower world
Can never cloud the eye—
When the mortal hath put brightly on
Its immortality!

TO H. A. B.

Deem not, beloved, that the glow
Of love with youth will know decay;
For, though the wing of Time may throw
A shadow o'er our way;
The sunshine of a cloudless faith,
The calmness of a holy trust,
Shall linger in our hearts till death
Consigns our "dust to dust!"

The fervid passions of our youth—
The fervour of affection's kiss—
Love, born of purity and truth—
All memories of bliss—
These still are ours, while looking back
Upon the past with dewy eyes;
O, dearest! on life's vanish'd track
How much of sunshine lies!

Men call us poor—it may be true
Amid the gay and glittering crowd;
We feel it, though our wants are few,
Yet envy not the proud.
The freshness of love's early flowers,
Heart-shelter'd through long years of want,
Pure hopes and quiet joys are ours,
That wealth could never grant.

Something of beauty from thy brow,
Something of lightness from thy tread,
Hath pass'd—yet thou art dearer now
Than when our vows were said:
A softer beauty round thee gleams,
Chasten'd by time, yet calmly bright;
And from thine eye of hazel beams
A deeper, tenderer light:

An emblem of the love which lives
Through every change, as time departs·
Which binds our souls in one, and gives
New gladness to our hearts!
Flinging a halo over life
Like that which gilds the life beyond!
Ah! well I know thy thoughts, dear wife!
To thoughts like these respond.

The mother, with her dewy eye,
Is dearer than the blushing bride
Who stood, three happy years gone by,
In beauty by my side!
Our Father, throned in light above,
Hath bless'd us with a fairy child—
A bright link in the chain of love—
The pure and undefiled:

Rich in the heart's best treasure, still
With a calm trust we'll journey on,
Link'd heart with heart, dear wife! until
Life's pilgrimage be done!
Youth—beauty—passion—these will pass
Like every thing of earth away—
The breath-stains on the polish'd glass
Less transient are than they.

But love dies not—the child of God—
The soother of life's many woes—
She scatters fragrance round the sod
Where buried hopes repose!
She leads us with her radiant hand
Earth's pleasant streams and pasture by,
Still pointing to a better land
Of bliss beyond the sky!

TO ———.

Hope, strewing with a liberal hand
Thy pathway with her choicest flowers,
Making the earth an Eden-land,
And gilding time's departing hours;
Lifting the clouds from life's blue sky,
And pointing to that sphere divine
Where joy's immortal blossoms lie
In the rich light of heaven—be thine!

Love, with its voice of silvery tone,
Whose music melts upon the heart
Like whispers from the world unknown,
When shadows from the soul depart—
Love, with its sunlight melting through
The mists that over earth are driven,
And giving earth itself the hue
And brightness of the upper-heaven—

Peace, hymning with her seraph-tones
Amid the stillness of thy soul,
Till every human passion owns
Her mighty but her mild control—
Devotion, with her lifted eye,
All radiant with the tears of bliss,
Looking beyond the bending sky
To worlds more glorious than this—

Duty, untiring in her toil
Earth's parch'd and sterile wastes among—
Zeal, delving in the rocky soil,
With words of cheer upon her tongue—
Faith, with a strong and daring hand
Rending aside the veil of heaven,
And claiming as her own the land
Whose glories to her view are given—

These, with the many lights that shine
Brightly life's pilgrim-path upon,—
These, with the bliss they bring, be thine,
Till purer bliss in heaven be won;
Till, gather'd with the loved of time,
Whose feet the "narrow way" have trod,
Thy soul shall drink of joys sublime,
And linger in the smile of God!

SONG.

Believe not the slander, my dearest Katrine!
For the ice of the world hath not frozen my heart;
In my innermost spirit there still is a shrine
Where thou art remember'd, all pure as thou art:
The dark tide of years, as it bears us along,
Though it sweep away hope in its turbulent flow,
Cannot drown the low voice of Love's eloquent song,
Nor chill with its waters my faith's early glow.

True, the world hath its snares, and the soul may grow faint
In its strifes with the follies and falsehoods of earth;
And amidst the dark whirl of corruption, a taint
May poison the thoughts that are purest at birth.
Temptations and trials, without and within,
From the pathway of virtue the spirit may lure;
But the soul shall grow strong in its triumphs o'er sin.
And the heart shall preserve its integrity pure.

The finger of Love, on my innermost heart,
Wrote thy name, O adored! when my feelings were young;
And the record shall 'bide till my soul shall depart,
And the darkness of death o'er my being be flung.
Then believe not the slander that says I forget,
In the whirl of excitement, the love that was thine;
Thou wert dear in my boyhood, art dear to me yet:
For my sunlight of life is the smile of Katrine!

THE BROOK.

"Like thee, O stream! to glide in solitude
Noiselessly on, reflecting sun or star,
Unseen by man, and from the great world's jar
Kept evermore aloof: methinks 't were good
To live thus lonely through the silent lapse
Of my appointed time." Not wisely said,
Unthinking Quietist! The brook hath sped
Its course for ages through the narrow gaps
Of rifted hills and o'er the reedy plain,
Or mid the eternal forests, not in vain;
The grass more greenly groweth on its brink,
And lovelier flowers and richer fruits are there,
And of its crystal waters myriads drink,
That else would faint beneath the torrid air.

THE TIMES.

Inaction now is crime. The old earth reels
Inebriate with guilt; and Vice, grown bold,
Laughs Innocence to scorn. The thirst for gold
Hath made men demons, till the heart that feels
The impulse of impartial love, nor kneels
In worship foul to Mammon, is contemn'd.
He who hath kept his purer faith, and stemm'd
Corruption's tide, and from the ruffian heels
Of impious tramplers rescued peril'd right,
Is call'd fanatic, and with scoffs and jeers
Maliciously assail'd. The poor man's tears
Are unregarded; the oppressor's might
Revered as law; and he whose righteous way
Departs from evil, makes himself a prey.

SOLITUDE.

The ceaseless hum of men, the dusty streets,
Crowded with multitudinous life; the din
Of toil and traffic, and the wo and sin,
The dweller in the populous city meets:
These have I left to seek the cool retreats
Of the untrodden forest, where, in bowers
Builded by Nature's hand, inlaid with flowers,
And roof'd with ivy, on the mossy seats
Reclining, I can while away the hours
In sweetest converse with old books, or give
My thoughts to God; or fancies fugitive
Indulge, while over me their radiant showers
Of rarest blossoms the old trees shake down,
And thanks to Him my meditations crown!

RAIN.

Dashing in big drops on the narrow pane,
And making mournful music for the mind,
While plays his interlude the wizard wind,
I hear the ringing of the frequent rain:
How doth its dreamy tone the spirit lull,
Bringing a sweet forgetfulness of pain,
While busy thought calls up the past again,
And lingers mid the pure and beautiful
Visions of early childhood! Sunny faces
Meet us with looks of love, and in the moans
Of the faint wind we hear familiar tones,
And tread again in old familiar places!
Such is thy power, O Rain! the heart to bless,
Wiling the soul away from its own wretchedness!

THE PILGRIM FATHERS.

Bold men were they, and true, that pilgrim-band,
Who plough'd with venturous prow the stormy sea,
Seeking a home for hunted Liberty
Amid the ancient forests of a land
Wild, gloomy, vast, magnificently grand!
Friends, country, hallow'd homes they left, to be
Pilgrims for Christ's sake, to a foreign strand—
Beset by peril, worn with toil, yet *free!*
Tireless in zeal, devotion, labour, hope;
Constant in faith; in justice how severe!
Though fools deride and bigot-skeptics sneer,
Praise to their names! If call'd like them to cope,
In evil times, with dark and evil powers,
O, be their faith, their zeal, their courage ours!

LOUIS LEGRAND NOBLE.

[Born, 181–.]

The Reverend Louis Legrand Noble was born in the valley of the Butternut Creek, in Otsego county, in New York. While he was a youth his father removed to the banks of the Wacamutquiock, now called the Huron, a small river in Michigan, and there, among scenes of remarkable wildness and beauty, he passed most of his time until the commencement of his college-life. In a letter to me, he says: "I was ever under a strong impulse to imbody in language my thoughts, feelings, fancies, as they sprung up in the presence of the rude but beautiful things around me: the prairies on fire, the sparkling lakes, the park-like forests, Indians on the hunt, guiding their frail canoes amid the rapids, or standing at night in the red light of their festival fires. I breathed the air of poetry."

Mr. Noble was admitted to orders in the Protestant Episcopal Church, in 1840. His principal poetical work is "Ne-mah-min," an Indian story, in three cantos, in which he has made good use of his experience of forest life. In 1853 he published in one volume, a Memoir of Mr. Cole, the painter.

THE CRIPPLE-BOY.

I.

Upon an Indian rush-mat, spread
Where burr-oak boughs a coolness shed,
Alone he sat, a cripple-child,
With eyes so large, so dark and wild,
And fingers, thin and pale to see,
Locked upon his trembling knee.
A-gathering nuts so blithe and gay,
The children early tripp'd away;
And he his mother had besought
Under the oak to have him brought;—
It was ever his seat when blackbirds sung
The wavy, rustling tops among;—
They calm'd his pain,—they cheer'd his loneliness—
The gales,—the music of the wilderness.

II.

Upon a prairie wide and wild
Look'd off that suffering cripple-child:
The hour was breezy, the hour was bright;—
O, 't was a lively, a lovely sight!
An eagle sailing to and fro
Around a flitting cloud so white—
Across the billowy grass below
Darting swift their shadows' light:—
And mingled noises sweet and clear,
Noises out of the ringing wood,
Were pleasing trouble in his ear,
A shock how pleasant to his blood:
O, happy world!—Beauty and Blessing slept
On everything but him—he felt, and wept.

III.

Humming a lightsome tune of yore,
Beside the open log-house door,
Tears upon his sickly cheek
Saw his mother, and so did speak;—
"What makes his mother's Henry weep?
You and I the cottage keep;
They hunt the nuts and clusters blue,
Weary lads for me and you;
And yonder see the quiet sheep;—
Why, now—I wonder why you weep!"—
"Mother, I wish that I could be
A sailor on the breezy sea!"
"A sailor on the stormy sea, my son!—
What ails the boy!—what have the breezes done!"

IV.

"I do!—I wish that I could be
A sailor on the rolling sea:
In the shadow of the sails
I would ride and rock all day,
Going whither blow the gales,
As I have heard a seaman say:
I would, I guess, come back again
For my mother now and then;
And the curling fire so bright,
When the prairie burns at night;
And tell the wonders I had seen
Away upon the ocean green;"—
"Hush! hush! talk not about the ocean so;
Better at home a hunter hale to go."

V.

Between a tear and sigh he smiled;
And thus spake on the cripple-child:—
"I would I were a hunter hale,
Nimbler than the nimble doe,
Bounding lightly down the dale,
But that will never be, I know!
Behind the house the woodlands lie;
A prairie wide and green before;
And I have seen them with my eye
A thousand times or more;
Yet in the woods I never stray'd,
Or on the prairie-border play'd;—
O, mother dear, that I could only be
A sailor-boy upon the rocking sea!"

VI.

You would have turned with a tear,
A tear upon your cheek;
She wept aloud, the woman dear,
And further could not speak:

The boy's it was a bitter lot
She always felt, I trow;
Yet never till then its bitterness
At heart had grieved her so.
Nature had waked the eternal wish;
—*Liberty*, far and wide!—
And now, to win him health, with joy,
She would that morn have died.
Till noon, she kept the shady door-way chair,
But never a measure of that ancient air.

VII.

Piped the March-wind; pinch'd and slow
The deer were trooping in the snow;
He saw them out of the cottage-door,
The lame boy sitting upon the floor:
"Mother, mother, how long will it be
Till the prairie go like a waving sea?
Will the bare woods ever be green, and when?
O, will it ever be summer again?"—
She look'd in silence on her child:
That large eye, ever so dark and wild,
O me, how bright!—it may have been
That he was grown so pale and thin.
It came, the emerald month, and sweetly shed
Beauty for grief, and garlands for the dead.

TO A SWAN

FLYING AT MIDNIGHT, IN THE VALE OF THE HURON.*

Oh, what a still, bright night! It is the sleep
Of beauteous Nature in her bridal hall.
See, while the groves shadow the shining lake,
How the full-moon does bathe their melting green!—
I hear the dew-drop twang upon the pool.
Hark, hark, what music! from the rampart hills,
How like a far-off bugle, sweet and clear,
It searches through the list'ning wilderness!—
A Swan—I know it by the trumpet-tone:
Winging her pathless way in the cool heavens,
Piping her midnight melody, she comes.
Beautiful bird! upon the dusk, still world
Thou fallest like an angel—like a lone
Sweet angel from some sphere of harmony.
Where art thou, where?—no speck upon the blue
My vision marks from whence thy music ranges.
And why this hour—this voiceless hour—is thine,
And thine alone, I cannot tell. Perchance,
While all is hush and silent but the heart,
E'en *thou* hast human sympathies for heaven,
And singest yonder in the holy deep
Because thou hast a pinion. If it be,
Oh, for a wing, upon the aerial tide
To sail with thee a minstrel mariner!
When to a rarer height thou wheelest up,
Hast thou that awful thrill of an ascension—
The lone, lost feeling in the vasty vault?
Oh, for thine ear, to hear the ascending tones
Range the ethereal chambers!—then to *feel*
A harmony, while from the eternal depth
Steals nought but the pure star-light evermore!
And then to list the echoes, faint and mellow,
Far, far below, breathe from the hollow earth,
For thee, soft, sweet petition, to return.
And hither, haply, thou wilt shape thy neck;
And settle, like a silvery cloud, to rest,
If thy wild image, flaring in the abyss,
Startle thee not aloft. Lone aeronaut,
That catchest, on thine airy looking-out,
Glassing the hollow darkness, many a lake,
Lay, for the night, thy lily bosom here.
There is the deep unsounded for thy bath,
The shallow for the shaking of thy quills,
The dreamy cove, or cedar-wooded isle,
With galaxy of water-lilies, where,
Like mild Diana 'mong the quiet stars,
'Neath over-bending branches thou wilt move,
Till early warblers shake the crystal shower,
And whistling pinions warn thee to thy voyage.
But where art thou?—lost,—spirited away
To bowers of light by thy own dying whispers?
Or does some billow of the ocean-air,
In its still roll around from zone to zone,
All breathless to the empyrean heave thee?—
There is a panting in the zenith—hush!—
The *Swan*—how strong her great wing times the silence!—
She passes over high and quietly.
Now peals the living clarion anew;
One vocal shower falls in and fills the vale.
What witchery in the wilderness it plays!—
Shrill snort the affrighted deer; across the lake
The loon, sole sentinel, screams loud alarm;—
The shy fox barks;—tingling in every vein
I feel the wild enchantment;—hark! they come,
The dulcet echoes from the distant hills,
Like fainter horns responsive; all the while,
From misty isles, soft-stealing symphonies.
Thou bright, swift river of the bark canoe,
Threading the prairie-ponds of Washtenung,
The day of romance wanes. Few summers more,
And the long night will pass away unwaked,
Save by the house-dog, or the village bell;
And she, thy minstrel queen, her ermine dip
In lonelier waters.
Ah! thou wilt not stoop:
Old Huron, haply, glistens on thy sky.
The chasing moon-beams, glancing on thy plumes,
Reveal thee now, a little beating blot,
Into the pale Aurora fading.
There!——
Sinks gently back upon her flowery couch
The startled Night;—tinkle the damp wood-vaults
While slip the dew-pearls from her leafy curtains.
That last soft whispering note, how spirit-like!
While vainly yet mine ear another waits,
A sad, sweet longing lingers in my heart.

* The river Huron rises in the interior of Michigan and flows into Lake Erie. Its clear waters gave it the name of its more mighty kinsman, Lake Huron.

THOMAS MACKELLAR.

(Born, 1812.)

This amiable poet is the son of a Scottish gentleman who, resigning a commission in the British navy, emigrated to New York, where he was married, and resided till his death. He was born in that city on the twelfth of August, 1812; in 1826 began to learn the printing business; in 1833 took charge of Mr. L. Johnson's extensive stereotype foundry, in Philadelphia, in which he is now a partner; and in 1844 published "Droppings from the Heart," in 1847 "Tam's Fortnight Ramble and other Poems," and in 1853 "Lines for the Gentle and Loving," in which works he has illustrated in a natural and pleasing manner strong domestic and religious affections and a love of nature, and frequently displayed much pathos and quiet humor. His favorite verse is the sonnet, which he manages very deftly.

LIFE'S EVENING.

The world to me is growing gray and old;
My friends are dropping one by one away;
Some live in far-off lands — some in the clay
Rest quietly, their mortal moments told.
My sire departed ere his locks were gray;
My mother wept, and soon beside him lay;
My elder kin have long since gone — and I
Am left — a leaf upon an autumn tree,
Among whose branches chilling breezes steal,
The sure precursors of the winter nigh:
And when my offspring at our altar kneel
To worship God, and sing our morning psalm,
Their rising stature whispers unto me
My life is gently waning to its evening calm.

THE SLEEPING WIFE.

My wife! how calmly sleepest thou!
A perfect peace is on thy brow:
Thine eyes beneath their fringed lid,
Like stars behind a cloud, are hid;
Thy voice is mute, and not a sound
Disturbs the tranquil air around;
I'll watch, and mark each line of grace
That God has drawn upon thy face.

My wife! my wife! thy bosom fair,
That heaves with breath more pure than air
Which dwells within the scented rose,
Is wrapped in deep and still repose;—
So deep, that I erewhile did start,
And lay my hand upon thy heart,
In sudden fear that stealthy death
Had slyly robbed thee of thy breath.

My wife! my wife! thy face now seems
To show the tenor of thy dreams;
Methinks thy gentle spirit plays
Amid the scenes of earlier days;
Thy thoughts, perchance, now dwell on him
Whom most thou lov'st; or in the dim
And shadowy future strive to pry,
With woman's curious, earnest eye.

Sleep on! sleep on! my dreaming wife!
Thou livest now another life,
With beings fill'd, of fancy's birth;—
I will not call thee back to earth:
Sleep on, until the car of morn
Above the eastern hills is borne;
Then thou wilt wake again, and bless
My sight with living loveliness

REMEMBER THE POOR.

Remember the Poor!
It fearfully snoweth,
And bitterly bloweth;
Thou couldst not endure
The tempest's wild power
Through night's dreary hour,
Then pity the poor!

Remember the poor!
The father is lying
In that hovel, dying
With sickness of heart.
No voice cheers his dwelling,
A Saviour's love telling,
Ere life shall depart.

Remember the poor!
The widow is sighing,
The orphans are crying,
Half starving for bread;
In mercy be speedy
To succor the needy,—
Their helper is dead!

Remember the poor!
The baby is sleeping,
Its cheeks wet with weeping,
On its mother's fond breast;
Whose cough, deep and hollow,
Foretells she'll soon follow
Her husband to rest!

Remember the poor!
To him who aid lendeth,
Whatever he spendeth
The Lord will repay;
And sweet thoughts shall cheer him,
And God's love be near him,
In his dying day!

MATTHEW C. FIELD.

[Born, 1812. Died, 1844.]

The author of the numerous compositions, in prose and verse, which appeared in the journals of the southern states under the signature of "Phazma," between the years 1834 and 1844, was born of Irish parentage, in London, in 1812, and when but four years of age was brought to this country, which was his home from that period until he died. He was of a feeble constitution, and in his later years a painful disease interrupted his occupations and induced a melancholy which is illustrated in the humorous sadness of many of his verses. In the hope of relief he made a journey from New Orleans to Santa Fé, and another, soon after, to the Rocky Mountains; and failing of any advantage from these, set out to visit some friends in Boston, trusting to the good influences of a voyage by sea; but died in the ship, before reaching Mobile, on the fifteenth of November, 1844, in the thirty-third year of his age. He was several years one of the editors of the New Orleans "Picayune," and was a brother of Mr. J. M. Field, of St. Louis, who is as nearly related in genius as by birth.

TO MY SHADOW.

Shadow, just like the thin regard of men,
 Constant and close to friends, while fortune's bright,
You leave me in the dark, but come again
 And stick to me as long as there is light!
Yet, Shadow, as good friends have often done,
You've never stepped between me and the sun;
 But ready still to back me I have found you—
Although, indeed, you're fond of changing sides;
 And, while I never yet could get around you,
Where'er I walk, my Shadow with me glides!
 That you should leave me in the dark, is meet
Enough, there being one thing to remark—
 Light calls ye forth, yet, lying at my feet,
I'm keeping you forever in the dark!

POOR TOM.

There's a new stone now in the old churchyard,
 And a few withered flowers enwreath it;
Alas! for the youth, by the fates ill-starr'd,
 Who sleeps in his shroud beneath it:
  Poor Tom! poor Tom!
In his early day to be pluck'd away,
 While the sunshine of life was o'er him,
And naught but the light of a gladdening ray
 Beamed out on the road before him.
  Poor Tom!

All the joy that love and affection sheds,
 Seemed to fling golden hope around him,
And the warmest hearts and the wisest heads
 Alike to their wishes found him.
  Poor Tom! poor Tom!
He is sleeping now 'neath the willow bough,
 Where the low-toned winds are creeping,
As if to bewail, so sad a tale,
 While the eyes of the night are weeping.
  Poor Tom!

Oh, the old churchyard, with its new white stone,
 Now I love, though I used to fear it;
And I linger oft mid its tombs alone,
 For a strange charm draws me near it.
  Poor Tom! poor Tom!
We were early friends—oh, time still tends
 All the links of our love to sever!
And alas! time breaks, but never mends,
 The chain that it snaps forever!
  Poor Tom! poor Tom!

In the old churchyard we have wandered oft,
 Lost in gentle and friendly musing;
And his eye was light, and his words were soft,
 Soul with soul, as we roved, infusing.
  Poor Tom! poor Tom!
And we wonder'd then, if, when we were men,
 Aught in life could our fond thoughts smother;
But alas! again—we dreamed not when
 Death should tear us from each other.
  Poor Tom!

On the very spot where the stone now stands,
 We have sat in the shade of the willow,
With a life-warm clasp of each other's hands,
 And this breast has been his pillow.
  Poor Tom! poor Tom!
Now poor Tom lies cold in the churchyard old,
 And his place may be filled by others;
But he still lives here with a firmer hold,
 For our souls were twined like brothers.
  Poor Tom!

There's a new stone now in the old churchyard,
 And a few withered flowers enwreath it;
Alas! for the youth by the fates ill-starr'd,
 Who sleeps in his shroud beneath it:
  Poor Tom! poor Tom!
In his early day to be plucked away,
 While the sunshine of life was o'er him,
And naught but the light of a gladdening ray
 Beamed out on the road before him.
  Poor Tom!

CHARLES T. BROOKS.

[Born, 1813.]

The Reverend Charles T. Brooks was born in Salem, Massachusetts, on the twentieth of June, 1813; graduated at Harvard University in 1832; completed his theological preparation in 1835; and was settled over the Unitarian church in Newport, Rhode Island, of which he has ever since been the pastor, in the beginning of 1837. His first poetical publication was a translation of Schiller's "William Tell," printed anonymously in Providence in 1838. Translations of "Mary Stuart" and "The Maid of Orleans" were made in a year or two after, but remain yet in manuscript. About the date of these last, he commenced versions of Jean Paul Richter's "Levana," "Jubel Senior," and "Titan," which have been since completed. In 1842 he published in Boston, in Mr. Ripley's series of "Specimens of Foreign Literature,"* a volume of "Songs and Ballads, from the German," of Uhland, Korner, Burger, and others. In 1845 he published a "Poem delivered before the Phi Beta Kappa Society of Harvard College;" in 1847, "Homage of the Arts," from Schiller, with miscellaneous gleanings from other German poets; in 1848, "Aquidneck and other Poems," embracing a "Poem on the hundreth Anniversary of the Redwood Library;" in 1853 the small collection called "Songs of Field and Flood," and in the same year a volume of "German Lyrics," the principal piece in which is that of Anastasius Grun, (count von Auerspero,) entitled "The Ship Cincinnatus," representing an American vessel with the figure-head of the noble Roman, sailing home from Pompeii.

Mr. Brooks has made himself thoroughly familiar with the spirit of German literature, and has been remarkably successful in most of his attempts to reproduce it in English. His original poems are chaste and elegant, equally modest in design and successful in execution.

"ALABAMA."†

Bruised and bleeding, pale and weary,
  Onward to the South and West,
Through dark woods and deserts dreary,
  By relentless foemen pressed,
Came a tribe where evening, darkling,
  Flushed a mighty river's breast;
And they cried, their faint eyes sparkling,
  "Alabama! Here we rest!"

By the stern steam-demon hurried,
  Far from home and scenes so blest;
By the gloomy care-dogs worried,
  Sleepless, houseless, and distressed,
Days and nights beheld me hieing
  Like a bird without a nest,
Till I hailed thy waters, crying,
  "Alabama! Here I rest!"

Oh! when life's last sun is blinking
  In the pale and darksome West,
And my weary frame is sinking,
  With its cares and woes oppressed,
May I, as I drop the burden
  From my sick and fainting breast,
Cry, beside the swelling Jordan,
  "Alabama! Here I rest!"

* Another volume from the German poets in this excellent series is by John S. Dwight, a translator of kindred scholarship and genius.

† There is a tradition, that a tribe of Indians, defeated and hard pressed by a more powerful foe, reached in their flight a river, where their chief set up a staff and exclaimed, "Alabama!" a word meaning, "Here we rest," which from that time became the river's name.

TO THE MISSISSIPPI.

Majestic stream! along thy banks,
In silent, stately, solemn ranks,
The forests stand, and seem with pride
To gaze upon thy mighty tide;
As when, in olden, classic time,
Beneath a soft, blue, Grecian clime,
Bent o'er the stage, in breathless awe,
Crowds thrilled and trembled, as they saw
Sweep by the pomp of human life,
The sounding flood of passion's strife,
And the great stream of history
Glide on before the musing eye.
There, row on row, the gazers rise;
Above, look down the arching skies;
O'er all those gathered multitudes
Such deep and voiceful silence broods,
Methinks one mighty heart I hear
Beat high with hope, or quake with fear;—
E'en so yon groves and forests seem
Spectators of this rushing stream,
In sweeping, circling ranks they rise,
Beneath the blue, o'erarching skies;
They crowd around and forward lean,
As eager to behold the scene—
To see, proud river! sparkling wide,
The long procession of thy tide,—
To stand and gaze, and feel with thee
All thy unuttered ecstasy.
It seems as if a heart did thrill
Within yon forests, deep and still,
So soft and ghost-like is the sound
That stirs their solitudes profound.

"OUR COUNTRY—RIGHT OR WRONG."

"Our country—right or wrong!"—
That were a traitor's song—
Let no true patriot's pen such words indite!
Who loves his native land,
Let him, with heart, voice, hand,
Say, "Country or no country: speed the right!"

"Our country—right or wrong!"—
O Christian men! how long
Shall He who bled on Calvary plead in vain!
How long, unheeded, call
Where War's gash'd victims fall,
While sisters, widows, orphans, mourn the slain!

"Our country—right or wrong!"—
O man of God be strong!
Take God's whole armor for the holy fray
Gird thee with truth; make right
Thy breastplate; in the might
Of God stand steadfast in the evil day!

"Our country—right or wrong!"
Each image of the throng
Of ghastly woes that rise upon thy sight,
O let it move thy heart,
Man! man! whoe'er thou art,
To say, "God guide our struggling country right!"

A SABBATH MORNING, AT PETTAQUAMSCUTT.

The Sabbath breaks—how heavenly clear!
Is it not always Sabbath here?
Such deep contentment seems to brood
O'er hill and meadow, field and flood.
No floating sound of Sabbath-bell
Comes mingling here with Ocean's swell;
No rattling wheels, no trampling feet,
Wend through the paved and narrow street
To the strange scene where sits vain pride
With meek devotion, side by side.
And surely here no temple-bell
Man needs, his quiet thoughts to tell
When he must rest from strife and care,
And own his God in praise and prayer.
For doth not nature's hymn arise,
Morn, noon, and evening, to the skies?
Is not broad Ocean's face—the calm
Of inland woods—a silent psalm?
Ay, come there not from earth and sea
Voices of choral harmony,
That tell the peopled solitude
How great is God,—how wise,—how good!
In Ocean's murmuring music swells
A chime as of celestial bells
The birds, at rest or on the wing,
With notes of angel-sweetness sing,
And insect-hum and breeze prolong
The bass of Nature's grateful song,
Is not each day a Sabbath then,
A day of rest for thoughtful men?
No idle Sabbath Nature keeps,
The God of Nature never sleeps;
And in this noontide of the year,
This pensive pause, I seem to hear
God say: "O man! would'st thou be blest,
Contented work is Sabbath rest."

SUNRISE ON THE SEA-COAST.

It was the holy hour of dawn:
By hands invisible withdrawn,
The curtain of the summer night
Had vanished; and the morning light,
Fresh from its hidden day-springs, threw
Increasing glory up the blue.
Oh sacred balm of summer dawn,
When odors from the new-mown lawn
Blend with the breath of sky and sea;
And, like the prayers of sanctity,
Go up to Him who reigns above,
An incense-offering of love!
Alone upon a rock I stood,
Far out above the ocean-flood,
Whose vast expanse before me lay,
Now silver-white, now leaden-gray,
As o'er its face, alternate, threw
The rays and clouds their varying hue.
I felt a deep, expectant hush
Through nature, as the growing flush
Of the red Orient seemed to tell
The approach of some great spectacle,
O'er which the birds, in heaven's far height,
Hung, as entranced, in mute delight.
But when the Sun, in royal state,
Through his triumphal golden gate,
Came riding forth in majesty
Out from the fleckéd eastern sky,
As comes a conqueror to his tent;
And, up and down the firmament,
The captive clouds of routed night,
Their garments fringed with golden light,
Bending around the azure arch,
Lent glory to the victor's march;
And when he flung his blazing glance
Across the watery expanse,—
Methought, along that rocky coast,
The foaming waves, a crested host,
As on their snowy plumes the beams
Of sunshine fell in dazzling gleams,
Thrilled through their ranks with wild delight,
And clapped their hands to hail the sight,
And sent a mighty shout on high
Of exultation to the sky.
Now all creation seemed to wake;
Each little leaf with joy did shake;
The trumpet-signal of the breeze
Stirred all the ripples of the seas:
Each in its gambols and its glee
A living creature seemed to be;
Like wild young steeds with snowy mane,
The white waves skimmed the liquid plain;
Glad Ocean, with ten thousand eyes,
Proclaimed its joy to earth and skies;
From earth and skies a countless throng
Of happy creatures swelled the song;
Praise to the Conquerer of night!
Praise to the King of Life and Light!

C. P. CRANCH.

(Born, 1813.)

The grandfather of Mr. Cranch was Judge Richard Cranch, of Quincy, Massachusetts, and his grandmother Mary Smith, a sister of the wife of the first President Adams. His father, Chief Justice William Cranch, of Washington, married a Miss Greenleaf, one of whose sisters was the wife of Noah Webster, the lexicographer, and another the wife of Judge Dawes, father of the author of "Athenia of Damascus," &c. Judge Cranch the younger removed to the District of Columbia in 1794, and Christopher Pease Cranch was born in Alexandria, on the eighth of March, 1813. His boyhood was passed on the Virginia side of the Potomac, but in 1826 the family settled in Washington, and two years afterward he entered Columbian College, where he was graduated in 1831. Having decided to enter the ministry of the Unitarian church, he now proceeded to Cambridge, where he passed three years in the divinity school connected with Harvard College, and in 1834 became a licentiate. He did not settle anywhere as a pastor, but preached a considerable time in Peoria, Illinois; Richmond, Virginia; Bangor, Maine; Washington, and other places.

He gradually withdrew from the clerical profession, and finally, about the year 1842, determined to devote himself entirely to painting, for which he had shown an early predilection and very decided talents. He was never a regular pupil of any one artist, but received friendly assistance from Mr. Durand and others, and always studied with enthusiasm from nature. In October, 1843, he was married to Miss Elizabeth de Windt, of Fishkill, on the Hudson, and from this period until 1847 resided principally in New York, in the assiduous practice of his art, in which he made very rapid improvement. He now proceeded to Italy, where for two or three years he was an industrious and successful student in the galleries, and produced many fine original landscape studies. In 1853 he went a second time to Europe, and has since made his home in Paris. His course as an artist has been marked by a strict regard to truth and nature, and he ranks among the first of our landscape painters. A taste for music is also one of his strong characteristics, and has been carefully cultivated.

Mr. Cranch was associated with George Ripley, Ralph Waldo Emerson, Margaret Fuller, and others of the school of "Boston transcendentalists," as a writer for "The Dial," and some of his earliest and best lyrical effusions appeared in that remarkable periodical. In 1854 he published in Philadelphia a small volume of his "Poems," which was sharply reviewed by old-fashioned critics; but it was not addressed to them: "Him we will seek," the poet says,

"and none but him,
Whose inward sense hath not grown dim;
Whose soul is steeped in Nature's tinct,
And to the Universal linkt:
Who loves the beauteous Infinite
With deep and ever new delight,
And carrieth, where'er he goes,
The inborn sweetness of the rose,
The perfume as of Paradise—
The talisman above all price—
The optic glass that wins from far
The meaning of the utmost star—
The key that opes the golden doors
Where earth and heaven have piled their stores—
The magic ring, the enchanter's wand—
The title-deed to Wonder-land—
The wisdom that o'erlooketh sense,
The clairvoyant of Innocence."

And the class who saw themselves reflected in these lines, and many others too, discovered merits as decided as they are peculiar in Mr. Cranch's poetry. He has imagination as well as fancy, great poetic sensibility, and a style that despite abundant conceits is very striking and attractive. He has published no second collection of his poems, but continues to be an occasional writer, and from time to time gives the public specimens of his abilities through the columns of "The Tribune," or some favorite magazine.

BEAUTY.

Say, where does beauty dwell?
I gazed upon the dance, where ladies bright
Were moving in the light
Of mirrors and of lamps; with music and with flowers,
Danced on the joyous hours;
And fairest bosoms
Heaved happily beneath the winter-rose's blossoms;
And it is well:
Youth hath its time—
Merry hearts will merrily chime.
The forms were fair to see,
The tones were sweet to the ear;
But there 's beauty more rare to me—
That beauty was not here.

I stood in the open air,
And gazed on nature there.
The beautiful stars were over my head,
The crescent moon hung o'er the west;
Beauty o'er river and hill was spread,
Wooing the feverish soul to rest;
Beauty breathed in the summer-breeze,
Beauty rock'd the whispering trees,
Was mirror'd in the sleeping billow,
Was bending in the swaying willow,

Flooding the skies, bathing the earth,
Giving all lovely things a birth:
All—all was fair to see—
All was sweet to the ear:
But there 's beauty more fair to me—
That beauty was not here.

I sat in my room alone.
My heart began a tone
Its soothing strains were such
As if a spirit's touch
Were visiting its chords.
Soon it gather'd words,
Pouring forth its feelings,
And its deep revealings:
Thoughts and fancies came
With their brightening flame.
Truths of deepest worth
Sprang embodied forth—
Deep and solemn mysteries,
Spiritual harmonies,
And the faith that conquers time
Strong, and lovely, and sublime.

Then the purposes of life
Stood apart from vulgar strife.
Labour in the path of duty
Gleam'd up like a thing of beauty.
Beauty shone in self-denial,
In the sternest hour of trial—
In a meek obedience
To the will of Providence—
In the lofty sympathies
That, forgetting selfish ease,
Prompted acts that sought the good
Of every spirit:—understood
The wants of every human heart,
Eager ever to impart
Blessings to the weary soul
That hath felt the better world's control.

Here is beauty such as ne'er
Met the eye or charm'd the ear.
In the soul's high duties then I felt
That the loftiest beauty ever dwelt.

MY THOUGHTS.

Many are the thoughts that come to me
In my lonely musing;
And they drift so strange and swift,
There 's no time for choosing
Which to follow, for to leave
Any, seems a losing.

When they come, they come in flocks,
As, on glancing feather,
Startled birds rise one by one,
In autumnal weather,
Waking one another up
From the sheltering heather.

Some so merry that I laugh,
Some are grave and serious,
Some so trite, their least approach
Is enough to weary us:
Others flit like midnight ghosts,
Shrouded and mysterious.

There are thoughts that o'er me steal,
Like the day when dawning;
Great thoughts wing'd with melody,
Common utterance scorning,
Moving in an inward tune,
And an inward morning.

Some have dark and drooping wings,
Children all of sorrow;
Some are as gay, as if to-day
Could see no cloudy morrow,
And yet like light and shade they each
Must from the other borrow.

One by one they come to me
On their destined mission;
One by one I see them fade
With no hopeless vision;
For they 've led me on a step
To their home Elysian.

THE HOURS.

The hours are viewless angels,
That still go gliding by,
And bear each minute's record up
To Him who sits on high;
And we, who walk among them,
As one by one departs,
See not that they are hovering
Forever round our hearts.

Like summer-bees, that hover
Around the idle flowers,
They gather every act and thought,
Those viewless angel-hours;
The poison or the nectar
The heart's deep flower-cups yield,
A sample still they gather swift
And leave us in the field.

And some flit by on pinions
Of joyous gold and blue,
And some flag on with drooping wings
Of sorrow's darker hue;
But still they steal the record,
And bear it far away;
Their mission-flight by day or night,
No magic power can stay.

And as we spend each minute
That God to us hath given,
The deeds are known before His throne,
The tale is told in heaven.
These bee-like hours we see not,
Nor hear their noiseless wings;
We only feel, too oft, when flown,
That they have left their stings.

So, teach me, Heavenly Father,
To meet each flying hour,
That as they go they may not show
My heart a poison flower!
So, when death brings its shadows,
The hours that linger last
Shall bear my hopes on angel-wings,
Unfetter'd by the past.

ON HEARING TRIUMPHANT MUSIC.

That joyous strain,
Wake—wake again!
O'er the dead stillness of my soul it lingers.
Ring out, ring out
The music-shout!
I hear the sounding of thy flying fingers,
And to my soul the harmony
Comes like a freshening sea.

Again, again!
Farewell, dull pain;
Thou heart-ache, rise not while those harp-strings quiver;
Sad feelings, hence!
I feel a sense
Of a new life come like a rushing river
Freshening the fountains parch'd and dry
That in my spirit lie.

That glorious strain!
Oh! from my brain
I see the shadows flitting like scared ghosts!
A light, a light
Shines in to-night
Round the good angels trooping to their posts—
And the black cloud is rent in twain
Before the ascending strain.

It dies away—
It will not stay—
So sweet—so fleeting. Yet to me it spake
Strange peace of mind
I could not find
Before that triumph-strain the silence brake.
So let it ever come to me
With an undying harmony.

STANZAS.

Thought is deeper than all speech;
Feeling deeper than all thought:
Souls to souls can never teach
What unto themselves was taught.

We are spirits clad in veils:
Man by man was never seen:
All our deep communing fails
To remove the shadowy screen.

Heart to heart was never known:
Mind with mind did never meet:
We are columns left alone,
Of a temple once complete.

Like the stars that gem the sky,
Far apart, though seeming near,
In our light we scatter'd lie;
All is thus but starlight here.

What is social company
But a babbling summer stream?
What our wise philosophy
But the glancing of a dream?

Only when the sun of love
Melts the scatter'd stars of thought,
Only when we live above
What the dim-eyed world hath taught,

Only when our souls are fed
By the fount which gave them birth,
And by inspiration led
Which they never drew from earth;

We, like parted drops of rain,
Swelling till they meet and run,
Shall be all absorbed again,
Melting, flowing into one.

MARGARET FULLER OSSOLI.

Oh, still sweet summer days! Oh, moonlight nights,
After so drear a storm how can ye shine!
Oh, smiling world of many-hued delights,
How canst thou 'round our sad hearts still entwine
The accustomed wreaths of pleasure! How, oh Day,
Wakest thou so full of beauty! Twilight deep,
How diest thou so tranquilly away!
And how, oh Night, bring'st thou the sphere of sleep.
For she is gone from us—gone, lost forever—
In the wild billows swallowed up and lost—
Gone, full of love, life, hope, and high endeavor,
Just when we would have welcom'd her the most.

Was it for this—oh, woman, true and pure,
That life thro' shade and light had form'd thy mind
To feel, imagine, reason, and endure—
To soar for truth, to labour for mankind?
Was it for this sad end thou borest thy part
In deeds and words for struggling Italy,—
Devoting thy large mind and larger heart
That Rome in later days might yet be free?
And, from that home driven out by tyranny,
Didst turn to see thy fatherland once more,
Bearing affection's dearest ties with thee—
And as the vessel bore thee to our shore,
And hope rose to fulfilment—on the deck
When friends seem'd almost beckoning unto thee:
Oh, God! the fearful storm—the splitting wreck—
The drowning billows of the dreary sea!

Oh, many a heart was stricken dumb with grief,
We who had known thee here—had met thee there
Where Rome threw golden light on every leaf
Life's volume turned in that enchanted air—
Oh, friend! how we recall the Italian days
Amid the Cæsar's ruined palace halls—
The Coliseum and the frescoed blaze
Of proud St. Peter's dome—the Sistine walls—
The lone Campagna and the village green—
The Vatican—the music and dim light
Of gorgeous temples—statues, pictures, seen
With thee: those sunny days return so bright,
Now thou art gone! Thou hast a fairer world
Than that bright clime. The dreams that fill'd thee here
Now find divine completion, and, unfurl'd,
Thy spirit wings, find out their own high sphere.

Farewell! thought-gifted, noble-hearted one!
We, who have known thee, know thou art not lost;
The star that set in storms still shines upon
The o'ershadowing cloud, and when we sorrow most,
In the blue spaces of God's firmament
Beams out with purer light than we have known,
Above the tempest and the wild lament
Of those who weep the radiance that is flown.

HENRY THEODORE TUCKERMAN.

[Born, 1813.]

The Tuckerman family is of German origin, and the name is still common in the states of Germany, where, however, it is spelled with a double *n*. In a history of the country of Braunselweig and Luneberg, by William Hanemann, published in Luneberg in 1827, allusion is made to one of the kindred of the Tuckermans in America, Peter Tuckerman, who is mentioned as the last abbot of the monastery of Riddagshausen. He was chosen by the chapter in 1621, and at the same time held the appointment of superintendent or court preacher at Wolfenbuttill. By the mother's side, Mr. Tuckerman is of Irish descent. The name of his mother's family is Keating. In Macaulay's recent history he thus speaks of one of her ancestors, as opposing a military deputy of James II., in his persecution of the Protestant English in Ireland, in 1686: "On all questions which arose in the privy council, Tyrconnel showed similar violence and partiality. John Keating, chief-justice of the common pleas, a man distinguished for ability, integrity, and loyalty, represented with great mildness that perfect equality was all that the general could reasonably ask for his own church." Mr. Tuckerman is a nephew of the late Rev. Dr. Joseph Tuckerman, a memoir of whom has recently appeared in England, and who is generally known and honoured as the originator of the "Ministry at Large," an institution of Christian benevolence and eminent utility. His mother was also related to and partly educated with another distinguished Unitarian clergyman, Joseph Stevens Buckminster, whose memory is yet cherished in Boston by all lovers of genius and character.

Mr. Tuckerman was born in Boston, on the twentieth of April, 1813. After preparing for college, the state of his health rendered it necessary for him to relinquish his studies and seek a milder climate. In September, 1833, he sailed from New York for Havre, and after a brief sojourn in Paris, proceeded to Italy, where he remained until the ensuing summer. In the spring after his return he gave the results of his observation to the public, in a volume entitled "The Italian Sketch-Book," of which a third and considerably augmented edition appeared in New York in 1849. Mr. Tuckerman resumed and for a time prosecuted his academical studies, but again experiencing the injurious effects of a sedentary life and continued mental application, he embarked in October, 1837, for the Mediterranean; visited Gibraltar and Malta, made the tour of Sicily, and after a winter's residence in Palermo, crossed over to the continent. The winter of 1838 he passed chiefly in Florence and returned to the United States in the course of the ensuing summer. In 1839 he published "Isabel, or Sicily, a Pilgrimage," in which, under the guise of a romance, he gives many interesting descriptions and reflections incident to a tour in Sicily. This work was reprinted in London, in 1846. In 1845 he finished his "Thoughts on the Poets," in which he has discussed the characteristics of the chief masters of modern song. This work has passed through several editions. In 1848 he gave to the press his "Artist Life, or Sketches of eminent American Painters;" in 1849, "Characteristics of Literature, illustrated by the Genius of Distinguished Men;" in 1850, "The Optimist," and a "Life of Commodore Talbot;" in 1851, a second series of "Characteristics of Literature;" in 1853 "The Diary of a Dreamer," "A Memorial of Greenough," and "Mental Portraits;" and in 1854, "A Month in England." A collection of his "Poems" appeared in 1851, but it embraces only a small proportion of those he had published in the magazines and newspapers.

Mr. Tuckerman's poems are in a great variety of measures; they are, for the most part, expressions of graceful and romantic sentiment, but are often fruits of his reflection and illustrations of his taste. The little piece called "Mary" is a delightful echo of emotions as common as culture of mind and refinement of feeling; and among his sonnets are some very pleasing examples of this kind of writing. In these works he has occasionally done injustice to his own fine powers by the carelessness with which he has adopted familiar ideas, images, and forms of expression, from other writers. Considering the nature of the poetic principle, the author of an Essay on American Poetry which appeared in 1841, observes:

> "He who looks on Lake George, or sees the sun rise on Mackinaw, or listens to the grand music of a storm, is divested, for a time, of a portion of the alloy of his nature."

The alteration Mr. Tuckerman makes in the paraphrase of this in his highly-finished production, "The Spirit of Poetry," published three years afterwards, is unquestionably an improvement:

> "Who that has rocked upon Lake George's tide,
> When its clear ripples in the moonlight glide ....
> And who Niagara's loveliness has known,
> The rainbow diadem, the emerald zone,
> Nor felt thy spell such baser thought control."

Hypercritical readers may fancy that the grammatical relations of the last word of the second line here copied demand that it should be written glide*d*, but it will not be denied that the substitution of "Niagara" for "a storm" renders the passage far more national, since storms may occur anywhere (except in Egypt), while the grand cataract is an orchestrion of whose sonorous music we have a fortunate monopoly. The change made in a line from JOHNSON, which Mr. TUCKERMAN introduces into the next page of this elegant poem, cannot, perhaps, be so easily defended:

"To raise the genius and to mend the heart,"

is made by him to read,

"Exalt the mind and renovate the heart."

"Exalt" is possibly a better word than "raise," but the poet doubtless substituted "renovate" for "mend" from an erroneous impression that it is from the more immediate vocabulary of common life, and hence to be preferred on the principles announced by Mr. WORDSWORTH; but though those useful industrials who attempt to obliterate the evidences of age in our seedy habiliments, frequently display in conspicuous letters the verb "renovate" upon their signboards, it should not be forgotten that they intend by it a larger promise than that of simply "mending," as Mr. TUCKERMAN seems to suppose.

Of Mr. TUCKERMAN'S character as an essayist, some more particular observations may be found in my "Prose Writers of America." He has resided for several years in the city of New York.

GIOVANNI.*

WHAT shade has fallen this loved threshold o'er
Without glad presage never crossed before?
Why through the past does startled memory range,
Then shrink to meet the desolating change?
Hushed is the dwelling, cold the hearthstone now.
Whose glow plays not upon thy manly brow:
For cordial grasp of hands the pleading eye,
For lettered talk the faintly smothered sigh,
For looks intent to solve, respond, or cheer,
Thine wan from pain, ours agonized with fear;
For bland philosophy and genial wit,
Wont round this group instinctively to flit,
Half-uttered prayers, the stillness of dismay
In dread suspense exhaust the winter day.
The keenest pang humanity can feel
Came in that hour of nature's mute appeal,
As waned expression to its last eclipse,
And speech grew palsied on thy frigid lips;
Yet thought and love before the parting sigh,
Converged and flickered in thy glazing eye.
The artist-friend, whose triumph thou believed
Ere fame ordained or genius had achieved,
Crouched by the form, now stilled in death's embrace,
Strove with dim eyes thy lineaments to trace.
"Yet can it be!" our hearts bewildered cried,
"That he, the idol of this home, has died?"
The leaf o'er which in calm delight he hung,
The plaintive rhyme that trembled from his tongue,
The honored effigies so fondly sought,
Of those who conquered in the realm of thought,
His elements of life—these all are here,
And more than these—the loved-ones round the bier.
Two whose gray hair with daily joy he crowned,
Two who in him fraternal guidance found.
When up the aisle familiar to thy tread,
Moved the long train by white-robed pastors led,
And at the altar, where thou oft hast bowed,
We tearful knelt, and laid thee in thy shroud;
When those deep tones on which with youthful pride,
For wisdom's banquet thou so well relied,
Breathed the last prayer that mortal rites delay,
In faltering accents o'er thy senseless clay;
The sternest wept, and even worldly men
Felt the poor refuge of ambition then.
The Christmas garlands still with verdure hung,
The temple where thy funeral hymn was sung,
And as it echoed, like a holy spell,
The blest assurance of a short farewell,
A flood of sunshine broke upon our sight,
And wreathed the mourners with supernal light;
In golden mists the peaceful cadence died,
And Nature hailed what Faith has prophesied!
Ah! might Grief nestle in this sacred air,
Shielded from view and unprofaned by care!
How grates the discord of the teeming street,
The rush of steeds, and tramp of busy feet;
How vain the stir, how pitiless the glare,
To those who sorrow's aching badges wear!
Yet even here our brother's worth appears,
To fill with honour his remembered years;
In yonder pile*—the wretch's last retreat,
Where Charity and Science nobly meet,
With steadfast heart, with love-inspired brain,
And patient zeal, he ministered to pain.
Welcome the vistas of the hills and sea,
Whose pure enchantments ever solaced thee,
As from the city's strife our dark array,
Emerged to meet the forest and the bay:
There is a balm in Nature's open face
That over anguish casts a soothing grace;
The winds mourn with us, and the fading day,
Serenely whispers—all must pass away;
Each herb and tree with promise are imbued,
Withered to bloom, despoiled to be renewed;
From every knoll a boundless void we see,
So, love bereft, appears the world to thee:
Here where the portals of the East arise,
And falls the earliest greeting from the skies,
Our heavy burden in the earth we lay,
Far heavier that our hearts must bear away!

* JOHN W. FRANCIS, jr., eldest son of the eminent and venerable JOHN W. FRANCIS, M.D., LL.D. of New York, died on the twentieth of January, 1855, of typhus fever, brought on by extreme devotion to medical studies and attendance upon the poor. He was a youth of rare promise and great accomplishments; and perhaps there was never another occasion when one so young received the tribute of funeral honours from so large and distinguished an assemblage as that which accompanied his remains to St. Thomas's Church, where appropriate services were conducted in a very impressive manner by Dr. HAWKS, an old personal friend of the family.

* The New York Hospital.

THE HOLY LAND.

THROUGH the warm noontide, I have roam'd
Where CESAR's palace-ruins lie,
And in the Forum's lonely waste
Oft listen'd to the night-wind's sigh.

I've traced the moss-lines on the walls
That Venice conjured from the sea,
And seen the Colosseum's dust
Before the breeze of autumn flee.

Along Pompeii's lava-street,
With curious eye, I've wander'd lone,
And mark'd Segesta's temple-floor
With the rank weeds of ages grown.

I've clamber'd Etna's hoary brow,
And sought the wild Campagna's gloom;
I've hail'd Geneva's azure tide,
And snatch'd a weed from VIRGIL's tomb.

Why all unsated yearns my heart
To seek once more a pilgrim shrine?
One other land I would explore—
The sacred fields of Palestine.

Oh, for a glance at those wild hills
That round Jerusalem arise!
And one sweet evening by the lake
That gleams beneath Judea's skies!

How anthem-like the wind must sound
In meadows of the Holy Land—
How musical the ripples break
Upon the Jordan's moonlit strand!

Behold the dew, like angels' tears,
Upon each thorn is gleaming now,
Blest emblems of the crown of love
There woven for the Sufferer's brow.

Who does not sigh to enter Nain,
Or in Capernaum to dwell;
Inhale the breeze from Galilee,
And rest beside Samaria's well?

Who would not stand beneath the spot
Where Bethlehem's star its vigil kept?
List to the plash of Siloa's pool,
And kiss the ground where JESUS wept?

Gethsemane who would not seek,
And pluck a lily by the way?
Through Bethany devoutly walk,
And on the mount of Olives pray?

How dear were one repentant night
Where MARY's tears of love were shed!
How blest, beside the Saviour's tomb,
One hour's communion with the dead!

What solemn joy to stand alone
On Calvary's celestial height!
Or kneel upon the mountain-slope
Once radiant with supernal light!

I cannot throw my staff aside,
Nor wholly quell the hope divine
That one delight awaits me yet—
A pilgrimage to Palestine.

TO AN ELM.

BRAVELY thy old arms fling
Their countless pennons to the fields of air,
And, like a sylvan king,
Their panoply of green still proudly wear.

As some rude tower of old,
Thy massive trunk still rears its rugged form,
With limbs of giant mould,
To battle sternly with the winter storm.

In Nature's mighty fane,
Thou art the noblest arch beneath the sky;
How long the pilgrim train
That with a benison have pass'd thee by!

Lone patriarch of the wood!
Like a true spirit thou dost freely rise,
Of fresh and dauntless mood,
Spreading thy branches to the open skies.

The locust knows thee well,
And when the summer-days his notes prolong,
Hid in some leafy cell,
Pours from thy world of green his drowsy song.

Oft, on a morn in spring,
The yellow-bird will seek thy waving spray,
And there securely swing,
To whet his beak, and pour his blithesome lay.

How bursts thy monarch wail,
When sleeps the pulse of Nature's buoyant life,
And, bared to meet the gale,
Wave thy old branches, eager for the strife!

The sunset often weaves
Upon thy crest a wreath of splendour rare,
While the fresh-murmuring leaves
Fill with cool sound the evening's sultry air.

Sacred thy roof of green
To rustic dance, and childhood's gambols free:
Gay youth and age serene
Turn with familiar gladness unto thee.

O, hither should we roam,
To hear Truth's herald in the lofty shade;
Beneath thy emerald dome
Might Freedom's champion fitly draw his blade.

With blessings at thy feet,
Falls the worn peasant to his noontide rest;
Thy verdant, calm retreat
Inspires the sad and soothes the troubled breast.

When, at the twilight hour,
Plays through thy tressil crown the sun's last gleam,
Under thy ancient bower
The schoolboy comes to sport, the bard to dream.

And when the moonbeams fall
Through thy broad canopy upon the g ass,
Making a fairy hall,
As o'er the sward the flitting shadows pass—

Then lovers haste to thee,
With hearts that tremble like that shifting light;
To them, O brave old tree,
Thou art Joy's shrine—a temple of delight!

MARY.

What though the name is old and oft repeated,
What though a thousand beings bear it now,
And true hearts oft the gentle word have greeted—
What though 'tis hallow'd by a poet's vow?
We ever love the rose, and yet its blooming
Is a familiar rapture to the eye;
And yon bright star we hail, although its looming
Age after age has lit the northern sky.

As starry beams o'er troubled billows stealing,
As garden odours to the desert blown,
In bosoms faint a gladsome hope revealing,
Like patriot music or affection's tone—
Thus, thus, for aye, the name of Mary spoken
By lips or text, with magic-like control,
The course of present thought has quickly broken,
And stirr'd the fountains of my inmost soul.

The sweetest tales of human weal and sorrow,
The fairest trophies of the limner's fame,
To my fond fancy, Mary, seem to borrow
Celestial halos from thy gentle name:
The Grecian artist glean'd from many faces,
And in a perfect whole the parts combined,
So have I counted o'er dear woman's graces
To form the Mary of my ardent mind.

And marvel not I thus call my ideal—
We inly paint as we would have things be—
The fanciful springs ever from the real,
As Aphrodite rose from out the sea.
Who smiled upon me kindly day by day,
In a far land where I was sad and lone?
Whose presence now is my delight away?
Both angels must the same bless'd title own.

What spirits round my weary way are flying,
What fortunes on my future life await,
Like the mysterious hymns the winds are sighing,
Are all unknown—in trust I bide my fate;
But if one blessing I might crave from Heaven,
'T would be that Mary should my being cheer,
Hang o'er me when the chord of life is riven,
Be my dear household word, and my last accent here.

"YOU CALL US INCONSTANT."

You call us inconstant—you say that we cease
Our homage to pay, at the voice of caprice;
That we dally with hearts till their treasures are ours,
As bees drink the sweets from a cluster of flowers;
For a moment's refreshment at love's fountain stay,
Then turn, with a thankless impatience, away.

And think you, indeed, we so cheerfully part
With hopes that give wings to the o'erwearied heart,
And throw round the future a promise so bright
That life seems a glory, and time a delight?
From our pathway forlorn can we banish the dove,
And yield without pain the enchantments of love?

You know not how chill and relentless a wave
Reflection will cast o'er the soul of the brave—
How keenly the clear rays of duty will beam,
And startle the heart from its passionate dream,
To tear the fresh rose from the garland of youth,
And lay it with tears on the altar of truth!

We pass from the presence of beauty, to think—
As the hunter will pause on the precipice brink—
"For me shall the bloom of the gladsome and fair
Be wasted away by the fetters of care!
Shall the old, peaceful nest, for my sake be forgot,
And the gentle and free know a wearisome lot?

"By the tender appeal of that beauty, beware
How you woo her thy desolate fortunes to share!
O pluck not a lily so shelter'd and sweet,
And bear it not off from its genial retreat.
Enrich'd with the boon thy existence would be,
But hapless the fate that unites her to thee!"

Thus, dearest, the spell that thy graces entwined,
No fickle heart breaks, but a resolute mind;
The pilgrim may turn from the shrine with a smile,
Yet, believe me, his bosom is wrung all the while,
And one thought alone lends a charm to the past—
That his love conquer'd selfishness nobly at last.

GREENOUGH'S WASHINGTON.

The quarry whence thy form majestic sprung
Has peopled earth with grace,
Heroes and gods that elder bards have sung,
A bright and peerless race;
But from its sleeping veins ne'er rose before
A shape of loftier name
Than his, who Glory's wreath with meekness wore,
The noblest son of Fame.
Sheathed is the sword that Passion never stain'd;
His gaze around is cast,
As if the joys of Freedom, newly-gain'd,
Before his vision pass'd;
As if a nation's shout of love and pride
With music fill'd the air,
And his calm soul was lifted on the tide
Of deep and grateful prayer;
As if the crystal mirror of his life
To fancy sweetly came,
With scenes of patient toil and noble strife,
Undimm'd by doubt or shame;
As if the lofty purpose of his soul
Expression would betray—
The high resolve Ambition to control,
And thrust her crown away!
Oh, it was well in marble firm and white
To carve our hero's form,
Whose angel guidance was our strength in fight,
Our star amid the storm!
Whose matchless truth has made his name divine,
And human freedom sure,
His country great, his tomb earth's dearest shrine,
While man and time endure!
And it is well to place his image there,
Beneath the dome he blest;
Let meaner spirits who its councils share,
Revere that silent guest!
Let us go up with high and sacred love
To look on his pure brow,
And as, with solemn grace, he points above,
Renew the patriot's vow!

ALONE ONCE MORE.

Alone once more!—but with such deep emotion,
Waking to life a thousand hopes and fears,
Such wild distrust—such absolute devotion,
My bosom seems a dreary lake of tears:

Tears that stern manhood long restrain'd from gush- [ing,
As mountains keep a river from the sea,
Until Spring's floods, impetuous'y rushing,
Channel a bed, and set its waters free!

What mockery to all true and earnest feeling,
This fatal union of the false and fair!
Eyes, lips, and voice, unmeasured bliss revealing,
With hearts whose lightness fills us with despair!

O God! some sorrows of our wondrous being
A patient mind can partly clear away;
Ambition cools when fortune's gifts are fleeing,
And men grow thoughtful round a brother's clay;

But to what end this waste of noble passion?
This wearing of a truthful heart to dust—
Adoring slaves of humour, praise, or fashion,
The vain recipients of a boundless trust?

Come home, fond heart, cease all instinctive plead- [ing,
As the dread fever of insane desire,
To some dark gulf thy warm affections leading,
When love must long survive, though faith expire!

Though wonted glory from the earth will vanish,
And life seem desolate, and hope beguile,
Love's cherish'd dream learn steadfastly to banish,
Till death thy spirit's conflict reconcile!

SONNETS.

I. TO ———.

What though our dream is broken! Yet again
Like a familiar angel it shall bear
Consoling treasures for these days of pain,
Such as they only who have grieved can share;
As unhived nectar for the bee to sip,
Lurks in each flower-cell which the spring-time [brings,
As music rests upon the quiet lip,
And power to soar yet lives in folded wings—
So let the love on which your spirits glide
Flow deep and strong beneath its bridge of sighs,
No shadow resting on the latent tide
Whose heavenward current baffles human eyes,
Until we stand upon the holy shore,
And realms it prophesied at length explore!

II. COURAGE AND PATIENCE.

Courage and patience! elements whereby
My soul shall yet her citadel maintain,
Baffled, perplex'd, and struggling oft to fly,
Far, far above this realm of wasting pain—
Come with your still and banded vigour now,
Fill my sad breast with energy divine,
Stamp a firm thought upon my aching brow,
Make my impulsive visions wholly thine!
Freeze my pent tears, chill all my tender dreams,
Brace my weak heart in panoply sublime,
Till dwelling only on thy martyr themes,
And turning from the richest lures of time,
Love, like an iceberg of the polar deep,
In adamantine rest is laid asleep!

III. ALL HEARTS ARE NOT DISLOYAL.

All hearts are not disloyal: let thy trust
Be deep, and clear, and all-confiding still,
For though Love's fruit turn on the lips to dust,
She ne'er betrays her child to lasting ill:
Through leagues of desert must the pilgrim go
Ere on his gaze the holy turrets rise;
Through the long, sultry day the stream must flow
Ere it can mirror twilight's purple skies.
Fall back unscathed from contact with the vain,
Keep thy robes white, thy spirit bold and free,
And calmly launch Affection's bark again,
Hopeful of golden spoils reserved for thee!
Though lone the way as that already trod,
Cling to thine own integrity and God!

IV. LIKE A FAIR SEA.

Like the fair sea that laves Italia's strand,
Affection's flood is tideless in my breast;
No ebb withdraws it from the chosen land,
Haven'd too richly for enamour'd quest:
Thus am I faithful to the vanish'd grace
Embodied once in thy sweet form and name,
And though love's charm no more illumes thy face,
In Memory's realm her olden pledge I claim.
It is not constancy to haunt a shrine
From which devotion's lingering spark has fled;
Insensate homage only wreaths can twine
Around the pulseless temples of the dead:
Thou from thy better self hast madly flown,
While to that self allegiance still I own.

V. FREEDOM.

Freedom! beneath thy banner I was born—
Oh let me share thy full and perfect life!
Teach me opinion's slavery to scorn,
And to be free from passion's bitter strife;
Free of the world, a self-dependent soul
Nourish'd by lofty aims and genial truth,
And made more free by Love's serene control,
The spell of beauty and the hopes of youth.
The liberty of Nature let me know,
Caught from her mountains, groves, and crystal streams,
Her starry host, and sunset's purple glow,
That woo the spirit with celestial dreams,
On Fancy's wing exultingly to soar,
Till life's harsh fetters clog the heart no more!

VI. DESOLATION.

Think ye the desolate must live apart,
By solemn vows to convent-walls confined?
Ah! no; with men may dwell the cloister'd heart,
And in a crowd the isolated mind;
Tearless behind the prison-bars of fate,
The world sees not how sorrowful they stand,
Gazing so fondly through the iron grate,
Upon the promised, yet forbidden land;
Patience, the shrine to which their bleeding feet,
Day after day, in voiceless penance turn;
Silence, the holy cell and calm retreat
In which unseen their meek devotions burn;
Life is to them a vigil that none share,
Their hopes a sacrifice, their love a prayer.

LUNA: AN ODE.

The south wind hath its balm, the sea its cheer,
And autumn woods their bright and myriad hues;
Thine is a joy that love and faith endear,
And awe subdues:
The wave-toss'd seamen and the harvest crew,
When on their golden sheaves the quivering dew
Hangs like pure tears—all fear beguile,
In glancing from their task to thy maternal smile!
The mist of hilltops undulating wreathes,
At thy enchanting touch, a magic woof,
And curling incense fainter odour breathes,
And in transparent clouds hangs round the vaulted roof.
Huge icebergs, with their crystal spires
Slow heaving from the northern main,
Like frozen monuments of high desires
Destin'd to melt in nothingness again—
Float in thy mystic beams,
As piles aerial down the tide of dreams!
A sacred greeting falls
With thy mild presence on the ruin'd fane,
Columns time-stain'd, dim frieze, and ivied walls,
As if a fond delight thou didst attain
To mingle with the Past,
And o'er her trophies lone a holy mantle cast!
Along the billow's snowy crest
Thy beams a moment rest,
And then in sparkling mirth dissolve away;
Through forest boughs, amid the wither'd leaves,
Thy light a tracery weaves,
And on the mossy clumps its rays fantastic play.
With thee, ethereal guide,
What reverent joy to pace the temple floor,
And watch thy silver tide
O'er statue, tomb, and arch, its solemn radiance pour!
Like a celestial magnet thou dost sway
The untamed waters in their ebb and flow,
The maniac raves beneath thy pallid ray,
And poet's visions glow.
Madonna of the stars! through the cold prison-grate
Thou stealest, like a nun on mercy bent,
To cheer the desolate,
And usher in Grief's tears when her mute pang is spent!
I marvel not that once thy altars rose
Sacred to human woes,
And nations deem'd thee arbitress of Fate,
To whom enamor'd virgins made their prayer,
Or widows in their first despair,
And wistful gazed upon thy queenly state,
As, with a meek assurance, gliding by,
In might and beauty unelate,
Into the bridal chambers of the sky!
And less I marvel that Endymion sigh'd
To yield his spirit unto thine,
And felt thee soul-allied,
Making his being thy receptive shrine!
A lofty peace is thine!—the tides of life
Flow gently when thy soothing orb appears,
And Passion's fever'd strife
From thy chaste glow imbibes the calmness of the spheres!
O twilight glory! that doth ne'er awake
Exhausting joy, but evenly and fond
Allays the immortal thirst it cannot slake,
And heals the chafing of the work-day bond;
Give me thy patient spell!—to bear
With an unclouded brow the secret pain
(That floods my soul as thy pale beams the air)
Of hopes that Reason quells, for Love to wake again!

TASSO TO LEONORA.

If to love solitude because my heart
May undisturbed upon thy image dwell,
And in the world to bear a cheerful part
To hide the fond thoughts that its pulses swell;
If to recall with credulous delight
Affection's faintest semblances in thee,
To feel thy breath upon my cheek at night,
And start in anguish that it may not be;
If in thy presence ceaselessly to know
Delicious peace, a feeling as of wings,
Content divine within my bosom glow,
A noble scorn of all unworthy things—
The quiet bliss that fills one's natal air,
When once again it fans the wanderer's brow,
The conscious spirit of the good and fair—
The wish to be forever such as now;
If in thy absence still to feel thee nigh,
Or with impatient longings waste the day,
If to be haunted by thy love-lit eye—
If for thy good devotedly to pray;
And chiefly sorrow that but half reveal'd
Can be the tenderness that in me lies,
That holiest pleasure must be all conceal'd—
Shrinking from heartless scoff or base surmise
If, as my being's crowning grace, to bless
The hour we recognised each other's truth,
And with calm joy unto my soul confess
That thou hast realized the dreams of youth—
My spirit's mate, long cherish'd, though unknown,
Friend of my heart bestow'd on me by God,
At whose approach all visions else have flown
From the vain path which I so long have trod;
If from thy sweet caress to bear new life
As one possess'd by a celestial spell,
That armeth me against all outward strife,
And ever breathes the watchword—all is well,
If with glad firmness, casting doubt aside,
To bare my heart to thee without disguise,
And yield it up as to my chosen bride,
Feeling that life vouchsafes no dearer prize;
If thus to blend my very soul with thine
By mutual consecration, watching o'er
The hallow'd bond with loyalty divine—
If this be love,—I love forevermore!

FROM THE SPIRIT OF POETRY.

THE LAW OF BEAUTY.

Read the great law in Beauty's cheering reign,
Blent with all ends through matter's wide domain;
She breathes Hope's language, and with boundless range
Sublimes all forms, smiles through each subtle change,
And with insensate elements combined
Ordains their constant ministry to mind.
The breeze awoke to waft the feather'd seed,
And the cloud-fountains with their dew to feed,

Upon its many errands might have flown,
Nor woke one river song or forest moan,
Stirr'd not the grass, nor the tall grain have bent,
Like shoreless billows tremulously spent;
Frost could the bosom of the lake have glass'd,
Nor paused to paint the woodlands as it pass'd;
The glossy seabird and the brooding dove
Might coyly peck with twinkling eye of love,
Nor catch upon their downy necks the dyes,
So like the mottled hues of summer skies:
Mists in the west could float, nor glory wear,
As if an angel's robes were streaming there;
The moon might sway the tides, nor yet impart
A solemn light to tranquillize the heart,
And leagues of sand could bar the ocean's swell,
Nor yield one crystal gleam or pearly shell.
The very sedge lends music to the blast,
And the thorn glistens when the storm is past;
Wild flowers nestle in the rocky cleft,
Moss decks the bough of leaf and life bereft,
O'er darkest clouds the moonbeams brightly steal,
The rainbow's herald is the thunder's peal;
Gay are the weeds that strew the barren shore,
And anthem-like the breaker's gloomy roar.
As love o'er sorrow spreads her genial wings
The ivy round a fallen column clings,
While on the sinking walls, where owlets cry,
The weather stains in tints of beauty lie.
The wasting elements adorn their prey
And throw a pensive charm around decay;
Thus ancient limners bade their canvas glow,
And group'd sweet cherubs o'er a martyr's wo.

COLUMBUS.

Heroic guide! whose wings are never furl'd,
By thee Spain's voyager sought another world;
What but poetic impulse could sustain
That dauntless pilgrim on the dreary main?
Day after day his mariners protest,
And gaze with dread along the pathless west;
Beyond that realm of waves, untrack'd before,
Thy fairy pencil traced the promised shore,
Through weary storms and faction's fiercer rage,
The scoffs of ingrates and the chills of age,
Thy voice renewed his earnestness of aim,
And whisper'd pledges of eternal fame;
Thy cheering smile atoned for fortune's frown,
And made his fetters garlands of renown.

FLORENCE.

Princes, when softened in thy sweet embrace,
Yearn for no conquest but the realm of grace,
And thus redeemed, Lorenzo's fair domain
Smiled in the light of Art's propitious reign.
Delightful Florence! though the northern gale
Will sometimes rave around thy lovely vale,
Can I forget how softly Autumn threw
Beneath thy skies her robes of ruddy hue,
Through what long days of balminess and peace,
From wintry bonds spring won thy mild release?
Along the Arno then I loved to pass,
And watch the violets peeping from the grass,
Mark the gray kine each chestnut grove between,
Startle the pheasants on the lawny green,
Or down long vistas hail the mountain snow,
Like lofty shrines the purple clouds below.
Within thy halls, when veil'd the sunny rays,
Marvels of art await the ardent gaze,
And liquid words from lips of beauty start,
With social joy to warm the stranger's heart.
How beautiful at moonlight's hallow'd hour,
Thy graceful bridges, and celestial tower!
The girdling hills enchanted seem to hang
Round the fair scene whence modern genius sprang
O'er the dark ranges of thy palace walls
The silver beam on dome and cornice falls;
The statues cluster'd in thy ancient square,
Like mighty spirits print the solemn air;
Silence meets beauty with unbroken reign,
Save when invaded by a choral strain,
Whose distant cadence falls upon the ear,
To fill the bosom with poetic cheer!

POETRY IMMORTAL.

For fame life's meaner records vainly strive,
While, in fresh beauty, thy high dreams survive.
Still Vesta's temple throws its classic shade
O'er the bright foam of Tivoli's cascade,
And to one Venus still we bow the knee,
Divine as if just issued from the sea;
In fancy's trance, yet deem on nights serene
We hear the revels of the fairy queen,
That Dian's smile illumes the marble fane,
And Ceres whispers in the rustling grain,
That Ariel's music has not died away,
And in his shell still floats the Culprit Fay.
The sacred beings of poetic birth
Immortal live to consecrate the earth.
San Marco's pavement boasts no doge's tread,
And all its ancient pageantry has fled;
Yet, as we muse beneath some dim arcade,
The mind's true kindred glide from ruin's shade;
In every passing eye that sternly beams
We start to meet the Shylock of our dreams;
Each maiden form, where virgin grace is seen,
Crosses our path with Portia's noble mien;
While Desdemona, beauteous as of yore,
Yields us the smile that once entranced the Moor
How Scotland's vales are peopled to the heart
By her bold minstrel's necromantic art!
Along this fern moved Jeannie's patient feet,
Where hangs yon mist rose Ellangowan's seat,
Here the sad bride first gave her love a tongue,
And there the chief's last shout of triumph rung
Beside each stream, down every glen they throng
The cherish'd offspring of creative song!
Long ere brave Nelson shook the Baltic shore,
The bard of Avon hallow'd Elsinore:
Perchance when moor'd the fleet, awaiting day,
To fix the battle's terrible array,
Some pensive hero, musing o'er the deep,
So soon to fold him in its dreamless sleep,
Heard the Dane's sad and self-communing tone
Blend with the water's melancholy moan,
Recall'd, with prayer and awe-suspended breath,
His wild and solemn questionings of death,
Or caught from land Ophelia's dying song,
Swept by the night-breeze plaintively along!

W. H. C. HOSMER.

[Born, 1814.]

One of the most truly American of our poets, that is, one of those whose characteristics are most directly and obviously results of a lifelong familiarity with the scenery, traditions, and institutions of our own country, is William Henry Cuyler Hosmer, of Avon, in western New York. His father, a distinguished lawyer, descended from a New England family which had furnished many eminent names to the bench and bar, emigrated at an early period from Connecticut; and his maternal ancestors were the first settlers among the Senecas, whose language he learned in infancy from his mother's lips, and whose mythology and public and private life he has understood as familiarly as if they were his natural inheritance. He was born at Avon, on the fifth of May, 1814, and was educated at the Temple Hill Academy, Geneseo, of which the learned Professor C. C. Felton, now of Harvard University, was the principal, and at Geneva College. For his literary productions he had already received the honorary degree of master of arts, from Hamilton College and the University of Vermont, before it was conferred in course by his alma mater. He subsequently studied the law, in the office of his father, and on being admitted to practice became his partner. The rank he has held in his profession is indicated by the fact that he succeeded the late Honorable John Young as master in chancery.

In 1836, while Wisconsin was still in almost undisturbed possession of the Indians, he spent some time in that territory, and for several months during the southern border war of 1838 and 1839, accompanied by his wife, to whom he had just been married, he was an invalid among the everglades of Florida. In these excursions he had ample opportunity of studying the Indian character as it is displayed in those regions, and of comparing it with that of the Iroquois.

Mr. Hosmer began to write verses at a very early age, and has been an industrious and a prolific author. In 1830 he composed a drama entitled "The Fall of Tecumseh." His first publication, except contributions to the journals and magazines, was "The Themes of Song," containing about six hundred and fifty lines; this appeared in 1834, and was followed by "The Pioneers of Western New York," in 1838; "The Prospects of the Age," in 1841; "Yonnondio, or the Warriors of the Genesee," in 1844; "The Months," in 1847; "Bird Notes," "Legends of the Senecas," and "Indian Traditions and Songs," in 1850; and a complete collection of his "Poetical Works," in two volumes, in 1853.

The longest if not the most important of these productions of Mr. Hosmer is "Yonnondio," a tale of the French domination in America in the seventeenth century. It is in octo-syllabic verse, occasionally varied to suit the requirements of his subject; the narrative is spirited and interesting; and all the details of Indian customs, costumes, superstitions, and character, as well as the delineations of external nature, studiously correct. It is a defect in the construction of the story, that no sufficient cause is presented for the conduct of one of the principal actors, De Grai: a quarrel on an unjust imputation affording no proper ground for his leaving France; generally, however, the dramatic proprieties of the piece are as well preserved as the descriptive; and it abounds with picturesque touches which betray a very careful observation, and unusual felicity in coloring. In the account of an Indian march, we are told:

"The red-breast, perch'd in arbour green,
Sad minstrel of the quiet scene,
While singing, for the dying sun,
As sings a broken-hearted one,
Raised not her mottled wing to fly,
As swept those silent warriors by;
The woodcock in his moist retreat,
Heard not the falling of their feet;
On his dark roost the gray owl slept;
Time with his drum the partridge kept;
Nor left the deer his watering place—
So hushed, so noiseless was their pace."

In a similar vein is the following finely finished passage describing the passage of an Indian maiden through the valley of the Genesee:

"Treading upon the grassy sod
As if her feet with moss were shod,
Fled on her errand, Wan-nut-hay;
Nor paused to list or look behind,
While groves, of outline undefined,
Before her darkly lay:
Boldly she plunged their depth's within
Though thorns pierced through her moccasin,
And the black clouds, unseal'd at last,
Discharged their contents thick and fast,
Drenching her locks and vesture slight,
And blinding with large drops her sight.

"The grizzly wolf was on the tramp
To gain the covert of his lair;
Fierce eyes glared on her from the swamp,
As if they asked her errand there;
The feathered hermit of the dell
Flew, hooting, to his oaken cell;
And grape-vines, tied in leafy coil
To gray-arm'd giants of the soil,
Swung, like a vessel's loosen'd shrouds,
Drifting beneath a bank of clouds.
From the pines' huge and quaking cones
Came sobbing and unearthly tones,
While trunks decayed, of measure vast,
Fought for the last time with the blast,
And near her fell with crushing roar,
That shook the cumbered forest floor."

There are scattered through the poem passages of reflection in their way not less creditable to the author. These lines, from the seventh canto, are excellent:

"Thou phantom, military fame!
How long will Genius laud thy name,
And curtain features from the sight,
More foul than those Khorassen's seer
Hid behind veil of silver bright,
Tempting his victim to draw near?
How long will thy misleading lamp
Through regions wrapped in smoke and fire,
To Slaughter's cavern, red and damp,
Guide beardless boy and gray-haired sire?
Up, fearless battlers for the right,
And flood old groaning earth with light!
Bid nations ponder well and pause,
When blade corrupt Ambition draws—
Oh! teach the world that Conquest wears
A darker brand than felon bears;
Prolific fount, from earliest time,
Of murder, orphanage, and crime!"

In a preface to his poems relating to the Indians, Mr. HOSMER reminds us of the extraordinary advantages he has enjoyed, "by their campfires, and in their councils," for becoming acquainted with their characteristics and traditions, and discusses eloquently the suitableness of his theme for poetical treatment.

To such poems, however, most readers will be apt to prefer the simpler effusions in which he has echoed the "Notes of the Birds," or painted the varying phenomena of "The Months." In these, too, he has faithfully subjected his muse to the requirements of truth. He accomplishes his task of description by felicities in selection and combination from nature. An AUDUBON or a MICHAUX would search in vain for an error in his plumage or foliage, and a COLE might give the finishing touches to the lights and shadows of his landscapes from the poet's observation of atmospheric effects or the changing influence of the seasons.

In 1854 Mr. HOSMER removed to the city of New York, where he occupies a place in the custom-house.

THE IMMORTALITY OF GENIUS.*

LANGUAGE provides poor symbols of expression
When roused Imagination, holding rein,
Sends airy forms of grace in vast procession
Across the poet's brain.

An Orphic tongue would be too weak an agent
To tell the tale of inspiration's hour;
To paint an outline of the gorgeous pageant,
A TITIAN have no power.

The meagre written record of the closet
Saves but a few, pale glimmering pearls—no more
When the lashed waves roll inland to deposit
Their wealth along the shore. ....

The queen of Beauty and her blushing daughters
In Crathis bathed—that old poetic stream—
And each dark ringlet from the sparkling waters
Imbibed an amber gleam.

Thus thoughts that send and will send on forever,
From the dim plains of long ago, a light,
Caught from Imagination's golden river
Their glow divinely bright.

When done with life, its fever, din, and jostle,
How scant and poor a portion after all
Of Nature's priest, and Art's renowned apostle
Lies hid beneath the pall.

Though grazing herd and hosts with clanging sabres
Their graves forgotten trample rudely o'er,
To tribes and nations, through their crowning labors,
They speak for evermore.

Oh, Genius! dowered with privilege immortal,
Thus from the wastes of time to stretch thy hand,
And, with a touch unfold the glittering portal
Of an enchanted land!

Death knows thee not, tho' long ago were blended
Thy visible forms with undistinguished clay;
The dead are they whose mission here is ended—
Thy voice is heard to-day.

Heard on the honeyed lip of JULIET melting—
In dreaming RICHARD's cry of guilty fear—
In shouts that rise above the night-storm pelting
From old distracted LEAR:

Heard in the organ-swell of MILTON pealing—
In GRAY's elegaic sorrow for the past—
In flute-notes from the muse of SPENSER stealing,
In DRYDEN's bugle's blast:

Heard in the matchless works of thy creation,
Spreaking from canvas, scroll, and marble lips,
In those deep awful tones of inspiration
That baffle death's eclipse.

* From a poem on "The Utility of Imagination."

THE SOLDIER OF THE CLOSET.*

NOT they alone work faithfully who labor
On the dull, dusty thoroughfare of life;
The clerkly pen can vanquish, when the sabre
Is useless in the strife.

In cloistered gloom the quiet man of letters
Launching his thoughts, like arrows from the bow,
Oft strikes the traitor and his base abettors,
Bringing their grandeur low.

Armed with a scroll, the birds of evil omen,
That curse a country, he can scare away,
Or, in the wake of error, marshal foemen
Impatient for the fray.

Scorn not the sons of Song! nor deem them only
Poor, worthless weeds upon the shore of time
Although they move in walks retired and lonely,
They have their tasks sublime.

When tyrants tread the hill-top and the valley,
Calling the birthright of the brave their own,
Around the tomb of Liberty they rally,
And roll away the stone!

* From "The Ideal"

BATTLE-GROUND OF DENONVILLE.

Oh! what secrets are revealed
In this ancient battle-field!
Round are scattered skull and bone,
Into light by workmen thrown
Who across this valley fair
For the train a way prepare.
Pictures brighten thick and fast
On the mirror of the past;
To poetic vision plain
Plume and banner float again;
Round are mangled bodies lying,
Some at rest, and others dying —
Thus the Swan-ne-ho-ont greet
Those who plant invading feet
On the chase-ground where their sires
Long have kindled council-fires.
Fragments of the deadly brand,
Lying in the yellow sand,
With the *fleur-de-lis* to tell
Of the Frank who clenched it well,
When his race encountered here
Tameless chasers of the deer —
Arrow-head and hatchet-blade,
War-club broken and decayed,
Belts in part resolved to dust,
Gun-locks red with gnawing rust.
Other sounds than pick and spade,
When this valley lay in shade,
Ringing on the summer air
Scared the panther from his lair;
Other sounds than axe and bar,
Pathway building for the car,
Buzzing saw, or hammer-stroke,
Echo wild from slumber woke,
When New France her lilies pale
Here unfolded to the gale —
Rifle-crack and musket-peal,
Whiz of shaft and clash of steel —
Painted forms from cover leaping,
Crimson swaths through foemen reaping,
While replied each savage throat,
To the rallying bugle-note,
With a wolf-howl long and loud,
That the stoutest veteran cowed,
Mingled in one fearful din
Where these graves are crumbling in.
Busy actors in the fray
Were their tenants on that day;
But each name, forgotten long,
Cannot now be wove in song.
They had wives, perchance, who kept
Weary watch for them, and wept
Bitter tears at last to learn
They would never more return;
And in hut as well as hall
Childless mothers mourned their fall.
In a vain attempt they died
To bring low Na-do-wa pride,
And extend the Bourbon's reign
O'er this broad and bright domain.
When the whirlwind of the fight
Sunk into a whisper light,
Rudely opened was the mould
For their bodies stiff and cold:
Brush and leaves were loosely piled
On their grave-couch in the wild,
That their place of rest the foe,
Drunk with blood, might never know.
When the settler for his hearth,
Cleared a spot of virgin earth;
And its smoke-thread on the breeze,
Curled above the forest trees,
Nor memorial sign, nor mound
Told that this was burial ground.
Since this bank received its dead,
Now unroofed to startled sight,
With its skeleton's all white,
More than eightscore years have fled.
Gather them with pious care,—
Let them not lie mouldering there,
Crushed beneath the grinding wheel,
And the laborer's heavy heel.
Ah! this fractured skull of man
Nursed a brain once quick to plan,
And these ribs that round me lie
Hearts enclosed that once beat high.
Here they fought, and here they fell,
Battle's roar their only knell,
And the soil that drank their gore
Should embrace the brave once more.

MENOMINEE DIRGE.

We bear the dead, we bear the dead,
In robes of otter habited,
From the quiet depths of the greenwood shade
To her lonely couch on the hill-top made.
There, there the sun when dies the day
Flings mournfully his parting ray —
In vain the winds lift her tresses black —
Ke-ton-ee-mi-coo, Wa-was-te-nac!*

When ploughs tear up the forest floor,
And hunters follow the deer no more,
When the red man's council hearth is cold
His glory, like a tale that's told,
Spare, white man! spare an oak to wave
Its bough above the maiden's grave,
And the dead will send a blessing back —
Ke-ton-ee-mi-coo, Wa-was-te-nac!

Another race are building fires
Above the bones of our buried sires —
Soon will the homes of our people be
Far from the bright Menominee;
But yearly to yon burial-place
Some mourning band of our luckless race
To smooth the turf will wander back —
Ke-ton-ee-mi-coo, Wa-was-te-nac!

On the wafting wings of yesternight,
The soul of our peerless one took flight;
She heard a voice from the clime of souls,
Sweeter than lays of orioles,
Say, "Come to that bright and blissful land
Where Death waves not his skeleton hand,
Where the sky with storm is never black".
Ke-ton-ee-mi-coo, Wa-was-te nac!

* Flower, farewell!

THE SWALLOW.

"La Rondinella, sopra il nido allegra,
Cantando salutava il nuovo giorno."

"The swallow is one of my favorite birds, and a rival of the nightingale; for he glads my sense of seeing, as the other does my sense of hearing."—Sir H. Davy.

Warm, cloudless days have brought a blithe new-comer,
Beloved by young and old,
That twitters out a welcome unto summer,
Arrayed in green and gold.

With sunlight on his plume, the happy swallow
Is darting swiftly by,
As if, with shaft dismissed by bright Apollo,
His speed he fain would try.

Now high above yon steeple wheels the rover,
In many a sportive ring:
Anon, the glassy lakelet skimming over,
He dips his dusky wing.

Old nests yet hang, though marred by winter's traces,
To rafter, beam and wall,
And his fond mate, to ancient breeding-places,
Comes at his amorous call.

Those mud-built domes were dear to me in childhood,
With feathers soft inlaid;
Dearer than the nests whose builders in the wild-wood
Were birds of man afraid.

To seedy floors of barns in thought I wander,
When swallows glads my sight,
And play with comrades in the church-yard yonder,
Shut out from air and light.

The "guests of summer" in and out are flying,
Their mansions to repair,
While on the fragrant hay together lying,
We bid adieu to care.

Barns that they haunt no thunderbolt can shatter,
Full many a hind believes;
No showers that bring a blighting mildew patter
Upon the golden sheaves.

Taught were our fathers that a curse would follow,
Beyond expression dread,
The cruel farmer who destroyed the swallow
That builded in his shed.

Oh! how I envied, in the school-house dreary,
The swallow's freedom wild,
Cutting the wind on pinion never weary,
Cleaving the clouds up piled.

And when the bird and his blithe mate beholding
Abroad in airy race,
Their evolutions filled my soul unfolding
With images of grace.

And, oh! what rapture, after wintry chidings,
And April's smile and tear,
Thrilled to the core, my bosom at the tidings,
"The swallow, boy, is here!"

Announcement of an angel on some mission
Of love without alloy,
Could not have sooner wakened a transition
From gloom to heart-felt joy.

For summer to the dreaming youth a heaven
Of bliss and beauty seems,
And in her sunshine less of earthly leaven
Clings to our thoughts and dreams.

In honor of the bird, with vain endeavor,
Why lengthen out my lay?
By Shakspeare's art he is embalmed forever,
Enshrined in song by Gray.

LAY OF A WANDERER.

A FLORIDIAN SCENE.

Where Pablo to the broad St. John
His dark and briny tribute pays,
The wild deer leads her dappled fawn,
Of graceful limb and timid gaze;
Rich sunshine falls on wave and land,
The gull is screaming overhead,
And on a beach of whiten'd sand
Lie wreathy shells with lips of red.

The jessamine hangs golden flowers
On ancient oaks in moss array'd,
And proudly the palmetto towers,
While mock-birds warble in the shade;
Mounds, built by mortal hands are near,
Green from the summit to the base,
Where, buried with the bow and spear,
Rest tribes, forgetful of the chase.

Cassada,* nigh the ocean shore,
Is now a ruin, wild and lone,
And on her battlements no more
Is banner waved or trumpet blown;
Those doughty cavaliers are gone
Who hurled defiance there to France,
While the bright waters of St. John
Reflected flash of sword and lance.

But when the light of dying day
Falls on the crumbling wrecks of time,
And the wan features of decay
Wear softened beauty like the clime,
My fancy summons from the shroud
The knights of old Castile again,
And charging thousands shout aloud —
"St. Jago strikes to-day for Spain!"

When mystic voices, on the breeze
That fans the rolling deep, sweep by,
The spirits of the Yemassees,
Who ruled the land of yore, seemed nigh;
For mournful marks, around where stood
Their palm-roofed lodges, yet are seen,
And in the shadows of the wood
Their monumental mounds are green.

* An old Spanish fort.

JEDIDIAH VINCENT HUNTINGTON.

[Born 1815. Died 1862.]

J. V. HUNTINGTON, of the distinguished Connecticut family of that name, was born in New York in 1815; was graduated bachelor of arts at the University of New York in 1835, and doctor of medicine at the University of Pennsylvania in 1838; practised his profession about two years in his native city, and then turned his attention to literature; wrote, for the "New York Review," an article on the Greek Anthology, which made him known among scholars, and various papers in the magazines; became professor of mental philosophy in St. Paul's College; in 1841 was ordained a clergyman in the Protestant Episcopal church; married his cousin (a daughter of the late Reverend JOSHUA HUNTINGTON, the memoirs of whose wife, Mrs. SUSAN HUNTINGTON, have had so wide a circulation as a religious biography); took a parish in Middlebury, Vermont, where his health failed; visited the South, and afterwards Europe, where he spent four years, mainly in Italy; in 1849 returned to this country, and reëngaged in the duties of the ministry, but at the end of a year renounced them by submitting to the church of Rome.

He published a volume of "Poems," in 1842; "The Divine Institution of the Festival System," a sermon, in 1843; "Lady Alice," a novel, in 1849; "The Sacrament of Repentance," a tract, in 1850; "Alban, or the History of a Young Puritan," a novel, in 1851; "America Discovered," a poem, in 1852; "The Forest," a sequel to "Alban," in the same year; "Alban," partly rewritten, in 1853; and "St. Vincent de Paul," a lecture, also in that year. His poems are chiefly meditative, and are finished in a style of scholarly elegance.

SONNETS

SUGGESTED BY THE CORONATION OF QUEEN VICTORIA.

AUGUST 4, 1838.

I. THE ABBEY.

WITHIN the minster's venerable pile
What pomps unwonted flash upon our eyes!
What galleries, in gold and crimson, rise
Between the antique pillars of the aisle,
Crowded with England's gayest life; the while
Beneath, her dead, unconscious glory lies;
Above, her ancient faith still seeks the skies;
And with apparent life doth well beguile
Our senses in that ever-growing roof;
Whence on the soul return those recollections
Of her great annals—built to be time-proof,
Which chiefly make this spot the fittest scene
Wherein to consecrate those new affections
We plight this day to Britain's virgin queen.

II. THE QUEEN.

How strange to see a creature young and fair
Assume the sceptre of these widespread lands!—
How in her femininely feeble hands
The orb of empire shall she ever bear!—
And crowns, they say, not more with gems than care
Are weighty: yet with calmest mien she stands;
August in innocence herself commands,
And will that stately burden lightly wear.
Claims surely inoffensive!—What is she?
Of ancient sovereignty a living shoot;
The latest blossom on a royal tree
Deep in the past extends whose famous root;
And realms from age to age securely free,
Gather of social peace its yet unfailing fruit.

III. THE CROWNING.

How dazzling flash the streams of colour'd light,
When on her sacred brow the crown is placed!
And straight her peers and dames with haughty haste
Their coronets assume, as is their right,
With sudden blaze making the temple bright.
Does man's enthusiasm run to waste,
By which a queen's investiture is graced
With deafening demonstrations of delight,
That from the cannon's roar protect the ear?
We may not dare to think so, for His sake
Whose word has link'd king's honour and GOD's fear.
Nor is it servile clamour that we make,
Who, born ourselves to reign, in her revere
The kingly nature that ourselves partake.

ON READING BRYANT'S POEM OF "THE WINDS."

YE Winds, whose various voices in his lay
That bard interpreted—your utterance mild,
Nor less your ministration fierce and wild,
Of those resistless laws which ye obey
In your apparent lawlessness—oh say!
Is not your will-less agency reviled
When it is liken'd unto what is styled
By such unwise the Spirit of the Day?
Not all the islands by tornadoes swept,
E'er knew such ruin as befalls a state
When not the winds of God, but mortal breath,
With threatening sweetness of melodious hate,
Assaults the fabrics reverent ages kept
To shelter ancient loyalty and faith.

TO EMMELINE: A THRENODIA.

I.

Sister! for as such I loved thee,
  May I not the privilege claim
As thy brother to lament thee,
  Though not mine that sacred name?

For though not indeed thy brother,
  Yet fraternal is the grief,
That in tears no solace meeting,
  Now in words would find relief.

Who did watch thy final conflict?
  Who did weep when it was o'er?
Whose the voice which then consoled
  One by thee belovéd more?

Lips that kiss'd thy cold white forehead
  Sure may sing thy requiem;
Hands that closed thy stiffening eyelids,
  Should it not be writ by them?

To perform those death-bed honours
  Soften'd much my deep regret;
But to celebrate thy virtues
  Is a task more soothing yet.

O'er thy features death-composed,
  As the life-like smile that play'd,
By its beauty so familiar
  Tears drew forth which soon it stay'd

So the memory of thy goodness
  Calms the grief that from it springs:
That which makes our loss the greatest,
  Sweetest consolation brings.

II.

When the Christian maiden findeth
  In the grave a maiden's rest,
We mourn not as did the heathen
  Over beauty unpossess'd.

As the tender Meleager,
  In that sweetly mournful strain,
Sung the fate of Clearista
  Borne to nuptial couch in vain:

How her virgin zone unloosed,
  She in Death's embraces slept;
As for vainly-woo'd Antibia
  Pure Anyte hopeless wept.

For the soul to Christ united
  Need regret no human bliss,
And there yet remains a marriage
  Better than the earthly is.

Wedded love is but the symbol
  Of a holier mystery,
Which unto the stainless only
  Ever shall unfolded be.

Life and Hope, when they embracing
  Seem like one, are Love on earth;
Death and Hope, so reuniting,
  Are the Love of heavenly birth.

Was it haply this foreknowing
  That thou so wouldst ever be?—
From pursuing ardours shrinking
  In thy saintly chastity.

III.

In thy fairy-like proportions
  Woman's dignity was yet,
And in all thy winning actions
  With the grace of childhood met.

With what light and airy motion
  Wert thou wont to glide or spring?
As if were that shape elastic
  Lifted by an unseen wing.

In what sweet and lively accents
  Flow'd or gush'd thy talk or song!
What pure thoughts and gentle feelings
  Did that current bear along!

But affliction prematurely
  On thy tender graces breathed,
And in sweet decay about thee
  Were the faded flowerets wreathed.

Blasts that smite with death the flower,
  Cull for use the ripen'd fruit;
Suns the plant that overpower,
  Cannot kill the buried root:

So the grief that dimm'd thy beauty
  Shower'd gifts of higher worth,
And the germ of both is hidden
  Safely now within the earth.

Nature, eldest, truest sybil,
  Writes upon her wither'd leaves,
Words of joy restored prophetic
  To the heart her law bereaves.

IV.

Greenly swell the clustering mountains
  Whence thy passing spirit went;
Clear the waters they embosom;
  Blue the skies above them bent.

Pass'd away the spirit wholly
  From the haunts to us so dear?
Or at will their forms assuming,
  In them doth it reappear?

For there is a new expression
  Now pervading all the place;
Rock and stream do look with meanings
  Such as wore thy living face.

Nor alone the face of Nature;
  Human features show it too;
Chiefly those by love illumin'd
  Of the heart-united few.

We upon each other gazing,
  Mystic shadows come and go,
Over each loved visage flitting,
  Why and whence we do not know.

In the old familiar dances
  Mingle thy accustom'd feet;
Blending with the song familiar
  Still are heard thy concords sweet.

Hence we know the world of spirits
  Is not far from each of us;
Scarce that veil forbids our entrance
  Which thou hast half lifted us.

CORNELIUS MATHEWS.

[Born, 1815.]

Mr. Mathews was born in New York in 1815; was graduated at Columbia College, in that city, in 1835; was admitted an attorney and counsellor in 1837; and has since devoted his attention chiefly to literature. A notice of his novels and essays may be found in "The Prose Writers of America," pages 543–554. His principal poetical compositions are, "Wakondah, the Master of Life," founded upon an Indian tradition, and "Man in the Republic, a series of Poems." Each of these works has appeared in several editions. There is a diversity of opinions as to the merits of Mr. Mathews. He has been warmly praised, and ridiculed with unsparing severity. The "North American Review," which indeed does not profess any consistency, has spoken of his "Man in the Republic" with both derision and respect, and for whatever condemnation others have expressed, his friends can perhaps cite as high authorities in approval. This may doubtless be said, both of his prose and verse, that it illustrates truly, to the extent of the author's abilities, directed by much and honest observation, the present, in our own country; or perhaps it may be said with more justice, in New York. The poems on "Man in the Republic" are entitled, "The Child," "The Father," "The Teacher," "The Statesman," "The Reformer," "The Masses," &c.

In the last edition, the author, referring to some friendly criticisms, observes: "I have carefully considered whatever has been objected to them, and where I could, in good conscience, and according to the motions of my own taste, have made amendment."

THE JOURNALIST.

As shakes the canvass of a thousand ships,
Struck by a heavy land-breeze far at sea—
Ruffle the thousand broad-sheets of the land,
Filled with the people's breath of potency.

A thousand images the hour will take,
From him who strikes, who rules, who speaks, who sings;
Many within the hour their grave to make—
Many to live far in the heart of things.

A dark-eyed spirit, he who coins the time,
To virtue's wrong, in base disloyal lies—
Who makes the morning's breath, the evening's tide,
The utterer of his blighting forgeries.

How beautiful who scatters, wide and free,
The gold-bright seeds of loved and loving truth!
By whose perpetual hand each day supplied,
Leaps to new life the nation's heart of youth.

To know the instant, and to speak it true,
Its pasing lights of joy, its dark, sad cloud—
To fix upon the unnumber'd gazers' view,
Is to thy ready hand's broad strength allowed.

There is an inwrought life in every hour,
Fit to be chronicled at large and told—
'Tis thine to pluck to light its secret power,
And on the air its many-coloured heart unfold.

The angel that in sand-dropp'd minutes lives,
Demands a message cautious as the ages—
Who stuns, with whirling words of hate, his ear,
That mighty power to boundless wrath enrages.

Shake not the quiet of a chosen land,
Thou grimy man over thine engine bending;
The spirit pent that breathes the life into its limbs,
Docile for love is tyrannous in rending.

Obey, rhinoceros! an infant's hand—
Leviathan! obey the fisher mild and young!
Vex'd ocean! smile, for on thy broad-beat sand
The little curlew pipes his shrilly song.

THE CITIZEN.

With plainness in thy daily pathway walk,
And disencumber'd of excess: no other
Jostling, servile to none, none overstalk,
For, right and left, who passes is thy brother.

Let him who in thy upward countenance looks,
Find there in meek and soften'd majesty
Thy Country writ, thy Brother, and thy God;
And be each motion onward, calm, and free.

Feel well with the poised ballot in thy hand,
Thine unmatch'd sovereignty of right and wrong,
'Tis thine to bless or blast the waiting land,
To shorten up its life or make it long.

Who looks on thee, with gladness should behold
A self-delivered, self-supported Man—
True to his being's mighty purpose—true
To this heaven-bless'd and God-imparted plan

Nowhere within the great globe's skyey round
Canst thou escape thy duty, grand and high—
A man unbadged, unbonneted, unbound—
Walk to the tropic, to the desert fly.

A full-fraught hope upon thy shoulder leans,
And beats with thine, the heart of half the world,
Ever behind thee walks the shining past,
Before thee burns the star-stripe, far unfurl'd.

THE REFORMER.

Man of the future! on the eager headland standing,
Gazing far off into the outer sea,
Thine eye, the darkness and the billows rough commanding,
Beholds a shore, bright as the heaven itself may be;
Where temples, cities, homes, and haunts of men,
Orchards and fields spread out in orderly array,
Invite the yearning soul to thither flee,
And there to spend in boundless peace its happier day.
By passion and the force of earnest thought,
Borne up and platformed at a height,
Where, 'gainst thy feet the force of earth and heaven are brought,
Yet, so into the frame of empire wrought,
Thou, stout man, canst not thence be sever'd,
Till ruled and rulers, fiends or men, are taught
And feel the truths by thee delivered.

Seize by its horns the shaggy Past,
Full of uncleanness; heave with mountain-cast
Its carcase down the black and wide abyss—
That opens day and night its gulfy precipice,
By faded empires, projects old and dead
Forever in its noisy hunger fed:
But rush not, therefore, with a brutish blindness,
Against the 'stablished bulwarks of the world;
Kind be thyself, although unkindness
Thy race to ruin dark and suffering long has hurl'd.
For many days of light, and smooth repose,
'Twixt storms and weathery sadness intervene;
Thy course is nature's: on thy triumph flows,
Assured, like hers, though noiseless and serene.

Wake not at midnight and proclaim it day,
When lightning only flashes o'er the way;
Pauses and starts, and strivings towards an end,
Are not a birth, although a god's birth they portend.
Be patient, therefore, like the old broad earth
That bears the guilty up, and through the night
Conducts them gently to the dawning light—
Thy silent hours shall have as great a birth.

THE MASSES.

When, wild and high, the uproar swells
From crowds that gather at the set of day,
When square and market roar in stormy play,
And fields of men, like lions, shake their fells
Of savage hair; when, quick and deep call out the bells
Through all the lower heaven ringing,
As if an earthquake's shock
The city's base shou'd rock,
And set its troubled turrets singing:
Remember, men! on massy strength relying,
There is a heart of right
Not always open to the light,
Secret and still, and force-defying.
In vast assemb'ies calm let order rule,
And every shout a cadence owning,
Make musical the vex'd wind's moaning,
And be as little children at singing-school.

But, when thick as night the sky is crusted o'er,
Stifling life's pulse, and making heaven an idle dream,
Arise! and cry, up through the dark, to God's own throne:
Your faces in a furnace-glow,
Your arms uplifted for the deathward blow—
Fiery and prompt as angry angels show;
Then draw the brand and fire the thunder gun!
Be nothing said and all things done,
Till every cobweb'd corner of the common weal
Is shaken free, and, creeping to its scabbard back, the steel,
Lets shine again God's rightful sun.

THE MECHANIC.

Oh, when thou walkest by the river's side,
Thy bulky figure outlined in the wave,
Or, on thine adze-staff resting, 'neath the ship
Thy strokes have shaped, or hearest loud and brave
The clangour of the boastful forge, think not
To strength of limb, to sinews large and tough,
Are given rights masterless and vantage-proof,
Which the pale scholar and his puny hand
Writing his thoughts upon the idle sand,
May not possess as full: oh, maddened, drink not
With greedy ear what selfish Passion pours!
His a sway peculiar is, no less than yours.

The inner world is his, the outer thine—
(And both are God's)—a world, maiden and new,
To shape and finish forth, of rock and wood,
Iron and brass, to fashion, mould, and hew—
In countless cunning forms to recreate,
Till the great God of order shall proclaim it "Good!"
Proportioned fair, as in its first estate.

It consecrates whate'er it strikes—each blow,
From the small whisper of the tinkling smith,
Up to the big-voiced sledge that heaving slow
Roars 'gainst the massy bar, and tears
Its entrail, glowing, as with angry teeth—
Anchors that hold a world should thus-wise grow.

In the First Builder's gracious spirit-work—
Through hall, through enginery, and temples meek,
In grandeur towered, or lapsing, beauty-sleek,
Let order and creative fitness shine:
Though mountains are no more to rear,
Though woods may rise again no more,
The noble task to reproduce is thine!
The spreading branch, the firm-set peak, may live
With thee, and in thy well-sped labours thrive.

The untried forces of the air, the earth, the sea,
Wait at thy bidding: oh, compel their powers
To uses holy! Let them ever be
Servants to tend and bless these new-found bowers,
And make them household-workers, free and swift,
On daily use—on daily service bent:
Her face again old Eden may uplift,
And God look down the open firmament.

WILLIAM JEWETT PABODIE.

[Born about 1815.]

Mr. Pabodie is a native of Providence, in Rhode Island. He was admitted to the bar in the spring of 1837, and has since, I believe, practised his profession in his native city. His principal work is "Calidore, a Legendary Poem," published in 1839. It possesses considerable merit, but is not so carefully finished as some of his minor pieces, nor is there any thing strikingly original in its fable or sentiments. His writings are more distinguished for elegance than for vigour.

GO FORTH INTO THE FIELDS.

Go forth into the fields,
Ye denizens of the pent city's mart!
Go forth and know the gladness nature yields
To the care-wearied heart.

Leave ye the feverish strife,
The jostling, eager, self-devoted throng;—
Ten thousand voices, waked anew to life,
Call you with sweetest song.

Hark! from each fresh-clad bough,
Or blissful soaring in the golden air,
Bright birds with joyous music bid you now
To spring's loved haunts repair.

The silvery gleaming rills
Lure with soft murmurs from the grassy lea,
Or gayly dancing down the sunny hills,
Call loudly in their glee!

And the young, wanton breeze,
With breath all odorous from her blossomy chase,
In voice low whispering 'mong th'embowering trees,
Woos you to her embrace.

Go—breathe the air of heaven,
Where violets meekly smile upon your way;
Or on some pine-crown'd summit, tempest riven,
Your wandering footsteps stay.

Seek ye the solemn wood,
Whose giant trunks a verdant roof uprear,
And listen, while the roar of some far flood
Thrills the young leaves with fear!

Stand by the tranquil lake,
Sleeping mid willowy banks of emerald dye,
Save when the wild bird's wing its surface break,
Checkering the mirror'd sky—

And if within your breast,
Hallow'd to nature's touch, one chord remain;
If aught save worldly honours find you blest,
Or hope of sordid gain,—

A strange delight shall thrill,
A quiet joy brood o'er you like a dove;
Earth's placid beauty shall your bosom fill,
Stirring its depths with love.

O, in the calm, still hours,
The holy Sabbath-hours, when sleeps the air,
And heaven, and earth deck'd with her beauteous flowers,
Lie hush'd in breathless prayer,—

Pass ye the proud fane by,
The vaulted aisles, by flaunting folly trod,
And, 'neath the temple of the uplifted sky,
Go forth and worship God!

TO THE AUTUMN FOREST.

Resplendent hues are thine!
Triumphant beauty—glorious as brief!
Burdening with holy love the heart's pure shrine,
Till tears afford relief.

What though thy depths be hush'd!
More eloquent in breathless silence thou,
Than when the music of glad songsters gush'd
From every green-robed bough.

Gone from thy walks the flowers!
Thou askest not their forms thy paths to fleck;—
The dazzling radiance of these sunlit bowers
Their hues could not bedeck.

I love thee in the spring,
Earth-crowning forest! when amid thy shades
The gentle south first waves her odorous wing,
And joy fills all thy glades.

In the hot summer-time,
With deep delight thy sombre aisles I roam,
Or, soothed by some cool brook's melodious chime,
Rest on thy verdant loam.

But, O, when autumn's hand
Hath mark'd thy beauteous foliage for the grave,
How doth thy splendour, as entranced I stand,
My willing heart enslave!

I linger then with thee,
Like some fond lover o'er his stricken bride;
Whose bright, unearthly beauty tells that she
Here may not long abide.

When my last hours are come,
Great God! ere yet life's span shall all be fill'd
And these warm lips in death be ever dumb,
This beating heart be still'd,—

Bathe thou in hues as blest—
Let gleams of Heaven about my spirit play!
So shall my soul to its eternal rest
In glory pass away!

ON THE DEATH OF A FRIEND.

Gone in the flush of youth!
Gone ere thy heart had felt earth's withering care;
Ere the stern world had soil'd thy spirit's truth,
Or sown dark sorrow there.

Fled like a dream away!
But yesterday mid life's auroral bloom—
To-day, sad winter, desolate and gray,
Sighs round thy lonely tomb.

Fond hearts were beating high,
Fond eyes were watching for the loved one gone,
And gentle voices, deeming thou wert nigh,
Talk'd of thy glad return.

They watch'd—not all in vain—
Thy form once more the wonted threshold pass'd;
But choking sobs, and tears like summer-rain,
Welcom'd thee home at last.

Friend of my youth, farewell!
To thee, we trust, a happier life is given;
One tie to earth for us hath loosed its spell,
Another form'd for heaven.

OUR COUNTRY.

Our country!—'t is a glorious land!
With broad arms stretch'd from shore to shore,
The proud Pacific chafes her strand,
She hears the dark Atlantic roar;
And, nurtured on her ample breast,
How many a goodly prospect lies
In Nature's wildest grandeur drest,
Enamell'd with her loveliest dyes.

Rich prairies, deck'd with flowers of gold,
Like sunlit oceans roll afar;
Broad lakes her azure heavens behold,
Reflecting clear each trembling star,
And mighty rivers, mountain-born,
Go sweeping onward, dark and deep,
Through forests where the bounding fawn
Beneath their sheltering branches leap.

And, cradled mid her clustering hills,
Sweet vales in dreamlike beauty hide,
Where love the air with music fills;
And calm content and peace abide;
For plenty here her fulness pours
In rich profusion o'er the land,
And, sent to seize her generous store,
There prowls no tyrant's hireling band.

Great God! we thank thee for this home—
This bounteous birthland of the free;
Where wanderers from afar may come,
And breathe the air of liberty!—
Still may her flowers untrampled spring,
Her harvests wave, her cities rise;
And yet, till Time shall fold his wing,
Remain Earth's loveliest paradise!

I HEAR THY VOICE, O SPRING!

I hear thy voice, O Spring!
Its flute-like tones are floating through the air,
Winning my soul with their wild ravishing,
From earth's heart-wearying care.

Divinely sweet thy song—
But yet, methinks, as near the groves I pass,
Low sighs on viewless wings are borne along,
Tears gem the springing grass.

For where are they, the young,
The loved, the beautiful, who, when thy voice,
A year agone, along these valleys rung,
Did hear thee and rejoice!

Thou seek'st for them in vain—
No more they 'll greet thee in thy joyous round;
Calmly they sleep beneath the murmuring main
Or moulder in the ground.

Yet peace, my heart—be still!
Look upward to yon azure sky and know,
To heavenlier music now their bosoms thrill,
Where balmier breezes blow.

For them hath bloom'd a spring,
Whose flowers perennial deck a holier sod,
Whose music is the song that seraphs sing
Whose light, the smile of God!

I STOOD BESIDE HIS GRAVE.

I stood beside the grave of him,
Whose heart with mine had fondly beat,
While memories, from their chambers dim,
Throng'd mournful, yet how sadly sweet!

It was a calm September eve,
The stars stole trembling into sight,
Save where the day, as loth to leave,
Still flush'd the heavens with rosy light.

The crickets in the grass were heard,
The city's murmur softly fell,
And scarce the dewy air was stirr'd,
As faintly toll'd the evening-bell.

O Death! had then thy summons come,
To bid me from this world away,—
How gladly had I hail'd the doom
That stretch'd me by his mouldering clay!

And twilight deepen'd into night,
And night itself grew wild and drear,—
For clouds rose darkly on the sight,
And winds sigh'd mournful on the ear:—

And yet I linger'd mid the fern,
Though gleam'd no star the eye to bless—
For, O, 't was agony to turn
And leave him to his loneliness!

EPES SARGENT.

[Born, 1816.]

The author of "Velasco" is a native of Gloucester, a town on the sea-coast of Massachusetts, and was born on the twenty-seventh of September, 1816. His father, a respectable merchant, of the same name, is still living, and resides in Boston. The subject of this sketch was educated in the schools of that city and the neighbourhood, where he lived until his removal to New York, in 1837. His earliest metrical compositions were printed in "The Collegian," a monthly miscellany edited by several of the students of Harvard College, of the junior and senior classes of 1830. One of his contributions to that work, entitled "Twilight Sketches," exhibits the grace of style, ease of versification, and variety of description, which are characteristic of his more recent effusions. It was a sketch of the Summer Gardens of St. Petersburg, and was written during a visit to that capital in the spring of 1828.

Mr. Sargent's reputation rests principally on his dramas, which bear a greater value in the closet than on the stage. His first appearance as a dramatic author was in the winter of 1836, when his "Bride of Genoa" was brought out at the Tremont Theatre, in Boston. This was a five-act play, founded on incidents in the career of Antonio Montaldo, a plebeian, who at the age of twenty-two, made himself doge of Genoa, in 1693, and who is described in the history of the times as a man of "forgiving temper," but daring and ambitious, with a genius adequate to the accomplishment of vast designs. In the delineation of his hero, the author has followed the historical record, though the other characters and incidents of the drama are entirely fictitious. It was successfully performed in Boston, and since in many of the first theatres of the country. His next production was of a much higher order, and as a specimen of dramatic art, has received warm commendation from the most competent judges. It was the tragedy of "Velasco," first performed at Boston, in November, 1837, Miss Ellen Tree in the character of Izidora, and subsequently at the principal theatres in New York, Philadelphia, Washington, and New Orleans. It was published in New York in 1839. "The general action of the piece," says the author in his preface, "is derived from incidents in the career of Rodrigo Diaz, the Cid, whose achievements constitute so considerable a portion of the historical and romantic literature of Spain." The subject had been variously treated by French and Spanish dramatists, among others, by Corneille, but Mr. Sargent was the first to introduce it successfully upon the English stage. It is a chaste and elegant performance, and probably has not been surpassed by any similar work by so youthful an author. It was written before Mr. Sargent was twenty-one years of age.

In the beginning of 1847 Mr. Sargent published in Boston a volume entitled "Songs of the Sea, and other Poems," and a new edition of his plays. The *quatorzains* written during a voyage to Cuba, in the spring of 1835, appear to be among the most elaborate of his sea pieces, but some of his nautical lyrics are more spirited.

Mr. Sargent has edited "The Modern Acting Drama," and several modern British poets; and recently has done the public an important service by preparing the best series of reading books, for schools, ever published in this country.

RECORDS OF A SUMMER-VOYAGE TO CUBA.

I.—THE DEPARTURE.

Again thy winds are pealing in mine ear!
Again thy waves are flashing in my sight!
Thy memory-haunting tones again I hear,
As through the spray our vessel wings her flight!
On thy cerulean breast, now swelling high,
Again, thou broad Atlantic, am I cast!
Six years, with noiseless tread, have glided by,
Since, an adventurous boy, I hail'd thee last,
The sea-birds o'er me wheel, as if to greet
An old companion; on my naked brow
The sparkling foam-drops not unkindly beat;
Flows through my hair the freshening breeze—and now
The horizon's ring enclasps me; and I stand
Gazing where fades from view, cloud-like, my fatherland!

II.—THE GALE.

The night came down in terror. Through the air
Mountains of clouds, with lurid summits, roll'd;
The lightning kindling with its vivid glare
Their outlines, as they rose, heap'd fold on fold,
The wind, in fitful sughs, swept o'er the sea;
And then a sudden lull, gentle as sleep,
Soft as an infant's breathing, seem'd to be
Lain, like enchantment, on the throbbing deep.
But, false the calm! for soon the strengthen'd gale
Burst, in one loud explosion, far and wide,
Drowning the thunder's voice! With every sail
Close-reef'd, our groaning ship heel'd on her side;
The torn waves comb'd the deck; while o'er the mast
The meteors of the storm a ghastly radiance cast!

III.—MORNING AFTER THE GALE.

Bravely our trim ship rode the tempest through;
And, when the exhausted gale had ceased to rave,
How broke the day-star on the gazer's view!
How flush'd the orient every crested wave!
The sun threw down his shield of golden light
In fierce defiance on the ocean's bed;
Whereat, the clouds betook themselves to flight,
Like routed hosts, with banners soil'd and red.
The sky was soon all brilliance, east and west;
All traces of the gale had pass'd away—
The chiming billows, by the breeze caress'd,
Toss'd lightly from their heads the feathery spray.
Ah! thus may Hope's auspicious star again
Rise o'er the troubled soul where gloom and grief have been!

IV.—TO A LAND-BIRD.

Thou wanderer from green fields and leafy nooks!
Where blooms the flower and toils the honey-bee;
Where odorous blossoms drift along the brooks,
And woods and hills are very fair to see—
Why hast thou left thy native bough to roam,
With drooping wing, far o'er the briny billow?
Thou canst not, like the osprey, cleave the foam,
Nor, like the petrel, make the wave thy pillow.
Thou 'rt like those fine-toned spirits, gentle bird,
Which, from some better land, to this rude life
Seem borne—they struggle, mid the common herd,
With powers unfitted for the selfish strife!
Haply, at length, some zephyr wafts them back
To their own home of peace, across the world's dull track.

V.—A THOUGHT OF THE PAST.

I woke from slumber at the dead of night,
Stirr'd by a dream which was too sweet to last—
A dream of boyhood's season of delight;
It flash'd along the dim shapes of the past!
And, as I mused upon its strange appeal,
Thrilling my heart with feelings undefined,
Old memories, bursting from time's icy seal,
Rush'd, like sun-stricken fountains, on my mind.
Scenes, among which was cast my early home,
My favourite haunts, the shores, the ancient woods,
Where, with my schoolmates, I was wont to roam,
Green, sloping lawns, majestic solitudes—
All rose before me, till, by thought beguiled,
Freely I could have wept, as if once more a child.

VI.—TROPICAL WEATHER.

We are afloat upon the tropic sea!
Here summer holdeth a perpetual reign:
How flash the waters in their bounding glee!
The sky's soft purple is without a stain!
Full in our wake the smooth, warm trade-winds blowing,
To their unvarying goal still faithful run;
And as we steer, with sails before them flowing,
Nearer the zenith daily climbs the sun.
The startled flying-fish around us skim,
Gloss'd, like the hummingbird, with rainbow dyes;
And, as they dip into the water's brim,
Swift in pursuit the preying dolphin hies.
All, all is fair; and, gazing round, we feel
The south's soft languor gently o'er our senses steal.

VII.—A CALM.

O! for one draught of cooling northern air!
That it might pour its freshness on me now;
That it might kiss my cheek and cleave my hair,
And part its currents round my fever'd brow!
Ocean, and sky, and earth! a blistering calm
Spread over all! how weary wears the day!
O, lift the wave, and bend the distant palm,
Breeze! wheresoe'er thy lagging pinions stray,
Triumphant burst upon the level deep,
Rock the fix'd hull and swell the clinging sail!
Arouse the opal clouds that o'er us sleep,
Sound thy shrill whistle! we will bid thee hail!
Though wrapt in all the storm-clouds of the north,
Yet from thy home of ice, come forth, O, breeze, come forth!

VIII.—A WISH.

That I were in some forest's green retreat,
Beneath a towering arch of proud old elms;
Where a clear streamlet gurgled at my feet—
Its wavelets glittering in their tiny helms!
Thick clustering vines, in many a rich festoon,
From the high, rustling branches should depend;
Weaving a net, through which the sultry noon
Might stoop in vain its fiery beams to send.
There, prostrate on some rock's gray sloping side,
Upon whose tinted moss the dew yet lay,
Would I catch glimpses of the clouds that ride
Athwart the sky—and dream the hours away;
While through the alleys of the sunless wood
The fanning breeze might steal, with wild-flowers' breath imbued.

IX.—TROPICAL NIGHT.

But, O! the night!—the cool, luxurious night,
Which closes round us when the day grows dim,
And the sun sinks from his meridian height
Behind the ocean's occidental rim!
Clouds, in thin streaks of purple, green, and red,
Lattice his parting glory, and absorb
The last bright emanations that are shed
In wide profusion, from his failing orb.
And now the moon, her lids unclosing, deigns
To smile serenely on the charmed sea,
That shines as if inlaid with lightning-chains,
From which it hardly struggled to be free.
Swan-like, with motion unperceived, we glide,
Touch'd by the downy breeze, and favour'd by the tide.

X.—THE PLANET JUPITER.

Ever, at night, have I look'd first for thee,
O'er all thy astral sisterhood supreme!
Ever, at night, have I look'd up to see
The diamond lustre of thy quivering beam;
Shining sometimes through pillowy clouds serene,
As they part from thee, like a loosen'd scroll;
Sometimes unveil'd, in all thy native sheen,
When no pale vapours underneath thee roll.
Bright planet! that art but a single ray
From our Creator's throne, illume my soul!
Thy influence shed upon my doubtful way
Through life's dark vista to the immortal goal—
Gleam but as now upon my dying eyes
And hope, from earth to thee, from thee to heaven shall rise.

XI.—TO EGERIA.

Leagues of blue ocean are between us spread;
And I cannot behold thee save in dreams!
I may not hear thy voice, nor list thy tread,
Nor see the light that ever round thee gleams.
Fairest and best! mid summer joys, ah, say,
Dost thou e'er think of one who thinks of thee—
The Atlantic-wanderer, who, day by day,
Looks for thine image in the deep, deep sea?
Long months, and years, perchance, will pass away,
Ere he shall gaze into thy face again;
He cannot know what rocks and quicksands may
Await him, on the future's shipless main;
But, thank'd be memory! there are treasures still,
Which the triumphant mind holds subject to its will.

XII.—CUBA.

What sounds arouse me from my slumbers light?
"*Land ho! all hands ahoy!*"—I'm on the deck.
'Tis early dawn. The day-star yet is bright.
A few white vapoury bars the zenith fleck.
And lo! along the horizon, bold and high,
The purple hills of Cuba! hail, all hail!
Isle of undying verdure, with thy sky
Of purest azure! Welcome, odorous gale!
O! scene of life and joy! thou art array'd
In hues of unimagined loveliness—
Sing louder, brave old mariner! and aid
My swelling heart its rapture to express;
For from enchanted memory never more [shore!
Shall fade this dawn sublime, this bright, celestial

THE DAYS THAT ARE PAST.

We will not deplore them, the days that are past;
The gloom of misfortune is over them cast;
They are lengthen'd by sorrow and sullied by care;
Their griefs were too many, their joys were too rare;
Yet, now that their shadows are on us no more,
Let us welcome the prospect that brightens before!

We have cherish'd fair hopes, we have plotted brave schemes,
We have lived till we find them illusive as dreams;
Wealth has melted like snow that is grasp'd in the hand,
And the steps we have climb'd have departed like sand;
Yet shall we despond while of health unbereft,
And honour, bright honour, and freedom are left?

O! shall we despond, while the pages of time
Yet open before us their records sublime! [gold,
While, ennobled by treasures more precious than
We can walk with the martyrs and heroes of old;
While humanity whispers such truths in the ear,
As it softens the heart like sweet music to hear?

O! shall we despond while, with visions still free,
We can gaze on the sky, and the earth, and the sea;
While the sunshine can waken a burst of delight,
And the stars are a joy and a glory by night:
While each harmony, running through nature, can raise
In our spirits the impulse of gladness and praise!

O! let us no longer then vainly lament
Over scenes that are faded and days that are spent:
But, by faith unforsaken, unawed by mischance,
On hope's waving banner still fix'd be our glance;
And, should fortune prove cruel and false to the last,
Let us look to the future and not to the past!

THE MARTYR OF THE ARENA.

Honour'd be the hero evermore,
Who at mercy's call has nobly died!
Echoed be his name from shore to shore,
With immortal chronicles allied!
Verdant be the turf upon his dust,
Bright the sky above, and soft the air!
In the grove set up his marble bust,
And with garlands crown it, fresh and fair.
In melodious numbers, that shall live
With the music of the rolling spheres,
Let the minstrel's inspiration give
His eulogium to the future years!
Not the victor in his country's cause,
Not the chief who leaves a people free,
Not the framer of a nation's laws
Shall deserve a greater fame than he!
Hast thou heard, in Rome's declining day,
How a youth, by Christian zeal impell'd,
Swept the sanguinary games away,
Which the Coliseum once beheld!
Fill'd with gazing thousands were the tiers,
With the city's chivalry and pride,
When two gladiators, with their spears,
Forward sprung from the arena's side.
Rang the dome with plaudits loud and long,
As, with shields advanced, the athletes met—
Was there no one in that eager throng
To denounce the spectacle of blood!
Aye, Telemachus, with swelling frame,
Saw the inhuman sport renew'd once more.
Few among the crowd could tell his name—
For a cross was all the badge he wore!
Yet, with brow elate and godlike mien,
Stepp'd he forth upon the circling sand;
And, while all were wondering at the scene,
Check'd the encounter with a daring hand.
"Romans!" cried he—"Let this reeking sod
Never more with human blood be stain'd!
Let no image of the living God
In unhallow'd combat be profaned!
Ah! too long has this colossal dome
Fail'd to sink and hide your brutal shows!
Here I call upon assembled Rome
Now to swear, they shall forever close!"
Parted thus, the combatants, with joy,
Mid the tumult, found the means to fly;
In the arena stood the undaunted boy,
And, with looks adoring, gazed on high.
Peal'd the shout of wrath on every side;
Every hand was eager to assail!
"Slay him! slay!" a hundred voices cried,
Wild with fury—but he did not quail!
Hears he, as entranced he looks above,
Strains celestial, that the menace drown?
Sees he angels, with their eyes of love,
Beckoning to him, with a martyr's crown!
Fiercer swell'd the people's frantic shout!
Launch'd against him flew the stones like rain!

Death and terror circled him about—
  But he stood and perish'd—not in vain!
Not in vain the youthful martyr fell!
  Then and there he crush'd a bloody creed!
And his high example shall impel
  Future heroes to as great a deed!
Stony answers yet remain for those
  Who would question and precede the time!
In their season, may they meet their foes,
  Like TELEMACHUS, with front sublime!

SUMMER IN THE HEART.

THE cold blast at the casement beats,
  The window-panes are white,
The snow whirls through the empty streets—
  It is a dreary night!
Sit down, old friend! the wine-cups wait,
  Fill to o'erflowing! fill!
Though Winter howleth at the gate,
  In our hearts 'tis summer still!

For we full many summer joys
  And greenwood sports have shared,
When, free and ever-roving boys,
  The rocks, the streams we dared!
And, as I look upon thy face—
  Back, back o'er years of ill,
My heart flies to that happy place,
  Where it is summer still!

Yes, though, like sere leaves on the ground,
  Our early hopes are strown,
And cherish'd flowers lie dead around,
  And singing birds are flown,—
The verdure is not faded quite,
  Not mute all tones that thrill;
For, seeing, hearing thee to-night,
  In my heart 'tis summer still!

Fill up! the olden times come back!
  With light and life once more
We scan the future's sunny track,
  From youth's enchanted shore!
The lost return. Through fields of bloom
  We wander at our will;
Gone is the winter's angry gloom—
  In our hearts 'tis summer still!

THE FUGITIVE FROM LOVE.

Is there but a single theme
For the youthful poet's dream?
Is there but a single wire
To the youthful poet's lyre?
Earth below and heaven above—
Can he sing of naught but love?

Nay! the battle's dust I see!
God of war! I follow thee!
And, in martial numbers, raise
Worthy pæans to thy praise.
Ah! she meets me on the field—
If I fly not, I must yield.

Jolly patron of the grape!
To thy arms I will escape!
Quick, the rosy nectar bring;
"Io BACCHE!" I will sing.
Ha! Confusion! every sip
But reminds me of her lip.

PALLAS! give me wisdom's page,
And awake my lyric rage;
Love is fleeting; love is vain;
I will try a nobler strain.
O, perplexity! my books
But reflect her haunting looks!

JUPITER! on thee I cry!
Take me and my lyre on high!
Lo! the stars beneath me gleam!
Here, O, poet! is a theme.
Madness! She has come above!
Every chord is whispering "Love!"

THE NIGHT-STORM AT SEA

'TIS a dreary thing to be
Tossing on the wide, wide sea,
When the sun has set in clouds,
And the wind sighs through the shrouds,
With a voice and with a tone
Like a living creature's moan

Look! how wildly swells the surge
Round the black horizon's verge!
See the giant billows rise
From the ocean to the skies!
While the sea-bird wheels his flight
O'er their streaming crests of white.

List! the wind is wakening fast!
All the sky is overcast!
Lurid vapours, hurrying, trail
In the pathway of the gale,
As it strikes us with a shock
That might rend the deep-set rock!

Falls the strain'd and shiver'd mast!
Spars are scatter'd by the blast!
And the sails are split asunder,
As a cloud is rent by thunder:
And the struggling vessel shakes,
As the wild sea o'er her breaks.

Ah! what sudden light is this,
Blazing o'er the dark abyss?
Lo! the full moon rears her form
Mid the cloud-rifts of the storm,
And, athwart the troubled air,
Shines, like hope upon despair!

Every leaping billow gleams
With the lustre of her beams,
And lifts high its fiery plume
Through the midnight's parting gloom
While its scatter'd flakes of gold
O'er the sinking deck are roll'd.

Father! low on bended knee,
Humbled, weak, we turn to thee.
Spare us, mid the fearful fight
Of the raging winds to-night!
Guide us o'er the threatening wave:
Save us!—thou alone canst save!

PHILIP PENDLETON COOKE.

[Born 1816. Died 1850.]

PHILIP PENDLETON COOKE was born in Martinsburg, Berkeley county, Virginia, on the twenty-sixth of October, 1816. His father, Mr. JOHN R. COOKE, was honourably distinguished at the bar, and his mother was of that family of PENDLETONS which has furnished so many eminent names to that part of the Union.

At fifteen he entered Princeton College, where he had a reputation for parts, though he did not distinguish himself, or take an honour, and could never tell how it happened that he obtained a degree, as he was not examined with his class. He liked fishing and hunting better than the books, and CHAUCER and SPENSER much more than the dull volumes in the "course of study." He had already made rhymes before he became a freshman, and the appearance of the early numbers of the "Knickerbocker Magazine" prompted him to new efforts in this way; he wrote for the "Knickerbocker," in his seventeenth year, "The Song of the Sioux Lover," and "The Consumptive," and in a village paper, about the same time, other humourous and sentimental verses.

When he left college his father was living at Winchester, and there he himself pursued the study of the law. He wrote pieces in verse and prose for the "Virginian," and "The Southern Literary Messenger," (then just started,) and projected novels and an extensive work in literary criticism. Before he was twenty-one he was married, admitted to the bar, and had a fair prospect of practice in Frederick, Jefferson, and Berkeley counties. "I am blessed by my fireside," he wrote, "here on the banks of the Shenandoah, in view and within a mile of the Blue Ridge; I go to county towns at the sessions of the courts, and hunt and fish, and make myself as happy with my companions as I can." "So," he writes to me in 1846, "have passed five, six, seven, eight years, and now I am striving, after long disuse of my literary veins, to get the rubbish of idle habits away, and work them again. My fruit-trees, rose-bushes, poultry, guns, fishing-tackle, good, hard-riding friends, a long-necked bottle on my sideboard, an occasional client, &c. &c., make it a little difficult to get from the real into the clouds again. It requires a resolute habit of self-concentration to enable a man to shut out these and all such real concerns, and give himself warmly to the nobler or more tender sort of writing—and I am slowly acquiring it."

The atmosphere in which he lived was not, it seems, altogether congenial—so far as literature was concerned—and I find in one of his letters: "What do you think of a good friend of mine, a most valuable and worthy and hard-riding one, saying gravely to me a short time ago, 'I would n't waste time on a damned thing like poetry; you might make yourself, with all your sense and judgment, a useful man in settling neighbourhood disputes and difficulties.' You have as much chance with such people, as a dolphin would have if in one of his darts he pitched in amongst the machinery of a mill. 'Philosophy would clip an angel's wings,' KEATS says, and pompous dulness would do the same. But these very persons I have been talking about are always ready, when the world generally has awarded the honours of successful authorship to any of our mad tribe, to come in and confirm the award, and *buy*, if not read, the popular book. And so they are not wholly without their uses in this world. But wo to him who seeks to *climb* amongst them! An author must avoid them until he is already mounted on the platform, and can look down on them, and make them ashamed to show their dulness by keeping their hands in their breeches pockets, while the rest of the world are taking theirs out to give money or to applaud with. I am wasting my letter with these people, but for fear you may think I am chagrined or cut by what I abuse them for, I must say that they suit one-half of my character, moods, and pursuits, in being good, kindly men, rare table companions, many of them great in field sports, and most of them rather deficient in letters than mind; and that, in an every-day sense of the words, I love and am beloved by them."

Soon afterwards he wrote: "Mr. KENNEDY'S assurance that you would find a publisher for my poems leaves me without any further excuse for not collecting them. If not the most devoted, truly you are the most serviceable, of my friends, but it is because Mr. KENNEDY has overpraised me to you. Your letter makes me feel as if I had always known you intimately, and I have a presentiment that you will counteract my idleness and good-for-nothingness, and that, hoisted on your shoulders I shall not be lost under the feet of the crowd, nor left behind in a fence corner. I am profoundly grateful for the kindness which dictated what you have done, and to show you that I will avail myself of it, I enclose a proem to the pieces of which I wrote you in my last."

The proem referred to was so beautiful that I asked and obtained permission to print it in a magazine of which I was at that time editor. The author's name was not given, and it excited much curiosity, as but two or three of our poets were thought capable of such a performance, and there was no reason why one of them should print any thing anonymously. It was most commonly, however, attributed to Mr. WILLIS, at which Mr. COOKE was highly gratified. The piece, which was entitled "Emily," contained about three hundred lines, and was a feigned history of the composition of tales designed to follow it, exquisitely told, and sprinkled all along with gems that could have come from only a mine of surpassing richness. It was a good while before the promised contents of the book were sent to me, and COOKE wrote of the delay to a friend: "Procrastination is a poison of my very marrow. Moreover, since 'the first wisping of the leaf,' my whole heart has been in the woods and on the waters—every rising sun that could be seen, *I have seen*, and I never came in from my sport until too much used up to do more than adopt this epitaph of Sardanapalus: 'Eat, drink,' &c. Moreover, (second,) Mr. KENNEDY and others were poking me in the ribs eternally about my poems; and I was driven to the labour of finishing them. I groaned and did it, and sent them to GRISWOLD, and have left the task of carrying them through the press to him; and only lie passive, saying with Don Juan, (in the slave-market of Adrianople, or some other place,) 'Would to God somebody would buy me.'"

At length through his cousin and friend, JOHN P. KENNEDY, (a name that makes one in charity with all mankind,) the MS. of all the poems was sent to me. It makes a book about the size of the printed volume, written with a regular elegance to match that of the old copyists. In an accompanying letter he says, "They are certainly not in the high key of a man warm with his subject, and doing the thing finely; I wrote them with the reluctance of a turkey-hunter kept from his sport, —only Mr. KENNEDY's urgent entreaty and remonstrance whipped me up to the labour. You will hardly perceive how they should be called 'Ballads.' You are somewhat responsible for the name. I designed (originally) to make them short poems of the old understood ballad cast. I sent you the proem, which you published as a preface to the 'Froissart Ballads.' Words in print bore a look of perpetuity (or rather of fixedness) about them, and what I would have changed if only my pen and portfolio had been concerned, your type deterred me from changing. The term 'Froissart Ballads,' however, is, after all, correct, even with the poems as they are. 'The Master of Bolton' is as much a *song* as the 'Lay of the Last Minstrel,' although I have no prologue, interludes, &c., to show how it was sung; and as for 'Orthone,' &c., Sir John Froissart may as easily be imagined chanting them as talking them."

In reply to some comments of mine upon these productions he remarks: "You will find them beneath your sanguine prognostic. They are mere narrative poems, designed for the crowd. Poetic speculation, bold inroads upon the debatable land, 'the wild weird clime, out of space, out of time,' I have not here attempted. I *will* hereafter merge myself in the nobler atmosphere; in the mean time I have stuck to the ordinary level, and endeavoured to write interesting stories in verse, with grace and spirit. I repeat my fear that in writing for the cold, I have failed to touch the quick and warm that in writing for a dozen hunting comrades, who have been in the habit of making my verse a *post prandium* entertainment, and never endured an audacity of thought or word, I have tamed myself out of your approbation."

The book was finally published, but though reveiwed very favourably by the late Judge BEVERLY TUCKER, in the "Southern Literary Messenger," and by Mr. POE, in the "American Review," and much quoted and praised elsewhere, it was, on the whole, not received according to its merits or my expectations. Yet the result aroused the author's ambition, and after a few weeks he remarked in a letter to me: "My literary life opens now. If the world manifest any disposition to hear my 'utterances,' it will be abundantly gratified. I am thirty: until forty literature shall be my calling—avoiding however to rely upon it pecuniarily, —then (after forty) politics will be a *sequitur*. It has occurred to me to turn my passion for hunting, and 'my crowding experiences' (gathered in fifteen or sixteen years of life in the merriest Virginia country society) of hunting, fishing, country races, character and want of character, woods, mountains, fields, waters, and the devil knows what, into a rambling book. Years ago I used to devour the 'Spirit of the Times.' Indeed, much of my passion for sports of all kinds grew out of reading the 'Spirit.' Like Albert Pike's poet, in 'Fantasms,' I

> 'Had not known the bent of my own mind,
> Until the mighty spell of "Porter" woke
> Its hidden passions:'

only Albert Pike, says 'Coleridge' and 'powers' for 'Porter' and 'passions.' Then I have a half-written novel in my MS. piles, with poems, tales, sketches, histories, commenced or arranged in my mind ready to be put in writing, *to order*. In a word, I am cocked and primed for authorship. My life here invites me urgently to literary employments. My house, servants, &c. &c.,—all that a country gentleman really wants of the goods of life,—are in sure possession to me and mine. I want honours, and some little more money. Be good enough, my dear sir, to let me know how I am to go about acquiring them."

I wrote with frankness what I thought was true, of possible pecuniary advantages from the course he proposed, and was answered: "What you say about the returns in money for an author's labours is dispiriting enough, and I at once give over an earnest purpose which I had formed of writing *books*. Thank God, I am not dependent on the booksellers, but have a moderate and sure support for my family, apart from the crowding hopes and fears which dependence on them would no doubt generate. But I must add (or forego some gratifications) two or three hundred dollars per annum to my ordinary means. I might easily make this by my profession, which I have deserted and neglected, but it would be as bad as the treadmill to me: I detest the law. On the other hand, I love the fever-fits of composition. The music of rhythm, coming from God knows where, like the airy melody in the Tempest, tingles pleasantly in my veins and fingers; I like to build the verse, cautiously, but with the excitement of a rapid writer, which I rein in and check; and then, we both know how glorious it is to make the gallant dash, and round off the stanza with the sonorous couplet, or with some rhyme as natural to its place as a leaf on a tree, but separated from its mate that peeps down to it over the inky ends of many intervening lines. . . . . That unepistolary sentence has considerably fatigued me. I was saying, or about to say, that I would be obliged to you for information as to the profitableness of writing for periodicals."

From this time Mr. COOKE wrote much, but in a desultory way, and seemed in a growing devotion to a few friends and in the happiness that was in his home to forget almost the dreams of ambition. Of this home he dwelt with a tender enthusiasm in his correspondence, and we have glimpses of it in some beautiful verses to his daughter, in which he has written with charming simplicity an interesting portion of his biography:

"TO MY DAUGHTER LILY.

"Six changeful years are gone, LILY,
Since you were born to be
A darling to your mother good,
A happiness to me;
A little, shivering, feeble thing
You were to touch and view,
But we could see a promise in
Your baby eyes of blue.

"You fastened on our hearts, LILY,
As day by day wore by,
And beauty grew upon your cheeks,
And deepened in your eye;
A year made dimples in your hands,
And plumped your little feet.
And you had learned some merry ways
Which we thought very sweet.

"And when the first sweet word, LILY,
Your wee mouth learned to say,
Your mother kissed it fifty times,
And marked the famous day.
I know not even now, my dear,
If it were quite a word,
But your proud mother surely knew,
For she the sound had heard.

"When you were four years old, LILY,
You were my little friend,
And we had walks and nightly plays,
And talks without an end.
You little ones are sometimes wise,
For you are undefiled;
A grave grown man will start to hear
The strange words of a child.

"When care pressed on our house, LILY,—
Pressed with an iron hand—
I hated mankind for the wrong
Which festered in the land;
But when I read your young frank face,—
Its meanings, sweet and good,
My charities grew clear again,
I felt my brotherhood.

"And sometimes it would be, LILY,
My faith in God grew cold,
For I saw virtue go in rags,
And vice in cloth of gold;
But in your innocence, my child,
And in your mother's love,
I learned those lessons of the heart
Which fasten it above.

"At last our cares are gone, LILY,
And peace is back again,
As you have seen the sun shine out
After the gloomy rain;
In the good land where we were born,
We may be happy still,
A life of love will bless our home—
The house upon the hill.

"Thanks to your gentle face, LILY!
Its innocence was strong
To keep me constant to the right,
When tempted by the wrong.
The litle ones were dear to Him
Who died upon the rood—
I ask his gentle care for you,
And for your mother good.

He commenced a historical novel to be called "Maurice Weterbern," in which the great battle of Lutzen was to end the adventures of his hero. "What it is you will some time or other see," he wrote to me; and, as if doubtful whether this were a safe prediction, added, "I am bestowing great *care*, but little *labor*, upon it." This he threw aside, and his love for that age appeared in "The Chevalier Merlin," suggested by the beautiful story of CHARLES the Twelfth, as given by VOLTAIRE, several chapters of which appeared in the "Southern Literary Messenger." In the same magazine he printed "John Carpe," "The Two Country Houses," and other tales: parts of a series in which he intended to dramatize the life and manners of Virginia. He also contributed to the "Literary Messenger" a few pieces of criticism, one of which was a reviewal of the poems of the late EDGAR A. POE. As for any applause these might win for him, he wrote to his friend JOHN R. THOMPSON: "I look upon these matters serenely, and will treat renown as Sir THOMAS MORE advises concerning guests: welcome its coming when it cometh, hinder not with oppressive eagerness its going, when it goeth. Furthermore I am of the temper to look placidly upon the profile of this same renown, if, instead of stopping, it went by to take up with another; therefore it would not ruffle me to see you win the honours of southern letters away from me."

Renewing his devotion to poetry, near the close of the year 1849, he wrote fragments of "The Women of Shakspeare," "The Chariot Race," and a political and literary satire. He projected works enough, in prose and verse, to occupy an industrious life of twenty years. In one of his letters he remarked, "I have lately spurred myself again into continuous composition, and mean to *finish* books." But in the midst of his reawakened activity and ambition, he suddenly died, on the twentieth of January, 1850, at the age of thirty-three.

Undoubtedly PHILIP PENDLETON COOKE was one of the truest poets of our country, and what he has left us was full of promise that he would vindicate, in other works, the rank with which he was accredited, by those admiring friends who estimated his abilities from his conversation more than from anything he had printed. His mind bloomed early, though it was late in maturing. Many of his most pleasing poems were written at ollege, or soon after his return, between his fifteenth and eighteenth years; but they had not the most noticeable characteristics of his later productions. The chivalric poetry occupied his attention early and long, and he was only banishing it for the more independent and beautiful growth of his own nature, when his untimely death destroyed the hopes of fruits which his youth foretold in such prodigality and perfection. Of his love poems, the little song entitled "Florence Vane," written when he was scarcely more than twenty, is perhaps the finest. In the lines "To my Daughter Lily," may be discovered the tenderness and warmth of his affections; in his "Ballads," the fiery and chivalrous phase of his intelligence; in "Ugolino," his pathos; and in "Life in the Autumn Woods," his love of nature. "Ugolino," was in his own opinion the best of all his poems, but it fell far short of his estimate of the capacities of the subject. "I have merely tried my hand in it," he said, "and can only praise what I have done as true to FROISSART. I shall do much better than this."

As a boy and as a young man, I understand, his life was always poetical—apart, original, and commanding affectionate respect. As he grew older, and married, he became practical in his views, reaching that point in the life of genius in which its beautiful ideals take the forms of duty or become the strength of wise resolves. Toward his family, including his father, mother, brothers, and sisters, he cherished a deep and unfaltering devotion. A short time before his last illness he introduced into his household morning and evening prayers. He died, as he had lived, a pure-minded gentleman, and humble Christian.

His voice has been described to me as musically joyous, sometimes varying to a sad sweetness, sometimes wild. His carriage was graceful and upright; his frame vigorous and elastic, trained as he was by constant hunting in the Blue Ridge; his hair was black and curling; his eye dark and bright; his expression calm and thoughtful; his manner impressed with dignity.

EMILY:

PROEM TO THE "FROISSART BALLADS."

YOUNG Emily has temples fair,
Caress'd by locks of dark brown hair.
A thousand sweet humanities
Speak wisely from her hazel eyes.
Her speech is ignorant of command,
And yet can lead you like a hand.
Her white teeth sparkle, when the eclipse
Is laughter-moved, of her red lips.
She moves, all grace, with gliding limbs
As a white-breasted cygnet swims.
In her sweet childhood, Emily
Was wild with natural gayety,
A little creature, full of laughter,
Who cast no thought before or after,
And knew not custom or its chains.
The dappled fawns upon the plains,
The birds that love the upper sky,
Lived not in lovelier liberty.
But with this natural merriment,
Mind, and the ripening years have blent
A thoughtfulness—not melancholy—
Which wins her life away from folly;
Checking somewhat the natural gladness,
But saved, by that it checks, from sadness—
Like clouds athwart a May-morn sailing,
Which take the golden light they are veiling.
She loves her kind, and shuns no duty,
Her virtues sanctify her beauty,
And all who know her say that she
Was born for man's felicity—
I know that she was born for mine.
Dearer than any joy of wine,
Or pomp, or gold, or man's loud praise,
Or purple power, art thou to me—
Kind cheerer of my clouded ways—
Young vine upon a rugged tree.

Maidens who love are full of hope,
And crowds hedge in its golden scope;
Wherefore they love green solitudes
And silence for their better moods.
I know some wilds, where tulip trees,
Full of the singing toil of bees,
Depend their loving branches over
Great rocks, which honeysuckles cover
In rich and liberal overflow.
In the dear time of long ago
When I had woo'd young Emily,
And she had told her love to me,
I often found her in these bowers,
Quite rapt away in meditation,
Or giving earnest contemplation
To leaf, or bird, or wild wood flowers,
And once I heard the maiden singing,
Until the very woods were ringing—
Singing an old song to the Hours!
I well remember that rare song,
It charged the Hours with cruel wrong—
Wrong to the verdure of the boughs—
Wrong to the lustre of fair brows,
Its music had a wondrous sound,
And made the greenwood haunted ground.
But I delay: one jocund morn—
A morn of that blithe time of spring,
When milky blossoms load the thorn,
And birds so prate, and soar, and sing,
That melody is everywhere,
On the glad earth, and in the air,—
On such a morn I went to seek
In our wild haunts for Emily,
I found her where a flowering tree
Gave odours and cool shade. Her cheek
A little rested on her hand;
Her rustic skill had made a band
Of rare device which garlanded
The beauty of her bending head;

Some maiden thoughts most kind and wise
Were dimly burning in her eyes.
When I beheld her—form and face
So lithe, so fair—the spirit race,
Of whom the better poets dream'd,
Came to my thought, and I half deem'd
My earth-born mistress, pure and good,
Was some such lady of the wood,
As she who work'd at spell, and snare,
With Huon of the dusky hair,
And fled, in likeness of a doe,
Before the fleet youth Angelo.
But these infirm imaginings
Flew quite away on instant wings.
I call'd her name. A swift surprise
Came whitely to her face, but soon
It fled before some daintier dyes,
And, laughing like a brook in June,
With sweet accost she welcomed me,
And I sat there with Emily.
The gods were very good to bless
My life with so much happiness.
The maiden on that lowly seat—
I sitting at her little feet!
Two happier lovers never met,
In dear and talk-charm'd privacy.
It was a golden day to me,
And its great bliss is with me yet,
Warming like wine my inmost heart—
For memories of happy hours
Are like the cordials press'd from flowers,
And madden sweetly. I impart
Naught of the love-talk I remember,
For May's young pleasures are best hid
From the cold prudence of December,
Which clips and chills all vernal wings;
And Love's own sanctities forbid,
Now as of old, such gossipings
In Hall, of what befalls in Bower,
But other matters of the hour,
Of which it breaks no faith to tell,
My homely rhyme shall chronicle.
As silently we sat alone—
Our love-talk spent—two mated birds
Began to prate in loving tone;
Quoth Emily, "They sure have words!
Didst hear them say '*My sweet*,' '*My dear*'?"
And as they chirp'd we laugh'd to he
Soon after this a southern wind
Came sobbing like a hunted hind
Into the quiet of the glen:
The maiden mused awhile, and then
Worded her thought right playfully.
"The winds," she said, "of land and sea,
My friend, are surely living things
That come and go on unseen wings.
The teeming air and prodigal,
Which droops its azure over all,
Is full of immortalities
That look on us with unseen eyes.
This sudden wind that hath come here,
With its hard sobs of pain or fear,
It may be, is a spirit kind,
That loves the bruised flowers to bind,
Whose task it is to shake the dew
From the sad violet's eye of blue,
Or chase the honey-making thieves
From off the rose, and shut its leaves
Against the cold of April eves.
Perhaps its dainty, pink-tipt hands
Have plied such tasks in far off lands
And now, perchance, some grim foe follows
The little wight to these green hollows."
Such gentle words had Emily
For the south wind in the tulip tree.
A runnel, hidden by the trees,
Gave out some natural melodies.
She said, "The brook, among the stones,
Is solemn in its undertones;
How like a hymn! the singing creature
Is worshipping the God of nature."
But I replied, "My dear—not so;
Thy solemn eyes, thy brow of snow,
And, more than these, thy maiden merit
Have won Undine, that gentle spirit,
To sing her songs of love to thee."
Swift answer'd merry Emily—
"Undine is but a girl, you know,
And would not pine for love of me;
She has been peering from the brook,
And glimpsed at you." She said and shook
With a rare fit of silvery laughter.
I was more circumspect thereafter,
And dealt in homelier talk. A man
May call a white-brow'd girl "Dian,"
But likes not to be turn'd upon,
And nick-named "Young Endymion."
My Emily loved very well,
At times, those ancient lays which tell
Rude natural tales; she had no lore
Of trouvere, or of troubadour,
Nor knew what difference there might be
Between the tongues of *oc* and *oui*;
But hearing old tales, loved them all
If truth but made them natural.
In our good talks, we oft went o'er
The little horde of my quaint lore,
Cull'd out of old melodious fable.
She little cared for Arthur's table,
For tales of doughty Launcelot,
Or Tristram, or of him who smote
The giant, Angoulafre hight,
And moan'd for love by day and night.
She little cared for such as these,
But if I cross'd the Pyrenees,
With the great peers of Charlemagne,
Descending toward the Spanish plain,
Her eye would lighten at the strain;
And it would moisten with a tear
The sad end of that tale to hear—
How all aweary, worn and white,
And urging his failing steed amain,
A courier from the south, one night,
Reach'd the great city of the Seine;
And how at that same time and hour,
The bride of Roland lay in Bower
Wakeful, and quick of ear to win
Some rumour of her Paladin—
And how it came in sudden cries,
That shook the earth and rent the skies:

And how the messenger of fate—
That courier who rode so late—
Was dragg'd on to her palace gate;
And how the lady sat in hall,
Moaning among her damsels all,
At the wild tale of Ronceval.
That story sounds like solemn truth,
And she would hear it with such ruth
As sympathetic hearts will pay
To real griefs of yesterday.
Pity look'd lovely in the maiden;
Her eyes were softer, when so laden
With the bright dew of tears unshed.
But I was somewhat envious
That other bards should move her thus,
And oft within myself had said,
"Yea—I will strive to touch her heart
With some fair songs of mine own art"—
And many days before the day
Whereof I speak, I made assay
At this bold labour. In the wells
Of Froissart's life-like chronicles
I dipp'd for moving truths of old.
A thousand stories, soft and bold,
Of stately dames, and gentlemen,
Which good Lord Berners, with a pen
Pompous in its simplicity,
Yet tipt with charming courtesy,
Had put in English words, I learn'd;
And some of these I deftly turn'd
Into the forms of minstrel verse.
I know the good tales are the worse—
But, sooth to say, it seems to me
My verse has sense and melody—
Even that its measure sometimes flows
With the brave pomp of that old prose.
Beneath our trysting tree, that day,
With dubious face, I read one lay;
Young Emily quite understood
My fears, and gave me guerdon good
In well-timed praise, and cheer'd me on,
Into full flow of heart and tone.
And when, in days of pleasant weather,
Thereafter, we were met together,
As our strong love oft made us meet,
I always took my cosy seat,
Just at the damsel's little feet,
And read my tales. It was no friend
To me—that day that heard their end.
It had become a play of love,
To watch the swift expression rove
Over the bright sky of her face—
To steal those upward looks, and trace
In every change of cheek and eye,
The influence of my poesy.
I made my verse for Emily—
I give it, reader, now to thee.
The tales which I have toil'd to tell
Of Dame in hall and knight in Selle,
Of faithful love, and courage high—
Sweet flower, strong staff of chivalry—
These tales indeed are old of date;
But why should time their force abate?
Shall we look back with vision dull
On the old brave and beautiful,
And, for they lived so long ago,
Be careless of their mirth or wo?
If sympathy knows but to-day—
If time quite wears its nerve away—
If deeds majestically bold,
In words of ancient music told,
Are only food for studious minds
And touch no hearts—if man but finds
An abstract virtue in the faith,
That clung to truth, and courted death,—
If he can lift the dusky pall
With dainty hand artistical
And smile at woes, because some years
Have swept between them and his tears—
I say, my friend, if this may be,
Then burn old books; antiquity
Is no more than a skeleton
Of painted vein and polish'd bone.
Reader! the minstrel brotherhood,
Earnest to soothe thy listening mood,
Were wont to style thee *Gentle*, *Good*,
Noble or *Gracious*:—they could bow
With loyal knee, yet open brow—
They knew to temper thy decision
With graces of a proud submission.
That wont is changed. Yet I, a man
Of this new land republican,
Where insolence wins upward better
Than courtesy—that old dead letter—
And toil claims pay with utterance sharp,
Follow the good Lords of the Harp,
And dub thee with each courtly phrase,
And ask indulgence for my lays.

LIFE IN THE AUTUMN WOODS.

Summer has gone,
And fruitful autumn has advanced so far
That there is warmth, not heat, in the broad sun,
And you may look, with naked eye, upon
The ardours of his car;
The stealthy frosts, whom his spent looks embolden,
Are making the green leaves golden.

What a brave splendour
Is in the October air! How rich, and clear,
And bracing, and all-joyous! we must render
Love to the spring-time, with its sproutings tender,
As to a child quite dear;
But autumn is a thing of perfect glory,
A manhood not yet hoary.

I love the woods,
In this good season of the liberal year;
I love to seek their leafy solitudes,
And give myself to melancholy moods,
With no intruder near,
And find strange lessons, as I sit and ponder,
In every natural wonder.

But not alone,
As Shakspeare's melancholy courtier loved Ardennes,
Love I the browning forest; and I own
I would not oft have mused, as he, but flown
To hunt with Amiens—

And little thought, as up the bold deer bounded,
Of the sad creature wounded.

A brave and good,
But world-worn knight*—soul wearied with his part
In this vext life—gave man for solitude,
And built a lodge, and lived in Wantley wood,
To hear the belling† Hart.
It was a gentle taste, but its sweet sadness
Yields to the Hunter's madness.

What passionate
And keen delight is in the proud swift chase!
Go out what time the lark at heaven's red gate
Soars joyously singing—quite infuriate
With the high pride of his place;
What time the unrisen sun arrays the morning
In its first bright adorning.

Hark! the quick horn—
As sweet to hear as any clarion—
Piercing with silver call the ear of morn;
And mark the steeds, stout Curtal and Topthorne
And Greysteil and the Don—
Each one of them his fiery mood displaying
With pawing and with neighing.

Urge your swift horse,
After the crying hounds in this fresh hour,
Vanquish high hills—stem perilous streams perforce,
On the free plain give free wings to your course,
And you will know the power
Of the brave chase—and how of griefs the sorest
A cure is in the forest.

Or stalk the deer;
The same red lip of dawn has kiss'd the hills,
The gladdest sounds are crowding on your ear,
There is a life in all the atmosphere:—
Your very nature fills
With the fresh hour, as up the hills aspiring
You climb with limbs untiring.

It is a fair
And goodly sight to see the antler'd stag,
With the long sweep of his swift walk repair
To join his brothers; or the plethoric Bear
Lying on some high crag,
With pinky eyes half closed, but broad head shaking,
As gad-flies keep him waking.

And these you see,
And seeing them, you travel to their death
With a slow stealthy step, from tree to tree,
Noting the wind however faint it be.
The hunter draws a breath
In times like these, which, he will say, repays him
For all care that waylays him.

A strong joy fills
(A joy beyond the tongue's expressive power)
My heart in autumn weather—fills and thrills!
And I would rather stalk the breezy hills,
Descending to my bower
Nightly, by the sweet spirit of Peace attended,
Than pine where life is splendid.

* Sir Thomas Wortley.

† *Belling* is an old word for the peculiar cry of the Hart. See a letter, written by George Ellis, in Lockhart's Life of Scott, giving an account of Sir Thomas Wortley and his reason for building his lodge.

FLORENCE VANE.

I loved thee long and dearly,
Florence Vane;
My life's bright dream and early
Hath come again;
I renew, in my fond vision,
My heart's dear pain,
My hopes, and thy derision,
Florence Vane.

The ruin, lone and hoary,
The ruin old
Where thou didst hark my story,
At even told,—
That spot—the hues Elysian
Of sky and plain—
I treasure in my vision,
Florence Vane.

Thou wast lovelier than the roses
In their prime;
Thy voice excell'd the closes
Of sweetest rhyme;
Thy heart was as a river
Without a main.
Would I had loved thee never,
Florence Vane!

But, fairest, coldest, wonder!
Thy glorious clay
Lieth the green sod under—
Alas, the day!
And it boots not to remember
Thy disdain—
To quicken love's pale ember,
Florence Vane.

The lilies of the valley
By young graves weep,
The daisies love to dally
Where maidens sleep;
May their bloom, in beauty vying,
Never wane
Where thine earthly part is lying,
Florence Vane

CHARLES G. EASTMAN.

[Born, ——.]

Mr. Eastman was educated at the University of Vermont, and has been for several years engaged as a journalist, at Burlington, Woodstock, and Montpelier. He now resides in the latter town, where he is editor of "The Vermont Patriot," the leading gazette of the democratic party in the state. In 1848 he published a collection of "Poems," nearly all of which had previously appeared in various literary miscellanies. They are chiefly lyrical, and the author displays in them a fondness for the French construction, with refrains and choruses, which he introduces naturally and effectively.

Some of his pieces in the manner of Praed, and other contemporary poets, are successful as imitations, but are scarcely equal in the qualities of poetry to his more independent compositions, in which he has reflected with equal truth and felicity the living features of the rural life of New England.

THE FARMER SAT IN HIS EASY CHAIR.

The farmer sat in his easy chair,
Smoking his pipe of clay,
While his hale old wife with busy care
Was clearing the dinner away;
A sweet little girl with fine blue eyes
On her grandfather's knee was catching flies.

The old man laid his hand on her head,
With a tear on his wrinkled face;
He thought how often her mother, dead,
Had sat in the self-same place:
As the tear stole down from his half-shut eye—
"Don't smoke," said the child; "how it makes you cry!"

The house-dog lay stretch'd out on the floor
Where the shade after noon used to steal;
The busy old wife by the open door
Was turning the spinning-wheel;
And the old brass clock on the manteltree
Had plodded along to almost three:

Still the farmer sat in his easy chair,
While close to his heaving breast
The moisten'd brow and the cheek so fair
Of his sweet grandchild were press'd;
His head, bent down, on her soft hair lay—
Fast asleep were they both, that summer day.

MILL MAY.

The strawberries grow in the mowing, Mill May,
And the bob-o'-link sings on the tree;
On the knolls the red clover is growing, Mill May,
Then come to the meadow with me!
We'll pick the ripe clusters among the deep grass,
On the knolls in the mowing, Mill May,
And the long afternoon together we'll pass,
Where the clover is growing, Mill May.

Come! come, ere the season is over, Mill May,
To the fields where the strawberries grow,
While the thick-growing stems and the clover, Mill May,
Shall meet us wherever we go;
We'll pick the ripe clusters among the deep grass,
On the knolls in the mowing, Mill May,
And the long afternoon together we'll pass,
Where the clover is growing Mill May.

The sun, stealing under your bonnet, Mill May,
Shall kiss a soft glow to your face,
And your lip the strawberry leave on it, Mill May,
A tint that the sea-shell would grace;
Then come! the ripe clusters among the deep grass
We'll pick in the mowing, Mill May,
And the long afternoon together we'll pass,
Where the clover is growing, Mill May.

HER GRAVE IS BY HER MOTHER'S.

Her grave is by her mother's,
Where the strawberries grow wild,
And there they've slept for many a year,
The mother and the child.

She was the frailest of us all,
And, from her mother's breast,
We hoped, and pray'd, and trembled, more
For her, than all the rest.

So frail, alas! she could not bear
The gentle breath of Spring,
That scarce the yellow butterfly
Felt underneath its wing.

How hard we strove to save her, love
Like ours alone can tell;
And only those know what we lost,
Who've loved the lost as well.

Some thirteen summers from her birth,
When th' reaper cuts the grain,
We laid her in the silent earth,
A flower without a stain.

We laid her by her mother,
Where the strawberries grow wild
And there they sleep together well,
The mother and the child!

JOHN G. SAXE.

[Born, 1816.]

John G. Saxe was born in Highgate, Franklin county, Vermont, on the second day of June, 1816. His youth was passed in rural occupations, until he was seventeen years of age, when he determined to study one of the liberal professions, and with this view entered the grammar school at St. Albans, and after the usual preliminary course, the college at Middlebury, where he was graduated bachelor of arts in the summer of 1839. He subsequently read law at Lockport, in New York, and at St. Albans, and was admitted to the bar at the latter place, in September, 1843.

He soon after removed to Burlington, where he conducted several years "The Sentinel," a leading democratic newspaper, and became district attorney and inspector of the customs. Since 1850, however, his attention has been principally devoted to literature, and he has been remarkably successful, not only in his printed productions, but in public readings of his humorous and satirical poems.

In 1846 he published "Progress," in which he ridicules in a very happy manner the grotesque and offensive theories by which sham philosophers have attempted to regenerate society, and other "novelties which disturb our peace," in literature, fashion, politics, religion, and morals. In 1849 appeared, in Boston, a collection of his "Poems," which has since passed through many editions. In this are included, besides "Progress," and all his shorter pieces, his "New Rape of the Lock," written in 1847, and "Proud Miss Mac Bride," written in 1848, both in the vein of Hood, but full of verbal felicities and humour, and original observation of manners. Among his unprinted satires are "The Times," "New England," "The Money King," and "The Press," which are of the average length of about one thousand lines.

Mr. Saxe excels most in fun, burlesque, and satire, fields upon the confines of the domain of poetry, in which we have many of the finest specimens of lyric expression, and which have furnished, from the times of Juvenal, a fair proportion of the noblest illustrations of creative energy. His verse is nervous, and generally highly finished; and in almost all cases it is admirably calculated for the production of the desired effects. One of the happiest exhibitions of his skill in language is the piece commencing—

> "Singing through the forests,
> Rattling over ridges,
> Shooting under arches,
> Rumbling over bridges;
> Whizzing through the mountains,
> Buzzing o'er the vale—
> Bless me! this is pleasant,
> Riding on a rail!"

The whole composition is an echo of the crowded railroad-car. In all his writings are displayed the same happy adaptation of sound to sense, and in all agreeable images, comic displays of wisdom, and wit equally genial and pointed.

THE PROUD MISS MACBRIDE.

A LEGEND OF GOTHAM.

O, terribly proud was Miss MacBride,
The very personification of pride,
As she minced along in fashion's tide,
Adown Broadway—on the proper side—
When the golden sun was setting;
There was pride in the head she carried so high,
Pride in her lip, and pride in her eye,
And a world of pride in the very sigh
That her stately bosom was fretting:

A sigh that a pair of elegant feet,
Sandal'd in satin, should kiss the street—
The very same that the vulgar greet
In common leather not over "neat"—
For such is the common booting;
(And Christian tears may well be shed,
That even among our gentlemen-bred,
The glorious Day of Morocco is dead,
And Day and Martin are reigning instead,
On a much inferior footing!)

O, terribly proud was Miss MacBride,
Proud of her beauty, and proud of her pride,
And proud of fifty matters beside—
That wouldn't have borne dissection;
Proud of her wit, and proud of her walk,
Proud of her teeth, and proud of her talk,
Proud of "knowing cheese from chalk,"
On a very slight inspection!—

Proud abroad, and proud at home,
Proud wherever she chanced to come—
When she was glad, and when she was glum
Proud as the head of a Saracen
Over the door of a tippling-shop!—
Proud as a duchess, proud as a fop,
"Proud as a boy with a bran-new top,"
Proud beyond comparison!

It seems a singular thing to say,
But her very senses led her astray
Respecting all humility;
In sooth, her dull, auricular drum
Could find in *humble* only a "hum,"
And heard no sound of "gentle" come,
In talking about gentility.

What *lowly* meant she did n't know,
For she always avoided "everything low,"
With care the most punctilious;
And, queerer still, the audible sound
Of "super-silly" she never had found
In the adjective supercilious!

The meaning of *meek* she never knew,
But imagined the phrase had something to do
With "Moses," a peddling German Jew,
Who, like all hawkers, the country through,
Was "a person of no position;"
And it seem'd to her exceedingly plain,
If the word was really known to pertain
To a vulgar German, it was n't germane
To a lady of high condition!

Even her graces—not her grace—
For that was in the "vocative case"—
Chill'd with the touch of her icy face,
Sat very stiffly upon her!
She never confess'd a favour aloud,
Like one of the simple, common crowd—
But coldly smiled, and faintly bow'd,
As who should say, "You do me proud,
And do yourself an honour!"

And yet the pride of Miss MacBride,
Although it had fifty hobbies to ride,
Had really no foundation;
But like the fabrics that gossips devise—
Those single stories that often arise
And grow till they reach a four-story size—
Was merely a fancy creation!

'Tis a curious fact as ever was known
In human nature, but often shown
Alike in castle and cottage,
That pride, like pigs of a certain breed,
Will manage to live and thrive on "feed"
As poor as a pauper's pottage!

That her wit should never have made her vain,
Was—like her face—sufficiently plain;
And, as to her musical powers,
Although she sang until she was hoarse,
And issued notes with a banker's force,
They were just such notes as we never endorse
For any acquaintance of ours!

Her birth, indeed, was uncommonly high—
For Miss MacBride first opened her eye
Through a skylight dim, on the light of the sky;
But pride is a curious passion—
And in talking about her wealth and worth,
She always forgot to mention her birth
To people of rank and fashion!

Of all the notable things on earth,
The queerest one is pride of birth,
Among our "fierce democracie!"
A bridge across a hundred years,
Without a prop to save it from sneers—
Not even a couple of rotten peers—
A thing for laughter, fleers, and jeers,
Is American aristocracy!

English and Irish, French and Spanish,
German, Italian, Dutch and Danish,
Crossing their veins until they vanish
In one conglomeration;
So subtle a tangle of blood, indeed,
No heraldry-Harvey will ever succeed
In finding the circulation!

Depend upon it, my snobbish friend,
Your family thread you can't ascend,
Without good reason to apprehend
You may find it wax'd at the farther end,
By some plebeian vocation;
Or, worse than that, your boasted line
May end in a loup of stronger twine,
That plagued some worthy relation!

But Miss MacBride had something beside
Her lofty birth to nourish her pride—
For rich was the old paternal MacBride,
According to public rumour;
And he lived "up town," in a splendid square,
And kept his daughter on dainty fare,
And gave her gems that were rich and rare,
And the finest rings and things to wear,
And feathers enough to plume her.

An honest mechanic was John MacBride,
As ever an honest calling plied,
Or graced an honest ditty;
For John had work'd in his early day,
In "pots and pearls," the legends say—
And kept a shop with a rich array
Of things in the soap and candle way,
In the lower part of the city!

No "*rara avis*" was honest John—
(That's the Latin for "sable-swan")—
Though in one of his fancy flashes,
A wicked wag, who meant to deride,
Call'd honest John "Old *Phœnix* MacBride,"
"Because he rose from his ashes!"

Little by little he grew to be rich,
By saving of candle-ends and "sich,"
Till he reach'd at last an opulent niche—
No very uncommon affair;
For history quite confirms the law
Express'd in the ancient Scottish saw—
A Mickle may come to be may'r!*

Alack for many ambitious beaux!
She hung their hopes upon her nose—
(The figure is quite Horatian!)
Until, from habit, the member grew
As very a hook as ever eye knew,
To the commonest observation.

A thriving tailor begg'd her hand,
But she gave "the fellow" to understand
By a violent manual action,
She perfectly scorn'd the best of his clan,
And reckon'd the ninth of any man
An exceedingly vulgar fraction!

Another, whose sign was a golden boot,
Was mortified with a bootless suit,
In a way that was quite appalling,
For, though a regular *sutor* by trade,
He wasn't a suitor to suit the maid,

* "Mickle, wi' thrift, may chance to be mair."—*Scotch Proverb.*

Who cut him off with a saw—and bade
"The cobbler keep to his calling!"

(The muse must let a secret out:
There isn't the faintest shadow of doubt
That folks who oftenest sneer and flout
At "the dirty, low mechanicals,"
Are they whose sires, by pounding their knees,
Or coiling their legs, or trades like these—
Contrived to win their children ease
From poverty's galling manacles.)

A rich tobacconist comes and sues,
And, thinking the lady would scarce refuse
A man of his wealth and liberal views,
Began, at once, with "If you *choose*—
And could you really love him—"
But the lady spoil'd his speech in a huff,
With an answer rough and ready enough,
To let him know she was up to snuff,
And altogether above him!

A young attorney, of winning grace,
Was scarce allow'd to "open his face,"
Ere Miss MacBride had closed his case
With true judicial celerity;
For the lawyer was poor, and "seedy" to boot,
And to say the lady discarded his *suit*,
Is merely a double verity!

The last of those who came to court,
Was a lively beau, of the dapper sort,
"Without any visible means of support,"
A crime by no means flagrant
In one who wears an elegant coat,
But the very point on which they vote
A ragged fellow "a vagrant!"

A courtly fellow was dapper Jim,
Sleek and supple, and tall and trim,
And smooth of tongue as neat of limb;
And maugre his meagre pocket,
You'd say from the glittering tales he told,
That Jim had slept in a cradle of gold,
With Fortunatus to rock it!

Now dapper Jim his courtship plied
(I wish the fact could be denied)
With an eye to the purse of the old MacBride,
And really "nothing shorter!"
For he said to himself, in his greedy lust,
"Whenever he dies—as die he must—
And yields to Heaven his vital trust,
He's very sure to 'come down with his dust,'
In behalf of his only daughter."

And the very magnificent Miss MacBride,
Half in love, and half in pride,
Quite graciously relented;
And, tossing her head, and turning her back,
No token of proper pride to lack—
To be a Bride, without the "Mac,"
With much disdain, consented!

Alas! that people who've got their box
Of cash beneath the best of locks,
Secure from all financial shocks,
Should stock their fancy with fancy stocks,
And madly rush upon Wall-street rocks,
Without the least apology!

Alas! that people whose money-affairs
Are sound, beyond all need of repairs,
Should ever tempt the bulls and bears
Of Mammon's fierce zoölogy!

Old John MacBride, one fatal day,
Became the unresisting prey
Of Fortune's undertakers;
And staking all on a single die,
His founder'd bark went high and dry
Among the brokers and breakers!

At his trade again, in the very shop
Where, years before, he let it drop,
He follows his ancient calling—
Cheerily, too, in poverty's spite,
And sleeping quite as sound at night,
As when, at fortune's giddy height,
He used to wake with a dizzy fright
From a dismal dream of falling.

But alas for the haughty Miss MacBride,
'T was such a shock to her precious pride!
She couldn't recover, although she tried
Her jaded spirits to rally;
'T was a dreadful change in human affairs,
From a Place "up town," to a nook "up stairs,"
From an avenue down to an alley!—

'T was little condolence she had, God wot—
From her "troops of friends," who hadn't forgot
The airs she used to borrow;
They had civil phrases enough, but yet
'T was plain to see that their "deepest regret"
Was a different thing from sorrow!

They own'd it couldn't have well been worse
To go from a full to an empty purse:
To expect a "reversion," and get a reverse,
Was truly a dismal feature;
But it wasn't strange—they whisper'd—at all!
That the summer of pride should have its fall
Was quite according to Nature!

And one of those chaps who make a pun,
As if it were quite legitimate fun
To be blazing away at every one
With a regular, double-loaded gun—
Remark'd that moral transgression
Always brings retributive stings
To candle-makers as well as kings:
For "making light of *cereous* things"
Was a very wick-ed profession!

And vulgar people—the saucy churls—
Inquired about "the price of pearls,"
And mock'd at her situation:
"She wasn't ruin'd—they ventured to hope-
Because she was poor, she needn't mope;
Few people were better off for soap,
And that was a consolation!"

And to make her cup of wo run over,
Her elegant, ardent plighted lover
Was the very first to forsake her;
"He quite regretted the step, 't was true—
The lady had pride enough 'for two,'
But that alone would never do
To quiet the butcher and baker!"

And now the unhappy Miss MacBride—
The merest ghost of her early pride—
  Bewails her lonely position;
Cramp'd in the very narrowest niche,
Above the poor, and below the rich—
  Was ever a worse condition?

MORAL.

Because you flourish in worldly affairs,
Don't be haughty, and put on airs,
  With insolent pride of station!
Don't be proud, and turn up your nose
At poorer people in plainer clo'es,
But learn, for the sake of your mind's repose,
That wealth's a bubble that comes—and goes!
And that all proud flesh, wherever it grows,
  Is subject to irritation!

EXTRACTS FROM "PROGRESS."

FASHION.

What impious mockery, when with soulless art
Fashion, intrusive, seeks to rule the heart;
Directs how grief may tastefully be borne;
Instructs Bereavement just how long to mourn;
Shows Sorrow how by nice degrees to fade,
And marks its measure in a riband's shade!
More impious still, when through her wanton laws
She desecrates Religion's sacred cause;
Shows how "the narrow road" is easiest trod,
And how genteelest, worms may worship God;
How sacred rites may bear a worldly grace,
And self-abasement wear a haughty face;
How sinners, long in Folly's mazes whirl'd,
With pomp and splendour may "renounce the world;"
How "with all saints hereafter to appear,"
Yet quite escape the vulgar portion here!

"THE PRESS."

O might the muse prolong her flowing rhyme,
(Too closely cramp'd by unrelenting Time,
Whose dreadful scythe swings heedlessly along,
And, missing speeches, clips the thread of song),
How would she strive in fitting verse to sing
The wondrous progress of the printing king!
Bibles and novels, treatises and songs,
Lectures on "rights," and strictures upon wrongs;
Verse in all metres, travels in all climes,
Rhymes without reason, sonnets without rhymes;
"Translations from the French," so vilely done,
The wheat escaping, leaves the chaff alone;
Memoirs, where dunces sturdily essay
To cheat Oblivion of her certain prey;
Critiques, where pedants vauntingly expose
Unlicensed verses in unlawful prose;
Lampoons, whose authors strive in vain to throw
Their headless arrows from a nerveless bow;
Poems by youths, who, crossing Nature's will,
Harangue the landscape they were born to till;
Huge tomes of law, that lead by rugged routes
Through ancient dogmas down to modern doubts,
Where judges oft, with well-affected ease,
Give learned reasons for absurd decrees,
Or, more ingenious still, contrive to found
Some just decision on fallacious ground—
Or blink the point, and haply, in its place,
Moot and decide some hypothetic case;
Smart epigrams, all sadly out of joint,
And pointless, save the "exclamation point,"
Which stands in state, with vacant wonder fraught,
The pompous tombstone of some pauper thought;
Ingenious systems based on doubtful facts,
"Tracts for the times," and most untimely tracts;
Polemic pamphlets, literary toys,
And "easy lessons" for uneasy boys;
Hebdomadal gazettes and daily news,
Gay magazines and quarterly reviews:
Small portion these of all the vast array
Of darken'd leaves that cloud each passing day,
And pour their tide unceasingly along,
A gathering, swelling, overwhelming throng!

"ASSOCIATION."

Hail, social progress! each new moon is rife
With some new theory of social life,
Some matchless scheme ingeniously design'd
From half their miseries to free mankind;
On human wrongs triumphant war to wage,
And bring anew the glorious golden age.
"Association" is the magic word
From many a social "priest and prophet" heard
"Attractive labour" is the angel given,
To render earth a sublunary heaven!
"Attractive labour!" ring the changes round,
And labour grows attractive in the sound;
And many a youthful mind, where haply lurk
Unwelcome fancies at the name of "work,"
Sees pleasant pastime in its longing view
Of "toil made easy" and "attractive" too—
And, fancy-rapt, with joyful ardour, turns
Delightful grindstones and seductive churns!......
Inventive France! what wonder-working schemes
Astound the world whene'er a Frenchman dreams!
What fine-spun theories—ingenious, new,
Sublime, stupendous, everything but true!
One little favour, O "imperial France:"
Still teach the world to cook, to dress, to dance;
Let, if thou wilt, thy boots and barbers roam,
But keep thy morals and thy creeds at home!

BEREAVEMENT.

Nay, weep not, dearest, though the child be dead,
  He lives again in heaven's unclouded life,
With other angels that have early fled
  From these dark scenes of sorrow, sin, and strife,
Nay, weep not, dearest, though thy yearning love
  Would fondly keep for earth its fairest flowers,
And e'en deny to brighter realms above
  The few that deck this dreary world of ours:
Though much it seems a wonder and a wo
  That one so loved should be so early lost—
And hallow'd tears may unforbidden flow,
  To mourn the blossom that we cherish'd most—
  Yet all is well: God's good design I see,
  That where our treasure is, our hearts may be!

HENRY B. HIRST.

[Born, 1817.]

Mr. Hirst was born in Philadelphia, on the twenty-third day of August, 1817. His father, Thomas Hirst, was a reputable merchant of that city, and held in high respect. When only eight years old he entered the law office of his brother, William L. Hirst, Esq., and at the age of eighteen he was registered as a student. His professional studies were now interrupted for a long period, and he engaged in mercantile pursuits, but at the age of twenty-five he made his application for admission, and graduated with the highest honors in the early part of 1843, and is now in successful practice at the Philadelphia Bar.

Mr. Hirst's first attempts at poetry, he informs me, were in his twenty-first or twenty-second year, about which time he became a contributor to Graham's Magazine. His poems were very successful and extensively copied. In 1845 he published in Boston his first volume, "The Coming of the Mammoth, the Funeral of Time, and other Poems," a book which certainly received all the praises to which it was entitled. It was not without graceful fancies, but its most striking characteristics were a clumsy extravagance of invention, and a vein of sentiment neither healthful nor poetical. It had the merit, however, of musical though somewhat mechanical versification, and its reception was such as to encourage the author to new and more ambitious efforts.

In the summer of 1848 he published "Endymion, a Tale of Greece," an epic poem, in four cantos. It was a long-meditated and carefully elaborated production, some parts of which had been kept the full Horatian period. It may be regarded, therefore, as an exhibition of his best abilities. He evinced a certain boldness in subjecting himself to a comparison with Keats, whose fine fancies, woven about it, will share the immortality of the Grecian fable. In the finish and musical flow of his rhythm, and in the distinctness and just proportion with which he has told his story, he has equalled Keats: but in nothing else. With passages of graphic and beautiful description, and a happy clearness in narrative, the best praise of Mr. Hirst's performance is, that it is a fine piece of poetical rhetoric. There is not much thought in the poem, and where there is any that arrests attention, it whispers of familiar readings.

The fault of the book is the want of a poetical delicacy of feeling; it is not classical; it is not beautiful; it is merely sensual; there is none of the diviner odour of poetry about it. Mr. Hirst's "chaste Diana" is a strumpet. The metre, though inappropriate, to such a poem, is unusual, and is managed by Mr. Hirst with singular skill. To illustrate his mastery of versification, and at the same time to present one of the most attractive passages of the poem, the following lines are quoted from the first canto:

Through a deep dell with mossy hemlocks girded
A dell by many a sylvan Dryad prest,—
Which Latmos' lofty crest
Flung half in shadow—where the red deer herded—
While mellow murmurs shook the forests gray—
Endymion took his way.....

Mount Latmos lay before him. Gently gleaming,
A roseate halo from the twilight dim
Hung round its crown. To him
The rough ascent was light; for, far off, beaming,
Orion rose—and Sirius, like a shield,
Shone on the azure field.....

At last he gain'd the top, and, crown'd with splendour,
The moon, arising from the Latmian sea,
Stepp'd o'er the heavenly lea,
Flinging her misty glances, meek and tender
As a young virgin's, o'er his marble brow
That glisten'd with their glow.

Beside him gush'd a spring that in a hollow
Had made a crystal lake, by which he stood
To cool his heated blood—
His blood yet fever'd, for the fierce Apollo
Throughout the long, the hot, the tropic day,
Embraced him with his ray.

Beside the lake whose waves were glassily gleaming,
A willow stood in Dian's rising rays,
And from the woodland ways
Its feather'd, lance-like leaves were gently streaming
Along the water, with their lucent tips
Kissing its silver lips.

And still the moon arose, serenely hovering,
Dove-like, above the horizon. Like a queen
She walk'd in light between
The stars—her lovely handmaids—softly covering
Valley and wold, and mountain-side and plain,
With streams of lucid rain.

Endymion watch'd her rise, his bosom burning
With princely thoughts; for though a shepherd's son,
He felt that fame is won
By high aspirings; and a lofty yearning,
From the bright blossoming of his boyish days,
Made his deeds those of praise.

Like her's, his track was tranquil: he had gather'd
By slow degrees the glorious, golden lore,
Hallowing his native shore;
And when at silent eve his flock was tether'd,
He read the stars, and drank, as from a stream,
Great knowledge from their gleam.

And so he grew a dreamer—one who, panting
For shadowy objects, languish'd like a bird
That, striving to be heard
Above its fellows, fails, the struggle haunting
Its memory ever, for ever the strife pursuing
To its own dark undoing.

In the summer of 1849 Mr. Hirst published in Boston a third volume, entitled "The Penance of Roland, a Romance of the Peiné Forte et Dure and other Poems," from which the extracts in the next pages are copied. Its contents are all well versified, and their rhetoric is generally poetical.

THE LAST TILT.

AT twilight, through the shadow, fled
An ancient, war-worn knight,
Array'd in steel, from head to heel,
And on a steed of white;
And, in the knight's despite,
The horse pursued his flight:
For the old man's cheek was pale,
And his hands strove at the rein,
With the clutch of phrensied pain;
And his courser's streaming mane
Swept, dishevell'd, on the gale.

"Dong—dong!" And the sound of a bell
Went wailing away over meadow and mere—
"SEVEN!"
Counted aloud by the sentinel clock
On the turret of Time; and the regular beat
Of his echoing feet
Fell, like lead, on the ear—
As he left the dead Hour on its desolate bier.

The old knight heard the mystic clock;
And the sound, like a funeral-bell,
Rang in his ears till their caverns were full
Of the knoll of the desolate knell.
And the steed, as aroused by a spell,
Sprang away with a withering yell,
While the old man strove again,
But each time with feebler force,
To arrest the spectral horse
In its mad, remorseless course,
But, alas! he strove in vain.

"Dong—dong!" And the sound of a bell
Went wailing away over meadow and mere—
"EIGHT!"
Counted aloud by the sentinel clock
On the turret of Time; and the regular beat
Of his echoing feet
Fell, like lead, on the ear—
As he left the dead Hour on its desolate bier.

The steed was white, and gaunt, and grim,
With lidless, leaden eyes,
That burn'd with the lurid, livid glare
Of the stars of Stygian skies;
And the wind, behind, with sighs,
Mimick'd his maniac cries,
While through the ebony gloom, alone,
Wan-visaged Saturn gazed
On the warrior—unamazed—
On the steed whose eyeballs blazed
With a lustre like his own.

"Dong—dong!" And the sound of a bell
Went wailing away over meadow and mere—
"NINE!"
Counted aloud by the sentinel clock
On the turret of Time; and the regular beat
Of his echoing feet
Fell, like lead, on the ear—
As he left the dead Hour on its desolate bier.

Athwart a swart and shadowy moor
The struggling knight was borne,
And far away, before him, gleam'd
A light like the gray of morn;
While the old man, weak, forlorn,
And wan, and travel-worn,
Gazed, mad with deathly fear:
For he dream'd it was the day,
Though the dawn was far away,
And he trembled with dismay
In the desert, dark and drear!

"Dong—dong!" And the sound of a bell
Went wailing away over meadow and mere—
"TEN!"
Counted aloud by the sentinel clock
On the turret of Time; and the regular beat
Of his echoing feet
Fell, like lead, on the ear—
As he left the dead Hour on its desolate bier.

In casque and cuirass, white as snow,
Came, merrily, over the wold,
A maiden knight, with lance and shield,
And a form of manly mould,
And a beard of woven gold:
When, suddenly, behold!—
With a loud, defiant cry,
And a tone of stern command,
The ancient knight, with lance in hand,
Rush'd, thundering, over the frozen land,
And bade him "Stand, or die!"

"Dong—dong!" And the sound of a bell
Went wailing away over meadow and mere—
"ELEVEN!"
Counted aloud by the sentinel clock
On the turret of Time; and the regular beat
Of his echoing feet
Fell, like lead, on the ear—
As he left the dead Hour on its desolate bier.

With his ashen lance in rest,
Career'd the youthful knight,
With a haughty heart, and an eagle eye,
And a visage burning bright—
For he loved the tilted fight—
And, under Saturn's light,
With a shock that shook the world,
The rude old warrior fell—and lay
A corpse—along the frozen clay!
As with a crash the gates of day
Their brazen valves unfurl'd.

"Dong—dong!" And the sound of a bell
Went wailing away over meadow and mere—
"TWELVE!"
Counted aloud by the sentinel clock
On the turret of Time; and the regular beat
Of his echoing feet
Fell, like lead, on the ear—
As he left the dead Year on his desolate bier!

BERENICE.

I WOULD that I could lay me at thy feet,
And with a bosom, warm with rapture, greet
The rose-like fragrance of thy odorous sighs,
Drinking, with dazzled eyes,
The radiant glory of a face

Which, even in dreams, adorns the Italian skies
Of passionate love—the Astarté of their space!

This, in some quiet, column'd chamber, where
The glare of sunlight dies, yet all is light;
With all around us ruddy, rich, and rare—
Books red with gold, and mirrors diamond-bright,
And choicest paintings, and rich flowers which bear
Their beauty, bloom, and fragrance, day and night,
And stately statues, white as gods, between
The scarlet blossoms and the leaves of green,
With all that Art creates, and Fancy rears,
And Genius snatches from supernal spheres.

All day, all day, dear love, would I lie there,
With elbow sunk in some soft ottoman,
Feeling far more than man,
Breathing the fragrance of the enchanted air
Swimming around thee; while, with book in hand,
I would unfold to thee the ancient sages—
Poet's, like CHAUCER's, quaint, delicious pages,
And wander thoughtfully through the poet's land—
Through it by night—a calm, unclouded night,
Full of sweet dreams.

By murmurous streams,
Sparkling with starry gleams,
We'd pause, entranced by Dian's amber light,
And watch the Nereid rising from the wave,
Or see the Oread lave
Her faultless feet in lucid ripples, white
As Indian ivory with the milky ray,
Trembling around their forms in liquid play.

Then to some tall old wood, beneath old trees,
Which, in the primal hours,
Gave birth to flowers
Fairer than those which jewell'd Grecian leas
What time the Dryads woo'd the summer breeze.
We'd seek some mossy bank, and sit, and scan
The stars, forgetting earth and man,
And all that is of earth, and watch the spheres,
And dream we heard their music; and, with tears
Born of our bliss, arise, and walk again,
Languid with passion's epicurean pain.

Treading the feather'd grasses,
Through misty, moonlit passes,
On, on, along some vernal, verdant plain
Our steps should falter, while the linnet's strain
Made music for our feet, and, keeping time,
Our hearts replied with gentle chime,
As our souls throbb'd responsive to the rhyme
Of perfect love, which Nature murmur'd round,
Making earth holy ground,
And as the gods who ruled all things we saw.

Then giving way to mad imaginings
Born of the time and place—
The perfume which pervaded space,
The natural emotions of our race—
We'd vow that love should be the only law
Henceforth for earth; that even the rudest things
Should love and be beloved: while we,
The ADAM and EVE, should sit enthroned, and see
All earth an Eden, and with thankful eyes
Reverence God in our new paradise.

THE LOST PLEIAD.

BEAUTIFUL sisters! tell me, do you ever
Dream of the loved and lost one, she who fell
And faded in Love's turbid, crimson river?
The sacred secret tell.
Calmly the purple heavens reposed around her,
As, chanting harmonies, she danced along:
Ere Eros in his silken meshes bound her,
Her being pass'd in song.

Once on a day she lay in dreamy slumber;
Beside her slept her golden-tonguéd lyre;
And radiant visions—fancies without number—
Fill'd breast and brain with fire.
She dream'd; and in her dreams saw bending o'er her
A form her fervid fancy deified;
And, waking, view'd the noble one before her,
Who woo'd her as his bride.

What words, what passionate words he breathed, beseeching,
Have long been lost in the descending years;
Nevertheless, she listen'd to his teaching,
Smiling between her tears.
And ever since that hour the happy maiden
Wanders unknown of any one but Jove;
Regretting not the lost Olympian Aidenn
In the Elysium—Love!

NO MORE.

NO MORE—no more! What vague, mysterious,
Inexplicable terrors in the sound!
What soul-disturbing secrecies abound
In those sad syllables! and what delirious,
Wild phantasies, what sorrowful and what serious
Mysteries lie hid in them! No More—No More!
Where is the silent and the solemn shore,
Wash'd by what soundless seas, where all imperious
He reigns? And over what his awful reign?
Who questions, maddens! what is veil'd in shade,
Let sleep in shadow. When No More was made,
Eternity felt his deity on the wane,
And Zeus rose shrieking, Saturn-like and hoar,
Before that dread Prometheus—No MORE!

ASTARTE.

THY lustre, heavenly star! shines ever on me.
I, trembling like Endymion over-bent
By dazzling Dian, when with wonderment
He saw her crescent light the Latmian lea:
And like a Naiad's sailing on the sea,
Floats thy fair form before me: the azure air
Is all ambrosial with thy hyacinth hair:
While round thy lips the moth in airy glee
Hovers, and hums in dim and dizzy dreams,
Drunken with odorous breath: thy argent eyes
(Twin planets swimming through Love's lustrous skies)
Are mirror'd in my heart's serenest streams—
Such eyes saw SHAKSPERE, flashing bold and bright
When queenly Egypt rode the Nile at night.

AUGUSTINE J. H. DUGANNE.

[Born about 1817.]

The largest work by Mr. Duganne which I have seen is a yellow-covered octavo called, "The Mysteries of Three Cities! Boston, New York, and Philadelphia! a True History of Men's Hearts and Habits!" and on the title-page, which is here faithfully copied, he is described as the author of "The Illegitimate," "Emily Harper," "The Pastor," "The Two Clerks," "Secret Guilt," "Fortunes of Pertinax," "etc. etc." He is therefore undoubtedly a voluminous writer in prose, for it may be inferred that all these productions are in that form; and he has published in verse "The Iron Harp," "Parnassus in Pillory," and "The Mission of Intellect," besides a great number of short pieces, in the newspapers, which are collected with the rest in a handsome octavo edition of his "Poetical Works." The argument of "Parnassus in Pillory" is thus announced:

"As in some butcher's barricaded stall,
A thousand prisoned rats gnaw, squeak, and crawl,
While at the entrance, held by stalwart hands,
A panting terrier strives to burst his bands;—
With eyes inflamed and glittering teeth displayed,
Half turns to bite the hand by which he's stayed;—
So writhes and pants my terrier muse to chase
The rats of letters from creation's face."

Satires of American poets have been sufficiently numerous. The best, in all respects, it need hardly be stated, is Mr. Lowell's "Fable for Critics." "American Bards," by Mr. Gorham A. Worth, "Truth, a New Year's Gift for Scribblers," by Mr. William J. Snelling, and "The Quacks of Helicon," by Mr. L. A Wilmer, are superior to any others of the second class. Mr. Duganne's "Parnassus in Pillory," cannot be regarded as equal to either of these, but it has some epigrammatic turns of expression, with occasional critical suggestions, neatly delivered, which render it very readable. If the works here referred to be compared with that amazing exhibition of satiric rage, "The Dunciad," of which most of our attempts in this class are imitations, in a greater or less degree, according to the abilities of their respective authors, no surprise will be felt that they have commanded so little attention. Several of them evince as much malice, but all together, except Mr. Lowell's ingenious performance, do not display as much poetry or wit, as the meanest page of Pope's ill-natured but incomparably polished and pointed attack on his contemporaries.

From his "Iron Harp," Mr. Duganne seems to belong to "the party of progress," and his favorite poet, it may be guessed, is Ebenezer Elliott. The most creditable illustration of his abilities is probably the following ode on Mr. Powers's statue of the Greek Slave.

ODE TO THE GREEK SLAVE.

O Greek! by more than Moslem fetters thrall'd!
O marble prison of a radiant thought,
Where life is half recall'd,
And beauty dwells, created, not enwrought—
Why hauntest thou my dreams, enrobed in light,
And atmosphered with purity, wherein
Mine own soul is transfigured, and grows bright,
As though an angel smiled away its sin?

O chastity of Art!
Behold! this maiden shape makes solitude
Of all the busy mart:
Beneath her soul's immeasurable woe,
All sensuous vision lies subdued,
And from her veiled eyes the flow
Of tears, is inward turned upon her heart;
While on the prisoning lips
Her eloquent spirit swoons,
And from the lustrous brow's eclipse
Falls patient glory, as from clouded moons!
Severe in vestal grace, yet warm
And flexile with the delicate glow of youth,
She stands, the sweet embodiment of Truth;
Her pure thoughts clustering around her form,
Like seraph garments, whiter than the snows
Which the wild sea upthrows.

O Genius! thou canst chain
Not marble only, but the human soul,
And melt the heart with soft control,
And wake such reverence in the brain,
That man may be forgiven,
If in the ancient days he dwelt
Idolatrous with sculptured life, and knelt
To Beauty more than Heaven!

Genius is worship! for its works adore
The Infinite Source of all their glorious thought,
So blessed Art, like Nature, is o'erfraught
With such a wondrous store
Of hallowed influence, that we who gaze
Aright on her creations, haply pray and praise!

Go, then, fair Slave! and in thy fetters teach
What Heaven inspired and Genius hath designed!—
Be thou Evangel of true Art, and preach
The freedom of the mind!

E. SPENCER MILLER.

[Born, 1817.]

Mr. E. SPENCER MILLER is a son of the late eminent theologian, the Reverend SAMUEL MILLER, D.D., of Princeton, New Jersey, where he was born on the third day of September, 1817. When nineteen years of age he was graduated at Nassau Hall, in his native town, and having studied the law, and been admitted to the bar, in Philadelphia, chose that city for his residence, and has attained to a distinguished position there in his profession.

Mr. MILLER has not hitherto been known to the public as a poet. The only book upon the title-page of which he has placed his name, is a stout octavo called "A Treatise on the Law of Partition, by Writ, in Pennsylvania," published in 1847; but while engaged in researches concerning this most unpoetical subject, in leisure hours his mind was teeming with those beautiful productions which were given to the world in 1849, in a modest anonymous volume entitled "Caprices." Among these poems are some that evince an imagination of unusual sensibility and activity, and in all are displayed culture and wise reflection. No one of our poets has made a first appearance in a book of greater promise, and it will be justly regretted if devotion to the law or to any other pursuit prevents its accomplished author from keeping that promise to the lovers of literature.

NIAGARA.

Ho, SPIRIT! I am with thee now;
My stride is by the rushing brow,
The mist is round me while I bow.

By summer streams, by land and sea,
Niagara. I have yearned to thee,
And dreamed what thou wouldst say to me.

In spells of vision I have stood,
And with the turmoil of thy flood
Have struggled into brotherhood.

The hour is mine; the dream is gone;
The sleep of Summer streams is done;
And I am by thy side alone.

The hour is mine; I feel thy spray;
I press along thy rainbow way;
God help my throbbing heart to-day.

The hour is mine; my feet are near;
I falter not, but wrestle here;
Eternal words are in mine ear.

I falter not; I feel the whole;
The mysteries of thy presence roll
In waves of tumult o'er my soul.

I merge myself, my race, my clime,
And as I tread thy paths sublime,
I seem to stand alone with Time;

To stand, all lost, with Time alone;
He makes thy sullen roar his own,
An infinite sad monotone:

Majestic dirge of strifes and sighs;
The voices of the year that rise
Between the two eternities:

Forever new, forever old,
Forever one, yet manifold,
Forever what all time hath told.

THE WIND.

I STIR the pulses of the mind,
And, with my passive cheek inclined,
I lay my ear along the wind.

It fans my face, it fans the tree,
It goes away and comes to me,
I feel it, but I cannot see.

Upon my chilly brow it plays,
It whispers of forgotten days,
It says whatever fancy says.

Away, away—by wood and plain,
About the park, and through the lane
It goes and comes to me again.

Away,—again away, it roams,
By fields of flocks and human homes,
And laden with their voices comes:

It comes and whispers in my ear,
So close I cannot choose but hear;
It speaks, and yet I do not fear;

Then, sweeping where the shadows lie,
Its murmur softens to a sigh
That pains me as it passes by,

And, in its sorrow, and reproof,
Goes wailing round the wall and roof,
So sad the swallow soars aloof.

Away,—the old cathedral bell
Is swinging over hill and dell;
Devoted men are praying well.

Away,—with every breath there come
The tones of toil's eternal hum,—
Man, legion-voiced, yet ever dumb. . .

Away, away,—by lake and lea,—
It cometh ever back to me,
I feel it, but I cannot see. . . .

"THE BLUE-BEARD CHAMBERS OF THE HEART."

Mould upon the ceiling,
  Mould upon the floor,
Windows barred and double barred,
  Opening nevermore;

Spiders in the corners,
  Spiders on the shelves,
Weaving frail and endless webs
  Back upon themselves;

Weaving, ever weaving,
  Weaving in the gloom,
Till the drooping drapery
  Trails about the room.

Waken not the echo,
  Nor the bat, that clings
In the curious crevices
  Of the pannelings.

Waken not the echo,
  It will haunt your ear
Wall and ceiling whispering
  Words you would not hear.

Hist! the spectres gather,
  Gather in the dark,
Where a breath has brushed away
  Dust from off a mark;

Dust of weary winters,
  Dust of solemn years,
Dust that deepens in the silence,
  As the minute wears.

On the shelf and wainscot,
  Window-bars and wall,
Covering infinite devices,
  With its stealthy fall.

Hist! the spectres gather,
  Break, and group again,
Wreathing, writhing, gibbering
  Round that fearful stain;—

Blood upon the panels,
  Blood upon the floor,
Blood that baffles wear and washing,
  Red for evermore.

See,— they pause and listen,
  Where the bat that clings,
Stirs within the crevices
  Of the pannelings.

See,—they pause and listen,
  Listen through the air;
How the eager life has struggled,
  That was taken there;

See.— they pause and listen,
  Listen in the gloom;
For a startled breath is sighing,
  Sighing through the room.

Sighing in the corners,
  Sighing on the floor,
Sighing through the window-bars,
  That open nevermore.

Waken not those whispers;
  They will pain your ears;
Waken not the dust that deepens
  Through the solemn years,—

Deepens in the silence,
  Deepens in the dark;
Covering closer, as it gathers,
  Many a fearful mark.

Hist! the spectres gather,
  Break and group again,
Wreathing, writhing, gibbering,
  Round that fearful stain:

Blood upon the panels,
  Blood upon the floor,
Blood that baffles wear and washing
  Red for evermore.

THE GLOW-WORM.

Deep within the night,
  Toiling on its way,
With its feeble lamp
  Giving out a ray.

Close about its path
  Sombre shadows meet,
And the light is cast
  Only at its feet.

Castle-top and grange
  Off within the dark;
What are they to it,
  Groping by its spark?

Castle-top and grange,
  Orchard, lane, and wood,
Human homes asleep,
  Precipice and flood,

What are they to it,
  Groping by its ray;
God hath given light,
  Light for all its way,

Light to know each step
  Of the toilsome ground;
Wherefore should it pry,
  Questioning, around? . .

In the night of time,
  Toiling through the dark,
Reason's feeble lamp
  Giveth out its spark.

Close about my path
  Hidden wonders lie,
Mysteries unseen,
  Shapes of destiny,

Beings of the air,
  Shadowless and weird,
Looking upon me,
  Uttering unheard,—

Sad and warning eyes
  Pleading from the past,
From the years to come
  Mournful glances cast,—

What are they to me,
  Toiling towards the day;
God hath given light,
  Light for all my way.

EXTRACT FROM "ABEL."

From these pure and happy places,
Outcast, striding forth alone;
Mournful eyes of all the ages
Turning backward to his own,

Striding forth alone, for ever,—
Burning brow, convulsive breath,
And the mark of God upon him,
Strange, mysterious mark of death.

Death,—relentless, stern intruder;
Never, in the years before,
Had its chill and pallid presence
Passed within life's iron door.

Death,—from out the pregnant future
Rise its tones of fear and pain,
Voices from the grave of Abel,
Echoes of the curse of Cain.

REST.

Rest?—there is no such thing;
A coward's baseless dream.
Time is a rushing flood,
And thou art in the stream.

Thou mayest fret and weep,
And turn upon thy side:
Remorseless currents hold
Thy being in their tide.

Rest?—Up and be a man;
Look out upon the night;
No star stands still in heaven,
In all thine aching sight. ....

Thy mind, a restless pool,
Where whirling eddies sweep
Hope's dreams and fancies round,
For ever, in its deep;

Thy frame, a battle-field,
Where every pulse and breath
Bring tidings from the ground,
Where life is meeting death.

Rest?—chafe no more in vain;
On, lest thy peers go by;
Thou wouldst not if thou couldst,
Evade thy destiny.

Insatiate nature craves
Some fuel for its fire,
Food for the appetite
Of unappeased desire.

Think what a helpless clog
These limbs of thine would be,
If motion never stirred
Their passive lethargy.

Think what a weary world,
Were all life's duties done,
And knowledge but a goal,
That was already won;

If this unquiet thought
Had roamed its region through,
And paused beyond the bourne,
With nothing else to do. ....

Around thee and above,
Within thee and apart,
Are countless goads and spurs
To rouse thy flagging heart. ....

Ambition, fear and love,
Pride, envy, discontents,
Those ministers of change,
Life's countless stimulants.

Ferment for evermore,
Within this passive form,
Unwearying as the wave,
That rolls in calm and storm. ..

Resistance,—pregnant law,
That all thy life attends,
And, in a hostile guise,
Leads action to its ends; ....

In thought's thin atmosphere,
Unhood thy fluttering soul;
Resistance bears it up,
And speeds it to its goal.

As thou hast seen a torch
Burn with a clearer glow,
When flung far up aloft,
Where fresher breezes blow;

So does my spirit burn,
Brighter, and yet more bright,
As higher currents meet,
And fan it in its flight.

Then onward in thy course;
When doubt obscures the way,
Trim better lamps, to light
Thy spirit to its day. ....

Want, sickness, danger, fear,
Are ever at thy hand,
To bring new forces out,
And train them to command.

Thou art not all a man,
Till thou hast known them all,
Till thou hast stood and faced
Whatever may appal.

Cui bono?—faithless words;
It is enough for thee,
To know that toil expands
Thy weak capacity. ....

Live one step further on,
And know that thou art, here,
A chrysalis, whose wings
Grow for another sphere;

That knowledge, being, power,
Are onward, infinite,
And every effort, now,
A progress in thy flight;

And see if thou, but one
Of all this race of men,
Can'st look around and ask
That faithless question then.

No! onward,—ever on;
Time's earnest moments roll;
Leave rest to sickly dreams,
Cui bono? to the fool.

Know this, for thee, the whole,
If thou canst comprehend,
Toil and Development
Are way, reward, and end.

FREDERIC S. COZZENS.

[Born 1818. Died 1869.]

The writer of the pleasant magazine papers under the signature of "Richard Haywarde" was born in New York in the year 1818. Richard Haywarde was the name of his father's maternal grandfather. He was born in Hampshire in England in 1693, and was one of the earlier Moravian missionaries to America. In 1740 he entertained some of the Brethren, who had come from the old world, at his house in Newport. In a little pamphlet published in 1808, giving an account of the Moravian settlements in this country, he is referred to familiarly as "Old father Haywarde." Leonard Cozzens, his great grandfather in another line, came from Wiltshire, in England, and settled in Newport in 1743. His grandfather, immediately after the battle of Lexington, joined the Newport volunteers, commanded by Captain Sears, and fought at Bunker Hill. He was himself educated in the city of New York, and has always resided there. He has been a curious student of American literature, and in the winter of 1854 delivered a lecture upon this subject. His volume entitled "Prismatics," printed in 1853, consists mainly of articles previously published in the "Knickerbocker Magazine," to which he has been a frequent contributor for several years. His more recent work, the "Sparrowgrass Papers," appeared originally in "The Knickerbocker" and "Putnam's Monthly." He is an importer and dealer in wines, of which he has written some admirable essays, both in "Putnam's Monthly," and in a little periodical which he publishes himself, under the title of "The Wine Press." In a certain fresh and whimsical humor, and a refined and agreeable sentiment, expressed in prose or verse, Mr. Cozzens always pleases. He is indeed, a delightful essayist, in a domain quite his own, and his poetry has an easy flow, and a natural vein of wit and pathos which render his signature one of the most welcome that can meet the eye of the desultory reader.

A BABYLONISH DITTY.

More than several years have faded
Since my heart was first invaded
By a brown-skinned, gray-eyed siren
  On the merry old "South-side;"
Where the mill-flume cataracts glisten,
And the agile blue fish listen
To the fleet of phantom schooners,
  Floating on the weedy tide. ....

There, amid the sandy reaches,
In among the pines and beeches,
Oaks, and various other kinds of
  Old primeval forest trees,
Did we wander in the noon-light
Or beneath the silver moon-light,
While in ledges sighed the sedges,
  To the salt salubrious breeze.

Oh, I loved her as a sister,
Often, oftentimes, I kissed her,
Holding prest against my vest
  Her slender, soft, seductive hand;
Often by my midnight taper,
Filled at least a quire of paper
With some graphic ode or sapphic
  "To the nymph of Baby Land."

Oft we saw the dim blue highlands,
Coney, Oak, and other islands,
(Motes that dot the dimpled bosom
  Of the sunny summer sea,)
Or, mid polished leaves of lotus,
Wheresoe'er our skiff would float us,
Anywhere, where none could note us,
  There we sought alone to be.

Thus, till summer was senescent,
And the woods were iridescent,
Dolphin tints and hectic tints
  Of what was shortly coming on,
Did I worship Amy Milton;
Fragile was the faith I built on!—
Then we parted, broken hearted
  I, when she left Babylon.

As upon the moveless water,
Lies the motionless frigata,—
Flings her spars and spidery outlines,
  Lightly on the lucid plain,—
But whene'er the fresh breeze bloweth
To more distant oceans goeth,
Never more the old haunt knoweth,
  Never more returns again,—

So is woman, evanescent,
Shifting with the shifting present,
Changing like the changing tide,
  And faithless as the fickle sea;
Lighter than the wind-blown thistle,
Falser than the fowler's whistle,
Was that coaxing piece of hoaxing —
  Amy Milton's love for me.

. . . .

Yes, thou transitory bubble!
Floating on this sea of trouble,
Though the sky be bright above thee,
  Soon will sunny days be gone;
Then, when thou 'rt by all forsaken,
Will thy bankrupt heart awaken
To these golden days of olden
  Times in happy Babylon!

GEORGE H. COLTON.

[Born, 1818. Died, 1847.]

George H. Colton, the fifth of nine children of a Congregational clergyman who had emigrated to that place from Connecticut, was born in Westford, about twelve miles north of Cooperstown, among the mountains of Otsego county, in New York, on the twenty-fifth of October, 1818. When about three years of age he was removed with his father's family to Royalton, near Lockport, where he remained three years, and then was carried to a new home in Elba, in the county of Essex. In this early period he attended indifferent district schools, but his chief means of education was the library of his father, in which he lingered, with an insatiable love of reading, so that before the close of his twelfth year he had made himself familiar with a large portion of English classical literature.

In 1830 he was sent to New Haven to pursue his studies under an elder brother, the Rev. John O. Colton, then a tutor in Yale College, which he himself entered in 1836, and left, with the degree of bachelor of arts, and next the highest honors of his class, in the summer of 1840. He soon after opened a grammar school in Hartford, but found teaching a disagreeable occupation, and gave it up. He had indeed determined already to devote himself entirely to literature. While an undergraduate he had been a frequent contributor to the college magazine, and in his senior year had written the first canto of a long poem entitled "Tecumseh, or the West Thirty Years Since." This work he now resumed, and completed, with great rapidity, that it might possess on its publication all the advantages which could arise from the political eminence of one of its principal characters, General Harrison, who was at that time a candidate for the presidency. It was brought out in New York in the spring of 1842.

"Tecumseh" is a narrative poem, founded on the history of the celebrated chief whose name is chosen for its title, and whose efforts to unite the various divisions of the red race into one grand confederacy, to regain their lost inheritance, though unsuccessful, constitute the most striking and sublime episode in the aboriginal history of this country. The measure of the main part of the poem, which extends through nine long cantos, and nearly fourteen thousand lines, is octo-syllabic. The versification is free, and generally correct, though in some cases marred by inexcusable carelessness, and phraseology more tame and unmeaning than, had he kept his manuscript the Horatian period, the author would have permitted to go before the critics. There are scattered through the work many passages of minute and skilful description of external nature, and interwoven with the main story is one of love, resulting, like most tales of the kind, in the perfect felicity of the parties. Considered as the production of an author but twenty-three years of age, commenced while he was still in college, and finished soon after, under circumstances most unfavorable for poetical composition, it was generally praised, but it was not successful; it was read by few, and the first and only American edition was sold very slowly.

In the autumn of 1844 Mr. Colton issued in New York the first number of "The American Review, a Whig Journal of Politics, Literature, Art, and Science," and of this work, which was issued monthly from the commencement of the following year, he remained editor and proprietor until his death, which occurred after a long and painful illness, induced by too severe mental and physical labor, on the evening of the first of December, 1847.

Mr. Colton was an accurate scholar, and a very rapid and industrious writer. Besides numerous papers, in prose and verse, printed in his own magazine, he contributed frequently to other periodicals, and a few weeks before his death wrote to me that his poems had accumulated so fast that he should print a new volume, nearly as large as "Tecumseh," in which the leading and title-giving piece would be "The Forsaken"—the story of a young girl, nurtured in the forest, and abandoned by a stranger, from the city, who had won her heart—which he had published in the eleventh volume of the "Democratic Review." Nearly all his poems are diffuse, and they all needed the file; but though he saw their defects, he had no patience for revision, and probably they would never have been improved. A severer style, however, might have been attained by him if he had lived, and the harassing cares of his profession had permitted him in new compositions to attempt those excellences of execution which no one more readily appreciated or confessed to be of higher importance.

The distinguishing and most poetical element in Mr. Colton's character was an intense love of nature. This is evident from his poems, and was much more so from his demeanor and conversation. Beautiful scenery and the more remarkable phenomena of the seasons, produced in him frequently a species of intoxication. "I shall never do myself justice," he said, referring to a discourse which he had delivered on the Eloquence of the Indians, "until I can write in the woods, and by the untrodden shores of the lakes. Let me become rich enough for this, and you shall see what I was made for."

EXTRACTS FROM "TECUMSEH."

TECUMSEH AND THE PROPHET.

NEVER did eye a form behold
At once more finished, firm, and bold.
Of larger mould and loftier mien
Than oft in hall or bower is seen,
And with a browner hue than seems
To pale maid fair, or lights her dreams,
He yet revealed a symmetry
Had charmed the Grecian sculptor's eye,—
A massive brow, a kindled face,
Limbs chiseled to a faultless grace,
  Beauty and strength in every feature,
While in his eyes there lived the light
Of a great soul's transcendant might—
  Hereditary lord by nature!
As stood he there, the stern, unmoved,
Except his eagle glance that roved,
And darkly limned against the sky
Upon that mound so lone and high,
He looked the sculptured god of wars,
Great Odin, or Egyptian Mars,
By crafty hand, from dusky stone,
Immortal wrought in ages gone,
And on some silent desert cast,
Memorial of the mighty Past.
And yet, though firm, though proud his glance,
There was upon his countenance
That settled shade which, oft in life,
Mounts upward from the spirit's strife,
As if upon his soul there lay
Some grief which would not pass away.
  The other's lineaments and air
Revealed him plainly brother born
  Of him, who on that summit bare
So sad, yet proudly, met the morn:
But, lighter built, his slender frame
Far less of grace, as strength, could claim;
And, with an eye that, sharp and fierce,
Would seem the gazer's breast to pierce,
And lowering visage, all the while
Inwrought of subtlety and guile,
Whose every glance, that darkly stole,
Bespoke the crafty cruel soul.
There was from all his presence shed
A power—a chill mysterious dread—
Which made him of those beings seem,
That shake us in the midnight dream.
Yet were his features, too, o'ercast
With mournfulness, as if the past
Had been one vigil, painful, deep and long
Of hushed Revenge still brooding over wrong.
No word was said: but long they stood,
And side by side, in thoughtful mood,
Watched the great curtains of the mist
  Up from the mighty landscape move;
'T was surely spirit-hands, they wist,
  Did lift them from above.
And when, unveiled to them alone
The solitary world was shown,
And dew from all the mound's green sod
Rose, like an incense, up to God,
Reclined, yet silent still, they bent
Their eyes on heaven's deep firmament-
As if were open to their view
The stars' sun-flooded homes of blue;
Or gazed, with mournful sternness, o'er
The rolling prairie stretched before—
While round them, fluttering on the breeze,
The sere leaves fell from faded trees.

THE DEATH OF TECUMSEH.

FORTH at the peal each charger sped,
The hard earth shook beneath their tread
The dim woods, all around them spread,
  Shone with their armor's light:
Yet in those stern, still lines, assailed,
No eye-ball shrunk, no bosom quailed,
  No foot was turned for flight;
But, thundering as their foemen came,
Each rifle flashed its deadly flame.
A moment, then recoil and rout,
With reeling horse and struggling shout,
  Confused that onset fair;
But, rallying each dark steed once more,
Like billows borne the low reefs o'er,
  With foamy crests in air,
Right on and over them they bore,
With gun and bayonet thrust before,
  And swift swords brandish'd bare.
Then madly was the conflict waged,
Then terribly red Slaughter raged!
How still is yet yon dense morass
  The bloody sun below!
Where'er you chosen horsemen pass
There stirs no bough nor blade of grass,
  There moves no secret foe!...
Sudden from tree and thicket green,
From trunk and mound and bushy screen,
Sharp lightning flashed with instant sheen,
  A thousand death-bolts sung!
Like ripened fruit before the blast,
Rider and horse to earth were cast,
  Its miry roots among;
Then wild—as if that earth were riven,
And, pour'd beneath the cope of heaven,
All hell to upper air were given—
  One fearful whoop was rung....
Then loud the crash of arms arose,
As when two forest whirlwinds close;
Then filled all heaven their shout and yell,
As if the forests on them fell!
I see, where swells the thickest fight,
With sword and hatchet brandish'd brigh',
And rifles flashing sulphurous light
  Through green leaves gleaming red—
I see a plume, now near, now far,
Now high, now low, like falling star
Wide waving o'er the tide of war,
  Where'er the onslaught's led....
Above the struggling storm I hear
A lofty voice the war-bands cheer—
Still, as they quail with doubt or fear,
  Yet loud and louder given—
And, rallying to the clarion cry,
With club and red axe raging high,
  And sharp knives sheathing low,
Fast back again, confusedly,
  They drive the staggering foe.

A FOREST SCENE.

Within a wood extending wide
By Thames's steeply winding side,
There sat upon a fallen tree,
Grown green through ages silently,
An Indian girl. The gradual change
Making all things most sweetly strange,
Had come again. The autumn sun,
Half up his morning journey, shone
With conscious lustre, calm and still;
By dell, and plain, and sloping hill
Stood mute the faded trees, in grief,
As various as their clouded leaf.
With all the hues of sunset skies
Were stamp'd the maple's mourning dyes
In meeker sorrow in the vale
The gentle ash was drooping pale
Brown-seared the walnut raised its head
The oak displayed a lifeless red;
And grouping bass and white-wood hoar
Sadly their yellow honors bore;
And silvered birch and poplar rose
With foliage gray and weeping boughs;
But elm and stubborn beach retained
Some verdant lines, though crossed and sta ned,
And by the river's side were seen
Hazel and willow, palely green,
While in the woods, by bank and stream
And hollows shut from daylight gleam,
Where tall trees wept their freshening dews,
Each shrub preserved its summer hues.
Nor this alone. From branch and trunk
The withered wild-vines coldly shrunk,
The woodland fruits hung ripe or dry,
The leaf-strewn brook flowed voiceless by;
And all throughout, nor dim nor bright,
There lived a rare and wondrous light,
Wherein the colored leaves around
Fell noiselessly; nor any sound,
Save chattering squirrels on the trees,
Or dropping nuts, when stirred the breeze,
Might there be heard; and, floating high,
Were light clouds borne alone the sky,
And, scarcely seen, in heaven's deep blue
One solitary eagle flew.

TO THE NIGHT-WIND IN AUTUMN.

Whence art thou, spirit wind—
Soothing with thy low voice the ear of Night,
And breathing o'er the wakeful, pensive mind
An influence of pleased yet sad delight?

Thou tell'st not of thy birth,
O viewless wanderer from land to land:
But, gathering all the secrets of the earth,
Where'er, unseen, thy airy wings expand,

At this hushed, holy hour,
When time seems part of vast eternity,
Thou dost reveal them with a magic power,
Saddening the soul with thy weird minstrelsy.

All nature seems to hear—
The woods, the waters, and each silent star;
What, that can thus enchain their earnest ear,
Bring'st thou of untold tidings from afar?

Is it of new, fair lands,
Of fresh-lit worlds that in the welkin burn,
Do new oäses gem Zahara's sands,
Or the lost Pleiads to the skies return?

Nay! 't is a voice of grief,
Of grief subdued, but deepened through long years,
The soul of Sorrow, seeking not relief—
Still gathering bitter knowledge without tears.

For thou, since earth was young,
And rose green Eden, purpled with the morn,
Its solemn wastes, and homes of men among,
Circling all zones, thy mourning flight hast borne.

Empires have risen, in might,
And peopled cities through the outspread earth,
And thou hast passed them at the hour of night,
Hearing their sounds of revelry and mirth.

Again thou hast gone by—
City and empire were alike o'erthrown,
Temple and palace, fallen confusedly,
In marble ruin on the desert strown.

In time-long solitudes,
Grand gray old mountains pierced the silent air,
Fair rivers roll'd, and stretch'd untravers'd woods:
'T was joy to hope that they were changeless there.

Lo! as the ages passed,
Thou found'st them struck with alteration dire,
The streams new channel'd, forests headlong cast,
The crumbling mountains scathed with storm and fire.

Gone but a few short hours,—
Beauty and bloom beguiled thy wanderings,
And thou mad'st love unto the virgin flowers,
Sighing through green trees and by mossy springs.

Now, on the earth's cold bed,
Fallen and faded, waste their forms away,
And all around the withered leaves are shed,
Mementos mute of Nature's wide decay.

Vain is the breath of morn;
Vainly the night-dews on their couches weep;
In vain thou call'st them at thy soft return—
No more awaking from their gloomy sleep. . . .

Oh, hush! oh, hush! sweet wind!
Thou melancholy soul, be still, I pray,
Nor pierce this heart, so long to grief resigned,
With plainings for the loved but lifeless clay!

Ah! now by thee I hear
The earnest, gentle voices, as of old;
They speak in accents tremulously clear—
The young, the beautiful, the noble souled.

The beautiful, the young,
The form of light, the wise, the honored head—
Thou bring'st the music of a lyre unstrung!—
Oh cease! with tears I ask it—they are *dead*.

While mortal joys depart,
While loved ones lie beneath the grave's green sod,
May we not fail to hear, with trembling heart,
In thy low tone the "still small voice of God"

ARTHUR CLEVELAND COXE.

[Born, 1818.]

Mr. Coxe is the eldest son of the Reverend Samuel H. Coxe, D. D., of Brooklyn. He was born in Mendham, in New Jersey, on the tenth day of May, 1818. At ten years of age he was sent to a gymnasium at Pittsfield, in Massachusetts, and he completed his studies preparatory to entering the University of New York, under the private charge of Doctor Bush, author of "The Life of Mohammed," etc. While in the university he distinguished himself by his devotion to classic learning, and particularly by his acquaintance with the Greek poets. In his freshman year he delivered a poem before one of the undergraduates' societies, on "The Progress of Ambition," and in the same period produced many spirited metrical pieces, some of which appeared in the periodicals* of the time. In the autumn of 1837 he published his first volume, "Advent, a Mystery," a poem in the dramatic form, to which was prefixed the following dedication:

Father, as he of old who reap'd the field,
The first young sheaves to Him did dedicate
Whose bounty gave whate'er the glebe did yield,
Whose smile the pleasant harvest might create—
So I to thee these numbers consecrate,
Thou who didst lead to Silo's pearly spring;
And if of hours well saved from revels late
And youthful riot, I these fruits do bring,
Accept my early vow, nor frown on what I sing.

This work was followed in the spring of 1838 by "Athwold, a Romaunt;" and in the summer of the same year were printed the first and second cantos of "Saint Jonathan, the Lay of a Scald." These were intended as introductory to a novel in the stanza of "Don Juan," and four other cantos were afterward written, but wisely destroyed by the author on his becoming a candidate for holy orders, an event not contemplated in his previous studies. He was graduated in July, and on the occasion delivered an eloquent valedictory oration.

From this period his poems assumed a devotional cast, and were usually published in the periodicals of the church. His "Athanasion" was pronounced before the alumni of Washington College, in Connecticut, in the summer of 1840. It is an irregular ode, and contains passages of considerable merit, but its sectarian character will prevent its receiving general applause. The following allusion to Bishop Berkeley is from this poem:

Oft when the eve-star, sinking into day,
Seems empire's planet on its westward way,
Comes, in soft light from antique window's groin,
Thy pure Ideal, mitred saint of Cloyne!
Taught, from sweet childhood, to revere in thee
Earth's every virtue, writ in poesie,
Nigh did I leap, on Clio's calmer line,
To see thy story with our own entwine.
On Yale's full walls, no pictured shape to me
Like Berkeley's seem'd, in priestly dignity,
Such as he stood, fatiguing, year by year,
In our behoof, dull prince and cavalier;
And dauntless still, as erst the Genoese;
Such as he wander'd o'er the Indy seas
To vex'd Bermoothes, witless that he went
Mid isles that beckon'd to a continent.
Such there he seem'd, the pure, the undefiled!
And meet the record! Though, perchance, I smile,
That those, in him, themselves will glorify,
Who reap his fields, but let his doctrine die,
Yet, let him stand: the world will note it well,
And Time shall thank them for the chronicle
By such confess'd, Columbus of new homes
For song, and Science with her thousand tomes.
Yes—pure apostle of our western lore,
Spoke the full heart, that now may breathe it more;
Still in those halls, where none without a sneer
Name the dear title of thy ghostly fear,
Stand up, bold bishop—in thy priestly vest;
Proof that the Church bore letters to the West!

In the autumn of the same year appeared Mr. Coxe's "Christian Ballads," a collection of religious poems, of which the greater number had previously been given to the public through the columns of "The Churchman." They are elegant, yet fervent expressions of the author's love for the impressive and venerable customs, ceremonies, and rites of the Protestant Episcopal Church.

While in the university, Mr. Coxe had, besides acquiring the customary intimacy with ancient literature, learned the Italian language; and he now, under Professor Nordheimer, devoted two years to the study of the Hebrew and the German. After passing some time in the Divinity School at Chelsea, he was admitted to deacon's orders, by the Bishop of New York, on the twenty-eighth of June, 1841. In the following July, on receiving the degree of Master of Arts from the University, he pronounced the closing oration, by appointment of the faculty; and in August he accepted a call to the rectorship of Saint Anne's church, then recently erected by Mr. Gouverneur Morris, on his domain of Morrisiana. He was married the same year to his third cousin, Miss Catherine Cleveland, daughter of Mr. Simeon Hyde.

Mr. Coxe was several years rector of St. John's Church, in Hartford; in 1851 he visited Europe, and in 1854 became minister of Grace Church, in Baltimore. He has published, besides the works already mentioned, in verse, "Saul, a Mystery," and "Halloween;" and in prose, "Sympathies of the Continent," "Impressions of England," "Sermons," and, from the French of the Abbe Laborde, "The New Dogma of Rome."

* Among them "The Blues" and "The Hebrew Muse," in "The American Monthly Magazine."

MANHOOD.

Boyhood hath gone, or ever I was 'ware:
Gone like the birds that have sung out their season,
And fly away, but never to return:
Gone—like the memory of a fairy vision;
Gone—like the stars that have burnt out in heaven:
Like flowers that open once a hundred years,
And have just folded up their golden petals:
Like maidenhood, to one no more a virgin;
Like all that's bright, and beautiful, and transient,
And yet, in its surpassing loveliness,
And quick dispersion into empty nothing,
Like its dear self alone, like life, like Boyhood.
Now, on the traversed scene I leave for ever,
Doth memory cast already her pale look,
And through the mellow light of by-gone summers,
Gaze, like the bride, that leaveth her home-valley,
And like the Patriarch, goes she knows not where.
She, with faint heart, upon the bounding hill-top
Turns her fair neck, one moment, unbeheld,
And through the sun-set, and her tearful eye,
Far as her father's dwelling, strains her sight,
To bless the roof-tree, and the lawn, and gardens,
Where romp her younger sisters, still at home.
I have just waken'd from a darling dream,
And fain would sleep once more. I have been roving
In a sweet isle, and thither would return.
I have just come, methinks, from Fairyland,
And yearn to see Mab's kingdom once again,
And roam its landscapes with her! Ah, my soul,
Thy holiday is over—play-time gone,
And a stern Master bids thee to thy task.
How shall I ever go through this rough world!
How find me older every setting sun;
How merge my boyish heart in manliness;
How take my part upon the tricksy stage,
And wear a mask to seem what I am not!
Ah me—but I forgot; the mimicry
Will not be long, ere all that I had feign'd,
Will be so real, that my mask will fall,
And Age act Self, uncostumed for the play.
Now my first step I take, adown the valley,
But ere I reach the foot, my pace must change;
And I toil on, as man has ever done,
Treading the causeway, smooth with endless travel,
Since first the giants of old Time descended,
And Adam leading down our mother Eve,
In ages elder than Antiquity.
This voice, so buoyant, must be all unstrung,
Like harps, that chord by chord grow musicless;
These hands must totter on a smooth-topp'd staff,
That late could whirl the ball-club vigorously:
This eye grow glassy, that can sparkle now,
And on the dear Earth's hues look doatingly:
And these brown locks, which tender hands have twined
In loving curls about their taper-fingers,
Must silver soon, and bear about such snows,
As freeze away all touch of tenderness.
And then, the end of every human story
Is ever this, whatever its beginning,
To wear the robes of being—in their rags;
To bear, like the old Tuscan's prisoners,
A corpse still with us, insupportable;
And then to sink in Earth, like dust to dust.
And hearse for ever from the gaze of men,
What long they thought—now dare to call—our relics!
Glory to him who doth subject the same,
In hope of Immortality! . . . .
I go from strength to strength, from joy to joy;
From being unto being! I will snatch
This germ of comfort from departing youth;
And when the pictured primer's thrown aside,
I'll hoard its early lessons in my heart.
I shall go on through all Eternity;
Thank God! I only am an embryo still;
The small beginning of a glorious soul;
An atom that shall fill Immensity;
The bell hath toll'd! my birth-hour is upon me!
The hour that made me child, has made me man,
And bids me put all childish things away.
Keep me from evil, that it may not grieve me!
And grant me, Lord, with this, the Psalmist's prayer,
Remember not the follies of my youth,
But in thy mercy, think upon me, Lord!

OLD CHURCHES.

Hast been where the full-blossom'd bay-tree is blowing,
With odours like Eden's around?
Hast seen where the broad-leaved palmetto is growing,
And wild vines are fringing the ground?
Hast sat in the shade of catalpas, at noon,
And ate the cool gourds of their clime;
Or slept where magnolias were screening the moon,
And the mocking-bird sung her sweet rhyme?

And didst mark, in thy journey, at dew-dropping eve
Some ruin peer high o'er thy way,
With rooks wheeling round it, and bushes to weave
A mantle for turrets so gray?
Did ye ask if some lord of the cavalier kind
Lived there, when the country was young?
And burn'd not the blood of a Christian, to find
How there the old prayer-bell had rung?

And did ye not glow, when they told ye—the Lord
Had dwelt in that thistle-grown pile;
And that bones of old Christians were under its sward,
That once had knelt down in its aisle?
And had ye no tear-drops your blushes to steep
When ye thought—o'er your country so broad,
The bard seeks in vain for a mouldering heap,
Save only these churches of God!

O ye that shall pass by those ruins agen,
Go kneel in their alleys and pray,
And not till their arches have echoed amen,
Rise up, and fare on in your way;
Pray God that those aisles may be crowded once more,
Those altars surrounded and spread,
While anthems and prayers are upsent as of yore,
As they take of the wine-cup and bread.

Ay, pray on thy knees, that each old rural fane
They have left to the bat and the mole,
May sound with the loud-pealing organ again,
And the full swelling voice of the soul.
Peradventure, when next thou shalt journey thereby,
Even-bells shall ring out on the air,
And the dim-lighted windows reveal to thine eye
The snowy-robed pastor at prayer.

THE HEART'S SONG.

In the silent midnight watches,
List—thy bosom-door!
How it knocketh, knocketh, knocketh,
Knocketh evermore!
Say not 'tis thy pulse's beating;
'Tis thy heart of sin:
'Tis thy Saviour knocks, and crieth
Rise, and let me in!

Death comes down with reckless footstep
To the hall and hut:
Think you Death will stand a-knocking
Where the door is shut?
Jesus waiteth—waiteth—waiteth;
But thy door is fast!
Grieved, away thy Saviour goeth:
Death breaks in at last.

Then 'tis thine to stand—entreating
Christ to let thee in:
At the gate of heaven beating,
Wailing for thy sin.
Nay, alas! thou foolish virgin,
Hast thou then forgot,
Jesus waited long to know thee,
But he knows thee not!

THE CHIMES OF ENGLAND.

The chimes, the chimes of Motherland,
Of England green and old,
That out from fane and ivied tower
A thousand years have toll'd;
How glorious must their music be
As breaks the hallow'd day,
And calleth with a seraph's voice
A nation up to pray!

Those chimes that tell a thousand tales,
Sweet tales of olden time!
And ring a thousand memories
At vesper, and at prime;
At bridal and at burial,
For cottager and king—
Those chimes—those glorious Christian chimes,
How blessedly they ring!

Those chimes, those chimes of Motherland,
Upon a Christmas morn,
Outbreaking, as the angels did,
For a Redeemer born;
How merrily they call afar,
To cot and baron's hall,
With holly deck'd and mistletoe,
To keep the festival!

The chimes of England, how they peal
From tower and gothic pile,
Where hymn and swelling anthem fill
The dim cathedral aisle;
Where windows bathe the holy light
On priestly heads that falls,
And stain the florid tracery
And banner-dighted walls!

And then, those Easter bells, in spring!
Those glorious Easter chimes;
How loyally they hail thee round,
Old queen of holy times!
From hill to hill, like sentinels,
Responsively they cry,
And sing the rising of the Lord,
From vale to mountain high.

I love ye—chimes of Motherland,
With all this soul of mine,
And bless the Lord that I am sprung
Of good old English line!
And like a son I sing the lay
That England's glory tells;
For she is lovely to the Lord,
For you, ye Christian bells!

And heir of her ancestral fame,
And happy in my birth,
Thee, too, I love, my forest-land,
The joy of all the earth;
For thine thy mother's voice shall be,
And here—where God is king,
With English chimes, from Christian spires,
The wilderness shall ring.

MARCH.

March—march—march!
Making sounds as they tread,
Ho-ho! how they step,
Going down to the dead!
Every stride, every tramp,
Every footfall is nearer;
And dimmer each lamp,
As darkness grows drearer;
But ho! how they march,
Making sounds as they tread;
Ho-ho! how they step,
Going down to the dead!

March—march—march!
Making sounds as they tread,
Ho-ho, how they laugh,
Going down to the dead!
How they whirl—how they trip,
How they smile, how they dally,
How blithesome they skip,
Going down to the valley;
Oh-ho, how they march,
Making sounds as they tread;
Ho-ho, how they skip,
Going down to the dead!

March—march—march!
Earth groans as they tread!
Each carries a skull;
Going down to the dead!
Every stride—every stamp,
Every footfall is bolder;
'Tis a skeleton's tramp,
With a skull on his shoulder!
But ho, how he steps
With a high-tossing head,
That clay-cover'd bone,
Going down to the dead!

WILLIAM W. LORD.

[Born about 1818.]

Mr. Lord is a native of Western New York, and is descended through both his parents from the New England Puritans. His father was a Presbyterian clergyman, and his mother, who now resides with her eldest son, the Rev. Dr. Lord of Buffalo, is a woman of refinement and cultivation. He had therefore the advantages of a good domestic training. He exhibited at a very early age a love of letters, and soon became familiar with Shakspeare and the other great writers of the Elizabethan age, and probably few men are now more familiar with English literature in all its departments. During his college life his health failed, and his friends, yielding to a desire for a sea voyage, committed him to the care of the master of a whale ship, owned by a family friend at New London. After being a few weeks at sea he grew weary of the monotony of a cabin passage, and, against the remonstrances of the captain, forced his way into the forecastle, where he soon became a sturdy seaman, and, during four years of service in the Pacific, endured all the hardships, privations and perils of that adventurous life, exhibiting on every occasion the boldest traits of character. On returning home he resolved to devote his time to the study of moral science, and with this view, in 1841, entered the theological school at Auburn; but the death of the Rev. Dr. Richards, president of that institution, occurring in 1843, he joined the senior class of the Princeton Theological Seminary, in which he completed his course of study, with much credit, early in the following year. He subsequently took orders in the Protestant Episcopal Church, and is now (1855) rector of an Episcopal Church in Vicksburg, Mississippi.

In 1845, Mr. Lord published his first volume of poems. They were all written the preceding year, and have marks of haste and carelessness, but such proofs of poetical taste and power as won praise from judicious critics. In 1851 appeared his "Christ in Hades," a poem of eight books, in blank verse, written with finished elegance, sustained elevation, and much original force. Its express character is indicated by its title. The pervading tone of his poetry is that of reverent meditation, but some of his shorter pieces are in a vein of graceful playfulness. He has been a laborious and successful student; is familiar with the ancient languages and literatures; has been a diligent reader of the best German writers; and has cultivated an acquaintance with the arts of design. Philosophy is his favourite study, however, and Coleridge and Wordsworth are his most familiar authors.

KEATS.*

Oh gold Hyperion, love-lorn Porphyro,
Ill-fated! from thine orb'd fire struck back
Just as the parting clouds began to glow,
And stars, like sparks, to bicker in thy track!
Alas! throw down, throw down, ye mighty dead,
The leaves of oak and asphodel
That ye were weaving for that honour'd head,—
In vain, in vain, your lips would seek a spell
In the few charmed words the poet sung,
To lure him upward in your seats to dwell,—
As vain your grief! O! why should one so young
Sit crown'd midst hoary heads with wreaths divine?
Though to his lips Hymettus' bees had clung,
His lips shall never taste the immortal wine,
Who sought to drain the glowing cup too soon,
For he hath perish'd, and the moon
Hath lost Endymion—but too well
The shaft that pierced him in her arms was sped:—
Into that gulf of dark and nameless dread,
Star-like he fell, but a wide splendour shed
Through its deep night, that kindled as he fell.

* From "An Ode to England."

TO MY SISTER.

And shall we meet in heaven, and know and love?
Do human feelings in that world above
Unchanged survive? blest thought! but ah, I fear
That thou, dear sister, in some other sphere,
Distant from mine, will find a brighter home,
Where I, unworthy found, may never come,
Or be so high above me glorified,
That I, a meaner angel, undescried,
Seeking thine eyes, such love alone shall see
As angels give to all bestowed on me;
And when my voice upon thy ear shall fall,
Hear only such reply as angels give to all.

Forgive me, sister, O forgive the love
Whose selfishness would reach the life above,
And even in heaven do its object wrong—
But should I see thee in the heavenly throng,
Bright as the star I love—the night's first star,
If, like that star, thou still must shine afar,
And in thy glory I must never see
A woman's, sister's look of love from thee,
Must never call thee by a sister's name,
I could but wish thee less, if thus, the same,
My sister still, dear Sarah! thou might'st be,
And I thy brother still, in that blest company

THE BROOK.

A little blind girl wandering,
While daylight pales beneath the moon,
And with a brook meandering,
To hear its gentle tune.

The little blind girl by the brook,
It told her something—you might guess,
To see her smile, to see her look
Of listening eagerness.

Though blind, a never silent guide
Flow'd with her timid feet along;
And down she wander'd by its side
To hear the running song.

And sometimes it was soft and low,
A creeping music in the ground;
And then, if something check'd its flow,
A gurgling swell of sound.

And now, upon the other side,
She seeks her mother's cot;
And still the noise shall be her guide,
And lead her to the spot.

For to the blind, so little free
To move about beneath the sun,
Small things like this seem liberty—
Something from darkness won.

But soon she heard a meeting stream,
And on the bank she follow'd still,
It murmur'd on, nor could she tell
It was another rill.

Ah! whither, whither, my little maid?
And wherefore dost thou wander here?
I seek my mother's cot, she said,
And surely it is near.

There is no cot upon this brook,
In yonder mountains dark and drear,
Where sinks the sun, its source it took,
Ah, wherefore art thou here?

Oh! sir, thou art not true nor kind,
It is the brook, I know its sound;
Ah! why would you deceive the blind?
I hear it in the ground.

And on she stepp'd, but grew more sad,
And weary were her tender feet,
The brook's small voice seem'd not so glad,
Its song was not so sweet.

Ah! whither, whither, my little maid?
And wherefore dost thou wander here?
I seek my mother's cot she said,
And surely it is near.

There is no cot upon this brook;
I hear its sound, the maid replied,
With dreamlike and bewilder'd look—
I have not left its side.

O go with me, the darkness nears,
The first pale star begins to gleam;
The maid replied with bursting tears,
It is the stream! It is the stream!

A RIME,

WHICH IS YET REASON, AND TEACHETH, IN A LIGHT MANNER, A GRAVE MATTER IN THE LERE OF LOVE.

As Love sat idling beneath a tree,
A Knight rode by on his charger free,
Stalwart and fair and tall was he,
With his plume and his mantle, a sight to see
And proud of his scars, right loftily,
He cried, Young boy, will you go with me?
But Love he pouted and shook his head,
And along fared the Warrior, ill-bested
Love is not won by chivalry.

Then came a Minstrel bright of blee,
Blue were his eyes as the heavens be,
And sweet as a song-bird's throat sung he
Of smiles and tears and ladie's eé,
Soft love and glorious chivalry,
Then cried, Sweet boy, will you go with me
Love wept and smiled, but shook his head,
And along fared the Minstrel ill-bested:
Love is not won by minstrelsy.

Then came a Bookman, wise as three,
Darker a scholar you shall not see
In Jewrie, Rome, or Araby,
But list, fair dames, what I rede to ye,
In love's sweet lere untaught was he,
For when he cried, Come, love, with me,
Tired of the parle he was nodding his head,
And along fared the Scholar ill-bested:
Love is not won by pedantry.

Then came a Courtier wearing the key
Of council and chambers high privity;
He could dispute yet seem to agree,
And soft as dew was his flatterie.
And with honied voice and low congee
Fair youth, he said, will you honour me?
In courteous wise Love shook his head,
And along fared the Courtier ill-bested:
Love is not won by courtesy.

Then came a Miser blinking his eé,
To view the bright boy beneath the tree;
His purse, which hung to his cringing knee,
The ransom held of a king's countreé;
And a handful of jewels and gold showed he,
And cried, Sweet child, will you go with me?
Then loud laugh'd Love as he shook his head
And along fared the Monger ill-bested:
Love is not won by merchandry.

O then to young Love beneath the tree,
Came one as young and as fair as he,
And as like to him as like can be,
And clapping his little wings for glee,
With nods and smiles and kisses free,
He whisper'd, Come, Oh come with me:
Love pouted and flouted and shook his head,
But along with that winsome youth he sped,
And love wins love, loud shouted he!

GEORGE W. DEWEY.

[Born, 1818.]

Mr. Dewey (whose father was a painter, from Westfield, in Massachusetts) was born in Baltimore, in 1818, and from an early age has resided in Philadelphia, to the journals and literary miscellanies of which city he has been a frequent contributor for several years. His numerous poems have a natural grace and tenderness which belong to the most genuine expressions of social feeling.

There is no published collection of Mr. Dewey's poems, or of his prose writings, which consist of moral essays, reviews, etc.

THE RUSTIC SHRINE.

"Their names were found cut upon a rural bench, overgrown with vines, which proved to be at once Love's shrine and cenotaph."—Legends of the Rhine.

A shadow of the cypress-bough
  Lies on my path to-day;
A melancholy—which in vain
  I strive to chase away.

The angel Memory hath flown
  To old and cherish'd things,
To bring the light of early years
  Around me on her wings:

And where the lovelorn birds complain
  Within their green abode,
Between two elms, a rustic seat
  Invites her from the road.

There shall she sit, as oft before,
  And sigh as oft again,
O'er names engraved, which long have braved
  The sunshine and the rain.

And one—it is the dearest name
  On Love's unnumber'd shrines—
So dear, that even envious Time
  Hath guarded it with vines;

And wreathed it with his choicest flowers,
  As if the bridal claim,
Which Fate denied unto her brow,
  Should still adorn her name!

Ah, well do I remember yet
  The day I carved that name!
The rattle of the locusts' drum
  Thrills o'er me now the same:

Adown the lane the wayward breeze
  Comes with a stealthy pace,
And brings the perfume of the fields
  To this deserted place.

Unto her blushing cheek again
  It comes—the blessed air!
Caressing, like a lover's hand,
  The tresses of her hair.

The brook runs laughing at her feet,
  O'erhead the wild-bird sings;
The air is fill'd with butterflies,
  As though the flowers had wings.

But this is Fancy's pilgrimage,
  And lures me back in vain!
The brook, the bench, the flowers, and vines
  I ne'er may see again:

For this is but an idle dream,
  That mocks me evermore—
And memory only fills the place
  The loved one fill'd of yore!

BLIND LOUISE.

She knew that she was growing blind—
  Foresaw the dreary night
That soon would fall, without a star,
  Upon her fading sight:

Yet never did she make complaint,
  But pray'd each day might bring
A beauty to her waning eyes—
  The loveliness of Spring!

She dreaded that eclipse which might
  Perpetually enclose
Sad memories of a leafless world—
  A spectral realm of snows.

She'd rather that the verdure left
  An evergreen to shine
Within her heart, as summer leaves
  Its memory on the pine.

She had her wish: for when the sun
  O'erhung his eastern towers,
And shed his benediction on
  A world of May-time flowers—

We found her seated, as of old,
  In her accustom'd place,
A midnight in her sightless eyes,
  And morn upon her face!

A MEMORY.

It was a bright October day—
  Ah, well do I remember!
One rose yet bore the bloom of May,
  Down toward the dark December

One rose that near the lattice grew,
  With fragrance floating round it;
Incarnardined, it blooms anew
  In dreams of her who found it.

Pale, wither'd rose, bereft and shorn
Of all thy primal glory,
All leafless now, thy piercing thorn
Reveals a sadder story.

It was a dreary winter day,
Too well do I remember!
They bore her frozen form away,
And gave her to December!

There were no perfumes on the air,
No bridal blossoms round her,
Save one pale lily in her hair
To tell how pure Death found her.

The thistle on the summer air
Hath shed its iris glory,
And thrice the willows weeping there
Have told the seasons' story,

Since she, who bore the blush of May,
Down toward the dark December
Pass'd like the thorn-tree's bloom away,
A pale, reluctant ember.

A BLIGHTED MAY.

Call not this the month of roses—
There are none to bud and bloom;
Morning light, alas! discloses
But the winter of the tomb.
All that should have deck'd a bridal
Rest upon the bier—how idle!
Dying in their own perfume.

Every bower is now forsaken—
There's no bird to charm the air!
From the bough of youth is shaken
Every hope that blossom'd there;
And my soul doth now enrobe her
In the leaves of sere October
Under branches swaying bare.

When the midnight falls beside me,
Like the gloom which in me lies,
To the stars my feelings guide me,
Seeking there thy sainted eyes;
Stars whose rays seem ever bringing
Down the soothing air, the singing
Of thy soul in paradise.

Oh that I might stand and listen
To that music ending never,
While those tranquil stars should glisten
On my life's o'erfrozen river,
Standing thus, forever seeming
Lost in what the world calls dreaming,
Dreaming, love, of thee, forever!

TO AN OLD ACQUAINTANCE.

Oh say, does the cottage yet peer from the shadow
Of ancestral elms on the side of the hill?—
Its doorway of woodbine, that look'd to the meadow,
And welcomed the sun as a guest on the sill;
The April-winged martin, with garrulous laughter,
Is he there where the mosses were thatching the eave!
And the dear little wren that crept under the rafter,
The earliest to come, and the latest to leave!
Oh say, is the hawthorn the hedgerow perfuming
Adown the old lane? are the willows still there,
Where briery thickets in springtime were blooming,
And breathing their life on the odorous air?
And runs yet the brook where the violets were weeping,
Where the white lily sat like a swan of the stream,
While under the laurel the shepherd-boy sleeping,
Saw only the glory of life in his dream!
Hath the reaper been there with his sickle relentless,
The stern reaper Death in the harvest of life!
Hath his foot crush'd the blossoms, till wither'd and scentless
They lay ere the frosts of the autumn were rife?
Ah yes, I can hear the sad villagers hymning
A requiem that swells from my heart on my ear,
And a gathering shadow of sorrow is dimming
Those scenes that must ever arise with a tear.

THE SHADY SIDE.

I sat and gazed upon thee, Rose,
Across the pebbled way,
And thought the very wealth of mirth
Was thine that winter day;
For, while I saw the truant rays
Within thy window glide,
Remember'd beams reflected came
Upon the shady side.

I sat and gazed upon thee, Rose,
And thought the transient beams
Were leaving on thy braided brow
The trace of golden dreams;
Those dreams, which like the ferry-barge
On youth's beguiling tide,
Will leave us when we reach old age,
Upon the shady side.

Ah! yes, methought while thus I gazed
Across the noisy way,
The stream of life between us flow'd
That cheerful winter day;
And that the bark whereon I cross'd
The river's rapid tide,
Had left me in the quietness
Upon the shady side.

Then somewhat of a sorrow, Rose,
Came crowding on my heart,
Revealing how that current sweeps
The fondest ones apart;
But while you stood to bless me there,
In beauty, like a bride,
I felt my own contentedness,
Though on the shady side.

The crowd and noise divide us, Rose,
But there will come a day
When you, with light and timid feet,
Must cross the busy way;
And when you sit, as I do now,
To happy thoughts allied,
May some bright angel shed her light
Upon the shady side!

WILLIAM WALLACE.

(Born, 1819.)

Mr. Wallace, the son of an eminent Presbyterian clergyman, who died during his childhood, was born in Lexington, Kentucky, in 1819. He received his general education at the Bloomington and South Hanover colleges in Indiana, and afterward studied the law, in his native city. When about twenty-two years of age, having already acquired considerable reputation in literature, by various contributions to western and southern journals, he came to the Atlantic states, and with the exception of a few months passed in Philadelphia, and a year and a half in Europe, he has since resided in New York, occupied in the practice of his profession and in the pursuits of literature.

The poetical compositions of Mr. Wallace are numerous, and they are for the most part distinguished for a sensuous richness of style, earnestness of temper, and much freedom of speculation. The longest of them is "Alban," a romance of New York, published in 1848, and intended to illustrate the influence of certain prejudices of society and principles of law upon individual character and destiny. This was followed in 1851 by the collection of his writings entitled "Meditations in America, and other Poems." The author is most at home in the serious and stately rhythm and solemn fancies of such pieces as "To the Hudson," which are the best measures of his powers.

REST.

The nation hath gone mad with action now.
Oh, many-troubled giant, with a heated brow,
And sultry heart, within whose wide
And lofty chambers stalketh Pride,
And hungry, pale Ambition, scenting power,
Wilt thou not let the wearied river steal
Through quiet hills for one short hour,
And dream, unvexèd by the eager keel,
Of that sweet peace he knew in times of old,
When only Nature sat near him and roll'd
Her simple songs amid her flowery fold?
And let the forest lift some unshorn plumes
Amid the ancient glooms:
For this it pleads with trembling hands,
Appealing to far Heaven from all the invading bands!
And leave the mountains for a time untrod—
And thou shalt see
Their dumb, gray lips yet struggling to be free,
So that they may shout backward to the sea—
"We also know and reverence our God."
Oh, Titan, of the eagle-eye and growing pain!
Wilt thou not rest on Alabama's plain?
O'er Huron lean and let his mirror show,
Unruffled by thy fiery feet,
That harmonies of light yet fall below—
That Heaven and Earth may meet:
Sleep, sleep, thou wide-brow'd power,
In Florida's magnolian bower,
And where New England's pilgrim-feet were prest,
Or by Ohio's softly wandering wave;
Or in the dusk halls of Kentucky's cave,
Or on the flowery and broad prairies rest
Of Illinois and Indiana,—slumber, in the west!
Your eagles took their lordly ease
On folded wing,
After disporting with the braggart Breeze,
And Thunder, watching by his cloudy spring
Whose cool stream tumbled to the thirsty seas.
The birds went all asleep on their high rocks,
Nor ruffled a feather in the rude fire-shocks.
Millions, a lesson ye can learn from these.
And see, the great woods slumber, and the lake
No longer is awake
Beneath the stars, that nod and start with sleep
In their white-clouded deep:
Fitfully the moon goes nodding through
The valleys of the vapory blue,
And dreams, forgetting all her queenly ills,
Of angels sleeping on Elysian hills:
The drowsy lake,
So sweet is slumber, would not yet awake;
But—like an infant two years old,
Before whose closèd eyes
Dreamily move the boys of paradise,
Singing their little psalms
Under the stately palms—
It stirreth softly lest rough motion might
Put out the moon's delicious light.
So rest! and Rest shall slay your many woes.
Is motion godlike? godlike is repose—
A mountain-stillness, of majestic might,
Whose peaks are glorious with the quiet light
Of suns, when Day is at his close.
Nor deem that quiet must ignoble be.
Jove laboured lustily once in airy fields;
And over the cloudy lea
He planted many a budding shoot
Whose liberal nature daily, nightly, yields
A store of starry fruit:
His labour done, the weary god went back
Up the broad mountain-track
To his great house; there he did wile away
With lightest thought a well-won holyday,
And all the powers croon'd softly an old tune,
Wishing their sire might sleep
Through all the sultry noon
And cold blue night; and very soon
They heard the awful thunderer breathing low and deep.
And in the hush that dropp'd adown the spheres,
And in the quiet of the awe-struck space,
The worlds learn'd worship at the birth of years

They look'd upon their Lord's calm, kingly face,
And bade Religion come and kiss each starry place.
At least, I must have peace, afar from strife—
No motion save enough to leave me life.
And I shall lay me gently in a nook
Where a small bay the sluggish tide receives,
And, reading, hear some bland old poet's book
Shake delicate music from its mystic leaves,
While under drowsy clouds the dull waves go,
And echo softly back the melody in their flow.
Will ye not also lend your souls to Song?
Ye! of the land where Nature's noblest rhyme,
Niagara, sounds the myth of Time;
And where the Mississippi darkly goes
Amid the trembling woods,
Gloomily murmuring legends of the floods
That troubled space before the worlds arose......
Or sleep. Why lose its wondrous world?
Look on its valleys, on its mountains look,
And cloudy streams;
Behold the arabesque land of dreams!
The golden mists are lazily curl'd;
And see in yonder glen,
Beside a little brook
Mid sleeping flocks, some sleeping men:
And one, who tries to watch, for danger's sake,
Nods and winks,
And vainly hums a tune to keep awake,
And now beside his brethren slowly sinks.
Ah, sleep like him! why lose its world?
Now when the banners of the day are furl'd
And safely put away:
Now when a languid glory binds
The long dim chambers of the darkling west,
While far below yon azure river winds
Like a blue vein on sleeping Beauty's breast.....
Then, millions, rest or dream with me:
Let not the struggle thus forever be.
Not from the gold that wounded Earth reveals;
Not from your iron wheels
That vex the valleys with their thunder-peals;
Not from the oceans pallid with your wings;
Not from the power that labour brings—
The enduring grandeur of a nation springs.
The wealth may perish as a fleeting breath—
The banner'd armament may find a death
Deep in the hungry waters—and the crown
Of empire from your tall brows topple down:
But that which rains true glory o'er
The low or lofty, and the rich or poor,
Shall never die—
Daughter of Truth and Ideality,
Large Virtue towering on the throne of will!
The nations drink the heroic from her eye,
And march triumphing over every ill.
Therefore with Silence sometimes sit apart
From rude Turmoil, and dignify the heart:
And in that noble hour
All hates shall be forgotten, and sweet Love
Shall gently win us like a mild-eyed dove
That shames the storm to silence; and a power,
Unknown before, shall lap us in delight,
As troubled waves are soothed by starry night.
Then manhood shall forget the vengeful thought
In action's fierce volcano wrought;
The poor old man shall bow his snow-white head
To bless the past, forgiving all his wrongs;
And feel the breathing of his childhood's songs
Once more around him shed.
The weary slave shall rest upon the chain,
And woo to his shut eyes
The ardent aspect of his native skies—
The forms of wife and children once again
Watching for his return along the palmy plain......
Nor in repose a tentless desert fear—
The gardenless wide waste of a blank heart:
Full many a rich oasis there shall start
Between horizons to illume and cheer:
Time's misty Nile shall slowly wander through
The slumberous plain that never knoweth storms;
Eternity's calm pyramidal forms
Shall meet our dreamy view,
Duskily towering mid the hazy blue,
And freezing contemplation in the giddy air.
Then all the weary myriads resting there—
Quiet beneath the hollow sky
As shapes that in a pictured landscape lie—
Shall know that bliss, that perfect, heavenly bliss
Which falls as moonlight music on a scene like this.

WORDSWORTH.

Sunset is on the dial: and I know
My hands are feeble and my head is white
With many snows, and in my dim old eyes
Light plays the miser with a frugal care,
And soon the curtain drops. But still I know,
The soul in sceptred majesty of will
Leaves not the royal dais.
The ancient winds
Still chant around me all the solemn themes
I learn'd when young; and in the hollow flower
I hear the murmur left there by the bee;
And jubilant rivers laugh and clap their hands
Amid the leaning hills that nurse them there;
And far away I see the mountains lift
Their silent tops to heaven, like thoughts
Too vast for speech; and over all, the sun
Stands by his flaming altar, and beholds,
As he beheld through many centuries gone,
The holocausts of light roll up to Heaven;
And when the evening calls her starry flock,
I know that Mazzaroth will sit and sing
Within his azure house; and I shall hear
The inmost melody of every star,
And know the meaning of the mystic sea:
And in the deep delight their presence gives
I shall be calm, and nevermore complain
That still the play—a venerable play,
World-wide—of this humanity goes on,
Still dark the plot, the issues unperceived.
So, with all things thus filling every sense,
The soul in sceptred majesty of will,
Sits on her royal dais.
Then why should I
My office yield, and let the general hymn
Unheeded harmonize the jangling space?
By action only doth Creation hold
Her charter—and, that gone, the worlds are dead:

Nor is't in souls which would the noblest find,
To rest contentedly upon old wreaths.
I will not rest and unmelodious die;
But with my full wreath round these thin, white
hairs,
And rhythmic lips, and vision kindling up,
March through the silent halls, and bravely pass
Right on into the land that lies beyond,
Where he, my brother-bard,* whose spirit seem'd
A mystical bright moon, whose influence wrought
The dull earth's ocean of dim sleep to life
And spectral motion—that majestic bard,
Who went before, choiring his lofty hymn,
Watches my coming on the Aiden hills.
But what the burden of that latest song
Will be, as yet I know not—nor the rhythm
That shall go beating with her silver feet
The sounding aisles of thought: but this I hope—
A listening world will hear that latest lay,
And seat it near the fireside of its heart
Forevermore, and by the embers' light
Look fondly on its face, as men of old
Look'd on the faces of the angel guests
Who tarried sometimes in their pastoral homes—
As this last hymn, befitting well the time
And circumstance, shall wear a holiest smile,
And show the might, the loveliness of song,
For Poetry is enthroned by his own right.
I hear his cadences in every breeze;
I see his presence fill the dark-blue lake,
Like an old melody; and I know
He is a living and immortal power.
No matter where he lifts his natural voice,
All men shall crown him as a gentle god
Who, wandering through his heritage of earth,
Makes pleasant music in the lowly huts
Where poor men ply their rugged toil; who smiles
Within the mellow sunbeams, when they pain;
The swelling upland, where October sits,
Holding her hands to catch the dropping fruit;
Who stands upon the hazy mountain-top,
Beautiful as the light; who, solemn, chants
Full many a rune in every sunless hall
Down in the deep, deep sea, and sways all things,
The angel of the world; who soars at will
Into the ample air, and walks the storm;
Or waves his wand upon the solemn stars,
Orion and the Pleiades, and rules
Their people by a gentle law; or stands
Imperial in the large red sun, and charms
The sky until its glorious passion finds
A language in the thunder and the cloud,
And in the rainbow, chorusing all hues,
And in the splendour of the broad, bright moon
That builds her Venice in a sea of air.
Most haply I shall sing some simple words,
Rich with the wealth experience gives to Time—
An antique tale of beauty and of tears:
Or I may wander in my thought afar
Where men have built their homes in forests vast,
And see the Atlantic rest his weary feet
And lift his large blue eyes on other stars:
Or hear the sire of many waters† hoarse
With counting centuries, and rolling through
The dim magnificence of stately woods,
Whose huge trunks sentinel a thousand leagues
His deep libation to the waiting sea;
Then would I join the choral preludes swelling
Between the wondrous acts of that great play
Which Time is prompting in another sphere:
Or I may wander in my thought after
To ruins gray of columns overthrown,
And then lift up a song of tender grief
Amid the glorious temples crumbling there—
The beautiful records of a world which was,
Majestic types of what a world must be:
Or I may turn to themes that have no touch
Of sorrow in them, piloted by Joy,
And raise the burial-stone from shrouded years,
And hear the laugh of youth clear ringing out,
Or feel once more a sweet religious awe,
Such as I felt when floated holy chimes
In boyhood's ear, and such as stern men feel
When, passing by cathedral doors, they hear
A dim-remembered psalm roll softly out
And fill their eyes with tears, they know not why:
Then shall I sing of children blooming o'er
The desolate wide heath of life, like flowers
Which daring men had stolen from paradise,
When near its gate the wearied cherub slept
And dream'd of heaven. Or to some pastoral vale
Shall pass my trembling feet? There shall I pour
To Nature, loved in all her many moods,
A chant sublimely earnest. I shall tell
To all the tribes with what a stately step
She walks the silent wilderness of air,
Which always puts its starry foliage on
At her serene approach, or in her lap
Scatters its harvest-wealth of golden suns:
And many a brook shall murmur in my verse;
And many an ocean join his cloudy bass;
And many a mountain tower aloft, whereon
The black storm crouches, with his deep-red eyes
Glaring upon the valleys stretch'd below:
And many a green wood rock the small, bright birds
To musical sleep beneath the large, full moon;
And many a star shall lift on high her cup
Of luminous cold chrysolite—set in gold
Chased subtily over by angelic art—
To catch the odorous dews which seraphs drink
In their wide wanderings; and many a sun
Shall press the pale lips of the timorous morn
Couch'd in the bridal east: and over all
Will brood the visible presence of the ONE
To whom my life has been a solemn chant.
Then let the sunset fall and flush Life's dial!
No matter how the years may smite my frame,
And cast a piteous blank upon my eyes
That seek in vain the old accustomed stars
Which skies hold over blue Winandermere;
Be sure that I, a crownèd bard, will sing
Until within the murmuring bark of verse
My spirit bears majestically away,
Charming to golden hues the gulf of death—
Well knowing that upon my honour'd grave,
Beside the widow'd lakes that wail for me,
Haply the dust of four great worlds will fall
And mingle—thither brought by pilgrims' feet.

* COLERIDGE

† The Mississippi.

THE MOUNDS OF AMERICA.*

Come to the mounds of death with me. They stretch
From deep to deep, sad, venerable, vast,
Graves of gone empires—gone without a sigh,
Like clouds from heaven. They stretch'd from deep to deep
Before the Roman smote his mail'd hand
On the gold portals of the dreaming East;
Before the pleiad, in white trance of song,
Beyond her choir of stars went wandering.

The great old trees, rank'd on these hills of death,
Have melancholy hymns about all this;
And when the moon walks her inheritance
With slow, imperial pace, the trees look up
And chant in solemn cadence. Come and hear.

"O patient Moon! go not behind a cloud,
But listen to our words. We, too, are old,
Though not so old as thou. The ancient towns,
The cities throned far apart like queens,
The shadowy domes, the realms majestical,
Slept in thy younger beams. In every leaf
We hold their dust, a king in every trunk.
We, too, are very old: the wind that wails
In our broad branches, from swart Ethiop come
But now, wail'd in our branches long ago,
Then come from darken'd Calvary. The hills
Lean'd ghastly at the tale that wan wind told;
The streams crept shuddering through the dark;
The torrent of the North, from morn till eve,
On his steep ledge hung pausing; and o'er all
Such silence fell, we heard the conscious rills
Drip slowly in the caves of central earth.
So were the continents by His crown'd grief
And glory bound together, ere the hand
Of Albion tamed the far Atlantic: so
Have we, whose aspect faced that time, the right
Of language unto all, while memory holds.

"O patient Moon! go not behind a cloud,
But hear our words. We know that thou didst see
The whole that we would utter—thou that wert
A worship unto realms beyond the flood—
But we are very lonesome on these mounds,
And speech doth make the burden of sad thought
Endurable; while these, the people new,
That take our land, may haply learn from us
What wonder went before them; for no word
E'er came from thee, so beautiful, so lone,
Throned in thy still domain, superbly calm
And silent as a god.
Here empires rose and died;
Their very dust, beyond the Atlantic borne
In the pale navies of the charter'd wind,
Stains the white Alp. Here the proud city ranged
Spire after spire, like star ranged after star,
Along the dim empyrean, till the air
Went mad with splendour, and the dwellers cried,
'Our walls have married Time!'—Gone are the marts,
The insolent citadels, the fearful gates,
The glorious domes that rose like summer clouds;
Gone are their very names! The royal ghost
Cannot discern the old imperial haunts,
But goes about perplexed like a mist
Between a ruin and the awful stars.
Nations are laid beneath our feet. The bard
Who stood in Song's prevailing light, as stands
The apocalyptic angel in the sun,
And rain'd melodious fire on all the realms;
The prophet pale, who shudder'd in his gloom,
As the white cataract shudders in its mist;
The hero shattering an old kingdom down
With one clear trumpet's peal; the boy, the sage,
Subject and lord, the beautiful, the wise—
Gone, gone to nothingness.
"The years glide on,
The pitiless years; and all alike shall fail,
State after state rear'd by the solemn sea,
Or where the Hudson goes unchallenged past
The ancient warder of the Palisades,
Or where, rejoicing o'er the enormous cloud,
Beam the blue Alleganies—all shall fail:
The Ages chant their dirges on the peaks;
The palls are ready in the peopled vales;
And nations fill one common sepulchre.
Nor goes the Earth on her dark way alone.
Each star in yonder vault doth hold the dead
In its funereal deeps: Arcturus broods
Over vast sepulchres that had grown old
Before the Earth was made: the universe
Is but one mighty cemetery,
Rolling around its central, solemn sun.

"O patient Moon! go not behind a cloud,
But listen to our words. We, too, must die—
And thou!—the vassal stars shall fail to hear
Thy queenly voice over the azure fields
Calling at sunset. They shall fade. The Earth
Shall look, and miss their sweet, familiar eyes,
And crouching die beneath the feet of God.
Then come the glories, then the nobler times,
For which the Orbs travail'd in sorrow; then
The mystery shall be clear, the burden gone;
And surely men shall know why nations came
Transfigured for the pangs; why not a spot
Of this wide world but hath a tale of wo;
Why all this glorious universe is Death's.

"Go, Moon! and tell the stars, and tell the suns,
Impatient of the wo, the strength of Him
Who doth consent to death; and tell the climes
That meet thy mournful eyes, one after one,
Through all the lapses of the lonesome night,
The pathos of repose, the might of Death!"

The voice is hush'd; the great old wood is still:
The moon, like one in meditation, walks
Behind a cloud. We, too, have theme for thought,
While, as a sun, God takes the west of Time
And smites the pyramid of Eternity.
The shadow lengthens over many worlds
Doom'd to the dark mausoleum and mound.

* "The mounds" are scattered over the whole of North America. Some of them are of vast size. They are full of skeletons (crumbling in the tomb), that evidently were deposited there many centuries since. The Indians cannot give us any account of the origin of the mounds, and they must have been erected by a people that lived in America at a very ancient period—a people (as the ruins of large cities, still faintly visible in the forests, naturally suggest) far advanced in civilization.

GREENWOOD CEMETERY.

Here are the houses of the dead. Here youth
And age and manhood, stricken in his strength,
Hold solemn state and awful silence keep,
While Earth goes murmuring in her ancient path,
And troubled Ocean tosses to and fro
Upon his mountainous bed impatiently,
And many stars make worship musical
In the dim-aisled abyss, and over all
The Lord of Life, in meditation sits
Changeless, alone, beneath the large white dome
Of Immortality.
I pause and think
Among these walks lined by the frequent tombs;
For it is very wonderful. Afar
The populous city lifts its tall, bright spires,
And snowy sails are glancing on the bay,
As if in merriment—but here all sleep;
They sleep, these calm, pale people of the past:
Spring plants her rosy feet on their dim homes—
They sleep!—Sweet Summer comes and calls, and calls
With all her passionate poetry of flowers
Wed to the music of the soft south wind—
They sleep!—The lonely Autumn sits and sobs
Between the cold white tombs, as if her heart
Would break—they sleep!—Wild Winter comes and chants
Majestical the mournful sagas learn'd
Far in the melancholy North, where God
Walks forth alone upon the desolate seas—
They slumber still!—Sleep on, O passionless dead!
Ye make our world sublime: ye have a power
And majesty the living never hold.
Here Avarice shall forget his den of gold!
Here Lust his beautiful victim, and hot Hate
His crouching foe. Ambition here shall lean
Against Death's shaft, veiling the stern, bright eye
That, over-bold, would take the height of gods,
And know Fame's nothingness. The sire shall come,
The matron and the child, through many years,
To this fair spot, whether the plum'd hearse
Moves slowly through the winding walks, or Death
For a brief moment pauses: all shall come
To feel the touching eloquence of graves:
And therefore it was well for us to clothe
The place with beauty. No dark terror here
Shall chill the generous tropic of the soul,
But Poetry and her starred comrade Art
Shall make the sacred country of the dead
Magnificent. The fragrant flowers shall smile
Over the low, green graves; the trees shall shake
Their soul-like cadences upon the tombs;
The little lake, set in a paradise
Of wood, shall be a mirror to the moon
What time she looks from her imperial tent
In long delight at all below; the sea
Shall lift some stately dirge he loves to breathe
Over dead nations, while calm sculptures stand
On every hill, and look like spirits there
That drink the harmony. Oh, it is well!
Why should a darkness scowl on any spot
Where man grasps immortality? Light, light,
And art, and poetry, and eloquence,
And all that we call glorious are its dower.

Oh, ye whose mouldering frames were brought and placed
By pious hands within these flowery slopes
And gentle hills, where are ye dwelling now?
For man is more than element. The soul
Lives in the body as the sunbeam lives
In trees or flowers that were but clay without.
Then where are ye, lost sunbeams of the mind?
Are ye where great Orion towers and holds
Eternity on his stupendous front?
Or where pale Neptune in the distant space
Shows us how far, in His creative mood,
With pomp of silence and concentred brows,
Walk'd forth the Almighty? Haply ye have gone
Where other matter roundeth into shapes
Of bright beatitude: or do ye know
Aught of dull space or time, and its dark load
Of aching weariness?
They answer not.
But He whose love created them of old,
To cheer his solitary realm and reign,
With love will still remember them.

HYMN TO THE HUDSON RIVER.

Lose not a memory of the glorious scenes,
Mountains, and palisades, and leaning rocks,
Steep white-wall'd towns and ships that lie beneath,
By which, like some serene, heroic soul
Revolving noble thoughts, thou calmly cam'st,
O mighty river of the North! Thy lip
Meets Ocean here, and in deep joy he lifts
His great white brow, and gives his stormy voice
A milder tone, and murmurs pleasantly
To every shore, and bids the insolent blast
To touch thee very gently; for thy banks
Held empires broad and populous as the leaves
That rustle o'er their grave—republics gone
Long, long ago, before the pale men came,
Like clouds into the dim and dusty past:
But there is dearer reason; for the rills
That feed thee, rise among the storied rocks
Where Freedom built her battle-tower; and blow
Their flutes of silver by the poor man's door;
And innocent childhood in the ripple dips
Its rosy feet; and from the round blue sky
That circles all, smiles out a certain Godhead.

Oh, lordly river! thou shalt henceforth be
A wanderer of the deep; and thou shalt hear
The sad, wild voices of the solemn North
Utter uncertain words in cloudy rhythm,
But full of terrible meaning, to the wave
That moans by Labrador; and thou shalt pause
To pay thy worship in the coral temples,
The ancient Meccas of the reverent sea;
And thou shalt start again on thy blue path
To kiss the southern isles; and thou shalt know
What beauty thrones the blue Symplegades,
What glory the long Dardanelles; and France
Shall listen to thy calm, deep voice, and learn
That Freedom must be calm if she would fix
Her mountain moveless in a heaving world;
And Greece shall hear thee chant by Marathon,

And Italy shall feel thy breathing on her shores,
Where Liberty once more takes up her lance;
And when thou hurriest back, full of high themes,
Great Albion shall joy through every cliff,
And lordly hall, and peasant-home, and old
Cathedral where earth's emperors sleep—whose crowns
Were laurel and whose sceptres pen and harp—
The mother of our race shall joy to hear
Thy low, sweet murmuring: her sonorous tongue
Is thine, her glory thine; for thou dost bear
On thy rejoicing tide, rejoicing at the task,
The manly Saxon sprung from her own loins
In far America.
Roll on! roll on,
Thou river of the North! Tell thou to all
The isles, tell thou to all the continents
The grandeur of my land. Speak of its vales
Where Independence wears a pastoral wreath
Amid the holy quiet of his flock;
And of its mountains with their cloudy beards
Toss'd by the breath of centuries; and speak
Of its tall cataracts that roll their bass
Among the choral of its midnight storms,
And of its rivers lingering through the plains,
So long, that they seem made to measure Time;
And of its lakes that mock the haughty sea;
And of its caves where banish'd gods might find
Night large enough to hide their crownless heads;
And of its sunsets, glorious and broad
Above the prairies spread like oceans on
And on, and on over the far dim leagues,
Till vision shudders o'er immensity.*
Roll on! roll on, thou river of the North!
Bear on thy wave the music of the crash
That tells a forest's fall, wide woods that hold
Beneath their cloister'd bark a registry
Where Time may almost find how old he is.†
Keep in thy memory the frequent homes,
That from the ruin rise, the triumphs these
Of real kings whose conquering march shines up
Into the wondering Oregon.
Oh, tell,
Thou glorious stream! to Europe's stately song,
Whose large white brows are fullest of the god—
To Asia's mighty hordes, whose dark eyes gaze
With wonder and unchangeable belief
On mountains where Jehovah sat, when Earth
Was fit to hold Jehovah on her thrones—.
To Afric, with her huge, rough brain on fire,
And Titan energy gone mad—tell thou to all,
That Freedom hath a home; that man arose
Ever as a mountain rises when its heart
Of flame is stirr'd, and its indignant breast
Heaves, and hurls off the enormous chain of ice
That marr'd its majesty. Say to the tribes,
"There is a hope, a love, a home for all;
The rivers woo them to their lucent lengths;
The woods to their green haunts; the prairies sigh
Throughout their broad and flowery solitudes
For some companionship. True, there are chains
On certain swarthy limbs. It shall not be
Forever. Yes! the fetter'd shall be loosed,
And liberty beam ample as the land!"

And, fearless river! tell to all the tribes
The might that lives in every human soul,
And what a feeble thing a tyrant is!
So speaking, that their hearts will bow
Before the beautiful, which holds the true,
As heaven in its sweet azure holds the sun;
So speaking, that they see the universe
Was made for Beauty's sake, and like a robe
It undulates around the inner soul.
A feeling and a harmony, a thought
That shows a deeper thought, until the soul
Trembles before the vision, and the voice,
Made musical by worship, whispers, "Joy!"
But utter all most calmly, with thy voice
Low as a seraph's near the eternal throne,
For mighty truths are always very calm

* A reference to American geography will show that there is no extravagance in these lines. Witness Niagara, the Mississippi river, Lake Superior, the Mammoth Cave in Kentucky the Grand Prairie of Illinois.

† The concentric circles of trees designate their age.

CHANT OF A SOUL.

My youth has gone—the glory, the delight
That gave new moons unto the night,
And put in every wind a tone
And presence that was not its own.
I can no more create,
What time the Autumn blows her solemn tromp,
And goes with golden pomp
Through our unmeasurable woods:
I can no more create, sitting in youthful state
Above the mighty floods,
And peopling glen, and wave, and air,
With shapes that are immortal. Then
The earth and heaven were fair,
While only less than gods seem'd all my fellow-men.

Oh! the delight, the gladness,
The sense yet love of madness,
The glorious choral exultations,
The far-off sounding of the banded nations,
The wings of angels at melodious sweeps
Upon the mountain's hazy steeps—
The very dead astir within their coffin'd deeps;
The dreamy veil that wrapp'd the star and sod—
A swathe of purple, gold, and amethyst;
And, luminous behind the billowy mist,
Something that look'd to my young eyes like God

Too late I learn I have not lived aright,
And hence the loss of that delight
Which put a moon into the moonless night.
I mingled in the human maze;
I sought their horrid shrine;
I knelt before the impure blaze;
I made their idols mine.
I lost mine early love—that land of balms
Most musical with solemn psalms
Sounding beneath the tall and graceful palms.

Who lives aright?
Answer me, all ye pyramids and piles
That look like calmest power in your still might.
Ye also do I ask, O continents and isles!

Blind though with blood ye be,
Your tongues, though torn with pain, I know are free.
Then speak, all ancient masses! speak
From patient obelisk to idle peak!
There is a heaving of the plains,
A trailing of a shroud,
A clash of bolts and chains—
A low, sad voice, that comes upon me like a cloud,
"Oh, misery! oh, misery!"—
Thou poor old Earth! no more, no more
Shall I draw speech from thee,
Nor dare thy crypts of legendary lore:
Let silence learn no tongue; let night fold every [shore.

Yet I have something left—the will,
That Mont Blanc of the soul, is towering still.
And I can bear the pain,
The storm, the old heroic chain;
And with a smile
Pluck wisdom from my torture, and give back
A love to Fate from this my mountain-rack.
I do believe the sad alone are wise;
I do believe the wrong'd alone can know
Why lives the world, why spread the burden'd skies,
And so from torture into godship grow.
Plainer and plainer beams this truth, the more
I hear the slow, dull dripping of my gore;
And now, arising from yon deep,
'T is plain as a white statue on a tall, dark steep.

Oh, suffering bards! oh, spirits black
With storm on many a mountain-rack!
Our early splendour's gone,
Like stars into a cloud withdrawn—
Like music laid asleep
In dried-up fountains—like a stricken dawn
Where sudden tempests sweep.
I hear the bolts around us falling,
And cloud to cloud forever calling:
Yet we must nor despair nor weep.
Did WE this evil bring?
Or from our fellows did the torture spring?
Titans! forgive, forgive!
Oh, know ye not 'tis victory but to live!
Therefore I say, rejoice with harp and voice!
We are the prophets of the beautiful.
And thou, O Earth! rejoice
With many waters rising like a voice.
Thou, too, art full of beauty: thou!
Though thorns are piercing thy pale brow,
And thy deep, awful eyes look dull.
Wherever beauty is, is hope;
And thou for HIS great sake hadst being:
From central deep to starry cope
Beauty is the all-seeing.
Oh, yet thou shalt be a majestic creature,
Redeem'd in form and every feature;
New moons on high, thy plains continuous bowers,
And in thy snow-white hand another Eden's flowers.

VOICES.

"Earth shall rejoice: we do rejoice,
Each with his harp and thorny crown;
And reverent hear, from dreary year to year,
Without a frown amid our patient fold
Upon the rocks beside the frozen fountains,
The avalanches of GOD'S judgments roll'd
With stately motion and far thunder down
Eternity's old mountains:
We hear, and calmly smile
Amid the mist on this our rocky pile."

Oh, suffering but heroic souls!
Your voices come to me like muffled rolls
Of brave but mournful thunders at their goals:
And, gaining strength, once more I cry aloud
From mine own stormy peak and clinging shroud,
"Still, still rejoice, with harp and voice!
I know not what our fate may be:
I only know that he who hath a time
Must also have eternity:
One billow proves and gives a whole wide sea.
On this I build my trust,
And not on mountain-dust,
Or murmuring woods, or starlit clime,
Or ocean with melodious chime,
Or sunset glories in the western sky:
Enough, I *am*, and shall not choose to die.
No matter what our future fate may be:
To live is in itself a majesty!
Oh! there we may again create
Fair worlds as in our youthful state;
Or Wo may build for us a fiery tomb
Like FARINATA's in the nether gloom.
Even then we will not lose the name of man
By idle moan or coward groan,
But say, 'It was so written in the mighty plan!'"

THE GODS OF OLD: AN ODE.

NOT realmless sit the ancient gods
Upon their misty thrones.
In that old glorious Grecian heaven
Of regal zones
A languor on their awful forms may lie,
And a deep grief on their large white brows,
King-dwellers of the sky!
But still they show the might of god,
In rustless panoply.
They cannot fade, though other creeds
Came burden'd with their curse,
And ONE's apotheosis was
A darken'd universe:
No tempest heralded the orient light;
No fiery portent walk'd the solemn night;
No conqueror's blood-red banner was unfurl'd;
No volcan shook its warning torch on high;
No earthquake tore the pulses of the world;
No pale suns wander'd through the swarthy sky;
Only the silent Spheres
Amid the darkness shed some joyous tears;
And then, as rainbows come, IT came
With morning's lambent flame.
The Stars look'd from their palaces, whose spires
And windows caught afar the prophet-glow,
And bade their choirs sing to the sweetest lyres,
"Peace and good will unto the orb below!"
The monarchs shudder'd and turn'd sick at heart;
And from their bright hands fell

Gemm'd sceptres with a thunderous sound
Before the miracle:
Ah! sick at soul—but they, the bards,
Song's calm immortals in the eclipse,
Throng'd up and held the nectar-cup
To their pale lips;
And each, with an eager, fond look, stirr'd
Certain melodious strings,
While the startled tempest-bearing bird,
Poised tremblingly his wings:
Then loftier still their harps resounded,
And louder yet their voices roll'd
Between the arches, and rebounded
Dreamily from the roof of gold:

"Ye cannot leave your throned spheres,
Though faith is o'er,
And a mightier ONE than JOVE appears
On Earth's expectant shore!"
Slowly the daring words went trampling through the halls—
"Not in the earth, nor hell, nor sky,
The IDEAL, O ye gods! can ever die,
But to the soul of man immortal calls.

"Still, JOVE, sublime, shall wrap
His awful forehead in Olympian shrouds,
Or take along the heavens' dark wilderness
His thunder-chase behind the hunted clouds:
And mortal eyes upturn'd shall behold
APOLLO's rustling robe of gold
Sweep through the corridors of the ancient sky
That kindling speaks its Deity:
And HE the ruler of the sunless land
Of restless ghosts shall fitfully illume
With smouldering fires that stir in cavern'd eyes
Hell's house of shuddering gloom:
Still the ethereal huntress, as of old,
Shall roam amid the sacred Latmos mountains,
And lave her virgin limbs in waters cold
That earth holds up for her in marble fountains:
And in his august dreams along the Italian* streams,
The poor old throneless god, with angry frown,
Will feebly grasp the air for his lost crown—
Then murmur sadly low of his great overthrow.
And wrapp'd in sounding mail shall he appear,
War's giant charioteer!—
And where the conflict reels,
Urge through the swaying lines his crashing wheels;
Or pause to list amid the horrent shades,
The deep, hoarse cry of battle's thirsty blades,
Led by the hungry spear—
Till at the weary combat's close,
They gave their passionate thanks,
Amid the panting ranks of conquer'd foes;
Then, drunken with their king's red wine,
Go swooning to repose around his purple shrine.

"And HE the trident-wielder still shall see
The adoring billows kneel around his feet,
While, at his call, the winds in ministry
Before their altar of the tempest meet:
Or—leaning gently o'er the Paphian isles,
Cheer'd by the music of some Triton's horn—
Lift up the shadowy curtains of the night
To their hid window-tops above,
And bathe thy drowsy eyelids with the light,
Voluptuous queen of love!
And thou, ah, thou,
Born of the white sea-foam
That dreams a-troubled still around thy home—
Awaking from thy slumbers, thou shalt press
Thy passionate lips on his resplendent brow
In some sweet, lone recess,
Where waters murmur and the dim leaves bow
And young ENDYMION
At midnight's pallid noon
Shall still be charm'd from his dewy sleep
By the foolish, lovesick Moon,
Who thrills to find him in some lovely vale
Before her silver lamp may fail:
And PAN shall play his pleasant reed
Down in the hush'd arcades,
And fauns shall prank the sward amid
Thessalia's sunny shades.

"Nor absent SHE whose eyes of azure throw*
Truth's sunburst on the world below:
Still shall she calmly watch the choral years
Circling fast the beamy spheres
That tremble as she marches through their plains,
While momently rolls out a sullen sound
From Error's hoary mountains tumbling round—
Heard by the Titan, who from his high rock,
Fill'd with immortal pains
That his immortal spirit still can mock,
Exultant sees—despite the oppressor's ire,
The frost, the heat, the vulture, and the storm—
Earth's ancient vales rejoicing in his fire,
The homes, the loves of men—those beings wrought
To many a beauteous form†
In the grand quiet of his own great thought:
And over all, bright, beautiful, serene,
And changeless in thy prime,
Thou, PSYCHE, glory-cinctured shalt be seen,
Whispering forever that one word sublime,
Down through the peopled gallery of Time—
'ETERNITY!'—in whose dread cycles stand
Men and their deities, alike on common land."

Like far-off stars that glimmer in a cloud,
Deathless, O gods! shall ye illume the past;
To ye the poet-voice will cry aloud,
Faithful among the faithless to the last—
"Ye must not die!"
Long as the dim robes of the ages trail
O'er Delphi's steep or Tempé's flowery vale—
Ye *shall not* die!
Though time and storm your calm old temples rend,
And, rightly, men to our "ONE ONLY" bend—
Ye were the things in which the ancient mind
Its darkling sense of Deity enshrined.
To Sinai still Olympus reverent calls,
And Ida leans to hear Mount Zion's voice:
Gods of the past! your shapes are in our halls;
Upon our clime your mighty presence falls,
And Christian hearts with Grecian souls rejoice.

* Saturn was banished to Italy

* "Thou, Pallas, Wisdom's blue-eyed queen!"

† According to the Greek mythology, Prometheus stole fire from heaven and created man, for which Jove punished him.

THOMAS WILLIAM PARSONS.

[Born, 1819.]

THOMAS WILLIAM PARSONS, son of Dr. T. W. PARSONS, was born in Boston on the eighteenth of August, 1819, and at nine years of age entered the Latin School in that city, where he remained during six years. After a brief interval of study at home, he travelled abroad, having sailed in company with his father for Malta and Messina, in the autumn of 1836. Prevented by the cholera, which was then raging in southern Italy, from visiting either of the Sicilies, he went from Malta in an Italian brig to Leghorn, having a tempestuous passage of fourteen days, during which the little vessel escaped wreck by putting into the island of Elba. He spent the winter partly in Pisa, but principally in Florence and Rome, proceeded to Paris, and thence to London; and near the close of 1837 returned home, where he commenced the study of medicine, which circumstances afterwards led him to relinquish.

In Florence Mr. PARSONS had accidentally became acquainted with a lady, Signora GUISEPPA DANTI, in whose house he dwelt during the whole period of his stay in that city. Whether from a coincidence of name, or from the delight, natural to a boy, of acquiring some insight into the "Divina Commedia" amid the gentle influences of the Etrurian Athens, Mr. PARSONS seems to have learned a passionate admiration for the poet in whose native city he was a resident. That the lady's instruction was not without its charm may be inferred from the following dedication to a translation of "The First Ten Cantos of the Inferno," which he published in Boston in 1843:

"TO GUISEPPA DANTI,
Under whose roof, in Florence,
The language of her immortal namesake
First grew familiar to her GRATEFUL GUEST."

In 1847 Mr. PARSONS made a second voyage to Europe in company with his friend, Professor DANIEL TREADWELL, and passed a year abroad.

His poems, written in the various intervals of business, have mostly appeared in periodicals. A few of them, collected in a volume, were published in Boston in 1855. His translation of the "Inferno" has been completed several years, but has not yet been given to the press.

That portion of his version of DANTE which Mr. PARSONS has published, is executed in a very masterly manner. The best critics have pronounced it the most successful reproduction of the spirit and power of the "Divina Commedia" in the English language. His original poems are variously admirable. They have the careful finish to which poets endeavoured to attain when it was deemed of importance not only that poetry should have meaning, but that both its writers and its readers should understand it. His verses are clear alike to the ear and the brain, and their old-fashioned music is in keeping with their vigorous sense, fine humour, sharp, but not ungenial wit, and delicate though always manly sentiment. His volume opens with a series of "Letters" supposed to have been written by a British traveller in this country to some of his friends in London. They are full of brilliant sarcasm and just reflection. In one of them, addressed to WALTER SAVAGE LANDOR, he has some lines which may have been intended as an apology for his love of Italian art, and preference of Italian before American subjects for poetical illustration. "Here," he says—

"Here, by the ploughman, as with daily tread
He tracks the furrows of his fertile ground,
Dark locks of hair, and thigh-bones of the dead,
Spear-heads, and skulls, and arrows oft are found.

"On such memorials unconcerned we gaze;
No trace returning of the glow divine,
Wherewith, dear WALTER! in our Eton days
We eyed a fragment from the Palentine.

"It fired us then to trace upon the map
The forum's line—proud empire's church-yard paths,
Ay, or to finger but a marble scrap
Or stucco piece from Diocletian's baths.

"Cellini's workmanship could nothing add
Nor any casket rich with gems and gold,
To the strange value every pebble had
O'er which perhaps the Tiber's wave had rolled.

"A like enchantment all thy land pervades,
Mellows the sunshine—softens every breeze—
O'erhangs the mouldering town, and chestnut shades,
And glows and sparkles in her storied seas. . .

"Art's rude beginnings, wheresoever found,
The same dull chord of feeling faintly strike;
The Druid's pillar, and the Indian mound,
And Uxmal's monuments, are mute alike.

"Nor here, although the gorgeous year hath brought
Crimson October's beautiful decay,
Can all this loveliness inspire a thought
Beyond the marvels of the fleeting day.

"For here the Present overpowers the Past;
No recollections to these woods belong,
(O'er which no minstrelsy its veil hath cast,)
To rouse our worship, or supply my song."

He has not however been altogether neglectful of American themes. His "Hudson River" is the noblest tribute any stream on this continent has received from a poet; and his lines "On the Death of Daniel Webster," are a display of genius suitable for their impressive occasion: far better than any thing else ever written in verse on the death of an American statesman.

Although not a graduate of any university, Mr. PARSONS was, at the instance of the late Rev. ANDREWS NORTON, elected a member of the Phi Beta Kappa Society of Harvard College, and in 1853 received the honorary degree of master of arts from that venerable institution.

CAMPANILE DE PISA.

Snow was glistening on the mountains, but the air was that of June,
Leaves were falling, but the runnels playing still their summer tune,
And the dial's lazy shadow hovered nigh the brink of noon.
On the benches in the market, rows of languid idlers lay,
When to Pisa's nodding belfry, with a friend, I took my way.

From the top we looked around us, and as far as eye might strain,
Saw no sign of life or motion in the town, or on the plain,
Hardly seemed the river moving, through the willows to the main;
Nor was any noise disturbing Pisa from her drowsy hour,
Save the doves that fluttered 'neath us, in and out and round the tower.

Not a shout from gladsome children, or the clatter of a wheel,
Nor the spinner of the suburb, winding his discordant reel,
Nor the stroke upon the pavement of a hoof or of a heel.
Even the slumberers, in the church-yard of the Campo Santo seemed
Scarce more quiet than the living world that underneath us dreamed.

Dozing at the city's portal, heedless guard the sentry kept,
More than oriental dulness o'er the sunny farms had crept,
Near the walls the ducal herdsman by the dusty road-side slept;
While his camels, resting round him, half alarmed the sullen ox,
Seeing those Arabian monsters pasturing with Etruria's flocks.

Then it was, like one who wandered, lately, singing by the Rhine,
Strains* perchance to maiden's hearing sweeter than this verse of mine,
That we bade Imagination lift us on her wing divine,
And the days of Pisa's greatness rose from the sepulchral past,
When a thousand conquering galleys bore her standard at the mast.

Memory for a moment crowned her sovereign mistress of the seas,
When she braved, upon the billows, Venice and the Genoese,
Daring to deride the Pontiff, though he shook his angry keys,
When her admirals triumphant, riding o'er the Soldan's waves,
Brought from Calvary's holy mountain fitting soil for knightly graves.

When the Saracen surrendered, one by one, his pirate isles,
And Ionia's marbled trophies decked Lungarno's Gothic piles,
Where the festal music floated in the light of ladies' smiles;
Soldiers in the busy court-yard, nobles in the halls above,
O, those days of arms are over—arms and courtesy and love!

Down in yonder square at sunrise, lo! the Tuscan troops arrayed,
Every man in Milan armor, forged in Brescia every blade:
Sigismondi is their captain—Florence! art thou not dismayed?
There 's Lanfranchi! there the bravest of Gherardesca stem,
Hugolino—with the bishop—but enough—enough of them.

Now, as on Achilles' buckler, next a peaceful scene succeeds;
Pious crowds in the cathedral duly tell their blessed beads;
Students walk the learned cloister—Ariosto wakes the reeds—
Science dawns—and Galileo opens to the Italian youth,
As he were a new Columbus, new discovered realms of truth.

Hark! what murmurs from the million in the bustling market rise!
All the lanes are loud with voices, all the windows dark with eyes;
Black with men the marble bridges, heaped the shores with merchandise;
Turks and Greeks and Libyan merchants in the square their councils hold,
And the Christian altars glitter gorgeous with Byzantine gold.

Look! anon the masqueraders don their holiday attire;
Every palace is illumined—all the town seems built of fire—
Rainbow-coloured lanterns dangle from the top of every spire.
Pisa's patron saint hath hallowed to himself the joyful day,
Never on the thronged Rialto showed the Carnival more gay.

Suddenly the bell beneath us broke the vision with its chime;
"Signors," quoth our gray attendant, "it is almost vesper time;"
Vulgar life resumed its empire—down we dropt from the sublime.
Here and there a friar passed us, as we paced the silent streets,
And a cardinal's rumbling carriage roused the sleepers from the seats.

* "The Belfry of Bruges."

THE SHADOW OF THE OBELISK.

Home returning from the music which had so entranced my brain,
That the way I scarce remember'd to the Pincian Hill again,
Nay, was willing to forget it underneath a moon so fair,
In a solitude so sacred, and so summer-like in air—
Came I to the side of Tiber, hardly conscious where I stood,
Till I marked the sullen murmur of the venerable flood.

Rome lay doubly dead around me, sunk in silence calm and deep;
'T was the death of desolation—and the nightly one of sleep.
Dreams alone, and recollections peopled now the solemn hour;
Such a spot and such a season well might wake the Fancy's power;
Yet no monumental fragment, storied arch or temple vast,
Mid the mean, plebeian buildings loudly whisper'd of the Past.

Tether'd by the shore, some barges hid the wave's august repose;
Petty sheds of humble merchants, nigh the Campus Martius rose;
Hardly could the dingy Thamis, when his tide is ebbing low,
Life's dull scene in colder colours to the homesick exile show.
Winding from the vulgar prospect, through a labyrinth of lanes,
Forth I stepp'd upon the Corso, where its greatness Rome retains.

Yet it was not ancient glory, though the midnight radiance fell
Soft on many a princely mansion, many a dome's majestic swell;
Though, from some hush'd corner gushing, oft a modern fountain gleam'd,
Where the marble and the waters in their freshness equal seem'd:
What though open courts unfolded columns of Corinthian mould?
Beautiful it was—but alter'd! naught bespake the Rome of old.

So, regardless of the grandeur, pass'd I tow'rds the Northern Gate;
All around were shining gardens—churches glittering, yet sedate,—
Heavenly bright the broad enclosure! but the o'erwhelming silence brought
Stillness to mine own heart's beating, with a moment's truce of thought,
And I started as I found me walking ere I was aware,
O'er the Obelisk's tall shadow, on the pavement of the Square.

Ghost-like seem'd it to address me, and convey'd me for a while,
Backward, through a thousand ages, to the borders of the Nile;
Where for centuries every morning saw it creeping, long and dun,
O'er the stones perchance of Memphis, or the City of the Sun.
Kingly turrets look'd upon it—pyramids and sculptured fanes:
Towers and palaces have moulder'd—but the shadow still remains.

Tired of that lone tomb of Egypt, o'er the seas the trophy flew;
Here the eternal apparition met the millions' daily view.
Virgil's foot has touch'd it often—it has kiss'd Octavia's face—
Royal chariots have rolled o'er it, in the frenzy of the race,
When the strong, the swift, the valiant, mid the throng'd arena strove,
In the days of good Augustus, and the dynasty of Jove.

Herds are feeding in the Forum, as in old Evander's time:
Tumbled from the steep Tarpeian all the towers that sprang sublime.
Strange! that what seem'd most inconstant should the most abiding prove;
Strange! that what is hourly moving no mutation can remove:
Ruin'd lies the cirque! the chariots, long ago, have ceased to roll—
Even the Obelisk is broken—but the shadow still is whole.

What is Fame! if mightiest empires leave so little mark behind,
How much less must heroes hope for, in the wreck of human kind!
Less than even this darksome picture, which I tread beneath my feet,
Copied by a lifeless moonbeam on the pebbles of the street;
Since if Cæsar's best ambition, living, was to be renown'd,
What shall Cæsar leave behind him, save the shadow of a sound?

ON A LADY SINGING.

Oft as my lady sang for me
That song of the lost one that sleeps by the sea,
Of the grave on the rock, and the cypress-tree,
Strange was the pleasure that over me stole,
For 't was made of old sadness that lives in my soul.

So still grew my heart at each tender word,
That the pulse in my bosom scarcely stirred,
And I hardly breathed, but only heard:
Where was I?—not in the world of men,
Until she awoke me with silence again.

Like the smell of the vine, when its early bloom
Sprinkles the green lane with sunny perfume,
Such a delicate fragrance filled the room:

Whether it came from the vine without,
Or arose from her presence, I dwell in doubt.

Light shadows played on the pictured wall
From the maples that fluttered outside the hall,
And hindered the daylight—yet ah! not all;
Too little for that all the forest would be,—
Such a sunbeam she was, and is, to me!

When my sense returned, as the song was o'er,
I fain would have said to her, "Sing it once more,"
But soon as she smiled my wish I forbore:
Music enough in her look I found,
And the hush of her lip seemed sweet as the sound.

HUDSON RIVER.

RIVERS that roll most musical in song
Are often lovely to the mind alone;
The wanderer muses, as he moves along
Their barren banks, on glories not their own.

When to give substance to his boyish dreams,
He leaves his own, far countries to survey,
Oft must he think, in greeting foreign streams,
"Their names alone are beautiful, not they."

If chance he mark the dwindled Arno pour
A tide more meagre than his native Charles;
Or views the Rhone when summer's heat is o'er,
Subdued and stagnant in the fen of Arles;

Or when he sees the slimy Tiber fling
His sullen tribute at the feet of Rome,
Oft to his thought must partial memory bring
More noble waves, without renown, at home:

Now let him climb the Catskill, to behold
The lordly Hudson, marching to the main,
And say what bard, in any land of old,
Had such a river to inspire his strain

Along the Rhine, gray battlements and towers
Declare what robbers once the realm possessed;
But here Heaven's handiwork surpasseth ours,
And man has hardly more than built his nest.

No storied castle overawes these heights,
Nor antique arches check the current's play,
Nor mouldering architrave the mind invites
To dream of deities long passed away.

No Gothic buttress, or decaying shaft
Of marble, yellowed by a thousand years,
Lifts a great landmark to the little craft,
A summer-cloud! that comes and disappears:

But cliffs, unaltered from their primal form,
Since the subsiding of the deluge rise,
And hold their savins to the upper storm,
While far below the skiff securely plies.

Farms, rich not more in meadows than in men
Of Saxon mould, and strong for every toil,
Spread o'er the plain, or scatter through the glen,
Bœotian plenty on a Spartan soil.

Then, where the reign of cultivation ends,
Again the charming wilderness begins;
From steep to steep one solemn wood extends,
Till some new hamlet's rise the boscage thins.

And these deep groves forever have remained
Touched by no axe—by no proud owner nursed:
As now they stand they stood when Pharaoh reign'd,
Lineal descendants of creation's first.

Thou Scottish Tweed,* a sacred streamlet now
Since thy last minstrel laid him down to die,
Where through the casement of his chamber thou
Didst mix thy moan with his departing sigh;

A few of Hudson's more majestic hills
Might furnish forests for the whole of thine,
Hide in thick shade all Humber's feeding rills,
And darken all the fountains of the Tyne.

Name all the floods that pour from Albion's heart,
To float her citadels that crowd the sea,
In what, except the meaner pomp of Art,
Sublimer Hudson! can they rival thee:

Could boastful Thames with all his riches buy,
To deck the strand which London loads with gold,
Sunshine so bright—such purity of sky—
As bless thy sultry season and thy cold?

No tales, we know, are chronicled of thee
In ancient scrolls; no deeds of doubtful claim
Have hung a history on every tree,
And given each rock its fable and a fame.

But neither here hath any conqueror trod,
Nor grim invader from barbarian climes;
No horrors feigned of giant or of god
Pollute thy stillness with recorded crimes.

Here never yet have happy fields, laid waste,
The ravished harvest and the blasted fruit,
The cottage ruined, and the shrine defaced,
Tracked the foul passage of the feudal brute.

"Yet, O, Antiquity!" the stranger sighs,
"Scenes wanting thee soon pall upon the view;
The soul's indifference dulls the sated eyes,
Where all is fair indeed—but all is new."

False thought! is age to crumbling walls confined,
To Grecian fragments and Egyptian bones?
Hath Time no monuments to raise the mind,
More than old fortresses and sculptured stones?

Call not this new which is the only land
That wears unchanged the same primeval face
Which, when just dawning from its Maker's hand,
Gladdened the first great grandsire of our race.

Nor did Euphrates with an earlier birth [south,
Glide past green Eden towards the unknown
Than Hudson broke upon the infant earth,
And kissed the ocean with his nameless mouth.

Twin-born with Jordan, Ganges, and the Nile!
Thebes and the pyramids to thee are young;
O! had thy waters burst from Britain's isle,
Till now perchance they had not flowed unsung

* "It was a beautiful day,—so warm that every window was wide open, and so still that the sound of all others most delicious to his ear—the gentle ripple of the Tweed over its pebbles,—was distinctly audible as we knelt around the bed: and his eldest son kissed and closed his eyes."—LOCKHART'S *Life of Sir Walter Scott.*

ON THE DEATH OF DANIEL WEBSTER,

TWENTY-FOURTH OF OCTOBER, 1852.

COMES there a frigate home? what mighty bark
  Returns with torn, but still triumphant sails?
Such peals awake the wondering Sabbath—hark!
  How the dread echoes die among the vales!

What ails the morning, that the misty sun
  Looks wan and troubled in the autumn air?
Dark over Marshfield!—'t was the minute gun:
  God! has it come that we foreboded there?

The woods at midnight heard an angel's tread;
  The sere leaves rustled in his withering breath;
The night was beautiful with stars; we said
  "This is the harvest moon,"—'t was thine, oh, Death!

Gone, then, the splendour of October's day!
  A single night, without the aid of frost,
Has turned the gold and crimson into gray,
  And the world's glory, with our own, is lost.

A little while, and we rode forth to greet
  His coming with glad music, and his eye
Drew many captives, as along the street
  His peaceful triumph passed, unquestioned, by.

Now there are moanings, by the desolate shore,
  That are not ocean's; by the patriot's bed,
Hearts throb for him whose noble heart no more—

Break off the rhyme—for sorrow cannot stop
  To trim itself with phrases for the ear,—
Too fast the tears upon the paper drop:

Fast as the leaves are falling on his bier,
  Thick as the hopes that cluster'd round his name,
While yet he walked with us, a pilgrim here.

He was our prophet, our majestic oak,
  That, like Dodona's, in Thesprotian land,
Whose leaves were oracles, divinely spoke.

We called him giant, for in every part
  He seemed colossal; in his port and speech,
In his large brain, and in his larger heart.

And when his name upon the roll we saw
  Of those who govern, then we felt secure,
Because we knew his reverence for the law.

So the young master* of the Roman realm
  Discreetly thought, we cannot wander far
From the true course, with Ulpian at the helm.

But slowly to this loss our sense awakes;
  To know what space it in the forum filled,
See what a gap the temple's ruin makes!

Kings have their dynasties, but not the mind;
  Cæsar leaves other Cæsars to succeed,
But Wisdom, dying, leaves no heir behind.

Who now shall stand the regent at the wheel?
  Who knows the dread machinery? who hath skill
Our course through oceans unsurveyed to feel?

Her mournful tidings Albion lately sent,
  How he, the victor in so many fields,
Fell, but not fighting, in the fields of Kent;

The chief whose conduct in the lofty scene
  Where England stood up for the world in arms,
Gave her victorious name to England's queen.

* ALEXANDER SEVERUS.

But peaceful Britain knows, amid her grief,
  She could spare now the soldier and his sword
What can our councils do without our chief?

Blest are the peace-makers!—and he was ours,—
  Winning, by force of argument, the right
Between two kindred, more than rival powers.

The richest stones require the gentlest hand
  Of a wise workman—be our brother's faults,
For all have faults, by wisdom gently scanned.

Resume the rhyme, and end the funeral strain;
  Dying, he asked for song,—he did not slight
The harmony of numbers,—let the main
  Sing round his grave, great anthems day and night.

The autumn rains are falling on his head,
  The snows of winter soon will shroud the shore,
The spring with violets will adorn his bed,
  And summer shall return,—but he no more!

We have no high cathedral for his rest,
  Dim with proud banners and the dust of years;
All we can give him is New England's breast
  To lay his head on,—and his country's tears.

ON A MAGDALEN BY GUIDO.

MARY, when thou wert a virgin,
  Ere the first, the fatal sin,
Stole into thy bosom's chamber,
  Leading six companions in;
Ere those eyes had wept an error,
  What thy beauty must have been!

Ere those lips had paled their crimson,
  Quivering with the soul's despair,
Ere with pain they oft had parted
  In thine agony of prayer,
Or, instead of pearls, the tear-drops
  Glistened in thy streaming hair.

While in ignorance of sorrow
  Still thy heart serenely dreamed,
And the morning light of girlhood
  On thy cheek's young garden beam'd,
Where th' abundant rose was blushing,
  Not of earth couldst thou have seem'd.

When thy frailty fell upon thee,
  Lovely wert thou, even then;
Shame itself could not disarm thee
  Of the charms that vanquished men,
Which of Salem's purest daughters
  Match'd the sullied Magdalen?

But thy Master's eye beheld thee
  Foul and all unworthy heaven;
Pitied, pardon'd, purged thy spirit
  Of its black, pernicious leaven;
Drove the devils from out the temple—
  All the dark and guilty seven.

Oh the beauty of repentance!
  Mary, tenfold fairer now
Art thou with those dewy eyelids,
  And that anguish on thy brow;
Ah, might every sinful sister
  Grow in beauty ev'n as thou

TO JAMES RUSSELL LOWELL,

IN RETURN FOR A TALBOTYPE PICTURE OF VENICE.

Poet and friend! if any gift could bring
A joy like that of listening while you sing,
'T were such as this,—memories of the days
When Tuscan airs inspired more tender lays:
When the gray Appennine, or Lombard plain,
Sunburnt, or spongy with autumnal rain,
Mingled perchance, as first they met your sight,
Some drops of disappointment with delight;
When, rudely wakened from the dream of years,
You heard Velino thundering in your ears,
And fancy drooped,—until Romagna's wine
Brought you new visions, thousand-fold more fine;
When first in Florence, hearkening to the flow
Of Arno's midnight music, hoarse below,
You thought of home, and recollected those
Who loved your verse, but hungered for your prose,
And more than all the sonnets that you made,
Longed for the letters—ah, too poorly paid!
Thanks for thy boon! I look, and I am there;
The soaring belfry guides me to the square;
The punctual doves, that wait the stroke of one,
Flutter above me and becloud the sun;
'T is Venice! Venice! and with joy I put
In Adria's wave, incredulous, my foot;
I smell the sea-weed, and again I hear
The click of oars, the screaming gondolier.
Ha! the Rialto—Dominic! a boat;
Now in a gondola to dream and float:
Pull the slight cord and draw the silk aside,
And read the city's history as we glide;
For strangely here, where all is strange, indeed,
Not he who runs, but he who swims, may read.
Mark now, albeit the moral make thee sad,
What stately palaces these merchants had!
Proud houses once!—Grimani and Pisani,
Spinelli, Foscari, Giustiniani;
Behold their homes and monuments in one!
They writ their names in water, and are gone.
My voyage is ended, all the round is past,—
See! the twin columns and the bannered mast,
The domes, the steeds, the lion's wingéd sign,
"Peace to thee, Mark! Evangelist of mine!"*
Poetic art! reserved for prosy times
Of great inventions and of little rhymes;
For us, to whom a wisely-ordering heaven
Ether for Lethe, wires for wings, has given;
Whom vapor work for, yet who scorn a ghost,
Amid enchantments, disenchanted most;
Whose light, whose fire, whose telegraph had been
In blessed Urban's liberal days a sin.
Sure, in Damascus, any reasoning Turk
Would count your Talbotype a sorcerer's work.
Strange power! that thus to actual presence brings
The shades of distant or departed things,
And calls dead Thebes or Athens up, or Arles,
To show like spectres on the banks of Charles!
But we receive this marvel with the rest;
Nothing is new or wondrous in the West;
Life 's all a miracle, and every age
To the great wonder-book but adds a page.

* The legend of the winged Lion of St. Mark, seen everywhere at Venice—"Pax tibi, Marce! Evangelista meus."

ON A BUST OF DANTE.

See, from this counterfeit of him
Whom Arno shall remember long,
How stern of lineament, how grim
The father was of Tuscan song.
There but the burning sense of wrong,
Perpetual care and scorn abide;
Small friendship for the lordly throng;
Distrust of all the world beside.

Faithful if this wan image be,
No dream his life was—but a fight;
Could any Beatrice see
A lover in that anchorite?
To that cold Ghibeline's gloomy sight
Who could have guess'd the visions came
Of beauty, veil'd with heavenly light,
In circles of eternal flame?

The lips, as Cumæ's cavern close,
The cheeks, with fast and sorrow thin,
The rigid front, almost morose,
But for the patient hope within,
Declare a life whose course hath been
Unsullied still, though still severe,
Which, through the wavering days of sin,
Keep itself icy-chaste and clear.

Not wholly such his haggard look
When wandering once, forlorn he stray'd,
With no companion save his book,
To Corvo's hush'd monastic shade;
Where, as the Benedictine laid
His palm upon the pilgrim-guest,
The single boon for which he prayed
The convent's charity was rest.*

Peace dwells not here—this rugged face
Betrays no spirit of repose;
The sullen warrior sole we trace,
The marble man of many woes.
Such was his mien when first arose
The thought of that strange tale divine,
When hell he peopled with his foes,
The scourge of many a guilty line.

War to the last he waged with all
The tyrant canker-worms of earth;
Baron and duke, in hold and hall,
Cursed the dark hour that gave him birth;
He used Rome's harlot for his mirth;
Pluck'd bare hypocrisy and crime;
But valiant souls of knightly worth
Transmitted to the rolls of Time.

O Time! whose verdicts mock our own,
The only righteous judge art thou;
That poor old exile, sad and lone,
Is Latium's other Virgil now:
Before his name the nations bow:
His words are parcel of mankind,
Deep in whose hearts, as on his brow,
The marks have sunk of Dante's mind.

* It is told of Dante that when he was roaming over Italy, he came to a certain monastery, where he was met by one of the friars, who blessed him, and asked him what was his desire—to which the weary stranger simply answered, "*Pace*."

J. R. Lowell.

JAMES RUSSELL LOWELL.

[Born, 1819.]

Mr. Lowell is a native of Boston, where his father is an eminent Congregational clergyman. He completed his education at Harvard College when about twenty years of age, and subsequently studied the law, but I believe with no intention of entering the courts. His first appearance as an author was in 1839, when he printed a class poem recited at Cambridge. It was a composition in heroic verse, which, though it betrayed marks of haste, contained many strokes of vigorous satire, much sharp wit, and occasional bursts of feeling. Two years afterward he published a volume of miscellaneous poems, under the title of "A Year's Life." This bore no relationship to his first production. It illustrated entirely different thoughts, feelings, and habits. It not only evinced a change of heart, but so entire a revolution in his mode of thinking as to seem the production of a different mind. The staple of one forms the satire of the other. Not more unlike are Carlyle's "Life of Schiller" and his "Sartor Resartus." Though "A Year's Life" was by no means deficient in merit, it had so many weak points as to be easily accessible to satirical criticism. The author's language was not pure. When he would "wreak his thoughts upon expression," in the absence of allowable words, he corrupted such as came nearest his meaning into terms which had an intelligible sound, but would not bear a close scrutiny. With all its faults, however, the book had gleams and flashes of genius, which justified warm praises and sanguine expectations. The new poet, it was evident, had an observing eye, and a suggestive imagination; he had caught the tone and spirit of the new and mystical philosophy; he had a large heart; and he aimed, not altogether unsuccessfully, to make Nature the representative and minister of his feelings and desires. If he failed in attempts to put thin abstractions and ever-fleeting shades of thought and emotion into palpable forms, the signs, in "A Year's Life," of the struggling of a larger nature than appeared in defined outlines, made for the author a watchful and hopeful audience.

In 1844 Mr. Lowell published a new volume, evincing very decided advancement in thought, and feeling, and execution. The longest of its contents, "A Legend of Brittany," is without any of the striking faults of his previous compositions, and in imagination and artistic finish is the best poem he has yet printed. A knight loves and betrays a maiden, and, to conceal his crime, murders her, and places her corpse for temporary concealment behind the altar of his church, whence he is prevented by a mysterious awe from removing it. Meanwhile a festival is held there, and when the people are all assembled, and the organ sounds, the templar hears the voice of the wronged spirit, complaining that she has no rest in heaven because of the state of the unbaptized infant in her womb, for which she implores the sacrament. Her prayer is granted, and the repentant lover dies of remorse. The illustration of this story gives occasion for the finest of Mr. Lowell's exhibitions of love, and the poem is in all respects beautiful and complete. In the same volume appeared the author's "Prometheus," "Rhœcus," and some of his most admired shorter pieces. He put forth in it his best powers, and though it embraced occasional redundancies, and he was sometimes so ill-satisfied with his poem as to give in its conclusion a versified exposition of its meaning in the form of a *moral*, it secured the general consent to his admission into the company of men of genius.

In 1845 appeared his "Conversations on some of the Old Poets," consisting of a series of criticisms and relevant discussions which evince careful study, delicate perception, and a generous catholicity of taste; but the book does not contain the best specimens of his criticism or of his prose diction.

He gave to the public a third collection of his poems in 1848. In this there is no improvement of versification, no finer fancy, or braver imagination, than in the preceding volume; but it illustrates a deeper interest in affairs, and a warm partisanship for the philanthropists and progressists of all classes. Among his subjects are "The Present Crisis," "Anti-Texas," "The Capture of Fugitive Slaves," "Hunger and Cold," "The Landlord," &c. He gives here the first examples of a peculiar humour, which he has since cultivated with success, and many passages of finished declamation and powerful invective. He had been married, in 1844, to Miss Maria White, whose abilities are shown in a graceful composition included in this volume, and by others which I have quoted in the "Female Poets of America."

In the same year Mr. Lowell published "A Fable for Critics, or a Glance at a Few of our Literary Progenies," a rhymed essay, critical and satirical, upon the principal living writers of the country. It abounds in ingenious turns of expression, and felicitous sketches of character; it is witty and humorous, and for the most part in a spirit of genial appreciation; but in a few instances the judgments indicate too narrow a range of sympathies, and the caustic severity of others has been attributed to desires of retaliation.

The "Fable for Critics" was soon followed by "The Biglow Papers," a collection of verses in the dialect of New England, with an introduction and notes, written in the character of a pedantic but sharp-witted and patriotic country parson. The book is a satire upon the defences of our recent war against Mexico, and it exhibits in various forms of indigenous and homely humour the indignation with which the contest was regarded by the best sort of people in the eastern states. The sectional peculiarities of idiom are perhaps exaggerated, but the entire work has an appearance of genuineness.

About the same time appeared Mr. LOWELL'S "Vision of Sir Launfal," a poem founded upon the legend of the search for the Holy Grail, (the cup out of which our Lord drank with his disciples at the last supper.) In the winter of 1854–5 he delivered a course of lectures before the Lowell Institute in Boston, on the British poets, which greatly increased his reputation; and on the retirement of Mr. LONGFELLOW from the professorship of modern languages in Harvard College, the following spring, was chosen to the vacant chair, and soon after sailed for Europe to spend there one or two years in preparation for its duties.

The growth of Mr. LOWELL'S fame has been steady and rapid from the beginning of his literary career, and no one of our younger authors has a prospect of greater eminence.

TO THE DANDELION.

DEAR common flower, that grow'st beside the way,
Fringing the dusty road with harmless gold,
First pledge of blithesome May,
Which children pluck, and, full of pride, uphold,
High-hearted buccaneers, o'erjoyed that they
An Eldorado in the grass have found,
Which not the rich earth's ample round
May match in wealth—thou art more dear to me
Than all the prouder summer-blooms may be.

Gold such as thine ne'er drew the Spanish prow
Through the primeval hush of Indian seas,
Nor wrinkled the lean brow
Of age, to rob the lover's heart of ease;
'T is the Spring's largess, which she scatters now
To rich and poor alike, with lavish hand,
Though most hearts never understand
To take it at GOD's value, but pass by
The offer'd wealth with unrewarded eye.

Thou art my trophies and mine Italy;
To look at thee unlocks a warmer clime;
The eyes thou givest me
Are in the heart, and heed not space or time;
Not in mid June the golden-cuirass'd bee
Feels a more summer-like, warm ravishment
In the white lily's breezy tint,
His conquer'd Sybaris, than I, when first
From the dark green thy yellow circles burst.

Then think I of deep shadows on the grass—
Of meadows where in sun the cattle graze,
Where, as the breezes pass,
The gleaming rushes lean a thousand ways—
Of leaves that slumber in a cloudy mass,
Or whiten in the wind—of waters blue
That from the distance sparkle through
Some woodland gap—and of a sky above,
Where one white cloud like a stray lamb doth move.

My childhood's earliest thoughts are link'd with thee;
The sight of thee calls back the robin's song,
Who, from the dark old tree
Beside the door, sang clearly all day long,
And I, secure in childish piety,
Listen'd as if I heard an angel sing
With news from heaven, which he did bring
Fresh every day to my untainted ears,
When birds and flowers and I were happy peers.

How like a prodigal doth Nature seem,
When thou, for all thy gold, so common art!
Thou teachest me to deem
More sacredly of every human heart,
Since each reflects in joy its scanty gleam
Of heaven, and could some wondrous secret show
Did we but pay the love we owe,
And with a child's undoubting wisdom look
On all these living pages of GOD's book.

TO THE MEMORY OF THOMAS HOOD

ANOTHER star 'neath Time's horizon dropp'd,
To gleam o'er unknown lands and seas!
Another heart that beat for freedom stopp'd:
What mournful words are these!

Oh! Love divine, thou claspest our tired earth,
And lullest it upon thy heart,
Thou knowest how much a gentle soul is worth,
To teach men what thou art.

His was a spirit that to all thy poor
Was kind as slumber after pain:
Why ope so soon thy heaven-deep Quiet's door
And call him home again?

Freedom needs all her poets: it is they
Who give her aspirations wings,
And to the wiser law of music sway
Her wild imaginings.

Yet thou hast call'd him, nor art thou unkind,
Oh! Love divine, for 't is thy will
That gracious natures leave their love behind
To work for Freedom still.

Let laurell'd marbles weigh on other tombs,
Let anthems peal for other dead,
Rustling the banner'd depth of minster-glooms
With their exulting spread:

His epitaph shall mock the short-lived stone,
No lichen shall its lines efface;
He needs these few and simple lines alone
To mark his resting-place:—

"Here lies a poet: stranger, if to thee
His claim to memory be obscure,
If thou wouldst learn how truly great was he,
Go, ask it of the poor."

SONNETS.

I. TO ——.

THROUGH suffering and sorrow thou hast pass'd
To show us what a woman true may be:
They have not taken sympathy from thee,
Nor made thee any other than thou wast;
Save as some tree, which, in a sudden blast,
Sheddeth those blossoms, that are weakly grown,
Upon the air, but keepeth every one
Whose strength gives warrant of good fruit at last;
So thou hast shed some blooms of gayety,
But never one of steadfast cheerfulness;
Nor hath thy knowledge of adversity
Robb'd thee of any faith in happiness,
But rather clear'd thine inner eyes to see
How many simple ways there are to bless.

II. THE FIERY TRIAL.

THE hungry flame hath never yet been hot
To him who won his name and crown of fire;
But it doth ask a stronger soul and higher
To bear, not longing for a prouder lot,
Those martyrdoms whereof the world knows not,—
Hope sneaped with frosty scorn, the faith of youth
Wasted in seeming vain defence of Truth,
Greatness o'ertopp'd with baseness, and fame got
Too late:—Yet this most bitter task was meant
For those right worthy in such cause to plead,
And therefore God sent poets, men content
To live in humbleness and body's need,
If they may tread the path where Jesus went,
And sow one grain of Love's eternal seed.

III.

I ASK not for those thoughts, that sudden leap
From being's sea, like the isle-seeming Kraken,
With whose great rise the ocean all is shaken
And a heart-tremble quivers through the deep;
Give me that growth which some perchance deem
Wherewith the steadfast coral-stems uprise, [sleep,
Which, by the toil of gathering energies,
Their upward way into clear sunshine keep,
Until, by Heaven's sweetest influences,
Slowly and slowly spreads a speck of green
Into a pleasant island in the seas,
Where, mid tall palms, the cane-roof'd home is seen,
And wearied men shall sit at sunset's hour,
Hearing the leaves and loving God's dear power.

IV. TO ——, ON HER BIRTH-DAY.

MAIDEN, when such a soul as thine is born,
The morning-stars their ancient music make,
And, joyful, once again their song awake,
Long silent now with melancholy scorn;
And thou, not mindless of so blest a morn,
By no least deed its harmony shalt break,
But shalt to that high chime thy footsteps take,
Through life's most darksome passes, unforlorn;
Therefore from thy pure faith thou shalt not fall,
Therefore shalt thou be ever fair and free,
And, in thine every motion, musical
As summer air, majestic as the sea,
A mystery to those who creep and craw!
Through Time, and part it from Eternity.

V. TO THE SAME.

MY Love, I have no fear that thou shouldst die;
Albeit I ask no fairer life than this,
Whose numbering-clock is still thy gentle kiss.
While Time and Peace with hands enlocked fly,—
Yet care I not where in Eternity
We live and love, well knowing that there is
No backward step for those who feel the bliss
Of Faith as their most lofty yearnings high:
Love hath so purified my heart's strong core,
Meseems I scarcely should be startled, even,
To find, some morn, that thou hadst gone before;
Since, with thy love, this knowledge too was given,
Which each calm day doth strengthen more and
more,
That they who love are but one step from Heaven.

IV. TO THE SPIRIT OF KEATS.

GREAT soul thou sittest with me in my room,
Uplifting me with thy vast, quiet eyes,
On whose full orbs, with kindly lustre, lies
The twilight warmth of ruddy ember-gloom:
Thy clear, strong tones will oft bring sudden bloom
Of hope secure, to him who lonely cries,
Wrestling with the young poet's agonies,
Neglect and scorn, which seem a certain doom;
Yes! the few words which, like great thunder-drops,
Thy large heart down to earth shook doubtfully,
Thrill'd by the inward lightning of its might,
Serene and pure, like gushing joy of light,
Shall track the eternal chords of Destiny,
After the moon-led pulse of ocean stops.

VII. TO ——.

OUR love is not a fading, earthly flower;
Its wing'd seed dropp'd down from Paradise,
And, nursed by day and night, by sun and shower,
Doth momently to fresher beauty rise:
To us the leafless autumn is not bare,
Nor winter's rattling boughs lack lusty green,
Our summer hearts make summer's fulness, where
No leaf, or bud, or blossom may be seen:
For nature's life in love's deep life doth lie,
Love,—whose forgetfulness is beauty's death,
Whose mystic keys these cells of Thou and I
Into the infinite freedom openeth,
And makes the body's dark and narrow grate
The wide-flung leaves of Heaven's palace-gate

VIII. IN ABSENCE.

THESE rugged, wintry days I scarce could bear,
Did I not know, that, in the early spring,
When wild March winds upon their errands sing,
Thou wouldst return, bursting on this still air,
Like those same winds, when, startled from their
They hunt up violets, and free swift brooks [lair,
From icy cares, even as thy clear looks
Bid my heart bloom, and sing, and break all care:
When drops with welcome rain the April day,
My flowers shall find their April in thine eyes,
Save there the rain in dreamy clouds doth stay,
As loath to fall out of those happy skies;
Yet sure, my love, thou art most like to May,
That comes with steady sun when April dies.

THE POET.

In the old days of awe and keen-eyed wonder,
The Poet's song with blood-warm truth was rife;
He saw the mysteries which circle under
The outward shell and skin of daily life.
Nothing to him were fleeting time and fashion,
His soul was led by the eternal law;
There was in him no hope of fame, no passion,
But with calm, godlike eyes, he only saw.
He did not sigh o'er heroes dead and buried,
Chief mourner at the Golden Age's hearse,
Nor deem that souls whom Charon grim had ferried
Alone were fitting themes of epic verse:
He could believe the promise of to-morrow,
And feel the wondrous meaning of to-day;
He had a deeper faith in holy sorrow
Than the world's seeming loss could take away.
To know the heart of all things was his duty,
All things did sing to him to make him wise,
And, with a sorrowful and conquering beauty,
The soul of all looked grandly from his eyes.
He gazed on all within him and without him,
He watch'd the flowing of Time's steady tide,
And shapes of glory floated all about him
And whisper'd to him, and he prophesied.
Than all men he more fearless was and freer,
And all his brethren cried with one accord,—
"Behold the holy man! Behold the Seer!
Him who hath spoken with the unseen Lord!"
He to his heart with large embrace had taken
The universal sorrow of mankind,
And, from that root, a shelter never shaken,
The tree of wisdom grew with sturdy rind.
He could interpret well the wondrous voices
Which to the calm and silent spirit come;
He knew that the One Soul no more rejoices
In the star's anthem than the insect's hum.
He in his heart was ever meek and humble,
And yet with kingly pomp his numbers ran,
As he foresaw how all things false should crumble
Before the free, uplifted soul of man:
And, when he was made full to overflowing
With all the loveliness of heaven and earth,
Out rush'd his song, like molten iron glowing,
To show God sitting by the humblest hearth.
With calmest courage he was ever ready
To teach that action was the truth of thought,
And, with strong arm and purpose firm and steady,
The anchor of the drifting world he wrought,
So did he make the meanest man partaker
Of all his brother-gods unto him gave;
All souls did reverence him and name him Maker,
And when he died heaped temples on his grave.
And still his deathless words of light are swimming
Serene throughout the great, deep infinite
Of human soul, unwaning and undimming,
To cheer and guide the mariner at night.
But now the Poet is an empty rhymer
Who lies with idle elbow on the grass,
And fits his singing, like a cunning timer,
To all men's prides and fancies as they pass.
Not his the song, which, in its metre holy,
Chimes with the music of the eternal stars,
Humbling the tyrant, lifting up the lowly,
And sending sun through the soul's prison-bars.
Maker no more,—O, no! unmaker rather,
For he unmakes who doth not all put forth
The power given by our loving Father
To show the body's dross, the spirit's worth.
Awake! great spirit of the ages olden!
Shiver the mists that hide thy starry lyre,
And let man's soul be yet again beholden
To thee for wings to soar to her desire.
O, prophesy no more to-morrow's splendor,
Be no more shame-faced to speak out for Truth,
Lay on her altar all the gushings tender,
The hope, the fire, the loving faith of youth!
O, prophesy no more the Maker's coming,
Say not his onward footsteps thou canst hear
In the dim void, like to the awful humming
Of the great wings of some new-lighted sphere!
O, prophesy no more, but be the Poet!
This longing was but granted unto thee
That, when all beauty thou couldst feel and know it,
That beauty in its highest thou couldst be.
O, thou who moanest, tost with sealike longings,
Who dimly hearest voices call on thee,
Whose soul is overfill'd with mighty throngings
Of love, and fear, and glorious agony,
Thou of the toil-strung hands and iron sinews
And soul by Mother Earth with freedom fed,
In whom the hero-spirit yet continues,
The old free nature is not chain'd or dead,
Arouse! let thy soul break in music-thunder,
Let loose the ocean that is in thee pent,
Pour forth thy hope, thy fear, thy love, thy wonder,
And tell the age what all its signs have meant.
Where'er thy wilder'd crowd of brethren jostles,
Where'er there lingers but a shade of wrong,
There still is need of martyrs and apostles,
There still are texts for never-dying song:
From age to age man's still aspiring spirit
Finds wider scope and sees with clearer eyes,
And thou in larger measure dost inherit
What made thy great forerunners free and wise.
Sit thou enthroned where the Poet's mountain
Above the thunder lifts its silent peak,
And roll thy songs down like a gathering fountain,
That all may drink and find the rest they seek.
Sing! there shall silence grow in earth and heaven,
A silence of deep awe and wondering;
For, listening gladly, bend the angels, even,
To hear a mortal like an angel sing.

Among the toil-worn poor my soul is seeking
For one to bring the Maker's name to light,
To be the voice of that almighty speaking
Which every age demands to do it right.
Proprieties our silken bards environ;
He who would be the tongue of this wide land
Must string his harp with chords of sturdy iron
And strike it with a toil-embrowned hand;
One who hath dwelt with Nature well-attended.
Who hath learnt wisdom from her mystic books,
Whose soul with all her countless lives hath blended,
So that all beauty awes us in his looks;
Who not with body's waste his soul hath pamper'd,
Who as the clear northwestern wind is free,

Who walks with Form's observances unhamper'd,
And follows the One Will obediently;
Whose eyes, like windows on a breezy summit,
Control a lovely prospect every way;
Who doth not sound God's sea with earthly plummet,
And find a bottom still of worthless clay;
Who heeds not how the lower gusts are working,
Knowing that one sure wind blows on above,
And sees, beneath the foulest faces lurking,
One God-built shrine of reverence and love;
Who sees all stars that wheel their shining marches
Around the centre fix'd of Destiny,
Where the encircling soul serene o'erarches
The moving globe of being, like a sky; [nearer
Who feels that God and Heaven's great deeps are
Him to whose heart his fellow-man is nigh,
Who doth not hold his soul's own freedom dearer
Than that of all his brethren, low or high;
Who to the right can feel himself the truer
For being gently patient with the wrong,
Who sees a brother in the evildoer,
And finds in Love the heart's blood of his song;—
This, this is he for whom the world is waiting
To sing the beatings of its mighty heart,
Too long hath it been patient with the grating
Of scrannel-pipes, and heard it misnamed Art.
To him the smiling soul of man shall listen,
Laying awhile its crown of thorns aside,
And once again in every eye shall glisten
The glory of a nature satisfied.
His verse shall have a great, commanding motion,
Heaving and swelling with a melody
Learnt of the sky, the river, and the ocean,
And all the pure, majestic things that be.
Awake, then, thou! we pine for thy great presence
To make us feel the soul once more sublime,
We are of far too infinite an essence
To rest contented with the lies of Time.
Speak out! and, lo! a hush of deepest wonder
Shall sink o'er all his many-voiced scene,
As when a sudden burst of rattling thunder
Shatters the blueness of a sky serene.

EXTRACT FROM A LEGEND OF BRITTANY.

Then swell'd the organ: up through choir and nave
The music trembled with an inward thrill
Of bliss at its own grandeur: wave on wave
Its flood of mellow thunder rose, until
The hush'd air shiver'd with the throb it gave,
Then, poising for a moment, it stood still,
And sank and rose again, to burst in spray
That wander'd into silence far away.

Like to a mighty heart the music seem'd,
That yearns with melodies it cannot speak,
Until, in grand despair of what it dream'd,
In the agony of effort it doth break,
Yet triumphs breaking; on it rush'd and stream'd
And wanton'd in its might, as when a lake,
Long pent among the mountains, bursts its walls
And in one crowding gush leaps forth and falls.

Deeper and deeper shudders shook the air,
As the huge bass kept gathering heavily,
Like thunder when it rouses in its lair,
And with its hoarse growl shakes the low-hung [sky:
It grew up like a darkness everywhere,
Filling the vast cathedral;—suddenly,
From the dense mass a boy's clear treble broke
Like lightning, and the full-toned choir awoke.

Through gorgeous windows shone the sun aslant,
Brimming the church with gold and purple mist,
Meet atmosphere to bosom that rich chant,
Where fifty voices in one strand did twist
Their varicolour'd tones, and left no want
To the delighted soul, which sank abyss'd
In the warm music-cloud, while, far below,
The organ heaved its surges to and fro.

As if a lark should suddenly drop dead
While the blue air yet trembled with its song,
So snapped at once that music's golden thread,
Struck by a nameless fear that leapt along
From heart to heart, and like a shadow spread
With instantaneous shiver through the throng,
So that some glanced behind, as half aware
A hideous shape of dread were standing there.

As, when a crowd of pale men gather round,
Watching an eddy in the leaden deep,
From which they deem'd the body of one drown'd
Will be cast forth, from face to face doth creep
An eager dread that holds all tongues fast bound,
Until the horror, with a ghastly leap,
Starts up, its dead blue arms stretch'd aimlessly,
Heaved with the swinging of the careless sea,—

So in the faces of all these there grew,
As by one impulse, a dark, freezing awe,
Which with a fearful fascination drew
All eyes toward the altar; damp and raw
The air grew suddenly, and no man knew
Whether perchance his silent neighbour saw
The dreadful thing, which all were sure would rise
To scare the strained lids wider from their eyes.

The incense trembled as it upward sent
Its slow, uncertain thread of wandering blue,
As 't were the only living element
In all the church, so deep the stillness grew;
It seem'd one might have heard it, as it went,
Give out an audible rustle, curling through
The midnight silence of that awe-struck air,
More hush'd than death, though so much life was
there.

THE SYRENS.

The sea is lonely, the sea is dreary,
The sea is restless and uneasy;
Thou seekest quiet, thou art weary,
Wandering thou knowest not whither;—
Our little isle is green and breezy,
Come and rest thee! O come hither!
Come to this peaceful home of ours,
Where evermore
The low west-wind creeps panting up the shore
To be at rest among the flowers:

Full of rest, the green moss lifts,
  As the dark waves o' the sea
Draw in and out of rocky rifts,
  Calling solemnly to thee
With voices deep and hollow,—
    "To the shore
  Follow! O follow!
To be at rest for evermore!
    For evermore!

  Look how the gray, old Ocean
From the depth of his heart rejoices,
Heaving with a gentle motion,
When he hears our restful voices;
List how he sings in an undertone,
Chiming with our melody;
And all sweet sounds of earth and air
Melt into one low voice alone,
That murmurs over the weary sea,—
And seems to sing from everywhere,—
"Here mayest thou harbour peacefully,
Here mayest thou rest from the aching oar;
  Turn thy curvèd prow ashore,
And in our green isle rest for evermore!
    For evermore!"
And Echo half wakes in the wooded hill,
  And, to her heart so calm and deep,
  Murmurs over in her sleep,
Doubtfully pausing and murmuring still,
    "Evermore!"
      Thus, on Life's weary sea,
      Heareth the marinere
      Voices sweet, from far and near,
      Ever singing low and clear,
      Ever singing longingly.

  Is it not better here to be,
Than to be toiling late and soon?
In the dreary night to see
Nothing but the blood-red moon
Go up and down into the sea;
Or, in the loneliness of day,
  To see the still seals only
Solemnly lift their faces gray,
  Making it yet more lonely?
Is it not better, than to hear
Only the sliding of the wave
Beneath the plank, and feel so near
A cold and lonely grave,
A restless grave, where thou shalt lie
Even in death unquietly?
Look down beneath thy wave-worn bark,
  Lean over the side and see
The leaden eye of the side-long shark
  Upturnèd patiently,
Ever waiting there for thee:
Look down and see those shapeless forms,
  Which ever keep their dreamless sleep
  Far down within the gloomy deep,
And only stir themselves in storms,
Rising like islands from beneath,
And snorting through the angry spray,
As the frail vessel perisheth
In the whirls of their unwieldy play:
  Look down! Look down!
Upon the seaweed, slimy and dark,
That waves its arms so lank and brown,
  Beckoning for thee!
Look down beneath thy wave-worn bark
  Into the cold depth of the sea!
    Look down! Look down!
      Thus, on Life's lonely sea,
      Heareth the marinere
      Voices sad, from far and near,
      Ever singing full of fear,
      Ever singing drearfully.

  Here all is pleasant as a dream;
The wind scarce shaketh down the dew,
The green grass floweth like a stream
    Into the ocean's blue:
      Listen! O listen!
Here is a gush of many streams,
  A song of many birds,
And every wish and longing seems
Lull'd to a number'd flow of words,—
    Listen! O listen!
Here ever hum the golden bees
Underneath full-blossom'd trees,
At once with glowing fruit and flowers crown'd;—
The sand is so smooth, the yellow sand,
That thy keel will not grate, as it touches the land;
All around, with a slumberous sound,
The singing waves slide up the strand,
And there, where the smooth, wet pebbles be,
The waters gurgle longingly,
As if they fain would seek the shore,
To be at rest from the ceaseless roar,
To be at rest for evermore,—
    For evermore.
      Thus, on Life's gloomy sea,
      Heareth the marinere
      Voices sweet, from far and near,
      Ever singing in his ear,
      "Here is rest and peace for thee!"

AN INCIDENT IN A RAILROAD CAR.

  He spoke of Burns: men rude and rough
  Press'd round to hear the praise of one
Whose heart was made of manly, simple stuff,
    As homespun as their own.

  And, when he read, they forward leaned,
  Drinking, with thirsty hearts and ears,
His brook-like songs whom glory never weaned
    From humble smiles and tears.

  Slowly there grew a tender awe,
  Sun-like, o'er faces brown and hard,
As if in him who read they felt and saw
    Some presence of the bard.

  It was a sight for sin and wrong
  And slavish tyranny to see,
A sight to make our faith more pure and strong
    In high humanity.

  I thought, these men will carry hence
  Promptings their former life above,
And something of a finer reverence
    For beauty, truth, and love.

God scatters love on every side,
Freely among his children all,
And always hearts are lying open wide,
Wherein some grains may fall.

There is no wind but soweth seeds
Of a more true and open life,
Which burst, unlook'd-for, into high-soul'd deeds
With wayside beauty rife.

We find within these souls of ours
Some wild germs of a higher birth,
Which in the poet's tropic heart bear flowers
Whose fragrance fills the earth.

Within the hearts of all men lie
These promises of wider bliss,
Which blossom into hopes that cannot die,
In sunny hours like this.

All that hath been majestical
In life or death, since time began,
Is native in the simple heart of all,
The angel heart of man.

And thus, among the untaught poor,
Great deeds and feelings find a home,
That cast in shadow all the golden lore
Of classic Greece and Rome.

O mighty brother-soul of man,
Where'er thou art, in low or high,
Thy skyey arches with exulting span
O'er-roof infinity!

All thoughts that mould the age begin
Deep down within the primitive soul,
And from the many slowly upward win
To one who grasps the whole:

In his broad breast the feeling deep
That struggled on the many's tongue,
Swells to a tide of thought, whose surges leap
O'er the weak thrones of wrong.

All thought begins in feeling,—wide
In the great mass its base is hid,
And, narrowing up to thought, stands glorified,
A moveless pyramid.

Nor is he far astray who deems
That every hope, which rises and grows broad
In the world's heart, by order'd impulse streams
From the great heart of God.

God wills, man hopes: in common souls
Hope is but vague and undefined,
Till from the poet's tongue the message rolls
A blessing to his kind.

Never did Poesy appear
So full of heaven to me, as when
I saw how it would pierce through pride and fear
To the lives of coarsest men.

It may be glorious to write
Thoughts that shall glad the two or three
High souls, like those far stars that come in sight
Once in a century;—

But better far it is to speak
One simple word, which now and then
Shall waken their free nature in the weak
And friendless sons of men;

To write some earnest verse or line,
Which, seeking not the praise of art,
Shall make a clearer faith and manhood shine
In the untutor'd heart.

He who doth this, in verse or prose,
May be forgotten in his day,
But surely shall be crown'd at last with those
Who live and speak for aye.

THE HERITAGE.

The rich man's son inherits lands,
And piles of brick, and stone, and gold,
And he inherits soft, white hands,
And tender flesh that fears the cold,
Nor dares to wear a garment old;
A heritage, it seems to me,
One scarce would wish to hold in fee.

The rich man's son inherits cares;
The bank may break, the factory burn,
A breath may burst his bubble shares,
And soft, white hands could hardly earn
A living that would serve his turn;
A heritage, it seems to me,
One scarce would wish to hold in fee.

The rich man's son inherits wants,
His stomach craves for dainty fare;
With sated heart, he hears the pants
Of toiling hinds with brown arms bare,
And wearies in his easy chair;
A heritage, it seems to me,
One scarce would wish to hold in fee.

What doth the poor man's son inherit?
Stout muscles and a sinewy heart,
A hardy frame, a hardier spirit;
King of two hands, he does his part
In every useful toil and art;
A heritage, it seems to me,
A king might wish to hold in fee.

What doth the poor man's son inherit?
Wishes o'erjoy'd with humble things,
A rank adjudged by toil-won merit,
Content that from employment springs,
A heart that in his labour sings;
A heritage, it seems to me,
A king might wish to hold in fee.

What doth the poor man's son inherit?
A patience learn'd by being poor,
Courage, if sorrow come, to bear it,
A fellow-feeling that is sure
To make the outcast bless his door;
A heritage, it seems to me,
A king might wish to hold in fee.

O, rich man's son! there is a toil,
That with all others level stands;
Large charity doth never soil,
But only whiten, soft, white hands,—
This is the best crop from thy lands;
A heritage, it seems to me,
Worth being rich to hold in fee.

O, poor man's son, scorn not thy state;
There is worse weariness than thine,
In merely being rich and great;
Toil only gives the soul to shine,
And makes rest fragrant and benign;
A heritage, it seems to me,
Worth being poor to hold in fee.

Both, heirs to some six feet of sod,
Are equal in the earth at last;
Both, children of the same dear God,
Prove title to your heirship vast
By record of a well-fill'd past;
A heritage, it seems to me,
Well worth a life to hold in fee.

TO THE FUTURE.

O, Land of Promise! from what Pisgah's height
Can I behold thy stretch of peaceful bowers?
Thy golden harvests flowing out of sight,
Thy nestled homes and sun-illumined towers?
Gazing upon the sunset's high-heap'd gold,
Its crags of opal and of crysolite,
Its deeps on deeps of glory that unfold
Still brightening abysses,
And blazing precipices,
Whence but a scanty leap it seems to heaven,
Sometimes a glimpse is given,
Of thy more gorgeous realm, thy more unstinted blisses.

O, Land of Quiet! to thy shore the surf
Of the perturbed Present rolls and sleeps;
Our storms breathe soft as June upon thy turf
And lure out blossoms: to thy bosom leaps,
As to a mother's, the o'er-wearied heart,
Hearing far off and dim the toiling mart,
The hurrying feet, the curses without numoer,
And, circled with the glow Elysian,
Of thine exulting vision,
Out of its very cares wooes charms for peace and slumber.

To thee the Earth lifts up her fetter'd hands
And cries for vengeance; with a pitying smile
Thou blessest her, and she forgets her bands,
And her old wo-worn face a little while
Grows young and noble; unto thee the Oppressor
Looks, and is dumb with awe;
The eternal law
Which makes the crime its own blindfold redresser,
Shadows his heart with perilous foreboding,
And he can see the grim-eyed Doom
From out the trembling gloom
Its silent-footed steeds toward his palace goading.

What promises hast thou for Poets' eyes,
Aweary of the turmoil and the wrong!
To all their hopes what overjoy'd replies!
What undream'd ecstasies for blissful song!
Thy happy plains no war-trumps brawling clangor
Disturbs, and fools the poor to hate the poor;
The humble glares not on the high with anger;
Love leaves no grudge at less, no greed for more;
In vain strives self the godlike sense to smother;
From the soul's deeps
It throbs and leaps;
The noble 'neath foul rags beholds his long lost brother.

To thee the Martyr looketh, and his fires
Unlock their fangs and leave his spirit free;
To thee the Poet 'mid his toil aspires,
And grief and hunger climb about his knee
Welcome as children: thou upholdest
The lone Inventor by his demon haunted;
The Prophet cries to thee when hearts are coldest,
And, gazing o'er the midnight's bleak abyss,
Sees the drowsed soul awaken at thy kiss,
And stretch its happy arms and leap up disenchanted.

Thou bringest vengeance, but so loving-kindly
The guilty thinks it pity; taught by thee
Fierce tyrants drop the scourges wherewith blindly
Their own souls they were scarring; conquerors see
With horror in their hands the accursed spear
That tore the meek One's side on Calvary,
And from their trophies shrink with ghastly fear;
Thou, too, art the Forgiver,
The beauty of man's soul to man revealing;
The arrows from thy quiver
Pierce error's guilty heart, but only pierce for healing.

O, whither, whither, glory-winged dreams,
From out Life's sweat and turmoil would ye bear me?
Shut, gates of Fancy, on your golden gleams,
This agony of hopeless contrast spare me!
Fade, cheating glow, and leave me to my night!
He is a coward who would borrow
A charm against the present sorrow
From the vague Future's promise of delight:
As life's alarums nearer roll,
The ancestral buckler calls,
Self-clanging, from the walls
In the high temple of the soul;
Where are most sorrows, there the poet's sphere is,
To feed the soul with patience,
To heal its desolations
With words of unshorn truth, with love that never wearies.

JAMES T. FIELDS.

[Born, 1820.]

Mr. Fields is a native of Portsmouth, New Hampshire, but has long resided in Boston. He is a partner in a well-known publishing and book-selling house in that city. His principal poems are "Commerce," read before the Boston Mercantile Library Association on its anniversary in 1838, when he was associated as poet with Edward Everett, who delivered on the occasion one of his most brilliant orations; and "The Post of Honour," read before the same society in 1848, when Daniel Webster preceded him as orator. For several years he has been an occasional contributor to the magazines, and a few of his poems, as "The Fair Wind," "Yankee Ships," and "Dirge for a Young Girl," have been copied from them into the newspapers of all parts of the Union. The general style of his serious pieces is pure, sweet, thoughtful, and harmonious; and though evidently unlaboured, they are characterized by much refinement of taste and an intuitive perception of metrical proprieties. His lyrics are clear, strong, and bright, in expression, and dashing in movement, and have that charm which comes from a "polished want of polish," in which spontaneous sensibility is allied with instinctive taste. The "Sleighing Song" has a clear, cold, merry sparkle, and a rapidity of metrical motion (the very verse seeming to go on runners), which bring the quick jingle of bells and the moon making diamonds out of snow-flakes, vividly home to the fancy. Perhaps his most characteristic poem, in respect to subtlety of sentiment and delicacy of illustration, is "A Bridal Melody." There is a mystical beauty in it which eludes a careless eye and untuned ear.

Besides his serious poems, he has produced some very original mirthful pieces, in which are adroit touches of wit, felicitous hits at current follies, and instances of quaint humour, laughing through prim and decorous lines, which evince a genius for *vers de société*.

The poems Mr. Fields has given us are evidently the careless products of a singularly sensitive and fertile mind—indications rather than exponents of its powers—furnishing evidence of a capacity which it is to be hoped the engagements of business will not wholly absorb.

In 1847 and the following year Mr. Fields visited Europe, and soon after his return a collection of his poems was published by Ticknor and Company, of Boston.

ON A PAIR OF ANTLERS,

BROUGHT FROM GERMANY.

Gift, from the land of song and wine—
 Can I forget the enchanted day,
When first along the glorious Rhine
 I heard the huntsman's bugle play,
And mark'd the early star that dwells
Among the cliffs of Drachenfels!

Again the isles of beauty rise;
 Again the crumbling tower appears,
That stands, defying stormy skies,
 With memories of a thousand years;
And dark old forests wave again,
And shadows crowd the dusky plain.

They brought the gift, that I might hear
 The music of the roaring pine—
To fill again my charmed ear
 With echoes of the Rodenstein—
With echoes of the silver horn,
Across the wailing waters borne.

Trophies of spoil! henceforth your place
 Is in this quiet home of mine;
Farewell the busy, bloody chase,
 Mute emblems now of "auld lang syne,"
When Youth and Hope went hand in hand
To roam the dear old German land.

BALLAD OF THE TEMPEST.

We were crowded in the cabin,
 Not a soul would dare to sleep—
It was midnight on the waters,
 And a storm was on the deep.

'T is a fearful thing in winter
 To be shatter'd in the blast,
And to hear the rattling trumpet
 Thunder, "Cut away the mast!"

So we shudder'd there in silence—
 For the stoutest held his breath,
While the hungry sea was roaring,
 And the breakers talked with Death

As thus we sat in darkness,
 Each one busy in his prayers—
"We are lost!" the captain shouted,
 As he stagger'd down the stairs.

But his little daughter whisper'd,
 As she took his icy hand,
"Isn't God upon the ocean,
 Just the same as on the land?"

Then we kiss'd the little maiden,
 And we spoke in better cheer,
And we anchor'd safe in harbor
 When the morn was shining clear.

A VALENTINE.

She that is fair, though never vain or proud,
More fond of home than fashion's changing crowd;
Whose taste refined even female friends admire,
Dress'd not for show, but robed in neat attire;
She who has learn'd, with mild, forgiving breast,
To pardon frailties, hidden or confess'd;
True to herself, yet willing to submit,
More sway'd by love than ruled by worldly wit:
Though young, discreet—though ready, ne'er unkind,
Blest with no pedant's, but a woman's mind:
She wins our hearts, toward her our thoughts incline,
So at her door go leave my Valentine.

ON A BOOK OF SEA-MOSSES,
SENT TO AN EMINENT ENGLISH POET.

To him who sang of Venice, and reveal'd
How wealth and glory cluster'd in her streets,
And poised her marble domes with wondrous skill,
We send these tributes, plunder'd from the sea.
These many-colour'd, variegated forms,
Sail to our rougher shores, and rise and fall
To the deep music of the Atlantic wave.
Such spoils we capture where the rainbows drop,
Melting in ocean. Here are broideries strange,
Wrought by the sea-nymphs from their golden hair,
And wove by moonlight. Gently turn the leaf:
From narrow cells, scoop'd in the rocks, we take
These fairy textures, lightly moor'd at morn.
Down sunny slopes, outstretching to the deep,
We roam at noon, and gather shapes like these.
Note now the painted webs from verdurous isles,
Festoon'd and spangled in sea-caves, and say
What hues of land can rival tints like those,
Torn from the scarfs and gonfalons of kings
Who dwell beneath the waters! Such our gift,
Cull'd from a margin of the western world,
And offer'd unto genius in the old.

FROM "THE POST OF HONOUR."

GLORY.

Unchanging Power! thy genius still presides
O'er vanquish'd fields, and ocean's purpled tides;
Sits like a spectre at the soldier's board,
Adds Spartan steps to many a broken sword;
For thee and thine combining squadrons form
To sweep the field with Glory's awful storm;
The intrepid warrior shouts thy deathless name,
And plucks new valour from thy torch of fame;
For him the bell shall wake its loudest song,
For him the cannon's thunder echo long,
For him a nation weave the unfading crown,
And swell the triumph of his sweet renown.
So Nelson watch'd, long ere Trafalgar's days,
Thy radiant orb, prophetic Glory, blaze—
Saw Victory wait, to weep his bleeding scars,
And plant his breast with Honour's burning stars.
So the young hero, with expiring breath,
Bequeaths fresh courage in the hour of death,
Bids his brave comrades hear the inspiring blast,
And nail their colours dauntless to the mast;
Then dies, like Lawrence, trembling on his lip
That cry of Honour, "Don't give up the ship!"

TRUE HONOUR.

The painter's skill life's lineaments may trace,
And stamp the impress of a speaking face;
The chisel's touch may make that marble warm
Which glows with all but breathing manhood's form—
But deeper lines, beyond the sculptor's art,
Are those which write their impress on the heart.
On Talfourd's page what bright memorials glow
Of all that's noblest, gentlest, best below!
Thou generous brother, guard of griefs conceal'd;
Matured by sorrow, deep but unreveal'd,
Let me but claim, for all thy vigils here,
The noiseless tribute to a heart sincere.
Though Dryburgh's walls still hold their sacred dust,
And Stratford's chancel shrines its hallow'd trust,
To Elia's grave the pilgrim shall repair,
And hang with love perennial garlands there.
And thou, great bard of never-dying name,
Thy filial care outshines the poet's fame;
For who, that wanders by the dust of Gray
While memory tolls the knell of parting day,
But lingers fondly at the hallow'd tomb,
That shrouds a parent in its pensive gloom,
To bless the son who pour'd that gushing tear,
So warm and earnest, at a mother's bier!
Wreaths for that line which woman's tribute gave,
"Last at the cross, and earliest at the grave."
Can I forget, a pilgrim o'er the sea,
The countless shrines of woman's charity?
In thy gay capital, bewildering France,
Where Pleasure's shuttle weaves the whirling dance,
Beneath the shelter of St. Mary's dome,
Where pallid Suffering seeks and finds a home,
Methinks I see that sainted sister now
Wipe Death's cold dewdrops from an infant's brow;
Can I forget that mild, seraphic grace,
With heaven-eyed Patience meeting in her face?
Ah! sure, if angels leave celestial spheres,
We saw an angel dry a mortal's tears.

WEBSTER.

Let blooming boys, from stagnant cloisters freed,
Sneer at old virtues and the patriot's creed;
Forget the lessons taught at Valour's side,
And all their country's honest fame deride.
All are not such: some glowing blood remains
To warm the icy current of our veins—
Some from the watch-towers still descry afar
The faintest glimmer of an adverse star.
When faction storms, when meaner statesmen quail,
Full high advanced, our eagle meets the gale!
On some great point where Honour takes her stand,
The Ehrenbreitstein of our native land—
See, in the front, to strike for Freedom's cause,
The mail'd defender of her rights and laws!
On his great arm behold a nation lean,
And parcel empire with the island queen;
Great in the council, peerless in debate,
Who follows Webster takes the field too late
Go track the globe, its changing climes explore,
From crippled Europe to the Arab's shore;
See Albion's lion guard her stormy seas,
See Gallia's lilies float on every breeze.
Roam through the world, but find no brighter names
Than those true honour for Columbia claims.

THE OLD YEAR.

The white dawn glimmered and he said "'tis day!"
The east was reddening and he sighed "Farewell"—
The herald Sun came forth and he was dead.

Life was in all his veins but yester-morn,
And ruddy health seemed laughing on his lips;—
Now he is dust and will not breathe again!

Give him a place to lay his regal head,
Give him a tomb beside his brothers gone,
Give him a tablet for his deeds and name.

Hear the new voice that claims the vacant throne,
Take the new hand outstretched to meet thy kiss,—
But give the Past—'tis all thou canst—thy tears!

SLEIGHING-SONG.

Oh swift we go, o'er the fleecy snow,
When moonbeams sparkle round;
When hoofs keep time to music's chime.
As merrily on we bound.

On a winter's night, when hearts are light,
And health is on the wind,
We loose the rein and sweep the plain,
And leave our cares behind.

With a laugh and song, we glide along
Across the fleeting snow;
With friends beside, how swift we ride
On the beautiful track below!

Oh, the raging sea has joy for me,
When gale and tempests roar;
But give me the speed of a foaming steed,
And I'll ask for the waves no more.

FAIR WIND.

Oh, who can tell, that never sail'd
Among the glassy seas,
How fresh and welcome breaks the morn
That ushers in a breeze!
"Fair wind! fair wind!" alow, aloft,
All hands delight to cry,
As, leaping through the parted waves,
The good ship makes reply.

While fore and aft, all staunch and tight,
She spreads her canvass wide,
The captain walks his realm, the deck,
With more than monarch's pride;
For well he knows the sea-bird's wings,
So swift and sure to-day,
Will waft him many a league to-night
In triumph on his way.

Then welcome to the rushing blast
That stirs the waters now—
Ye white-plumed heralds of the deep,
Make music round her prow!
Good sea-room in the roaring gale,
Let stormy trumpets blow;
But chain ten thousand fathoms down
The sluggish calm below!

DIRGE FOR A YOUNG GIRL.

Underneath the sod, low lying,
Dark and drear,
Sleepeth one who left, in dying,
Sorrow here.

Yes, they're ever bending o'er her,
Eyes that weep;
Forms, that to the cold grave bore her,
Vigils keep.

When the summer moon is shining
Soft and fair,
Friends she loved in tears are twining
Chaplets there.

Rest in peace, thou gentle spirit,
Throned above;
Souls like thine with God inherit
Life and love!

LAST WISHES OF A CHILD.

"All the hedges are in bloom,
And the warm west wind is blowing,
Let me leave this stifled room—
Let me go where flowers are growing.

"Look! my cheek is thin and pale,
And my pulse is very low;
Ere my sight begins to fail,
Take my hand and let us go;

"Was not that the robin's song
Piping through the casement wide?
I shall not be listening long—
Take me to the meadow-side!

"Bear me to the willow-brook—
Let me hear the merry mill—
On the orchard I must look,
Ere my beating heart is still.

"Faint and fainter grows my breath—
Bear me quickly down the lane;
Mother dear, this chill is death—
I shall never speak again!"

Still the hedges are in bloom,
And the warm west wind is blowing,
Still we sit in silent gloom—
O'er her grave the grass is growing.

A BRIDAL MELODY.

She stood, like an angel just wander'd from heaven,
A pilgrim benighted away from the skies,
And little we deem'd that to mortals were given
Such visions of beauty as came from her eyes.

She look'd up and smiled on the many glad faces,
The friends of her childhood, who stood by her side;
But she shone o'er them all, like a queen of the Graces,
When blushing she whisper'd the vow of a bride.

We sang an old song, as with garlands we crown'd her,
And each left a kiss on her delicate brow;
And we pray'd that a blessing might ever surround her,
And the future of life be unclouded as now.

THOMAS DUNN ENGLISH.

[Born, 1819.]

Thomas Dunn English was born in Philadelphia on the twenty-ninth of June, 1819; received the degree of Doctor of Medicine, from the University of Pennsylvania, in 1839; and afterwards studying the law, was admitted to the bar in 1842. He wrote "Walter Woolfe, or the Doom of the Drinker," a novel, in 1842; "Mdcccxlii. or the Power of the S. F.," a political romance, in 1846; and, with G. G. Foster, an octavo volume on the then recent European revolutions, in 1848. He has edited "The Aristidean," a monthly magazine; "The John Donkey," a comic weekly; "The Philadelphia Lancet," "The New York Aurora," and a few other journals, besides writing largely for "De Bow's Review," the "American Review," and "Sartain's Magazine." Since 1852 he has resided in south-western Virginia.

Dr. English published a collection of his "Poems," in New York, in 1855. Several of them are written in a style of vigorous declamation, upon subjects to which such a style is suitable. The stirring lyric of "The Gallows Goers," is the best of his productions, and there are few more effective examples of partisan verse. It was much quoted during the agitation of the death-punishment question in several of the states between 1845 and 1850. Of a more poetical character are various love songs, written carelessly, but with freshness and apparent earnestness. Of one of these, entitled "Dora Lee," the concluding verses display in a creditable manner his abilities for description:

"Oh, cabin brown! low-roofed and fast decaying!
 No kin of mine now dwell within your walls;
Around your ruins now the gray fox straying
 His step arrests, and to his fellow calls.
The mountain, o'er whose top the winds are blowing,
 Still rears its form as loftily to the gaze;
The waterfall yet roars; the stream is flowing
 As wildly as it flowed in other days:
The eagle soars as he was wont; his screaming
 Is heard o'erhead, as loudly as when I,
Shading my vision from the sun's hot beaming,
 Looked up to note his dark form on the sky.
Yet I shall see him not; nor hill nor valley,
 Nor waterfall, nor river rushing on;
Although they rise around continually,
 'T is that they are in constant memory drawn.
There are they figured, deeply as an etching
 Worked on soft metal by strong hand could be;
And in the foreground of that life-like sketching
 She stands most life-like—long lost Dora Lee."

Dr. English is of that large and busy class known as "reformers," and seldom writes without some other purpose than the making of verses. His poems commonly refer to the experiences of humble life, which they reflect with distinctness and fidelity.

BEN BOLT.

Do n't you remember sweet Alice, Ben Bolt?
 Sweet Alice whose hair was so brown,
Who wept with delight when you gave her a smile,
 And trembled with fear at your frown?
In the old churchyard in the valley, Ben Bolt,
 In a corner obscure and alone,
They have fitted a slab of the granite so gray,
 And Alice lies under the stone.

Under the hickory tree, Ben Bolt,
 Which stood at the foot of the hill,
Together we 've lain in the noonday shade,
 And listened to Appleton's mill:
The mill-wheel has fallen to pieces, Ben Bolt,
 The rafters have tumbled in,
And a quiet which crawls round the walls as you
 gaze,
 Has followed the olden din.

Do you mind the cabin of logs, Ben Bolt,
 At the edge of the pathless wood,
And the button-ball tree with its motley limbs,
 Which nigh by the door-step stood?
The cabin to ruin has gone, Ben Bolt,
 The tree you would seek in vain;
And where once the lords of the forest waved,
 Grows grass and the golden grain.

And do n't you remember the school, Ben Bolt,
 With the master so cruel and grim,
And the shaded nook in the running brook,
 Where the children went to swim?
Grass grows on the master's grave, Ben Bolt,
 The spring of the brook is dry,
And of all the boys who were schoolmates then,
 There are only you and I.

There is change in the things I loved, Ben Bolt,
 They have changed from the old to the new;
But I feel in the deeps of my spirit the truth,
 There never was change in you.
Twelvemonths twenty have past, Ben Bolt,
 Since first we were friends—yet I hail
Thy presence a blessing, thy friendship a truth,
 Ben Bolt, of the salt-sea gale.

* In the preface to his poems, Dr. English notices quite unnecessarily an unfounded charge of plagiarism in connection with this popular song. No such charge ever deserves or receives attention unless accompanied by specifications and citations, such as were quite impossible in this case.

J. M. LEGARE.

[Born, 18—.]

Mr. Legare is of Charleston, South Carolina, and is of the family of the late eminent scholar and orator Hugh S. Legare. He published, in Boston, in 1848, "Orta Undis, and other Poems," in Latin and English, and he has since contributed to the literary miscellanies many compositions of various but progressive excellence. His favourite themes are of love and nature, and his writings are often pervaded by a religious feeling. His taste is elegant, and his tone chivalrous and manly. His verse is occasionally abrupt and harsh—perhaps from attempted condensation.

THANATOKALLOS.

I think we faint and weep more than is manly;
I think we more mistrust than Christians should.
Because the earth we cling to interposes
And hides the lower orbit of the sun,
We have no faith to know the circle perfect,
And that a day will follow on the night:
Nay, more, that when the sun we see, is setting,
He is but rising on another people,
And not his face but ours veil'd in darkness.
We are less wise than were the ancient heathen
Who temper'd feasting with a grisly moral.
With higher hope, we shrink from thoughts of dying,
And dare not read, while yet of death unbidden,
As gipsies in the palm, those seams, and circles,
And time-worn lineaments, which kings in purple
Have trembled to behold, but holy men,
Interpreting aright, like martyr'd Stephen,
In singleness of heart have sunk to sleep;
God's children weary with an evening ramble.
Unthinking custom from our very cradle
Makes us most cowards where we should be bold.
The house is closed and hush'd; a gloom funereal
Pervades the rooms once cheerful with the light;
Sobs and outcries from those we love infect us
With strange disquiet, making play unsought
Before they take us on the knee and tell us
We must no more be joyful, for a dread
And terrible calamity has smitten one.
And then, poor innocents, with frighted hearts
Within the awful chamber are we led
To look on death; the hard, impassive face,
The formal shroud, which the stiff feet erect
Into the semblance of a second forehead,
Swathed and conceal'd; the tumbler whence he drank
Who ne'er shall drink again; the various adjuncts
Of a sick room; the useless vials
Half emptied only, on the hearth the lamp,
Even the fly that buzzes round and settles
Upon the dead man's mouth, and walking thence
Into his nostril, starts him not from slumber.
All portions of the dreary, changeless scene
In the last drama, with unwholesome stillness
Succeeding to the weepings and complaints
Of Heaven's own justice, and loud cries for succour
That fill the dying ear not wholly dead,
Distract the fluttering spirit, and invest
A death-bed with a horror not its own.
I thought of these things sadly, and I wonder'd
If in this thanatopsis, soul as clay
Took part and sorrow'd. While I this debated,
I knew my soul was loosing from my hold,
And that the pines around, assuming shape
Of mournful draperies, shut out the day.
Then I lost sight and memory for a moment,
Then stood erect beside my usual couch,
And saw my longwhile tenement, a pallid
And helpless symbol of my former self.
The hands laid heavily across the breast,
The eyelids down, the mouth with final courage
That aim'd a smile for sake of her who watch'd,
But lapsed into a pang and so congeal'd,
Half sweet, half suffering: Aria to Caecinna.
Poor sinful clod, erewhile the spirit's master
Not less than servant, with desire keen
Alloying love, and oft with wants and achings
Leading the mind astray from noblest deeds
To sell its birthright for an Esau's portion.
I all forgave, for I was all forgiven.
Phosphor had brought a day too broad for twilight
Or mist upon its confines. All the old
Sad mysteries that raise gigantic shadows
Betwixt our mortal faces and God's throne,
Had fainted in its splendour; pride and sin,
Sorrow and pain, and every mortal ill,
In the deserted tenement remain'd,
A palace outwardly, a vault within.
And so, because she thought it still a palace
And not a prison with the prisoner fled,
She stood before the gates accustom'd. Weeping,
Laid her moist cheek upon its breast, and cried,
"My lord! my life!" to what had ceased from living
And could no more command with word or eyes.
It moved my pity sorely, for these fingers,
Now lock'd in agonizing prayer, once turn'd
Gently the pages of his life who slumber'd;
And this brave mouth, with words of faith and cheer

Strew'd flowers in the path he needs must tread;
That as a conqueror and not a captive,
Dragg'd at the heavy chariot-wheels of Time,
And through an arch triumphal, where for others
A narrow portal opens in the sod,
Silent, and sad, and void of outlet, he
The kingdom of his LORD might enter in.
Thus she made dying sweet and full of beauty
As life itself. There was no harsh transition;
He that slept twofold, woke a single nature
Beatified and glad. But she who stay'd,
Poor little Roman heart, no longer brave
Now that the eyes were shut forevermore,
Which made all virtues sweeter for their praise,
Saw not the joy and greatness of the change.
And I drew near her, as a spirit may
Not to the mortal ear, but that the words
Seem'd teachings of her bruised and lowly soul:
"Is this the poet of thy summer days,
The thoughtful husband of maturer years?
Are these the lips whose kindly words could reach
The deepness of thy nature? If they be,
Let them resume their own, nor tarry. Nay,
Thou *knowest* all that thou didst ever love
Is lifted out, and all that thou didst hate
Lived in the flesh, and with the flesh remains.
What matters it to thee if this decays,
And mingling with the sod, is trampled on
Of clownish feet, by gleaming share upturn'd,
Or feeds a rose, or roots a noisome weed?
How canst thou halve thy heart, half to the grave,
Half to high Heaven yield? Thank GOD instead,
That he who was so dear to thee, released
From sin and care, at length has found great peace."
While she thus mused, her silent tears were stay'd,
And kneeling down, with her sweet, patient face
Lifted toward heaven, itself sufficient prayer—
"LORD GOD!" she cried, "thou knowest best how weak
And frail I am, and faithless; give me strength
To take the rod thou sendest for a staff,
And falter never more in this lone journey!"
Then she went forth and gather'd freshest flowers,
And strew'd them on the dead: young violets
Upon the breast, verbena round the temples,
Loose rose-leaves o'er the mouth, to hide the pang,
And in his hand a lily newly open'd,
In token of her faith and his transition.
And in her eyes there reign'd such quietude,
That those who saw her, said, "An angel surely
Has spoken with her, or her reason's moved
By sufferings prolong'd." But none might say
She loved but lightly, or with levity
Look'd forward to the common lot of all.

MAIZE IN TASSEL.

THE blades of maize are broad and green,
The farm-roof scarcely shows between
The long and softly-rustling rows
Through which the farmer homeward goes.
The blue smoke curling through the trees,
The children round their mother's knees,
He sees, and thanks GOD while he sees.

He holds one in his sturdy hands
Aloft, when at the threshold stands
(None noticed whence) a stranger. "Dame,"
The stranger said, as half with shame
He made request; "astray and poor,
By hunger guided to your door,
I"—"Hush," she answer'd, "say no more!"

The farmer set the prattler down—
(Soft heart, although his hands were brown!)
With words of welcome brought and pour'd
Cool water from the spring: the board
The wife set out. What mellow light
Made the mean hovel's walls as white
As snow! how sweet their bread that night!

Long while their humble lot had been
To dwell with poverty: between
Them all one pallet and a bed
Were shared. But to the latter led,
The guest in peaceful slumber lay,
While, with what broken sleep they may,
The dame and host await the day.

So pass'd the night. At length the dawn
Arrived, and show'd the stranger gone.
To none had e'er been closed their door
Who ask'd for alms; yet none before
Had so much lack'd in courtesy.
So spoke the wife. Her husband, he
Sat musing by most anxiously—

Of sterner need. A drought that year
Prevail'd, and though the corn in ear
Began to swell, must perish all
Unless a kindly rain should fall.
GOD send it straight!—or toil from morn
To eve, the hoard of buried corn,
Ay, food itself, were lost and gone.

Such thoughts now bring him to the door:
Perchance some cloud sails up before
The morning breeze. None—none; in vain
His eyes explore the blue again:
With sighs to earth returns his gaze.
Ha! what is here!—to GOD be praise!
See, see the glad drops on the maize!

No mist had dimm'd the night, and yet
The furrows all lay soft and wet,
As if with frequent showers; nay,
More—all bloom that shuns the day,
And tassel tall, and ear and blade,
With heavy drops were downward weighed,
And a swift stream the pathway fray'd.

Long while might I prolong this strain,
Relating thence how great his gain;
How he who held not from the poor,
Now saw his corncribs running o'er;
And how his riches grew amain,
And on his hillside ripen'd grain
When parch'd was that within the plain.

But who the guest was of that night
Conjecture thou—I dare not write.
We know that angels, with the mien
Of men, of men the guests have been;
That he who giveth to the poor,
Lends to the Lord. (I am not sure—)
The promise here deep meaning bore.

ERASTUS W. ELLSWORTH.

(Born 1822.)

ERASTUS W. ELLSWORTH was born in East Windsor, Connecticut, in November, 1822. His father was at that time a merchant, doing business in New York, in which city our author passed his boyhood until 1833, when the family retired to a farm, in his native town, where they have ever since resided. He was graduated at Amherst College, in 1844, and soon after commenced the study of the law, but a predilection for natural philosophy induced the devotion of much of his time to experimental studies, chiefly relating to machinery and mechanical inventions, and in 1845 he took out two patents, one for a drawing or copying instrument, and the other for a device for making a syphon discharge a portion of its contents at the highest point, or curve, thus making it available for elevating water or other fluids. Both these inventions are now in practical though not extensive use; and their reception led him to abandon his legal studies, and to enter an extensive foundry and machine shop, where he remained, among tools and machinery, until he acquired a competent knowledge of the art and mystery of making steam-engines. If his profession is now demanded, he calls himself a machinist, but he has never since the completion of his novitiate given the trade much attention

His first published poem, entitled "The Yankee," appeared in 1849, and he has since been an occasional contributor to the literary journals. His best and longest poem, the finest structure in English verse from the suggestive materials furnished by the classical legend, is "Ariadne," originally printed in the "International Magazine" for 1852. It reminds us, in some passages, of "Comus," but its peculiar merits as a specimen of poetical art are decided and conspicuous. In the spring of 1855 he published his first volume, containing not a complete collection, nor perhaps the best selection that might have been offered of his fugitive pieces, but such as exhibited in the most striking manner the variety of his tastes and talents. The leading poem is entitled "The Chimes," the main idea of which is, that poets derive a portion of their inspiration from each others' songs, and for its illustration he pays Mr. LONGFELLOW a delicate compliment by imitating the melody of one of his beautiful productions. His success led to a ridiculous but offensively-stated charge of plagiarism in one of the monthly magazines.

Of Mr. ELLSWORTH's shorter poems one of the most thoughtful and impressive is, "What is the Use?" It might be abridged without injury, but it is a performance to be pondered and remembered.

WHAT IS THE USE?

I SAW a man, by some accounted wise,
For some things said and done before their eyes,
Quite overcast, and in a restless muse,
Pacing a path about,
And often giving out:
"What is the use?"

Then I, with true respect: What meanest thou
By those strange words, and that unsettled brow?
Health, wealth, the fair esteem of ample views,
To these things thou art born.
But he as one forlorn:
"What is the use?"

"I have surveyed the sages and their books,
Man, and the natural world of woods and brooks,
Seeking that perfect good that I would choose;
But find no perfect good,
Settled and understood.
What is the use?

"Life, in a poise, hangs trembling on the beam,
Even in a breath bounding to each extreme
Of joy and sorrow; therefore I refuse
All beaten ways of bliss,
And only answer this:
What is the use?

"The hoodwinked world is seeking happiness.
'Which way?' they cry, 'here?' 'no!' 'there?' 'who can guess?'
And so they grope and grope, and grope, and cruise
On, on, till life is lost,
At blindman's with a ghost.
What is the use?

"Love first, with most, then wealth, distinction, fame,
Quicken the blood and spirit on the game.
Some try them all, and all alike accuse—
'I have been all,' said one,
'And find that all is none.'
What is the use?

"In woman's love we sweetly are undone,
Willing to attract, but harder to be won,
Harder to keep is she whose love we choose.
Loves are like flowers that grow
In soils on fire below.
What is the use?

"Some pray for wealth, and seem to pray aright;
They heap until themselves are out of sight;
Yet stand, in charities, not over shoes,
And ask of their old age
As an old ledger page,
What is the use?....

"'The strife for fame and the high praise of power,
Is as a man, who, panting up a tower,
Bears a great stone, then, straining all his thews,
Heaves it, and sees it make
A splashing in a lake.
What is the use?....

"Should some new star, in the fair evening sky
Kindle a blaze, startling so keen an eye
Of flamings eminent, athwart the dews,
Our thoughts would say; No doubt
That star will soon burn out.
What is the use?

"Who'll care for me, when I am dead and gone?
Not many now, and surely, soon, not one;
And should I sing like an immortal Muse,
Men, if they read the line,
Read for their good, not mine;
What is the use?....

"Spirit of Beauty! Breath of golden lyres!
Perpetual tremble of immortal wires!
Divinely torturing rapture of the Muse!
Conspicuous wretchedness!
Thou starry, sole success!—
What is the use!

"Doth not all struggle tell, upon its brow,
That he who makes it is not easy now,
But hopes to be? Vain hope that dost abuse!
Coquetting with thine eyes,
And fooling him who sighs.
What is the use?

"Go pry the lintels of the pyramids;
Lift the old kings' mysterious coffin lids—
This dust was theirs whose names these stones confuse,
These mighty monuments
Of mighty discontents.
What is the use?

"Did not he sum it all, whose Gate of Pearls
Blazed royal Ophir, Tyre, and Syrian girls—
The great, wise, famous monarch of the Jews?
Though rolled in grandeur vast,
He said of all, at last:
What is the use?

"O! but to take, of life, the natural good,
Even as a hermit caverned in a wood,
More sweetly fills my sober-suited views,
Than sweating to attain
Any luxurious pain.
What is the use?

"Give me a hermit's life, without his beads—
His lantern-jawed, and moral-mouthing creeds;
Systems and creeds the natural heart abuse.
What need of any book,
Or spiritual crook?
What is the use?

"I love, and God is love; and I behold
Man, Nature, God, one triple chain of gold—
Nature in all sole oracle and muse.
What should I seek, at all,
More than is natural?
What is the use?"

Seeing this man so heathenly inclined—
So wilted in the mood of a good mind,
I felt a kind of heat of earnest thought;
And studying in reply,
Answered him, eye to eye:

Thou dost amaze me that thou dost mistake
The wandering rivers for the fountain lake.
What is the end of living?—happiness?
An end that none attain,
Argues a purpose vain.

Plainly, this world is not a scope for bliss,
But duty. Yet we see not all that is,
Or may be, some day, if we love the light.
What man is, in desires,
Whispers where man aspires.

But what and where are we? what now—to-day?
Souls on a globe that spins our lives away—
A multitudinous world, where Heaven and Hell,
Strangely in battle met,
Their gonfalons have set.

Dust though we are, and shall return to dust,
Yet being born to battles, fight we must;
Under which ensign is our only choice.
We know to wage our best,
God only knows the rest.

Then since we see about us sin and dole,
And some things good, why not, with hand and soul,
Wrestle and succor out of wrong and sorrow—
Grasping the swords of strife,
Making the most of life?

Yea, all that we can wield is worth the end,
If sought as God's and man's most loyal friend
Naked we come into the world, and take
Weapons of various skill—
Let us not use them ill.

As for the creeds, Nature is dark at best;
And darker still is the deep human breast.
Therefore consider well of creeds and books,
Lest thou mayst somewhat fail
Of things beyond the vail.

Nature was dark to the dim starry age
Of wistful Job; and that Athenian sage,
Pensive in piteous thought of Faith's distress
For still she cried, with tears:
"More light, ye crystal spheres!"

But rouse thee, man! Shake off this hideous death!
Be man! Stand up! Draw in a mighty breath!
This world has quite enough emasculate hands,
Dallying with doubt and sin.
Come—here is work—begin!

Come, here is work—and a rank field—begin.
Put thou thine edge to the great weeds of sin;
So shalt thou find the use of life, and see
Thy Lord, at set of sun,
Approach and say: "Well done!"

This at the last: They clutch the sapless fruit,
Ashes and dust of the Dead Sea, who suit
Their course of life to compass happiness;
But be it understood
That, to be greatly good,
All is the use.

THOMAS BUCHANAN READ.

[Born, 1822.—Died, 1872.]

Mr. Read was born in Chester county, Pennsylvania, on the twelfth of March, 1822. His family having separated, in consequence of the death of his father, he in 1839 went to Cincinnati, where he was employed in the studio of Clevenger the sculptor, and here his attention was first directed to painting, which he chose for his profession, and soon practised with such skill as to arrest the favourable notice of some of the most eminent persons of the city and adjoining country, several of whom, including the late President Harrison, sat to him for portraits, which he carried as specimens of his abilities to New York, when he settled in that city in 1841, while still under twenty years of age. After a few months he removed to Boston, where he remained until 1846, and then went to Philadelphia, where he practised his profession, occasionally writing for the periodicals, until 1850, in which year he made his first visit to Europe. After spending a few months in Great Britain and on the continent, he returned, in 1852, passed the following winter in Cincinnati, and in the summer of 1853 went abroad a second time, accompanied by his family, and settled in Florence, where he has since resided, in friendly intercourse with an agreeable society of artists and men of letters. Here, in July, 1855, his wife and daughter died suddenly of a prevailing epidemic.

Mr. Read's earliest literary performances were a series of lyrics published in the "Boston Courier" in 1843 and 1844. In 1847 he printed in Boston the first collection of his "Poems;" in 1848, in Philadelphia, "Lays and Ballads;" in 1849, in the same city, "The Pilgrims of the Great Saint Bernard," a prose romance, in the successive numbers of a magazine; in 1853 an illustrated edition of his "Poems," comprising, with some new pieces, all he wished to preserve of his other volumes; and in 1855 the longest of his works, "The New Pastoral," in thirty-seven books.

Familiar experiences enable him to invest his descriptions with a peculiar freshness. His recollections are of the country, and of the habits of the primitive Pennsylvania farmers, in many respects the most picturesque and truly pastoral to be found in these active and practical times. A school of American pastoral poetry is yet to be established. The fresh and luxuriant beauty of our inland scenery has been sung in noble verse by Bryant and Whittier, and with less power in the sweet and plaintive strains of Carlos Wilcox, and the striking productions of Street and Gallagher; but the life of an American farmer has not yet received a just degree of attention from our poets. Mr. Read has made it the subject of a work in every way creditable to his talents and taste. He had already touched on this ground very successfully in his "Stranger on the Sill," "The Deserted Road," and other illustrations of country life, the graphic and healthful sentiment of which was generally recognised. In the "New Pastoral" he has still further and more happily displayed his capacities for this kind of writing. Its principal theatre is a neighborhood in one of the most beautiful regions of Pennsylvania, beside the Susquehanna. "I have seen," he says:

> "In lands less free, less fair, but far more known,
> The streams which flow through history.... and yet
> Nor Rhine, like Bacchus crowned, and reeling through
> His hills, nor Danube, marred with tyranny,
> His dull waves moaning on Hungarian shores;
> Nor rapid Po, his opaque waters pouring
> Athwart the fairest, fruitfullest, and worst
> Enslaved of European lands; nor Seine,
> Winding uncertain through inconstant France,
> Are half so fair as thy broad stream, whose breast
> Is gemmed with many isles, and whose proud name
> Shall yet become among the names of rivers,
> A synonym for beauty."

The poem consists of a series of sketches of rustic and domestic life, mostly of primitive simplicity, and so truthful as to be not less valuable as history than attractive as poetry.

Mr. Read's distinguishing characteristic is a delicate and varied play of fancy. His more ambitious productions display its higher exercise, rather than that of a distinct and creative imagination; he is a lark, flickering aloft in the pure air of song, not an eagle, courting its storms and undazzled by its meridian splendour. And, to extend the comparison, his muse most delights in common and humble subjects. The flowers that spring by the dusty wayside, the cheerful murmur of the meadow brook, the village tavern, and rustic mill, and all quiet and tender impulses and affections, are his favourite sources of inspiration. He excels in homely description, marked frequently by quaintness of epithet and quiet and natural pathos.

His verse, though sometimes irregular, is always musical. Indeed, in the easy flow of his stanzas and in the melody of their cadences, he seems to follow some chime of sound within his brain. This is the pervading expression of his poems, many of which might more properly be called songs. Though he has written in the dramatic form with freedom and unaffected feeling, and extremely well in didactic and descriptive blank verse, his province is evidently the lyrical.

Like most of our poets, in his earlier poems Mr Read wrote from the inspiration of foreign song and story, and he seems but lately to have perceived that the most appropriate field for the exercise of his powers is to be found at home.

THE BRICKMAKER.

I.

Let the blinded horse go round
Till the yellow clay be ground,
And no weary arms be folded
Till the mass to brick be moulded.

In no stately structures skill'd,
What the temple we would build?
Now the massive kiln is risen—
Call it palace—call it prison;
View it well: from end to end
Narrow corridors extend—
Long, and dark, and smother'd aisles:
Choke its earthy vaults with piles
Of the resinous yellow pine;
Now thrust in the fetter'd Fire—
Hearken! how he stamps with ire,
Treading out the pitchy wine;
Wrought anon to wilder spells,
Hear him shout his loud alarms;
See him thrust his glowing arms
Through the windows of his cells.

But his chains at last shall sever;
Slavery lives not forever;
And the thickest prison wall
Into ruin yet must fall.
Whatsoever falls away
Springeth up again, they say;
Then, when this shall break asunder,
And the fire be freed from under,
Tell us what imperial thing
From the ruin shall upspring?

There shall grow a stately building—
Airy dome and column'd walls;
Mottoes writ in richest gilding
Blazing through its pillar'd halls.

In those chambers, stern and dreaded,
They, the mighty ones, shall stand;
There shall sit the hoary-headed
Old defenders of the land.

There shall mighty words be spoken,
Which shall thrill a wondering world;
Then shall ancient bonds be broken,
And new banners be unfurl'd.

But anon those glorious uses
In these chambers shall lie dead,
And the world's antique abuses,
Hydra-headed, rise instead.

But this wrong not long shall linger—
The old capitol must fall;
For, behold! the fiery finger
Flames along the fated wall.

II.

Let the blinded horse go round
Till the yellow clay be ground,
And no weary arms be folded
Till the mass to brick be moulded—
Till the heavy walls be risen,
And the fire is in his prison:
But when break the walls asunder,
And the fire is freed from under,
Say again what stately thing
From the ruin shall upspring?

There shall grow a church whose steeple
To the heavens shall aspire;
And shall come the mighty people
To the music of the choir.

On the infant, robed in whiteness,
Shall baptismal waters fall,
While the child's angelic brightness
Sheds a halo over all.

There shall stand enwreathed in marriage
Forms that tremble—hearts that thrill—
To the door Death's sable carriage
Shall bring forms and hearts grown still!

Deck'd in garments richly glistening,
Rustling wealth shall walk the aisle;
And the poor without stand listening,
Praying in their hearts the while.

There the veteran shall come weekly
With his cane, oppress'd and poor,
Mid the horses standing meekly,
Gazing through the open door.

But these wrongs not long shall linger—
The presumptuous pile must fall;
For, behold! the fiery finger
Flames along the fated wall

III.

Let the blinded horse go round
Till the yellow clay be ground;
And no weary arms be folded
Till the mass to brick be moulded:
Say again what stately thing
From the ruin shall upspring?

Not the hall with column'd chambers,
Starr'd with words of liberty,
Where the freedom-canting members
Feel no impulse of the free:

Not the pile where souls in error
Hear the words, "Go, sin no more!"
But a dusky thing of terror,
With its cells and grated door.

To its inmates each to-morrow
Shall bring in no tide of joy.
Born in darkness and in sorrow,
There shall stand the fated boy.

With a grief too loud to smother,
With a throbbing, burning head,
There shall groan some desperate mother,
Nor deny the stolen bread!

There the veteran, a poor debtor,
Mark'd with honourable scars,
Listening to some clanking fetter,
Shall gaze idly through the bars:

Shall gaze idly, not demurring,
Though with thick oppression bow'd,
While the many, doubly erring,
Shall walk honour'd through the crowd.

Yet these wrongs not long shall linger—
The benighted pile must fall;
For, behold! the fiery finger
Flames along the fated wall!

IV.

Let the blinded horse go round
Till the yellow clay be ground;
And no weary arms be folded
Till the mass to brick be moulded—
Till the heavy walls be risen
And the fire is in his prison.
Capitol, and church, and jail,
Like our kiln at last shall fail;
Every shape of earth shall fade;
But the heavenly temple, made
For the sorely tried and pure,
With its Builder shall endure!

THE STRANGER ON THE SILL.

Between broad fields of wheat and corn
Is the lowly home where I was born;
The peach-tree leans against the wall,
And the woodbine wanders over all;
There is the shaded doorway still,
But a stranger's foot has cross'd the sill.

There is the barn—and, as of yore,
I can smell the hay from the open door,
And see the busy swallow's throng,
And hear the peewee's mournful song;
But the stranger comes—oh! painful proof—
His sheaves are piled to the heated roof.

There is the orchard—the very trees
Where my childhood knew long hours of ease,
And watch'd the shadowy moments run
Till my life imbibed more shade than sun;
The swing from the bough still sweeps the air,
But the stranger's children are swinging there.

There bubbles the shady spring below,
With its bulrush brook where the hazels grow;
'T was there I found the calamus-root,
And watch'd the minnows poise and shoot,
And heard the robin lave his wing,
But the stranger's bucket is at the spring.

Oh, ye who daily cross the sill,
Step lightly, for I love it still;
And when you crowd the old barn eaves,
Then think what countless harvest sheaves
Have pass'd within that scented door
To gladden eyes that are no more!

Deal kindly with these orchard trees;
And when your children crowd their knees,
Their sweetest fruit they shall impart,
As if old memories stirr'd their heart:
To youthful sport still leave the swing,
And in sweet reverence hold the spring.

The barn, the trees, the brook, the birds,
The meadows with their lowing herds,
The woodbine on the cottage wall—
My heart still lingers with them all.
Ye strangers on my native sill,
Step lightly, for I love it still!

A SONG.

Bring me the juice of the honey fruit,
The large translucent, amber-hued,
Rare grapes of southern isles, to suit
The luxury that fills my mood.

And bring me only such as grow
Where rarest maidens tend the bowers,
And only fed by rain and dew
Which first had bathed a bank of flowers.

They must have hung on spicy trees
In airs of far, enchanted vales,
And all night heard the ecstasies
Of noble-throated nightingales:

So that the virtues which belong
To flowers may therein tasted be,
And that which hath been thrill'd with song
May give a thrill of song to me.

For I would wake that string for thee
Which hath too long in silence hung,
And sweeter than all else should be
The song which in thy praise is sung.

THE DESERTED ROAD.

Ancient road, that wind'st deserted
Through the level of the vale,
Sweeping toward the crowded market
Like a stream without a sail;

Standing by thee, I look backward,
And, as in the light of dreams,
See the years descend and vanish
Like thy whitely-tented teams.

Here I stroll along the village
As in youth's departed morn;
But I miss the crowded coaches,
And the driver's bugle-horn—

Miss the crowd of jovial teamsters
Filling buckets at the wells,
With their wains from Conestoga,
And their orchestras of bells.

To the mossy wayside tavern
Comes the noisy throng no more;
And the faded sign, complaining,
Swings unnoticed at the door;

While the old, decrepit tollman,
Waiting for the few who pass,
Reads the melancholy story
In the thickly-springing grass.

Ancient highway, thou art vanquish'd
The usurper of the vale
Rolls in fiery, iron rattle,
Exultations on the gale.

Thou art vanquish'd and neglected;
But the good which thou hast done,
Though by man it be forgotten,
Shall be deathless as the sun.

Though neglected, gray, and grassy,
Still I pray that my decline
May be through as vernal valleys
And as blest a calm as thine.

THE CLOSING SCENE.

Within his sober realm of leafless trees
 The russet year inhaled the dreamy air;
Like some tann'd reaper in his hour of ease,
 When all the fields are lying brown and bare.

The gray barns looking from their hazy hills
 O'er the dim waters widening in the vales,
Sent down the air a greeting to the mills,
 On the dull thunder of alternate flails.

All sights were mellow'd and all sounds subdued,
 The hills seem'd farther and the streams sang low;
As in a dream the distant woodman hewed
 His winter log with many a muffled blow.

The embattled forests, erewhile armed in gold,
 Their banners bright with every martial hue,
Now stood, like some sad beaten host of old,
 Withdrawn afar in Time's remotest blue.

On slumb'rous wings the vulture held his flight;
 The dove scarce heard its sighing mate's complaint;
And like a star slow drowning in the light,
 The village church-vane seem'd to pale and faint.

The sentinel-cock upon the hill-side crew—
 Crew thrice, and all was stiller than before,—
Silent till some replying warder blew
 His alien horn, and then was heard no more.

Where erst the jay, within the elm's tall crest,
 Made garruious trouble round her unfledg'd young,
And where the oriole hung her swaying nest,
 By every light wind like a censer swung:—

Where sang the noisy masons of the eaves,
 The busy swallows circling ever near,
Foreboding, as the rustic mind believes,
 An early harvest and a plenteous year;—

Where every bird which charm'd the vernal feast,
 Shook the sweet slumber from its wings at morn,
To warn the reaper of the rosy east,—
 All now was songless, empty and forlorn.

Alone from out the stubble piped the quail,
 And croak'd the crow thro' all the dreamy gloom;
Alone the pheasant, drumming in the vale,
 Made echo to the distant cottage loom.

There was no bud, no bloom upon the bowers;
 The spiders wove their thin shrouds night by night;
The thistle-down, the only ghost of flowers,
 Sailed slowly by, pass'd noiseless out of sight.

Amid all this, in this most cheerless air,
 And where the woodbine shed upon the porch
Its crimson leaves, as if the Year stood there
 Firing the floor with his inverted torch;

Amid all this, the centre of the scene,
 The white-haired matron with monotonous tread,
Plied the swift wheel, and with her joyless mien,
 Sat, like a Fate, and watched the flying thread.

She had known Sorrow,—he had walk'd with her,
 Oft supp'd and broke the bitter ashen crust;
And in the dead leaves still she heard the stir
 Of his black mantle trailing in the dust.

While yet her cheek was bright with summer bloom,
 Her country summon'd and she gave her all;
And twice War bow'd to her his sable plume,—
 Regave the swords to rust upon her wall.

Regave the swords,—but not the hand that drew
 And struck for Liberty its dying blow,
Nor him who, to his sire and country true,
 Fell 'mid the ranks of the invading foe.

Long, but not loud, the droning wheel went on,
 Like the low murmur of a hive at noon;
Long, but not loud, the memory of the gone
 Breath'd thro' her lips a sad and tremulous tune.

At last the thread was snapp'd: her head was bow'd;
 Life dropt the distaff through his hands serene;
And loving neighbours smooth'd her careful shroud,
 While death and winter closed the autumn scene.

AN INVITATION.

TO GEORGE HAMMERSLEY.

Come thou, my friend;—the cool autumnal eves
 About the hearth have drawn their magic rings;
There, while his song of peace the cricket weaves,
 The simmering hickory sings.

The winds unkennell'd round the casements whine,
 The shelter'd hound makes answer in his dream,
And in the hayloft, hark, the cock at nine,
 Crows from the dusty beam.

The leafless branches chafe the roof all night,
 And through the house the troubled noises go,
While, like a ghostly presence, thin and white,
 The frost foretells the snow.

The muffled owl within the swaying elm
 Thrills all the air with sadness as he swings,
Till sorrow seems to spread her shadowy realm
 About all outward things.

Come, then, my friend, and this shall seem no more,
 Come when October walks his red domain,
Or when November from his windy floor
 Winnows the hail and rain:

And when old Winter through his fingers numb
 Blows till his breathings on the windows gleam;
And when the mill-wheel spiked with ice is dumb
 Within the neighboring stream:

Then come, for nights like these have power to wake
 The calm delight no others may impart,
When round the fire true souls communing make
 A summer in the heart.

And I will weave athwart the mystic gloom,
 With hand grown weird in strange romance for
  thee
Bright webs of fancy from the golden loom
 Of charméd Poesy.

And let no censure in thy looks be shown,
 That I, with hands adventurous and bold,
Should grasp the enchanted shuttle which was
  thrown
 Through mightier warps of old.

MY HERMITAGE.

WITHIN a wood, one summer's day,
And in a hollow, ancient trunk,
I shut me from the world away,
To live as lives a hermit monk.

My cell was a ghostly sycamore,
The roots and limbs were dead with age;
Decay had carved the gothic door
Which looked into my hermitage.

My library was large and full,
Where, ever as a hermit plods,
I read until my eyes are dull
With tears; for all those tomes were God's.

The vine that at my doorway swung
Had verses writ on every leaf,
The very songs the bright bees sung
In honey-seeking visits brief—

Not brief—though each stayed never long—
So rapidly they came and went
No pause was left in all their song,
For while they borrowed still they lent.

All day the woodland minstrels sang—
Small feet were in the leaves astir—
And often o'er my doorway rang
The tap of a blue-winged visiter.

Afar the stately river swayed,
And poured itself in giant swells,
While here the brooklet danced and played,
And gayly rung its liquid bells.

The springs gave me their crystal flood,
And my contentment made it wine—
And oft I found what kingly food
Grew on the world-forgotten vine

The moss, or weed, or running flower,
Too humble in their hope to climb,
Had in themselves the lovely power
To make me happier for the time.

And when the starry night came by,
And stooping looked into my cell,
Then all between the earth and sky
Was circled in a holier spell.

A height and depth, and breadth sublime
O'erspread the scene, and reached the stars,
Until Eternity and Time
Seemed drowning their dividing bars.

And voices which the day ne'er hears,
And visions which the sun ne'er sees,
From earth and from the distant spheres,
Came on the moonlight and the breeze.

Thus day and night my spirit grew
In love with that which round me shone,
Until my calm heart fully knew
The joy it is to be alone.

The time went by—till one fair dawn
I saw against the eastern fires
A visionary city drawn,
With dusky lines of domes and spires.

The wind in sad and fitful spells
Blew o'er it from the gates of morn,
Till I could clearly hear the bells
That rung above a world forlorn.

And well I listened to their voice,
And deeply pondered what they said—
Till I arose—there was no choice—
I went while yet the east was red.

My wakened heart for utterance yearned—
The clamorous wind had broke the spell—
I heeds must teach what I had learned
Within my simple woodland cell.

PASSING THE ICEBERGS.

A FEARLESS shape of brave device,
Our vessel drives through mist and rain.
Between the floating fleets of ice—
The navies of the northern main.

These arctic ventures, blindly hurled
The proofs of Nature's olden force,—
Like fragments of a crystal world
Long shattered from its skiey course.

These are the buccaneers that fright
The middle sea with dream of wrecks,
And freeze the south winds in their flight,
And chain the Gulf-stream to their decks.

At every dragon prow and helm
There stands some Viking as of yore;
Grim heroes from the boreal realm
Where Odin rules the spectral shore.

And oft beneath the sun or moon
Their swift and eager falchions glow—
While, like a storm-vexed wind, the rune
Comes chafing through some beard of snow

And when the far north flashes up
With fires of mingled red and gold,
They know that many a blazing cup
Is brimming to the absent bold.

Up signal there, and let us hail
Yon looming phantom as we pass!
Note all her fashion, hull, and sail,
Within the compass of your glass.

See at her mast the steadfast glow
Of that one star of Odin's throne;
Up with our flag, and let us show
The Constellation on our own.

And speak her well; for she might say,
If from her heart the words could thaw,
Great news from some far frozen bay,
Or the remotest Esquimaux.

Might tell of channels yet untold,
That sweep the pole from sea to sea
Of lands which God designs to hold
A mighty people yet to be:—

Of wonders which alone prevail
Where day and darkness dimly meet,—
Of all which spreads the arctic sail;
Of FRANKLIN and his venturous fleet:

How, haply, at some glorious goal
His anchor holds—his sails are furled;
That Fame has named him on her scroll,
"Columbus of the Polar World."

Or how his ploughing barques wedge on
Thro' splintering fields, with battered shares,
Lit only by that spectral dawn,
The mask that mocking darkness wears;—

Or how, o'er embers black and few,
The last of shivered masts and spars,
He sits amid his frozen crew
In council with the norland stars.

No answer but the sullen flow
Of ocean heaving long and vast;—
An argosy of ice and snow,
The voiceless North swings proudly past.

A DIRGE FOR A DEAD BIRD.

The cage hangs at the window,
There's the sunshine on the sill;
But where the form and where the voice
That never till now were still?

The sweet voice hath departed
From its feathery home of gold,
The little form of yellow dust
Lies motionless and cold!

Oh, where amid the azure
Hath thy sweet spirit fled?
I hold my breath and think I hear
Its music overhead.

Death has not hushed thy spirit,
Its joy shall vanish never;
The slightest thrill of pleasure born
Lives on and lives forever!

Throughout the gloomy winter
Thy soul shed joy in ours,
As it told us of the summer-time
Amid the land of flowers.

But now thy songs are silent,
Except what memory brings;
For thou hast folded death within
The glory of thy wings!

And here thy resting-place shall be
Beneath the garden bower;
A bush shall be thy monument,
Thy epitaph a flower!

MIDNIGHT.

The moon looks down on a world of snow,
And the midnight lamp is burning low,
And the fading embers mildly glow
In their bed of ashes soft and deep;
All, all is still as the hour of death;
I only hear what the old clock saith,
And the mother and infant's easy breath,
That flows from the holy land of Sleep.

Say on, old clock—I love you well,
For your silver chime, and the truths you tell,
Your every stroke is but the knell
Of hope, or sorrow, buried deep;
Say on—but only let me hear
The sound most sweet to my listening ear,
The child and the mother breathing clear
Within the harvest-fields of Sleep.

Thou watchman, on thy lonely round,
I thank thee for that warning sound;
The clarion cock and the baying hound
Not less their dreary vigils keep;
Still hearkening. I will love you all,
While in each silent interval
I hear those dear breasts rise and fall
Upon the airy tide of Sleep.

Old world, on time's benighted stream
Sweep down till the stars of morning beam
From orient shores—nor break the dream
That calms my love to pleasure deep;
Roll on, and give my Bud and Rose
The fulness of thy best repose,
The blessedness which only flows
Along the silent realms of Sleep.

THE NAMELESS.

Come fill, my merry friends, to-night,
And let the winds unheeded blow,
And we will wake the deep delight
Which true hearts only know.
And ere the passing wine be done,
Come drink to those most fair and dear,
And I will pledge a cup to one
Who shall be nameless here.

Come fill, nor let the flagon stand,
Till pleasure's voice shall drown the wind,
Nor heed old Winter's stormy hand
Which shakes the window-blind.
And down the midnight hour shall run
The brightest moments of the year;
While I will fill, my friends, to one
Who shall be nameless here.

Pledge you to lips that smile in sleep,
Whose dreams have strewed your path with [flowers,
And to those sacred eyes that weep
Whene'er your fortune lowers;
And charm the night, ere it be done,
With names that are forever dear,
While I must pour and quaff to one
Who shall be nameless here.

To her I proudly poured the first
Inspiring beaker of the Rhine,
And still it floods my veins as erst
It filled the German vine.
And when her memory, like the sun,
Shall widen down my dying year,
My latest cup will be to one
Who shall be nameless here.

GEORGE H. BOKER.

[Born, 1823.]

George Henry Boker was born in Philadelphia in 1823, and was graduated bachelor of arts at Nassau Hall, Princeton, when nineteen years of age. After travelling some time in Europe, and making himself familiar with contemporaneous literatures among their creators, he settled in his native city, to devote a life of opulent leisure to the cultivation of letters and to the enjoyment of the liberal arts and of society.

His first appearance as an author was in a small volume published in 1847, under the title of "The Lesson of Life, and other Poems." In this were indications of a manly temper and a cultivated taste, but it had the customary faults of youthful compositions in occasional feebleness of epithet, indistinctness, diffuseness, and a certain kind of romanticism that betrays a want of experience of the world. Its reception however by judicious critics, who saw amid its faults the signs of a fine understanding, justified new efforts; and turning his attention to the drama, he produced in the following year "Calaynos, a Tragedy," which gave him large increase of reputation in the best audience of this country. The plot of this play illustrates the hatred of the Moors by the Castilians. Calaynos, a nobleman of a sincere and generous nature, whose youth has been passed in the study of philosophy and in acts of kindness, and whose Saracen taint of blood is concealed from his wife, Donna Alda, until made known in the progress of the history, proposes to leave his retirement for a journey to Seville. There is a superstition among the neighbouring peasants that a visit to Seville is dangerous to the race of Calaynos, and Oliver, his secretary, whose practical sagacity alone is necessary to the perfection of the master's character, has also a presentiment of evil on this occasion, and endeavours to dissuade him from his purpose; upon which Calaynos discloses that the principal object of his journey is to see an early friend, Don Luis, who has become involved in difficulties and whose estates will be sacrificed unless he receives by a certain day considerable assistance in money. Arriving in Seville with Oliver, Calaynos discharges the obligations of Don Luis, who so wins upon his affection that he persuades him to become his guest. The party in the next act are at the castle of Calaynos, where Don Luis discovers that Calaynos is of Moorish origin, and having fallen in love with the wife of his benefactor, in a secret interview he informs her of her disgrace. It is difficult to appreciate the intensity of the prejudice which made this revelation so important; and it is an objection to the play for acting purposes, that out of Spain and Portugal few audiences could sympathize with it, though the historical student will perceive that Mr. Boker has not at all exaggerated it. Donna Alda, struggling between love and pride, calls upon her husband, faints, and is borne from the scene in the arms of Don Luis; and the act closes with Calaynos's discovery of his friend's ingratitude and his wife's perfidy. In the month which passes before the opening of the last act, Calaynos has become old through grief. His secretary, returned from a pursuit of the fugitives, informs him that Donna Alda had fled from the residence of her seducer; she is discovered, seeking shelter from a storm under the walls of the castle, brought in, recognised, and dies, referring to a written exposure of the villany of Don Luis. Calaynos, convinced of her innocence, hastens to Seville, and slays the destroyer of his happiness in the midst of his debaucheries. This simple story is managed with much skill, and so as to produce a cumulative interest to its close. The characters, besides those already referred to, are some half dozen gentlemen to make side speeches and care about the details of the plot. They are distinctly drawn, in most cases with finely contrasted idiosyncracies (though the hero and heroine converse somewhat too much in the same style), and they are all excellently sustained. The action is less dramatic than the dialogue, which in some parts evinces great power, and, more frequently, those happy turns of expression which disclose a chief element of the dramatic faculty.

The next production of Mr. Boker was "Anne Boleyn, a Tragedy," which in many respects surpasses "Calaynos," evincing more skill in the use of language, more force in the display of passion, and a finer vein of poetical feeling, with the same admirable contrasts of character, and unity and directness of conduct.

"Calaynos" and "Anne Boleyn" have been followed by "The Betrothal," "Francesca di Rimini," and other plays, and a small volume published in 1853 under the title of "The Podesta's Daughter, and other Poems." In the present year (1856) he has given to the public a collection of his Dramatic and Miscellaneous Poems, in two volumes, from the press of Ticknor and Fields.

In his minor productions Mr. Boker has displayed a richness of invention, a copiousness of illustration, and a vigour and finish of style, that amply vindicate his right to be classed among the small number of our writers of verses who are poets. The attraction of these pieces, like that of his more ambitious performances, consists more in their general cast than in the strength or grace of particular ideas, or a fit elegance of phrase. It is a fault indeed, less conspicuous in his minor poems than in his tragedies, that modelling himself after some of the older masters of English verse, there is an occasional want of ease in the structure of his sentences, and in his selection of words an insensibility to the more delicate charms of language: a fault that is not likely to outlast the full development of his genius. It would be easy to point out in "Calaynos" many passages which are spoiled by inversions altogether unnecessary to the perfection of the rhythm, or by other departures from the rule of nature, which are results of no carelessness, but evidently of an erroneous and it is to be hoped very transient fancy in regard to the effect of a colloquial simplicity in poetical writing.

THE SONG OF THE EARTH.

PRELUDE—CHORUS OF PLANETS.

Hark to our voices, O mother of nations!
Why art thou dim when thy sisters are radiant?
Why veil'st thy face in a mantle of vapour,
Gliding obscure through the depths of the night?
Wake from thy lethargy. Hear'st thou our music,
Harmonious, that reaches the confines of space?
Join in our chorus, join in our jubilee,
Make the day pine with thy far-piercing melody—
Pine that his kingdom of blue sky and sunshine
Never re-echoes such marvellous tones.
No, thou art silent, O mystical sister,
Silent and proud that thou bear'st on thy bosom
The wonderful freight of the God-lighted soul.
We hear thee, we hear thee, beneath thy thick mantle,
The war of the winds through thy leaf-laden forests,
And round aisles of thy pillar'd and hill-piercing
Caverns sonorous; hear the dread avalanche
Torn from its quivering mountainous summit,
Ribbèd with massy rocks, crested with pine-trees,
Thundering enormous upon thy fair valleys;
Hear the dull roar of thy mist-spouting cataracts;
Hear the faint plash of thy salt, seething billows,
Lifting their heads multitudinous, or shoreward
Climbing the cliffs that overhang them with trembling,
And tossing their spray in exultant defiance
Over the weed-bearded guardians of ocean.
Sister, we listen; thy strains are enlinking,
Melodiously blending to ravishing harmony;
Clouds are departing, we see thee, we yearn to thee,
Noblest of planets, creation's full glory!
Bending we hearken, thou mother of nations,
Hark to the sky-rending voice of humanity.

SONG OF THE EARTH.

Oh vex me not, ye ever-burning planets;
Nor sister call me, ye who me afflict.
I am unlike ye: ye may revelling sing,
Careless and joyful, roaming sunlit ether,
Urged with but one emotion, chanting still
Through lapsing time the purpose of your birth,
Each with a several passion; but to me
Are mix'd emotions, vast extremes of feeling—
Now verdant in the fruitful smile of Heaven,
Now waste and blacken'd in the scowl of Hell.
Ye know me not, nor can ye sympathize
With one like me, for wisdom is not yours
Ye sing for joy; but wisdom slowly comes
From the close whispers of o'erburden'd pain.
I am alone in all the universe!
To me is pain; I can distinguish sin;
But ye with constant though unweeting glance
Rain good or ill, and smile alike at both,
Nor understand the mystery of your natures.
To me is wisdom—wisdom bought with wo,
Ages on ages past, when first I stray'd,
With haughty scorn and self-reliant pride,
From purity and God. For once, like you,
God spoke me face to face, me soulless led
From joy to joy; yet he was mystical—
Too obvious for thought—I knew him not:
But now, through sin, I understand like him
The heart of things—the steep descents of guilt,
And the high pinnacles of heaven-lit virtue.
Bend down, ye stars, bend from your silver thrones,
Ye joyful wanderers of ether bright;
For I, soul-bearer of the universe,
Would teach your ignorance with the lips of song!
O Mercury, hot planet, burying deep
Thy forehead in the sunlight, list to me!
I groan beneath thy influence. Thou dost urge
The myriad hands of Labour, and with toil
Dost mar my features; day by day dost work
Thy steady changes on mine ancient face,
Till all the host of heaven blank wonder look,
Nor know the fresh, primeval-moulded form
That like the Aphrodite, rose from chaos,
Smiling through dews upon the first morn's sun.
The leaf-crown'd mountain's brows thou hurlest down
Into the dusty valley, and dost still
The free, wild singing of the cleaving streams
To murmurs dying lazily within
The knotted roots of pool-engender'd lilies,
That sluggish nod above the slimy dams.
All day the axe I hear rending through trunks,
Moss-grown and reverend, of cluster'd oaks.
All day the circling scythe sweeps off
The ruddy bloom of vain-aspiring fields,
Clipping to stubbles grim the vernal flowers.
Thou portionest my meadows, and dost make
Each fruitful slope a spot for sweaty toil.
Thou tearest up my bosom; far within
My golden veins the grimed miner's pick
Startles the babbling echoes. Ancient rocks,
My hardy bones, are rent with nitrous fire,
To rear thy marts, to bridge the leaping streams,
Or to usurp the ocean's olden right,
That selfish trade may dry-shod walk to power.
The very ocean, grim, implacable,
Thou loadest with the white-wing'd fleets of commerce,
Crossing, like wheeling birds, each other's tracks;
Until the burden'd giant, restless grown,
Bounds from his sleep, and in the stooping clouds
Nods his white head, while splinter'd navies melt
To scatter'd fragments in his sullen froth!
Malignant star, I feel thy wicked power:

My children's busy thoughts are full of thee:
Thou 'st chill'd the loving spirit in their hearts,
And on their lips hast placed the selfish finger—
They dare not know each other. All that is,
All that God bless'd my teeming bosom with,
Is priced and barter'd; ay, the very worth
Of man himself is weigh'd with senseless gold—
Therefore I hate thee, bright-brow'd wanderer!

Daughter of the sober twilight,
Lustrous planet, ever hanging
In the mottled mists that welcome
Coming morning, or at evening
Peeping through the ruddy banners
Of the clouds that wave a parting,
From their high aerial summits,
To the blazing god of day—
'T is for thee I raise my pæan,
Steady-beaming Venus! kindler,
In the stubborn hearts of mortals,
Of the sole surviving passion
That enlinks a lost existence
With the dull and ruthless present.
Far adown the brightening future,
Prophetess, I see thee glancing—
See thee still amid the twilight
Of the ages rolling onward,
Promising to heart-sick mortals
Triumph of thy gracious kingdom;
When the hand of power shall weaken,
And the wronger right the wrongèd,
And the pure, primeval Eden
Shall again o'erspread with blossoms
Sunny hill and shady valley.
'T is to thee my piny mountains
Wave aloft their rustling branches,
'T is to thee my opening flowerets
Send on high their luscious odours,
'T is to thee my leaping fountains
Prattle through their misty breathings,
And the bass of solemn ocean
Chimes accordant in the chorus.
Every fireside is thy altar,
Streaming up its holy incense;
Every mated pair of mortals,
Happily link'd, are priest and priestess,
Pouring to thee full libations
From their overbrimming spirits.
Clash the loud-resounding cymbals,
Light the rosy torch of Hymen;
Bands of white-robed youths and maidens
Whirl aloft the votive myrtle!
Raise the choral hymn to Venus—
Young-eyed Venus, ever youthful,
Ever on true hearts bestowing
Pleasures new that never pall!
Brightest link 'tween man and Heaven,
Soul of virtue, life of goodness,
Cheering light in pain and sorrow,
Pole-star to the struggling voyager
Wreck'd on life's relentless billows,
Fair reward of trampled sainthood,
Beaming from the throne Eternal
Lonely hope to sinful mankind—
Still among the mists of morning,
Still among the clouds of evening,
While the years drive ever onward,
Hang thy crescent lamp of promise,
Venus, blazing star of Love!
O Mars, wide heaven is shuddering 'neath the stride
Of thy mail'd foot, most terrible of planets;
I see thee struggling with thy brazen front
To look a glory from amid the crust
Of guilty blood that dims thy haughty face:
The curse of crime is on thee.—Look, behold!

See where thy frenzied votaries march;
Hark to the brazen blare of the bugle,
Hark to the rattling clatter of the drums,
The measured tread of the steel-clad footmen!
Hark to the labouring horses' breath,
Painfully tugging the harness'd cannon;
The shrill, sharp clank of the warriors' swords,
As their chargers bound when the trumpets sound
Their alarums through the echoing mountains!
See the flashing of pennons and scarfs,
Shaming the gorgeous blazon of evening,
Rising and falling mid snowy plumes
That dance like foam on the crested billows!
Bright is the glitter of burnish'd steel,
Stirring the clamour of martial music;
The clank of arms has a witchery
That wakes the blood in a youthful bosom;
And who could tell from this pleasant show,
That flaunts in the sun like a May-day festal,
For what horrid rites are the silken flags,
For what horrid use are the gleaming sabres,
What change shall mar, when the battles join,
This marshall'd pageant of shallow glory?
For then the gilded flags shall be rent,
The sabres rust with the blood of foemen,
And the courteous knight shall howl like a wolf,
When he scents the gory steam of battle.

The orphan's curse is on thee, and the tears
Of widow'd matrons plead a fearful cause.
Each thing my bosom bears, that thou hast touch'd,
Is loud against thee. Flowers and trampled grass,
And the long line of waste and barren fields,
Erewhile o'erflowing with a sea of sweets,
Look up all helpless to the pitying heavens,
Showing thy bloody footprints in their wounds,
And shrieking through their gaunt and leafless trees,
That stand with imprecating arms outspread—
They fiercely curse thee with their desolation;
Each cheerless hearthstone in the home of man,
Where Ruin grins, and rubs his bony palms,
Demands its lost possessor. Thou hast hurl'd
Man's placid reason from its rightful throne,
And in its place rear'd savage force, to clip
Debate and doubt with murder. Therefore, Mars,
I sicken in thy angry glance, and loathe
The dull red glitter of thy bloody spear!

I know thy look, majestic Jupiter!
I see thee moving mid the stars of heaven,
Girt with thy train of ministering satellites.
Proud planet, I confess thy influence:
My heart grows big with gazing in thy face;
Unwonted power pervades my eager frame;
My bulk aspiring towers above itself,
And restless pants to rush on acts sublime,
At which the wondering stars might stand agaze,

And the whole universe from end to end,
Conscious of me, should tremble to its core!
Spirit heroical, imperious passion,
That sharply sets the pliant face of youth,
That blinds the shrinking eyes of pallid fear,
And plants the lion's heart in modest breasts—
I know that thou hast led, with regal port,
The potent spirits of humanity
Before the van of niggard Time, and borne,
With strides gigantic, man's advancing race
From power to power; till, like a host of gods,
They mock my elements, and drag the secrets
Of my mysterious forces up to light,
Giving them bounds determinate and strait,
And of their natures, multiform and huge,
Talking to children in familiar way.
The hero's sword, the poet's golden string,
The tome-illuming taper of the sage,
Flash 'neath thy influence; from thee alone,
Ambitious planet, comes the marvellous power
That in a cherub's glowing form can veil
A heart as cold as Iceland, and exalt
To deity the demon Selfishness.
O planet, mingle with thy chilling rays,
That stream inspiring to the hero's soul,
One beam of love for vast humanity,
And thou art godlike. Must it ever be,
That brightest flowers of action and idea
Spring from the same dark soil of selfish lust?
Must man receive the calculated gifts
Of shrewd Ambition's self-exalting hand,
And blindly glorify an act at which
The host of heaven grow red with thoughtful shame?
Shall Knowledge hasten with her sunny face,
And weeping Virtue lag upon the path!
Shall man exultant boast advance of power,
Nor see arise, at every onward stride,
New forms of sin to shadow every truth?
Roll on, roll on, in self-supported pride,
Prodigious influence of the hero's soul;
I feel thy strength, and tremble in thy glare!

O many-ringed Saturn, turn away
The chilling terrors of thy baleful glance!
Thy gloomy look is piercing to my heart—
I wither 'neath thy power! My springs dry up,
And shrink in horror to their rocky beds;
The brooks that whisper'd to the lily-bells
All day the glory of their mountain homes,
And kiss'd the dimples of the wanton rose,
At the deed blushing to their pebbly strands,
Cease their sweet merriment, and glide afraid
Beneath the shelter of the twisted sedge.
The opening bud shrinks back upon its shell,
As if the North had puff'd his frozen breath
Full in its face. The billowing grain and grass,
Rippling with windy furrows, stand becalm'd;
Nor 'mong their roots, nor in their tiny veins,
Bestirs the fruitful sap. The very trees,
Broad, hardy sons of crags and sterile plains,
That roar'd defiance to the Winter's shout,
And battled sternly through his cutting sleet,
Droop in their myriad leaves; while nightly birds,
That piped their shrilling treble to the moon,
Hang silent from the boughs, and peer around,
Awed by mysterious sympathy. From thee,
From thee, dull planet, comes this lethargy
That numbs in mid career meek Nature's power,
And stills the prattle of her plumèd train.
O icy Saturn, proud in ignorance,
Father of sloth, dark, deadening influence,
That dims the eye to all that's beautiful,
And twists the haughty lip with killing scorn
For love and holiness—from thee alone
Springs the cold, crushing power that presses down
The infinite in man. From thee, dull star,
The cautious fear that checks the glowing heart,
With sympathetic love world-wide o'erfreighted,
And sends it panting back upon itself,
To murmur in its narrow hermitage.
The boldest hero staggers in thy frown,
And drops his half-form'd projects all aghast:
The poet shrinks before thy phantom glare,
Ere the first echo greets his timid song;
The startled sage amid the embers hurls
The gather'd wisdom of a fruitful life.—
Oh, who may know from what bright pinnacles
The mounting soul might look on coming time,
Had all the marvellous thoughts of genius—
Blasted to nothingness by thy cold sneer—
Burst through the bud and blossom'd into fruit?
Benumbing planet, on our system's skirt,
Whirl from thy sphere, and round some lonely sun,
Within whose light no souls their ordeals pass,
Circle and frown amid thy frozen belts;
For I am sick of thee, and stately man
Shrinks to a pigmy in thy fearful stare!

FINALE—CHORUS OF STARS.

Heir of Eternity, mother of souls,
Let not thy knowledge betray thee to folly!
Knowledge is proud, self-sufficient, and lone,
Trusting, unguided, its steps in the darkness.
Thine is the learning that mankind may win,
Glean'd in the pathway between joy and sorrow;
Ours is the wisdom that hallows the child,
Fresh from the touch of his awful Creator,
Dropp'd, like a star, on thy shadowy realm,
Falling in splendour, but falling to darken.
Ours is the simple religion of faith,
The wisdom of trust in God who o'errules us—
Thine is the complex misgivings of thought,
Wrested to form by imperious Reason.
We are forever pursuing the light—
Thou art forever astray in the darkness.
Knowledge is restless, imperfect, and sad—
Faith is serene, and completed, and joyful.
Chide not the planets that rule o'er thy ways;
They are God's creatures; nor, proud in thy reason,
Vaunt that thou knowest his counsels and him:
Boaster, though sitting in midst of the glory,
Thou couldst not fathom the least of his thoughts.
Bow in humility, bow thy proud forehead,
Circle thy form in a mantle of clouds,
Hide from the glittering cohorts of evening
Wheeling in purity, singing in chorus;
Howl in the depths of thy lone, barren mountains,
Restlessly moan on the deserts of ocean,
Wail o'er thy fall in the desolate forests,
Lost star of paradise, straying alone!

A BALLAD OF SIR JOHN FRANKLIN.

"The ice was here, the ice was there,
The ice was all around."—COLERIDGE.

O, WHITHER sail you, Sir JOHN FRANKLIN?
Cried a whaler in Baffin's Bay.
To know if between the land and the pole
I may find a broad sea-way.

I charge you back, Sir JOHN FRANKLIN,
As you would live and thrive;
For between the land and the frozen pole
No man may sail alive.

But lightly laughed the stout Sir JOHN,
And spoke unto his men:
Half England is wrong, if he is right;
Bear off to westward then.

O, whither sail you, brave Englishman?
Cried the little Esquimaux.
Between your land and the polar star
My goodly vessels go.

Come down, if you would journey there,
The little Indian said;
And change your cloth for fur clothing,
Your vessel for a sled.

But lightly laughed the stout Sir JOHN,
And the crew laughed with him too:—
A sailor to change from ship to sled,
I ween, were something new!

All through the long, long polar day,
The vessels westward sped;
And wherever the sail of Sir JOHN was blown,
The ice gave way and fled.

Gave way with many a hollow groan,
And with many a surly roar,
But it murmured and threatened on every side;
And closed where he sailed before.

Ho! see ye not, my merry men,
The broad and open sea?
Bethink ye what the whaler said,
Think of the little Indian's sled!
The crew laughed out in glee.

Sir JOHN, Sir JOHN, 't is bitter cold,
The scud drives on the breeze,
The ice comes looming from the north,
The very sunbeams freeze.

Bright summer goes, dark winter comes—
We cannot rule the year;
But long e'er summer's sun goes down,
On yonder sea we 'll steer.

The dripping icebergs dipped and rose,
And floundered down the gale;
The ships were staid, the yards were manned,
And furled the useless sail.

The summer 's gone, the winter 's come,
We sail not on yonder sea:
Why sail we not, Sir JOHN FRANKLIN?
A silent man was he.

The summer goes, the winter comes—
We cannot rule the year:
I ween, we cannot rule the ways,
Sir JOHN, wherein we'd steer.

The cruel ice came floating on,
And closed beneath the lee,
Till the thickening waters dashed no more;
'T was ice around, behind, before—
My GOD! there is no sea!

What think you of the whaler now?
What of the Esquimaux?
A sled were better than a ship,
To cruise through ice and snow.

Down sank the baleful crimson sun,
The northern light came out,
And glared upon the ice-bound ships,
And shook its spears about.

The snow came down, storm breeding storm,
And on the decks was laid:
Till the weary sailor, sick at heart,
Sank down beside his spade.

Sir JOHN, the night is black and long,
The hissing wind is bleak,
The hard, green ice is strong as death:—
I prithee, Captain, speak!

The night is neither bright nor short,
The singing breeze is cold,
The ice is not so strong as hope—
The heart of man is bold!

What hope can scale this icy wall,
High o'er the main flag-staff?
Above the ridges the wolf and bear
Look down with a patient, settled stare,
Look down on us and laugh.

The summer went, the winter came—
We could not rule the year;
But summer will melt the ice again,
And open a path to the sunny main,
Whereon our ships shall steer.

The winter went, the summer went,
The winter came around:
But the hard green ice was strong as death,
And the voice of hope sank to a breath,
Yet caught at every sound.

Hark! heard ye not the noise of guns?
And there, and there, again!
'T is some uneasy iceberg's roar,
As he turns in the frozen main.

Hurrah! hurrah! the Esquimaux
Across the ice-fields steal:
GOD give them grace for their charity!
Ye pray for the silly seal.

Sir JOHN, where are the English fields,
And where are the English trees,
And where are the little English flowers
That open in the breeze?

Be still, be still, my brave sailors!
You shall see the fields again,
And smell the scent of the opening flowers,
The grass and the waving grain.

Oh! when shall I see my orphan child?
My Mary waits for me.
Oh! when shall I see my old mother,
And pray at her trembling knee?

Be still, be still, my brave sailors!
Think not such thoughts again.
But a tear froze slowly on his cheek;
He thought of Lady JANE.

Ah! bitter, bitter grows the cold,
The ice grows more and more;
More settled stare the wolf and bear,
More patient than before.

Oh! think you, good Sir JOHN FRANKLIN,
We 'll ever see the land?
'T was cruel to send us here to starve,
Without a helping hand.

'T was cruel, Sir JOHN, to send us here,
So far from help or home,
To starve and freeze on this lonely sea:
I ween, the Lords of the Admiralty
Would rather send than come.

Oh! whether we starve to death alone,
Or sail to our own country,
We have done what man has never done—
The truth is founded, the secret won—
We passed the Northern Sea!

ODE TO ENGLAND.

OH, days of shame! oh, days of wo!
Of helpless shame, of helpless wo!
The times reveal thy nakedness,
Thy utter weakness, deep distress.
There is no help in all the land;
Thy eyes may wander to and fro,
Yet find no succour. Every hand
Has weighed the guinea, poised the gold,
Chaffered and bargained, bought and sold,
Until the sinews, framed for war,
Can grasp the sword and shield no more.
Their trembling palms are stretched to thee;
Purses are offered, heaping hoards—
The plunder of the land and sea—
Are proffered, all too eagerly,
But thou must look abroad for swords.

These are the gods ye trusted in;
For these ye crept from sin to sin;
Made honor cheap, made station dear,
Made wealth a lord, made truth a drudge,
Made venal interest the sole judge
Of principles as high and clear
As heaven itself.
With glittering pelf
Ye gilt the coward, knave, and fool,
Meted the earth out with a rule
Of gold, weighed nations in your golden scales,
And surely this law never fails—
What else may change, this law stands fast -
"The golden standard is the thing
To which the beggar, lord and king
And all that's earthly, come at last."
O mighty gods! O noble trust!
They are your all; ye cannot look
Back to the faith ye once forsook;
The past is dry and worthless dust;
Gold, gold is all! Ye cannot fill
Your brains with legends vague and thin;
Hang up your arms amidst their rust:
These are the gods ye trusted in;
They can deliver you and will!

Oh, bitter waking! mocking dream!
The gilt has worn away,
The idols are but clay,
Their pride is overthrown, their glories only seem!
The land is full of fear,
Men pale at what they hear,
The widowed matrons sob, the orphan'd children cry,
There's desolation every where, there's not one comfort nigh!
The nations stands agaze,
In dubious amaze,
To see Britannia's threatening form,
That loomed gigantic 'mid the splendid haze
Through which they saw her tower—
As, at the morning hour,
The spectral figure strides across her misty hills—
Shrink to a pigmy when the storm
Rends the delusive cloud,
And shows her weak and bowed,
A feeble crone that hides for shelter from her ills.

O mother of our race! can nothing break
This leaden apathy of thine?
Think of the long and glorious line
Of heroes, who beside the Stygian lake
Hearken for news from thee!
Apart their forms I see,
With muffled heads and tristful faces bowed—
Heads once so high, faces so calm and proud!
The Norman fire burns low
In WILLIAM's haughty heart;
The mirth has passed away
From Cœur de Lion's ample brow;
In sorrowful dismay
The warlike EDWARDS and the HENRIES stand,
Stung with a shameful smart;
While the eighth HARRY, with his close-clutched hand,
Smothers the passion in his ireful soul;
Or his fierce eye-balls roll
Where his bold daughter beats her sharp foot-tip,
And gnaws her quivering lip.
While the stern, crownless king who strode between
Father and son, and put them both aside,
With straight terrific glare,
As a lion from his lair,
Asks with his eyes such questions keen
As his crowned brothers neither dare
To answer or abide.
How shall he make reply,
The shadow that draws nigh,
The latest comer, the great Duke,
Whose patient valour, blow by blow,
Wrought at a Titan's overthrow,
And gave his pride its first and last rebuke?
What shall he say when this heroic band
Catch at his welcome hand,
And trembling, half in fear,
Half in their eagerness to hear,
"What of our England?" ask

Ah! shameful, shameful task!
To tell to souls like these
Of her languid golden ease,
Of her tame dull history!
How she frowns upon the free,
How she ogles tyranny;
How with despots she coquets;
How she swears and then forgets:
How she plays at fast and loose
With right and gross abuse;
How she fawns upon her foes;
And lowers upon her friends;
Growing weaker, day by day,
In her mean and crooked way,
Piling woes upon her woes,
As tottering she goes
Down the path where falsehood ends.
Methinks I see the awful brow
Of Cromwell wrinkle at the tale forlorn,
See the hot flushes on his forehead glow,
Hear his low growl of scorn!
Is this the realm these souls bequeathed to you,
That with all its many faults,
Its hasty strides and tardy halts,
To the truth was ever true!
Oh! shame not the noble dead,
Who through storm and slaughter led,
With toil and care and pain,
Winning glory, grain by grain,
Till no land that history knows
With such unutterable splendor glows!

Awake! the spirit yet survives
To baffle fate and conquer foes!
If not among your lords it lives,
Your chartered governors, if they
Have not the power to lead, away,
Away with lords! and give the men
Whom nature gives the right to sway,
Who love their country with a fire
That, for her darkness burns the higher—
Give these the rule! Abase your ken,
Look downward to your heart for those
In whom your ancient life blood flows,
And let their souls aspire!
Somewhere, I trust in God, remain,
Untainted by the golden stain,
Men worthy of an English sire;
Bold men who dare, in wrong's despite,
Speak truth, and strike a blow for right;
Men who have ever but their trust,
Neither in rank nor gold,
Nor aught that's bought and sold,
But in high aims, and God the just!
Seek through the land,
On every hand,
Rear up the strong, the feeble lop;
Laugh at the star and civic fur,
The blazoned shield and gartered knee—
The gewgaws of man's infancy;
And if the search be vain,
Give it not o'er too suddenly—
I swear the soul still lives in thee!—
Down to the lowest atoms drop,
Down to the very dregs, and stir
1855. The People to the top!

LIDA.

Lida, lady of the land,
Called by men "the blue-eyed wonder,"
Hath a lily forehead fanned
By locks the sunlight glitters under.
She hath all that's scattered round,
Through a race of winning creatures,
All—except the beauty found
By Johnny Gordon in my features.

Lida, lady of the land,
Hath full many goodly houses;
Fields and parks, on every hand,
Where your foot the roebuck rouses;
She hath orchards, garden-plots,
Valleys deep and mountains swelling,
All—except yon nest of cots,
Johnny Gordon's humble dwelling.

Lida, lady of the land,
Hath treasures, more than she remembers,
Heaps of dusty gems that stand
Like living coals among the embers:
She hath gold whose touch would bring
A lordship to a lowly peasant;
All—except this little ring,
Johnny Gordon's humble present.

Lida, lady of the land,
Hath a crowd of gallant suitors;
Squires who fly at her command,
Knights her slightest motion tutors:
She hath barons kneeling mute,
To hear the fortune of their proffers;
All—except the honest suit
Johnny Gordon humbly offers.

Lida, lady of the land,
Keep your wondrous charms untroubled,
May your wide domain expand,
May your gems and gold be doubled!
Keep your lords on bended knee!
Take all earth, and leave us lonely,
All—except you take from me
Humble Johnny Gordon only!

SONNET.

Not when the buxom form which nature wears
Is pregnant with the lusty warmth of spring;
Nor when hot summer, sunk with what she bears,
Lies panting in her flowery offering;
Nor yet when dusty Autumn sadly fares
In tattered garb, through which the shrewd winds sing,
To bear her treasures to the griping snares
Hard Winter set for the poor bankrupt thing
Not even when winter, heir of all the year,
Deals, like a miser, round his niggard board
The brimming plenty of his luscious hoard;
No, not in nature, change she howsoe'er,
Can I find perfect type or worthy peer
Of the fair maid in whom my heart is stored.

JOHN R. THOMPSON.

[Born, 1823.]

John R. Thompson was born in Richmond, Virginia, on the twenty-third of October, 1823. He was graduated at the University of Virginia, near Charlottesville; studied law in the office of Mr. James A. Seddon; returned to the University law school, and took the degree of bachelor of laws under Judge Henry St. George Tucker; and in 1845 came to the bar. A strong predilection for literature induced him near the close of the year 1847 to take charge of "The Southern Literary Messenger" magazine, which he has since conducted, in a manner eminently creditable to his abilities, taste, and temper. Besides his large and various contributions to this periodical, he has made frequent public addresses at colleges, delivered several ingenious and highly finished lectures, and written occasional papers for the literary journals of the north and south. He is one of the most accomplished and most useful writers of the southern states.

EXTRACT FROM "THE GREEK SLAVE."

It is not that the sculptor's patient toil
Gives sweet expression to the poet's dream —
It is not that the cold and rigid stone
Is taught to mock the human face divine —
That silently we stand before her form
And feel as in a holy presence there.
But in those fair, calm lineaments of hers,
All pure and passionless, we catch the glow
The bright intelligence of soul infused,
And tender memories of gentle things,
And sorrowing innocence and hopeful trust. ....
In some secluded vale of Arcady,
In playful gambols o'er its sunny slopes,
Had nature led her childish feet to stray;
Or she had watched the blue Egean wave
Dash on the sands of "sea-born Salamis;"
Or, in her infant sports, had sank to sleep,
Beneath the wasting shadow of that porch,
Whose sculptured gods, upon its crumbling front,
Reveal the glories of a bygone age.
There, watered by affection's richest dews
This lovely floweret, day by day grew up
In beauty and in fragrance. ....
Now, a slave,
Fettered and friendless in the market-place
Of that imperial city of the east,
Whose thousand minarets at eve resound
With the muezzin's sunset call to prayer,
She stands exposed to the unhallowed gaze
And the rude jests of every passer-by.
There in her loveliness, disrobed, for sale,
Girt with no vesture save her purity,
A ray of placid resignation beams
In every line of her sweet countenance,
And on the lip a half-disdainful curl
Proclaims the helpless victim in her chains
Victorious in a maiden's modesty!
There does the poor dejected slave display
A mien the fabled goddess could not wear,
A look and gesture that might well beseem
Some seraph from that bright meridian shore,
Where walk the angels of the Christian's creed. ....

Sweet visions cheer'd the sculptor's lonely hours,
And glorious images of heavenly mould
Came trooping at his call, as blow by blow,
The marble yielded to his constant toil,
And when he gave his last informing touch
And raised the chisel from that radiant brow,
And gazed upon the work of his own hands,
So cunningly struck out from shapeless stone,
His eye dilated with a conscious joy,
That patient effort with enduring life
Had clothed his beauteous and majestic child.
Such are thy triumphs, genius! such rewards
As far outweigh all perishable gifts,
Ingots of silver and barbaric gold
And all the trophies of tiaraed pride.

TO MISS AMELIE LOUISE RIVES,

ON HER DEPARTURE FOR FRANCE.

Lady! that bark will be more richly freighted,
That bears thee proudly on to foreign shores,
Than argosies of which old poets prated,
With Colchian fleece or with Peruvian ores;
And should the prayers of friendship prove availing,
That trusting hearts now offer up for thee,
'T will ride the crested wave with braver sailing
Than ever pinnace on the Pontic sea.

The sunny land thou seekest o'er the billow
May boast indeed the honors of thy birth,
And they may keep a vigil round thy pillow
Whom thou dost love most dearly upon earth
Yet, shall there not remain with thee a vision—
Some lingering thought of happy faces here—
Fonder and fairer than the dreams elysian
Wherein thy future's radiant hues appear?

The high and great shall render thee obeisance,
In halls bedecked with tapestries of gold,
And mansions shall be brighter for thy presence,
Where swept the stately Medicis of old;
Still amid the pomp of all this courtly lustre
I cannot think that thou wilt all forget
The pleasing fantasies that thickly cluster
Around the walls of the old homestead yet!

CHARLES G. LELAND.

[Born, 1824.]

The author of "Meister Karl's Sketch Book" was born in Philadelphia on the fifteenth of August, 1824. He is descended, according to the "Genæological Register," from the same family as the English antiquary, John Leland, who lived in the time of the eighth Henry, and his first American ancestor was Henry Leland, who died in Sherburne, Massachusetts, in 1580. He was graduated at Princeton College, in 1846, and soon after went to Europe, and studied some time at the universities of Heidelberg, Munich, and Paris, devoting special attention to modern languages, æsthetics, history, and philosophy, under Gervinus, Thiersch, Schlosser, and other teachers.

Mr. Leland in 1845 became a contributor to the "Knickerbocker" magazine, in which he has since published a great number of articles; and he has written much for other periodicals, chiefly on subjects of foreign literature and art. His "Sketch Book of Me Meister Karl," first given to the public through the pages of the "Knickerbocker," is an extraordinary production, full of natural sentiment, wit, amiable humor, incidents of foreign travel, description, moralizing, original poetry, odd extracts, and curious learning, all combined so as to display effectively the author's information, vivacity, and independence, and to illustrate the life of a student of the most catholic temper and ambition, who thinks it worth his while occasionally to indulge in studies from nature as well as from books, and enjoys a life of action quite as well as one of speculation.

His "Poetry and mystery of Dreams" is the only work in English in which are collected the displays of feeling and opinion that the ingenious and learned in various ages have made respecting the activity of the mind during sleep. In its preparation he carefully examined the writings of Artemidorus, Astrampsychius, Nicephorus of Constantinople, and Achmet, the Arabian, as well as the authors of modern Europe who have treated systematically or incidentally of oneirology or the related mental phenomena. His last book, "Pictures of Travel," translated from the German of Henry Heine, is an admirable rendering of that great wit's "Reisebilder," in which the spirit of the original is given with a point and elegance rarely equalled in English versions of German poetry, while the whole is singularly literal and exact.

Mr. Leland's poems are for the most part in a peculiar vein of satirical humor. He has an invincible dislike of the sickly extravagances of small sentimentalists, and the absurd assumptions of small philanthropists. He is not altogether incredulous of progress, but does not look for it from that boastful independence, characterizing the new generation, which rejects the authority and derides the wisdom of the past. He is of that healthy intellectual constitution which promises in every department the best fruits to his industry.

THELEME.*

I sat one night on a palace step,
  Wrapped up in a mantle thin;
And I gazed with a smile on the world without,
  With a growl at my world within,
Till I heard the merry voices ring
  Of a lordly companie,
And straight to myself I began to sing
  "It is there that I ought to be."

And long I gazed through a lattice raised
  Which smiled from the old gray wall,
And my glance went in, with the evening breeze,
  And ran o'er the revellers all;
And I said, "If they saw me, 't would cool their [mirth,
  Far more than this wild breeze free,
But a merrier party was ne'er on earth,
  And among them I fain would be."

And oh! but they all were beautiful,
  Fairer than fairy-dreams,
And their words were sweet as the wind harp's tone
  When it rings o'er summer streams;
And they pledged each other with noble mien,
  "True heart with my life to thee!"
"Alack!" quoth I, "but my soul is dry,
  And among them I fain would be!"

And the gentlemen were noble souls,
  Good fellows both sain and sound,
I had not deemed that a band like this
  Could over the world be found;
And they spoke of brave and beautiful things,
  Of all that was dear to me;
And I thought, "Perhaps they would like me well
  If among them I once might be!"

And lovely were the ladies too,
  Who sat in the light-bright hall,
And one there was, oh, dream of life!
  The loveliest 'mid them all;
She sat alone by an empty chair,
  The queen of the feast was she,
And I said to myself, "By that lady fair
  I certainly ought to be."

* "'If you think,' said the monk, 'that I have done you any service, give me leave to found an abbey after my own fancy.' The notion pleased Gargantua very well, who thereupon offered him all the country of Thelemé."—Rabelais, *Book* I. c. lvii.

And aloud she spoke, "We have waited long
For one who in fear and doubt
Looks wistfully into our hall of song
As he sits on the steps without;
I have sung to him long in silent dreams,
I have led him o'er land and sea,
Go welcome him in as his rank beseems,
And give him a place by me!"

They opened the door, yet I shrunk with shame,
As I sat in my mantle thin,
But they haled me out with a joyous shout,
And merrily led me in—
And gave me a place by my bright-haired love,
As she wept with joy and glee,
And I said to myself, "By the stars above.
I am just where I ought to be!"

Farewell to thee, life of joy and grief!
Farewell to ye, care, and pain!
Farewell, thou vulgar and selfish world!
For I never will know thee again.
I live in a land where good fellows abound,
In Thelemé, by the sea;
They may long for a "happier life" that will,—
I am just where I ought to be!

A DREAM OF LOVE.

I DREAMED I lay beside the dark blue Rhine,
In that old tower where once Sir ROLAND dwelt;
Methought his gentle lady-love was mine,
And mine the cares and pain which once he felt.
Dim, cloudy centuries had rolled away,
E'en to that minstrel age—the olden time,
When ROLAND's lady bid him woo no more,
And he, aweary, sought the eastern clime.

Methought that I, like him, had wandered long,
In those strange lands of which old legends tell;
Then home I turned to my own glancing Rhine,
And found my lady in a convent cell;
And I, like him, had watched through weary years,
And dwelt unseen hard by her convent's bound,
In that old tower, which yet stands pitying
The cloister-isle, enclosed by water round.

I long had watched—for in the early morn,
To ope her lattice, came that lady oft;
And earnestly I gazed, yet naught I saw,
Save one small hand and arm, white, fair, and [soft.
And when, at eve, the long, dark shadows fell
O'er rock and valley, vineyard, town, and tower,
Again she came—again that small white hand
Would close her lattice for the vesper hour.

I lingered still, e'en when the silent night
Had cast its sable mantle o'er the shrine,
To see her lonely taper's softened light
Gleam, far reflected, o'er the quiet Rhine;
But most I loved to see her form, at times,
Obscure those beams—for then her shade would [fall,
And I beheld it, evenly portrayed—
A living profile, on that window small.

And thus I lived in love—though not in hope—
And thus I watched that maiden many a year,
When, lo! I saw, one morn, a funeral train—
Alas! they bore my lady to her bier!

And she was dead—yet grieved I not therefore,
For now in Heaven she knew the love I felt,
Death could not kill affection, nor destroy
The holy peace wherein I long had dwelt.

Oh, gentle lady! this was but a dream!
And in a dream I bore all this for thee.
If thus in sleep love's pangs assail my soul,
Think, lady, what my waking hours must be!

MANES.

THERE'S a time to be jolly, a time to repent,
A season for folly, a season for Lent.
The first as the worst we too often regard,
The rest as the best, but our judgment is hard.

There are snows in December and roses in June,
There's darkness at midnight and sunshine at noon:
But were there no sorrow, no storm-cloud or rain,
Who'd care for the morrow with beauty again?

The world is a picture both gloomy and bright,
And grief is the shadow, and pleasure the light,
And neither should smother the general tone;
For where were the other if either were gone!

The valley is lovely, the mountain is drear,
Its summit is hidden in mist all the year;
But gaze from the heaven, high over all weather,
And mountain and valley are lovely together.

I have learned to love LUCY, though faded she be,
If my next love be lovely, the better for me;
By the end of next summer, I'll give you my oath,
It was best, after all, to have flirted with both.

In London or Munich, Vienna, or Rome,
The sage is contented, and finds him a home,
He learns all that is bad, and does all that is good,
And will bite at the apple, by field or by flood.

THE THREE FRIENDS.

I HAVE three friends, three glorious friends, three dearer could not be;
And every night, when midnight tolls, they meet to laugh with me.
The first was shot by Carlist thieves, three years ago, in Spain;
The second drowned, near Alicante, and I alive remain.

I love to see their thin white forms come stealing through the night,
And grieve to see them fade away in the early morning light.
The first with gnomes in the Under-land is leading a lordly life,
The second has married a mermaiden, a beautiful water-wife.

And since I have friends in the earth and sea—with a few, I trust, on high,
'T is a matter of small account to me, the way that I may die.
For whether I sink in the foaming flood, or swing on the triple tree,
Or die in my grave as a Christian should, is much the same to me.

Engraved at J M Butlers establishment from a Daguerreotype by Brady

Bayard Taylor.

BAYARD TAYLOR.

(Born, 1825.)

BAYARD TAYLOR was born on the eleventh of January, 1825, at Kennet Square, near the Brandywine, in Pennsylvania, and in that rural and classical region he lived until his departure for Europe in the summer of 1844. Having passed two years in Great Britain, Switzerland, Germany, Italy, and France, he returned to the United States, and after publishing an account of his travels, under the title of "Views a-Foot," he settled in New York, where except while absent on his travels he has since been occupied as one of the editors of "The Tribune," in which journal the greater part of his recent productions have been first printed.

Though not egotistical, there is scarcely an author more easily detected in his works. And this is not from any of those tricks of style in which alone consists the individuality of so many; but his sincere, frank, and enthusiastic spirit, grateful while aspiring, calm while struggling, and humble while attaining; and his life, which moves in order in the crowd and jar of society, in the solitude where Nature is seen with reverence, "up heights of rough ascent," and over streams and chasms, by shapely ways constructed by his will and knowledge. We do not remember any book of travels in which an author appears altogether so amiable and interesting as he in his "Views a-Foot." He always lingers in the background, or steps forward modestly but to solicit more earnestly our admiration for what has kindled his own: but undesignedly, or against his design even, he continually engrosses our interest, as if he were the hero of a novel; and as we pass from scene to scene with him, we think of the truth and poetry of each only to sympathize in his surprise, and joy, and wonder.

BAYARD TAYLOR'S first move in literature was a small volume of poems, of which the longest, and the longest he has yet published, was upon an incident in Spanish history. This was written when he was about eighteen years of age, and my acquaintance with him commenced when he arrived in the city with his manuscripts. We read "Ximena" together; and, while negotiations were in progress for its publication, discussed the subject of Americanism in letters. I urged upon his consideration the themes I thought best adapted to the development and illustration of his genius.

Here was a young author, born and nurtured in one of the most characteristic and beautiful of our rural districts, so removed from the associations that vitiate the national feeling and manner, and altogether of a growth so indigenous, that he was one of the fittest types of our people, selecting the materials for his first production from scenes and actions which are more picturesque, more romantic, or in any way more suitable for the purposes of art, only as they have been made so by art, and are seen through the media of art, in preference to the fresh valleys and mountains and forests, and lakes and rivers and cataracts, and high resolve, and bold adventure, and brave endurance, which have more distinctly marked, and varied, and ennobled our history than all other histories, in events crowding so fast upon each other, that our annals seem but a rehearsal of all that had been before, with years for centuries—divided by the Declaration of Independence, which is our gospel—beyond which the colonies are ancient nations, and this side of which our states have swept, with steamboats, and railroads, and telegraphs, the whole breadth of Time; and ere the startled empires are aware, are standing before them all, beckoning them to the last and best condition, which is the fulfilment of farthest-reaching prophecy. In such a choice, he had not only to enter into a competition with the greatest geniuses of the countries and ages he invaded, but, worse than this, to be a parasite of their inspiration, or to animate old forms, disciplined to a mere routine, with the new life to which he was born—sacrificing altogether his native strength, or attempting its exhibition in fetters.

Genius creates, but not like the Divine energy, from nothing. Genius creates from knowledge; and the fullness of knowledge necessary to its uses can be acquired, not from any second-hand glimpses through books, or pictures, or discourse, but from experience in the midst of its subjects, the respiration of their atmosphere, a daily contact with their forms, and a constant sympathy with their nature. This pervading intelligence gives no transient tone to the feelings, but enters into the essence of character, and becomes a part of life. He who would set aside the spirit of his age and country, to take upon himself another being, must approach his task with extraordinary powers and an indomitable will, or he will fail utterly. It is undoubtedly true that, to be American, it is not needful in all cases to select subjects which are so geographically; but this admission does not justify an indiscriminate use of foreign life, or a reckless invasion or assumption of foreign sentiment. There must be some relationship of condition and aspiration. Of all writers who have yet written, MILTON was the most American. All the works of CHANNING embrace less that is national to us than a page of the "Defence of the People of England;" and a library larger than that which was at Alexandria, of such books as IRVING'S, would not contain as much Americanism as a paragraph of the "Areopagitica." But the Genius of America was born in England, and his strength was put forth in those conflicts of the commonwealth which ended in the exile of the young Hercules. During the Cromwellian era, England offers almost as appropriate a field for illustration by the American as Massachusetts under HUTCHINSON, except in the accessories of nature, which should enter into the compositions of art. Not so Spain or Russia, at the extremes of Europe, without affinities with each other or with us. There is very little in the life or nature, or past or present or future, of either of these nations, with which the American can have any real sympathy; and for an American author, whose heart keeps time with his country's, to attempt the illustration of any character from either, while his own domain, far more rich in suggestion and material, lies waste, is a thing scarcely possible to the apprehension of a common understanding. In a remote and shadowy antiquity, like that of Egypt, or in such a darkness as envelops Mexico or Peru, or our own continent before its last discovery, the case is different: we are at liberty, with conditions, to make these the scenes of our conventionalities, because there is scarcely a record to contradict the suggestions of the imagination.

Mr. TAYLOR happily went abroad just after the publication of his story of the Sierra Morena, and though he had then travelled but little in his native country, and Europe, "seen with a staff and knapsack," opened all her gates before him with circumstances to produce the most vivid and profound impressions, his love of home grew stronger, and he felt at length the truth which might never have come to him if he had remained here, that for him the holiest land for the intellect, as well as the affections, was that in which he was born. The fables of genius and the records of history may kindle the fancy and give activity to the imagination, but they cannot rouse the passions, which must best dispose the illustrations of fancy, and can alone give vitality and attractive beauty to the fruits of a creative energy. In all his later writings the influence of the inspirations which belong to his country and his age are more and more apparent, and in his volume entitled "Rhymes of Travel, Ballads, and other Poems," published in New York in 1848, the most spirited, natural, and altogether successful compositions, are those which were suggested by the popular impulses and the peculiar adventure which had distinguished the recent life of the republic. "El Canalo," "The Bison Track," and "The fight of Paso del Mar," belong entirely to the years in which they were written, but the inspiration of which they are fruits was not more genuine than that from which we have "The Continents," "In Italy," or "The Requiem in the North."

The discovery, soon after Mr. TAYLOR became connected with the "Tribune," that California was underlaid with gold, turned all eyes in that direction, and he was among the first to leave New York for San Francisco. Starting in June, 1849, he sailed for Chagres, crossed the Isthmus to Panama, arrived in the Pacific territory, visited the gold placers, explored the forests and mountains of the interior, went to Mazatlan, travelled by land to Mexico, and returned home by way of Vera Cruz and Mobile, having been absent between eight and nine months, and met with a variety of stirring and romantic adventures such as is seldom crowded within so short a space of time in the experience of one individual. He published, soon after, his "Eldorado, or Adventures in the Path of Empire."

In 1851 appeared his "Book of Romances, Lyrics and Songs," which greatly increased his reputation as a poet. It contained "The Metempsychosis of the Pine," and "Kubleh," two of his finest poems.

There is a little episode in his life which has already been referred to in print, and may therefore be repeated, however sacred is its nature, since it would be difficult to convey by different means as just an impression of his character. The readers of poetry, which more than any other kind of literature is apt to be an emanation from the heart as well as the brain, wish always to know something of the interior life of an author, more than his books disclose, and the appreciation of his works is deeper as they may be connected with his peculiar temper or vicissitudes. In his boyhood, BAYARD TAYLOR discovered in a fair young angel of the place where he was born, that portion of himself which, according to the old mystery, should crown each nature with perfection and happiness. When he aspired, she was at the far-away end of the high-reaching vista, holding in her hand the hoped-for crown. In a letter which he sent from Rome, we see what substance his dreams were of, while a hundred ages hovered about his bed to bind his soul:

IN ITALY.

DEAR Lillian, all I wished is won!
I sit beneath Italia's sun,
Where olive orchards gleam and quiver
Along the banks of Arno's river.

Through laurel leaves, the dim green light
Falls on my forehead as I write,
And the sweet chimes of vespers, ringing,
Blend with the contadina's singing.

Rich is the soil with Fancy's gold;
The stirring memories of old
Rise thronging in my haunted vision,
And wake my spirit's young ambition.

But, as the radiant sunsets close
Above Val'd Arno's bowers of rose,
My soul forgets the olden glory
And deems our love a dearer story.

Thy words, in Memory's ear, outchime
The music of the Tuscan rhyme;
Thou standest here—the gentle-hearted—
Amid the shades of bards departed!

Their garlands of immortal bay,
I see before thee fade away,
And turn from Petrarch's passion-glances
To my own dearer heart-romances!

Sad is the opal glow that fires
The midnight of the cypress spires,
And cold the scented wind that closes
The hearts of bright Etruscan roses.

The fair Italian dream I chased,
A single thought of thee effaced;
For the true clime of song and sun
Lies in the heart which mine hath won!

There are a thousand evil things that mar each plan of joy; the marriage was deferred, perhaps for the poet to make his way in the world; and when he came back from California there was perceived another cause for deferring it; she was in ill health, and all that could be done for her was of no avail; and the suggestion came, the doubt and finally the terrible conviction, that she had the consumption, and was dying. He watched her suffering day by day, and when hope was quite dead, that he might make little journeys with her, and minister to her gently as none could but one whose light came from her eyes, he married her; while her sun was setting placed his hand in her's, that he might go with her down into the night. There are not many such marriages; there were never any holier since the father of mankind looked up into the face of our mother. She lived a few days, a few weeks perhaps, and then he came back to his occupations, and it was never mentioned that there had been any such events in his life.

In the summer of 1851, his health had become so much impaired that he felt the need of relaxation from labor, and change of scene, and started on his journey round the world. He sailed from Philadelphia on the twenty-eighth of August, and after a short stay in London proceeded to Egypt by way of the Rhine, Vienna, Trieste, and Smyrna. He reached Alexandria on the fourth of November, and immediately left for Cairo, in order to make preparations for the tour into Central Africa. He started from Cairo on the seventeenth of the month, in company with a German gentleman, bound for the first cataract, and after visiting all the Egyptian temples on the Nile, on the fifteenth of December reached Assouan, where the German left him to return. Accompanied by a faithful dragoman, and an Arab servant, he followed the Nile to Korosko, in Nubia, where he took camels to cross the great Nubian desert, and after a journey of nine days, through a waste of sand, and porphyry mountains, reached the Nile again at Abou Hammed, on the Ethiopian frontier, and continued his journey with camels to El Mekheyref, the capital of Dar Berber, where he arrived on the third of January, 1852. Here he took a boat for Khartoum, visiting on the way the ruins of ancient Meroë, and the town of Shendy, formerly the capital of a powerful Ethiopian kingdom. He arrived at Khartoum, the capital of Egyptian Soudân, at the juncture of the Blue with the White Nile, on the twelfth of January. The chiefs of all the Arab tribes between the Nile and the Red Sea, as far south as Abyssinia, were then in that city, and he was enabled to make their acquaintance, and to learn much of the unknown countries they inhabit. After remaining there ten days, he took a boat and ascended the White Nile as far as the islands of the Shilook negroes, between the twelfth and thirteenth degrees of north latitude, where, on account of the lateness of the season, and the fears of his boatmen, who refuse. o proceed, he was obliged to commence his retur.a. He penetrated a greater distance in that direction, however, than any other traveller except D'ARNAUD, WERNE, and Dr. KNOBLECHER, and carried the American flag a thousand miles farther into Africa than any one had done before him. He left Khartoum again on the fifth of February, and in fifteen days crossed the Beyooda Desert, west of the Nile, to the ruins of Napata, the ancient capital of Ethiopia, whence he went to Dongola, and passing through the countries of Măhass and Sakkôt, reached the second cataract on the ninth of March; made a rapid descent of the Nile, and was again in Cairo on the first of April, having travelled about four thousand miles.

He went from Alexandria to Beyrout, and made the circuit of Palestine and Syria, visiting Jerusalem, the Dead Sea, Damascus, and the cedars of Lebanon. Leaving Beyrout again on the twenty-eighth of May, he sailed northward along the coast to the mouth of the Orontes: and thence penetrated inland to Antioch and Aleppo, after a stay of six days in which city he proceeded to the Plain of Issus, and Tarsus in Cilicia, and crossing the range of the Taurus into Cappadocia, visited Konieh, the ancient Iconium, passed through the forests of Phrygia to Kiutahya, by the old Greek city of Œzani and the Bithynian Olympus to Broussa, and on the thirteenth of July entered Constantinople, where he continued until the sixth of August, witnessing in that period the great Mohammedan festival of the Bairam.

He took a ship from Constantinople for Malta and Sicily, and was at the foot of Mount Etna when the eruption of 1852 broke out. From Sicily he passed through Italy, the Tyrol, and Germany, renewing his acquaintance with scenes and persons described in his "Views a-Foot," and reached London by the middle of October. He next sailed from Southampton for Gibraltar, and spent a month in the south of Spain, visiting Seville, Cordova, and Granada, and returning to Gibraltar took the overland route to Alexandria, crossed to Suez, and proceeded to Bombay, where he arrived on the twenty-seventh of December. A journey of seven hundred and eighty miles brought him to Agra, whence he went to Delhi, and thence to the range of the Himalayas. Having visited Lucknow, the capital of the kingdom of Oude, Allahabad, and Benares, the holy city of the Ganges, he travelled to Calcutta, and there embarked for Hong Kong, by way of Penang and Singapore, and shortly after his arrival in China, was attached to the American legation, and accompanied the minister, Mr. HUMPHREY MARSHALL, to Shanghai, where he remained nearly two months.

When the American expedition under Commodore PERRY reached Shanghai, he was allowed to enter the naval service, with the rank of master's mate, for the purpose of accompanying it; and sailed on the seventeenth of May, 1853, for Loo Choo, where he was attached to a party which explored the interior of the island, never before visited by white men. In June, he proceeded to the Bonin Islands, in the Pacific, eight hundred miles east of Loo Choo, and explored them, and returning, sailed for Japan, and came to anchor in the bay of Yeddo on the eighth of July. After witnessing all the negotiations which took place, and participating in the landing, he returned with the squadron to Loo Choo and China, and remained a month at Macao. He then, with the permission of Commodore PERRY, resigned his place in the navy, passed a short time at Canton, and on the fifth of September took passage for New York; and after a voyage of one hundred and one days, during which he stopped at Java and St. Helena, arrived home on the twentieth of December, having been absent two years and four months and travelled more than fifty thousand miles. His spirited, graphic and entertaining history of this journey is given in three works entitled "The Lands of the Saracen," "A Journey to Central Africa," and "India, Loo Choo, and Japan."

Mr. TAYLOR has probably travelled more extensively than any man of his years in the world, and the records of his adventures have the best charms of works in their class; but eminent as he is as a writer of travels, his highest and most enduring distinction will be from his poetry. As a picturesque, passionate and imaginative poet his excellence has been more and more conspicuous every year since he printed his little volume of juvenile effusions containing "Ximena, a Story of the Sierra Morena." The fame he has won among the masses as a tourist has undoubtedly been in the way of his proper reputation in literary art; but his travels will hereafter be to his poems no more than those of SMOLLET are to his extraordinary novels.

Besides his works already mentioned he has published "The American Legend," a poem delivered before the Phi Beta Kappa Society of Harvard University, in 1850; and "Poems of the Orient," which appeared in 1854, and embrace only such pieces as were written while he was on his passage round the world, and present the more poetical phases of that portion of his experiences. They are glowing with the warm light of the east, and passages rich, sensuous and impetuous as the Arab sings in dreams, with others gentle and tender and exquisitely modulated as ever were murmured by the meditative and sentimental Persian. The profound influence of oriental life, nature, and reminiscence, upon his imagination, are vindicated in a sonnet of

NUBIA.

"A LAND of Dreams and Sleep—a poppied land,
With skies of endless calm above her head,
The drowsy warmth of Summer noonday shed
Upon her hills, and silence stern and grand
Throughout her Desert's temple-burying sand,
Before her threshold, in their ancient place,
With closed lips, and fixed, majestic face,
Noteless of time, her dumb colossi stand.
O, pass them not with light irreverent tread;
Respect the dream that builds her fallen throne;
And soothes her to oblivion of her woes.
Hush! for she does but sleep; she is not dead:
Action and Toil have made the world their own,
But she hath built an altar to REPOSE."

The whole book exhibits an advance in general cultivation, an increased mastery of the difficulties and resources of rhythm, a deeper sympathy with nature, and no deficiency of that genuineness, that fidelity to his own character, which is among the most eminent attractions of his previous performances. In a proem, addressed to his friend R. H. STODDARD, he describes the growth and tendencies of his intellectual passion:

"I pitch my tent upon the naked sands.
And the tall palm, that plumes the orient lands,
Can with its beauty satisfy my heart.
You, in your starry trances, breathe the air
Of lost Elysium, pluck the snowy bells
Of lotus and Olympian asphodels,
And bid us their diviner odors share.
I at the threshold of that world have lain,
Gazed on its glory, heard the grand acclaim
Wherewith its trumpets hail the sons of Fame,
And striven its speech to master—but in vain.
And now I turn, to find a late content
In Nature, making mine her myriad shows;
Better contented with one living rose
Than all the gods' ambrosia; sternly bent
On wresting from her hand the cup, whence flow
The flavors of her ruddiest life—the change
Of climes and races—the unshackled range
Of all experience;—that my songs may show
The warm red blood that beats in hearts of men,
And those who read them in the festering den
Of cities, may behold the open sky,
And hear the rhythm of the winds that blow,
Instinct with Freedom. Blame me not, that I
Find in the forms of Earth a deeper joy
Than in the dreams which lured me as a boy,
And leave the heavens, where you are wandering still
With bright APOLLO, to converse with PAN."

Here is his poetical creed, which is in perfect correspondence with his organization, and admirably adapted for the development of his finest powers.

In the following pages are examples of his emotion and art in different periods. I reluctantly omit "The Romance of the Maize," in which he has embodied a fine Indian superstition, his noble "Ode to Shelley," and several others, exhibiting a still wider range of feeling and invention.

METEMPSYCHOSIS OF THE PINE.

As when the haze of some wan moonlight makes
Familiar fields a land of mystery,
Where all is changed, and some new presence wakes
In flower, and bush, and tree,—

Another life the life of Day o'erwhelms;
The Past from present consciousness takes hue,
And we remember vast and cloudy realms
Our feet have wandered through:

So, oft, some moonlight of the mind makes dumb
The stir of outer thought: wide open seems
The gate where through strange sympathies have come,
The secret of our dreams;

The source of fine impressions, shooting deep
Below the failing plummet of the sense;
Which strike beyond all Time, and backward sweep
Through all intelligence.

We touch the lower life of beast and clod,
And the long process of the ages see
From blind old Chaos, ere the breath of God
Moved it to harmony.

All outward wisdom yields to that within,
Whereof nor creed nor canon holds the key;
We only feel that we have ever been
And evermore shall be;

And thus I know, by memories unfurled
In rarer moods, and many a nameless sign,
That once in Time, and somewhere in the world,
I was a towering Pine,

Rooted upon a cape that overhung
The entrance to a mountain gorge; whereon
The wintry shadow of a peak was flung,
Long after rise of sun.

Behind, the silent snows; and wide below,
The rounded hills made level, lessening down
To where a river washed with sluggish flow
A many-templed town.

There did I clutch the granite with firm feet,
There shake my boughs above the roaring gulf,
When mountain whirlwinds through the passes beat,
And howled the mountain wolf.

There did I louder sing than all the floods
Whirled in white foam adown the precipice,
And the sharp sleet that stung the naked woods
Answer with sullen hiss:

But when the peaceful clouds rose white and high
On blandest airs that April skies could bring,
Through all my fibres thrilled the tender sigh,
The sweet unrest of Spring.

She, with warm fingers laced in mine, did melt
In fragrant balsam my reluctant blood;
And with a smart of keen delight I felt
The sap in every bud,

And tingled through my rough old bark, and fast
Pushed out the younger green, that smoothed my tones,
When last year's needles to the wind I cast,
And shed my scaly cones.

I held the eagle, till the mountain mist
Rolled from the azure paths he came to soar,
And like a hunter, on my gnarled wrist
The dappled falcon bore.

Poised o'er the blue abyss, the morning lark
Sang, wheeling near in rapturous carouse,
And hart and hind, soft-pacing through the dark,
Slept underneath my boughs.

Down on the pasture-slopes the herdsman lay,
And for the flock his birchen trumpet blew;
There ruddy children tumbled in their play,
And lovers came to woo.

And once an army, crowned with triumph came
Out of the hollow bosom of the gorge,
With mighty banners in the wind aflame,
Borne on a glittering surge

Of tossing spears, a flood that homeward rolled,
While cymbals timed their steps of victory,
And horn and clarion from their throats of gold
Sang with a savage glee.

I felt the mountain-walls below me shake,
Vibrant with sound, and through my branches poured
The glorious gust: my song thereto did make
Magnificent accord.

Some blind harmonic instinct pierced the rind
Of that slow life which made me straight and high,
And I became a harp for every wind,
A voice for every sky;

When fierce autumnal gales began to blow,
Roaring all day in concert, hoarse and deep;
And then made silent with my weight of snow,—
A spectre on the steep;

Filled with a whispering gush, like that which flows
Through organ-stops, when sank the sun's red disk
Beyond the city, and in blackness rose
Temple and obelisk;

Or breathing soft, as one who sighs in prayer,
Mysterious sounds of portent and of might,
What time I felt the wandering waves of air
Pulsating through the night.

And thus for centuries my rhythmic chant
Rolled down the gorge or surged about the hill:
Gentle, or stern, or sad, or jubilant,
At every season's will.

No longer Memory whispers whence arose
The doom that tore me from my place of pride:
Whether the storms that load the peak with snows,
And start the mountain-slide,

Let fall a fiery bolt to smite my top,
Upwrenched my roots, and o'er the precipice
Hurled me, a dangling wreck, erelong to drop
Into the wild abyss;

Or whether hands of men, with scornful strength
And force from Nature's rugged armory lent,
Sawed through my heart and rolled my tumbling length
Sheer down the steep descent.

All sense departed, with the boughs I wore;
And though I moved with mighty gales at strife,
A mast upon the seas, I sang no more,
And music was my life.

Yet still that life awakens, brings again
Its airy anthems, resonant and long,
Till Earth and Sky, transfigured, fill my brain
With rhythmic sweeps of song.

Thence am I made a poet: thence are sprung
Those motions of the soul, that sometimes reach
Beyond all grasp of Art,—for which the tongue
Is ignorant of speech.

And if some wild, full-gathered harmony
Roll its unbroken music through my line,
Believe there murmurs, faintly though it be
The Spirit of the Pine.

EL CANALO.*

Now saddle El Canalo!—the freshening wind of morn
Down in the flowery vega is stirring through the corn;
The thin smoke of the ranches grows red with coming day,
And the steed's impatient stamping is eager for the way!

My glossy-limb'd Canalo, thy neck is curved in pride,
Thy slender ears prick'd forward, thy nostril straining wide,
And as thy quick neigh greets me, and I catch thee by the mane,
I'm off with the winds of morning—the chieftain of the plain!

I feel the swift air whirring, and see along our track,
From the flinty-paved sierra, the sparks go streaming back;
And I clutch my rifle closer, as we sweep the dark defile,
Where the red guerilla watches for many a lonely mile.

They reach not El Canalo; with the swiftness of a dream
We've pass'd the bleak Nevada, and Tulé's icy stream;
But where, on sweeping gallop, my bullet backward sped,
The keen-eyed mountain vultures will circle o'er the dead!

On! on, my brave Canalo! we've dash'd the sand and snow
From peaks upholding heaven, from deserts far below—
We've thunder'd through the forest, while the crackling branches rang,
And trooping elks, affrighted, from lair and covert sprang!

We've swum the swollen torrent, we've distanced in the race
The baying wolves of Pinos, that panted with the chase;
And still thy mane streams backward, at every thrilling bound,
And still thy measured hoof-stroke beats with its morning sound!

The seaward winds are wailing through Santa Barbara's pines,
And like a sheathless sabre, the far Pacific shines;
Hold to thy speed, my arrow!—at nightfall thou shalt lave
Thy hot and smoking haunches beneath his silver wave!

My head upon thy shoulder, along the sloping sand
We'll sleep as trusty brothers, from out the mountain land;
The pines will sound in answer to the surges on the shore,
And in our dreams, Canalo, we'll make the journey o'er!

* El Canalo, or the cinnamon-coloured, is the name of the choicest breed of the Californian horse.

THE BISON-TRACK.

STRIKE the tent! the sun has risen; not a cloud has ribb'd the dawn,
And the frosted prairie brightens to the westward, far and wan:
Prime afresh the trusty rifle—sharpen well the hunting-spear—
For the frozen sod is trembling, and a noise of hoofs I hear!

Fiercely stamp the tether'd horses, as they snuff the morning's fire,
And their flashing heads are tossing, with a neigh of keen desire;
Strike the tent—the saddles wait us! let the bridle-reins be slack,
For the prairie's distant thunder has betray'd the bison's track!

See! a dusky line approaches; hark! the onward-surging roar,
Like the din of wintry breakers on a sounding wall of shore!
Dust and sand behind them whirling, snort the foremost of the van,
And the stubborn horns are striking, through the crowded caravan.

Now the storm is down upon us—let the madden'd horses go!
We shall ride the living whirlwind, though a hundred leagues it blow!
Though the surgy manes should thicken, and the red eyes' angry glare
Lighten round us as we gallop through the sand and rushing air!

Myriad hoofs will scar the prairie, in our wild, resistless race,
And a sound, like mighty waters, thunder down the desert space:
Yet the rein may not be tighten'd, nor the rider's eye look back—
Death to him whose speed should slacken, on the madden'd bison's track!

Now the trampling herds are threaded, and the chase is close and warm
For the giant bull that gallops in the edges of the storm:
Hurl your lassoes swift and fearless—swing your rifles as we run!
Ha! the dust is red behind him: shout, my brothers, he is won!

Look not on him as he staggers—'tis the last shot he will need;
More shall fall, among his fellows, ere we run the bold stampede—
Ere we stem the swarthy breakers—while the wolves, a hungry pack,
Howl around each grim-eyed carcass, on the bloody bison-track!

BEDOUIN SONG.

From the Desert I come to thee
On a stallion shod with fire;
And the winds are left behind
In the speed of my desire.
Under thy window I stand,
And the midnight hears my cry:
I love thee, I love but thee,
With a love that shall not die
Till the sun grows cold,
And the stars are old,
And the leaves of the Judgment
Book unfold!

Look from thy window and see
My passion and my pain;
I lie on the sands below,
And I faint in thy disdain.
Let the night-winds touch thy brow
With the heat of my burning sigh,
And melt thee to hear the vow
Of a love that shall not die
Till the sun grows cold,
And the stars are old,
And the leaves of the Judgment
Book unfold!

My steps are nightly driven,
By the fever in my breast,
To hear from thy lattice breathed
The word that shall give me rest.
Open the door of thy heart,
And open thy chamber door,
And my kisses shall teach thy lips
The love that shall fade no more
Till the sun grows cold,
And the stars are old,
And the leaves of the Judgment
Book unfold!

THE ARAB TO THE PALM.

Next to thee, O fair gazelle,
O Beddowee girl, beloved so well;

Next to the fearless Nedjidee,
Whose fleetness shall bear me again to thee;

Next to ye both I love the Palm,
With his leaves of beauty, his fruit of balm;

Next to ye both I love the Tree
Whose fluttering shadow wraps us three
With love, and silence, and mystery!

Our tribe is many, our poets vie
With any under the Arab sky;
Yet none can sing of the Palm but I.

The marble minarets that begem
Cairo's citadel-diadem
Are not so light as his slender stem.

He lifts his leaves in the sunbeam's glance
As the Almehs lift their arms in dance—

A slumberous motion, a passionate sign,
That works in the cells of the blood like wine

Full of passion and sorrow is he,
Dreaming where the beloved may be.

And when the warm south-winds arise,
He breathes his longing in fervid sighs—

Quickening odors, kisses of balm,
That drop in the lap of his chosen palm.
The sun may flame and the sands may stir,
But the breath of his passion reaches her.

O Tree of Love, by that love of thine,
Teach me how I shall soften mine!

Give me the secret of the sun,
Whereby the wooed is ever won!

If I were a King, O stately Tree,
A likeness, glorious as might be,
In the court of my palace I'd build for thee!

With a shaft of silver, burnished bright,
And leaves of beryl and malachite·

With spikes of golden bloom a-blaze,
And fruits of topaz and chrysoprase:

And there the poets, in thy praise,
Should night and morning frame new lays—

New measures sung to tunes divine;
But none, O Palm, should equal mine!

KUBLEH;

A STORY OF THE ASSYRIAN DESERT.

The black eyed children of the Desert drove
Their flocks together at the set of sun.
The tents were pitched; the weary camels bent
Their suppliant necks, and knelt upon the sand;
The hunters quartered by the kindled fires
The wild boars of the Tigris they had slain
And all the stir and sound of evening ran
Throughout the Shammar camp. The dewy air
Bore its full burden of confused delight
Across the flowery plain, and while afar,
The snows of Koordish Mountains in the ray
Flashed roseate amber, Nimroud's ancient mound
Rose broad and black against the burning West.
The shadows deepened and the stars came out,
Sparkling in violet ether; one by one
Glimmered the ruddy camp-fires on the plain,
And shapes of steed and horseman moved among
The dusky tents with shout and jostling cry,
And neigh and restless prancing. Children ran
To hold the thongs while every rider drove
His quivering spear in the earth, and by his door
Tethered the horse he loved. In midst of all
Stood Shammeriyah, whom they dared not touch,—
The foal of wondrous Kubleh, to the Sheik
A dearer wealth than all his Georgian girls.
But when their meal was o'er,—when the red fires
Blazed brighter, and the dogs no longer bayed,—
When Shammar hunters with the boys sat down
To cleanse their bloody knives, came Alimàr,
The poet of the tribe, whose songs of love
Are sweeter than Bassora's nightingales,—
Whose songs of war can fire the Arab blood

Like war itself: who knows not Alimar?
Then ask'd the men: "O poet, sing of Kubleh!"
And boys laid down the knives half burnish'd, saying:
"Tell us of Kubleh, whom we never saw—
Of wondrous Kubleh!" Closer flock'd the group
With eager eyes about the flickering fire,
While Alimar, beneath the Assyrian stars,
Sang to the listening Arabs:
"God is great!
O Arabs, never yet since Mahmoud rode
The sands of Yemen, and by Mecca's gate
The wingéd steed bestrode, whose mane of fire
Blazed up the zenith, when, by Allah call'd,
He bore the prophet to the walls of heaven,
Was like to Kubleh, Sofuk's wondrous mare:
Not all the milk-white barbs, whose hoofs dash'd flame
In Bagdad's stables, from the marble floor—
Who, swath'd in purple housings, pranced in state
The gay bazaars, by great Al-Raschid back'd:
Not the wild charger of Mongolian breed
That went o'er half the world with Tamerlane:
Nor yet those flying coursers, long ago
From Ormuz brought by swarthy Indian grooms
To Persia's kings—the foals of sacred mares,
Sired by the fiery stallions of the sea!
"Who ever told, in all the Desert Land,
The many deeds of Kubleh? Who can tell
Whence came she, whence her like shall come again?
O Arabs, like a tale of Scherezade
Heard in the camp, when javelin shafts are tried
On the hot eve of battle, is her story.
"Far in the Southern sands, the hunters say,
Did Sofuk find her, by a lonely palm.
The well had dried; her fierce, impatient eye
Glared red and sunken, and her slight young limbs
Were lean with thirst. He check'd his camel's pace,
And while it knelt, untied the water-skin,
And when the wild mare drank, she follow'd him.
Thence none but Sofuk might the saddle gird
Upon her back, or clasp the brazen gear
About her shining head, that brook'd no curb
From even him; for she, alike, was royal.
"Her form was lighter, in its shifting grace,
Than some impassion'd Almée's, when the dance
Unbinds her scarf, and golden anklets gleam
Through floating drapery, on the buoyant air.
Her light, free head was ever held aloft;
Between her slender and transparent ears
The silken forelock toss'd; her nostril's arch,
Thin-drawn, in proud and pliant beauty spread,
Snuffing the desert winds. Her glossy neck
Curved to the shoulder like an eagle's wing,
And all her matchless lines of flank and limb
Seem'd fashion'd from the flying shapes of air
By hands of lightning. When the war-shouts rang
From tent to tent, her keen and restless eye
Shone like a blood-red ruby, and her neigh
Rang wild and sharp above the clash of spears.
"The tribes of Tigris and the Desert knew her:
Sofuk before the Shammar bands she bore
To meet the dread Jebours, who waited not
To bid her welcome; and the savage Koord,
Chased from his bold irruption on the plain,
Has seen her hoofprints in his mountain snow.
Lithe as the dark-eyed Syrian gazelle,
O'er ledge and chasm and barren steep, amid
The Sindjar hills, she ran the wild ass down.
Through many a battle's thickest brunt she storm'd,
Reeking with sweat and dust, and fetlock-deep
In curdling gore. When hot and lurid haze
Stifled the crimson sun, she swept before
The whirling sand-spout, till her gusty mane
Flared in its vortex, while the camels lay
Groaning and helpless on the fiery waste.
"The tribes of Taurus and the Caspian knew her:
The Georgian chiefs have heard her trumpet-neigh
Before the walls of Teflis. Pines that grow
On ancient Caucasus, have harbour'd her,
Sleeping by Sofuk in their spicy gloom.
The surf of Trebizond has bathed her flanks,
When from the shore she saw the white-sail'd bark
That brought him home from Stamboul. Never yet,
O Arabs, never yet was like to Kubleh!
"And Sofuk loved her. She was more to him
Than all his snowy-bosom'd odalisques.
For many years, beside his tent she stood,
The glory of the tribe.
"At last she died:
Died, while the fire was yet in all her limbs—
Died for the life of Sofuk, whom she loved.
The base Jebours—on whom be Allah's curse!—
Came on his path, when far from any camp,
And would have slain him, but that Kubleh sprang
Against the javelin-points and bore them down,
And gain'd the open desert. Wounded sore,
She urged her light limbs into maddening speed
And made the wind a laggard. On and on
The red sand slid beneath her, and behind
Whirl'd in a swift and cloudy turbulence,
As when some star of Eblis, downward hurl'd
By Allah's bolt, sweeps with its burning hair
The waste of darkness. On and on, the bleak,
Bare ridges rose before her, came and pass'd;
And every flying leap with fresher blood
Her nostril stain'd, till Sofuk's brow and breast
Were fleck'd with crimson foam. He would have turn'd
To save his treasure, though himself were lost,
But Kubleh fiercely snapp'd the brazen rein.
At last, when through her spent and quivering frame
The sharp throes ran, our distant tents arose,
And with a neigh, whose shrill excess of joy
O'ercame its agony, she stopp'd and fell.
The Shammar men came round her as she lay,
And Sofuk raised her head and held it close
Against his breast. Her dull and glazing eye
Met his, and with a shuddering gasp she died.
Then like a child his bursting grief made way
In passionate tears, and with him all the tribe
Wept for the faithful mare.
"They dug her grave
Amid Al-Hather's marbles, where she lies
Buried with ancient kings; and since that time
Was never seen, and will not be again,
O Arabs, though the world be doom'd to live
As many moons as count the desert sands,
The like of wondrous Kubleh. God is great!"

CHARMIAN.

O DAUGHTER of the Sun!
  Who gave the keys of passion unto thee?
Who taught the powerful sorcery
  Wherein my soul, too willing to be won,
Still feebly struggles to be free,
  But more than half undone?
Within the mirror of thine eyes,
Full of the sleep of warm Egyptian skies —
The sleep of lightning, bound in airy spell,
And deadlier, because invisible,—
  I see the reflex of a feeling
Which was not, till I looked on thee:
  A power, involved in mystery,
That shrinks, affrighted, from its own revealing.

Thou sitt'st in stately indolence,
  Too calm to feel a breath of passion start
The listless fibres of thy sense,
  The fiery slumber of thy heart.
Thine eyes are wells of darkness, by the vail
  Of languid lids half-sealed: the pale
And bloodless olive of thy face,
  And the full, silent lips that wear
A ripe serenity of grace,
  Are dark beneath the shadow of thy hair.
Not from the brow of templed ATHOR beams
Such tropic warmth along the path of dreams;
Not from the lips of hornéd ISIS flows
Such sweetness of repose!
For thou art Passion's self, a goddess too,
And aught but worship never knew;
  And thus thy glances, calm and sure,
Look for accustomed homage, and betray
  No effort to assert thy sway:
Thou deem'st my fealty secure.

O Sorceress! those looks unseal
  The undisturbéd mysteries that press
Too deep in nature for the heart to feel
  Their terror and their loveliness.
Thine eyes are torches that illume
  On secret shrines their unforeboded fires,
And fill the vaults of silence and of gloom
  With the unresting life of new desires.
I follow where their arrowy ray
Pierces the vail I would not tear away,
And with a dread delicious awe behold
Another gate of life unfold,
Like the rapt neophyte who sees
Some march of grand Osirian mysteries.
The startled chambers I explore,
  And every entrance open lies,
Forced by the magic thrill that runs before
  Thy slowly-lifted eyes.
I tremble to the centre of my being
  Thus to confess the spirit's poise o'erthrown,
And all its guiding virtues blown
  Like leaves before the whirlwind's fury fleeing.

But see! one memory rises in my soul,
  And, beaming steadily and clear,
Scatters the lurid thunder-clouds that roll
  Through Passion's sultry atmosphere.
An alchemy more potent borrow
  From thy dark eyes, enticing Sorceress,
For on the casket of a sacred Sorrow
  Their shafts fell powerless.
Nay, frown not, ATHOR, from thy mystic shrine:
  Strong Goddess of Desire, I will not be
One of the myriad slaves thou callest thine,
  To cast my manhood's crown of royalty
  Before thy dangerous beauty: I am free!

THE POET IN THE EAST.

THE poet came to the land of the East,
  When Spring was in the air:
The earth was dressed for a wedding feast,
  So young she seemed, and fair;
And the poet knew the land of the East—
  His soul was native there.

All things to him were the visible forms
  Of early and precious dreams—
Familiar visions that mocked his quest
  Beside the western streams,
Or gleamed in the gold of the cloud unrolled
  In the sunset's dying beams.

He looked above in the cloudless calm,
  And the Sun sat on his throne;
The breath of gardens deep in balm,
  Was all about him blown,
And a brother to him was the princely Palm,
  For he cannot live alone.

His feet went forth on the myrtled hills,
  And the flowers their welcome shed;
The meads of milk-white asphodel
  They knew the Poet's tread,
And far and wide, in a scarlet tide,
  The poppy's bonfire spread.

And, half in shade and half in sun,
  The Rose sat in her bower,
With a passionate thrill in her crimson heart
  She had waited for the hour!
And, like a bride's, the Poet kissed
  The lips of the glorious flower.

Then the Nightingale who sat above
  In the boughs of the citron-tree,
Sang: We are no rivals, brother mine,
  Except in minstrelsy;
For the rose you kissed with the kiss of love,
  Is faithful still to me.

And further sang the Nightingale:
  Your bower not distant lies.
I heard the sound of a Persian lute
  From the jasmined window rise,
And like two stars, through the lattice-bars,
  I saw the Sultana's eyes.

The Poet said; I will here abide,
  In the Sun's unclouded door;
Here are the wells of all delight
  On the lost Arcadian shore:
Here is the light on sea and land,
  And the dream deceives no more.

KILIMANDJARO.

HAIL to thee, monarch of African mountains,
Remote, inaccessible, silent, and lone—
Who, from the heart of the tropical fervors,
Liftest to heaven thine alien snows,
Feeding forever the fountains that make thee
Father of Nile and Creator of Egypt!

The years of the world are engraved on thy forehead;
Time's morning blushed red on thy first-fallen snows;
Yet lost in the wilderness, nameless, unnoted,
Of Man unbeholden, thou wert not till now.
Knowledge alone is the being of Nature,
Giving a soul to her manifold features,
Lighting through paths of the primitive darkness
The footsteps of Truth and the vision of Song.
Knowledge has born thee anew to Creation,
And long-baffled Time at thy baptism rejoices.
Take, then, a name, and be filled with existence,
Yea, be exultant in sovereign glory,
While from the hand of the wandering poet
Drops the first garland of song at thy feet.

Floating alone, on the flood of thy making,
Through Africa's mystery, silence, and fire,
Lo! in my palm, like the Eastern enchanter,
I dip from the waters a magical mirror,
And thou art revealed to my purified vision.
I see thee, supreme in the midst of thy co-mates,
Standing alone 'twixt the Earth and the Heavens,
Heir of the Sunset and Herald of Morn.
Zone above zone, to thy shoulders of granite,
The climates of Earth are displayed, as an index,
Giving the scope of the Book of Creation.
There, in the gorges that widen, descending
From cloud and from cold into summer eternal,
Gather the threads of the ice-gendered fountains—
Gather to riotous torrents of crystal,
And, giving each shelvy recess where they dally
The blooms of the North and its evergreen turfage,
Leap to the land of the lion and lotus!
There, in the wondering airs of the Tropics
Shivers the Aspen, still dreaming of cold:
There stretches the Oak, from the loftiest ledges,
His arms to the far-away lands of his brothers,
And the Pine-tree looks down on his rival the Palm.

Bathed in the tenderest purple of distance,
Tinted and shadowed by pencils of air,
Thy battlements hang o'er the slopes and the forests,
Seats of the Gods in the limitless ether,
Looming sublimely aloft and afar.
Above them, like folds of imperial ermine,
Sparkle the snow-fields that furrow thy forehead—
Desolate realms, inaccessible, silent,
Chasms and caverns where Day is a stranger,
Garners where storeth his treasures the Thunder,
The Lightning his falchion, his arrows the Hail!

Sovereign Mountain, thy brothers give welcome:
They, the baptized and the crownéd of ages,
Watch-towers of Continents, altars of Earth,
Welcome thee now to their mighty assembly.
Mont Blanc, in the roar of his mad avalanches
Hails thy accession; superb Orizaba,
Belted with beech and ensandalled with palm;
Chimborazo, the lord of the regions of noonday,—
Mingle their sounds in magnificent chorus
With greeting august from the Pillars of Heaven,
Who, in the urns of the Indian Ganges,
Filter the snows of their sacred dominions,
Unmarked with a footprint, unseen but of God.

Lo! unto each is the seal of his lordship,
Nor questioned the right that his majesty giveth;
Each in his awful supremacy forces
Worship and reverence, wonder and joy.
Absolute all, yet in dignity varied,
None has a claim to the honors of story,
Or the superior splendors of song,
Greater than thou, in thy mystery mantled—
Thou, the sole monarch of African mountains,
Father of Nile and Creator of Egypt!

AN ORIENTAL IDYL.

A SILVER javelin which the hills
Have hurled upon the plain below,
The fleetest of the Pharpar's rills,
Beneath me shoots in flashing flow.

I hear the never-ending laugh
Of jostling waves that come and go,
And suck the bubbling pipe, and quaff
The sherbet cooled in mountain snow.

The flecks of sunshine gleam like stars
Beneath the canopy of shade;
And in the distant, dim bazaars
I scarcely hear the hum of trade.

No evil fear, no dream forlorn,
Darkens my heaven of perfect blue;
My blood is tempered to the morn—
My very heart is steeped in dew.

What Evil is I cannot tell;
But half I guess what Joy may be;
And, as a pearl within its shell,
The happy spirit sleeps in me.

I feel no more the pulse's strife,—
The tides of Passion's ruddy sea,—
But live the sweet, unconscious life
That breathes from yonder jasmine-tree.

Upon the glittering pageantries
Of gay Damascus streets I look
As idly as a babe that sees
The painted pictures of a book.

Forgotten now are name and race;
The Past is blotted from my brain;
For Memory sleeps, and will not trace
The weary pages o'er again.

I only know the morning shines,
And sweet the dewy morning air,
But does it play with tendrilled vines?
Or does it lightly lift my hair?

Deep-sunken in the charmed repose,
This ignorance is bliss extreme:
And whether I be Man, or Rose,
O, pluck me not from out my dream!

HASSAN TO HIS MARE.

Come, my beauty! come, my desert darling!
  On my shoulder lay thy glossy head!
Fear not, though the barley-sack be empty,
  Here 's the half of Hassan's scanty bread.

Thou shalt have thy share of dates, my beauty!
  And thou know'st my water-skin is free:
Drink and welcome, for the wells are distant,
  And my strength and safety lie in thee.

Bend thy forehead now, to take my kisses!
  Lift in love thy dark and splendid eye:
Thou art glad when Hassan mounts the saddle—
  Thou art proud he owns thee: so am I.

Let the Sultan bring his boasted horses,
  Prancing with their diamond-studded reins;
They, my darling, shall not match thy fleetness
  When they course with thee the desert-plains!

Let the Sultan bring his famous horses,
  Let him bring his golden swords to me —
Bring his slaves, his eunuchs, and his harem;
  He would offer them in vain for thee.

We have seen Damascus, O my beauty!
  And the splendor of the Pashas there;
What's their pomp and riches? Why, I would not
  Take them for a handful of thy hair!

Khaled sings the praises of his mistress,
  And, because I've none he pities me:
What care I if he should have a thousand,
  Fairer than the morning? *I* have thee.

He will find his passion growing cooler
  Should her glance on other suitors fall:
Thou wilt ne'er, my mistress and my darling,
  Fail to answer at thy master's call.

By-and-by some snow-white Nedjid-stallion
  Shall to thee his spring-time ardor bring;
And a foal, the fairest of the Desert,
  To thy milky dugs shall crouch and cling.

Then, when Khaled shows to me his children,
  I shall laugh, and bid him look at thine;
Thou wilt neigh, and lovingly caress me,
  With thy glossy neck laid close to mine.

THE PHANTOM.

Again I sit within the mansion,
  In the old, familiar seat;
And shade and sunshine chase each other
  O'er the carpet at my feet.

But the sweet-brier's arms have wrestled upwards
  In the summers that are past,
And the willow trails its branches lower
  Than when I saw them last.

They strive to shut the sunshine wholly
  From out the haunted room;
To fill the house, that once was joyful,
  With silence and with gloom

And many kind, remembered faces
  Within the doorway come—
Voices, that wake the sweeter music
  Of one that now is dumb.

They sing, in tones as glad as ever,
  The songs she loved to hear;
They braid the rose in summer garlands,
  Whose flowers to her were dear.

And still, her footsteps in the passage,
  Her blushes at the door,
Her timid words of maiden welcome,
  Come back to me once more.

And all forgetful of my sorrow,
  Unmindful of my pain,
I think she has but newly left me,
  And soon will come again.

She stays without, perchance, a moment,
  To dress her dark-brown hair;
I hear the rustle of her garments—
  Her light step on the stair!

O, fluttering heart! control thy tumult,
  Lest eyes profane should see
My cheeks betray the rush of rapture
  Her coming brings to me!

She tarries long: but lo, a whisper
  Beyond the open door
And, gliding through the quiet sunshine,
  A shadow on the floor!

Ah! 'tis the whispering pine that calls me,
  The vine, whose shadow strays;
And my patient heart must still await her,
  Nor chide her long delays.

But my heart grows sick with weary waiting
  As many a time before:
Her foot is ever at the threshold,
  Yet never passes o'er.

"MOAN YE WILD WINDS."

Moan, ye wild winds! around the pane,
And fall, thou drear December rain!
Fill with your gusts the sullen day,
Tear the last clinging leaves away!
Reckless as yonder naked tree,
No blast of yours can trouble me.

Give me your chill and wild embrace,
And pour your baptism on my face;
Sound in mine ears the airy moan
That sweeps in desolate monotone,
Where on the unsheltered hill-top beat
The marches of your homeless feet!

Moan on, ye winds! and pour, thou rain!
Your stormy sobs and tears are vain,
If shed for her, whose fading eyes
Will open soon on Paradise:
The eye of Heaven shall blinded be,
Or ere ye cease, if shed for me.

RICHARD COE.

[Born, 1821.]

Richard Coe is of a Quaker family, and was born in Philadelphia, on the thirteenth of February, 1821. He was educated for the mercantile business, and has been for many years engaged in trade in his native city. In 1851 he published a volume of "Poems," which attracted favorable attention by their simplicity and grace, as much as by their fine religious spirit, and in 1853, "The Old Farm Gate," a book of prose and verse, designed for youthful readers; and he writes occasionally for the Philadelphia literary magazines. His pieces are marked by refinement of feeling, and have frequently a quaintness reminding us of some of the older religious poets.

SMILES AND TEARS.

"Art thou happy, little child,
  On this clear bright summer's day—
In the garden sporting wild,
  Art thou happy? tell me, pray."
"If I had that pretty thing,
  That has flown to yonder tree,
I would laugh, and dance, and sing—
  Oh! how happy I should be!"
Then I caught the butterfly,
  Placed it in his hands securely—
Now, methought, his pretty eye
  Never more will look demurely.
"Art thou happy, now?" said I;
Tears were sparkling in his eye:
Lo! the butterfly was dead—
In his hands its life had sped!

"Art thou happy, maiden fair,
  On this pleasant summer's day,
Culling flowerets so rare,
  Art thou happy? tell me, pray."
"If my Henry were but here,
  To enjoy the scene with me—
He whose love is so sincere—
  Oh! how happy I should be!"
Soon I heard her lover's feet,
  Sounding on the gravel lightly,
To his loving words so sweet,
  Tender glances answer brightly!
"Art thou happy, now?" I said;
Down she hung her lovely head:
"Henry leaves for foreign skies"—
Tears were in the maiden's eyes.

"Art thou happy, mother mild,
  On this balmy summer's day,
Gazing on thy cherub child—
  Art thou happy? tell me, pray."
"If my baby-boy were well,"
  Thus the mother spake to me,
"Gratitude my heart would swell—
  Oh! how happy I should be!"
Then the cordial I supplied,
  Soon the babe restored completely;
Cherub-faced and angel-eyed,
  On his mother smiled he sweetly.
"Art thou happy, now?" I said,
"Would his father were not dead!"—
Thus she answered me with sighs,
Scalding tear-drops in her eyes.

"Art thou happy, aged man,
  On this glorious summer's day,
With a cheek all pale and wan,
  Art thou happy? tell me, pray."
"If I were but safe above,"
  Spake the old man unto me,
"To enjoy my Saviour's love—
  Oh! how happy I should be!"
Then the angel Death came down,
  And he welcomed him with gladness.
On his brow so pale and wan,
  Not a trace was seen of sadness:
"Art thou happy, now?" I cried;
"Yes!" he answered, as he died:
Tears of joy were in his eyes,
Dew-drops from the upper skies!

EMBLEMS.

Falleth now from off a tree,
    A wither'd leaf:
This the lesson taught to me—
    Life is brief!
    Hear it say,
"Mortal, soon thou'lt follow me
    To decay!"

Droppeth now from off my head,
    A silver hair:
  Plainer preacher never said,
    "For death prepare!"
    Fill'd with gloom,
We follow Time with solemn tread,
    To the tomb.

Mounteth now on wings of air,
    To the sky,
A little dewdrop, pure and clear:
    Far up on high,
    Hear it say—
"All above the earth is fair;
    Watch and pray!
Night or sorrow come not here—
    'T is perfect day!"

R. H. STODDARD.

[Born, 1825.]

RICHARD HENRY STODDARD, although young, stands in a foremost rank among American poets. His place he has himself won. With no commanding antecedents to support him, he has, step by step, fought his way to a position which is alike creditable to his indomitable energy and his genius. He was born in the month of July, 1825, in Hingham, Massachusetts. His father was a sea-captain, who, while the poet was yet in his early youth, sailed for Sweden: his last voyage, for tidings of his fate were never after heard. Idleness not being the fashion in our country, Mr. STODDARD was, as soon as his age permitted, placed in an iron foundry, for the purpose of learning the trade. Here he worked for some years, dreaming in the intervals of his toil, and even then moulding his thoughts into the symmetry of verse, while he moulded the molten metal into shapes of grace. In 1847, the earliest blossoms of his genius appeared, and some verses in the "Union Magazine" gave evidence that his mind as well as his body was toiling. The first was, however, the stronger of the two, for in 1848, after publishing a small volume entitled "Footprints," which contained some pieces of merit, his health gave way, and he surrendered his mechanical occupation.

His career as a literary man now commenced. He wrote for the magazines and newspapers, and supported himself by his pen. In the autumn of 1851 he published his second collection of poems: second, as regards date, and first as far as the requisites of art are concerned. In 1852 he gave to the public a little book of poetic prose, under the name of "Adventures in Fairy Land," and in the autumn of the same year married Miss ELIZABETH D. BARSTOW, of Mattapoisett, Massachusetts, a poetess whose recent occasional contributions to the periodicals have marked individuality, and justify predictions of remarkable and peculiar excellence should she continue to cultivate her capacities for literature.* Mr. STODDARD was about that time appointed to a place in the New York custom-house, which he continues to fill. Since the completion of his second volume of poems he has furnished a considerable number to "Putnam's Monthly," and "Graham's Magazine," and to the last two of greater length than any of his other productions, called "The Burden of Unrest," and "The Squire of Low Degree."

The poems he has published since the appearance of his last book are more numerous and generally in a better style of art than his previous performances, and it is understood that he has in manuscript one upon a classical subject in the composition of which he has exercised with suitable care his best abilities. His prose compositions, except the volume of fairy stories before mentioned, consist of a few clever magazine tales, a series of literary biographies, and occasional criticisms of books in one of the prominent New York journals.

Mr. STODDARD's mind is essentially poetical. All his works are stamped with earnestness, and whether he fails or not in realizing his ideal, we can see that he does nothing lightly. His style is characterized by purity and grace of expression. He is a master of rhythmical melody, and his mode of treating a subject is sometimes exquisitely subtle. In his poems there is no rude writing, no course sketching the power of which makes us forget the carelessness of the outline. All is finished and highly glazed. The coloring is warm, the costumes harmonious, the grouping symmetrical. He paints cabinet pictures, and spares no pains in the manipulation.

Independent of what may be called the external features of his poetry, it almost always possesses a spiritual meaning. Every sound and sight in nature is to him a symbol which represents some phase of internal experience, or at least strikes some spiritual chord. The trees that wave at his window, the moon that silvers his roof, are not to him swaying trees and a white moon merely, but things that play an intimate part in his existence. Thus, in all his poems, will be found the echo of an internal to an external nature, and a harmony resulting from the intimate union of both.

The danger to which Mr. STODDARD is most exposed is that of occasional but unquestionably altogether unconscious imitation, sometimes merely in his cadences, and sometimes in the main conception and purpose of his pieces. Different as is his beautiful poem of "A Household Dirge," from Mr. PIERPONT's touching lamentation, "I cannot make him Dead," the careful reader will not fail to perceive that it is a continuation of the same sad song, set to a different air. In another piece, he makes use of Miss ALICE CAREY's exquisite "Pictures of Memory," and in that very remarkable effusion, "The Burden of Unrest," will be found not a few reflections from Mr. TENNYSON's "Locksley Hall." The indisputable genius of Mr. STODDARD is so apparent in many strikingly original poems, that these careless immoralities of his muse scarcely deserve an allusion, and they are referred to only lest in arresting the attention of casual readers of his poems injustice should now and then be done to his singular merits in lyrics which are in every respect and entirely of his own creation.

* See "Female Poets of America," fifth edition, 1855.

HYMN TO THE BEAUTIFUL.

My heart is full of tenderness and tears,
And tears are in mine eyes, I know not why;
With all my grief, content to live for years,
Or even this hour to die.
My youth is gone, but that I heed not now;
My love is dead, or worse than dead can be;
My friends drop off like blossoms from a bough,
But nothing troubles me,
Only the golden flush of sunset lies
Within my heart like fire, like dew within my eyes!

Spirit of Beauty! whatsoe'er thou art,
I see thy skirts afar, and feel thy power;
It is thy presence fills this charméd hour,
And fills my charméd heart;
Nor mine alone, but myriads feel thee now,
That know not what they feel, nor why they bow;
Thou canst not be forgot,
For all men worship thee, and know it not;
Nor men alone, but babes with wondrous eyes,
New-comers on the earth, and strangers from the skies!

We hold the keys of Heaven within our hands,
The gift and heirloom of a former state,
And lie in infancy at Heaven's gate,
Transfigured in the light that streams along the lands!
Around our pillows golden ladders rise,
And up and down the skies,
With wingéd sandals shod,
The angels come, and go, the messengers of God!
Nor do they, fading from us, e'er depart,—
It is the childish heart;
We walk as heretofore,
Adown their shining ranks, but see them nevermore!
Not Heaven is gone, but we are blind with tears,
Groping our way along the downward slope of years!

From earliest infancy my heart was thine;
With childish feet I trod thy temple aisles;
Not knowing tears, I worshipped thee with smiles,
Or if I ever wept, it was with joy divine!
By day, and night, on land, and sea, and air,—
I saw thee everywhere!
A voice of greeting from the wind was sent;
The mists enfolded me with soft white arms;
The birds did sing to lap me in content,
The rivers wove their charms,
And every little daisy in the grass
Did look up in my face, and smile to see me pass!

Not long can Nature satisfy the mind,
Nor outward fancies feed its inner flame;
We feel a growing want we cannot name,
And long for something sweet, but undefined;
The wants of Beauty other wants create,
Which overflow on others soon or late;
For all that worship thee must ease the heart,
By Love, or Song, or Art:
Divinest Melancholy walks with thee,
Her thin white cheek forever leaned on thine;
And Music leads her sister Poesy,
In exultation shouting songs divine!
But on thy breast Love lies,—immortal child!—
Begot of thine own longings, deep and wild:
The more we worship him, the more we grow
Into thy perfect image here below;
For here below, as in the spheres above,
All Love is Beauty, and all Beauty, Love!

Not from the things around us do we draw
Thy light within; within the light is born;
The growing rays of some forgotten morn,
And added canons of eternal law.
The painter's picture, the rapt poet's song,
The sculptor's statue, never saw the Day;
Not shaped and moulded after aught of clay,
Whose crowning work still does its spirit wrong,
Hue after hue divinest pictures grow,
Line after line immortal songs arise,
And limb by limb, out-starting stern and slow,
The statue wakes with wonder in its eyes!
And in the master's mind
Sound after sound is born, and dies like wind,
That echoes through a range of ocean caves,
And straight is gone to weave its spell upon the waves!
The mystery is thine,
For thine the more mysterious human heart,
The temple of all wisdom, Beauty's shrine,
The oracle of Art!

Earth is thine outer court, and Life a breath,
Why should we fear to die, and leave the earth?
Not thine alone the lesser key of Birth,—
But all the keys of Death;
And all the worlds, with all that they contain
Of Life, and Death, and Time, are thine alone;
The universe is girdled with a chain,
And hung below the throne
Where Thou dost sit, the universe to bless,—
Thou sovereign smile of God, eternal loveliness!

SPRING.

The trumpet winds have sounded a retreat,
Blowing o'er land and sea a sullen strain;
Usurping March, defeated, flies again,
And lays his trophies at the Winter's feet!
And lo!—where April, coming in his turn,
In changeful motleys, half of light and shade,
Leads his belated charge, a delicate maid,
A nymph with dripping urn.

Hail! hail! thrice hail!—thou fairest child of Time,
With all thy retinue of laughing hours,
Thou paragon from some diviner clime,
And ministrant of its benignest powers,
Who hath not caught the glancing of thy wing,
And peeped beneath thy mask, delicious Spring?
Sometimes we see thee on the pleasant morns
Of lingering March, with wreathéd crook of gold,
Leading the Ram from out his starry fold,
A leash of light around his jagged horns!
Sometimes in April, goading up the skies
The Bull, whose neck Apollo's silvery flies
Settle upon, a many-twinkling swarm;
And when May-days are warm,
And drawing to a close,
And Flora goes

With Zephyr from his palace in the west,
Thou dost upsnatch the Twins from cradled rest,
And strain them to thy breast,
And haste to meet the expectant, bright new comer,
The opulent queen of Earth, the gay, voluptuous Summer!

Unmuffled now, shorn of thy veil of showers,
Thou tripp'st along the mead with shining hair
Blown back, and scarf out-fluttering on the air,
White-handed, strewing the fresh sward with flowers!
The green hills lift their foreheads far away;
But where thy pathway runs the sod is pressed
By fleecy lambs, behind the budding spray;
And troops of butterflies are hovering round,
And the small swallow drops upon the ground
Beside his mate and nest!
A little month ago, the sky was gray;
Snow tents were pitched along the mountain-side,
Where March encamped his stormy legions wide,
And shook his standard o'er the fields of Day!
But now the sky is blue, the snow is flown,
And every mountain is an emerald throne,
And every cloud a dais fringed with light,
And all below is beautiful and bright!
The forest waves its plumes,—the hedges blow,—
The south wind scuds along the meadowy sea
Thick-flecked with daisied foam,—and violets grow
Blue-eyed, and cowslips star the bloomy lea:
The skylark floods the scene with pleasant rhyme;
The ousel twitters in the swaying pine;
And wild bees hum about the beds of thyme,
And bend the clover-bells and eglantine;
The snake casts off his skin in mossy nooks;
The long-eared rabbits near their burrows play;
The dormouse wakes; and see! the noisy rooks
Sly foraging, about the stacks of hay!

What sights! what sounds! what rustic life and mirth!
Housed all the winter long from bitter cold,
Huddling in chimney-corners, young and old
Come forth and share the gladness of the Earth.
The ploughmen whistle as the furrows trail
Behind their glittering shares, a billowy row;
The milkmaid sings a ditty while her pail
Grows full and frothy; and the cattle low;
The hounds are yelping in the misty wood,
Starting the fox: the jolly huntsmen cheer;
And winding horns delight the listening ear,
And startle Echo in her solitude;
The teamster drives his wagon down the lane,
Flattening a broader rut in weeds and sand;
The angler fishes in the shady pool;
And loitering down the road with cap in hand,
The truant chases butterflies,—in vain,
Heedless of bells that call the village lads to school!

Methinks the world is sweeter than of yore,
More fresh, and fine, and more exceeding fair;
There is a presence never felt before,
The soul of inspiration everywhere;
Incarnate Youth in every idle limb,
My vernal days, my prime, return anew;
My trancéd spirit breathes a silent hymn,
My heart is full of dew!

THE WITCH'S WHELP.

Along the shore the slimy brine-pits yawn,
Covered with thick green scum; the billows rise,
And fill them to the brim with clouded foam,
And then subside, and leave the scum again;
The ribbéd sand is full of hollow gulfs,
Where monsters from the waters come and lie:
Great serpents bask at noon among the rocks,
To me no terror; coil on coil they roll
Back to their holes, before my flying feet;
The Dragon of the Sea, my mother's god,
Enormous Setebos, comes here to sleep;
Him I molest not; when he flaps his wing
A whirlwind rises, when he swims the deep
It threatens to engulf the trembling isle.
Sometimes when winds do blow, and clouds are dark,
I seek the blasted wood, whose barkless trunks
Are bleached with summer suns; the creaking trees
Stoop down to me, and swing me right and left
Through crashing limbs, but not a jot care I:
The thunder breaks o'erhead, and in their lairs
The panthers roar; from out the stormy clouds
With hearts of fire, sharp lightnings rain around
And split the oaks; not faster lizards run
Before the snake up the slant trunks than I;
Not faster down, sliding with hands and feet.
I stamp upon the ground, and adders rouse
Sharp-eyed, with poisonous fangs; beneath the leaves
They couch, or under rocks, and roots of trees
Felled by the winds; through briery undergrowth
They slide with hissing tongues, beneath my feet
To writhe, or in my fingers squeezed to death.
There is a wild and solitary pine,
Deep in the meadows; all the island birds
From far and near fly there, and learn new songs;
Something imprisoned in its wrinkled bark
Wails for its freedom; when the bigger light
Burns in mid-heaven, and dew elsewhere is dried,
There it still falls; the quivering leaves are tongues,
And load the air with syllables of wo.
One day I thrust my spear within a cleft
No wider than its point, and something shrieked,
And falling cones did pelt me sharp as hail:
I picked the seeds that grew between their plates,
And strung them round my neck, with sea-mew eggs.
Hard by are swamps and marshes, reedy fens
Knee-deep in water; monsters wade therein
Thick-set with plated scales; sometimes in troops
They crawl on slippery banks; sometimes they lash
The sluggish waves, among themselves at war;
Often I heave great rocks from off the crags,
And crush their bones; often I push my spear
Deep in their drowsy eyes, at which they howl
And chase me inland; then I mount their humps
And prick them back again, unwieldy, slow:
At night the wolves are howling round the place,
And bats sail there athwart the silver light,
Flapping their wings; by day in hollow trees
They hide, and slink into the gloom of dens.
We live, my mother Sycorax and I,
In caves with bloated toads and crested snakes;

She can make charms, and philters, and brew
storms,
And call the great Sea Dragon from his deeps:
Nothing of this know I, nor care to know;
Give me the milk of goats in gourds or shells,
The flesh of birds and fish, berries, and fruit,
Nor want I more, save all day long to lie,
And hear, as now, the voices of the sea.

A HOUSEHOLD DIRGE.

"A six years' loss to Paradise,—
And ne'er on earth the child grew older."
T. B. Read.

I've lost my little May at last!
She perished in the spring,
When earliest flowers began to bud,
And earliest birds to sing;
I laid her in a country grave,
A green and soft retreat,
A marble tablet o'er her head,
And violets at her feet.

I would that she were back again,
In all her childish bloom;
My joy and hope have followed her,
My heart is in her tomb!
I know that she is gone away,
I know that she is fled,
I miss her everywhere, and yet
I cannot think her dead!

I wake the children up at dawn,
And say a single prayer,
And draw them round the morning meal,
But one is wanting there!
I see a little chair apart,
A little pinafore,
And Memory fills the vacancy,
As Time will—nevermore!

I sit within my quiet room,
Alone, and write for hours,
And miss the little maid again
Among the window flowers,
And miss her with her toys beside
My desk in silent play;
And then I turn and look for her,
But she has flown away!

I drop my idle pen, and hark,
And catch the faintest sound;
She must be playing hide-and-seek
In shady nooks around;
She'll come and climb my chair again,
And peep my shoulders o'er;
I hear a stifled laugh,—but no,
She cometh nevermore!

I waited only yester-night
The evening service read,
And lingered for my idol's kiss
Before she went to bed;
Forgetting she had gone before,
In slumbers soft and sweet,
A monument above her head,
And violets at her feet.

LEONATUS.

The fair boy Leonatus,
The page of Imogen:
It was his duty evermore
To tend the Lady Imogen;
By peep of day he might be seen
Tapping against her chamber door,
To wake the sleepy waiting-maid;
She woke, and when she had arrayed
The Princess, and the twain had prayed,
(They prayed with rosaries of yore,)
They called him, pacing to and fro;
And cap in hand, and bowing low,
He entered, and began to feed
The singing birds with fruit and seed.

The brave boy Leonatus,
The page of Imogen:
He tripped along the kingly hall,
From room to room, with messages;
He stopped the butler, clutched his keys,
(Albeit he was broad and tall,)
And dragged him down the vaults, where win
In bins lay beaded and divine,
To pick a flask of vintage fine;
Came up, and clomb the garden wall,
And plucked from out the sunny spots
Peaches, and luscious apricots,
And filled his golden salver there,
And hurried to his Lady fair.

The gallant Leonatus,
The page of Imogen:
He had a steed from Arab ground,
And when the lords and ladies gay
Went hawking in the dews of May,
And hunting in the country round,
And Imogen did join the band,
He rode him like a hunter grand,
A hooded hawk upon his hand,
And by his side a slender hound:
But when they saw the deer go by
He slipped the leash, and let him fly,
And gave his fiery barb the rein,
And scoured beside her o'er the plain.

The strange boy Leonatus,
The page of Imogen:
Sometimes he used to stand for hours
Within her room, behind her chair;
The soft wind blew his golden hair
Across his eyes, and bees from flowers
Hummed round him, but he did not stir
He fixed his earnest eyes on her,
A pure and reverent worshipper,
A dreamer building airy towers:
But when she spoke he gave a start,
That sent the warm blood from his heart
To flush his cheeks, and every word
The fountain of his feelings stirred.

The sad boy Leonatus,
The page of Imogen:
He lost all relish and delight,
For all things that did please before;
By day he wished the day was o'er,

By night he wished the same of night:
He could not mingle in the crowd,
He loved to be alone, and shroud
His tender thoughts, and sigh aloud,
And cherish in his heart its blight.
At last his health began to fail,
His fresh and glowing cheeks to pale;
And in his eyes the tears unshed
Did hang like dew in violets dead.

The timid Leonatus,
The page of Imogen:
"What ails the boy!" said Imogen:
He stammer'd, sigh'd, and answer'd "Naught."
She shook her head, and then she thought
What all his malady could mean;
It might be love; her maid was fair,
And Leon had a loving air;
She watched them with a jealous care,
And played the spy, but naught was seen:
And then she was aware at first,
That she, not knowing it, had nursed
His memory till it grew a part—
A heart within her very heart!

The dear boy Leonatus,
The page of Imogen:
She loved, but owned it not as yet;
When he was absent she was lone,
She felt a void before unknown,
And Leon filled it when they met;
She called him twenty times a day,
She knew not why, she could not say;
She fretted when he went away,
And lived in sorrow and regret;
Sometimes she frowned with stately mien,
And chid him like a little queen;
And then she soothed him meek and mild,
And grew as trustful as a child.

The neat scribe Leonatus,
The page of Imogen:
She wondered that he did not speak,
And own his love, if love indeed
It was that made his spirit bleed;
And she bethought her of a freak
To test the lad; she bade him write
A letter that a maiden might,
A billet to her heart's delight;
He took the pen with fingers weak,
Unknowing what he did, and wrote,
And folded up and sealed the note:
She wrote the superscription sage,
"For Leonatus, Lady's Page!"

The happy Leonatus,
The page of Imogen:
The page of Imogen no more,
But now her love, her lord, her life,
For she became his wedded wife,
As both had hoped and dreamed before.
He used to sit beside her feet,
And read romances rare and sweet,
And, when she touched her lute, repeat
Impassioned madrigals of yore,
Uplooking in her face the while,
Until she stooped with loving smile,
And pressed her melting mouth to his,
That answered in a dreamy bliss—
The joyful Leonatus,
The lord of Imogen!

A DIRGE.

A few frail summers had touched thee,
As they touch the fruit;
Not so bright as thy hair, the sunshine,
Not so sweet as thy voice the lute.
Hushed the voice, shorn the hair, all is over:
An urn of white ashes remains;
Nothing else save the tears in our eyes,
And our bitterest, bitterest pains!

We garland the urn with white roses,
Burn incense and gums on the shrine,
Play old tunes with the saddest of closes,
Dear tunes that were thine!
But in vain, all in vain;
Thou art gone—we remain!

THE SHADOW OF THE HAND

You were very charming, Madam,
In your silks and satins fine;
And you made your lovers drunken,
But it was not with your wine!
There were court gallants in dozens,
There were princes of the land,
And they would have perished for you
As they knelt and kissed your hand—
For they saw no stain upon it,
It was such a snowy hand!

But for me—I knew you better,
And, while you were flaunting there,
I remembered some one lying,
With the blood on his white hair!
He was pleading for you, Madam,
Where the shriven spirits stand;
But the Book of Life was darkened,
By the Shadow of a Hand!
It was tracing your perdition,
For the blood upon your hand!

A SERENADE.

The moon is muffled in a cloud,
That folds the lover's star,
But still beneath thy balcony
I touch my soft guitar.

If thou art waking, Lady dear,
The fairest in the land,
Unbar thy wreathéd lattice now,
And wave thy snowy hand.

She hears me not; her spirit lies
In trances mute and deep;—
But Music turns the golden key
Within the gate of Sleep!

Then let her sleep, and if I fail
To set her spirit free!
My song shall mingle in her dream,
And she will dream of me!

THE YELLOW MOON.

The yellow moon looks slantly down,
Through seaward mists, upon the town;
And like a dream the moonshine falls
Between the dim and shadowy walls.

I see a crowd in every street,
But cannot hear their falling feet;
They float like clouds through shade and light,
And seem a portion of the night.

The ships have lain, for ages fled,
Along the waters, dark and dead;
The dying waters wash no more
The long black line of spectral shore.

There is no life on land or sea,
Save in the quiet moon and me;
Nor ours is true, but only seems,
Within some dead old world of dreams!

INVOCATION TO SLEEP.

Draw the curtains round your bed,
And I 'll shade the wakeful light;
'T will be hard for you to sleep,
If you have me still in sight:—
But you must though, and without me,
For I have a song to write:
Then sleep, love, sleep!
The flowers have gone to rest,
And the birds are in the nest:
'T is time for you to join them beneath the wings of Sleep!

Wave thy poppies round her, Sleep!
Touch her eye-lids, flood her brain;
Banish Memory, Thought, and Strife,
Bar the portals of her life,
Till the morning comes again!
Let no enemy intrude
On her helpless solitude:
Fear and Pain, and all their train—
Keep the evil hounds at bay,
And all evil dreams away!
Thou, thyself, keep thou the key,
Or intrust it unto me,
Sleep! Sleep! Sleep!
A lover's eyes are bright
In the darkest night;
And jealous even of dreams, almost of thee, dear Sleep!

I must sit, and think, and think,
Till the stars begin to wink:
(For the web of Song is wrought
Only in the looms of Thought!)
She must lie, and sleep, and sleep,
(Be her slumbers calm and deep!)
Till the dews of morning weep;
Therefore bind your sweetest sprite
To her service and delight,
All the night,
Sleep! Sleep! Sleep!
And I'll whisper in her ear,
(Even in dreams it will be dear!)
What she loveth so to hear,
Tiding sweeter than the flowers,
All about this love of ours,
And its rare increase:
Singing in the starry peace,
Ditties delicate, and free,
Dedicate to her, and thee,
Sleep! Sleep! Sleep!
For I owe ye both a boon,
And I mean to grant it soon,
In my golden numbers that breathe of Love and Sleep!

AT THE WINDOW.

Beneath the heavy curtains,
My face against the pane,
I peer into the darkness,
And scan the night in vain.

The vine o'erruns the lattice,
And lies along its roof,
So thick with leaves and clusters,
It keeps the moon aloof.

By yonder pear-tree splintered,
The ghostly radiance falls,
But fails to pierce the branches,
Or touch the sombre walls.

No moon, no starlight gleaming,
The dark encircles me;
And what is more annoying,
My neighbor cannot see.

She stands beneath her curtains,
Her face against the pane,
Nor knows that I am watching
For her to-night again!

AT REST.

With folded hands the lady lies
In flowing robes of white,
A globéd lamp beside her couch,
A round of tender light.

With such a light above her head,
A little year ago,
She walked adown the shadowy vale,
Where the blood-red roses grow!

A shape or shadow joined her there,
To pluck the royal flower,
But from her breast the lily stole,
Which was her only dower.

That gone, all went: her false love first,
And then her peace of heart;
The hard world frowned, her friends grew cold,
She hid in tears apart:

And now she lies upon her couch,
Amid the dying light:
Nor wakes to hear the little voice
That moans throughout the night!

WILLIAM ALLEN BUTLER.

[Born, 1825.]

Mr. Butler is a son of Benjamin F. Butler, recently Attorney-General of the United States, and long conspicuous in public affairs. He was born in Albany, in 1825, and was educated at the New York University, where he graduated in 1843. From July, 1846, to December, 1848, he travelled in Europe, and he has since been associated with his father in the practice of the law, in the city of New York.

The principal literary compositions of Mr. Butler are a class-poem entitled "The Future," published in 1846; occasional contribution to the "Democratic Review" and "Literary World," and a small volume of the character of "Rejected Addresses," entitled "Barnum's Parnassus." He has wit and humor, and a natural and flexible style, abounding in felicities of expression. In general he writes hastily, and finishes a piece at a sitting.

THE NEW ARGONAUTS.

To-day the good ship sails,
Across the sparkling sea—
To-day the northern gales
Are blowing swift and free;
Speed, speed her distant way,
To that far land of gold:
A richer prize we seek than they,
The Argonauts of old!

Who goes with us? who quits the tiresome shore,
And sails where Fortune beckons him away;
Where in that marvellous land, in virgin ore,
The wealth of years is gather'd in a day?
Here, toil and trouble are our portion still,
And still with want our weary work is paid;
Slowly the shillings drop into the till,
Small are the profits of our tedious trade;
There, Nature proffers with unstinted hands,
The countless wealth the wide domain confines,
Sprinkles the mountain-streams with golden sands,
And calls the adventurer to exhaustless mines.
Come, then, with us! what are the charms of home,
What are the ties of friends or kindred worth?
Thither, oh thither, let our footsteps roam—
There is the Eden of our fallen earth!

Well do we hold the fee of those broad lands
Wrested from feebler hands,
By our own sword and spear;
Well may the weeping widow be consoled,
And orphan'd hearts their ceaseless grief withhold;
Well have our brothers shed their life-blood here.
Say, could we purchase at a price too dear,
These boundless acres of uncounted gold?
Come, then! it is to-day,
To-day the good ship sails,
And swift upon her way
Blow out the northern gales.
A twelvemonth more, and we
Our homeward course shall hold,
With richer freight within than theirs,
The Argonauts of old!

Alas! for honest labour from honest ends averted;
Alas! for firesides left, and happy homes deserted
Brightly the bubble glitters; bright in the distance
The land of promise gleams;
But ah, the phantom fortunes of existence
Live but in dreams!
Behold the end afar:
Beyond the bright, deceptive cloud,
Beneath what dim, malignant star,
Sails on the eager crowd!
Some in mid-ocean lie—
Some gain the wish'd-for shore,
And grasp the golden ore,
But sicken as they grasp, and where they sicken, die!
There have they found beside the mountain streams,
On desolate crags where the wild eagle screams,
In dark ravines where western forests wave—
Gold, and a grave!
Some for the spendthrift's eager touch,
Some for the miser's hoarded store,
Some for the robber's grasp, the murderer's clutch,
Heap up the precious ore,
Dear bought with life's lost strength, and the heart's wither'd core!

Oh, cursèd love of gold!
Age follows age,
And still the world's slow records are unroll'd,
Page after page;
And the same tale is told—
The same unholy deeds, the same sad scenes unfold!
Where the assassin's knife is sharpen'd,
In the dark;
Where lies the murder'd man in the midnight,
Cold and stark;
Where the slave groans and quivers under
The driver's lash;
Where the keen-eyed son of trade is bartering
Honour for cash;
Where the sons wish the fathers dead, of their wealth
To be partakers;
Where the maiden of sixteen weds the old man
For his acres;
Where the gambler stakes his all on the last throw
Of the dice;
Where the statesman for his country and its glory
Sets a price!
There are thy altars rear'd, thy trophies told,
Oh, cursed love of gold!

THE INCOGNITA OF RAPHAEL.*

Long has the summer sunlight shone
On the fair form, the quaint costume;
Yet nameless still, she sits unknown,
A lady in her youthful bloom.

Fairer for this! no shadows cast
Their blight upon her perfect lot;
Whate'er her future, or her past,
In this bright moment matters not.

No record of her high descent
There needs, nor memory of her name:
Enough that RAPHAEL's colours blent
To give her features deathless fame!

'Twas his anointing hand that set
The crown of beauty on her brow;
Still lives its earlier radiance yet,
As at the earliest, even now.

'Tis not the ecstasy that glows
In all the rapt CECILIA's grace;
Nor yet the holy, calm repose,
He painted on the Virgin's face.

Less of the heavens, and more of earth,
There lurk within these earnest eyes,
The passions that have had their birth,
And grown beneath Italian skies.

What mortal thoughts, and cares, and dreams,
What hopes, and fears, and longings rest,
Where falls the folded veil, or gleams
The golden necklace on her breast.

What mockery of the painted glow
May shade the secret soul within;
What griefs from passion's overflow,
What shame that follows after sin!

Yet calm as heaven's serenest deeps
Are those pure eyes, those glances pure;
And queenly is the state she keeps,
In beauty's lofty trust secure.

And who has stray'd, by happy chance,
Through all those grand and pictured halls,
Nor felt the magic of her glance,
As when a voice of music calls!

Not soon shall I forget the day—
Sweet day, in spring's unclouded time,
While on the glowing canvass lay
The light of that delicious clime—

I mark'd the matchless colours wreathed
On the fair brow, the peerless cheek,
The lips, I fancied, almost breathed
The blessings that they could not speak.

Fair were the eyes with mine that bent
Upon the picture their mild gaze,
And dear the voice that gave consent
To all the utterance of my praise.

Oh, fit companionship of thought;
Oh, happy memories, shrined apart;
The rapture that the painter wrought,
The kindred rapture of the heart!

* The portrait to which these verses refer is in the Pitti Palace at Florence. It is one of the gems of that admirable collection.

UHLAND.

It is the poet UHLAND, from whose wreathings
Of rarest harmony I here have drawn,
To lower tones and less melodious breathings,
Some simple strains, of youth and passion born.

His is the poetry of sweet expression,
Of clear, unfaltering tune, serene and strong;
Where gentlest thoughts and words, in soft procession,
Move to the even measures of his song.

Delighting ever in his own calm fancies,
He sees much beauty where most men see naught,
Looking at Nature with familiar glances,
And weaving garlands in the groves of thought.

He sings of youth, and hope, and high endeavour,
He sings of love—O crown of poesy!—
Of fate, and sorrow, and the grave, forever
The end of strife, the goal of destiny.

He sings of fatherland, the minstrel's glory,
High theme of memory and hope divine,
Twining its fame with gems of antique story,
In Suabian songs and legends of the Rhine;

In ballads breathing many a dim tradition,
Nourish'd in long belief or minstrel rhymes,
Fruit of the old Romance, whose gentle mission
Pass'd from the earth before our wiser times.

Well do they know his name among the mountains,
And plains, and valleys, of his native land;
Part of their nature are the sparkling fountains
Of his clear, thought, with rainbow fancies spann'd.

His simple lays oft sings the mother cheerful
Beside the cradle in the dim twilight;
His plaintive notes low breathes the maiden tearful
With tender murmurs in the ear of night.

The hillside swain, the reaper in the meadows,
Carol his ditties through the toilsome day;
And the lone hunter in the Alpine shadows
Recalls his ballads by some ruin gray.

O precious gift! O wondrous inspiration!
Of all high deeds, of all harmonious things,
To be the oracle, while a whole nation
Catches the echo from the sounding strings.

Out of the depths of feeling and emotion
Rises the orb of song, serenely bright,
As who beholds, across the tracts of ocean,
The golden sunrise bursting into light.

Wide is its magic world—divided neither
By continent, nor sea, nor narrow zone:
Who would not wish sometimes to travel thither
In fancied fortunes to forget his own?

HENRY W. PARKER.

[Born, 1825.]

The Reverend Henry W. Parker is a native of Danby, New York, and was born in 1825. His mother is a niece of the late Noah Webster, and his father, the Reverend Samuel Parker, of Ithaca, travelled in Oregon, and published in 1837 an account of his tour, a very interesting book, in which the practicability of a railroad through the Rocky Mountains was first suggested.

Mr. Parker passed his early years in Ithaca, a place of singular beauty, at the head of Cayuga Lake, and was graduated at Amherst College in 1843. He subsequently studied divinity, and is now pastor of a Presbyterian church in Brooklyn. His wife, to whom he was married in 1852, is the author of a work entitled "Stars of the Western World," and he has himself written much in "The North American Review" and other periodicals, besides a volume of "Poems," published at Auburn, in 1850, and "The Story of a Soul," a poem read before the literary societies of Hamilton College, in 1851.

Mr. Parker has a luxuriant fancy, a ready apprehension of the picturesque in nature, a meditative tenderness, and uncommon facility of versification. In some of his pieces there is humor, but this is a quality he does not seem to cherish.

VISION OF SHELLEY'S DEATH.

The wind had darkly touched the outer bay,
A looming storm shut out the sultry day,
And whiter grew the distant billows' play.

The nearer calm a single sail beguiled,
And at the helm, with features fair and mild,
Sat one whom men have called the Eternal Child.

A breath—a breeze—the tempest strikes the sail;
It fills, it stoops, and, swift and free as frail,
It flies a broad-winged arrow from the gale.

A precious boat! may angels speed it right!
The world, in shell so thin and form so slight,
Hath all its hold upon a mind of might.

He lay reclined in noonday dreams no more,
He gazed no longer at the purple shore,
Nor mused on roofing skies, and ocean's floor.

The wizard storm invoked a truer dream—
Had kindled in his eye its proudest gleam,
And given his eagle soul a grander theme.

No sign of craven fear his lips reveal;
He only feels the joy that heroes feel,
When lightnings flash and jarring thunders peal.

The boat dipt low; his foot was on the helm;
The deck a throne, the storm his genial realm,
He dared the powers that nature's king o'erwhelm.

The gentle eye that turned from man away,
Now flashed in answer to the flashing spray,
And glanced in triumph o'er the foaming bay.

And as aloft the boat a moment hung,
Then down the plunging wave was forward flung,
His own wild song, "The Fugitives," he sung:

Said he, "And seest thou, and hearest thou?"
Cried he, "And fearest thou, and fearest thou?
A pilot bold, I trow, should follow now." ....

The sail was torn and trailing in the sea,
The water flooded o'er the dipping lee,
And clomb the mast in maddest revelry.

It righted, with the liquid load, and fast
Went down; the mariners afloat were cast,
And louder roared and laughed the mocking blast.

A moment, and no trace of man or spar
Is left to strew the path that, near and far,
Is whirled in foam beneath the tempest's car. ....

A moment more, and one pale form appeared,
And faintly looked the eyes; no storm careered,
And all the place with mystic light was sphered.

Around him slept a circling space of wave;
It seemed the crystal pavement of a cave,
And all about he heard the waters rave.

He saw them waving like a silken tent—
Beheld them fall, as rocks of beryl rent,
And rage like lions from a martyr pent.

A sudden life began to thrill his veins;
A strange new force his sinking weight sustains,
Until he seemed released from mortal chains.

He looked above—a glory floating down—
A dazzling face and form—a kingly crown—
With blinding beauty all his senses drown.

As tearful eyes may see the light they shun,
As veiling mists reveal the clear-shaped sun,
He knew the crucified, transfigured One.

In that still pause of trembling, blissful sight,
He woke as from a wild and life-long night,
And through his soul there crept a holy light.

A blot seemed fading from his troubled brain,
A doubt of God—a madness and a pain—
Till upward welled his trustful youth again;

Till upward every feeling pure was drawn,
As nightly dews are claimed again at dawn,
And whence they gently come are gently gone

He gazed upon those mercy-beaming eyes,
Till recognition chased away surprise,
And he had faith from heaven to slowly rise—

To rise and kneel upon the glassy tide,
While down the Vision floated to his side,
And stooped to hear what less he said than sighed

"Oh Truth, Love, Gentleness! I wooed and won
Your essences, nor knew that ye are One;
Oh crownéd Truth, receive thine erring son!" ...

The gentle one, whose thought alone was wrong—
The Eternal Child amidst a cherub throng,
Was wafted to the Home of Love and Song.

THE DEAD-WATCH.

Each saddened face is gone, and tearful eye
Of mother, brother, and of sisters fair;
With ghostly sound their distant footfalls die
Thro' whispering hall, and up the rustling stair.
In yonder room the newly dead doth sleep;
Begin we thus, my friend, our watch to keep.

And now both feed the fire and trim the lamp;
Pass cheerly, if we can, the slow-paced hours;
For, all without is cold, and drear, and damp,
And the wide air with storm and darkness lowers;
Pass cheerly, if we may, the live-long night,
And chase pale phantoms, paler fear, to flight.

We will not talk of death, of pall and knell —
Leave that, the mirth of brighter hours to check;
But tales of life, love, beauty, let us tell,
Or of stern battle, sea, and stormy wreck;
Call up the visions gay of other days —
Our boyhood's sports and merry youthful ways.

Hark to the distant bell! — an hour is gone!
Enter yon silent room with footsteps light;
Our brief, appointed du y must be done —
To bathe the face, and stay death's rapid blight:
To bare the rigid face, and dip the cloth
That hides a mortal, "crushed before the moth."

The bathing liquid scents the chilly room;
How spectral white are shroud and vailing lace
On yonder side-board, in the fearful gloom!
Take off the muffler from the sleeper's face —
You spoke, my friend, of sunken cheek and eye —
Ah, what a form of beauty here doth lie!

Never hath Art, from purest wax or stone,
So fair an image, and so lustrous, wrought;
It is as if a beam from heaven had shown
A weary angel in sweet slumber caught! —
The smiling lip, the warmly tinted cheek,
And all so calm, so saint-like, and so meek!

She softly sleeps, and yet how unlike sleep;
No fairy dreams flit o'er that marble face,
As ripples play along the breezy deep,
As shadows o'er the field each other chase;
The spirit dreams no more, but wakes in light,
And freely wings its flashing seraph flight.

She sweetly sleeps, her lips and eyelids sealed;
No ruby jewel heaves upon her breast,
With her quick breath now hidden, now revealed,
As setting stars long tremble in the west;
But white and still as drifts of moonlit snow,
Her folded cerements and her flushless brow.

Oh, there is beauty in the winter moon,
And beauty in the brilliant summer flower,
And in the liquid eye and luring tone
Of radiant Love's and rosy Laughter's hour;
But where is beauty, in this blooming world,
Like Death upon a maiden's lip impearled!

Vail we the dead, and close the open door;
Perhaps the spirit, ere it soar above,
Would watch its clay alone, and hover o'er
The face it once had kindled into love;
Commune we hence, oh friend, this wakef l night,
Of death made lovely by so blest a sight

SONNETS.

SUMMER LIGHTS.

No more the tulips hold their torches up,
And chestnuts silver candelabra bear.
The spring, dethroned, has left her festive cup
Of honey-dew, and other blossoms flare
To light another feast with tinted glare.
Summer has ta'en the sceptre, and the trees,
In low obeisance bow their weight of green;
The locusts bloom with swarms of snowy bees
That make the fragrant branches downward lean;
Each snow-ball bush with full-blown moons is hung,
And all around, like red suns setting low,
Large peonies shed a burning crimson glow,
While, worlds of foliage on the shoulders swung
Of Atlantean trunks, the orchards darkly grow.

SUMMER'S ESSENCE.

A tide of song and leaf, of bloom and feather –
A sea of summer's freshest, fullest splendor,
Has come with June's serenely crystal weather.
Whate'er of beauty, mornings clear and tende
And golden eves and dewy nights, engender,
I s met in one bewildering bliss together —
Delicious fragrance, foliage deep and massy,
Unfolding roses, silver locust flowers,
And darkling silences of waters glassy,
Soft crescents, loving stars and nightly showers,
Rich shades and lemon lights in vistas grassy,
And sweetest twitterings through all the hours,
And opal clouds that float in slumber bland,
And distances that soften into fairy-land.

A STREET.

By day, soft clouded in a twilight gloom,
And letting sunlight through its arches pour,
The street is like a lofty banquet room,
And every sunny leaf a golden bloom,
And sunny spots upon the level floor,
As if with tiger-robes 't were covered o'er.
By night, the gas-lights half in foliage hid,
Seem birds of flame that flutter silver wings
And shake in concert with the katydid.
It is a leafy palace made for kings
To meet their thousand lords in festivals —
A temple with its wreathed and pillared walls —
A street that slowly grew a Mammoth Cave
Stalagmited with trunks through all the nave.

SNOW IN THE VILLAGE.

Not thus on street and garden, roof and spire,
The snow, for ages, here was yearly spread;
It tipt the Indian's plume of bloody red,
And melted, hissing, in his council-fire;
It gave an impress to the panther's tread,
And all the monster feet that filled the wood.
But now the snow of whiter towns and faces
Has drifted o'er the glorious solitude;
And death and silence, like a winter, brood
Upon the vanished brute and human races
So let oblivion come, till it effaces.
Oh weary soul, thy summer's maddest mood,
Thus o'er thy woes let silence softly fall,
And Winter, with a holy beauty, vail them all.

JOHN ESTEN COOKE.

[Born, 1830.]

John Esten Cooke, son of John Rogers and Maria Pendleton Cooke, and brother of the author of "Froissart Ballads," was born in Winchester, Frederic county, Virginia, on the third of November, 1830; was taken to Glengary, his father's estate, near that town, and lived there until the destruction of the house by fire, in 1839, when the family removed to Richmond, which has ever since been his home. Having studied the law, in the office of his father, he was admitted to the bar, and continues in the practice of the profession.

Mr. Cooke's first work was "Leather Stocking and Silk," which appeared in 1853. It is a story of provincial life in Virginia, as it is represented in the traditions which cluster around Martinsburg. It is remarkable for picturesque grouping and dramatic situations, for simple touches of nature, and gentle pathos. This was followed in 1854 by "The Virginia Comedians, or the Old Days of the Old Dominion," in which is presented a carefully studied and finely colored picture of Virginia society just before the revolution. The book is thoroughly democratic and American, and abounds with natural delineations of character, brilliant dialogue, and graphic description. In the same year he produced "The Youth of Jefferson," in all respects, perhaps, his best novel. It is founded on some of the statesman's early letters, and is a graceful and romantic drama, the personages of which are distinctly drawn, and in their different ways all interesting. In 1855 he published "Ellie, or the Human Comedy."

Mr. Cooke's poems have appeared in the "Literary Messenger" and other southern periodicals. The longest and most remarkable of them has but the unexpressive title of "Stanzas," and its subject and style will remind the reader of a noble work of the most popular living poet of England. It is, however, an original performance, simple, natural, and touching, and every verse vindicates its genuineness as an expression of feeling. His minor pieces are cabinet pictures, executed with taste and skill.

EXTRACTS FROM "STANZAS."

I.

For long I thought the dreadful day
Which robbed me of my joy and peace,
Had palsied me with such disease
As never more could pass away:

But Nature whispered low and sweet:
"Oh heart! struck down with deep despair,
The goal is near, these trials are
But beckoning's to the Saviour's feet."

And then, "Even put your grief in words,
The soul expends itself, as tears
Flow after storms; the hopes of years
Rise stronger than the binding cords.

"Oh Soul! these are the trials meet
To fit thee for the nobler strife
With Evil through the bounds of Life:
Pure steel is from the furnace-heat.

"Shrink not! a nobler self is wrought
From out the shock, more grand and fair:
March on, oh Heart! through toil and care—
The grand result is cheaply bought!"

II.

I hear around me echoing feet—
The din of cities, never still—
The clinking purse we toil to fill—
The quick accost when merchants meet—

The wagons rattling o'er the way—
The drayman calling to his horse—
The auctioneer, with utterance hoarse
Cry in yon house of dusky gray—

The clash of arméd minds, aloof,
Resound through legislative halls—
The indignant echo of the walls—
The nothingness that shakes the roof,

And, near the bustle of the courts
Where law's condottieri wage
The fight, with passion, well-paid rage—
Below, the ships draw toward the ports.

From all I turn with weary heart
To that green mountain land of thine,
Where tranquil suns unclouded shine,
And to the abode where now thou art.

III.

The deep alarum of the drum
Resounds in yonder busy street,
The horses move on restless feet,
And every urchin cries, "They come!"

With which the trumpet blares aloud
And brazen-throated horns reply:
The incense of the melody
Floats upward like a golden cloud.

And like the boy's my soul is fired,
And half I grasp the empty air,
With dreams of lists and ladies fair,
As in the days when I aspired.

The trumpet dies, a distant roar,
  The drum becomes a murmuring voice—
  No more in battle I rejoice,
But fall to dreaming as before—

Of other skies and greener trees,
  And mountain peaks of purple gloom—
  And of the dim and shadowy tomb,
Where that great spirit rests in peace.

IV.

The sunset died that tender day,
  Across the mountains bright and pure,
  And bathed with golden waves the shore
Of evening, and the fringéd spray,

And stately ships which glided by,
  With whitest sails toward the dim
  Untravelled seas beyond the rim
Of peaks that melted in the sky.

He sat upon the trellised porch,
  And still the conversation ranged
  From olden things all gone or changed,
To grand, eternal Truth—a torch

That spread around a steady light,
  And mocked the strength of hostile hands
  And pointed man to other lands
Of hope beyond Thought's farthest flight.

That noble forehead, broad and calm,
  Was flushed with evening's holy ray,
  His eye gave back the light of day—
His words poured out a soothing balm;

His low sweet tones fell on the ear
  Like music in the quiet watch
  Of midnight, when the spirits catch
At golden memories, ever dear.

And now recalling that dim eve,
  And him who spake those noble words,
  Though trembling still in all its chords,
My heart is calmed, and I believe.

V.

I thought to pass away from earth
  And join thee, with that other heart
  Loved even more than thee, a part
Of other worlds, through heavenlier birth—

Of whom I do not speak my thought
  So dear she is, because the eye
  O'erflows with wo, and with a cry
I tear the symbols I have wrought.

No word shall be of that one grief,
  Because it lies too deep for words,
  And this sad trifling which affords
Some respite, could be no relief.

VI.

Come from the fields, thy dwelling place,
  Oh spirit of the Past! and steep
  My wounded soul in dreamy sleep,
And fit its sandals for the race

Of flashing, hurrying life; and spread
  A soft oblivion o'er the ills
  With which the fainting bosom fills,
And calm the throbbing heart and head:

So shall I gather strength again
  To stem the tide of worldly strife,
  To bear the weariness of life,
And feel that all things are not vain.

CLOUDS.

I KNOW not whither past the crimson zone
  Of evening sail those ships of snow and gold—
  The beauteous clouds that seem to hover and fold
Their wings—like birds that having all day flown
Against the blue sky, now at set of sun
  Play for a moment gayly on their soft
  And burnished pinions wide: then from aloft
Sink down below the horizon and are gone!
I know not where they fold their shining wings
  In very truth; nor what far happy land
  They come together in—a radiant band,
The brightest, purest, of all earthly things!
But well I know that land lies broad and fair
Beyond the evening: Oh! that I were there!

MAY.

HAS the old glory passed
  From tender May—
That never the echoing blast
Of bugle horns merry, and fast
Dying away like the past,
  Welcomes the day?

Has the old Beauty gone
  From golden May—
That not any more at dawn
Over the flowery lawn,
Or knolls of the forest withdrawn,
  Maids are at play!

Is the old freshness dead
  Of the fairy May?—
Ah! the sad tear-drops unshed!
Ah! the young maidens unwed!
Golden locks—cheeks rosy red!
  Ah! where are they?

MEMORIES.

  THE flush of sunset dies
Far on ancestral trees:
On the bright-booted bees:
On cattle-dotting leas!
  And a mist is in my eyes—
For in a stranger land
Halts the quick-running sand,
Shaken by no dear hand!

  How plain is the flowering grass—
The sunset-flooded door;
I hear the river's roar
Say clearly "Nevermore."
  I see the cloud-shadows pass
Over my mountain meres;
Gone are the rose-bright years:
Drowned in a sea of tears.

WILLIAM CROSWELL DOANE.

[Born, 1832.]

The Reverend WILLIAM C. DOANE, A.M., second son of the Right Reverend GEORGE W. DOANE, D.D., LL.D., was born in Boston, in March, 1832; graduated at Burlington College, in 1850; ordained deacon, by his father, in March, 1853; and is now assistant minister of St. Mary's Church, Burlington, of which his father is the rector, and adjunct professor of English literature and instructor in Anglo-Saxon, in Burlington College. His poetical productions have been published in "The Missionary," of which he was the editor, and in other newspapers. They are meditative, graceful, and fanciful, and promise a great excellence.

GREY CLIFF, NEWPORT.*

WHAT strivest thou for, oh thou most mighty ocean,
Rolling thy ceaseless sweeping surfs ashore?
Canst thou not stay that restless wild commotion?
Must that low murmur moan for evermore?
Yet thou art better than our hearts, though yearning
Still for some unattainéd, unknown land;
Thou still art constant, evermore returning,
With each fresh wind, to kiss our waiting strand.
Oh, heart! if restless, like the yearning ocean,
Like it be all thy waves, of one emotion!

Whither, with canvas wings, oh ship, art sailing—
Homeward or outward-bound, to shore or sea?
What thought within thy strong sides is prevailing,
Hope or despair, sorrow or careless glee?
Thou, too, art like our hearts, which gayly seeming,
With hope sails set, to catch each fresh'ning breeze,
In truth art sad, with tears and trials teeming—
Perhaps to sail no more on life's wild seas.
Oh, heart! while sailing, like a ship, remember,
Thou, too, may'st founder, in a rough December!

Why, your white arms, ye windmills, are ye crossing
In sad succession to the evening breeze,
As though within your gray old heads were tossing
Thoughts of fatigue, and longings after ease?—
But ye are better than our hearts, for grieving,
Over your cares, ye work your destined way,
While they, their solemn duties weakly leaving,
In helpless sorrow weep their lives away.
Oh, heart! if like those hoary giants mourning,
Why not be taught, by their instructive warning!

* My sister's home.

MY FATHER'S FIFTY-THIRD BIRTH-DAY.

A YEAR of stir, and storm, and strife,
Has mixed the snows of time
With the sharp hail of thickening cares
Upon thy brow sublime.

But yet the firm undaunted step
That marks the might of truth—
The eye undimmed, the fearless heart,
Are thine, as in thy youth.

And as the tree that feels the gale
The fiercest and the first,
Glistens the soonest in the sun,
Through scattered storm-clouds burst,—

So, when the false world's strife is done
And time has passed away,
The brightest beam of heaven's own light
About thy head shall play!

SHELLS.

FAR out at sea a tiny boat
Has set its tiny sail,
And, swiftly, see it onward float,
As freshens still the gale.
A rainbow in it must have slept
To lend it tints so fair,
Or loveliest angel o'er it wept—
A pearl in every tear.
Fairer than pen of mine can tell
Sails on that fearless tiny shell.

Deep in the chambers of the sea,
Where storied mermaids dwell,
A palace stood: and seemed to me,
Its every stone a shell;
And oh, what glorious hues were they
That sparkled on my eyes,
Of blue and gold, and red and gray,
Like tints of western skies!
As violets sweet in loveliest dells,
So blushed unseen those beauteous shells

Thus, on the sea, and 'neath its waves
Those tinctured sea-gems lie,
Like tombstones set to mark the graves
Of low-born men and high;
And, when they rest upon the shore,
In wealth's luxuriant ease,
They sound to us the solemn roar
They learned beneath the seas,—
As exiles, though afar they roam,
Still sing the songs they learned at home.*

* "Pleased they remember their august abodes,
And murmur, as the ocean murmurs there."
WALTER SAVAGE LANDOR

ROBERT TRAIL SPENCE LOWELL.

[Born 1816.]

"POEMS." 1864.

THE RELIEF OF LUCKNOW.

OH! that last day in Lucknow fort!
We knew that it was the last;
That the enemy's mines had crept surely in,
And the end was coming fast.

To yield to that foe meant worse than death;
And the men and we all worked on:
It was one day more, of smoke and roar,
And then it would all be done.

There was one of us, a Corporal's wife,
A fair, young, gentle thing,
Wasted with fever in the siege,
And her mind was wandering.

She lay on the ground in her Scottish plaid,
And I took her head on my knee;
"When my father comes hame frae the pleugh," she said,
"Oh! please then waken me."

She slept like a child on her father's floor,
In the flecking of woodbine-shade,
When the house-dog sprawls by the half-open door,
And the mother's wheel is stayed.

It was smoke and roar and powder-stench,
And hopeless waiting for death;
But the soldier's wife, like a full-tired child,
Seemed scarce to draw her breath.

I sank to sleep, and I had my dream
Of an English village-lane,
And wall and garden;—a sudden scream
Brought me back to the roar again.

There Jessie Brown stood listening,
And then a broad gladness broke
All over her face, and she took my hand
And drew me near and spoke:

"*The Highlanders!* Oh! dinna ye hear?
The slogan far awa?
The McGregor's? Ah! I ken it weel;
It's the grandest o' them a'.

"God bless thae bonny Highlanders!
We're saved! We're saved!" she cried;
And fell on her knees, and thanks to God
Poured forth, like a full flood-tide.

Along the battery-line her cry
Had fallen among the men:
And they started; for they were there to die;
Was life so near them then?

They listened, for life; and the rattling fire
Far off, and the far-off roar
Were all;—and the Colonel shook his head,
And they turned to their guns once more.

Then Jessie said, "That slogan's dune;
But can ye no hear them, noo,
'*The Campbells are comin'*?' It's no a dream;
Our succors hae broken through!"

We heard the roar and the rattle afar,
But the pipes we could not hear;
So the men plied their work of hopeless war,
And knew that the end was near.

It was not long ere it must be heard;
A shrilling, ceaseless sound;
It was no noise of the strife afar,
Or the sappers underground.

It *was* the pipes of the Highlanders,
And now they played "*Auld Lang Syne:*"
It came to our men like the voice of God,
And they shouted along the line.

And they wept and shook one another's hands,
And the women sobbed in a crowd;
And every one knelt down where we stood,
And we all thanked God aloud.

That happy day, when we welcomed them,
Our men put Jessie first;
And the General took her hand, and cheers
From the men, like a volley, burst.

And the pipers' ribbons and tartan streamed,
Marching round and round our line;
And our joyful cheers were broken with tears,
For the pipes played "*Auld Lang Syne.*"

THE BARREN FIELD.

HERE I labor, weak and lone,
Ever, ever sowing seed;
Ever tending what is sown:
Little is my gain, indeed.

Weary day and restless night
Follow in an endless round;
Wastes my little human might:
Soon my place will not be found.

Why so stubborn is my field?
Why does little fruit appear?
What an hundred-fold should yield,
Now goes barren all the year

Rank weeds crowd and jostle there,
Nodding vainly in the sun:
But the plants for which I care,
I may tell them one by one.

After all the sun and rain,
Weak and yellow drooping things,
From the lean earth, turned in vain,
These are all my labor wrings!

Oh, my Lord, the field is Thine:
Why do I, with empty pride,
Call the little garden mine,
When my work is Thine, beside?

If I claim it for my own,
Thou wilt give me its poor gain;
And, at harvest, I, alone,
May bring fruits to Thee in vain.

If I give myself to Thee
For Thy work, all poor and mean,
As Thou pleasest it shall be,
If I much or little glean:

Yet Thou wilt not spurn my toil,
Or my offering, at the last,
If, from off this meagre soil,
At Thy feet my all is cast.

Other work for man is none,
But to do the Master's will;
Wet with rain, or parched with sun,
Meekly I Thy garden till.

LOVE DISPOSED OF.

Here goes Love! Now cut him clear,
A weight about his neck:
If he linger longer here,
Our ship will be a wreck.
Overboard! Overboard!
Down let him go!
In the deep he may sleep,
Where the corals grow.

He said he'd woo the gentle breeze,
A bright tear in her eye;
But she was false or hard to please,
Or he has told a lie.
Overboard! Overboard!
Down in the sea
He may find a truer mind,
Where the mermaids be.

He sang us many a merry song
While the breeze was kind:
But he has been lamenting long
The falseness of the wind.
Overboard! Overboard!
Under the wave
Let him sing where smooth shells ring
In the ocean's cave.

He may struggle; he may weep;
We'll be stern and cold;
His grief will find, within the deep,
More tears than can be told.

He has gone overboard!
We will float on;
We shall find a truer wind
Now that he is gone.

A BURIAL-HYMN.

TO BE SUNG ON THE WAY TO THE GRAVE.

We bring Thee, Lord, this little dust
To lay in earth away:
In thy sure watch we meekly trust
To keep it for the Day.

Thy will be done! This dust, all dead,
Must lose its fairer form,
And graces in the deep grave shed,
That almost yet are warm.

We thank Thee for the little while
Our child lived here in love,
To glad a narrow place with smile
As from Thy house above.

And more, oh! we must thank Thee more,
That dew of upper day
Baptized his earthly being o'er,
And spirit hallowed clay.

AN ANTHEM-CAROL FOR CHRISTMAS.

Out of highest heaven dropping,
Like tinkling rain upon the sea
Came sweet music, swelling, stopping,
'Twas the angels' symphony.
"Glory be to God on high!"
Ran like lightning round the sky:
Then, like rain-drops, fell agen,
"Peace on earth, good-will to men!"

THE WARNED ONE.

Silent watcher, seest thou aught
On the far-off ocean's brim?
Has thine eye a meaning caught
In the mist-world's changeful whim?
Gaze full long, and gaze full deep:
There is that which chaseth sleep
In the spirit-forms that rise
Far before thy fated eyes:
Be thou, watcher, timely wise.

Blessed are those sons of men
For whose sake a light is set
Out beside things far-off, yet,
So to bring them within ken;
Showing them in ghastly white,
While beyond is depth of night:
Blessed are they, if they know
What these things far-moving are,
Coming, coming, sure if slow,
They give warning thus, afar.

WILLIAM WETMORE STORY.

[Born, 1819.]

"*Graffiti d'Italia.*" 1868.

CLEOPATRA

[DEDICATED TO J. L. M.]

HERE, Charmian, take my bracelets,
  They bar with purple stain
My arms; turn over my pillows—
  They are hot where I have lain:
Open the lattice wider,
  A gauze o'er my bosom throw,
And let me inhale the odours
  That over the garden blow.

I dreamed I was with my Anthony,
  And in his arms I lay:
Ah, me! the vision has vanished—
  The music has died away.
The flame and the perfume have perished—
  As this spiced aromatic pastille
That wound the blue smoke of its odour
  Is now but an ashy hill.

Scatter upon me rose-leaves,
  They cool me after my sleep,
And with sandal odours fan me
  Till into my veins they creep;
Reach down the lute and play me
  A melancholy tune,
To rhyme with the dream that has vanished,
  And the slumbering afternoon.

There, drowsing in golden sunlight,
  Loiters the slow smooth Nile,
Through slender papyri, that cover
  The wary crocodile.
The lotus lolls on the water,
  And opens its heart of gold,
And over its broad leaf-pavement
  Never a ripple is rolled.
The twilight breeze is too lazy
  Those feathery palms to wave,
And yon little cloud is as motionless
  As a stone above a grave.

Ah, me! this lifeless nature
  Oppresses my heart and brain!
Oh! for a storm and thunder—
  For lightning and wild fierce rain!
Fling down that lute—I hate it!
  Take rather his buckler and sword,
And crash them and clash them together
  Till this sleeping world is stirred.

Hark! to my Indian beauty—
  My cockatoo, creamy white,
With roses under his feathers—
  That flashes across the light.
Look! listen! as backward and forward
  To his hoop of gold he clings,
How he trembles, with crest uplifted,
  And shrieks as he madly swings!
Oh, cockatoo, shriek for Anthony!
  Cry, "Come, my love, come home!"
Shriek, "Anthony! Anthony! Anthony!"
  Till he hears you even in Rome.

There—leave me, and take from my chamber
  That stupid little gazelle,
With its bright black eyes so meaningless,
  And its silly tinkling bell!
Take him,—my nerves he vexes—
  The thing without blood or brain—
Or, by the body of Isis,
  I'll snap his thin neck in twain!

Leave me to gaze at the landscape
  Mistily stretching away,
Where the afternoon's opaline tremors
  O'er the mountains quivering play;
Till the fiercer splendor of sunset
  Pours from the west its fire,
And melted, as in a crucible,
  Their earthly forms expire;
And the bald blear skull of the desert
  With glowing mountains is crowned,
That burning like molten jewels
  Circle its temples round.

I will lie and dream of the past time
  Æons of thought away,
And through the jungle of memory
  Loosen my fancy to play;
When a smooth and velvety tiger,
  Ribbed with yellow and black,
Supple and cushion-footed,
  I wandered, where never the track
Of a human creature had rustled
  The silence of mighty woods,
And, fierce in a tyrannous freedom,
  I knew but the law of my moods.
The elephant, trumpeting, started,
  When he heard my footsteps near,
And the spotted giraffes fled wildly
  In a yellow cloud of fear.
I sucked in the noontide splendour,
  Quivering along the glade,
Or yawning, panting, and dreaming,
  Basked in the tamarisk shade,
Till I heard my wild mate roaring,
  As the shadows of night came on,
To brood in the trees' thick branches,
  And the shadow of sleep was gone;
Then I roused, and roared in anger,
  And unsheathed from my cushioned feet

My curving claws, and stretched me,
  And wandered my mate to greet.
We toyed in the amber moonlight,
  Upon the warm flat sand,
And struck at each other our massive arms—
  How powerful he was and grand!
His yellow eyes flashed fiercely
  As he crouched and gazed at me,
And his quivering tail, like a serpent,
  Twitched curving nervously.
Then like a storm he seized me,
  With a wild triumphant cry,
And we met, as two clouds in heaven,
  When the thunders before them fly.
We grappled and struggled together,
  For his love like his rage was rude;
And his teeth in the swelling folds of my neck
  At times, in our play, drew blood.

Often another suitor—
  For I was flexile and fair—
Fought for me in the moonlight,
  While I lay crouching there,
Till his blood was drained by the desert;
  And, ruffled with triumph and power,
He licked me and lay beside me
  To breathe him a vast half-hour.
Then down to the fountain we loitered,
  Where the antelopes came to drink;
Like a bolt we sprang upon them,
  Ere they had time to shrink.
We drank their blood and crushed them,
  And tore them limb from limb,
And the hungriest lion doubted,
  Ere he disputed with him.

That was a life to live for!
  Not this weak human life,
With its frivolous bloodless passions,
  Its poor and petty strife!

Come, to my arms, my hero,
  The shadows of twilight grow,
And the tiger's ancient fierceness
  In my veins begins to flow.
Come not cringing to sue me!
  Take me with triumph and power,
As a warrior wins a fortress!
  I will not shrink nor cower.
Come, as you came in the desert,
  Ere we were women and men,
When the tiger passions were in us,
  And love as you loved me then!

PRAXITELES AND PHRYNE.

[DEDICATED TO R. B.]

A THOUSAND silent years ago,
  The twilight faint and pale
Was drawing o'er the sunset glow
  Its soft and shadowy veil;

When from his work the Sculptor stayed
  His hand, and, turned to one
Who stood beside him, half in shade,
  Said, with a sigh, "'Tis done.

"Thus much is saved from chance and change,
  That waits for me and thee;
Thus much—how little! from the range
  Of Death and Destiny.

"Phryne, thy human lips shall pale,
  Thy rounded limbs decay,—
Nor love nor prayers can aught avail
  To bid thy beauty stay;

"But there thy smile for centuries
  On marble lips shall live,—
For Art can grant what love denies,
  And fix the fugitive.

"Sad thought! nor age nor death shall fade
  The youth of this cold bust;
When this quick brain and hand that made,
  And thou and I are dust!

"When all our hopes and fears are dead,
  And both our hearts are cold,
And love is like a tune that's played,
  And Life a tale that's told,

"This senseless stone, so coldly fair,
  That love nor life can warm,
The same enchanting look shall wear,
  The same enchanting form.

"Its peace no sorrow shall destroy;
  Its beauty age shall spare
The bitterness of vanished joy,
  The wearing waste of care.

"And there upon that silent face
  Shall unborn ages see
Perennial youth, perennial grace,
  And sealed serenity.

"And strangers, when we sleep in peace,
  Shall say, not quite unmoved,
So smiled upon Praxiteles
  The Phryne whom he loved."

SNOWDROP.

WHEN, full of warm and eager love,
  I clasp you in my fond embrace,
You gently push me back and say,
  "Take care, my dear, you'll spoil my lace."

You kiss me just as you would kiss
  Some woman friend you chanced to see;
You call me "dearest"—All love's forms
  Are yours, not its reality.

Oh Annie! cry, and storm, and rave!
  Do anything with passion in it!
Hate me one hour, and then turn round
  And love me truly, just one minute.

WALTER WHITMAN.

[Born 1819.]

"LEAVES OF GRASS." 1871.

I CELEBRATE myself:
And what I assume you shall assume;
For every atom belonging to me, as good belongs to you.

I loafe and invite my Soul;
I lean and loafe at my ease, observing a spear of summer grass.

Houses and rooms are full of perfumes—the shelves are crowded with perfumes;
I breathe the fragrance myself, and know it and like it;
The distillation would intoxicate me also, but I shall not let it.

The atmosphere is not a perfume—it has no taste of the distillation—it is odorless;
It is for my mouth forever—I am in love with it;
I will go to the bank of the wood, and become undisguised and naked;
I am mad for it to be in contact with me.

A child once said, *What is the grass?* fetching it to me with full hands;
How could I answer the child? I do not know what it is, any more than he.

I guess it must be the flag of my disposition, out of hopeful green stuff woven.

Or I guess it is the handkerchief of the Lord,
A scented gift and remembrancer, designedly dropt,
Bearing the owner's name some way in the corners, that we may see and remark, and say, *Whose?*

Or I guess the grass is itself a child, the produced babe of the vegetation.

Or I guess it is a uniform hieroglyphic;
And it means, Sprouting alike in broad zones and narrow zones,
Growing among black folks as among white;
Kanuck, Tuckahoe, Congressman, Cuff, I gave them the same, I receive the same.

And now it seems to me the beautiful uncut hair of graves.

Tenderly will I use you, curling grass;
It may be you transpire from the breasts of young men;
It may be if I had known them I would have loved them;
It may be you are from old people, and from women, and from offspring taken soon out of their mothers' laps;
And here you are the mothers' laps.

This grass is very dark to be from the white heads of old mothers;
Darker than the colorless beards of old men;
Dark to come from under the faint red roofs of mouths.

O I perceive after all so many uttering tongues!
And I perceive they do not come from the roofs of mouths for nothing.

I wish I could translate the hints about the dead young men and women,
And the hints about old men and mothers, and the offspring taken soon out of their laps.

What do you think has become of the young men and old men?
And what do you think has become of the women and children?
They are alive and well somewhere;
The smallest sprout shows there is really no death;
And if ever there was, it led forward life, and does not wait at the end to arrest it,
And ceased the moment life appeared.

All goes onward and outward—nothing collapses;
And to die is different from what any one supposed, and luckier.

The big doors of the country barn stand open and ready;
The dried grass of the harvest-time loads the slow-drawn wagon;
The clear light plays on the brown gray and green intertinged;
The armfuls are packed to the sagging mow.

I am there—I help—I came stretched atop of the load;
I felt its soft jolts—one leg reclined on the other;
I jump from the cross-beams, and seize the clover and timothy,
And roll head over heels, and tangle my hair full of wisps.

Alone, far in the wilds and mountains, I hunt,
Wandering, amazed at my own lightness and glee;
In the late afternoon choosing a safe spot to pass the night,
Kindling a fire and broiling the fresh-killed game;
Falling asleep on the gathered leaves, with my dog and gun by my side.

The Yankee clipper is under her sky-sails—she cuts the sparkle and scud;
My eyes settle the land—I bend at her prow, or shout joyously from the deck.

The boatman and clam-diggers arose early and stopt for me;
I tucked my trowser-ends in my boots, and went and had a good time:
(You should have been with us that day round the chowder-kettle.)

I saw the marriage of the trapper in the open air, in the far west—the bride was a red girl;
Her father and his friends sat near, cross-legged and dumbly smoking—they had moccasins to their feet, and large thick blankets hanging from their shoulders;
On a bank lounged the trapper—he was dressed mostly in skins—his luxuriant beard and curls protected his neck—he held his bride by the hand;
She had long eyelashes—her head was bare—her coarse straight locks descended upon her voluptuous limbs and reached to her feet.

The runaway slave came to my house and stopt outside;
I heard his motions crackling the twigs of the woodpile;
Through the swung half-door of the kitchen I saw him limpsy and weak,
And went where he sat on a log, and led him in and assured him,
And brought water and filled a tub, for his sweated body and bruised feet,
And gave him a room that entered from my own, and gave him some coarse clean clothes,
And remember perfectly well his revolving eyes and his awkwardness,
And remember putting plasters on the galls of his neck and ankles;
He staid with me a week before he was recuperated and passed north:
(I had him sit next me at table—my fire-lock cleaned in the corner.)

I am he that walks with the tender and growing night;
I call to the earth and sea, half-held by the night.

Press close, bare-bosomed night! Press close, magnetic, nourishing night!
Night of south winds! night of the large few stars!
Still, nodding night! mad, naked, summer night.

Smile, O voluptuous, cool-breathed earth!
Earth of the slumbering and liquid trees;
Earth of departed sunset! earth of the mountains, misty-topt!
Earth of the vitreous pour of the full moon, just tinged with blue!
Earth of shine and dark, mottling the tide of the river!
Earth of the limpid gray of clouds, brighter and clearer for my sake!
Far-swooping elbowed earth! rich apple-blossomed earth!
Smile, for your lover comes!

Prodigal, you have given me love! Therefore I to you give love!
O unspeakable, passionate love!

The past and present wilt—I have filled them, emptied them,
And proceed to fill my next fold of the future.

Listener up there! Here, you! What have you to confide to me?
Look in my face, while I snuff the sidle of evening;
Talk honestly—no one else hears you, and I stay only a minute longer.

Do I contradict myself?
Very well, then, I contradict myself;
(I am large—I contain multitudes.)

I concentre toward them that are nigh—I wait on the door-slab.

Who has done his day's work? Who will soonest be through with his supper?
Who wishes to walk with me?

Will you speak before I am gone? Will you prove already too late?

The spotted hawk swoops by and accuses me—he complains of my gab and my loitering.

I too am not a bit tamed—I too am untranslatable;
I sound my barbaric yawp over the roofs of the world.

The last scud of day holds back for me;
It flings my likeness after the rest, and true as any, on the shadowed wilds;
It coaxes me to the vapor and the dusk.

I depart as air—I shake my white locks at the runaway sun;
I effuse my flesh in eddies, and drift it in lacy jags.

I bequeathe myself to the dirt, to grow from the grass I love;
If you want me again, look for me under your boot-soles.

You will hardly know who I am, or what I mean;
But I shall be good health to you nevertheless,
And filter and fibre your blood.

Failing to fetch me at first, keep encouraged;
Missing me one place, search another:
I stop somewhere, waiting for you.

JOSIAH GILBERT HOLLAND.

[Born 1819.]

"BITTER-SWEET." 1858.

A SONG OF DOUBT.

The day is quenched, and the sun is fled;
God has forgotten the world!
The moon is gone, and the stars are dead;
God has forgotten the world!

Evil has won the horrid feud
Of ages with The Throne;
Evil stands on the neck of Good,
And rules the world alone.

There is no good; there is no God;
And Faith is a heartless cheat
Who bares the back for the Devil's rod,
And scatters thorns for the feet.

What are prayers in the lips of death,
Filling and chilling with hail?
What are prayers but wasted breath
Beaten back by the gale?

The day is quenched, and the sun is fled;
God has forgotten the world!
The moon is gone, and the stars are dead;
God has forgotten the world!

A SONG OF FAITH.

Day will return with a fresher boon;
God will remember the world!
Night will come with a newer moon;
God will remember the world!

Evil is only the slave of Good;
Sorrow the servant of Joy;
And the soul is mad that refuses food
Of the meanest in God's employ.

The fountain of joy is fed by tears,
And love is lit by the breath of sighs;
The deepest griefs and the wildest fears
Have holiest ministries.

Strong grows the oak in the sweeping storm;
Safely the flower sleeps under the snow;
And the farmer's heart is never warm
Till the cold wind starts to blow.

Day will return with a fresher boon;
God will remember the world!
Night will come with a newer moon;
God will remember the world!

"LIFE EVERMORE IS FED BY DEATH."

Life evermore is fed by death,
In earth and sea and sky;
And, that a rose may breathe its breath,
Something must die.

Earth is a sepulchre of flowers,
Whose vitalizing mould
Through boundless transmutation towers,
In green and gold.

The oak tree, struggling with the blast,
Devours its father tree,
And sheds its leaves and drops its mast,
That more may be.

The falcon preys upon the finch,
The finch upon the fly,
And nought will loose the hunger-pinch
But death's wild cry.

The milk-haired heifer's life must pass
That it may fill your own,
As passed the sweet life of the grass
She fed upon.

The power enslaved by yonder cask
Shall many burdens bear;
Shall nerve the toiler at his task,
The soul at prayer.

From lowly woe springs lordly joy;
From humbler good diviner;
The greater life must aye destroy
And drink the minor.

From hand to hand life's cup is passed
Up Being's piled gradation,
Till men to angels yield at last
The rich collation.

"THUS IS IT OVER ALL THE EARTH."

Thus is it over all the earth!
That which we call the fairest,
And prize for its surpassing worth,
Is always rarest.

Iron is heaped in mountain piles,
And gluts the laggard forges;
But gold-flakes gleam in dim defiles
And lonely gorges.

The snowy marble flecks the land
  With heaped and rounded ledges,
But diamonds hide within the sand
    Their starry edges.

The finny armies clog the twine
  That sweeps the lazy river,
But pearls come singly from the brine,
    With the pale diver.

God gives no value unto men
  Unmatched by meed of labor;
And Cost of Worth has ever been
    The closest neighbor.

Wide is the gate and broad the way
  That open to perdition,
And countless multitudes are they
    Who seek admission.

Bnt strait the gate, the path unkind,
  That lead to life immortal,
And few the careful feet that find
    The hidden portal.

All common good has common price;
  Exceeding good, exceeding;
Christ bought the keys of Paradise
    By cruel bleeding;

And every soul that wins a place
  Upon its hills of pleasure,
Must give its all, and beg for grace
    To fill the measure.

Were every hill a precious mine,
  And golden all the mountains;
Were all the rivers fed with wine
    By tireless fountains;

Life would be ravished of its zest,
  And shorn of its ambition,
And sink into the dreamless rest
    Of inanition.

Up the broad stairs that Value rears
  Stand motives beck'ning earthward,
To summon men to nobler spheres,
    And lead them worthward.

BABY SONG.

What is the little one thinking about?
Very wonderful things, no doubt.
    Unwritten history!
    Unfathomed mystery!
Yet he laughs and cries, and eats and drinks,
And chuckles and crows, and nods and winks,
As if his head were as full of kinks
And curious riddles as any sphinx!
  Warped by colic, and wet by tears,
  Punctured by pins, and tortured by fears,
  Our little nephew will lose two years;
    And he'll never know
    Where the summers go;—
  He need not laugh, for he'll find it so!
Who can tell what a baby thinks?
Who can follow the gossamer links
  By which the manikin feels his way
Out from the shore of the great unknown,
Blind, and wailing, and alone,
  Into the light of day?—
Out from the shore of the unknown sea,
Tossing in pitiful agony,—
Of the unknown sea that reels and rolls,
Specked with the barks of little souls—
Barks that were launched on the other side,
And slipped from Heaven on an ebbing tide!
  What does he think of his mother's eyes?
What does he think of his mother's hair?
  What of the cradle-roof that flies
Forward and backward through the air?
  What does he think of his mother's breast—
Bare and beautiful, smooth and white,
Seeking it ever with fresh delight—
  Cup of his life and couch of his rest?
What does he think when her quick embrace
Presses his hand and buries his face
Deep where the heart-throbs sink and swell
With a tenderness she can never tell,
  Though she murmur the words
  Of all the birds—
Words she has learned to murmur well?
    Now he thinks he'll go to sleep!
    I can see the shadow creep
    Over his eyes in soft eclipse,
    Over his brow and over his lips,
    Out to his little finger-tips!
    Softly sinking, down he goes!
    Down he goes! Down he goes!
    See! He is hushed in sweet repose!

A MOTHER'S SONG

Hither, Sleep! A motner wants thee!
  Come with velvet arms!
Fold the baby that she grants thee
  To thy own soft charms!

Bear him into Dreamland lightly!
  Give him sight of flowers!
Do not bring him back till brightly
  Break the morning hours!

Close his eyes with gentle fingers!
  Cross his hands of snow!
Tell the angels where he lingers
  They must whisper low!

I will guard thy spell unbroken
  If thou hear my call;
Come then, Sleep! I wait the token
  Of thy downy thrall.

Now I see his sweet lips moving;
  He is in thy keep;
Other milk the babe is proving
  At the breast of Sleep!

HERMAN MELVILLE.

[Born 1819.]

"BATTLE PIECES." 1866.

SHERIDAN AT CEDAR CREEK.

SHOE the steed with silver
  That bore him to the fray,
When he heard the guns at dawning—
    Miles away;
When he heard them calling, calling—
    Mount! nor stay;
      Quick, or all is lost;
      They've surprised and stormed the post,
      They push your routed host—
Gallop! retrieve the day.

House the horse in ermine—
  For the foam-flake blew
White through the red October;
  He thundered into view;
They cheered him in the looming,
  Horseman and horse they knew.
      The turn of the tide began,
      The rally of bugles ran,
      He swung his hat in the van;
The electric hoof-spark flew.

Wreathe the steed and lead him—
  For the charge he led
Touched and turned the cypress
  Into amaranths for the head
Of Philip, king of riders,
  Who raised them from the dead.
      The camp (at dawning lost),
      By eve, recovered—forced,
      Rang with laughter of the host
At belated Early fled.

Shroud the horse in sable—
  For the mounds they heap!
There is firing in the Valley,
  And yet no strife they keep;
It is the parting volley,
  It is the pathos deep.
      There is glory for the brave
      Who lead, and nobly save,
      But no knowledge in the grave
Where the nameless followers sleep.

BATTLE OF STONE RIVER, TENNESSEE.

A View from Oxford Cloisters.

WITH Tewksbury and Barnet heath
  In days to come the field shall blend,
The story dim and date obscure;
  In legend all shall end.
Even now, involved in forest shade
  A Druid-dream the strife appears,
The fray of yesterday assumes
  The haziness of years.
      In North and South still beats the vein
      Of Yorkist and Lancastrian.

Our rival Roses warred for Sway—
  For Sway, but named the name of Right;
And Passion, scorning pain and death,
  Lent sacred fervor to the fight.
Each lifted up a broidered cross,
  While crossing blades profaned the sign;
Monks blessed the fratricidal lance,
  And sisters scarfs could twine.
      Do North and South the sin retain
      Of Yorkist and Lancastrian?

But Rosecrans in the cedarn glade,
  And, deep in denser cypress gloom,
Dark Breckinridge, shall fade away
    Or thinly loom.
The pale throngs who in forest cowed
  Before the spell of battle's pause,
Forefelt the stillness that shall dwell
  On them and on their wars.
      North and South shall join the train
      Of Yorkist and Lancastrian.

But where the sword has plunged so deep,
  And then been turned within the wound
By deadly Hate; where Climes contend
    On vasty ground—
No warning Alps or seas between,
  And small the curb of creed or law,
And blood is quick, and quick the brain;
  Shall North and South their rage deplore,
      And reunited thrive amain
      Like Yorkist and Lancastrian?

AN UNINSCRIBED MONUMENT

On one of the Battle-fields of the Wilderness

SILENCE and Solitude may hint
  (Whose home is in yon piney wood)
What I, though tableted, could never tell—
The din which here befell,
  And striving of the multitude.
The iron cones and spheres of death
  Set round me in their rust,
    These, too, if just,
Shall speak with more than animated breath
  Thou who beholdest, if thy thought,
Not narrowed down to personal cheer,
Take in the import of the quiet here—
  The after-quiet—the calm full fraught;
Thou too wilt silent stand—
Silent as I, and lonesome as the land.

THE VICTOR OF ANTIETAM.

When tempest winnowed grain from bran,
And men were looking for a man
Authority called you to the van,
McClellan:
Along the line the plaudit ran,
As later when Antietam's cheers began.

Through storm-cloud and eclipse must move
Each Cause and Man, dear to the stars and Jove;
Nor always can the wisest tell
Deferred fulfillment from the hopeless knell—
The struggler from the floundering ne'er-do-well.
A pall-cloth on the Seven Days fell,
McClellan—
Unprosperously heroical!
Who could Antietam's wreath foretell?

Authority called you; then in mist
And loom of jeopardy—dismissed.
But staring peril soon appalled;
You, the Discarded, she recalled—
Recalled you, nor endured delay:
And forth you rode upon a blasted way,
Arrayed Pope's rout, and routed Lee's array,
McClellan:
Your tent was choked with captured flags that day,
McClellan.
Antietam was a telling fray.

Recalled you; and she heard your drum
Advancing through the ghastly gloom.
You manned the wall, you propped the Dome,
You stormed the powerful stormer home,
McClellan:
Antietam's cannon long shall boom.

At Alexandria, left alone,
McClellan—
Your veterans sent from you, and thrown
To fields and fortunes all unknown—
What thoughts were yours, revealed to none,
While faithful still you labored on—
Hearing the far Manassas gun!
McClellan,
Only Antietam could atone.

You fought in the front (an evil day,
McClellan)—
The fore-front of the first assay;
The Cause went sounding, groped its way;
The leadsmen quarrelled in the bay;
Quills thwarted swords; divided sway;
The rebel flushed in his lusty May:
You did your best, as in you lay,
McClellan.
Antietam's sun-burst sheds a ray.

Your medalled soldiers love you well,
McClellan:
Name your name, their true hearts swell;
With you they shook dread Stonewall's spell,
With you they braved the blended yell
Of rebel and maligner fell;
With you in shame or fame they dwell,
McClellan:
Antietam-braves a brave can tell.

And when your comrades (now so few,
McClellan—
Such ravage in deep files they rue)
Meet round the board, and sadly view
The empty places; tribute due
They render to the dead—and you!
Absent and silent o'er the blue;
The one-armed lift the wine to *you*,
McClellan,
And great Antietam's cheers renew.

THE MOUND BY THE LAKE.

The grass shall never forget this grave.
When homeward footing it in the sun
After the weary ride by rail,
The stripling soldiers passed her door,
Wounded perchance, or wan and pale,
She left her household work undone—
Duly the wayside table spread,
With evergreens shaded, to regale
Each travel-spent and grateful one.
So warm her heart—childless—unwed,
Who like a mother comforted.

THE RETURNED VOLUNTEER TO HIS RIFLE.

Over this hearth—my father's seat—
Repose, to patriot-memory dear,
Thou tried companion, whom at last I greet
By steepy banks of Hudson here.
How oft I told thee of this scene—
The Highlands blue — the river's narrowing sheen.
Little at Gettysburg we thought
To find such haven; but God kept it green.
Long rest! with belt, and bayonet, and canteen.

SHILOH.

A Requiem.

Skimming lightly, wheeling still,
The swallows fly low
O'er the field in clouded days,
The forest-field of Shiloh—
Over the field where April rain
Solaced the parched ones stretched in pain,
Through the pauses of night—
That followed the Sunday fight
Around the church of Shiloh—
The church so lone, the log-built one,
That echoed to many a parting groan
And natural prayer
Of dying foemen mingled there—
Foemen at morn, but friends at eve—
Fame or country least their care:
(What like a bullet can undeceive!)
But now they lie low,
While over them the swallows skim,
And all is hushed at Shiloh.

HENRY HOWARD BROWNELL.

[Born 18—.]

"WAR LYRICS." 1866.

THE COLOR-BEARER.

(Vicksburg, May 22, 1863.)

Let them go!—they are brave, I know—
  But a berth like this, why, it suits me best;
I can't carry back the Old Colors to-day,
We've come together a long rough way—
  Here's as good a spot as any to rest.

No look, I reckon, to hold them long;
  So here, in the turf, with my bayonet,
To dig for a bit, and plant them strong—
  (Look out for the point—we may want it yet!)

Dry work!—but the old canteen holds fast
  A few drops of water—not over-fresh—
So, for a drink!—it may be the last—
  My respects to you, Mr. Secesh!

No great show for the snakes to sight;
  Our boys keep 'em busy yet, by the powers!—
Hark, what a row going on, to the Right!
  Better luck there, I hope, than ours.

Half an hour!—(and you'd swear 'twas three)—
  Here, by the bully old staff, I've sat—
Long enough, as it seems to me,
  To lose as many lives as a cat.

Now and then, they sputter away;
  A puff and a crack, and I hear the ball.
Mighty poor shooting, I should say—
  Not bad fellows, may be, after all.

My chance, of course, isn't worth a dime—
  But I thought 'twould be over, sudden and quick—
Well, since it seems that we're not on time,
  Here's for a touch of the Kilikinick.

Cool as a clock!—and what is strange,
  Out of this dream of death and alarm,
(This wild, hard week of battle and change,)
Out of the rifle's deadly range—
  My thoughts are all at the dear old farm.

'Tis green as a sward, by this, I know—
  The orchard is just beginning to set,
They mowed the home-lot a week ago—
  The corn must be late, for that piece is wet.

I can think of one or two, that would wipe
  A drop or so from a soft blue eye,
To see me sit and puff at my pipe,
  With a hundred death's heads grinning hard by.

And I wonder when this has all passed o'er,
  And the tattered old stars in triumph wave on
Through street and square, with welcoming roar,
  If ever they'll think of us who are gone?

How we marched together, sound or sick,
  Sank in the trench o'er the heavy spade—
How we charged on the guns, at double-quick,
Kept rank for Death to choose and to pick—
  And lay on the bed no fair hands made.

Ah, well!—at last, when the nation's free,
  And flags are flapping from bluff to bay,
In old St. Lou what a time there'll be!
I mayn't be there, the Hurrah to see—
  But if the Old Rag goes back to-day,
They never shall say 'twas carried by me!

THE BURIAL OF THE DANE.

Blue gulf all around us,
  Blue sky overhead—
Muster all on the quarter,
  We must bury the dead!

It is but a Danish sailor,
  Rugged of front and form;
A common son of the forecastle,
  Grizzled with sun and storm.

His name and the strand he hailed from
  We know—and there's nothing more!
But perhaps his mother is waiting
  In the lonely Island of Fohr.

Still, as he lay there dying,
  Reason drifting awreck,
"'Tis my watch," he would mutter,
  "I must go upon deck!"

Aye, on deck—by the foremast!—
  But watch and look-out are done;
The Union-Jack laid o'er him,
  How quiet he lies in the sun!

Slow the ponderous engine,
  Stay the hurrying shaft!
Let the roll of the ocean
  Cradle our giant craft—
Gather around the grating,
  Carry your messmate aft!

Stand in order, and listen
  To the holiest page of prayer!
Let every foot be quiet,
  Every head be bare—
The soft trade-wind is lifting
  A hundred locks of hair.

Our captain reads the service,
  (A little spray on his cheeks,)
The grand old words of burial,
  And the trust a true heart seeks—
"We therefore commit his body
  To the deep"—and, as he speaks,

Launched from the weather-railing,
Swift as the eye can mark,
The ghastly, shotted hammock
Plunges, away from the shark,
Down, a thousand fathoms,
Down into the dark!

A thousand summers and winters
The stormy Gulf shall roll
High o'er his canvas coffin,—
But, silence to doubt and dole!
There's a quiet harbor somewhere
For the poor a-weary soul.

Free the fettered engine,
Speed the tireless shaft!
Loose to'gallant and topsail,
The breeze is fair abaft!

Blue sea all around us,
Blue sky bright o'erhead—
Every man to his duty!
We have buried our dead.

Steamship Cahawba, at Sea, Jan. 20th, 1858.

THE SPHINX.

They glare—those stony eyes!
That in the fierce sun-rays
Showered from these burning skies,
Through untold centuries
Have kept their sleepless and unwinking gaze.

Since what unnumbered year
Hast thou kept watch and ward,
And o'er the buried Land of Fear
So grimly held thy guard?
No faithless slumber snatching—
Still couched in silence brave—
Like some fierce hound long watching
Above her master's grave.

No fabled Shape art thou!
On that thought-freighted brow
And in those smooth weird lineaments we find,
Though traced all darkly, even now,
The relics of a Mind:
And gather dimly thence
A vague, half-human sense—
The strange and sad Intelligence
That sorrow leaves behind.

Dost thou in anguish thus
Still brood o'er Œdipus?
And weave enigmas to mislead anew,
And stultify the blind
Dull heads of human kind,
And inly make thy moan
That, 'mid the hated crew,
Whom thou so long couldst vex,
Bewilder, and perplex—
Thou yet couldst find a subtler than thine own?

Even now, methinks that those
Dark, heavy lips, which close
In such a stern repose,
Seem burdened with some Thought unsaid,
And hoard within their portals dread
Some fearful Secret there—
Which to the listening earth
She may not whisper forth—
Not even to the air!

Of awful wonders hid
In yon dread pyramid,
The home of magic Fears;
Of chambers vast and lonely,
Watched by the Genii only,
Who tend their Masters' long-forgotten biers;
And treasures that have shone
On cavern walls alone
For thousand, thousand years.

Those sullen orbs wouldst thou eclipse,
And ope those massy, tomb-like lips,
Many a riddle thou couldst solve
Which all blindly men revolve.

Would She but tell! She knows
Of the old Pharaohs,
Could count the Ptolemies' long line;
Each mighty Myth's original hath seen,
Apis, Anubis—Ghosts that haunt between
The Bestial and Divine—
(Such, He that sleeps in Philœ—He that stands
In gloom, unworshipped, 'neath his rock-hewn fane—
And They who, sitting on Memnonian sands,
Cast their long shadows o'er the desert plain:)
Hath marked Nitocris pass,
And Ozymandias
Deep-versed in many a dark Egyptian wile;
The Hebrew Boy hath eyed
Cold to the master's bride;
And that Medusan stare hath frozen the smile
Of Her all love and guile,
For whom the Cæsar sighed,
And the World-Loser died—
The Darling of the Nile.

ALONE.

A sad old house by the sea.
Were we happy, I and thou,
In the days that used to be?
There is nothing left me now

But to lie, and think of thee,
With folded hands on my breast,
And list to the weary sea
Sobbing itself to rest.

QUI'L MOURUT.

Not a sob, not a tear be spent
For those who fell at his side—
But a moan and a long lament
For him—who might have died!

Who might have lain, as Harold lay,
A King, and in state enow—
Or slept with his peers, like Roland
In the Straits of Roncesvaux.

JOHN TOWNSEND TROWBRIDGE.

[Born 1827.]

"THE VAGABONDS, AND OTHER POEMS." 1869.

THE VAGABONDS.

We are two travellers, Roger and I.
 Roger's my dog.—Come here, you scamp!
Jump for the gentlemen,—mind your eye!
 Over the table,—look out for the lamp!—
The rogue is growing a little old;
 Five years we've tramped through wind and weather,
And slept out-doors when nights were cold,
 And ate and drank—and starved—together.

We've learned what comfort is, I tell you!
 A bed on the floor, a bit of rosin,
A fire to thaw our thumbs (poor fellow!
 The paw he holds up there's been frozen),
Plenty of catgut for my fiddle
 (This out-door business is bad for strings),
Then a few nice buckwheats hot from the griddle,
 And Roger and I set up for kings!

No, thank ye, Sir—I never drink;
 Roger and I are exceedingly moral,—
Aren't we, Roger?—See him wink!—
 Well, something hot, then,—we won't quarrel.
He's thirsty, too,—see him nod his head?
 What a pity, Sir, that dogs can't talk!
He understands every word that's said,—
 And he knows good milk from water-and-chalk.

The truth is, Sir, now I reflect,
 I've been so sadly given to grog,
I wonder I've not lost the respect
 (Here's to you, Sir!) even of my dog.
But he sticks by. through thick and thin;
 And this old coat, with its empty pockets,
And rags that smell of tobacco and gin,
 He'll follow while he has eyes in his sockets.

There isn't another creature living
 Would do it, and prove, through every disaster,
So fond, so faithful, and so forgiving,
 To such a miserable, thankless master!
No, Sir!—see him wag his tail and grin!
 By George! it makes my old eyes water!
That is, there's something in this gin
 That chokes a fellow. But no matter!

We'll have some music, if you're willing,
 And Roger (hem! what a plague a cough is, Sir!)
Shall march a little—Start, you villain!
 Paws up! Eyes front! Salute your officer!
'Bout face! Attention! Take your rifle!
 (Some dogs have arms, you see!) Now hold your
Cap while the gentlemen give a trifle,
 To aid a poor old patriot soldier!

March! Halt! Now show how the rebel shakes
 When he stands up to hear his sentence
Now tell us how many drams it takes
 To honor a jolly new acquaintance.
Five yelps,—that's five; he's mighty knowing!
 The night's before us, fill the glasses!—
Quick, Sir! I'm ill,—my brain is going!—
 Some brandy,—thank you,—there!—it passes!

Why not reform? That's easily said;
 But I've gone through such wretched treatment,
Sometimes forgetting the taste of bread,
 And scarce remembering what meat meant,
That my poor stomach's past reform;
 And there are times when, mad with thinking,
I'd sell out heaven for something warm
 To prop a horrible inward sinking.

Is there a way to forget to think?
 At your age, Sir, home, fortune, friends,
A dear girl's love,—but I took to drink;—
 The same old story; you know how it ends.
If you could have seen these classic features,—
 You needn't laugh, Sir; they were not then
Such a burning libel on God's creatures:
 I was one of your handsome men!

If you had seen HER, so fair and young,
 Whose head was happy on this breast!
If you could have heard the songs I sung
 When the wine went round, you wouldn't have guessed
That ever I, Sir, should be straying
 From door to door, with fiddle and dog,
Ragged and penniless, and playing
 To you to-night for a glass of grog!

She's married since,—a parson's wife:
 'Twas better for her that we should part,—
Better the soberest, prosiest life
 Than a blasted home and a broken heart.
I have seen her? Once: I was weak and spent
 On the dusty road: a carriage stopped
But little she dreamed as on she went,
 Who kissed the coin that her fingers dropped!

You've set me talking, Sir; I'm sorry;
 It makes me wild to think of the change!
What do you care for a beggar's story?
 Is it amusing? you find it strange?
I had a mother so proud of me!
 'Twas well she died before—Do you know
If the happy spirits in heaven can see
 The ruin and wretchedness here below?

Another glass, and strong, to deaden
 This pain; then Roger and I will start.
I wonder has he such a lumpish, leaden,
 Aching thing in place of a heart?

He is sad sometimes, and would weep, if he could,
No doubt, remembering things that were,—
A virtuous kennel, with plenty of food,
And himself a sober, respectable cur.

I'm better now; that glass was warming.—
You rascal! limber your lazy feet!
We must be fiddling and performing
For supper and bed, or starve in the street.—
Not a very gay life to lead, you think?
But soon we shall go where lodgings are free,
And the sleepers need neither victuals nor drink;—
The sooner the better for Roger and me!

OUR LADY.

Our lady lives on the hillside here,
Amid shady avenues, terraced lawns,
And fountains that leap like snow-white deer,
With flashing antlers, and silver fawns;
And the twinkling wheels of the rich and great
Hum in and out of the high-arched gate;
And willing worshippers throng and wait,
Where she wearily sits and yawns.

I remember her pretty and poor,—
Now she has servants, jewels, and land:
She gave her heart to a poet-wooer,—
To a wealthy suitor she bartered her hand.
A very desirable mate to choose,—
Believing in viands, in good port-juice,
In solid comfort and solid use,—
Things simple to understand.

She loves poetry, music, and art,—
He dines, and races, and smokes, and shoots;
She walks in an ideal realm apart,—
He treads firm ground in his prosperous boots:
A wise design; for you see, 'tis clear,
Their paths do not lie so unsuitably near
As that ever either should interfere
With the other's chosen pursuits.

By night, as you roam through the rich saloons,
When music's purple and crimson tones
Float, in invisibly fine festoons,
O'er the buzz and hum of these human drones,
You are ready to swear that no happier pair
Have lived than your latter-day Adam there,
And our sweet, pale Eve, of the dark-furrowed hair,
Thick sown with glittering stones.

But I see, in the midst of the music and talk,
A shape steal forth from the glowing room,
And pass by a lonely cypress walk,
Far down through the ghostly midnight gloom,
Sighing and sorrowful, wringing its hands,
And bruising its feet on the pointed sands,
Till, white, despairing, and dumb it stands,
In the shadowy damp of a tomb.

The husband sprawls in his easy-chair,
And smirks, and smacks, and tells his jest,
And strokes his chin with a satisfied air,
And hooks his thumbs in his filagreed vest;
And the laugh rings round, and still she seems
To sit smiling there, and nobody deems
That her soul has gone down to that region of dreams,
A weary, disconsolate guest.

Dim ghosts of happiness haunt the grot,
Phantoms of buried hopes untold,
And ashen memories strew the spot
Where her young heart's love lies coffined and cold.
With her burden of sin she kneeleth within,
And kisses, and presses, with fingers thin,
Brow, mouth, and bosom, and beautiful chin
Of the dead that groweth not old.

He is ever there, with his dark wavy hair,
Unchanged through years of anguish and tears;
His hands are pressed on his passionate breast,
His eyes still plead with foreboding and fears.
O, she dwells not at all in that stately hall!
But, day and night, 'neath the cypresses tall,
She opens the coffin, uplifteth the pall,
And the living dead appears!

MIDWINTER.

The speckled sky is dim with snow,
The light flakes falter and fall slow;
Athwart the hill-top, rapt and pale,
Silently drops a silvery veil;
And all the valley is shut in
By flickering curtains gray and thin.

But cheerily the chickadee
Singeth to me on fence and tree;
The snow sails round him, as he sings,
White as the down of angels' wings.

I watch the slow flakes as they fall
On bank and brier and broken wall;
Over the orchard, waste and brown,
All noiselessly they settle down,
Tipping the apple-boughs, and each
Light quivering twig of plum and peach.

On turf and curb and bower-roof
The snow-storm spreads its ivory woof;
It paves with pearl the garden-walk;
And lovingly round tattered stalk
And shivering stem its magic weaves
A mantle fair as lily-leaves.

The hooded beehive, small and low,
Stands like a maiden in the snow;
And the old door-slab is half hid
Under an alabaster lid.

All day it snows: the sheeted post
Gleams in the dimness like a ghost;
All day the blasted oak has stood
A muffled wizard of the wood;
Garland and airy cap adorn
The sumach and the wayside thorn,
And clustering spangles lodge and shine
In the dark tresses of the pine.

The ragged bramble, dwarfed and old,
Shrinks like a beggar in the cold;
In surplice white the cedar stands,
And blesses him with priestly hands.

Still cheerily the chickadee
Singeth to me on fence and tree:
But in my inmost ear is heard
The music of a holier bird;
And heavenly thoughts, as soft and white
As snow-flakes, on my soul alight,
Clothing with love my lonely heart,
Healing with peace each bruised part,
Till all my being seems to be
Transfigured by their purity.

MIDSUMMER.

Around this lovely valley rise
The purple hills of Paradise.

O softly on yon banks of haze
Her rosy face the summer lays!

Becalmed along the azure sky,
The argosies of cloudland lie,
Whose shores, with many a shining rift,
Far off their pearl-white peaks uplift.

Through all the long midsummer-day
The meadow-sides are sweet with hay.
I seek the coolest sheltered seat,
Just where the field and forest meet,—
Where grow the pine-trees tall and bland,
The ancient oaks austere and grand,
And fringy roots and pebbles fret
The ripples of the rivulet.

I watch the mowers, as they go
Through the tall grass, a white-sleeved row;
With even stroke their scythes they swing,
In tune their merry whetstones ring.
Behind the nimble youngsters run,
And toss the thick swaths in the sun.
The cattle graze, while, warm and still,
Slopes the broad pasture, basks the hill,
And bright, where summer breezes break,
The green wheat crinkles like a lake.

The butterfly and humble-bee
Come to the pleasant woods with me;
Quickly before me runs the quail,
Her chickens skulk behind the rail;
High up the lone wood-pigeon sits,
And the woodpecker pecks and flits.
Sweet woodland music sinks and swells,
The brooklet rings its tinkling bells,

The swarming insects drone and hum,
The partridge beats his throbbing drum.
The squirrel leaps among the boughs,
And chatters in his leafy house.
The oriole flashes by; and, look!
Into the mirror of the brook,
Where the vain bluebird trims his coat,
Two tiny feathers fall and float.

As silently, as tenderly,
The down of peace descends on me.
O, this is peace! I have no need
Of friend to talk, of book to read;
A dear Companion here abides;
Close to my thrilling heart He hides;
The holy silence is His Voice:
I lie and listen, and rejoice.

EVENING AT THE FARM.

Over the hill the farm-boy goes.
His shadow lengthens along the land,
A giant staff in a giant hand;
In the poplar-tree, above the spring,
The katydid begins to sing;
The early dews are falling;—
Into the stone-heap darts the mink;
The swallows skim the river's brink;
And home to the woodland fly the crows,
When over the hill the farm-boy goes,
Cheerily calling,
"Co', boss! co', boss! co'! co'! co'!"
Farther, farther, over the hill,
Faintly calling, calling still,
"Co', boss! co', boss! co'! co'!"

Into the yard the farmer goes,
With grateful heart, at the close of day:
Harness and chain are hung away;
In the wagon-shed stand yoke and plough,
The straw's in the stack, the hay in the mow,
The cooling dews are falling;—
The friendly sheep his welcome bleat,
The pigs come grunting to his feet,
And the whinnying mare her master knows,
When into the yard the farmer goes,
His cattle calling,—
"Co', boss! co', boss! co'! co'! co'!"
While still the cow-boy, far away,
Goes seeking those that have gone astray,—
"Co', boss! co', boss! co'! co'!"

Now to her task the milkmaid goes.
The cattle come crowding through the gate,
Looing, pushing, little and great;
About the trough, by the farm-yard pump,
The frolicsome yearlings frisk and jump,
While the pleasant dews are falling;—
The new milch heifer is quick and shy,
But the old cow waits with tranquil eye,
And the white stream into the bright pail flows,
When to her task the milkmaid goes,
Soothingly calling,
"So, boss! so, boss! so! so! so!"
The cheerful milkmaid takes her stool,
And sits and milks in the twilight cool,
Saying, "So! so, boss! so! so!"

To supper at last the farmer goes.
The apples are pared, the paper read,
The stories are told, then all to bed.
Without, the cricket's ceaseless song
Makes shrill the silence all night long;
The heavy dews are falling.
The housewife's hand has turned the lock;
Drowsily ticks the kitchen clock;
The household sinks to deep repose,
But still in sleep the farm-boy goes
Singing, calling,—
"Co', boss! co', boss! co'! co'! co'!"
And oft the milkmaid, in her dreams,
Drums in the pail with the flashing streams,
Murmuring, "So, boss! so!"

PAUL H. HAYNE.

[Born 1831.]

"POEMS." 1855.

THE PORTRAIT.

THE laughing Hours before her feet,
And scattering spring-time roses,
And the voices in her soul are sweet
As Music's mellowed closes;
All Hopes and Passions, heavenly-born,
In her, have met together,
And Joy diffuses round her morn
A mist of golden weather.

As o'er her cheek of delicate dyes,
The blooms of childhood hover,
So do the tranced and sinless eyes,
All childhood's heart discover;
Full of a dreamy happiness,
With rainbow fancies laden,
Whose arch of promise glows to bless
Her spirit's beauteous Adenne.

She is a being born to raise
Those undefiled emotions,
That link us with our sunniest days,
And most sincere devotions;
In her, we see renewed and bright,
That phase of earthly story,
Which glimmers in the morning light,
Of God's exceeding glory.

Why, in a life of mortal cares,
Appear these heavenly faces?
Why, on the verge of darkened years,
These amaranthine graces?
'Tis but to cheer the soul that faints
With pure and blest evangels,
To prove, if Heaven is rich with Saints,
That Earth may have her Angels.

Enough! 'tis not for me to pray
That on her life's sweet river,
The calmness of a virgin day
May rest, and rest forever;
I know a guardian Genius stands
Beside those waters lowly,
And labors with immortal hands
To keep them pure and holy.

LINES.

THIS is the place—I pray thee, friend,
Leave me alone with that dread GRIEF,
Whose raven wings o'erarch the grave,
Closed on a life how sad and brief.

Already the young violets bloom
On the light sod that shrouds her form,
And summer's awful sunshine strikes
Incongruous on the spirit's storm.

She died, and did not know that I,
Whose heart is breaking in this gloom,
Had shrined her love, as pilgrims shrine
A blossom from some saintly tomb.

And ah! indeed it *was* a tomb,
The tomb of Hope, so ghastly-gray,
Whence sprung that flower of love that grew
Serenely on the Hope's decay;

A pallid flower that bloomed alone,
With no warm light to keep it fair,
But nurtured by the tears that fell,
E'en from the clouds of our despair—

She perished, and her patient soul
Passed to God's rest, nor did she know
I kept the faith,—we could not plight
In honor, or in peace below.

But, Edith! now, all, all is clear,
You see the flame of that fierce fate,
Which blazed between my life and yours,
And left both—desolate.

And well you comprehend that now
My heart is breaking where I stand
But 'mid the ruin, shrines its faith,
A relic from love's Holy Land.

LINES.

THOU! who hast wakened secret springs,
Deep in the verdure of my soul,
And stirred on many a fairy knoll,
In its dim shadows, purple wings

Of new and fresh Desires, that rise,
Like eagles to the morning sun,
Thrilled with the hope to look upon
The splendor of the inner skies;

Thy wondrous being, fair and good,
Revolves before me in the might
Of music, and the tender light
Of consummated womanhood.

As wandering orbs that meet in space,
Our spirits met, their wild career,
Transformed in the homeless air
To circles of eternal grace.

And each renewed in bliss to move,
And each rejoicing to have met
A world of such sweet glory set,
In so divine a Heaven of love.

O Souls! that breathe in mutual light,
Which, if divided or withdrawn,
Would leave indeed a doubtful dawn,
More dreary than the dreariest night,

Give us your subtlest sympathy,
For ours, that intellectual life,
Which blends even dissonance and strife
Into majestic harmony.

Through this charmed sphere to pass with thee,
Where Truth and Beauty wedded are,
And rounded to a silver star,
Poised on its own Eternity;

Is all I ask, or hope, or dream,
More can a mortal life time yield?
A foresight of an ampler field,
Outspread, where nobler glories gleam.

ON ——.

Thy cheek hath lost its happy flush and bloom,
Thine eye its light;
And the fresh fragrance of life's flowery morn,
Alas! hath vanished quite.

Pale the sweet garden, where a season since
The rose did blow;
And haunted only by a tender shade,
A flitting, ghostly glow:

Solemn and spiritual, and very sad,
Like the far smile
That beams from the Madonna's face divine,
In some dim convent aisle.

The Earth to thee smiles only from her tombs—
Thou standest lone,
Where in thy darkened and o'erclouded path,
Expiring joys are strewn:

Joys that have withered suddenly and dropped
From stately stems
Of thy green Hopes, once beautiful, and crowned
With dewy diadems:

And standing there all desolate and lorn,
Thy spirit grieves,
As grieve the winds of Autumn, at the fall
Of Summer's wealth of leaves.

I gaze upon thy face, serene and fixed,
Pallid and calm;
Tranced with a vision of the land of rest,
The Pilgrim's conquering palm.

Yet sometimes, turned from glory, thy sad soul
Dissolves in tears—
When, like a loosened Falcon, Memory mounts
Thy Heaven of youthful years.

Thy far-off Heaven of vanished years and youth,
Where past delights
Shine in cold distance, like the freezing stars
Of the pale Arctic night.

Fading, and oh! how faint and desolate,
Thy form doth seem,
And hour by hour thy wan face waxeth dim,
And shadowy as a dream.

The dream will melt from our horizon soon,
In higher skies.
Already meanings, mystical and strange,
Float in thine eyes.

And through those gentle lights, thy gentle soul
Too well I know,
Is passing up in dimness and in tears
From mortal wrong and wo.

THE GOLDEN AGE.

A ship with lofty prow came down
To Latium's strand—
A God had burst from severed chains,
To rule the land.

Plenty and smiling Peace sprung up
Beneath his tread—
Earth blossomed like Hesperian fields—
Discord was dead.

Heaven, with its calm, supernal light,
Had blessed the spot—
And Misery in the enchanted realm
Durst enter not.

Life passed away like holy dreams
On spring-tide eves—
And melted as the sunset melts
From violet leaves.

From haunted wood-shades genii flew,
In twilight dim—
Nature and human hearts drank deep
Their 'wildering hymn.

Earth, air, and heaven entrancèd were—
A cloudless clime
Hung, like transparent dews, around
That Golden Time.

Those golden years have passed, to come
In purer light—
Their hopes that sleep, but are not dead,
Will chase the night.

Time from the dungeon vault of Sin
Will strongly burst,
And glorious in his wrath cast off
His chains accurst.

A God will reach from viewless realms
This mortal shore,
And dark-robed Misery flee his face
Forevermore.

EDMUND CLARENCE STEDMAN.

[Born 1833.]

"THE BLAMELESS PRINCE, AND OTHER POEMS." 1869.

ILIUM FUIT.

ONE by one they died,—
Last of all their race;
Nothing left but pride,
Lace, and buckled hose.
Their quietus made,
On their dwelling-place
Ruthless hands are laid:
Down the old house goes!

See the ancient manse
Meet its fate at last!
Time, in his advance,
Age nor honor knows;
Axe and broadaxe fall,
Lopping off the Past:
Hit with bar and maul,
Down the old house goes!

Sevenscore years it stood:
Yes, they built it well,
Though they built of wood,
When that house arose.
For its cross-beams square
Oak and walnut fell;
Little worse for wear,
Down the old house goes!

Rending board and plank,
Men with crow-bars ply,
Opening fissures dank,
Striking deadly blows.
From the gabled roof
How the shingles fly!
Keep you here aloof,—
Down the old house goes!

Holding still its place,
There the chimney stands,
Stanch from top to base,
Frowning on its foes.
Heave apart the stones,
Burst its iron bands!
How it shakes and groans!
Down the old house goes!

Round the mantel-piece
Glisten Scripture tiles;
Henceforth they shall cease
Painting Egypt's woes,
Painting David's fight,
Fair Bathsheba's smiles,
Blinded Samson's might,—
Down the old house goes!

On these oaken floors
High-shoed ladies trod;
Through those panelled doors
Trailed their furbelows:
Long their day has ceased;
Now, beneath the sod,
With the worms they feast,—
Down the old house goes!

Many a bride has stood
In yon spacious room;
Here her hand was wooed
Underneath the rose;
O'er that sill the dead
Reached the family-tomb:
All, that were, have fled,—
Down the old house goes!

Once, in yonder hall,
Washington, they say,
Led the New-Year's ball,
Stateliest of beaux.
O that minuet,
Maids and matrons gay!
Are there such sights yet?
Down the old house goes!

British troopers came
Ere another year,
With their coats aflame,
Mincing on their toes;
Daughters of the house
Gave them haughty cheer,
Laughed to scorn their vows,—
Down the old house goes!

Doorway high the box
In the grass-plot spreads;
It has borne its locks
Through a thousand snows;
In an evil day,
From those garden-beds
Now 'tis hacked away,—
Down the old house goes!

Lo! the sycamores,
Scathed and scrawny mates,
At the mansion doors
Shiver, full of woes;
With its life they grew,
Guarded well its gates;
Now their task is through,—
Down the old house goes!

On this honored site
Modern trade will build,—
What unseemly fright
Heaven only knows!
Something peaked and high,
Smacking of the guild:
Let us heave a sigh,—
Down the old house goes!

PAN IN WALL STREET.

A. D. 1867.

JUST where the Treasury's marble front
  Looks over Wall Street's mingled nations,—
Where Jews and Gentiles most are wont
  To throng for trade and last quotations,—
Where, hour by hour, the rates of gold
  Outrival, in the ears of people,
The quarter-chimes, serenely tolled
  From Trinity's undaunted steeple;—

Even there I heard a strange, wild strain
  Sound high above the modern clamor,
Above the cries of greed and gain,
  The curbstone war, the auction's hammer,—
And swift, on Music's misty ways,
  It led, from all this strife for millions,
To ancient, sweet do-nothing days
  Among the kirtle-robed Sicilians.

And as it stilled the multitude,
  And yet more joyous rose, and shriller,
I saw the minstrel where he stood
  At ease against a Doric pillar:
One hand a droning organ played,
  The other held a Pan's-pipe (fashioned
Like those of old) to lips that made
  The reeds give out that strain impassioned.

'Twas Pan himself had wandered here
  A-strolling through this sordid city,
And piping to the civic ear
  The prelude of some pastoral ditty!
The demigod had crossed the seas,—
  From haunts of shepherd, nymph, and satyr,
And Syracusan times,—to these
  Far shores and twenty centuries later.

A ragged cap was on his head:
  But—hidden thus—there was no doubting
That, all with crispy locks o'erspread,
  His gnarlèd horns were somewhere sprouting;
His club-feet, cased in rusty shoes,
  Were crossed, as on some frieze you see them,
And trousers, patched of divers hues,
  Concealed his crooked shanks beneath them.

He filled the quivering reeds with sound,
  And o'er his mouth their changes shifted,
And with his goat's-eyes looked around
  Where'er the passing current drifted;
And soon, as on Trinacrian hills
  The nymphs and herdsmen ran to hear him,
Even now the tradesmen from their tills,
  With clerks and porters, crowded near him.

The bulls and bears together drew
  From Jauncey Court and New Street Alley,
As erst, if pastorals be true,
  Came beasts from every wooded valley;
The random passers stayed to list,—
  A boxer Ægon, rough and merry,—
A Broadway Daphnis, on his tryst
  With Naïs at the Brooklyn Ferry.

A one-eyed Cyclops halted long
  In tattered cloak of army pattern,
And Galatea joined the throng,—
  A blowsy, apple-vending slattern;
While old Silenus staggered out
  From some new-fangled lunch-house handy,
And bade the piper, with a shout,
  To strike up Yankee Doodle Dandy!

A newsboy and a peanut-girl
  Like little Fauns began to caper:
His hair was all in tangled curl,
  Her tawny legs were bare and taper;
And still the gathering larger grew,
  And gave its pence and crowded nigher,
While aye the shepherd-minstrel blew
  His pipe, and struck the gamut higher.

O heart of Nature, beating still
  With throbs her vernal passion taught her,—
Even here, as on the vine-clad hill,
  Or by the Arethusan water!
New forms may fold the speech, new lands
  Arise within these ocean-portals,
But Music waves eternal wands,—
  Enchantress of the souls of mortals!

So thought I,—but among us trod
  A man in blue, with legal baton,
And scoffed the vagrant demigod,
  And pushed him from the step I sat on.
Doubting I mused upon the cry,
  "Great Pan is dead!"—and all the people
Went on their ways:—and clear and high
  The quarter sounded from the steeple.

THE DOORSTEP

THE conference-meeting through at last,
  We boys around the vestry waited
To see the girls come tripping past,
  Like snow-birds willing to be mated.

Not braver he that leaps the wall
  By level musket-flashes litten,
Than I, who stepped before them all
  Who longed to see me get the mitten.

But no, she blushed and took my arm!
  We let the old folks have the highway,
And started toward the Maple Farm
  Along a kind of lovers' by-way.

I can't remember what we said,
  'Twas nothing worth a song or story;
Yet that rude path by which we sped
  Seemed all transformed and in a glory.

The snow was crisp beneath our feet,
  The moon was full, the fields were gleaming;
By hood and tippet sheltered sweet,
  Her face with youth and health was beaming

The little hand outside her muff,—
  O sculptor! if you could but mould it!
So lightly touched my jacket-cuff,
  To keep it warm I had to hold it.

To have her with me there alone,—
  'Twas love and fear and triumph blended.
At last we reached the foot-worn stone
  Where that delicious journey ended.

The old folks, too, were almost home:
  Her dimpled hand the latches fingered,
We heard the voices nearer come,
  Yet on the doorstep still we lingered.

She shook her ringlets from her hood,
  And with a "Thank you, Ned," dissembled,
But yet I knew she understood
  With what a daring wish I trembled.

A cloud passed kindly overhead,
  The moon was slyly peeping through it,
Yet hid its face, as if it said,
  "Come, now or never! do it! *do it!*"

My lips till then had only known
  The kiss of mother and of sister,
But somehow, full upon her own
  Sweet, rosy, darling mouth,—I kissed her!

Perhaps 'twas boyish love, yet still,
  O listless woman, weary lover!
To feel once more that fresh, wild thrill,
  I'd give,—but who can live youth over?

TOUJOURS AMOUR.

Prithee tell me, Dimple-Chin,
At what age does Love begin?
Your blue eyes have scarcely seen
Summers three, my fairy queen,
But a miracle of sweets,
Soft approaches, sly retreats,
Show the little archer there,
Hidden in your pretty hair;
When didst learn a heart to win?
Prithee tell me, Dimple-Chin!

  "Oh!" the rosy lips reply,
  "I can't tell you if I try.
'Tis so long I can't remember:
  Ask some younger lass than I!"

Tell, O tell me, Grizzled-Face,
Do your heart and head keep pace?
When does hoary Love expire,
When do frosts put out the fire?
Can its embers burn below
All that chill December snow?
Care you still soft hands to press,
Bonny heads to smooth and bless?
When does love give up the chase?
Tell, O tell me, Grizzled-Face!

  "Ah!" the wise old lips reply,
  "Youth may pass and strength may die;
But of Love I can't foretoken:
  Ask some older sage than I!"

LAURA, MY DARLING.

Laura, my darling, the roses have blushed
At the kiss of the dew, and our chamber is
    hushed;
Our murmuring babe to your bosom has clung,
And hears in his slumber the song that you sung;
I watch you asleep with your arms round him
    thrown,
Your links of dark tresses wound in with his own,
And the wife is as dear as the gentle young bride
Of the hour when you first, darling, came to my
    side.

Laura, my darling, our sail down the stream
Of Youth's summers and winters has been like a
    dream;
Years have but rounded your womanly grace,
And added their spell to the light of your face;
Your soul is the same as though part were not
    given
To the two, like yourself, sent to bless me from
    heaven,—
Dear lives, springing forth from the life of my life,
To make you more near, darling, mother, and wife!

Laura, my darling, there's hazel-eyed Fred,
Asleep in his own tiny cot by the bed,
And little King Arthur, whose curls have the art
Of winding their tendrils so close round my
    heart,—
Yet fairer than either, and dearer than both,
Is the true one who gave me in girlhood her troth:
For we, when we mated for evil and good,—
What were we, darling, but babes in the wood?

Laura, my darling, the years which have flown
Brought few of the prizes I pledged to my own.
I said that no sorrow should roughen her way,—
Her life should be cloudless, a long summer's day.
Shadow and sunshine, thistles and flowers,
Which of the two, darling, most have been ours?
Yet to-night, by the smile on your lips, I can see
You are dreaming of me, darling, dreaming of me.

Laura, my darling, the stars, that we knew
In our youth, are still shining as tender and true;
The midnight is sounding its slumberous bell,
And I come to the one who has loved me so well.
Wake, darling, wake, for my vigil is done;
What shall dissever our lives which are one?
Say, while the rose listens under her breath,
"Naught until death, darling, naught until
    death!"

WHAT THE WINDS BRING.

Which is the Wind that brings the cold?
  The North Wind, Freddy, and all the snow;
And the sheep will scamper into the fold
  When the North begins to blow.

Which is the Wind that brings the heat?
  The South Wind, Katy; and corn will grow,
And peaches redden for you to eat,
  When the South begins to blow.

Which is the Wind that brings the rain?
  The East Wind, Arty; and farmers know
That cows come shivering up the lane
  When the East begins to blow.

Which is the Wind that brings the flowers?
  The West Wind, Bessy; and soft and low
The birdies sing in the summer hours
  When the West begins to blow.

GEORGE ARNOLD.

[Born 1834. Died 1865.]

"DRIFT, AND OTHER POEMS." 1866.

THE JOLLY OLD PEDAGOGUE.

'Twas a jolly old pedagogue, long ago,
  Tall and slender, and sallow and dry;
His form was bent, and his gait was slow,
His long, thin hair was as white as snow,
  But a wonderful twinkle shone in his eye;
And he sang every night as he went to bed,
  "Let us be happy down here below;
The living should live, though the dead be dead,"
  Said the jolly old pedagogue, long ago.

He taught his scholars the rule of three,
  Writing, and reading, and history, too;
He took the little ones up on his knee,
For a kind old heart in his breast had he,
  And the wants of the littlest child he knew;
"Learn while you're young," he often said,
  "There is much to enjoy, down here below;
Life for the living, and rest for the dead!"
  Said the jolly old pedagogue, long ago.

With the stupidest boys he was kind and cool,
  Speaking only in gentlest tones;
The rod was hardly known in his school. . .
Whipping, to him, was a barbarous rule,
  And too hard work for his poor old bones;
Beside, it was painful, he sometimes said:
  "We should make life pleasant, down here below;
The living need charity more than the dead,"
  Said the jolly old pedagogue, long ago.

He lived in the house by the hawthorn lane,
  With roses and woodbine over the door;
His rooms were quiet, and neat, and plain,
But a spirit of comfort there held reign,
  And made him forget he was old and poor;
"I need so little," he often said;
  "And my friends and relatives here below
Won't litigate over me when I am dead,"
  Said the jolly old pedagogue, long ago.

But the pleasantest times that he had, of all,
  Were the sociable hours he used to pass,
With his chair tipped back to a neighbor's wall,
Making an unceremonious call,
  Over a pipe and a friendly glass:
This was the finest pleasure, he said,
  Of the many he tasted, here below;
"Who has no cronies, had better be dead!"
  Said the jolly old pedagogue, long ago.

Then the jolly old pedagogue's wrinkled face
  Melted all over in sunshiny smiles;
He stirred his glass with an old-school grace,
Chuckled, and sipped, and prattled apace,
  Till the house grew merry, from cellar to tiles:
"I'm a pretty old man," he gently said,
  "I have lingered a long while, here below;
But my heart is fresh, if my youth is fled!"
  Said the jolly old pedagogue, long ago.

He smoked his pipe in the balmy air,
  Every night when the sun went down,
While the soft wind played in his silvery hair,
Leaving its tenderest kisses there,
  On the jolly old pedagogue's jolly old crown
And, feeling the kisses, he smiled, and said,
  'Twas a glorious world, down here below;
"Why wait for happiness till we are dead?"
  Said the jolly old pedagogue, long ago.

He sat at his door, one midsummer night,
  After the sun had sunk in the west,
And the lingering beams of golden light
Made his kindly old face look warm and bright,
  While the odorous night-wind whispered
      "Rest!"
Gently, gently, he bowed his head. . .
  There were angels waiting for him, I know;
He was sure of happiness, living or dead,
  This jolly old pedagogue, long ago.

BEER.

  Here,
  With my beer
I sit,
While golden moments flit:
  Alas!
  They pass
Unheeded by:
And, as they fly,
I,
Being dry,
  Sit, idly sipping here
  My beer.

O, finer far
Than fame, or riches, are
The graceful smoke-wreaths of this free cigar!
  Why
  Should I
  Weep, wail, or sigh?
  What if luck has passed me by?
What if my hopes are dead,—
My pleasures fled?
  Have I not still
  My fill
Of right good cheer,—
Cigars and beer?

  Go, whining youth,
  Forsooth!
Go, weep and wail,
Sigh and grow pale,

Weave melancholy rhymes
On the old times,
Whose joys like shadowy ghosts appear,—
But leave to me my beer!
Gold is dross,—
Love is loss,—
So, if I gulp my sorrows down,
Or see them drown
In foamy draughts of old nut-brown,
Then do I wear the crown,
Without the cross!

GONE.

The summer was long and sweet,
The roses blossomed for me
Over a porch where fairy feet
Went pattering merrily.

All summer the roses smiled,
Hiding their thorns from sight;
All summer my passionate heart beat wild
With a feverish love and delight.

Now, autumn's rain-drops beat
On the casement, drearily;—
The summer I found so long and sweet
Has faded forever from me!

Under each thorny bough
The roses are withering fast,
And my passionate heart beats slower, now,
For the fever of love is past!

SERENADE.

I hear the dry-voiced insects call,
And "Come," they say, "the night grows brief!"
I hear the dew-drops pattering fall
From leaf to leaf,—from leaf to leaf.

Your night-lamp glimmers fitfully;
I watch below, you sleep above;
Yet on your blind I seem to see
Your shadow, love,—your shadow, love!

The roses in the night-wind sway,
Their petals glistening with the dew;
As they are longing for the day,
I long for you,—I long for you!

But you are in the land of dreams;
Your eyes are closed, your gentle breath
So faintly comes, your slumber seems
Almost like death,—almost like death!

Sleep on; but may my music twine
Your sleep with strands of melody,
And lead you, gentle love of mine,
To dream of me,—to dream of me!

THE MATRON YEAR.

The leaves that made our forest pathways shady
Begin to rustle down upon the breeze;
The year is fading, like a stately lady
Who lays aside her youthful vanities:

Yet, while the memory of her beauty lingers,
She cannot wear the livery of the old,
So Autumn comes, to paint with frosty fingers
Some leaves with hues of crimson and of gold.

The Matron's voice filled all the hills and valleys
With full-toned music, when the leaves were young;
While now, in forest dells and garden-alleys,
A chirping, reedy song at eve is sung;
Yet sometimes, too, when sunlight gilds the morning,
A carol bursts from some half-naked tree,
As if, her slow but sure decadence scorning,
She woke again the olden melody.

With odorous May-buds, sweet as youthful pleasures,
She made her beauty bright and debonair:
But now, the sad earth yields no floral treasures,
And twines no roses for the Matron's hair:
Still can she not all lovely things surrender;
Right regal is her drapery even now,—
Gold, purple, green, inwrought with every splendor,
And clustering grapes in garlands on her brow!

In June, she brought us tufts of fragrant clover
Rife with the wild bee's cheery monotone,
And, when the earliest bloom was past and over,
Offered us sweeter scents from fields new-mown:
Now, upland orchards yield, with pattering laughter,
Their red-cheeked bounty to the groaning wain,
And heavy-laden racks go creeping after,
Piled high with sheaves of golden-bearded grain.

Erelong, when all to love and life are clinging,
And festal holly shines on every wall,
Her knell shall be the New-Year bells, outringing;
The drifted snow, her stainless burial-pall:
She fades and fails, but proudly and sedately,
This Matron Year, who has such largess given,
Her brow still tranquil, and her presence stately,
As one who, losing earth, holds fast to heaven!

JUBILATE.

Gray distance hid each shining sail,
By ruthless breezes borne from me;
And, lessening, fading, faint and pale,
My ships went forth to sea.

Where misty breakers rose and fell
I stood and sorrowed hopelessly;
For every wave had tales to tell
Of wrecks far out at sea.

To-day, a song is on my lips:
Earth seems a paradise to me:
For God is good, and, lo, my ships
Are coming home from sea!

JOHN AYLMERE DORGAN.

(Born 1835. Died 1867.)

"STUDIES." 1864.

FATE.

THESE withered hands are weak,
But they shall do my bidding, though so frail;
These lips are thin and white, but shall not fail
The appointed words to speak.

Thy sneer I can forgive,
Because I know the strength of destiny;
Until my task is done I cannot die,
And then I would not live.

THE EXILE.

SHADOWS of lost delight, arise!
And move my darksome soul to tears:
Renew the light of faded skies,
The rapture of the fallen spheres:
For I will give to-night to these;
To-morrow to the stormy seas—
Beyond them, it may be, is peace!

Even as I speak the past returns;
I dwell again in Paradise;
Around the ardent spring-tide burns,
Above us laugh the happy skies;
All things in gladness onward move,
And earth beneath and heaven above
Are full of love, and only love.

Of all that joy a part are we,
Of all that love we share the bliss;
And know the years to come shall be
As full of happiness as this:
I drain my madness to the lees;
To-morrow to the stormy seas—
Beyond them, it may be, is peace!

For all the rapture was my own,
And all the falsehood hers; and so
The dream that lit the earth is gone,
And I the dreamer sadly go:
No more of mournful memories;
To-morrow to the stormy seas—
Beyond them, it may be, is peace!

A FAREWELL.

FAINT splendors of the night of June,
Sweet radiance of the summer moon,
Upon thy pathway dwell.
Farewell, Estelle! Farewell!

Dim fragrance of the violet,
And of the briar-rose dew-wet,
Breathe from the shadowy dell.
Farewell, Estelle! Farewell!

Far murmurs of the summer trees,
And voices low of dreamy seas,
Around thee sink and swell.
Farewell, Estelle! Farewell!

And ever sweet, by thee be heard
The hum of bee, and song of bird,
And sound of holy bell.
Farewell, Estelle! Farewell!

IT MIGHT HAVE BEEN.

MY wasted cheeks are wet
With tears of vain regret
For all I should remember not,
And all I would forget.

Oh, how shall these avenge us,
With look, or word, or kiss,
For all the bliss that might have been,
And all the pain that is.

THE KISS.

THE lyre I bear, so sweet of sound—
I dash it on the frozen ground,
For idle are its golden chords,
And vain of song the burning words.

I kiss thee; let my kiss avail,
Where speech and music both must fail
To tell the love, which else from thee
A secret evermore must be.

REMORSE.

I DIE. I know that men will haunt my grave—
Great men to weep a kindred spirit fled—
Whose souls in hours of mirthfulness and gloom
Upon my verses fed;

I know the critics shall be kind at last,
I know the world shall deem that not in vain
I lived; but I—alas, oh barren past!
Would I could live again

THEODORE TILTON.

[Born 1835.]

"THE SEXTON'S TALE." 1867.

THE PARSON'S COURTSHIP.

THE story, as I heard it told,
 I fashion into idle rhyme,
To show that, though the heart grows old,
 Yet love abides in golden prime.

An aged parson, on his mare,
 Was riding where his heart inclined,
Yet wore a sober look and air,
 As one who had a troubled mind.

For, when he passed the graveyard gate,
 His eyes grew dim with sudden tears
In looking at a slab of slate,
 Where lay his wife of other years.

She, dying, said it wronged the dead
 To make a wedding on a grave:
The words kept ringing in his head,
 And great bewilderment they gave.

He longed to make a second choice,
 For every Sunday in the choir
He heard the Widow Churchill's voice,
 Until she grew his heart's desire.

The parson's passion, unconfessed,
 Like smouldered heat within him burned,
Which never once the widow guessed,
 Or haply it had been returned.

With hazel branch the mare was switched,
 And cantered down the winding road,
And underneath a tree was hitched,
 At Captain Churchill's old abode.

The dame was busy sifting flour,
 Nor heard the comer till he said,
"Be praise to that Almighty Power
 Who giveth man his daily bread!"

The widow—caught by such a guest
 In just her linsey-woolsey gown,
Instead of in her Sunday best—
 Dropped bashfully her eyelids down.

Then spake her suitor to her face—
 "I have a solemn word to say,
Whereto is need of heavenly grace;
 So, Widow Churchill, let us pray!"

Devoutly did the couple kneel—
 The parson at the rocking-chair,
The widow at the spinning-wheel—
 And this the burden of the prayer:—

He mourned for uncommitted sin,
 Implored a grace on all mankind,
And asked that love might enter in
 And sweetly move the widow's mind.

Uprising from his prayerful knees,
 "I seek a wife," the parson said,
"And, finding thee, if God shall please,
 Nor thou deny, then let us wed!"

The widow started with surprise
 (For women old are women still),
And answered, lifting not her eyes,
 "I seek to do the heavenly will."

The heavenly will was plain indeed,
 And pointed to the flowery yoke,
For love is not the human need
 Of young alone, but aged folk.

One day, when asters were in bloom,
 There came a throng from far and near,
To wish the joy of bride and groom,
 And eat and drink the wedding-cheer.

That night, beside the bridal bed,
 Up spoke the bride in tender tone,
"I hold a message from the dead,
 And time has come to make it known:

"The years are twelve, this very day,
 Since she whose title now is mine,
The night before she passed away,
 Bequeathed to me this written line:—

"'To thee, O friend of all my life,
 I vow before my strength be spent,
That should he wed another wife,
 If thou art she, I rest content.'"

He gazed upon the well-known hand,
 Thought backward of the bygone years,
Thought forward of the heavenly land,
 And answered not a word for tears.

A hallowed honeymoon they passed,
 And both grew young in growing old,
Till, sweetly fading out at last,
 They left the tale that I have told.

NO AND YES.

I WATCHED her at her spinning,
And this was my beginning
Of wooing and of winning.

So cruel, so uncaring,
So scornful was her bearing,
She set me half despairing.

Yet sorry wit one uses,
Who loves, and thinks he loses
Because a maid refuses.

Love prospers in the making
By help of all its aching,
And quaking, and heart-breaking.

A woman's first denying
Betokens her complying
Upon a second trying.

When first I said in pleading,
"Behold, my love lies bleeding!"—
She shook her head unheeding.

But when again I told her,
And blamed her growing colder,
She dropped against my shoulder.

Then, with her eyes of splendor,
She gave a look so tender,
I knew she would surrender!

So down the lane I led her,
And while her cheek grew redder,
I sued outright to wed her.

Good end from bad beginning!
My wooing came to winning!
And still I watch her spinning!

THE FLY.

A RHYME FOR CHILDREN.

Baby Bye,
Here's a Fly:
Let us watch him, you and I.
How he crawls
Up the walls—
Yet he never falls!
I believe, with those six legs,
You and I could walk on eggs!
There he goes,
On his toes,
Tickling Baby's nose!

Spots of red
Dot his head:
Rainbows on his wings are spread!
That small speck
Is his neck;
See him nod and beck!
I can show you, if you choose,
Where to look to find his shoes:
Three small pairs
Made of hairs—
These he always wears.

Black and brown
Is his gown;
He can wear it upside down!
It is laced
Round his waist;
I admire his taste.
Pretty as his clothes are made,
He will spoil them, I'm afraid,
If to-night
He gets sight
Of the candle-light!

In the sun
Webs are spun:
What if he gets into one!
When it rains
He complains
On the window-panes.
Tongues to talk have you and I:
God has given the little Fly
No such things;
So he sings
With his buzzing wings.

He can eat
Bread and meat;
See his mouth between his feet!
On his back
Hangs a sack,
Like a peddler's pack.
Does the Baby understand?
Then the Fly shall kiss her hand!
Put a crumb
On her thumb:
Maybe he will come!

Round and round,
On the ground,
On the ceiling he is found.
Catch him? No:
Let him go:
Never hurt him so!
Now you see his wings of silk
Drabbled in the Baby's milk!
Fie, oh fie!
Foolish Fly!
How will he get dry?

All wet flies
Twist their thighs.
So they wipe their heads and eyes.
Cats, you know,
Wash just so:
Then their whiskers grow.
Flies have hair too short to comb!
Flies go barehead out from home!
But the Gnat
Wears a hat:
Do you laugh at that?

Flies can see
More than we—
So how bright their eyes must be!
Little Fly,
Mind your eye—
Spiders are near by!
Now a secret let me tell:
Spiders will not treat you well!
So I say
Heed your way!
Little Fly, good day!

JOHN JAMES PIATT.

[Born 1835.]

"WESTERN WINDOWS." 1869.

MARIAN'S FIRST HALF-YEAR.

MAIDEN Marian, born in May,
When the earth with flowers was gay,
And the Hours by day and night
Wore the jewels of delight:
Half-a-year has vanish'd by
Like a wondrous pageantry—
Mother May with fairy flowers,
June with dancing leaf-crown'd Hours,
July red with harvest-rust,
Swarthy August white with dust,
Mild September clothed in gold,
Wise October, hermit old—
And the world, so new and strange,
Circled you in olden change,
Since the miracle-morn of birth
Made your May-day on the earth.
Half-a-year, sweet child, has brought
To your eyes the soul of thought;
To your lips, with cries so dumb,
Baby-syllables have come,
Dreams of fairy language known
To your mother's heart alone—
Ante-Hebrew words complete
(To old Noah obsolete);
You have learn'd expressions strange,
Miracles of facial change,
Winning gestures, supplications,
Stamp'd entreaties, exhortations—
Oratory eloquent
Where no more is said than meant:
You have lived philosophies
Older far than Socrates—
Holiest life you've understood
Better than oldest wise and good:
Such as erst in Eden's light
Shunn'd not God's nor angels' sight;
You have caught with subtler eyes
Close Pythagorean ties
In the bird and in the tree,
And in every thing you see;
You have found and practise well
(Moulding life of principle)
Epicurean doctrines old
Of the Hour's fruit of gold:
Lifted, Moses-like, you stand,
Looking, where the Promised Land
Dazzles far away your sight—
Milk-and-honey's your delight!
  Maiden Marian, born in May,
Half-a-year has pass'd away;
Half-a-year of cannon-pealing,
('Twas your era of good-feeling,)
You have scarce heard dreader sound
Than those privateers around,
Buzzing flies, a busy brood,
Lovers of sweet babyhood—
Than the hum of lullaby
Rock'd to dreamland tenderly;
Half-a-year of dreadest sights
Through bright days and fairy nights,
You have seen no dreader thing
Than the marvel of a wing,
Than the leaves whose shadows warm
Play'd in many a phantom swarm
On the floor, the table under,
Lighting your small face with wonder!
  Maiden Marian, born in May,
Half-a-year has pass'd away:
'Tis a dark November day;
Lifted by our window, lo!
Washington is whirl'd in snow!
But, within, the fluttering flame
Keeps you summer-warm the same,
And your mother (while I write),
Crimson'd by the ember light,
Murmurs sweeter things to you
Than I'd write a half-year through;
Baby lyrics, lost to art,
Found within a mother's heart.
  Maiden Marian, born in May,
I'll not question Time to-day,
For the mysteries of your morrows,
Girlhood's joys or woman's sorrows,
But (while—side by side, alone—
We recall your summer flown,
And, with eyes that cannot look,
Hold his claspèd Mystery-Book)
I will trust when May is here
He shall measure you a year,
With another half-year sweet
Make the ring of light complete:
We will date our New-Years thence,
Full of summer songs and sense—
All the years begun that day
Shall be born and die in May!

THE BLACKBERRY FARM.

NATURE gives with freëst hands
Richest gifts to poorest lands:
When the lord has sown his last
And his field's to desert pass'd,
She begins to claim her own,
And—instead of harvests flown,
Sunburnt sheaves and golden ears—
Sends her hardier pioneers;
Barbarous brambles, outlaw'd seeds,
The first families of weeds
Fearing neither sun nor wind,
With the flowers of their kind
(Outcasts of the garden-bound),
Colonize the expended ground,
Using (none her right gainsay)
Confiscations of decay:

Thus she clothes the barren place,
Old disgrace, with newer grace.
Title-deeds, which cover lands
Ruled and reap'd by buried hands,
She—disowning owners old,
Scorning their "to have and hold"—
Takes herself; the mouldering fence
Hides with her munificence;
O'er the crumbled gatepost twines
Her proprietary vines;
On the doorstep of the house
Writes in moss "Anonymous,"
And, that beast and bird may see,
"This is Public property;"
To the bramble makes the sun
Bearer of profusion:
Blossom-odors breathe in June
Promise of her later boon,
And in August's brazen heat
Grows the prophecy complete—
Lo, her largess glistens bright,
Blackness diamonded with light!
Then, behold, she welcomes all
To her annual festival:
"Mine the fruit, but yours as well,"
Speaks the Mother Miracle;
"Rich and poor are welcome; come,
Make to-day millennium
In my garden of the sun:
Black and white to me are one.
This my freehold use content—
Here no landlord rides for rent;
I proclaim my jubilee,
In my Black Republic, free.
Come," she beckons; "Enter, through
Gates of gossamer, doors of dew
(Lit with Summer's tropic fire),
My Liberia of the brier."

LEAVES AT MY WINDOW.

I watch the leaves that flutter in the wind,
Bathing my eyes with coolness and my heart
Filling with springs of grateful sense anew,
Before my window—in the sun and rain.
And now the wind is gone and now the rain,
And all a motionless moment breathe, and now
Playful the wind comes back—again the shower,
Again the sunshine! Like a golden swarm
Of butterflies the leaves are fluttering,
The leaves are dancing, singing—all alive
(For Fancy gives her breath to every leaf)
For the blithe moment. Beautiful to me,
Of all inanimate things most beautiful,
And dear as flowers their kindred, are the leaves
In all their summer life; and, when a child,
I loved to lie through sunny afternoons
With half-shut eyes (familiar eyes with things
Long unfamiliar, knowing Fairyland
And all the unhidden mysteries of the Earth)
Using my kinship in those earlier days
With Nature and the humbler people, dear
To her green life, in every shade and sun.
The leaves had myriad voices, and their joy
One with the birds' that sang among them seem'd;
And, oftentimes, I lay in breezy shade
Till, creeping with the loving stealth he takes
In healthy temperaments, the blessèd Sleep
(Thrice blessèd and thrice blessing now, because
Of sleepless things that will not give us rest)
Came with his weird processions—dreams that
wore
All happy masks—blithe fairies numberless,
Forever passing, never more to pass,
The Spirits of the Leaves. Awaking then,
Behold the sun was swimming in my face
Through mists of his creations, swarming gold,
And all the leaves in sultry languor lay
Above me, for I waken'd when they dropp'd
Asleep, unmoving. Now, when Time has ceased
His holiday, and I am prison'd close
In his harsh service, master'd by his Hours,
The leaves have not forgotten me: behold,
They play with me like children who, awake,
Find one most dear asleep and waken him
To their own gladness from his sultry dream;
But nothing sweeter do they give to me
Than thoughts of one who, far away, perchance
Watches, like me, the leaves, and thinks of me
While o'er her window, sunnily, the shower
Touches all boughs to music, and the rose
Beneath swings lovingly toward the pane,
And she, whom Nature gave the freshest sense
For all her delicate life, rejoices in
The joy of birds that use the sun to sing
With breasts o'er-full of music. "Little Birds,"
She sings, "sing to my little Bird below!"
And with her child-like fancy, half-belief,
She hears them sing and makes believe they obey,
And the child, wakening, listens motionless.

ROSE AND ROOT.

A FABLE OF TWO LIVES.

The Rose, aloft in sunny air,
Beloved alike by bird and bee,
Takes for the dark Root little care,
That toils below it ceaselessly.

I put my question to the flower:
"Pride of the Summer, garden-queen,
Why livest thou thy little hour?"
And the Rose answer'd, "I am seen."

I put my question to the Root—
"I mine the earth content," it said,
"A hidden miner underfoot;
I know a Rose is overhead."

MY SHADOW'S STATURE.

Whene'er, in morning airs, I walk abroad,
Breasting upon the hills the buoyant wind,
Up from the vale my shadow climbs behind,
An earth-born giant climbing toward his god;
Against the sun, on heights before untrod,
I stand: faint glorified, but undefined,
Far down the slope in misty meadows blind,
I see my ghostly follower slowly plod.
"O stature of my shade," I muse and sigh,
"How great art thou, how small am I the while!"
Then the vague giant blandly answers, "True,
But though thou art small thy head is in the sky,
Crown'd with the sun and all the Heaven's smile—
My head is in the shade and valley too."

WILLIAM WINTER.

[Born 1836.]

"MY WITNESS." 1871.

THE WHITE FLAG.

Bring poppies for a weary mind
  That saddens in a senseless din,
And let my spirit leave behind
  A world of riot and of sin,—
In action's torpor deaf and blind.

Bring poppies—that I may forget!
  Bring poppies—that I may not learn!
But bid the audacious sun to set,
  And bid the peaceful starlight burn
O'er buried memory and regret.

Then shall the slumb'rous grasses grow
  Above the bed wherein I sleep;
While winds I love shall softly blow,
  And dews I love shall softly weep,
O'er rest and silence hid below.

Bring poppies,—for this work is vain!
  I cannot mould the clay of life.
A stronger hand must grasp the rein,
  A stouter arm annul the strife,
A braver heart defy the pain.

Youth was my friend,—but Youth had wings,
  And he has flown unto the day,
And left me, in a night of things,
  Bewildered, on a lonesome way,
And careless what the future brings.

Let there be sleep! nor any more
  The noise of useless deed or word;
While the free spirit wanders o'er
  A sea where not one wave is stirred,
A sea of dreams, without a shore.

Dark Angel, counselling defeat,
  I see thy mournful, tender eyes;
I hear thy voice, so faint, so sweet,
  And very dearly should I prize
Thy perfect peace, thy rest complete.

But is it rest to vanish hence,
  To mix with earth or sea or air?
Is death indeed a full defence
  Against the tyranny of care?
Or is it cruellest pretence?

And if an hour of peace draws nigh,
  Shall we, who know the arts of war,
Turn from the field and basely fly,
  Nor take what fate reserves us for,
Because we dream 'twere sweet to die?

What shall the untried warriors do,
  If we, the battered veterans, fail?
How strive and suffer and be true,
  In storms that make our spirits quail,
Except our valor lead them through?

Though for ourselves we droop and tire,
  Let us at least for them be strong.
'Tis but to bear familiar fire;
  Life at the longest is not long,
And peace at last will crown desire.

So, Death, I will not hear thee speak!
  But I will labor—and endure
All storms of pain that time can wreak. . .
  My flag be white because 'tis pure,
And not because my soul is weak!

LOVE'S QUESTION.

Because love's sigh is but a sigh,
  Doth it the less love's heart disclose?
Because the rose must fade and die,
  Is it the less the lovely rose?
Because black night must shroud the day,
Shall the brave sun no more be gay?

Because chill autumn frights the birds,
  Shall we distrust that spring will come?
Because sweet words are only words,
  Shall love for evermore be dumb?
Because our bliss is fleeting bliss,
Shall we who love forbear to kiss?

Because those eyes of gentle mirth
  Must some time cease my heart to thrill,
Because the sweetest voice on earth
  Sooner or later must be still,
Because its idol is unsure,
Shall my strong love the less endure?

Ah no! let lovers breathe their sighs,
  And roses bloom, and music sound,
And passion burn on lips and eyes,
  And pleasure's merry world go round:
Let golden sunshine flood the sky,
And let me love, or let me die!

LOVE'S QUEEN.

He loves not well whose love is bold!
  I would not have thee come too nigh.
The sun's gold would not seem pure gold
  Unless the sun were in the sky:
To take him thence and chain him near
Would make his beauty disappear.

He keeps his state,—do thou keep thine,
  And shine upon me from afar!
So shall I bask in light divine
  That falls from Love's own guiding-star.
So shall thy eminence be high,
And so my passion shall not die.

But all my life shall reach its hands
  Of lofty longing toward thy face,
And be as one who speechless stands
  In rapture at some perfect grace.
My love, my hope, my all, shall be
To look to heaven and look to thee.

Thine eyes shall be the heavenly lights;
  Thy voice shall be the summer breeze,
What time its sways, on moonlit nights,
  The murmuring tops of leafy trees;
And I will touch thy beauteous form
In June's red roses, rich and warm.

But thou thyself shalt come not down
  From that pure region far above;
But keep thy throne and wear thy crown,
  Queen of my heart and queen of love!
A monarch in thy realm complete,
And I a monarch—at thy feet!

AFTER ALL.

1862.

The apples are ripe in the orchard,
  The work of the reaper is done,
And the golden woodlands redden
  In the blood of the dying sun.

At the cottage-door the grandsire
  Sits, pale, in his easy-chair,
While a gentle wind of twilight
  Plays with his silver hair.

A woman is kneeling beside him;
  A fair young head is prest,
In the first wild passion of sorrow,
  Against his aged breast.

And far from over the distance
  The faltering echoes come,
Of the flying blast of trumpet
  And the rattling roll of drum.

Then the grandsire speaks, in a whisper,—
  "The end no man can see;
But we give him to his country,
  And we give our prayers to Thee." . . .

The violets star the meadows,
  The rose-buds fringe the door,
And over the grassy orchard
  The pink-white blossoms pour.

But the grandsire's chair is empty,
  The cottage is dark and still,
There's a nameless grave on the battle-field,
  And a new one under the hill.

And a pallid, tearless woman
  By the cold hearth sits alone;
And the old clock in the corner
  Ticks on with a steady drone.

AZRAEL.

Come with a smile, when come thou must,
  Evangel of the world to be,
And touch and glorify this dust,—
  This shuddering dust that now is me,—
  And from this prison set me free!

Long in those awful eyes I quail,
  That gaze across the grim profound:
Upon that sea there is no sail,
  Nor any light nor any sound
  From the far shore that girds it round

Only—two still and steady rays,
  That those twin orbs of doom o'ertop;
Only—a quiet, patient gaze
  That drinks my being, drop by drop,
  And bids the pulse of Nature stop.

Come with a smile, auspicious friend,
  To usher in the eternal day!
Of these weak terrors make an end,
  And charm the paltry chains away
  That bind me to this timorous clay!

And let me know my soul akin
  To sunrise and the winds of morn,
And every grandeur that has been
  Since this all-glorious world was born,
  Nor longer droop in my own scorn.

Come, when the way grows dark and chil'
  Come, when the baffled mind is weak,
And in the heart that voice is still
  Which used in happier days to speak,
  Or only whispers sadly meek.

Come with a smile that dims the sun!
  With pitying heart and gentle hand!
And waft me, from a work that's done,
  To peace that waits on thy command,
  In God's mysterious better land.

THE HEART'S ANCHOR.

Think of me as your friend, I pray,
  And call me by a loving name:
I will not care what others say,
  If only you remain the same.
I will not care how dark the night,
  I will not care how wild the storm;
Your love will fill my heart with light,
  And shield me close and keep me warm.

Think of me as your friend, I pray,
  For else my life is little worth:
So shall your memory light my way,
  Although we meet no more on earth.
For while I know your faith secure,
  I ask no happier fate to see:
Thus to be loved by one so pure
  Is honor rich enough for me.

THOMAS BAILEY ALDRICH.

[Born 1836.]

"POEMS." 1865.

THE BLUEBELLS OF NEW ENGLAND.

THE roses are a regal troop,
  And humble folks the daisies;
But, Bluebells of New England,
  To you I give my praises,—
To you, fair phantoms in the sun,
  Whom merry Spring discovers,
With bluebirds for your laureates,
  And honey-bees for lovers.

The south-wind breathes, and lo! you throng
  This rugged land of ours:
I think the pale blue clouds of May
  Drop down, and turn to flowers!
By cottage-doors along the roads
  You show your winsome faces,
And, like the spectre lady, haunt
  The lonely woodland places.

All night your eyes are closed in sleep,
  Kept fresh for day's adorning:
Such simple faith as yours can see
  God's coming in the morning!
You lead me by your holiness
  To pleasant ways of duty:
You set my thoughts to melody,
  You fill me with your beauty.

And you are like the eyes I love,
  So modest and so tender,
Just touch'd with daybreak's glorious light,
  And evening's quiet splendor.
Long may the heavens give you rain,
  The sunshine its caresses,
Long may the woman that I love
  Entwine you in her tresses.

PALABRAS CARIÑOSAS.

GOOD-NIGHT! I have to say good-night
To such a host of peerless things!
Good-night unto that fragile hand
All queenly with its weight of rings;
Good-night to fond up-lifted eyes,
Good-night to chestnut braids of hair,
Good-night unto the perfect mouth,
And all the sweetness nestled there,—
  The snowy hand detains me, then
  I'll have to say Good-night again!

But there will come a time, my love,
When, if I read our stars aright,
I shall not linger by this porch
With my adieus. Till then, good-night!
You wish the time were now? And I.
You do not blush to wish it so?
You would have blush'd yourself to death
To own so much a year ago,—
  What, both these snowy hands! ah, then,
  I'll have to say Good-night again!

THE FADED VIOLET.

WHAT thought is folded in thy leaves!
What tender thought, what speechless pain!
I hold thy faded lips to mine,
Thou darling of the April rain!

I hold thy faded lips to mine,
Though scent and azure tint are fled,—
O dry, mute lips! ye are the type
Of something in me cold and dead:

Of something wilted like thy leaves;
Of fragrance flown, of beauty gone;
Yet, for the love of those white hands
That found thee, April's earliest-born,—

That found thee when thy dewy mouth
Was purpled as with stains of wine,—
For love of her who love forgot,
I hold thy faded lips to mine.

That thou shouldst live when I am dead,
When hate is dead, for me, and wrong,
For this, I use my subtlest art,
For this, I fold thee in my song.

TIGER-LILIES.

I LIKE not lady-slippers,
Nor yet the sweet-pea blossoms,
Nor yet the flaky roses,
    Red, or white as snow;
I like the chaliced lilies,
The heavy Eastern lilies,
The gorgeous tiger-lilies,
    That in our garden grow!

For they are tall and slender;
Their mouths are dashed with carmine,
And when the wind sweeps by them,
    On their emerald stalks
They bend so proud and graceful,—
They are Circassian women,
The favorites of the Sultan,
    Adown our garden walks!

And when the rain is falling,
I sit beside the window
And watch them glow and glisten,—
    How they burn and glow!
O for the burning lilies,
The tender Eastern lilies,
The gorgeous tiger-lilies,
    That in our garden grow!

WHEN THE SULTAN GOES TO ISPAHAN.

When the Sultan Shah-Zaman
Goes to the city Ispahan,
Even before he gets so far
As the place where the clustered palm-trees are,
At the last of the thirty palace-gates,
The pet of the harem, Rose-in-Bloom,
Orders a feast in his favorite room,—
Glittering squares of colored ice,
Sweetened with syrup, tinctured with spice,
Creams, and cordials, and sugared dates,
Syrian apples, Othmanee quinces,
Limes, and citrons, and apricots,
And wines that are known to Eastern princes;
And Nubian slaves, with smoking pots
Of spicèd meats and costliest fish
And all that the curious palate could wish,
Pass in and out of the cedarn doors:
Scattered over mosaic floors
Are anemones, myrtles, and violets,
And a musical fountain throws its jets
Of a hundred colors into the air.
The dusk Sultana loosens her hair,
And stains with the henna-plant the tips
Of her pearly nails, and bites her lips
Till they bloom again,—but, alas, *that* rose
Not for the Sultan buds and blows!
Not for the Sultan Shah-Zaman
When he goes to the city Ispahan.

Then at a wave of her sunny hand,
The dancing-girls of Samarcand
Float in like mists from Fairy-land!
And to the low voluptuous swoons
Of music rise and fall the moons
Of their full brown bosoms. Orient blood
Runs in their veins, shines in their eyes:
And there, in this Eastern Paradise,
Filled with the fumes of sandal-wood,
And Khoten musk, and aloes and myrrh,
Sits Rose-in-Bloom on a silk divan,
Sipping the wines of Astrakhan;
And her Arab lover sits with her.
That's when the Sultan Shah-Zaman
Goes to the city Ispahan.

Now, when I see an extra light,
Flaming, flickering on the night
From my neighbor's casement opposite,
I know as well as I know to pray,
I know as well as a tongue can say,
That the innocent Sultan Shah-Zaman
Has gone to the city Ispahan.

THE MOORLAND.

The moorland lies a dreary waste:
The night is dark with drizzling rain;
In yonder yawning cave of cloud
The snaky lightning writhes with pain.

O sobbing rain, outside my door,
O wailing phantoms, make your moan;
Go through the night in blind despair,—
Your shadowy lips have touched my own.

No more the robin breaks its heart
Of music in the pathless woods!
The ravens croak for such as I,
The plovers screech above their broods.

All mournful things are friends of mine,
(That weary sound of falling leaves!)
Ah, there is not a kindred soul
For me on earth, but moans and grieves

I cannot sleep this lonesome night:
The ghostly rain goes by in haste,
And, further than the eye can reach,
The moorland lies a dreary waste.

SONG.

Out from the depths of my heart
Had arisen this single cry,
Let me behold my belovèd,
Let me behold her, and die.

At last, like a sinful soul,
At the portals of Heaven I lie,
Never to walk with the blest,
Ah, never! . . . only to die.

DEAD.

A sorrowful woman said to me,
"Come in and look on our child."
I saw an Angel at shut of day,
And it never spoke,—but smiled.

I think of it in the city's streets,
I dream of it when I rest,—
The violet eyes, the waxen hands,
And the one white rose on the breast!

HESPERIDES.

If thy soul, Herrick, dwelt with me,
This is what my songs would be:
Hints of our sea-breezes, blent
With odors from the Orient;
Indian vessels deep with spice;
Star-showers from the Norland ice;
Wine-red jewels that seem to hold
Fire, but only burn with cold;
Antique goblets, strangely wrought,
Filled with the wine of happy thought;
Bridal measures, vain regrets,
Laburnum buds and violets;
Hopeful as the break of day;
Clear as crystal; new as May;
Musical as brooks that run
O'er yellow shallows in the sun;
Soft as the satin fringe that shades
The eyelids of thy fragrant maids;
Brief as thy lyrics, Herrick, are,
And polished as the bosom of a star.

FRANCIS BRET HARTE.

[Born 1837.]

"POEMS." 1871.

"JIM."

SAY there! P'r'aps
  Some on you chaps
Might know Jim Wild?
Well,—no offence:
Thar ain't no sense
  In gittin' riled!

Jim was my chum
  Up on the Bar:
That's why I come
  Down from up yar,
Lookin' for Jim.
Thank ye, sir! *You*
Ain't of that crew,—
  Blest if you are!

Money?—Not much:
  That ain't my kind;
I ain't no such.
  Rum?—I don't mind,
Seein' it's you.

Well, this yer Jim,
Did you know him?—
Jess 'bout your size;
Same kind of eyes?—
Well, that is strange:
  Why, it's two year
  Since he came here,
Sick, for a change.
Well, here's to us:
        Eh?
The h—— you say!
        Dead?—
That little cuss?

What makes you star,—
You over thar?
Can't a man drop
's glass in yer shop
But you must rar'?
  It wouldn't take
  D—— much to break
You and your bar.

        Dead!
Poor—little—Jim!
—Why, thar was me,
Jones, and Bob Lee,
Harry and Ben,—
No-account men:
Then to take *him!*

Well, thar—Good-by,—
No more, sir,—I—
        Eh?
What's that you say?—
Why, dern it!—sho!—
No? Yes! By Jo!
        Sold!
Sold! Why, you limb,
You ornery,
        Derned old
Long-legged Jim!

PLAIN LANGUAGE FROM TRUTHFUL JAMES.

TABLE MOUNTAIN, 1870.

WHICH I wish to remark,—
  And my language is plain,—
That for ways that are dark
  And for tricks that are vain,
The heathen Chinee is peculiar.
  Which the same I would rise to explain.

Ah Sin was his name;
  And I shall not deny
In regard to the same
  What that name might imply,
But his smile it was pensive and childlike,
  As I frequent remarked to Bill Nye.

It was August the third;
  And quite soft was the skies;
Which it might be inferred
  That Ah Sin was likewise;
Yet he played it that day upon William
  And me in a way I despise.

Which we had a small game,
  And Ah Sin took a hand:
It was Euchre. The same
  He did not understand;
But he smiled as he sat by the table,
  With the smile that was childlike and bland.

Yet the cards they were stocked
  In a way that I grieve,
And my feelings were shocked
  At the state of Nye's sleeve:
Which was stuffed full of aces and bowers,
  And the same with intent to deceive.

But the hands that were played
  By that heathen Chinee,
And the points that he made,
  Were quite frightful to see,—
Till at last he put down a right bower,
  Which the same Nye had dealt unto me.

Then I looked up at Nye,
  And he gazed upon me;

And he rose with a sigh,
  And said, "Can this be?
We are ruined by Chinese cheap labor,"—
  And he went for that heathen Chinee.

In the scene that ensued
  I did not take a hand,
But the floor it was strewed
  Like the leaves on the strand
With the cards that Ah Sin had been hiding,
  In the game "he did not understand."

In his sleeves, which were long,
  He had twenty-four packs,—
Which was coming it strong,
  Yet I state but the facts;
And we found on his nails, which were taper,
  What is frequent in tapers,—that's wax.

Which is why I remark,
  And my language is plain,
That for ways that are dark,
  And for tricks that are vain,
The heathen Chinee is peculiar,—
  Which the same I am free to maintain.

THE SOCIETY UPON THE STANISLAUS.

I reside at Table Mountain, and my name is Truthful James;
I am not up to small deceit, or any sinful games;
And I'll tell in simple language what I know about the row
That broke up our society upon the Stanislow.

But first I would remark, that it is not a proper plan
For any scientific gent to whale his fellow-man,
And, if a member don't agree with his peculiar whim,
To lay for that same member for to "put a head" on him.

Now nothing could be finer or more beautiful to see
Than the first six months' proceedings of that same society,
Till Brown of Calaveras brought a lot of fossil bones
That he found within a tunnel near the tenement of Jones.

Then Brown he read a paper, and he reconstructed there,
From those same bones, an animal that was extremely rare;
And Jones then asked the Chair for a suspension of the rules,
Till he could prove that those same bones was one of his lost mules.

Then Brown he smiled a bitter smile, and said he was at fault.
It seemed he had been trespassing on Jones's family vault;
He was a most sarcastic man, this quiet Mr. Brown,
And on several occasions he had cleaned out the town.

Now I hold it is not decent for a scientific gent
To say another is an ass,—at least, to all intent;
Nor should the individual who happens to be meant
Reply by heaving rocks at him to any great extent.

Then Abner Dean of Angel's raised a point of order—when
A chunk of old red sandstone took him in the abdomen,
And he smiled a kind of sickly smile, and curled up on the floor,
And the subsequent proceedings interested him no more.

For, in less time than I write it, every member did engage
In a warfare with the remnants of a palæozoic age;
And the way they heaved those fossils in their anger was a sin,
Till the skull of an old mammoth caved the head of Thompson in.

And this is all I have to say of these improper games,
For I live at Table Mountain, and my name is Truthful James;
And I've told in simple language what I know about the row
That broke up our society upon the Stanislow.

GRIZZLY.

Coward,—of heroic size,
In whose lazy muscles lies
Strength we fear and yet despise;
Savage,—whose relentless tusks
Are content with acorn husks;
Robber,—whose exploits ne'er soared
O'er the bee's or squirrel's hoard;
Whiskered chin, and feeble nose,
Claws of steel on baby toes,—
Here, in solitude and shade,
Shambling, shuffling, plantigrade,
Be thy courses undismayed!

Here, where Nature makes thy bed,
Let thy rude, half-human tread
  Point to hidden Indian springs,
Lost in ferns and fragrant grasses,
  Hovered o'er by timid wings,
Where the wood duck lightly passes,
Where the wild-bee holds her sweets,—
Epicurean retreats,
Fit for thee, and better than
Fearful spoils of dangerous man.

In thy fat-jowled deviltry
Friar Tuck shall live in thee;
Thou mayst levy tithe and dole;
  Thou shalt spread the woodland cheer,
From the pilgrim taking toll;
  Match thy cunning with his fear;
Eat, and drink, and have thy fill;
Yet remain an outlaw still!

WILLIAM DEAN HOWELLS.

[Born 1837.]

"THE ATLANTIC MONTHLY." 1860–1871.

ANDENKEN.

I.

THROUGH the silent streets of the city,
 In the night's unbusy noon,
Up and down in the pallor
 Of the languid summer moon,

I wander and think of the village,
 And the house in the maple-gloom,
And the porch with the honeysuckles
 And the sweet-brier all abloom.

My soul is sick with the fragrance
 Of the dewy sweet-brier's breath:
Oh, darling! the house is empty,
 And lonesomer than death!

If I call, no one will answer;
 If I knock, no one will come;—
The feet are at rest forever,
 And the lips are cold and dumb.

The summer moon is shining
 So wan and large and still,
And the weary dead are sleeping
 In the graveyard under the hill.

II.

We looked at the wide, white circle
 Around the autumn moon,
And talked of the change of weather,—
 It would rain to-morrow, or soon.

And the rain came on the morrow,
 And beat the dying leaves
From the shuddering boughs of the maples
 Into the flooded eaves.

The clouds wept out their sorrow;
 But in my heart the tears
Are bitter for want of weeping,
 In all these autumn years.

III.

It is sweet to lie awake musing
 On all she has said and done,
To dwell on the words she uttered,
 To feast on the smiles I won,

To think with what passion at parting
 She gave me my kisses again,—
Dear adieux, and tears and caresses,—
 Oh, love! was it joy or pain?

To brood, with a foolish rapture,
 On the thought that it must be
My darling this moment is waking
 With tenderest thoughts of me!

O sleep! are thy dreams any sweeter?
 I linger before thy gate:
We must enter at it together,
 And my love is loath and late.

IV.

The bobolink sings in the meadow,
 The wren in the cherry-tree:
Come hither, thou little maiden,
 And sit upon my knee;

And I will tell thee a story
 I read in a book of rhyme;—
I will but feign that it happened
 To me, one summer-time,

When we walked through the meadow,
 And she and I were young;—
The story is old and weary
 With being said and sung.

The story is old and weary;—
 Ah, child! is it known to thee?
Who was it that last night kissed thee
 Under the cherry-tree?

V.

Like a bird of evil presage,
 To the lonely house on the shore
Came the wind with a tale of shipwreck,
 And shrieked at the bolted door,

And flapped its wings in the gables,
 And shouted the well-known names,
And buffeted the windows
 Afeard in their shuddering frames.

It was night, and it is daytime,—
 The morning sun is bland,
The white-cap waves come rocking, rocking,
 In to the smiling land.

The white-cap waves come rocking, rocking,
 In the sun so soft and bright,
And toss and play with the dead man
 Drowned in the storm last night.

VI.

I remember the burning brushwood,
 Glimmering all day long
Yellow and weak in the sunlight,
 Now leaped up red and strong,

And fired the old dead chestnut,
 That all our years had stood,
Gaunt and gray and ghostly,
 Apart from the sombre wood;

And, flushed with sudden summer,
 The leafless boughs on high

Blossomed in dreadful beauty
 Against the darkened sky.

We children sat telling stories,
 And boasting what we should be,
When we were men like our fathers,
 And watched the blazing tree,

That showered its fiery blossoms,
 Like a rain of stars, we said,
Of crimson and azure and purple.
 That night, when I lay in bed,

I could not sleep for seeing,
 Whenever I closed my eyes,
The tree in its dazzling splendor
 Against the darkened skies.

I cannot sleep for seeing,
 With closèd eyes to-night,
The tree in its dazzling splendor
 Dropping its blossoms bright;

And old, old dreams of childhood
 Come thronging my weary brain,
Dear foolish beliefs and longings;—
 I doubt, are they real again?

It is nothing, and nothing, and nothing,
 That I either think or see;—
The phantoms of dead illusions
 To-night are haunting me.

PLEASURE-PAIN.

"Das Vergnügen ist Nichts als ein höchst angenehmer Schmerz."—Heinrich Heine.

I.

Full of beautiful blossoms
 Stood the tree in early May:
Came a chilly gale from the sunset,
 And blew the blossoms away,—

Scattered them through the garden,
 Tossed them into the mere;
The sad tree moaned and shuddered,
 "Alas! the fall is here."

But all through the glowing summer
 The blossomless tree throve fair,
And the fruit waxed ripe and mellow,
 With sunny rain and air;

And when the dim October
 With golden death was crowned,
Under its heavy branches
 The tree stooped to the ground.

In youth there comes a west wind,
 Blowing our bloom away,—
A chilly breath of Autumn
 Out of the lips of May.

We bear the ripe fruit after,—
 Ah, me! for the thought of pain!
We know the sweetness and beauty
 And the heart-bloom never again.

II.

One sails away to sea,—
 One stands on the shore and cries;
The ship goes down the world, and the light
 On the sullen water dies.

The whispering shell is mute,—
 And after is evil cheer:
She shall stand on the shore and cry in vain
 Many and many a year.

But the stately, wide-winged ship
 Lies wrecked on the unknown deep;
Far under, dead in his coral bed,
 The lover lies asleep.

III.

In the wainscot ticks the death-watch,
 Chirps the cricket in the floor,
In the distance dogs are barking,
 Feet go by outside my door.

From her window honeysuckles
 Stealing in upon the gloom,
Spice and sweets embalm the silence
 Dead within the lonesome room.

And the ghost of that dead silence
 Haunts me ever, thin and chill,
In the pauses of the death-watch,
 When the cricket's cry is still.

IV.

She stands in silks of purple,
 Like a splendid flower in bloom,
She moves, and the air is laden
 With delicate perfume.

The over-vigilant mamma
 Can never let her be:
She must play this march for another,
 And sing that song for me.

I wonder if she remembers
 The song I made for her:
"The hopes of love are frailer
 Than lines of gossamer:"

Made when we strolled together
 Through fields of happy June,
And our hearts kept time together,
 With birds and brooks in tune,—

And I was so glad of loving,
 That I must mimic grief,
And, trusting in love forever,
 Must fable unbelief.

I did not hear the prelude,—
 I was thinking of these old things.
She is fairer and wiser and older
 Than—— What is it she sings?

"The hopes of love are frailer
 Than lines of gossamer."
Alas! the bitter wisdom
 Of the song I made for her!

V.

All the long August afternoon,
  The little drowsy stream
Whispers a melancholy tune,
As if it dreamed of June
  And whispered in its dream.

The thistles show beyond the brook
  Dust on their down and bloom,
And out of many a weed-grown nook
The aster-flowers look
  With eyes of tender gloom.

The silent orchard aisles are sweet
  With smell of ripening fruit.
Through the sere grass, in shy retreat,
Flutter, at coming feet,
  The robins strange and mute.

There is no wind to stir the leaves,
  The harsh leaves overhead;
Only the querulous cricket grieves,
And shrilling locust weaves
  A song of summer dead.

BEFORE THE GATE.

They gave the whole long day to idle laughter,
  To fitful song and jest,
To moods of soberness as idle, after,
  And silences, as idle too as the rest.

But when at last upon their way returning,
  Taciturn, late, and loath,
Through the broad meadow in the sunset burning,
  They reached the gate, one sweet spell hindered them both.

Her heart was troubled with a subtile anguish
  Such as but women know
That wait, and lest love speak or speak not languish,
  And what they would, would rather they would not so;

Till he said,—man-like nothing comprehending
  Of all the wondrous guile
That women won win themselves with, and bending
  Eyes of relentless asking on her the while,—

"Ah, if beyond this gate the path united
  Our steps as far as death,
And I might open it!—" His voice, affrighted
  At its own daring, faltered under his breath.

Then she—whom both his faith and fear enchanted
  Far beyond words to tell,
Feeling her woman's finest wit had wanted
  The art he had that knew to blunder so well—
Shyly drew near, a little step, and mocking,
  "Shall we not be too late
For tea?" she said. "I'm quite worn out with walking;
  Yes, thanks, your arm. And will you—open the gate?"

THE FIRST CRICKET.

Ah me! is it then true that the year has waxed unto waning,
  And that so soon must remain nothing but lapse and decay,—
Earliest cricket, that out of the midsummer midnight complaining,
  All the faint summer in me takest with subtle dismay?

Though thou bringest no dream of frost to the flowers that slumber,
  Though no tree for its leaves, doomed of thy voice, maketh moan;
With the unconscious earth's boded evil my soul thou dost cumber,
  And in the year's lost youth makest me still lose my own.

Answerest thou, that when nights of December are blackest and bleakest,—
  And when the fervid grate feigns me a May in my room,
And by my hearthstone gay, as now sad in my garden, thou creakest,—
  Thou wilt again give me all,—dew and fragrance and bloom?

Nay, little poet! full many a cricket I have that is willing,
  If I but take him down out of his place on my shelf,
Me blither lays to sing than the blithest known to thy shrilling,
  Full of the rapture of life, May, morn, hope, and—himself:

Leaving me only the sadder; for never one of my singers
  Lures back the bee to his feast, calls back the bird to his tree.
Hast thou no art can make me believe, while the summer yet lingers,
  Better than bloom that has been red leaf and sere that must be?

THE POET'S FRIENDS.

The Robin sings in the elm;
  The cattle stand beneath,
Sedate and grave, with great brown eyes,
  And fragrant meadow-breath.

They listen to the flattered bird,
  The wise-looking, stupid things!
And they never understand a word
  Of all the Robin sings.

HENRY TIMROD.

[Born 18—. Died 1867.]

"WAR POETRY OF THE SOUTH." 1866.

THE COTTON-BOLL.

WHILE I recline
At ease beneath
This immemorial pine,
Small sphere!—
By dusky fingers brought this morning here,
And shown with boastful smiles,—
I turn thy cloven sheath,
Through which the soft white fibres peer,
That, with their gossamer bands,
Unite, like love, the sea-divided lands,
And slowly, thread by thread,
Draw forth the folded strands,
Than which the trembling line,
By whose frail help yon startled spider fled
Down the tall spear-grass from his swinging bed,
Is scarce more fine;
And as the tangled skein
Unravels in my hands,
Betwixt me and the noon-day light
A veil seems lifted, and for miles and miles
The landscape broadens on my sight,
As, in the little boll, there lurked a spell
Like that which, in the ocean shell,
With mystic sound,
Breaks down the narrow walls that hem us round,
And turns some city lane
Into the restless main,
With all his capes and isles!

Yonder bird,—
Which floats, as if at rest,
In those blue tracts above the thunder, where
No vapors cloud the stainless air,
And never sound is heard,
Unless at such rare time
When, from the City of the Blest,
Rings down some golden chime,—
Sees not from his high place
So vast a cirque of summer space
As widens round me in one mighty field,
Which, rimmed by seas and sands,
Doth hail its earliest daylight in the beams
Of gray Atlantic dawns;
And, broad as realms made up of many lands,
Is lost afar
Behind the crimson hills and purple lawns
Of sunset, among plains which roll their streams
Against the Evening Star!
And lo!
To the remotest point of sight,
Although I gaze upon no waste of snow,
The endless field is white;
And the whole landscape glows,
For many a shining league away,
With such accumulated light
As Polar lands would flash beneath a tropic day!
Nor lack there (for the vision grows,
And the small charm within my hands—
More potent even than the fabled one,
Which oped whatever golden mystery
Lay hid in fairy wood or magic vale,
The curious ointment of the Arabian tale—
Beyond all mortal sense
Doth stretch my sight's horizon, and I see
Beneath its simple influence,
As if, with Uriel's crown,
I stood in some great temple of the Sun,
And looked, as Uriel, down)—
Nor lack there pastures rich and fields all green
With all the common gifts of God,
For temperate airs and torrid sheen
Weave Edens of the sod;
Through lands which look one sea of billowy gold
Broad rivers wind their devious ways;
A hundred isles in their embraces fold
A hundred luminous bays;
And through yon purple haze
Vast mountains lift their plumèd peaks cloud-crowned;
And, save where up their sides the ploughman creeps,
An unknown forest girds them grandly round,
In whose dark shades a future navy sleeps!
Ye stars, which though unseen, yet with me gaze
Upon this loveliest fragment of the earth!
Thou Sun, that kindlest all thy gentlest rays
Above it, as to light a favorite hearth!
Ye clouds, that in your temples in the West
See nothing brighter than its humblest flowers!
And, you, ye Winds, that on the ocean's breast
Are kissed to coolness ere ye reach its bowers!
Bear witness with me in my song of praise,
And tell the world that, since the world began,
No fairer land hath fired a poet's lays,
Or given a home to man!

But these are charms already widely blown!
His be the meed whose pencil's trace
Hath touched our very swamps with grace,
And round whose tuneful way
All Southern laurels bloom;
The Poet of "The Woodlands," unto whom
Alike are known
The flute's low breathing and the trumpet's tone,
And the soft west-wind's sighs;
But who shall utter all the debt,
O Land! wherein all powers are met
That bind a people's heart,
The world doth owe thee at this day,
And which it never can repay,
Yet scarcely deigns to own!
Where sleeps the poet who shall fitly sing
The source wherefrom doth spring

That mighty commerce which, confined
To the mean channels of no selfish mart,
Goes out to every shore
Of this broad earth, and throngs the sea with ships
That bear no thunders; hushes hungry lips
In alien lands;
Joins with a delicate web remotest strands;
And gladdening rich and poor,
Doth gild Parisian domes,
Or feed the cottage-smoke of English homes,
And only bounds its blessings by mankind?
In offices like these, thy mission lies,
My Country! and it shall not end
As long as rain shall fall and Heaven bend
In blue above thee; though thy foes be hard
And cruel as their weapons, it shall guard
Thy hearthstones as a bulwark; make thee great
In white and bloodless state;
And, haply, as the years increase—
Still working through its humbler reach
With that large wisdom which the ages teach—
Revive the half-dead dream of universal peace!

As men who labor in that mine
Of Cornwall, hollowed out beneath the bed
Of ocean, when a storm rolls overhead,
Hear the dull booming of the world of brine
Above them, and a mighty muffled roar
Of winds and waters, and yet toil calmly on,
And split the rock, and pile the massive ore,
Or carve a niche, or shape the archèd roof;
So I, as calmly, weave my woof
Of song, chanting the days to come,
Unsilenced, though the quiet summer air
Stirs with the bruit of battles, and each dawn
Wakes from its starry silence to the hum
Of many gathering armies. Still,
In that we sometimes hear,
Upon the Northern winds the voice of woe
Not wholly drowned in triumph, though I know
The end must crown us, and a few brief years
Dry all our tears,
I may not sing too gladly. To Thy will
Resigned, O Lord! we cannot all forget
That there is much even Victory must regret.
And, therefore, not too long
From the great burden of our country's wrong
Delay our just release!
And, if it may be, save
These sacred fields of peace
From stain of patriot or of hostile blood!
Oh, help us, Lord! to roll the crimson flood
Back on its course, and, while our banners wing
Northward, strike with us! till the Goth shall cling
To his own blasted altar-stones, and crave
Mercy; and we shall grant it, and dictate
The lenient future of his fate
There, where some rotting ships and trembling quays
Shall one day mark the Port which ruled the Western seas.

SPRING.

SPRING, with that nameless pathos in the air
Which dwells with all things fair,
Spring, with her golden suns and silver rain,
Is with us once again.

Out in the lonely woods the jasmine burns
Its fragrant lamps, and turns
Into a royal court with green festoons
The banks of dark lagoons.

In the deep heart of every forest tree
The blood is all aglee,
And there's a look about the leafless bowers
As if they dreamed of flowers.

Yet still on every side appears the hand
Of Winter in the land,
Save where the maple reddens on the lawn,
Flushed by the season's dawn;

Or where, like those strange semblances we find
That age to childhood bind,
The elm puts on, as if in Nature's scorn,
The brown of Autumn corn.

As yet the turf is dark, although you know
That not a span below,
A thousand germs are groping through the gloom,
And soon will burst their tomb.

Already, here and there, on frailest stems
Appear some azure gems,
Small as might deck, upon a gala-day,
The forehead of a fay.

In gardens you may see, amid the dearth,
The crocus breaking earth;
And near the snowdrop's tender white and green,
The violet in its screen.

But many gleams and shadows need must pass
Along the budding grass,
And weeks go by, before the enamored South
Shall kiss the rose's mouth.

Still there's a sense of blossoms yet unborn
In the sweet airs of morn;
One almost looks to see the very street
Grow purple at his feet.

At times a fragrant breeze comes floating by,
And brings, you know not why,
A feeling as when eager crowds await
Before a palace gate

Some wondrous pageant; and you scarce would start,
If from a beech's heart
A blue-eyed Dryad, stepping forth, should say,
"Behold me! I am May!"

Ah! who would couple thoughts of war and crime
With such a blessed time!
Who in the west-wind's aromatic breath
Could hear the call of Death!

Yet not more surely shall the Spring awake
The voice of wood and brake,
Than she shall rouse, for all her tranquil charms
A million men to arms.

There shall be deeper hues upon her plains
  Than all her sunlight rains,
And every gladdening influence around,
  Can summon from the ground.

Oh! standing on this desecrated mould,
  Methinks that I behold,
Lifting her bloody daisies up to God,
  Spring, kneeling on the sod,

And calling with the voice of all her rills
  Upon the ancient hills,
To fall and crush the tyrants and the slaves
  Who turn her meads to graves.

CHARLESTON.

Calm as that second summer which precedes
  The first fall of the snow,
In the broad sunlight of heroic deeds,
  The city bides the foe.

As yet, behind their ramparts, stern and proud,
  Her bolted thunders sleep—
Dark Sumter, like a battlemented cloud,
  Looms o'er the solemn deep.

No Calpe frowns from lofty cliff or scaur
  To guard the holy strand;
But Moultrie holds in leash her dogs of war,
  Above the level sand.

And down the dunes a thousand guns lie couched,
  Unseen, beside the flood—
Like tigers in some Orient jungle crouched,
  That wait and watch for blood.

Meanwhile, through streets still echoing with trade,
  Walk grave and thoughtful men,
Whose hands may one day wield the patriot's blade
  As lightly as the pen.

And maidens, with such eyes as would grow dim
  Over a bleeding hound,
Seem each one to have caught the strength of him
  Whose sword she sadly bound.

Thus girt without and garrisoned at home,
  Day patient following day,
Old Charleston looks from roof, and spire, and dome,
  Across her tranquil bay.

Ships, through a hundred foes, from Saxon lands
  And spicy Indian ports,
Bring Saxon steel and iron to her hands,
  And summer to her courts.

But still, along yon dim Atlantic line,
  The only hostile smoke
Creeps like a harmless mist above the brine,
  From some frail, floating oak.

Shall the spring dawn, and she still clad in smiles,
  And with an unscathed brow,
Rest in the strong arms of her palm-crowned isles,
  As fair and free as now?

We know not; in the temple of the Fates
  God has inscribed her doom;
And, all untroubled in her faith, she waits
  The triumph or the tomb.

THE UNKNOWN DEAD.

The rain is plashing on my sill,
But all the winds of Heaven are still;
And so, it falls with that dull sound
Which thrills us in the churchyard ground,
When the first spadeful drops like lead
Upon the coffin of the dead.
Beyond my streaming window-pane,
I cannot see the neighboring vane,
Yet from its old familiar tower
The bell comes, muffled, through the shower.
What strange and unsuspected link
Of feeling touched has made me think—
While with a vacant soul and eye
I watch that gray and stony sky—
Of nameless graves on battle-plains,
Washed by a single winter's rains,
Where, some beneath Virginian hills,
And some by green Atlantic rills,
Some by the waters of the West,
A myriad unknown heroes rest?
Ah! not the chiefs who, dying, see
Their flags in front of victory,
Or, at their life-blood's noblest cost
Pay for a battle nobly lost,
Claim from their monumental beds
The bitterest tears a nation sheds.
Beneath yon lonely mound—the spot,
By all save some fond few, forgot—
Lie the true martyrs of the fight,
Which strikes for freedom and for right.
Of them, their patriot zeal and pride,
The lofty faith that with them died,
No grateful page shall further tell
Than that so many bravely fell;
And we can only dimly guess
What worlds of all this world's distress,
What utter woe, despair, and dearth,
Their fate has brought to many a hearth.
Just such a sky as this should weep
Above them, always, where they sleep;
Yet, haply, at this very hour,
Their graves are like a lover's bower;
And Nature's self, with eyes unwet,
Oblivious of the crimson debt
To which she owes her April grace,
Laughs gayly o'er their burial-place.

FORCEYTHE WILLSON.

[Born 18—. Died 1867.]

"THE OLD SERGEANT, AND OTHER POEMS." 1867.

THE OLD SERGEANT.

Jan. 1, 1863.

THE Carrier cannot sing to-day the ballads
With which he used to go,
Rhyming the glad rounds of the happy New Years
That are now beneath the snow:

For the same awful and portentous Shadow
That overcast the earth,
And smote the land last year with desolation,
Still darkens every hearth.

And the carrier hears Beethoven's mighty death-march
Come up from every mart;
And he hears and feels it breathing in his bosom,
And beating in his heart.

And to-day, a scarred and weather-beaten veteran,
Again he comes along,
To tell the story of the Old Year's struggles
In another New Year's song.

And the song is his, but not so with the story;
For the story, you must know,
Was told in prose to Assistant-Surgeon Austin,
By a soldier of Shiloh:

By Robert Burton, who was brought up on the *Adams*,
With his death-wound in his side;
And who told the story to the Assistant-Surgeon,
On the same night that he died.

But the singer feels it will better suit the ballad,
If all should deem it right,
To tell the story as if what it speaks of
Had happened but last night.

"Come a little nearer, Doctor,—thank you,—let me take the cup:
Draw your chair up,—draw it closer,—just another little sup!
May-be you may think I'm better; but I'm pretty well used up,—
Doctor, you've done all you could do, but I'm just a going up!

"Feel my pulse, sir, if you want to, but it ain't much use to try"—
"Never say that," said the Surgeon, as he smothered down a sigh;
"It will never do, old comrade, for a soldier to say die!"
"What you *say* will make no difference, Doctor, when you come to die."

"Doctor, what has been the matter?" "You were very faint, they say;
You must try to get to sleep now." "Doctor, have I been away!"
"Not that anybody knows of!" "Doctor—Doctor, please to stay!
There is something I must tell you, and you won't have long to stay!

"I have got my marching orders, and I'm ready now to go;
Doctor, did you say I fainted?—but it couldn't ha' been so,—
For as sure as I'm a Sergeant, and was wounded at Shiloh,
I've this very night been back there, on the old field of Shiloh!

"This is all that I remember: The last time the Lighter came,
And the lights had all been lowered, and the noises much the same,
He had not been gone five minutes before something called my name:
'ORDERLY SERGEANT—ROBERT BURTON!'—just that way it called my name.

"And I wondered who could call me so distinctly and so slow,
Knew it couldn't be the Lighter,—he could not have spoken so—
And I tried to answer, 'Here, sir!' but I couldn't make it go;
For I couldn't move a muscle, and I couldn't make it go!

"Then I thought: It's all a nightmare, all a humbug and a bore;
Just another foolish *grape-vine* *—and it won't come any more;
But it came, sir, notwithstanding, just the same way as before:
'ORDERLY SERGEANT—ROBERT BURTON!'—even plainer than before.

"That is all that I remember, till a sudden burst of light,
And I stood beside the River, where we stood that Sunday night,
Waiting to be ferried over to the dark bluffs opposite,
When the river was perdition and all hell was opposite!—

"And the same old palpitation came again in all its power,
And I heard a Bugle sounding, as from some celestial Tower;

* *Canard.*

And the same mysterious voice said: 'It is the eleventh hour!
  Orderly Sergeant—Robert Burton—it is the eleventh hour!'

"Doctor Austin!—what *day* is this?" "It is Wednesday night, you know."
'Yes,—to-morrow will be New Year's, and a right good time below!
What *time* is it, Doctor Austin?" "Nearly twelve." "Then don't you go!
  Can it be that all this happened—all this—not an hour ago!

'There was where the gunboats opened on the dark rebellious host;
And where Webster semicircled his last guns upon the coast;
There were still the two log-houses, just the same, or else their ghost,—
  And the same old transport came and took me over—or its ghost!

"And the old field lay before me all deserted far and wide;
There was where they fell on Prentiss,—there McClernand met the tide;
There was where stern Sherman rallied, and where Hurlbut's heroes died,—
  Lower down, where Wallace charged them, and kept charging till he died.

"There was where Lew Wallace showed them he was of the canny kin,
There was where old Nelson thundered, and where Rousseau waded in;
There McCook sent 'em to breakfast, and we all began to win—
  There was where the grape-shot took me, just as we began to win.

"Now, a shroud of snow and silence over everything was spread;
And but for this old blue mantle and the old hat on my head
I should not have even doubted, to this moment, I was dead,—
  For my footsteps were as silent as the snow upon the dead!

"Death and silence!—Death and silence: all around me as I sped!
And behold, a mighty Tower, as if builded to the dead,—
To the Heaven of the heavens, lifted up its mighty head,
  Till the Stars and Stripes of Heaven all seemed waving from its head!

"Round and mighty-based it towered—up into the infinite—
And I knew no mortal mason could have built a shaft so bright;
For it shone like solid sunshine; and a winding stair of light,
  Wound around it and around it till it wound clear out of sight!

"And, behold, as I approached it—with a rapt and dazzled stare,—
Thinking that I saw old comrades just ascending the great Stair,—
Suddenly the solemn challenge broke of—'Halt, and who goes there!'
  'I'm a friend,' I said, 'if you are.'—'Then advance, sir, to the Stair!'

"I advanced!—That sentry, Doctor, was Elijah Ballantyne!—
First of all to fall on Monday, after we had formed the line!—
'Welcome, my old Sergeant, welcome! Welcome by that countersign!'
  And he pointed to the scar there, under this old cloak of mine!

"As he grasped my hand, I shuddered, thinking only of the grave;
But he smiled and pointed upward with a bright and bloodless glaive:
'That's the way, sir, to Head-quarters.' 'What Head-quarters!'—'Of the Brave.'
  'But the great Tower?'—'That,' he answered, 'Is the way, sir, of the Brave!'

"Then a sudden shame came o'er me at his uniform of light;
At my own so old and tattered, and at his so new and bright;
'Ah!' said he, 'you have forgotten the New Uniform to-night,—
Hurry back, for you must be here at just twelve o'clock to-night!'

"And the next thing I remember, you were sitting *there*, and I—
Doctor—did you hear a footstep? Hark!—God bless you all! Good-by!
Doctor, please to give my musket and my knapsack, when I die,
  To my Son—my Son that's coming,—he won't get here till I die!

"Tell him his old father blessed him as he never did before,—
And to carry that old musket"—Hark! a knock is at the door!—
"Till the Union—" See! it opens!—"Father! Father! speak once more!"—
  "*Bless you!*"—gasped the old, gray Sergeant, and he lay and said no more!

AUTUMN SONG.

In Spring the Poet is glad,
  And in Summer the Poet is gay;
But in Autumn the Poet is sad,
  And has something sad to say:

For the Wind moans in the Wood,
  And the Leaf drops from the Tree;
And the cold Rain falls on the graves of the Good,
  And the cold Mist comes up from the Sea:

And the Autumn Songs of the Poet's soul
  Are set to the passionate grief,
Of Winds that sough and Bells that toll
  The Dirge of the Falling Leaf.

JOHN HAY.

[Born 1839.]

"PIKE COUNTY BALLADS AND OTHER POEMS." 1871.

LITTLE BREECHES.

I DON'T go much on religion,
  I never ain't had no show;
But I've got a middlin' tight grip, sir,
  On the handful o' things I know.
I don't pan out on the prophets
  And free-will, and that sort of thing,—
But I b'lieve in God and the angels,
  Ever sence one night last spring.

I come into town with some turnips,
  And my little Gabe come along,—
No four-year-old in the county
  Could beat him for pretty and strong,
Peart and chipper and sassy,
  Always ready to swear and fight,—
And I'd larnt him to chaw terbacker
  Jest to keep his milk-teeth white.

The snow come down like a blanket
  As I passed by Taggart's store;
I went in for a jug of molasses
  And left the team at the door.
They scared at something and started,—
  I heard one little squall,
And hell-to-split over the prairie
  Went team, Little Breeches and all.

Hell-to-split over the prairie!
  I was almost froze with skeer;
But we rousted up some torches,
  And sarched for 'em far and near.
At last we struck horses and wagon,
  Snowed under a soft white mound,
Upsot, dead beat,—but of little Gabe
  No hide nor hair was found.

And here all hope soured on me,
  Of my fellow-critter's aid,—
I jest flopped down on my marrow-bones,
  Crotch-deep in the snow, and prayed.

* * * *

By this the torches was played out,
  And me and Isrul Parr
Went off for some wood to a sheepfold
  That he said was somewhar thar.

We found it at last, and a little shed
  Where they shut up the lambs at night.
We looked in and seen them huddled thar,
  So warm and sleepy and white;
And THAR sot Little Breeches and chirped,
  As peart as ever you see,
"I want a chaw of terbacker,
  And that's what's the matter of me."

How did he git thar? Angels.
  He could never have walked in that storm.
They jest scooped down and toted him
  To whar it was safe and warm.
And I think that saving a little child,
  And bringing him to his own,
Is a derned sight better business
  Than loafing around The Throne.

JIM BLUDSO,

OF THE PRAIRIE BELLE.

WALL, no! I can't tell whar he lives,
  Becase he don't live, you see;
Leastways, he's got out of the habit
  Of livin' like you and me.
Whar have you been for the last three year
  That you haven't heard folks tell
How Jimmy Bludso passed in his checks
  The night of the Prairie Belle?

He weren't no saint,—them engineers
  Is all pretty much alike,—
One wife in Natchez-under-the-Hill
  And another one here, in Pike;
A keerless man in his talk was Jim,
  And an awkward hand in a row,
But he never flunked, and he never lied,—
  I reckon he never knowed how.

And this was all the religion he had,—
  To treat his engine well;
Never be passed on the river;
  To mind the pilot's bell;
And if ever the Prairie Belle took fire,—
  A thousand times he swore,
He'd hold her nozzle agin the bank
  Till the last soul got ashore.

All boats has their day on the Mississip,
  And her day come at last,—
The Movaster was a better boat,
  But the Belle she *wouldn't* be passed.
And so she come tearin' along that night—
  The oldest craft on the line—
With a nigger squat on her safety-valve,
  And her furnace crammed, rosin and pine.

The fire burst out as she clared the bar,
  And burnt a hole in the night,
And quick as a flash she turned, and made
  For that willer-bank on the right.
There was runnin' and cursin', but Jim yelled
    out,
  Over all the infernal roar,
"I'll hold her nozzle agin the bank
  Till the last galoot's ashore."

Through the hot, black breath of the burnin'
boat
Jim Bludso's voice was heard,
And they all had trust in his cussedness,
And knowed he would keep his word.
And, sure's you're born, they all got off
Afore the smokestacks fell,—
And Bludso's ghost went up alone
In the smoke of the Prairie Belle.

He weren't no saint,—but at jedgment
I'd run my chance with Jim,
'Longside of some pious gentlemen
That wouldn't shook hands with him.
He seen his duty, a dead-sure thing,—
And went for it thar and then;
And Christ ain't going to be too hard
On a man that died for men.

A WOMAN'S LOVE.

A SENTINEL angel sitting high in glory
Heard this shrill wail ring out from Purgatory:
"Have mercy, mighty angel, hear my story!

"I loved,—and, blind with passionate love, I
fell.
Love brought me down to death, and death to
Hell.
For God is just, and death for sin is well.

"I do not rage against his high decree,
Nor for myself do ask that grace shall be;
But for my love on earth who mourns for me.

"Great Spirit! Let me see my love again
And comfort him one hour, and I were fain
To pay a thousand years of fire and pain."

Then said the pitying angel, "Nay, repent
That wild vow! Look, the dial-finger's bent
Down to the last hour of thy punishment!"

But still she wailed, "I pray thee, let me go!
I cannot rise to peace and leave him so.
O, let me soothe him in his bitter woe!'

The brazen gates ground sullenly ajar,
And upward, joyous, like a rising star,
She rose and vanished in the ether far.

But soon adown the dying sunset sailing,
And like a wounded bird her pinions trailing,
She fluttered back, with broken-hearted wailing.

She sobbed, "I found him by the summer sea
Reclined, his head upon a maiden's knee,—
She curled his hair and kissed him. Woe is me!"

She wept, "Now let my punishment begin!
I have been fond and foolish. Let me in
To expiate my sorrow and my sin."

The angel answered, "Nay, sad soul, go higher!
To be deceived in your true heart's desire
Was bitterer than a thousand years of fire!"

IN A GRAVEYARD.

In the dewy depths of the graveyard
I lie in the tangled grass,
And watch, in the sea of azure,
The white cloud-islands pass.

The birds in the rustling branches
Sing gayly overhead;
Gray stones like sentinel spectres
Are guarding the silent dead.

The early flowers sleep shaded
In the cool green noonday glooms;
The broken light falls shuddering
On the cold white face of the tombs.

Without, the world is smiling
In the infinite love of God,
But the sunlight fails and falters
When it falls on the churchyard sod.

On me the joyous rapture
Of a heart's first love is shed,
But it falls on my heart as coldly
As sunlight on the dead.

THROUGH THE LONG DAYS.

THROUGH the long days and years
What will my loved one be,
Parted from me?
Through the long days and years.

Always as then she was,
Loveliest, brightest, best,
Blessing and blest,—
Always as then she was.

Never on earth again
Shall I before her stand,
Touch lip or hand,—
Never on earth again.

But while my darling lives
Peaceful I journey on,
Not quite alone,—
Not while my darling lives.

REMORSE.

SAD is the thought of sunniest days
Of love and rapture perished,
And shine through memory's tearful haze
The eyes once fondliest cherished.
Reproachful is the ghost of toys
That charmed while life was wasted.
But saddest is the thought of joys
That never yet were tasted.

Sad is the vague and tender dream
Of dead love's lingering kisses,
To crushed hearts haloed by the gleam
Of unreturning blisses;
Deep mourns the soul in anguished pride
For the pitiless death that won them,—
But the saddest wail is for lips that died
With the virgin dew upon them.

ROBERT KELLEY WEEKS.

[Born 1840.]

"EPISODES AND LYRIC PIECES." 1870.

THE RETURN OF PARIS.

I STUMBLED thrice, and twice I fell and lay
Moaning and faint, and yet I did not pray
To any God or Goddess of them all;
Because I never doubted, climb or crawl,
That I should reach the fountain and the tall
One old familiar pine-tree, where I lay
Prone on my face, with outstretched hands, you say,
Fallen once again—this time against the goal.
And now, what shall I pray for? since my whole
Wish is accomplished, and I have your face
Once more by mine in the remembered place,
And the cool hand laid on my head aright,
A little while before I die to-night.
For surely I am dying: not a vein
But has received the poison and the pain
Of Philoctetes' arrow.—Oh! I heard
The hissing of the vengeance long deferred,
And felt it smite me, and not smite me dead;
And all at once the very words you said
Too long ago returned to me once more—
When, as you shall be, you are wounded sore,
Come back to me, and I will cure you then,
Whom none but I can cure: and once again,
Sweet! I am with you, and am cured by you,
And by you only; and yet it is true
That I must die, Œnone. So it is,
And better that it is so! Hark to this.
How good it were, if we could live once more
The old sweet life we found so sweet before—
Here in the mountain where we were so glad,
Ere I was cruel and ere you were sad!
How good it were could we begin again
The old sweet life just where we left it then!
A song, love;—but my singing voice is gone—
The one song that I made, the only one
After I left you to be mad so long;
(A marvellous thing to have made no other song!)
The only one—which, many months ago,
Came to me strangely with a soft and slow
Movement of music, which at first was sad,
But sad and sweet, and after only sad,
And then most bitter, as its death gave birth
To a low laughter of uneasy mirth—
Made of blent noises that the night-winds bore,
The lapse of waves upon the dusky shore,
The creaking of the tackle, and the stir
Of threatening banners where the camp-fires were
About the armies, that no such a charm
As a regretful love song could disarm,
And bring to life the heroes that were slain,
And make the war as if it were a vain
Noise in the night that at the morn is not,
And all the Past a dream that it begot.
The wind was right to laugh my song away!
And then I thought—if only for a day
I might be with her, only for so long
As to be pardoned or (forgive the wrong)
Cursed by her there, and so get leave to die!
And here we are, Œnone, you and I!
Yes, we are here! why ever otherwhere?

Ah! why indeed? And yet, love, let me dare
Uncover my whole heart to you once more;
I think I never was so blest before—
Never so happy as I am to-day.
Not even, indeed, when in the early May
We found each other, and were quite too glad
To know the value of the love we had.
But now I seem to know it in my need,
Inhaling the full sweetness of it—freed
Now, for the first time, from its perfect flower;
Ah! quite too sweet to overlast its hour!
What more now shall I pray for? To be let
Live and not die? Ah! if we could forget
All but the Present and outlaw the Past!
And yet I know not—could the Present last
If quite cut off from all that gave it birth,
And not be changed, if changed to alien earth,
Into a Future that we know not of?
We will not ask: we have attained to Love—
Whatever grown from—which not all the years
Past or to come, nor memories nor fears,
Can rob us of forever, nor make less.
No praying then—but only thankfulness!

No sound floats hither from the smoky plain:
Turn me a little—never mind the pain—
I see it now. And that was Ilion then!
The accursed city in the mouths of men,
Whose mouths are swift to interweave its name
With mine forever for a word of shame.
I never loved it, and it loved me not—
The fatal firebrand that itself begot
And tried to quench and could not—there it smokes!
And there the shed blood of its people soaks
Into the soil that they loved more than life.

Let the Gods answer who decreed the strife!
But you, great-hearted, whom indeed I loved—
Brother and friend, by whom, if unapproved,
I was loved sometime in the upper air—
Will you turn from me when I meet you there
And greet you, Hector, in the other world?
Will you turn from me, with lips coldly curled,
And frank eyes hardened?—

I accept the sign!
Lo you! Œnone, where the gloomy line
Of the slow clouds is broken, and a bright
Gleam, like a smile, steals softly into sight
And grows to a glory in the increasing sky!
Nay, you are right, love! What have you and I

To do with Past or Future, who have for boon
So rich a Present, to exhaust so soon
Between the daylight and the afterglow?
The last cloud passes, and how calm I grow!
And now—if I should close my eyes, my love,
And seem to sleep a little, and not move
Until the sky has got its perfect gold,
You will not think me dying while I hold
Your hand thus closely? Kiss me now. Again!
Past chance of change—just where we left it then.

ŒNONE.

I had him last! I had him first and last!
His morning beauty and his evening charm!
Oh, Love! triumphant over all the Past,
What Death can daunt you, or what Future harm?

AD FINEM.

I WOULD not have believed it then,
If any one had told me so—
Ere you shall see his face again
A year and more shall go.

And let them come again to-day
To pity me and prophesy,
And I will face them all, and say
To all of them, You lie!

False prophets all, you lie, you lie!
I will believe no word but his;
Will say December is July,
That Autumn April is,

Rather than say he has forgot,
Or will not come who bade me wait,
Who wait him and accuse him not
Of being very late.

He said that he would come in Spring,
And I believed—believe him now,
Though all the birds have ceased to sing
And bare is every bough;

For Spring is not till he appear,
Winter is not when he is nigh—
The only Lord of all my year,
For whom I live—and die!

A PAUSE.

To have the imploring hands of her
Clasped on his shoulder, and his cheek
Brushed over slowly by the stir
Of thrilling hair, and not to speak;

To see within the unlifted eyes
More than the fallen fringes prove
Enough to hide, to see the rise
Of tear-drops in them, and not move;

Would this be strange? And yet at last,
What weary man may not do this,
Seeing when the long pursuit is past,
To only cease how sweet it is?

To only cease and be as one
Who, when the fever leaves him, lies
Careless of what is come or gone,
Which yet he cannot realize;

For all his little thought is spent
In wondering what it was that gave
To be so quiet and content,
While yet he is not in the grave.

IN NUBIBUS.

THIS is a dream I had of her
When in the middle seas we were.

Sunlight possessed the clouds again,
Well emptied of unfruitful rain,
When, leaning o'er the vessel's side,
I watched the bubbles rise and glide
And break and pass away beneath;
And heard the creamy waters seethe,
As when an undecided breeze
Plays in the branches of the trees
Just ere the leaves begin to fall;
And as I listened, slowly all
The elm-tree branches on the Green
Rose up before me; and between
The stately trees on either side
I saw the pathway, smooth and wide,
In which I once had walked with her;
And in it men and women were,
Who came and went no otherwise
Than vague cloud-shadows to my eyes,
And whispering bubbles to my ear,
Who neither cared to see nor hear,
And straight forgot them every one.

But when the last of them was gone,
And now from end to end the walk
Was empty of them and their talk,
A listening, longing silence fell
Upon the elm-trees like a spell
Of expectation and desire,
And quick I saw the impulsive fire
Of sunset overflush the white
And waiting clouds with rosy light;
And then a breeze ran all along
The pathway, as if from a song—
Imparting freshness as it ran,
Till all the autumn leaves began
Midsummer murmurs in the air,
And suddenly I saw her there—
And felt my heart leap up, and then
As suddenly shrink back again
To see that she was not alone;
But with her walking there was one
Whose face turned sidewise, as it were
The better so to hark to her,
Showed not enough to let me know
What man it was I envied so:
And yet I could not go away,
But fascinated still to stay,
And wait till they should pass me by,
I stood and watched them cloudily,
And saw them coming near and near,
And nearer yet till I could hear
Her voice and recognize his face;
And, save that a transmitted grace
Made it not easy to be known,
So went the dream—it was my own.

SAMUEL WILLOUGHBY DUFFIELD.

[Born 1843.]

"WARP AND WOOF." 1870.

A SMALL WARBLER.

A LITTLE bird with the blackest eyes
Sits on a twig and nods at me;
Very merry he seems to be,
And wise.

I wish I knew what the fellow thinks,
Saucily shaking his cunning head—
Whether it cannot all be said
By winks.

I wish I were of the craft as well,
Careless of morrows which come too soon,
Hearing the tales a golden noon
Can tell.

For I should tarry among the leaves,
Breathing no other than balmy air,
Seeing my harvest everywhere
In sheaves.

And then I should tax my brain no more,
Thick though the snowflakes chose to fall,
Knowing I have beyond them all
A shore.

ON MY BACK.

HERE in the shade amid the clover,
You shall discover me, friend of mine;
Oak-leaf and maple bending over,
Tangled with tendrils of the vine.

This is my fortress—here I battle
Evil which grows from the city's thought;
Here I forget the ceaseless rattle,
Hurry, and toil, which men have wrought.

These are the pages which the summer—
Diligent student!—thums and turns,
Reading in haste, like some late comer—
Into whose soul the wisdom burns.

Come to me, then. No poet's measure
Holds to the full this golden day,
Rich in what gifts of countless treasure
Winter, the miser, hid away.

Hark! to his wife the thrush is calling:
All the blue sky is thrilled with song;
Now and then through the tree-tops falling,
Full of a mirth most glad and strong.

Here to the shade amid the clover
Come, and discover me, friend of mine;
Oak-leaf and maple bending over,
Tangled with tendrils of the vine.

TWO OF A TRADE.

THE dragon-fly and I together
Sail up the stream in the summer weather;
He at the stern, all green and gold,
And I at the oars, our course to hold.

Above the floor of the level river
The bent blades dip and spring and quiver;
And the dragon-fly is here and there,
Along the water and in the air.

And thus we go as the sunshine mellows,
A pair of nature's merriest fellows;
For the Spanish cedar is light and true,
And instead of one, it has carried two.

And thus we sail without care or sorrow,
With trust for to-day and hope for to-morrow;
He at the stern, all green and gold,
And I at the oars, our course to hold.

THE LOST SONG.

THERE went a bird away from me,
In the stormy winter, across the sea;
One sudden day,
All chill and gray,
Unto new lands it flew away.

It took from hence beneath its wing
One of the songs I used to sing—
A song more sweet
Than I can meet,
Wandering on with weary feet.

But spring has come, and now once more
Hither it flutters as before—
More dear to me
Than these can be,
Because it has flown across the sea.

EDWARD ROWLAND SILL.

[Born 1841.]

"THE HERMITAGE, AND OTHER POEMS." 1868.

SLEEPING.

HUSHED within her quiet bed
She is lying, all the night,
In her pallid robe of white,
Eyelids on the pure eyes pressed,
Soft hands folded on the breast,—
And you thought I meant it—dead ?

Nay! I smile at your shocked face :
In the morning she will wake,
Turn her dreams to sport, and make
All the household glad and gay
Yet for many a merry day,
With her beauty and her grace.

But some Summer 'twill be said—
"She is lying, all the night,
In her pallid robe of white,
Eyelids on the tired eyes pressed,
Hands that cross upon the breast ;"
We shall understand it—dead !

Yet 'twill only be a sleep :
When, with songs and dewy light,
Morning blossoms out of Night,
She will open her blue eyes
'Neath the palms of Paradise,
While we foolish ones shall weep.

MORNING.

I ENTERED once, at break of day,
A chapel, lichen-stained and gray,
Where a congregation dozed and heard
An old monk read from a written Word.
No light through the window-panes could pass,
For shutters were closed on the rich-stained glass ;
And in a gloom like the nether night
The monk read on by a taper's light.
Ghostly with shadows, that shrank and grew
As the dim light flared, were aisle and pew ;
And the congregation that dozed around,
Listened without a stir or sound—
Save one, who rose with wistful face,
And shifted a shutter from its place.
Then light flashed in like a flashing gem—
For dawn had come unknown to them—
And a slender beam, like a lance of gold,
Shot to a crimson curtain-fold,
Over the bended head of him
Who pored and pored by the taper dim ;
And it kindled over his wrinkled brow
Such words—"The law which was till now :"
And I wondered that, under that morning ray,
When night and shadow were scattered away,
The monk should bow his locks of white
By a taper's feebly flickering light—
Should pore and pore, and never seem
To notice the golden morning-beam.

THE FUTURE.

WHAT may we take into the vast Forever ?
That marble door
Admits no fruit of all our long endeavor,
No fame-wreathed crown we wore,
No garnered lore.

What can we bear beyond the unknown portal ?
No gold, no gains
Of all our toiling : in the life immortal
No hoarded wealth remains,
Nor gilds, nor stains.

Naked from out that far abyss behind us
We entered here :
No word came with our coming, to remind us
What wondrous world was near,
No hope, no fear.

Into the silent, starless Night before us,
Naked we glide :
No hand has mapped the constellations o'er us,
No comrade at our side,
No chart, no guide.

Yet fearless toward that midnight, black and hollow,
Our footsteps fare :
The beckoning of a Father's hand we follow—
His love alone is there,
No curse, no care.

A POET'S APOLOGY.

TRUTH cut on high in tablets of hewn stone,
Or on great columns gorgeously adorned,
Perchance were left alone,
Passed by and scorned ;
But Truth enchased upon a jewel rare,
A man would keep, and next his bosom wear.

So, many an hour, I sit and carve my gems—
Ten spoiled, for one in purer beauty set :
Not for kings' diadems—
Some amulet
That may be worn o'er hearts that toil and plod,—
Though but one pearl that bears the name of God.

Index of Names of Authors.